MY FAVORITE THING IS MONSTERS

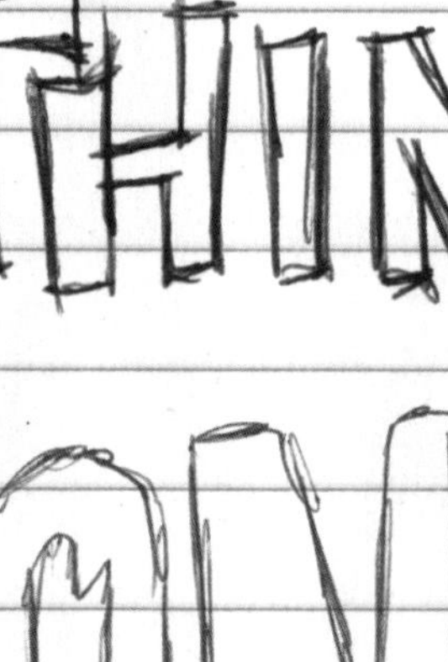

BOOK ONE

EMIL FERRIS

FANTAGRAPHICS BOOKS

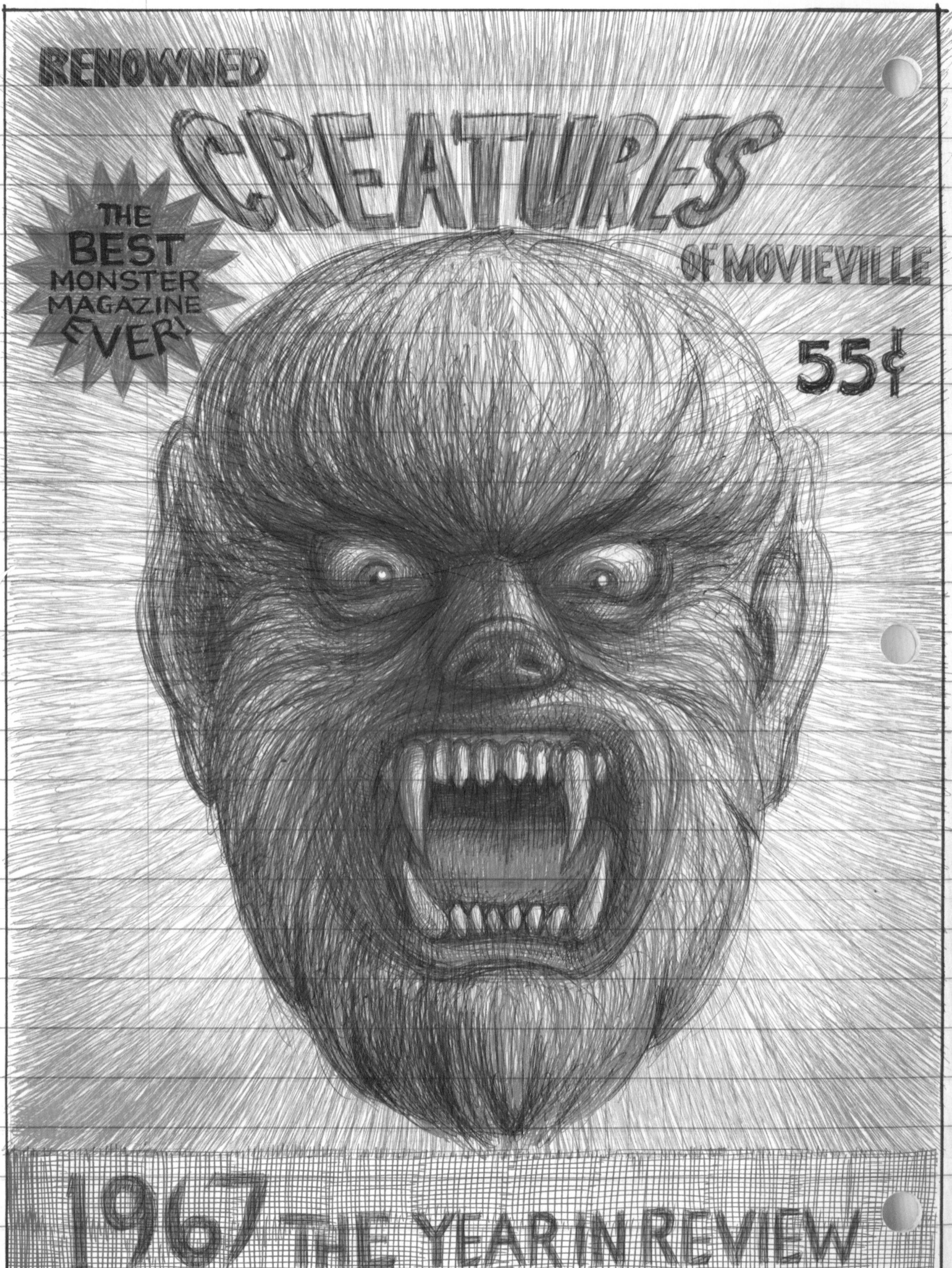
RENOWNED
CREATURES
OF MOVIEVILLE
THE BEST MONSTER MAGAZINE EVER!
55¢
1967 THE YEAR IN REVIEW

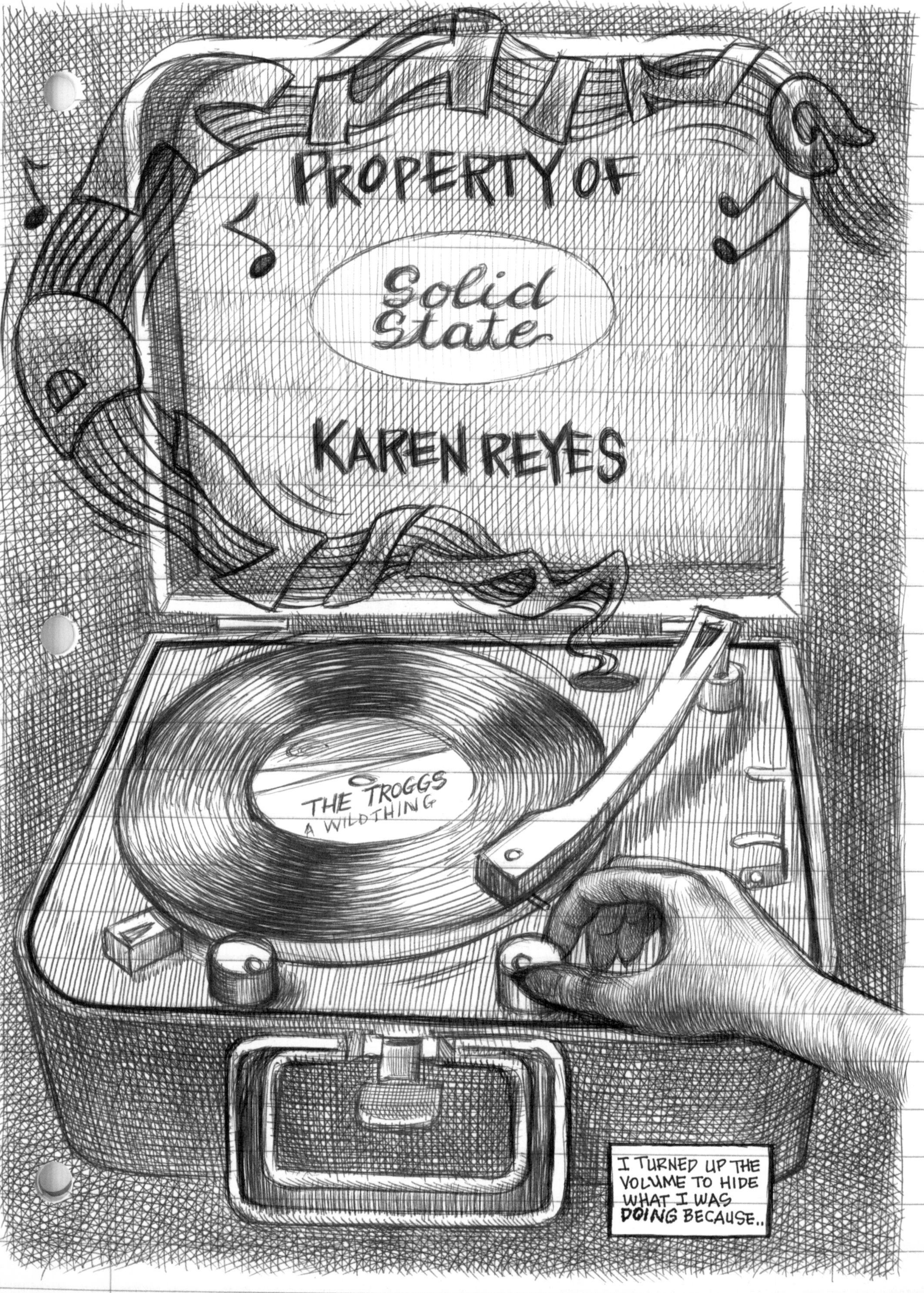
PROPERTY OF
Solid State
KAREN REYES
THE TROGGS
A WILD THING
I TURNED UP THE VOLUME TO HIDE WHAT I WAS DOING BECAUSE..

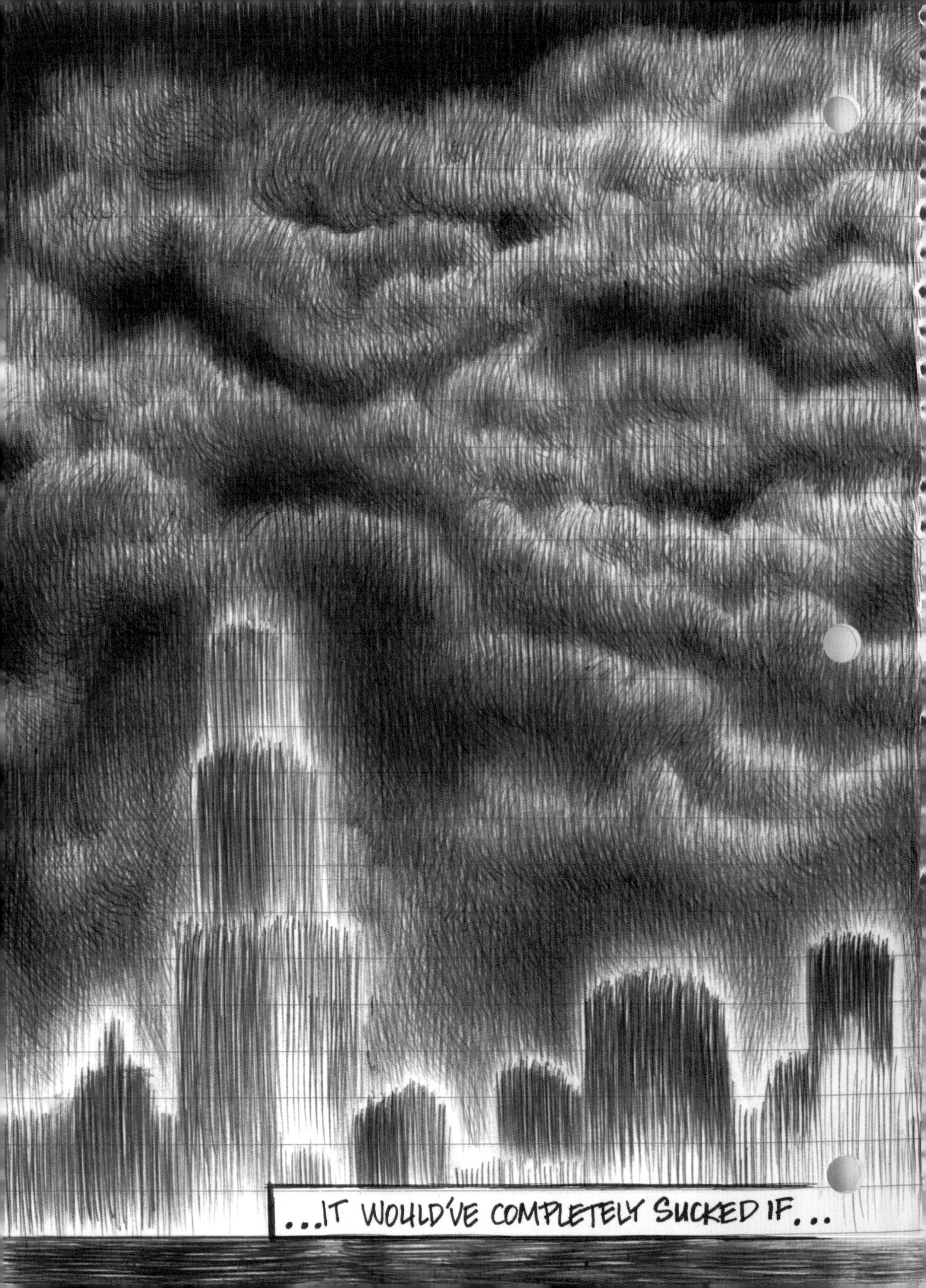
...IT WOULD'VE COMPLETELY SUCKED IF...

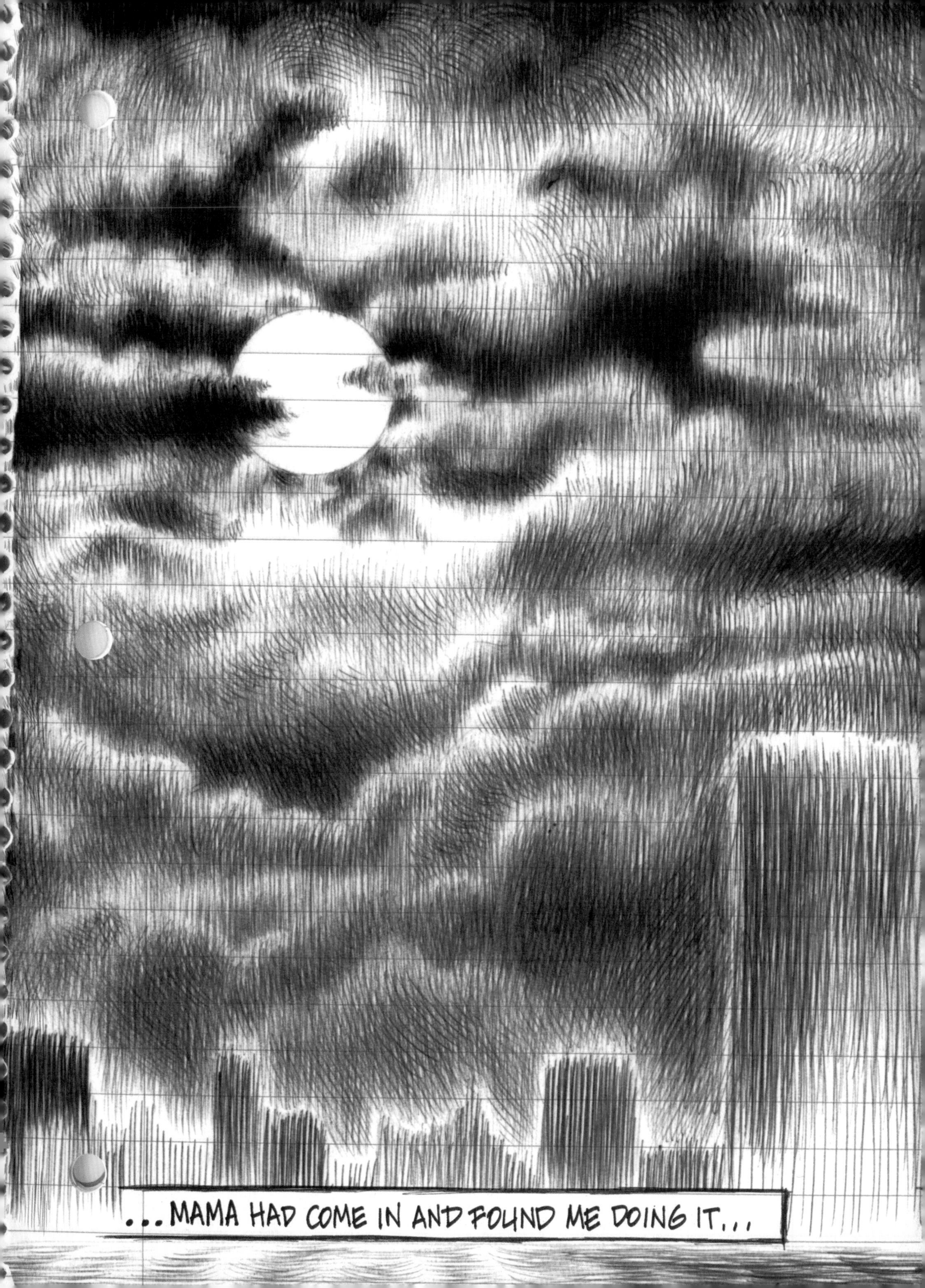
...MAMA HAD COME IN AND FOUND ME DOING IT...

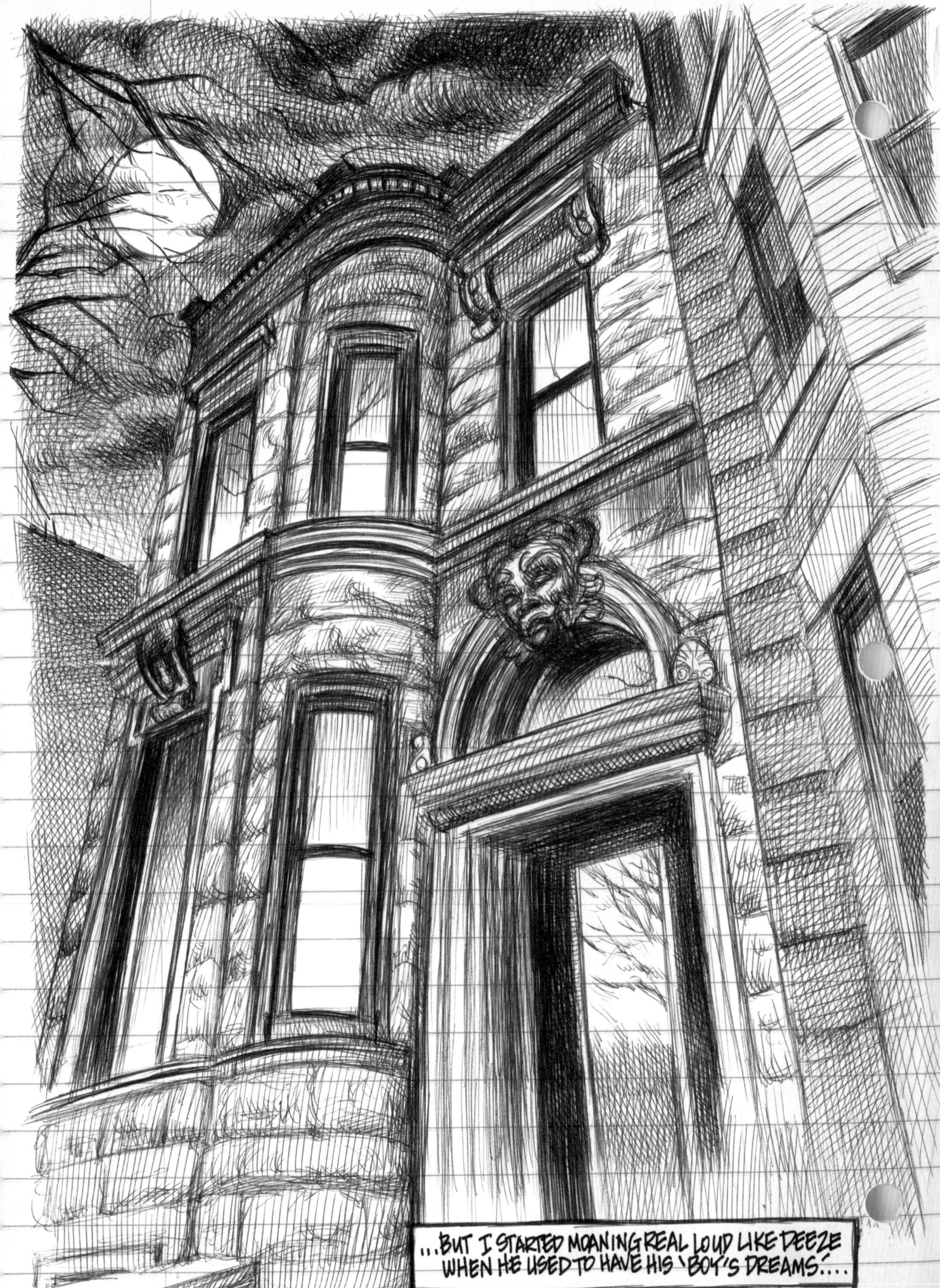
...BUT I STARTED MOANING REAL LOUD LIKE DEEZE WHEN HE USED TO HAVE HIS 'BOY'S DREAMS'....

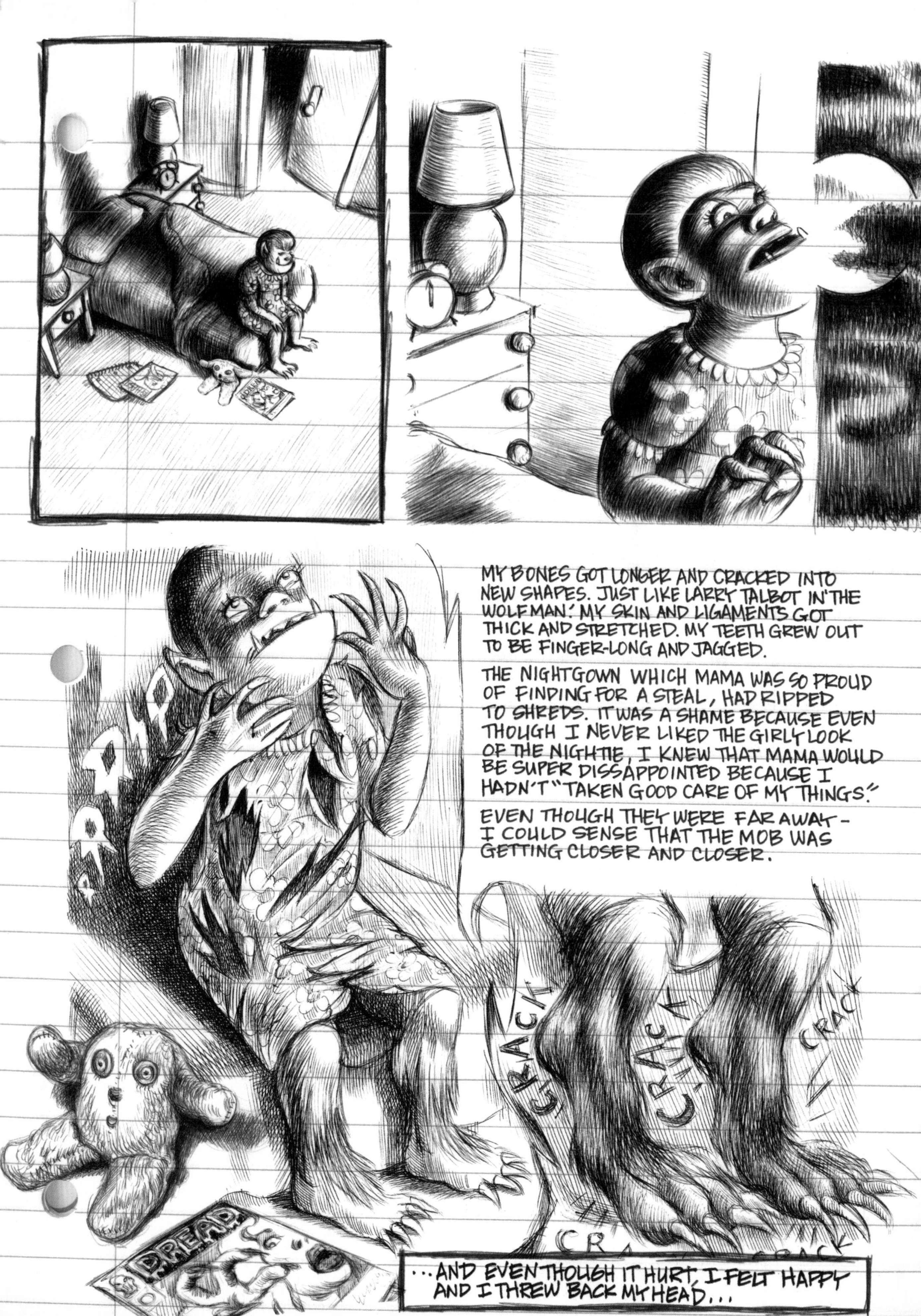
MY BONES GOT LONGER AND CRACKED INTO NEW SHAPES. JUST LIKE LARRY TALBOT IN "THE WOLFMAN." MY SKIN AND LIGAMENTS GOT THICK AND STRETCHED. MY TEETH GREW OUT TO BE FINGER-LONG AND JAGGED.
THE NIGHTGOWN WHICH MAMA WAS SO PROUD OF FINDING FOR A STEAL, HAD RIPPED TO SHREDS. IT WAS A SHAME BECAUSE EVEN THOUGH I NEVER LIKED THE GIRLY LOOK OF THE NIGHTIE, I KNEW THAT MAMA WOULD BE SUPER DISSAPPOINTED BECAUSE I HADN'T "TAKEN GOOD CARE OF MY THINGS."
EVEN THOUGH THEY WERE FAR AWAY - I COULD SENSE THAT THE MOB WAS GETTING CLOSER AND CLOSER.
CRACK
CRACK
CRACK
DREAD
...AND EVEN THOUGH IT HURT, I FELT HAPPY AND I THREW BACK MY HEAD...

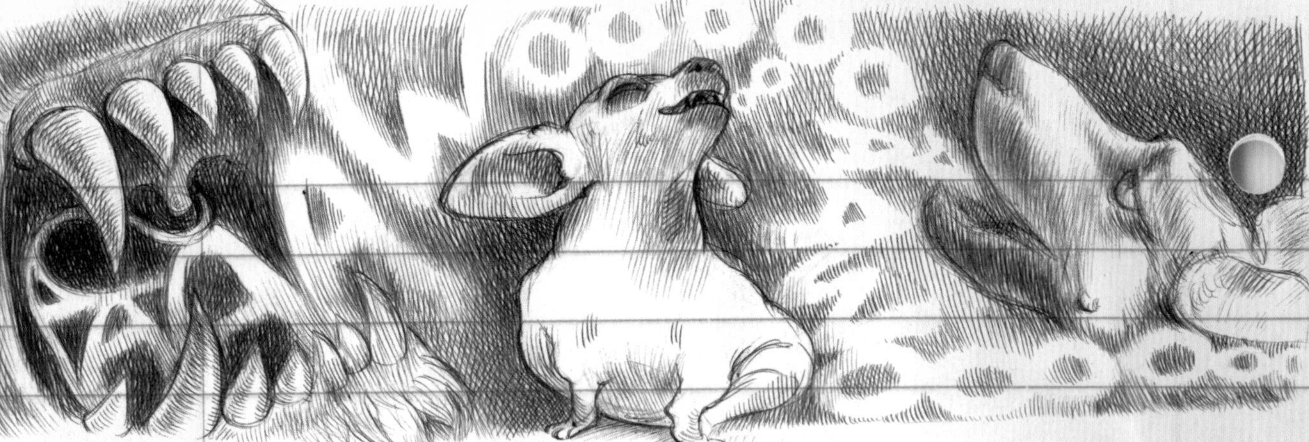

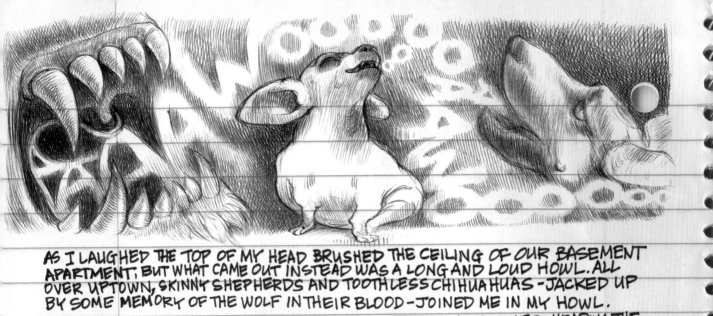

AS I LAUGHED THE TOP OF MY HEAD BRUSHED THE CEILING OF OUR BASEMENT APARTMENT; BUT WHAT CAME OUT INSTEAD WAS A LONG AND LOUD HOWL. ALL OVER UPTOWN, SKINNY SHEPHERDS AND TOOTHLESS CHIHUAHUAS - JACKED UP BY SOME MEMORY OF THE WOLF IN THEIR BLOOD - JOINED ME IN MY HOWL.

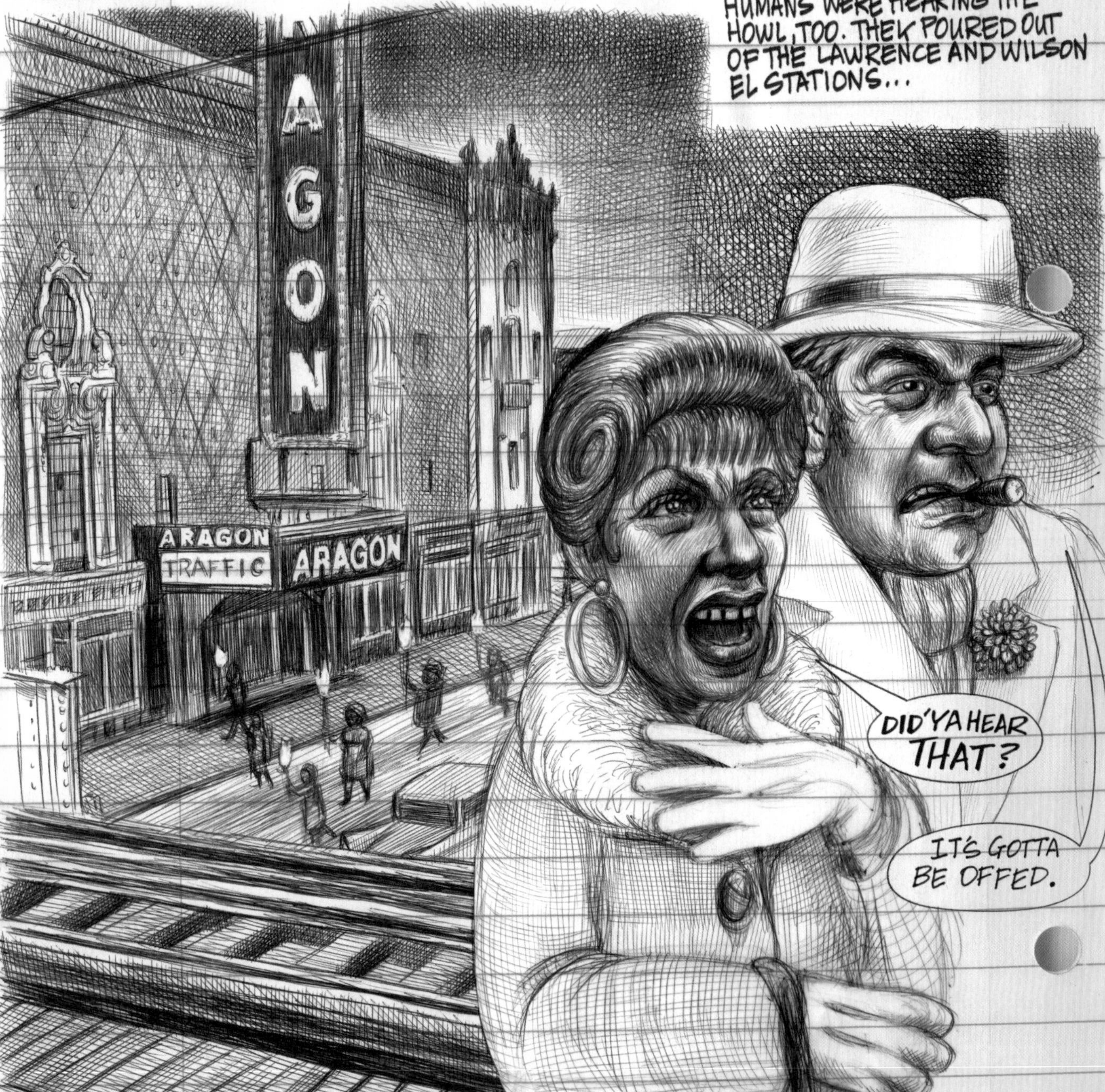
HUMANS WERE HEARING THE HOWL, TOO. THEY POURED OUT OF THE LAWRENCE AND WILSON EL STATIONS...
ARAGON
ARAGON
TRAFFIC
ARAGON
DID'YA HEAR THAT?
IT'S GOTTA BE OFFED.

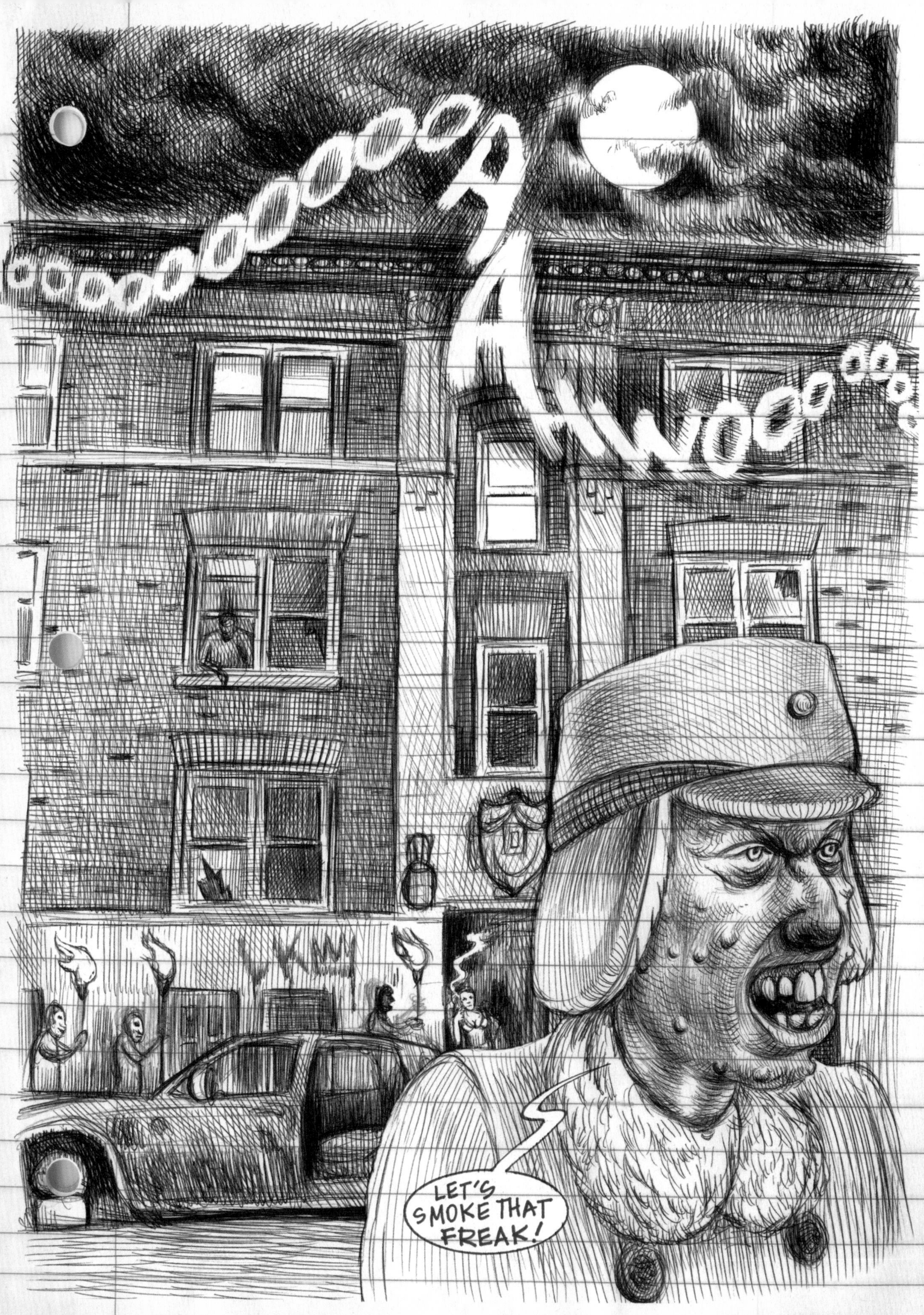
LET'S SMOKE THAT FREAK!

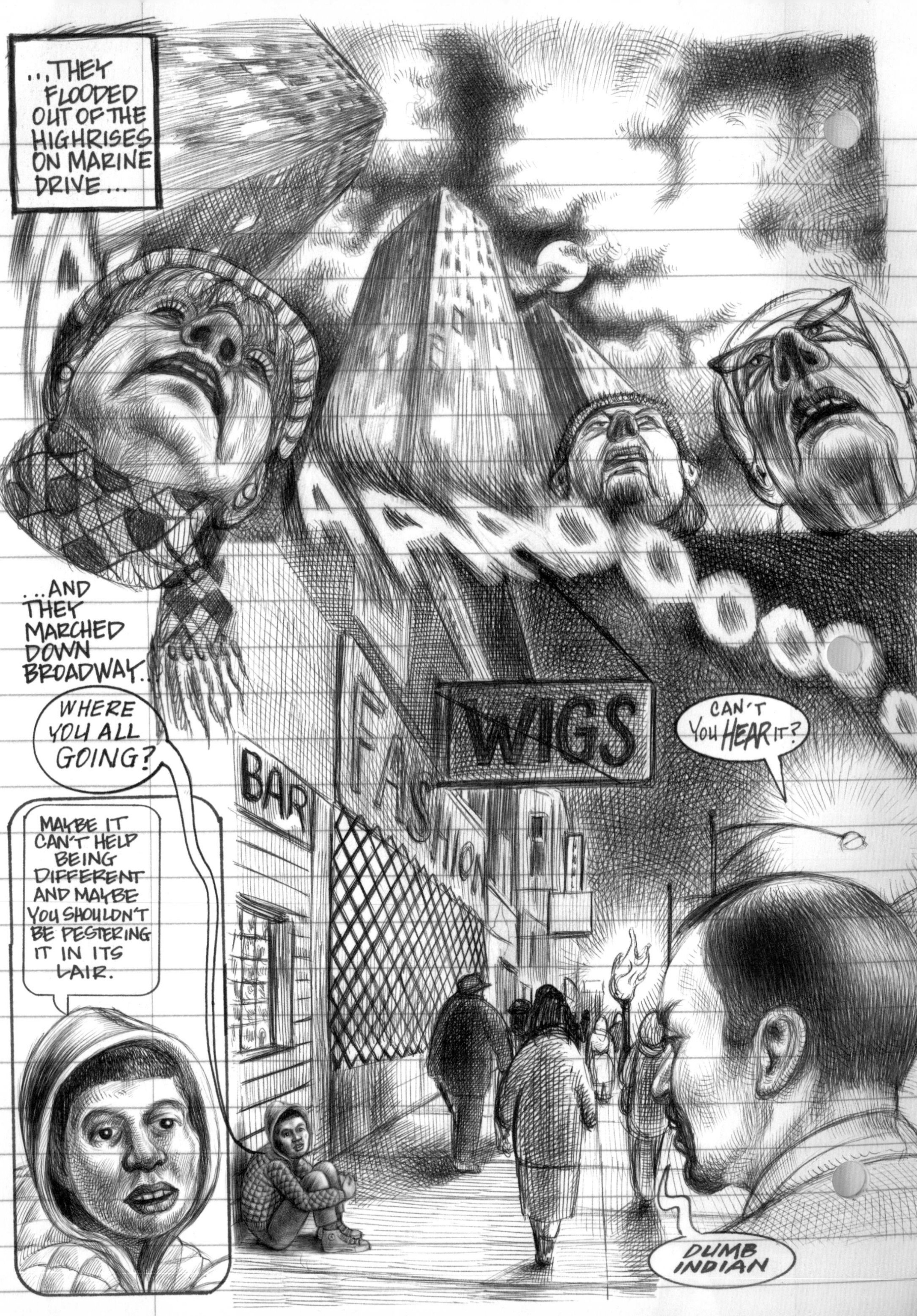
...THEY FLOODED OUT OF THE HIGHRISES ON MARINE DRIVE...
AAAOOOOOOO
...AND THEY MARCHED DOWN BROADWAY...
WHERE YOU ALL GOING?
CAN'T YOU HEAR IT?
WIGS
FASHION
BAR
MAYBE IT CAN'T HELP BEING DIFFERENT AND MAYBE YOU SHOULDN'T BE PESTERING IT IN ITS LAIR.
DUMB INDIAN

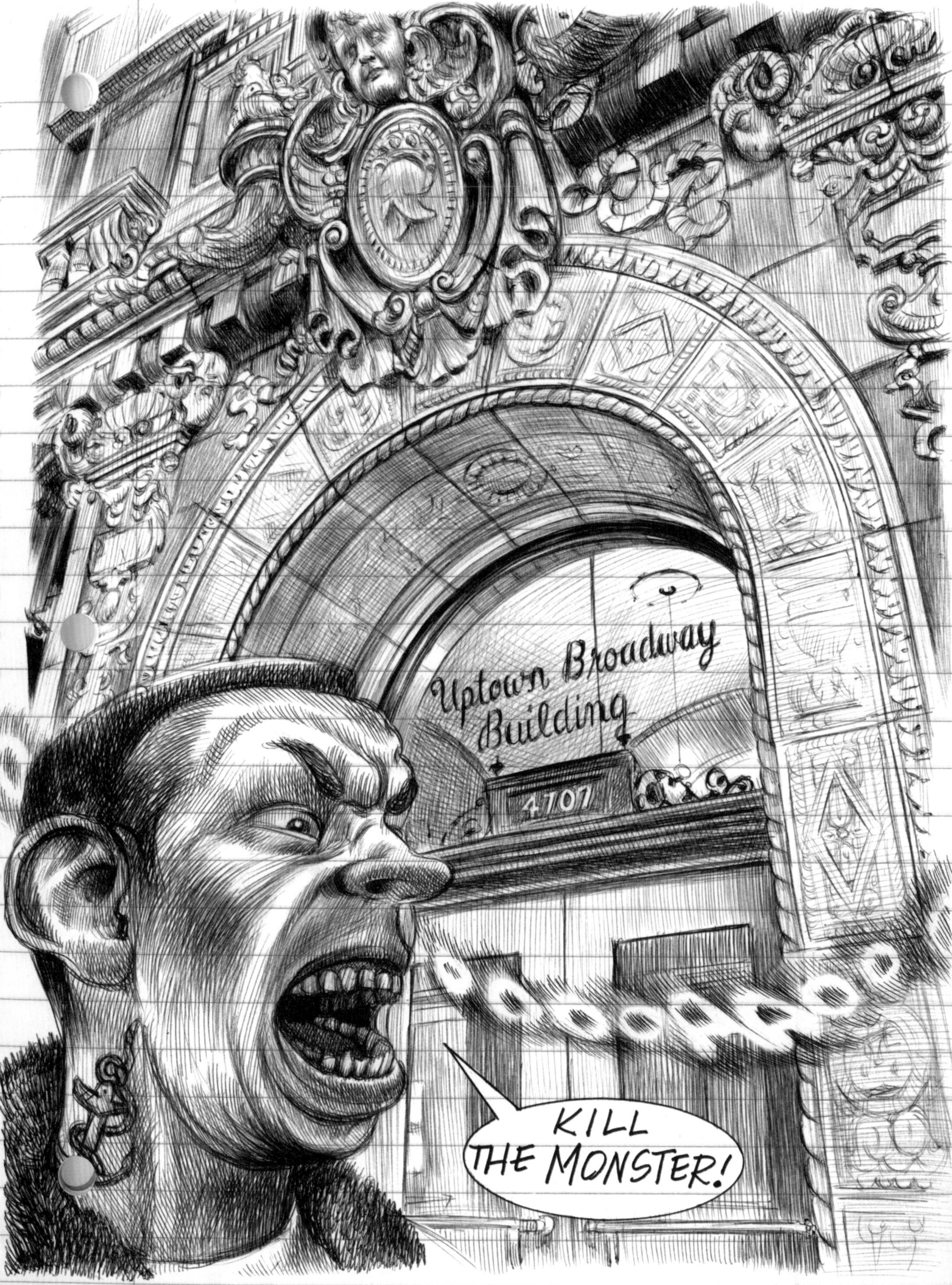
Uptown Broadway Building
4707
KILL THE MONSTER!

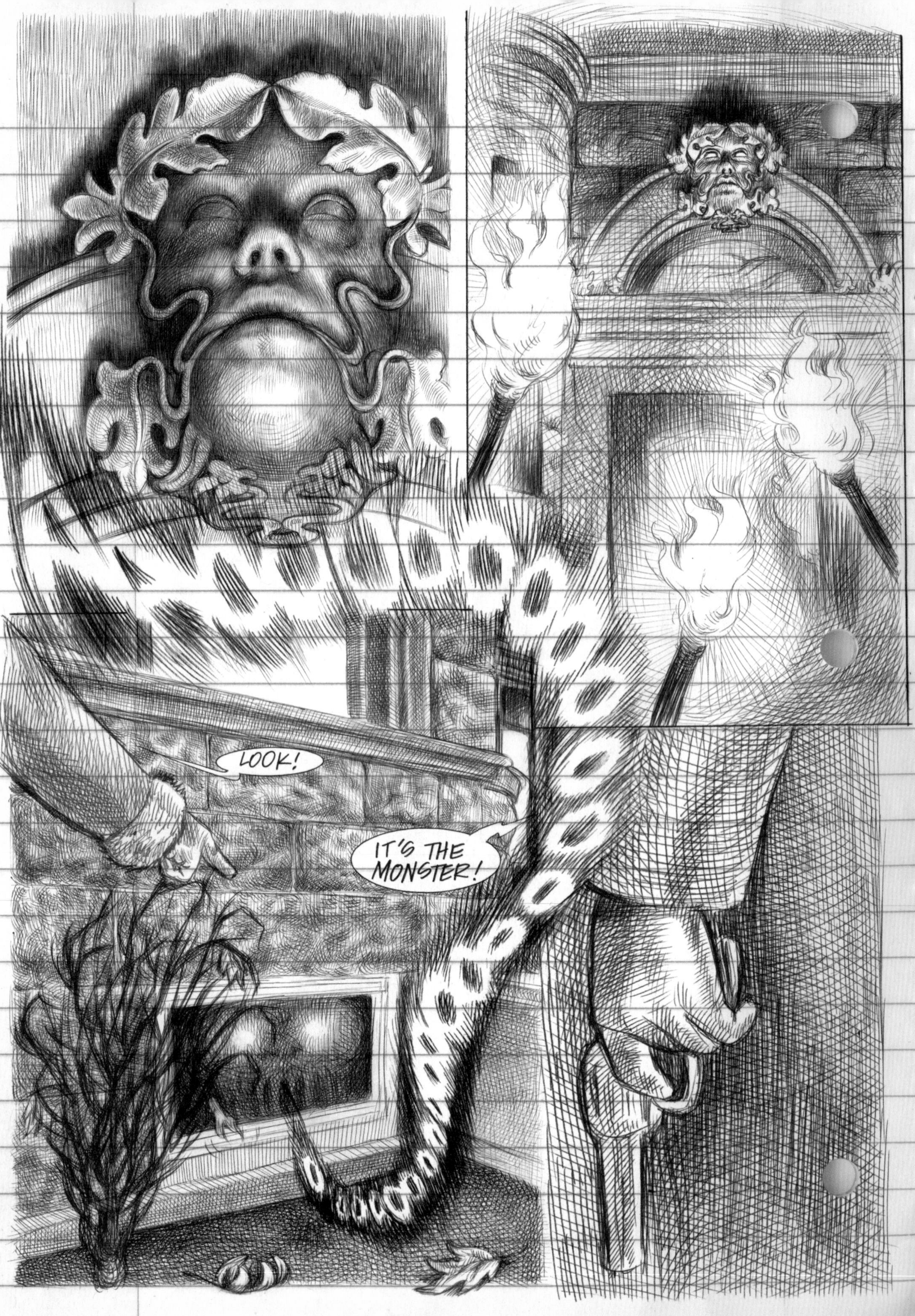
LOOK!
IT'S THE MONSTER!

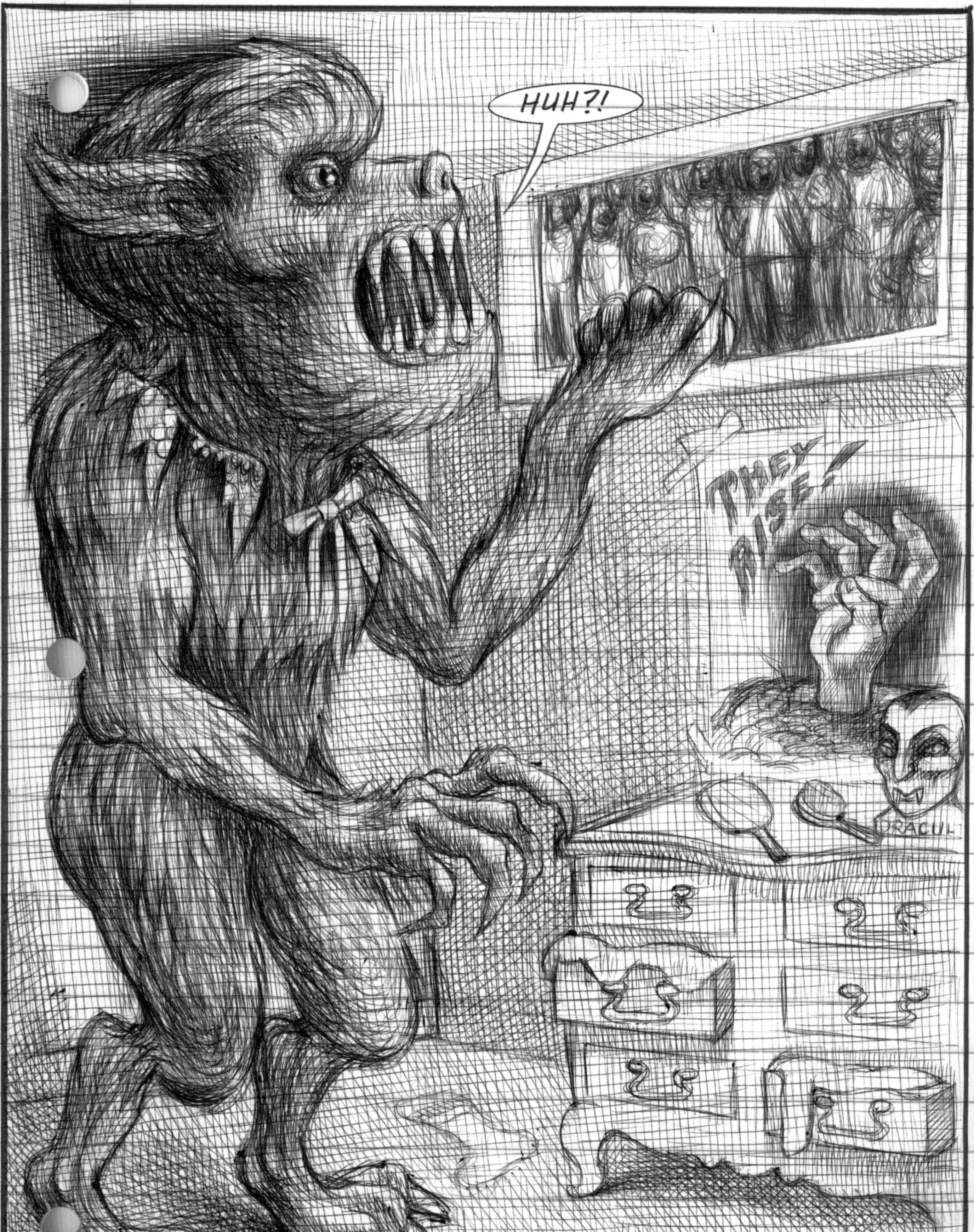
HUH?!
THEY RISE!!
DRACUL

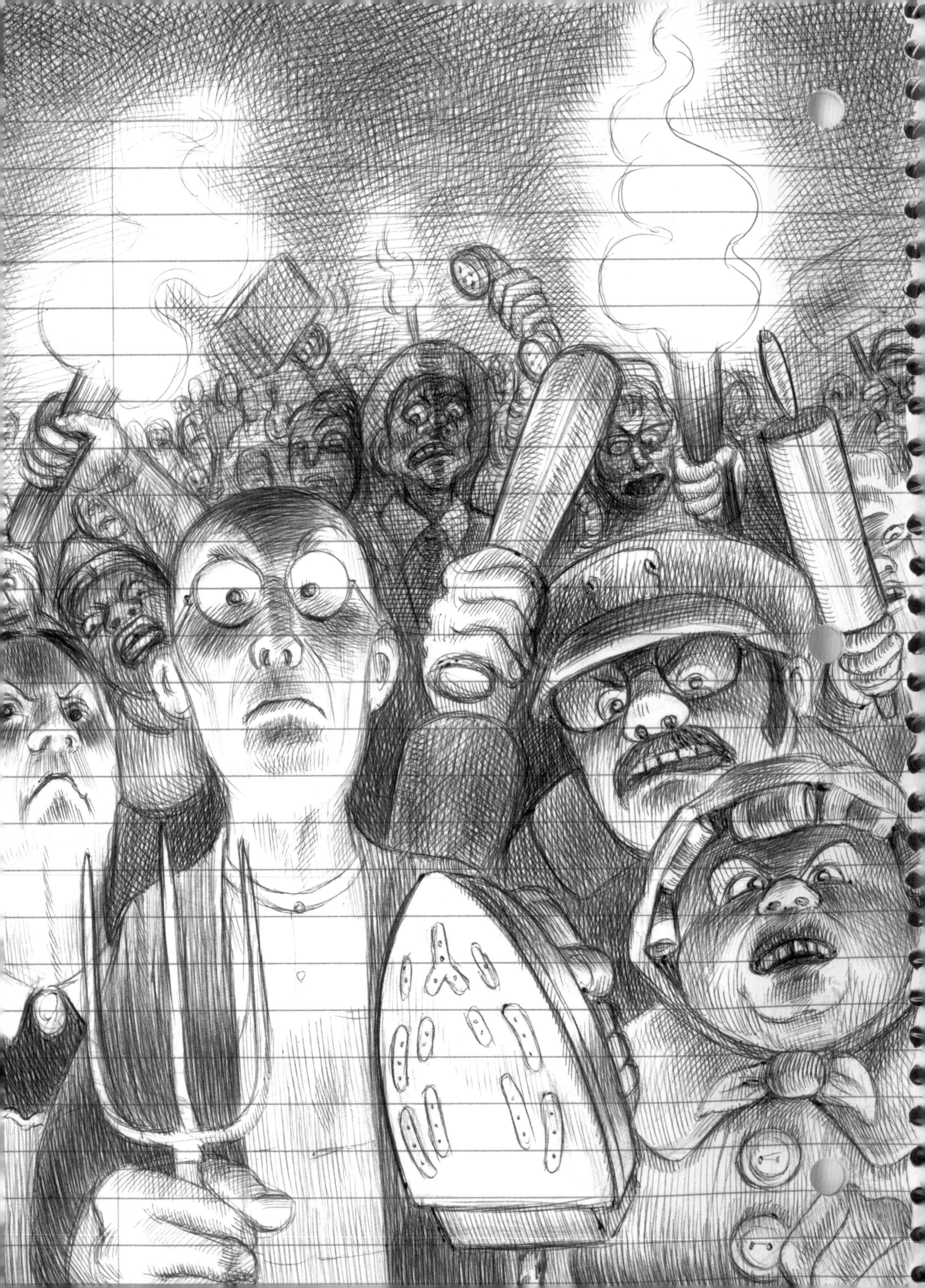

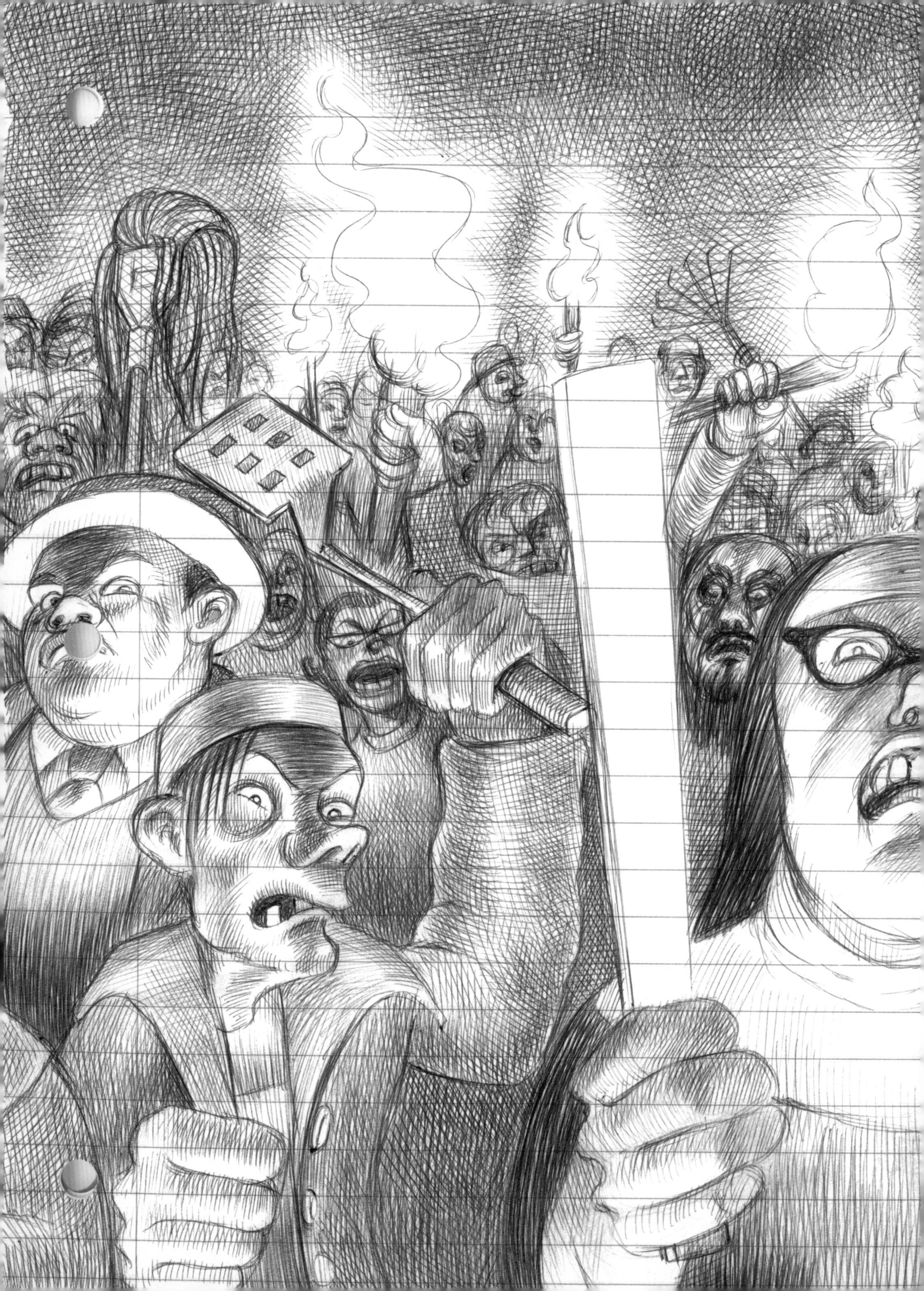

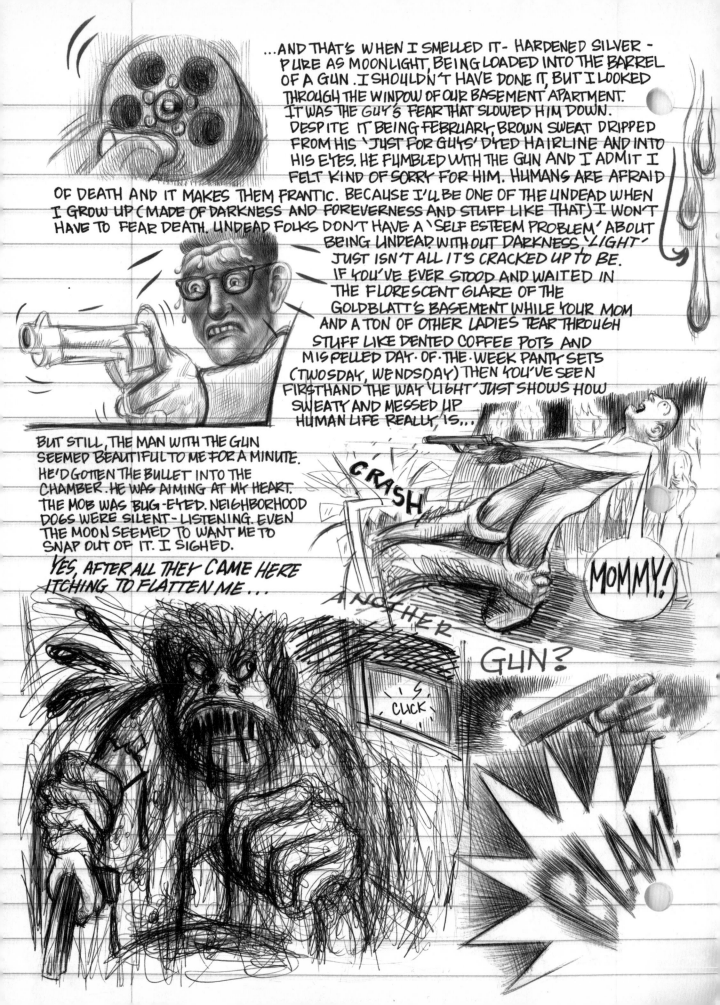

...AND THAT'S WHEN I SMELLED IT- HARDENED SILVER - PURE AS MOONLIGHT, BEING LOADED INTO THE BARREL OF A GUN. I SHOULDN'T HAVE DONE IT, BUT I LOOKED THROUGH THE WINDOW OF OUR BASEMENT APARTMENT. IT WAS THE GUY'S FEAR THAT SLOWED HIM DOWN. DESPITE IT BEING FEBRUARY, BROWN SWEAT DRIPPED FROM HIS 'JUST FOR GUYS' D'YED HAIRLINE AND INTO HIS EYES. HE FUMBLED WITH THE GUN AND I ADMIT I FELT KIND OF SORRY FOR HIM. HUMANS ARE AFRAID OF DEATH AND IT MAKES THEM FRANTIC. BECAUSE I'LL BE ONE OF THE UNDEAD WHEN I GROW UP (MADE OF DARKNESS AND FOREVERNESS AND STUFF LIKE THAT) I WON'T HAVE TO FEAR DEATH. UNDEAD FOLKS DON'T HAVE A 'SELF ESTEEM PROBLEM' ABOUT BEING UNDEAD. WITHOUT DARKNESS 'LIGHT' JUST ISN'T ALL IT'S CRACKED UP TO BE. IF YOU'VE EVER STOOD AND WAITED IN THE FLORESCENT GLARE OF THE GOLDBLATT'S BASEMENT WHILE YOUR MOM AND A TON OF OTHER LADIES TEAR THROUGH STUFF LIKE DENTED COFFEE POTS AND MISPELLED DAY·OF·THE·WEEK PANTY SETS (TWOSDAY, WENDSDAY) THEN YOU'VE SEEN FIRSTHAND THE WAY 'LIGHT' JUST SHOWS HOW SWEATY AND MESSED UP HUMAN LIFE REALLY IS...

BUT STILL, THE MAN WITH THE GUN SEEMED BEAUTIFUL TO ME FOR A MINUTE. HE'D GOTTEN THE BULLET INTO THE CHAMBER. HE WAS AIMING AT MY HEART. THE MOB WAS BUG-EYED. NEIGHBORHOOD DOGS WERE SILENT - LISTENING. EVEN THE MOON SEEMED TO WANT ME TO SNAP OUT OF IT. I SIGHED.

YES, AFTER ALL THEY CAME HERE ITCHING TO FLATTEN ME...

CRASH

MOMMY!

ANOTHER GUN?

·CLICK·

BLAM!

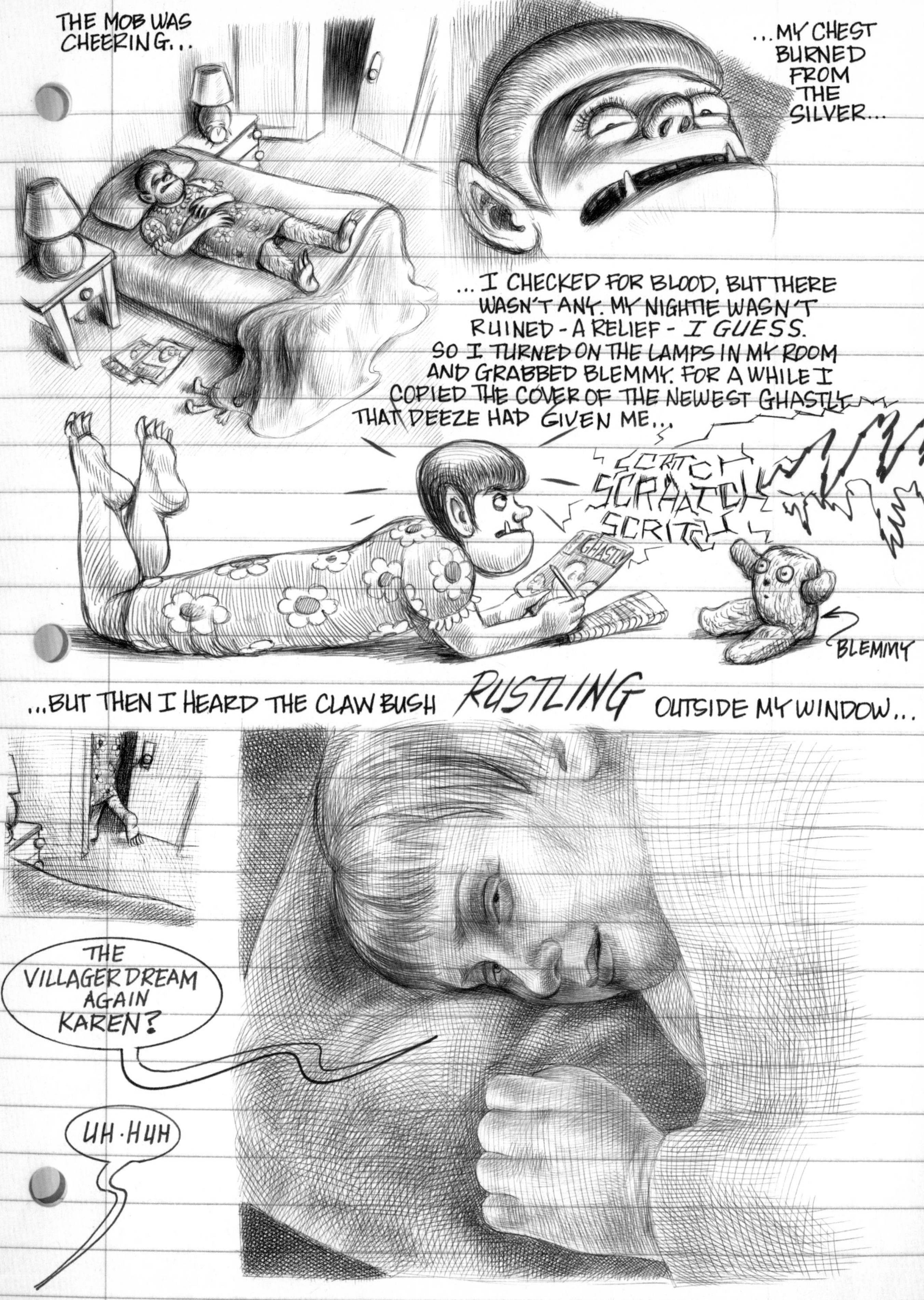
THE MOB WAS CHEERING...
...MY CHEST BURNED FROM THE SILVER...
...I CHECKED FOR BLOOD, BUT THERE WASN'T ANY. MY NIGHTIE WASN'T RUINED - A RELIEF - I GUESS. SO I TURNED ON THE LAMPS IN MY ROOM AND GRABBED BLEMMY. FOR A WHILE I COPIED THE COVER OF THE NEWEST GHASTLY THAT DEEZE HAD GIVEN ME...
SCRITCH
SCRAATCH
SCRITCH
GHASTLY
BLEMMY
...BUT THEN I HEARD THE CLAW BUSH RUSTLING OUTSIDE MY WINDOW...
THE VILLAGER DREAM AGAIN KAREN?
UH-HUH

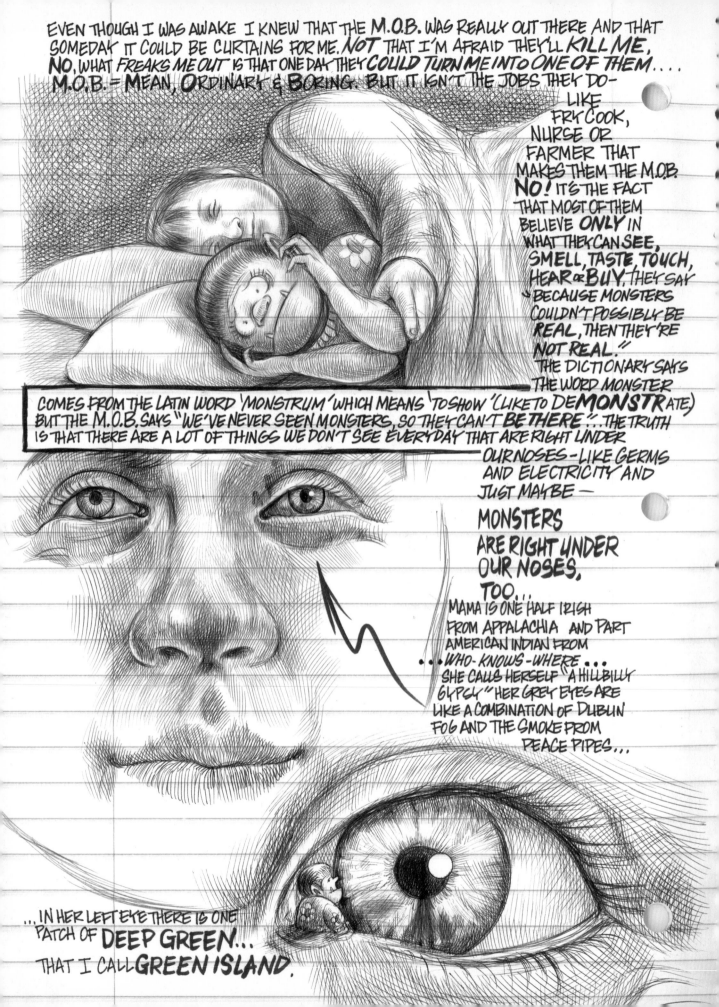

EVEN THOUGH I WAS AWAKE I KNEW THAT THE M.O.B. WAS REALLY OUT THERE AND THAT SOMEDAY IT COULD BE CURTAINS FOR ME. *NOT* THAT I'M AFRAID THEY'LL *KILL ME*, NO, WHAT *FREAKS ME OUT* IS THAT ONE DAY THEY *COULD TURN ME INTO ONE OF THEM....* M.O.B. = **M**EAN, **O**RDINARY & **B**ORING. BUT IT ISN'T THE JOBS THEY DO —

LIKE FRY COOK, NURSE OR FARMER THAT MAKES THEM THE M.O.B. **NO!** IT'S THE FACT THAT MOST OF THEM BELIEVE **ONLY** IN WHAT THEY CAN SEE, SMELL, TASTE, TOUCH, HEAR OR **BUY**, THEY SAY "BECAUSE MONSTERS COULDN'T POSSIBLY BE REAL, THEN THEY'RE NOT REAL."

THE DICTIONARY SAYS THE WORD MONSTER COMES FROM THE LATIN WORD 'MONSTRUM' WHICH MEANS 'TO SHOW' (LIKE TO DE**MONSTR**ATE) BUT THE M.O.B. SAYS "WE'VE NEVER SEEN MONSTERS, SO THEY CAN'T *BE THERE*"...THE TRUTH IS THAT THERE ARE A LOT OF THINGS WE DON'T SEE EVERYDAY THAT ARE RIGHT UNDER OUR NOSES — LIKE GERMS AND ELECTRICITY AND JUST MAYBE —

MONSTERS ARE RIGHT UNDER OUR NOSES, TOO...

MAMA IS ONE HALF IRISH FROM APPALACHIA AND PART AMERICAN INDIAN FROM ...WHO- KNOWS -WHERE ... SHE CALLS HERSELF "A HILLBILLY GYPSY" HER GREY EYES ARE LIKE A COMBINATION OF DUBLIN FOG AND THE SMOKE FROM PEACE PIPES...

...IN HER LEFT EYE THERE IS ONE PATCH OF **DEEP GREEN**... THAT I CALL **GREEN ISLAND**.

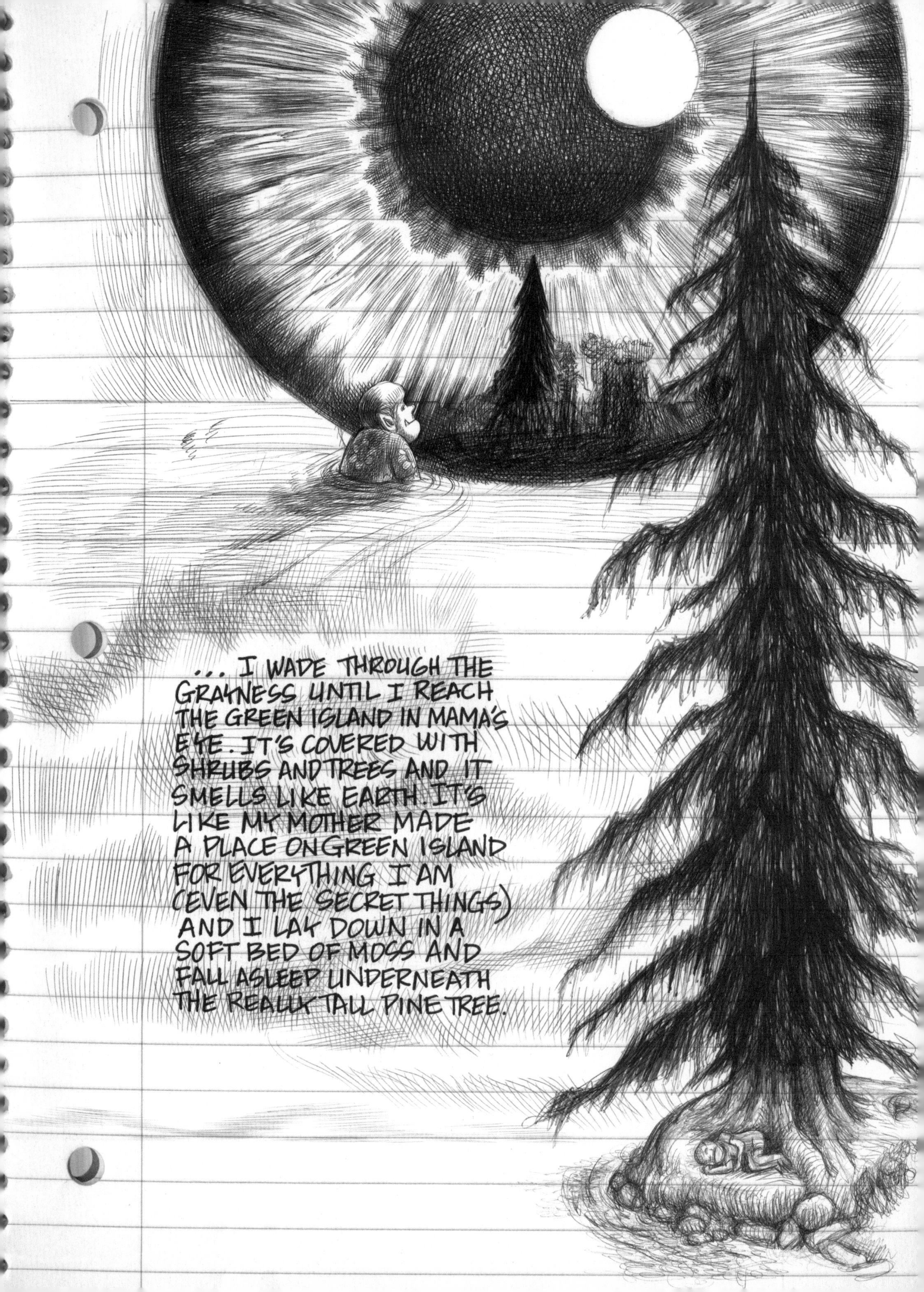
... I WADE THROUGH THE GRAYNESS UNTIL I REACH THE GREEN ISLAND IN MAMA'S EYE. IT'S COVERED WITH SHRUBS AND TREES AND IT SMELLS LIKE EARTH. IT'S LIKE MY MOTHER MADE A PLACE ON GREEN ISLAND FOR EVERYTHING I AM (EVEN THE SECRET THINGS) AND I LAY DOWN IN A SOFT BED OF MOSS AND FALL ASLEEP UNDERNEATH THE REALLY TALL PINE TREE.

EVERY MONTH DEEZE BUYS ME COPIES OF DREAD, SPECTRAL AND GHASTLY.

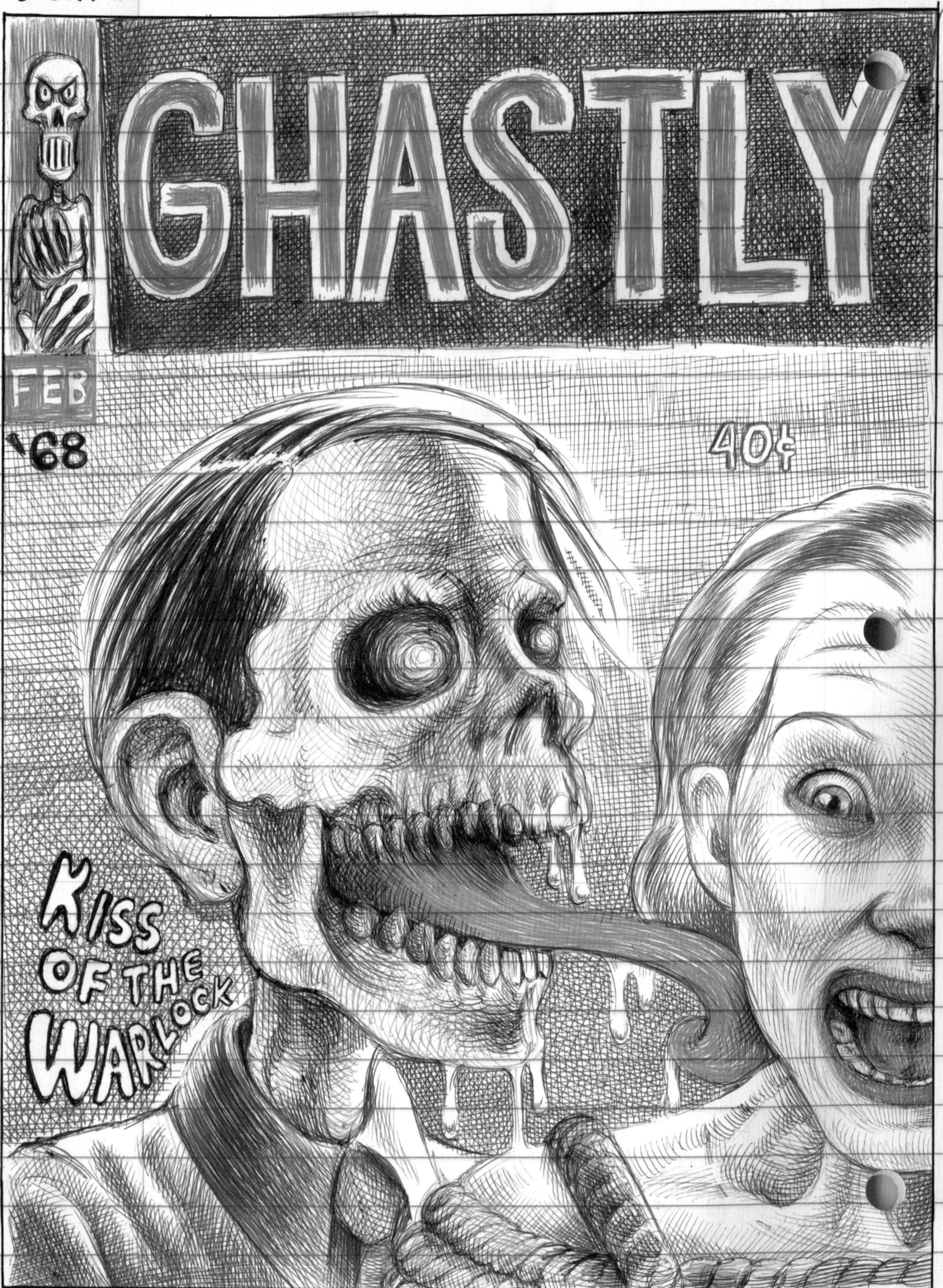
GHASTLY
FEB
'68
40¢
KISS OF THE WARLOCK

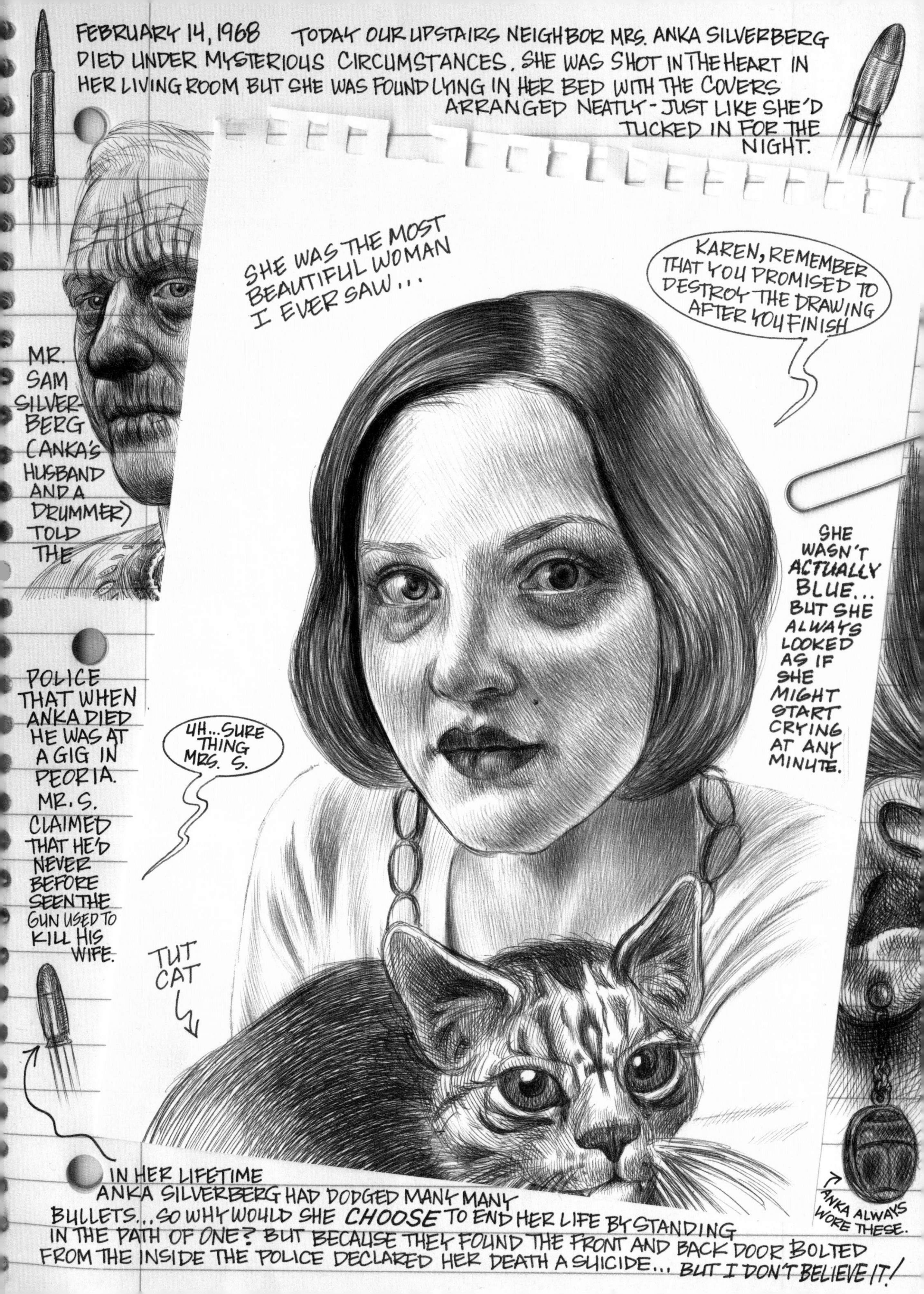
FEBRUARY 14, 1968 TODAY OUR UPSTAIRS NEIGHBOR MRS. ANKA SILVERBERG DIED UNDER MYSTERIOUS CIRCUMSTANCES. SHE WAS SHOT IN THE HEART IN HER LIVING ROOM BUT SHE WAS FOUND LYING IN HER BED WITH THE COVERS ARRANGED NEATLY - JUST LIKE SHE'D TUCKED IN FOR THE NIGHT.
MR. SAM SILVERBERG (ANKA'S HUSBAND AND A DRUMMER) TOLD THE POLICE THAT WHEN ANKA DIED HE WAS AT A GIG IN PEORIA. MR. S. CLAIMED THAT HE'D NEVER BEFORE SEEN THE GUN USED TO KILL HIS WIFE.
SHE WAS THE MOST BEAUTIFUL WOMAN I EVER SAW...
KAREN, REMEMBER THAT YOU PROMISED TO DESTROY THE DRAWING AFTER YOU FINISH
UH... SURE THING MRS. S.
SHE WASN'T ACTUALLY BLUE... BUT SHE ALWAYS LOOKED AS IF SHE MIGHT START CRYING AT ANY MINUTE.
TUT CAT
IN HER LIFETIME ANKA SILVERBERG HAD DODGED MANY MANY BULLETS... SO WHY WOULD SHE CHOOSE TO END HER LIFE BY STANDING IN THE PATH OF ONE? BUT BECAUSE THEY FOUND THE FRONT AND BACK DOOR BOLTED FROM THE INSIDE THE POLICE DECLARED HER DEATH A SUICIDE... BUT I DON'T BELIEVE IT!
ANKA ALWAYS WORE THESE.

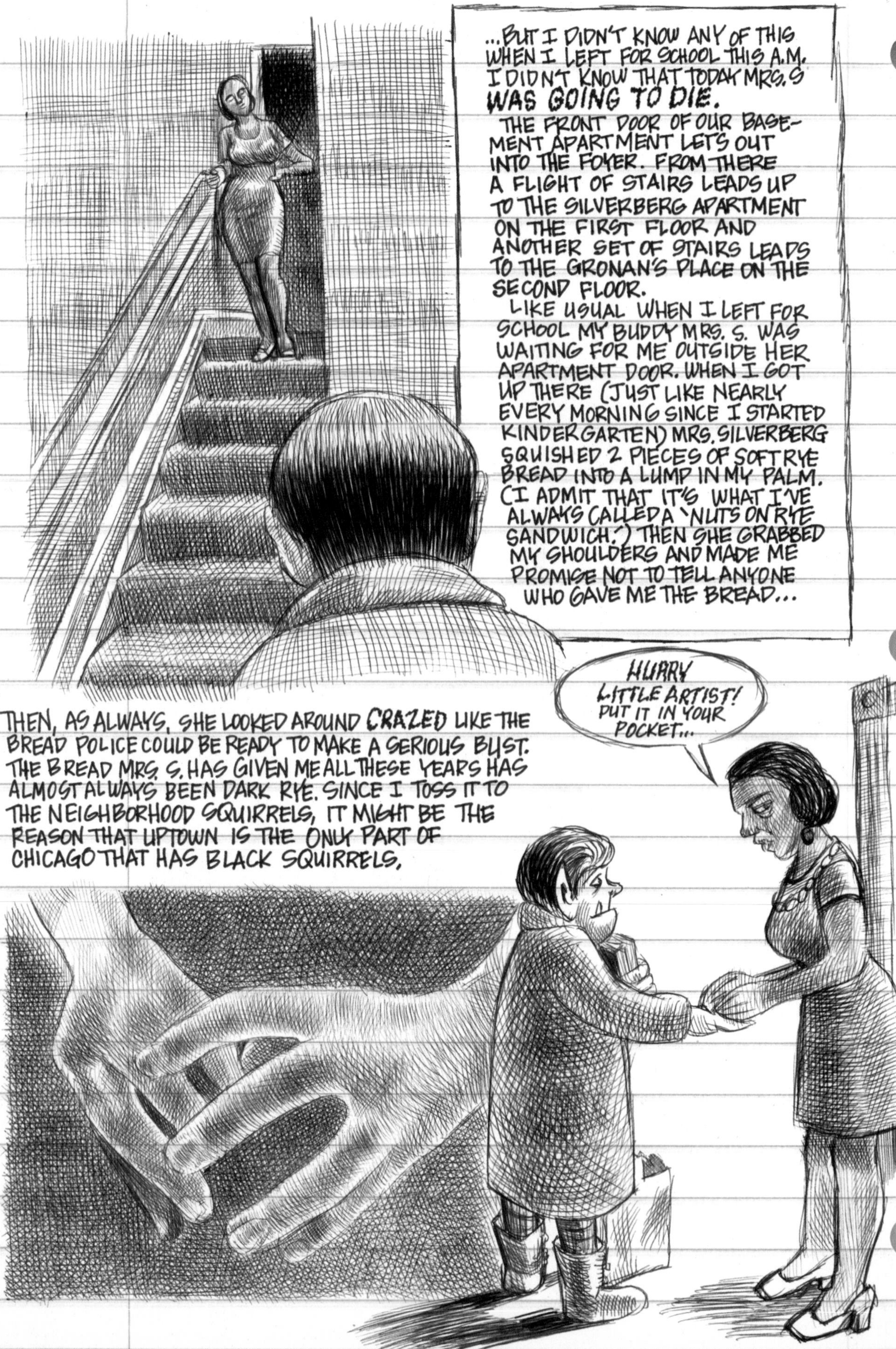
...BUT I DIDN'T KNOW ANY OF THIS WHEN I LEFT FOR SCHOOL THIS A.M. I DIDN'T KNOW THAT TODAY MRS. S WAS GOING TO DIE.
THE FRONT DOOR OF OUR BASEMENT APARTMENT LETS OUT INTO THE FOYER. FROM THERE A FLIGHT OF STAIRS LEADS UP TO THE SILVERBERG APARTMENT ON THE FIRST FLOOR AND ANOTHER SET OF STAIRS LEADS TO THE GRONAN'S PLACE ON THE SECOND FLOOR.
LIKE USUAL WHEN I LEFT FOR SCHOOL MY BUDDY MRS. S. WAS WAITING FOR ME OUTSIDE HER APARTMENT DOOR. WHEN I GOT UP THERE (JUST LIKE NEARLY EVERY MORNING SINCE I STARTED KINDERGARTEN) MRS. SILVERBERG SQUISHED 2 PIECES OF SOFT RYE BREAD INTO A LUMP IN MY PALM. (I ADMIT THAT IT'S WHAT I'VE ALWAYS CALLED A 'NUTS ON RYE SANDWICH.') THEN SHE GRABBED MY SHOULDERS AND MADE ME PROMISE NOT TO TELL ANYONE WHO GAVE ME THE BREAD...
THEN, AS ALWAYS, SHE LOOKED AROUND CRAZED LIKE THE BREAD POLICE COULD BE READY TO MAKE A SERIOUS BUST. THE BREAD MRS. S. HAS GIVEN ME ALL THESE YEARS HAS ALMOST ALWAYS BEEN DARK RYE. SINCE I TOSS IT TO THE NEIGHBORHOOD SQUIRRELS, IT MIGHT BE THE REASON THAT UPTOWN IS THE ONLY PART OF CHICAGO THAT HAS BLACK SQUIRRELS.
HURRY LITTLE ARTIST! PUT IT IN YOUR POCKET...

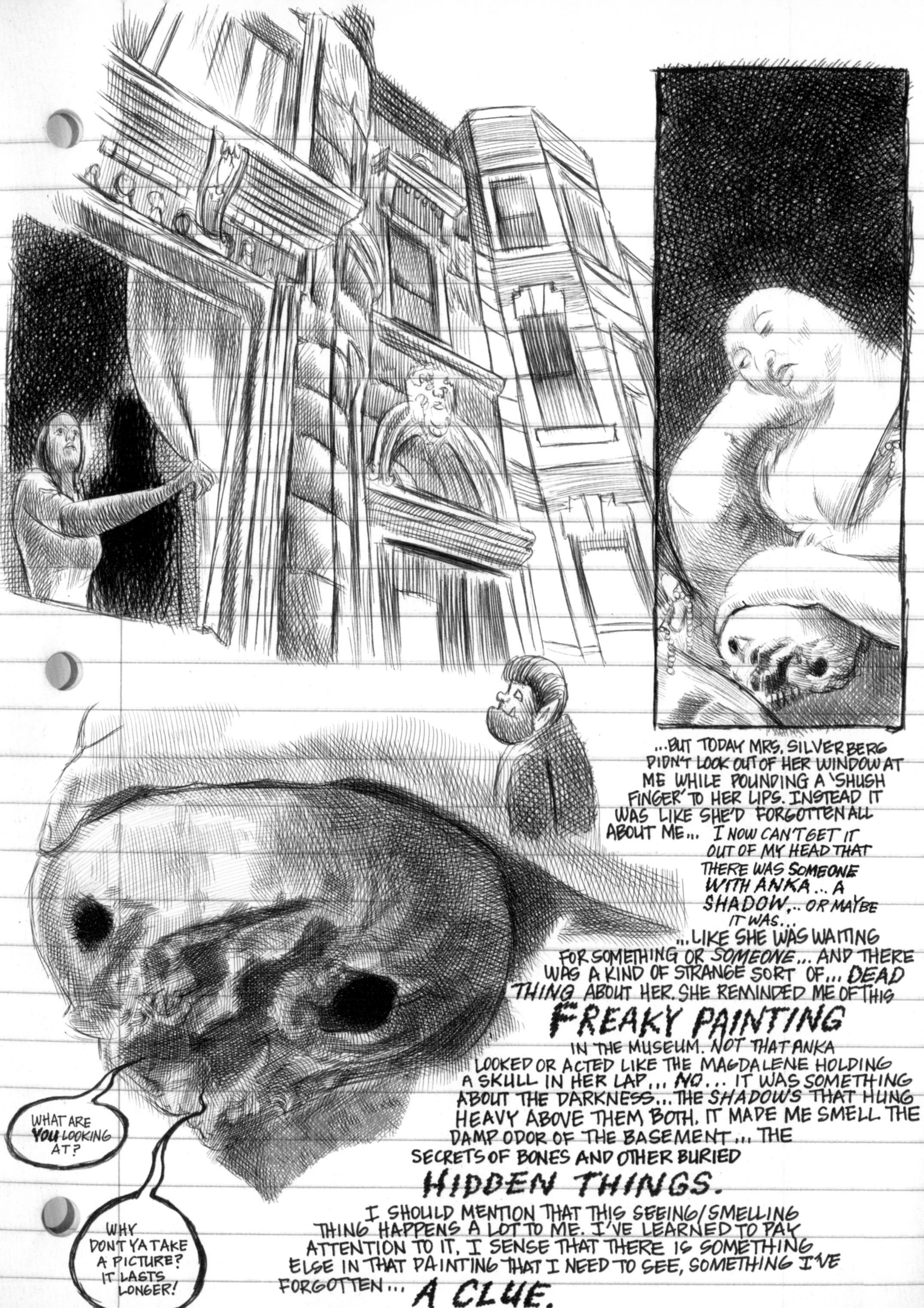
...BUT TODAY MRS. SILVERBERG DIDN'T LOOK OUT OF HER WINDOW AT ME WHILE POUNDING A 'SHUSH FINGER' TO HER LIPS. INSTEAD IT WAS LIKE SHE'D FORGOTTEN ALL ABOUT ME... I NOW CAN'T GET IT OUT OF MY HEAD THAT THERE WAS SOMEONE WITH ANKA... A SHADOW,... OR MAYBE IT WAS...
...LIKE SHE WAS WAITING FOR SOMETHING OR SOMEONE... AND THERE WAS A KIND OF STRANGE SORT OF... DEAD THING ABOUT HER. SHE REMINDED ME OF THIS
FREAKY PAINTING
IN THE MUSEUM. NOT THAT ANKA LOOKED OR ACTED LIKE THE MAGDALENE HOLDING A SKULL IN HER LAP... NO... IT WAS SOMETHING ABOUT THE DARKNESS... THE SHADOWS THAT HUNG HEAVY ABOVE THEM BOTH. IT MADE ME SMELL THE DAMP ODOR OF THE BASEMENT... THE SECRETS OF BONES AND OTHER BURIED
HIDDEN THINGS.
WHAT ARE YOU LOOKING AT?
WHY DON'T YA TAKE A PICTURE? IT LASTS LONGER!
I SHOULD MENTION THAT THIS SEEING/SMELLING THING HAPPENS A LOT TO ME. I'VE LEARNED TO PAY ATTENTION TO IT. I SENSE THAT THERE IS SOMETHING ELSE IN THAT PAINTING THAT I NEED TO SEE, SOMETHING I'VE FORGOTTEN... A CLUE.

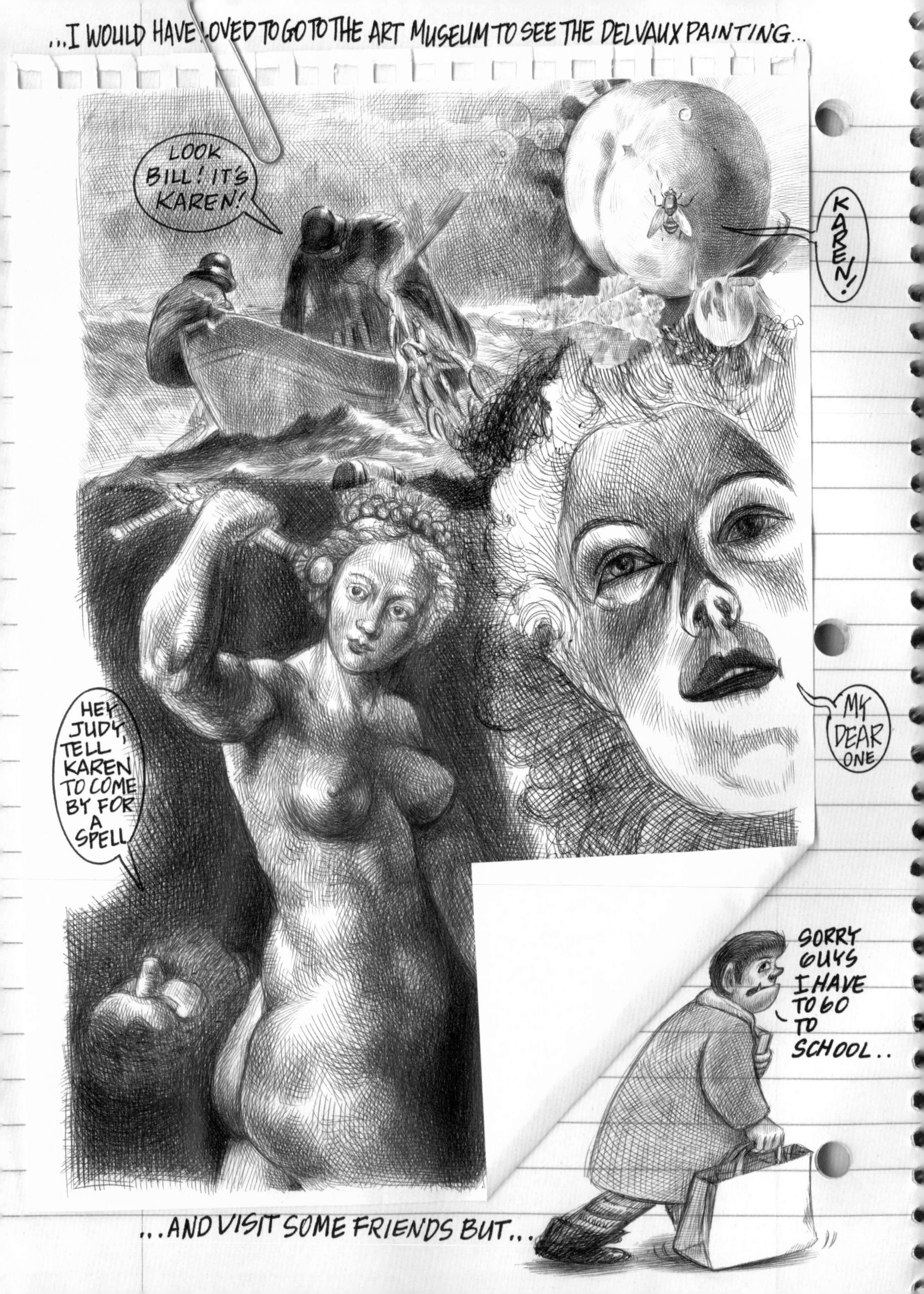
...I WOULD HAVE LOVED TO GO TO THE ART MUSEUM TO SEE THE DELVAUX PAINTING...
LOOK BILL! IT'S KAREN!
KAREN!
HEY JUDY, TELL KAREN TO COME BY FOR A SPELL
MY DEAR ONE
SORRY GUYS I HAVE TO GO TO SCHOOL..
...AND VISIT SOME FRIENDS BUT...

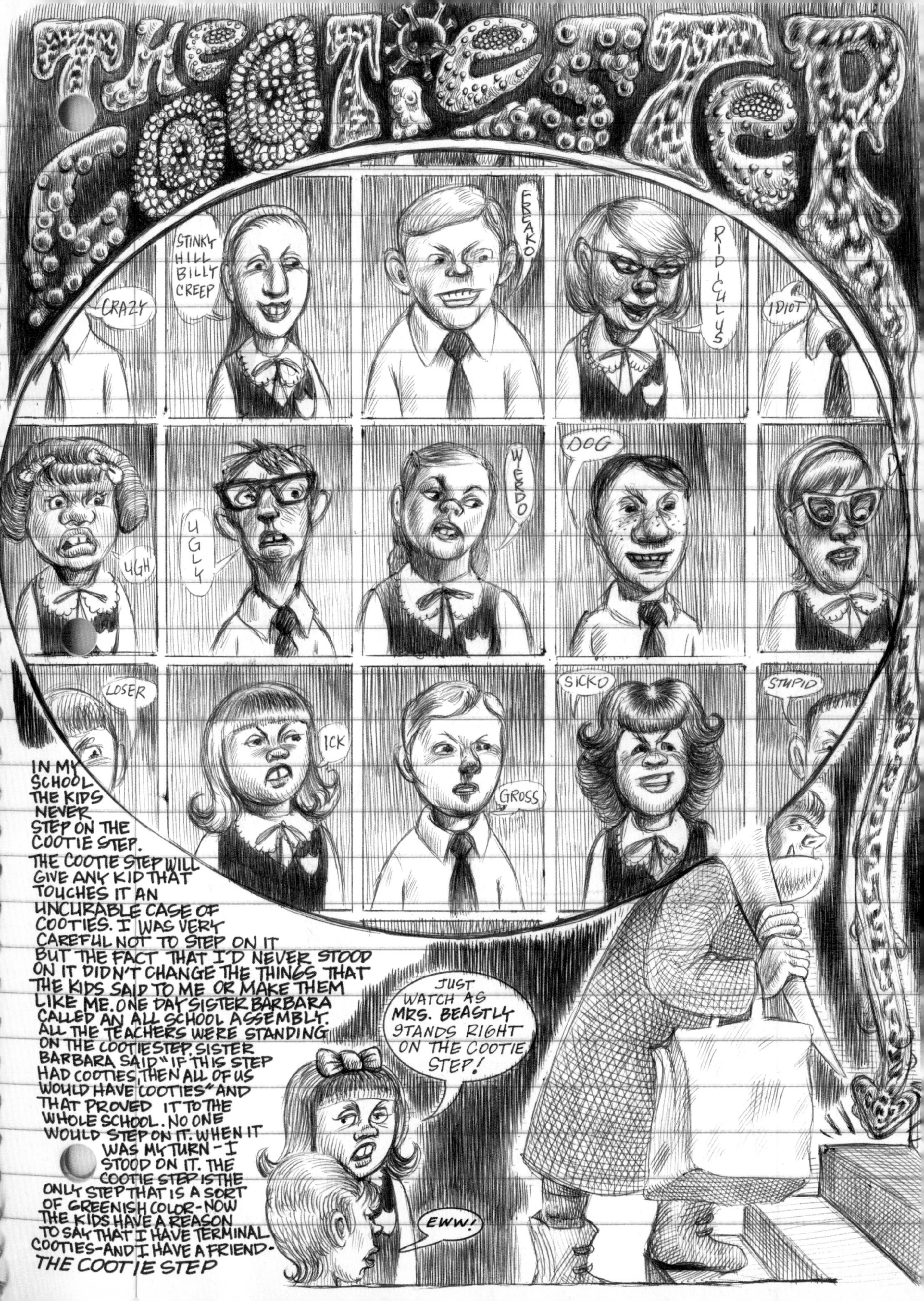
THE COOTIE STEP
CRAZY
STINKY HILL BILLY CREEP
FREAKO
RIDICULUS
IDIOT
UGH
UGLY
WIERDO
DOG
LOSER
ICK
GROSS
SICKO
STUPID
IN MY SCHOOL THE KIDS NEVER STEP ON THE COOTIE STEP. THE COOTIE STEP WILL GIVE ANY KID THAT TOUCHES IT AN UNCURABLE CASE OF COOTIES. I WAS VERY CAREFUL NOT TO STEP ON IT BUT THE FACT THAT I'D NEVER STOOD ON IT DIDN'T CHANGE THE THINGS THAT THE KIDS SAID TO ME OR MAKE THEM LIKE ME. ONE DAY SISTER BARBARA CALLED AN ALL SCHOOL ASSEMBLY. ALL THE TEACHERS WERE STANDING ON THE COOTIE STEP. SISTER BARBARA SAID "IF THIS STEP HAD COOTIES, THEN ALL OF US WOULD HAVE COOTIES" AND THAT PROVED IT TO THE WHOLE SCHOOL. NO ONE WOULD STEP ON IT. WHEN IT WAS MY TURN - I STOOD ON IT. THE COOTIE STEP IS THE ONLY STEP THAT IS A SORT OF GREENISH COLOR - NOW THE KIDS HAVE A REASON TO SAY THAT I HAVE TERMINAL COOTIES - AND I HAVE A FRIEND - THE COOTIE STEP
JUST WATCH AS MRS. BEASTLY STANDS RIGHT ON THE COOTIE STEP!
EWW!

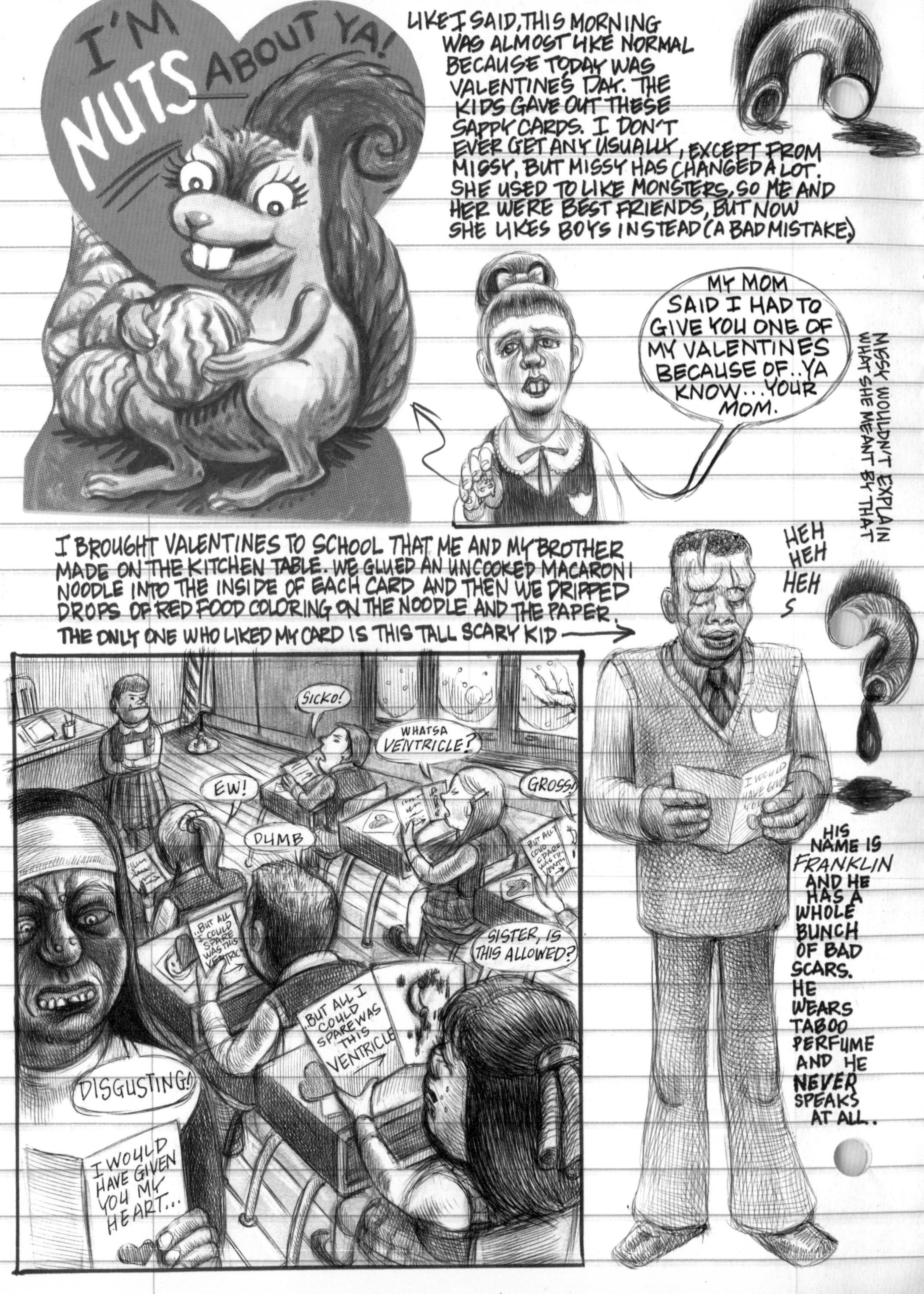
I'M NUTS ABOUT YA!
LIKE I SAID, THIS MORNING WAS ALMOST LIKE NORMAL BECAUSE TODAY WAS VALENTINE'S DAY. THE KIDS GAVE OUT THESE SAPPY CARDS. I DON'T EVER GET ANY USUALLY, EXCEPT FROM MISSY, BUT MISSY HAS CHANGED A LOT. SHE USED TO LIKE MONSTERS, SO ME AND HER WERE BEST FRIENDS, BUT NOW SHE LIKES BOYS INSTEAD (A BAD MISTAKE)
MY MOM SAID I HAD TO GIVE YOU ONE OF MY VALENTINES BECAUSE OF.. YA KNOW... YOUR MOM.
MISSY WOULDN'T EXPLAIN WHAT SHE MEANT BY THAT
I BROUGHT VALENTINES TO SCHOOL THAT ME AND MY BROTHER MADE ON THE KITCHEN TABLE. WE GLUED AN UNCOOKED MACARONI NOODLE INTO THE INSIDE OF EACH CARD AND THEN WE DRIPPED DROPS OF RED FOOD COLORING ON THE NOODLE AND THE PAPER.
THE ONLY ONE WHO LIKED MY CARD IS THIS TALL SCARY KID
HEH HEH HEHS
SICKO!
WHATSA VENTRICLE?
EW!
GROSS!
DUMB
..BUT ALL I COULD SPARE WAS THIS VENTRIC
SISTER, IS THIS ALLOWED?
BUT ALL I COULD SPARE WAS THIS VENTRICLE
DISGUSTING!
I WOULD HAVE GIVEN YOU MY HEART...
HIS NAME IS FRANKLIN AND HE HAS A WHOLE BUNCH OF BAD SCARS. HE WEARS TABOO PERFUME AND HE NEVER SPEAKS AT ALL.

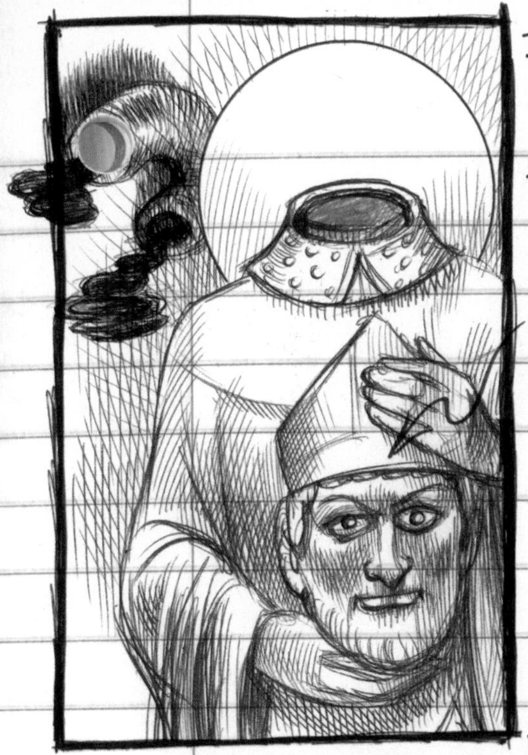

I GOT INTO TROUBLE BECAUSE MY CARDS "WERE TOO WEIRD AND TOO GORY" **OK.** TWO WEEKS AGO WE LEARNED ABOUT THE "*CEPHALOPHORE*" SAINTS LIKE St. DENIS **HERE** WHO CARRY THEIR OWN HEADS... IF YOU LOVE THE KIND OF STUFF I DO, BEING ***CATHOLIC*** IS THE WAY TO GO... *THAT IS*... IF YOU CAN OVERLOOK THE ***NUNS.*** THEY SAID MY CARDS DID NOT FIT THE **VALENTINE'S DAY** *TRADITION*... TRUTHFULLY I'VE NEVER GOTTEN INTO THIS HOLIDAY BECAUSE THERE ARE *NO* MONSTERS IN VALENTINE'S DAY. HALLOWEEN IS GROOVY... THE EASTER BUNNY IS A TERRIFYING MUTANT... St. PATRICK'S DAY HAS THAT SUPER CREEPY LITTLE LEPRECHAUN. EVEN CHRISTMAS HAS THOSE *ELVES* THAT, I GUESS ARE... *CREATURE-ISH* BUT ALL VALENTINE'S HAS IS THAT WINK-EYED NAKED BABY "CUPID" WITH HIS TEENY BOW AND ARROW... ***PATHETIC*** AND ALSO KIND OF 'CHESTER THE MOLESTER' *S.I.C.K.* (IF YOU ASK ME.) WHEN I CAME BACK FROM THE BATHROOM I FOUND A MYSTERY ON MY DESK - A HOME MADE VALENTINE'S CARD THAT SAYS "*KAREN, YOU ARE REALLY GHOUL,*" ON THE INSIDE. THERE'S NO NAME ON THE CARD... SO IT IS FROM A **SECRET ADMIRER!**

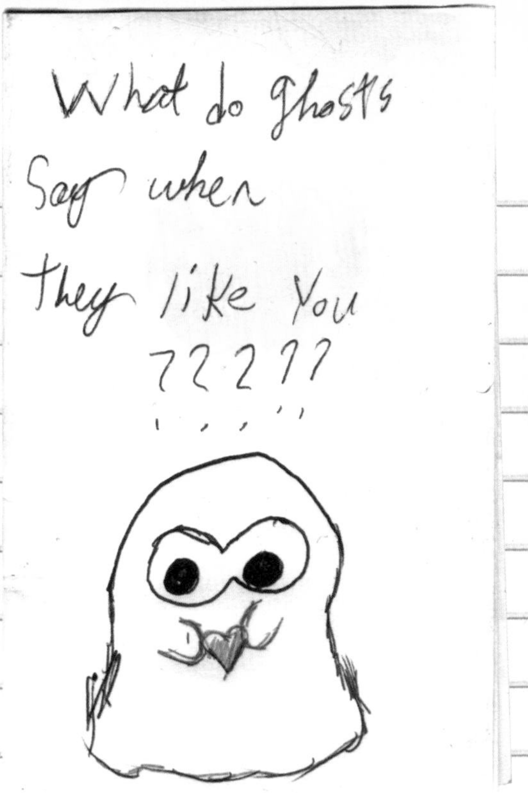
What do ghosts
say when
they like you
????

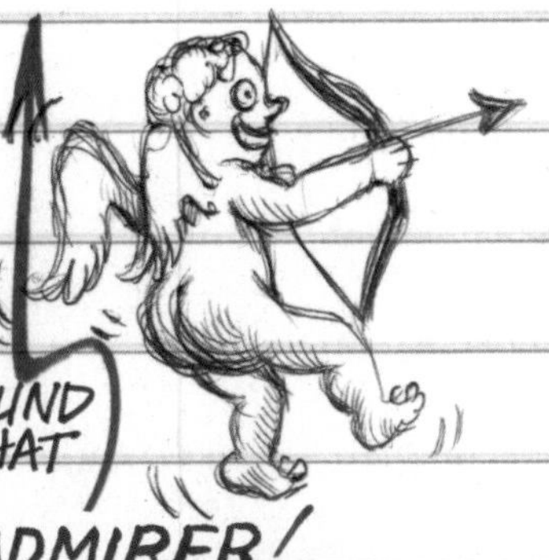

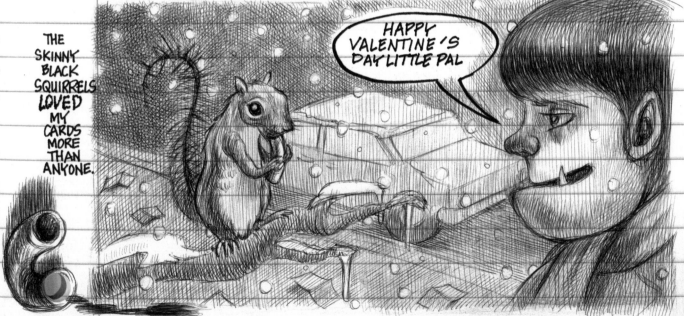

THE SKINNY BLACK SQUIRRELS ***LOVED*** MY CARDS MORE THAN ANYONE.

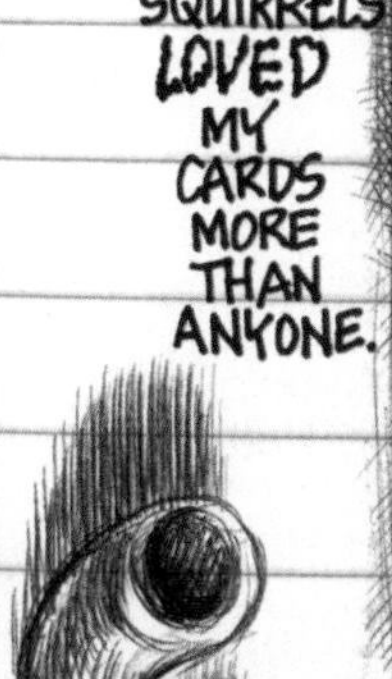

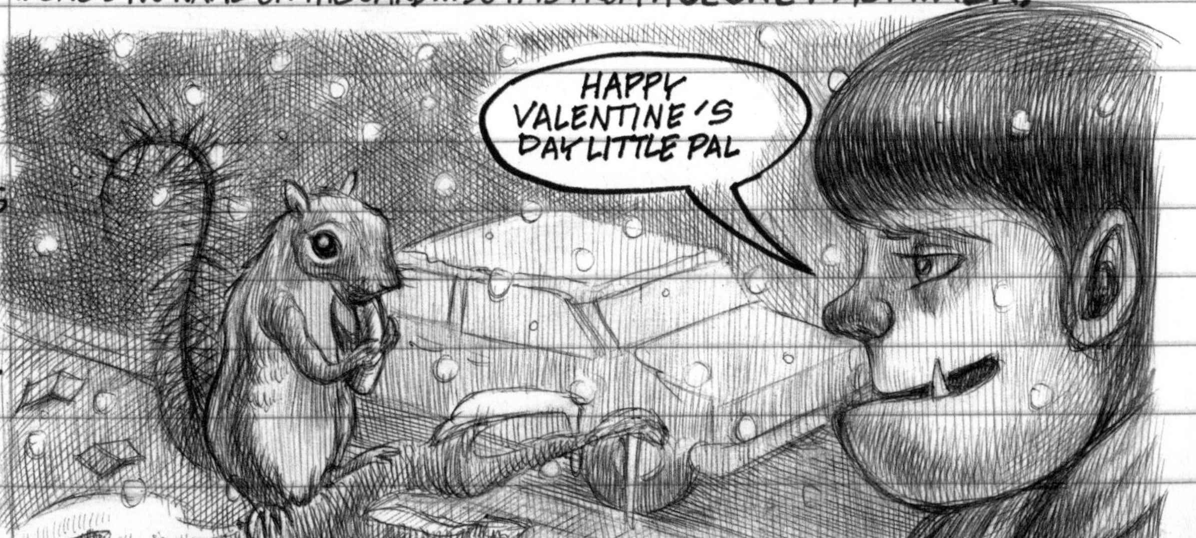
HAPPY VALENTINE'S DAY LITTLE PAL

DURING SCHOOL I RISKED GETTING MY NOTEBOOK CONFISCATED BY DRAWING SOME MONSTERS AND WHILE I WALKED HOME I THOUGHT ABOUT THE NEW ***COOLER,*** VALENTINE'S MASCOTS I COOKED UP...

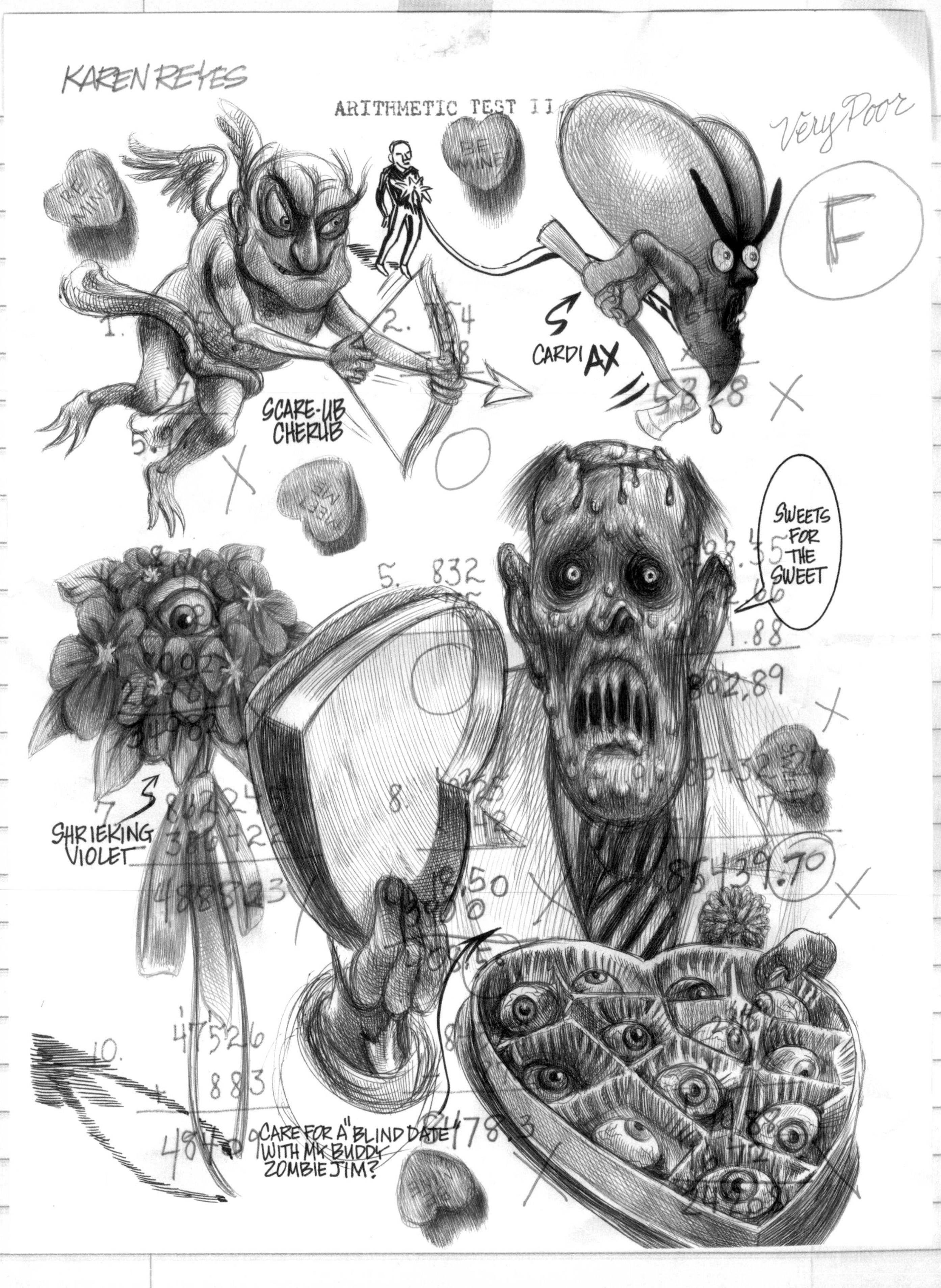
KAREN REYES
ARITHMETIC TEST II
Very Poor
F
BE MINE
CARDI AX
SCARE-UB CHERUB
SWEETS FOR THE SWEET
SHRIEKING VIOLET
CARE FOR A "BLIND DATE" WITH MY BUDDY ZOMBIE JIM?

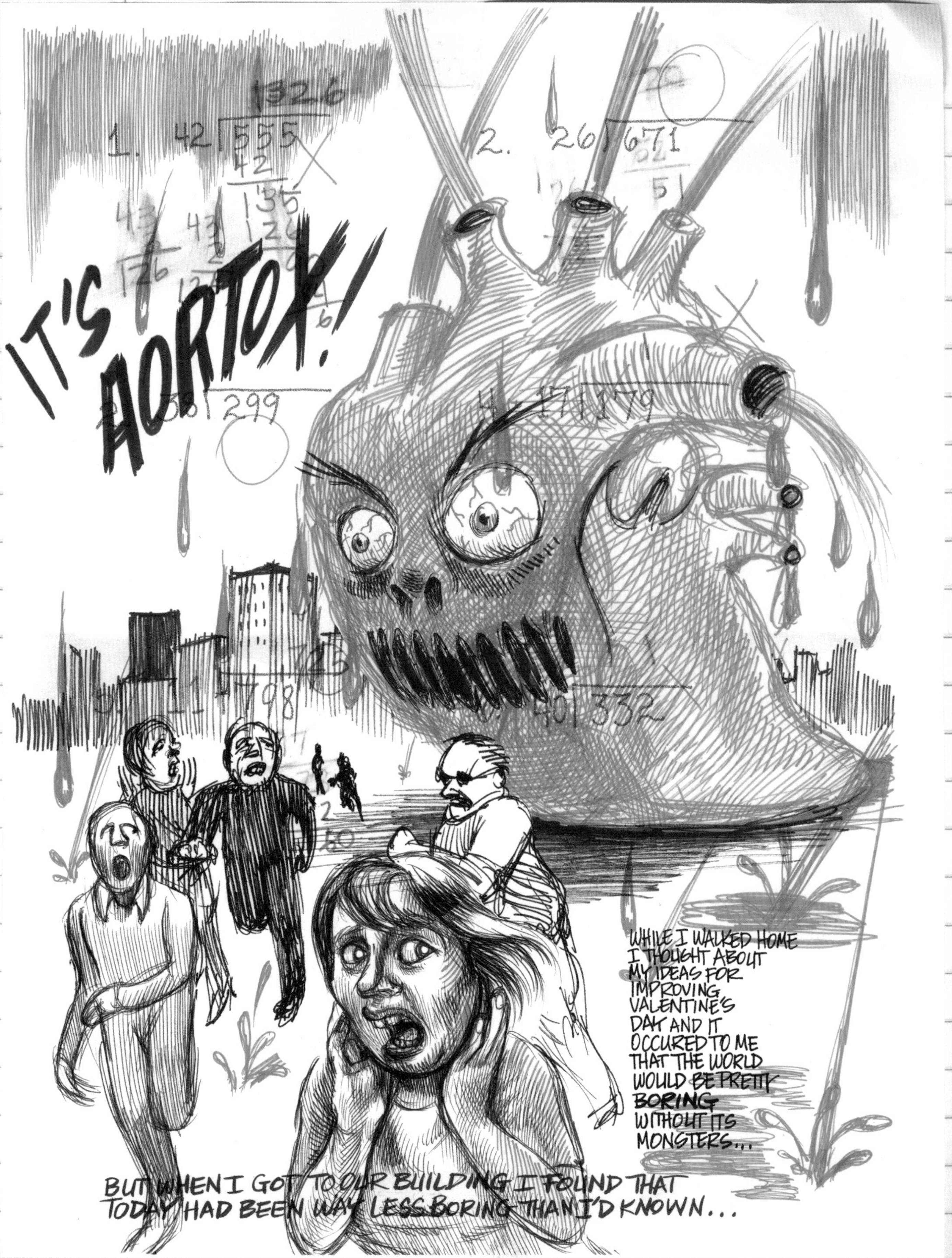
IT'S AORTOX!
WHILE I WALKED HOME I THOUGHT ABOUT MY IDEAS FOR IMPROVING VALENTINE'S DAY AND IT OCCURED TO ME THAT THE WORLD WOULD BE PRETTY BORING WITHOUT ITS MONSTERS...
BUT WHEN I GOT TO OUR BUILDING I FOUND THAT TODAY HAD BEEN WAY LESS BORING THAN I'D KNOWN...

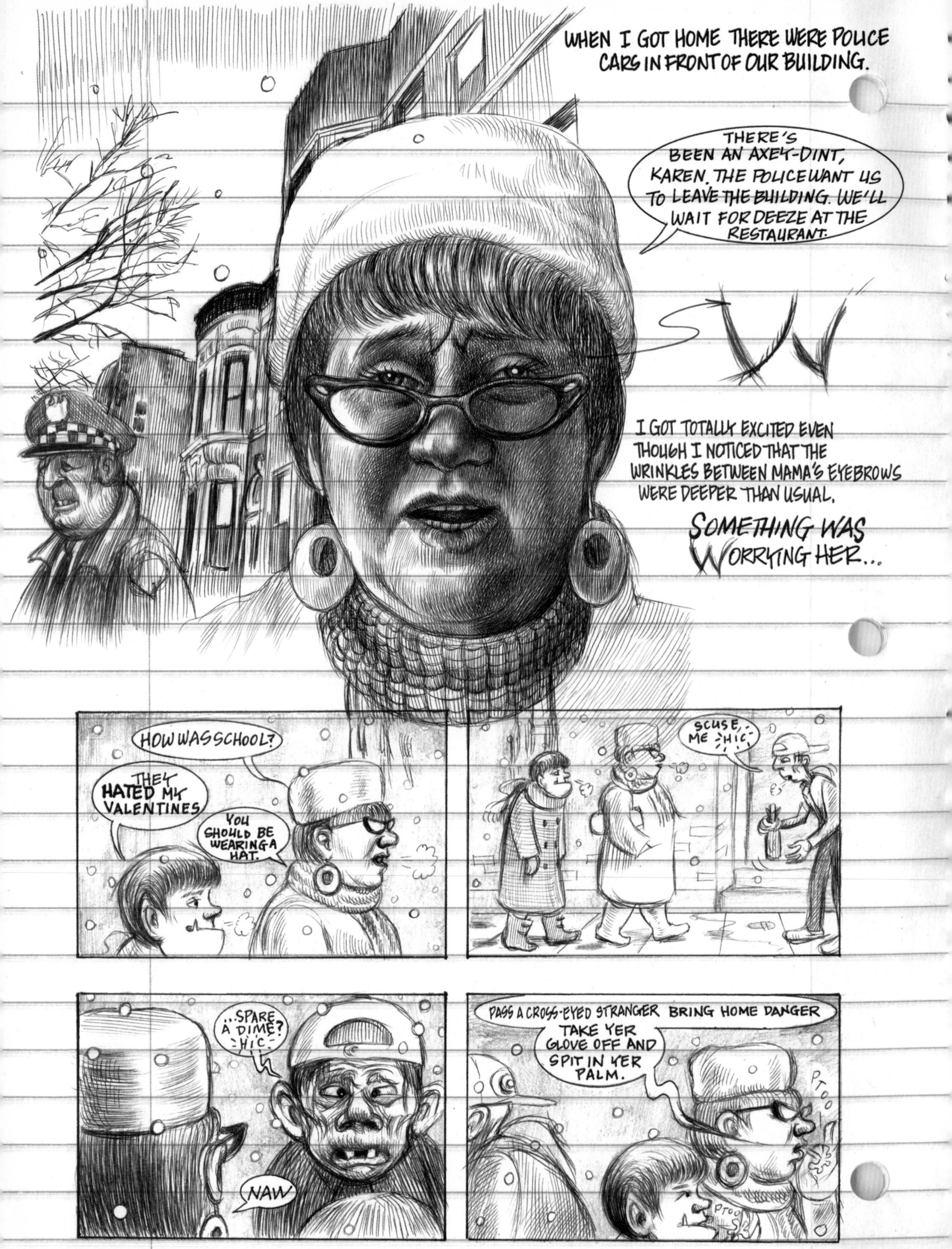
WHEN I GOT HOME THERE WERE POLICE CARS IN FRONT OF OUR BUILDING.
THERE'S BEEN AN AXEY-DINT, KAREN. THE POLICE WANT US TO LEAVE THE BUILDING. WE'LL WAIT FOR DEEZE AT THE RESTAURANT.
SW
I GOT TOTALLY EXCITED EVEN THOUGH I NOTICED THAT THE WRINKLES BETWEEN MAMA'S EYEBROWS WERE DEEPER THAN USUAL.
SOMETHING WAS WORRYING HER...
HOW WAS SCHOOL?
THEY HATED MY VALENTINES
YOU SHOULD BE WEARING A HAT.
SCUSE, ME HIC
...SPARE A DIME? HIC
NAW
PASS A CROSS-EYED STRANGER BRING HOME DANGER
TAKE YER GLOVE OFF AND SPIT IN YER PALM.
PTOO
PTOO

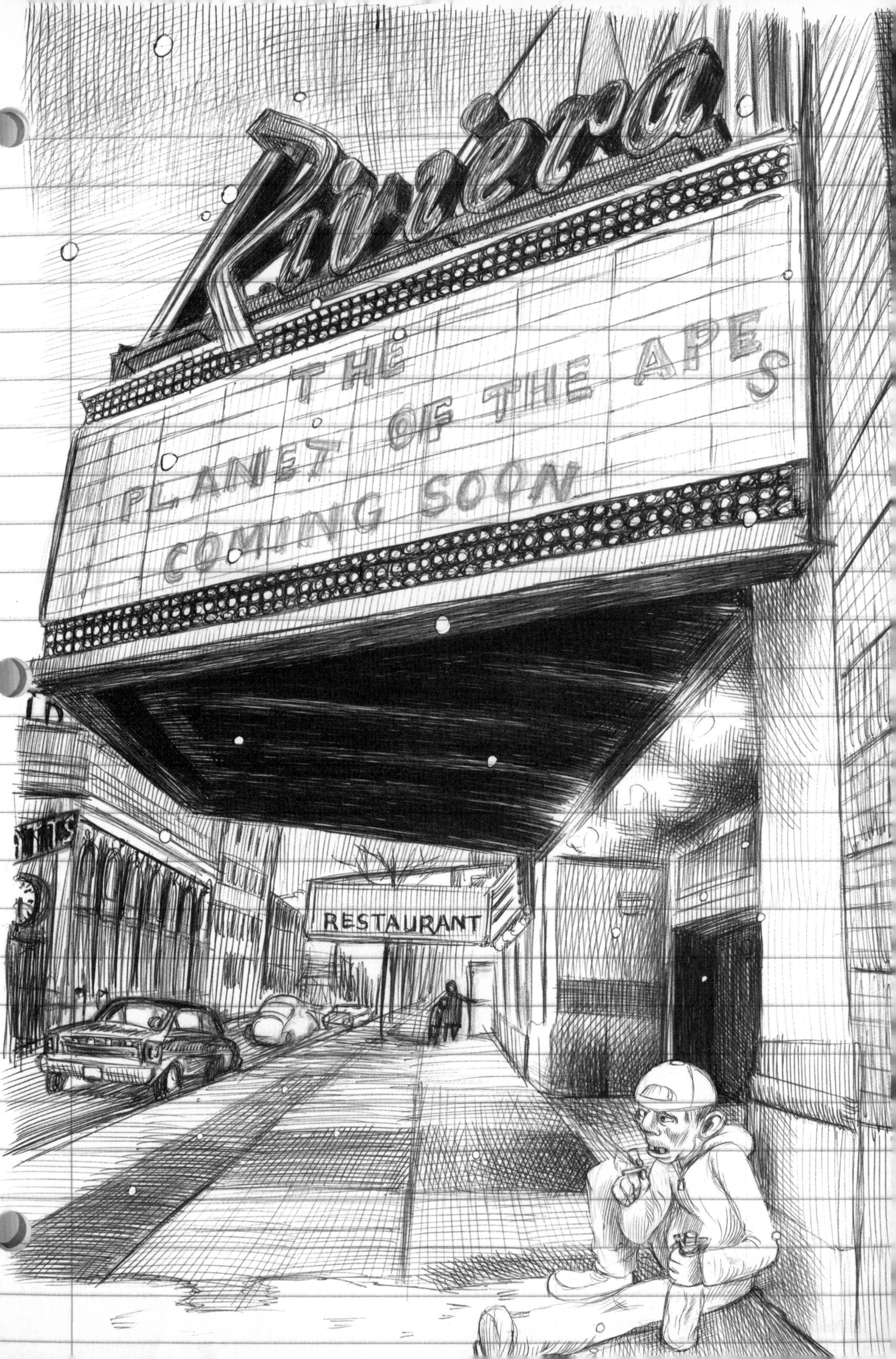
Riviera
THE
PLANET OF THE APES
COMING SOON
RESTAURANT

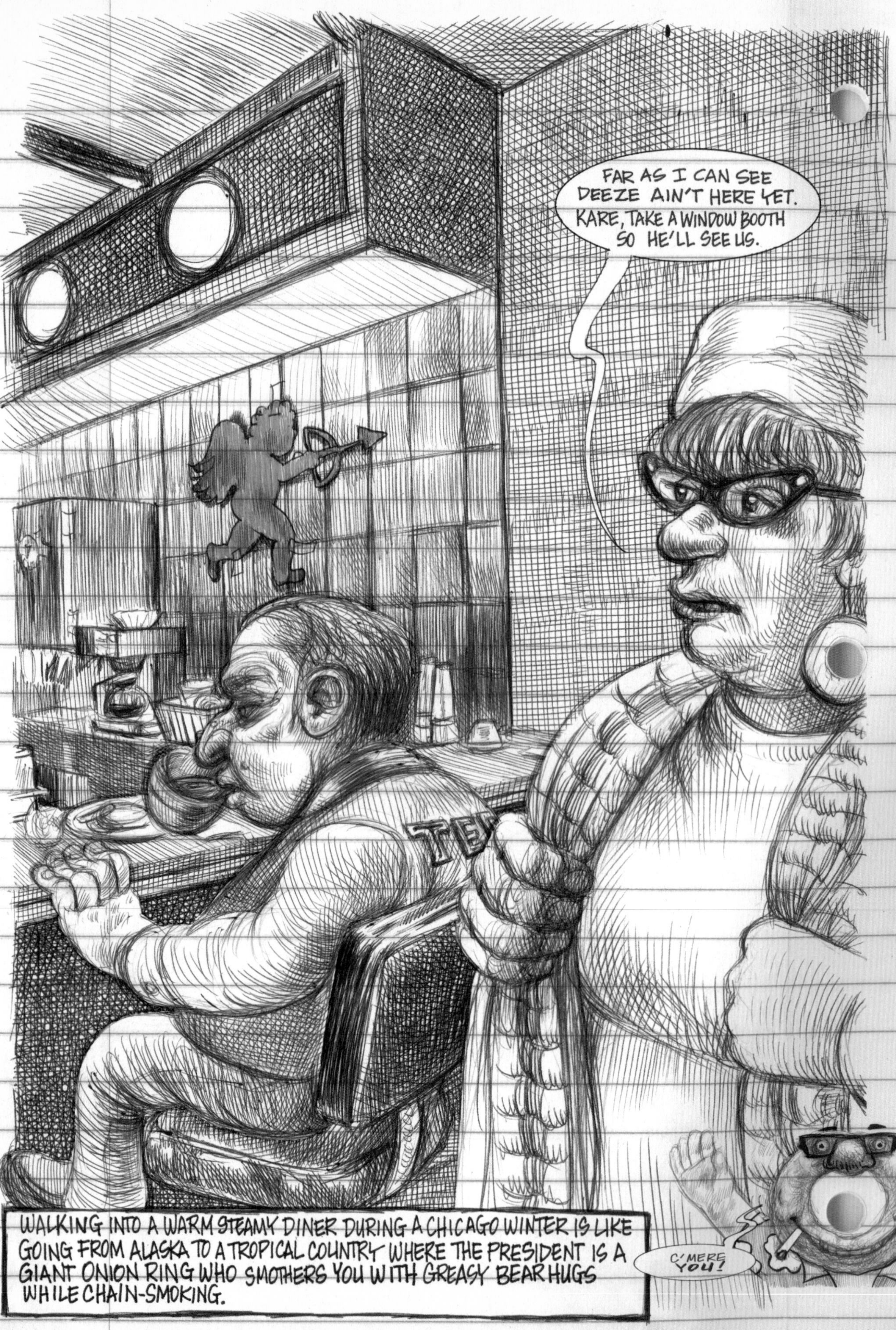
FAR AS I CAN SEE DEEZE AIN'T HERE YET. KARE, TAKE A WINDOW BOOTH SO HE'LL SEE US.
WALKING INTO A WARM STEAMY DINER DURING A CHICAGO WINTER IS LIKE GOING FROM ALASKA TO A TROPICAL COUNTRY WHERE THE PRESIDENT IS A GIANT ONION RING WHO SMOTHERS YOU WITH GREASY BEAR HUGS WHILE CHAIN-SMOKING.
C'MERE YOU!

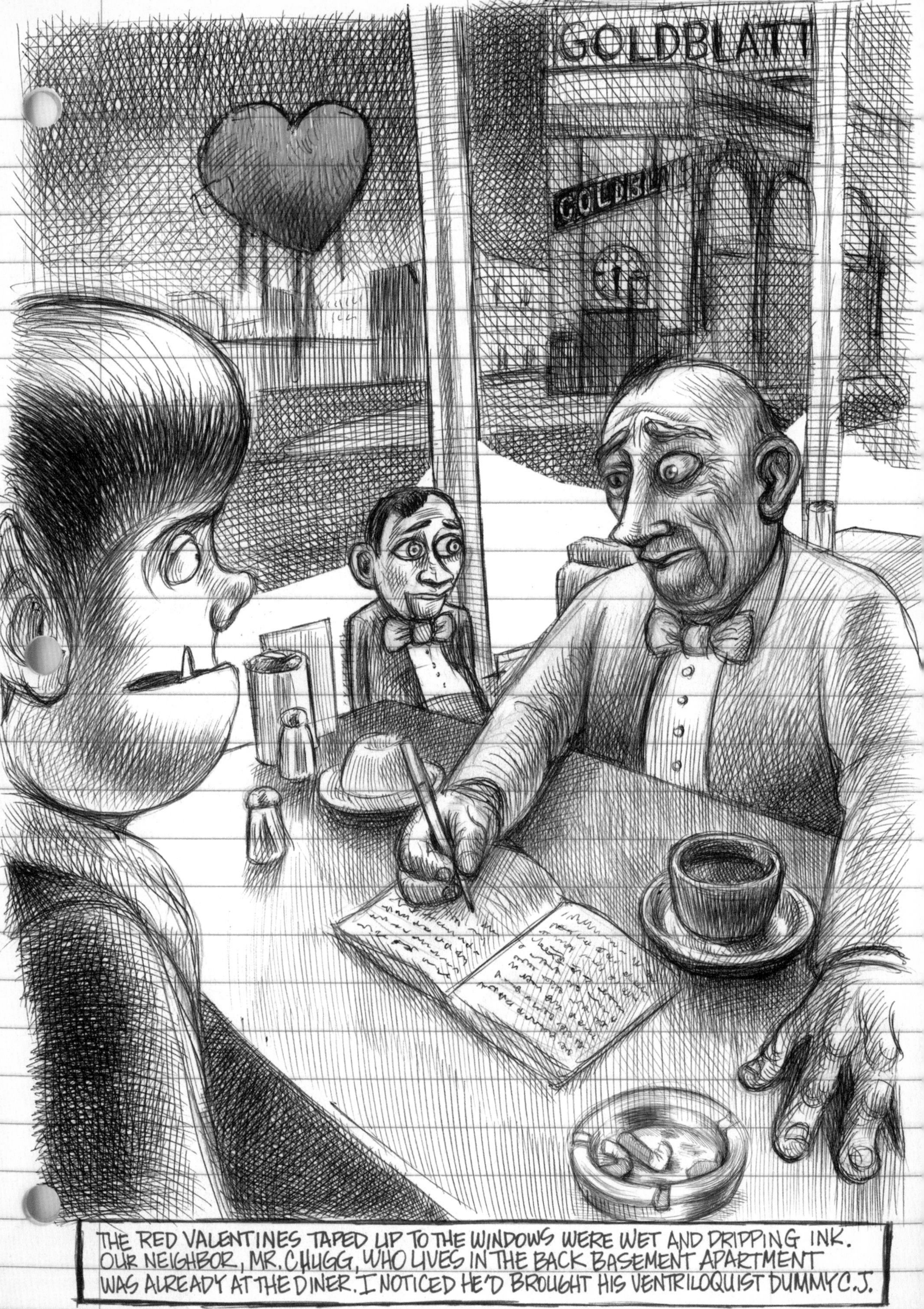
GOLDBLATT
THE RED VALENTINES TAPED UP TO THE WINDOWS WERE WET AND DRIPPING INK. OUR NEIGHBOR, MR. CHUGG, WHO LIVES IN THE BACK BASEMENT APARTMENT WAS ALREADY AT THE DINER. I NOTICED HE'D BROUGHT HIS VENTRILOQUIST DUMMY C.J.

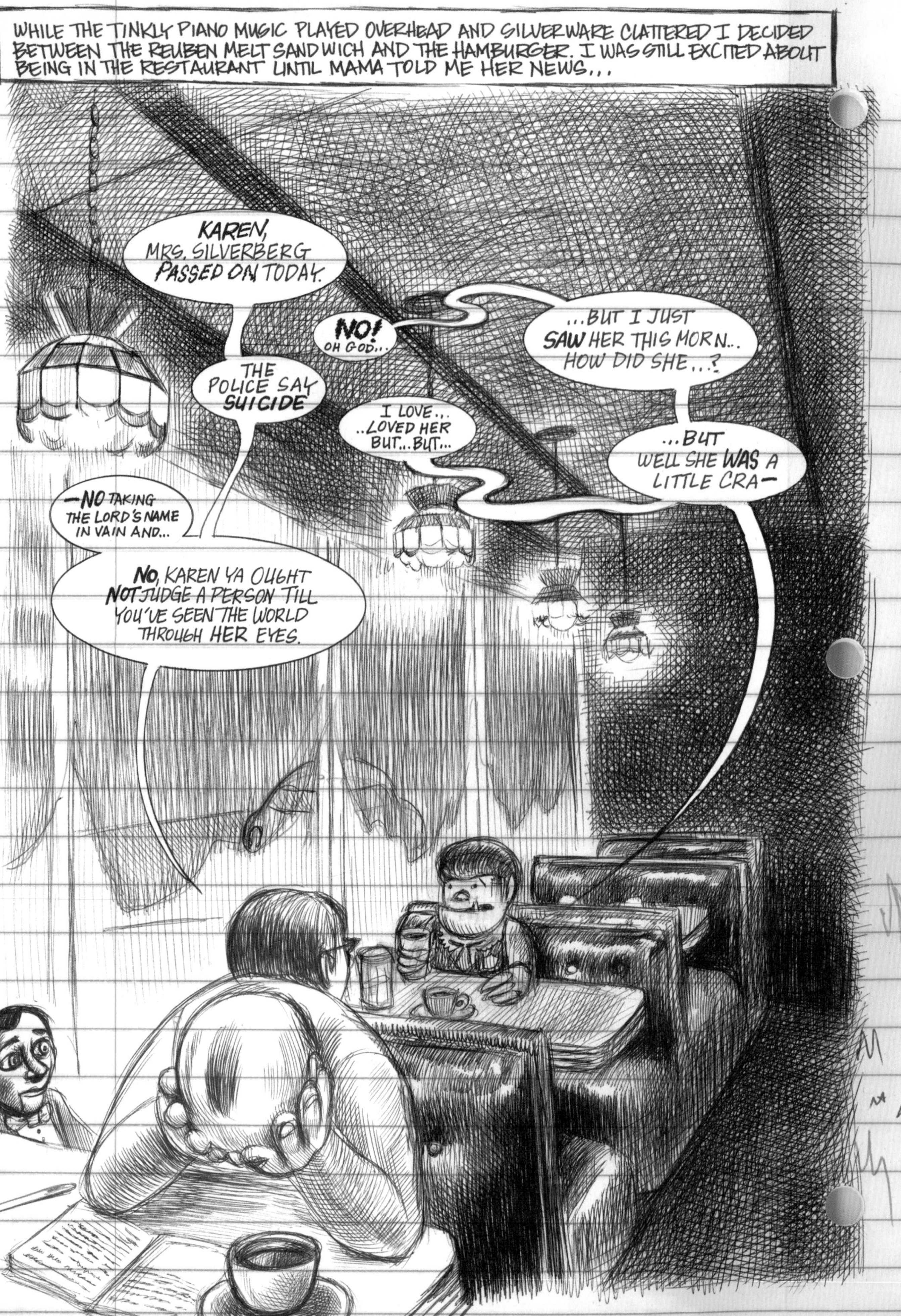
WHILE THE TINKLY PIANO MUSIC PLAYED OVERHEAD AND SILVERWARE CLATTERED I DECIDED BETWEEN THE REUBEN MELT SANDWICH AND THE HAMBURGER. I WAS STILL EXCITED ABOUT BEING IN THE RESTAURANT UNTIL MAMA TOLD ME HER NEWS...
KAREN, MRS. SILVERBERG PASSED ON TODAY.
NO! OH GOD...
...BUT I JUST SAW HER THIS MORN.. HOW DID SHE...?
THE POLICE SAY SUICIDE
I LOVE.. ..LOVED HER BUT...BUT...
...BUT WELL SHE WAS A LITTLE CRA-
-NO TAKING THE LORD'S NAME IN VAIN AND...
NO, KAREN YA OUGHT NOT JUDGE A PERSON TILL YOU'VE SEEN THE WORLD THROUGH HER EYES.

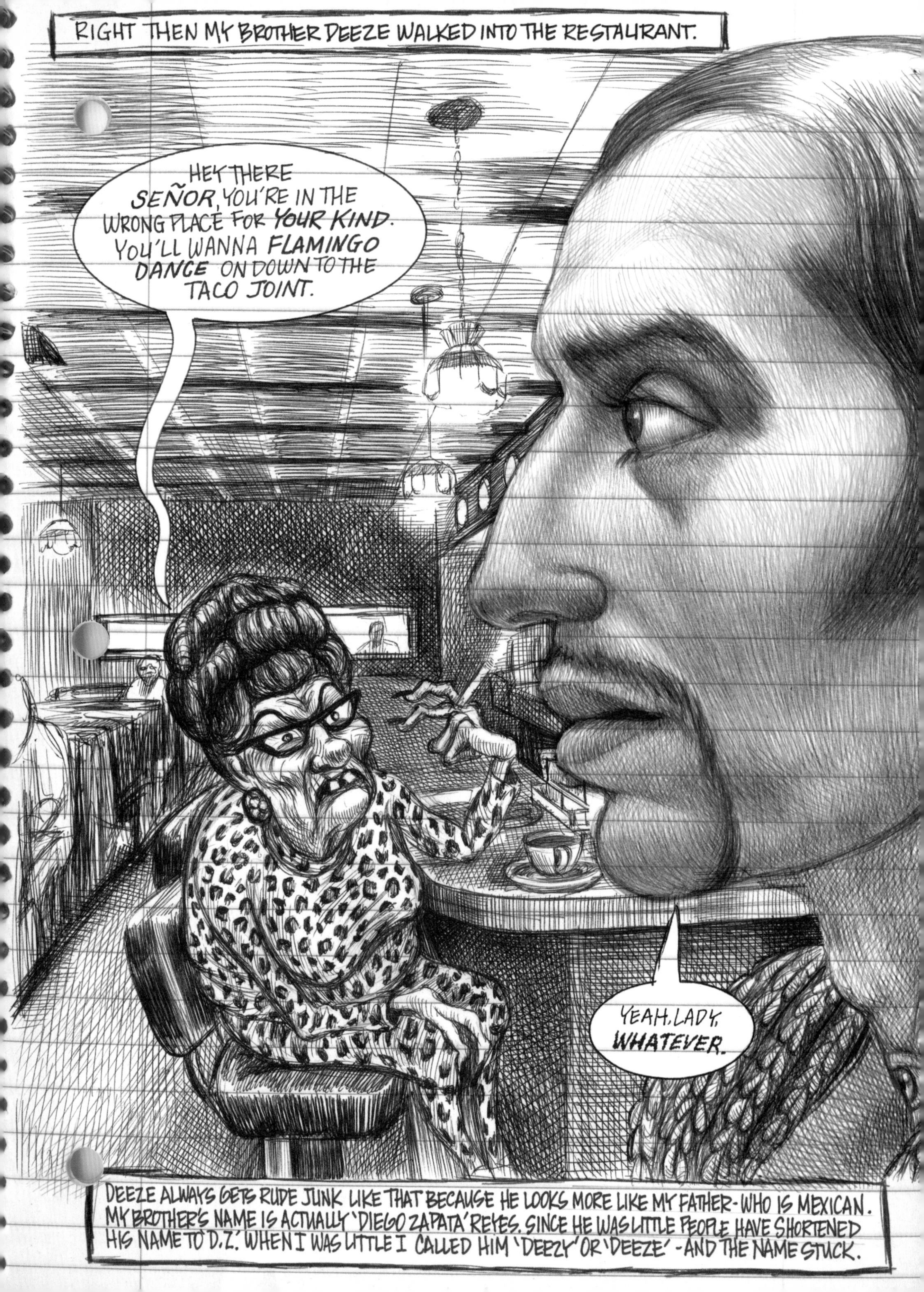
RIGHT THEN MY BROTHER DEEZE WALKED INTO THE RESTAURANT.
HEY THERE SEÑOR, YOU'RE IN THE WRONG PLACE FOR YOUR KIND. YOU'LL WANNA FLAMINGO DANCE ON DOWN TO THE TACO JOINT.
YEAH, LADY, WHATEVER.
DEEZE ALWAYS GETS RUDE JUNK LIKE THAT BECAUSE HE LOOKS MORE LIKE MY FATHER- WHO IS MEXICAN. MY BROTHER'S NAME IS ACTUALLY 'DIEGO ZAPATA' REYES. SINCE HE WAS LITTLE PEOPLE HAVE SHORTENED HIS NAME TO 'D.Z.' WHEN I WAS LITTLE I CALLED HIM 'DEEZY' OR 'DEEZE' - AND THE NAME STUCK.

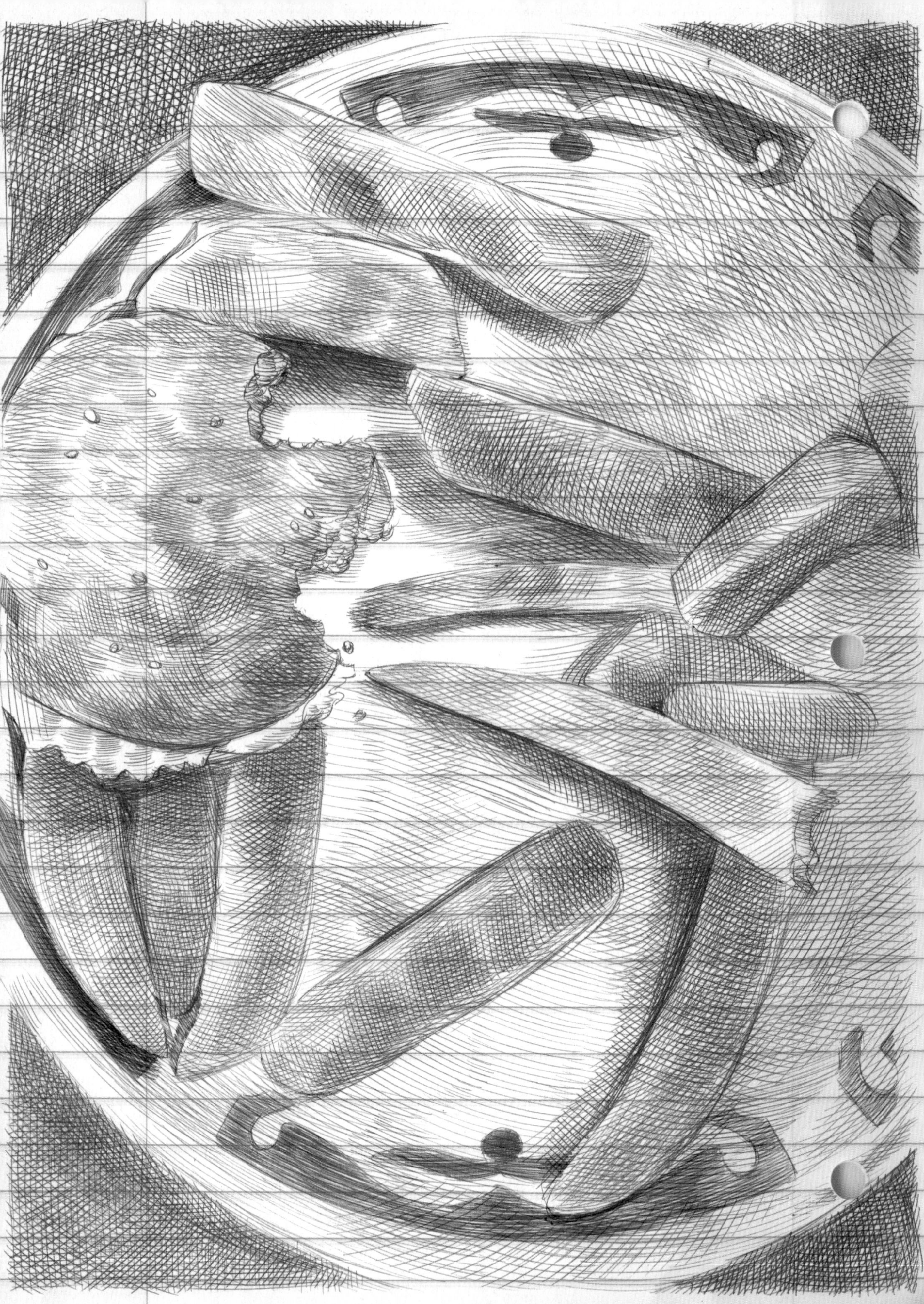

RIGHT WHEN DEEZE CAME INTO THE RESTAURANT, BUT SECONDS BEFORE HE SAT IN THE BOOTH, MAMA SAID SOMETHING (HALF TO ME AND HALF TO HERSELF) ABOUT HOW WHEN THE POLICE ALLOWED HER TO USE OUR PHONE TO CALL DEEZE'S JOB... *HE HADN'T BEEN THERE.*
"*I SUPPOSE THE POLICE MUSTA TOLD HIM WHAT HAPPENED...*"
AND THAT'D ACCOUNT FOR WHY HE LOOKS SO **DOWN IN THE MOUTH**."
I COULD TELL THAT MAMA HAD THINGS TO TELL DEEZE ABOUT ANKA'S DEATH THAT SHE DIDN'T WANT ME TO HEAR.
MAMA IS FOND OF SAYING, "LITTLE PITCHERS HAVE BIG EARS,"
BUT I KNEW THAT IF I WAS DRAWING AND ACTING **NOT** INTERESTED IN WHAT MAMA SAID, SHE'D SPILL THE BEANS RIGHT IN FRONT OF ME... SO I STARTED DRAWING MY UNEATEN BURGER.

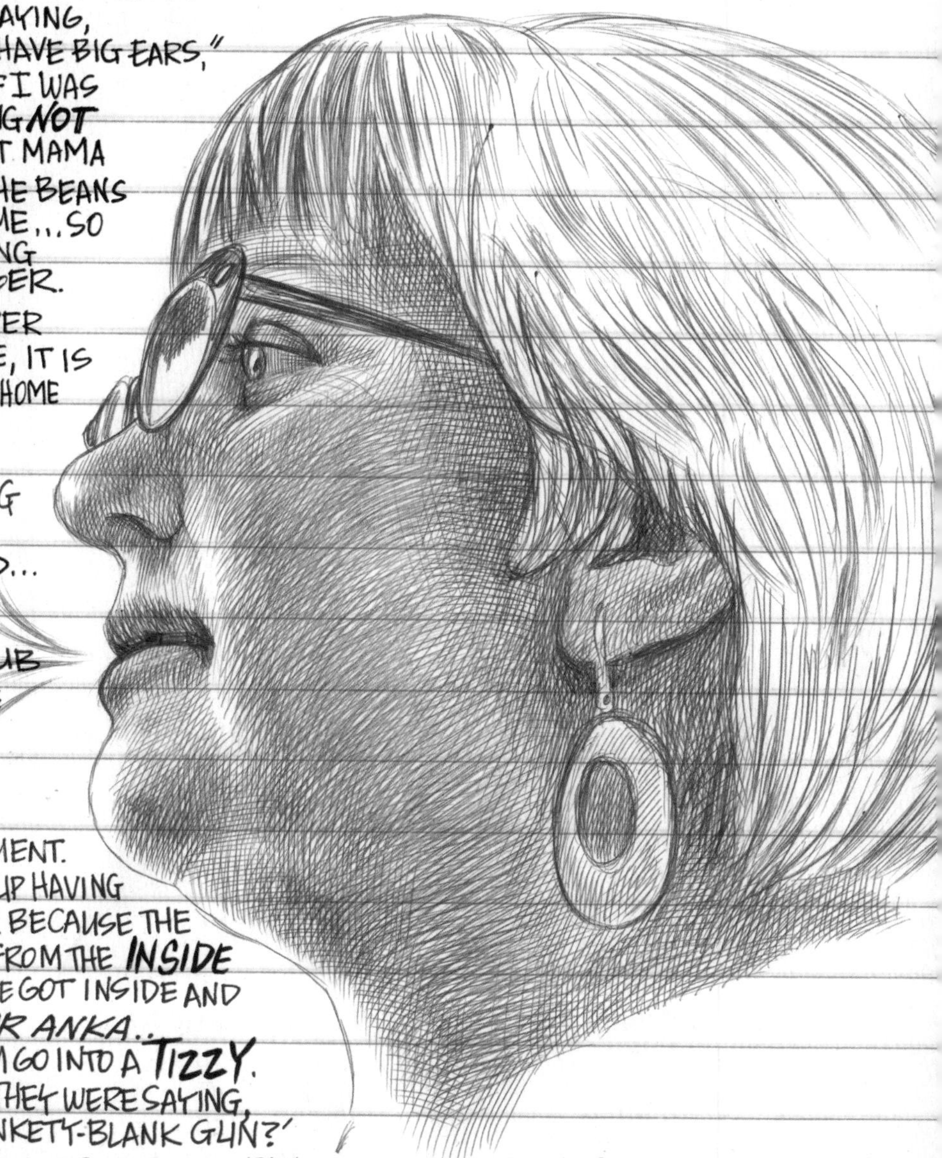

IN A KIND OF WHISPER MAMA SAID, "DEEZE, IT IS STRANGE. WHEN I GOT HOME *FROM... WORK* THE POLICE WERE THERE AT THE BUILDING ... THE GUNSHOT HAD BEEN REPORTED... THEY'D LOCATED MR. GRONAN AT THE GREEN MAN PUB AND HE CAME HOME AND TRIED TO USE HIS SET OF KEYS FOR THE SILVERBERG APARTMENT.

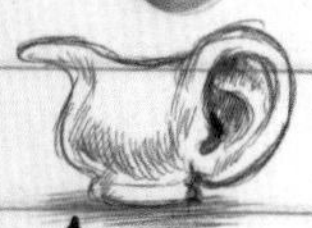

I NEVER *HAVE* UNDERSTOOD THE SAYING ABOUT PITCHERS AND EARS.

BUT THE POLICE ENDED UP HAVING TO USE A CROW BAR BECAUSE THE DOOR WAS BOLTED FROM THE **INSIDE** AND WHEN THE POLICE GOT INSIDE AND FOUND ANKA... *POOR ANKA*...
I OVERHEARD THEM GO INTO A **TIZZY**.
'THERE'S NO GUN!' THEY WERE SAYING, 'WHERE'S THE BLANKETY-BLANK GUN?'
THEY ENDED UP CALLING IT SUICIDE, SO THEY MUST'VE FOUND THE GUN... BUT IF SHE'D SHOT HERSELF IN HER HEART, HOW FAR AWAY COULD THE GUN HAVE GOTTEN?... AND THEN THERE'S ANKA'S CAT.
WHILE I WAS STANDING OUTSIDE THE FRONT DOOR I HEARD THE COPS YELLING, 'CATCH IT! CATCH IT!' AND OUT SHOT ANKA'S CAT, 'KING TUT.'
IT STOPPED AND LOOKED UP AT ME LIKE IT WAS SAYING 'SHE'S DEAD, MY *PERSON* IS DEAD' (AND AT THIS POINT MAMA'S VOICE GOT SO WHISPERY AND BROKEN.) ANKA'S CAT WAS STREAKED WITH HER BLOOD BUT THE POLICE SAID THAT THE CAT HAD COME OUT OF A CLOSET THAT'D BEEN SHUT TIGHT WHEN THEY BROKE INTO THE APARTMENT. AN OFFICER OPENED THE CLOSET AND TUT RACED OUT... SO THEY *SAY* IT WAS SUICIDE BUT I JUST DON'T KNOW... KAREN, ARE YOU GONNA **DRAW** YOUR DINNER OR ARE YOU GONNA **EAT** IT?... YOU CAN'T DO BOTH, HONEY."

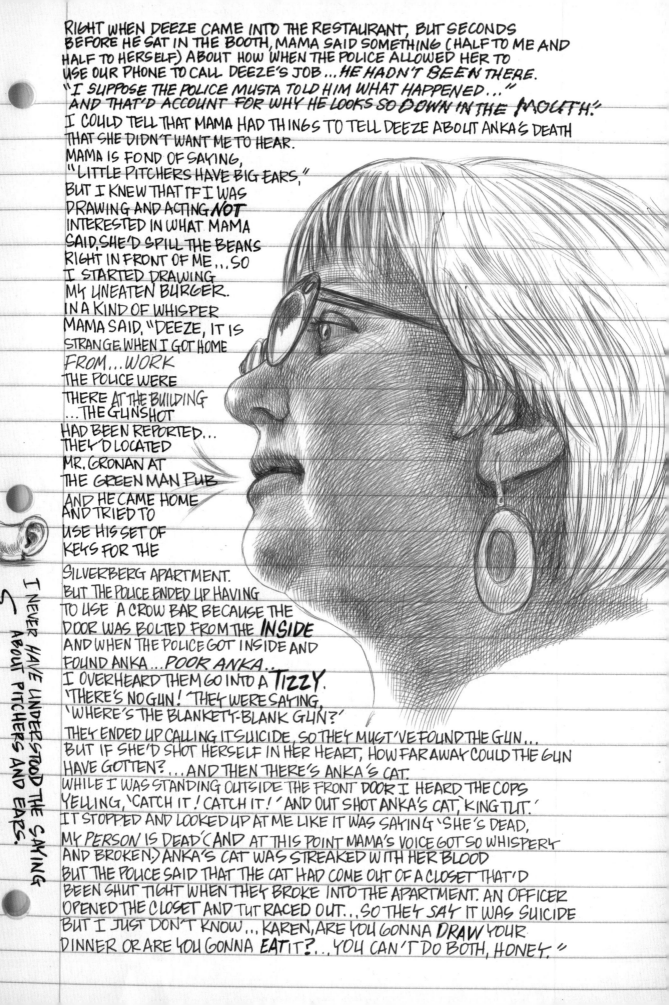

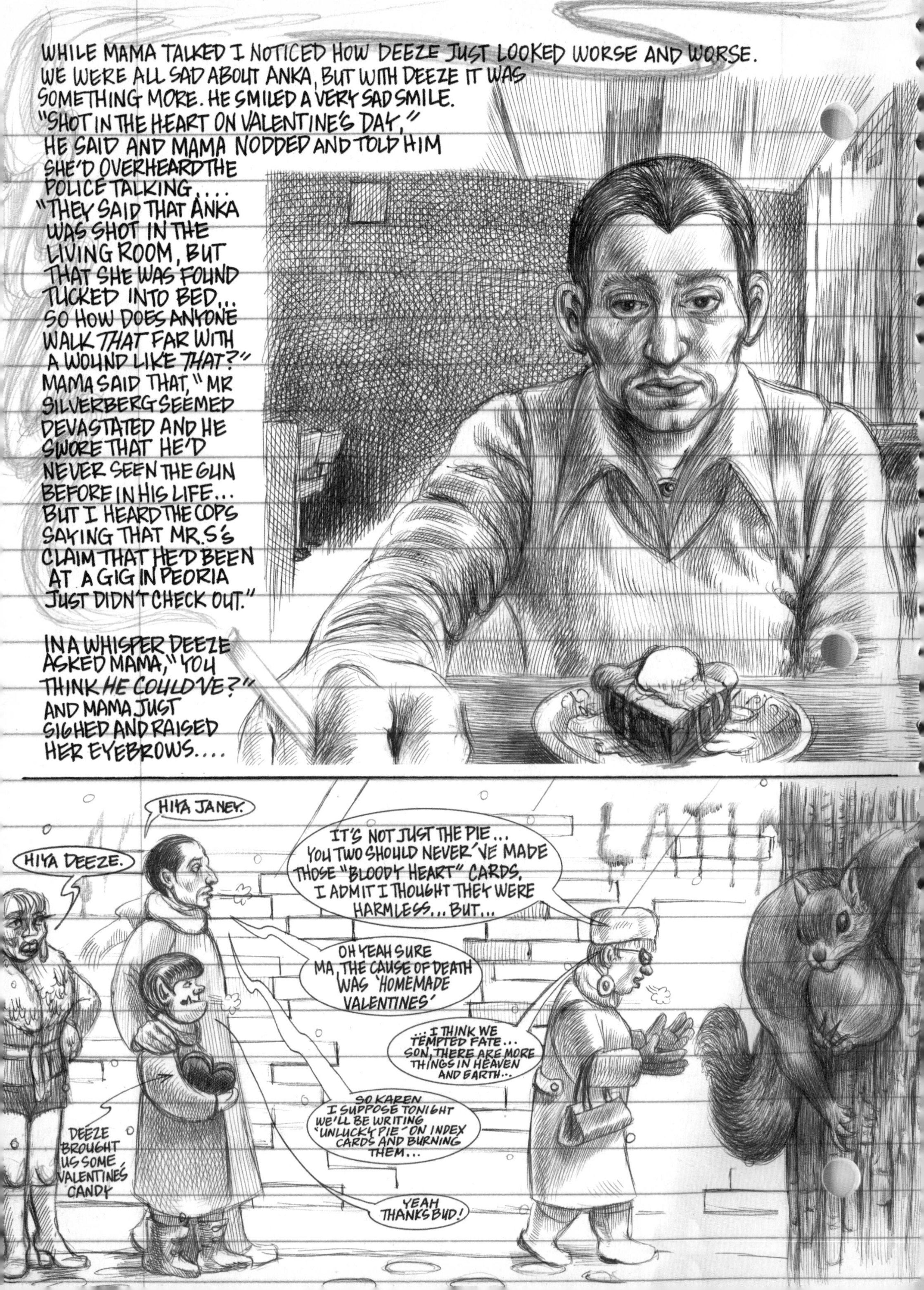
WHILE MAMA TALKED I NOTICED HOW DEEZE JUST LOOKED WORSE AND WORSE. WE WERE ALL SAD ABOUT ANKA, BUT WITH DEEZE IT WAS SOMETHING MORE. HE SMILED A VERY SAD SMILE. "SHOT IN THE HEART ON VALENTINE'S DAY," HE SAID AND MAMA NODDED AND TOLD HIM SHE'D OVERHEARD THE POLICE TALKING.... "THEY SAID THAT ANKA WAS SHOT IN THE LIVING ROOM, BUT THAT SHE WAS FOUND TUCKED INTO BED... SO HOW DOES ANYONE WALK *THAT* FAR WITH A WOUND LIKE *THAT*?" MAMA SAID THAT, "MR SILVERBERG SEEMED DEVASTATED AND HE SWORE THAT HE'D NEVER SEEN THE GUN BEFORE IN HIS LIFE... BUT I HEARD THE COPS SAYING THAT MR. S's CLAIM THAT HE'D BEEN AT A GIG IN PEORIA JUST DIDN'T CHECK OUT."
IN A WHISPER DEEZE ASKED MAMA, "YOU THINK *HE COULD'VE*?" AND MAMA JUST SIGHED AND RAISED HER EYEBROWS....
HIYA DEEZE.
HIYA JANEY.
IT'S NOT JUST THE PIE... YOU TWO SHOULD NEVER'VE MADE THOSE "BLOODY HEART" CARDS. I ADMIT I THOUGHT THEY WERE HARMLESS... BUT...
OH YEAH SURE MA, THE CAUSE OF DEATH WAS 'HOMEMADE VALENTINES'
...I THINK WE TEMPTED FATE... SON, THERE ARE MORE THINGS IN HEAVEN AND EARTH...
SO KAREN I SUPPOSE TONIGHT WE'LL BE WRITING 'UNLUCKY PIE' ON INDEX CARDS AND BURNING THEM...
YEAH THANKS BUD!
DEEZE BROUGHT US SOME VALENTINE'S CANDY

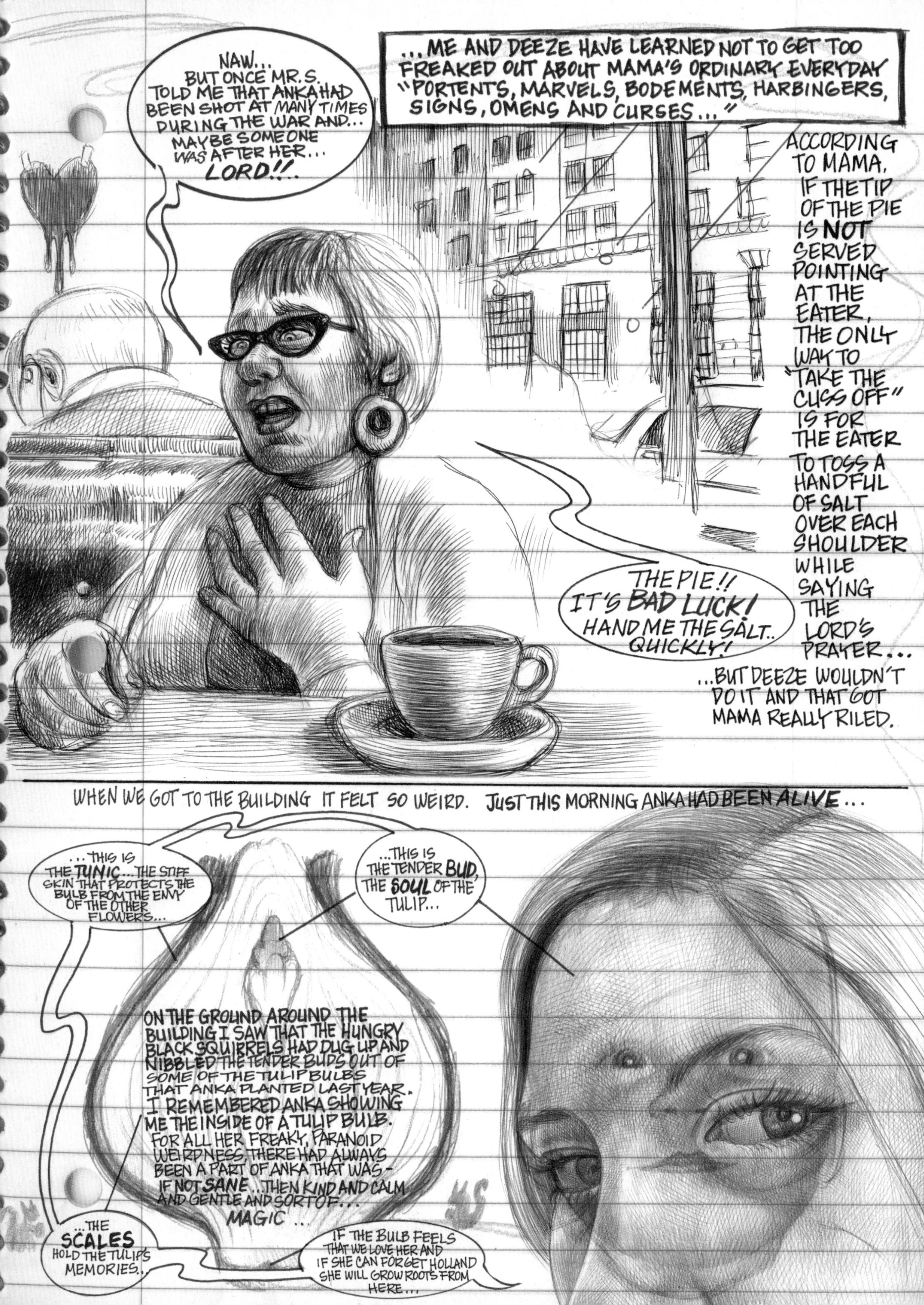

NAW... BUT ONCE MR. S. TOLD ME THAT ANKA HAD BEEN SHOT AT MANY TIMES DURING THE WAR AND... MAYBE SOMEONE WAS AFTER HER... LORD!!..
...ME AND DEEZE HAVE LEARNED NOT TO GET TOO FREAKED OUT ABOUT MAMA'S ORDINARY EVERYDAY "PORTENTS, MARVELS, BODEMENTS, HARBINGERS, SIGNS, OMENS AND CURSES..."
ACCORDING TO MAMA, IF THE TIP OF THE PIE IS NOT SERVED POINTING AT THE EATER, THE ONLY WAY TO "TAKE THE CUSS OFF" IS FOR THE EATER TO TOSS A HANDFUL OF SALT OVER EACH SHOULDER WHILE SAYING THE LORD'S PRAYER...
THE PIE!! IT'S BAD LUCK! HAND ME THE SALT.. QUICKLY!
...BUT DEEZE WOULDN'T DO IT AND THAT GOT MAMA REALLY RILED.
WHEN WE GOT TO THE BUILDING IT FELT SO WEIRD. JUST THIS MORNING ANKA HAD BEEN ALIVE...
...THIS IS THE TUNIC... THE STIFF SKIN THAT PROTECTS THE BULB FROM THE ENVY OF THE OTHER FLOWERS...
...THIS IS THE TENDER BUD, THE SOUL OF THE TULIP...
ON THE GROUND AROUND THE BUILDING I SAW THAT THE HUNGRY BLACK SQUIRRELS HAD DUG UP AND NIBBLED THE TENDER BUDS OUT OF SOME OF THE TULIP BULBS THAT ANKA PLANTED LAST YEAR. I REMEMBERED ANKA SHOWING ME THE INSIDE OF A TULIP BULB. FOR ALL HER FREAKY, PARANOID WEIRDNESS, THERE HAD ALWAYS BEEN A PART OF ANKA THAT WAS - IF NOT SANE... THEN KIND AND CALM AND GENTLE AND SORT OF... MAGIC...
...THE SCALES HOLD THE TULIP'S MEMORIES...
IF THE BULB FEELS THAT WE LOVE HER AND IF SHE CAN FORGET HOLLAND SHE WILL GROW ROOTS FROM HERE...

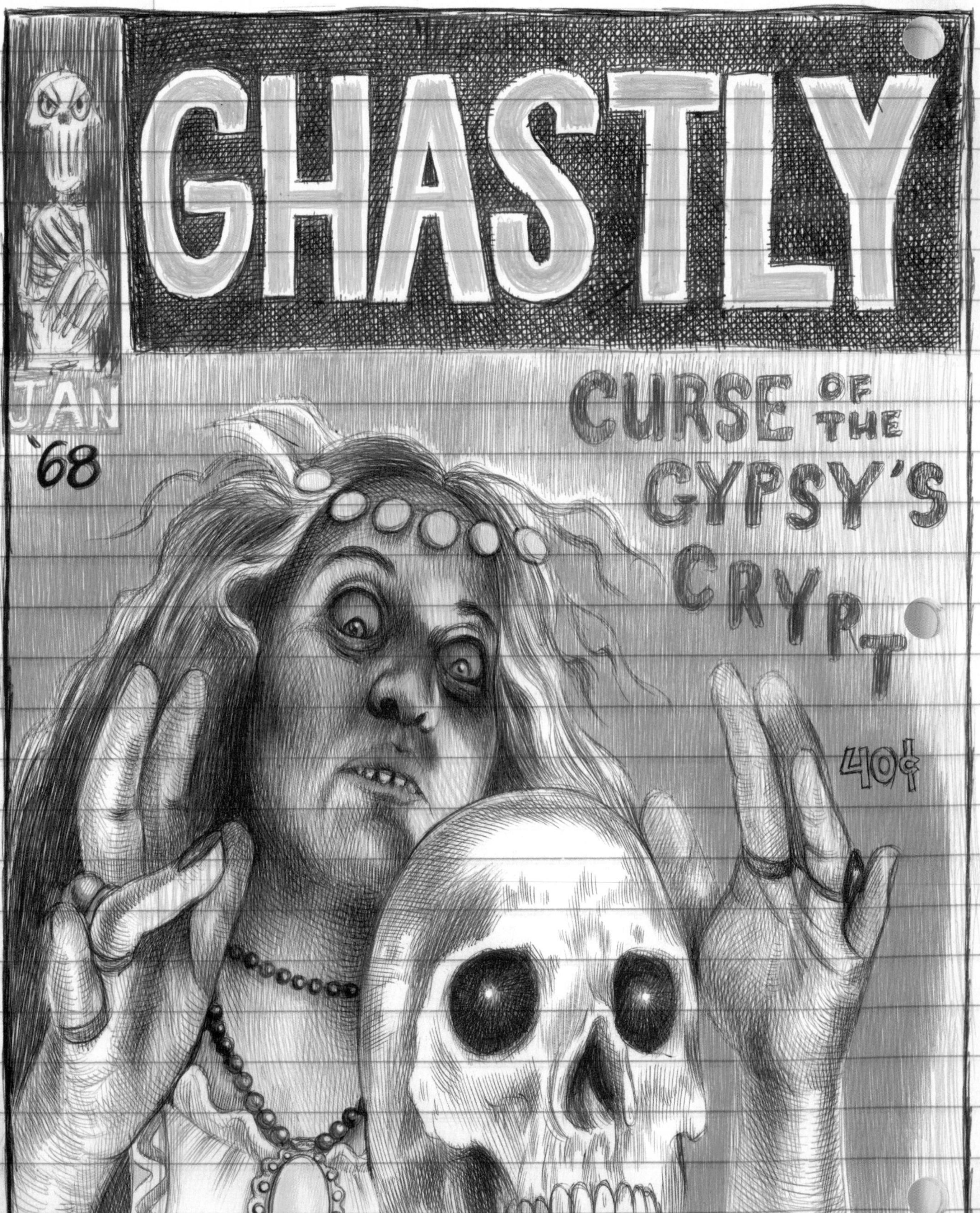
GHASTLY
JAN
'68
CURSE OF THE GYPSY'S CRYPT
40¢

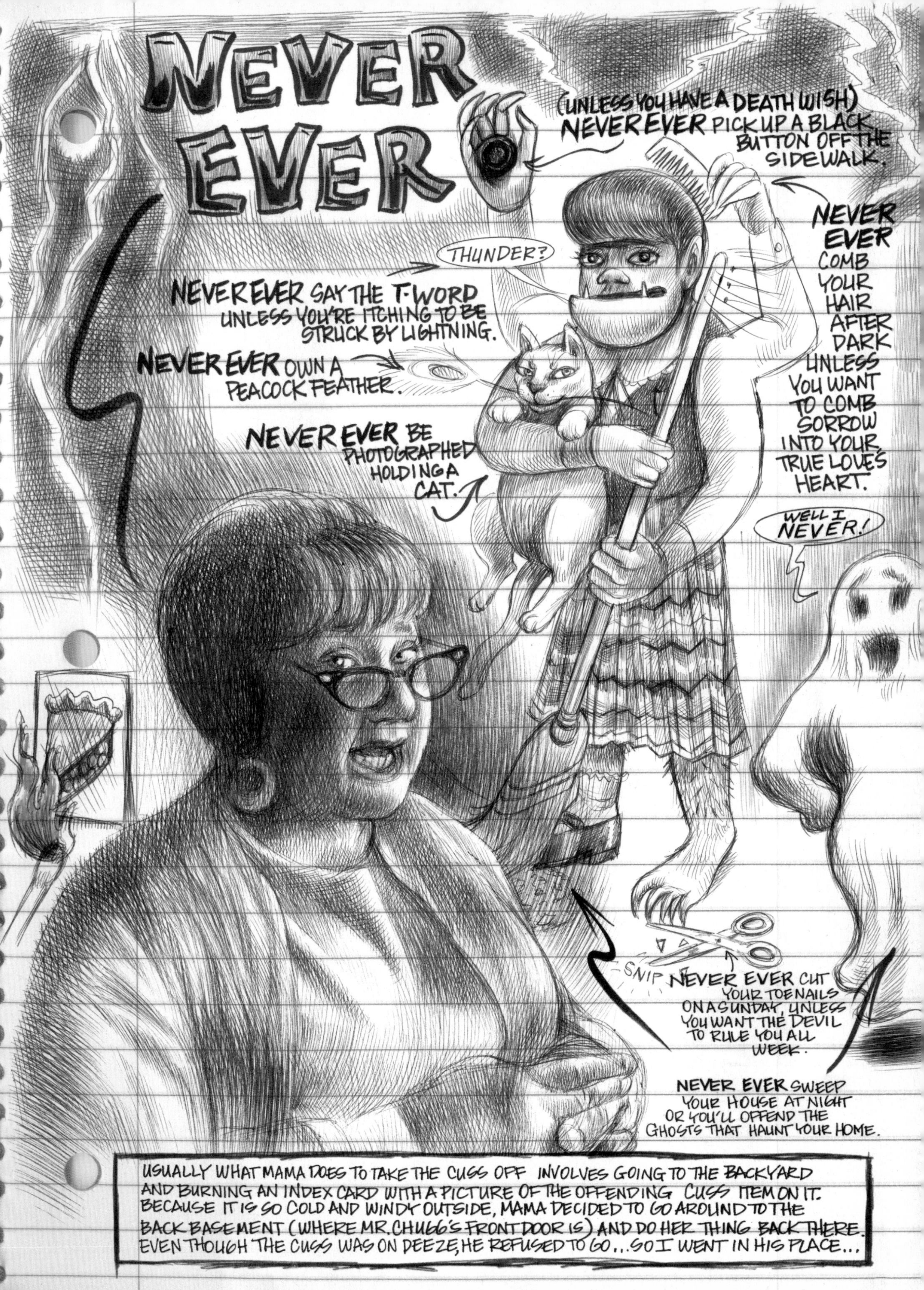
NEVER EVER
(UNLESS YOU HAVE A DEATH WISH) NEVER EVER PICK UP A BLACK BUTTON OFF THE SIDEWALK.
THUNDER?
NEVER EVER SAY THE T-WORD UNLESS YOU'RE ITCHING TO BE STRUCK BY LIGHTNING.
NEVER EVER OWN A PEACOCK FEATHER.
NEVER EVER BE PHOTOGRAPHED HOLDING A CAT.
NEVER EVER COMB YOUR HAIR AFTER DARK UNLESS YOU WANT TO COMB SORROW INTO YOUR TRUE LOVE'S HEART.
WELL I NEVER!
SNIP
NEVER EVER CUT YOUR TOENAILS ON A SUNDAY, UNLESS YOU WANT THE DEVIL TO RULE YOU ALL WEEK.
NEVER EVER SWEEP YOUR HOUSE AT NIGHT OR YOU'LL OFFEND THE GHOSTS THAT HAUNT YOUR HOME.
USUALLY WHAT MAMA DOES TO TAKE THE CUSS OFF INVOLVES GOING TO THE BACKYARD AND BURNING AN INDEX CARD WITH A PICTURE OF THE OFFENDING CUSS ITEM ON IT. BECAUSE IT IS SO COLD AND WINDY OUTSIDE, MAMA DECIDED TO GO AROUND TO THE BACK BASEMENT (WHERE MR. CHUGG'S FRONT DOOR IS) AND DO HER THING BACK THERE. EVEN THOUGH THE CUSS WAS ON DEEZE, HE REFUSED TO GO... SO I WENT IN HIS PLACE...

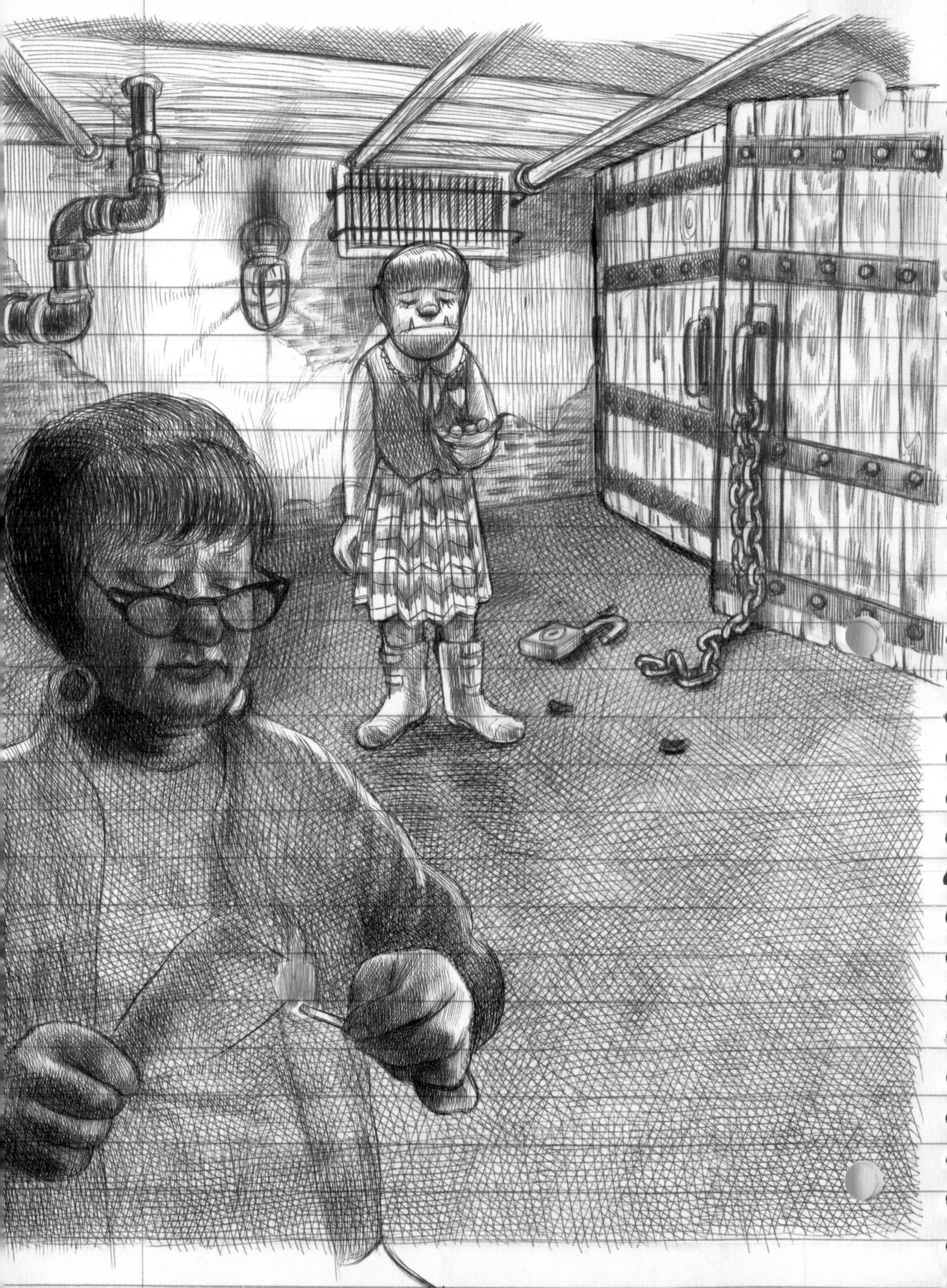

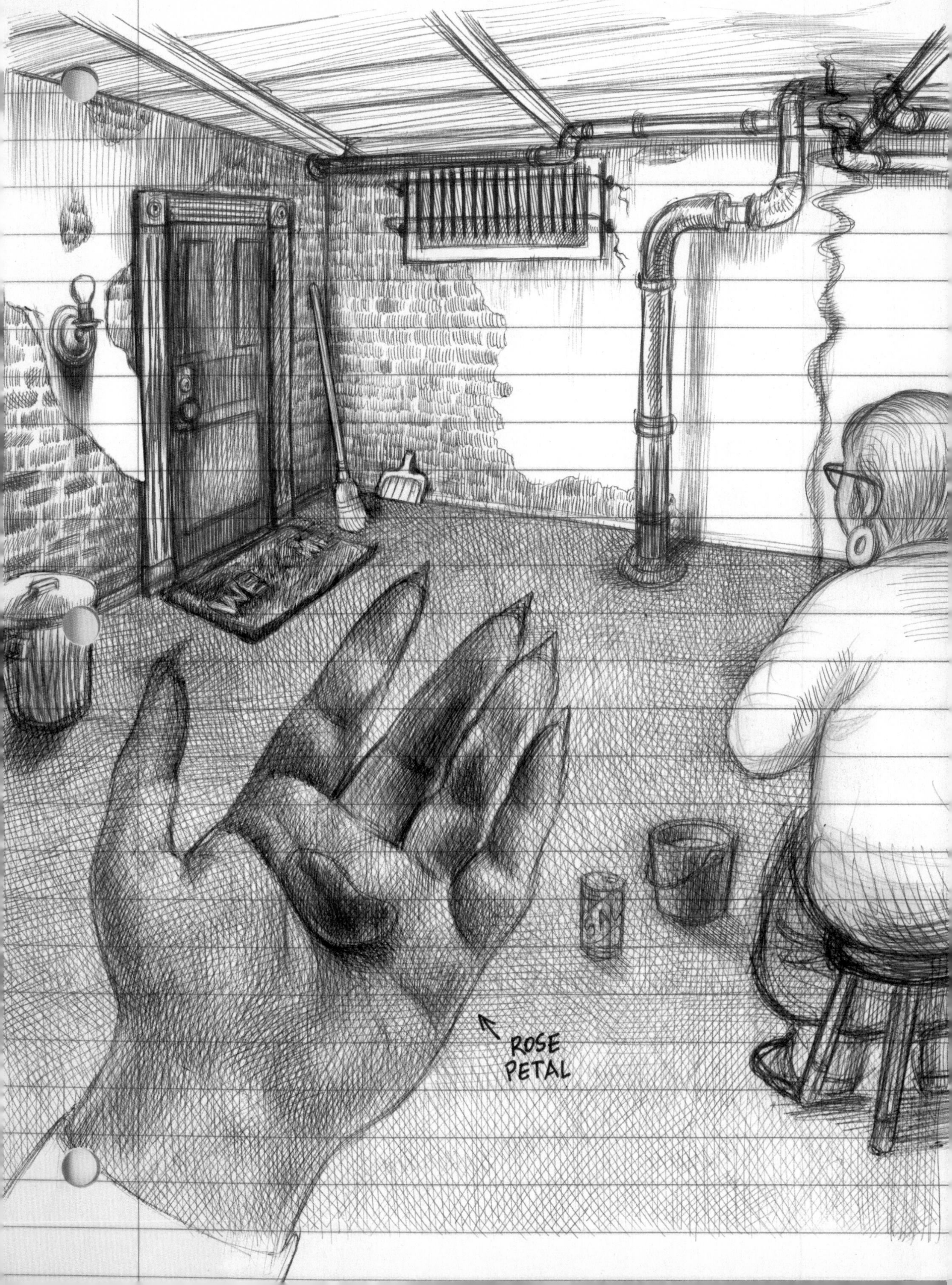
ROSE
PETAL

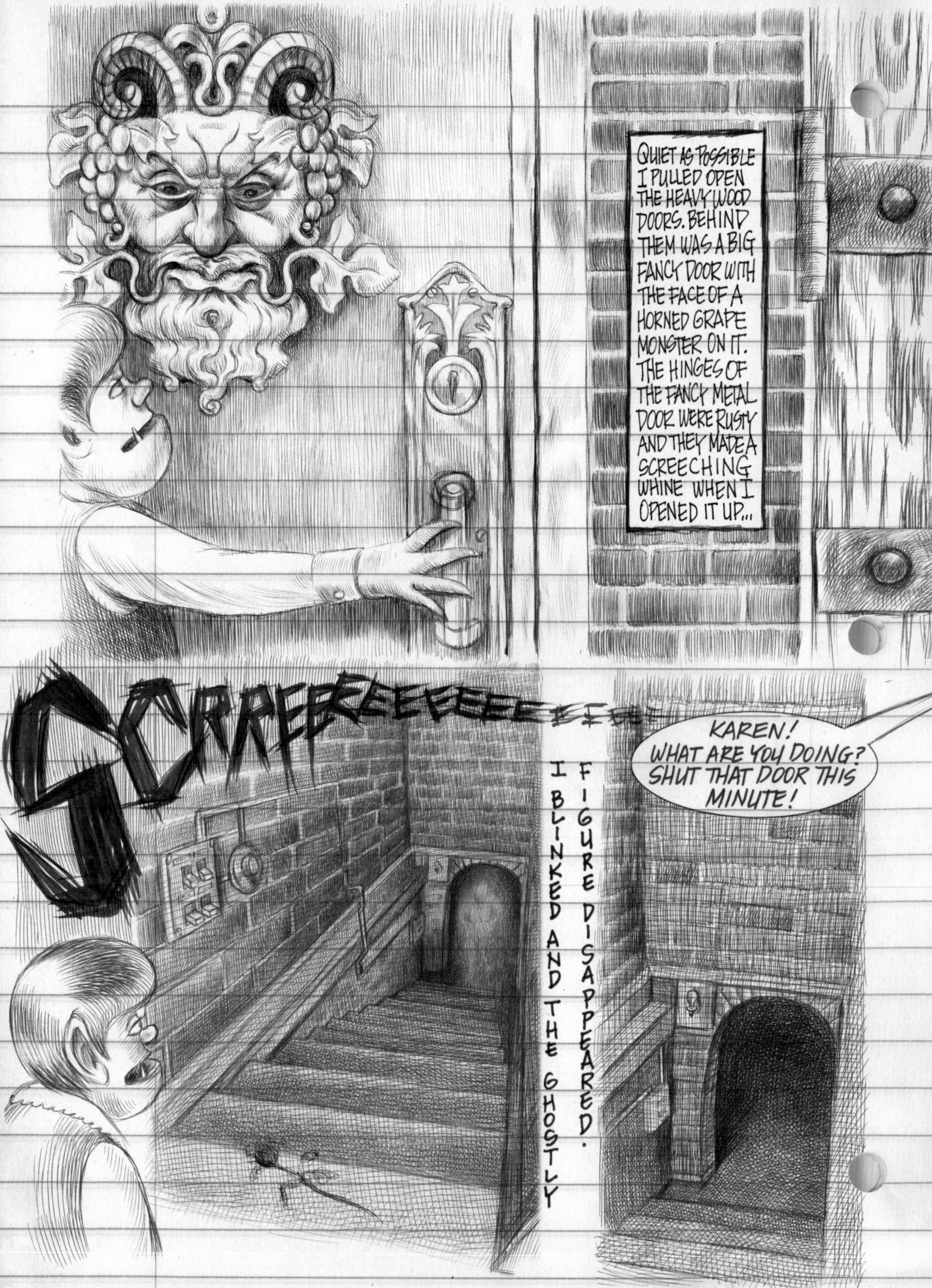
QUIET AS POSSIBLE I PULLED OPEN THE HEAVY WOOD DOORS. BEHIND THEM WAS A BIG FANCY DOOR WITH THE FACE OF A HORNED GRAPE MONSTER ON IT. THE HINGES OF THE FANCY METAL DOOR WERE RUSTY AND THEY MADE A SCREECHING WHINE WHEN I OPENED IT UP...
SCRREEEEEEEEEEEEEEEE
I BLINKED AND THE GHOSTLY FIGURE DISAPPEARED.
KAREN! WHAT ARE YOU DOING? SHUT THAT DOOR THIS MINUTE!

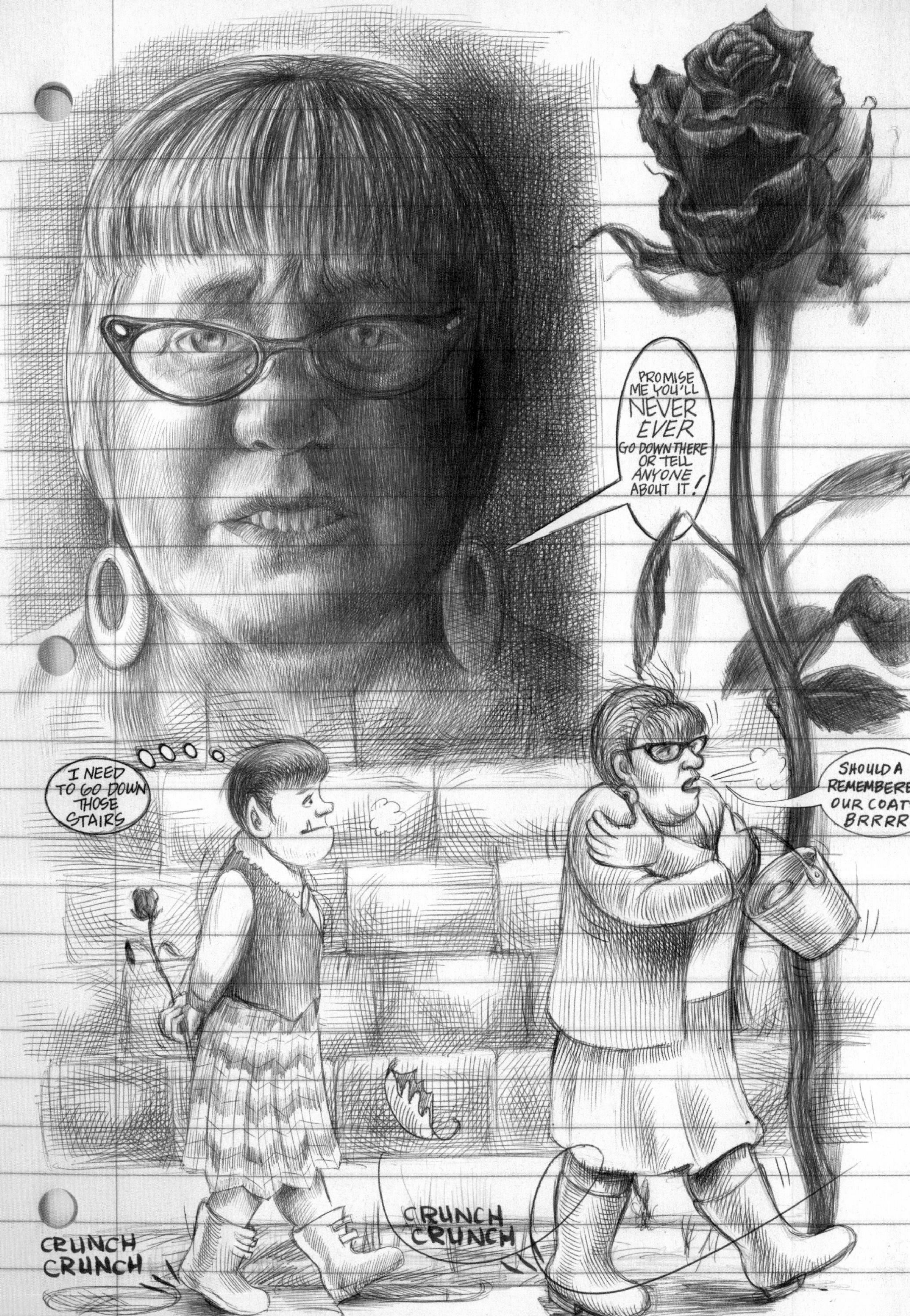
PROMISE ME YOU'LL NEVER EVER GO DOWN THERE OR TELL ANYONE ABOUT IT!
I NEED TO GO DOWN THOSE STAIRS
SHOULD A REMEMBERED OUR COATS BRRRR
CRUNCH CRUNCH
CRUNCH CRUNCH

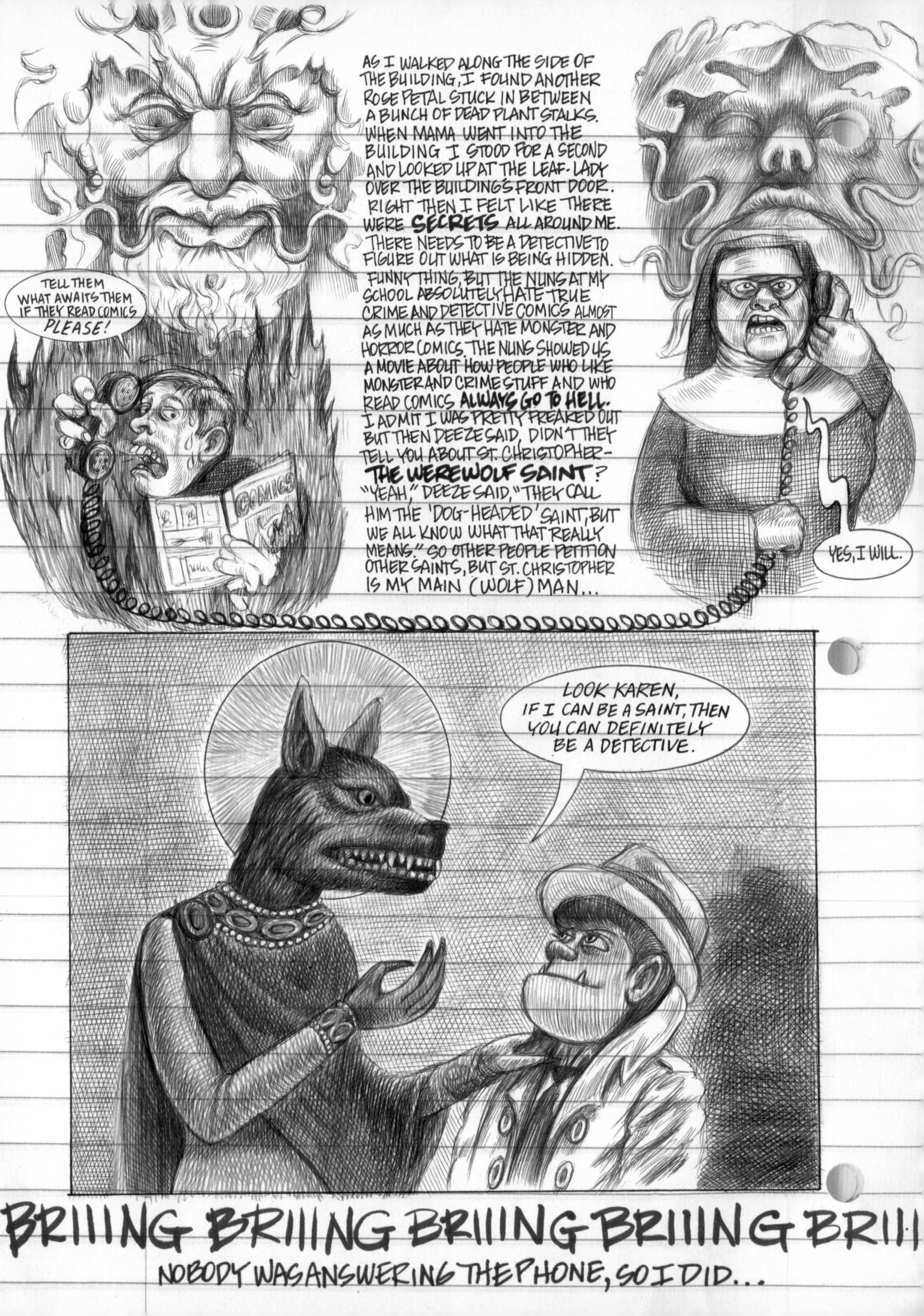

AS I WALKED ALONG THE SIDE OF THE BUILDING, I FOUND ANOTHER ROSE PETAL STUCK IN BETWEEN A BUNCH OF DEAD PLANT STALKS. WHEN MAMA WENT INTO THE BUILDING I STOOD FOR A SECOND AND LOOKED UP AT THE LEAF-LADY OVER THE BUILDING'S FRONT DOOR. RIGHT THEN I FELT LIKE THERE WERE **SECRETS** ALL AROUND ME. THERE NEEDS TO BE A DETECTIVE TO FIGURE OUT WHAT IS BEING HIDDEN. FUNNY THING, BUT THE NUNS AT MY SCHOOL ABSOLUTELY HATE TRUE CRIME AND DETECTIVE COMICS ALMOST AS MUCH AS THEY HATE MONSTER AND HORROR COMICS. THE NUNS SHOWED US A MOVIE ABOUT HOW PEOPLE WHO LIKE MONSTER AND CRIME STUFF AND WHO READ COMICS **ALWAYS GO TO HELL.** I ADMIT I WAS PRETTY FREAKED OUT BUT THEN DEEZE SAID, DIDN'T THEY TELL YOU ABOUT ST. CHRISTOPHER- **THE WEREWOLF SAINT**? "YEAH," DEEZE SAID, "THEY CALL HIM THE 'DOG-HEADED' SAINT, BUT WE ALL KNOW WHAT THAT REALLY MEANS." SO OTHER PEOPLE PETITION OTHER SAINTS, BUT ST. CHRISTOPHER IS MY MAIN (WOLF) MAN...
TELL THEM WHAT AWAITS THEM IF THEY READ COMICS PLEASE!
COMICS
YES, I WILL.
LOOK KAREN, IF I CAN BE A SAINT, THEN YOU CAN DEFINITELY BE A DETECTIVE.
BRIIING BRIIING BRIIING BRIIING BRIII
NOBODY WAS ANSWERING THE PHONE, SO I DID...

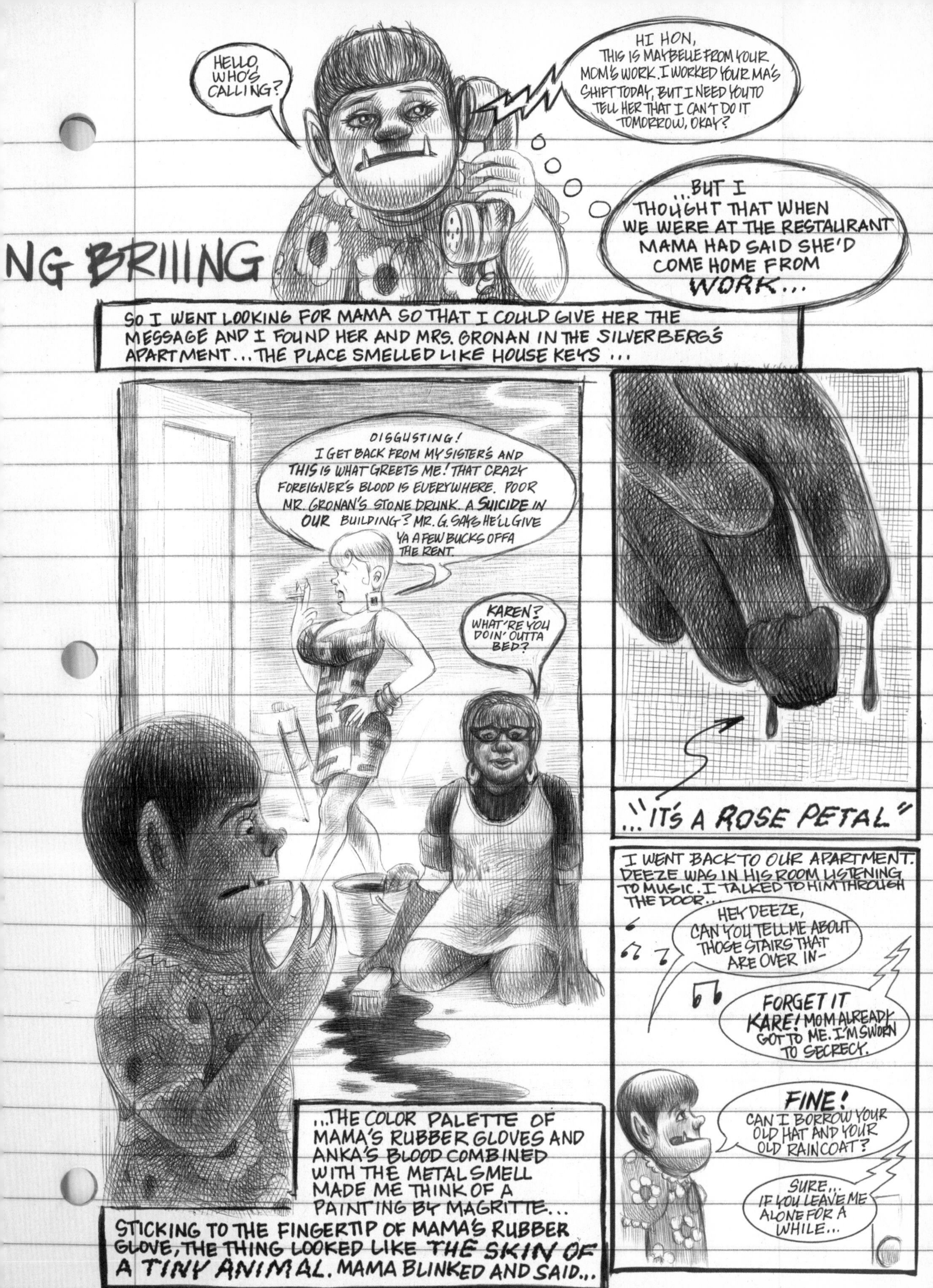
HELLO, WHO'S CALLING?
HI HON, THIS IS MAYBELLE FROM YOUR MOM'S WORK. I WORKED YOUR MA'S SHIFT TODAY, BUT I NEED YOU TO TELL HER THAT I CAN'T DO IT TOMORROW, OKAY?
...BUT I THOUGHT THAT WHEN WE WERE AT THE RESTAURANT MAMA HAD SAID SHE'D COME HOME FROM WORK...
NG BRIIING
SO I WENT LOOKING FOR MAMA SO THAT I COULD GIVE HER THE MESSAGE AND I FOUND HER AND MRS. GRONAN IN THE SILVERBERG'S APARTMENT... THE PLACE SMELLED LIKE HOUSE KEYS...
DISGUSTING! I GET BACK FROM MY SISTER'S AND THIS IS WHAT GREETS ME! THAT CRAZY FOREIGNER'S BLOOD IS EVERYWHERE. POOR MR. GRONAN'S STONE DRUNK. A SUICIDE IN OUR BUILDING? MR. G. SAYS HE'LL GIVE YA A FEW BUCKS OFFA THE RENT.
KAREN? WHAT'RE YOU DOIN' OUTTA BED?
...THE COLOR PALETTE OF MAMA'S RUBBER GLOVES AND ANKA'S BLOOD COMBINED WITH THE METAL SMELL MADE ME THINK OF A PAINTING BY MAGRITTE...
STICKING TO THE FINGERTIP OF MAMA'S RUBBER GLOVE, THE THING LOOKED LIKE THE SKIN OF A TINY ANIMAL. MAMA BLINKED AND SAID...
..."IT'S A ROSE PETAL"
I WENT BACK TO OUR APARTMENT. DEEZE WAS IN HIS ROOM LISTENING TO MUSIC. I TALKED TO HIM THROUGH THE DOOR...
HEY DEEZE, CAN YOU TELL ME ABOUT THOSE STAIRS THAT ARE OVER IN-
FORGET IT KARE! MOM ALREADY GOT TO ME. I'M SWORN TO SECRECY.
FINE! CAN I BORROW YOUR OLD HAT AND YOUR OLD RAINCOAT?
SURE... IF YOU LEAVE ME ALONE FOR A WHILE...

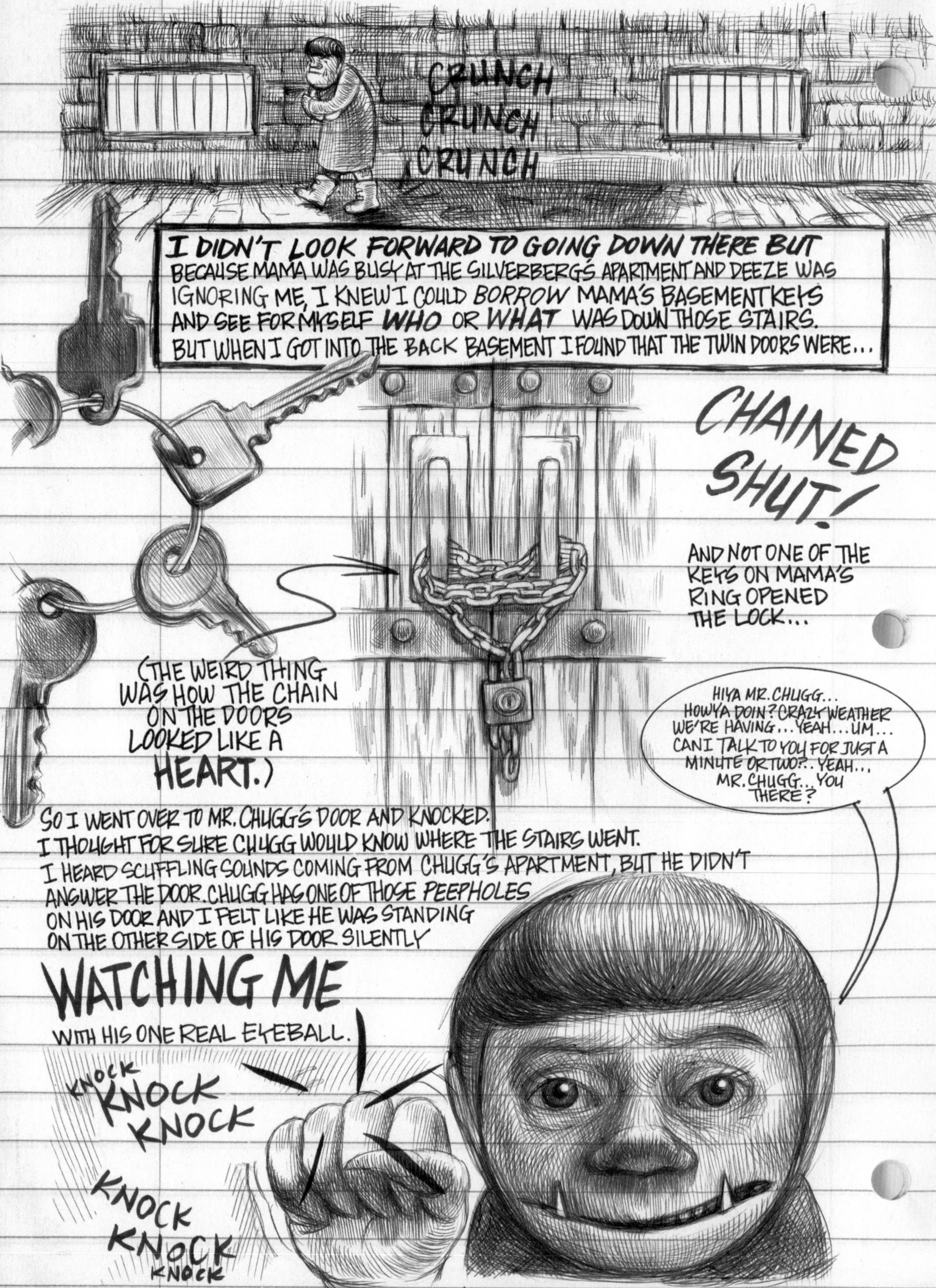
CRUNCH
CRUNCH
CRUNCH
I DIDN'T LOOK FORWARD TO GOING DOWN THERE BUT BECAUSE MAMA WAS BUSY AT THE SILVERBERG'S APARTMENT AND DEEZE WAS IGNORING ME, I KNEW I COULD BORROW MAMA'S BASEMENT KEYS AND SEE FOR MYSELF WHO OR WHAT WAS DOWN THOSE STAIRS. BUT WHEN I GOT INTO THE BACK BASEMENT I FOUND THAT THE TWIN DOORS WERE…
CHAINED SHUT!
AND NOT ONE OF THE KEYS ON MAMA'S RING OPENED THE LOCK…
(THE WEIRD THING WAS HOW THE CHAIN ON THE DOORS LOOKED LIKE A HEART.)
HIYA MR. CHUGG… HOWYA DOIN? CRAZY WEATHER WE'RE HAVING… YEAH… UM… CAN I TALK TO YOU FOR JUST A MINUTE OR TWO?.. YEAH… MR. CHUGG… YOU THERE?
SO I WENT OVER TO MR. CHUGG'S DOOR AND KNOCKED. I THOUGHT FOR SURE CHUGG WOULD KNOW WHERE THE STAIRS WENT. I HEARD SCUFFLING SOUNDS COMING FROM CHUGG'S APARTMENT, BUT HE DIDN'T ANSWER THE DOOR. CHUGG HAS ONE OF THOSE PEEPHOLES ON HIS DOOR AND I FELT LIKE HE WAS STANDING ON THE OTHER SIDE OF HIS DOOR SILENTLY
WATCHING ME
WITH HIS ONE REAL EYEBALL.
KNOCK KNOCK KNOCK
KNOCK KNOCK KNOCK

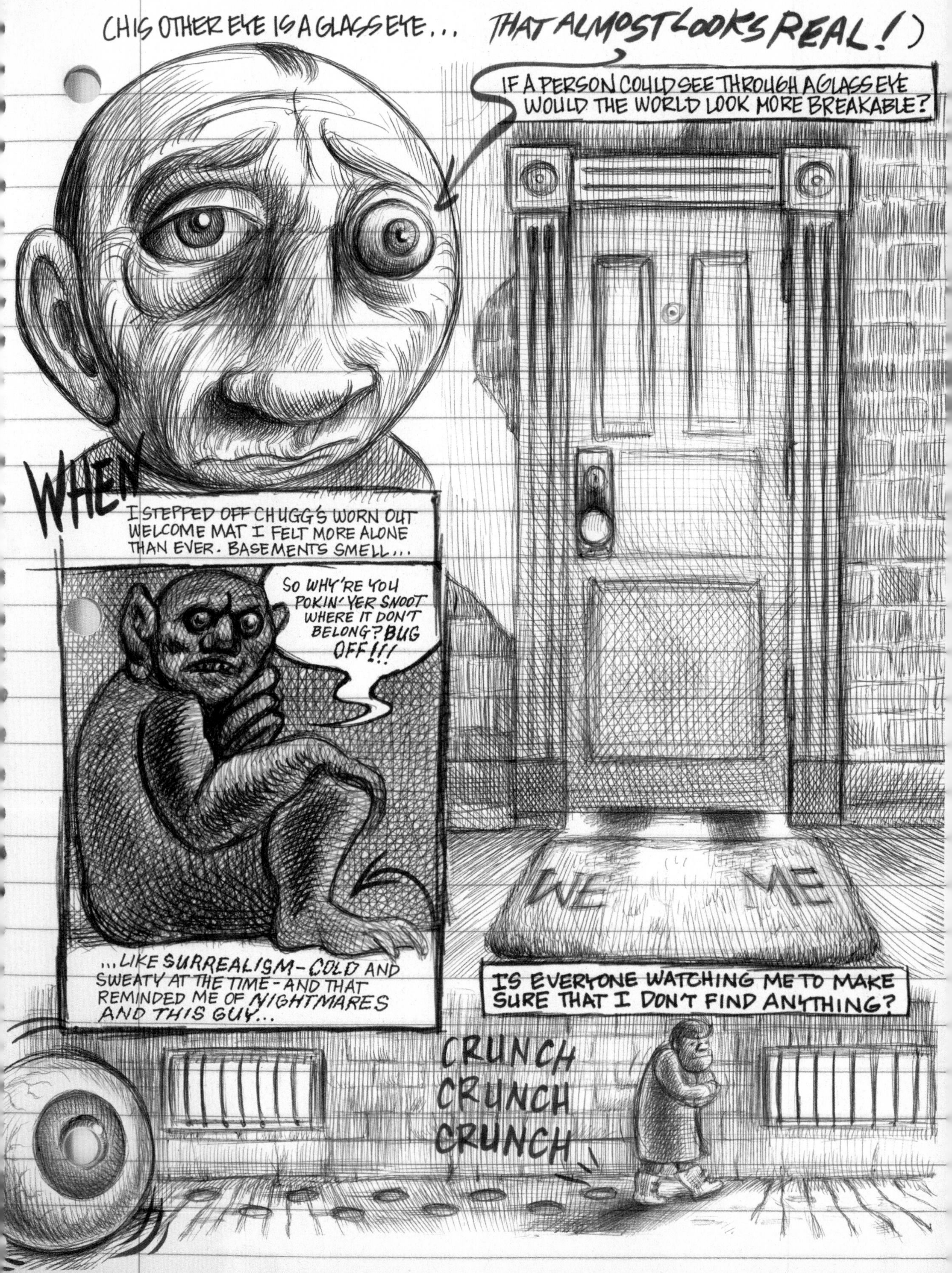
(HIS OTHER EYE IS A GLASS EYE... THAT ALMOST LOOKS REAL!)
IF A PERSON COULD SEE THROUGH A GLASS EYE WOULD THE WORLD LOOK MORE BREAKABLE?
WHEN I STEPPED OFF CHUGG'S WORN OUT WELCOME MAT I FELT MORE ALONE THAN EVER. BASEMENTS SMELL...
SO WHY'RE YOU POKIN' YER SNOOT WHERE IT DON'T BELONG? BUG OFF!!!
...LIKE SURREALISM - COLD AND SWEATY AT THE TIME - AND THAT REMINDED ME OF NIGHTMARES AND THIS GUY...
WE ME
IS EVERYONE WATCHING ME TO MAKE SURE THAT I DON'T FIND ANYTHING?
CRUNCH
CRUNCH
CRUNCH

LAST YEAR DEEZE DROVE US TO THE DETROIT INSTITUTE OF ARTS... ONE OF THE COOLEST PAINTINGS WE SAW WAS THIS ONE. →

'THE NIGHT MARE' BY HENRY FUSELI, 1781.

DEEZE SAYS THAT IT IS FULL OF SYMBOLS AND THAT IT IS ROMANTICISM, BUT IT DOESN'T EXACTLY LOOK LIKE MAMA'S ROMANCE NOVELS...

THERE IS A SWOONING LADY IN THE PAINTING– LIKE ON THE ROMANCE COVERS–BUT THE MONSTERY CREATURE ON HER BODY LOOKS WAY GROOVIER (AND MORE INTELLIGENT AND MORE RESPECTFUL) THAN THE BEEFY IDIOTS RIPPING THE LADIES SHIRTS ON THE ROMANCE NOVEL COVERS.

MY BROTHER CLAIMS THAT THE PAINTING IS 'SEXY.'

HE SAYS I *COULD* THINK OF IT AS HISTORY'S FIRST HORROR COMIC COVER...

...AND CONSIDERING THE WHOLE ARITHMETIC OF BOOBS + MONSTERS = *HORROR*, I GUESS HE'S PROBABLY RIGHT...

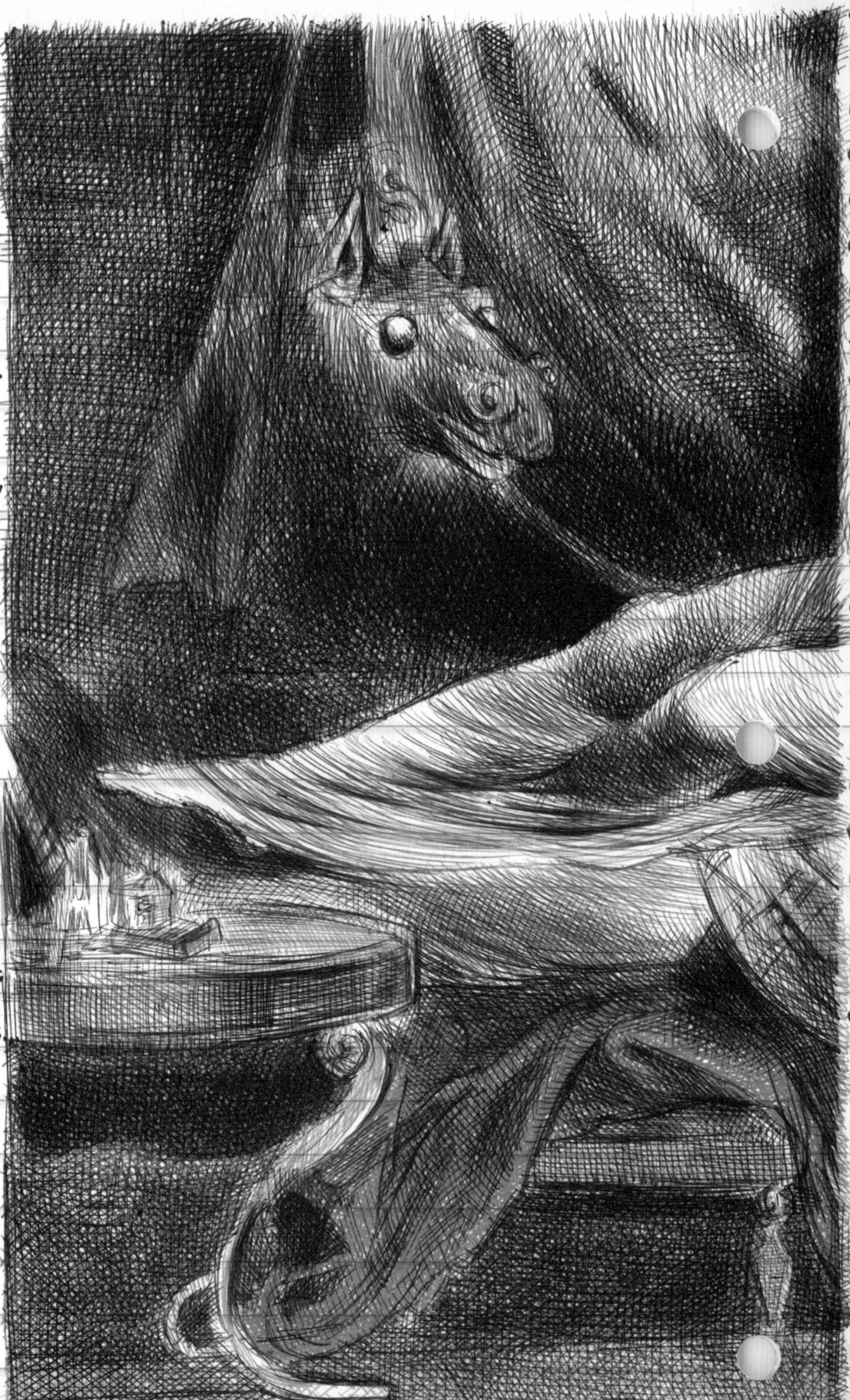

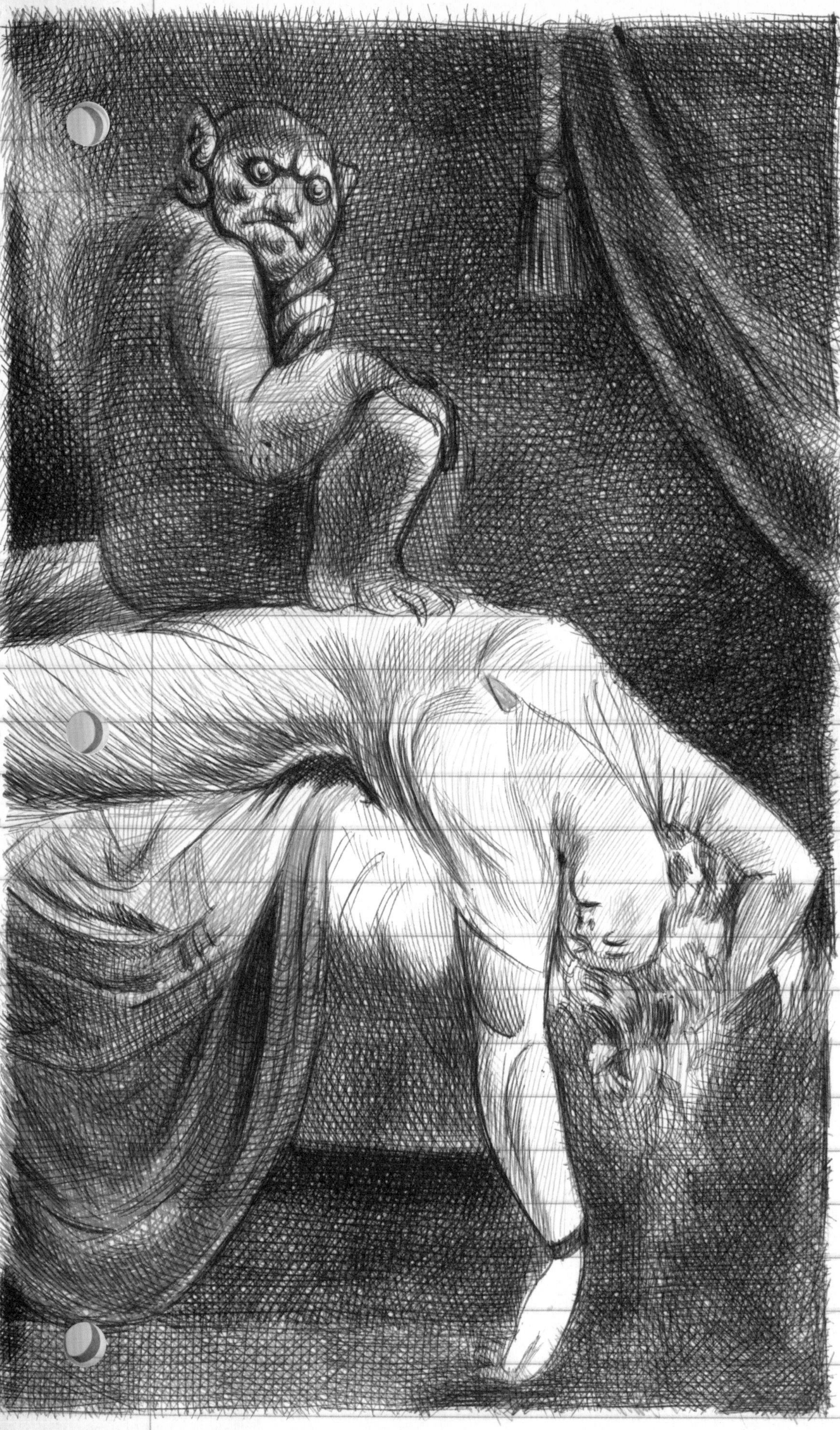

ACCORDING TO DEEZE THIS PAINTING INSPIRED ONE OF THE FIRST HORROR WRITERS, *MARY SHELLEY*, WHO LATER WROTE 'FRANKENSTEIN.'

WE STOOD IN FRONT OF IT FOR A LONG TIME (FRANKLY I THINK IT REALLY TURNED DEEZE *ON*.) HE SAID, "THAT HORSEY IS *TOTALLY INTO* WATCHING!" (WHICH WAS **GROSS**!)

FOR SOME REASON WHILE WE WERE IN FRONT OF FUSELI'S MASTERPIECE, I THOUGHT ABOUT ANKA.

SOMETIMES SHE SCREAMS IN THE MIDDLE OF THE NIGHT AND MR. SILVERBERG COMES DOWN AND APOLOGIZES.

"ONLY A BAD DREAM," HE SAYS, BUT WHEN I LOOK AT THE PAINTING I SEE THE WAY THE BEDSPREAD LOOKS LIKE... ***BLOOD***, AND THE WAY THE STITCHED MATTRESS LOOKS LIKE THE RIBS OF A CORPSE...

SURE, THE DEMON IS A *PROBLEM* BUT SOMETHING FROM HER PAST IS TORTURING THE LADY IN THE PAINTING.

WHERE WAS EVERYONE
WHEN ANKA DIED?

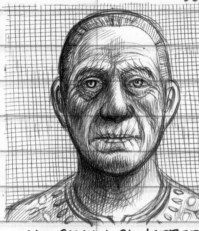

MR. SAMUEL SILVERBERG
...SAID THAT WHEN ANKA DIED HE'D BEEN AT A GIG IN PEORIA — BUT THE POLICE HADN'T AGREED.

MR. 'LAUGHING JACK' GRONAN
...HAD BEEN LOCATED AT THE 'GREEN MAN CLUB' WITHIN MINUTES OF ANKA'S DEATH.

MRS. SYLVIA GRONAN
...SAID THAT WHEN ANKA DIED SHE'D BEEN AT HER SISTER'S IN MILWAUKEE.

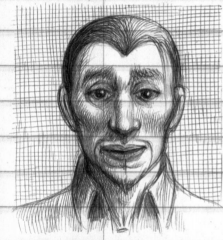

DIEGO ZAPATA 'DEEZE' REYES
MAMA HAD "LEFT A MESSAGE" FOR HIM AT HIS JOB AFTER ANKA WAS SHOT...WHY HADN'T SHE SPOKEN TO HIM?

MARVELA 'MAMA' REYES
...SAID SHE'D BEEN AT HER JOB BUT THAT TURNED OUT NOT TO BE THE TRUTH....

MR. SEAMUS CHUGG
I DON'T KNOW WHERE HE WAS WHEN ANKA DIED.

AN UNKNOWN SUSPECT
(SOMEONE I DON'T YET KNOW OF)

ALL THE QUESTIONS THAT FLOATED THROUGH MY MIND KEPT ME FROM SLEEPING. SO I WENT TO THE KITCHEN TO WARM UP SOME MILK. OUR KITCHEN SHARES A WALL WITH MR. CHUGG'S APARTMENT. I COULD HEAR HIM TALKING TO HIS DUMMIES, WHICH IS PRETTY NORMAL FOR HIM, BUT THE WEIRD THING IS THAT THEY WERE TALKING BACK...

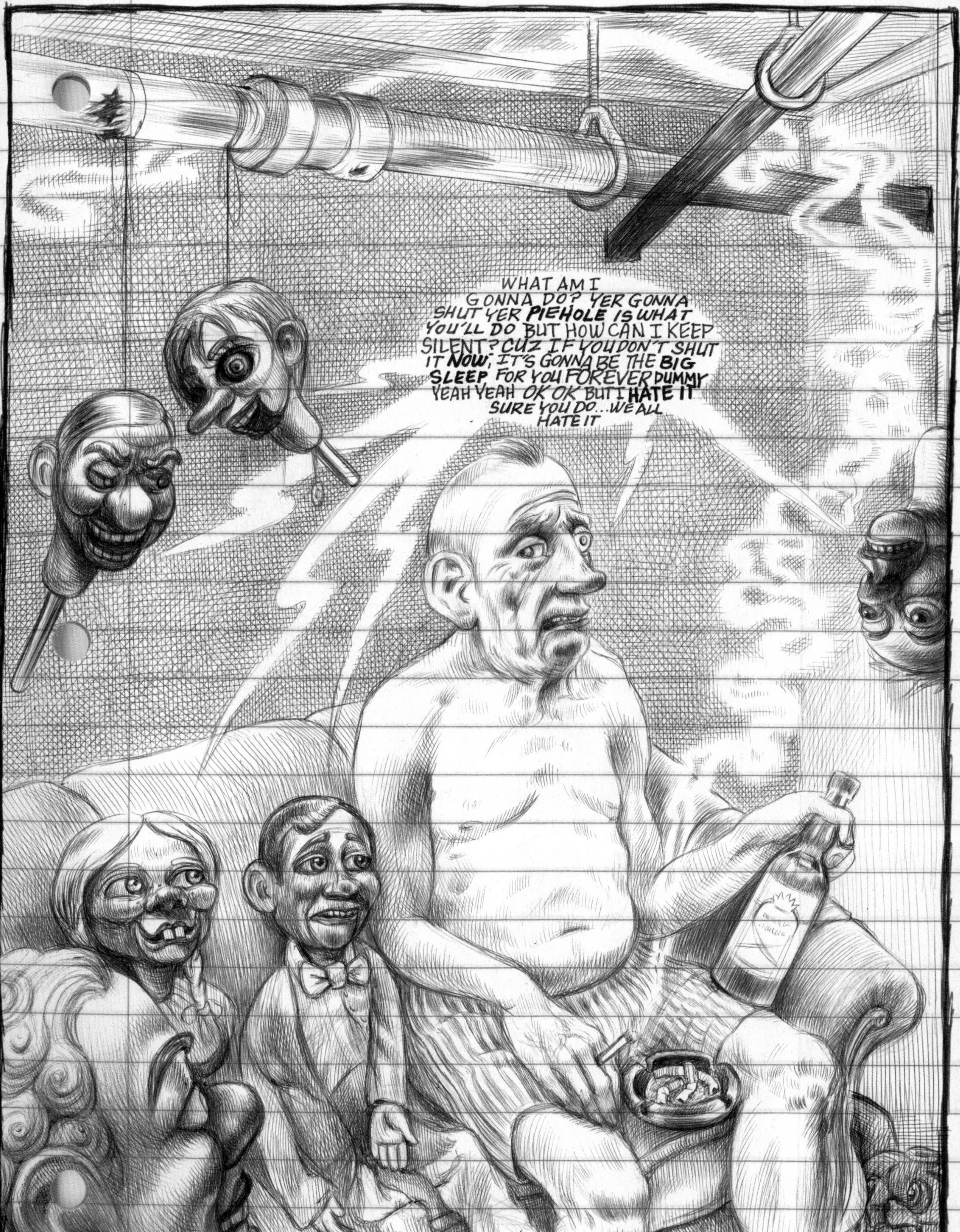
WHAT AM I GONNA DO? YER GONNA SHUT YER PIEHOLE IS WHAT YOU'LL DO BUT HOW CAN I KEEP SILENT? CUZ IF YOU DON'T SHUT IT NOW, IT'S GONNA BE THE BIG SLEEP FOR YOU FOREVER DUMMY YEAH YEAH OK OK BUT I HATE IT SURE YOU DO... WE ALL HATE IT

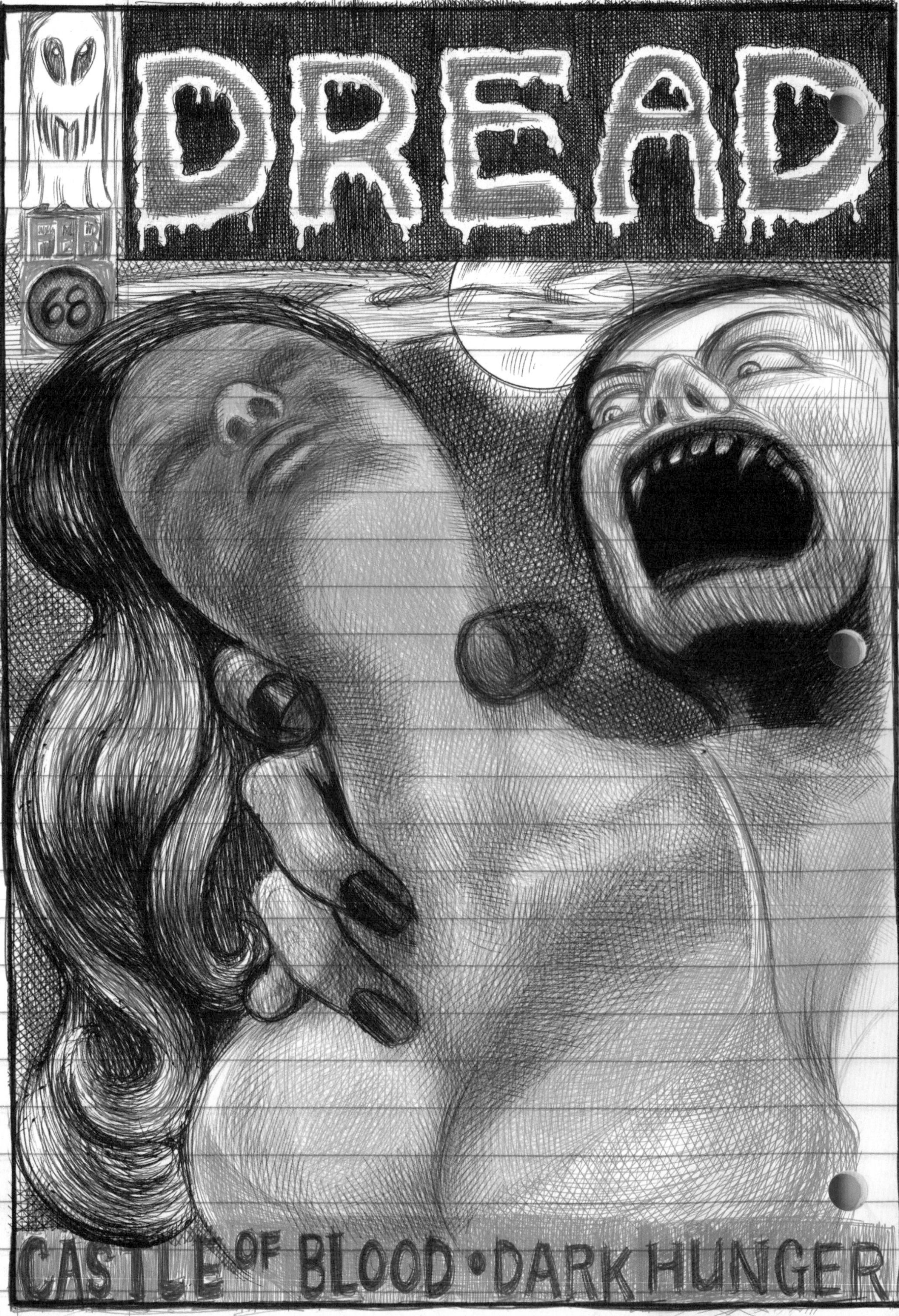
DREAD
FEB
68
CASTLE OF BLOOD • DARK HUNGER

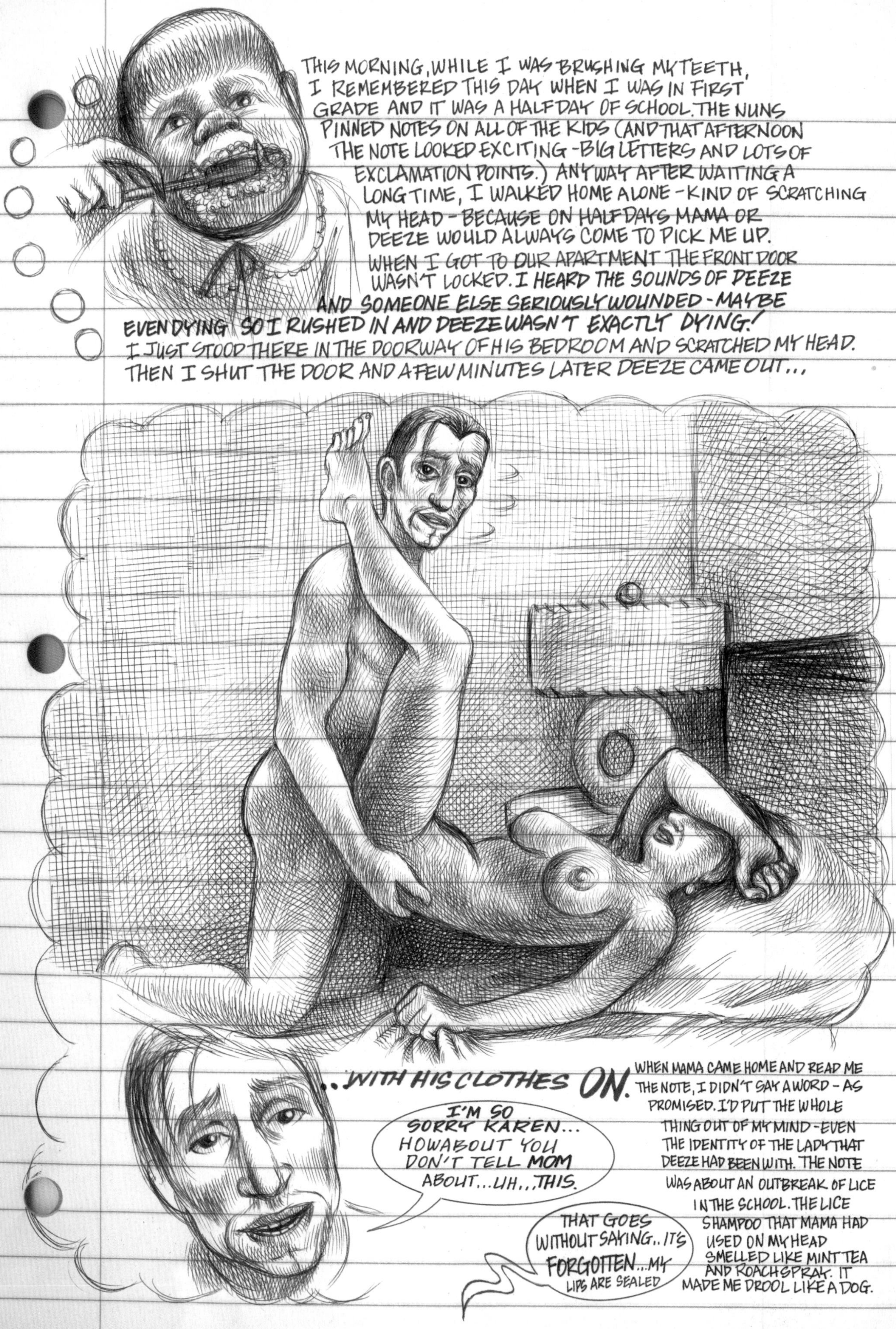

THIS MORNING, WHILE I WAS BRUSHING MY TEETH, I REMEMBERED THIS DAY WHEN I WAS IN FIRST GRADE AND IT WAS A HALF DAY OF SCHOOL. THE NUNS PINNED NOTES ON ALL OF THE KIDS (AND THAT AFTERNOON THE NOTE LOOKED EXCITING - BIG LETTERS AND LOTS OF EXCLAMATION POINTS.) ANYWAY AFTER WAITING A LONG TIME, I WALKED HOME ALONE - KIND OF SCRATCHING MY HEAD - BECAUSE ON HALF DAYS MAMA OR DEEZE WOULD ALWAYS COME TO PICK ME UP. WHEN I GOT TO OUR APARTMENT THE FRONT DOOR WASN'T LOCKED. I HEARD THE SOUNDS OF DEEZE AND SOMEONE ELSE SERIOUSLY WOUNDED - MAYBE EVEN DYING SO I RUSHED IN AND DEEZE WASN'T EXACTLY DYING!
I JUST STOOD THERE IN THE DOORWAY OF HIS BEDROOM AND SCRATCHED MY HEAD. THEN I SHUT THE DOOR AND A FEW MINUTES LATER DEEZE CAME OUT...
...WITH HIS CLOTHES ON.
I'M SO SORRY KAREN... HOW ABOUT YOU DON'T TELL MOM ABOUT... UH... THIS.
THAT GOES WITHOUT SAYING.. IT'S FORGOTTEN... MY LIPS ARE SEALED
WHEN MAMA CAME HOME AND READ ME THE NOTE, I DIDN'T SAY A WORD - AS PROMISED. I'D PUT THE WHOLE THING OUT OF MY MIND - EVEN THE IDENTITY OF THE LADY THAT DEEZE HAD BEEN WITH. THE NOTE WAS ABOUT AN OUTBREAK OF LICE IN THE SCHOOL. THE LICE SHAMPOO THAT MAMA HAD USED ON MY HEAD SMELLED LIKE MINT TEA AND ROACH SPRAY. IT MADE ME DROOL LIKE A DOG.

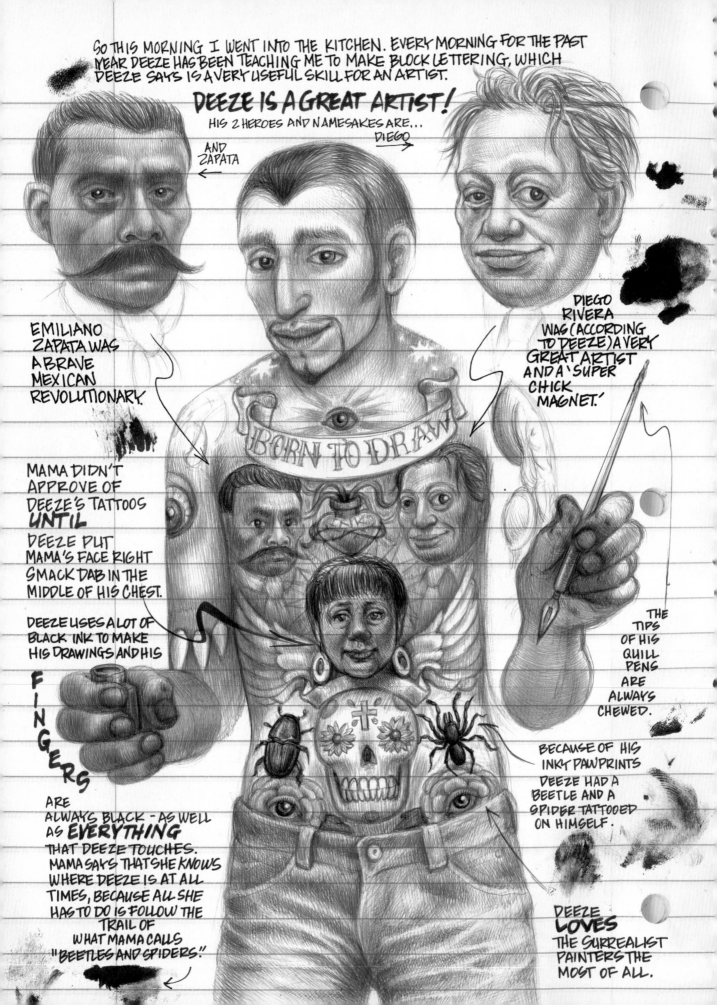

SO THIS MORNING I WENT INTO THE KITCHEN. EVERY MORNING FOR THE PAST YEAR DEEZE HAS BEEN TEACHING ME TO MAKE BLOCK LETTERING, WHICH DEEZE SAYS IS A VERY USEFUL SKILL FOR AN ARTIST.

DEEZE IS A GREAT ARTIST!

HIS 2 HEROES AND NAMESAKES ARE...

DIEGO

AND ZAPATA

EMILIANO ZAPATA WAS A BRAVE MEXICAN REVOLUTIONARY.

DIEGO RIVERA WAS (ACCORDING TO DEEZE) A VERY GREAT ARTIST AND A 'SUPER CHICK MAGNET.'

MAMA DIDN'T APPROVE OF DEEZE'S TATTOOS UNTIL DEEZE PUT MAMA'S FACE RIGHT SMACK DAB IN THE MIDDLE OF HIS CHEST.

DEEZE USES A LOT OF BLACK INK TO MAKE HIS DRAWINGS AND HIS

FINGERS

ARE ALWAYS BLACK - AS WELL AS EVERYTHING THAT DEEZE TOUCHES. MAMA SAYS THAT SHE KNOWS WHERE DEEZE IS AT ALL TIMES, BECAUSE ALL SHE HAS TO DO IS FOLLOW THE TRAIL OF WHAT MAMA CALLS "BEETLES AND SPIDERS!"

BORN TO DRAW

THE TIPS OF HIS QUILL PENS ARE ALWAYS CHEWED.

BECAUSE OF HIS INKY PAWPRINTS DEEZE HAD A BEETLE AND A SPIDER TATTOOED ON HIMSELF.

DEEZE LOVES THE SURREALIST PAINTERS THE MOST OF ALL.

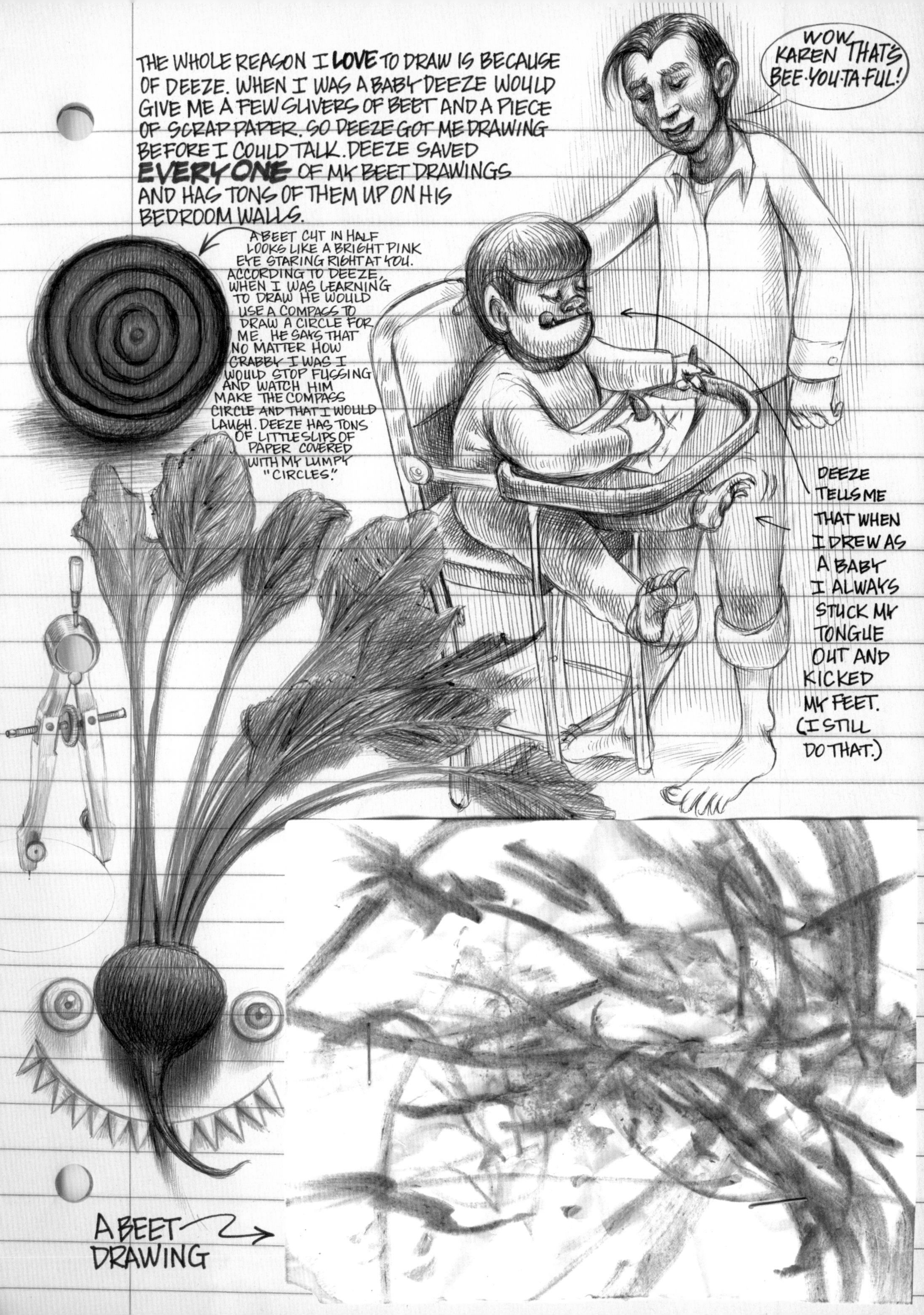
THE WHOLE REASON I LOVE TO DRAW IS BECAUSE OF DEEZE. WHEN I WAS A BABY DEEZE WOULD GIVE ME A FEW SLIVERS OF BEET AND A PIECE OF SCRAP PAPER. SO DEEZE GOT ME DRAWING BEFORE I COULD TALK. DEEZE SAVED EVERY ONE OF MY BEET DRAWINGS AND HAS TONS OF THEM UP ON HIS BEDROOM WALLS.
WOW KAREN THAT'S BEE-YOU-TA-FUL!
A BEET CUT IN HALF LOOKS LIKE A BRIGHT PINK EYE STARING RIGHT AT YOU. ACCORDING TO DEEZE, WHEN I WAS LEARNING TO DRAW HE WOULD USE A COMPASS TO DRAW A CIRCLE FOR ME. HE SAYS THAT NO MATTER HOW CRABBY I WAS I WOULD STOP FUSSING AND WATCH HIM MAKE THE COMPASS CIRCLE AND THAT I WOULD LAUGH. DEEZE HAS TONS OF LITTLE SLIPS OF PAPER COVERED WITH MY LUMPY "CIRCLES."
DEEZE TELLS ME THAT WHEN I DREW AS A BABY I ALWAYS STUCK MY TONGUE OUT AND KICKED MY FEET. (I STILL DO THAT.)
A BEET DRAWING

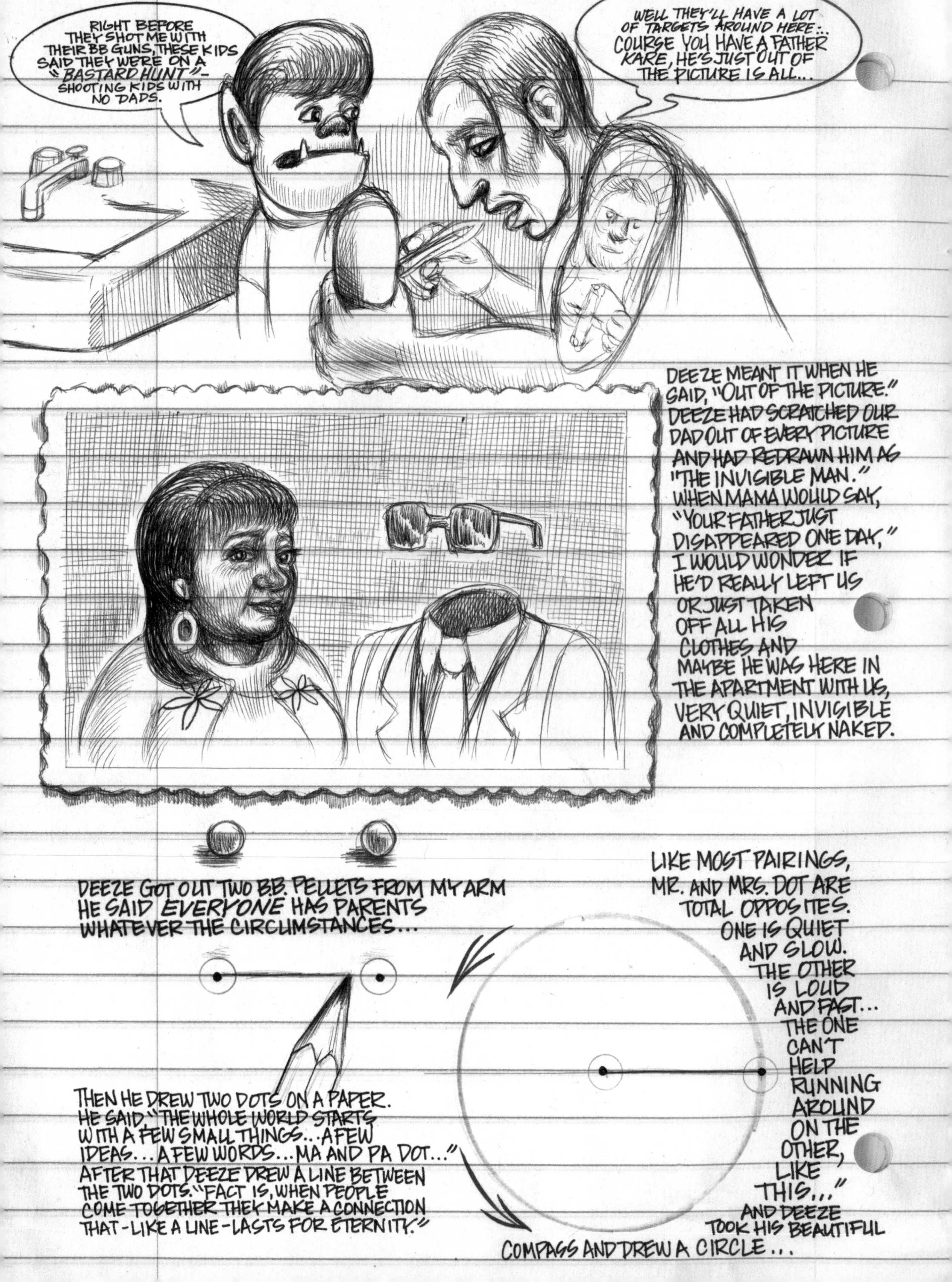
RIGHT BEFORE THEY SHOT ME WITH THEIR BB GUNS, THESE KIDS SAID THEY WERE ON A "BASTARD HUNT"- SHOOTING KIDS WITH NO DADS.
WELL THEY'LL HAVE A LOT OF TARGETS AROUND HERE... COURSE YOU HAVE A FATHER KARE, HE'S JUST OUT OF THE PICTURE IS ALL...
DEEZE MEANT IT WHEN HE SAID, "OUT OF THE PICTURE." DEEZE HAD SCRATCHED OUR DAD OUT OF EVERY PICTURE AND HAD REDRAWN HIM AS "THE INVISIBLE MAN." WHEN MAMA WOULD SAY, "YOUR FATHER JUST DISAPPEARED ONE DAY," I WOULD WONDER IF HE'D REALLY LEFT US OR JUST TAKEN OFF ALL HIS CLOTHES AND MAYBE HE WAS HERE IN THE APARTMENT WITH US, VERY QUIET, INVISIBLE AND COMPLETELY NAKED.
DEEZE GOT OUT TWO B.B. PELLETS FROM MY ARM HE SAID EVERYONE HAS PARENTS WHATEVER THE CIRCUMSTANCES...
THEN HE DREW TWO DOTS ON A PAPER. HE SAID, "THE WHOLE WORLD STARTS WITH A FEW SMALL THINGS... A FEW IDEAS... A FEW WORDS... MA AND PA DOT..." AFTER THAT DEEZE DREW A LINE BETWEEN THE TWO DOTS. "FACT IS, WHEN PEOPLE COME TOGETHER THEY MAKE A CONNECTION THAT-LIKE A LINE-LASTS FOR ETERNITY."
LIKE MOST PAIRINGS, MR. AND MRS. DOT ARE TOTAL OPPOSITES. ONE IS QUIET AND SLOW. THE OTHER IS LOUD AND FAST... THE ONE CAN'T HELP RUNNING AROUND ON THE OTHER, LIKE THIS..." AND DEEZE TOOK HIS BEAUTIFUL COMPASS AND DREW A CIRCLE...

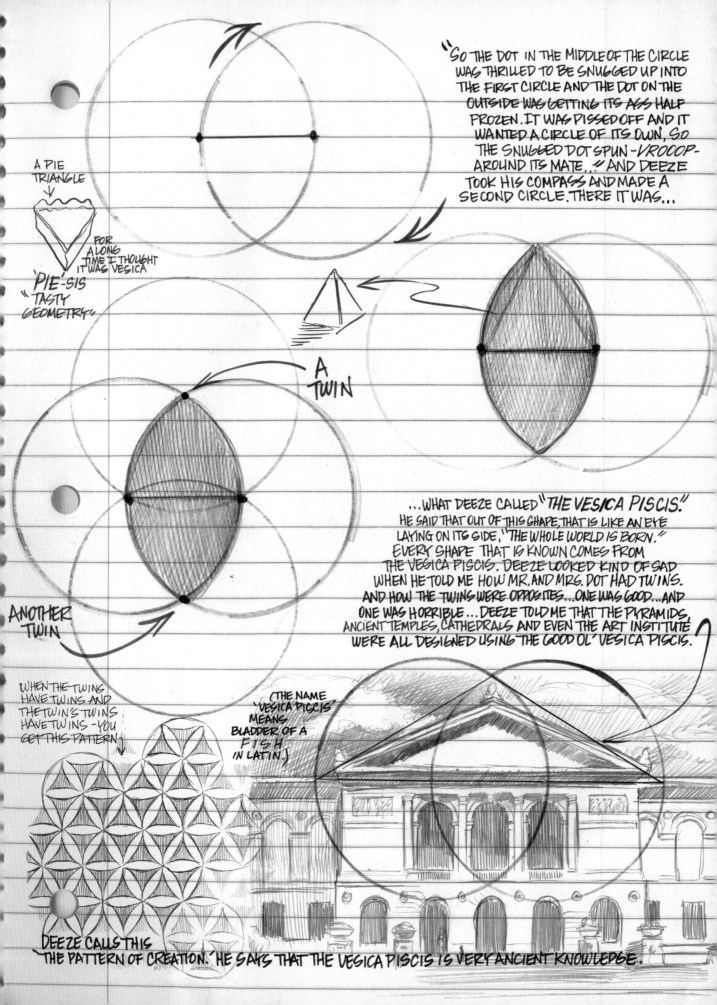

"SO THE DOT IN THE MIDDLE OF THE CIRCLE WAS THRILLED TO BE SNUGGED UP INTO THE FIRST CIRCLE AND THE DOT ON THE OUTSIDE WAS GETTING ITS ASS HALF FROZEN. IT WAS PISSED OFF AND IT WANTED A CIRCLE OF ITS OWN, SO THE SNUGGED DOT SPUN -VROOOP- AROUND ITS MATE..." AND DEEZE TOOK HIS COMPASS AND MADE A SECOND CIRCLE. THERE IT WAS...

A PIE TRIANGLE

FOR A LONG TIME I THOUGHT IT WAS VESICA

'PIE-SIS' "TASTY GEOMETRY"

A TWIN

...WHAT DEEZE CALLED "THE VESICA PISCIS." HE SAID THAT OUT OF THIS SHAPE, THAT IS LIKE AN EYE LAYING ON ITS SIDE, "THE WHOLE WORLD IS BORN." EVERY SHAPE THAT IS KNOWN COMES FROM THE VESICA PISCIS. DEEZE LOOKED KIND OF SAD WHEN HE TOLD ME HOW MR. AND MRS. DOT HAD TWINS. AND HOW THE TWINS WERE OPPOSITES...ONE WAS GOOD... AND ONE WAS HORRIBLE... DEEZE TOLD ME THAT THE PYRAMIDS, ANCIENT TEMPLES, CATHEDRALS AND EVEN THE ART INSTITUTE WERE ALL DESIGNED USING THE GOOD OL' VESICA PISCIS.

ANOTHER TWIN

WHEN THE TWINS HAVE TWINS AND THE TWIN'S TWINS HAVE TWINS -YOU GET THIS PATTERN

(THE NAME 'VESICA PISCIS' MEANS BLADDER OF A FISH IN LATIN.)

DEEZE CALLS THIS 'THE PATTERN OF CREATION.' HE SAYS THAT THE VESICA PISCIS IS VERY ANCIENT KNOWLEDGE.

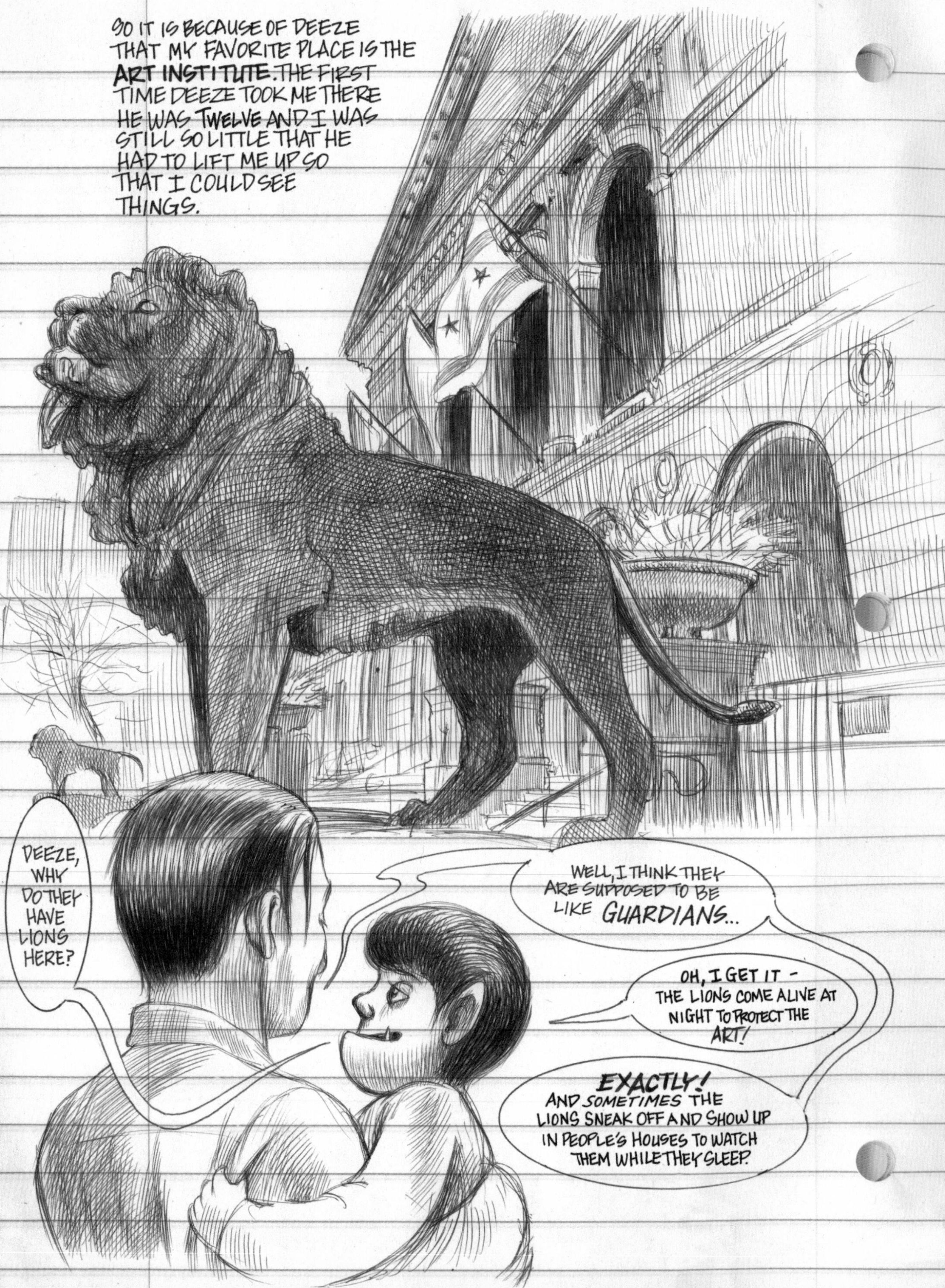
SO IT IS BECAUSE OF DEEZE THAT MY FAVORITE PLACE IS THE ART INSTITUTE. THE FIRST TIME DEEZE TOOK ME THERE HE WAS TWELVE AND I WAS STILL SO LITTLE THAT HE HAD TO LIFT ME UP SO THAT I COULD SEE THINGS.
DEEZE, WHY DO THEY HAVE LIONS HERE?
WELL, I THINK THEY ARE SUPPOSED TO BE LIKE GUARDIANS...
OH, I GET IT - THE LIONS COME ALIVE AT NIGHT TO PROTECT THE ART!
EXACTLY! AND SOMETIMES THE LIONS SNEAK OFF AND SHOW UP IN PEOPLE'S HOUSES TO WATCH THEM WHILE THEY SLEEP.

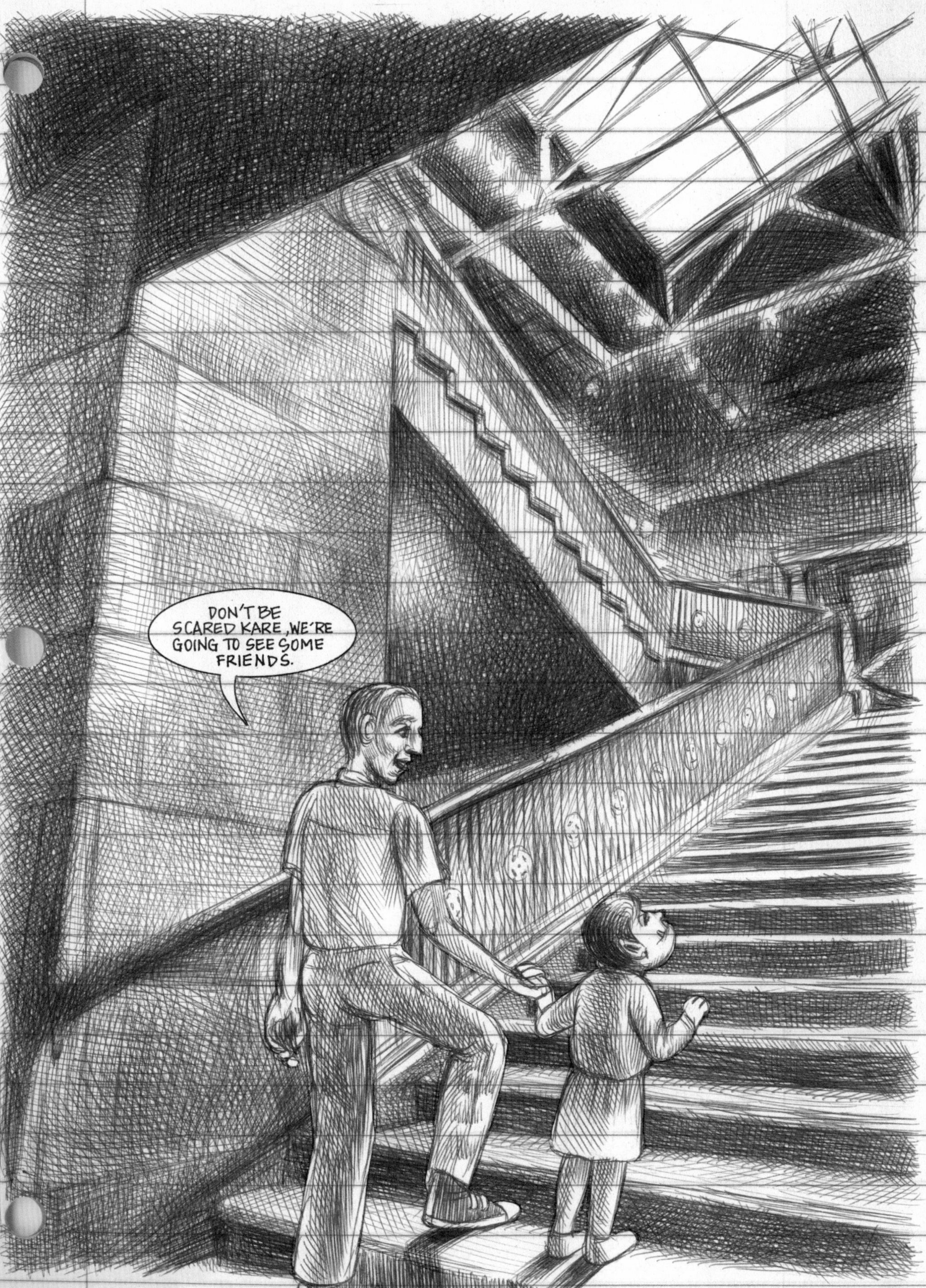
DON'T BE SCARED KARE, WE'RE GOING TO SEE SOME FRIENDS.

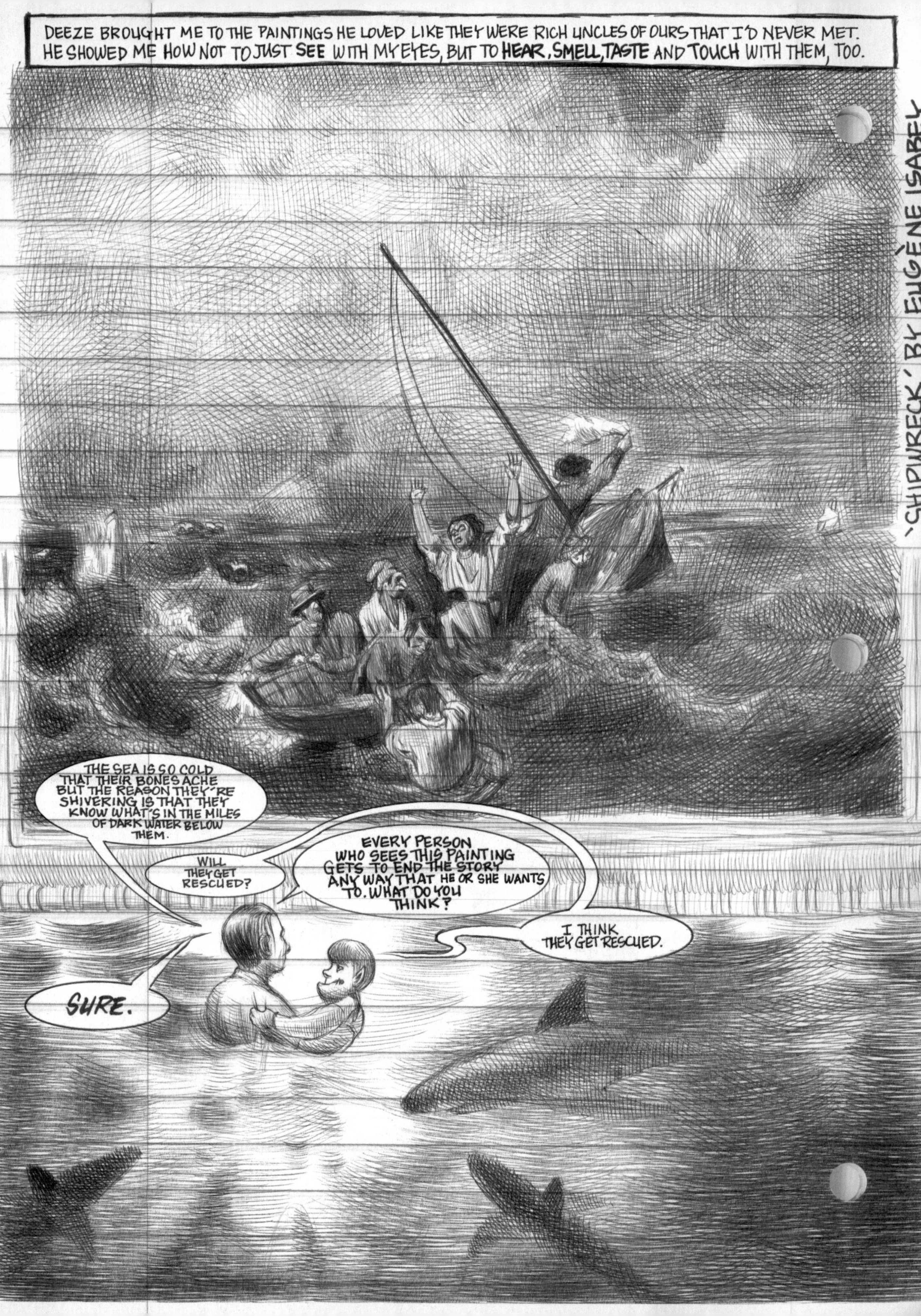
DEEZE BROUGHT ME TO THE PAINTINGS HE LOVED LIKE THEY WERE RICH UNCLES OF OURS THAT I'D NEVER MET. HE SHOWED ME HOW NOT TO JUST SEE WITH MY EYES, BUT TO HEAR, SMELL, TASTE AND TOUCH WITH THEM, TOO.
'SHIPWRECK' BY EUGÈNE ISABEY
THE SEA IS SO COLD THAT THEIR BONES ACHE BUT THE REASON THEY'RE SHIVERING IS THAT THEY KNOW WHAT'S IN THE MILES OF DARK WATER BELOW THEM.
WILL THEY GET RESCUED?
EVERY PERSON WHO SEES THIS PAINTING GETS TO END THE STORY ANY WAY THAT HE OR SHE WANTS TO. WHAT DO YOU THINK?
I THINK THEY GET RESCUED.
SURE.

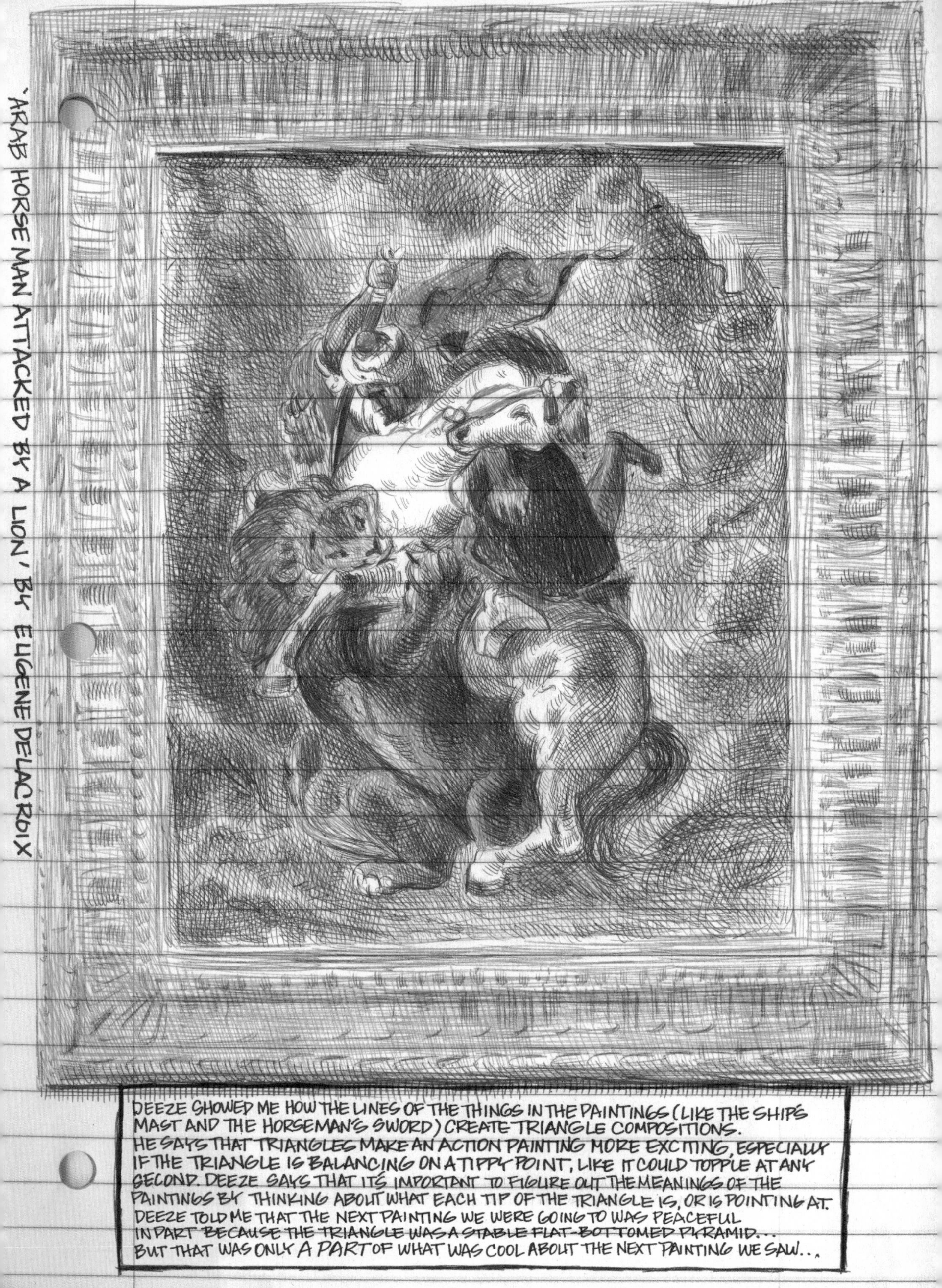

'ARAB HORSEMAN ATTACKED BY A LION' BY EUGENE DELACROIX

DEEZE SHOWED ME HOW THE LINES OF THE THINGS IN THE PAINTINGS (LIKE THE SHIPS MAST AND THE HORSEMAN'S SWORD) CREATE TRIANGLE COMPOSITIONS.
HE SAYS THAT TRIANGLES MAKE AN ACTION PAINTING MORE EXCITING, ESPECIALLY IF THE TRIANGLE IS BALANCING ON A TIPPY POINT, LIKE IT COULD TOPPLE AT ANY SECOND. DEEZE SAYS THAT IT'S IMPORTANT TO FIGURE OUT THE MEANINGS OF THE PAINTINGS BY THINKING ABOUT WHAT EACH TIP OF THE TRIANGLE IS, OR IS POINTING AT.
DEEZE TOLD ME THAT THE NEXT PAINTING WE WERE GOING TO WAS PEACEFUL IN PART BECAUSE THE TRIANGLE WAS A STABLE FLAT-BOTTOMED PYRAMID... BUT THAT WAS ONLY A PART OF WHAT WAS COOL ABOUT THE NEXT PAINTING WE SAW...

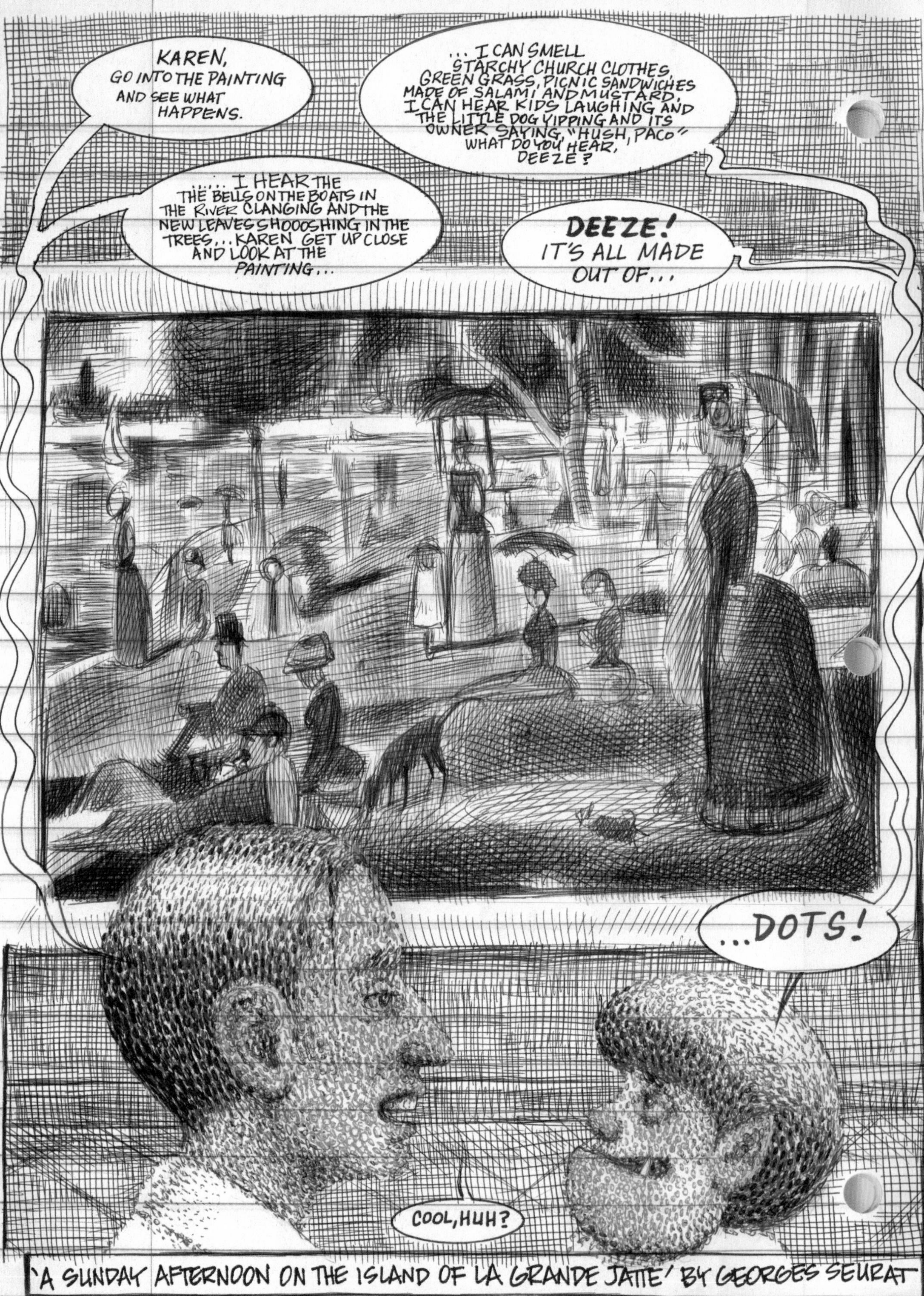
KAREN, GO INTO THE PAINTING AND SEE WHAT HAPPENS.
... I CAN SMELL STARCHY CHURCH CLOTHES, GREEN GRASS, PICNIC SANDWICHES MADE OF SALAMI AND MUSTARD. I CAN HEAR KIDS LAUGHING AND THE LITTLE DOG YIPPING AND ITS OWNER SAYING, "HUSH, PACO" WHAT DO YOU HEAR, DEEZE?
...... I HEAR THE THE BELLS ON THE BOATS IN THE RIVER CLANGING AND THE NEW LEAVES SHOOOSHING IN THE TREES... KAREN GET UP CLOSE AND LOOK AT THE PAINTING...
DEEZE! IT'S ALL MADE OUT OF...
...DOTS!
COOL, HUH?
'A SUNDAY AFTERNOON ON THE ISLAND OF LA GRANDE JATTE' BY GEORGES SEURAT

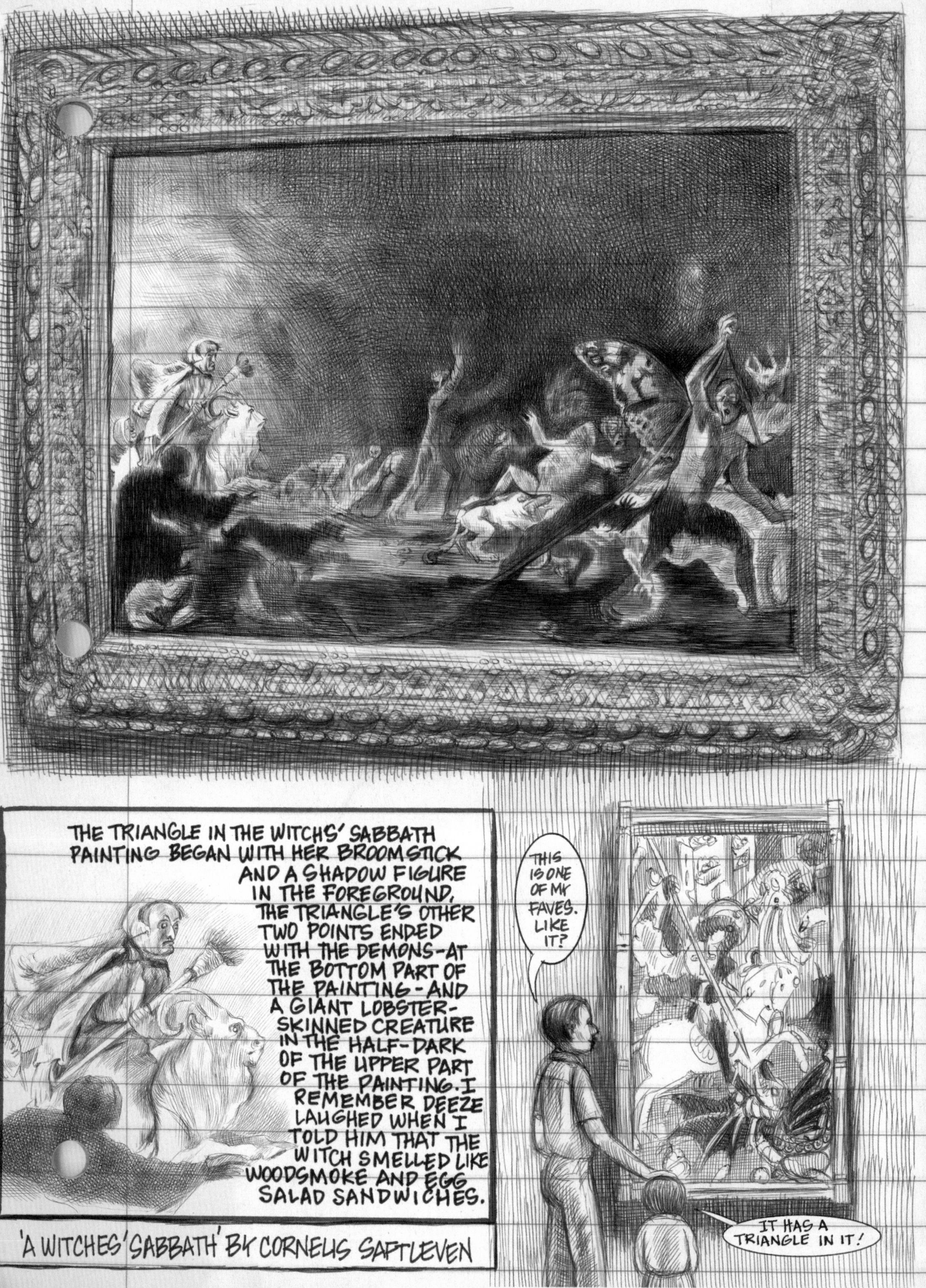
THE TRIANGLE IN THE WITCHS' SABBATH PAINTING BEGAN WITH HER BROOMSTICK AND A SHADOW FIGURE IN THE FOREGROUND, THE TRIANGLE'S OTHER TWO POINTS ENDED WITH THE DEMONS-AT THE BOTTOM PART OF THE PAINTING-AND A GIANT LOBSTER-SKINNED CREATURE IN THE HALF-DARK OF THE UPPER PART OF THE PAINTING. I REMEMBER DEEZE LAUGHED WHEN I TOLD HIM THAT THE WITCH SMELLED LIKE WOODSMOKE AND EGG SALAD SANDWICHES.
'A WITCHES' SABBATH' BY CORNELIS SAFTLEVEN
THIS IS ONE OF MY FAVES. LIKE IT?
IT HAS A TRIANGLE IN IT!

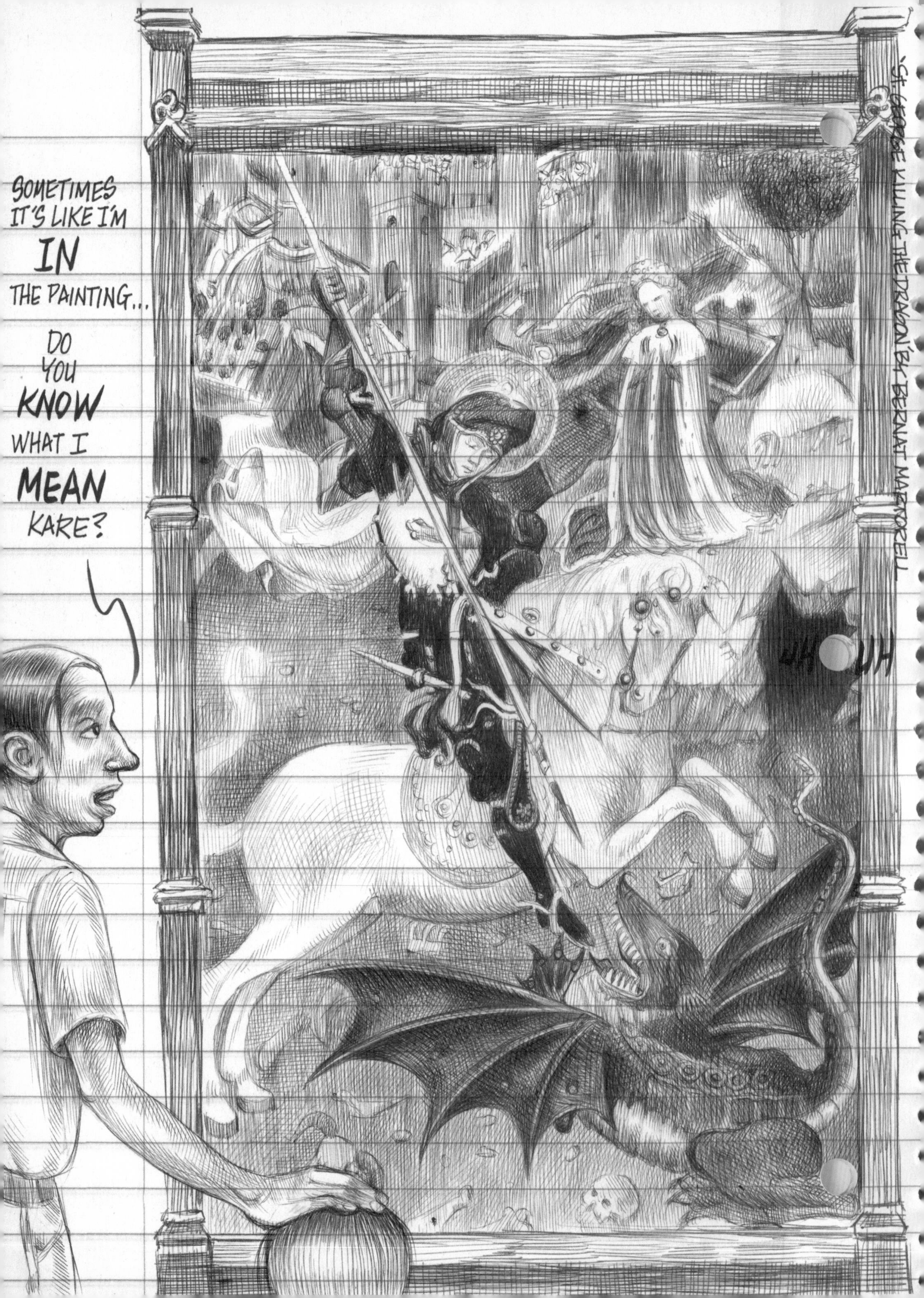
'ST GEORGE KILLING THE DRAGON' BY BERNAT MARTORELL
SOMETIMES IT'S LIKE I'M IN THE PAINTING... DO YOU KNOW WHAT I MEAN KARE?

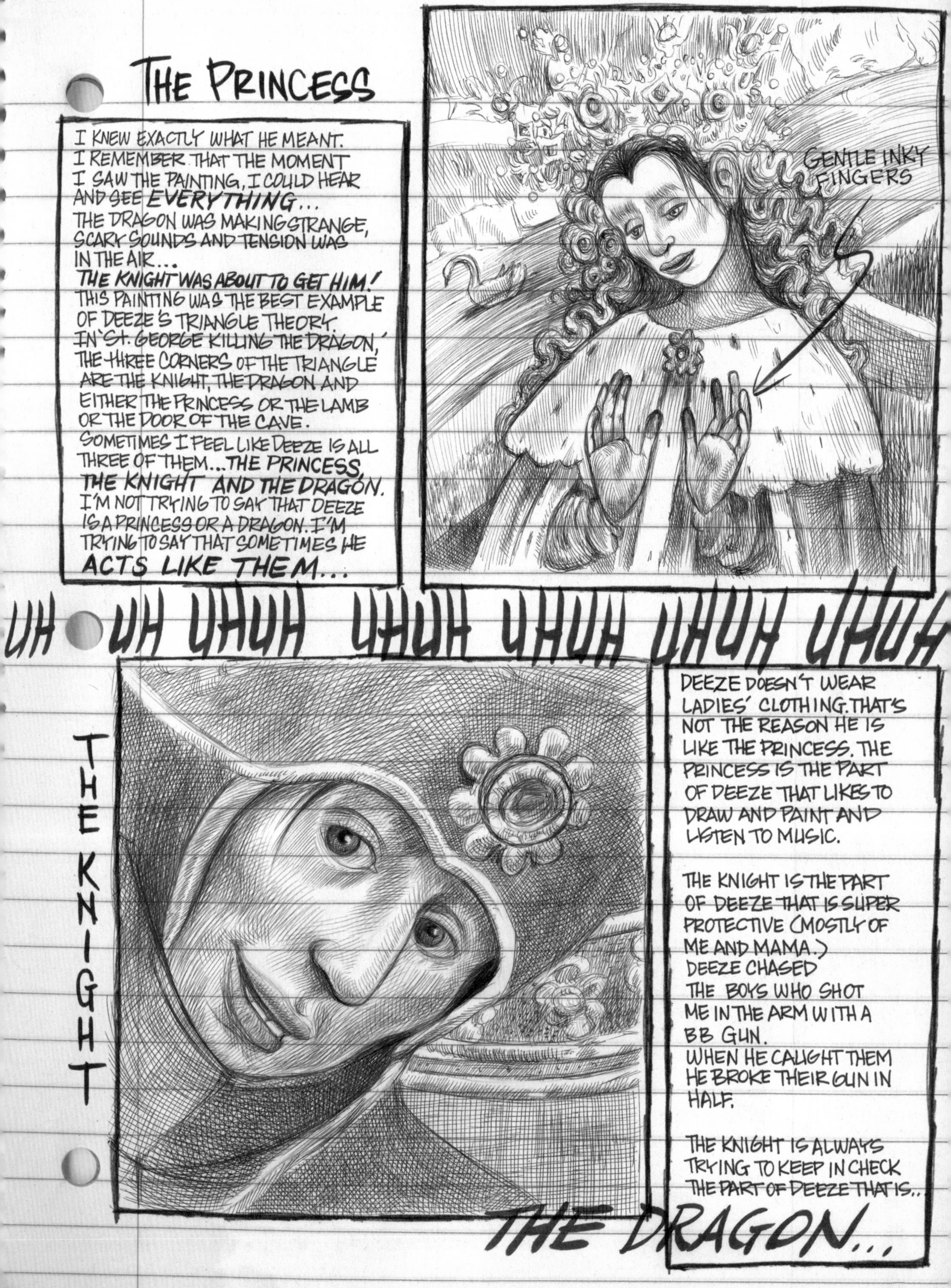
THE PRINCESS
I KNEW EXACTLY WHAT HE MEANT. I REMEMBER THAT THE MOMENT I SAW THE PAINTING, I COULD HEAR AND SEE EVERYTHING... THE DRAGON WAS MAKING STRANGE, SCARY SOUNDS AND TENSION WAS IN THE AIR... THE KNIGHT WAS ABOUT TO GET HIM! THIS PAINTING WAS THE BEST EXAMPLE OF DEEZE'S TRIANGLE THEORY. IN 'ST. GEORGE KILLING THE DRAGON,' THE THREE CORNERS OF THE TRIANGLE ARE THE KNIGHT, THE DRAGON AND EITHER THE PRINCESS OR THE LAMB OR THE DOOR OF THE CAVE. SOMETIMES I FEEL LIKE DEEZE IS ALL THREE OF THEM... THE PRINCESS, THE KNIGHT AND THE DRAGON. I'M NOT TRYING TO SAY THAT DEEZE IS A PRINCESS OR A DRAGON. I'M TRYING TO SAY THAT SOMETIMES HE ACTS LIKE THEM...
GENTLE INKY FINGERS
UH UH UHUH UHUH UHUH UHUH UHUH
THE KNIGHT
DEEZE DOESN'T WEAR LADIES' CLOTHING. THAT'S NOT THE REASON HE IS LIKE THE PRINCESS. THE PRINCESS IS THE PART OF DEEZE THAT LIKES TO DRAW AND PAINT AND LISTEN TO MUSIC.
THE KNIGHT IS THE PART OF DEEZE THAT IS SUPER PROTECTIVE (MOSTLY OF ME AND MAMA.) DEEZE CHASED THE BOYS WHO SHOT ME IN THE ARM WITH A BB GUN. WHEN HE CAUGHT THEM HE BROKE THEIR GUN IN HALF.
THE KNIGHT IS ALWAYS TRYING TO KEEP IN CHECK THE PART OF DEEZE THAT IS...
THE DRAGON...

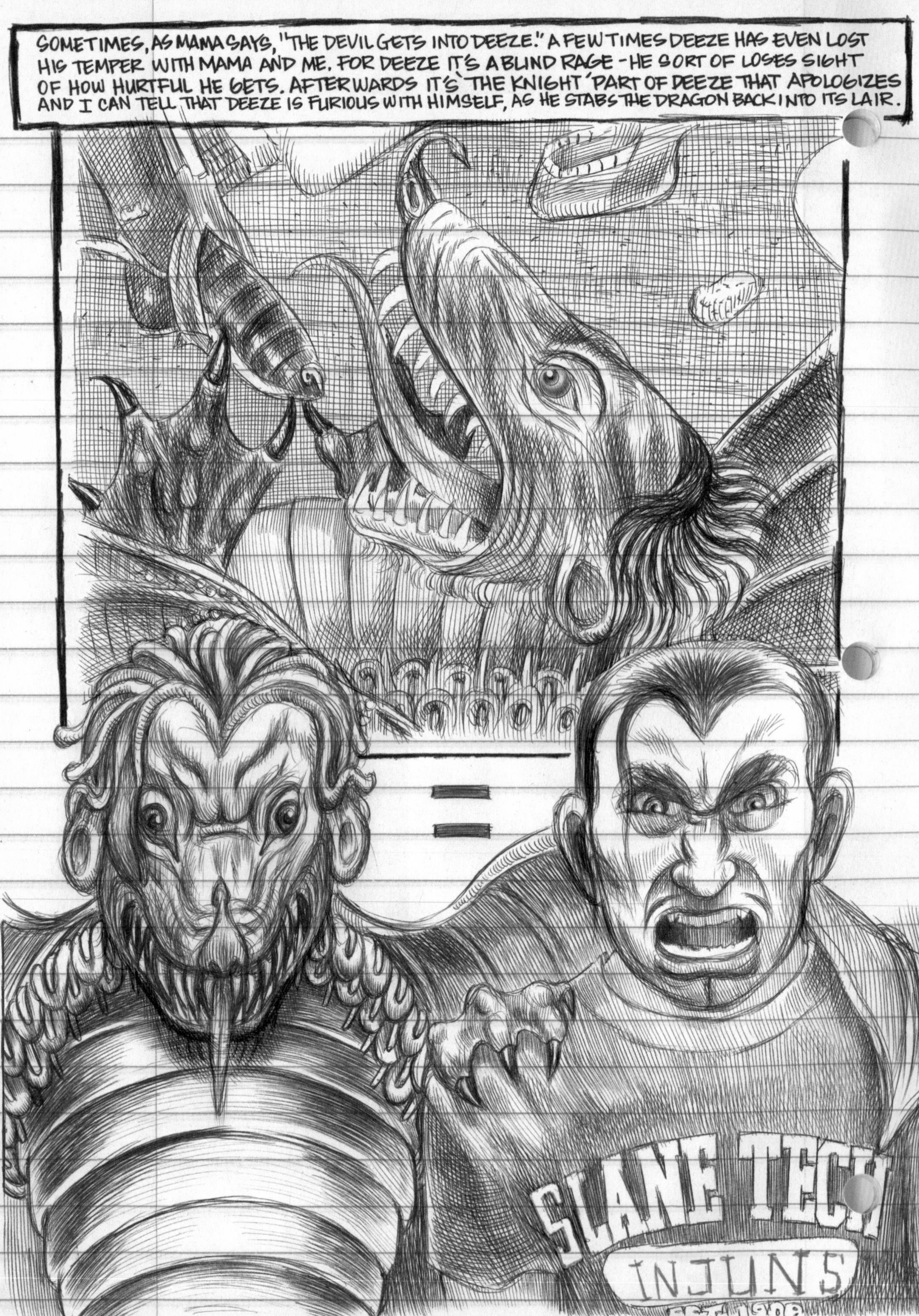
SOMETIMES, AS MAMA SAYS, "THE DEVIL GETS INTO DEEZE." A FEW TIMES DEEZE HAS EVEN LOST HIS TEMPER WITH MAMA AND ME. FOR DEEZE IT'S A BLIND RAGE - HE SORT OF LOSES SIGHT OF HOW HURTFUL HE GETS. AFTERWARDS IT'S "THE KNIGHT" PART OF DEEZE THAT APOLOGIZES AND I CAN TELL THAT DEEZE IS FURIOUS WITH HIMSELF, AS HE STABS THE DRAGON BACK INTO ITS LAIR.
SLANE TECH
INJUNS

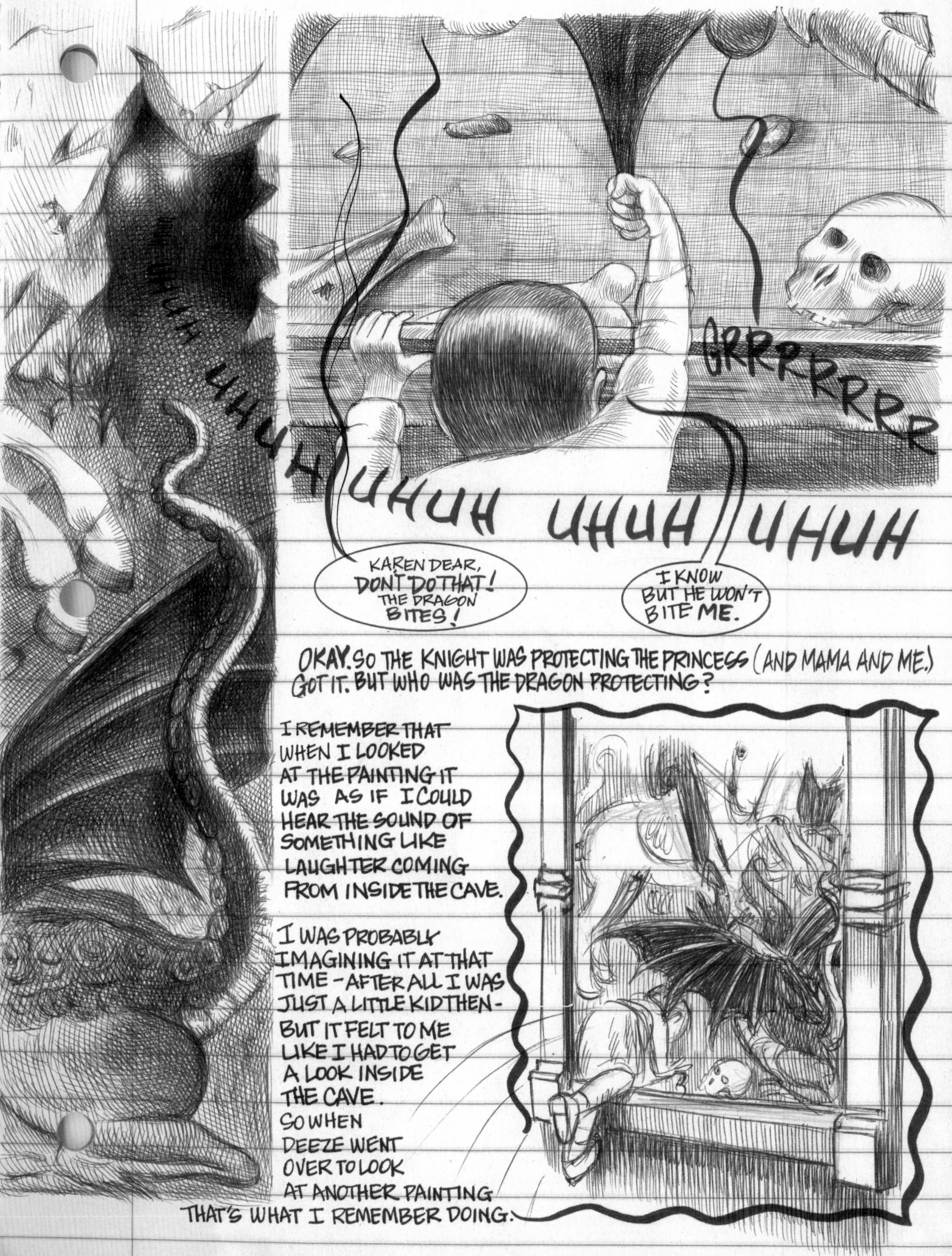

UHUH UHUH UHUH
GRRRRRRRRR
UHUH UHUH UHUH
KAREN DEAR, DON'T DO THAT! THE DRAGON BITES!
I KNOW BUT HE WON'T BITE ME.
OKAY. SO THE KNIGHT WAS PROTECTING THE PRINCESS (AND MAMA AND ME.) GOT IT. BUT WHO WAS THE DRAGON PROTECTING?
I REMEMBER THAT WHEN I LOOKED AT THE PAINTING IT WAS AS IF I COULD HEAR THE SOUND OF SOMETHING LIKE LAUGHTER COMING FROM INSIDE THE CAVE.
I WAS PROBABLY IMAGINING IT AT THAT TIME - AFTER ALL I WAS JUST A LITTLE KID THEN - BUT IT FELT TO ME LIKE I HAD TO GET A LOOK INSIDE THE CAVE.
SO WHEN DEEZE WENT OVER TO LOOK AT ANOTHER PAINTING
THAT'S WHAT I REMEMBER DOING.

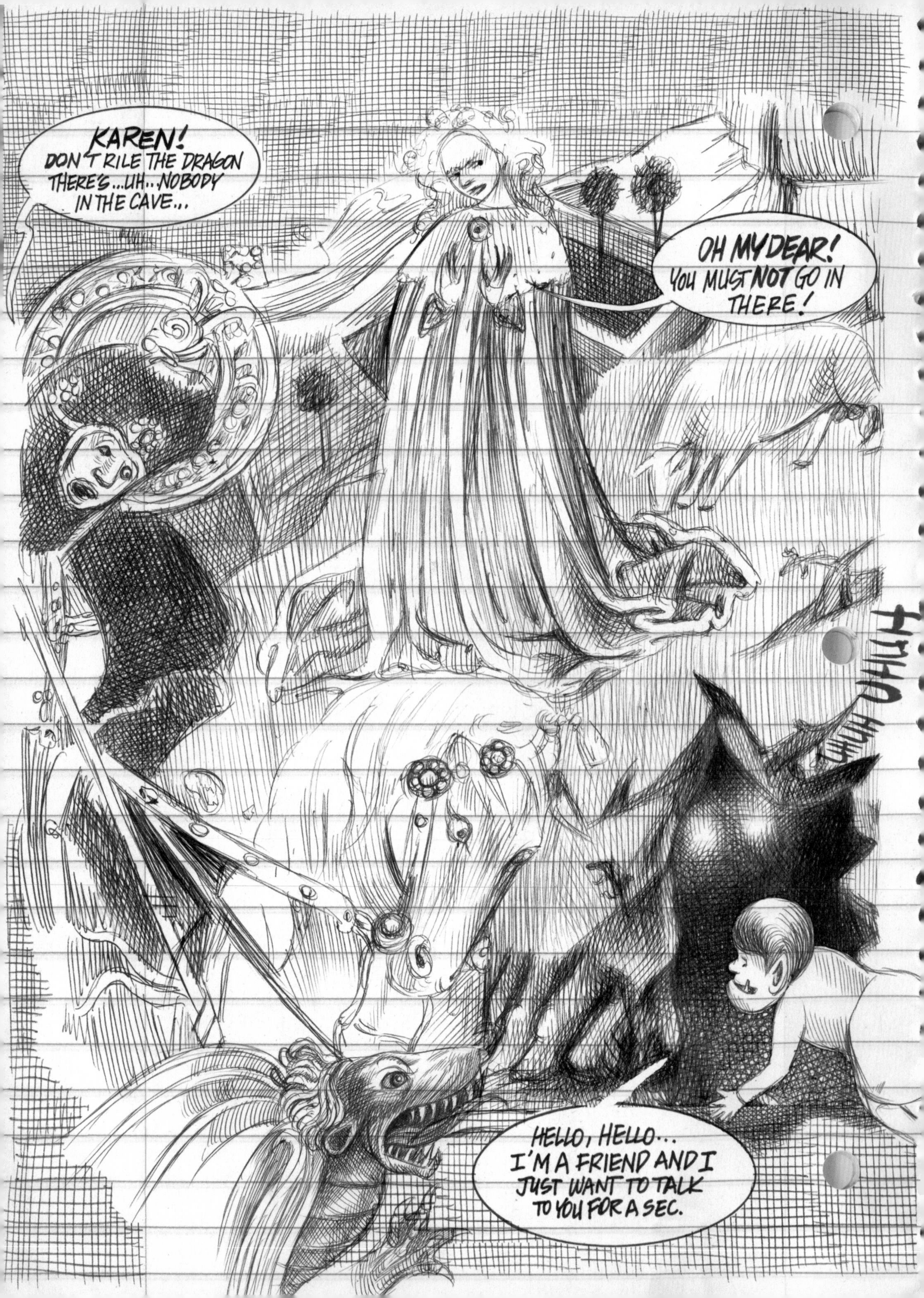
KAREN! DON'T RILE THE DRAGON THERE'S...UH...NOBODY IN THE CAVE...
OH MY DEAR! YOU MUST NOT GO IN THERE!
HELLO, HELLO... I'M A FRIEND AND I JUST WANT TO TALK TO YOU FOR A SEC.

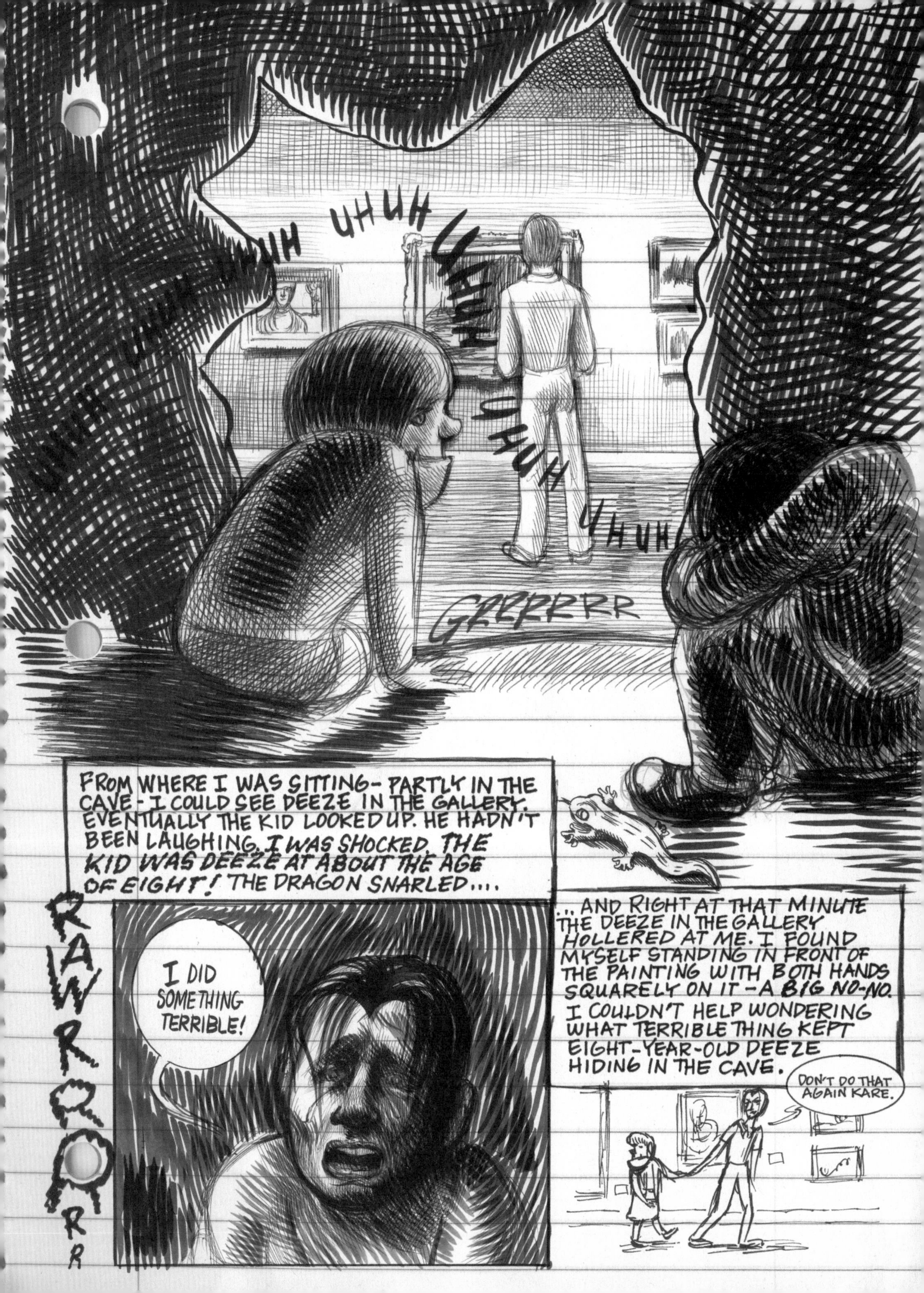

UHUH UHUH UHUH UHUH UHUH UHUH UHUH UHUH
GRRRRRR
FROM WHERE I WAS SITTING - PARTLY IN THE CAVE - I COULD SEE DEEZE IN THE GALLERY. EVENTUALLY THE KID LOOKED UP. HE HADN'T BEEN LAUGHING. I WAS SHOCKED. THE KID WAS DEEZE AT ABOUT THE AGE OF EIGHT! THE DRAGON SNARLED....
RAWRRRRR
I DID SOMETHING TERRIBLE!
... AND RIGHT AT THAT MINUTE THE DEEZE IN THE GALLERY HOLLERED AT ME. I FOUND MYSELF STANDING IN FRONT OF THE PAINTING WITH BOTH HANDS SQUARELY ON IT - A BIG NO-NO. I COULDN'T HELP WONDERING WHAT TERRIBLE THING KEPT EIGHT-YEAR-OLD DEEZE HIDING IN THE CAVE.
DON'T DO THAT AGAIN KARE.

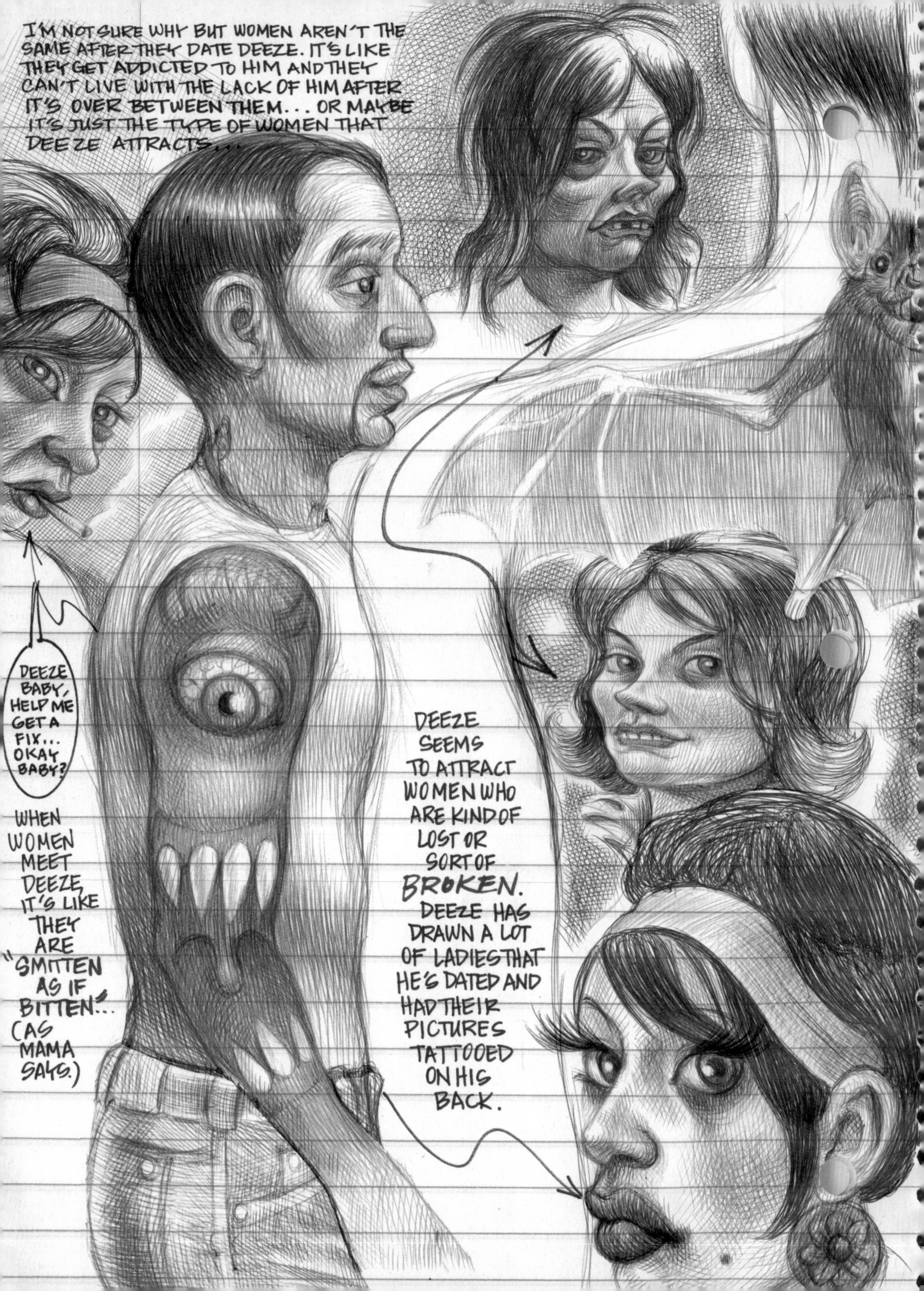
I'M NOT SURE WHY BUT WOMEN AREN'T THE SAME AFTER THEY DATE DEEZE. IT'S LIKE THEY GET ADDICTED TO HIM AND THEY CAN'T LIVE WITH THE LACK OF HIM AFTER IT'S OVER BETWEEN THEM... OR MAYBE IT'S JUST THE TYPE OF WOMEN THAT DEEZE ATTRACTS...
DEEZE BABY, HELP ME GET A FIX... OKAY BABY?
WHEN WOMEN MEET DEEZE, IT'S LIKE THEY ARE "SMITTEN AS IF BITTEN"... (AS MAMA SAYS.)
DEEZE SEEMS TO ATTRACT WOMEN WHO ARE KIND OF LOST OR SORT OF BROKEN. DEEZE HAS DRAWN A LOT OF LADIES THAT HE'S DATED AND HAD THEIR PICTURES TATTOOED ON HIS BACK.

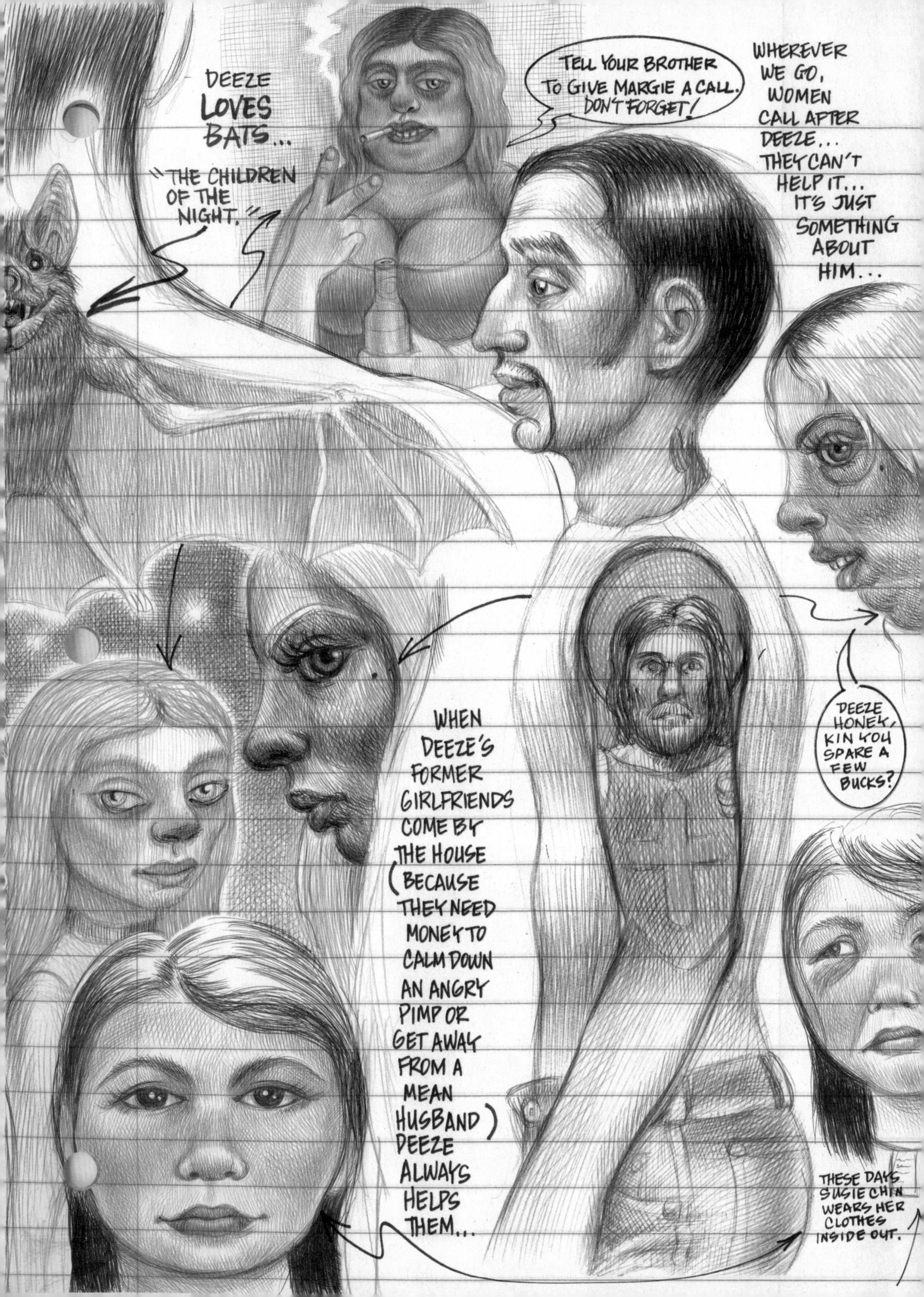
DEEZE LOVES BATS...
"THE CHILDREN OF THE NIGHT."
TELL YOUR BROTHER TO GIVE MARGIE A CALL. DON'T FORGET!
WHEREVER WE GO, WOMEN CALL AFTER DEEZE... THEY CAN'T HELP IT... IT'S JUST SOMETHING ABOUT HIM...
DEEZE HONEY, KIN YOU SPARE A FEW BUCKS?
WHEN DEEZE'S FORMER GIRLFRIENDS COME BY THE HOUSE (BECAUSE THEY NEED MONEY TO CALM DOWN AN ANGRY PIMP OR GET AWAY FROM A MEAN HUSBAND) DEEZE ALWAYS HELPS THEM...
THESE DAYS SUSIE CHIN WEARS HER CLOTHES INSIDE OUT.

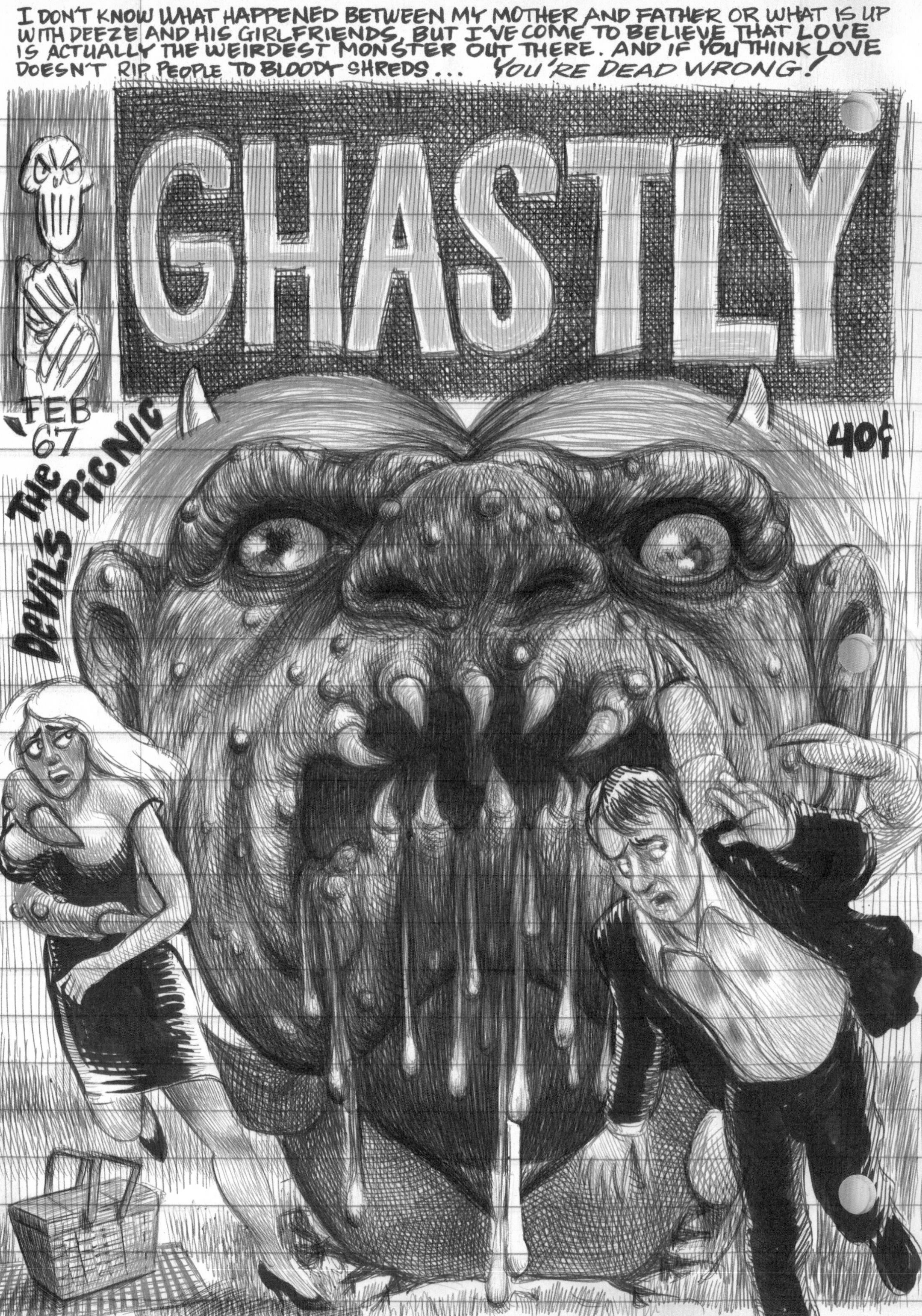
I DON'T KNOW WHAT HAPPENED BETWEEN MY MOTHER AND FATHER OR WHAT IS UP WITH DEEZE AND HIS GIRLFRIENDS, BUT I'VE COME TO BELIEVE THAT LOVE IS ACTUALLY THE WEIRDEST MONSTER OUT THERE. AND IF YOU THINK LOVE DOESN'T RIP PEOPLE TO BLOODY SHREDS... YOU'RE DEAD WRONG!
GHASTLY
FEB '67
THE DEVIL'S PICNIC
40¢

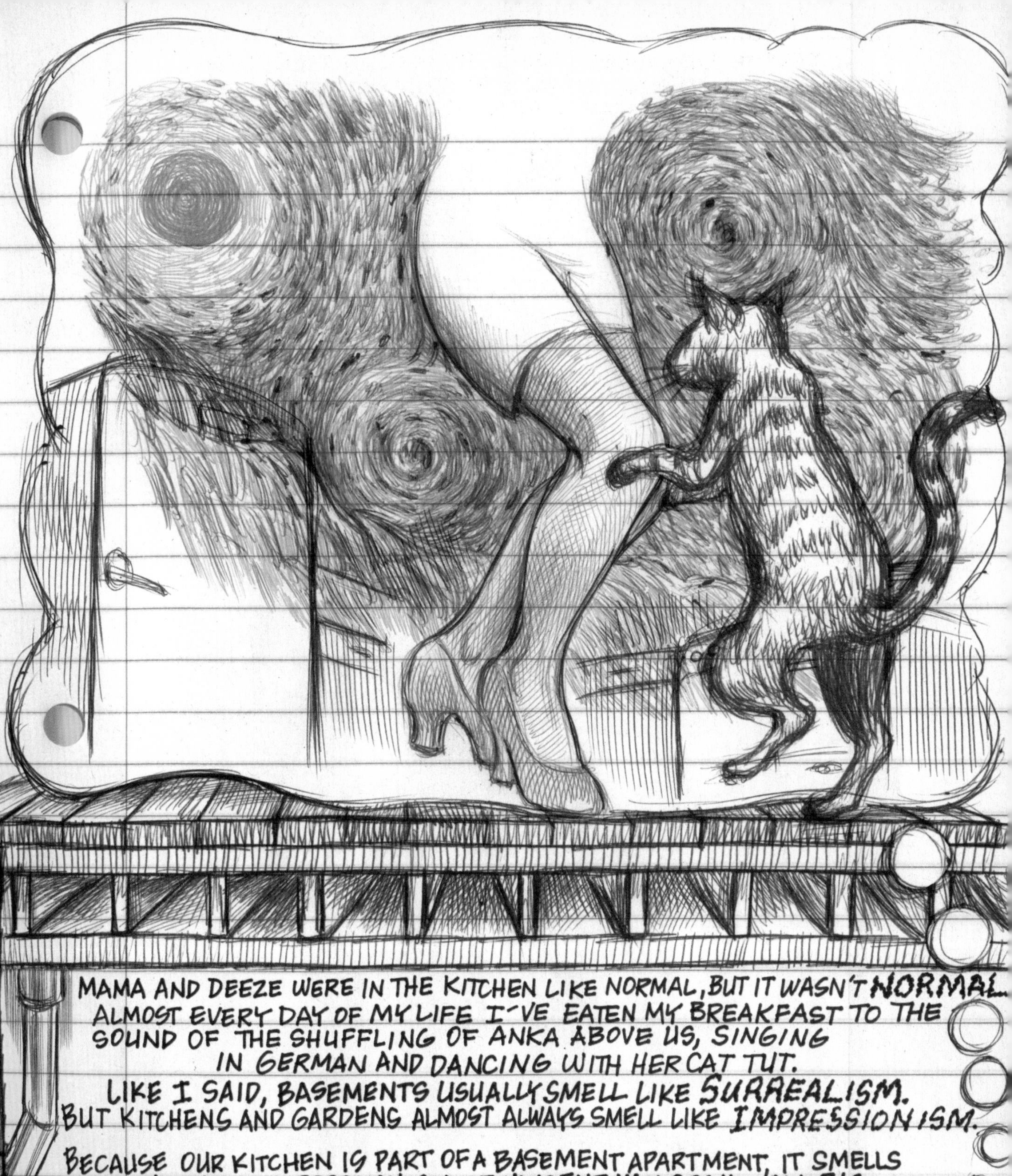

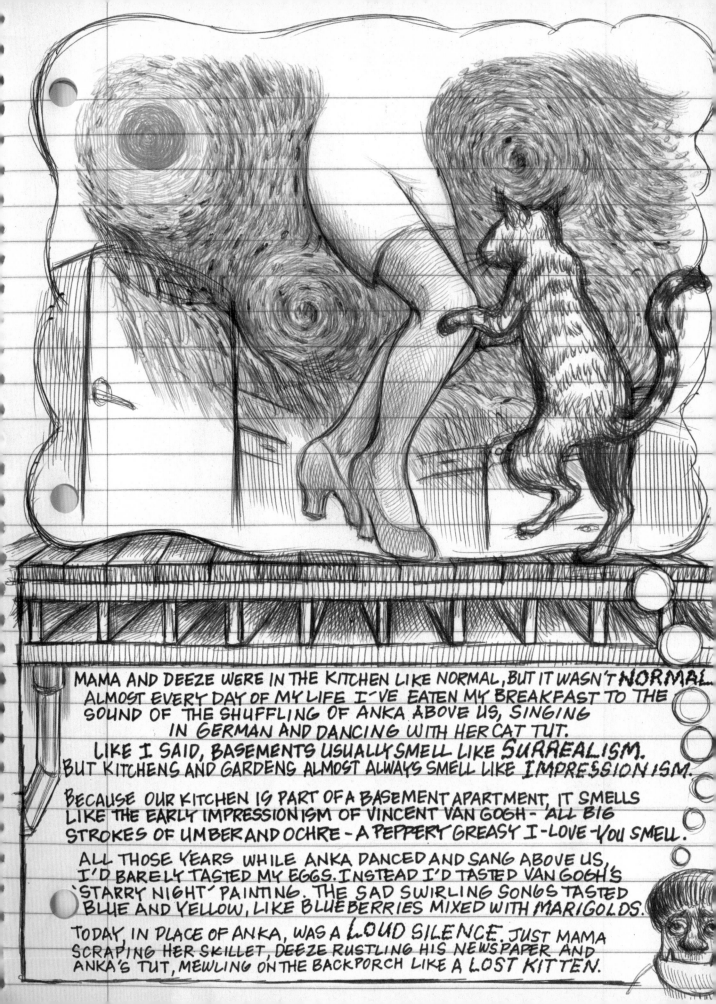

MAMA AND DEEZE WERE IN THE KITCHEN LIKE NORMAL, BUT IT WASN'T **NORMAL**. ALMOST EVERY DAY OF MY LIFE I'VE EATEN MY BREAKFAST TO THE SOUND OF THE SHUFFLING OF ANKA ABOVE US, SINGING IN GERMAN AND DANCING WITH HER CAT TUT.

LIKE I SAID, BASEMENTS USUALLY SMELL LIKE *SURREALISM*. BUT KITCHENS AND GARDENS ALMOST ALWAYS SMELL LIKE *IMPRESSIONISM*.

BECAUSE OUR KITCHEN IS PART OF A BASEMENT APARTMENT, IT SMELLS LIKE THE EARLY IMPRESSIONISM OF VINCENT VAN GOGH - ALL BIG STROKES OF UMBER AND OCHRE - A PEPPERY GREASY I-LOVE-YOU SMELL.

ALL THOSE YEARS WHILE ANKA DANCED AND SANG ABOVE US, I'D BARELY TASTED MY EGGS. INSTEAD I'D TASTED VAN GOGH'S 'STARRY NIGHT' PAINTING. THE SAD SWIRLING SONGS TASTED BLUE AND YELLOW, LIKE BLUEBERRIES MIXED WITH *MARIGOLDS*.

TODAY, IN PLACE OF ANKA, WAS A *LOUD SILENCE*. JUST MAMA SCRAPING HER SKILLET, DEEZE RUSTLING HIS NEWSPAPER AND ANKA'S TUT, MEWLING ON THE BACKPORCH LIKE A *LOST KITTEN*.

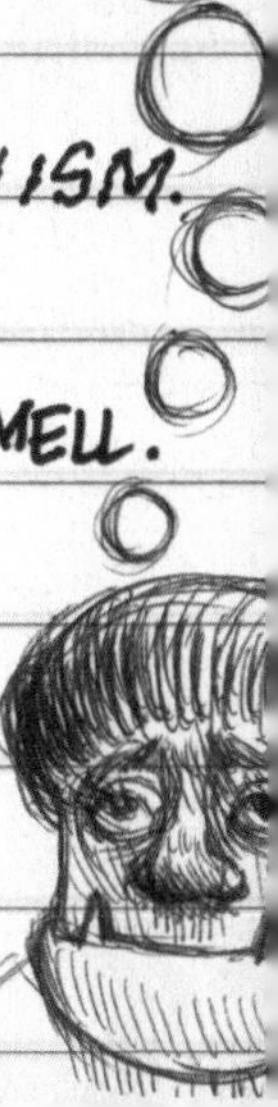

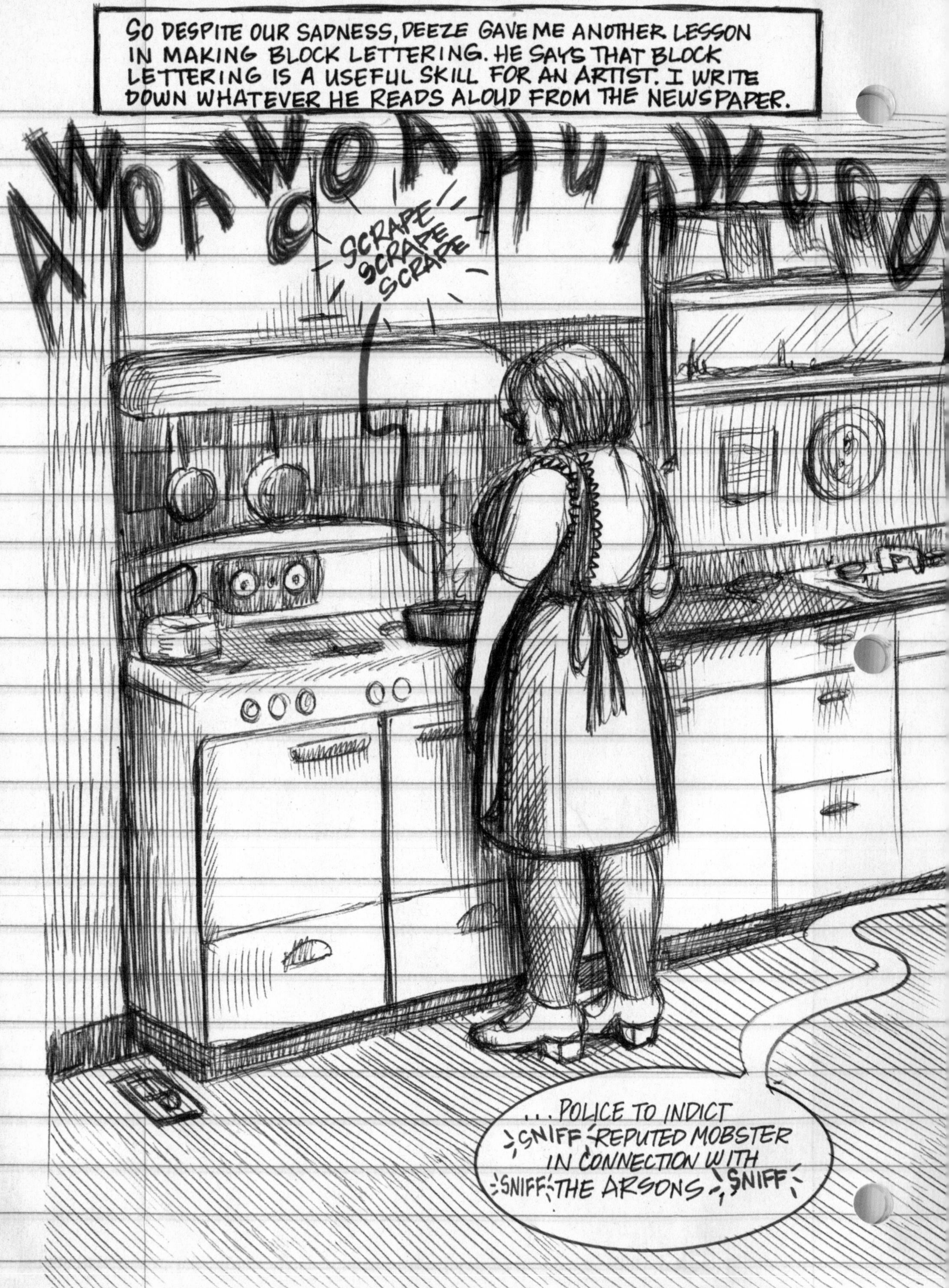
SO DESPITE OUR SADNESS, DEEZE GAVE ME ANOTHER LESSON IN MAKING BLOCK LETTERING. HE SAYS THAT BLOCK LETTERING IS A USEFUL SKILL FOR AN ARTIST. I WRITE DOWN WHATEVER HE READS ALOUD FROM THE NEWSPAPER.
AWOAWOOOAHUAWOOOO
SCRAPE SCRAPE SCRAPE
...POLICE TO INDICT *SNIFF* REPUTED MOBSTER IN CONNECTION WITH *SNIFF* THE ARSONS *SNIFF*

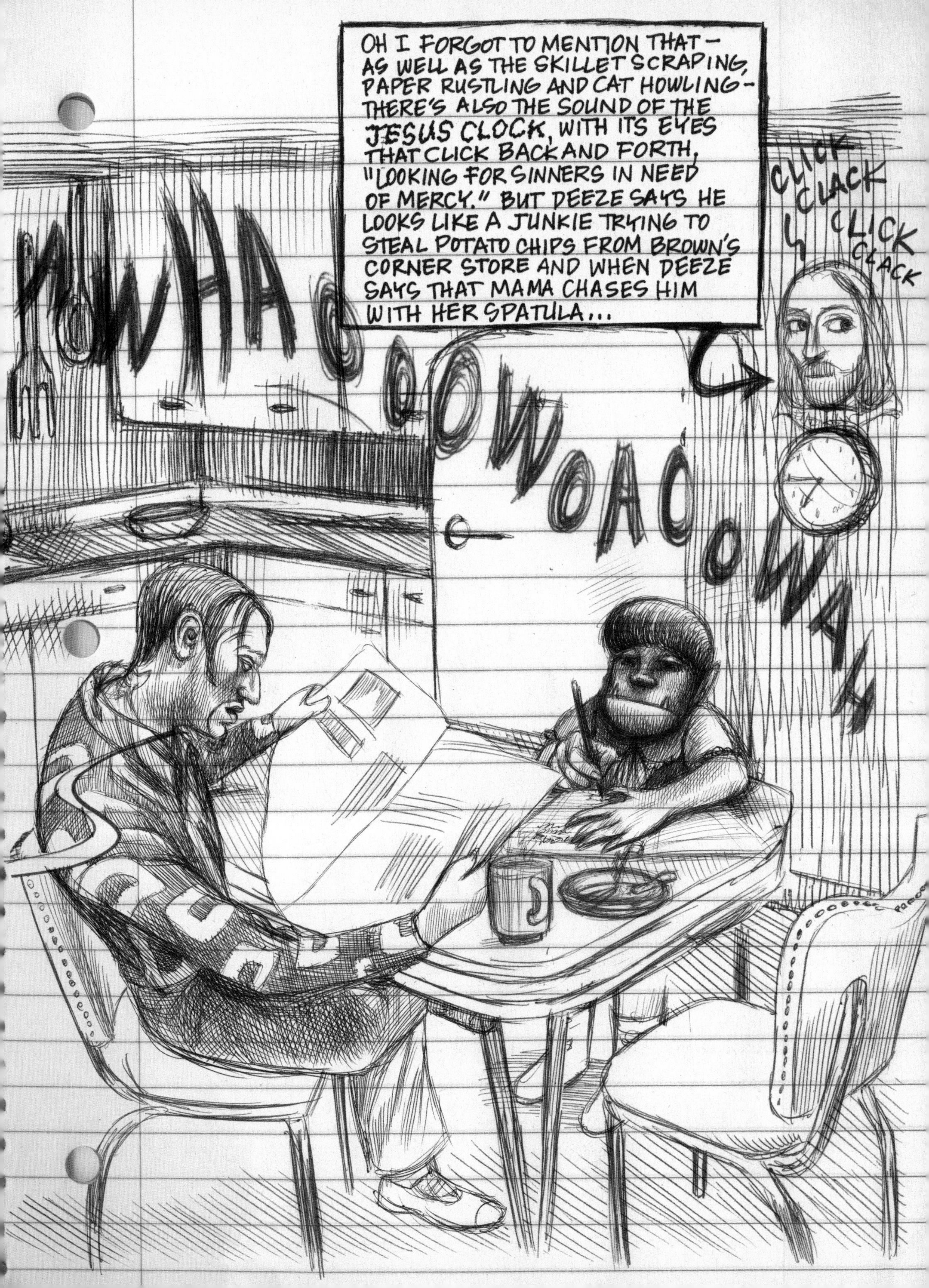
OH I FORGOT TO MENTION THAT— AS WELL AS THE SKILLET SCRAPING, PAPER RUSTLING AND CAT HOWLING— THERE'S ALSO THE SOUND OF THE JESUS CLOCK, WITH ITS EYES THAT CLICK BACK AND FORTH, "LOOKING FOR SINNERS IN NEED OF MERCY." BUT DEEZE SAYS HE LOOKS LIKE A JUNKIE TRYING TO STEAL POTATO CHIPS FROM BROWN'S CORNER STORE AND WHEN DEEZE SAYS THAT MAMA CHASES HIM WITH HER SPATULA...
CLICK CLACK
CLICK CLACK
WHAOOOWOWOAOOOWAH

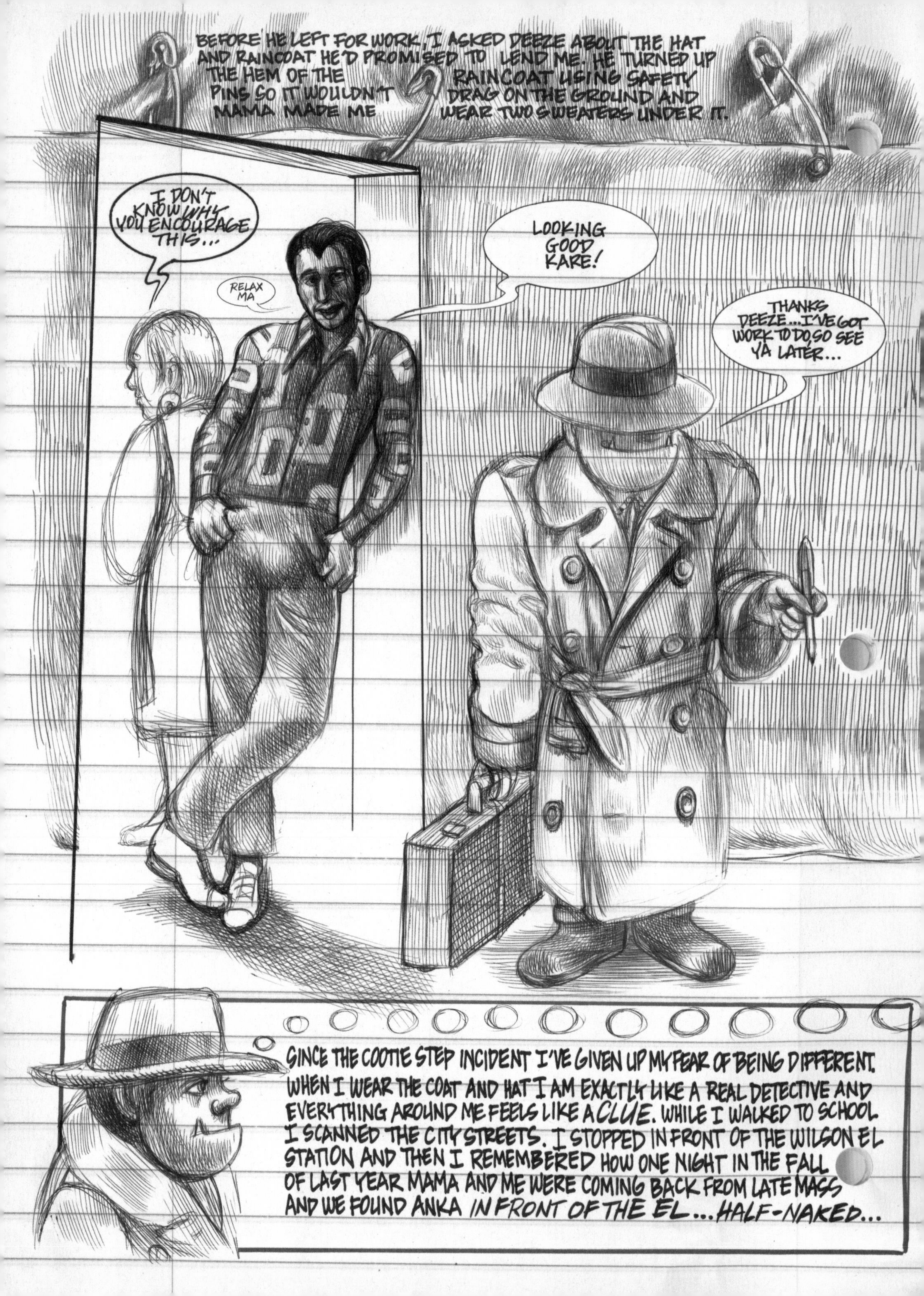
BEFORE HE LEFT FOR WORK, I ASKED DEEZE ABOUT THE HAT AND RAINCOAT HE'D PROMISED TO LEND ME. HE TURNED UP THE HEM OF THE RAINCOAT USING SAFETY PINS SO IT WOULDN'T DRAG ON THE GROUND AND MAMA MADE ME WEAR TWO SWEATERS UNDER IT.
I DON'T KNOW WHY YOU ENCOURAGE THIS...
RELAX MA
LOOKING GOOD KARE!
THANKS DEEZE... I'VE GOT WORK TO DO, SO SEE YA LATER...
SINCE THE COOTIE STEP INCIDENT I'VE GIVEN UP MY FEAR OF BEING DIFFERENT. WHEN I WEAR THE COAT AND HAT I AM EXACTLY LIKE A REAL DETECTIVE AND EVERYTHING AROUND ME FEELS LIKE A CLUE. WHILE I WALKED TO SCHOOL I SCANNED THE CITY STREETS. I STOPPED IN FRONT OF THE WILSON EL STATION AND THEN I REMEMBERED HOW ONE NIGHT IN THE FALL OF LAST YEAR MAMA AND ME WERE COMING BACK FROM LATE MASS AND WE FOUND ANKA IN FRONT OF THE EL... HALF-NAKED...

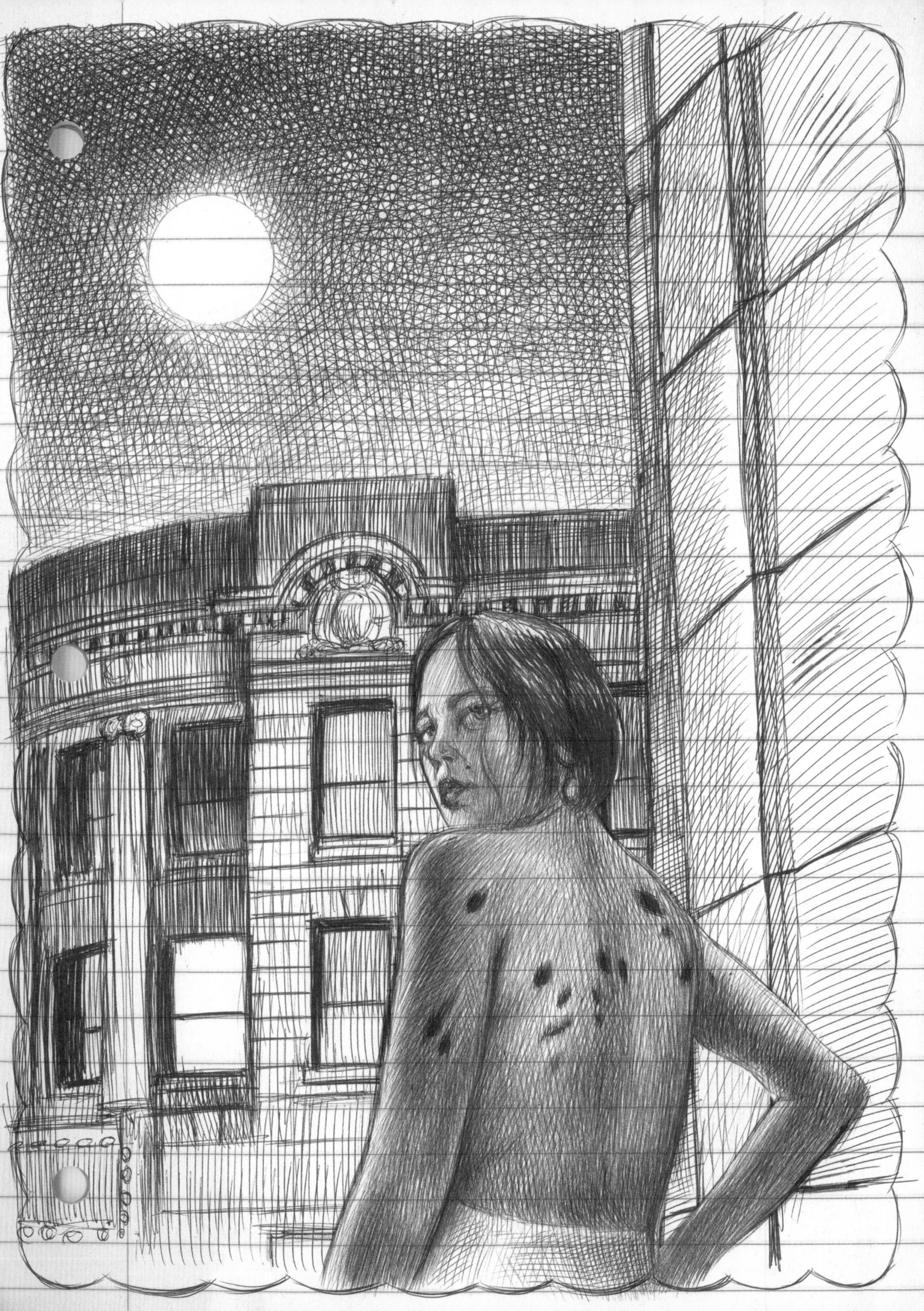

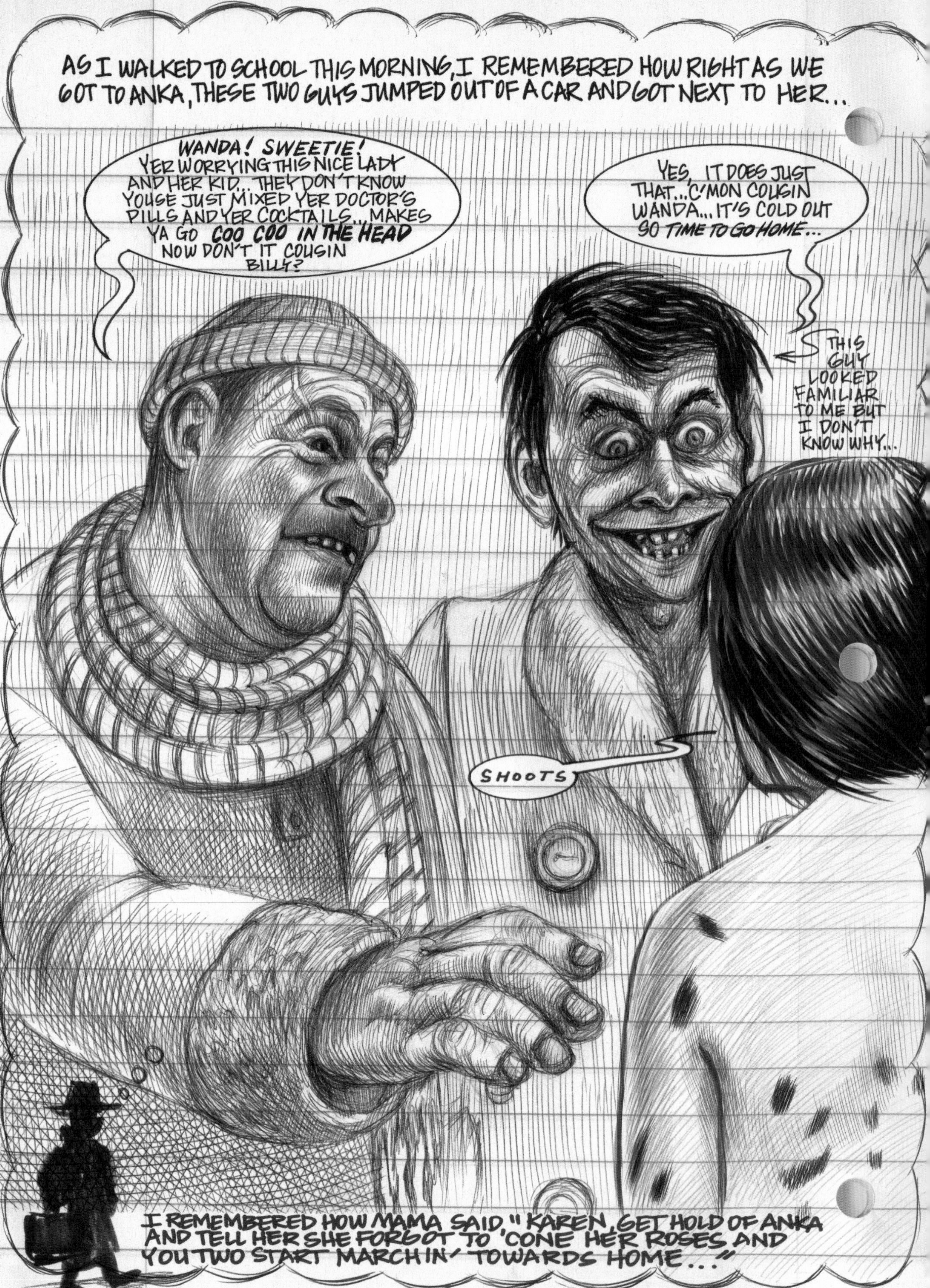
AS I WALKED TO SCHOOL THIS MORNING, I REMEMBERED HOW RIGHT AS WE GOT TO ANKA, THESE TWO GUYS JUMPED OUT OF A CAR AND GOT NEXT TO HER...
WANDA! SWEETIE! YER WORRYING THIS NICE LADY AND HER KID... THEY DON'T KNOW YOUSE JUST MIXED YER DOCTOR'S PILLS AND YER COCKTAILS... MAKES YA GO COO COO IN THE HEAD NOW DON'T IT COUSIN BILLY?
YES, IT DOES JUST THAT... C'MON COUSIN WANDA... IT'S COLD OUT SO TIME TO GO HOME...
THIS GUY LOOKED FAMILIAR TO ME BUT I DON'T KNOW WHY...
SHOOTS
I REMEMBERED HOW MAMA SAID, "KAREN, GET HOLD OF ANKA AND TELL HER SHE FORGOT TO 'CONE HER ROSES AND YOU TWO START MARCHIN' TOWARDS HOME..."

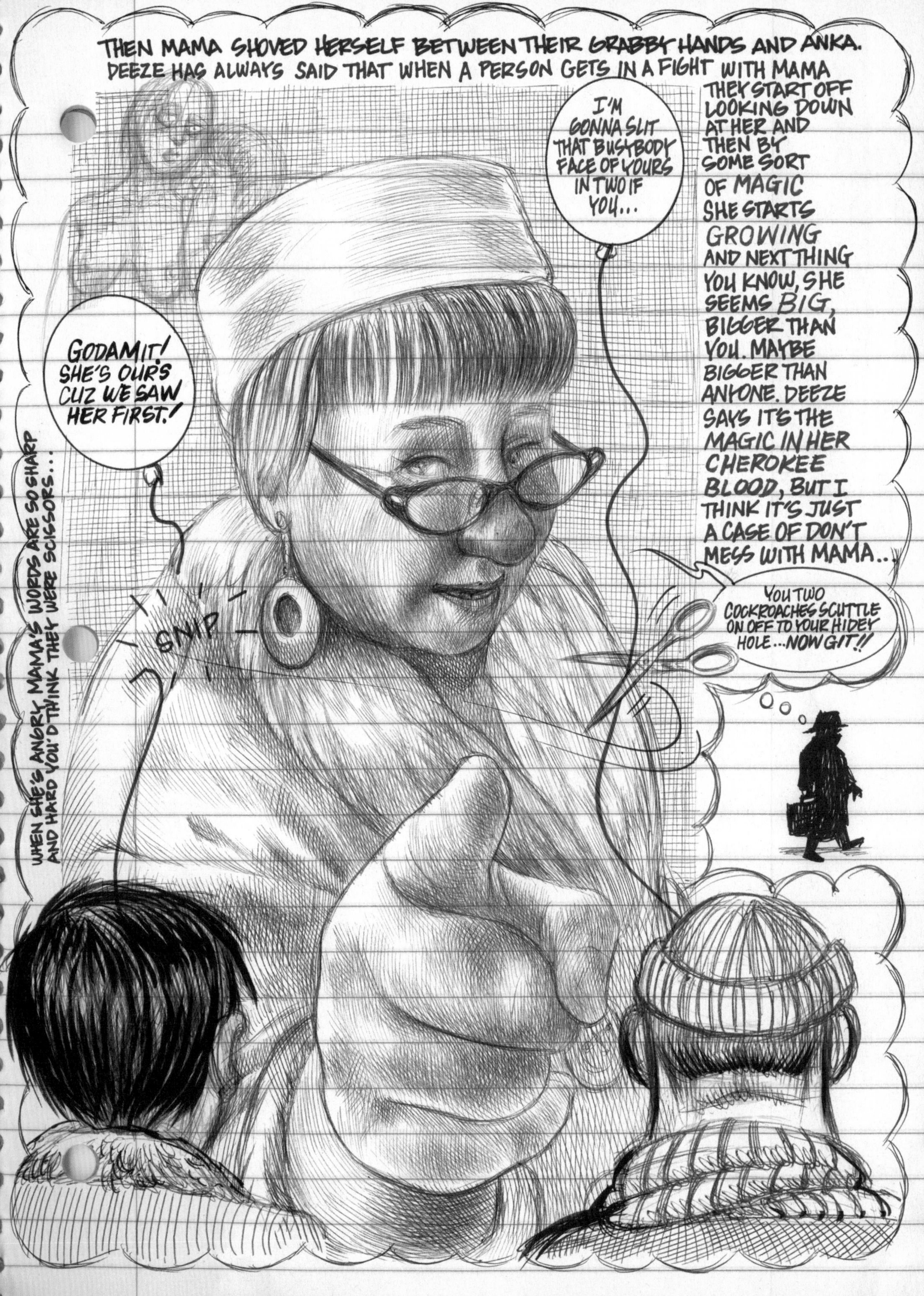

THEN MAMA SHOVED HERSELF BETWEEN THEIR GRABBY HANDS AND ANKA.
DEEZE HAS ALWAYS SAID THAT WHEN A PERSON GETS IN A FIGHT WITH MAMA THEY START OFF LOOKING DOWN AT HER AND THEN BY SOME SORT OF MAGIC SHE STARTS GROWING AND NEXT THING YOU KNOW, SHE SEEMS BIG, BIGGER THAN YOU. MAYBE BIGGER THAN ANYONE. DEEZE SAYS IT'S THE MAGIC IN HER CHEROKEE BLOOD, BUT I THINK IT'S JUST A CASE OF DON'T MESS WITH MAMA...
I'M GONNA SLIT THAT BUSYBODY FACE OF YOURS IN TWO IF YOU...
GODAMIT! SHE'S OUR'S CUZ WE SAW HER FIRST!
WHEN SHE'S ANGRY, MAMA'S WORDS ARE SO SHARP AND HARD YOU'D THINK THEY WERE SCISSORS...
SNIP
YOU TWO COCKROACHES SCUTTLE ON OFF TO YOUR HIDEY HOLE...NOW GIT!!

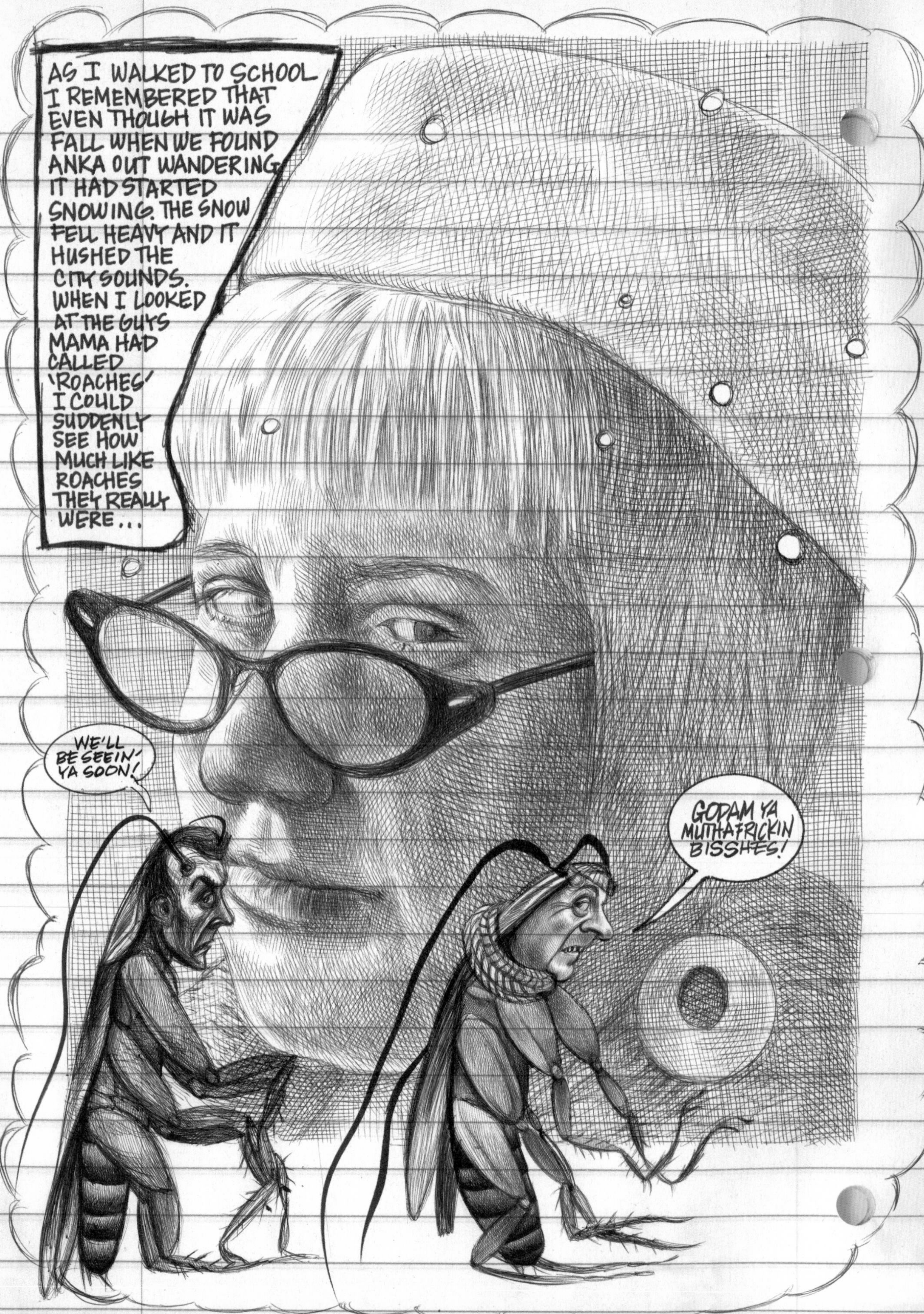
AS I WALKED TO SCHOOL I REMEMBERED THAT EVEN THOUGH IT WAS FALL WHEN WE FOUND ANKA OUT WANDERING IT HAD STARTED SNOWING. THE SNOW FELL HEAVY AND IT HUSHED THE CITY SOUNDS. WHEN I LOOKED AT THE GUYS MAMA HAD CALLED 'ROACHES' I COULD SUDDENLY SEE HOW MUCH LIKE ROACHES THEY REALLY WERE...
WE'LL BE SEEIN' YA SOON!
GODAM YA MUTHAFRICKIN BISSHES!

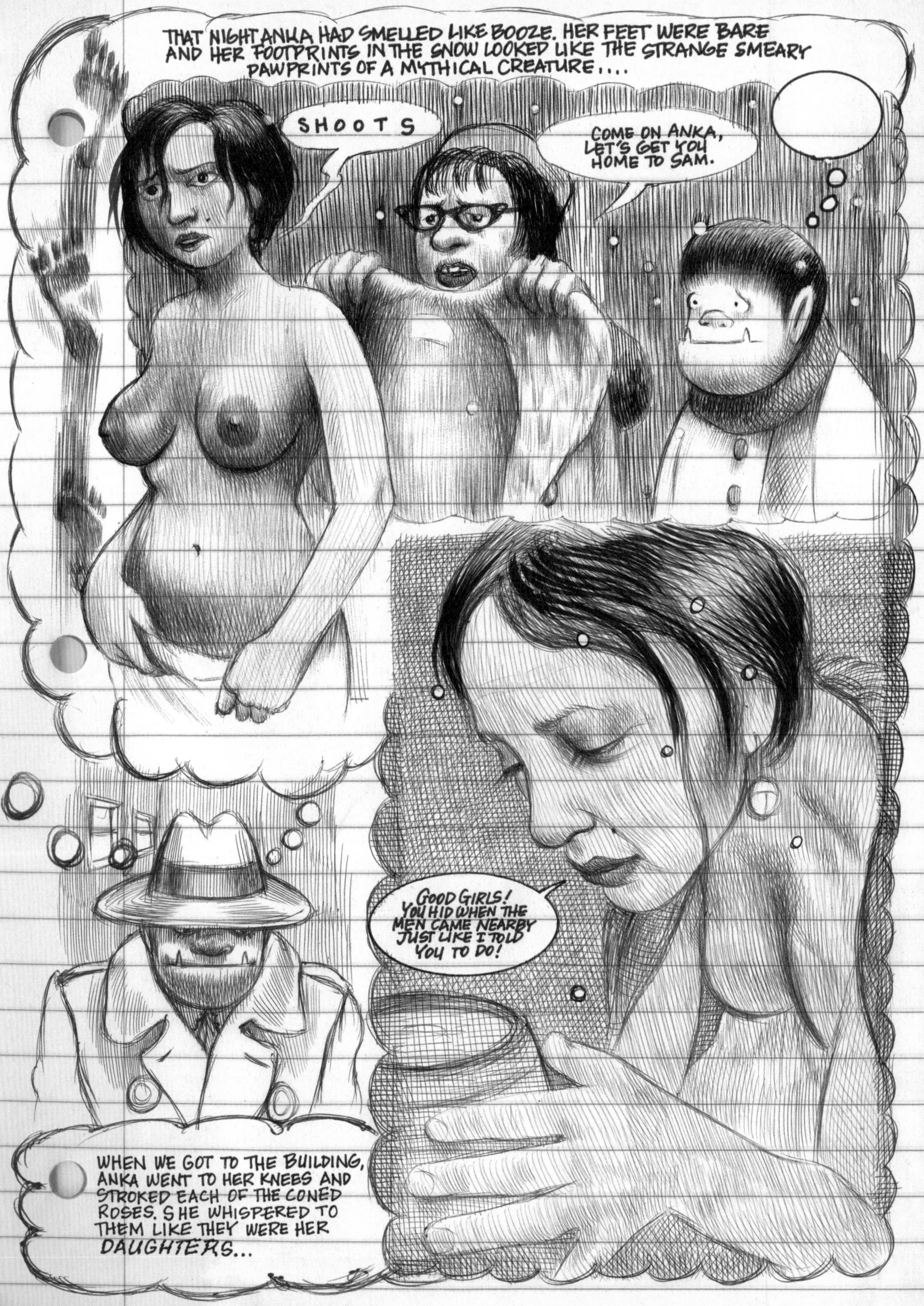
THAT NIGHT ANKA HAD SMELLED LIKE BOOZE. HER FEET WERE BARE AND HER FOOTPRINTS IN THE SNOW LOOKED LIKE THE STRANGE SMEARY PAWPRINTS OF A MYTHICAL CREATURE....
SHOOTS
COME ON ANKA, LET'S GET YOU HOME TO SAM.
GOOD GIRLS! YOU HID WHEN THE MEN CAME NEARBY JUST LIKE I TOLD YOU TO DO!
WHEN WE GOT TO THE BUILDING, ANKA WENT TO HER KNEES AND STROKED EACH OF THE CONED ROSES. SHE WHISPERED TO THEM LIKE THEY WERE HER DAUGHTERS...

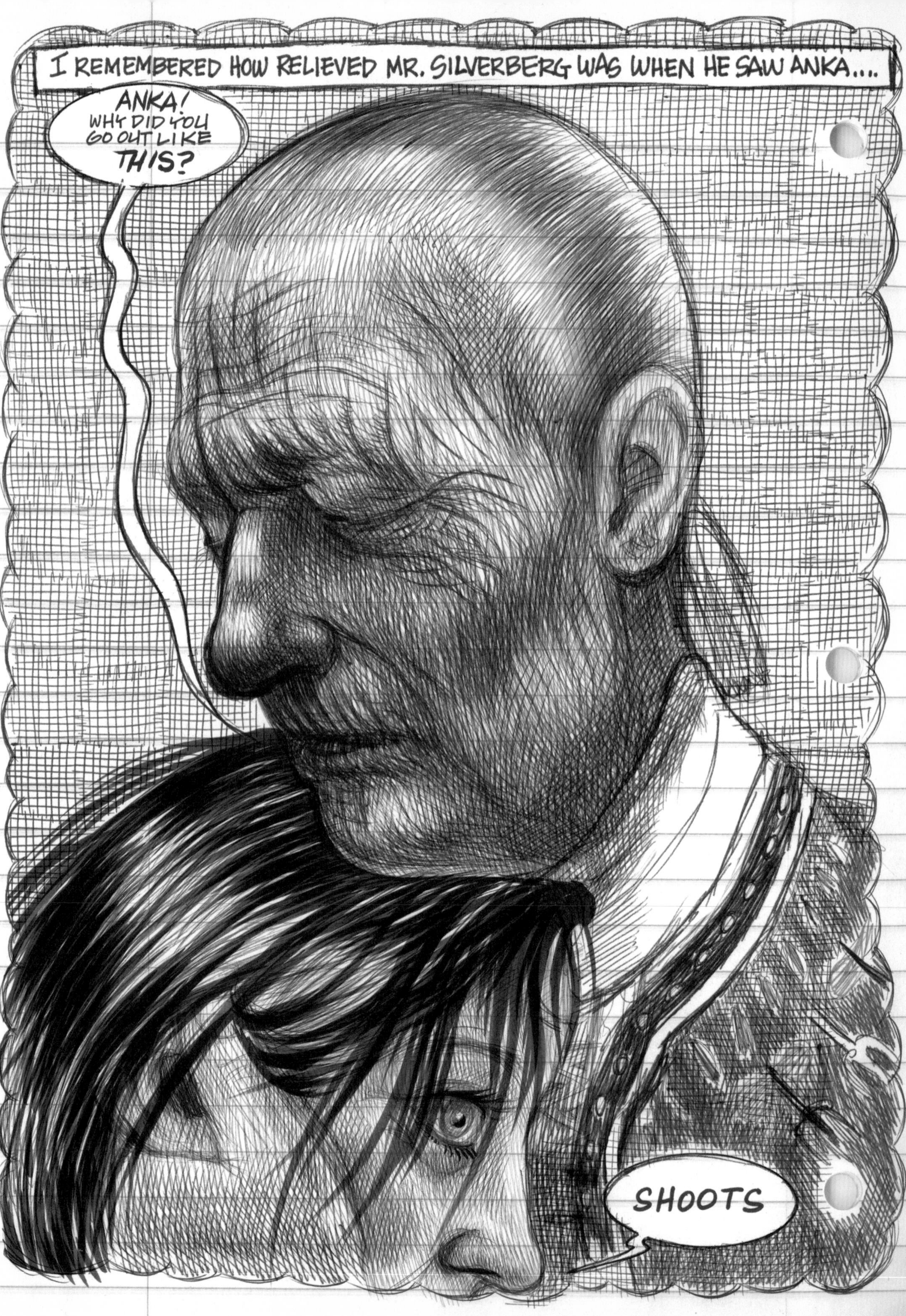
I REMEMBERED HOW RELIEVED MR. SILVERBERG WAS WHEN HE SAW ANKA....
ANKA! WHY DID YOU GO OUT LIKE THIS?
SHOOTS

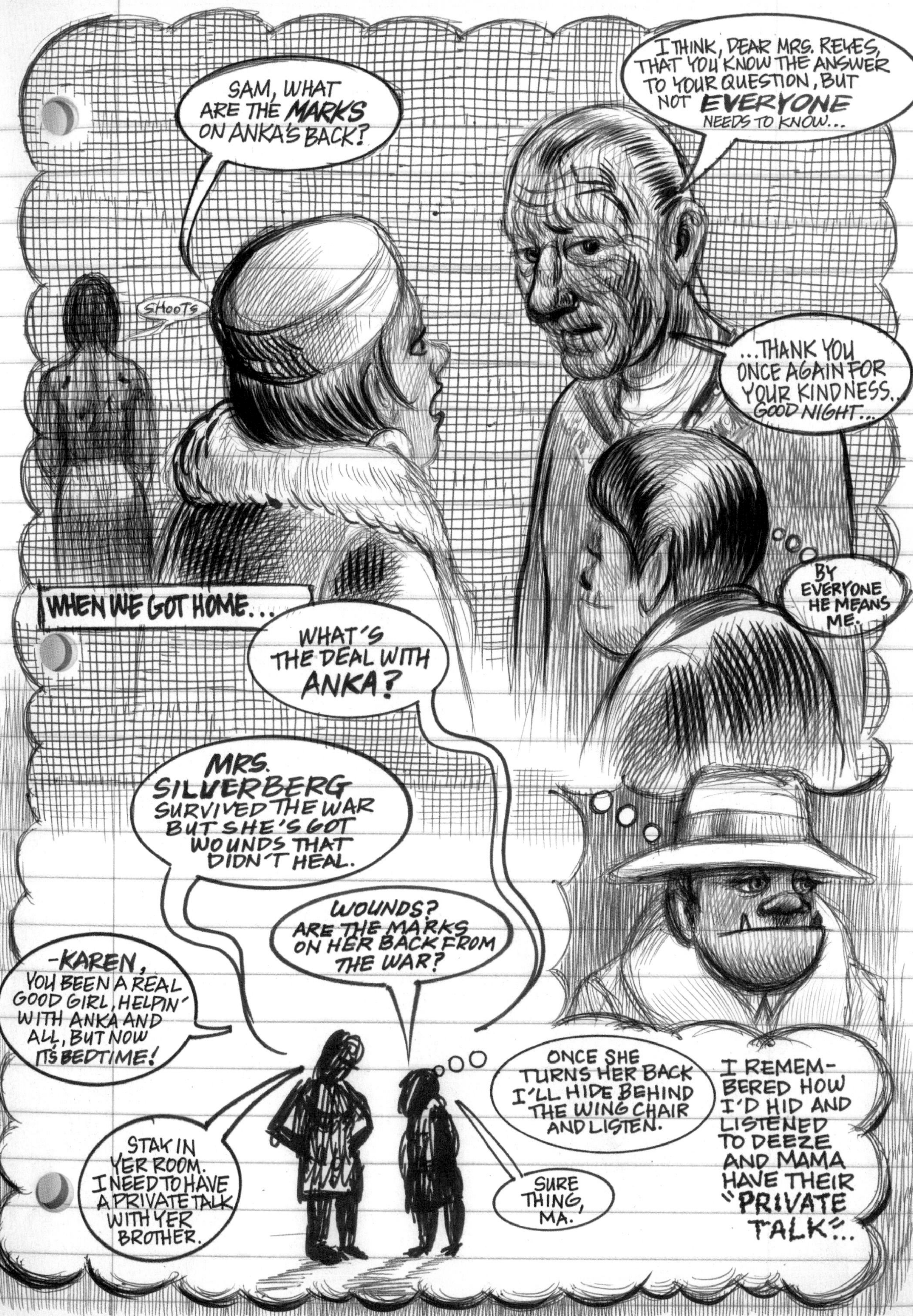
SAM, WHAT ARE THE MARKS ON ANKA'S BACK?
I THINK, DEAR MRS. REYES, THAT YOU KNOW THE ANSWER TO YOUR QUESTION, BUT NOT EVERYONE NEEDS TO KNOW...
SHOOTS
...THANK YOU ONCE AGAIN FOR YOUR KINDNESS.. GOOD NIGHT...
BY EVERYONE HE MEANS ME.
WHEN WE GOT HOME...
WHAT'S THE DEAL WITH ANKA?
MRS. SILVERBERG SURVIVED THE WAR BUT SHE'S GOT WOUNDS THAT DIDN'T HEAL.
WOUNDS? ARE THE MARKS ON HER BACK FROM THE WAR?
-KAREN, YOU BEEN A REAL GOOD GIRL, HELPIN' WITH ANKA AND ALL, BUT NOW IT'S BEDTIME!
STAY IN YER ROOM. I NEED TO HAVE A PRIVATE TALK WITH YER BROTHER.
SURE THING, MA.
ONCE SHE TURNS HER BACK I'LL HIDE BEHIND THE WING CHAIR AND LISTEN.
I REMEMBERED HOW I'D HID AND LISTENED TO DEEZE AND MAMA HAVE THEIR "PRIVATE TALK"...

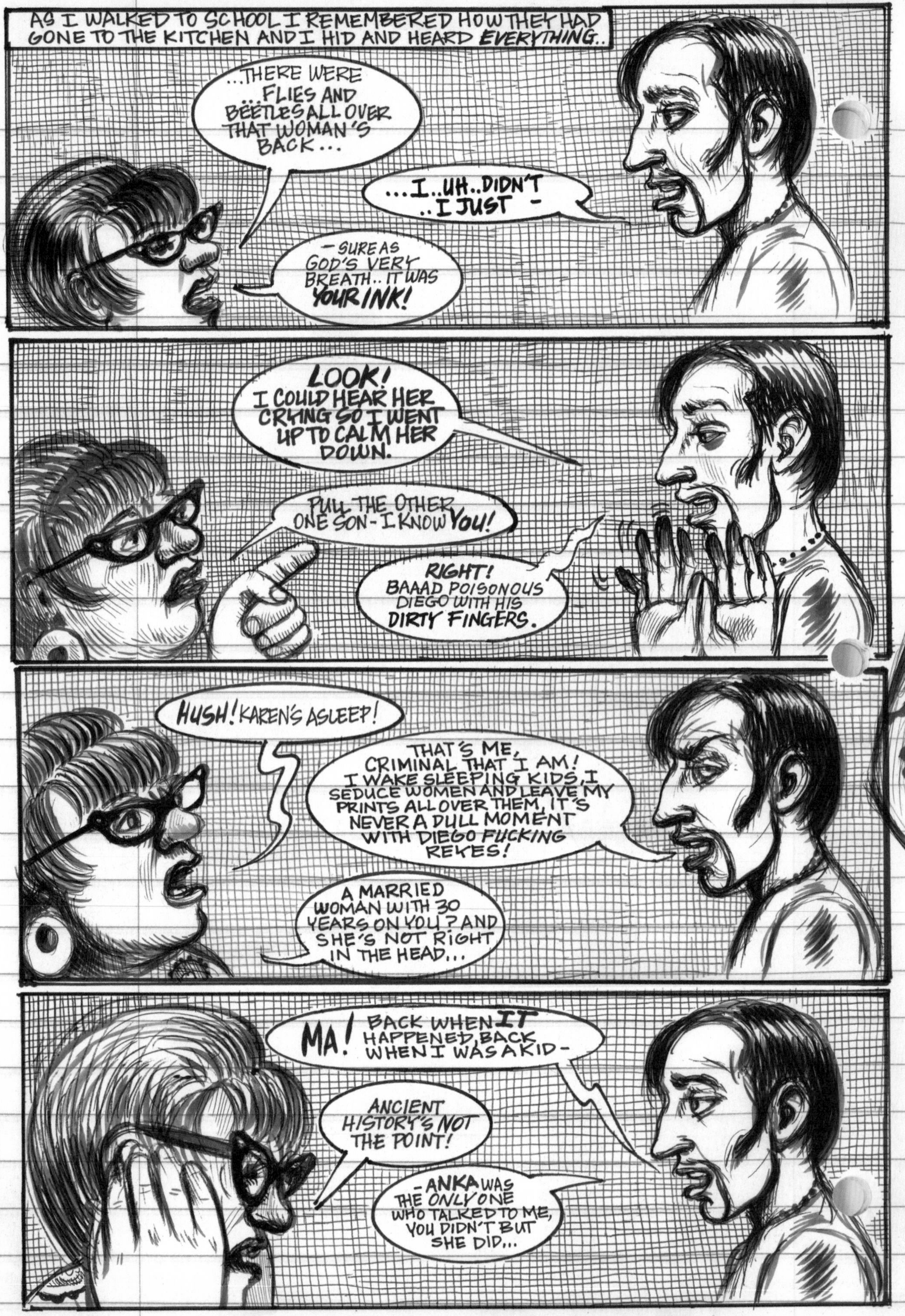

AS I WALKED TO SCHOOL I REMEMBERED HOW THEY HAD GONE TO THE KITCHEN AND I HID AND HEARD EVERYTHING..
...THERE WERE ...FLIES AND BEETLES ALL OVER THAT WOMAN'S BACK...
...I..UH..DIDN'T ..I JUST -
- SURE AS GOD'S VERY BREATH.. IT WAS YOUR INK!
LOOK! I COULD HEAR HER CRYING SO I WENT UP TO CALM HER DOWN.
PULL THE OTHER ONE SON - I KNOW YOU!
RIGHT! BAAAD POISONOUS DIEGO WITH HIS DIRTY FINGERS.
HUSH! KAREN'S ASLEEP!
THAT'S ME, CRIMINAL THAT I AM! I WAKE SLEEPING KIDS, I SEDUCE WOMEN AND LEAVE MY PRINTS ALL OVER THEM, IT'S NEVER A DULL MOMENT WITH DIEGO FUCKING REYES!
A MARRIED WOMAN WITH 30 YEARS ON YOU? AND SHE'S NOT RIGHT IN THE HEAD...
MA! BACK WHEN IT HAPPENED, BACK WHEN I WAS A KID -
ANCIENT HISTORY'S NOT THE POINT!
- ANKA WAS THE ONLY ONE WHO TALKED TO ME, YOU DIDN'T BUT SHE DID...

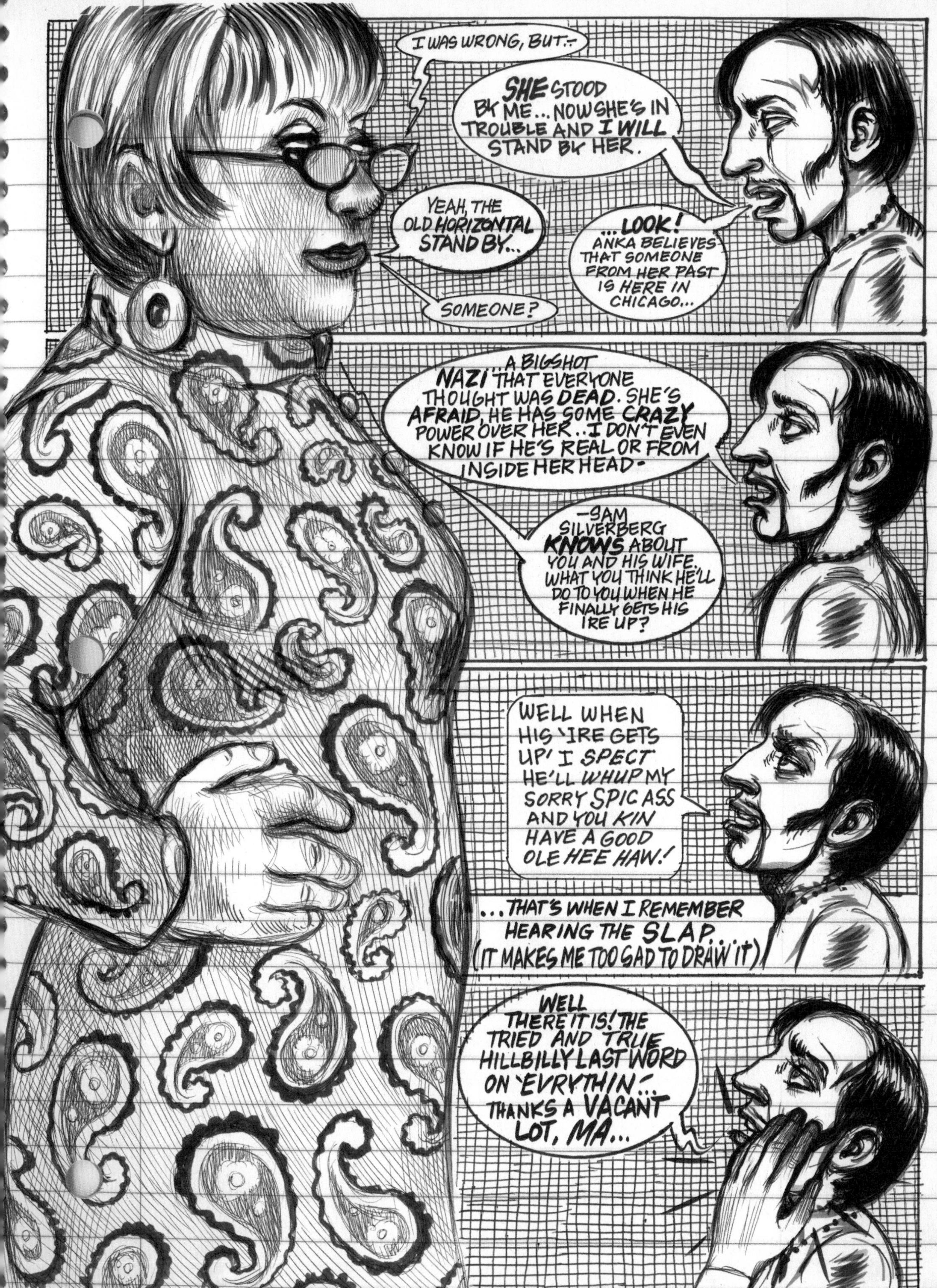
I WAS WRONG, BUT...
SHE STOOD BY ME... NOW SHE'S IN TROUBLE AND I WILL STAND BY HER.
YEAH, THE OLD HORIZONTAL STAND BY...
...LOOK! ANKA BELIEVES THAT SOMEONE FROM HER PAST IS HERE IN CHICAGO...
SOMEONE?
...A BIGSHOT NAZI THAT EVERYONE THOUGHT WAS DEAD. SHE'S AFRAID, HE HAS SOME CRAZY POWER OVER HER.. I DON'T EVEN KNOW IF HE'S REAL OR FROM INSIDE HER HEAD-
-SAM SILVERBERG KNOWS ABOUT YOU AND HIS WIFE. WHAT YOU THINK HE'LL DO TO YOU WHEN HE FINALLY GETS HIS IRE UP?
WELL WHEN HIS 'IRE GETS UP' I SPECT HE'LL WHUP MY SORRY SPIC ASS AND YOU KIN HAVE A GOOD OLE HEE HAW!
...THAT'S WHEN I REMEMBER HEARING THE SLAP... (IT MAKES ME TOO SAD TO DRAW IT)
WELL THERE IT IS! THE TRIED AND TRUE HILLBILLY LAST WORD ON 'EVRYTHIN'... THANKS A VACANT LOT, MA...

SOMETIMES YOU DON'T LET YOURSELF KNOW WHAT YOU KNOW. (WHICH IS PROBABLY WHY I'D NEVER FACED THE IDENTITY OF THE WOMAN WHO I'D SEEN IN BED WITH DEEZE BACK WHEN I WAS A KID.)

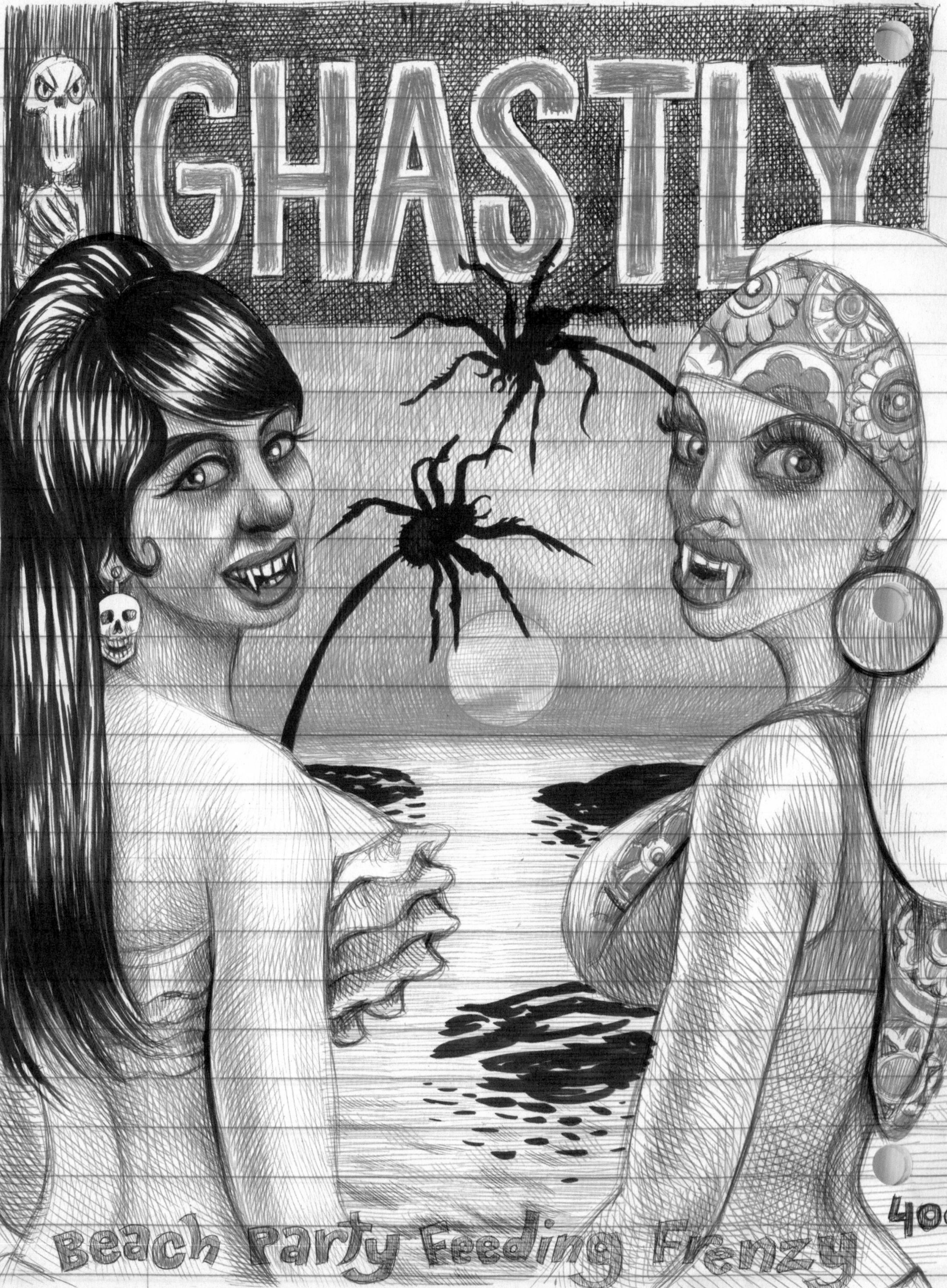

GHASTLY
40¢
Beach Party Feeding Frenzy

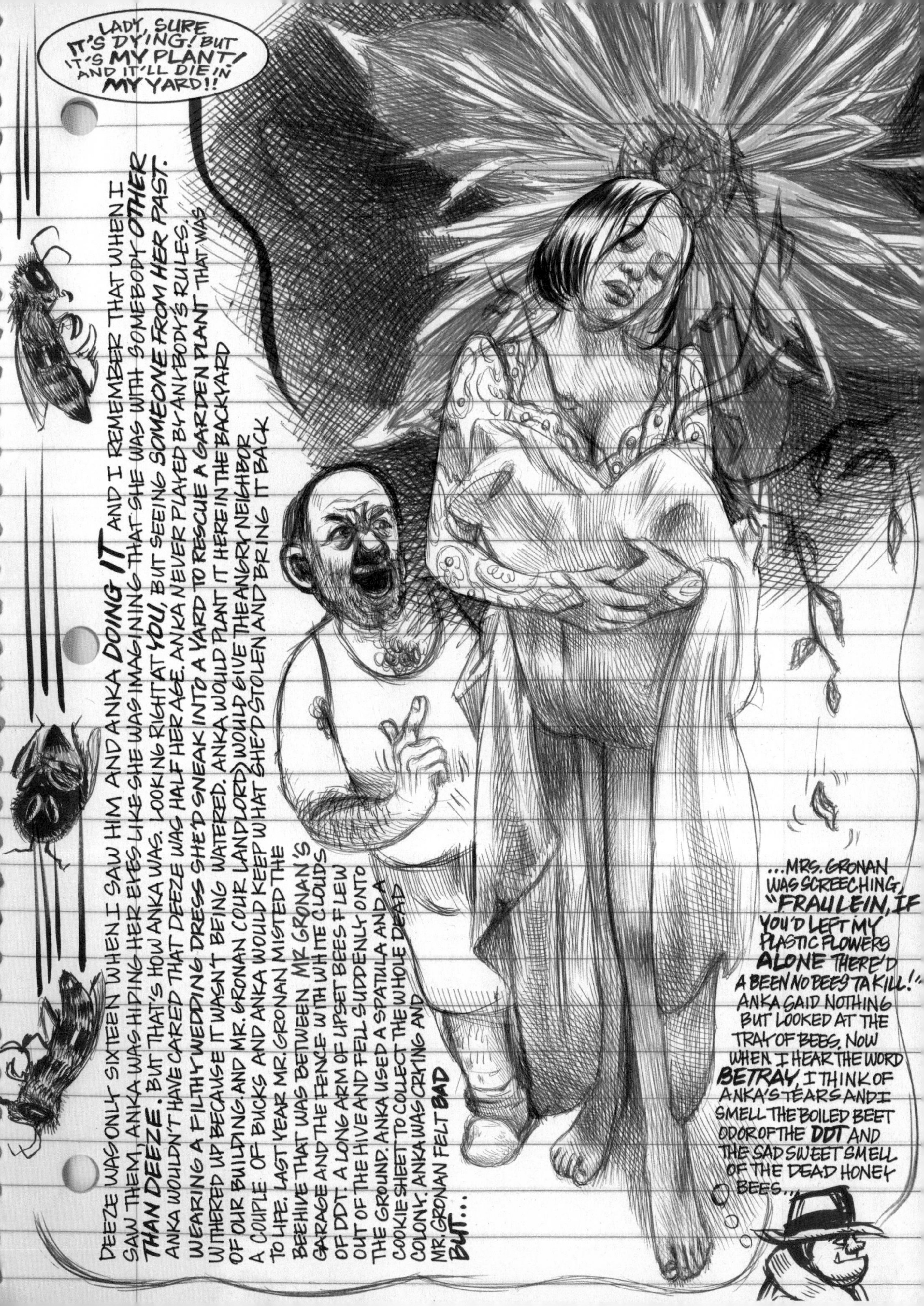

LADY, SURE IT'S DYING! BUT IT'S MY PLANT! AND IT'LL DIE IN MY YARD!!
DEEZE WAS ONLY SIXTEEN WHEN I SAW HIM AND ANKA DOING IT AND I REMEMBER THAT WHEN I SAW THEM, ANKA WAS HIDING HER EYES LIKE SHE WAS IMAGINING THAT SHE WAS WITH SOMEBODY OTHER THAN DEEZE. BUT THAT'S HOW ANKA WAS. LOOKING RIGHT AT YOU, BUT SEEING SOMEONE FROM HER PAST. ANKA WOULDN'T HAVE CARED THAT DEEZE WAS HALF HER AGE. ANKA NEVER PLAYED BY ANYBODY'S RULES. WEARING A FILTHY WEDDING DRESS SHE'D SNEAK INTO A YARD TO RESCUE A GARDEN PLANT THAT WAS WITHERED UP BECAUSE IT WASN'T BEING WATERED. ANKA WOULD PLANT IT HERE IN THE BACKYARD OF OUR BUILDING. AND MR. GRONAN (OUR LANDLORD) WOULD GIVE THE ANGRY NEIGHBOR A COUPLE OF BUCKS AND ANKA WOULD KEEP WHAT SHE'D STOLEN AND BRING IT BACK TO LIFE. LAST YEAR MR. GRONAN MISTED THE BEEHIVE THAT WAS BETWEEN MR GRONAN'S GARAGE AND THE FENCE WITH WHITE CLOUDS OF DDT. A LONG ARM OF UPSET BEES FLEW OUT OF THE HIVE AND FELL SUDDENLY ONTO THE GROUND. ANKA USED A SPATULA AND A COOKIE SHEET TO COLLECT THE WHOLE DEAD COLONY. ANKA WAS CRYING AND MR. GRONAN FELT BAD BUT...
...MRS. GRONAN WAS SCREECHING, "FRAULEIN, IF YOU'D LEFT MY PLASTIC FLOWERS ALONE THERE'D A BEEN NO BEES TA KILL!" ANKA SAID NOTHING BUT LOOKED AT THE TRAY OF BEES. NOW WHEN I HEAR THE WORD BETRAY, I THINK OF ANKA'S TEARS AND I SMELL THE BOILED BEET ODOR OF THE DDT AND THE SAD SWEET SMELL OF THE DEAD HONEY BEES...

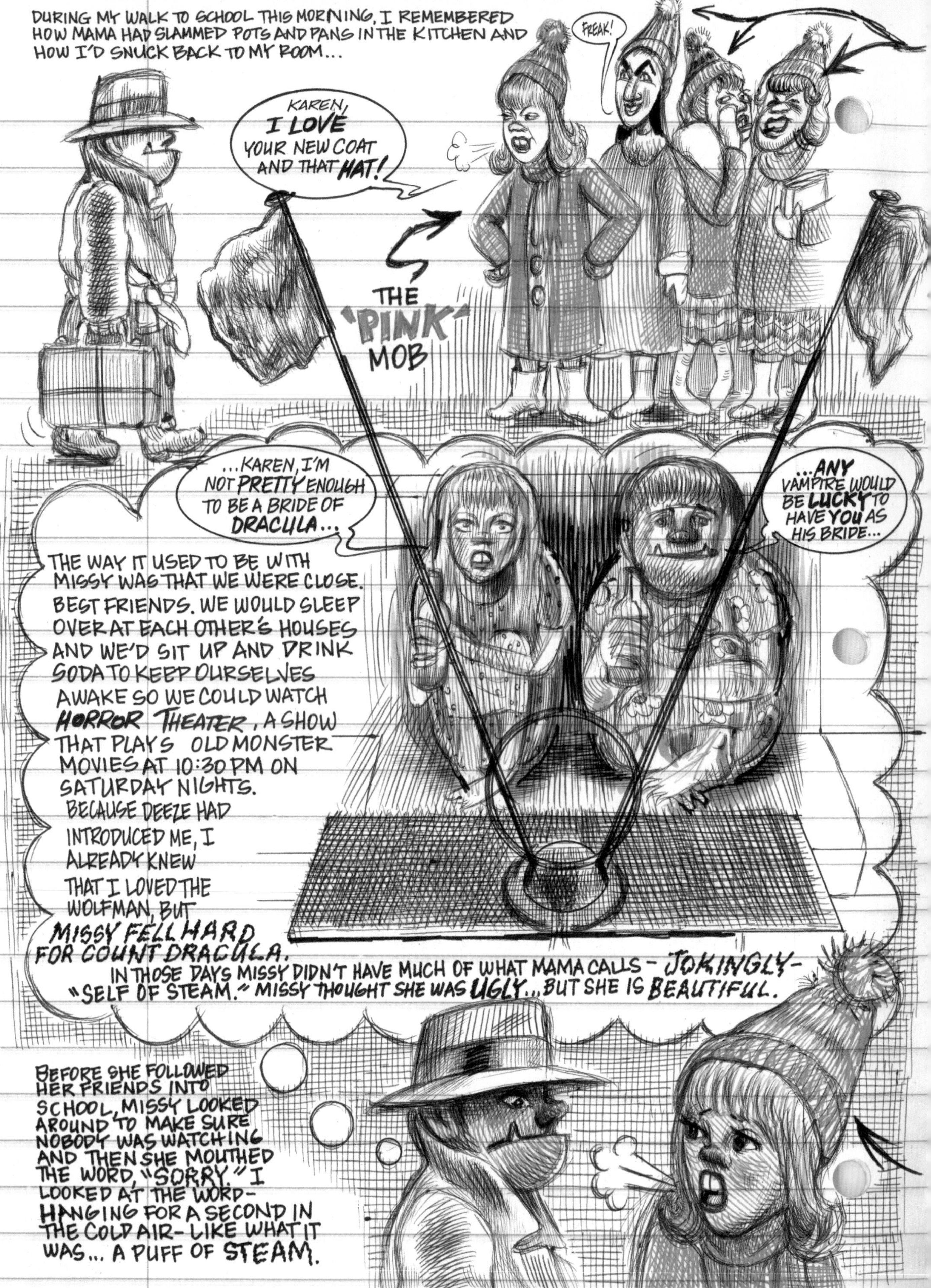

DURING MY WALK TO SCHOOL THIS MORNING, I REMEMBERED HOW MAMA HAD SLAMMED POTS AND PANS IN THE KITCHEN AND HOW I'D SNUCK BACK TO MY ROOM...
FREAK!
KAREN, I LOVE YOUR NEW COAT AND THAT HAT!
THE "PINK" MOB
...KAREN, I'M NOT PRETTY ENOUGH TO BE A BRIDE OF DRACULA...
...ANY VAMPIRE WOULD BE LUCKY TO HAVE YOU AS HIS BRIDE...
THE WAY IT USED TO BE WITH MISSY WAS THAT WE WERE CLOSE. BEST FRIENDS. WE WOULD SLEEP OVER AT EACH OTHER'S HOUSES AND WE'D SIT UP AND DRINK SODA TO KEEP OURSELVES AWAKE SO WE COULD WATCH HORROR THEATER, A SHOW THAT PLAYS OLD MONSTER MOVIES AT 10:30 PM ON SATURDAY NIGHTS.
BECAUSE DEEZE HAD INTRODUCED ME, I ALREADY KNEW THAT I LOVED THE WOLFMAN, BUT MISSY FELL HARD FOR COUNT DRACULA.
IN THOSE DAYS MISSY DIDN'T HAVE MUCH OF WHAT MAMA CALLS - JOKINGLY - "SELF OF STEAM." MISSY THOUGHT SHE WAS UGLY... BUT SHE IS BEAUTIFUL.
BEFORE SHE FOLLOWED HER FRIENDS INTO SCHOOL, MISSY LOOKED AROUND TO MAKE SURE NOBODY WAS WATCHING AND THEN SHE MOUTHED THE WORD, "SORRY." I LOOKED AT THE WORD- HANGING FOR A SECOND IN THE COLD AIR- LIKE WHAT IT WAS... A PUFF OF STEAM.

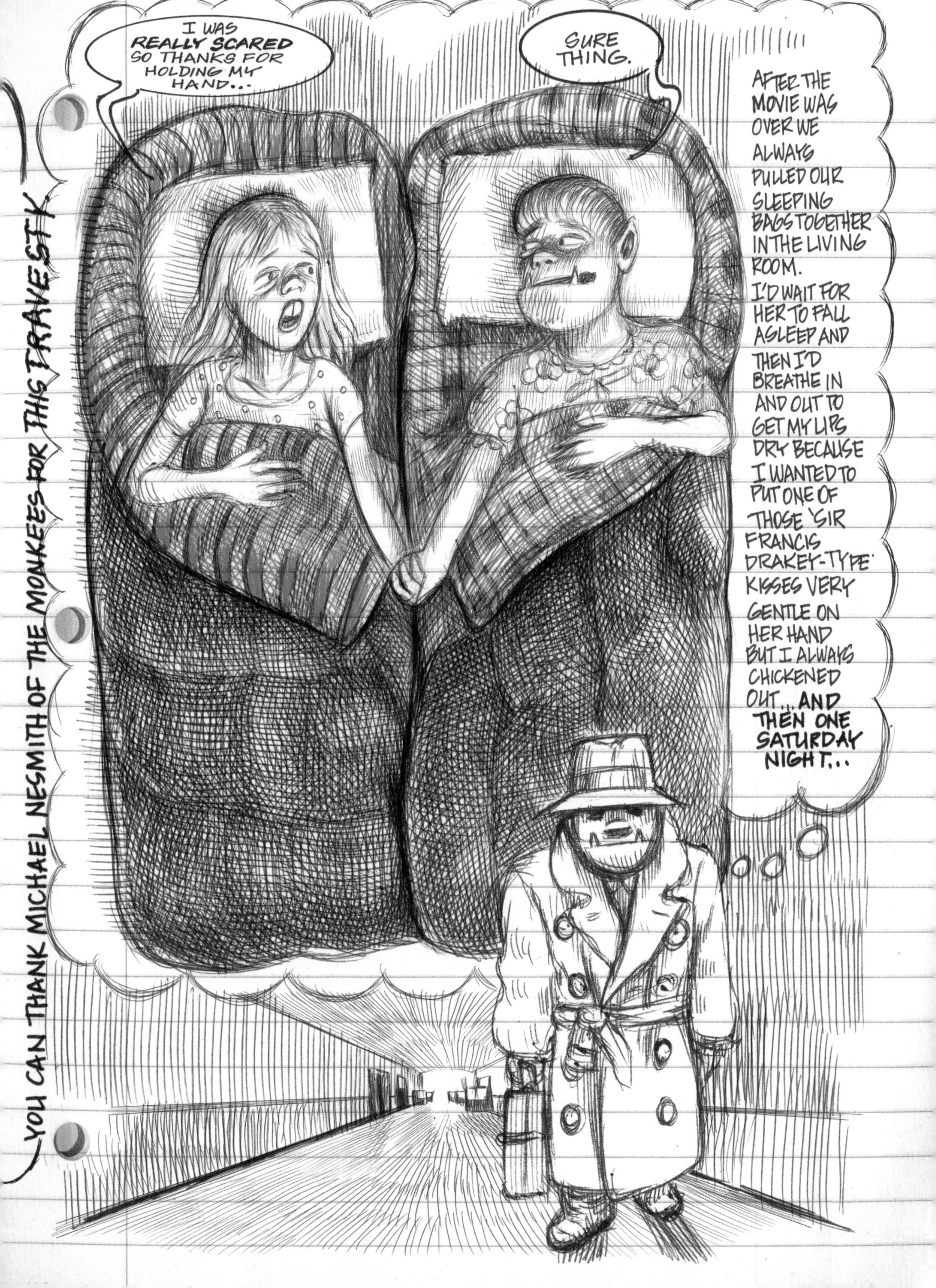

I WAS REALLY SCARED SO THANKS FOR HOLDING MY HAND...
SURE THING.
AFTER THE MOVIE WAS OVER WE ALWAYS PULLED OUR SLEEPING BAGS TOGETHER IN THE LIVING ROOM.
I'D WAIT FOR HER TO FALL ASLEEP AND THEN I'D BREATHE IN AND OUT TO GET MY LIPS DRY BECAUSE I WANTED TO PUT ONE OF THOSE 'SIR FRANCIS DRAKEY-TYPE' KISSES VERY GENTLE ON HER HAND BUT I ALWAYS CHICKENED OUT... AND THEN ONE SATURDAY NIGHT...
YOU CAN THANK MICHAEL NESMITH OF THE MONKEES FOR THIS TRAVESTY

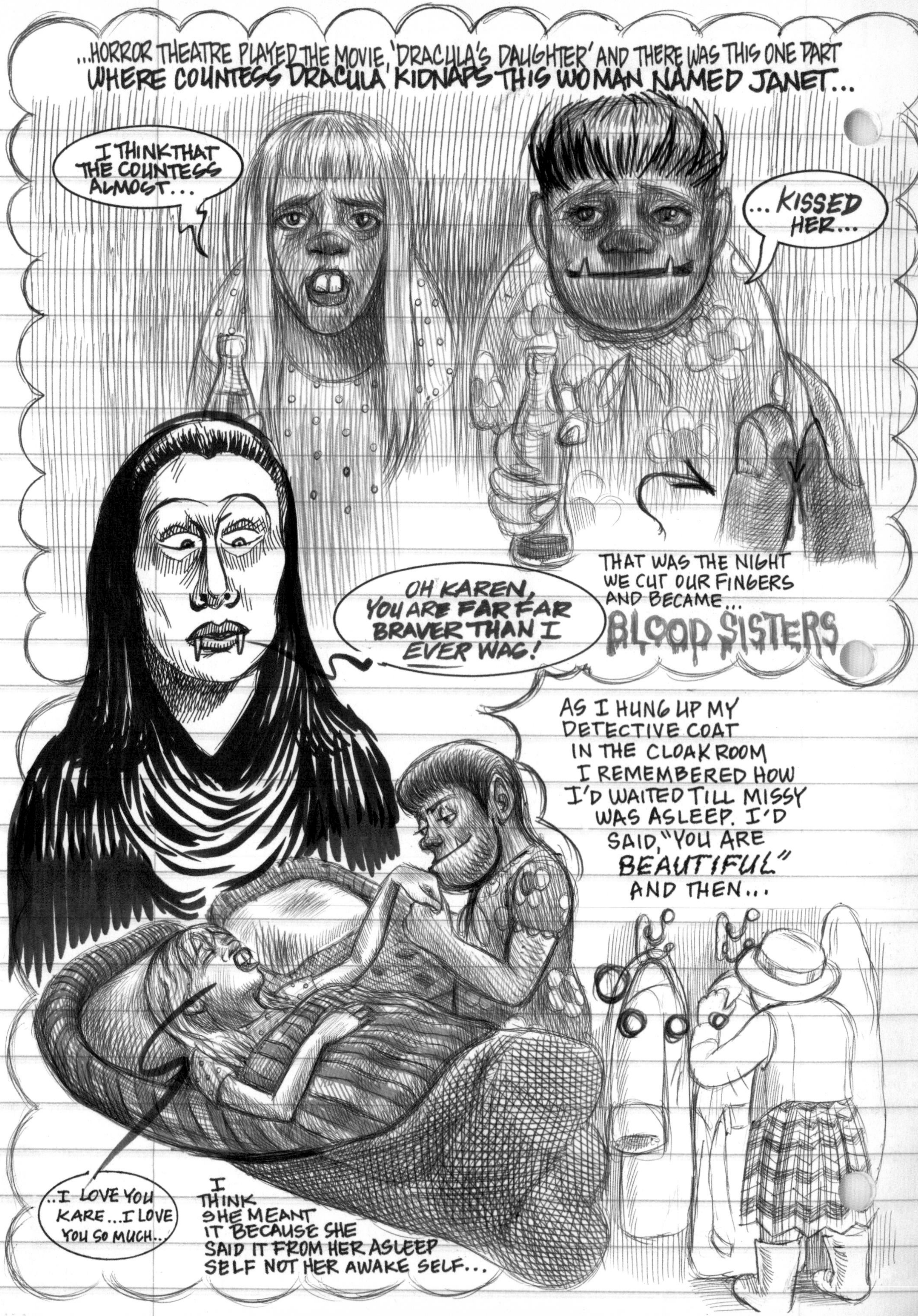
...HORROR THEATRE PLAYED THE MOVIE, 'DRACULA'S DAUGHTER' AND THERE WAS THIS ONE PART WHERE COUNTESS DRACULA KIDNAPS THIS WOMAN NAMED JANET...
I THINK THAT THE COUNTESS ALMOST...
...KISSED HER...
OH KAREN, YOU ARE FAR FAR BRAVER THAN I EVER WAS!
THAT WAS THE NIGHT WE CUT OUR FINGERS AND BECAME...
BLOOD SISTERS
AS I HUNG UP MY DETECTIVE COAT IN THE CLOAK ROOM I REMEMBERED HOW I'D WAITED TILL MISSY WAS ASLEEP. I'D SAID, "YOU ARE BEAUTIFUL" AND THEN...
..I LOVE YOU KARE...I LOVE YOU SO MUCH...
I THINK SHE MEANT IT BECAUSE SHE SAID IT FROM HER ASLEEP SELF NOT HER AWAKE SELF...

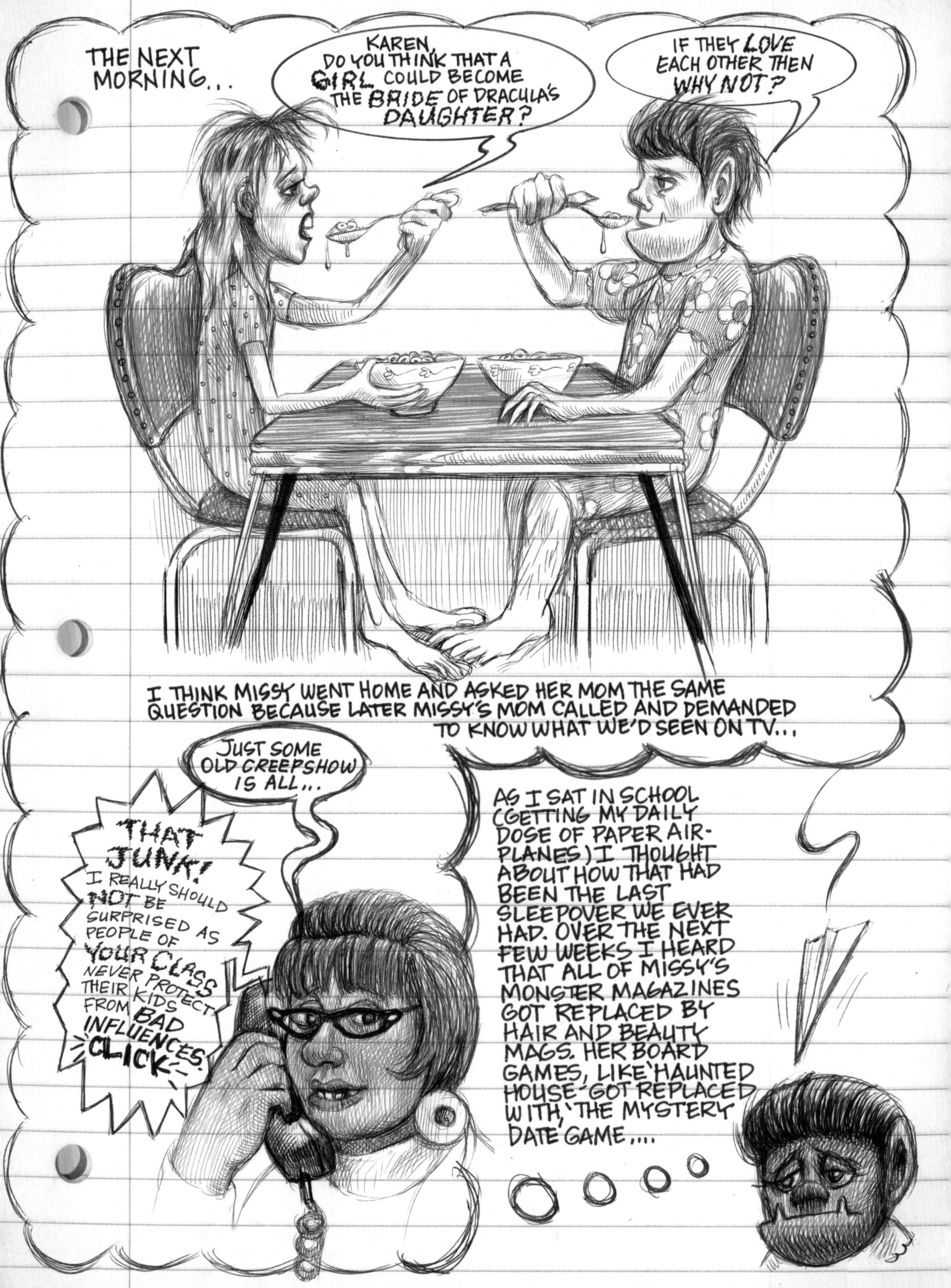

THE NEXT MORNING...
KAREN, DO YOU THINK THAT A GIRL COULD BECOME THE BRIDE OF DRACULA'S DAUGHTER?
IF THEY LOVE EACH OTHER THEN WHY NOT?
I THINK MISSY WENT HOME AND ASKED HER MOM THE SAME QUESTION BECAUSE LATER MISSY'S MOM CALLED AND DEMANDED TO KNOW WHAT WE'D SEEN ON TV...
JUST SOME OLD CREEPSHOW IS ALL...
THAT JUNK! I REALLY SHOULD NOT BE SURPRISED AS PEOPLE OF YOUR CLASS NEVER PROTECT THEIR KIDS FROM BAD INFLUENCES.
CLICK
AS I SAT IN SCHOOL (GETTING MY DAILY DOSE OF PAPER AIR-PLANES) I THOUGHT ABOUT HOW THAT HAD BEEN THE LAST SLEEPOVER WE EVER HAD. OVER THE NEXT FEW WEEKS I HEARD THAT ALL OF MISSY'S MONSTER MAGAZINES GOT REPLACED BY HAIR AND BEAUTY MAGS. HER BOARD GAMES, LIKE 'HAUNTED HOUSE' GOT REPLACED WITH 'THE MYSTERY DATE' GAME....

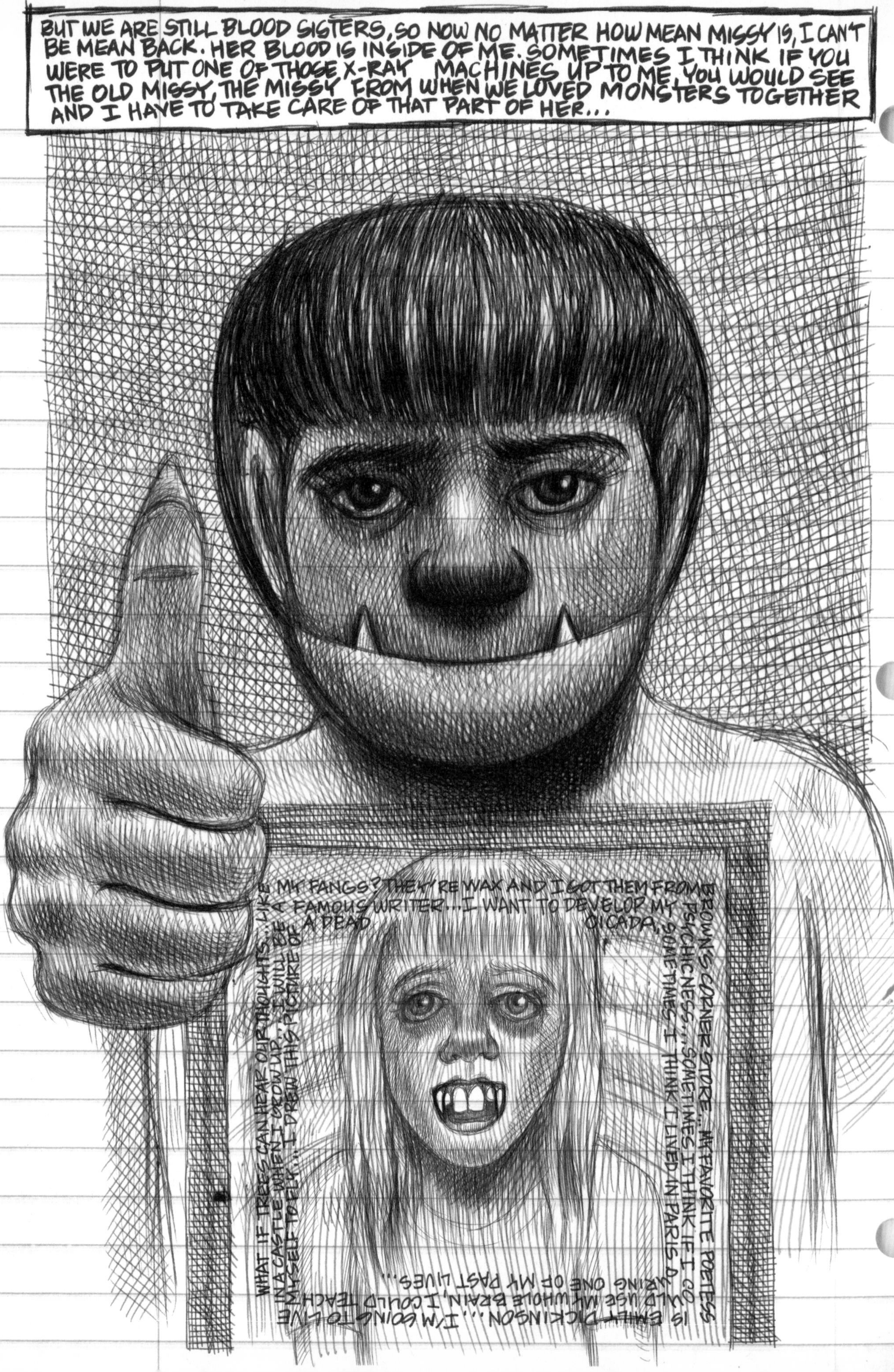
BUT WE ARE STILL BLOOD SISTERS, SO NOW NO MATTER HOW MEAN MISSY IS, I CAN'T BE MEAN BACK. HER BLOOD IS INSIDE OF ME. SOMETIMES I THINK IF YOU WERE TO PUT ONE OF THOSE X-RAY MACHINES UP TO ME, YOU WOULD SEE THE OLD MISSY, THE MISSY FROM WHEN WE LOVED MONSTERS TOGETHER AND I HAVE TO TAKE CARE OF THAT PART OF HER...
WHAT IF TREES CAN HEAR OUR THOUGHTS...LIKE MY FANGS? THEY'RE WAX AND I GOT THEM FROM BROWN'S CORNER STORE... MY FAVORITE POETESS IS EMILY DICKINSON... I'M GOING TO LIVE IN A CASTLE WHEN I GROW UP... I WILL BE A FAMOUS WRITER... I WANT TO DEVELOP MY PSYCHICNESS... SOMETIMES I THINK IF I COULD USE MY WHOLE BRAIN, I COULD TEACH MYSELF TO FLY... I DREW THIS PICTURE OF A DEAD CICADA, SOMETIMES I THINK I LIVED IN PARIS DURING ONE OF MY PAST LIVES...

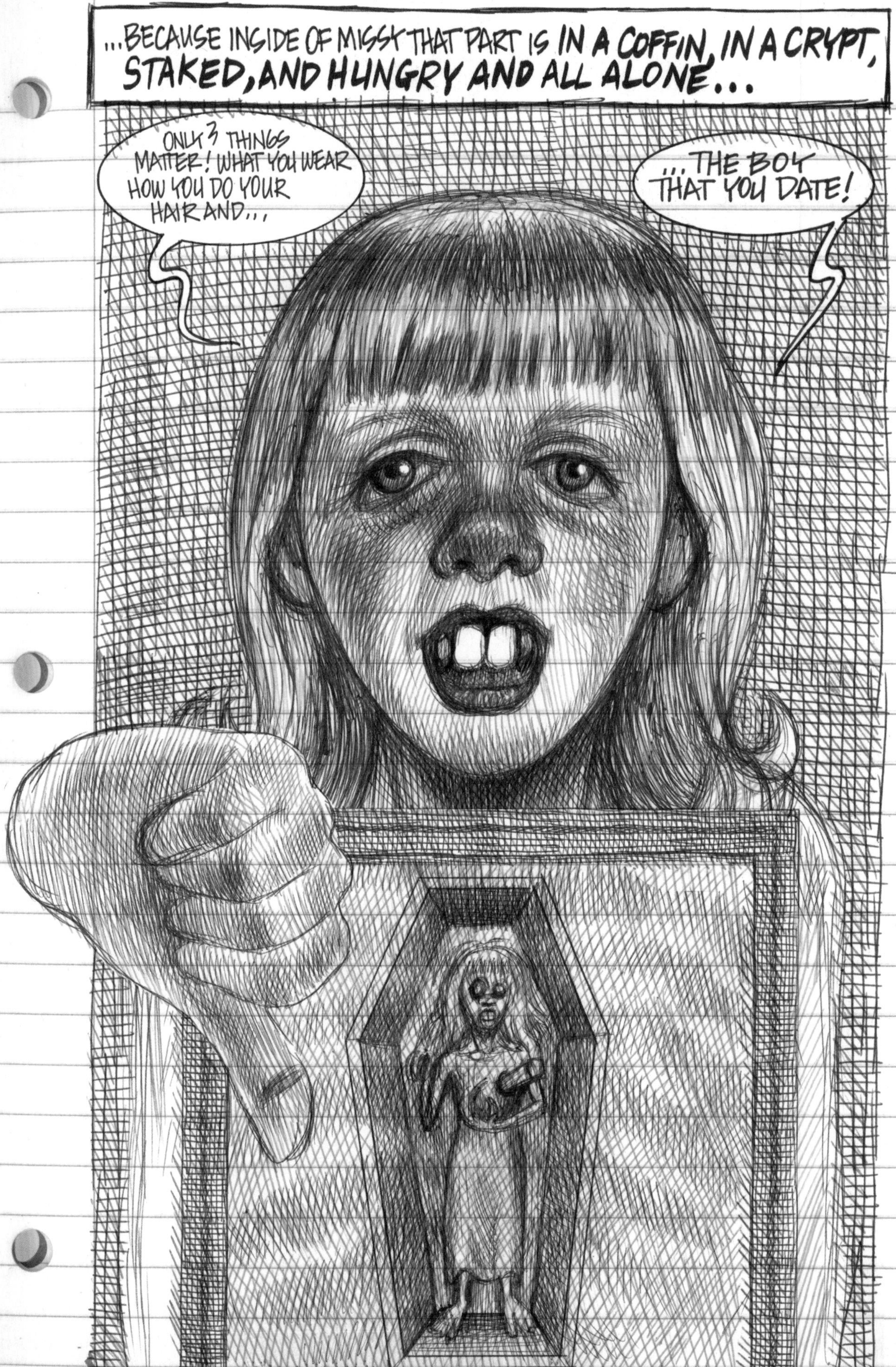
...BECAUSE INSIDE OF MISSY THAT PART IS IN A COFFIN, IN A CRYPT, STAKED, AND HUNGRY AND ALL ALONE...
ONLY 3 THINGS MATTER! WHAT YOU WEAR HOW YOU DO YOUR HAIR AND...,
...THE BOY THAT YOU DATE!

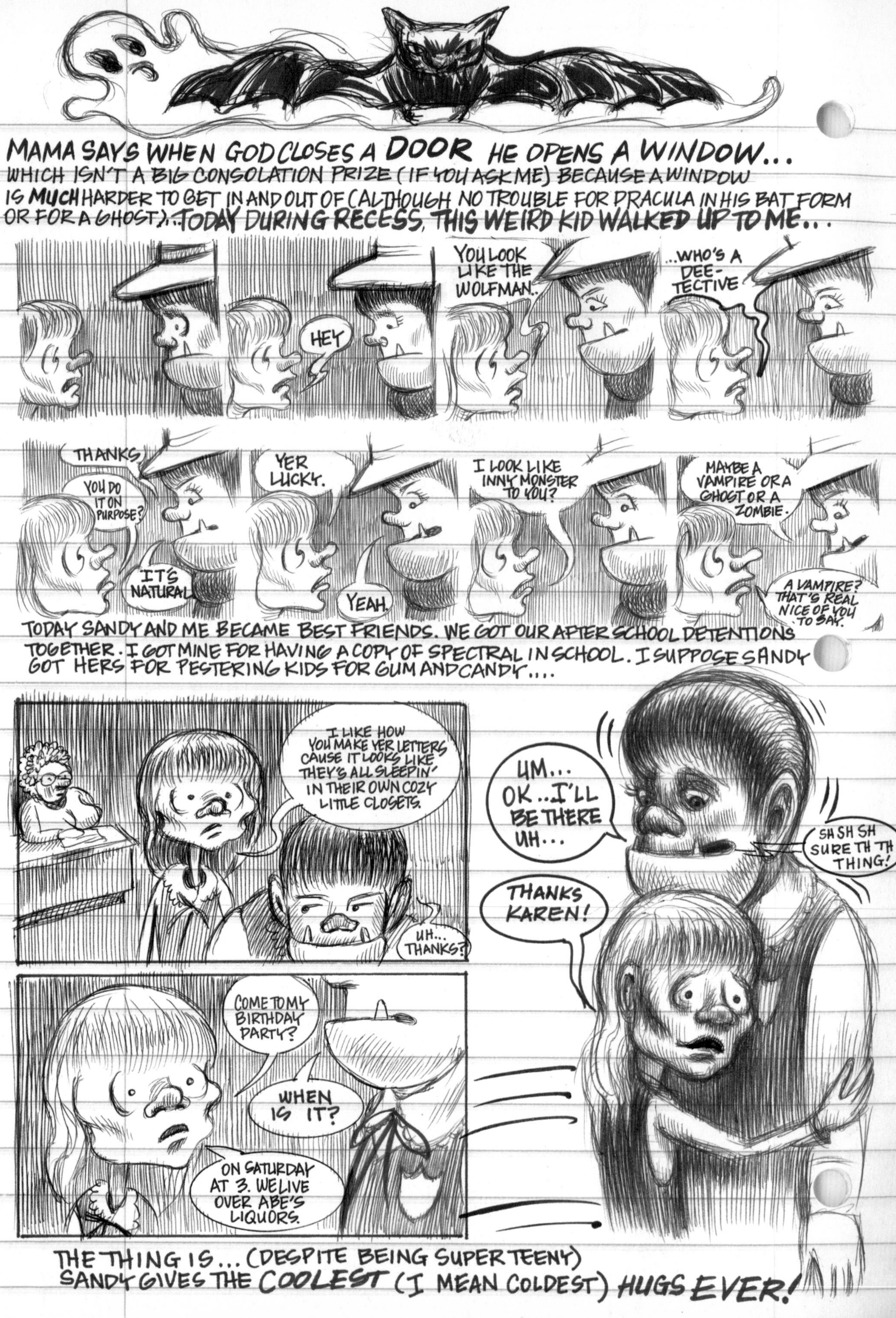
MAMA SAYS WHEN GOD CLOSES A DOOR HE OPENS A WINDOW...
WHICH ISN'T A BIG CONSOLATION PRIZE (IF YOU ASK ME) BECAUSE A WINDOW IS MUCH HARDER TO GET IN AND OUT OF (ALTHOUGH NO TROUBLE FOR DRACULA IN HIS BAT FORM OR FOR A GHOST)...TODAY DURING RECESS, THIS WEIRD KID WALKED UP TO ME...
HEY
YOU LOOK LIKE THE WOLFMAN..
...WHO'S A DEE-TECTIVE
THANKS
YOU DO IT ON PURPOSE?
IT'S NATURAL
YER LUCKY.
YEAH.
I LOOK LIKE INNY MONSTER TO YOU?
MAYBE A VAMPIRE OR A GHOST OR A ZOMBIE.
A VAMPIRE? THAT'S REAL NICE OF YOU TO SAY.
TODAY SANDY AND ME BECAME BEST FRIENDS. WE GOT OUR AFTER SCHOOL DETENTIONS TOGETHER. I GOT MINE FOR HAVING A COPY OF SPECTRAL IN SCHOOL. I SUPPOSE SANDY GOT HERS FOR PESTERING KIDS FOR GUM AND CANDY....
I LIKE HOW YOU MAKE YER LETTERS CAUSE IT LOOKS LIKE THEY'S ALL SLEEPIN' IN THEIR OWN COZY LITTLE CLOSETS.
UH... THANKS?
COME TO MY BIRTHDAY PARTY?
WHEN IS IT?
ON SATURDAY AT 3. WE LIVE OVER ABE'S LIQUORS.
UM... OK...I'LL BE THERE UH...
SH SH SH SURE TH TH THING!
THANKS KAREN!
THE THING IS... (DESPITE BEING SUPER TEENY) SANDY GIVES THE COOLEST (I MEAN COLDEST) HUGS EVER!

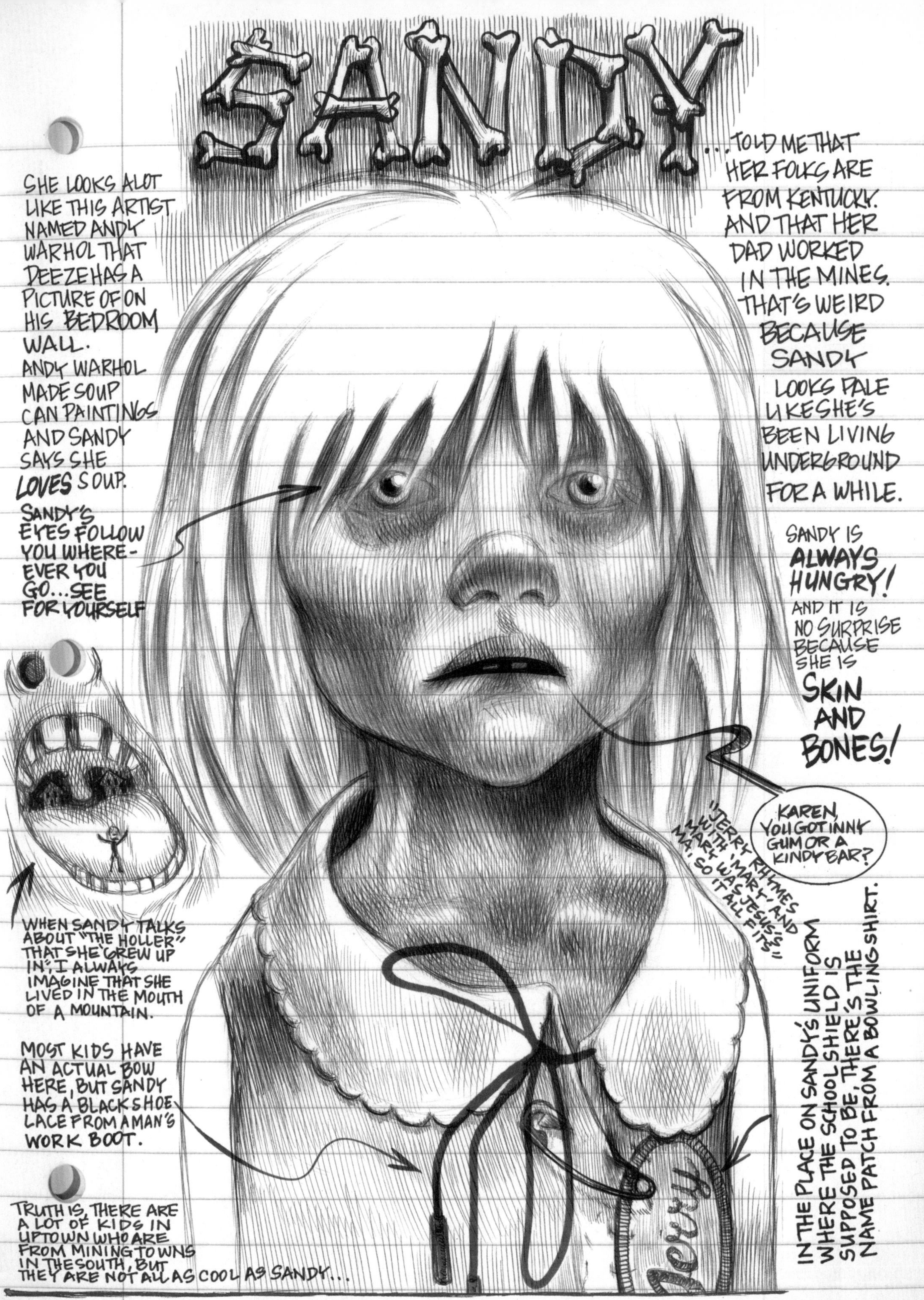
SANDY
...TOLD ME THAT HER FOLKS ARE FROM KENTUCKY. AND THAT HER DAD WORKED IN THE MINES. THAT'S WEIRD BECAUSE SANDY LOOKS PALE LIKE SHE'S BEEN LIVING UNDERGROUND FOR A WHILE.
SHE LOOKS ALOT LIKE THIS ARTIST NAMED ANDY WARHOL THAT DEEZE HAS A PICTURE OF ON HIS BEDROOM WALL. ANDY WARHOL MADE SOUP CAN PAINTINGS AND SANDY SAYS SHE LOVES SOUP.
SANDY'S EYES FOLLOW YOU WHERE-EVER YOU GO...SEE FOR YOURSELF
SANDY IS ALWAYS HUNGRY! AND IT IS NO SURPRISE BECAUSE SHE IS SKIN AND BONES!
KAREN, YOU GOT INNY GUM OR A KINDY BAR?
"JERRY" RHYMES WITH 'MARY' AND MARY WAS JESUS'S MA, SO IT ALL FITS."
WHEN SANDY TALKS ABOUT "THE HOLLER" THAT SHE "GREW UP IN", I ALWAYS IMAGINE THAT SHE LIVED IN THE MOUTH OF A MOUNTAIN.
MOST KIDS HAVE AN ACTUAL BOW HERE, BUT SANDY HAS A BLACK SHOE LACE FROM A MAN'S WORK BOOT.
IN THE PLACE ON SANDY'S UNIFORM WHERE THE SCHOOL SHIELD IS SUPPOSED TO BE, THERE'S THE NAME PATCH FROM A BOWLING SHIRT.
Jerry
TRUTH IS, THERE ARE A LOT OF KIDS IN UPTOWN WHO ARE FROM MINING TOWNS IN THE SOUTH, BUT THEY ARE NOT ALL AS COOL AS SANDY...

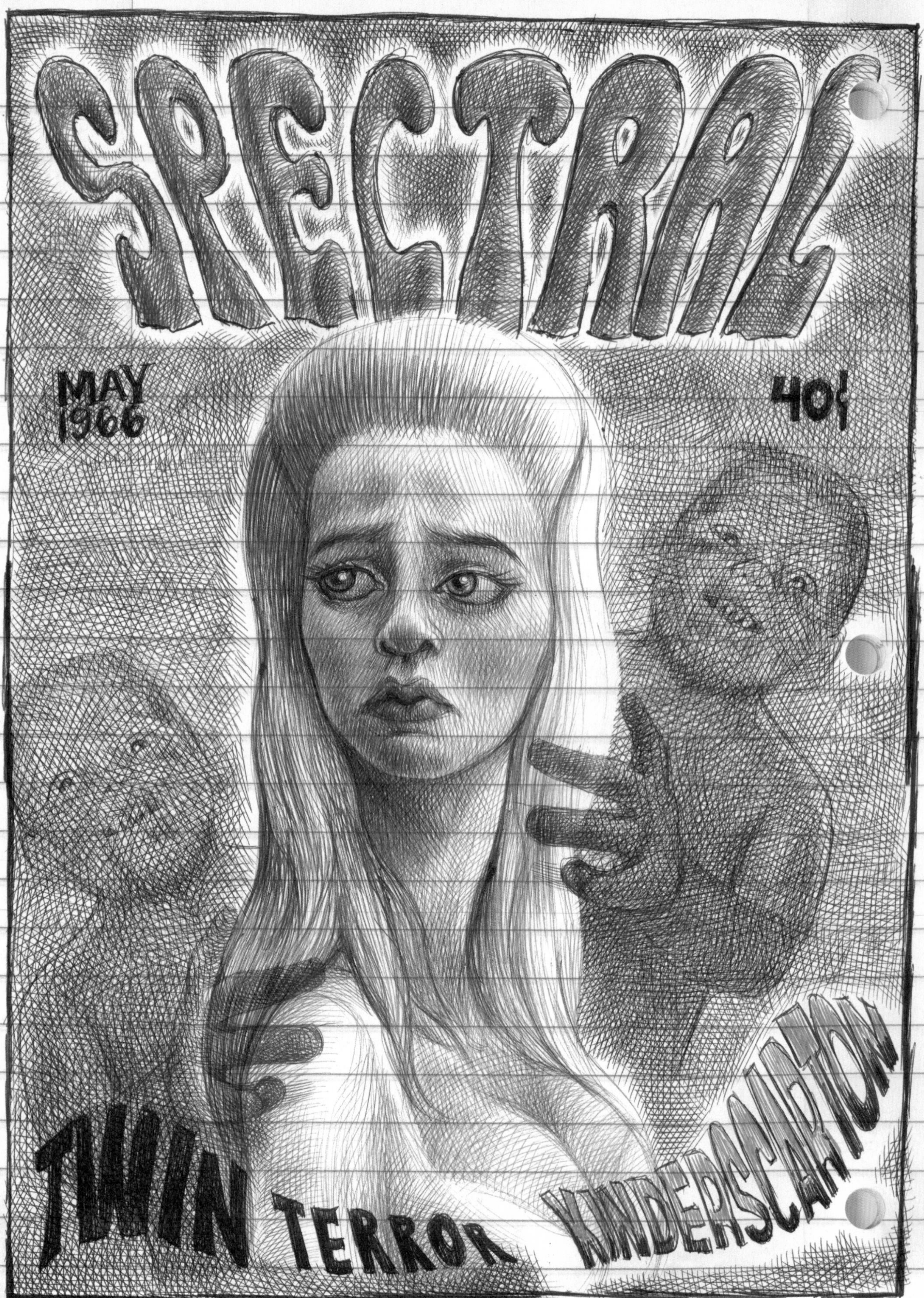
SPECTRAL
MAY 1966
40¢
TWIN TERROR
KINDERSCARTON

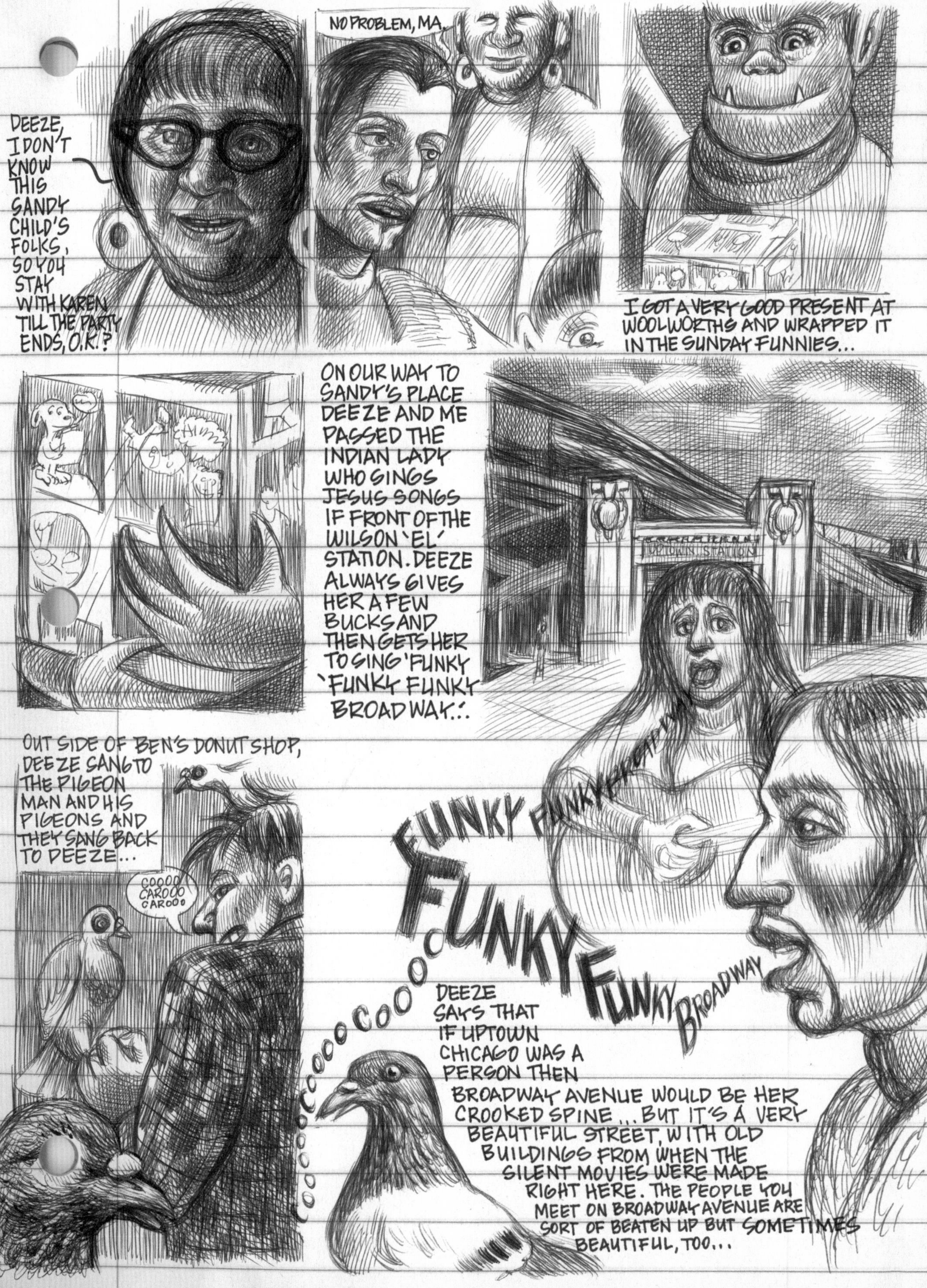
DEEZE, I DON'T KNOW THIS SANDY CHILD'S FOLKS, SO YOU STAY WITH KAREN TILL THE PARTY ENDS, O.K.?
NO PROBLEM, MA.
I GOT A VERY GOOD PRESENT AT WOOLWORTHS AND WRAPPED IT IN THE SUNDAY FUNNIES...
ON OUR WAY TO SANDY'S PLACE DEEZE AND ME PASSED THE INDIAN LADY WHO SINGS JESUS SONGS IF FRONT OF THE WILSON 'EL' STATION. DEEZE ALWAYS GIVES HER A FEW BUCKS AND THEN GETS HER TO SING 'FUNKY FUNKY FUNKY BROADWAY.'.
UPTOWN STATION
OUT SIDE OF BEN'S DONUT SHOP, DEEZE SANG TO THE PIGEON MAN AND HIS PIGEONS AND THEY SANG BACK TO DEEZE...
COOOO CAROOO CAROOO
FUNKY FUNKY BROADWAY
FUNKY FUNKY FUNKY BROADWAY
DEEZE SAYS THAT IF UPTOWN CHICAGO WAS A PERSON THEN BROADWAY AVENUE WOULD BE HER CROOKED SPINE... BUT IT'S A VERY BEAUTIFUL STREET, WITH OLD BUILDINGS FROM WHEN THE SILENT MOVIES WERE MADE RIGHT HERE. THE PEOPLE YOU MEET ON BROADWAY AVENUE ARE SORT OF BEATEN UP BUT SOMETIMES BEAUTIFUL, TOO...

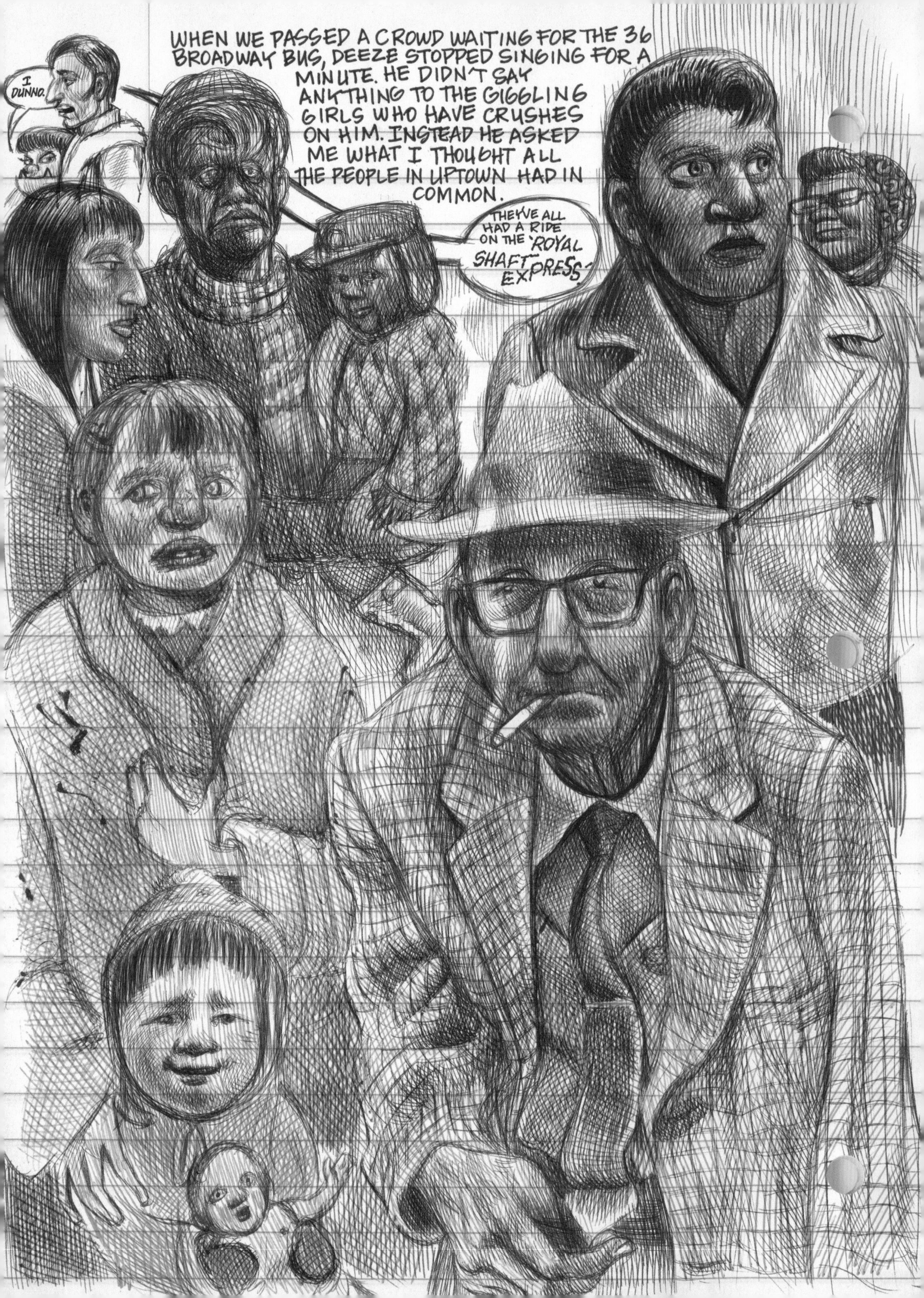
WHEN WE PASSED A CROWD WAITING FOR THE 36 BROADWAY BUS, DEEZE STOPPED SINGING FOR A MINUTE. HE DIDN'T SAY ANYTHING TO THE GIGGLING GIRLS WHO HAVE CRUSHES ON HIM. INSTEAD HE ASKED ME WHAT I THOUGHT ALL THE PEOPLE IN UPTOWN HAD IN COMMON.
I DUNNO.
THEY'VE ALL HAD A RIDE ON THE 'ROYAL SHAFT EXPRESS.'

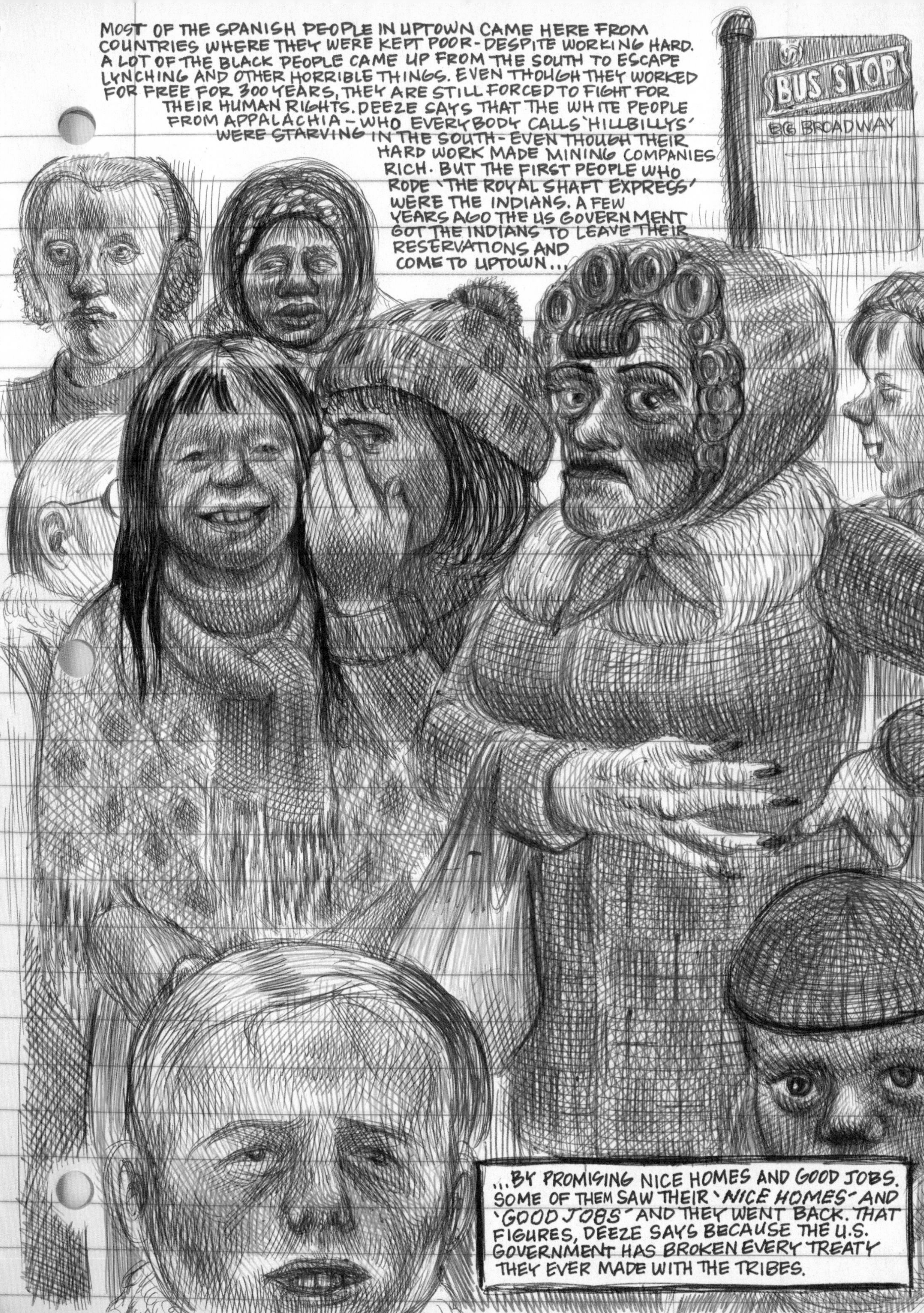
MOST OF THE SPANISH PEOPLE IN UPTOWN CAME HERE FROM COUNTRIES WHERE THEY WERE KEPT POOR - DESPITE WORKING HARD. A LOT OF THE BLACK PEOPLE CAME UP FROM THE SOUTH TO ESCAPE LYNCHING AND OTHER HORRIBLE THINGS. EVEN THOUGH THEY WORKED FOR FREE FOR 300 YEARS, THEY ARE STILL FORCED TO FIGHT FOR THEIR HUMAN RIGHTS. DEEZE SAYS THAT THE WHITE PEOPLE FROM APPALACHIA - WHO EVERYBODY CALLS 'HILLBILLYS' WERE STARVING IN THE SOUTH - EVEN THOUGH THEIR HARD WORK MADE MINING COMPANIES RICH. BUT THE FIRST PEOPLE WHO RODE 'THE ROYAL SHAFT EXPRESS' WERE THE INDIANS. A FEW YEARS AGO THE US GOVERNMENT GOT THE INDIANS TO LEAVE THEIR RESERVATIONS AND COME TO UPTOWN...
BUS STOP
BIG BROADWAY
...BY PROMISING NICE HOMES AND GOOD JOBS. SOME OF THEM SAW THEIR '*NICE HOMES*' AND '*GOOD JOBS*' AND THEY WENT BACK. THAT FIGURES, DEEZE SAYS BECAUSE THE U.S. GOVERNMENT HAS BROKEN EVERY TREATY THEY EVER MADE WITH THE TRIBES.

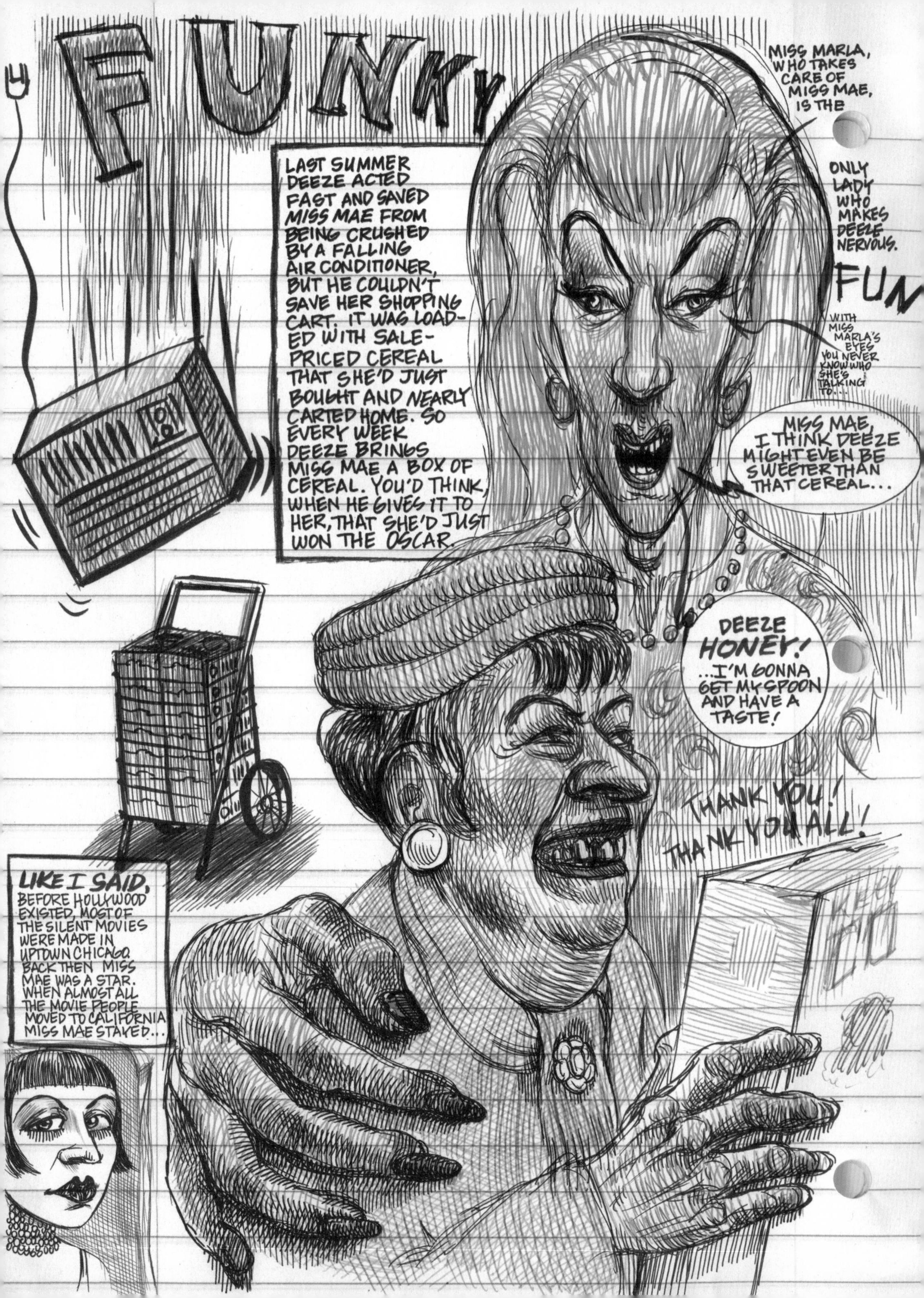
FUNKY
LAST SUMMER DEEZE ACTED FAST AND SAVED MISS MAE FROM BEING CRUSHED BY A FALLING AIR CONDITIONER, BUT HE COULDN'T SAVE HER SHOPPING CART. IT WAS LOADED WITH SALE-PRICED CEREAL THAT SHE'D JUST BOUGHT AND NEARLY CARTED HOME. SO EVERY WEEK DEEZE BRINGS MISS MAE A BOX OF CEREAL. YOU'D THINK, WHEN HE GIVES IT TO HER, THAT SHE'D JUST WON THE OSCAR.
MISS MARLA, WHO TAKES CARE OF MISS MAE, IS THE ONLY LADY WHO MAKES DEEZE NERVOUS.
FUN
WITH MISS MARLA'S EYES YOU NEVER KNOW WHO SHE'S TALKING TO...
MISS MAE, I THINK DEEZE MIGHT EVEN BE SWEETER THAN THAT CEREAL...
DEEZE HONEY! ...I'M GONNA GET MY SPOON AND HAVE A TASTE!
THANK YOU! THANK YOU ALL!
LIKE I SAID, BEFORE HOLLYWOOD EXISTED, MOST OF THE SILENT MOVIES WERE MADE IN UPTOWN CHICAGO. BACK THEN MISS MAE WAS A STAR. WHEN ALMOST ALL THE MOVIE PEOPLE MOVED TO CALIFORNIA MISS MAE STAYED...

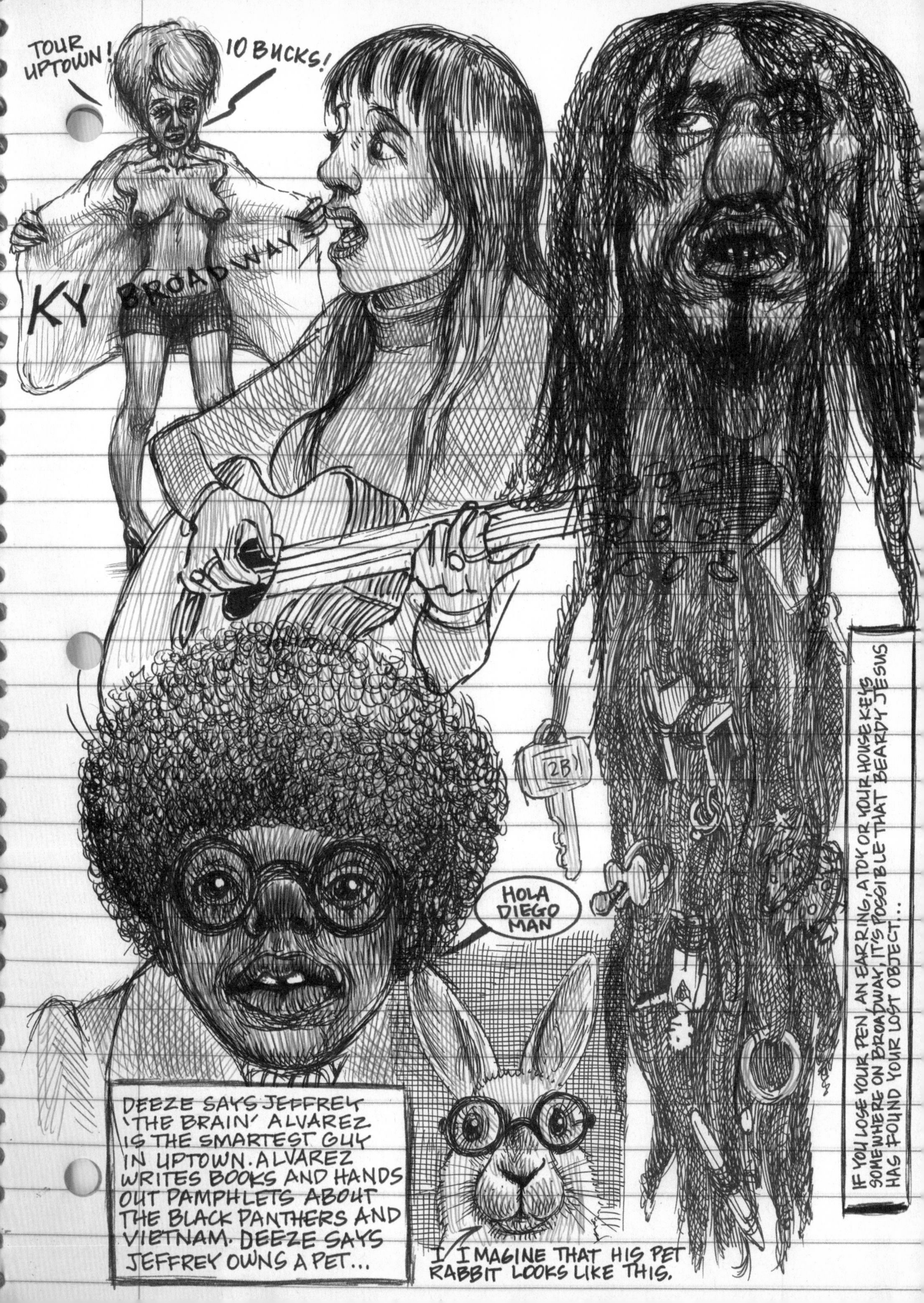
TOUR UPTOWN!
10 BUCKS!
KY BROADWAY
2B
HOLA DIEGO MAN
IF YOU LOSE YOUR PEN, AN EARRING, A TOK OR YOUR HOUSE KEYS SOMEWHERE ON BROADWAY, IT'S POSSIBLE THAT BEARDY JESUS HAS FOUND YOUR LOST OBJECT...
DEEZE SAYS JEFFREY 'THE BRAIN' ALVAREZ IS THE SMARTEST GUY IN UPTOWN. ALVAREZ WRITES BOOKS AND HANDS OUT PAMPHLETS ABOUT THE BLACK PANTHERS AND VIETNAM. DEEZE SAYS JEFFREY OWNS A PET...
I IMAGINE THAT HIS PET RABBIT LOOKS LIKE THIS.

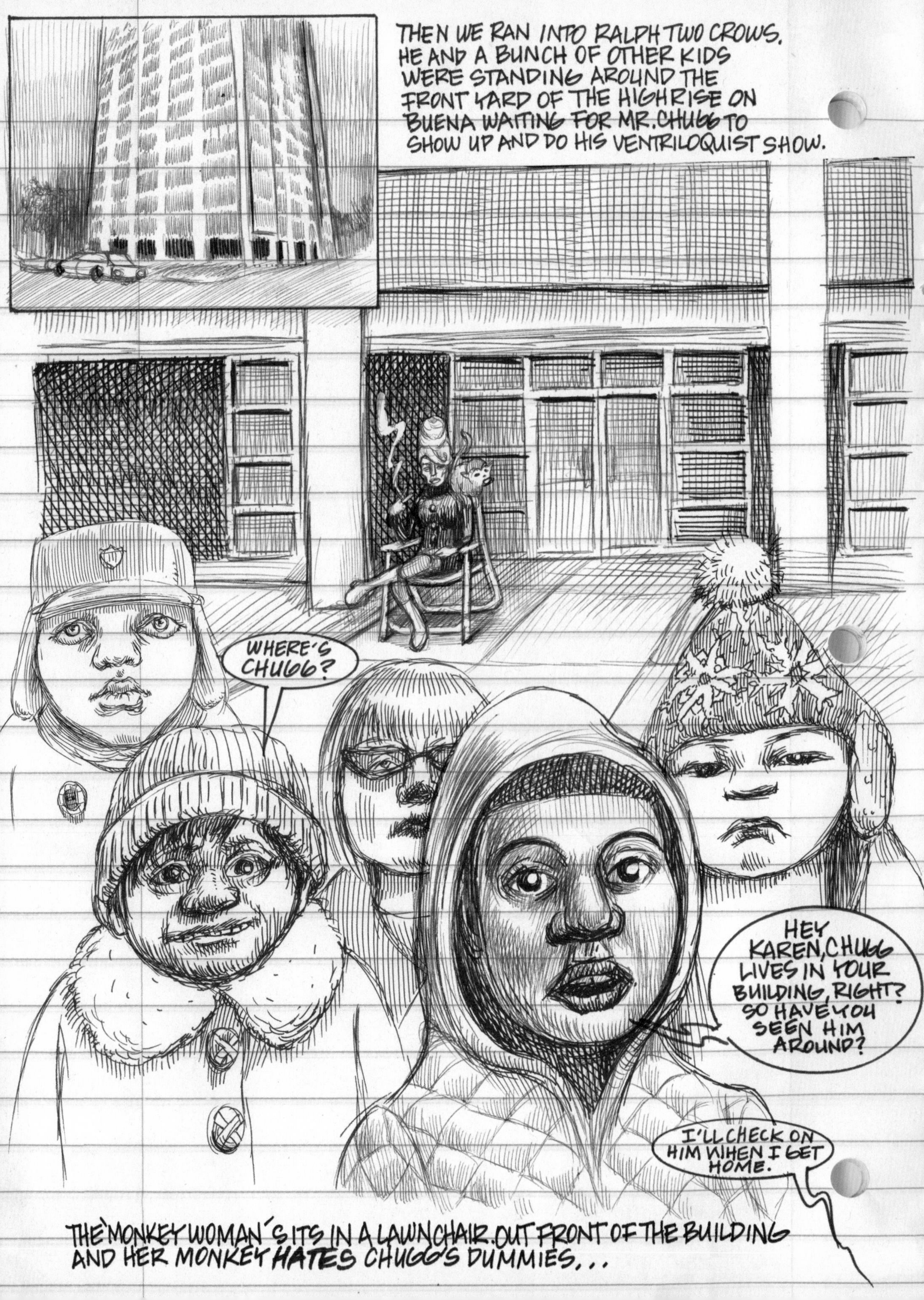
THEN WE RAN INTO RALPH TWO CROWS. HE AND A BUNCH OF OTHER KIDS WERE STANDING AROUND THE FRONT YARD OF THE HIGHRISE ON BUENA WAITING FOR MR. CHUGG TO SHOW UP AND DO HIS VENTRILOQUIST SHOW.
WHERE'S CHUGG?
HEY KAREN, CHUGG LIVES IN YOUR BUILDING, RIGHT? SO HAVE YOU SEEN HIM AROUND?
I'LL CHECK ON HIM WHEN I GET HOME.
THE 'MONKEY WOMAN' SITS IN A LAWNCHAIR OUT FRONT OF THE BUILDING AND HER MONKEY HATES CHUGG'S DUMMIES...

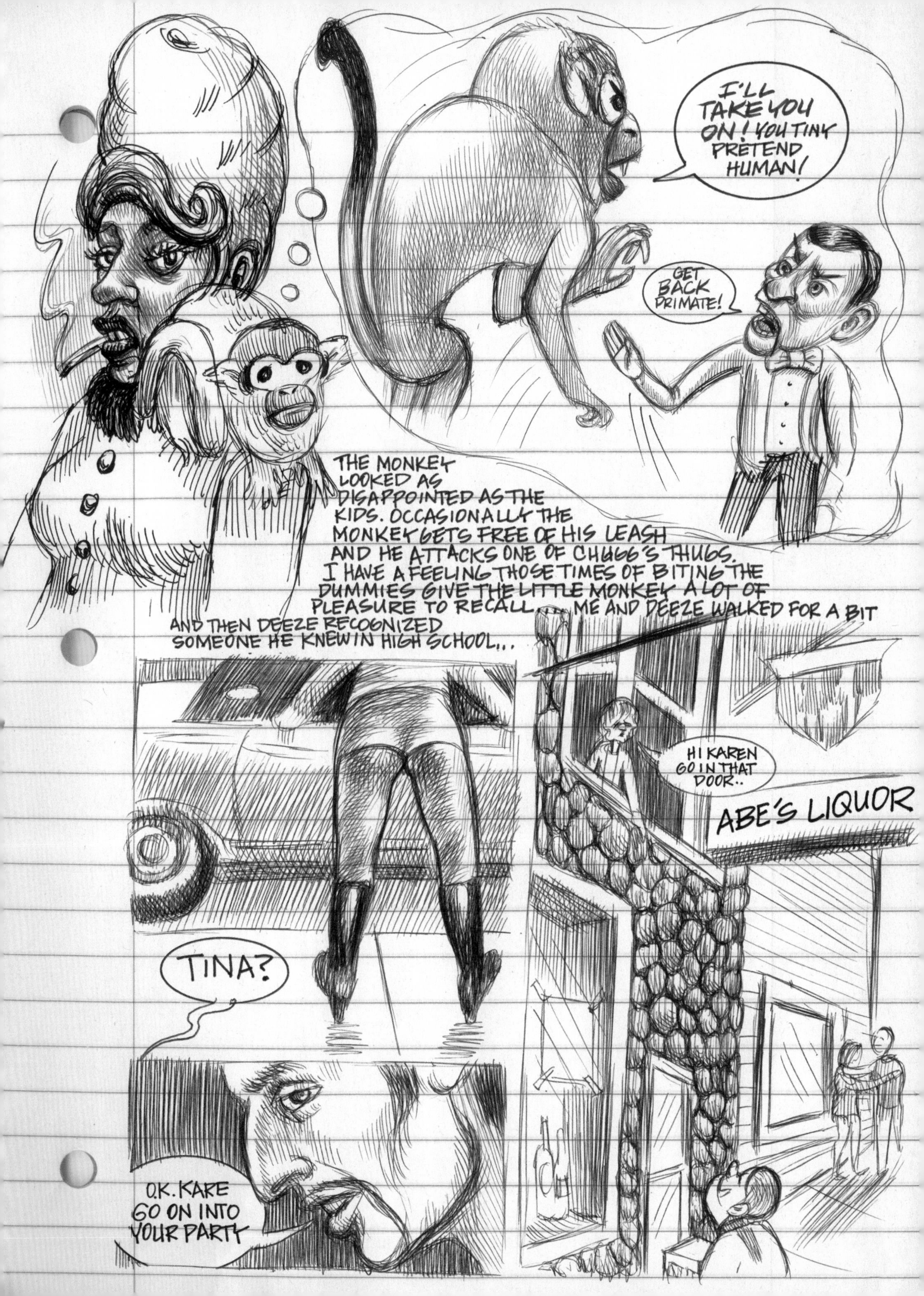
I'LL TAKE YOU ON! YOU TINY PRETEND HUMAN!
GET BACK PRIMATE!
THE MONKEY LOOKED AS DISAPPOINTED AS THE KIDS. OCCASIONALLY THE MONKEY GETS FREE OF HIS LEASH AND HE ATTACKS ONE OF CHUGG'S THUGS. I HAVE A FEELING THOSE TIMES OF BITING THE DUMMIES GIVE THE LITTLE MONKEY A LOT OF PLEASURE TO RECALL.... ME AND DEEZE WALKED FOR A BIT AND THEN DEEZE RECOGNIZED SOMEONE HE KNEW IN HIGH SCHOOL...
TINA?
O.K. KARE GO ON INTO YOUR PARTY
HI KAREN GO IN THAT DOOR..
ABE'S LIQUOR

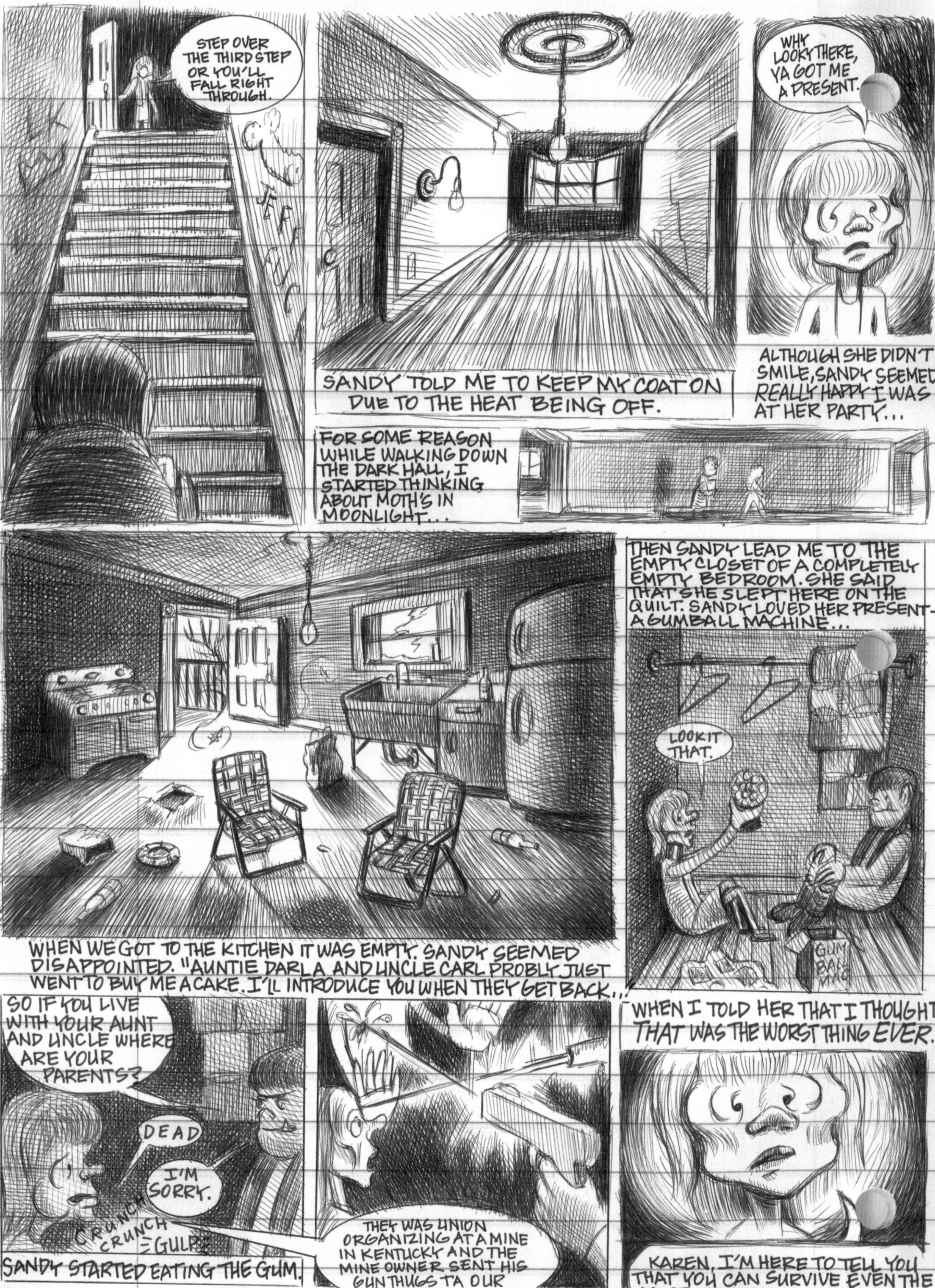
STEP OVER THE THIRD STEP OR YOU'LL FALL RIGHT THROUGH.
SANDY TOLD ME TO KEEP MY COAT ON DUE TO THE HEAT BEING OFF.
WHY LOOKY THERE, YA GOT ME A PRESENT.
ALTHOUGH SHE DIDN'T SMILE, SANDY SEEMED REALLY HAPPY I WAS AT HER PARTY...
FOR SOME REASON WHILE WALKING DOWN THE DARK HALL, I STARTED THINKING ABOUT MOTH'S IN MOONLIGHT...
WHEN WE GOT TO THE KITCHEN IT WAS EMPTY. SANDY SEEMED DISAPPOINTED. "AUNTIE DARLA AND UNCLE CARL PROBLY JUST WENT TO BUY ME A CAKE. I'LL INTRODUCE YOU WHEN THEY GET BACK..."
THEN SANDY LEAD ME TO THE EMPTY CLOSET OF A COMPLETELY EMPTY BEDROOM. SHE SAID THAT SHE SLEPT HERE ON THE QUILT. SANDY LOVED HER PRESENT- A GUMBALL MACHINE...
LOOKIT THAT.
GUM BALL MAC
SO IF YOU LIVE WITH YOUR AUNT AND UNCLE WHERE ARE YOUR PARENTS?
DEAD
I'M SORRY.
CRUNCH CRUNCH
GULP
SANDY STARTED EATING THE GUM.
THEY WAS UNION ORGANIZING AT A MINE IN KENTUCKY AND THE MINE OWNER SENT HIS GUN THUGS TA OUR HOME.
WHEN I TOLD HER THAT I THOUGHT THAT WAS THE WORST THING EVER...
KAREN, I'M HERE TO TELL YOU THAT YOU CAN SURVIVE EVEN THE MOST TERRBULL THINGS...

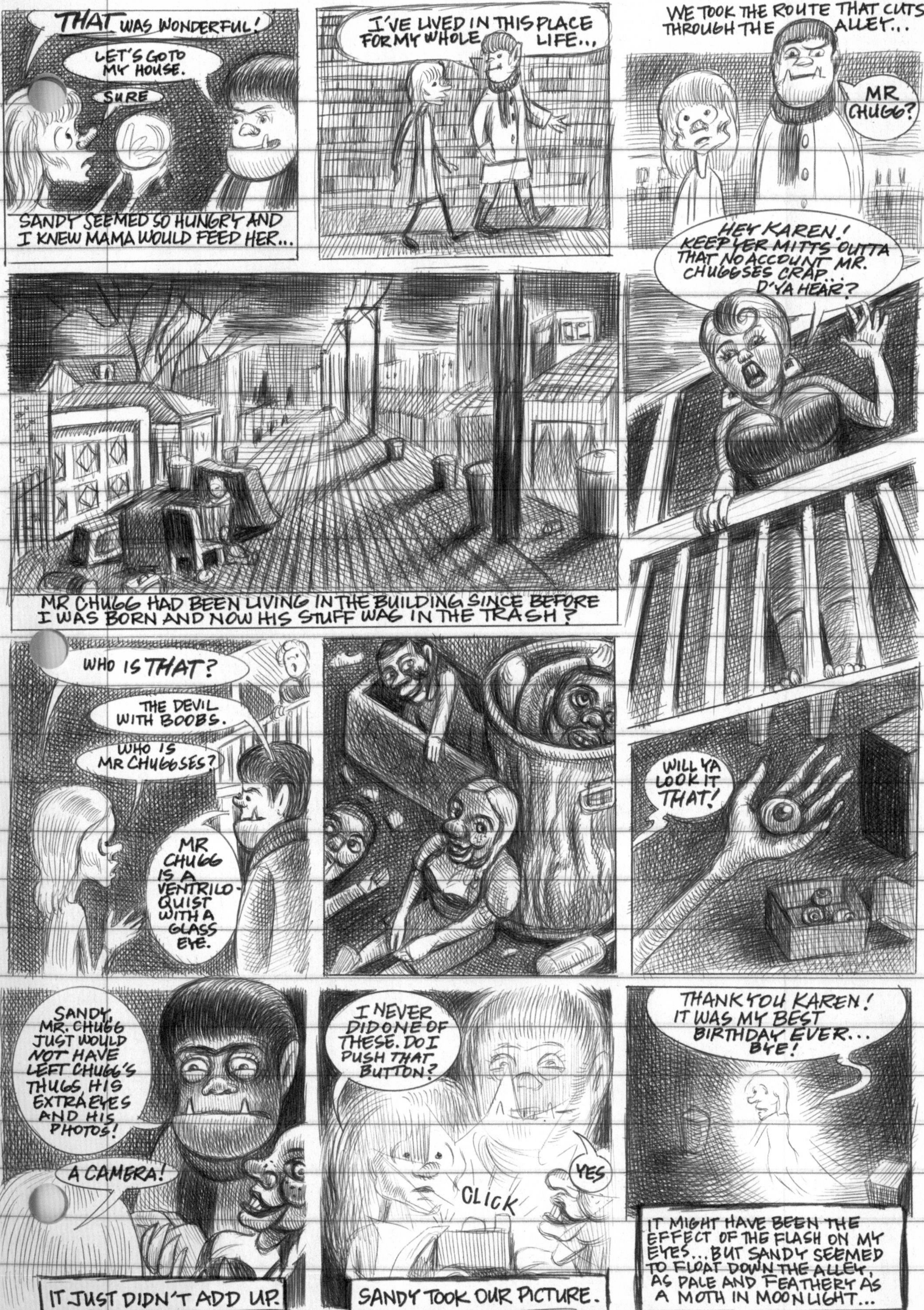
THAT WAS WONDERFUL!
LET'S GO TO MY HOUSE.
SURE
SANDY SEEMED SO HUNGRY AND I KNEW MAMA WOULD FEED HER...
I'VE LIVED IN THIS PLACE FOR MY WHOLE LIFE...
WE TOOK THE ROUTE THAT CUTS THROUGH THE ALLEY...
MR CHUGG?
MR CHUGG HAD BEEN LIVING IN THE BUILDING SINCE BEFORE I WAS BORN AND NOW HIS STUFF WAS IN THE TRASH?
HEY KAREN! KEEP YER MITTS OUTTA THAT NO ACCOUNT MR. CHUGGSES CRAP... D'YA HEAR?
WHO IS THAT?
THE DEVIL WITH BOOBS.
WHO IS MR CHUGGSES?
MR CHUGG IS A VENTRILOQUIST WITH A GLASS EYE.
WILL YA LOOK IT THAT!
SANDY, MR. CHUGG JUST WOULD NOT HAVE LEFT CHUGG'S THUGS, HIS EXTRA EYES AND HIS PHOTOS!
A CAMERA!
IT JUST DIDN'T ADD UP.
I NEVER DID ONE OF THESE. DO I PUSH THAT BUTTON?
YES
CLICK
SANDY TOOK OUR PICTURE.
THANK YOU KAREN! IT WAS MY BEST BIRTHDAY EVER... BYE!
IT MIGHT HAVE BEEN THE EFFECT OF THE FLASH ON MY EYES... BUT SANDY SEEMED TO FLOAT DOWN THE ALLEY, AS PALE AND FEATHERY AS A MOTH IN MOONLIGHT...

SINCE I CAME HOME WITHOUT DEEZE, MAMA FIGURED OUT THAT HE HADN'T STAYED WITH ME AT SANDY'S PARTY. I TRIED TO 'TELL A TALL TALE' AS MAMA SAYS, BUT SHE SAW RIGHT THROUGH IT. WHEN DEEZE GOT HOME (KINDA DRUNK) MAMA TOLD ME TO GO TO MY BEDROOM. INSTEAD I HID AND LISTENED...

YEAH GOOD LUCK WITH THAT MA—

DEEZE YER GONNA NEED TO GROW UP BECAUSE I MAY NOT...

SON! I'M SICK VERY SICK

MAMA SAID SOME WORDS THAT I COULDN'T HEAR AND AFTER A FEW MINUTES DEEZE'S VOICE WAS SO UPSET THAT I WENT INTO THE KITCHEN AND RIGHT AWAY I COULD SEE THAT WAS A MISTAKE. THEY SAW ME AND I COULDN'T GET AWAY. MY BROTHER WAS KNEELING IN FRONT OF MAMA WHO WAS SITTING ON A CHAIR. HE HAD HIS ARM AROUND HER AND THEY BOTH MOTIONED FOR ME. CLEARLY THE PLAN WAS FOR US ALL TO HUG EACH OTHER FOR A MILLION YEARS AND TRUTHFULLY I COULDN'T THINK OF ANYTHING I WANTED TO DO LESS, NOT GET POKED WITH A SHARP STICK OR PUT A LIT CIGARETTE UP MY NOSE OR CLIMB A RICKETY LADDER OVER A BIG VAT OF ACID. THIS GROUP HUG STUFF IS ALWAYS WHAT PEOPLE DO RIGHT BEFORE THEY DROP A BOMB ON YOU...

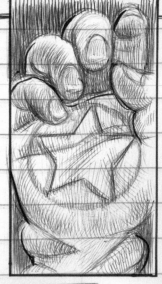

I LOOKED DOWN INTO MAMA'S PALM RIGHT BEFORE I WAS SWALLOWED INTO THE 'HUG OF DEATH.' MAYBE WHAT I SAW IN HER PALM WAS A SHADOW CAST FROM THE CEILING FIXTURE, BUT TO ME IT LOOKED JUST LIKE THE SIGN OF THE PENTAGRAM THAT SHOWS UP IN THE PALM OF THE 'NEXT VICTIM' - LIKE IN THE WOLFMAN MOVIE... AND IT TOTALLY FREAKED ME OUT!

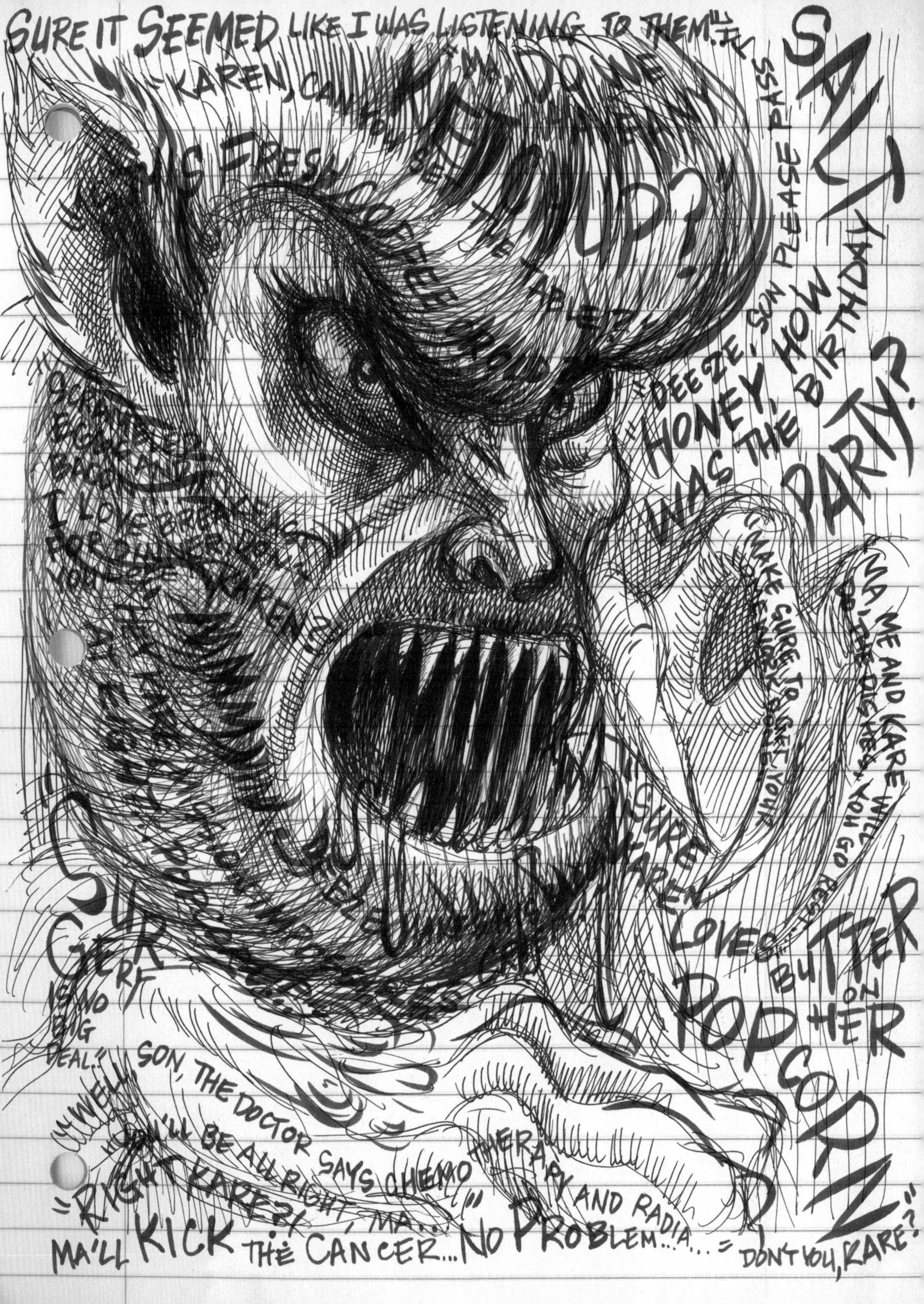
SURE IT SEEMED LIKE I WAS LISTENING TO THEM...
KAREN, CAN YOU SET THE TABLE?
KETCHUP?
PLEASE PASS SALT
DEEZE, SON PLEASE PASS
HONEY, HOW WAS THE BIRTHDAY PARTY?
MA, ME AND KARE WILL GO
MAKE SURE TO
SURE KAREN LOVES BUTTER ON HER POPCORN
SURGERY IS NO BIG DEAL!
WELL SON, THE DOCTOR SAYS CHEMO THERAPY AND RADIA...A...
YOU'LL BE ALL RIGHT, MA...
RIGHT KARE?!
MA'LL KICK THE CANCER... NO PROBLEM...
DON'T YOU, KARE?

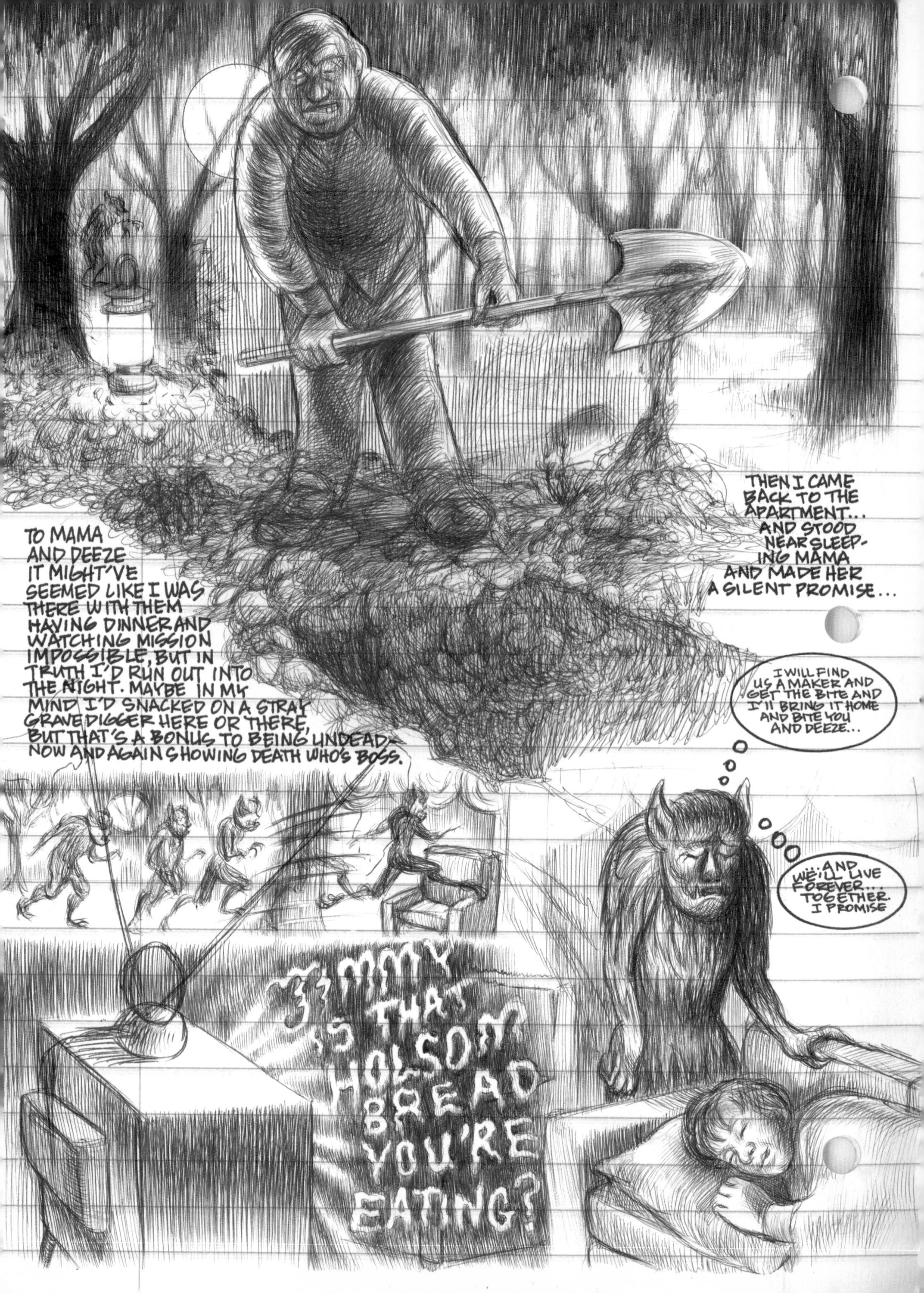

TO MAMA AND DEEZE IT MIGHT'VE SEEMED LIKE I WAS THERE WITH THEM HAVING DINNER AND WATCHING MISSION IMPOSSIBLE, BUT IN TRUTH I'D RUN OUT INTO THE NIGHT. MAYBE IN MY MIND I'D SNACKED ON A STRAY GRAVE DIGGER HERE OR THERE, BUT THAT'S A BONUS TO BEING UNDEAD- NOW AND AGAIN SHOWING DEATH WHO'S BOSS.
THEN I CAME BACK TO THE APARTMENT... AND STOOD NEAR SLEEPING MAMA AND MADE HER A SILENT PROMISE...
I WILL FIND US A MAKER AND GET THE BITE AND I'LL BRING IT HOME AND BITE YOU AND DEEZE...
...AND WE'LL LIVE FOREVER... TOGETHER. I PROMISE
JIMMY IS THAT HOLSOM BREAD YOU'RE EATING?

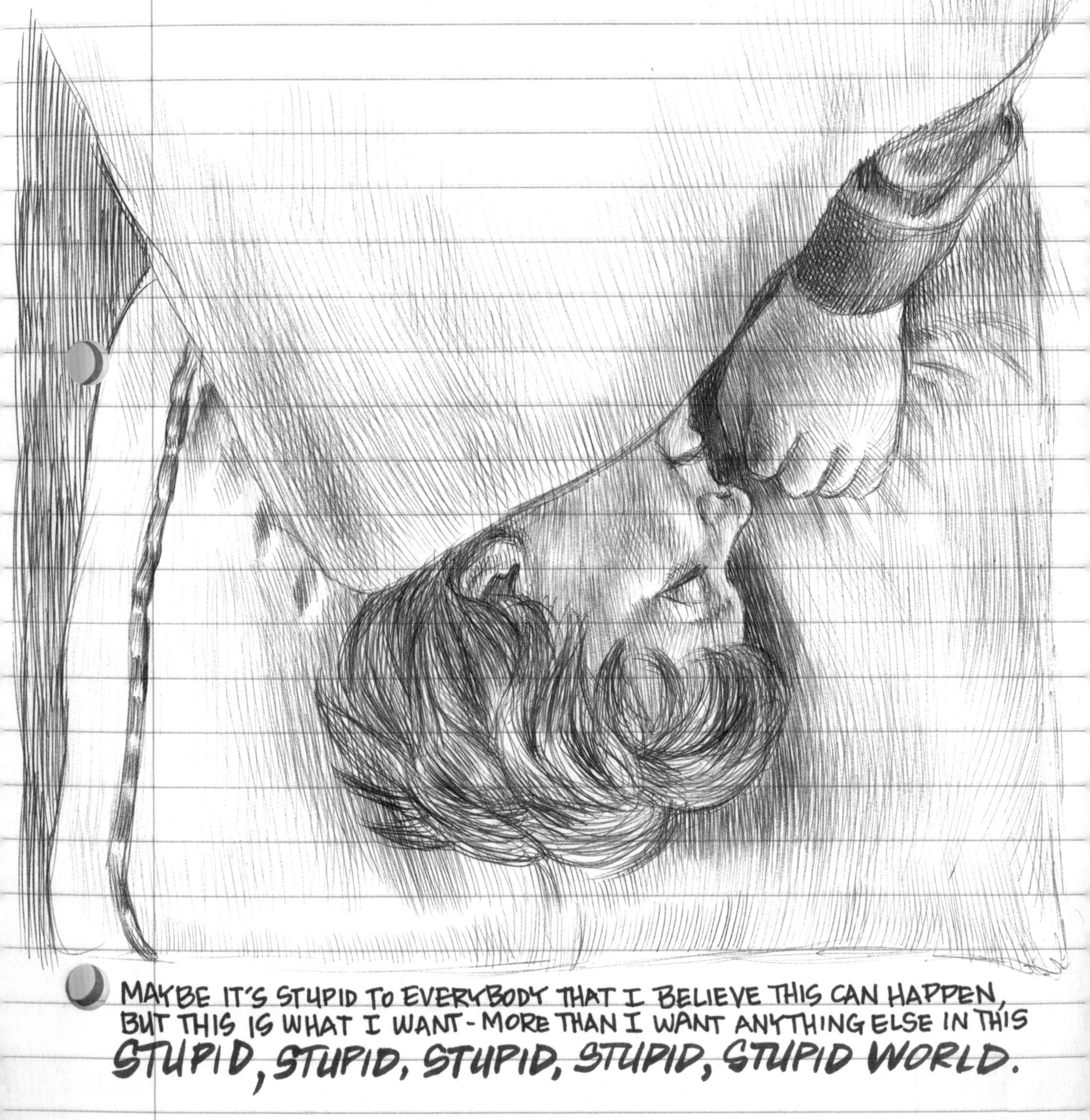

MAYBE IT'S STUPID TO EVERYBODY THAT I BELIEVE THIS CAN HAPPEN, BUT THIS IS WHAT I WANT - MORE THAN I WANT ANYTHING ELSE IN THIS **STUPID, STUPID, STUPID, STUPID, STUPID WORLD.**

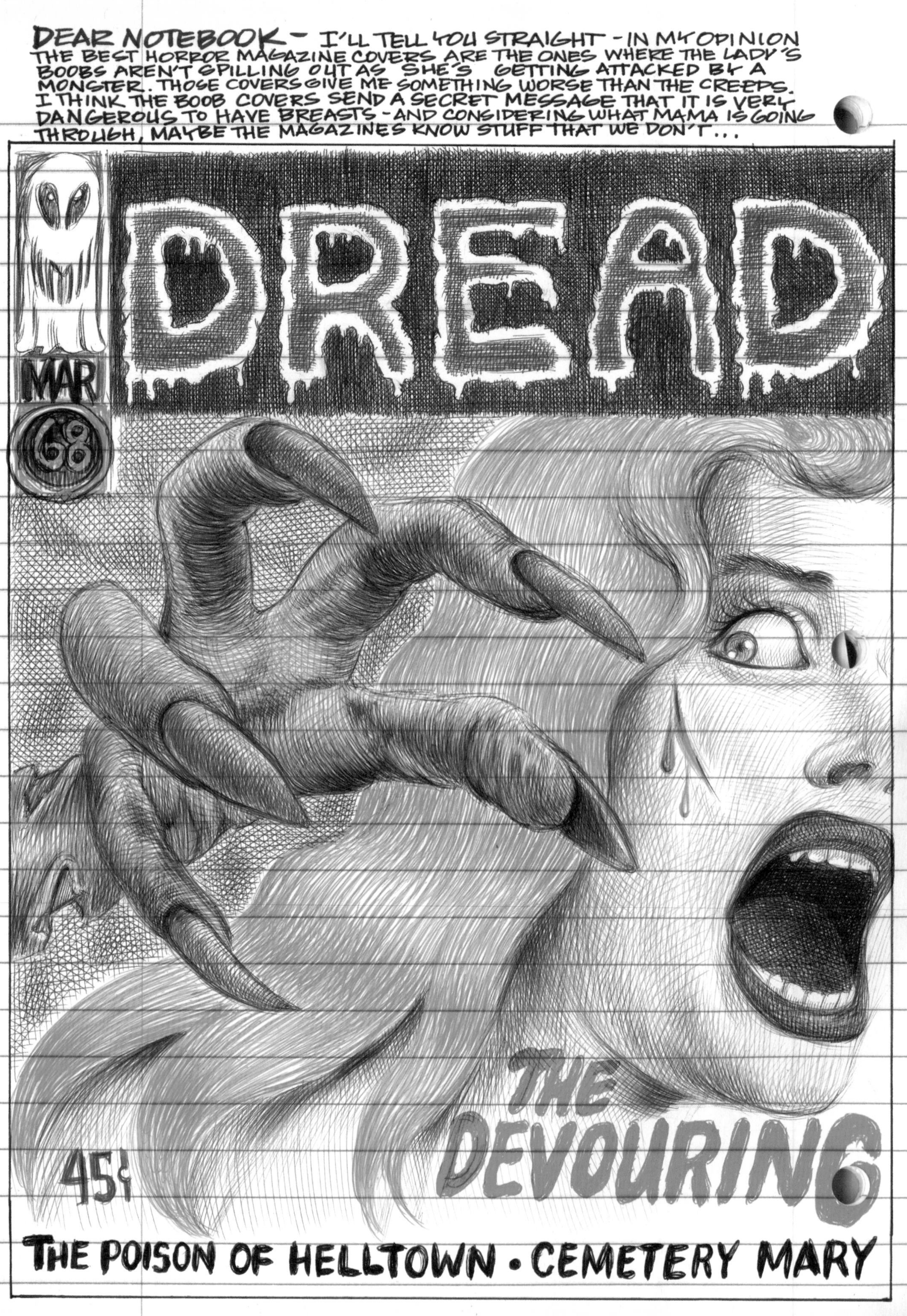
DEAR NOTEBOOK — I'LL TELL YOU STRAIGHT — IN MY OPINION THE BEST HORROR MAGAZINE COVERS ARE THE ONES WHERE THE LADY'S BOOBS AREN'T SPILLING OUT AS SHE'S GETTING ATTACKED BY A MONSTER. THOSE COVERS GIVE ME SOMETHING WORSE THAN THE CREEPS. I THINK THE BOOB COVERS SEND A SECRET MESSAGE THAT IT IS VERY DANGEROUS TO HAVE BREASTS — AND CONSIDERING WHAT MAMA IS GOING THROUGH, MAYBE THE MAGAZINES KNOW STUFF THAT WE DON'T...
DREAD
MAR
68
THE DEVOURING
45¢
THE POISON OF HELLTOWN • CEMETERY MARY

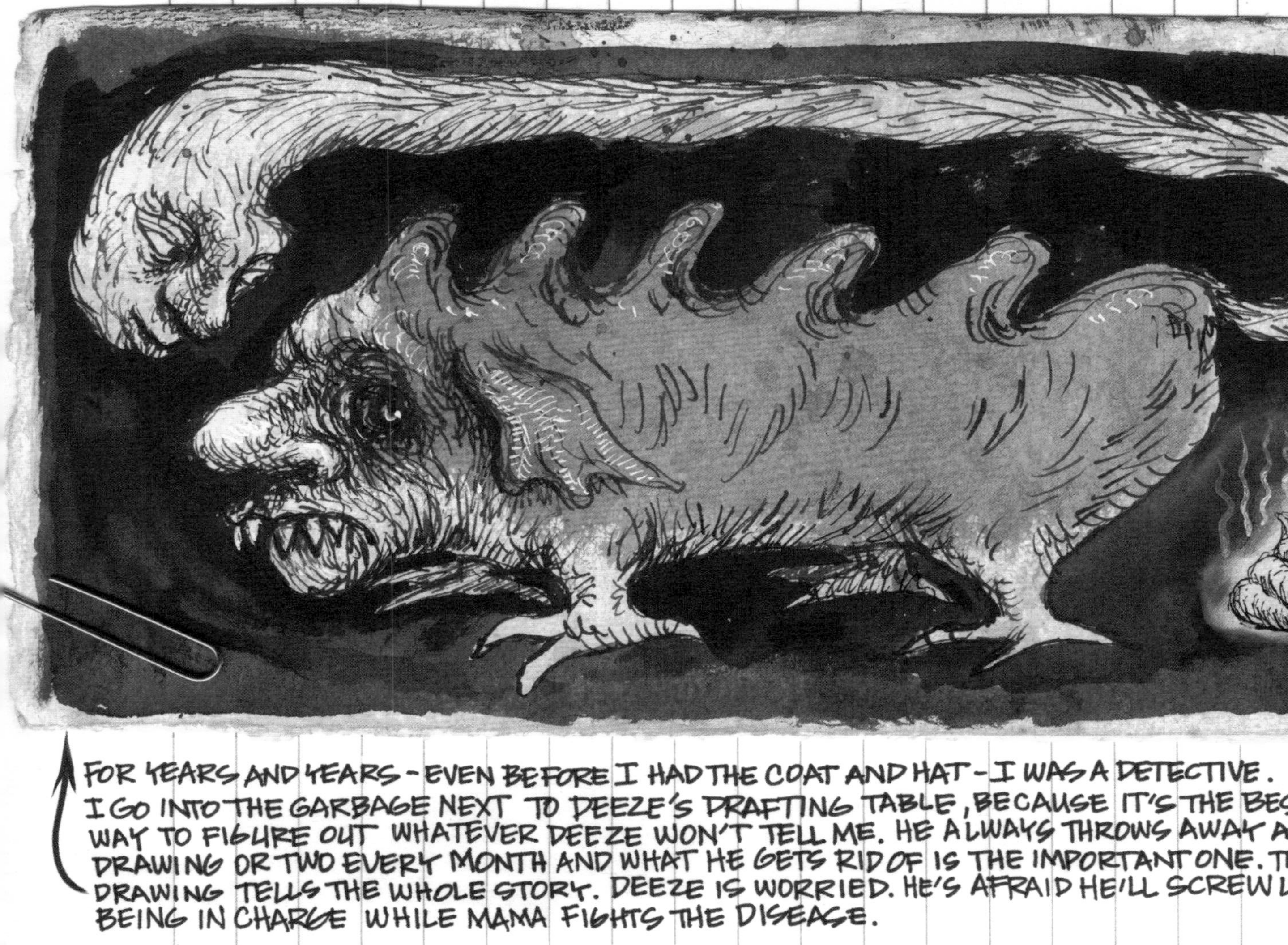

FOR YEARS AND YEARS - EVEN BEFORE I HAD THE COAT AND HAT - I WAS A DETECTIVE. I GO INTO THE GARBAGE NEXT TO DEEZE'S DRAFTING TABLE, BECAUSE IT'S THE BEST WAY TO FIGURE OUT WHATEVER DEEZE WON'T TELL ME. HE ALWAYS THROWS AWAY A DRAWING OR TWO EVERY MONTH AND WHAT HE GETS RID OF IS THE IMPORTANT ONE. THIS DRAWING TELLS THE WHOLE STORY. DEEZE IS WORRIED. HE'S AFRAID HE'LL SCREW UP BEING IN CHARGE WHILE MAMA FIGHTS THE DISEASE.

THIS SATURDAY MORNING WHEN I TURNED ON THE TV TO SEE THE MONKEES, SCOOBY DOO, SPIDER MAN AND AMERICAN BANDSTAND (OUR NORMAL SATURDAY LINE-UP THAT DEEZE LIKES TO LISTEN TO WHILE HE DRAWS AND MAKE SMART ALECK REMARKS ABOUT) DEEZE WENT **NUTS!** HE HOLLERED AT ME, "**THE T.V. HAS TO STAY OFF!**"

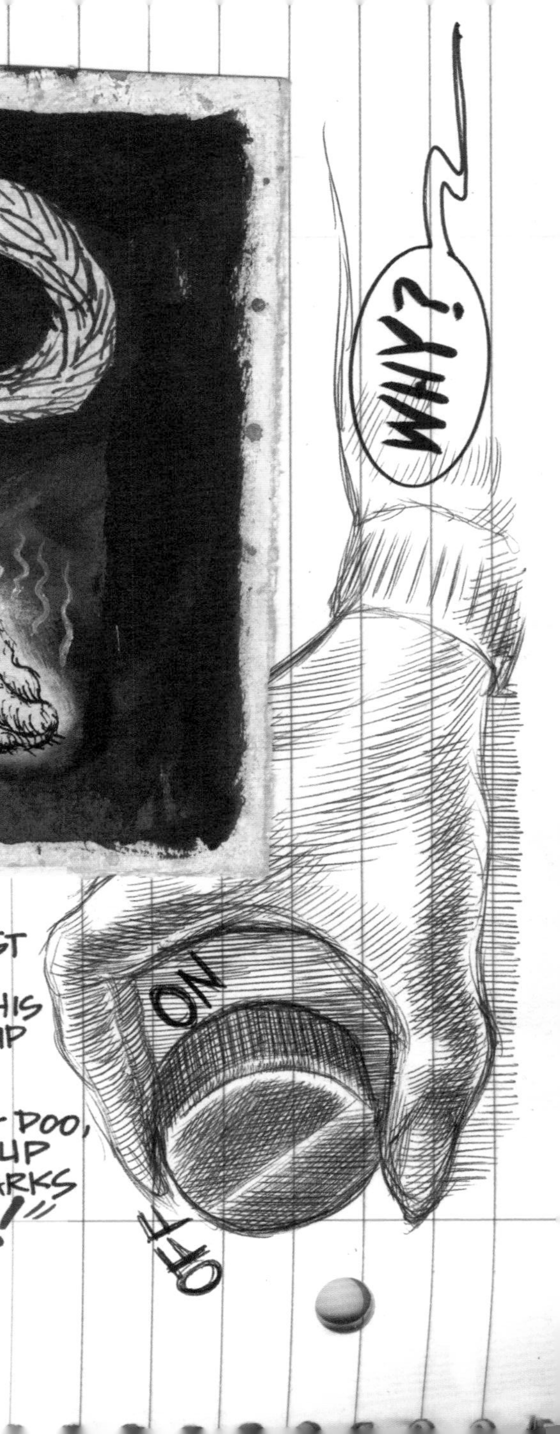
WHY?
ON
OFF

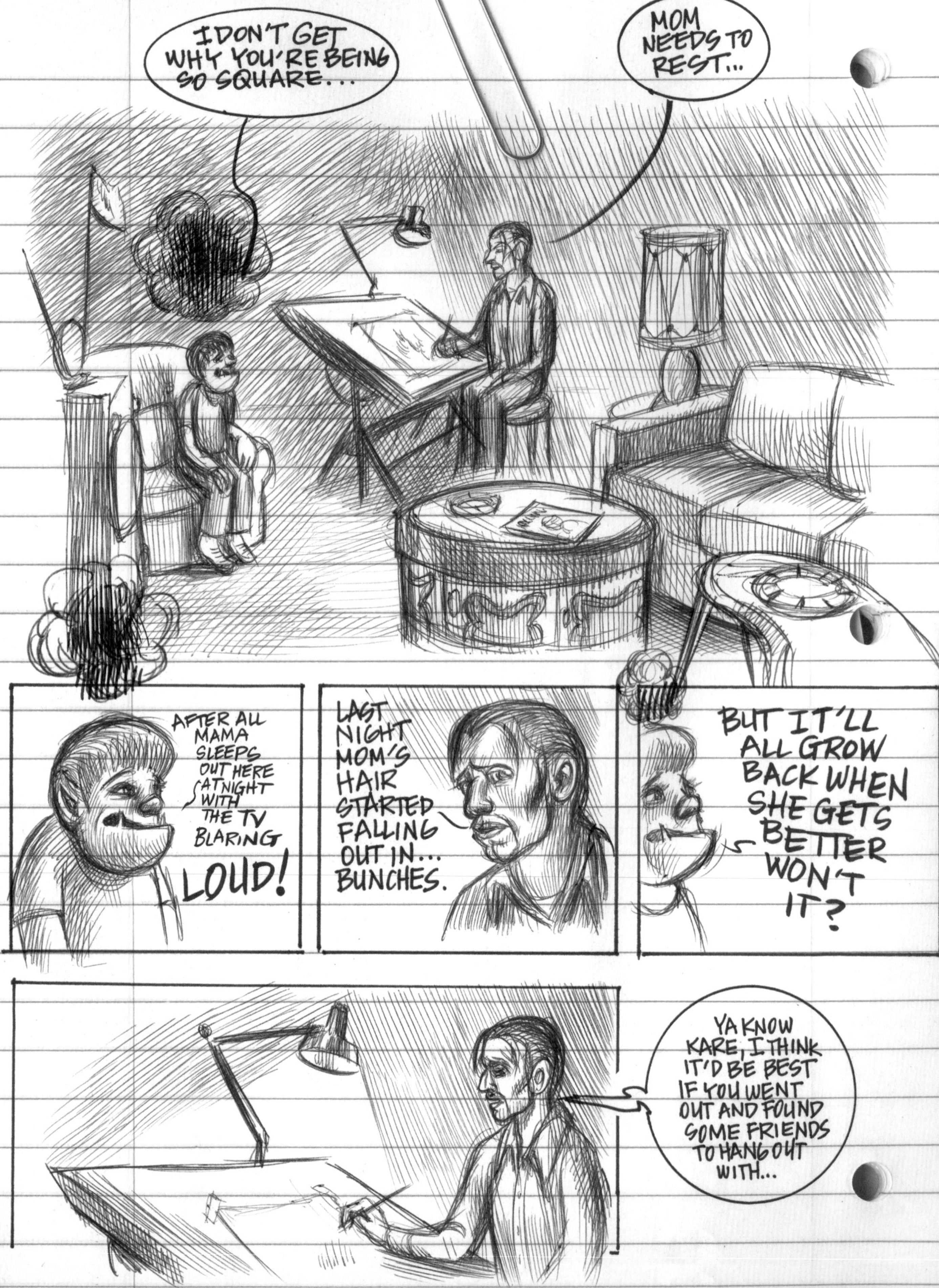

I DON'T GET WHY YOU'RE BEING SO SQUARE...
MOM NEEDS TO REST...
AFTER ALL MAMA SLEEPS OUT HERE AT NIGHT WITH THE TV BLARING LOUD!
LAST NIGHT MOM'S HAIR STARTED FALLING OUT IN... BUNCHES.
BUT IT'LL ALL GROW BACK WHEN SHE GETS BETTER WON'T IT?
YA KNOW KARE, I THINK IT'D BE BEST IF YOU WENT OUT AND FOUND SOME FRIENDS TO HANG OUT WITH...

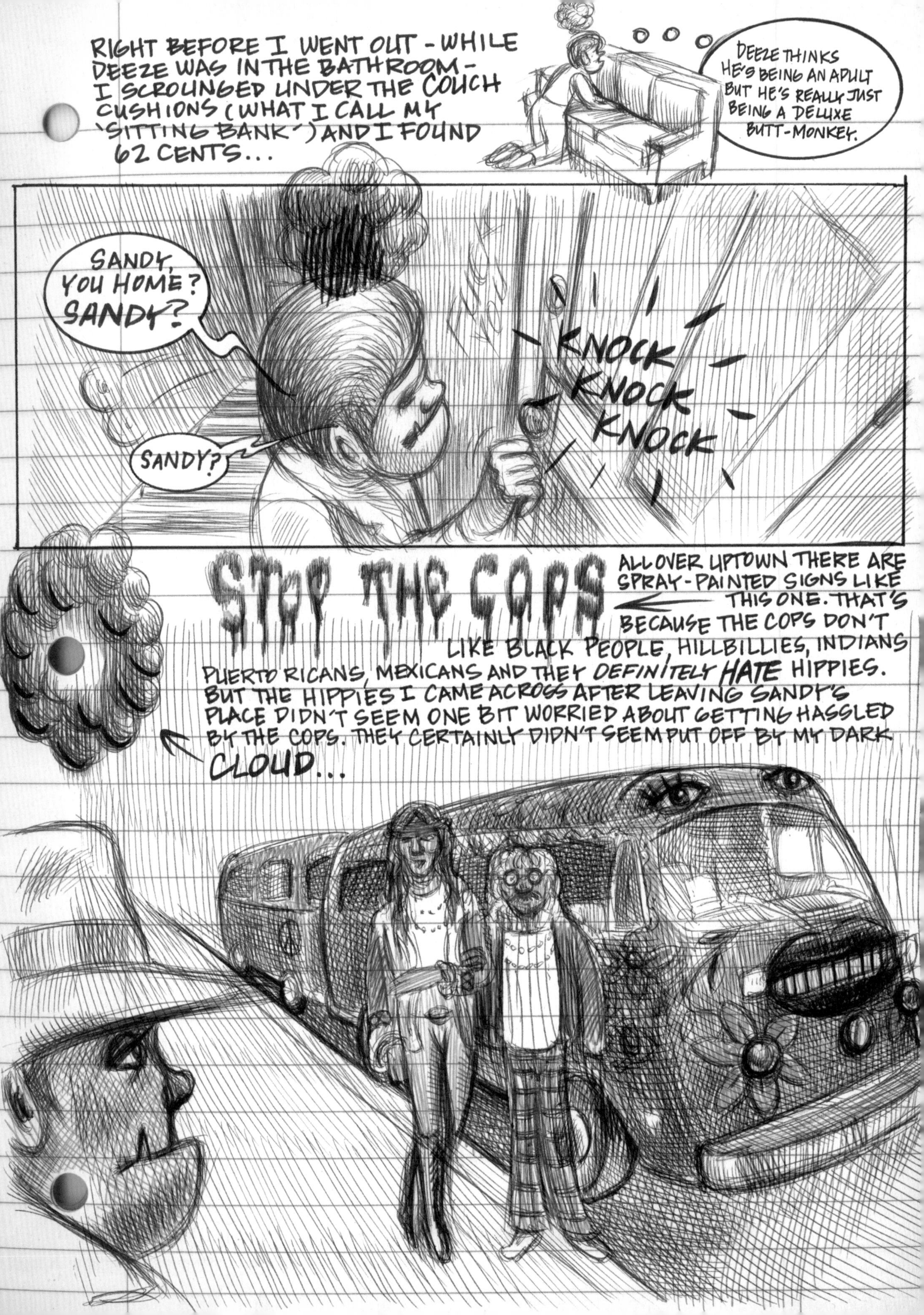
RIGHT BEFORE I WENT OUT - WHILE DEEZE WAS IN THE BATHROOM - I SCROUNGED UNDER THE COUCH CUSHIONS (WHAT I CALL MY 'SITTING BANK') AND I FOUND 62 CENTS...
DEEZE THINKS HE'S BEING AN ADULT BUT HE'S REALLY JUST BEING A DELUXE BUTT-MONKEY.
SANDY, YOU HOME? SANDY?
SANDY?
KNOCK KNOCK KNOCK
STOP THE COPS
ALL OVER UPTOWN THERE ARE SPRAY-PAINTED SIGNS LIKE THIS ONE. THAT'S BECAUSE THE COPS DON'T LIKE BLACK PEOPLE, HILLBILLIES, INDIANS PUERTO RICANS, MEXICANS AND THEY DEFINITELY HATE HIPPIES. BUT THE HIPPIES I CAME ACROSS AFTER LEAVING SANDY'S PLACE DIDN'T SEEM ONE BIT WORRIED ABOUT GETTING HASSLED BY THE COPS. THEY CERTAINLY DIDN'T SEEM PUT OFF BY MY DARK CLOUD...

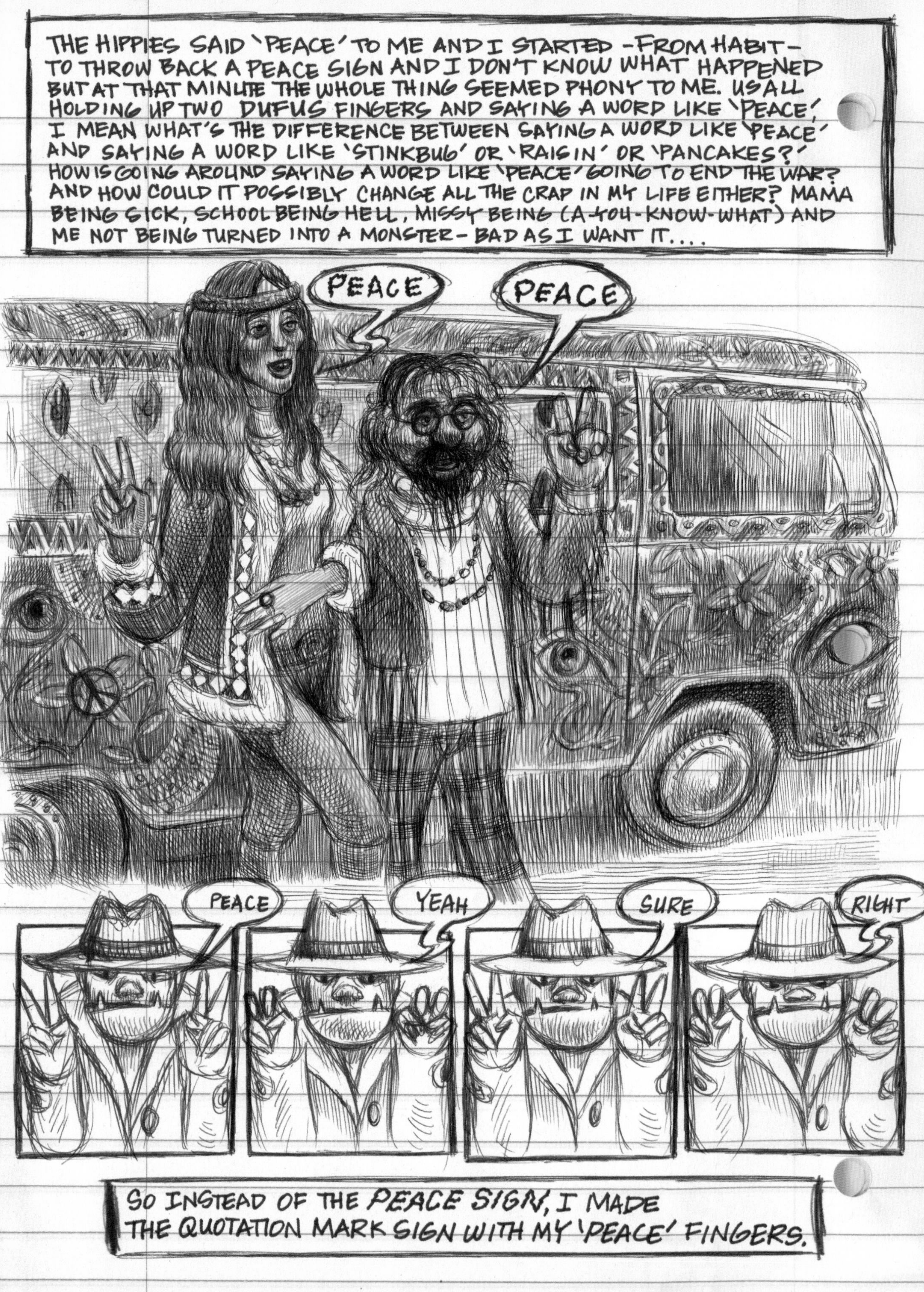
THE HIPPIES SAID 'PEACE' TO ME AND I STARTED -FROM HABIT- TO THROW BACK A PEACE SIGN AND I DON'T KNOW WHAT HAPPENED BUT AT THAT MINUTE THE WHOLE THING SEEMED PHONY TO ME. US ALL HOLDING UP TWO DUFUS FINGERS AND SAYING A WORD LIKE 'PEACE', I MEAN WHAT'S THE DIFFERENCE BETWEEN SAYING A WORD LIKE 'PEACE' AND SAYING A WORD LIKE 'STINKBUG' OR 'RAISIN' OR 'PANCAKES?' HOW IS GOING AROUND SAYING A WORD LIKE 'PEACE' GOING TO END THE WAR? AND HOW COULD IT POSSIBLY CHANGE ALL THE CRAP IN MY LIFE EITHER? MAMA BEING SICK, SCHOOL BEING HELL, MISSY BEING (A-YOU-KNOW-WHAT) AND ME NOT BEING TURNED INTO A MONSTER- BAD AS I WANT IT....
PEACE
PEACE
PEACE
YEAH
SURE
RIGHT
SO INSTEAD OF THE PEACE SIGN, I MADE THE QUOTATION MARK SIGN WITH MY 'PEACE' FINGERS.

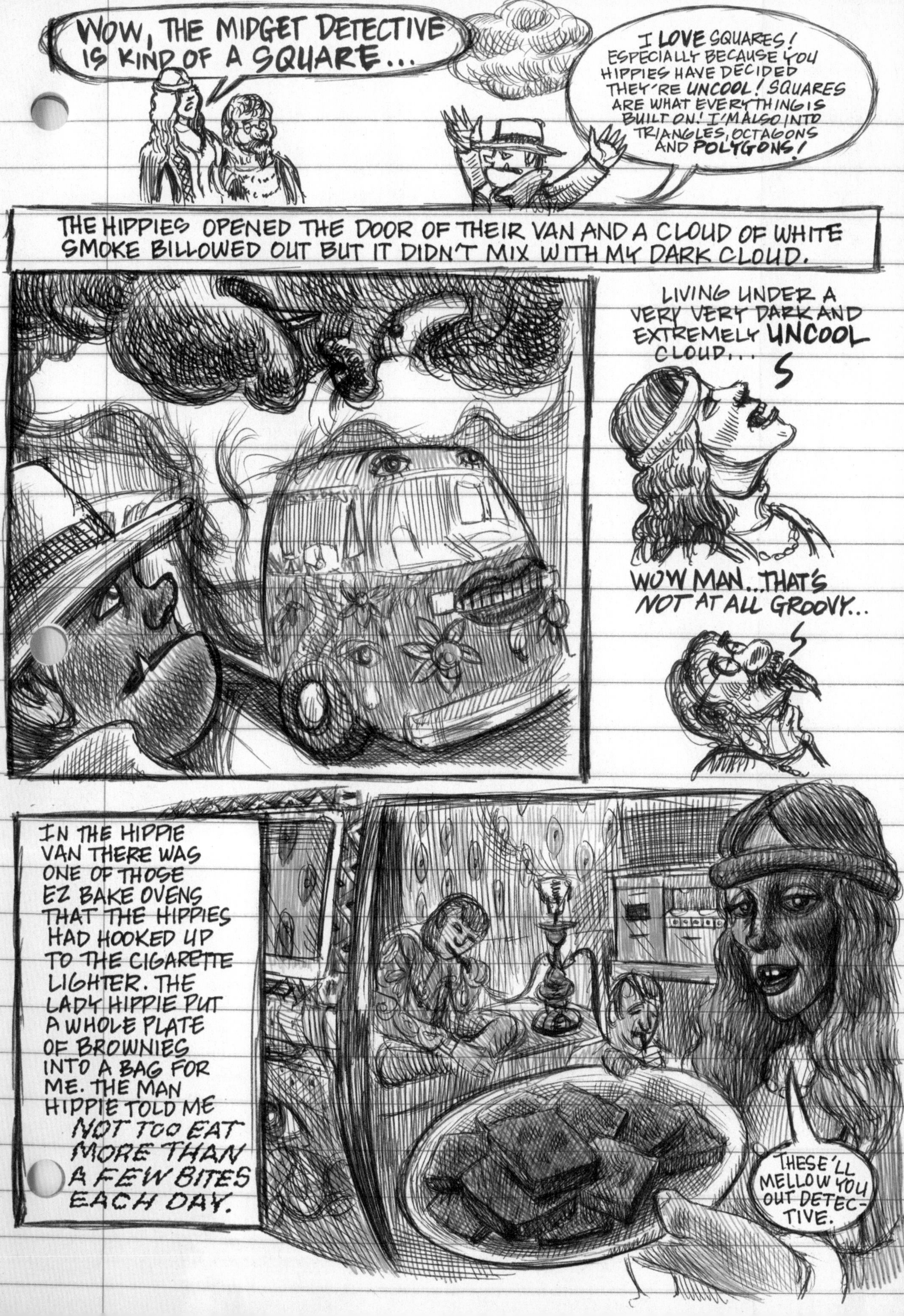

WOW, THE MIDGET DETECTIVE IS KIND OF A SQUARE...
I LOVE SQUARES! ESPECIALLY BECAUSE YOU HIPPIES HAVE DECIDED THEY'RE UNCOOL! SQUARES ARE WHAT EVERYTHING IS BUILT ON! I'M ALSO INTO TRIANGLES, OCTAGONS AND POLYGONS!
THE HIPPIES OPENED THE DOOR OF THEIR VAN AND A CLOUD OF WHITE SMOKE BILLOWED OUT BUT IT DIDN'T MIX WITH MY DARK CLOUD.
LIVING UNDER A VERY VERY DARK AND EXTREMELY UNCOOL CLOUD...
WOW MAN...THAT'S NOT AT ALL GROOVY...
IN THE HIPPIE VAN THERE WAS ONE OF THOSE EZ BAKE OVENS THAT THE HIPPIES HAD HOOKED UP TO THE CIGARETTE LIGHTER. THE LADY HIPPIE PUT A WHOLE PLATE OF BROWNIES INTO A BAG FOR ME. THE MAN HIPPIE TOLD ME NOT TOO EAT MORE THAN A FEW BITES EACH DAY.
THESE'LL MELLOW YOU OUT DETECTIVE.

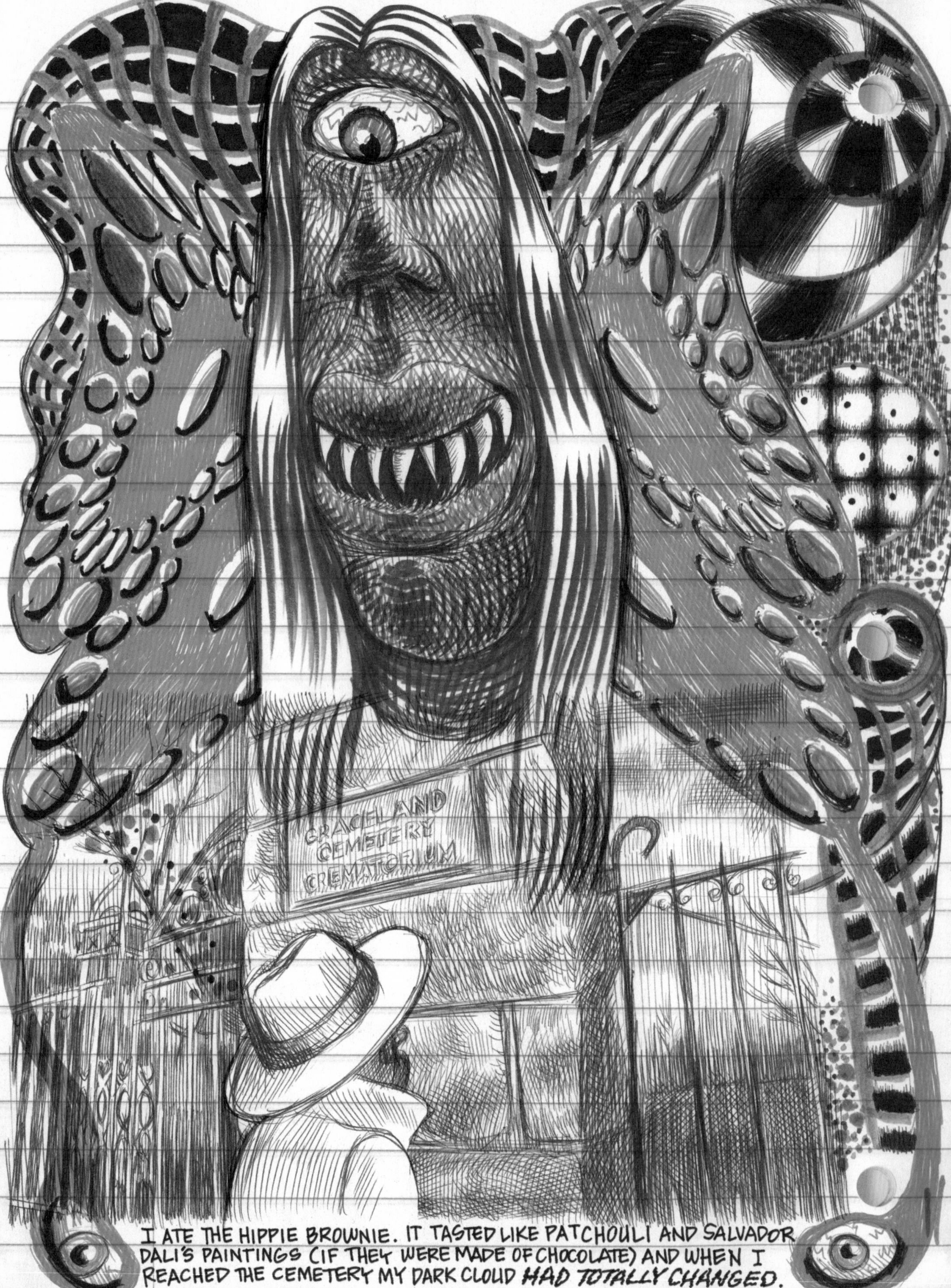
GRACELAND CEMETERY CREMATORIUM
I ATE THE HIPPIE BROWNIE. IT TASTED LIKE PATCHOULI AND SALVADOR DALI'S PAINTINGS (IF THEY WERE MADE OF CHOCOLATE) AND WHEN I REACHED THE CEMETERY MY DARK CLOUD *HAD TOTALLY CHANGED.*

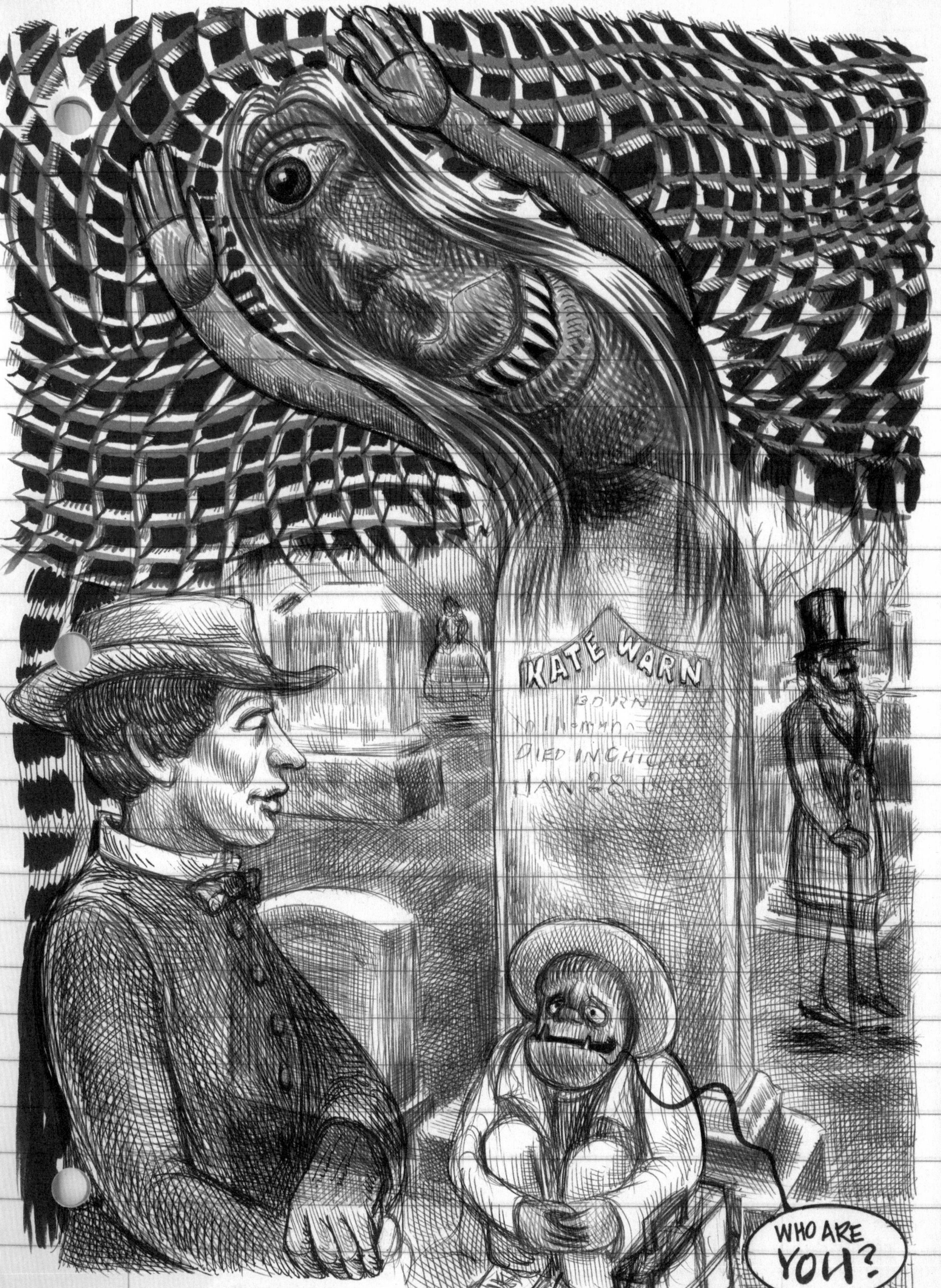
KATE WARN
BORN
WHO ARE YOU?

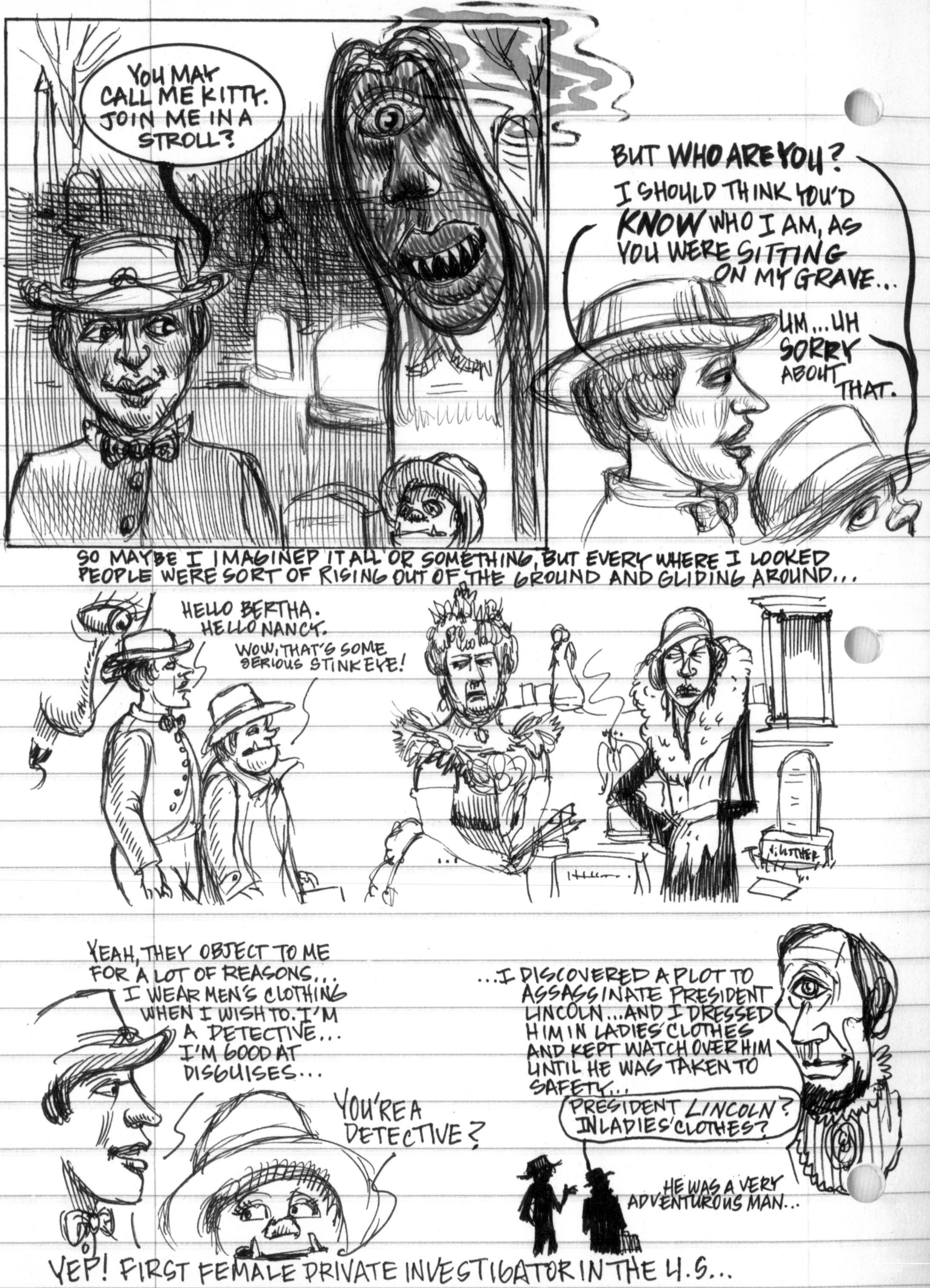
YOU MAY CALL ME KITTY. JOIN ME IN A STROLL?
BUT WHO ARE YOU?
I SHOULD THINK YOU'D KNOW WHO I AM, AS YOU WERE SITTING ON MY GRAVE...
UM...UH SORRY ABOUT THAT.
SO MAYBE I IMAGINED IT ALL OR SOMETHING, BUT EVERY WHERE I LOOKED PEOPLE WERE SORT OF RISING OUT OF THE GROUND AND GLIDING AROUND...
HELLO BERTHA. HELLO NANCY.
WOW, THAT'S SOME SERIOUS STINKEYE!
YEAH, THEY OBJECT TO ME FOR A LOT OF REASONS... I WEAR MEN'S CLOTHING WHEN I WISH TO. I'M A DETECTIVE... I'M GOOD AT DISGUISES...
YOU'RE A DETECTIVE?
...I DISCOVERED A PLOT TO ASSASSINATE PRESIDENT LINCOLN...AND I DRESSED HIM IN LADIES' CLOTHES AND KEPT WATCH OVER HIM UNTIL HE WAS TAKEN TO SAFETY...
PRESIDENT LINCOLN? IN LADIES' CLOTHES?
HE WAS A VERY ADVENTUROUS MAN...
YEP! FIRST FEMALE PRIVATE INVESTIGATOR IN THE U.S...

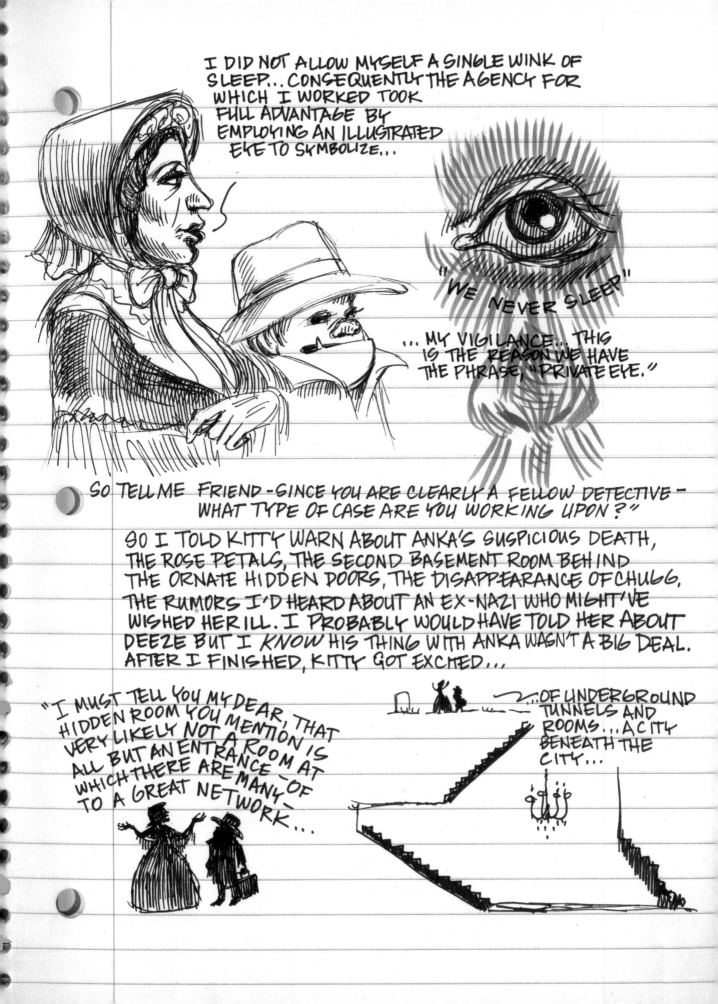

I DID NOT ALLOW MYSELF A SINGLE WINK OF SLEEP... CONSEQUENTLY THE AGENCY FOR WHICH I WORKED TOOK FULL ADVANTAGE BY EMPLOYING AN ILLUSTRATED EYE TO SYMBOLIZE...

"WE NEVER SLEEP"

... MY VIGILANCE... THIS IS THE REASON WE HAVE THE PHRASE, "PRIVATE EYE."

SO TELL ME FRIEND -SINCE YOU ARE CLEARLY A FELLOW DETECTIVE - WHAT TYPE OF CASE ARE YOU WORKING UPON ?"

SO I TOLD KITTY WARN ABOUT ANKA'S SUSPICIOUS DEATH, THE ROSE PETALS, THE SECOND BASEMENT ROOM BEHIND THE ORNATE HIDDEN DOORS, THE DISAPPEARANCE OF CHUGG, THE RUMORS I'D HEARD ABOUT AN EX-NAZI WHO MIGHT'VE WISHED HER ILL. I PROBABLY WOULD HAVE TOLD HER ABOUT DEEZE BUT I KNOW HIS THING WITH ANKA WASN'T A BIG DEAL. AFTER I FINISHED, KITTY GOT EXCITED...

"I MUST TELL YOU MY DEAR, THAT HIDDEN ROOM YOU MENTION IS VERY LIKELY NOT A ROOM AT ALL BUT AN ENTRANCE -OF WHICH THERE ARE MANY- TO A GREAT NETWORK...

...OF UNDERGROUND TUNNELS AND ROOMS... A CITY BENEATH THE CITY...

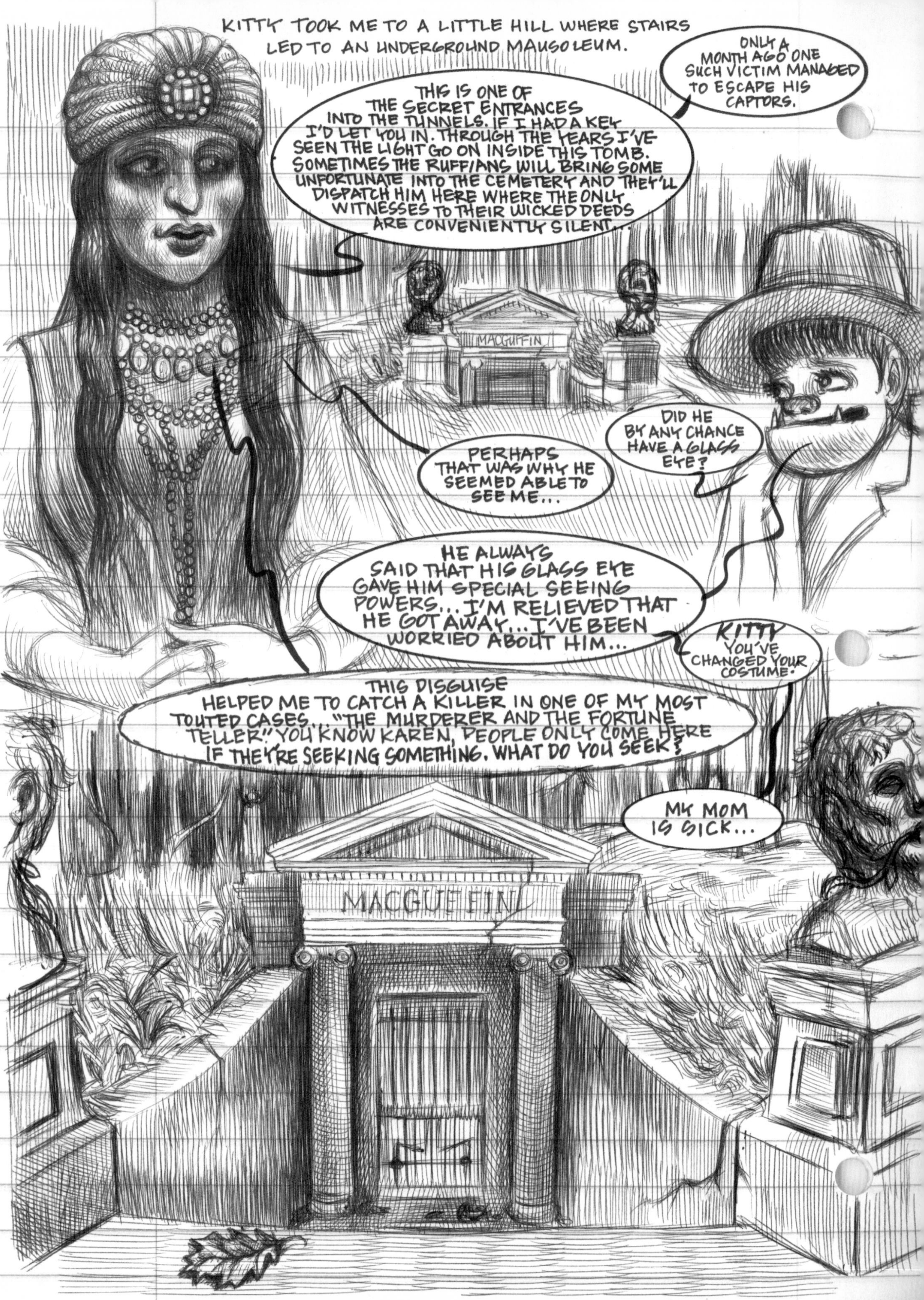
KITTY TOOK ME TO A LITTLE HILL WHERE STAIRS LED TO AN UNDERGROUND MAUSOLEUM.
THIS IS ONE OF THE SECRET ENTRANCES INTO THE TUNNELS. IF I HAD A KEY I'D LET YOU IN. THROUGH THE YEARS I'VE SEEN THE LIGHT GO ON INSIDE THIS TOMB. SOMETIMES THE RUFFIANS WILL BRING SOME UNFORTUNATE INTO THE CEMETERY AND THEY'LL DISPATCH HIM HERE WHERE THE ONLY WITNESSES TO THEIR WICKED DEEDS ARE CONVENIENTLY SILENT...
ONLY A MONTH AGO ONE SUCH VICTIM MANAGED TO ESCAPE HIS CAPTORS.
MACGUFFIN
DID HE BY ANY CHANCE HAVE A GLASS EYE?
PERHAPS THAT WAS WHY HE SEEMED ABLE TO SEE ME...
HE ALWAYS SAID THAT HIS GLASS EYE GAVE HIM SPECIAL SEEING POWERS... I'M RELIEVED THAT HE GOT AWAY... I'VE BEEN WORRIED ABOUT HIM...
KITTY YOU'VE CHANGED YOUR COSTUME.
THIS DISGUISE HELPED ME TO CATCH A KILLER IN ONE OF MY MOST TOUTED CASES... "THE MURDERER AND THE FORTUNE TELLER." YOU KNOW KAREN, PEOPLE ONLY COME HERE IF THEY'RE SEEKING SOMETHING. WHAT DO YOU SEEK?
MY MOM IS SICK...
MACGUFFIN

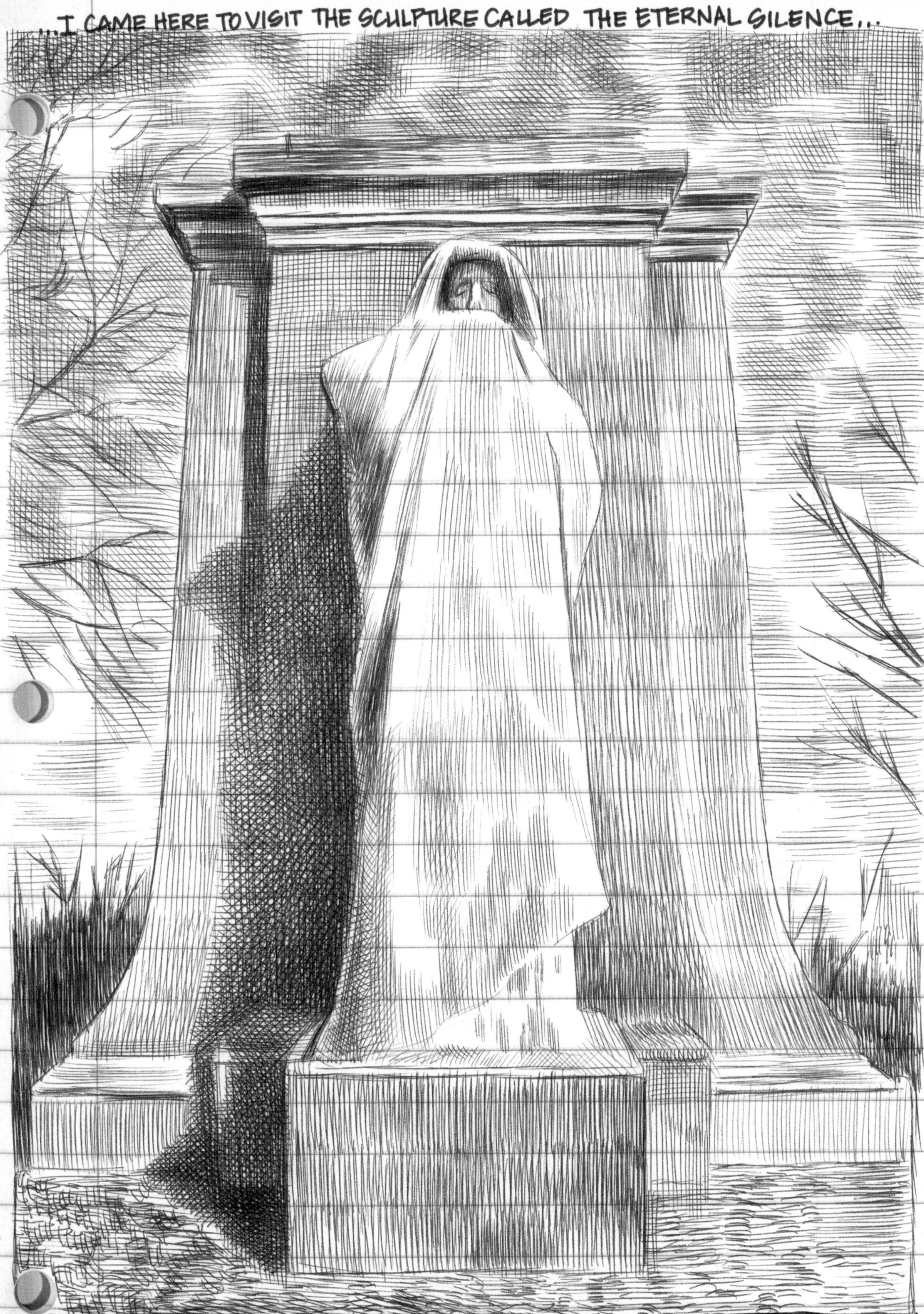
...I CAME HERE TO VISIT THE SCULPTURE CALLED THE ETERNAL SILENCE...
...BECAUSE EVERY KID IN UPTOWN KNOWS THAT IF YOU'RE BRAVE ENOUGH TO STARE STRAIGHT INTO THE FACE OF THE CLOAKED GUY, FOR A LONG TIME WITHOUT BLINKING, YOU'LL SEE A VISION OF YOUR DEATH...

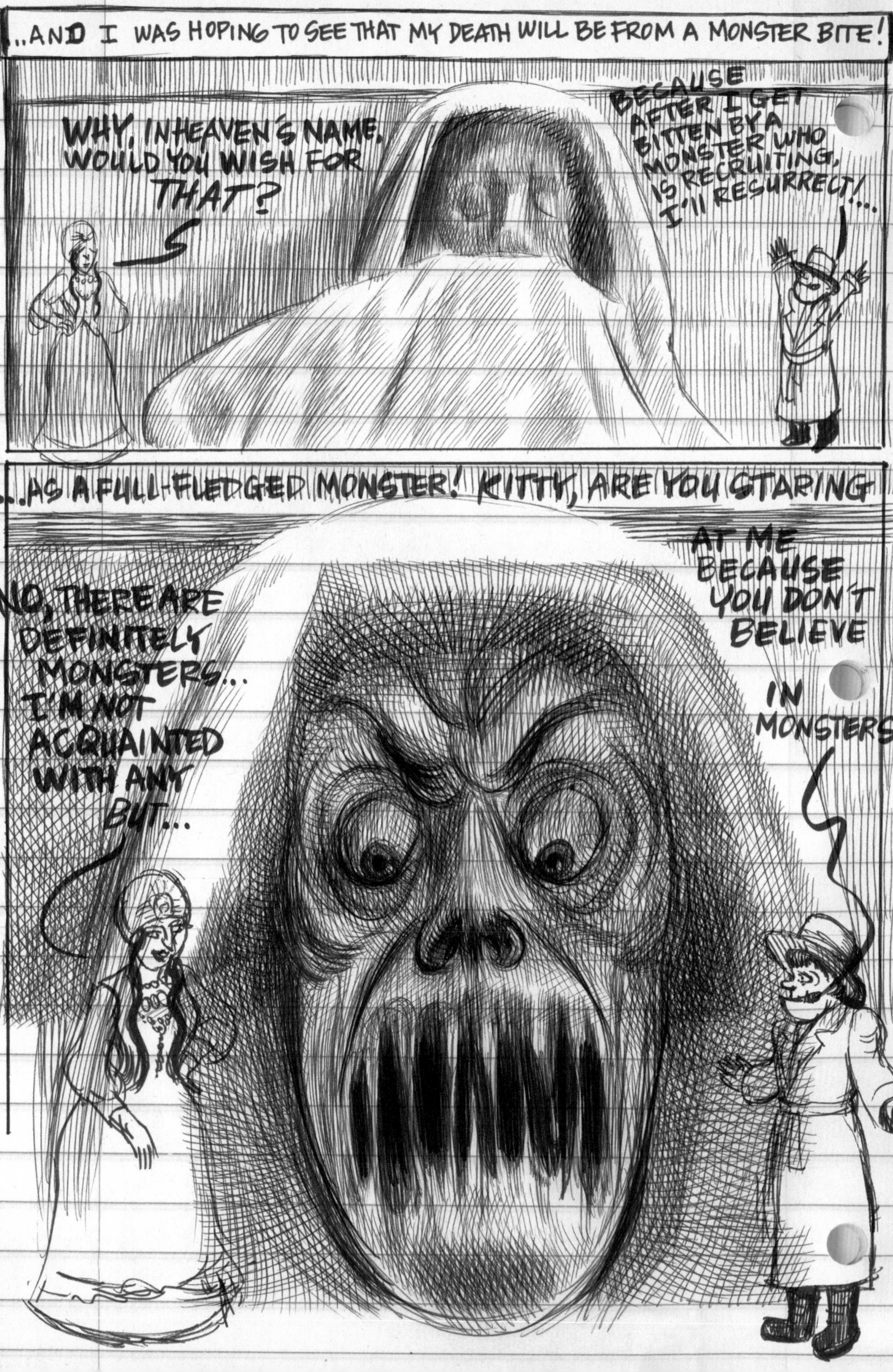
...AND I WAS HOPING TO SEE THAT MY DEATH WILL BE FROM A MONSTER BITE!
WHY, IN HEAVEN'S NAME, WOULD YOU WISH FOR THAT?
BECAUSE AFTER I GET BITTEN BY A MONSTER WHO IS RECRUITING, I'LL RESURRECT!...
...AS A FULL-FLEDGED MONSTER! KITTY, ARE YOU STARING
AT ME BECAUSE YOU DON'T BELIEVE IN MONSTERS?
NO, THERE ARE DEFINITELY MONSTERS... I'M NOT ACQUAINTED WITH ANY BUT...

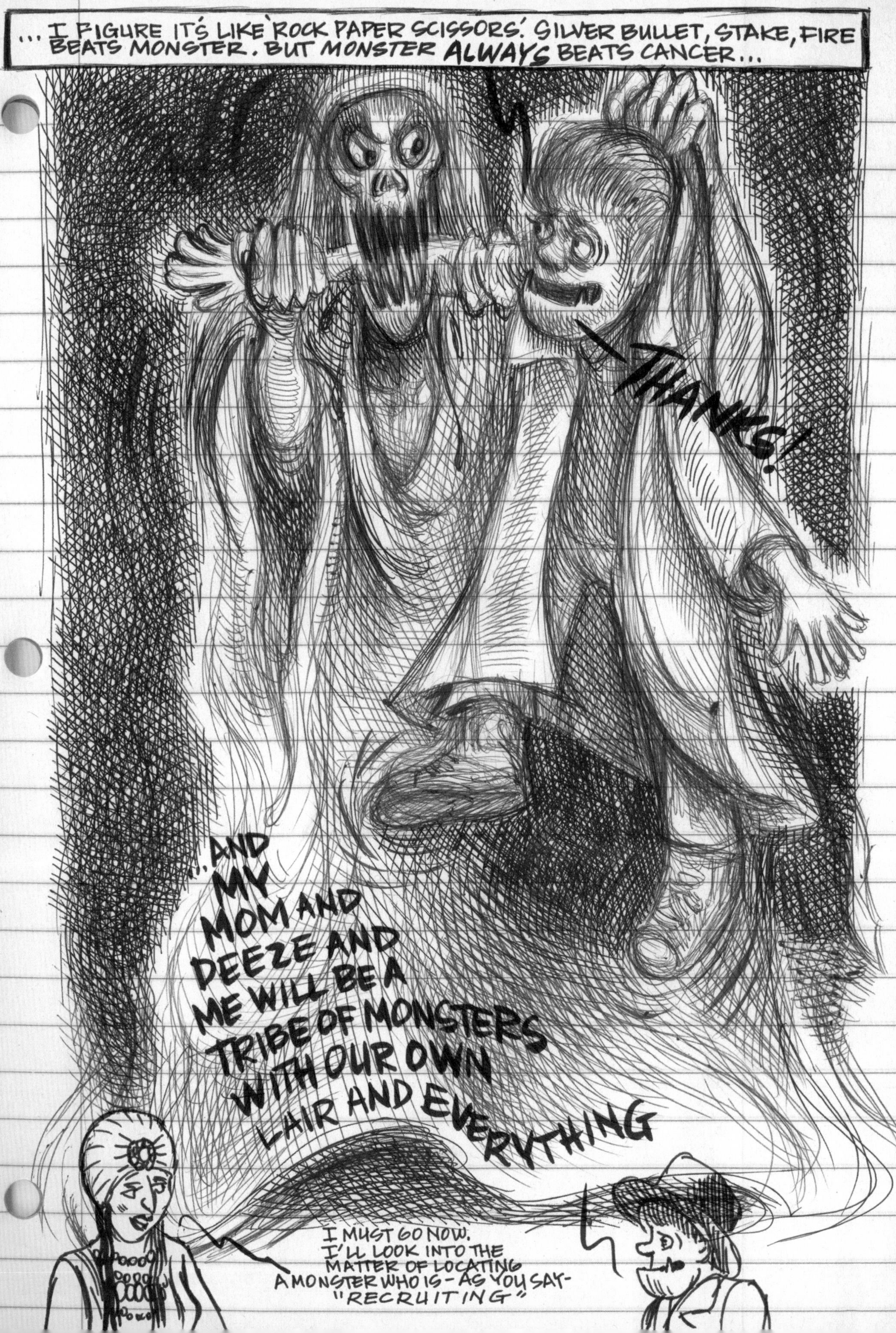
... I FIGURE IT'S LIKE 'ROCK PAPER SCISSORS.' SILVER BULLET, STAKE, FIRE BEATS MONSTER. BUT MONSTER ALWAYS BEATS CANCER...
THANKS!
...AND MY MOM AND DEEZE AND ME WILL BE A TRIBE OF MONSTERS WITH OUR OWN LAIR AND EVERYTHING
I MUST GO NOW. I'LL LOOK INTO THE MATTER OF LOCATING A MONSTER WHO IS - AS YOU SAY - "RECRUITING"

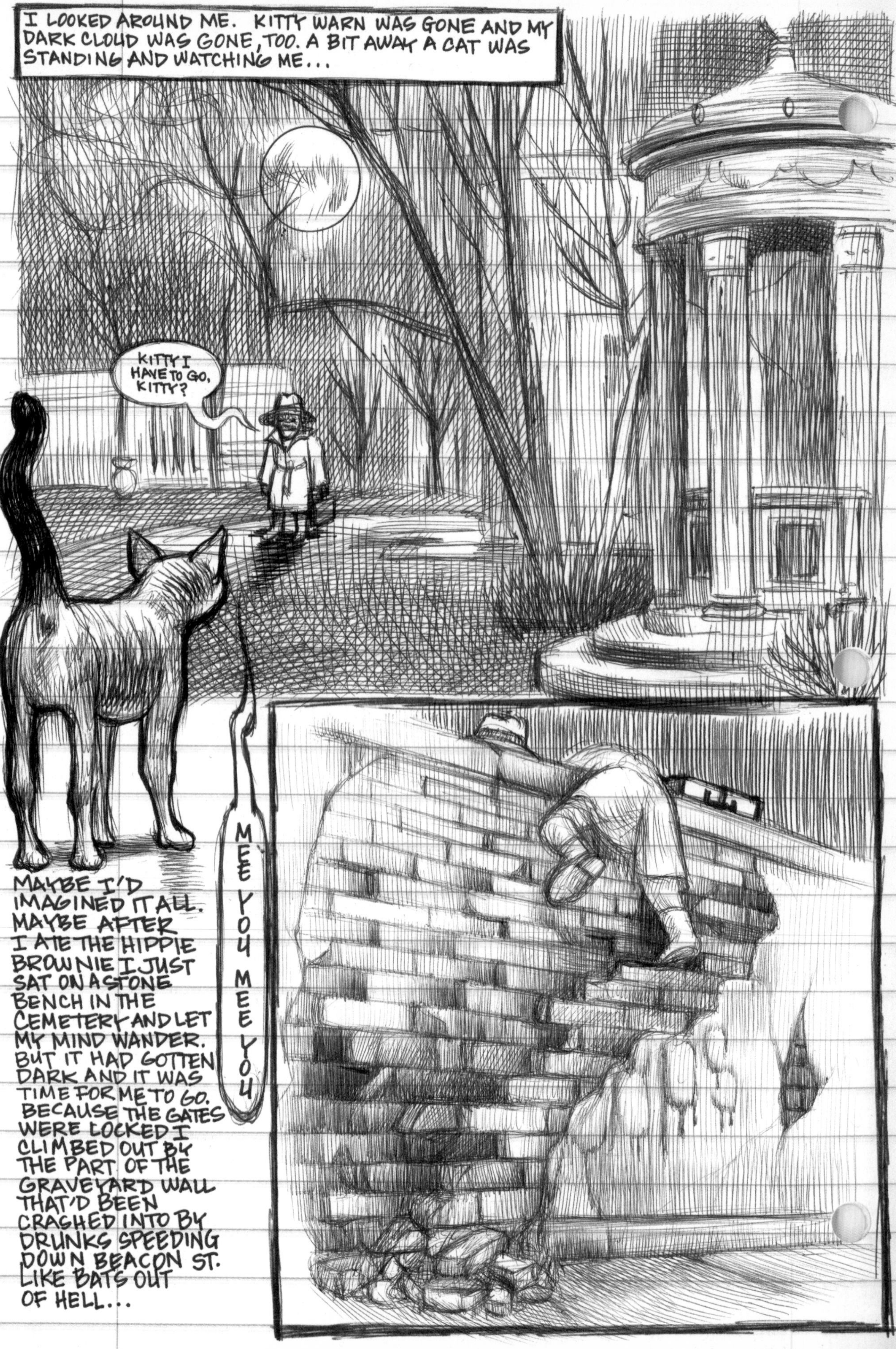
I LOOKED AROUND ME. KITTY WARN WAS GONE AND MY DARK CLOUD WAS GONE, TOO. A BIT AWAY A CAT WAS STANDING AND WATCHING ME...
KITTY I HAVE TO GO, KITTY?
MEE YOU MEE YOU
MAYBE I'D IMAGINED IT ALL. MAYBE AFTER I ATE THE HIPPIE BROWNIE I JUST SAT ON A STONE BENCH IN THE CEMETERY AND LET MY MIND WANDER. BUT IT HAD GOTTEN DARK AND IT WAS TIME FOR ME TO GO. BECAUSE THE GATES WERE LOCKED I CLIMBED OUT BY THE PART OF THE GRAVEYARD WALL THAT'D BEEN CRASHED INTO BY DRUNKS SPEEDING DOWN BEACON ST. LIKE BATS OUT OF HELL...

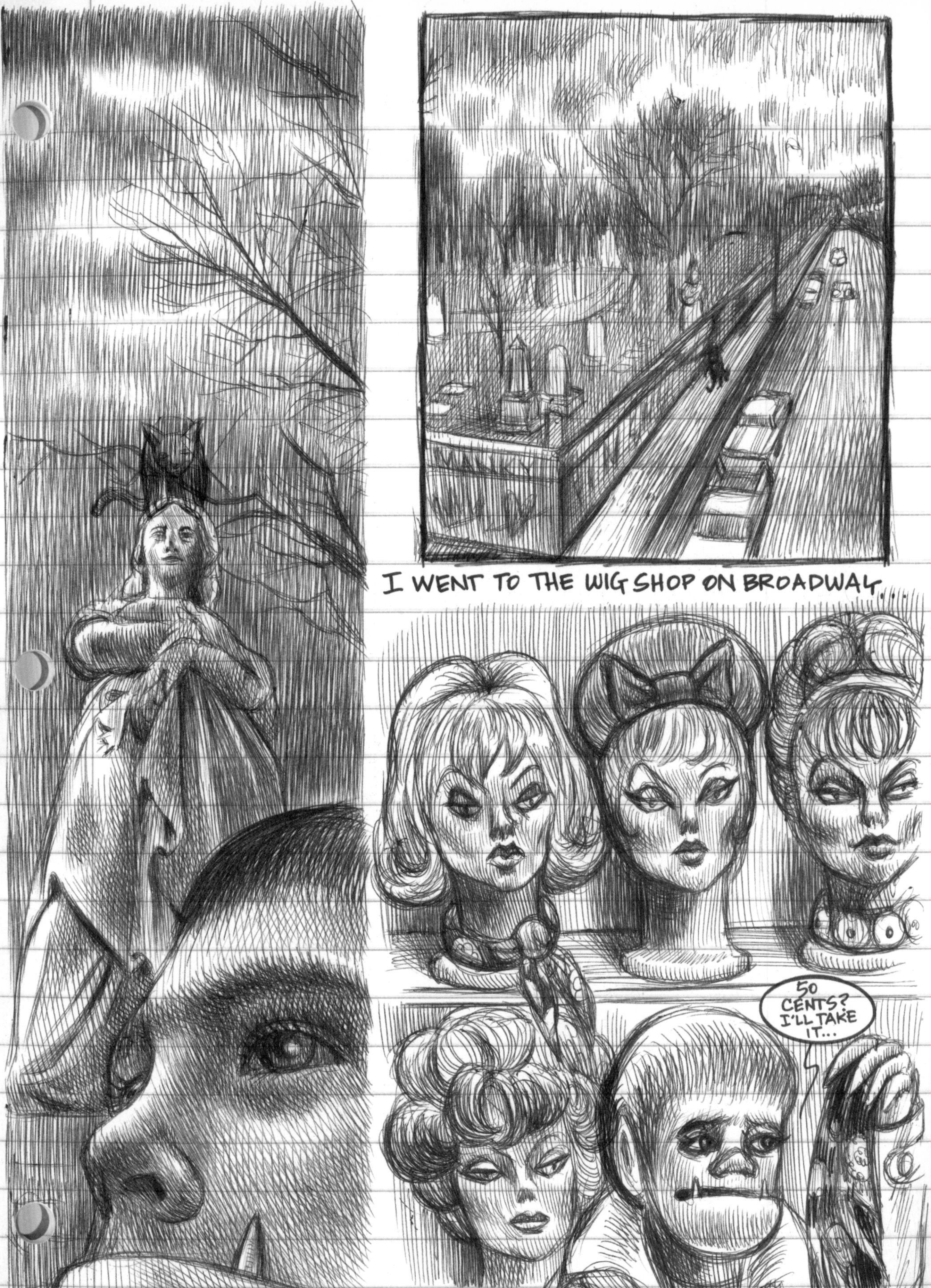
I WENT TO THE WIG SHOP ON BROADWAY...
50 CENTS? I'LL TAKE IT...

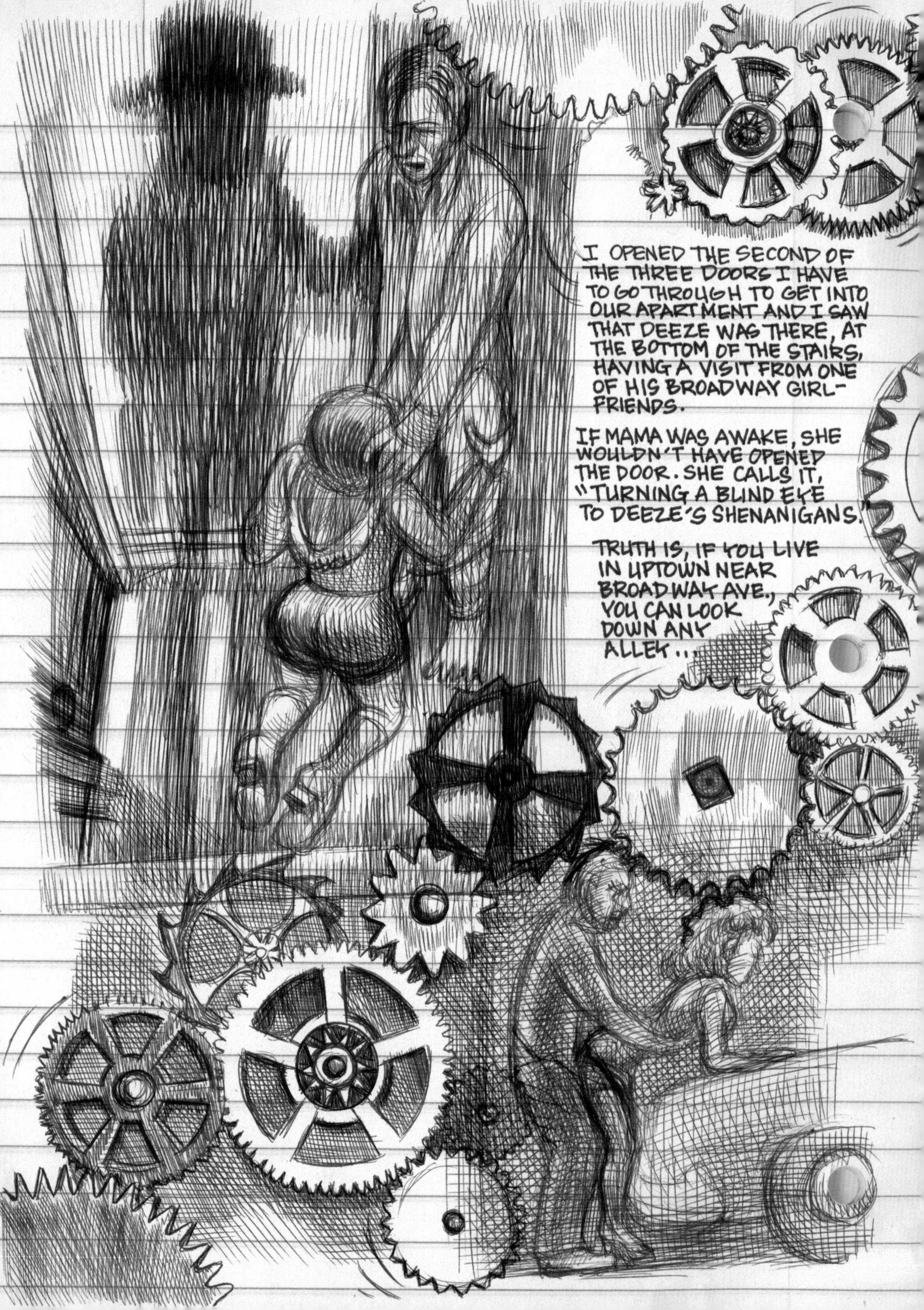
I OPENED THE SECOND OF THE THREE DOORS I HAVE TO GO THROUGH TO GET INTO OUR APARTMENT AND I SAW THAT DEEZE WAS THERE, AT THE BOTTOM OF THE STAIRS, HAVING A VISIT FROM ONE OF HIS BROADWAY GIRL-FRIENDS.
IF MAMA WAS AWAKE, SHE WOULDN'T HAVE OPENED THE DOOR. SHE CALLS IT, "TURNING A BLIND EYE TO DEEZE'S SHENANIGANS."
TRUTH IS, IF YOU LIVE IN UPTOWN NEAR BROADWAY AVE., YOU CAN LOOK DOWN ANY ALLEY...

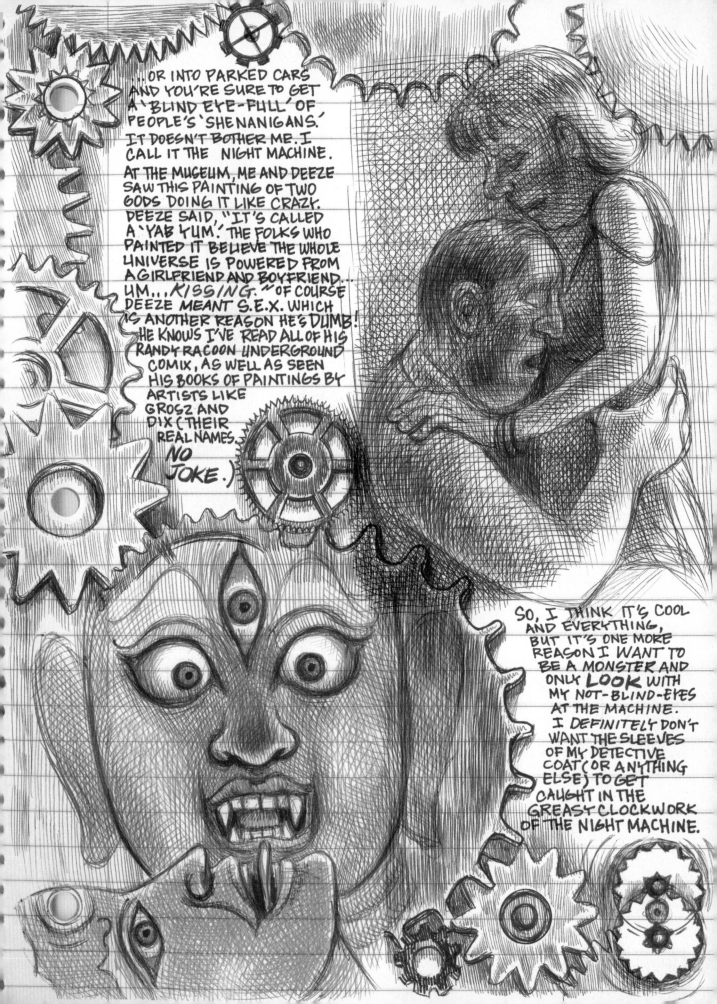

...OR INTO PARKED CARS AND YOU'RE SURE TO GET A 'BLIND EYE-FULL' OF PEOPLE'S 'SHENANIGANS.' IT DOESN'T BOTHER ME. I CALL IT THE NIGHT MACHINE.

AT THE MUSEUM, ME AND DEEZE SAW THIS PAINTING OF TWO GODS DOING IT LIKE CRAZY. DEEZE SAID, "IT'S CALLED A 'YAB YUM.' THE FOLKS WHO PAINTED IT BELIEVE THE WHOLE UNIVERSE IS POWERED FROM A GIRLFRIEND AND BOYFRIEND... UM....*KISSING*." OF COURSE DEEZE MEANT S.E.X. WHICH IS ANOTHER REASON HE'S DUMB! HE KNOWS I'VE READ ALL OF HIS RANDY RACOON UNDERGROUND COMIX, AS WELL AS SEEN HIS BOOKS OF PAINTINGS BY ARTISTS LIKE GROSZ AND DIX (THEIR REAL NAMES. *NO JOKE*.)

SO, I THINK IT'S COOL AND EVERYTHING, BUT IT'S ONE MORE REASON I WANT TO BE A MONSTER AND ONLY *LOOK* WITH MY NOT-BLIND-EYES AT THE MACHINE. I DEFINITELY DON'T WANT THE SLEEVES OF MY DETECTIVE COAT (OR ANYTHING ELSE) TO GET CAUGHT IN THE GREASY CLOCKWORK OF THE NIGHT MACHINE.

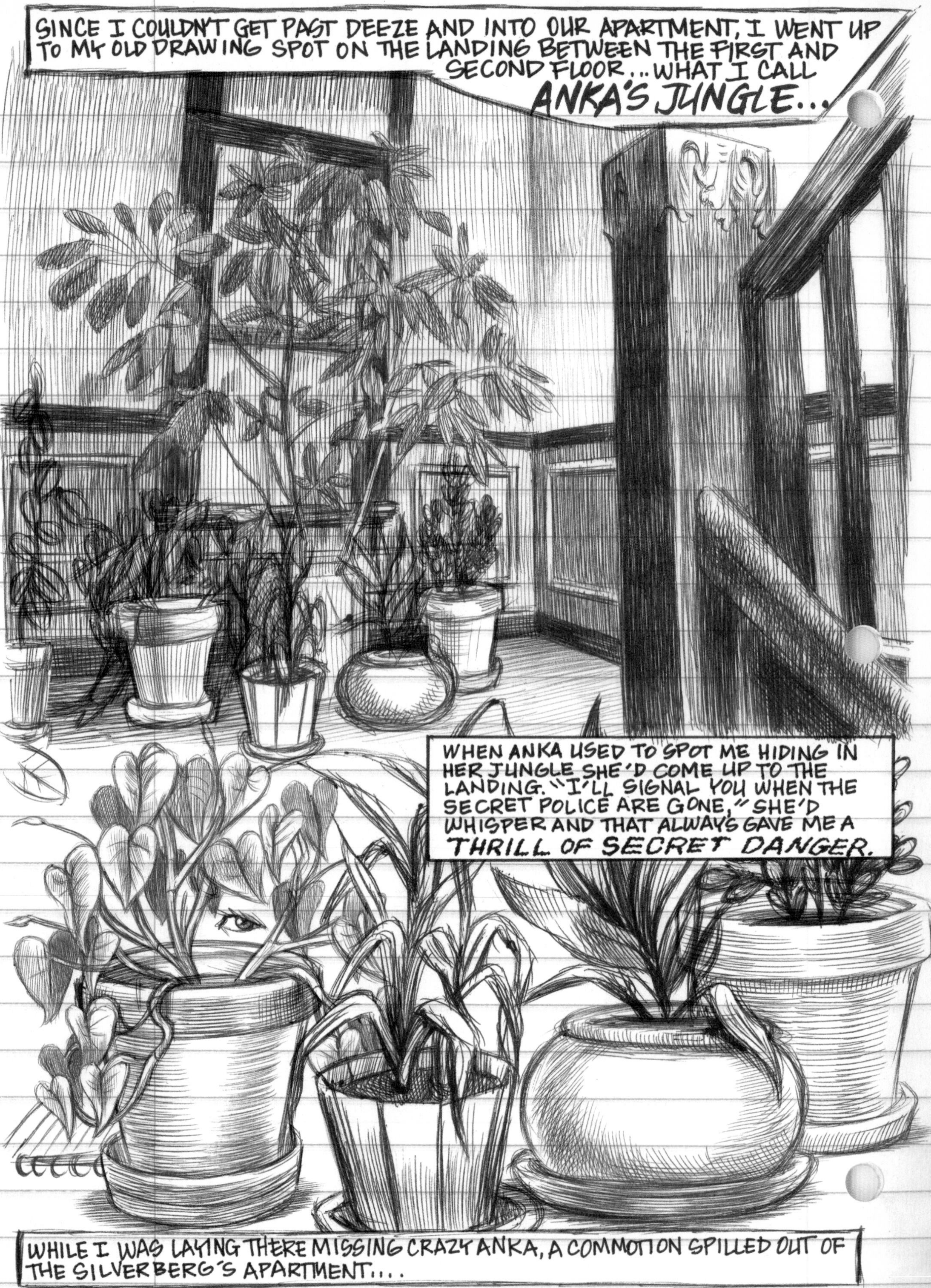
SINCE I COULDN'T GET PAST DEEZE AND INTO OUR APARTMENT, I WENT UP TO MY OLD DRAWING SPOT ON THE LANDING BETWEEN THE FIRST AND SECOND FLOOR... WHAT I CALL ANKA'S JUNGLE...
WHEN ANKA USED TO SPOT ME HIDING IN HER JUNGLE SHE'D COME UP TO THE LANDING. "I'LL SIGNAL YOU WHEN THE SECRET POLICE ARE GONE," SHE'D WHISPER AND THAT ALWAYS GAVE ME A THRILL OF SECRET DANGER.
WHILE I WAS LAYING THERE MISSING CRAZY ANKA, A COMMOTION SPILLED OUT OF THE SILVERBERG'S APARTMENT...

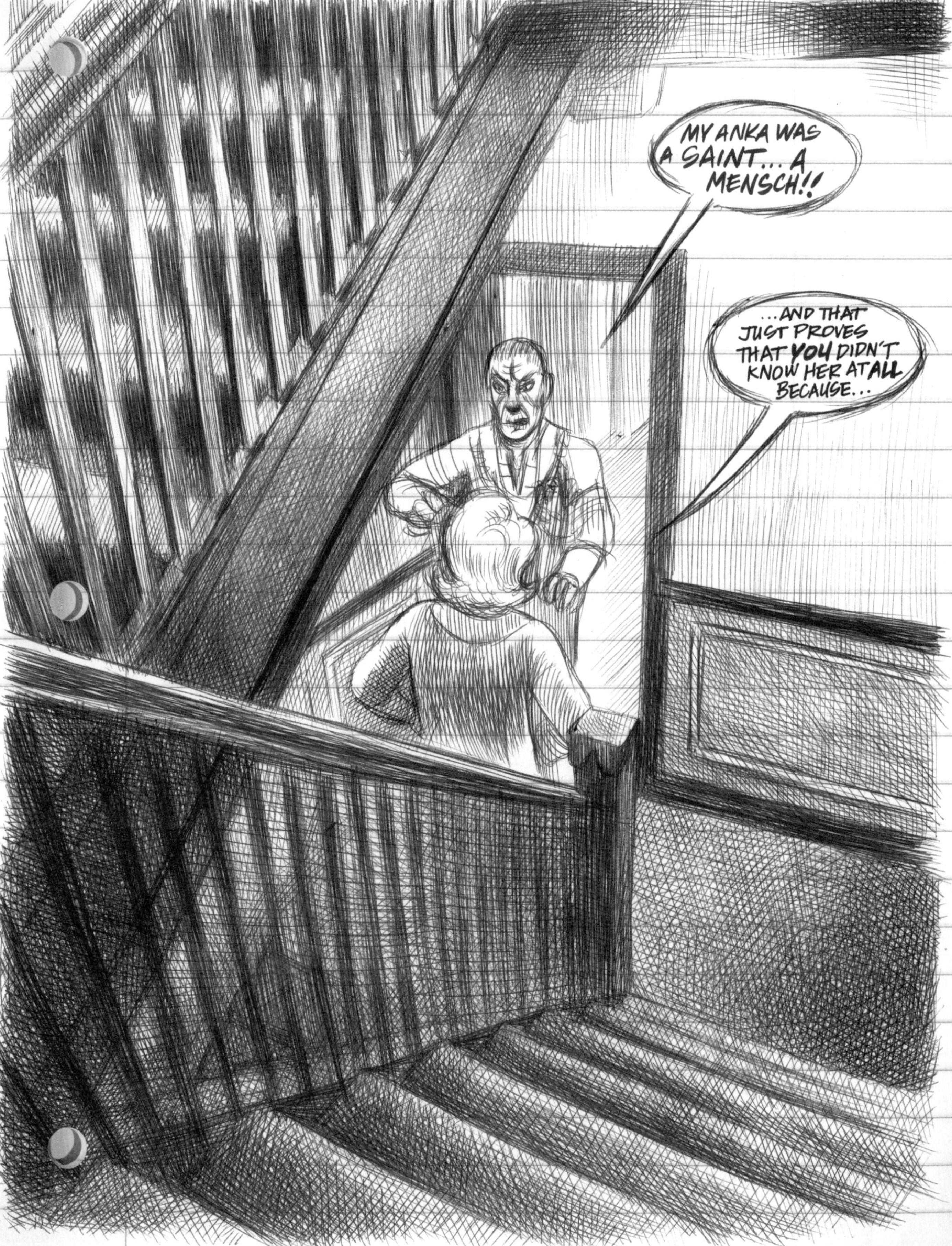
MY ANKA WAS A SAINT... A MENSCH!!
...AND THAT JUST PROVES THAT YOU DIDN'T KNOW HER AT ALL BECAUSE...

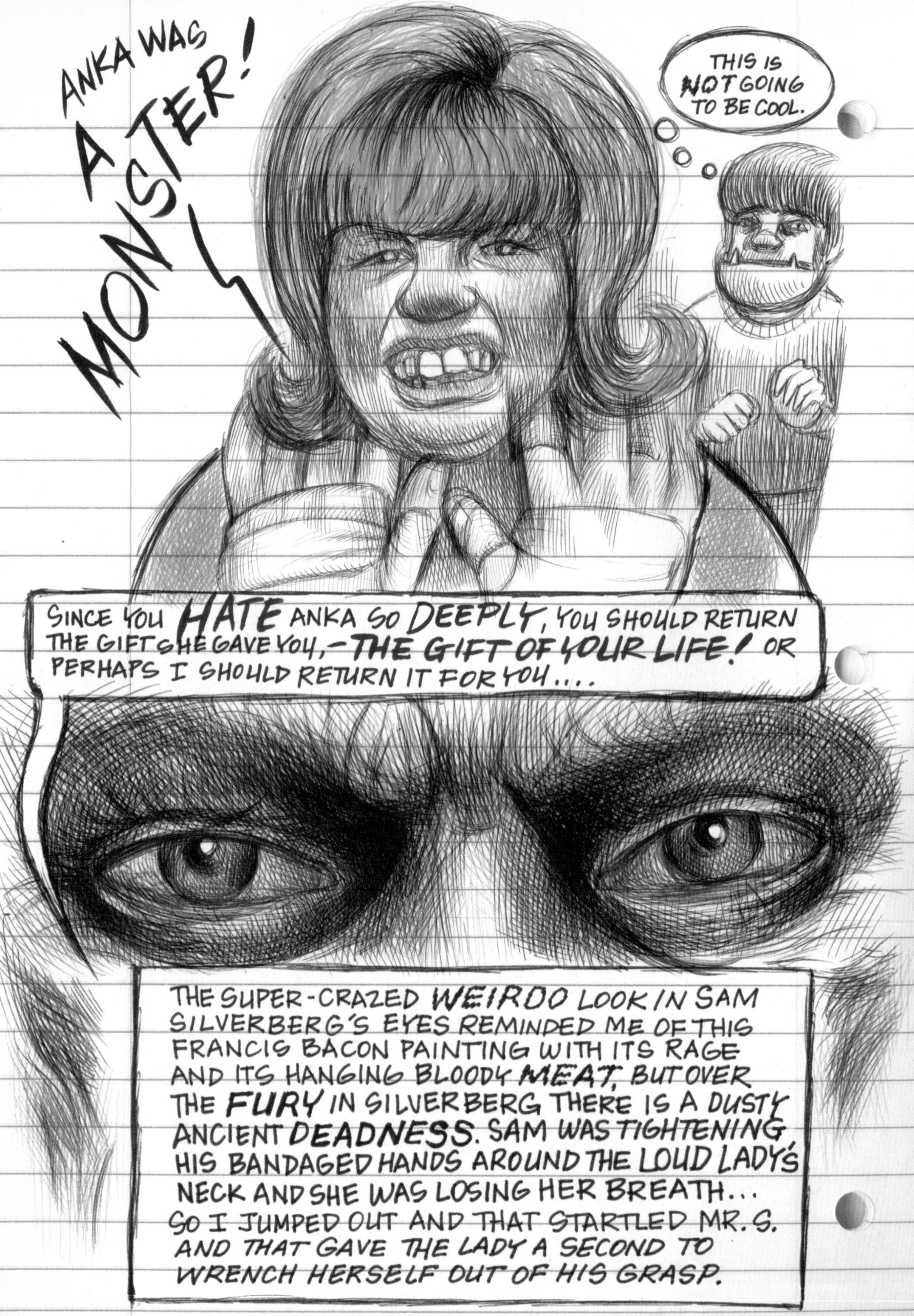
ANKA WAS A MONSTER!
THIS IS NOT GOING TO BE COOL.
SINCE YOU HATE ANKA SO DEEPLY, YOU SHOULD RETURN THE GIFT SHE GAVE YOU, - THE GIFT OF YOUR LIFE! OR PERHAPS I SHOULD RETURN IT FOR YOU....
THE SUPER-CRAZED WEIRDO LOOK IN SAM SILVERBERG'S EYES REMINDED ME OF THIS FRANCIS BACON PAINTING WITH ITS RAGE AND ITS HANGING BLOODY MEAT, BUT OVER THE FURY IN SILVERBERG THERE IS A DUSTY ANCIENT DEADNESS. SAM WAS TIGHTENING HIS BANDAGED HANDS AROUND THE LOUD LADY'S NECK AND SHE WAS LOSING HER BREATH... SO I JUMPED OUT AND THAT STARTLED MR. S. AND THAT GAVE THE LADY A SECOND TO WRENCH HERSELF OUT OF HIS GRASP.

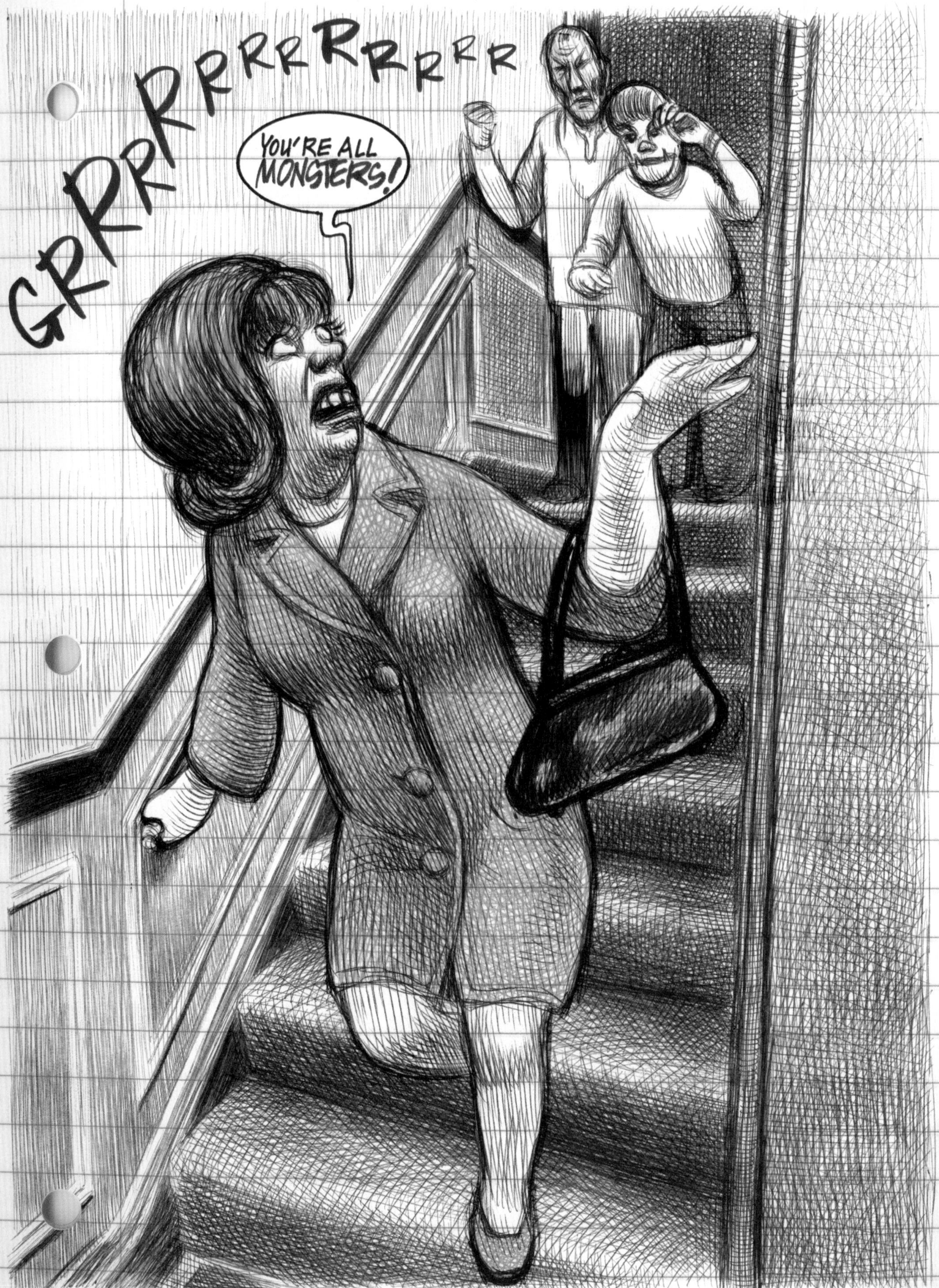
GRRRRRRRRRRRRRR
YOU'RE ALL MONSTERS!

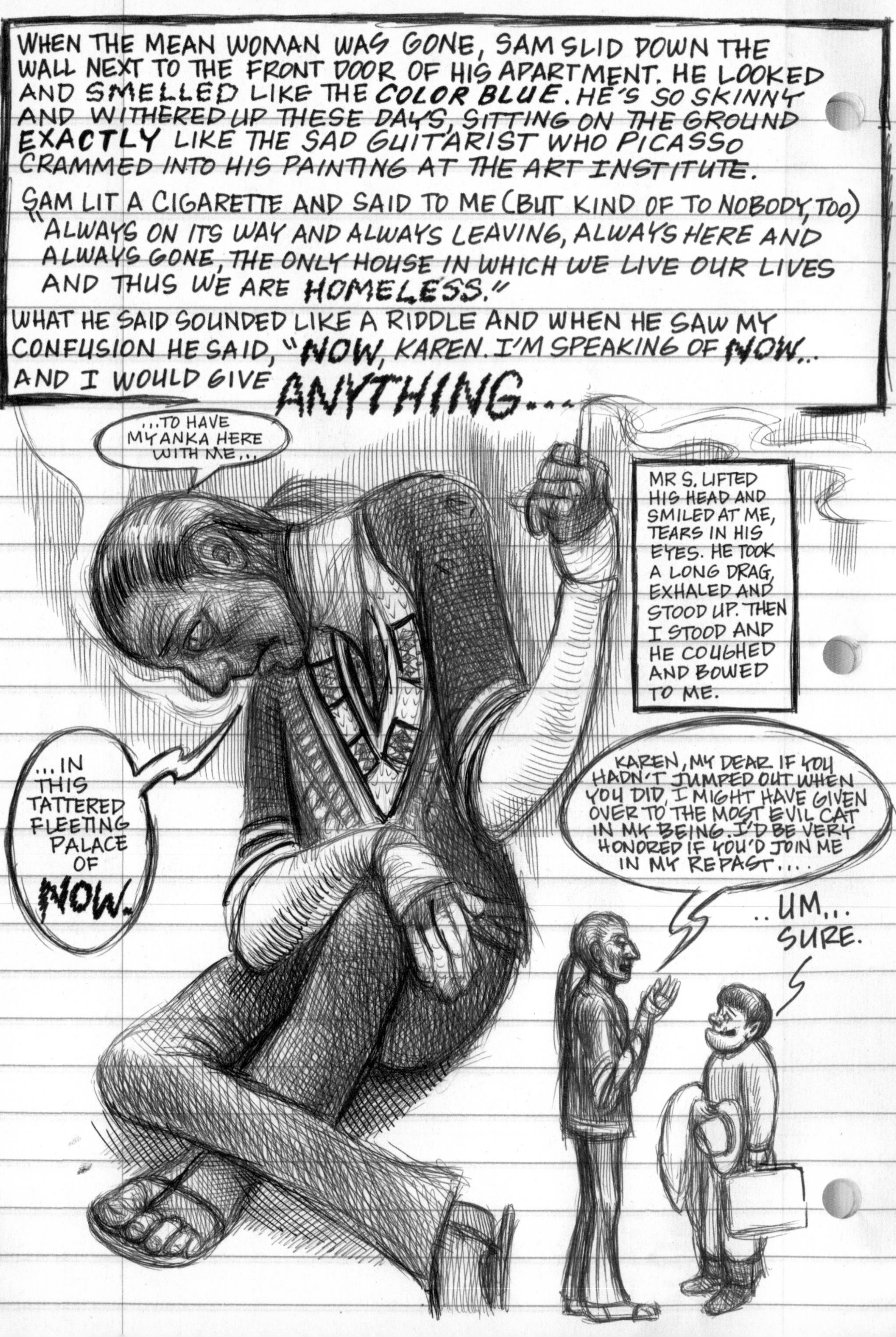
WHEN THE MEAN WOMAN WAS GONE, SAM SLID DOWN THE WALL NEXT TO THE FRONT DOOR OF HIS APARTMENT. HE LOOKED AND SMELLED LIKE THE COLOR BLUE. HE'S SO SKINNY AND WITHERED UP THESE DAYS, SITTING ON THE GROUND EXACTLY LIKE THE SAD GUITARIST WHO PICASSO CRAMMED INTO HIS PAINTING AT THE ART INSTITUTE.
SAM LIT A CIGARETTE AND SAID TO ME (BUT KIND OF TO NOBODY, TOO) "ALWAYS ON ITS WAY AND ALWAYS LEAVING, ALWAYS HERE AND ALWAYS GONE, THE ONLY HOUSE IN WHICH WE LIVE OUR LIVES AND THUS WE ARE HOMELESS."
WHAT HE SAID SOUNDED LIKE A RIDDLE AND WHEN HE SAW MY CONFUSION HE SAID, "NOW, KAREN. I'M SPEAKING OF NOW... AND I WOULD GIVE ANYTHING...
...TO HAVE MY ANKA HERE WITH ME...
MR S. LIFTED HIS HEAD AND SMILED AT ME, TEARS IN HIS EYES. HE TOOK A LONG DRAG, EXHALED AND STOOD UP. THEN I STOOD AND HE COUGHED AND BOWED TO ME.
...IN THIS TATTERED FLEETING PALACE OF NOW.
KAREN, MY DEAR IF YOU HADN'T JUMPED OUT WHEN YOU DID, I MIGHT HAVE GIVEN OVER TO THE MOST EVIL CAT IN MY BEING. I'D BE VERY HONORED IF YOU'D JOIN ME IN MY REPAST...
..UM... SURE.

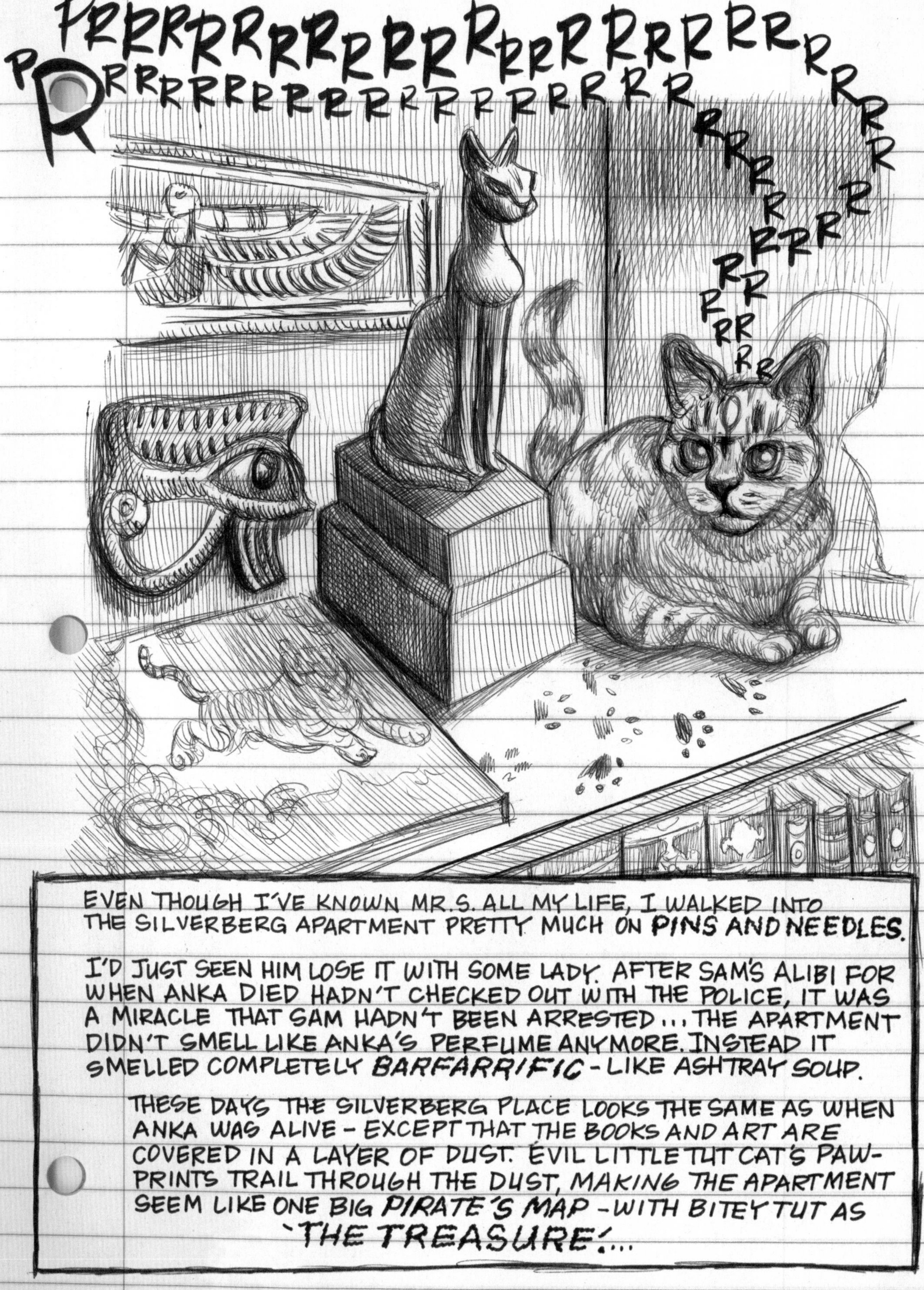
PRRRRRRRRRRRRRRRRRRRRRRRRRRRRRRR
PRRRRRRRRRRRRRRRRRRRRRRRRRRRRRR
EVEN THOUGH I'VE KNOWN MR. S. ALL MY LIFE, I WALKED INTO THE SILVERBERG APARTMENT PRETTY MUCH ON PINS AND NEEDLES.
I'D JUST SEEN HIM LOSE IT WITH SOME LADY. AFTER SAM'S ALIBI FOR WHEN ANKA DIED HADN'T CHECKED OUT WITH THE POLICE, IT WAS A MIRACLE THAT SAM HADN'T BEEN ARRESTED... THE APARTMENT DIDN'T SMELL LIKE ANKA'S PERFUME ANYMORE. INSTEAD IT SMELLED COMPLETELY BARFARRIFIC - LIKE ASHTRAY SOUP.
THESE DAYS THE SILVERBERG PLACE LOOKS THE SAME AS WHEN ANKA WAS ALIVE - EXCEPT THAT THE BOOKS AND ART ARE COVERED IN A LAYER OF DUST. EVIL LITTLE TUT CAT'S PAW-PRINTS TRAIL THROUGH THE DUST, MAKING THE APARTMENT SEEM LIKE ONE BIG PIRATE'S MAP - WITH BITEY TUT AS "THE TREASURE!"...

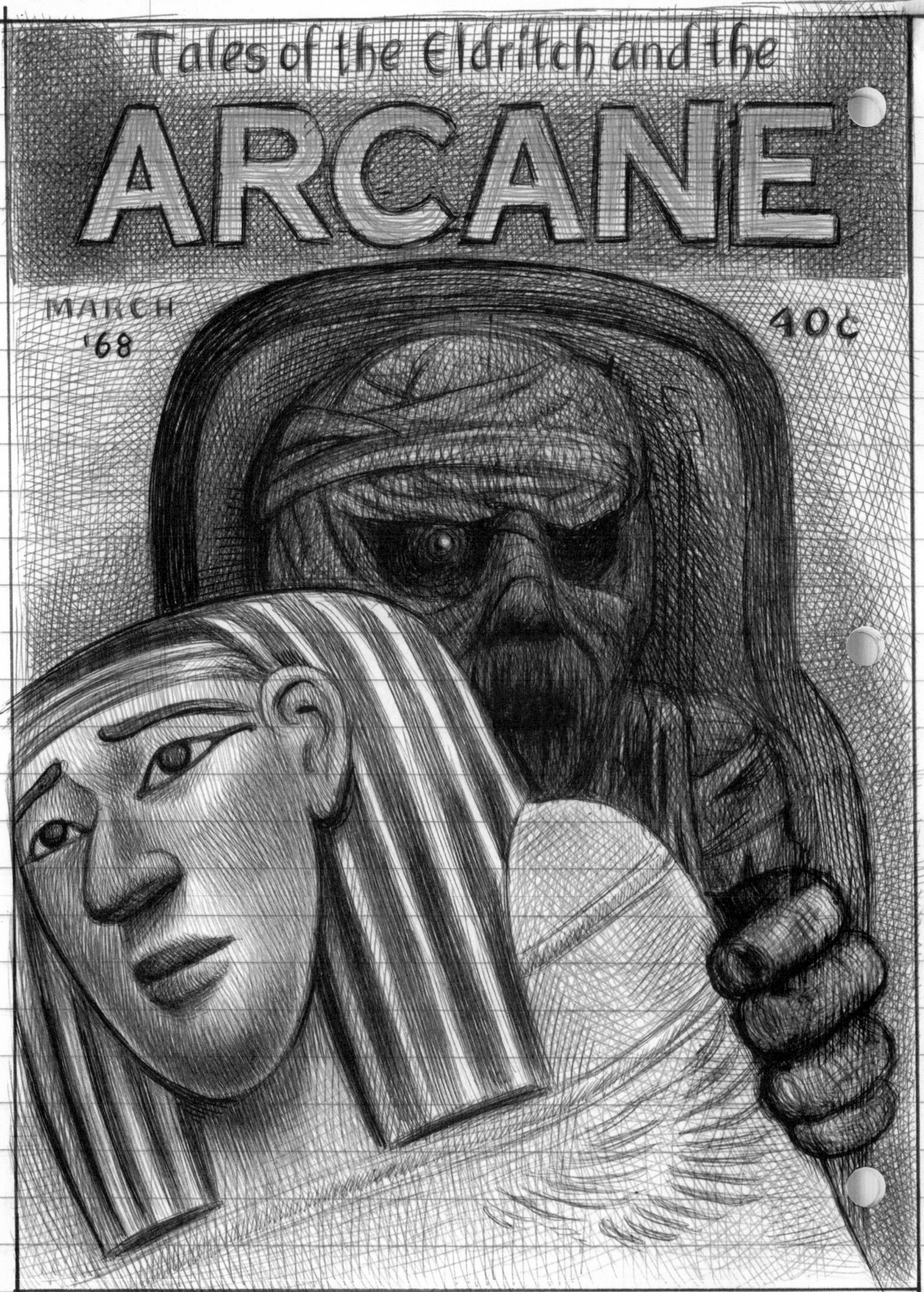
Tales of the Eldritch and the
ARCANE
MARCH '68
40¢

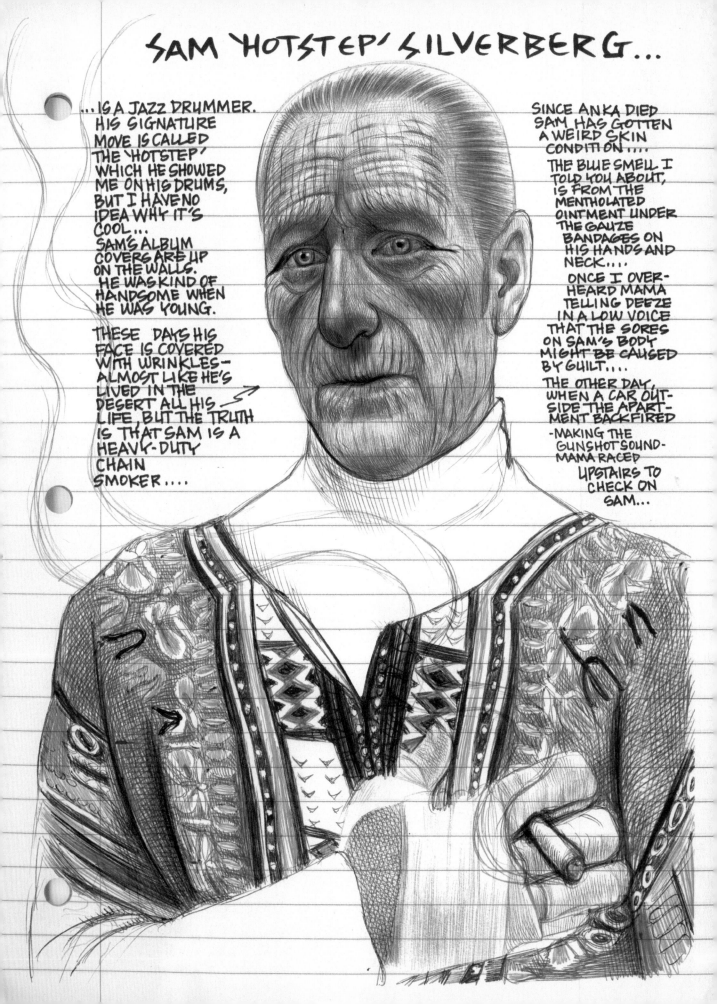

SAM 'HOTSTEP' SILVERBERG...

...IS A JAZZ DRUMMER. HIS SIGNATURE MOVE IS CALLED THE 'HOTSTEP' WHICH HE SHOWED ME ON HIS DRUMS, BUT I HAVE NO IDEA WHY IT'S COOL...
SAM'S ALBUM COVERS ARE UP ON THE WALLS. HE WAS KIND OF HANDSOME WHEN HE WAS YOUNG.

THESE DAYS HIS FACE IS COVERED WITH WRINKLES – ALMOST LIKE HE'S LIVED IN THE DESERT ALL HIS LIFE, BUT THE TRUTH IS THAT SAM IS A HEAVY-DUTY CHAIN SMOKER....

SINCE ANKA DIED SAM HAS GOTTEN A WEIRD SKIN CONDITION....

THE BLUE SMELL I TOLD YOU ABOUT, IS FROM THE MENTHOLATED OINTMENT UNDER THE GAUZE BANDAGES ON HIS HANDS AND NECK....

ONCE I OVER-HEARD MAMA TELLING DEEZE IN A LOW VOICE THAT THE SORES ON SAM'S BODY MIGHT BE CAUSED BY GUILT....

THE OTHER DAY, WHEN A CAR OUT-SIDE THE APART-MENT BACKFIRED
–MAKING THE GUNSHOT SOUND– MAMA RACED UPSTAIRS TO CHECK ON SAM...

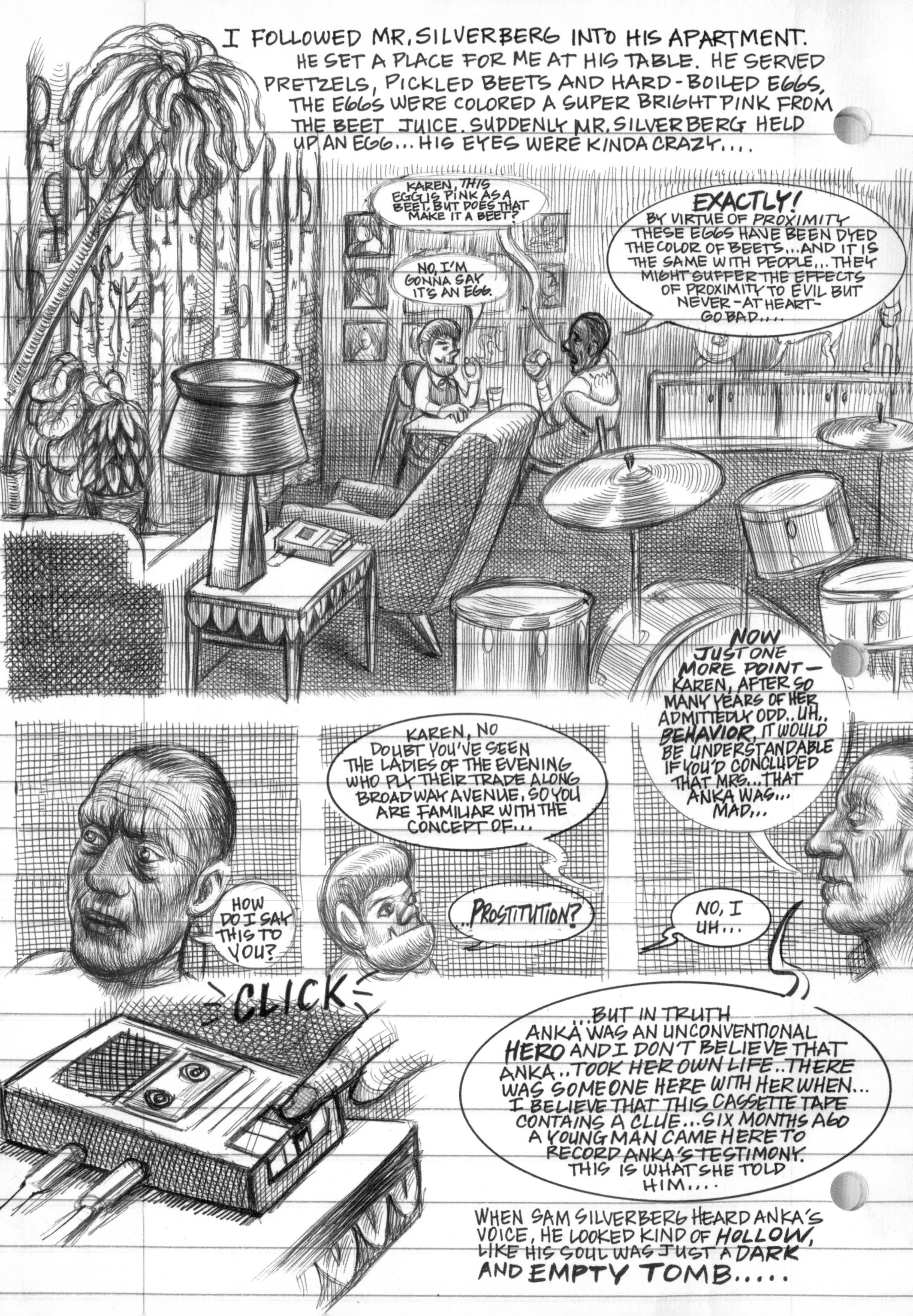

I FOLLOWED MR. SILVERBERG INTO HIS APARTMENT. HE SET A PLACE FOR ME AT HIS TABLE. HE SERVED PRETZELS, PICKLED BEETS AND HARD-BOILED EGGS. THE EGGS WERE COLORED A SUPER BRIGHT PINK FROM THE BEET JUICE. SUDDENLY MR. SILVERBERG HELD UP AN EGG... HIS EYES WERE KINDA CRAZY....
KAREN, THIS EGG IS PINK AS A BEET, BUT DOES THAT MAKE IT A BEET?
NO, I'M GONNA SAY IT'S AN EGG.
EXACTLY! BY VIRTUE OF PROXIMITY THESE EGGS HAVE BEEN DYED THE COLOR OF BEETS...AND IT IS THE SAME WITH PEOPLE... THEY MIGHT SUFFER THE EFFECTS OF PROXIMITY TO EVIL BUT NEVER - AT HEART - GO BAD....
HOW DO I SAY THIS TO YOU?
KAREN, NO DOUBT YOU'VE SEEN THE LADIES OF THE EVENING WHO PLY THEIR TRADE ALONG BROADWAY AVENUE, SO YOU ARE FAMILIAR WITH THE CONCEPT OF...
...PROSTITUTION?
NOW JUST ONE MORE POINT — KAREN, AFTER SO MANY YEARS OF HER ADMITTEDLY ODD.. UH.. BEHAVIOR, IT WOULD BE UNDERSTANDABLE IF YOU'D CONCLUDED THAT MRS... THAT ANKA WAS... MAD...
NO, I UH...
CLICK
...BUT IN TRUTH ANKA WAS AN UNCONVENTIONAL HERO AND I DON'T BELIEVE THAT ANKA.. TOOK HER OWN LIFE.. THERE WAS SOMEONE HERE WITH HER WHEN... I BELIEVE THAT THIS CASSETTE TAPE CONTAINS A CLUE... SIX MONTHS AGO A YOUNG MAN CAME HERE TO RECORD ANKA'S TESTIMONY. THIS IS WHAT SHE TOLD HIM....
WHEN SAM SILVERBERG HEARD ANKA'S VOICE, HE LOOKED KIND OF HOLLOW, LIKE HIS SOUL WAS JUST A DARK AND EMPTY TOMB.....

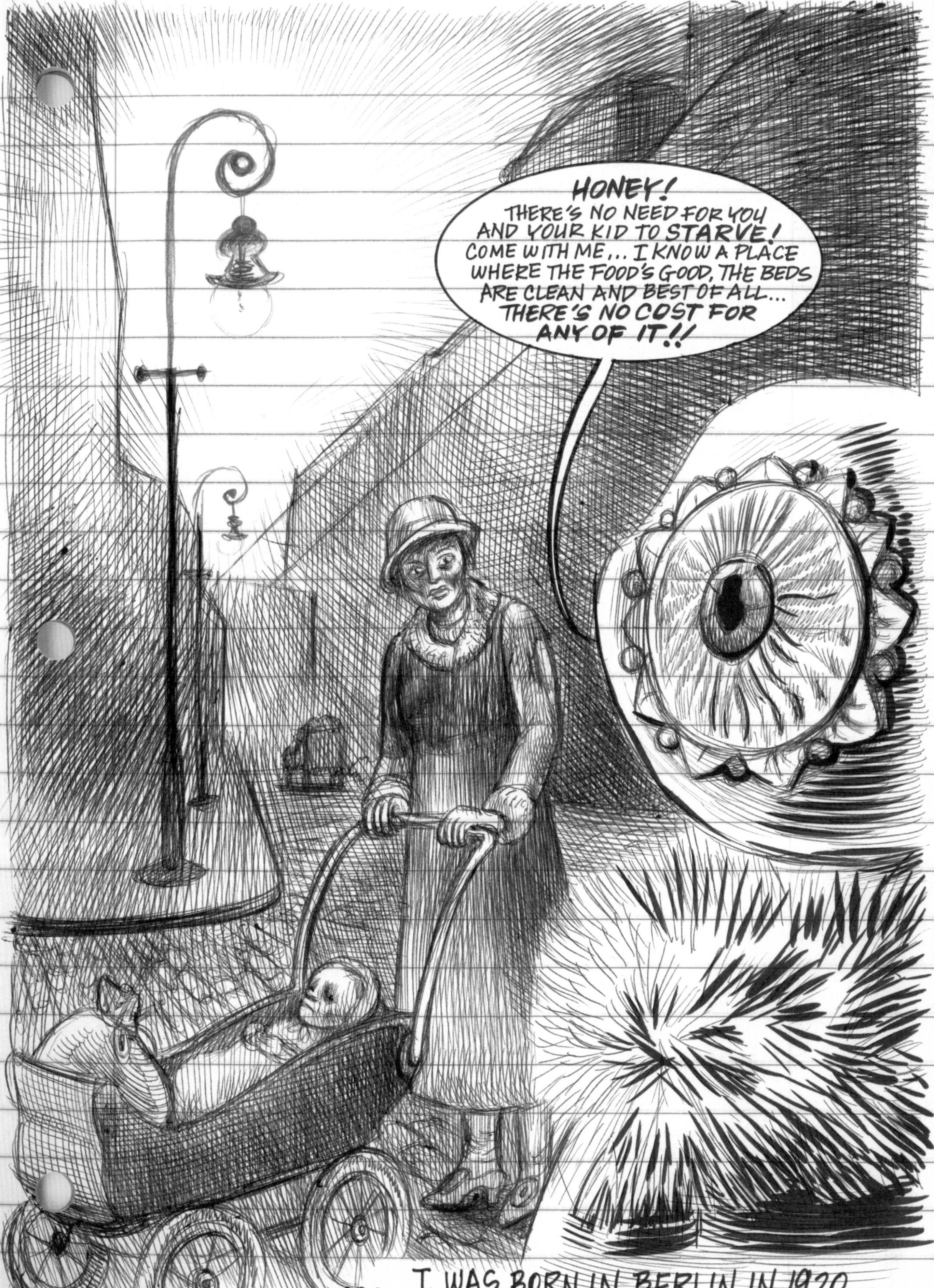
HONEY! THERE'S NO NEED FOR YOU AND YOUR KID TO STARVE! COME WITH ME,.. I KNOW A PLACE WHERE THE FOOD'S GOOD, THE BEDS ARE CLEAN AND BEST OF ALL... THERE'S NO COST FOR ANY OF IT!!
.... I WAS BORN IN BERLIN IN 1920...

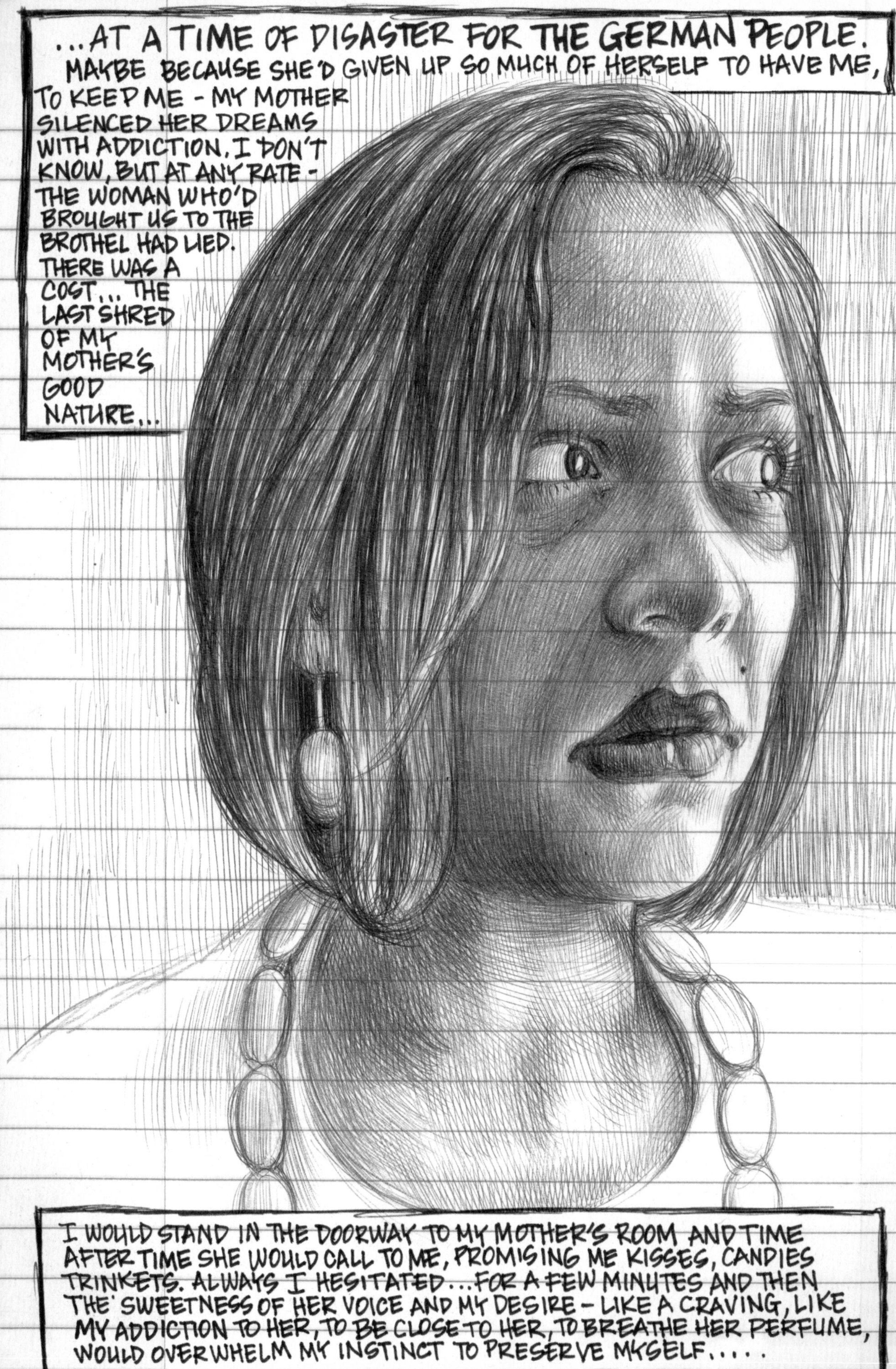
...AT A TIME OF DISASTER FOR THE GERMAN PEOPLE.
MAYBE BECAUSE SHE'D GIVEN UP SO MUCH OF HERSELF TO HAVE ME, TO KEEP ME - MY MOTHER SILENCED HER DREAMS WITH ADDICTION, I DON'T KNOW, BUT AT ANY RATE - THE WOMAN WHO'D BROUGHT US TO THE BROTHEL HAD LIED. THERE WAS A COST... THE LAST SHRED OF MY MOTHER'S GOOD NATURE...
I WOULD STAND IN THE DOORWAY TO MY MOTHER'S ROOM AND TIME AFTER TIME SHE WOULD CALL TO ME, PROMISING ME KISSES, CANDIES TRINKETS. ALWAYS I HESITATED... FOR A FEW MINUTES AND THEN THE SWEETNESS OF HER VOICE AND MY DESIRE - LIKE A CRAVING, LIKE MY ADDICTION TO HER, TO BE CLOSE TO HER, TO BREATHE HER PERFUME, WOULD OVERWHELM MY INSTINCT TO PRESERVE MYSELF....

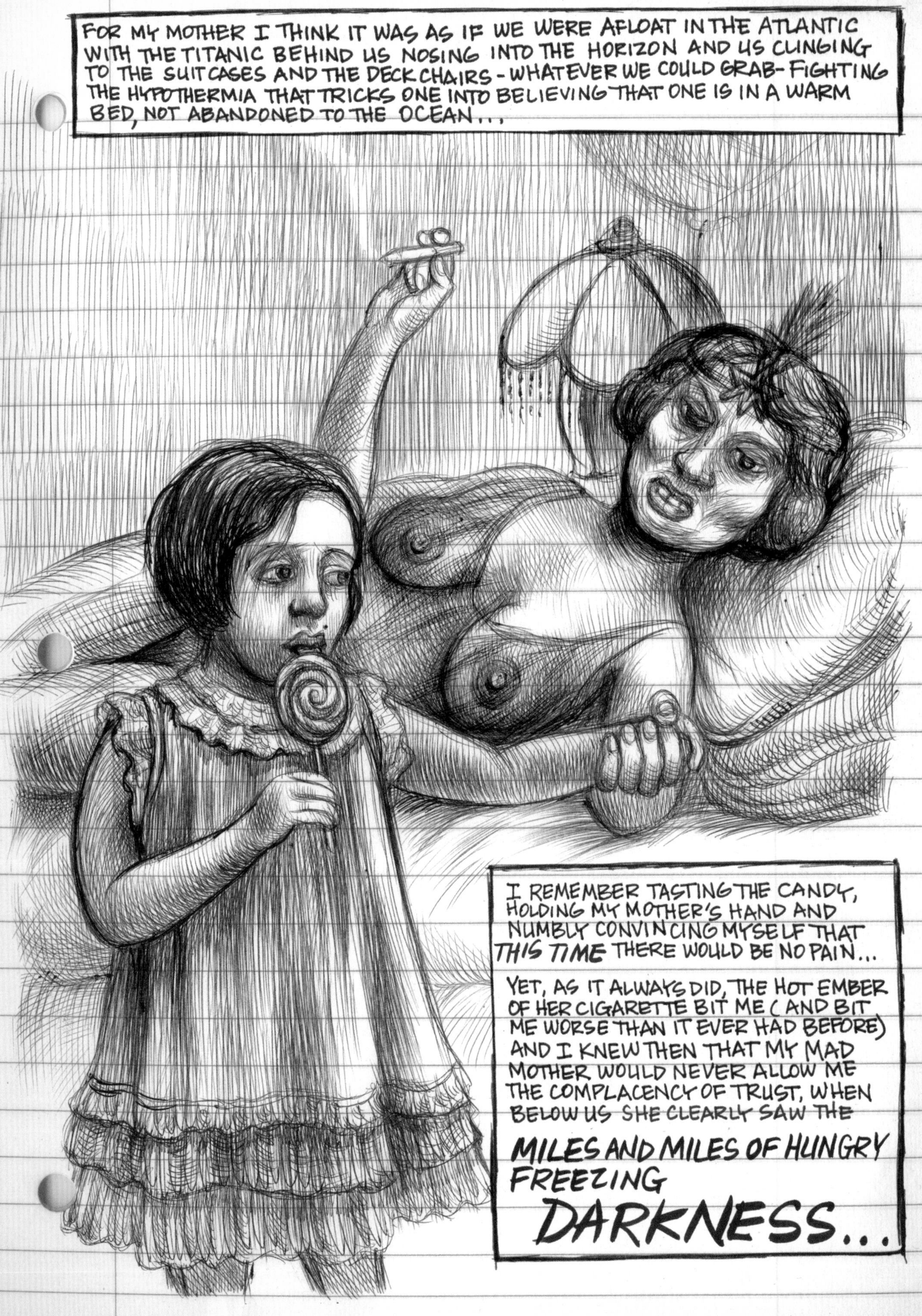
FOR MY MOTHER I THINK IT WAS AS IF WE WERE AFLOAT IN THE ATLANTIC WITH THE TITANIC BEHIND US NOSING INTO THE HORIZON AND US CLINGING TO THE SUITCASES AND THE DECK CHAIRS - WHATEVER WE COULD GRAB - FIGHTING THE HYPOTHERMIA THAT TRICKS ONE INTO BELIEVING THAT ONE IS IN A WARM BED, NOT ABANDONED TO THE OCEAN...
I REMEMBER TASTING THE CANDY, HOLDING MY MOTHER'S HAND AND NUMBLY CONVINCING MYSELF THAT *THIS TIME* THERE WOULD BE NO PAIN...
YET, AS IT ALWAYS DID, THE HOT EMBER OF HER CIGARETTE BIT ME (AND BIT ME WORSE THAN IT EVER HAD BEFORE) AND I KNEW THEN THAT MY MAD MOTHER WOULD NEVER ALLOW ME THE COMPLACENCY OF TRUST, WHEN BELOW US SHE CLEARLY SAW THE
MILES AND MILES OF HUNGRY FREEZING
DARKNESS...

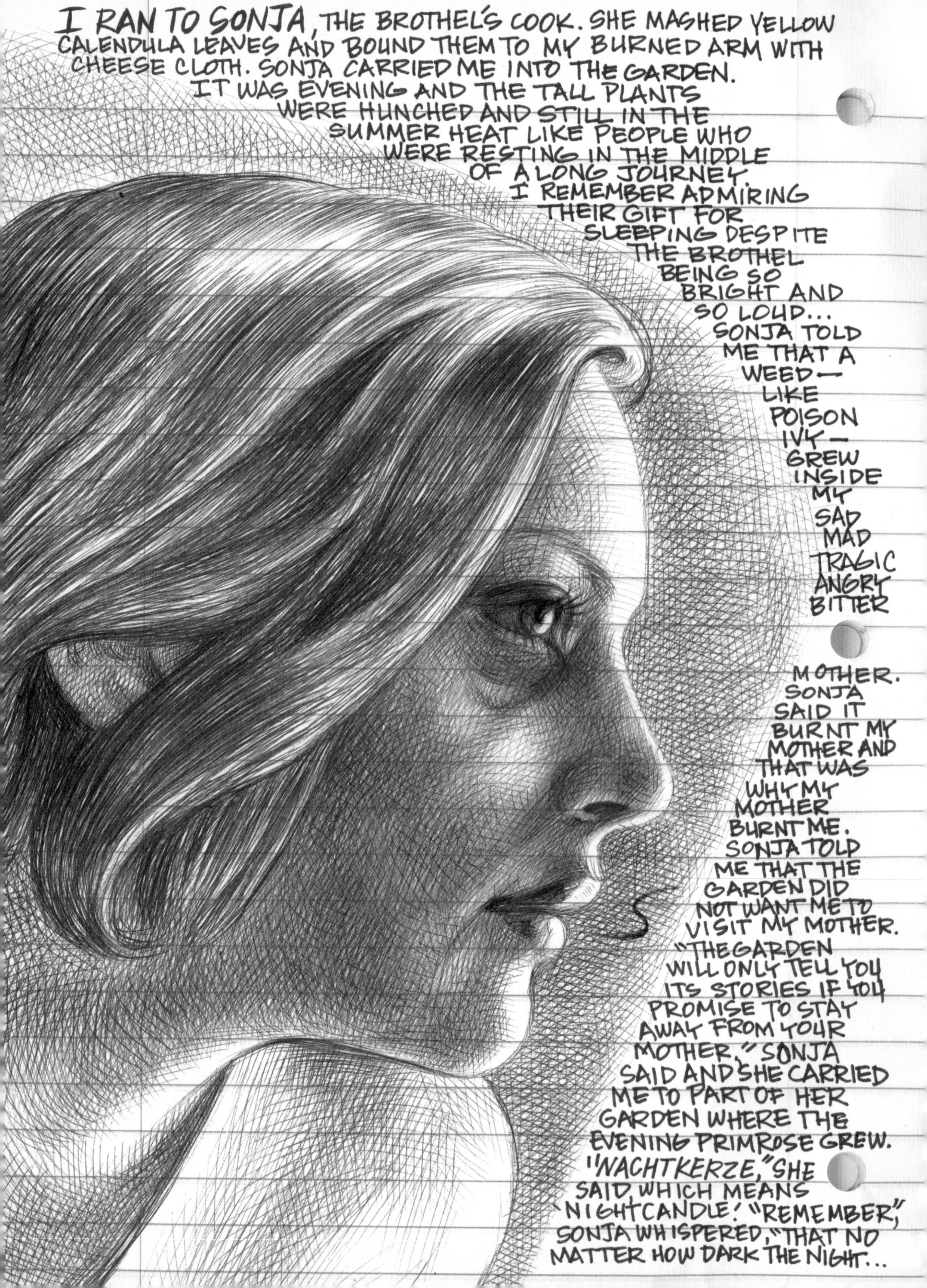
I RAN TO SONJA, THE BROTHEL'S COOK. SHE MASHED YELLOW CALENDULA LEAVES AND BOUND THEM TO MY BURNED ARM WITH CHEESE CLOTH. SONJA CARRIED ME INTO THE GARDEN. IT WAS EVENING AND THE TALL PLANTS WERE HUNCHED AND STILL IN THE SUMMER HEAT LIKE PEOPLE WHO WERE RESTING IN THE MIDDLE OF A LONG JOURNEY. I REMEMBER ADMIRING THEIR GIFT FOR SLEEPING DESPITE THE BROTHEL BEING SO BRIGHT AND SO LOUD... SONJA TOLD ME THAT A WEED— LIKE POISON IVY— GREW INSIDE MY SAD MAD TRAGIC ANGRY BITTER MOTHER. SONJA SAID IT BURNT MY MOTHER AND THAT WAS WHY MY MOTHER BURNT ME. SONJA TOLD ME THAT THE GARDEN DID NOT WANT ME TO VISIT MY MOTHER. "THE GARDEN WILL ONLY TELL YOU ITS STORIES IF YOU PROMISE TO STAY AWAY FROM YOUR MOTHER," SONJA SAID AND SHE CARRIED ME TO PART OF HER GARDEN WHERE THE EVENING PRIMROSE GREW. "NACHTKERZE," SHE SAID WHICH MEANS 'NIGHTCANDLE.' "REMEMBER," SONJA WHISPERED, "THAT NO MATTER HOW DARK THE NIGHT...

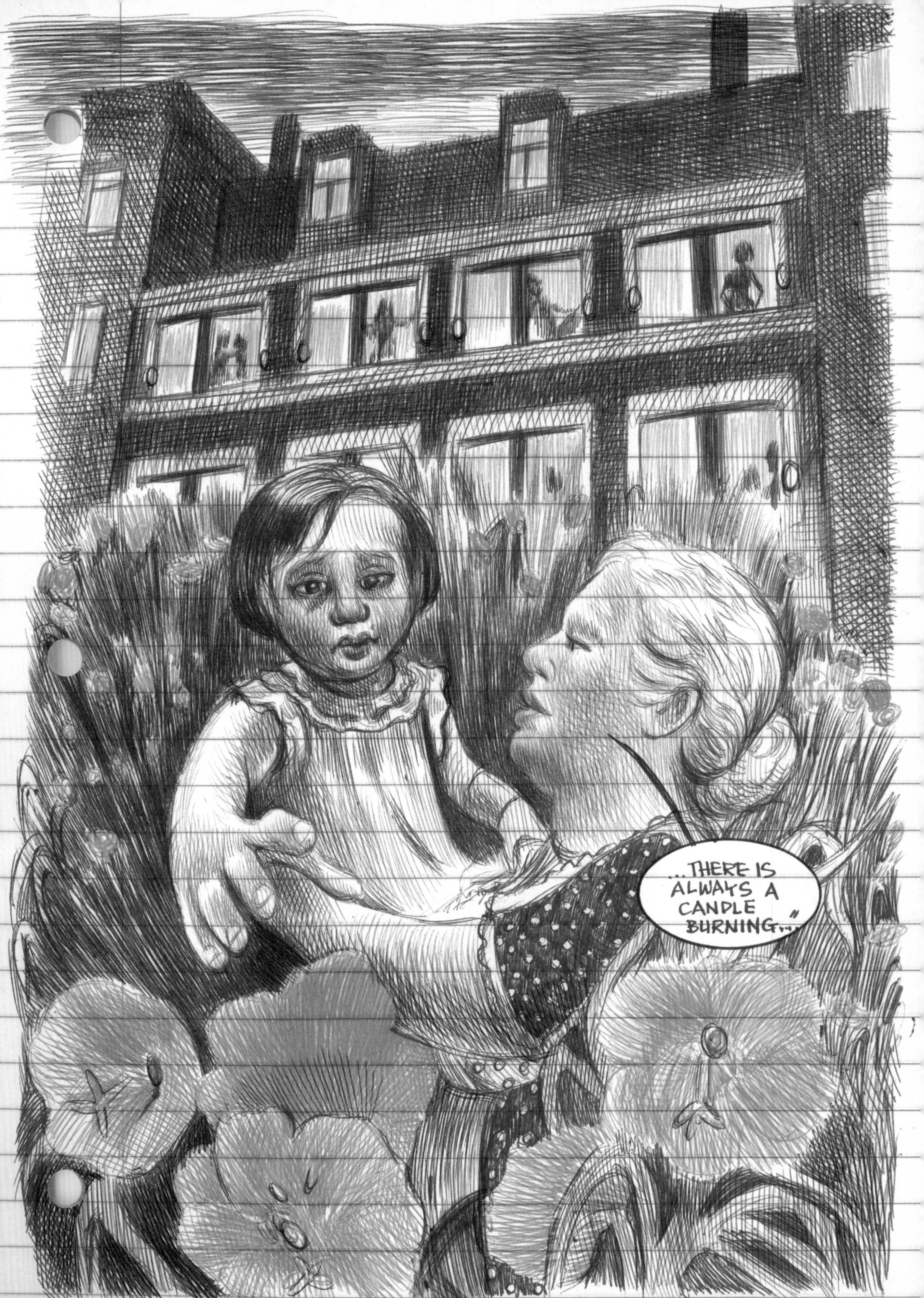
...THERE IS ALWAYS A CANDLE BURNING..."

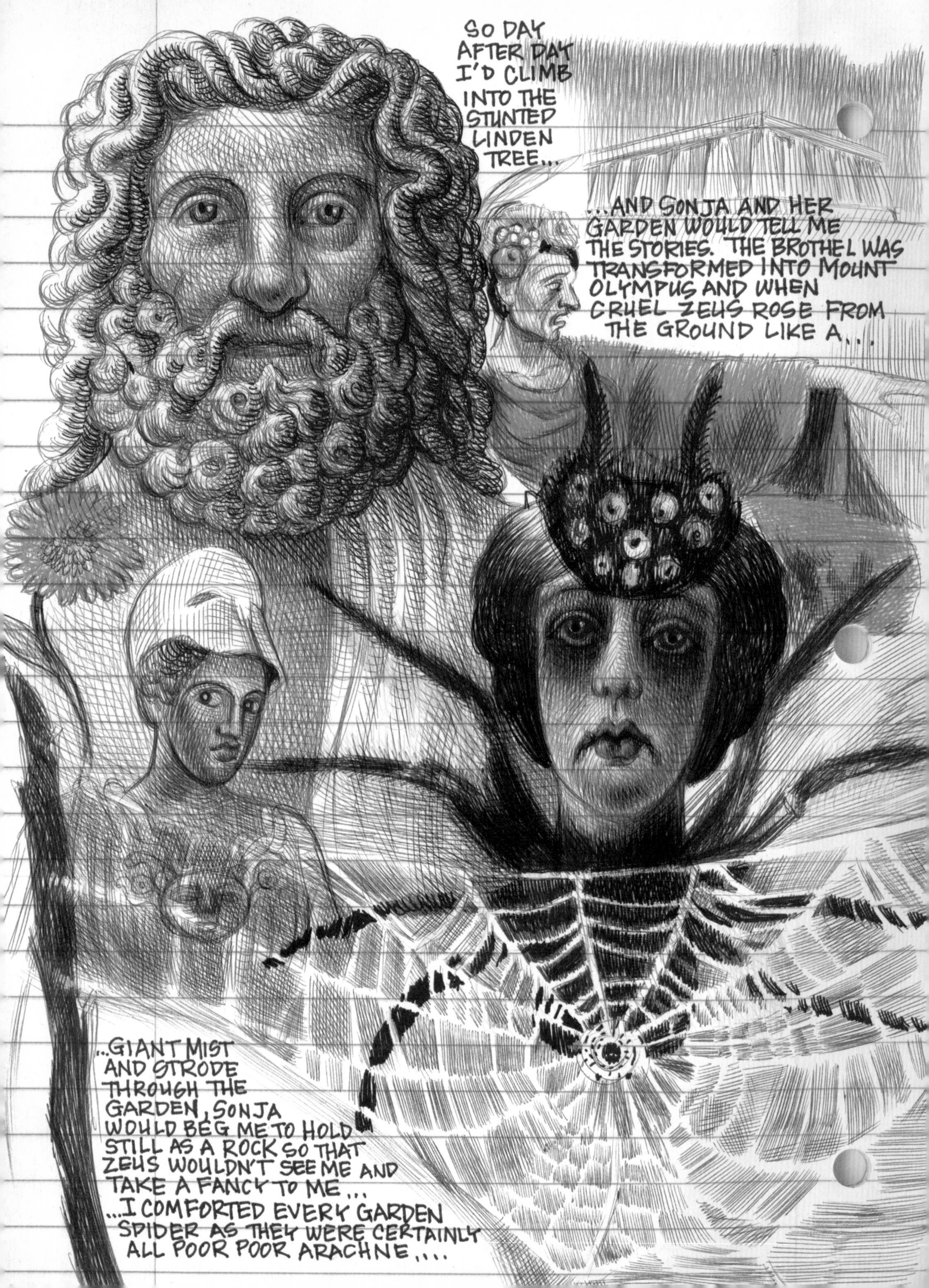
SO DAY AFTER DAY I'D CLIMB INTO THE STUNTED LINDEN TREE...
...AND SONJA AND HER GARDEN WOULD TELL ME THE STORIES. THE BROTHEL WAS TRANSFORMED INTO MOUNT OLYMPUS AND WHEN CRUEL ZEUS ROSE FROM THE GROUND LIKE A...
...GIANT MIST AND STRODE THROUGH THE GARDEN, SONJA WOULD BEG ME TO HOLD STILL AS A ROCK SO THAT ZEUS WOULDN'T SEE ME AND TAKE A FANCY TO ME...
...I COMFORTED EVERY GARDEN SPIDER AS THEY WERE CERTAINLY ALL POOR POOR ARACHNE....

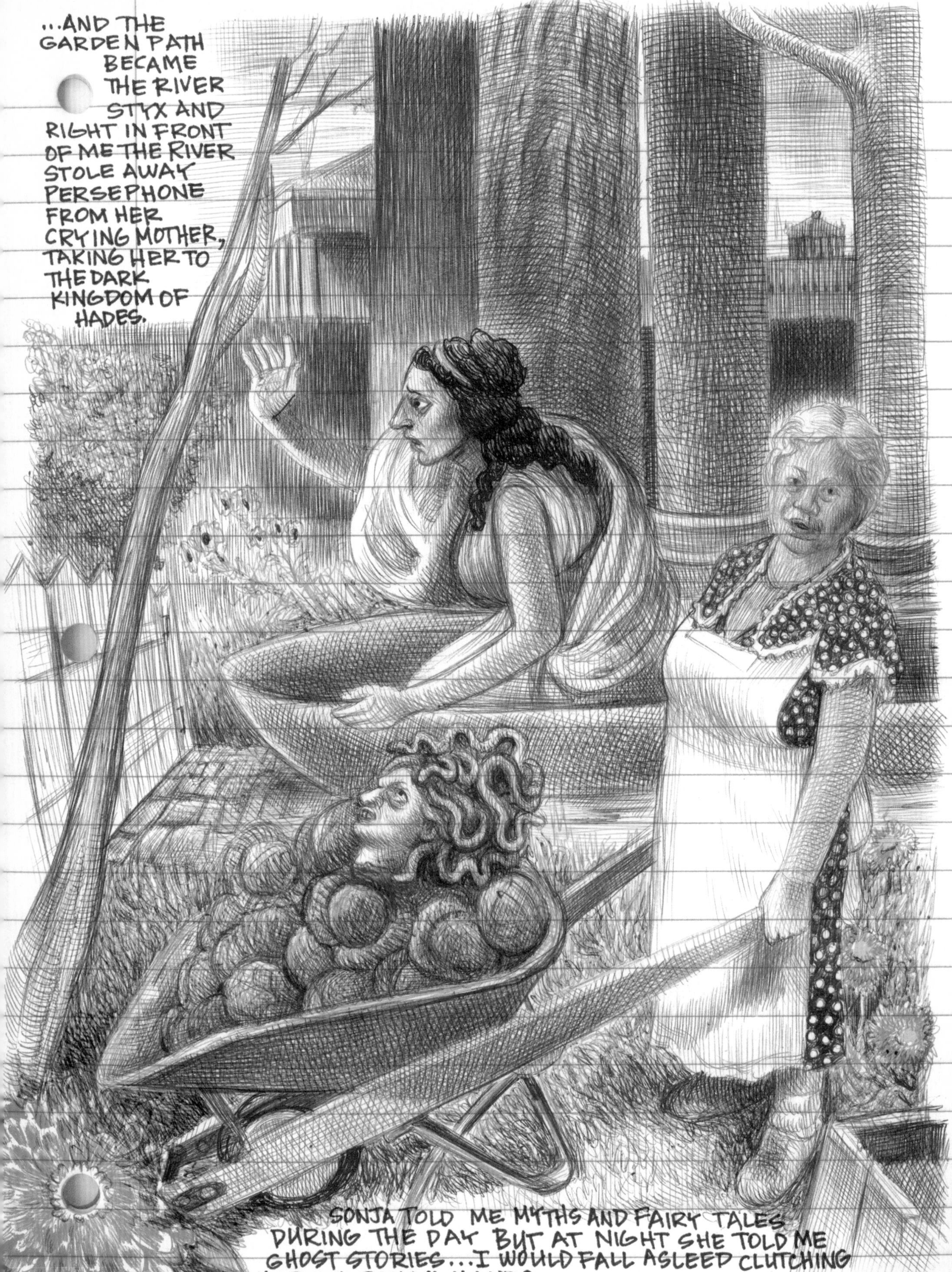
...AND THE GARDEN PATH BECAME THE RIVER STYX AND RIGHT IN FRONT OF ME THE RIVER STOLE AWAY PERSEPHONE FROM HER CRYING MOTHER, TAKING HER TO THE DARK KINGDOM OF HADES.
SONJA TOLD ME MYTHS AND FAIRY TALES DURING THE DAY BUT AT NIGHT SHE TOLD ME GHOST STORIES...I WOULD FALL ASLEEP CLUTCHING HER BIG ROUGH HANDS...

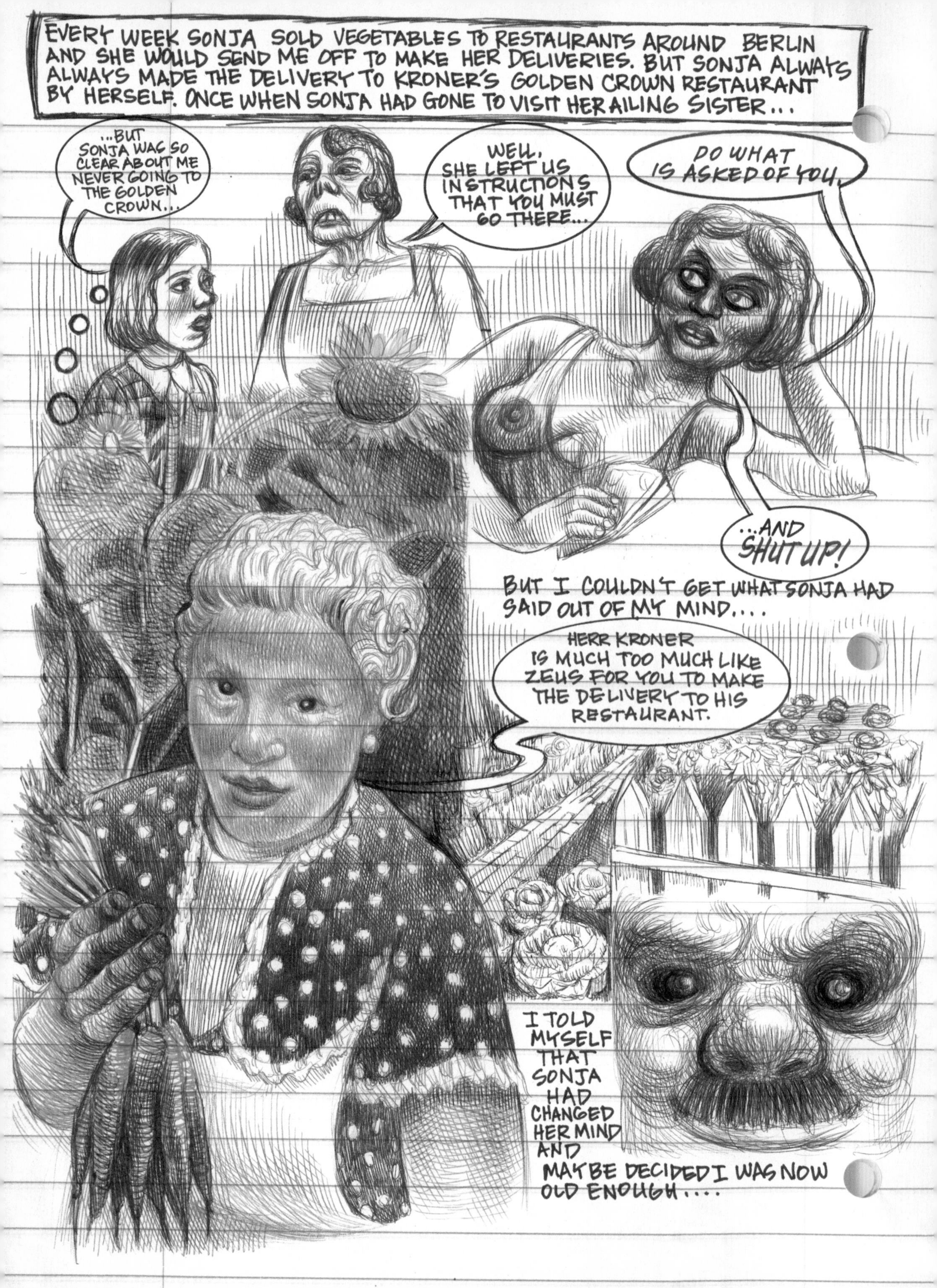
EVERY WEEK SONJA SOLD VEGETABLES TO RESTAURANTS AROUND BERLIN AND SHE WOULD SEND ME OFF TO MAKE HER DELIVERIES. BUT SONJA ALWAYS ALWAYS MADE THE DELIVERY TO KRONER'S GOLDEN CROWN RESTAURANT BY HERSELF. ONCE WHEN SONJA HAD GONE TO VISIT HER AILING SISTER...
...BUT SONJA WAS SO CLEAR ABOUT ME NEVER GOING TO THE GOLDEN CROWN...
WELL, SHE LEFT US INSTRUCTIONS THAT YOU MUST GO THERE...
DO WHAT IS ASKED OF YOU.
...AND SHUT UP!
BUT I COULDN'T GET WHAT SONJA HAD SAID OUT OF MY MIND....
HERR KRONER IS MUCH TOO MUCH LIKE ZEUS FOR YOU TO MAKE THE DELIVERY TO HIS RESTAURANT.
I TOLD MYSELF THAT SONJA HAD CHANGED HER MIND AND MAYBE DECIDED I WAS NOW OLD ENOUGH....

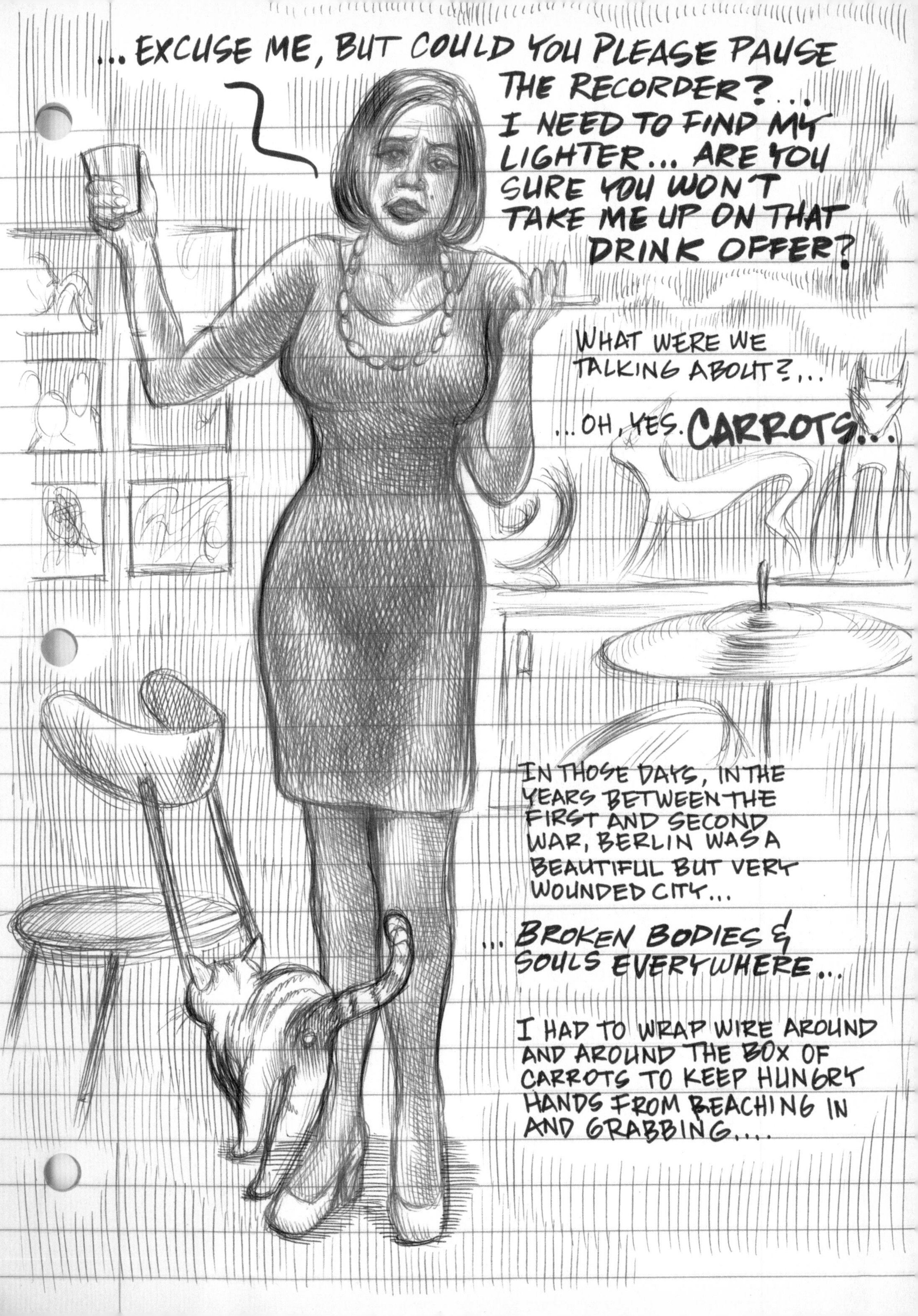

...EXCUSE ME, BUT COULD YOU PLEASE PAUSE THE RECORDER?... I NEED TO FIND MY LIGHTER... ARE YOU SURE YOU WON'T TAKE ME UP ON THAT DRINK OFFER?
WHAT WERE WE TALKING ABOUT?...
...OH, YES. CARROTS...
IN THOSE DAYS, IN THE YEARS BETWEEN THE FIRST AND SECOND WAR, BERLIN WAS A BEAUTIFUL BUT VERY WOUNDED CITY...
...BROKEN BODIES & SOULS EVERYWHERE...
I HAD TO WRAP WIRE AROUND AND AROUND THE BOX OF CARROTS TO KEEP HUNGRY HANDS FROM REACHING IN AND GRABBING...

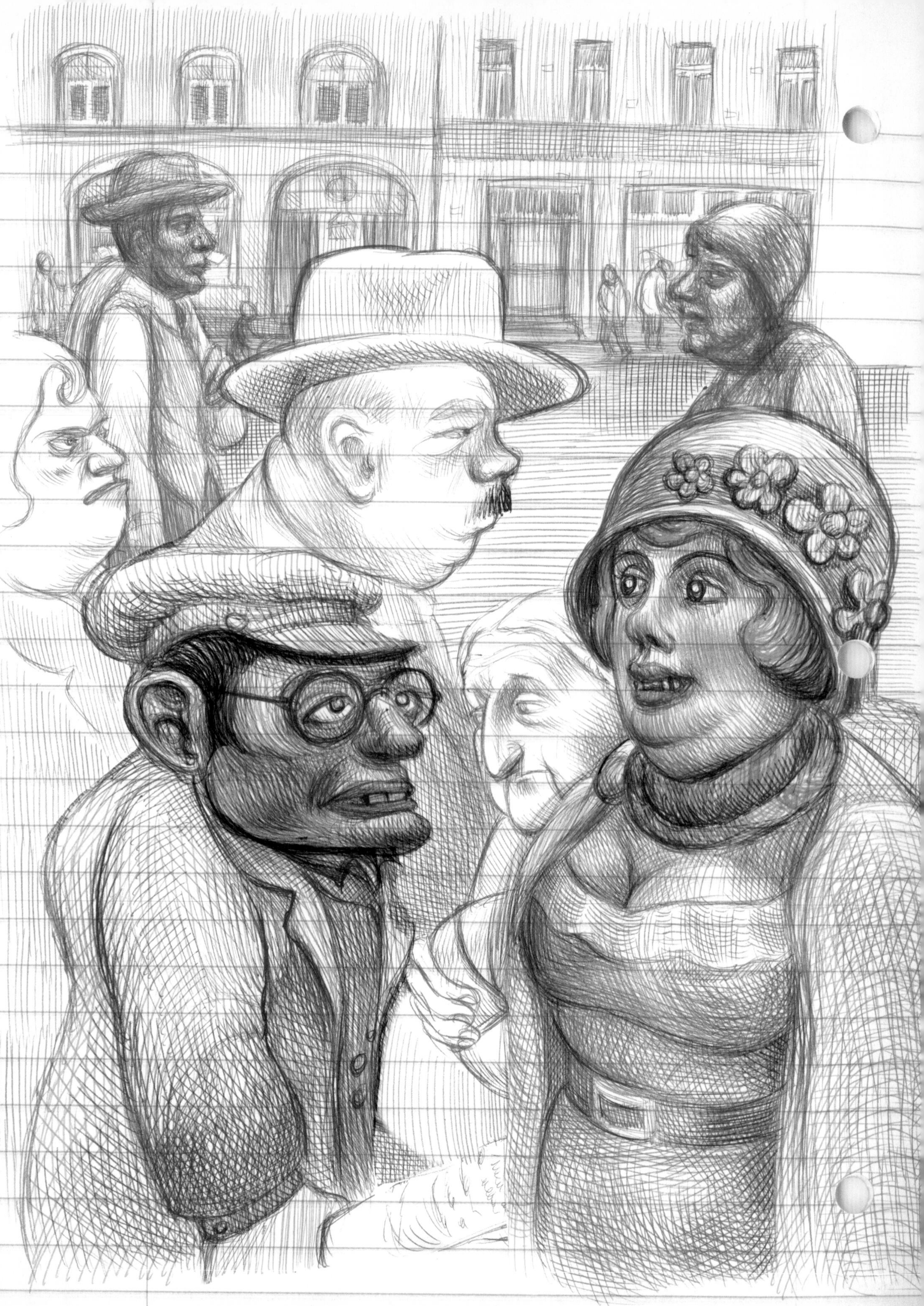

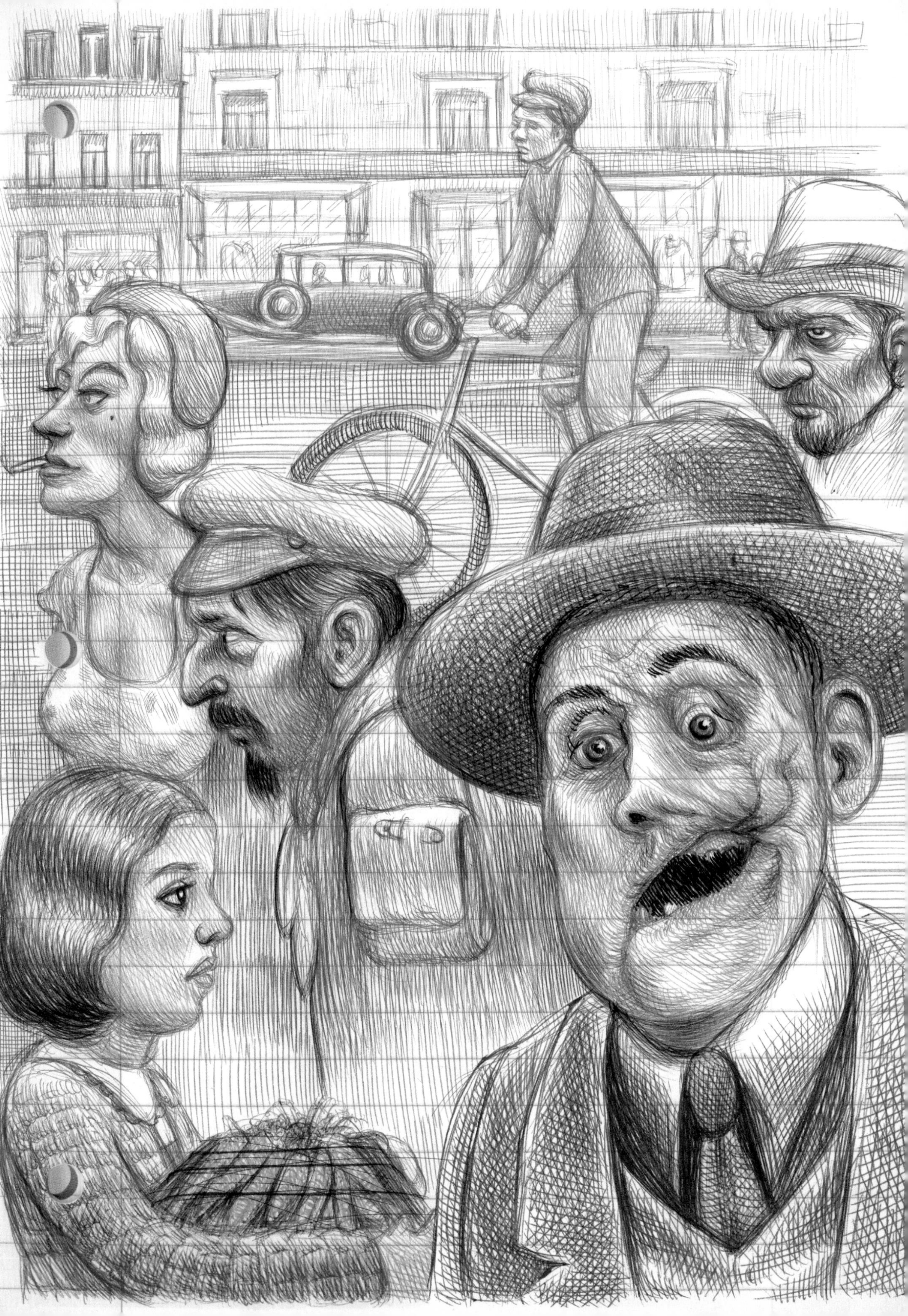

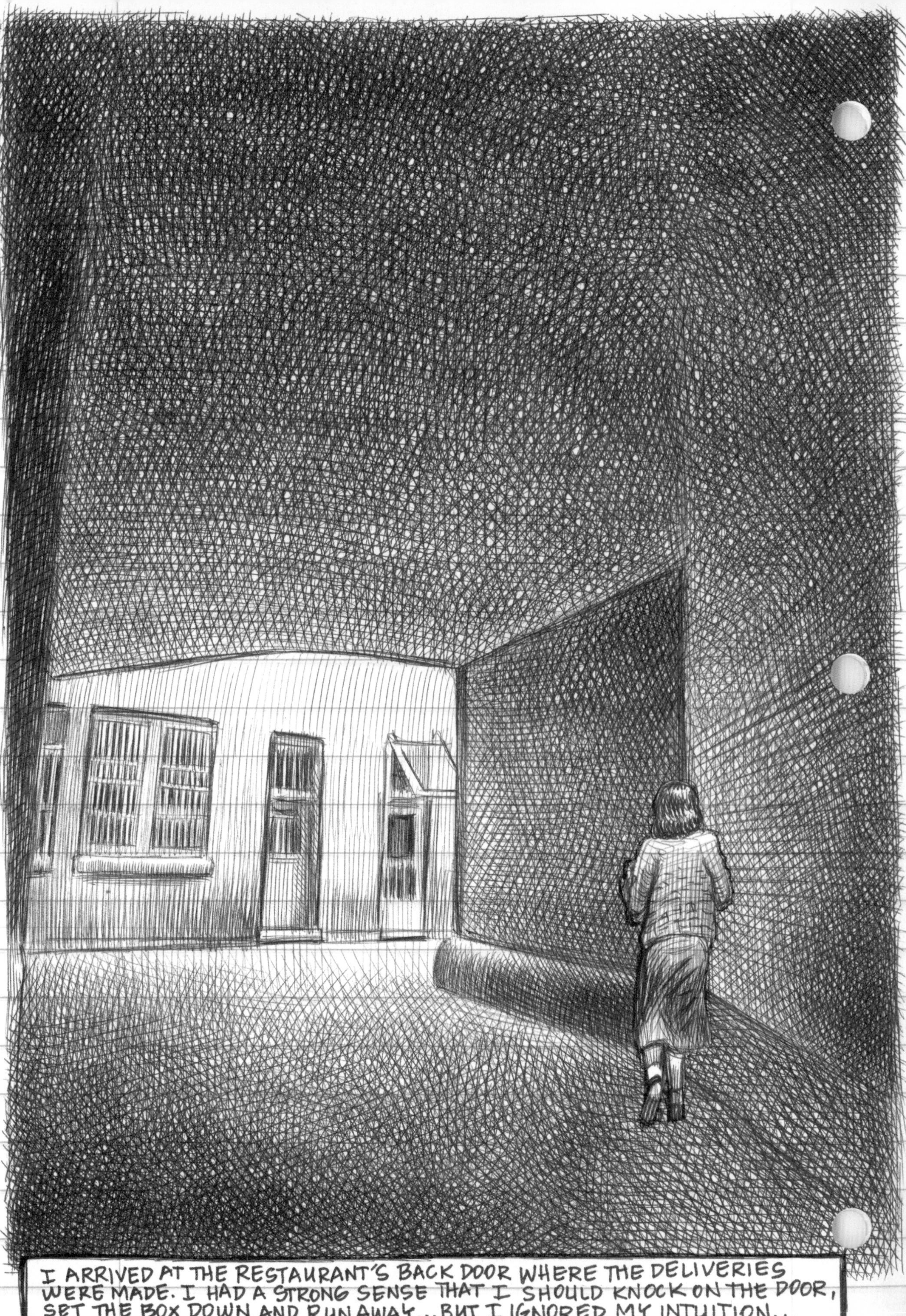
I ARRIVED AT THE RESTAURANT'S BACK DOOR WHERE THE DELIVERIES WERE MADE. I HAD A STRONG SENSE THAT I SHOULD KNOCK ON THE DOOR, SET THE BOX DOWN AND RUN AWAY... BUT I IGNORED MY INTUITION...

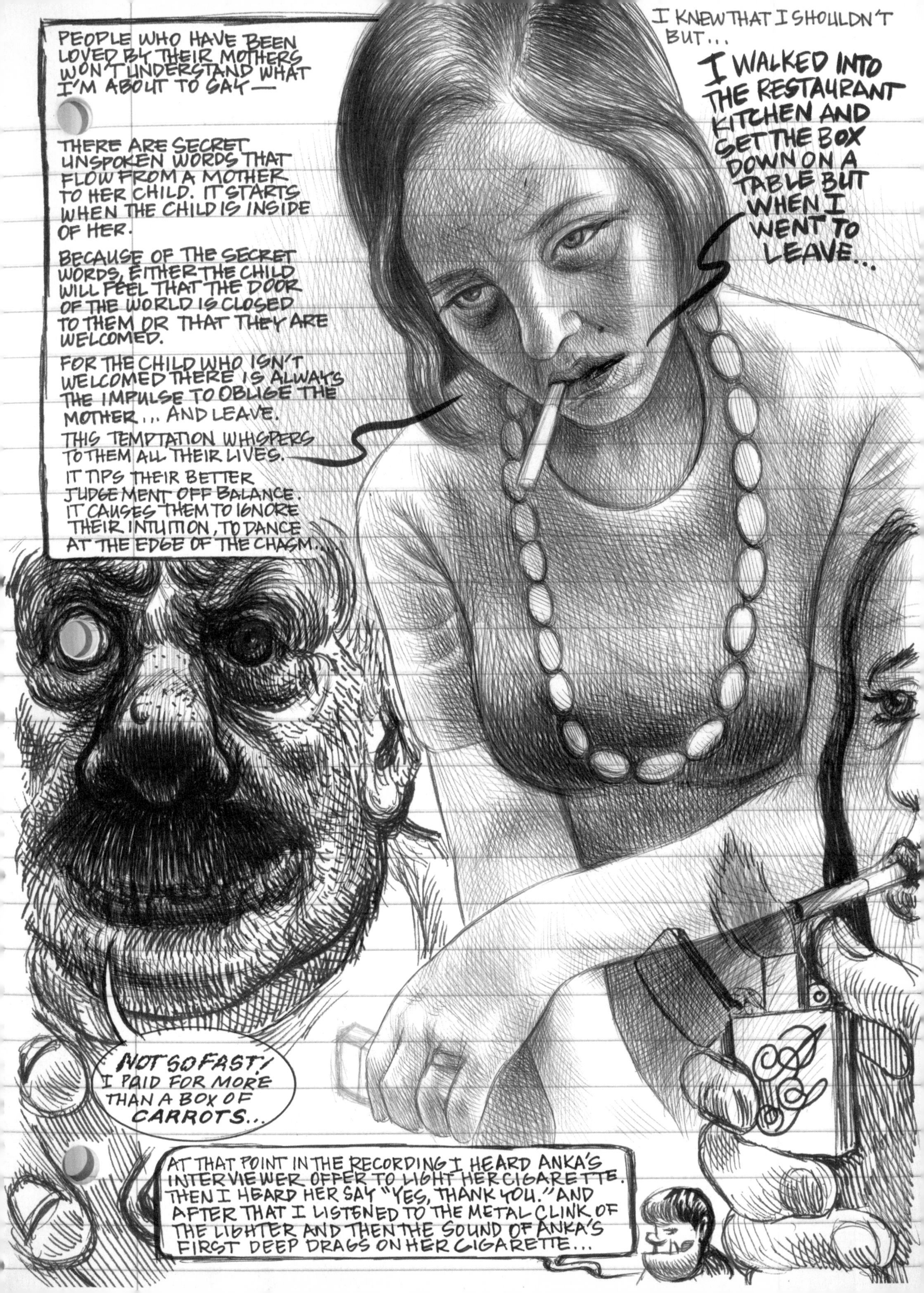
PEOPLE WHO HAVE BEEN LOVED BY THEIR MOTHERS WON'T UNDERSTAND WHAT I'M ABOUT TO SAY—
THERE ARE SECRET UNSPOKEN WORDS THAT FLOW FROM A MOTHER TO HER CHILD. IT STARTS WHEN THE CHILD IS INSIDE OF HER.
BECAUSE OF THE SECRET WORDS, EITHER THE CHILD WILL FEEL THAT THE DOOR OF THE WORLD IS CLOSED TO THEM OR THAT THEY ARE WELCOMED.
FOR THE CHILD WHO ISN'T WELCOMED THERE IS ALWAYS THE IMPULSE TO OBLIGE THE MOTHER... AND LEAVE.
THIS TEMPTATION WHISPERS TO THEM ALL THEIR LIVES.
IT TIPS THEIR BETTER JUDGEMENT OFF BALANCE.
IT CAUSES THEM TO IGNORE THEIR INTUITION, TO DANCE AT THE EDGE OF THE CHASM...
I KNEW THAT I SHOULDN'T BUT...
I WALKED INTO THE RESTAURANT KITCHEN AND SET THE BOX DOWN ON A TABLE BUT WHEN I WENT TO LEAVE...
NOT SO FAST! I PAID FOR MORE THAN A BOX OF CARROTS...
AT THAT POINT IN THE RECORDING I HEARD ANKA'S INTERVIEWER OFFER TO LIGHT HER CIGARETTE. THEN I HEARD HER SAY "YES, THANK YOU." AND AFTER THAT I LISTENED TO THE METAL CLINK OF THE LIGHTER AND THEN THE SOUND OF ANKA'S FIRST DEEP DRAGS ON HER CIGARETTE...

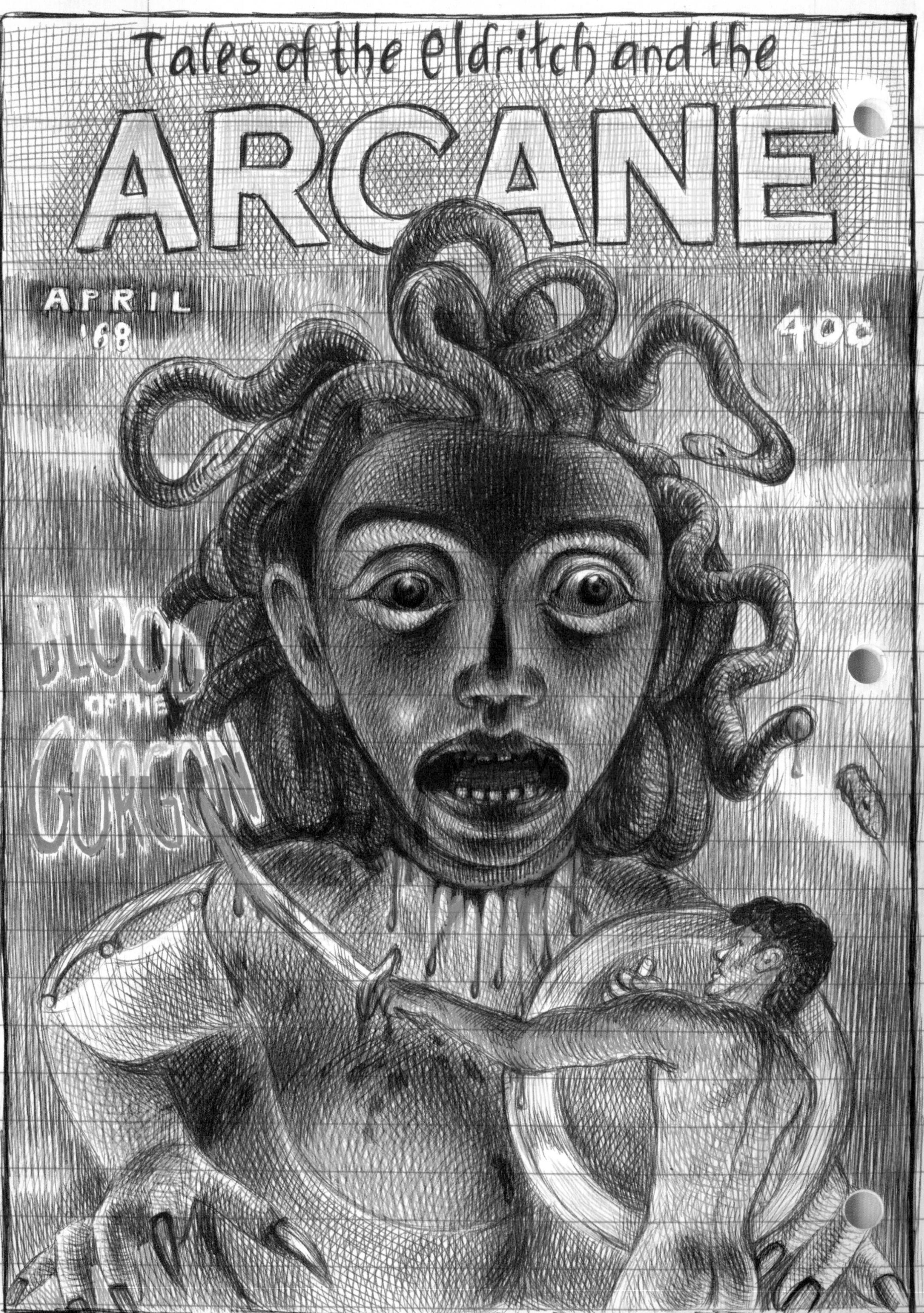
Tales of the eldritch and the
ARCANE
APRIL '68
40¢
BLOOD OF THE GORGON

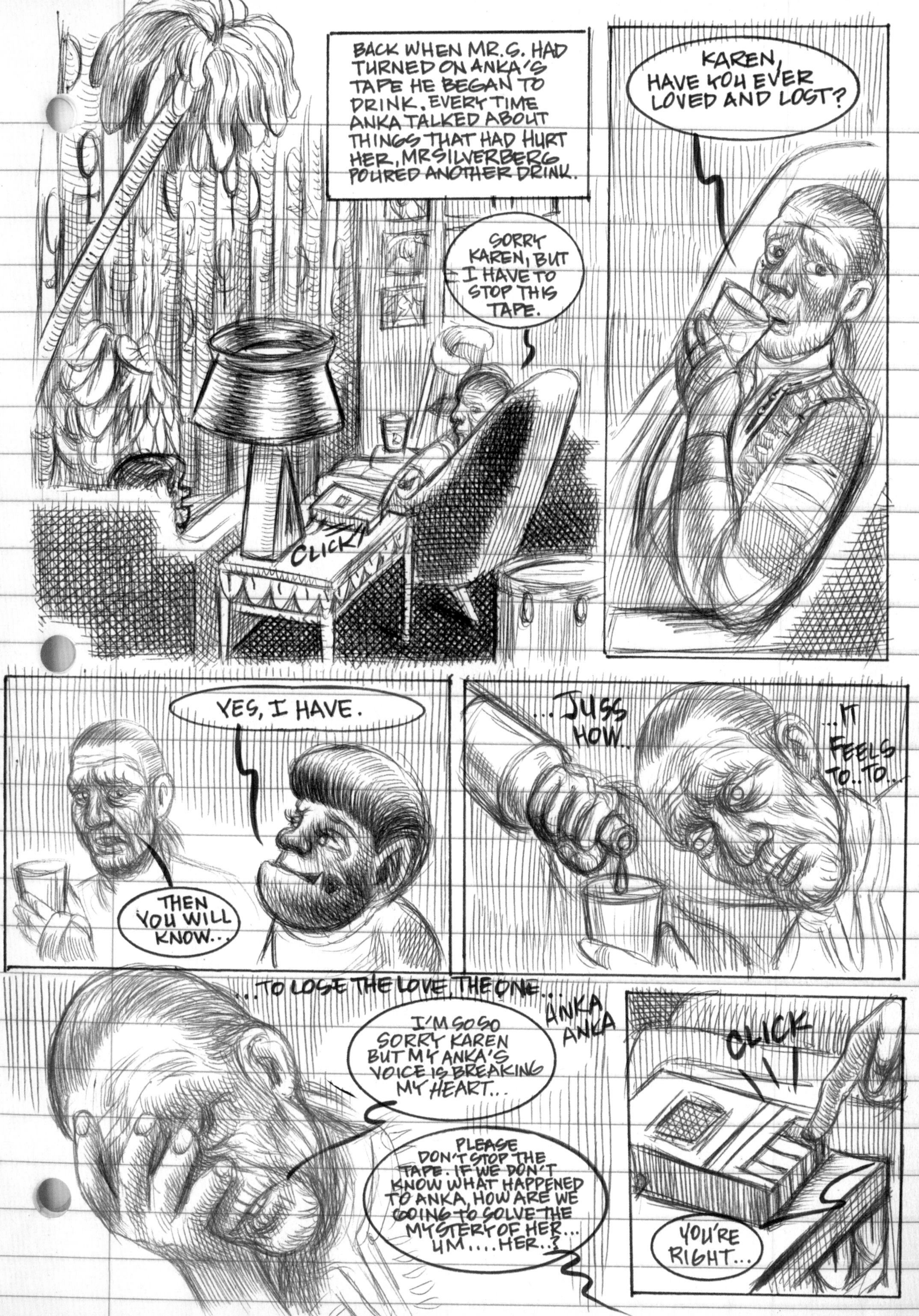
BACK WHEN MR. S. HAD TURNED ON ANKA'S TAPE HE BEGAN TO DRINK. EVERY TIME ANKA TALKED ABOUT THINGS THAT HAD HURT HER, MR SILVERBERG POURED ANOTHER DRINK.
SORRY KAREN, BUT I HAVE TO STOP THIS TAPE.
CLICK
KAREN, HAVE YOU EVER LOVED AND LOST?
YES, I HAVE.
THEN YOU WILL KNOW...
...JUSS HOW...
...IT FEELS TO...TO...
...TO LOSE THE LOVE, THE ONE...
ANKA ANKA
I'M SO SO SORRY KAREN BUT MY ANKA'S VOICE IS BREAKING MY HEART...
PLEASE DON'T STOP THE TAPE. IF WE DON'T KNOW WHAT HAPPENED TO ANKA, HOW ARE WE GOING TO SOLVE THE MYSTERY OF HER... UM.... HER...?
CLICK
YOU'RE RIGHT...

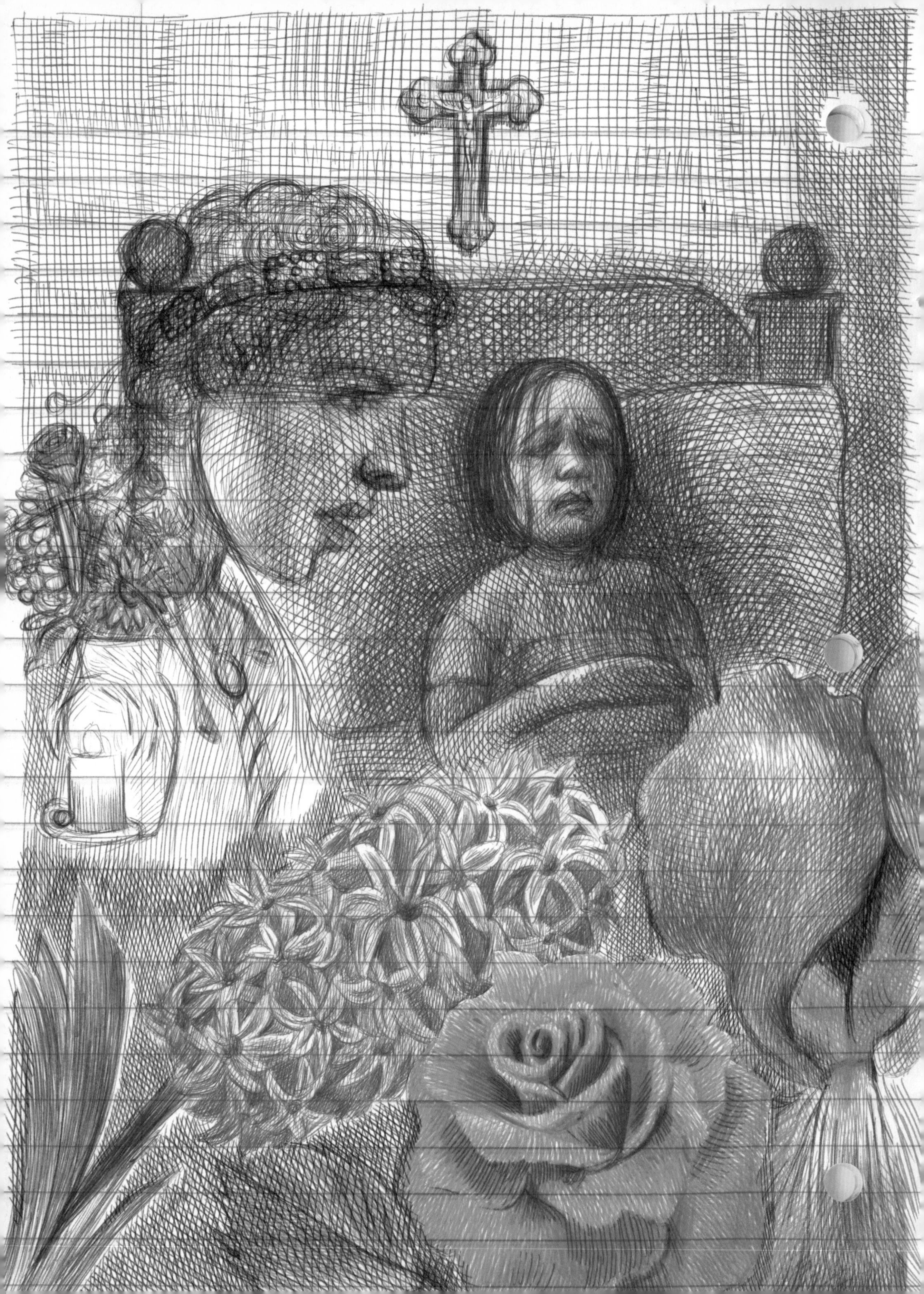

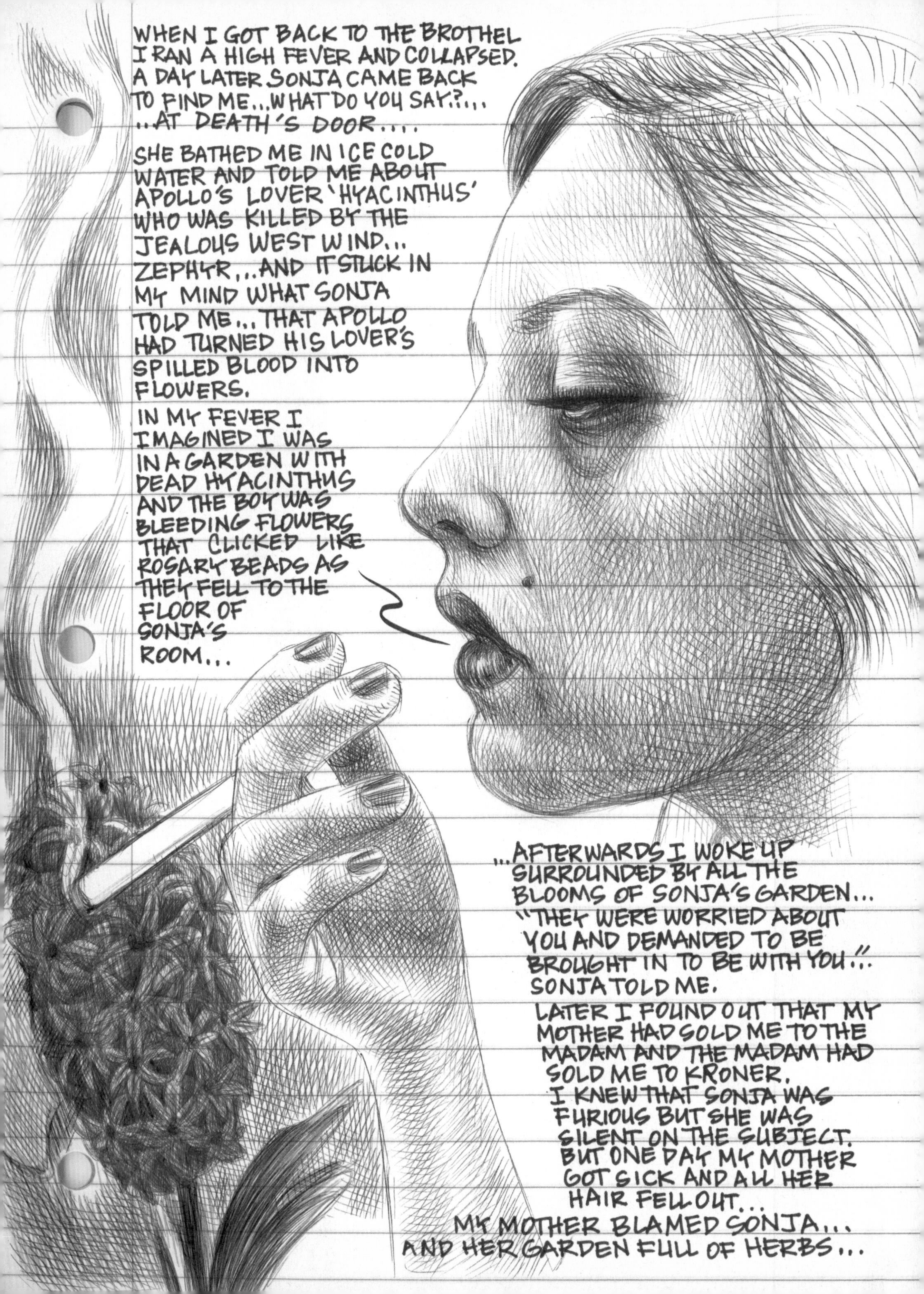
WHEN I GOT BACK TO THE BROTHEL I RAN A HIGH FEVER AND COLLAPSED. A DAY LATER SONJA CAME BACK TO FIND ME... WHAT DO YOU SAY?... ..AT DEATH'S DOOR....
SHE BATHED ME IN ICE COLD WATER AND TOLD ME ABOUT APOLLO'S LOVER 'HYACINTHUS' WHO WAS KILLED BY THE JEALOUS WEST WIND... ZEPHYR... AND IT STUCK IN MY MIND WHAT SONJA TOLD ME... THAT APOLLO HAD TURNED HIS LOVER'S SPILLED BLOOD INTO FLOWERS.
IN MY FEVER I IMAGINED I WAS IN A GARDEN WITH DEAD HYACINTHUS AND THE BOY WAS BLEEDING FLOWERS THAT CLICKED LIKE ROSARY BEADS AS THEY FELL TO THE FLOOR OF SONJA'S ROOM...
...AFTERWARDS I WOKE UP SURROUNDED BY ALL THE BLOOMS OF SONJA'S GARDEN... "THEY WERE WORRIED ABOUT YOU AND DEMANDED TO BE BROUGHT IN TO BE WITH YOU!" SONJA TOLD ME.
LATER I FOUND OUT THAT MY MOTHER HAD SOLD ME TO THE MADAM AND THE MADAM HAD SOLD ME TO KRONER.
I KNEW THAT SONJA WAS FURIOUS BUT SHE WAS SILENT ON THE SUBJECT. BUT ONE DAY MY MOTHER GOT SICK AND ALL HER HAIR FELL OUT...
MY MOTHER BLAMED SONJA... AND HER GARDEN FULL OF HERBS...

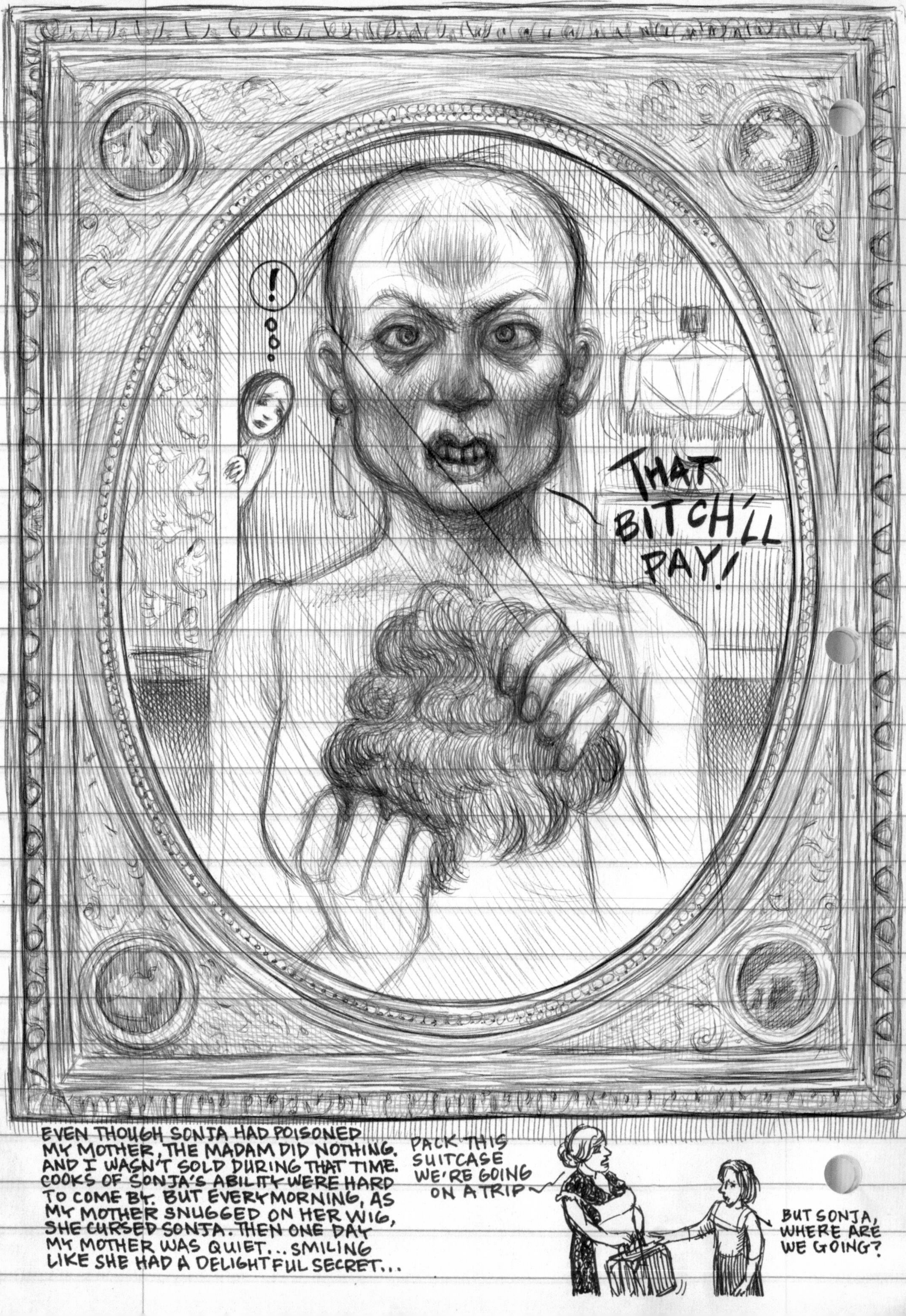
THAT BITCH'LL PAY!
EVEN THOUGH SONJA HAD POISONED MY MOTHER, THE MADAM DID NOTHING. AND I WASN'T SOLD DURING THAT TIME. COOKS OF SONJA'S ABILITY WERE HARD TO COME BY. BUT EVERY MORNING, AS MY MOTHER SNUGGED ON HER WIG, SHE CURSED SONJA. THEN ONE DAY MY MOTHER WAS QUIET... SMILING LIKE SHE HAD A DELIGHTFUL SECRET...
PACK THIS SUITCASE WE'RE GOING ON A TRIP
BUT SONJA, WHERE ARE WE GOING?

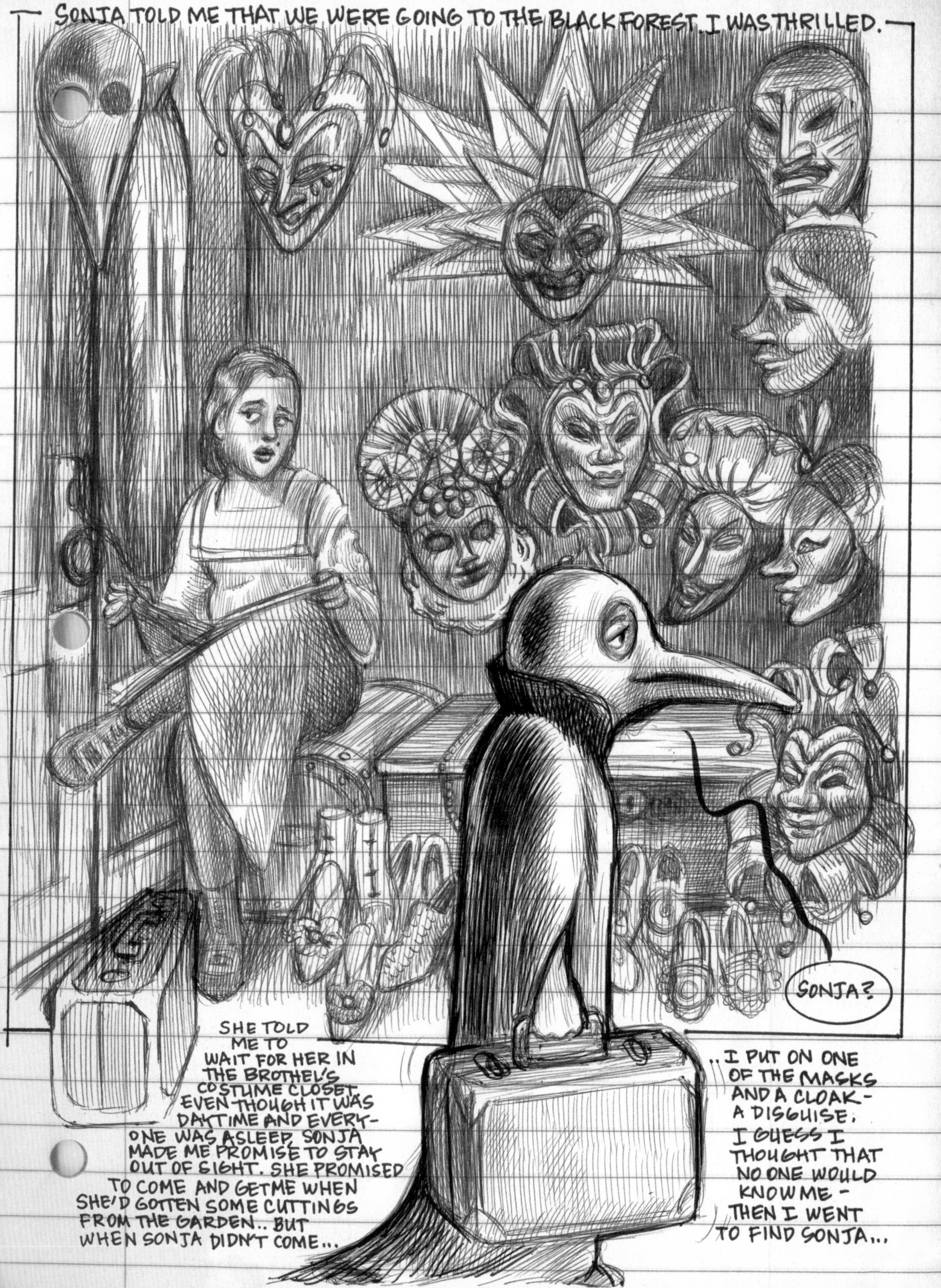
SONJA TOLD ME THAT WE WERE GOING TO THE BLACK FOREST. I WAS THRILLED.
SONJA?
SHE TOLD ME TO WAIT FOR HER IN THE BROTHEL'S COSTUME CLOSET EVEN THOUGH IT WAS DAYTIME AND EVERYONE WAS ASLEEP. SONJA MADE ME PROMISE TO STAY OUT OF SIGHT. SHE PROMISED TO COME AND GET ME WHEN SHE'D GOTTEN SOME CUTTINGS FROM THE GARDEN.. BUT WHEN SONJA DIDN'T COME...
.. I PUT ON ONE OF THE MASKS AND A CLOAK - A DISGUISE. I GUESS I THOUGHT THAT NO ONE WOULD KNOW ME - THEN I WENT TO FIND SONJA...

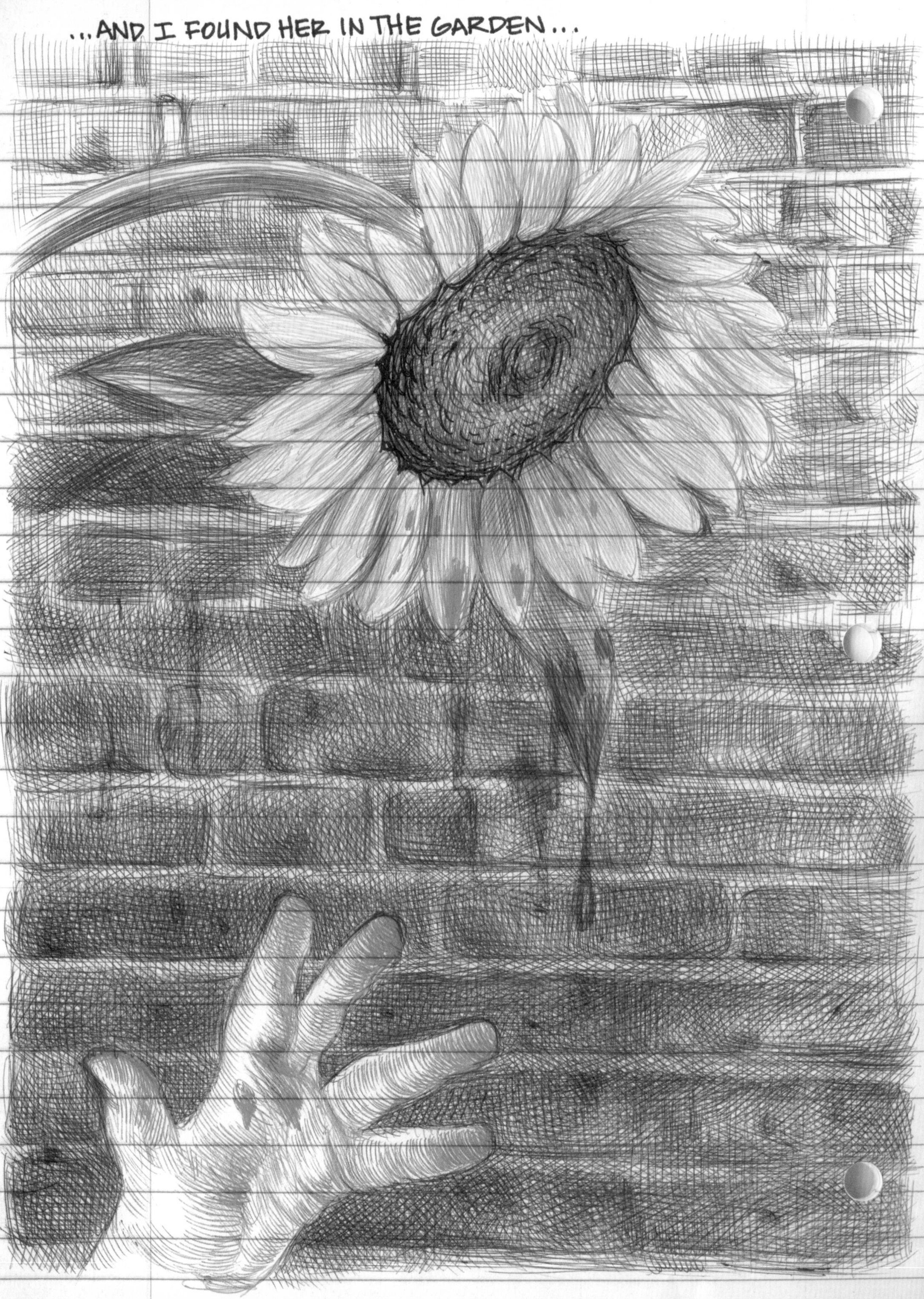
...AND I FOUND HER IN THE GARDEN...

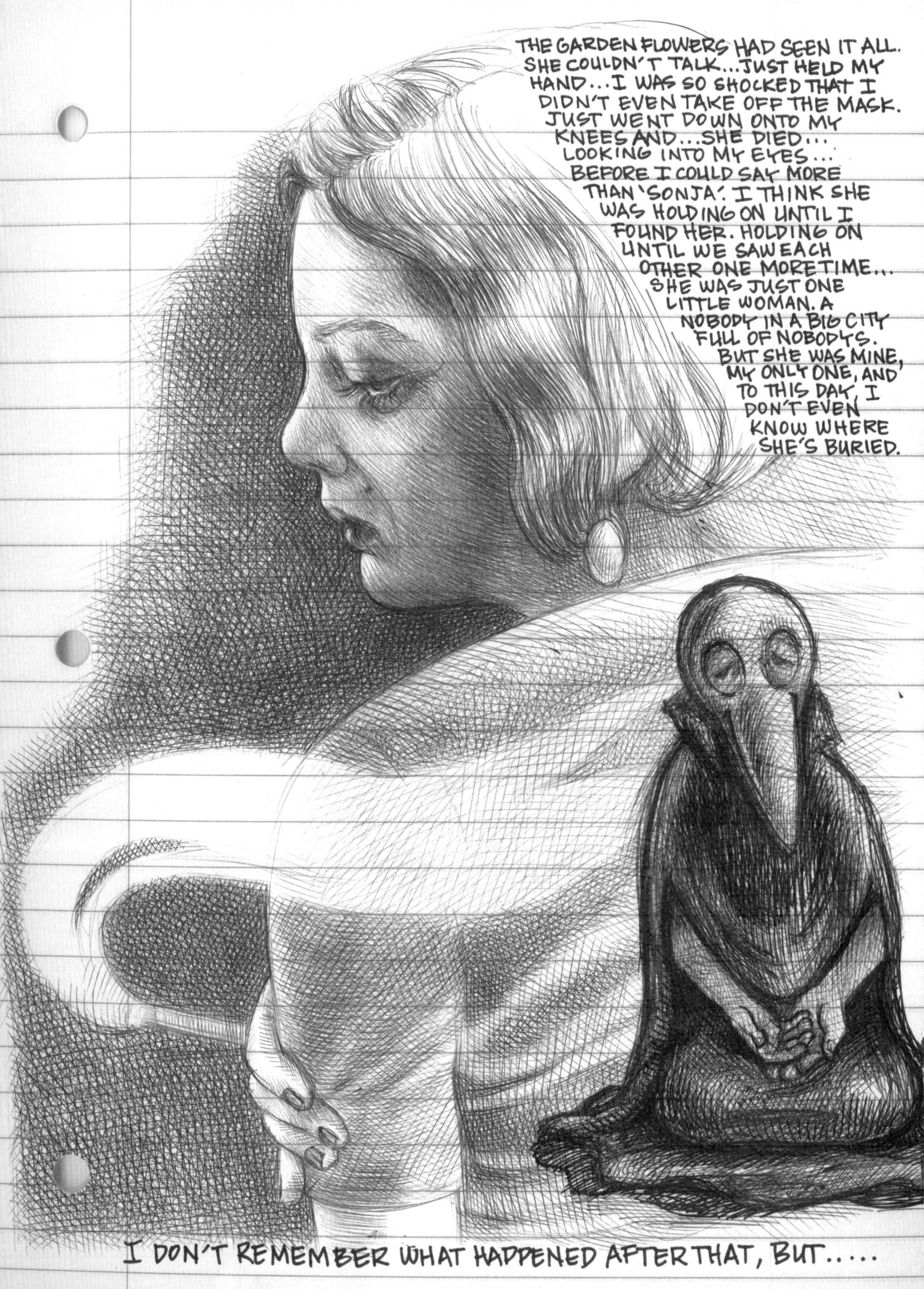
THE GARDEN FLOWERS HAD SEEN IT ALL. SHE COULDN'T TALK... JUST HELD MY HAND... I WAS SO SHOCKED THAT I DIDN'T EVEN TAKE OFF THE MASK. JUST WENT DOWN ONTO MY KNEES AND... SHE DIED... LOOKING INTO MY EYES... BEFORE I COULD SAY MORE THAN 'SONJA'. I THINK SHE WAS HOLDING ON UNTIL I FOUND HER. HOLDING ON UNTIL WE SAW EACH OTHER ONE MORE TIME... SHE WAS JUST ONE LITTLE WOMAN. A NOBODY IN A BIG CITY FULL OF NOBODYS. BUT SHE WAS MINE, MY ONLY ONE, AND TO THIS DAY, I DON'T EVEN KNOW WHERE SHE'S BURIED.
I DON'T REMEMBER WHAT HAPPENED AFTER THAT, BUT.....

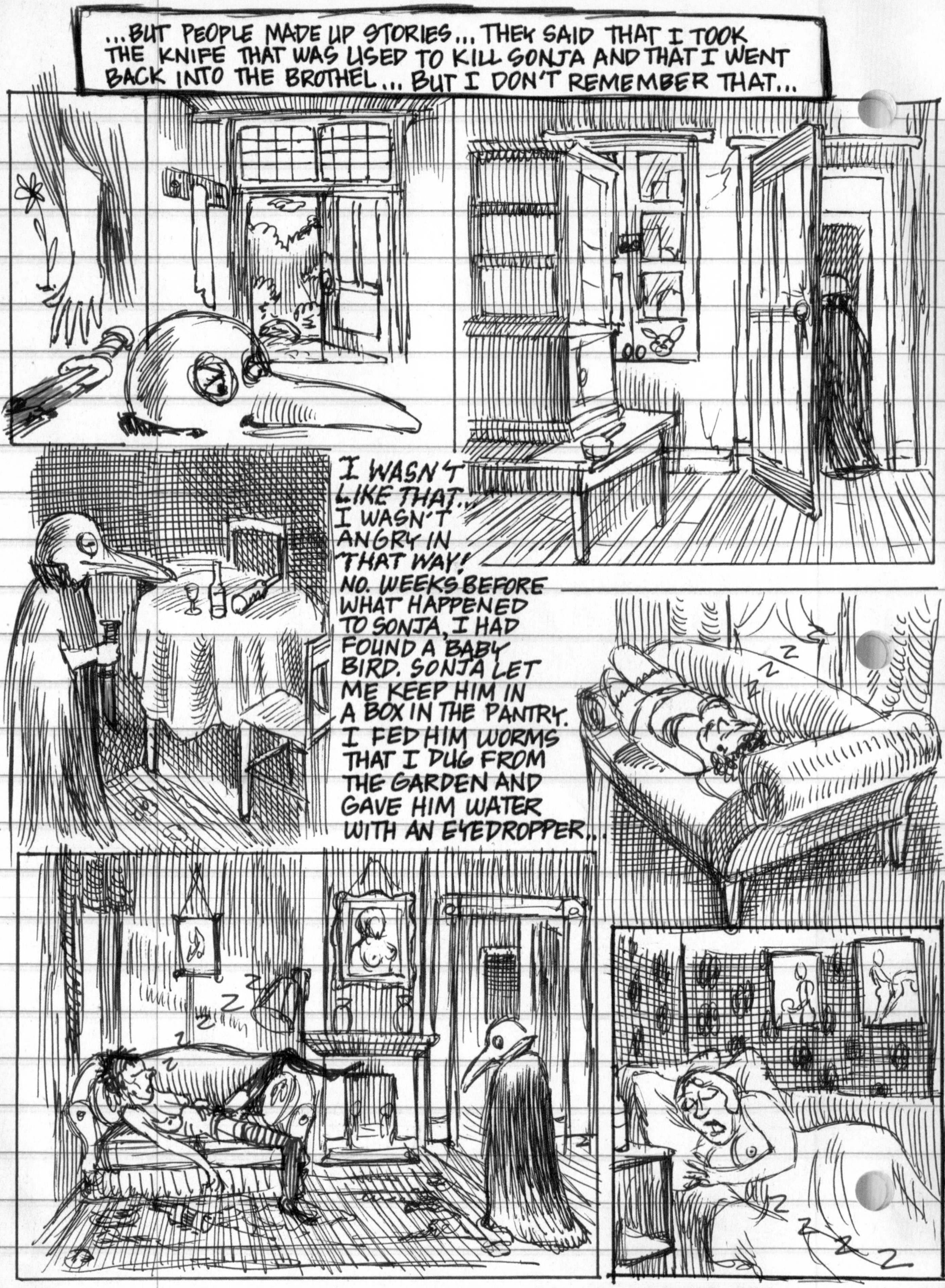
...BUT PEOPLE MADE UP STORIES... THEY SAID THAT I TOOK THE KNIFE THAT WAS USED TO KILL SONJA AND THAT I WENT BACK INTO THE BROTHEL... BUT I DON'T REMEMBER THAT...
I WASN'T LIKE THAT... I WASN'T ANGRY IN THAT WAY!
NO. WEEKS BEFORE WHAT HAPPENED TO SONJA, I HAD FOUND A BABY BIRD. SONJA LET ME KEEP HIM IN A BOX IN THE PANTRY. I FED HIM WORMS THAT I DUG FROM THE GARDEN AND GAVE HIM WATER WITH AN EYEDROPPER...

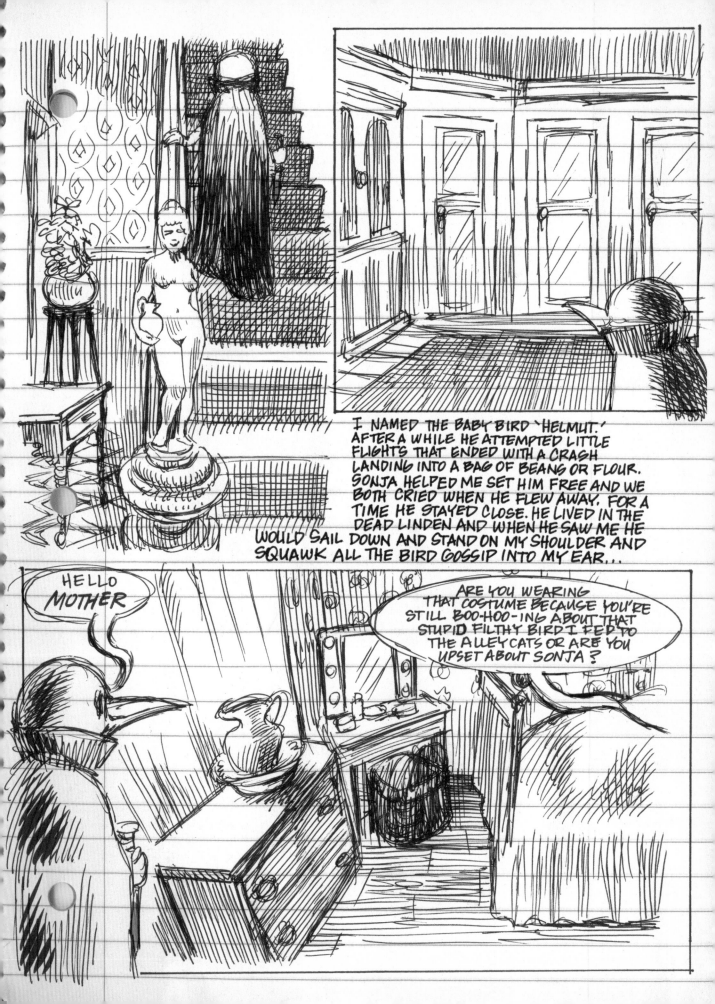

I NAMED THE BABY BIRD 'HELMUT.'
AFTER A WHILE HE ATTEMPTED LITTLE
FLIGHTS THAT ENDED WITH A CRASH
LANDING INTO A BAG OF BEANS OR FLOUR.
SONJA HELPED ME SET HIM FREE AND WE
BOTH CRIED WHEN HE FLEW AWAY. FOR A
TIME HE STAYED CLOSE. HE LIVED IN THE
DEAD LINDEN AND WHEN HE SAW ME HE
WOULD SAIL DOWN AND STAND ON MY SHOULDER AND
SQUAWK ALL THE BIRD GOSSIP INTO MY EAR...

HELLO MOTHER

ARE YOU WEARING
THAT COSTUME BECAUSE YOU'RE
STILL BOO-HOO-ING ABOUT THAT
STUPID FILTHY BIRD I FED TO
THE ALLEY CATS OR ARE YOU
UPSET ABOUT SONJA?

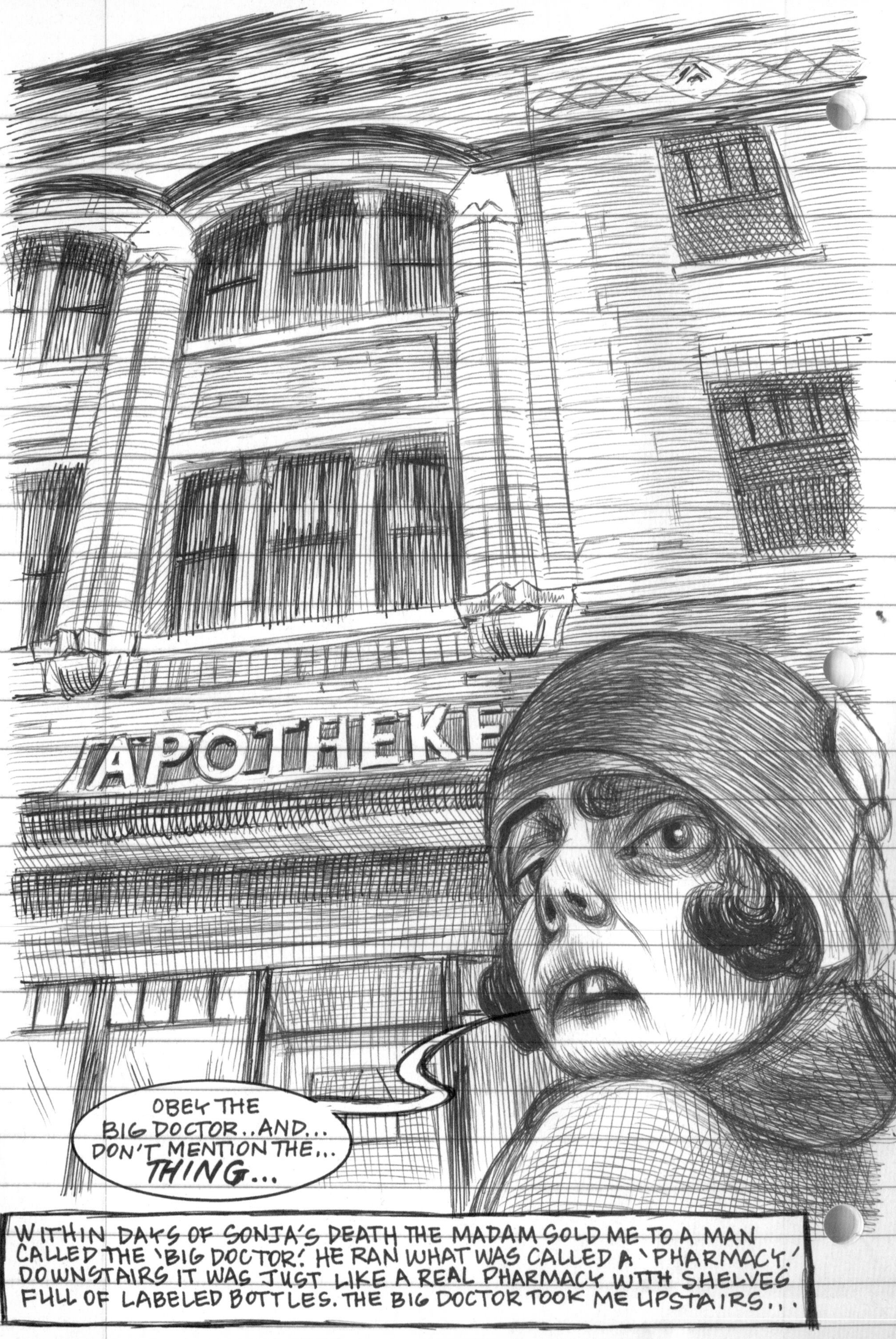
APOTHEKE
OBEY THE BIG DOCTOR..AND... DON'T MENTION THE... THING...
WITHIN DAYS OF SONJA'S DEATH THE MADAM SOLD ME TO A MAN CALLED THE 'BIG DOCTOR.' HE RAN WHAT WAS CALLED A 'PHARMACY.' DOWNSTAIRS IT WAS JUST LIKE A REAL PHARMACY WITH SHELVES FULL OF LABELED BOTTLES. THE BIG DOCTOR TOOK ME UPSTAIRS...

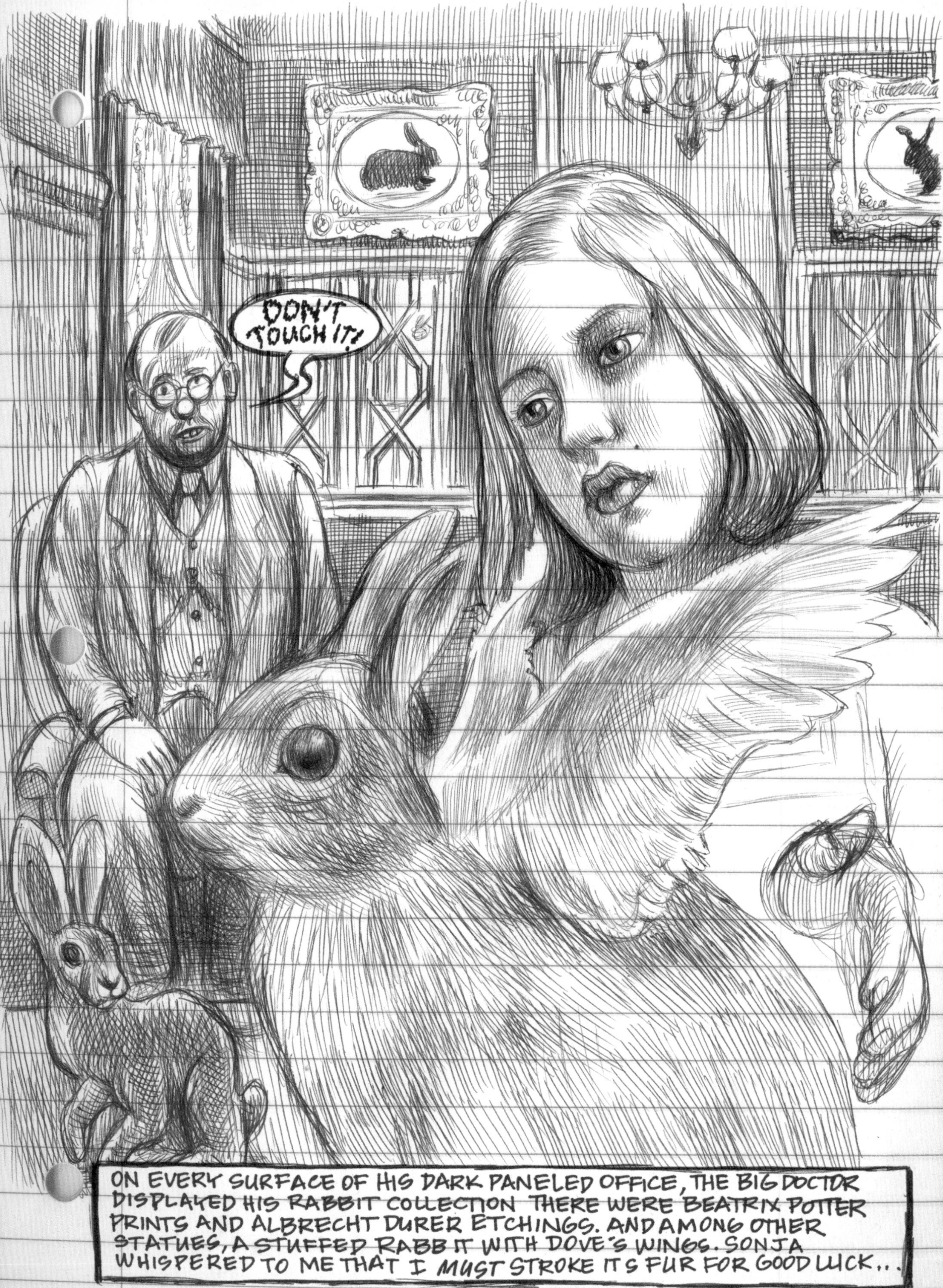
DON'T TOUCH IT!
ON EVERY SURFACE OF HIS DARK PANELED OFFICE, THE BIG DOCTOR
DISPLAYED HIS RABBIT COLLECTION THERE WERE BEATRIX POTTER
PRINTS AND ALBRECHT DURER ETCHINGS. AND AMONG OTHER
STATUES, A STUFFED RABBIT WITH DOVE'S WINGS. SONJA
WHISPERED TO ME THAT I *MUST* STROKE ITS FUR FOR GOOD LUCK...

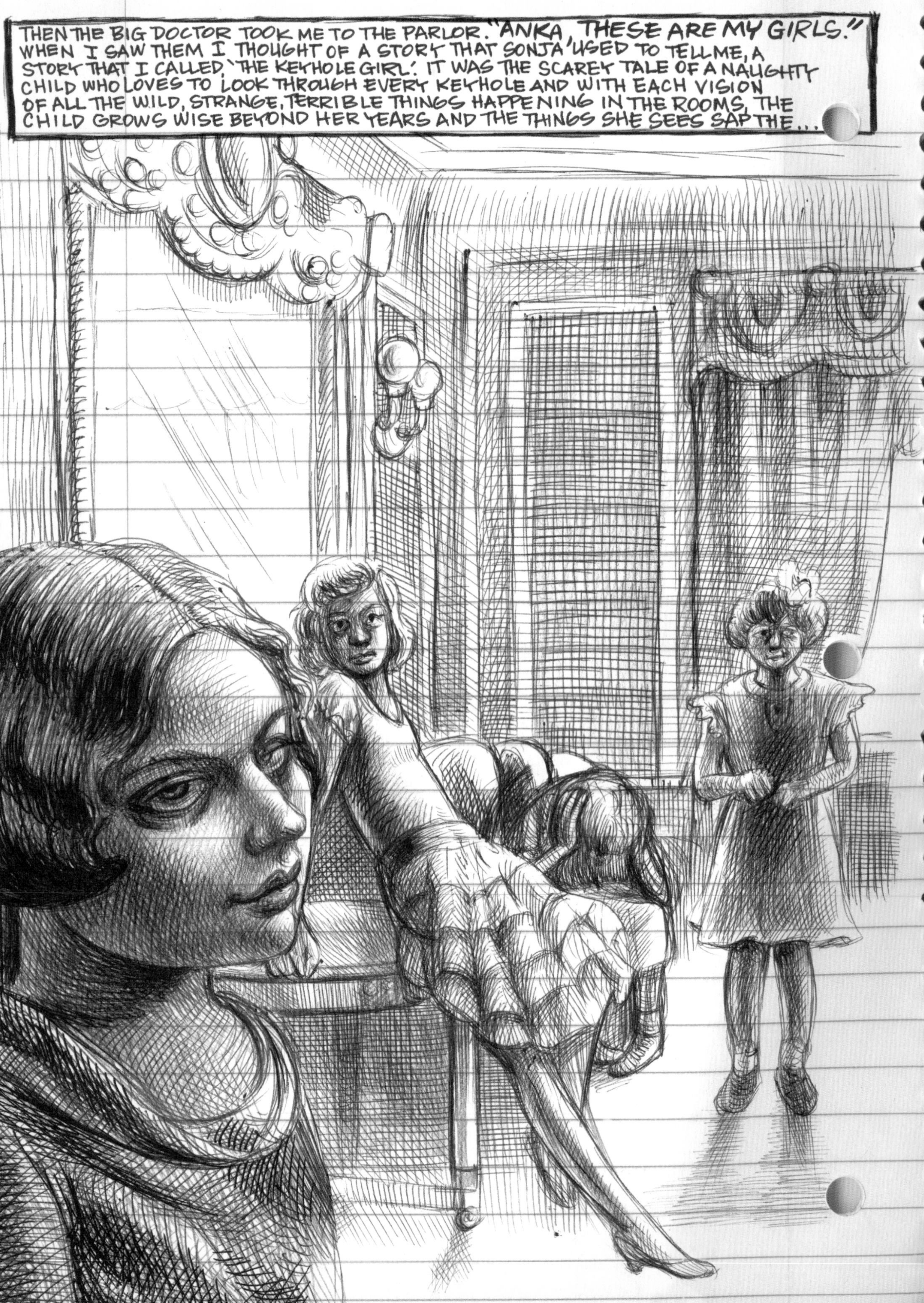
THEN THE BIG DOCTOR TOOK ME TO THE PARLOR. "ANKA, THESE ARE MY GIRLS." WHEN I SAW THEM I THOUGHT OF A STORY THAT SONJA USED TO TELL ME, A STORY THAT I CALLED 'THE KEYHOLE GIRL'. IT WAS THE SCAREY TALE OF A NAUGHTY CHILD WHO LOVES TO LOOK THROUGH EVERY KEYHOLE AND WITH EACH VISION OF ALL THE WILD, STRANGE, TERRIBLE THINGS HAPPENING IN THE ROOMS, THE CHILD GROWS WISE BEYOND HER YEARS AND THE THINGS SHE SEES SAP THE...

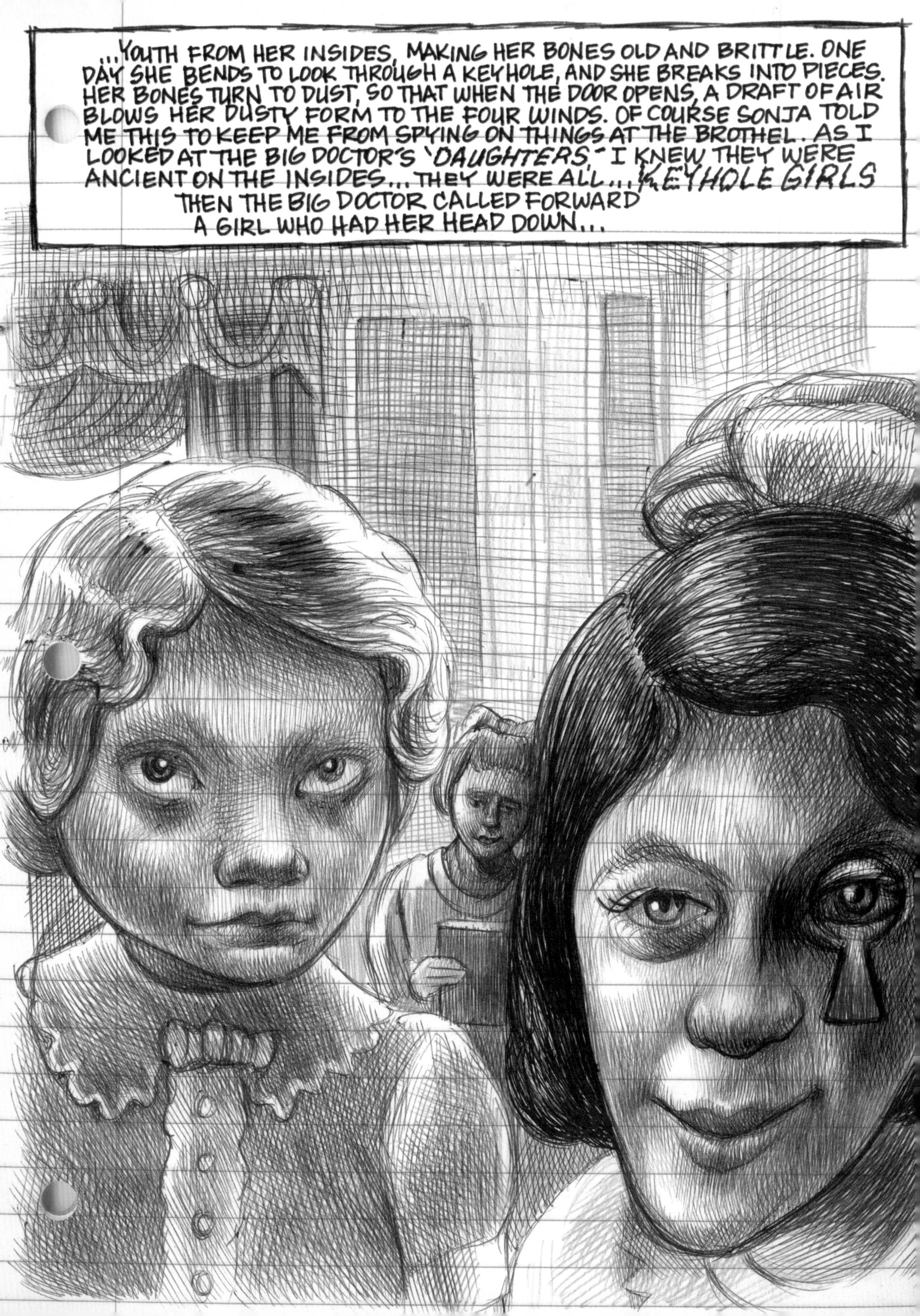
...YOUTH FROM HER INSIDES, MAKING HER BONES OLD AND BRITTLE. ONE DAY SHE BENDS TO LOOK THROUGH A KEYHOLE, AND SHE BREAKS INTO PIECES. HER BONES TURN TO DUST, SO THAT WHEN THE DOOR OPENS, A DRAFT OF AIR BLOWS HER DUSTY FORM TO THE FOUR WINDS. OF COURSE SONJA TOLD ME THIS TO KEEP ME FROM SPYING ON THINGS AT THE BROTHEL. AS I LOOKED AT THE BIG DOCTOR'S 'DAUGHTERS,' I KNEW THEY WERE ANCIENT ON THE INSIDES... THEY WERE ALL... KEYHOLE GIRLS
THEN THE BIG DOCTOR CALLED FORWARD A GIRL WHO HAD HER HEAD DOWN...

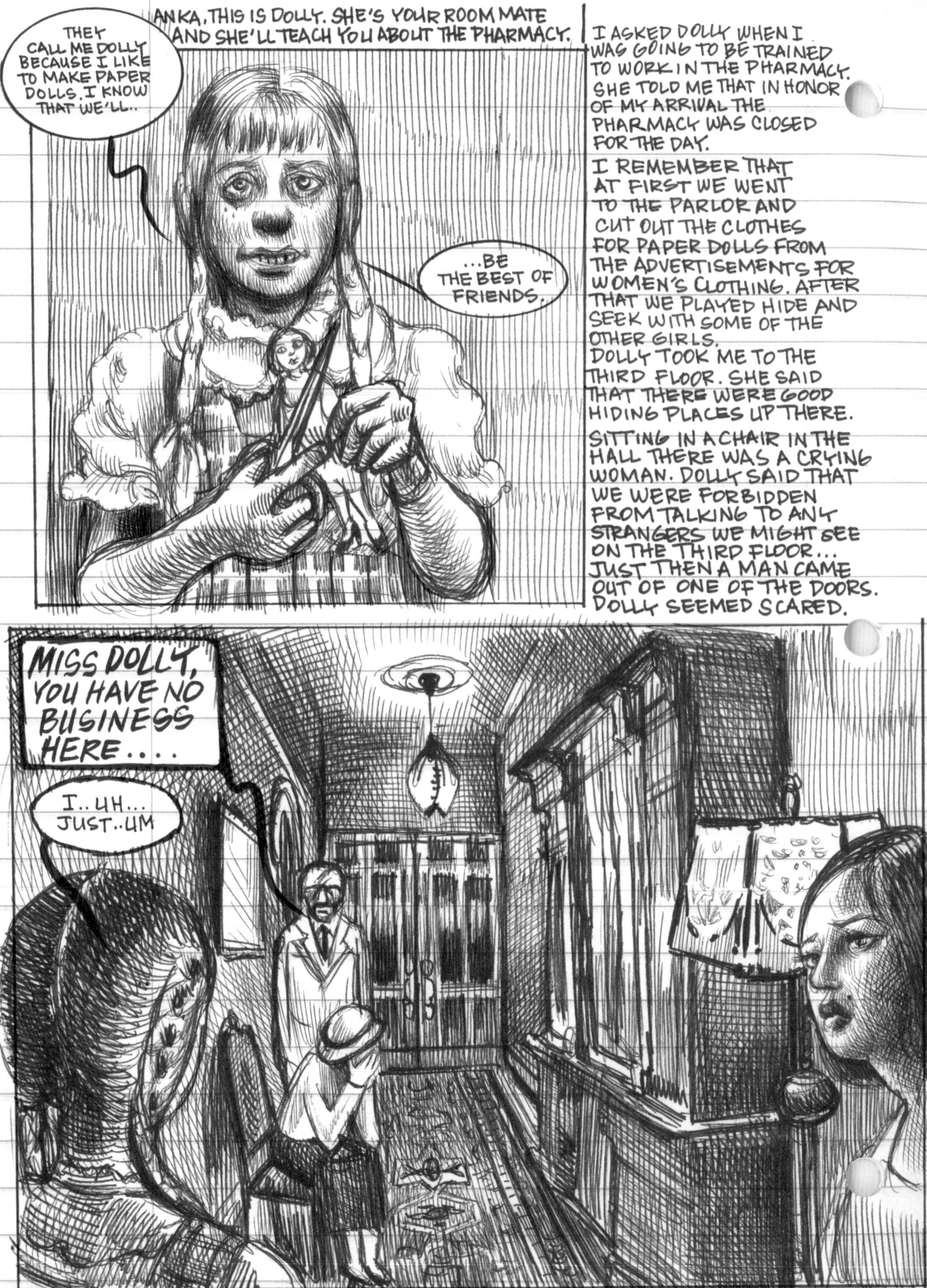
ANKA, THIS IS DOLLY. SHE'S YOUR ROOM MATE AND SHE'LL TEACH YOU ABOUT THE PHARMACY.
THEY CALL ME DOLLY BECAUSE I LIKE TO MAKE PAPER DOLLS. I KNOW THAT WE'LL..
...BE THE BEST OF FRIENDS.
I ASKED DOLLY WHEN I WAS GOING TO BE TRAINED TO WORK IN THE PHARMACY. SHE TOLD ME THAT IN HONOR OF MY ARRIVAL THE PHARMACY WAS CLOSED FOR THE DAY.
I REMEMBER THAT AT FIRST WE WENT TO THE PARLOR AND CUT OUT THE CLOTHES FOR PAPER DOLLS FROM THE ADVERTISEMENTS FOR WOMEN'S CLOTHING. AFTER THAT WE PLAYED HIDE AND SEEK WITH SOME OF THE OTHER GIRLS. DOLLY TOOK ME TO THE THIRD FLOOR. SHE SAID THAT THERE WERE GOOD HIDING PLACES UP THERE.
SITTING IN A CHAIR IN THE HALL THERE WAS A CRYING WOMAN. DOLLY SAID THAT WE WERE FORBIDDEN FROM TALKING TO ANY STRANGERS WE MIGHT SEE ON THE THIRD FLOOR... JUST THEN A MAN CAME OUT OF ONE OF THE DOORS. DOLLY SEEMED SCARED.
MISS DOLLY, YOU HAVE NO BUSINESS HERE....
I.. UH... JUST.. UM

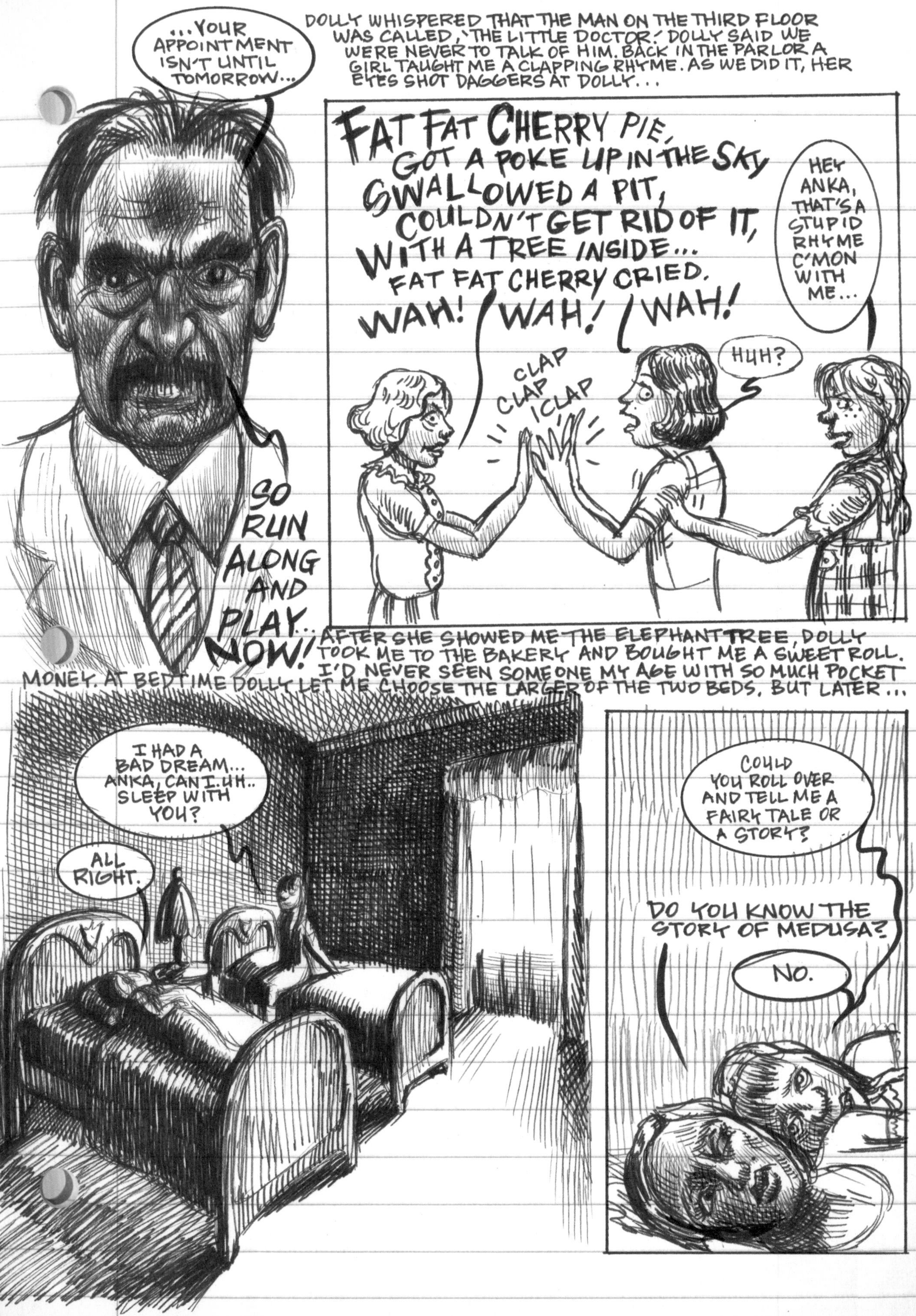
...YOUR APPOINTMENT ISN'T UNTIL TOMORROW...
SO RUN ALONG AND PLAY... NOW!
DOLLY WHISPERED THAT THE MAN ON THE THIRD FLOOR WAS CALLED, 'THE LITTLE DOCTOR.' DOLLY SAID WE WERE NEVER TO TALK OF HIM. BACK IN THE PARLOR A GIRL TAUGHT ME A CLAPPING RHYME. AS WE DID IT, HER EYES SHOT DAGGERS AT DOLLY...
FAT FAT CHERRY PIE, GOT A POKE UP IN THE SKY SWALLOWED A PIT, COULDN'T GET RID OF IT, WITH A TREE INSIDE... FAT FAT CHERRY CRIED.
WAH! WAH! WAH!
CLAP CLAP CLAP
HEY ANKA, THAT'S A STUPID RHYME C'MON WITH ME...
HUH?
AFTER SHE SHOWED ME THE ELEPHANT TREE, DOLLY TOOK ME TO THE BAKERY AND BOUGHT ME A SWEET ROLL. I'D NEVER SEEN SOMEONE MY AGE WITH SO MUCH POCKET MONEY. AT BEDTIME DOLLY LET ME CHOOSE THE LARGER OF THE TWO BEDS, BUT LATER...
I HAD A BAD DREAM... ANKA, CAN I..UH.. SLEEP WITH YOU?
ALL RIGHT.
COULD YOU ROLL OVER AND TELL ME A FAIRY TALE OR A STORY?
DO YOU KNOW THE STORY OF MEDUSA?
NO.

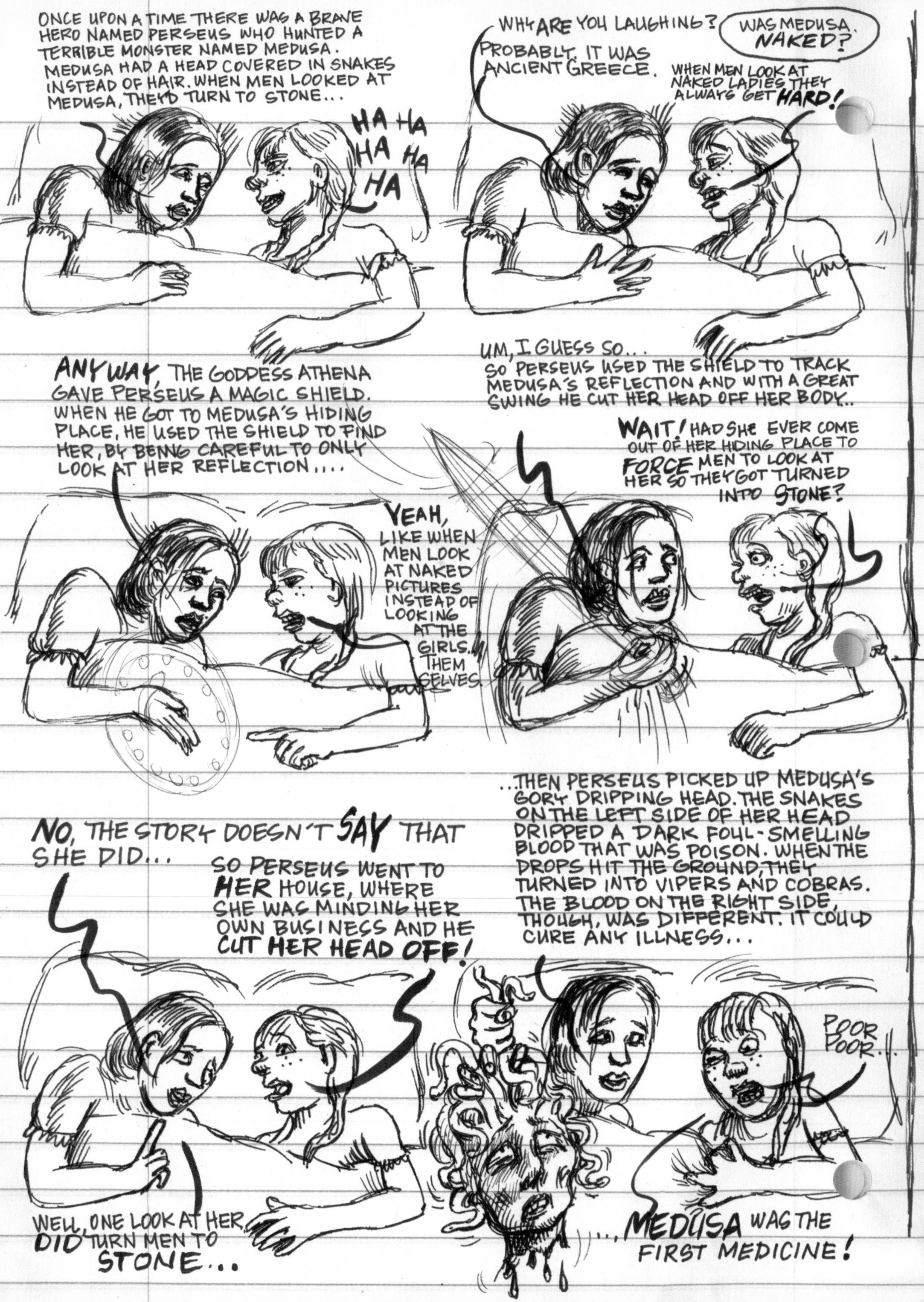

ONCE UPON A TIME THERE WAS A BRAVE HERO NAMED PERSEUS WHO HUNTED A TERRIBLE MONSTER NAMED MEDUSA. MEDUSA HAD A HEAD COVERED IN SNAKES INSTEAD OF HAIR. WHEN MEN LOOKED AT MEDUSA, THEY'D TURN TO STONE...
HA HA HA HA HA
WHY ARE YOU LAUGHING?
WAS MEDUSA NAKED?
PROBABLY. IT WAS ANCIENT GREECE.
WHEN MEN LOOK AT NAKED LADIES THEY ALWAYS GET HARD!
ANYWAY, THE GODDESS ATHENA GAVE PERSEUS A MAGIC SHIELD. WHEN HE GOT TO MEDUSA'S HIDING PLACE, HE USED THE SHIELD TO FIND HER, BY BEING CAREFUL TO ONLY LOOK AT HER REFLECTION....
YEAH, LIKE WHEN MEN LOOK AT NAKED PICTURES INSTEAD OF LOOKING AT THE GIRLS THEM SELVES.
UM, I GUESS SO... SO PERSEUS USED THE SHIELD TO TRACK MEDUSA'S REFLECTION AND WITH A GREAT SWING HE CUT HER HEAD OFF HER BODY..
WAIT! HAD SHE EVER COME OUT OF HER HIDING PLACE TO FORCE MEN TO LOOK AT HER SO THEY GOT TURNED INTO STONE?
NO, THE STORY DOESN'T SAY THAT SHE DID...
SO PERSEUS WENT TO HER HOUSE, WHERE SHE WAS MINDING HER OWN BUSINESS AND HE CUT HER HEAD OFF!
WELL, ONE LOOK AT HER DID TURN MEN TO STONE...
...THEN PERSEUS PICKED UP MEDUSA'S GORY DRIPPING HEAD. THE SNAKES ON THE LEFT SIDE OF HER HEAD DRIPPED A DARK FOUL-SMELLING BLOOD THAT WAS POISON. WHEN THE DROPS HIT THE GROUND, THEY TURNED INTO VIPERS AND COBRAS. THE BLOOD ON THE RIGHT SIDE, THOUGH, WAS DIFFERENT. IT COULD CURE ANY ILLNESS...
POOR POOR...
...MEDUSA WAS THE FIRST MEDICINE!

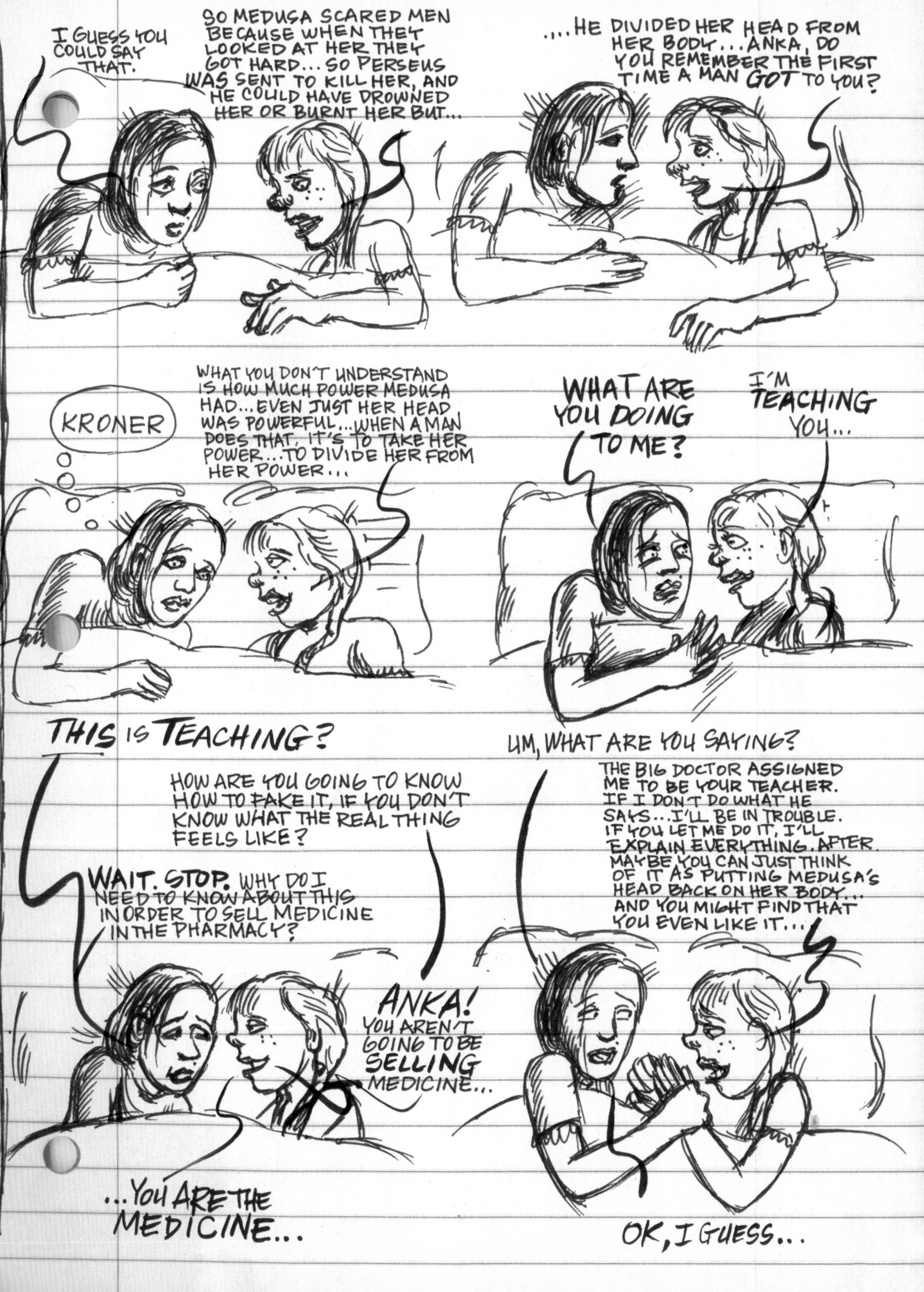
I GUESS YOU COULD SAY THAT.
SO MEDUSA SCARED MEN BECAUSE WHEN THEY LOOKED AT HER THEY GOT HARD... SO PERSEUS WAS SENT TO KILL HER, AND HE COULD HAVE DROWNED HER OR BURNT HER BUT...
....HE DIVIDED HER HEAD FROM HER BODY... ANKA, DO YOU REMEMBER THE FIRST TIME A MAN GOT TO YOU?
KRONER
WHAT YOU DON'T UNDERSTAND IS HOW MUCH POWER MEDUSA HAD... EVEN JUST HER HEAD WAS POWERFUL... WHEN A MAN DOES THAT, IT'S TO TAKE HER POWER... TO DIVIDE HER FROM HER POWER...
WHAT ARE YOU DOING TO ME?
I'M TEACHING YOU...
THIS is TEACHING?
HOW ARE YOU GOING TO KNOW HOW TO FAKE IT, IF YOU DON'T KNOW WHAT THE REAL THING FEELS LIKE?
WAIT. STOP. WHY DO I NEED TO KNOW ABOUT THIS IN ORDER TO SELL MEDICINE IN THE PHARMACY?
ANKA! YOU AREN'T GOING TO BE SELLING MEDICINE...
...YOU ARE THE MEDICINE...
UM, WHAT ARE YOU SAYING?
THE BIG DOCTOR ASSIGNED ME TO BE YOUR TEACHER. IF I DON'T DO WHAT HE SAYS... I'LL BE IN TROUBLE. IF YOU LET ME DO IT, I'LL EXPLAIN EVERYTHING. AFTER. MAYBE YOU CAN JUST THINK OF IT AS PUTTING MEDUSA'S HEAD BACK ON HER BODY... AND YOU MIGHT FIND THAT YOU EVEN LIKE IT...
OK, I GUESS...

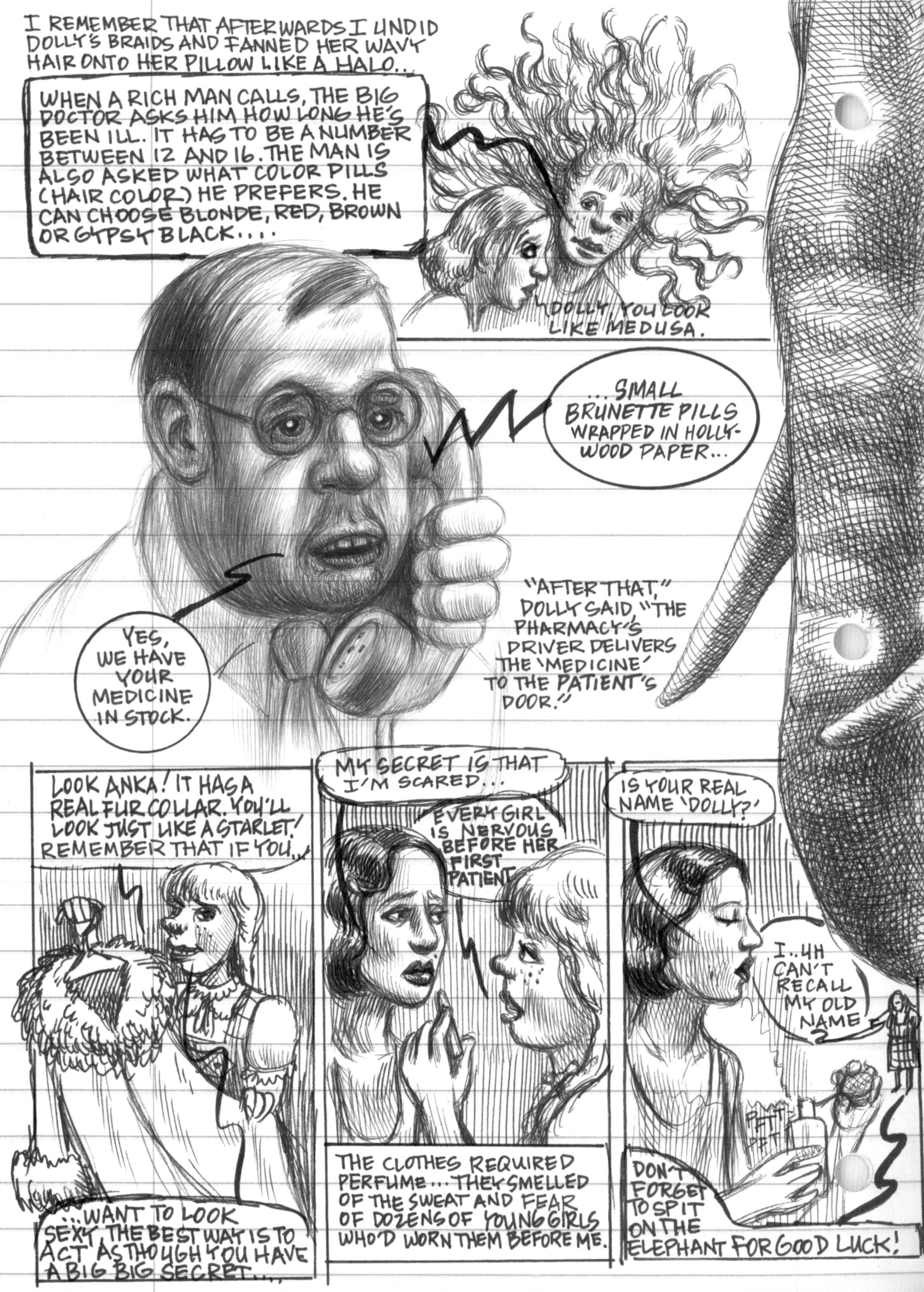
I REMEMBER THAT AFTERWARDS I UNDID DOLLY'S BRAIDS AND FANNED HER WAVY HAIR ONTO HER PILLOW LIKE A HALO...
WHEN A RICH MAN CALLS, THE BIG DOCTOR ASKS HIM HOW LONG HE'S BEEN ILL. IT HAS TO BE A NUMBER BETWEEN 12 AND 16. THE MAN IS ALSO ASKED WHAT COLOR PILLS (HAIR COLOR) HE PREFERS. HE CAN CHOOSE BLONDE, RED, BROWN OR GYPSY BLACK....
DOLLY, YOU LOOK LIKE MEDUSA.
...SMALL BRUNETTE PILLS WRAPPED IN HOLLY-WOOD PAPER...
YES, WE HAVE YOUR MEDICINE IN STOCK.
"AFTER THAT," DOLLY SAID, "THE PHARMACY'S DRIVER DELIVERS THE 'MEDICINE' TO THE PATIENT'S DOOR."
LOOK ANKA! IT HAS A REAL FUR COLLAR. YOU'LL LOOK JUST LIKE A STARLET! REMEMBER THAT IF YOU...
...WANT TO LOOK SEXY, THE BEST WAY IS TO ACT AS THOUGH YOU HAVE A BIG BIG SECRET...
MY SECRET IS THAT I'M SCARED...
EVERY GIRL IS NERVOUS BEFORE HER FIRST PATIENT.
THE CLOTHES REQUIRED PERFUME... THEY SMELLED OF THE SWEAT AND FEAR OF DOZENS OF YOUNG GIRLS WHO'D WORN THEM BEFORE ME.
IS YOUR REAL NAME 'DOLLY?'
I...UH CAN'T RECALL MY OLD NAME
PFFT PFFT
DON'T FORGET TO SPIT ON THE ELEPHANT FOR GOOD LUCK!

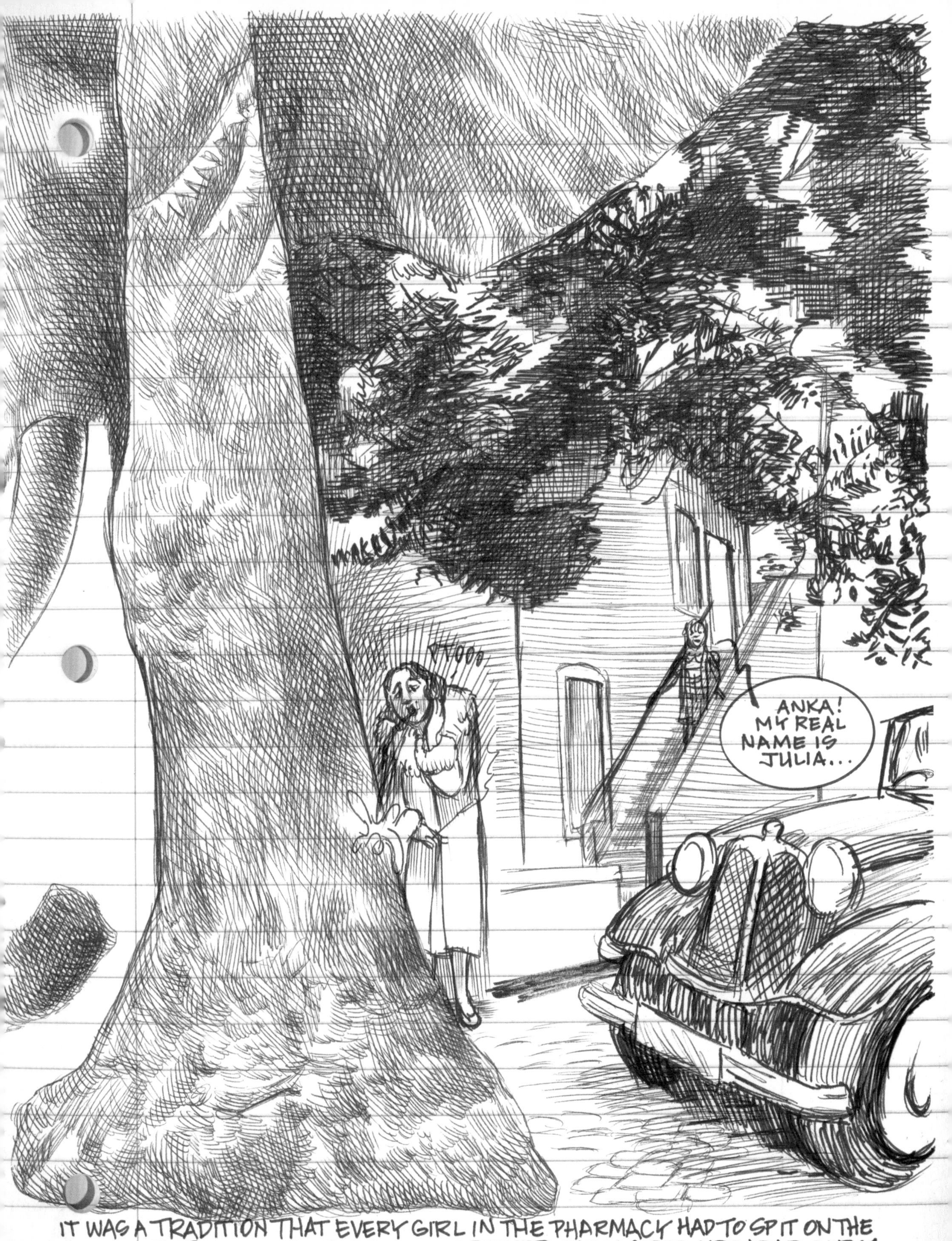
PTOOO
ANKA! MY REAL NAME IS JULIA...

IT WAS A TRADITION THAT EVERY GIRL IN THE PHARMACY HAD TO SPIT ON THE ELEPHANT TREE BEHIND THE BUILDING BEFORE SHE VISITED HER 'PATIENTS'. THERE WAS A DESPERATION IN JULIA'S VOICE THAT I DIDN'T UNDERSTAND AT THE TIME.

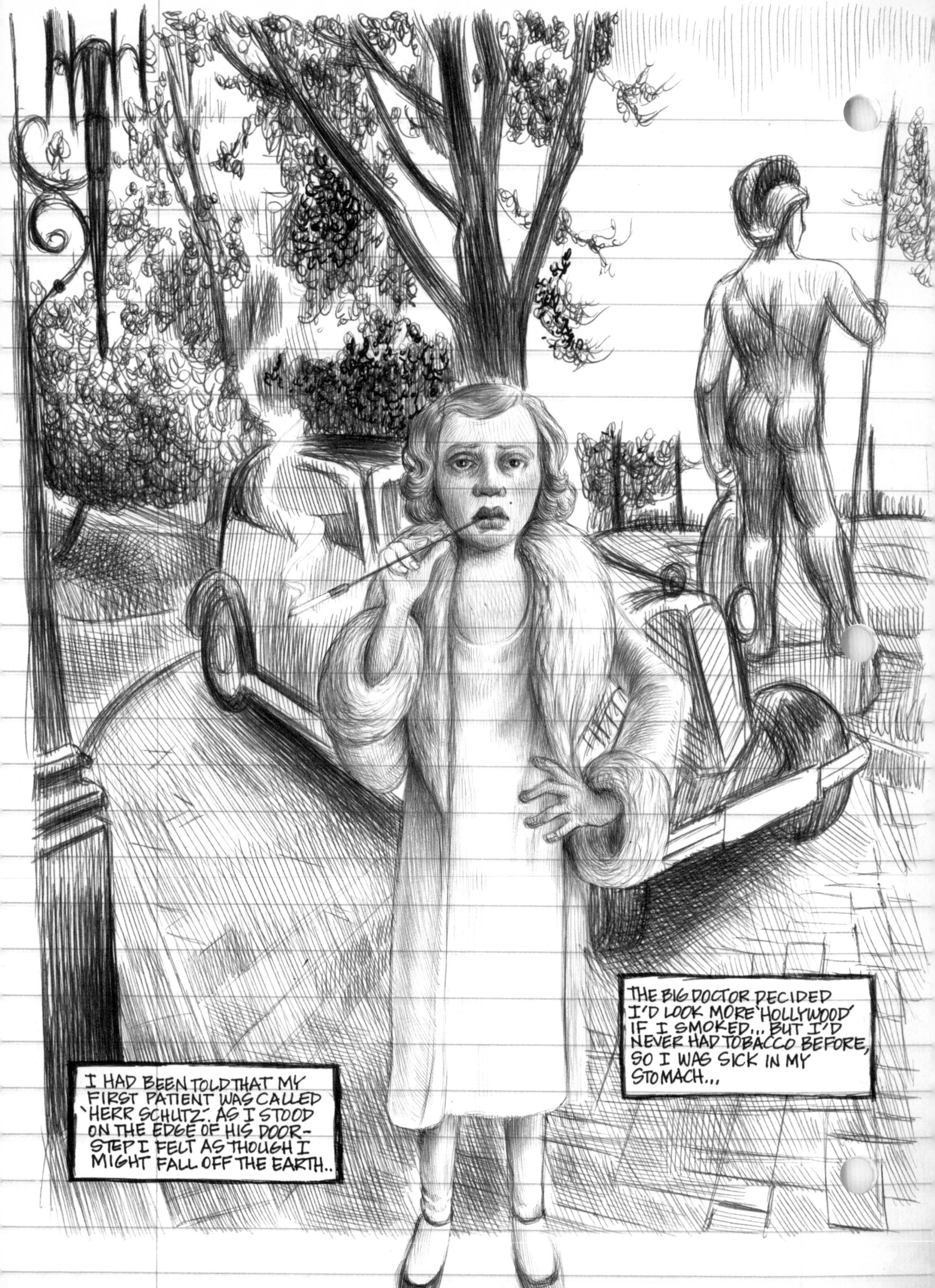
I HAD BEEN TOLD THAT MY FIRST PATIENT WAS CALLED 'HERR SCHUTZ'. AS I STOOD ON THE EDGE OF HIS DOOR-STEP I FELT AS THOUGH I MIGHT FALL OFF THE EARTH..
THE BIG DOCTOR DECIDED I'D LOOK MORE 'HOLLYWOOD' IF I SMOKED... BUT I'D NEVER HAD TOBACCO BEFORE, SO I WAS SICK IN MY STOMACH...

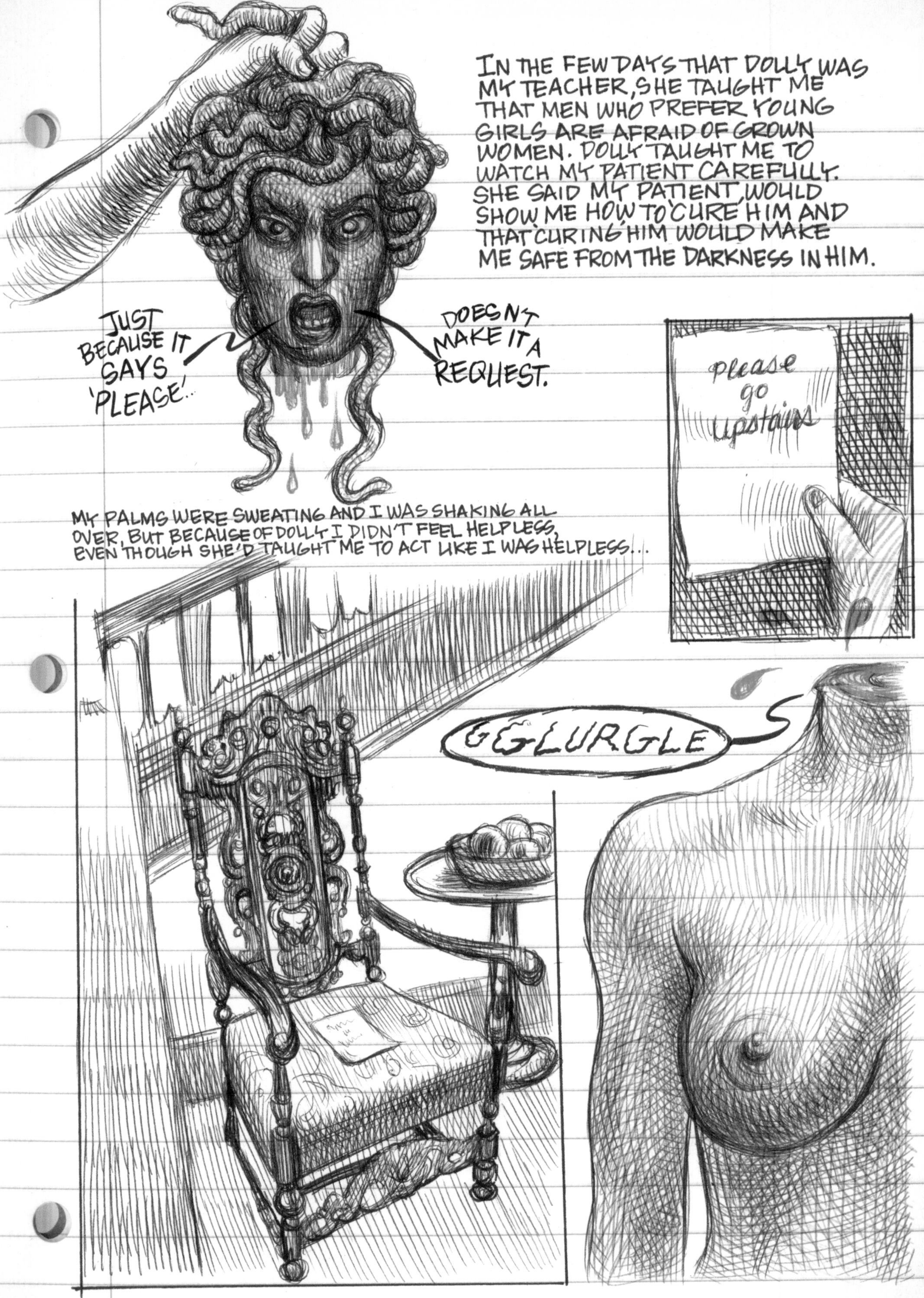
IN THE FEW DAYS THAT DOLLY WAS MY TEACHER, SHE TAUGHT ME THAT MEN WHO PREFER YOUNG GIRLS ARE AFRAID OF GROWN WOMEN. DOLLY TAUGHT ME TO WATCH MY PATIENT CAREFULLY. SHE SAID MY PATIENT WOULD SHOW ME HOW TO 'CURE' HIM AND THAT 'CURING' HIM WOULD MAKE ME SAFE FROM THE DARKNESS IN HIM.
JUST BECAUSE IT SAYS 'PLEASE'...
DOESN'T MAKE IT A REQUEST.
please go upstairs
MY PALMS WERE SWEATING AND I WAS SHAKING ALL OVER, BUT BECAUSE OF DOLLY I DIDN'T FEEL HELPLESS, EVEN THOUGH SHE'D TAUGHT ME TO ACT LIKE I WAS HELPLESS...
GGLURGLE

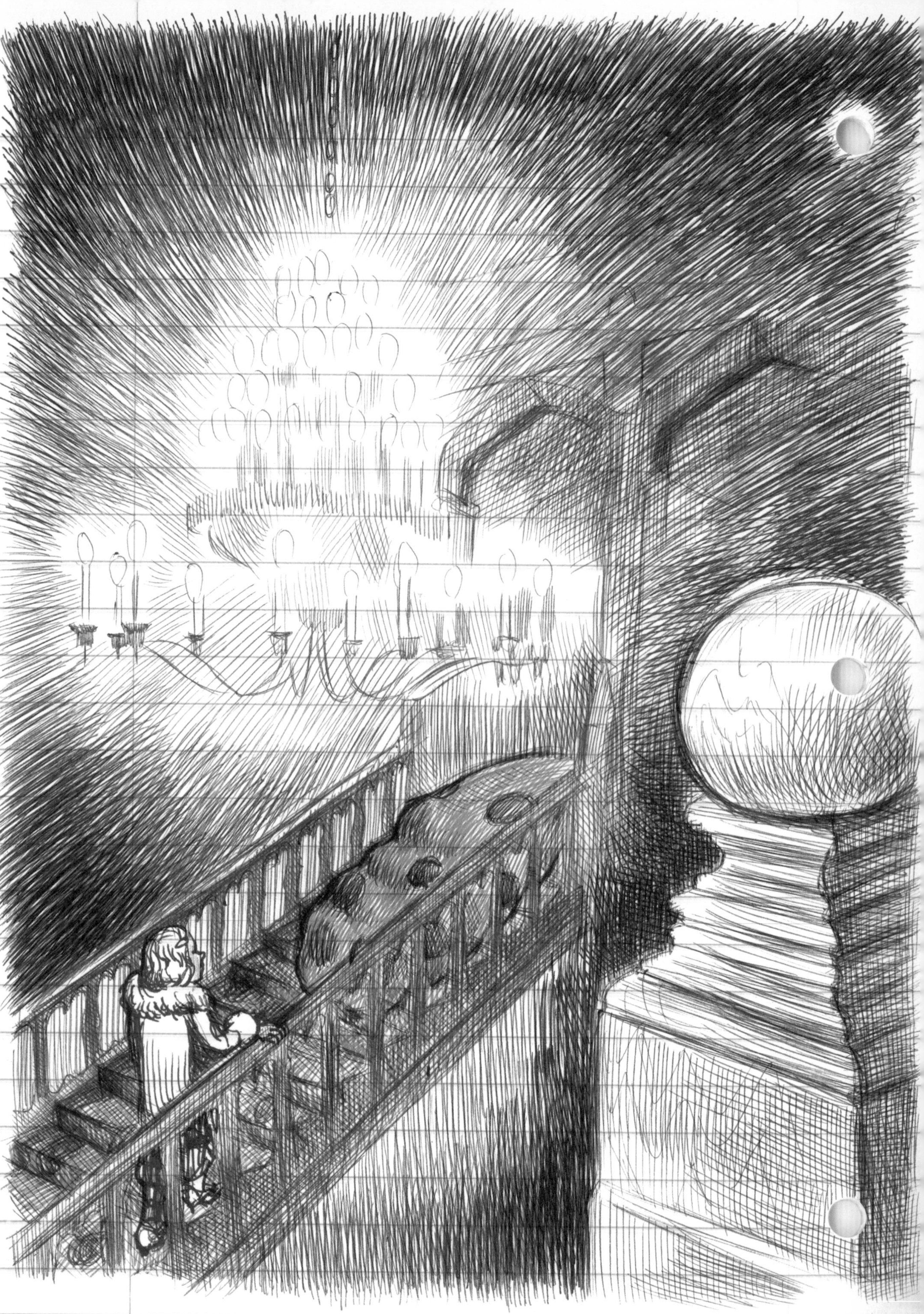

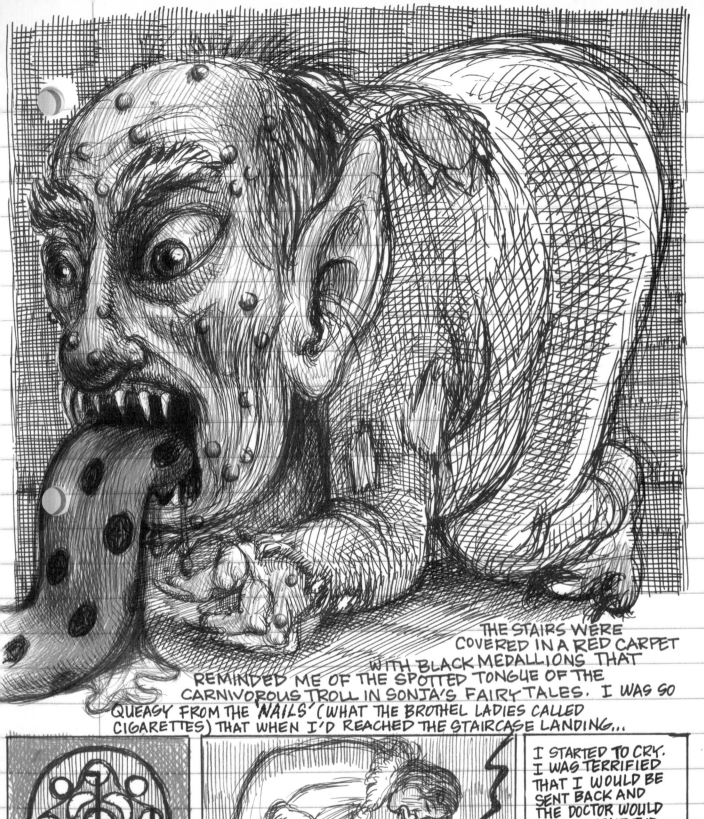

THE STAIRS WERE COVERED IN A RED CARPET WITH BLACK MEDALLIONS THAT REMINDED ME OF THE SPOTTED TONGUE OF THE CARNIVOROUS TROLL IN SONJA'S FAIRY TALES. I WAS SO QUEASY FROM THE 'NAILS' (WHAT THE BROTHEL LADIES CALLED CIGARETTES) THAT WHEN I'D REACHED THE STAIRCASE LANDING...

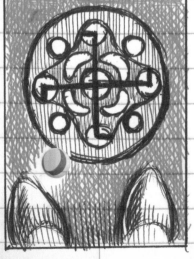

WHAT DO WE HAVE HERE?

I STARTED TO CRY. I WAS TERRIFIED THAT I WOULD BE SENT BACK AND THE DOCTOR WOULD BE TOLD THAT I'D FAILED TO 'CURE' THE PATIENT OR MAYBE WORSE, HE'D BE TOLD THAT I'D MADE THE MAN SICKER AND I'D BE THROWN ONTO THE STREET...

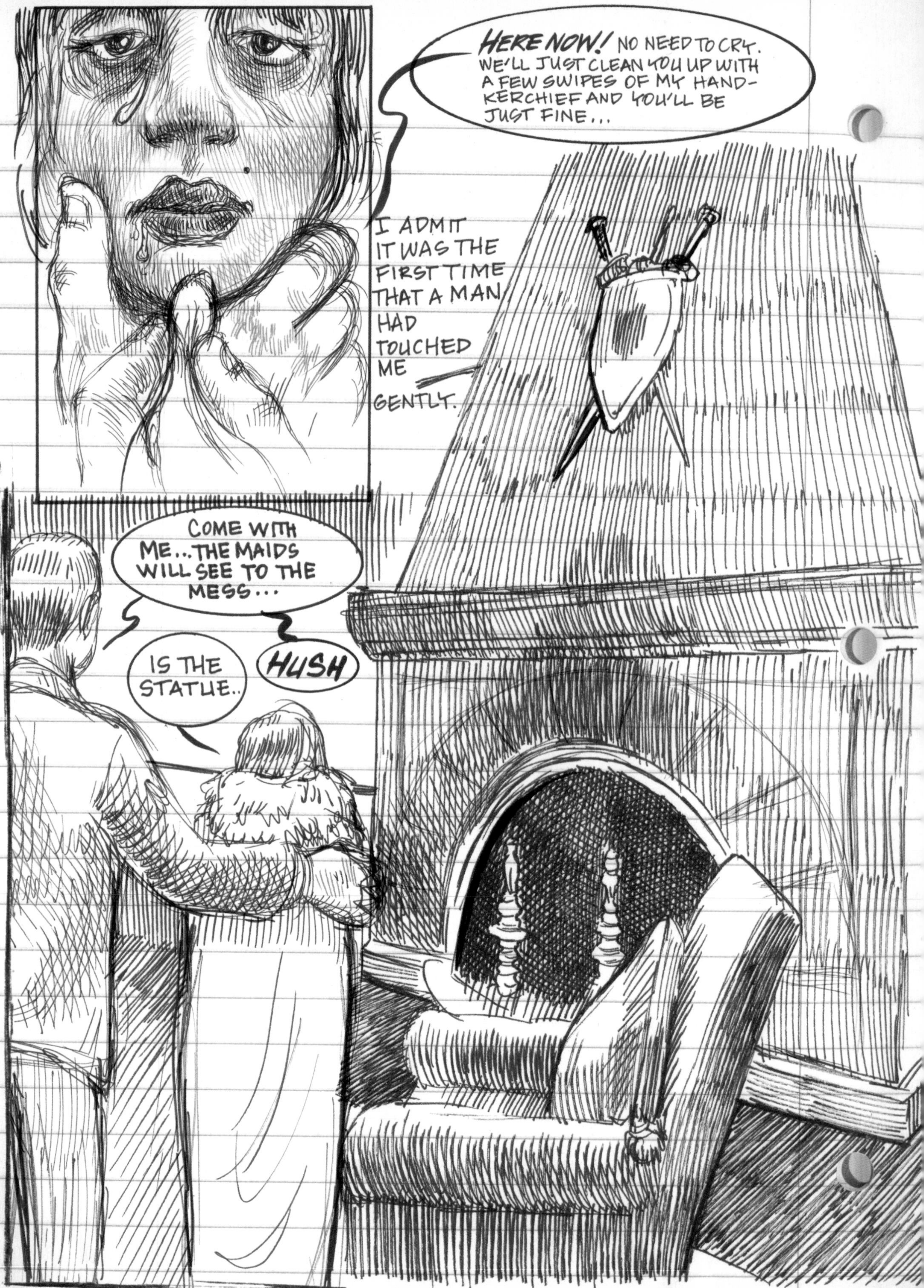
HERE NOW! NO NEED TO CRY. WE'LL JUST CLEAN YOU UP WITH A FEW SWIPES OF MY HANDKERCHIEF AND YOU'LL BE JUST FINE...
I ADMIT IT WAS THE FIRST TIME THAT A MAN HAD TOUCHED ME
GENTLY.
COME WITH ME...THE MAIDS WILL SEE TO THE MESS...
IS THE STATUE..
HUSH

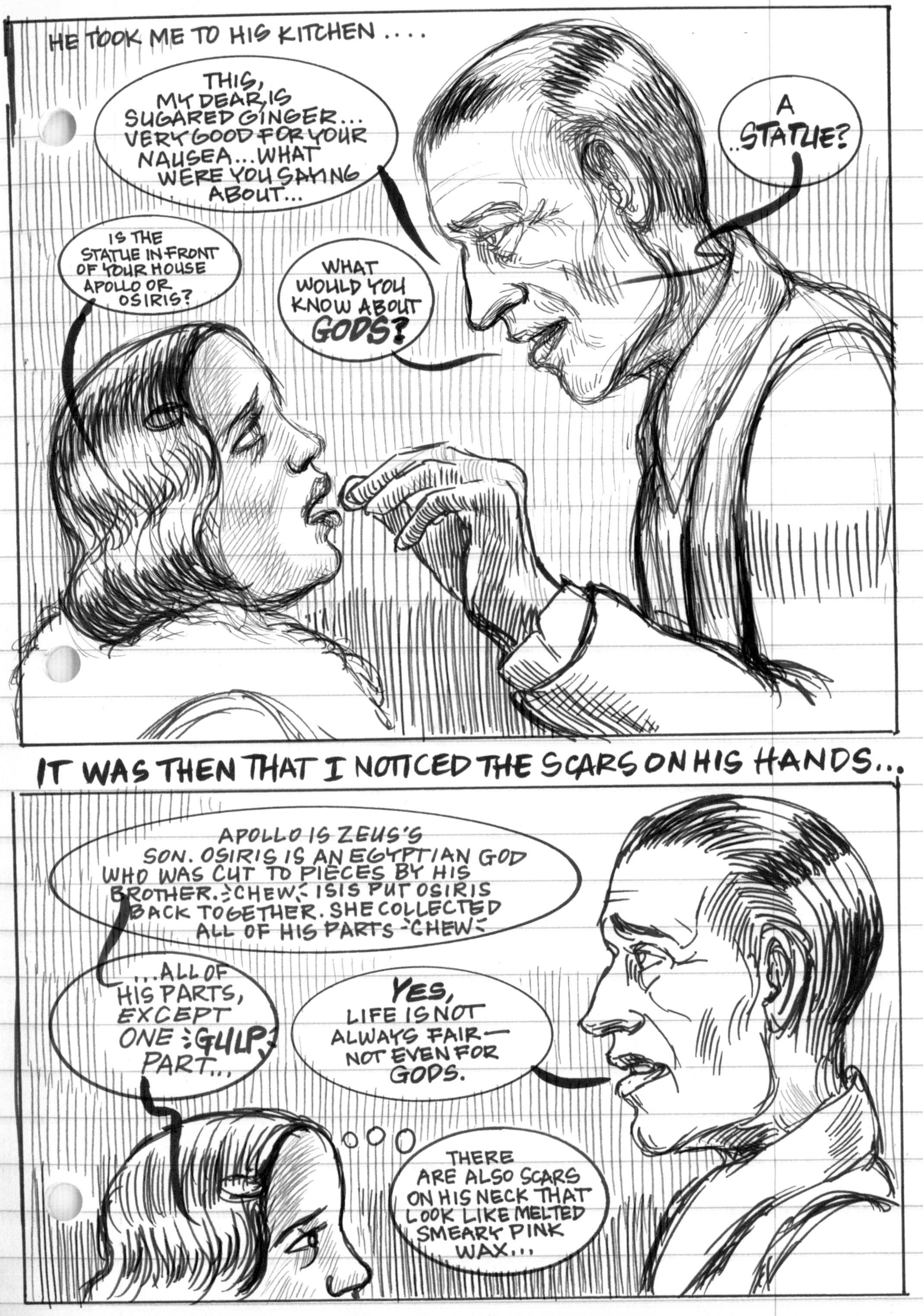
HE TOOK ME TO HIS KITCHEN....
THIS, MY DEAR, IS SUGARED GINGER... VERY GOOD FOR YOUR NAUSEA... WHAT WERE YOU SAYING ABOUT...
A ..STATUE?
IS THE STATUE IN FRONT OF YOUR HOUSE APOLLO OR OSIRIS?
WHAT WOULD YOU KNOW ABOUT GODS?
IT WAS THEN THAT I NOTICED THE SCARS ON HIS HANDS...
APOLLO IS ZEUS'S SON. OSIRIS IS AN EGYPTIAN GOD WHO WAS CUT TO PIECES BY HIS BROTHER. CHEW ISIS PUT OSIRIS BACK TOGETHER. SHE COLLECTED ALL OF HIS PARTS CHEW
...ALL OF HIS PARTS, EXCEPT ONE GULP PART...
YES, LIFE IS NOT ALWAYS FAIR— NOT EVEN FOR GODS.
THERE ARE ALSO SCARS ON HIS NECK THAT LOOK LIKE MELTED SMEARY PINK WAX...

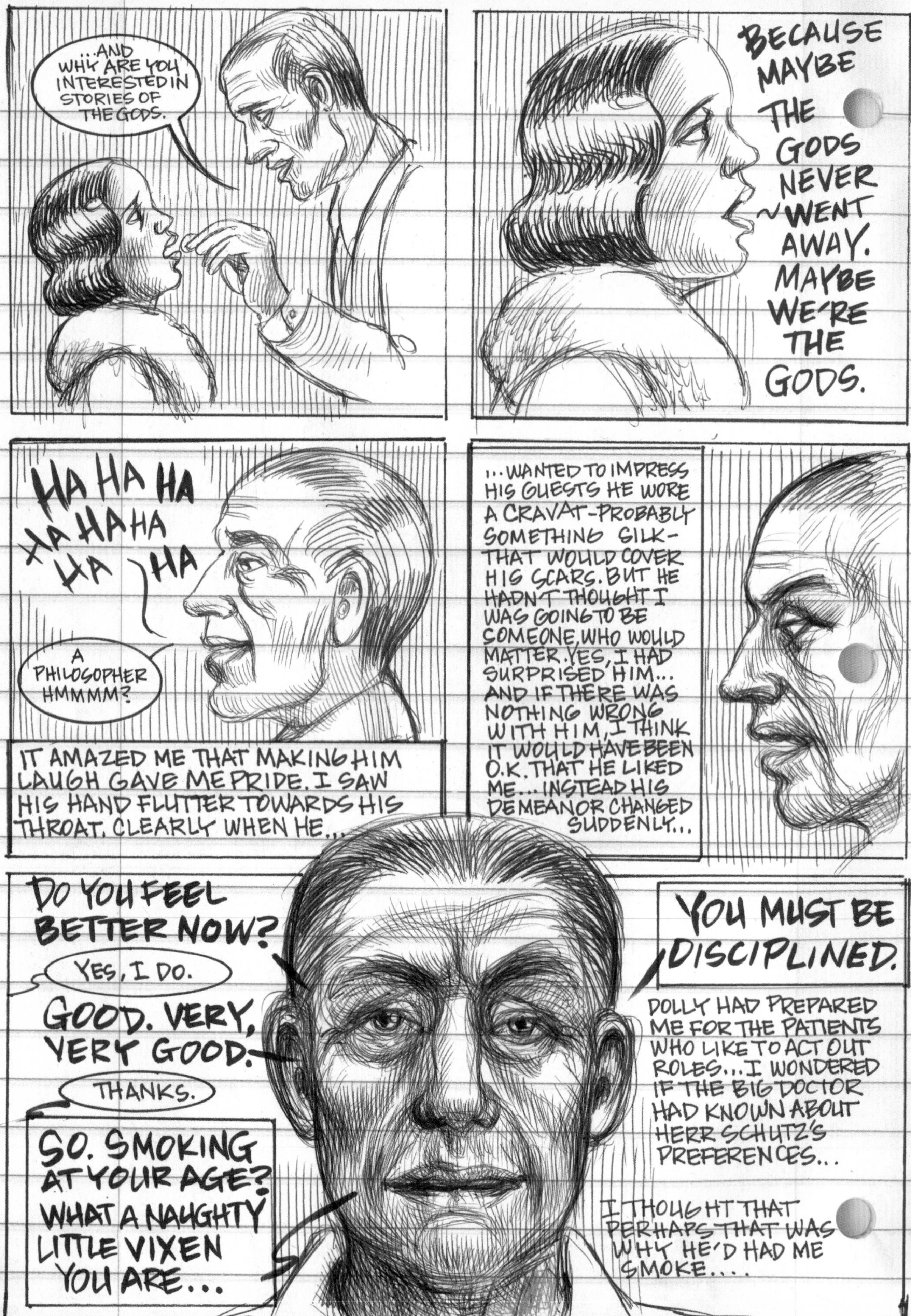
...AND WHY ARE YOU INTERESTED IN STORIES OF THE GODS.
BECAUSE MAYBE THE GODS NEVER WENT AWAY. MAYBE WE'RE THE GODS.
HA HA HA HA HA HA HA HA
A PHILOSOPHER HMMMM?
IT AMAZED ME THAT MAKING HIM LAUGH GAVE ME PRIDE. I SAW HIS HAND FLUTTER TOWARDS HIS THROAT. CLEARLY WHEN HE...
...WANTED TO IMPRESS HIS GUESTS HE WORE A CRAVAT-PROBABLY SOMETHING SILK-THAT WOULD COVER HIS SCARS. BUT HE HADN'T THOUGHT I WAS GOING TO BE SOMEONE, WHO WOULD MATTER. YES, I HAD SURPRISED HIM... AND IF THERE WAS NOTHING WRONG WITH HIM, I THINK IT WOULD HAVE BEEN O.K. THAT HE LIKED ME... INSTEAD HIS DEMEANOR CHANGED SUDDENLY...
DO YOU FEEL BETTER NOW?
YES, I DO.
GOOD. VERY, VERY GOOD.
THANKS.
SO. SMOKING AT YOUR AGE? WHAT A NAUGHTY LITTLE VIXEN YOU ARE...
YOU MUST BE DISCIPLINED.
DOLLY HAD PREPARED ME FOR THE PATIENTS WHO LIKE TO ACT OUT ROLES... I WONDERED IF THE BIG DOCTOR HAD KNOWN ABOUT HERR SCHUTZ'S PREFERENCES...
I THOUGHT THAT PERHAPS THAT WAS WHY HE'D HAD ME SMOKE...

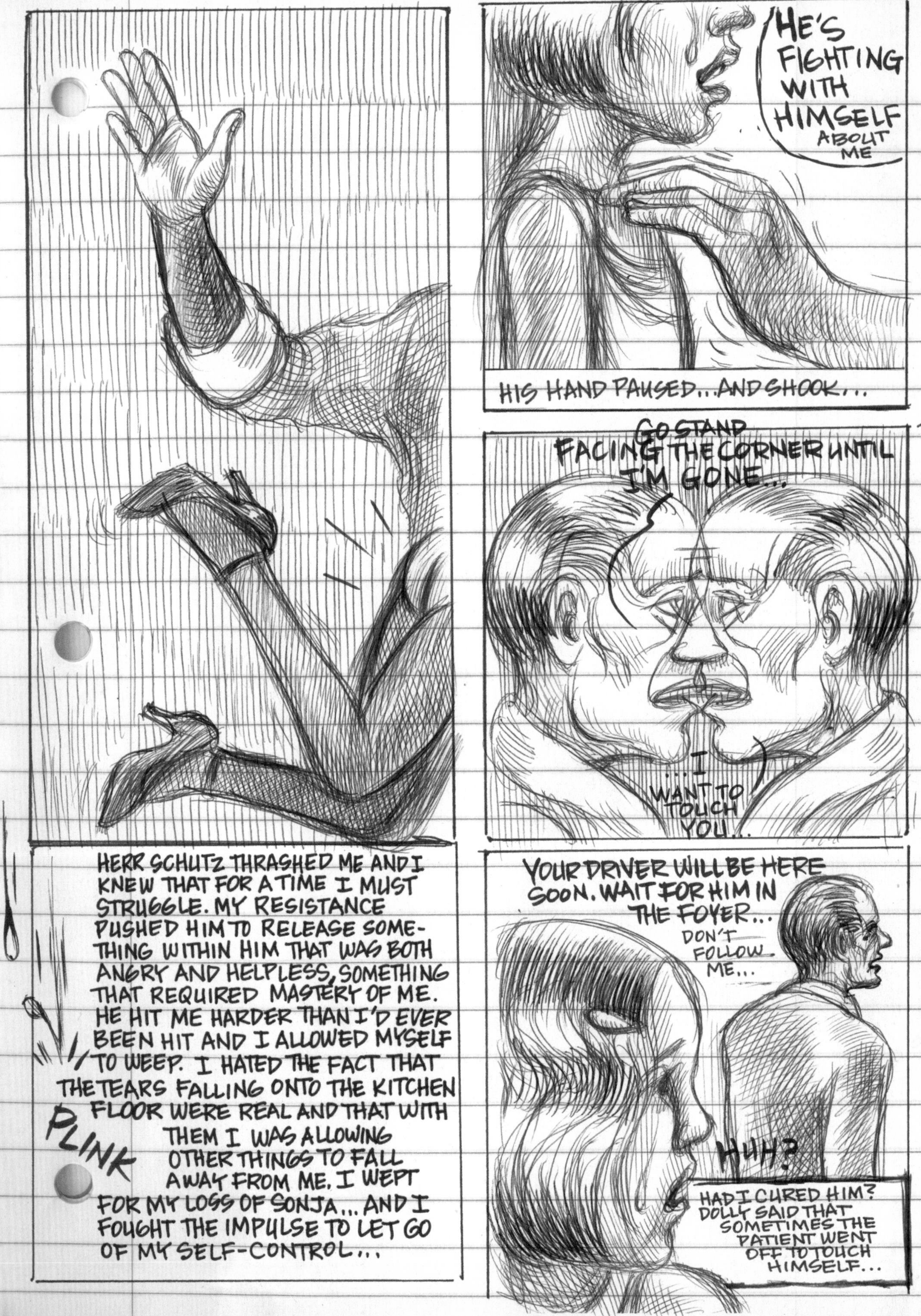
HE'S FIGHTING WITH HIMSELF ABOUT ME
HIS HAND PAUSED... AND SHOOK...
GO STAND FACING THE CORNER UNTIL I'M GONE...
...I WANT TO TOUCH YOU...
HERR SCHUTZ THRASHED ME AND I KNEW THAT FOR A TIME I MUST STRUGGLE. MY RESISTANCE PUSHED HIM TO RELEASE SOMETHING WITHIN HIM THAT WAS BOTH ANGRY AND HELPLESS, SOMETHING THAT REQUIRED MASTERY OF ME. HE HIT ME HARDER THAN I'D EVER BEEN HIT AND I ALLOWED MYSELF TO WEEP. I HATED THE FACT THAT THE TEARS FALLING ONTO THE KITCHEN FLOOR WERE REAL AND THAT WITH THEM I WAS ALLOWING OTHER THINGS TO FALL AWAY FROM ME. I WEPT FOR MY LOSS OF SONJA... AND I FOUGHT THE IMPULSE TO LET GO OF MY SELF-CONTROL...
PLINK
YOUR DRIVER WILL BE HERE SOON. WAIT FOR HIM IN THE FOYER...
DON'T FOLLOW ME...
HUH?
HAD I CURED HIM? DOLLY SAID THAT SOMETIMES THE PATIENT WENT OFF TO TOUCH HIMSELF...

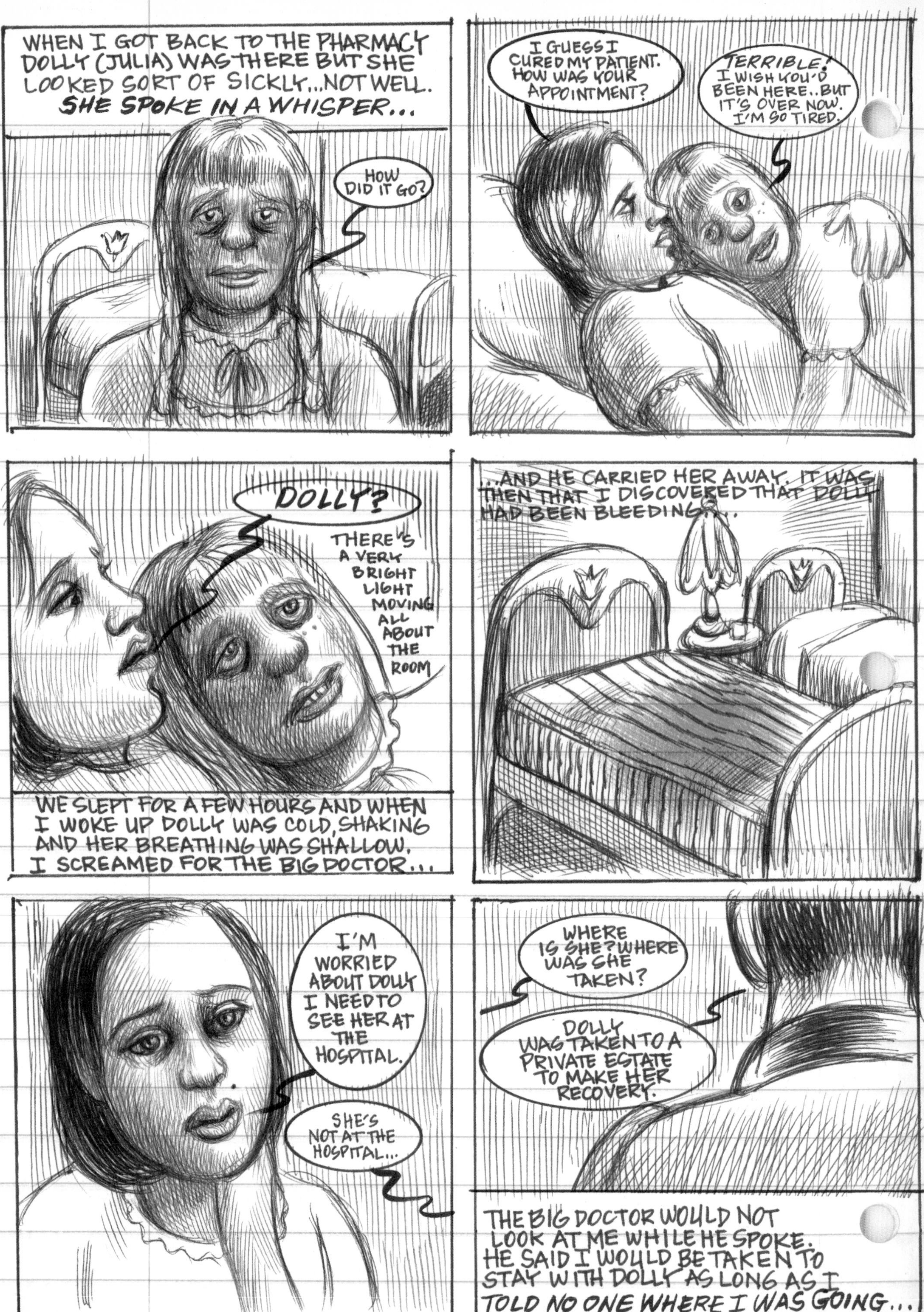
WHEN I GOT BACK TO THE PHARMACY DOLLY (JULIA) WAS THERE BUT SHE LOOKED SORT OF SICKLY...NOT WELL. SHE SPOKE IN A WHISPER...
HOW DID IT GO?
I GUESS I CURED MY PATIENT. HOW WAS YOUR APPOINTMENT?
TERRIBLE! I WISH YOU'D BEEN HERE..BUT IT'S OVER NOW. I'M SO TIRED.
DOLLY?
THERE'S A VERY BRIGHT LIGHT MOVING ALL ABOUT THE ROOM
WE SLEPT FOR A FEW HOURS AND WHEN I WOKE UP DOLLY WAS COLD, SHAKING AND HER BREATHING WAS SHALLOW. I SCREAMED FOR THE BIG DOCTOR...
...AND HE CARRIED HER AWAY. IT WAS THEN THAT I DISCOVERED THAT DOLLY HAD BEEN BLEEDING...
I'M WORRIED ABOUT DOLLY I NEED TO SEE HER AT THE HOSPITAL.
SHE'S NOT AT THE HOSPITAL...
WHERE IS SHE? WHERE WAS SHE TAKEN?
DOLLY WAS TAKEN TO A PRIVATE ESTATE TO MAKE HER RECOVERY.
THE BIG DOCTOR WOULD NOT LOOK AT ME WHILE HE SPOKE. HE SAID I WOULD BE TAKEN TO STAY WITH DOLLY AS LONG AS I TOLD NO ONE WHERE I WAS GOING...

THE BROTHEL'S DRIVER DROVE ME A LONG DISTANCE OUTSIDE OF BERLIN, TO AN OLD ABBEY THAT SAT IN A FORESTED AREA....

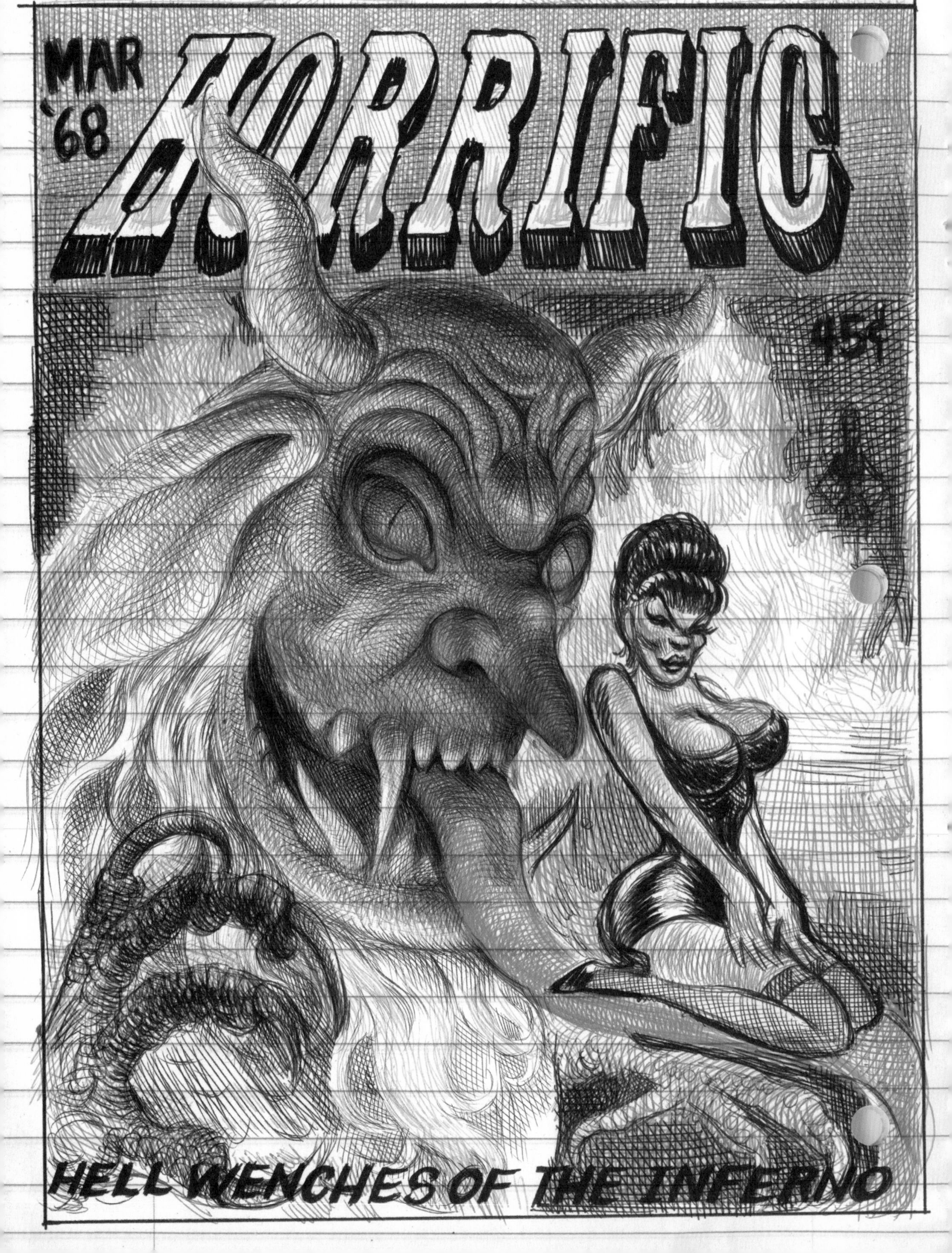
MAR '68
HORRIFIC
45¢
HELL WENCHES OF THE INFERNO

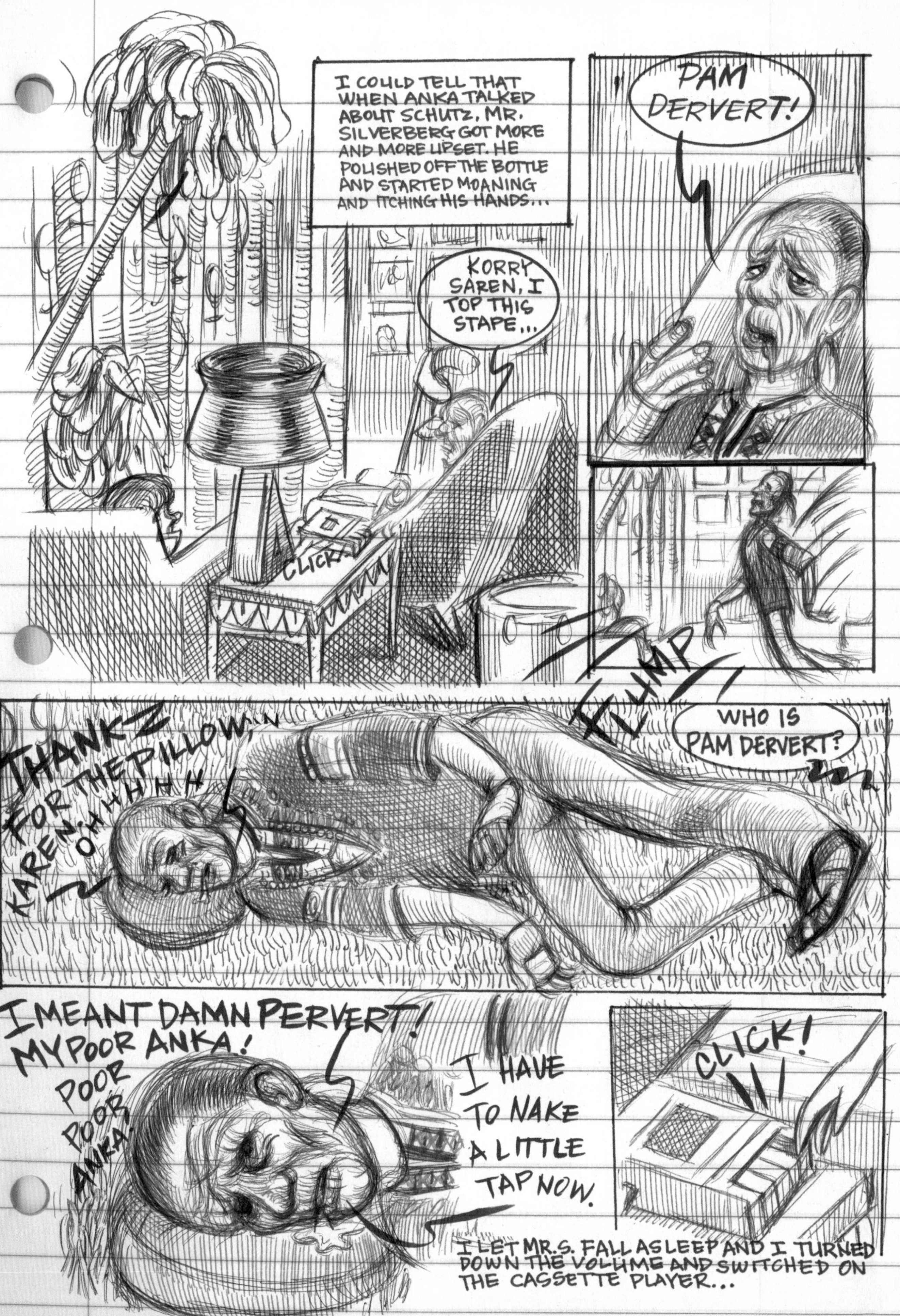
I COULD TELL THAT WHEN ANKA TALKED ABOUT SCHUTZ, MR. SILVERBERG GOT MORE AND MORE UPSET. HE POLISHED OFF THE BOTTLE AND STARTED MOANING AND ITCHING HIS HANDS...
KORRY SAREN, I TOP THIS STAPE...
CLICK
PAM DERVERT!
FLUMP
THANKZ FOR THE PILLOW, KAREN. OHHHHH
WHO IS PAM DERVERT?
I MEANT DAMN PERVERT! MY POOR ANKA! POOR POOR ANKA.
I HAVE TO NAKE A LITTLE TAP NOW.
CLICK!
I LET MR. S. FALL ASLEEP AND I TURNED DOWN THE VOLUME AND SWITCHED ON THE CASSETTE PLAYER...

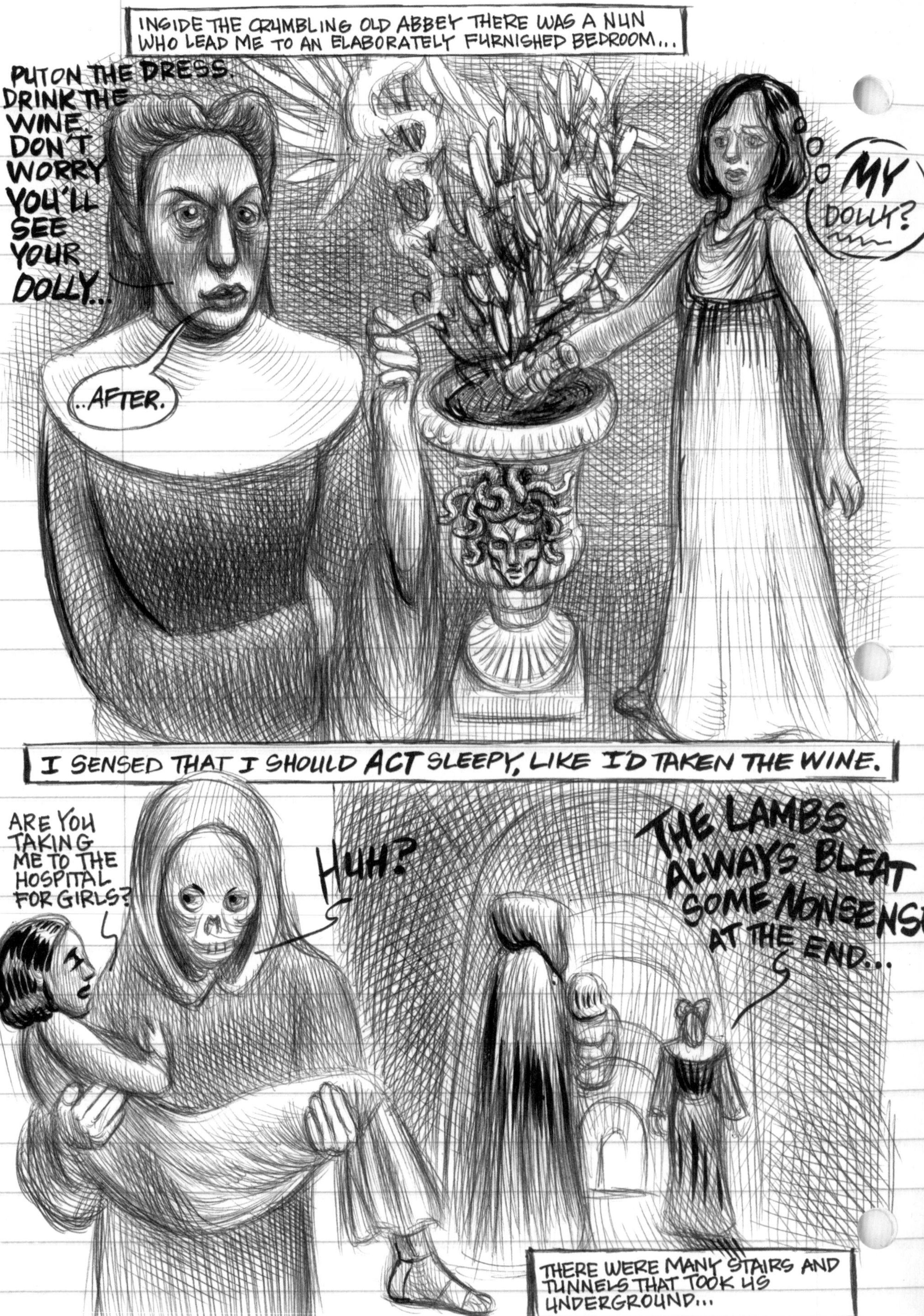
INSIDE THE CRUMBLING OLD ABBEY THERE WAS A NUN WHO LEAD ME TO AN ELABORATELY FURNISHED BEDROOM...
PUT ON THE DRESS. DRINK THE WINE. DON'T WORRY YOU'LL SEE YOUR DOLLY...
...AFTER.
MY DOLLY?
I SENSED THAT I SHOULD ACT SLEEPY, LIKE I'D TAKEN THE WINE.
ARE YOU TAKING ME TO THE HOSPITAL FOR GIRLS?
HUH?
THE LAMBS ALWAYS BLEAT SOME NONSENSE AT THE END...
THERE WERE MANY STAIRS AND TUNNELS THAT TOOK US UNDERGROUND...

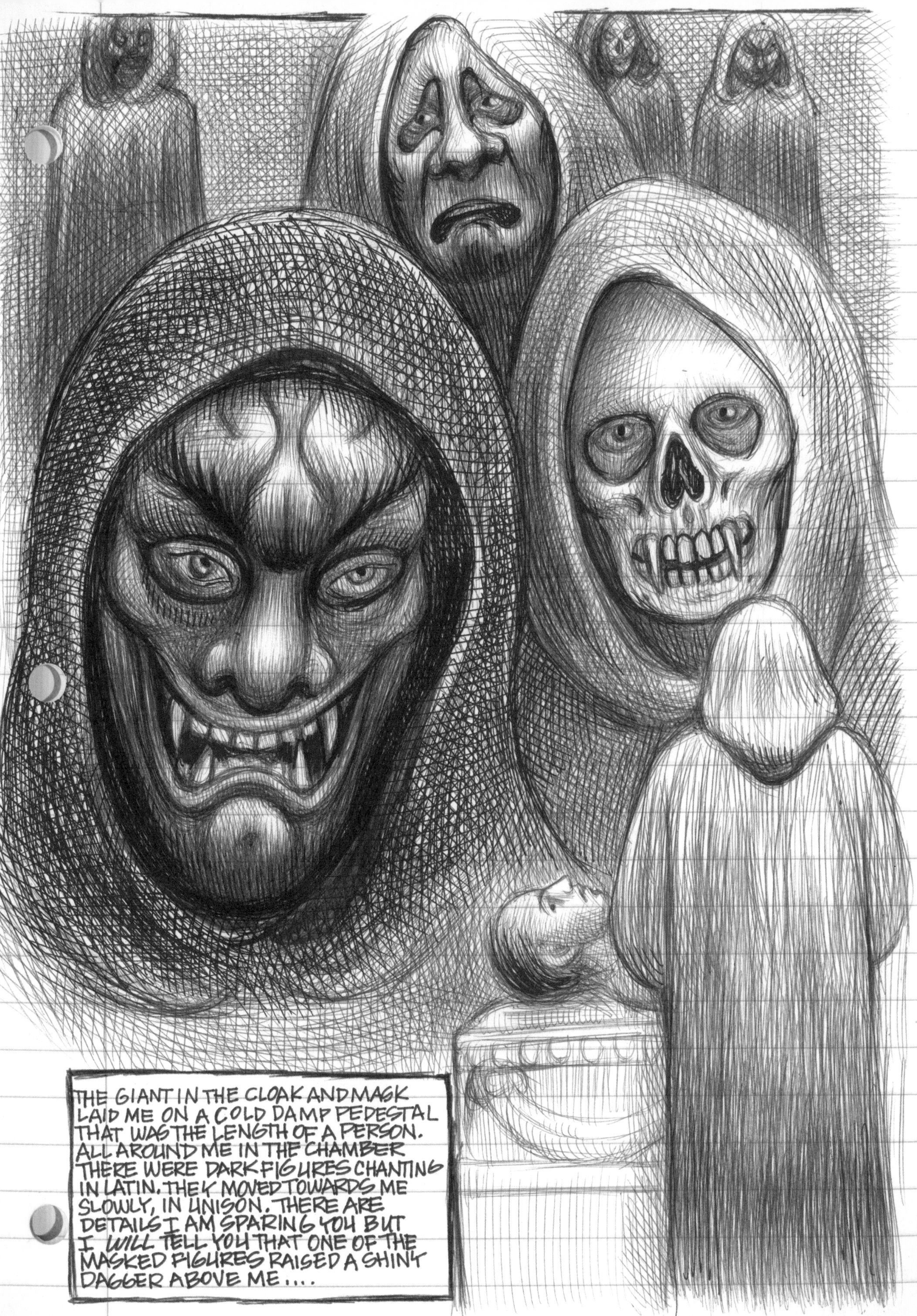
THE GIANT IN THE CLOAK AND MASK LAID ME ON A COLD DAMP PEDESTAL THAT WAS THE LENGTH OF A PERSON. ALL AROUND ME IN THE CHAMBER THERE WERE DARK FIGURES CHANTING IN LATIN. THEY MOVED TOWARDS ME SLOWLY, IN UNISON. THERE ARE DETAILS I AM SPARING YOU BUT I *WILL* TELL YOU THAT ONE OF THE MASKED FIGURES RAISED A SHINY DAGGER ABOVE ME....

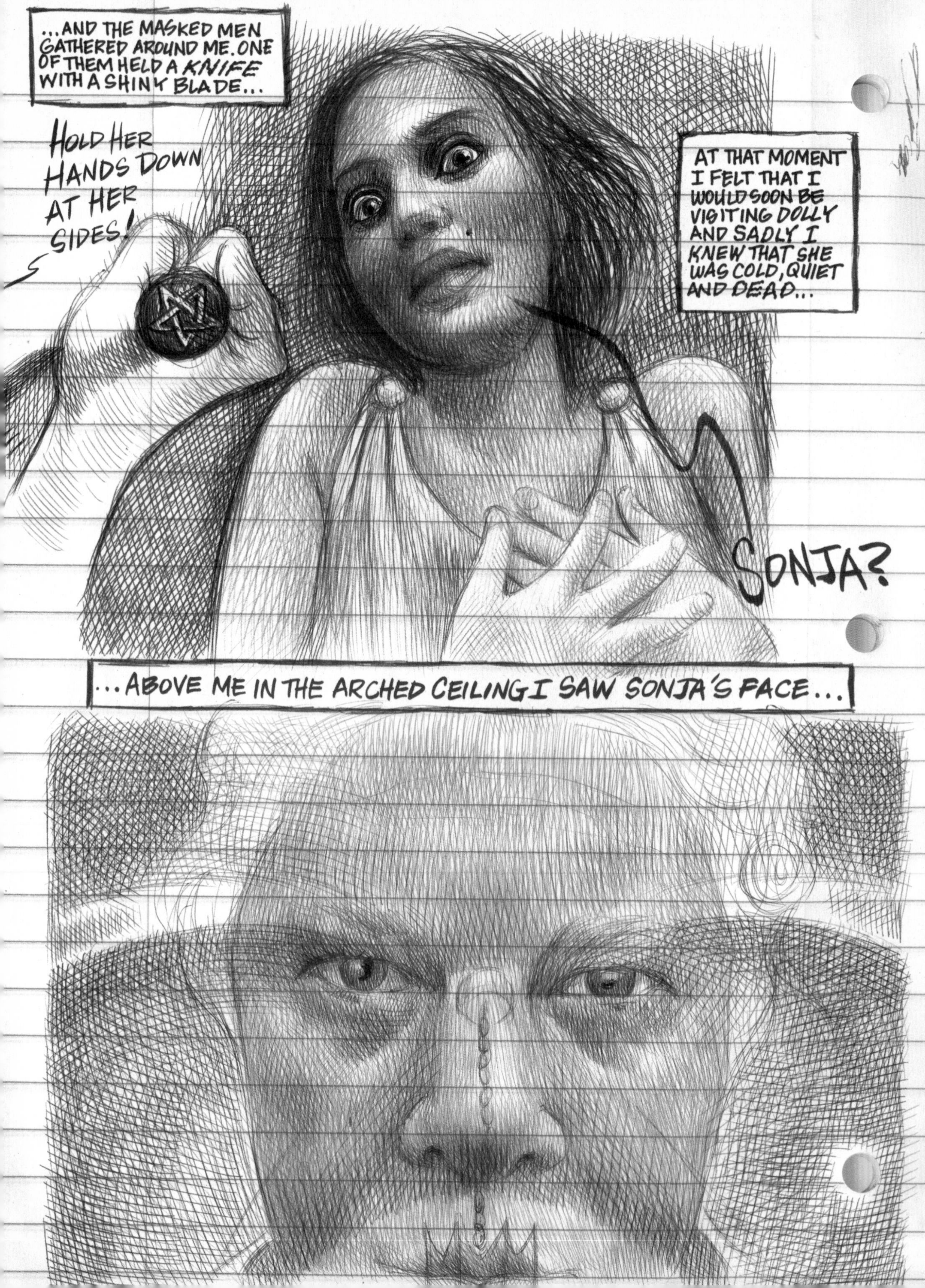
...AND THE MASKED MEN GATHERED AROUND ME. ONE OF THEM HELD A KNIFE WITH A SHINY BLADE...
HOLD HER HANDS DOWN AT HER SIDES!
AT THAT MOMENT I FELT THAT I WOULD SOON BE VISITING DOLLY AND SADLY I KNEW THAT SHE WAS COLD, QUIET AND DEAD...
SONJA?
...ABOVE ME IN THE ARCHED CEILING I SAW SONJA'S FACE...

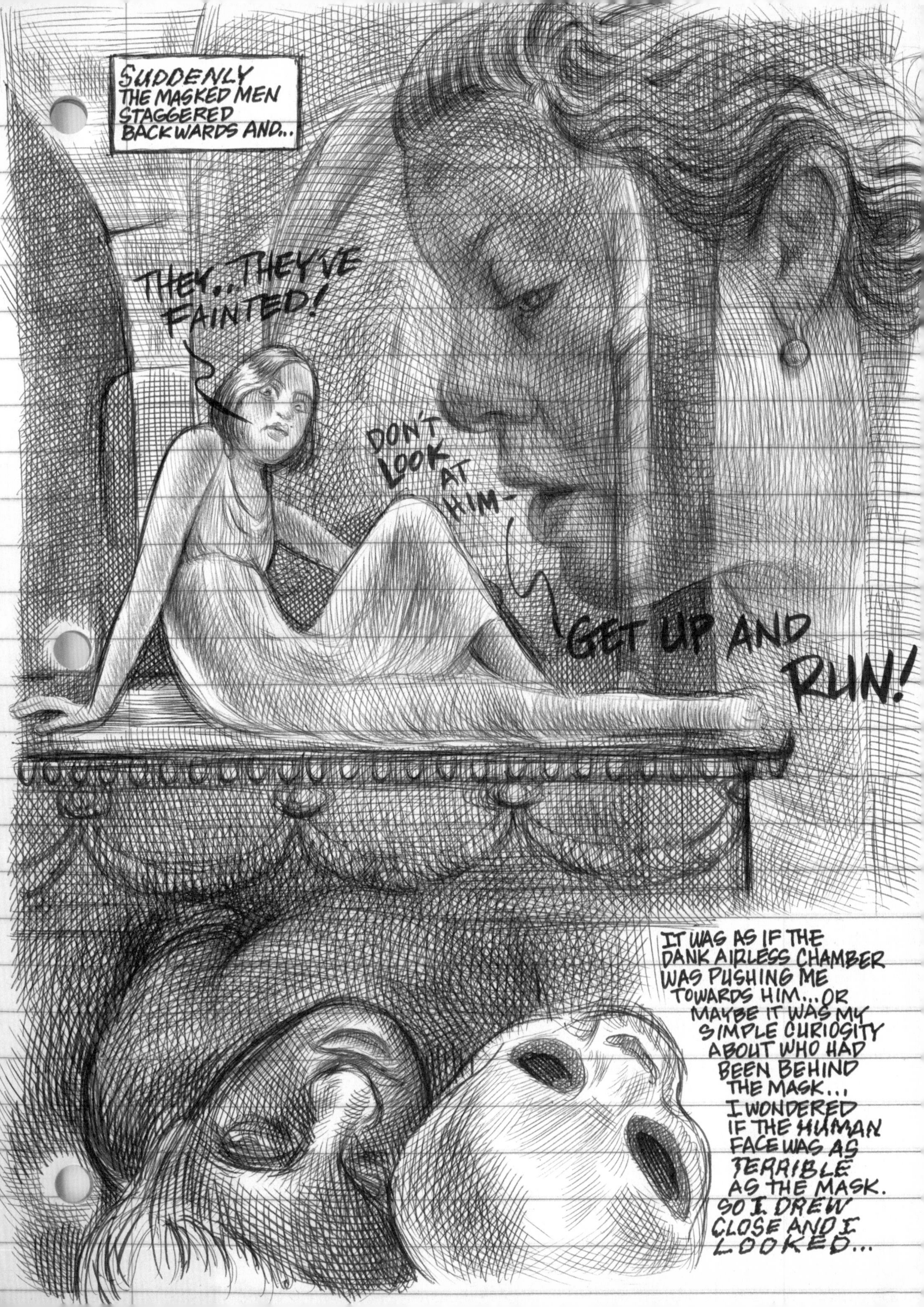
SUDDENLY THE MASKED MEN STAGGERED BACKWARDS AND...
THEY... THEY'VE FAINTED!
DON'T LOOK AT HIM-
GET UP AND RUN!
IT WAS AS IF THE DANK AIRLESS CHAMBER WAS PUSHING ME TOWARDS HIM... OR MAYBE IT WAS MY SIMPLE CURIOSITY ABOUT WHO HAD BEEN BEHIND THE MASK... I WONDERED IF THE HUMAN FACE WAS AS TERRIBLE AS THE MASK. SO I DREW CLOSE AND I LOOKED...

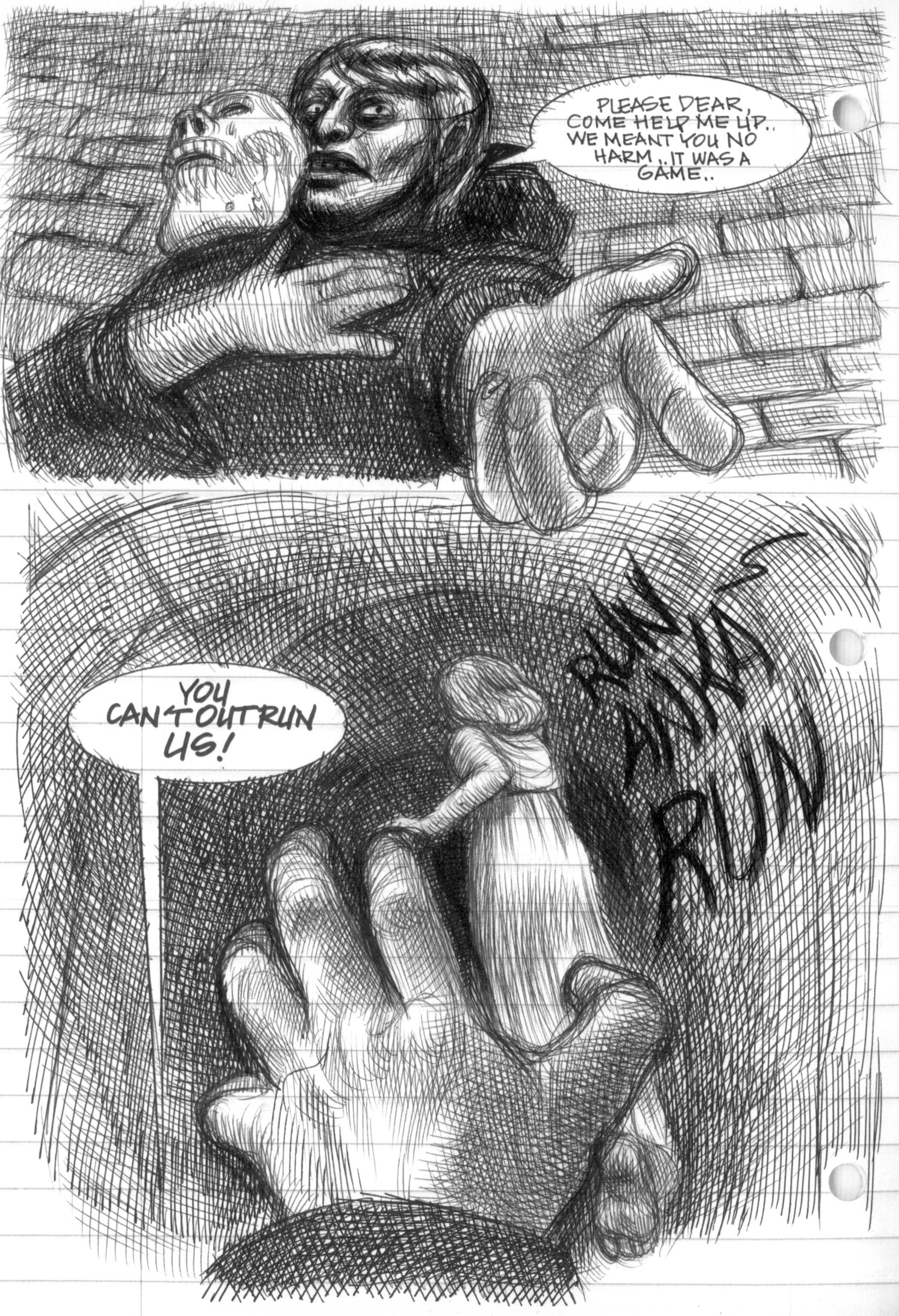
PLEASE DEAR, COME HELP ME UP.. WE MEANT YOU NO HARM.. IT WAS A GAME..
YOU CAN'T OUTRUN US!
RUN AWAY RUN

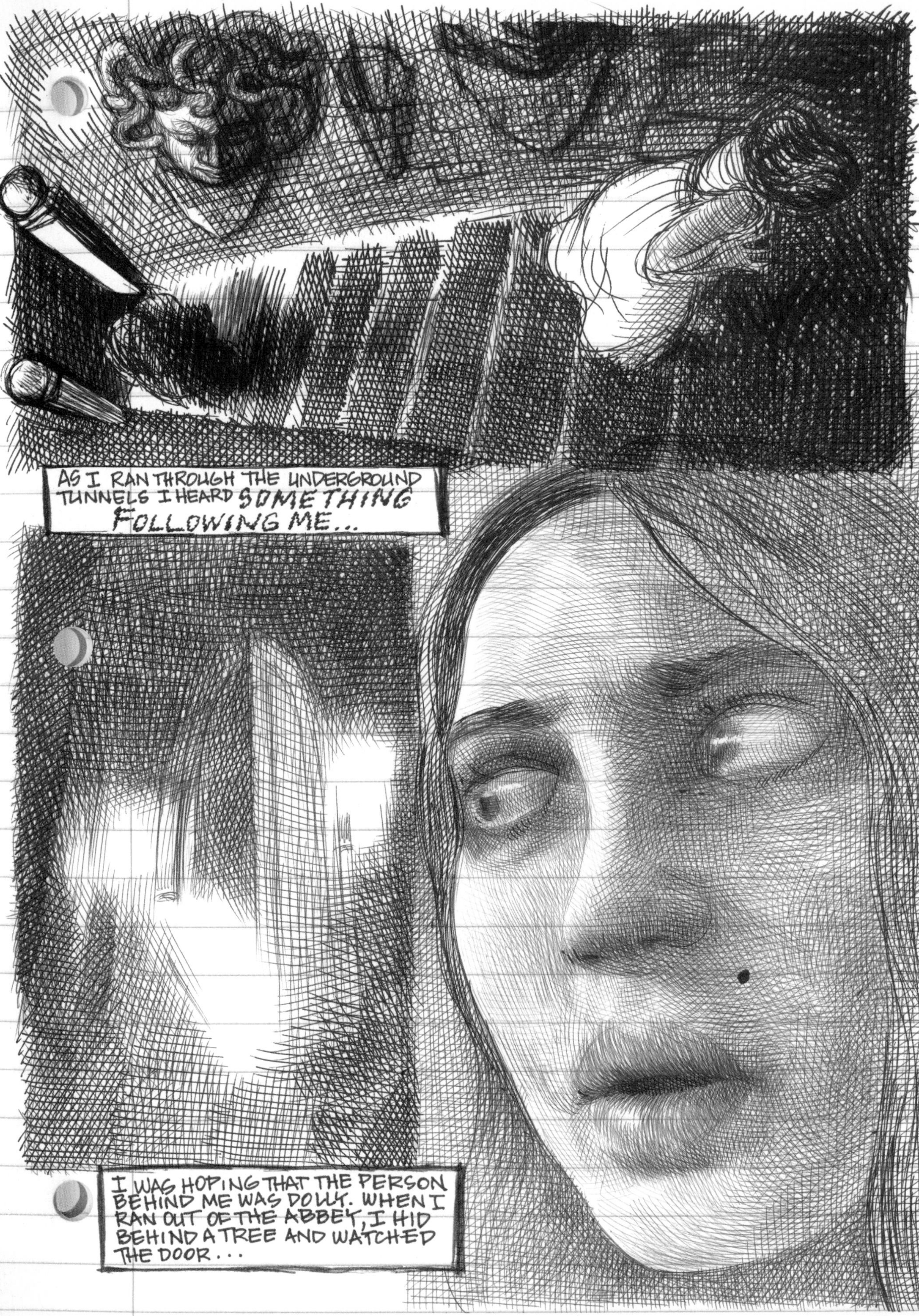
AS I RAN THROUGH THE UNDERGROUND TUNNELS I HEARD SOMETHING FOLLOWING ME...
I WAS HOPING THAT THE PERSON BEHIND ME WAS DOLLY. WHEN I RAN OUT OF THE ABBEY, I HID BEHIND A TREE AND WATCHED THE DOOR...

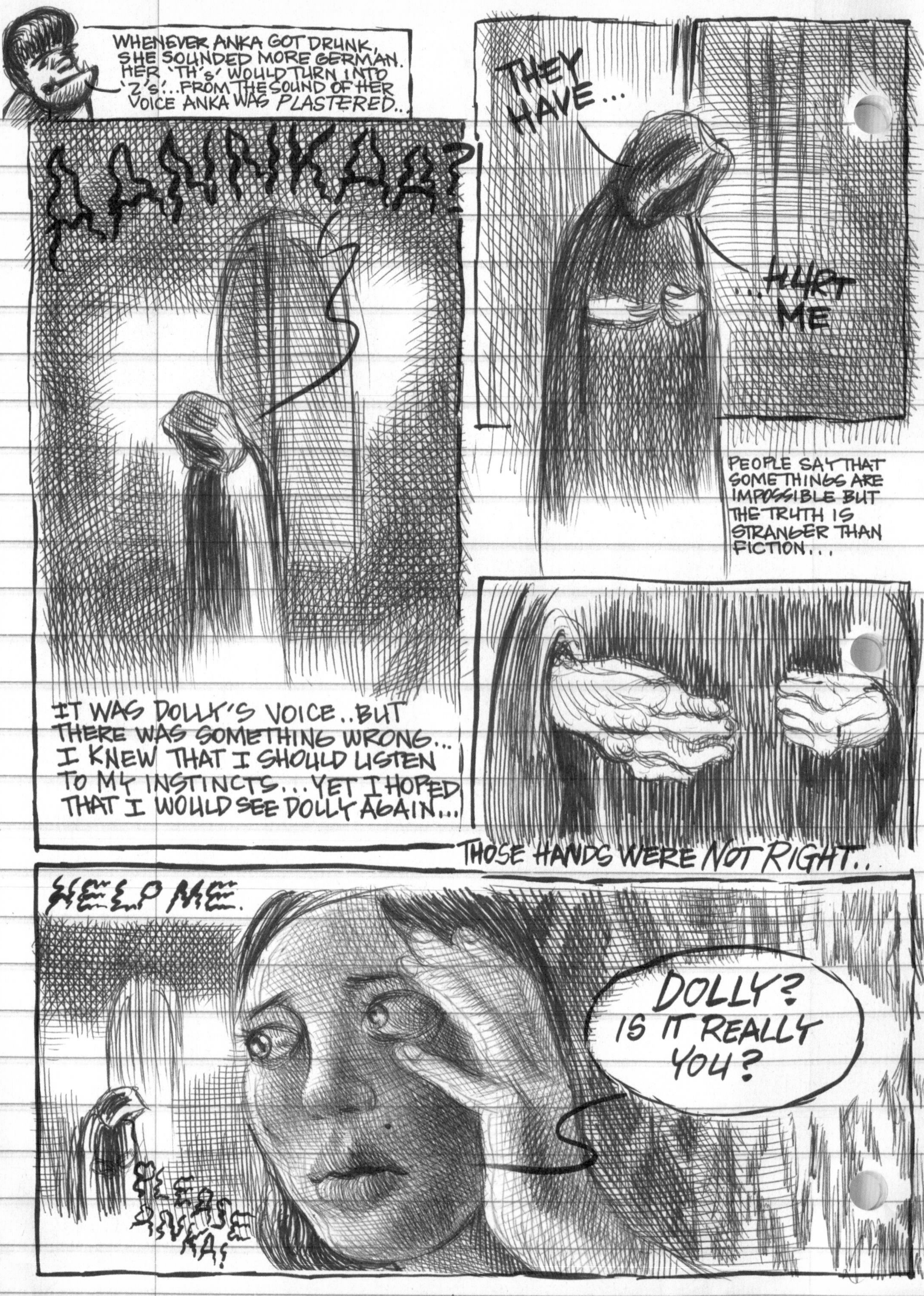
WHENEVER ANKA GOT DRUNK, SHE SOUNDED MORE GERMAN. HER 'TH's' WOULD TURN INTO 'Z's'... FROM THE SOUND OF HER VOICE ANKA WAS PLASTERED...
AAANNKAA?
IT WAS DOLLY'S VOICE.. BUT THERE WAS SOMETHING WRONG... I KNEW THAT I SHOULD LISTEN TO MY INSTINCTS... YET I HOPED THAT I WOULD SEE DOLLY AGAIN...
THEY HAVE...
...HURT ME
PEOPLE SAY THAT SOMETHINGS ARE IMPOSSIBLE BUT THE TRUTH IS STRANGER THAN FICTION...
THOSE HANDS WERE NOT RIGHT..
HELP ME.
DOLLY? IS IT REALLY YOU?
PLEASE ANKA!

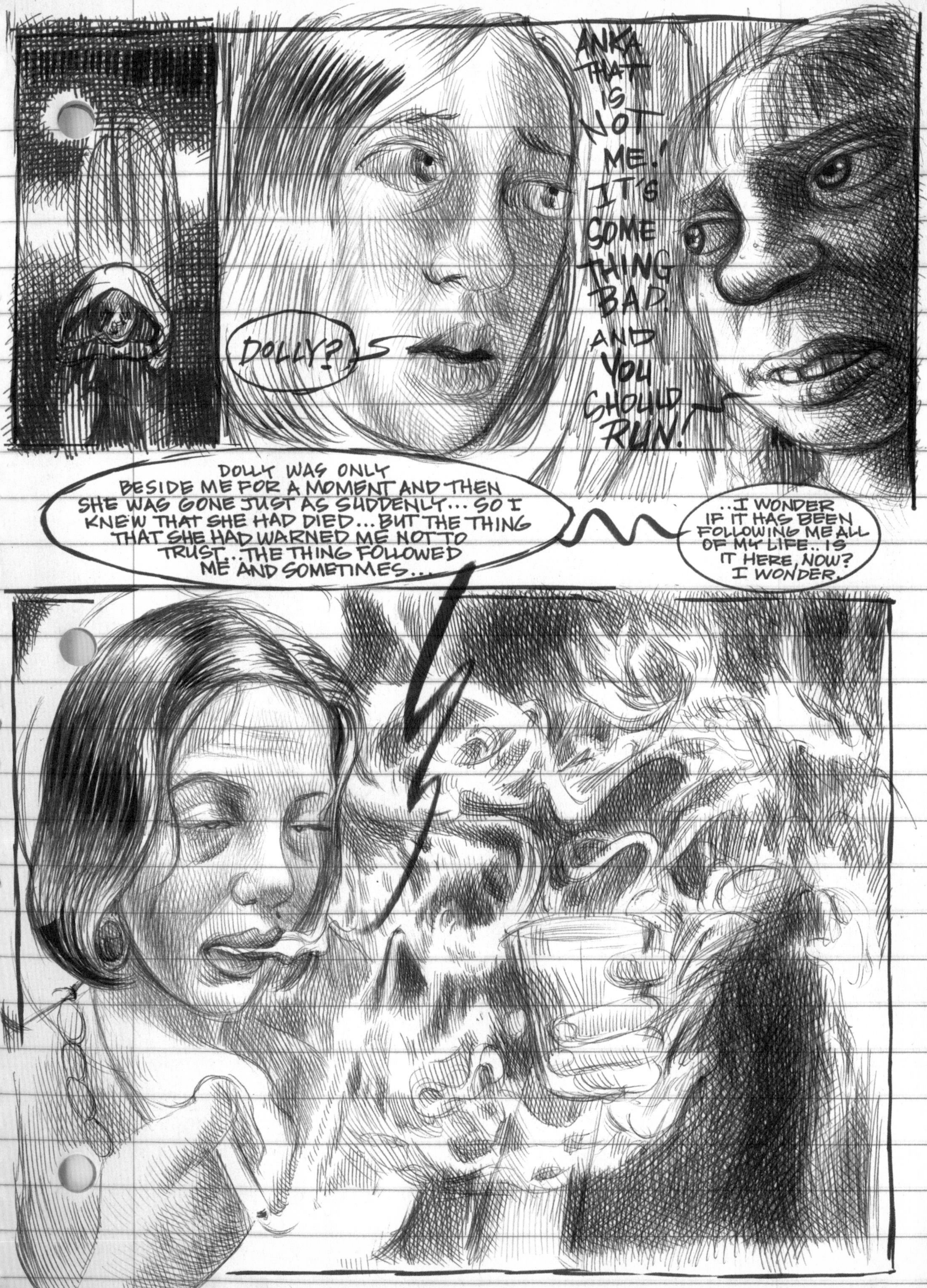
DOLLY?
ANKA THAT IS NOT ME! IT'S SOMETHING BAD. AND YOU SHOULD RUN!
DOLLY WAS ONLY BESIDE ME FOR A MOMENT AND THEN SHE WAS GONE JUST AS SUDDENLY... SO I KNEW THAT SHE HAD DIED... BUT THE THING THAT SHE HAD WARNED ME NOT TO TRUST... THE THING FOLLOWED ME AND SOMETIMES...
...I WONDER IF IT HAS BEEN FOLLOWING ME ALL OF MY LIFE.. IS IT HERE, NOW? I WONDER.

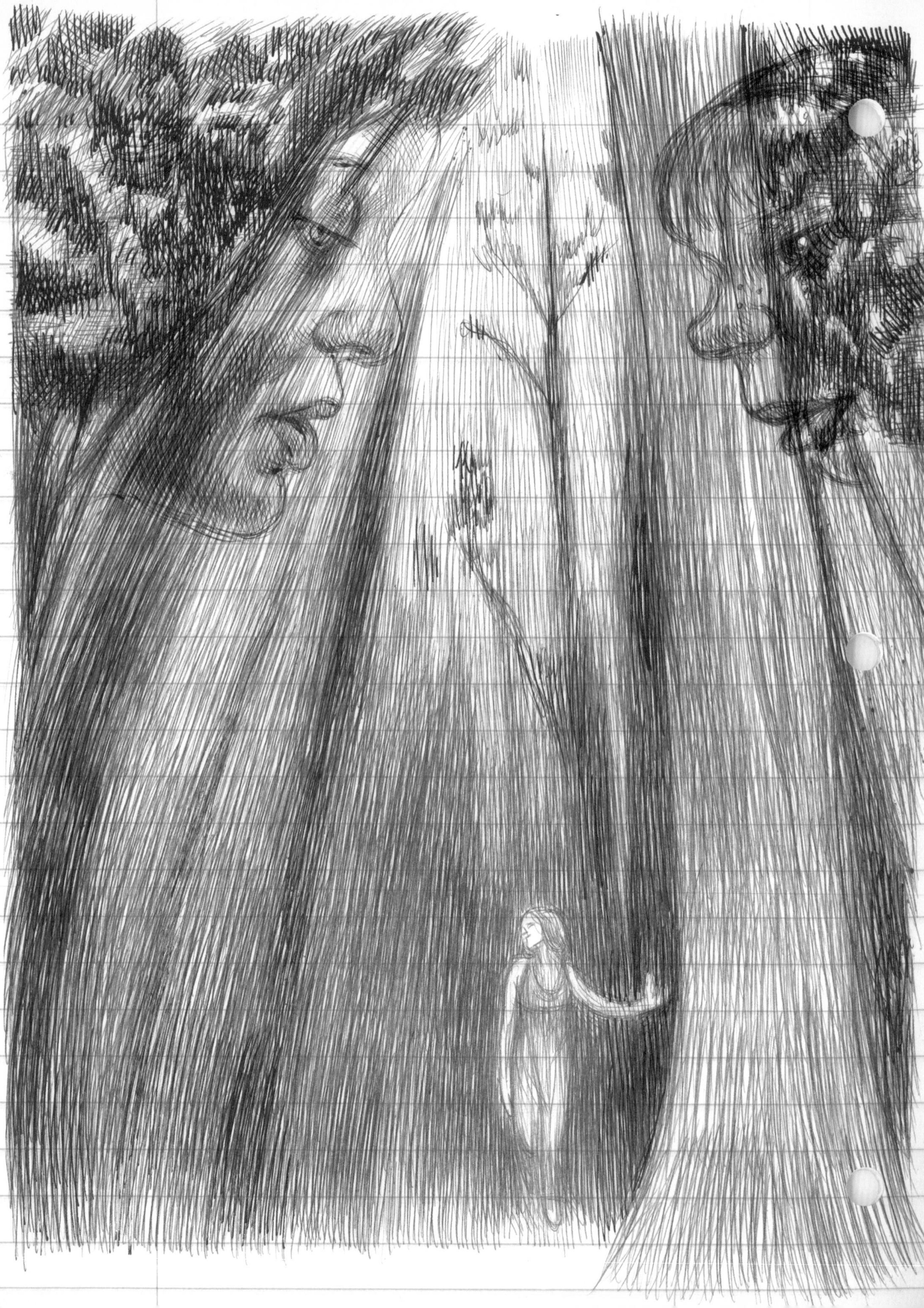

I WAS LEAD TO A HOUSE IN THE WOODS...

I POUNDED ON THE DOOR AND AN OLD COUPLE ANSWERED. THEY LOOKED AT MY COSTUME AND I COULD TELL THAT THEY KNEW FROM WHERE I HAD ESCAPED...

AFTER THE WAR MANY THINGS WERE SAID ABOUT GERMANS BUT TRUTHFULLY THERE WERE MANY GERMANS WHO RISKED THEIR LIVES TO PROTECT OTHERS. I WONDER IF AMERICANS WERE IN THE SAME PLACE WOULD THEY BE AS COURAGEOUS?

SHE SAID SHE WOULD DRUG THE DEMON'S WINE AND SHE FINALLY DID IT!

AND WHEN THEY WAKEN?

THE GIRL MUST BE SAFE.

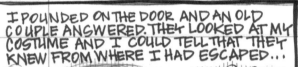

THE OLD COUPLE FED ME AND LET ME WARM AT THEIR FIRE AND THEN...

YOU CAN NOT GO BACK TO WHO SENT YOU TO THAT PLACE...

WHERE WILL I GO?

...THEY SENT YOU THERE AND THEY KNEW YOU'D NEVER COME BACK. YOU WOULD NOT BE SAFE WITH US EITHER...

APPROACH THIS PROBLEM LIKE IT IS A GAME OF CHECKERS...

...YOU MUST HAVE A STRATEGY IN ORDER TO SURVIVE...

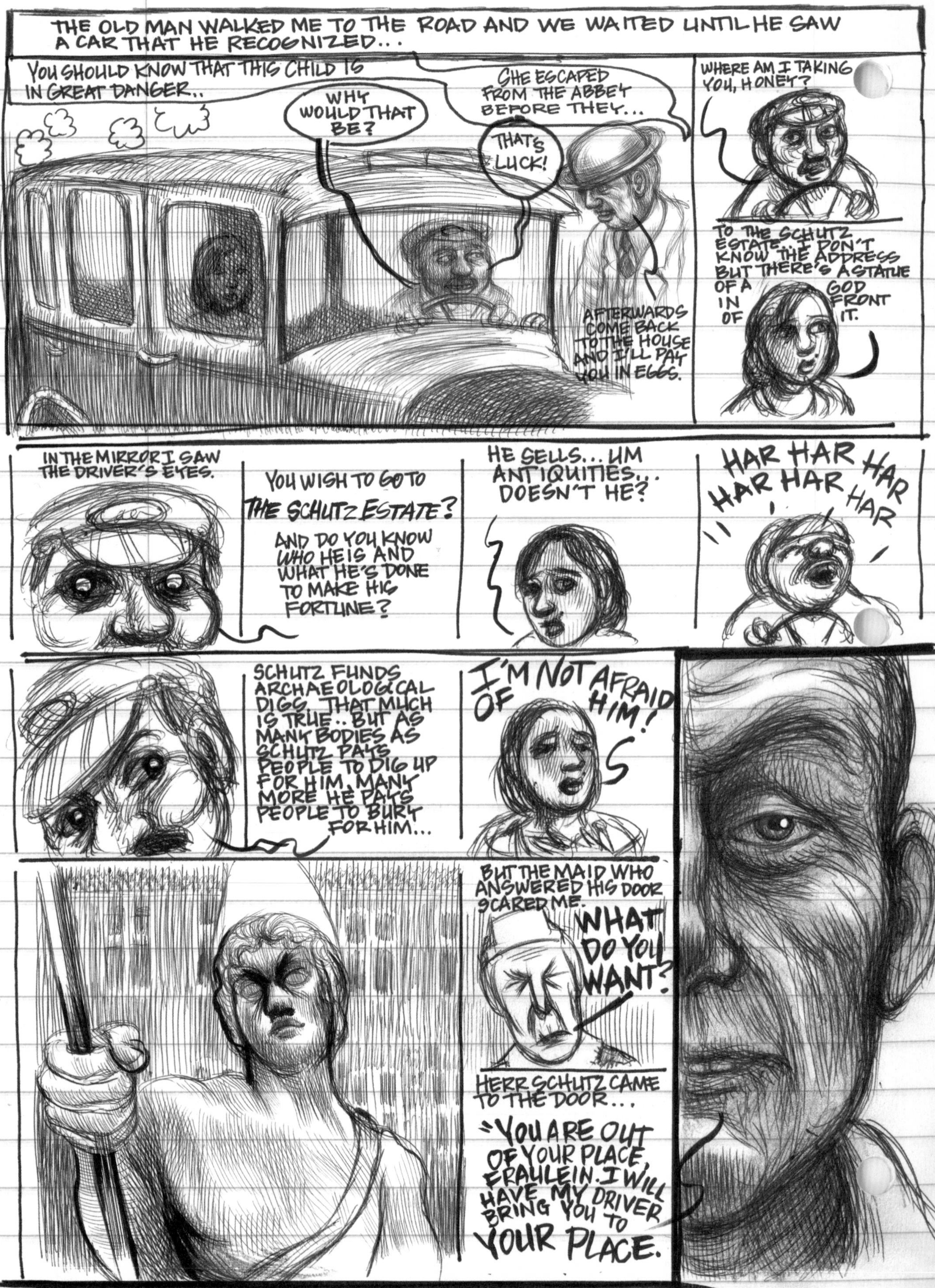
THE OLD MAN WALKED ME TO THE ROAD AND WE WAITED UNTIL HE SAW A CAR THAT HE RECOGNIZED...
YOU SHOULD KNOW THAT THIS CHILD IS IN GREAT DANGER..
WHY WOULD THAT BE?
SHE ESCAPED FROM THE ABBEY BEFORE THEY...
THAT'S LUCK!
AFTERWARDS COME BACK TO THE HOUSE AND I'LL PAY YOU IN EGGS.
WHERE AM I TAKING YOU, HONEY?
TO THE SCHUTZ ESTATE. I DON'T KNOW THE ADDRESS BUT THERE'S A STATUE OF A GOD IN FRONT OF IT.
IN THE MIRROR I SAW THE DRIVER'S EYES.
YOU WISH TO GO TO THE SCHUTZ ESTATE?
AND DO YOU KNOW WHO HE IS AND WHAT HE'S DONE TO MAKE HIS FORTUNE?
HE SELLS... UM ANTIQUITIES... DOESN'T HE?
HAR HAR HAR HAR HAR HAR
SCHUTZ FUNDS ARCHAEOLOGICAL DIGS. THAT MUCH IS TRUE.. BUT AS MANY BODIES AS SCHUTZ PAYS PEOPLE TO DIG UP FOR HIM, MANY MORE HE PAYS PEOPLE TO BURY FOR HIM...
I'M NOT AFRAID OF HIM!
BUT THE MAID WHO ANSWERED HIS DOOR SCARED ME.
WHAT DO YOU WANT?
HERR SCHUTZ CAME TO THE DOOR...
"YOU ARE OUT OF YOUR PLACE, FRAULEIN. I WILL HAVE MY DRIVER BRING YOU TO YOUR PLACE.

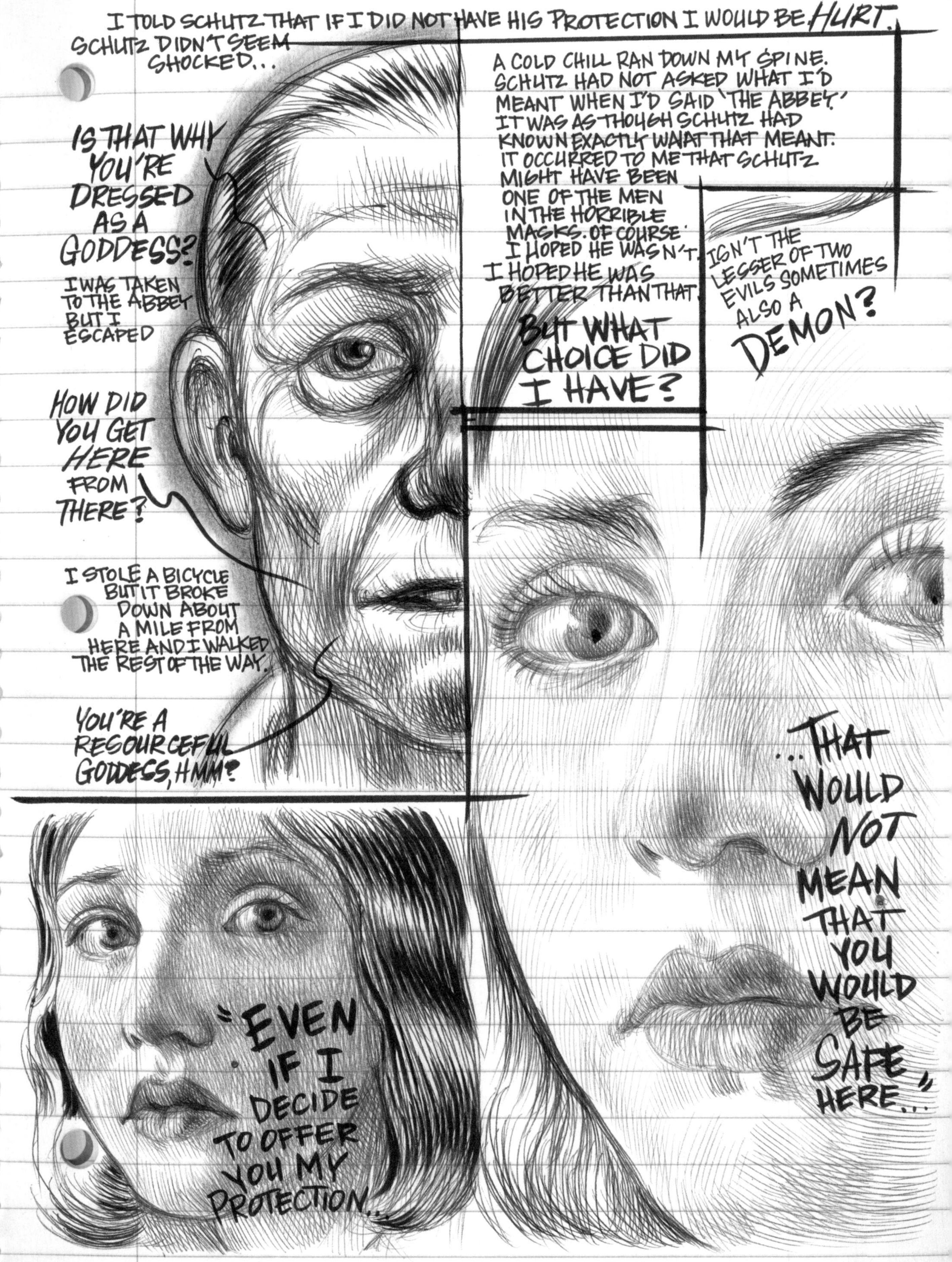
I TOLD SCHUTZ THAT IF I DID NOT HAVE HIS PROTECTION I WOULD BE *HURT*.
SCHUTZ DIDN'T SEEM SHOCKED...
IS THAT WHY YOU'RE DRESSED AS A GODDESS?
I WAS TAKEN TO THE ABBEY BUT I ESCAPED
HOW DID YOU GET *HERE* FROM THERE?
I STOLE A BICYCLE BUT IT BROKE DOWN ABOUT A MILE FROM HERE AND I WALKED THE REST OF THE WAY.
YOU'RE A RESOURCEFUL GODDESS, HMM?
A COLD CHILL RAN DOWN MY SPINE. SCHUTZ HAD NOT ASKED WHAT I'D MEANT WHEN I'D SAID 'THE ABBEY.' IT WAS AS THOUGH SCHUTZ HAD KNOWN EXACTLY WHAT THAT MEANT. IT OCCURRED TO ME THAT SCHUTZ MIGHT HAVE BEEN ONE OF THE MEN IN THE HORRIBLE MASKS. OF COURSE I HOPED HE WASN'T. I HOPED HE WAS BETTER THAN THAT.
BUT WHAT CHOICE DID I HAVE?
ISN'T THE LESSER OF TWO EVILS SOMETIMES ALSO A DEMON?
"EVEN IF I DECIDE TO OFFER YOU MY PROTECTION...
...THAT WOULD *NOT* MEAN THAT YOU WOULD BE SAFE HERE..."

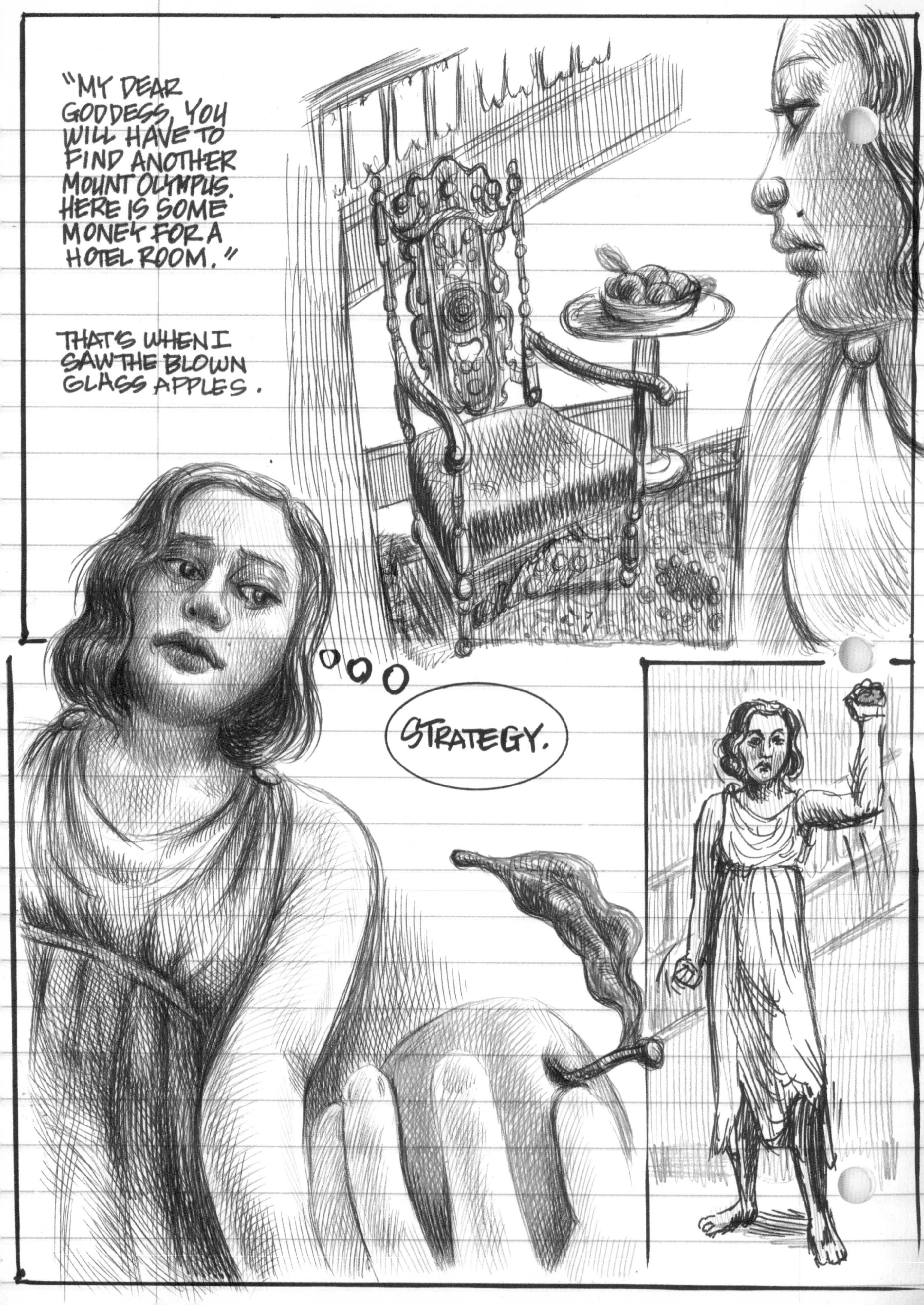
"MY DEAR GODDESS, YOU WILL HAVE TO FIND ANOTHER MOUNT OLYMPUS. HERE IS SOME MONEY FOR A HOTEL ROOM."
THAT'S WHEN I SAW THE BLOWN GLASS APPLES.
STRATEGY.

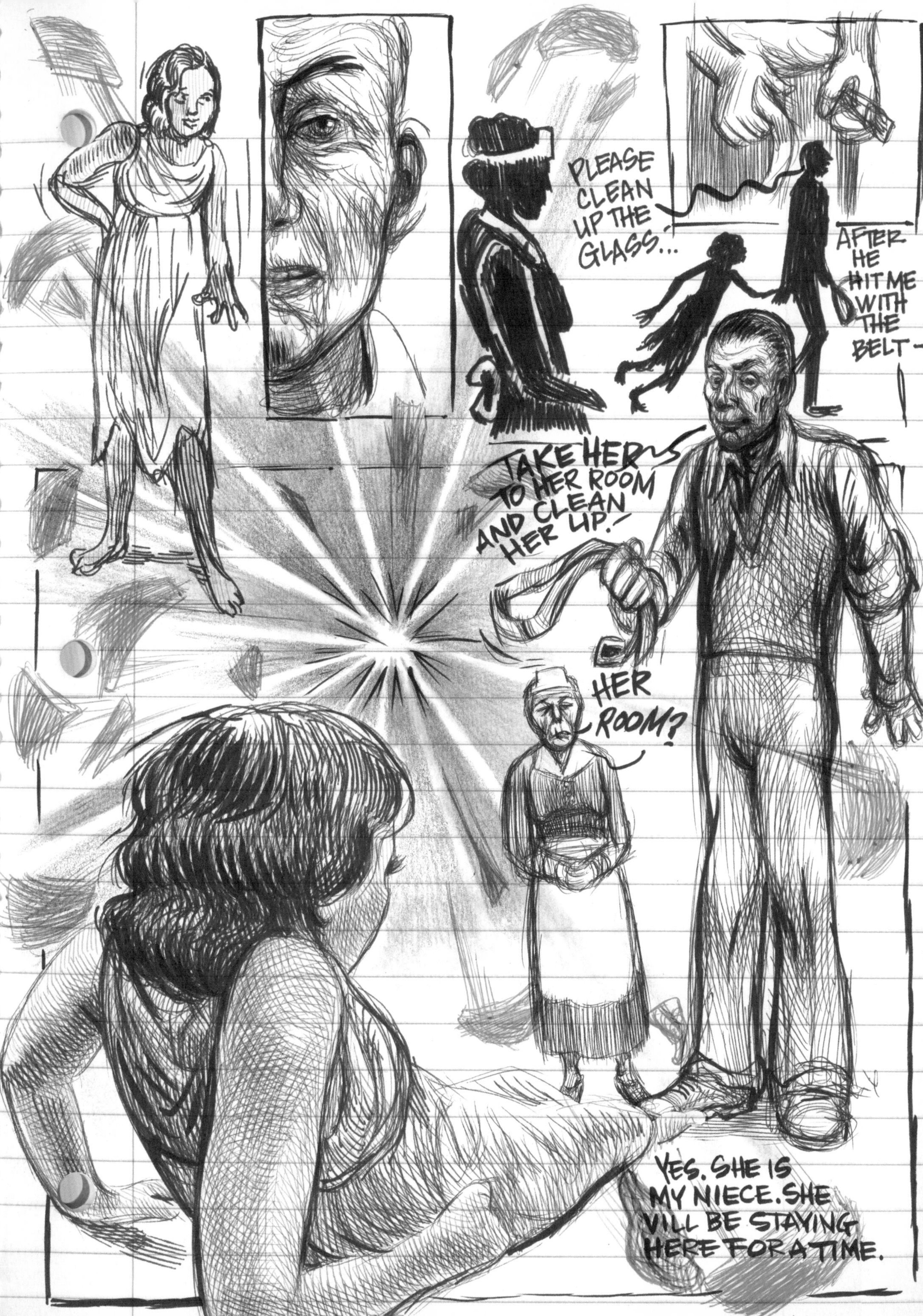
PLEASE CLEAN UP THE GLASS...
AFTER HE HIT ME WITH THE BELT-
TAKE HER TO HER ROOM AND CLEAN HER UP!
HER ROOM?
YES. SHE IS MY NIECE. SHE VILL BE STAYING HERE FOR A TIME.

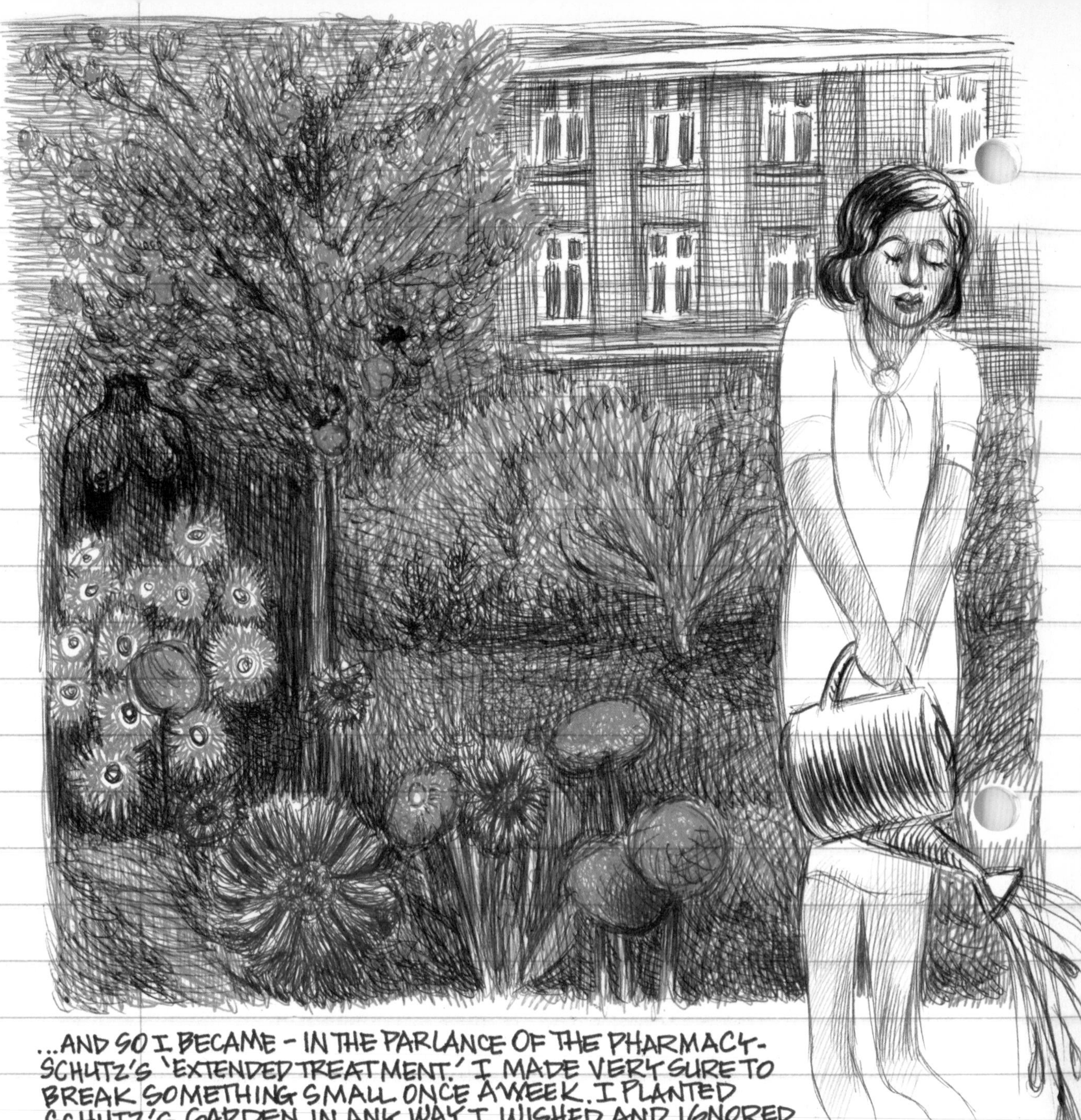

...AND SO I BECAME – IN THE PARLANCE OF THE PHARMACY – SCHUTZ'S 'EXTENDED TREATMENT.' I MADE VERY SURE TO BREAK SOMETHING SMALL ONCE A WEEK. I PLANTED SCHUTZ'S GARDEN IN ANY WAY I WISHED AND IGNORED WHATEVER TERRIBLE THINGS LURKED BEHIND ME.

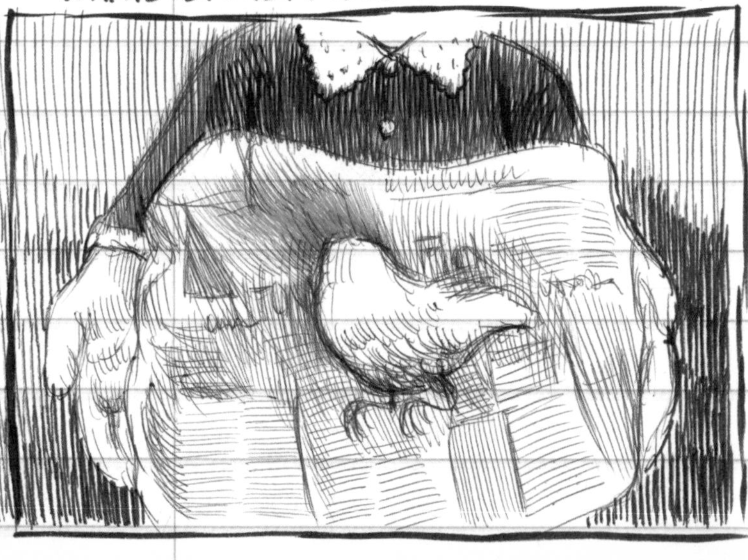

THEN ONE DAY A HEADLESS DOVE WAS LEFT AT THE DOOR. ON THE FOLLOWING DAY THE DOVE'S SKULL WAS DELIVERED WRAPPED IN A PAGE THAT WAS TORN FROM ONE OF THE BOOKS IN SCHUTZ'S LIBRARY...

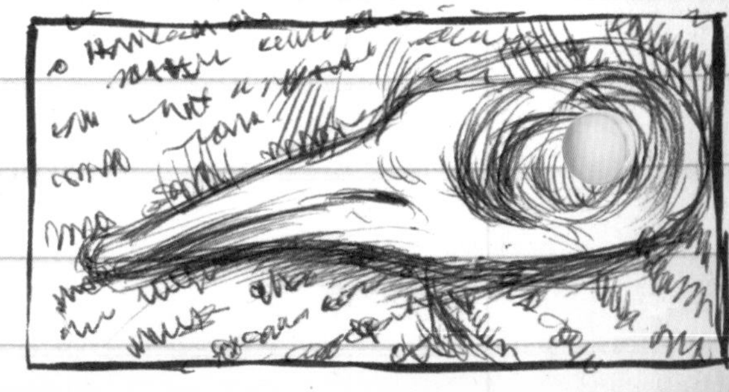

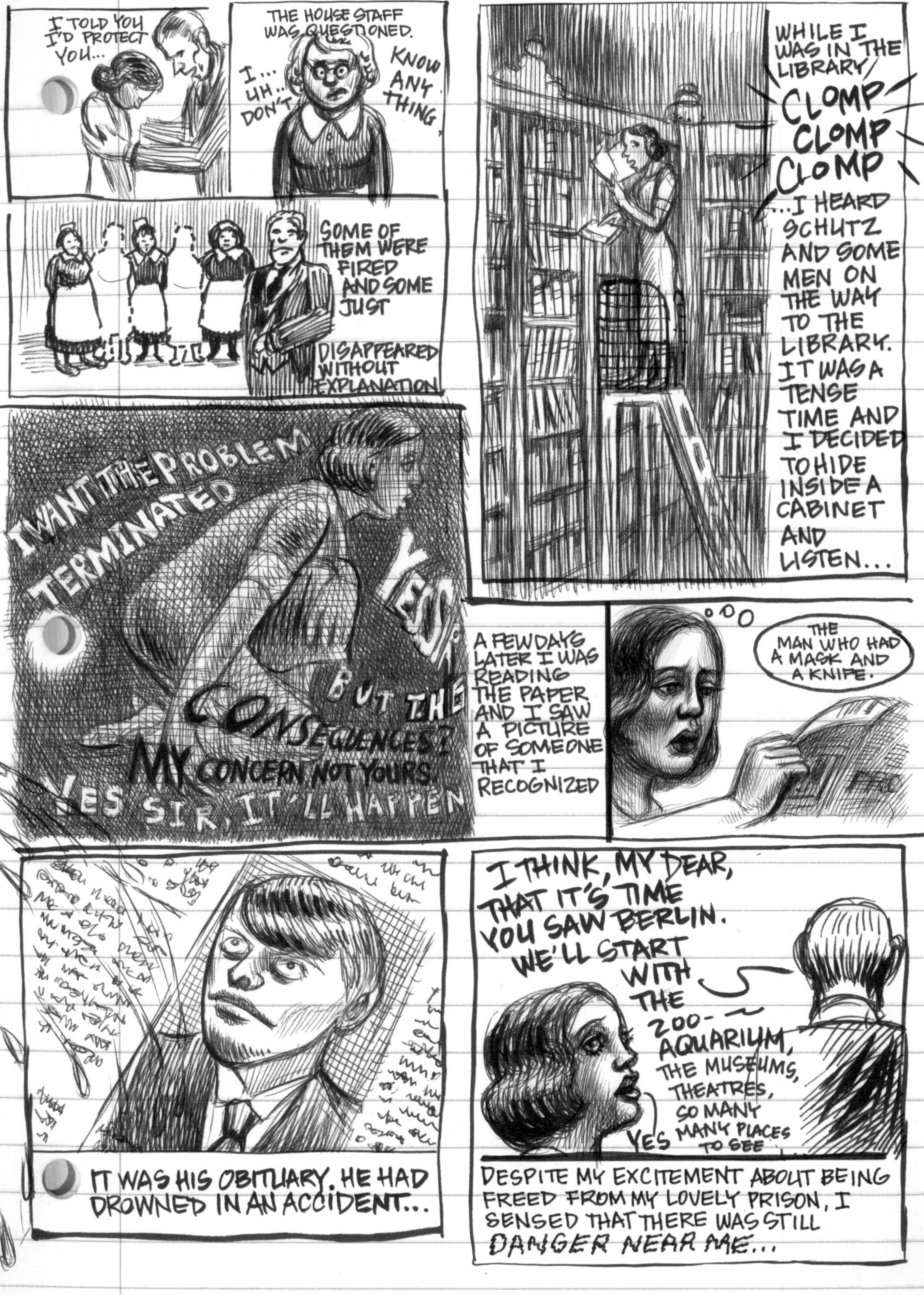
I TOLD YOU I'D PROTECT YOU...
THE HOUSE STAFF WAS QUESTIONED.
I... UH... DON'T
KNOW ANY THING
WHILE I WAS IN THE LIBRARY
CLOMP CLOMP CLOMP
...I HEARD SCHUTZ AND SOME MEN ON THE WAY TO THE LIBRARY. IT WAS A TENSE TIME AND I DECIDED TO HIDE INSIDE A CABINET AND LISTEN...
SOME OF THEM WERE FIRED AND SOME JUST
DISAPPEARED WITHOUT EXPLANATION
I WANT THE PROBLEM TERMINATED
YES
BUT THE CONSEQUENCES?
MY CONCERN NOT YOURS.
YES SIR, IT'LL HAPPEN
A FEW DAYS LATER I WAS READING THE PAPER AND I SAW A PICTURE OF SOMEONE THAT I RECOGNIZED
THE MAN WHO HAD A MASK AND A KNIFE.
IT WAS HIS OBITUARY. HE HAD DROWNED IN AN ACCIDENT...
I THINK, MY DEAR, THAT IT'S TIME YOU SAW BERLIN. WE'LL START WITH THE ZOO-AQUARIUM, THE MUSEUMS, THEATRES, SO MANY MANY PLACES TO SEE
YES
DESPITE MY EXCITEMENT ABOUT BEING FREED FROM MY LOVELY PRISON, I SENSED THAT THERE WAS STILL DANGER NEAR ME...

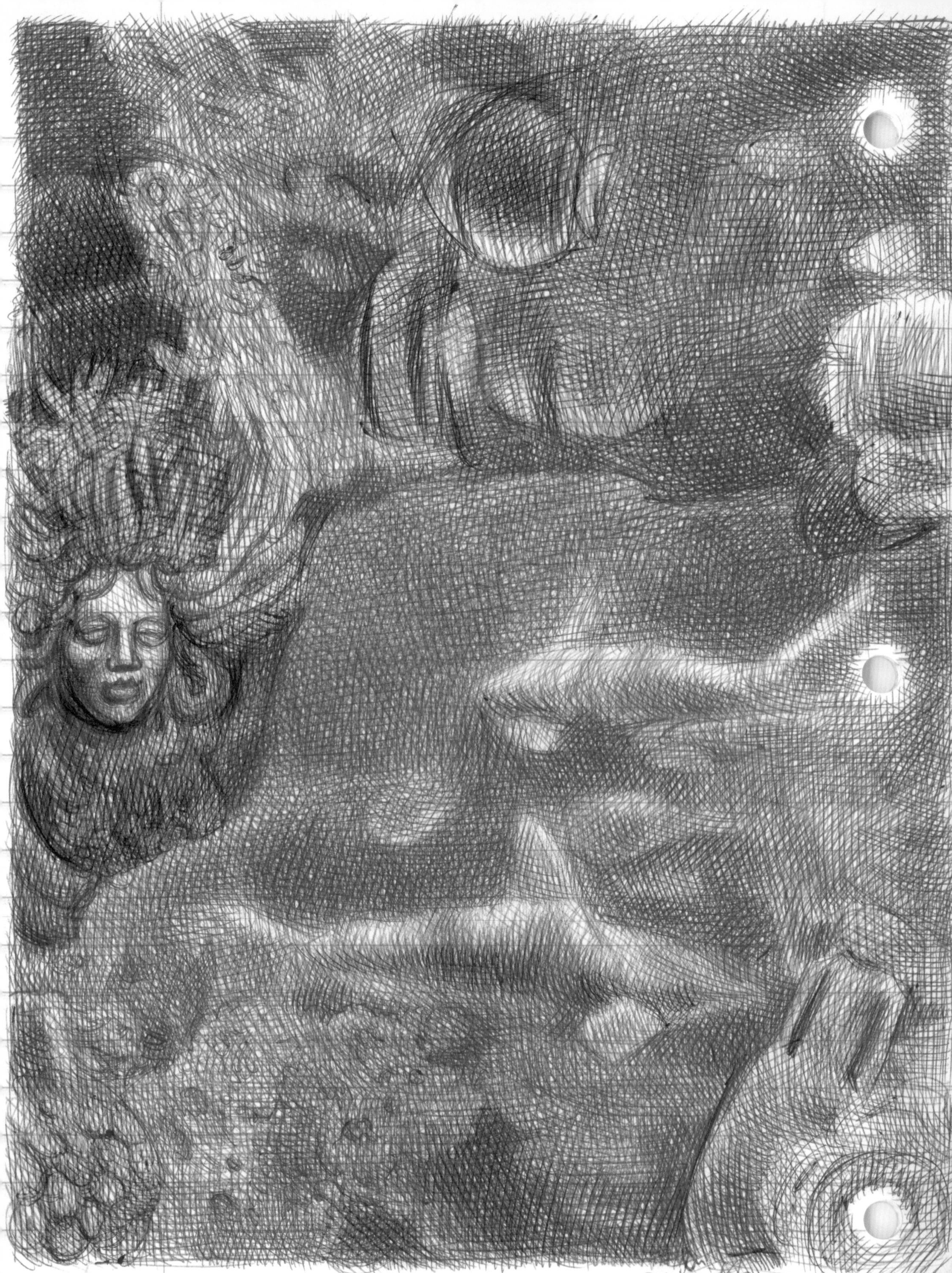

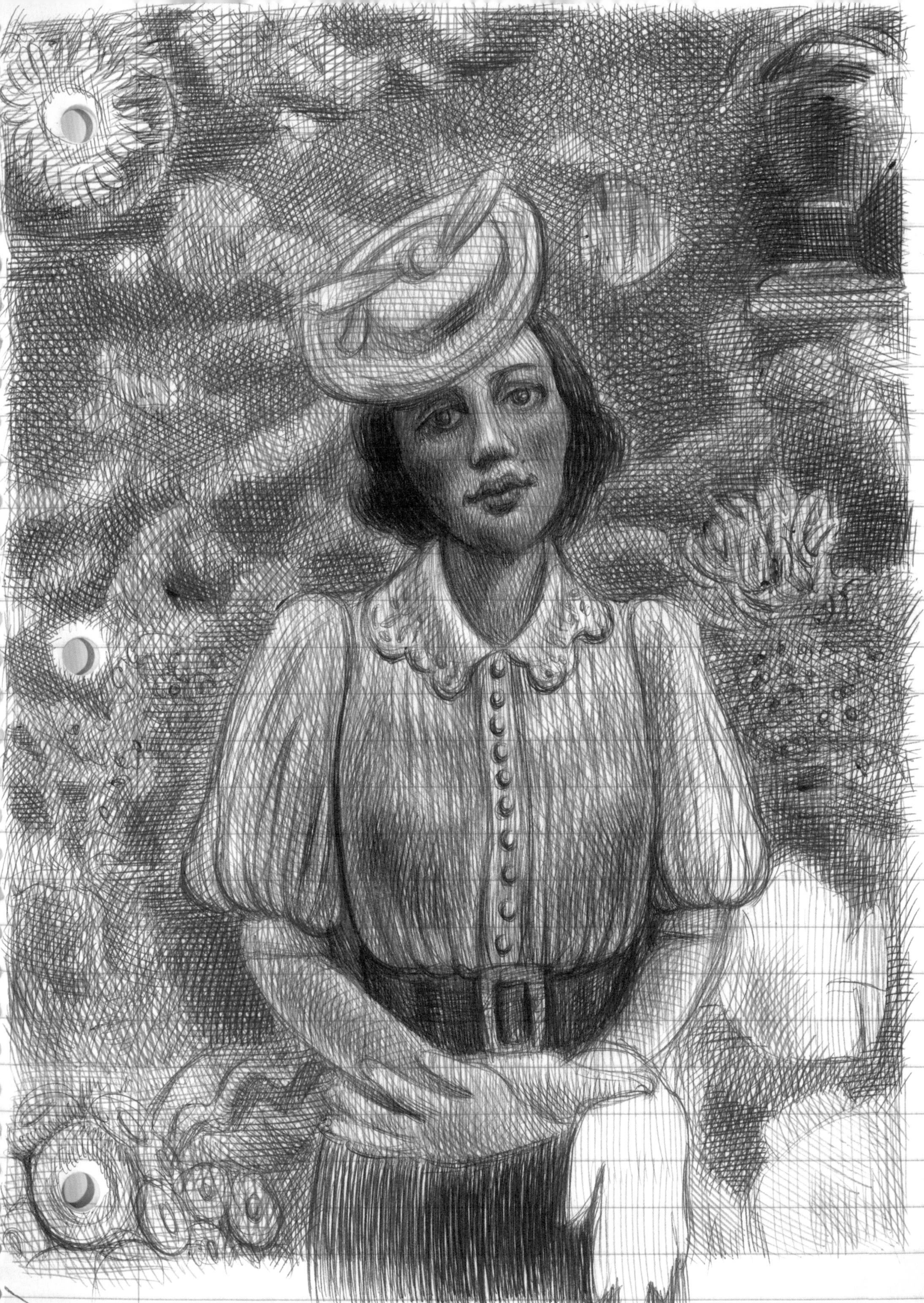

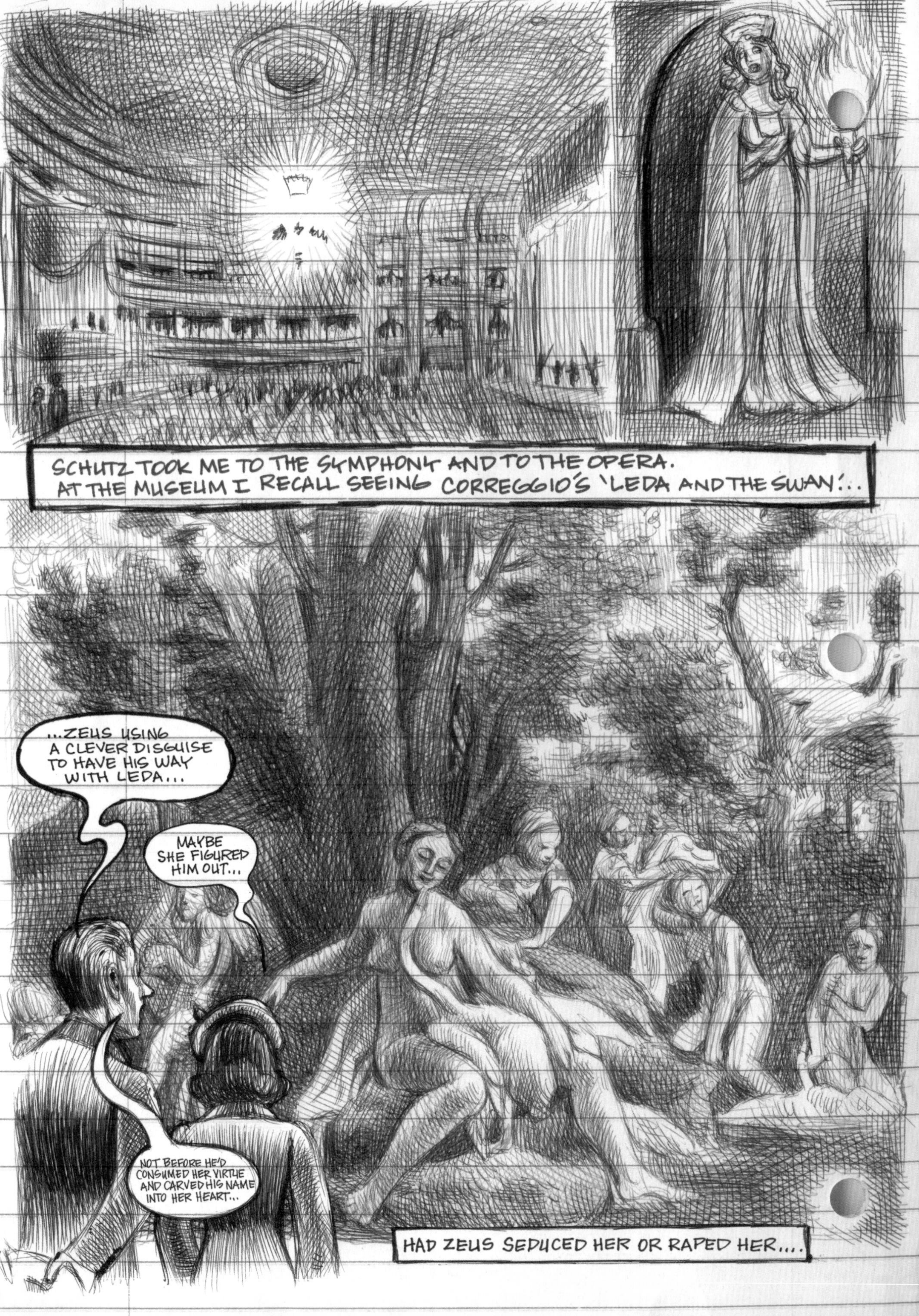
SCHUTZ TOOK ME TO THE SYMPHONY AND TO THE OPERA.
AT THE MUSEUM I RECALL SEEING CORREGGIO'S 'LEDA AND THE SWAN'...
...ZEUS USING A CLEVER DISGUISE TO HAVE HIS WAY WITH LEDA...
MAYBE SHE FIGURED HIM OUT...
NOT BEFORE HE'D CONSUMED HER VIRTUE AND CARVED HIS NAME INTO HER HEART...
HAD ZEUS SEDUCED HER OR RAPED HER....

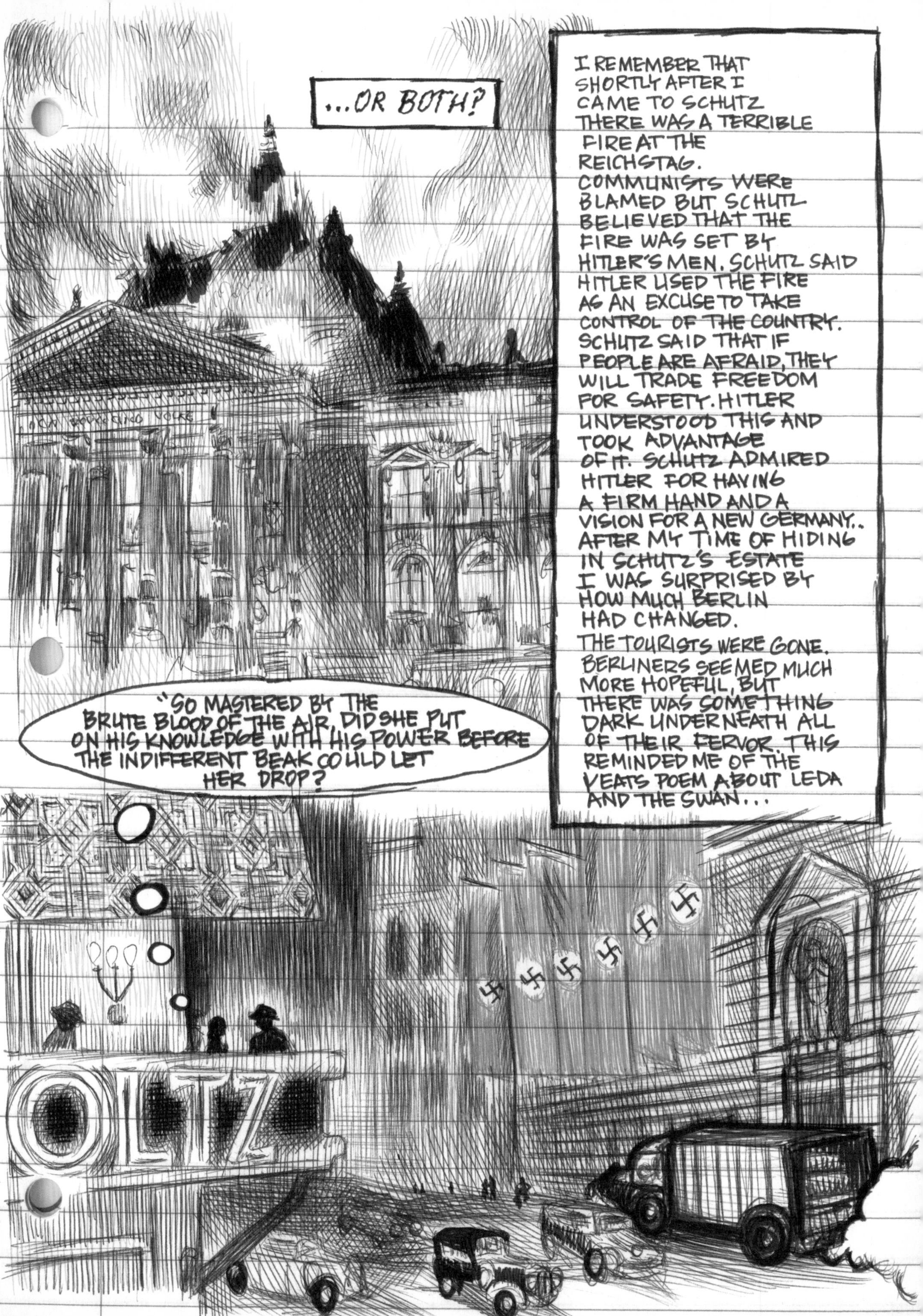
...OR BOTH?
I REMEMBER THAT SHORTLY AFTER I CAME TO SCHUTZ THERE WAS A TERRIBLE FIRE AT THE REICHSTAG. COMMUNISTS WERE BLAMED BUT SCHUTZ BELIEVED THAT THE FIRE WAS SET BY HITLER'S MEN. SCHUTZ SAID HITLER USED THE FIRE AS AN EXCUSE TO TAKE CONTROL OF THE COUNTRY. SCHUTZ SAID THAT IF PEOPLE ARE AFRAID, THEY WILL TRADE FREEDOM FOR SAFETY. HITLER UNDERSTOOD THIS AND TOOK ADVANTAGE OF IT. SCHUTZ ADMIRED HITLER FOR HAVING A FIRM HAND AND A VISION FOR A NEW GERMANY.. AFTER MY TIME OF HIDING IN SCHUTZ'S ESTATE I WAS SURPRISED BY HOW MUCH BERLIN HAD CHANGED. THE TOURISTS WERE GONE. BERLINERS SEEMED MUCH MORE HOPEFUL, BUT THERE WAS SOMETHING DARK UNDERNEATH ALL OF THEIR FERVOR. THIS REMINDED ME OF THE YEATS POEM ABOUT LEDA AND THE SWAN...
"SO MASTERED BY THE BRUTE BLOOD OF THE AIR, DID SHE PUT ON HIS KNOWLEDGE WITH HIS POWER BEFORE THE INDIFFERENT BEAK COULD LET HER DROP?

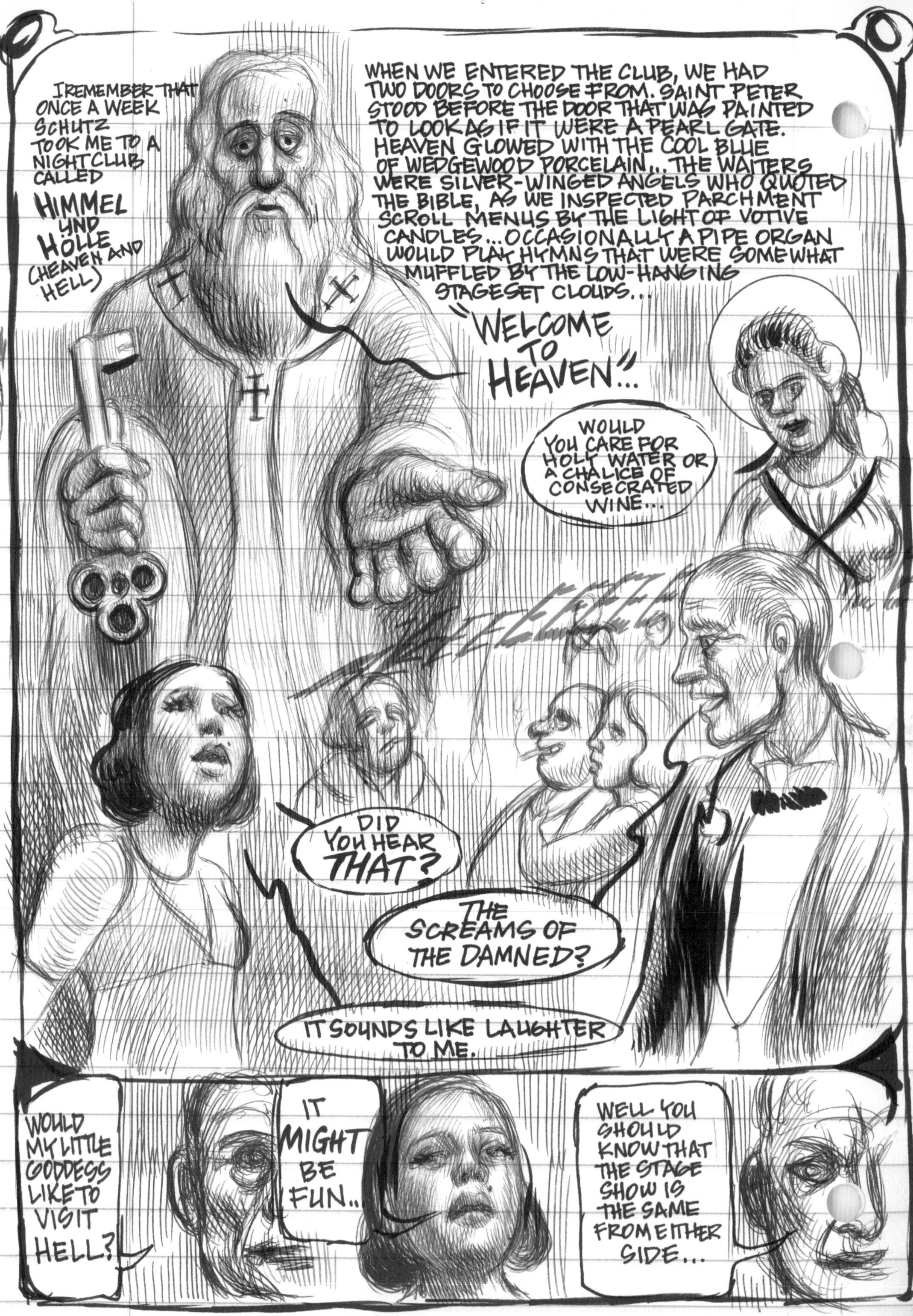
I REMEMBER THAT ONCE A WEEK SCHUTZ TOOK ME TO A NIGHTCLUB CALLED HIMMEL UND HÖLLE (HEAVEN AND HELL)
WHEN WE ENTERED THE CLUB, WE HAD TWO DOORS TO CHOOSE FROM. SAINT PETER STOOD BEFORE THE DOOR THAT WAS PAINTED TO LOOK AS IF IT WERE A PEARL GATE. HEAVEN GLOWED WITH THE COOL BLUE OF WEDGEWOOD PORCELAIN... THE WAITERS WERE SILVER-WINGED ANGELS WHO QUOTED THE BIBLE, AS WE INSPECTED PARCHMENT SCROLL MENUS BY THE LIGHT OF VOTIVE CANDLES... OCCASIONALLY A PIPE ORGAN WOULD PLAY HYMNS THAT WERE SOMEWHAT MUFFLED BY THE LOW-HANGING STAGESET CLOUDS...
"WELCOME TO HEAVEN"...
WOULD YOU CARE FOR HOLY WATER OR A CHALICE OF CONSECRATED WINE...
DID YOU HEAR THAT?
THE SCREAMS OF THE DAMNED?
IT SOUNDS LIKE LAUGHTER TO ME.
WOULD MY LITTLE GODDESS LIKE TO VISIT HELL?
IT MIGHT BE FUN...
WELL YOU SHOULD KNOW THAT THE STAGE SHOW IS THE SAME FROM EITHER SIDE...

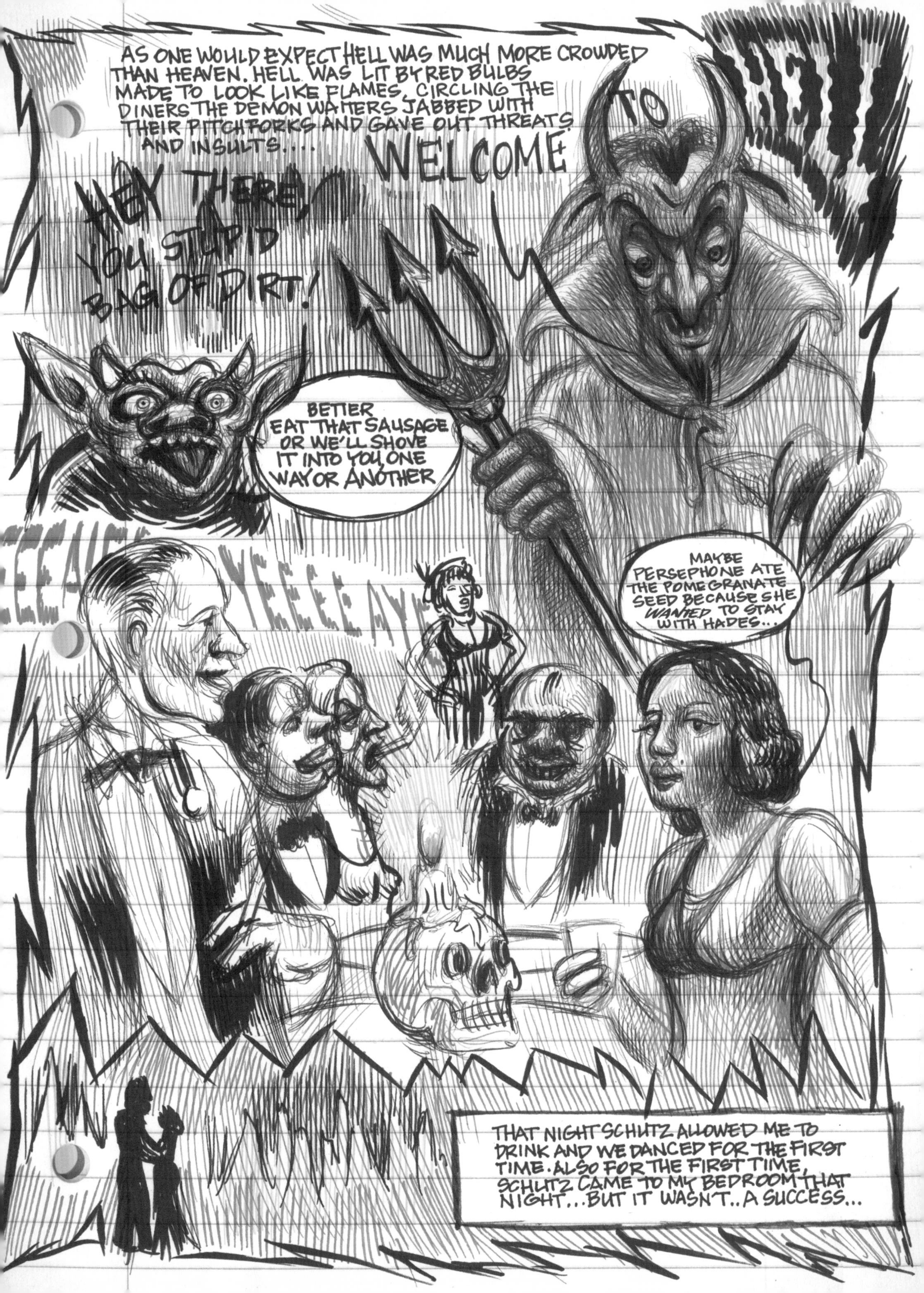
AS ONE WOULD EXPECT HELL WAS MUCH MORE CROWDED THAN HEAVEN. HELL WAS LIT BY RED BULBS MADE TO LOOK LIKE FLAMES, CIRCLING THE DINERS THE DEMON WAITERS JABBED WITH THEIR PITCHFORKS AND GAVE OUT THREATS AND INSULTS...
WELCOME TO HELL!
HEY THERE, YOU STUPID BAG OF DIRT!
BETTER EAT THAT SAUSAGE OR WE'LL SHOVE IT INTO YOU, ONE WAY OR ANOTHER
EEEAYEE YEEEEAYE
MAYBE PERSEPHONE ATE THE POMEGRANATE SEED BECAUSE SHE WANTED TO STAY WITH HADES...
THAT NIGHT SCHUTZ ALLOWED ME TO DRINK AND WE DANCED FOR THE FIRST TIME. ALSO FOR THE FIRST TIME, SCHUTZ CAME TO MY BEDROOM THAT NIGHT... BUT IT WASN'T.. A SUCCESS...

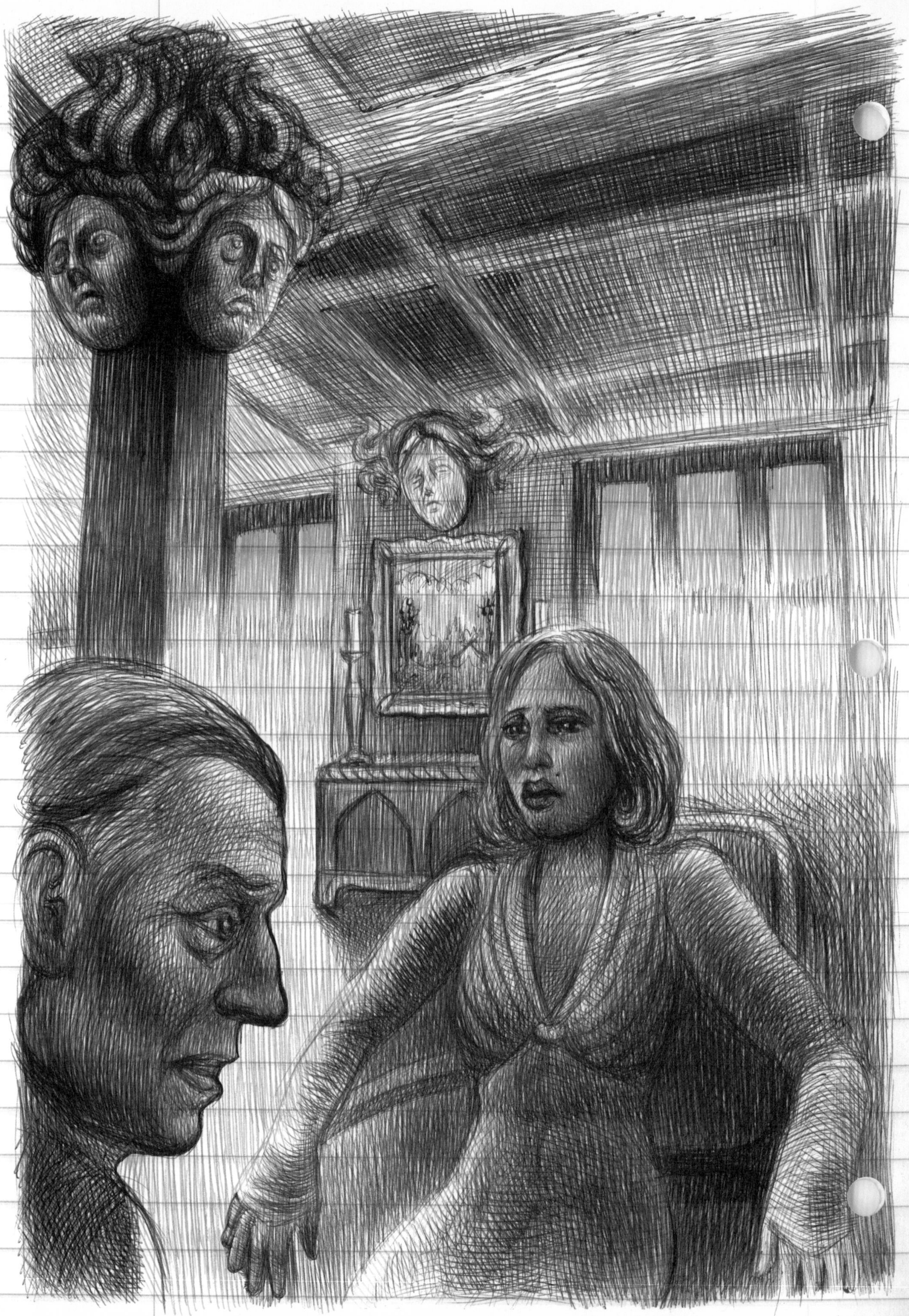

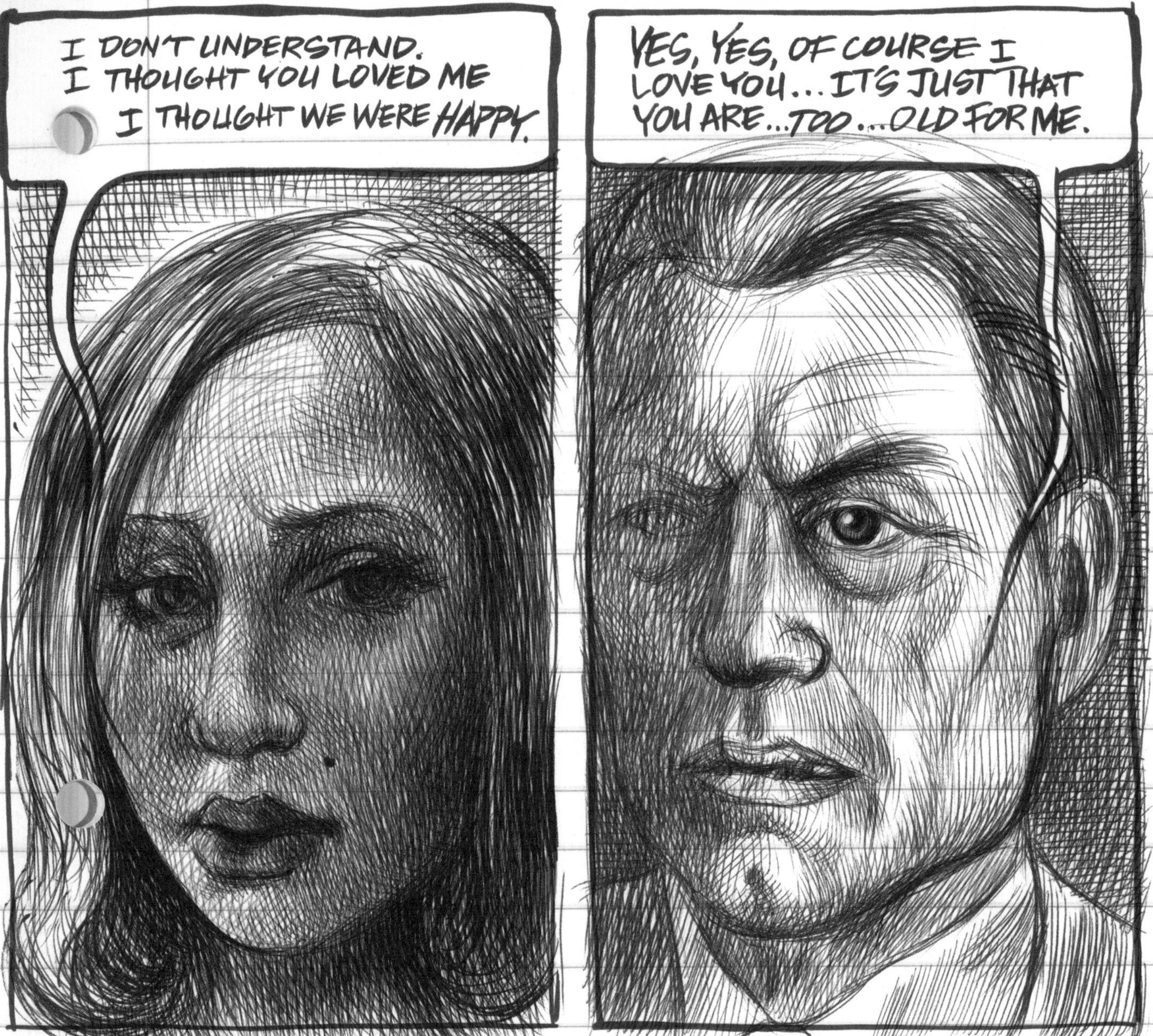
I DON'T UNDERSTAND. I THOUGHT YOU LOVED ME I THOUGHT WE WERE *HAPPY.*
YES, YES, OF COURSE I LOVE YOU... IT'S JUST THAT YOU ARE...*TOO*...*OLD* FOR ME.

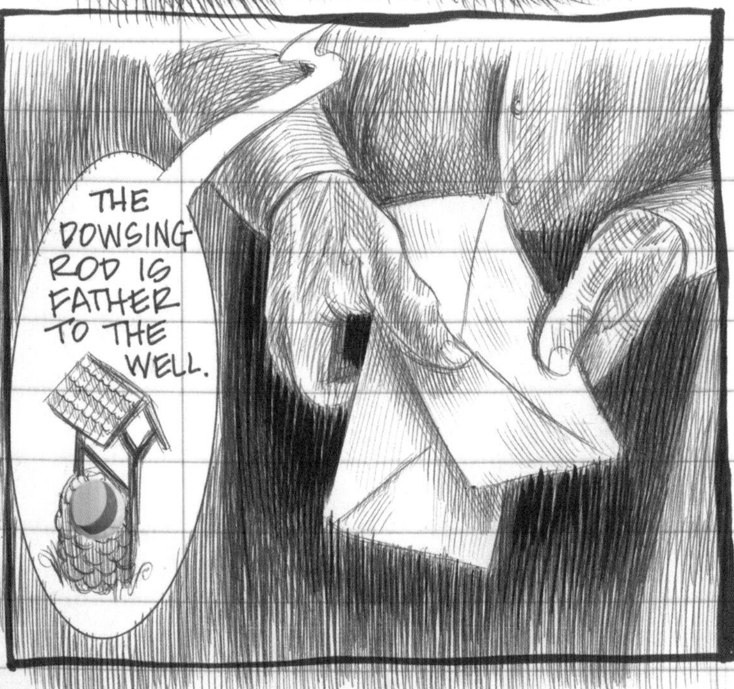
THE DOWSING ROD IS FATHER TO THE WELL.

SCHUTZ GAVE ME TWO ENVELOPES. ONE HAD MONEY IN IT. THE OTHER CONTAINED A LETTER OF RECOMMENDATION, SO THAT – AS SCHUTZ SAID – I COULD GO TO UNIVERSITY. HE SAID THAT IT WAS "TIME FOR ME TO HAVE A LIFE OF MY OWN." AND THAT ALTHOUGH HE PREFERRED YOUNGER GIRLS THAN ME... WE WOULD BE "FOREVER LINKED."
I QUIETLY REJECTED THE IDEA THAT ANY CONNECTION BETWEEN MYSELF AND SCHUTZ WOULD OUTLAST OUR PARTING, BUT I TOOK THE MONEY AND THE LETTER. SCHUTZ HAD BEEN THE ONLY MAN I'D EVER KNOWN. I PACKED AND LEFT THE ESTATE AND I FOUND AN APARTMENT...

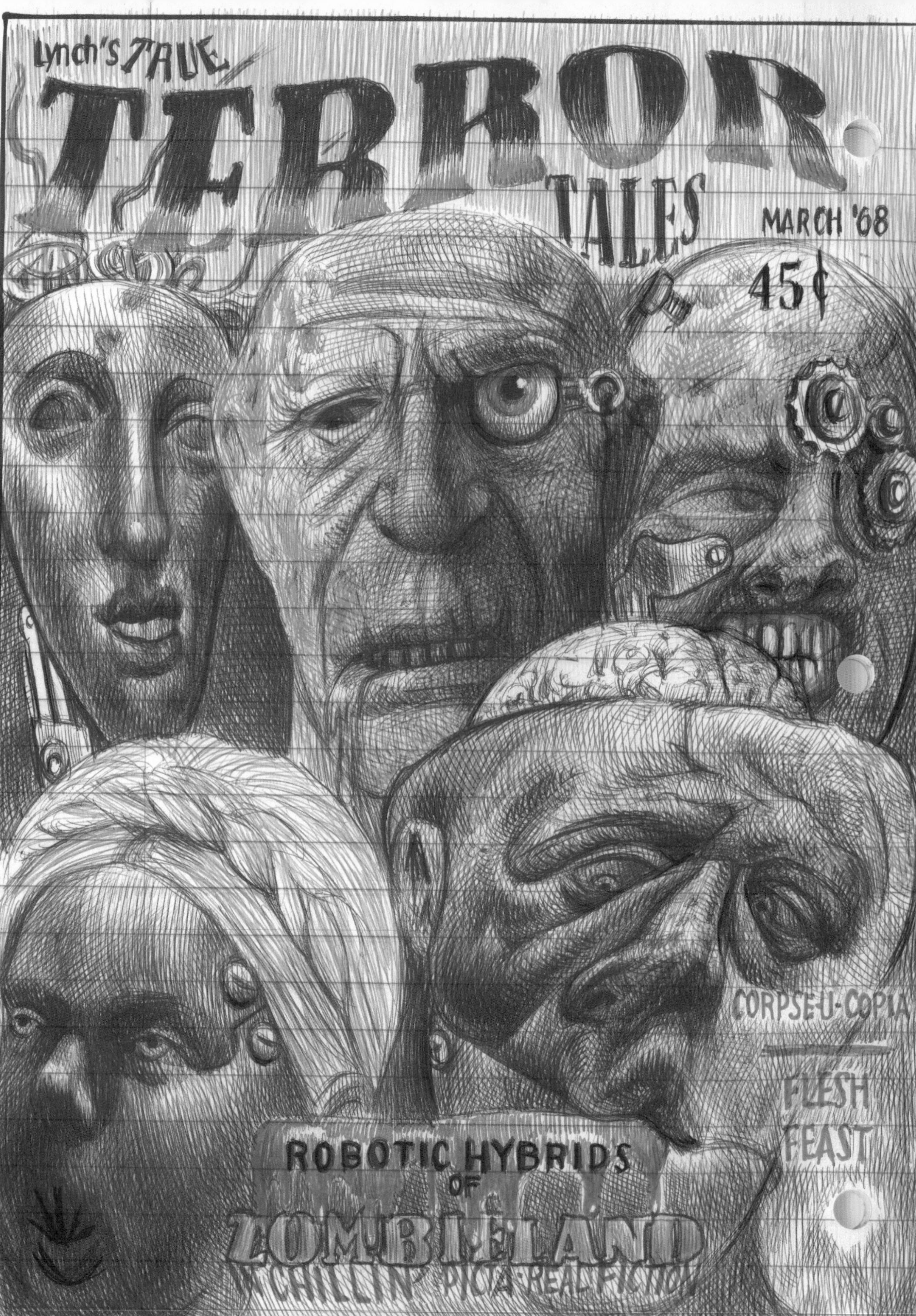
Lynch's TRUE
TERROR
TALES
MARCH '68
45¢
CORPSE-U-COPIA
FLESH
FEAST
ROBOTIC HYBRIDS
OF
ZOMBIELAND
CHILLIN' PIC-A-REAL FICTIO

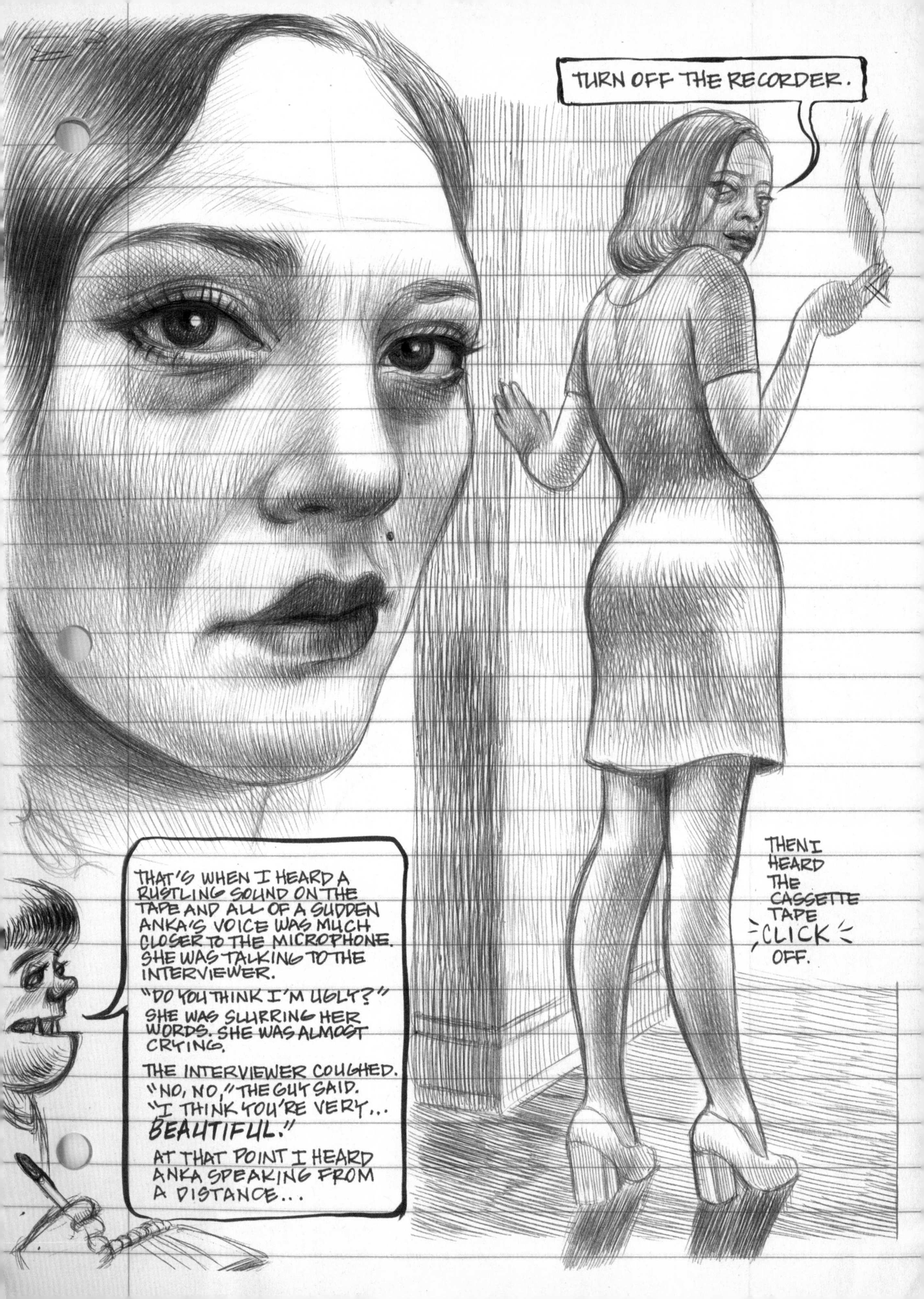
TURN OFF THE RECORDER.
THAT'S WHEN I HEARD A RUSTLING SOUND ON THE TAPE AND ALL OF A SUDDEN ANKA'S VOICE WAS MUCH CLOSER TO THE MICROPHONE. SHE WAS TALKING TO THE INTERVIEWER.
"DO YOU THINK I'M UGLY?" SHE WAS SLURRING HER WORDS. SHE WAS ALMOST CRYING.
THE INTERVIEWER COUGHED. "NO, NO," THE GUY SAID. "I THINK YOU'RE VERY... BEAUTIFUL."
AT THAT POINT I HEARD ANKA SPEAKING FROM A DISTANCE...
THEN I HEARD THE CASSETTE TAPE CLICK OFF.

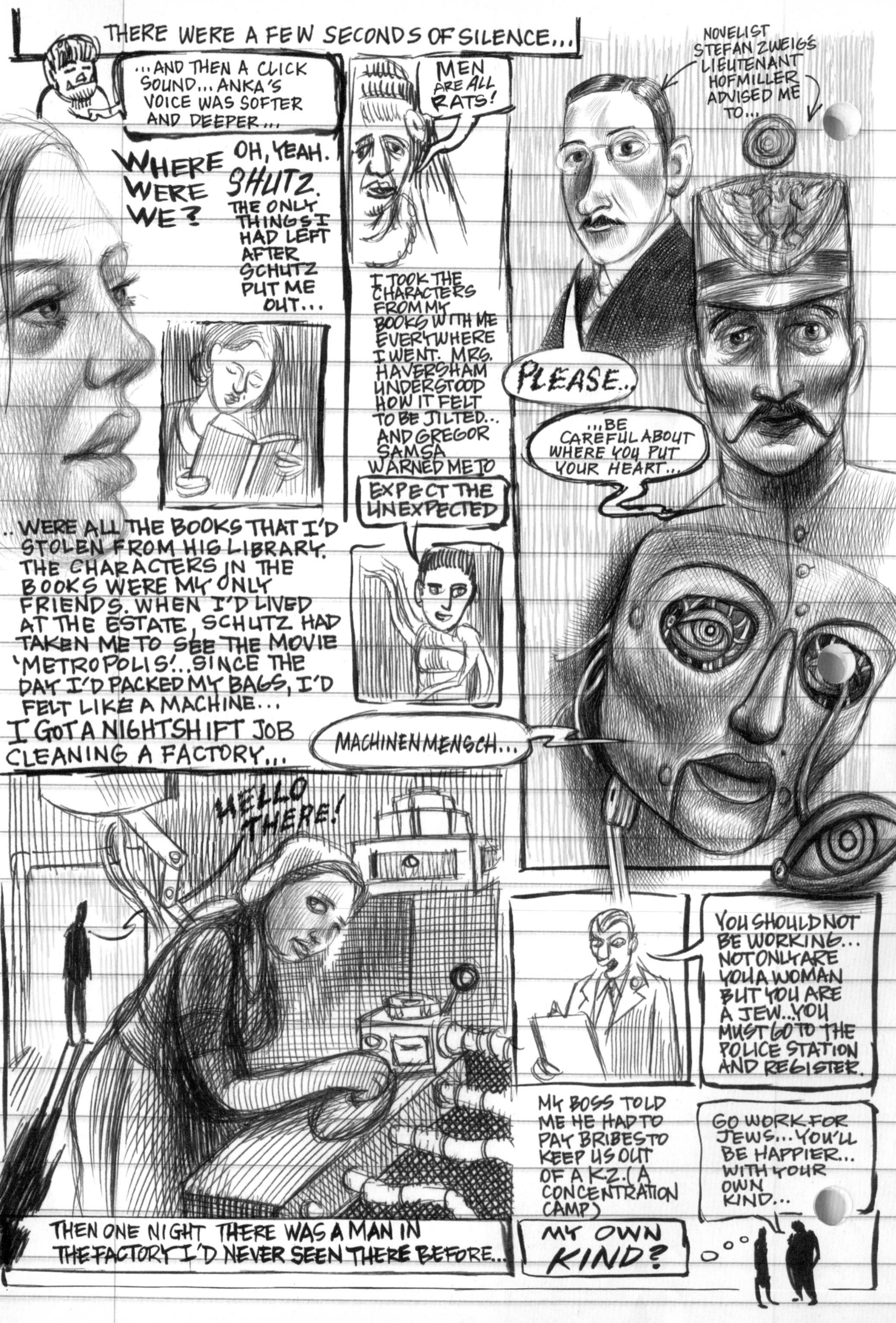
THERE WERE A FEW SECONDS OF SILENCE...
...AND THEN A CLICK SOUND... ANKA'S VOICE WAS SOFTER AND DEEPER...
WHERE WERE WE?
OH, YEAH. SHUTZ. THE ONLY THINGS I HAD LEFT AFTER SCHUTZ PUT ME OUT...
MEN ARE ALL RATS!
... WERE ALL THE BOOKS THAT I'D STOLEN FROM HIS LIBRARY. THE CHARACTERS IN THE BOOKS WERE MY ONLY FRIENDS. WHEN I'D LIVED AT THE ESTATE, SCHUTZ HAD TAKEN ME TO SEE THE MOVIE 'METROPOLIS'... SINCE THE DAY I'D PACKED MY BAGS, I'D FELT LIKE A MACHINE...
I TOOK THE CHARACTERS FROM MY BOOKS WITH ME EVERYWHERE I WENT. MRS. HAVERSHAM UNDERSTOOD HOW IT FELT TO BE JILTED... AND GREGOR SAMSA WARNED ME TO
EXPECT THE UNEXPECTED
NOVELIST STEFAN ZWEIG'S LIEUTENANT HOFMILLER ADVISED ME TO...
PLEASE...
...BE CAREFUL ABOUT WHERE YOU PUT YOUR HEART...
MACHINENMENSCH...
I GOT A NIGHTSHIFT JOB CLEANING A FACTORY...
HELLO THERE!
THEN ONE NIGHT THERE WAS A MAN IN THE FACTORY I'D NEVER SEEN THERE BEFORE...
YOU SHOULD NOT BE WORKING... NOT ONLY ARE YOU A WOMAN BUT YOU ARE A JEW... YOU MUST GO TO THE POLICE STATION AND REGISTER.
MY BOSS TOLD ME HE HAD TO PAY BRIBES TO KEEP US OUT OF A KZ. (A CONCENTRATION CAMP)
GO WORK FOR JEWS... YOU'LL BE HAPPIER... WITH YOUR OWN KIND...
MY OWN KIND?

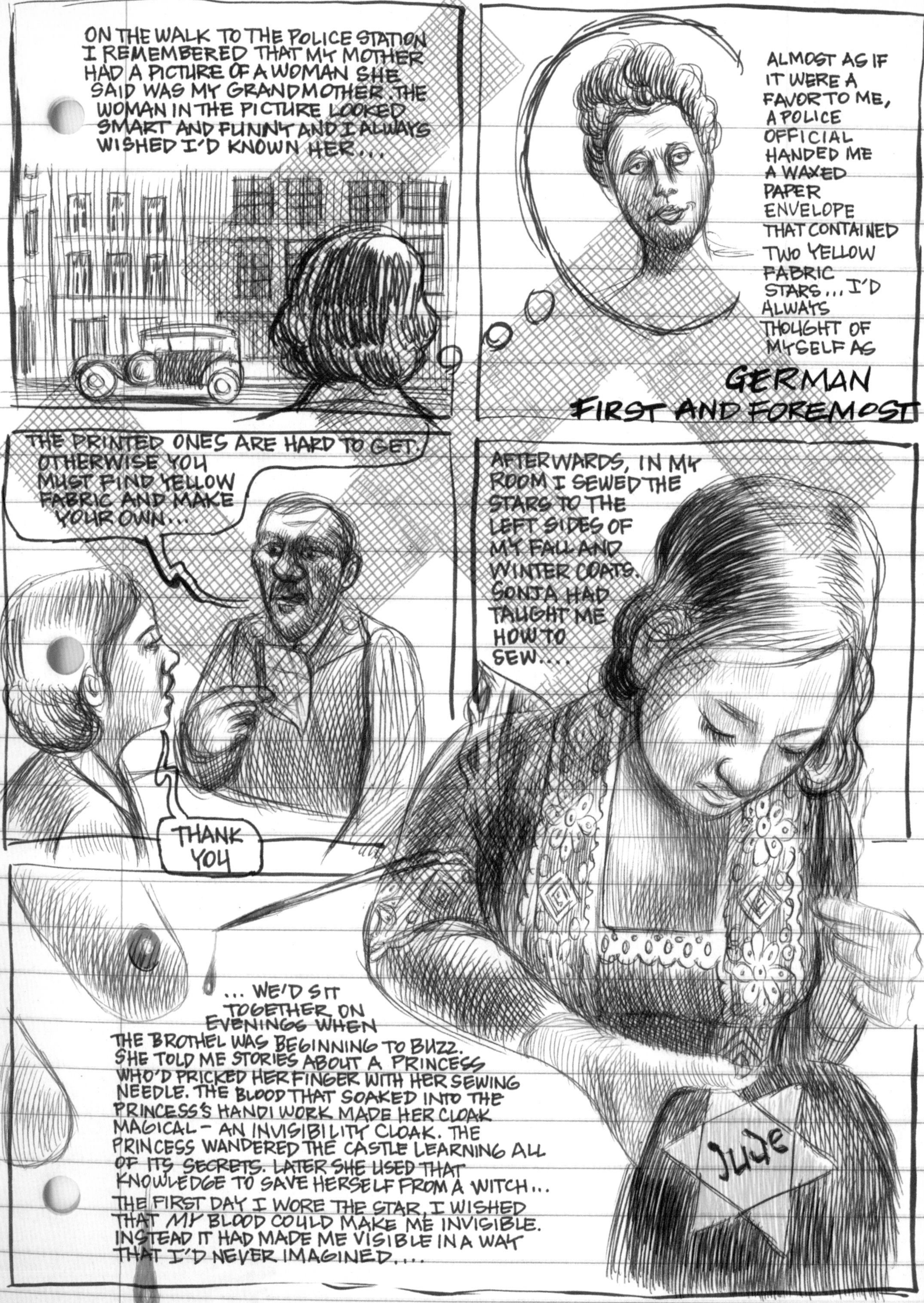
ON THE WALK TO THE POLICE STATION I REMEMBERED THAT MY MOTHER HAD A PICTURE OF A WOMAN SHE SAID WAS MY GRANDMOTHER. THE WOMAN IN THE PICTURE LOOKED SMART AND FUNNY AND I ALWAYS WISHED I'D KNOWN HER...
ALMOST AS IF IT WERE A FAVOR TO ME, A POLICE OFFICIAL HANDED ME A WAXED PAPER ENVELOPE THAT CONTAINED TWO YELLOW FABRIC STARS... I'D ALWAYS THOUGHT OF MYSELF AS
GERMAN FIRST AND FOREMOST
THE PRINTED ONES ARE HARD TO GET. OTHERWISE YOU MUST FIND YELLOW FABRIC AND MAKE YOUR OWN...
THANK YOU
AFTERWARDS, IN MY ROOM I SEWED THE STARS TO THE LEFT SIDES OF MY FALL AND WINTER COATS. SONJA HAD TAUGHT ME HOW TO SEW....
... WE'D SIT TOGETHER ON EVENINGS WHEN THE BROTHEL WAS BEGINNING TO BUZZ. SHE TOLD ME STORIES ABOUT A PRINCESS WHO'D PRICKED HER FINGER WITH HER SEWING NEEDLE. THE BLOOD THAT SOAKED INTO THE PRINCESS'S HANDIWORK MADE HER CLOAK MAGICAL - AN INVISIBILITY CLOAK. THE PRINCESS WANDERED THE CASTLE LEARNING ALL OF ITS SECRETS. LATER SHE USED THAT KNOWLEDGE TO SAVE HERSELF FROM A WITCH...
THE FIRST DAY I WORE THE STAR, I WISHED THAT MY BLOOD COULD MAKE ME INVISIBLE. INSTEAD IT HAD MADE ME VISIBLE IN A WAY THAT I'D NEVER IMAGINED...
JUDE

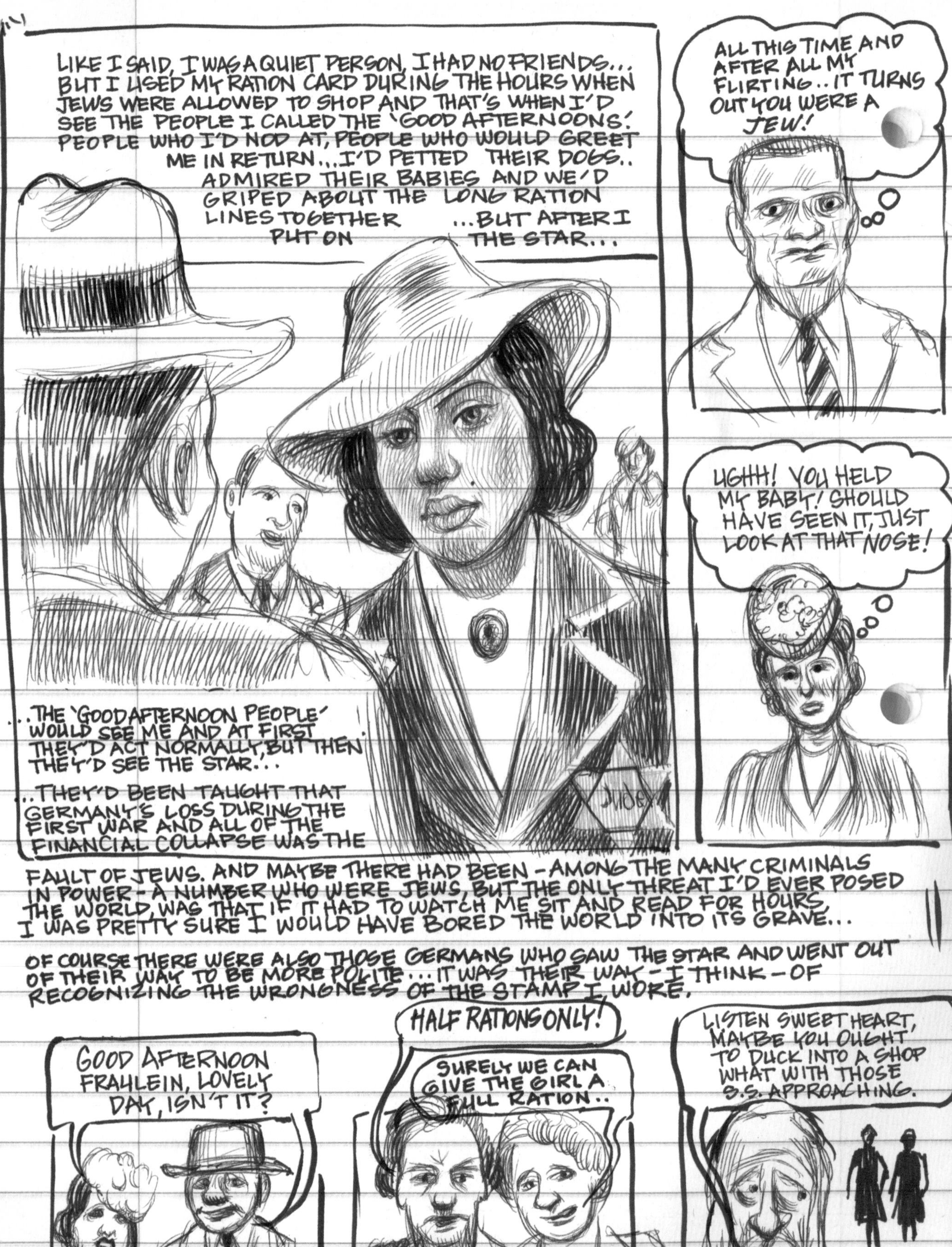
LIKE I SAID, I WAS A QUIET PERSON, I HAD NO FRIENDS... BUT I USED MY RATION CARD DURING THE HOURS WHEN JEWS WERE ALLOWED TO SHOP AND THAT'S WHEN I'D SEE THE PEOPLE I CALLED THE 'GOOD AFTERNOONS.' PEOPLE WHO I'D NOD AT, PEOPLE WHO WOULD GREET ME IN RETURN... I'D PETTED THEIR DOGS.. ADMIRED THEIR BABIES AND WE'D GRIPED ABOUT THE LONG RATION LINES TOGETHER ...BUT AFTER I PUT ON THE STAR...
ALL THIS TIME AND AFTER ALL MY FLIRTING.. IT TURNS OUT YOU WERE A JEW!
UGHH! YOU HELD MY BABY! SHOULD HAVE SEEN IT, JUST LOOK AT THAT NOSE!
..THE 'GOOD AFTERNOON PEOPLE' WOULD SEE ME AND AT FIRST THEY'D ACT NORMALLY, BUT THEN THEY'D SEE THE STAR...
..THEY'D BEEN TAUGHT THAT GERMANY'S LOSS DURING THE FIRST WAR AND ALL OF THE FINANCIAL COLLAPSE WAS THE FAULT OF JEWS. AND MAYBE THERE HAD BEEN - AMONG THE MANY CRIMINALS IN POWER - A NUMBER WHO WERE JEWS, BUT THE ONLY THREAT I'D EVER POSED THE WORLD, WAS THAT IF IT HAD TO WATCH ME SIT AND READ FOR HOURS, I WAS PRETTY SURE I WOULD HAVE BORED THE WORLD INTO ITS GRAVE...
OF COURSE THERE WERE ALSO THOSE GERMANS WHO SAW THE STAR AND WENT OUT OF THEIR WAY TO BE MORE POLITE... IT WAS THEIR WAY - I THINK - OF RECOGNIZING THE WRONGNESS OF THE STAMP I WORE.
GOOD AFTERNOON FRAULEIN, LOVELY DAY, ISN'T IT?
HALF RATIONS ONLY!
SURELY WE CAN GIVE THE GIRL A FULL RATION..
LISTEN SWEETHEART, MAYBE YOU OUGHT TO DUCK INTO A SHOP WHAT WITH THOSE S.S. APPROACHING.

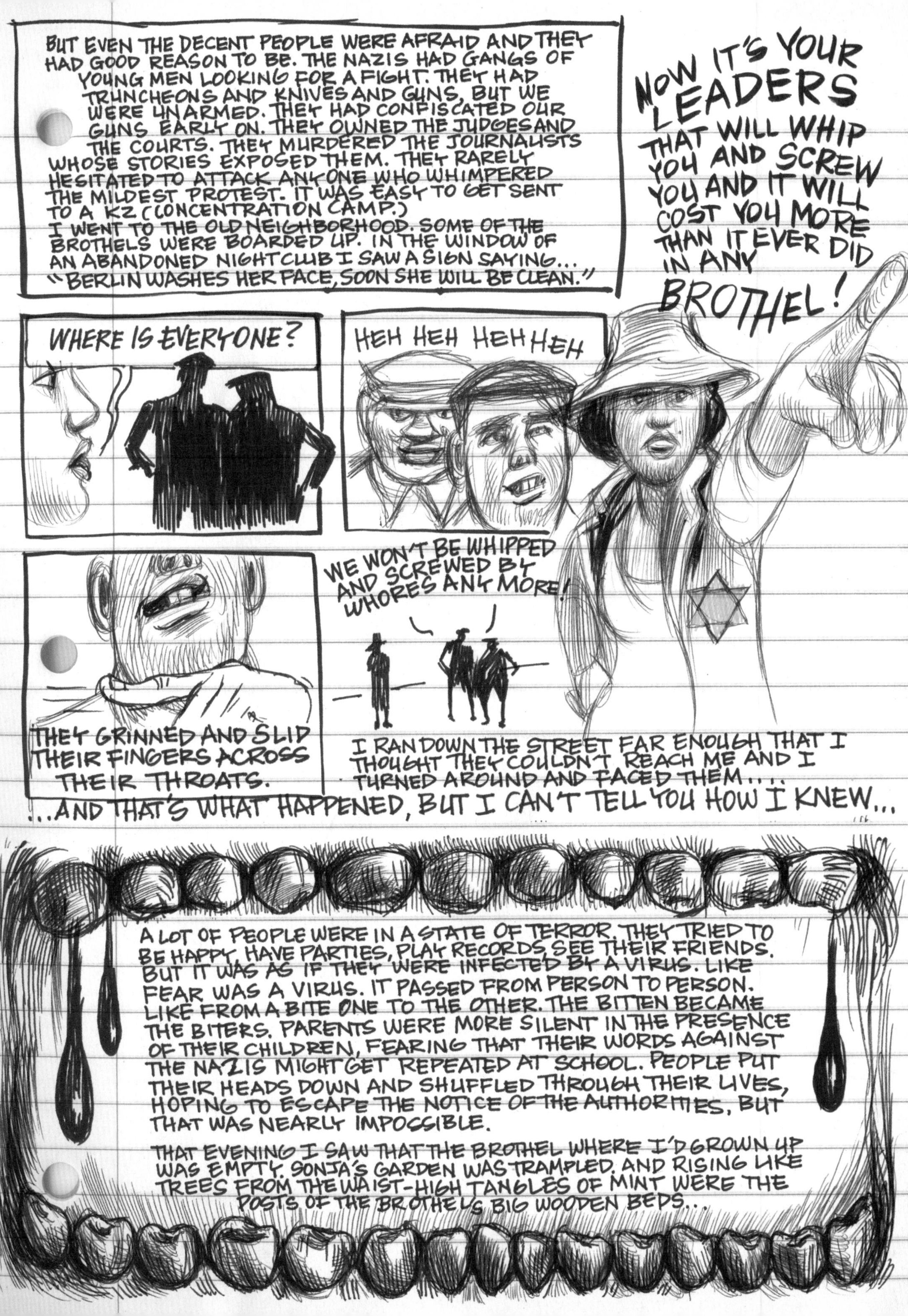
BUT EVEN THE DECENT PEOPLE WERE AFRAID AND THEY HAD GOOD REASON TO BE. THE NAZIS HAD GANGS OF YOUNG MEN LOOKING FOR A FIGHT. THEY HAD TRUNCHEONS AND KNIVES AND GUNS, BUT WE WERE UNARMED. THEY HAD CONFISCATED OUR GUNS EARLY ON. THEY OWNED THE JUDGES AND THE COURTS. THEY MURDERED THE JOURNALISTS WHOSE STORIES EXPOSED THEM. THEY RARELY HESITATED TO ATTACK ANYONE WHO WHIMPERED THE MILDEST PROTEST. IT WAS EASY TO GET SENT TO A KZ (CONCENTRATION CAMP.)
I WENT TO THE OLD NEIGHBORHOOD. SOME OF THE BROTHELS WERE BOARDED UP. IN THE WINDOW OF AN ABANDONED NIGHTCLUB I SAW A SIGN SAYING... "BERLIN WASHES HER FACE, SOON SHE WILL BE CLEAN."
NOW IT'S YOUR LEADERS THAT WILL WHIP YOU AND SCREW YOU AND IT WILL COST YOU MORE THAN IT EVER DID IN ANY BROTHEL!
WHERE IS EVERYONE?
HEH HEH HEH HEH
WE WON'T BE WHIPPED AND SCREWED BY WHORES ANY MORE!
THEY GRINNED AND SLID THEIR FINGERS ACROSS THEIR THROATS.
I RAN DOWN THE STREET FAR ENOUGH THAT I THOUGHT THEY COULDN'T REACH ME AND I TURNED AROUND AND FACED THEM...
...AND THAT'S WHAT HAPPENED, BUT I CAN'T TELL YOU HOW I KNEW...
A LOT OF PEOPLE WERE IN A STATE OF TERROR. THEY TRIED TO BE HAPPY, HAVE PARTIES, PLAY RECORDS, SEE THEIR FRIENDS. BUT IT WAS AS IF THEY WERE INFECTED BY A VIRUS. LIKE FEAR WAS A VIRUS. IT PASSED FROM PERSON TO PERSON. LIKE FROM A BITE ONE TO THE OTHER. THE BITTEN BECAME THE BITERS. PARENTS WERE MORE SILENT IN THE PRESENCE OF THEIR CHILDREN, FEARING THAT THEIR WORDS AGAINST THE NAZIS MIGHT GET REPEATED AT SCHOOL. PEOPLE PUT THEIR HEADS DOWN AND SHUFFLED THROUGH THEIR LIVES, HOPING TO ESCAPE THE NOTICE OF THE AUTHORITIES, BUT THAT WAS NEARLY IMPOSSIBLE.
THAT EVENING I SAW THAT THE BROTHEL WHERE I'D GROWN UP WAS EMPTY. SONJA'S GARDEN WAS TRAMPLED, AND RISING LIKE TREES FROM THE WAIST-HIGH TANGLES OF MINT WERE THE POSTS OF THE BROTHEL'S BIG WOODEN BEDS...

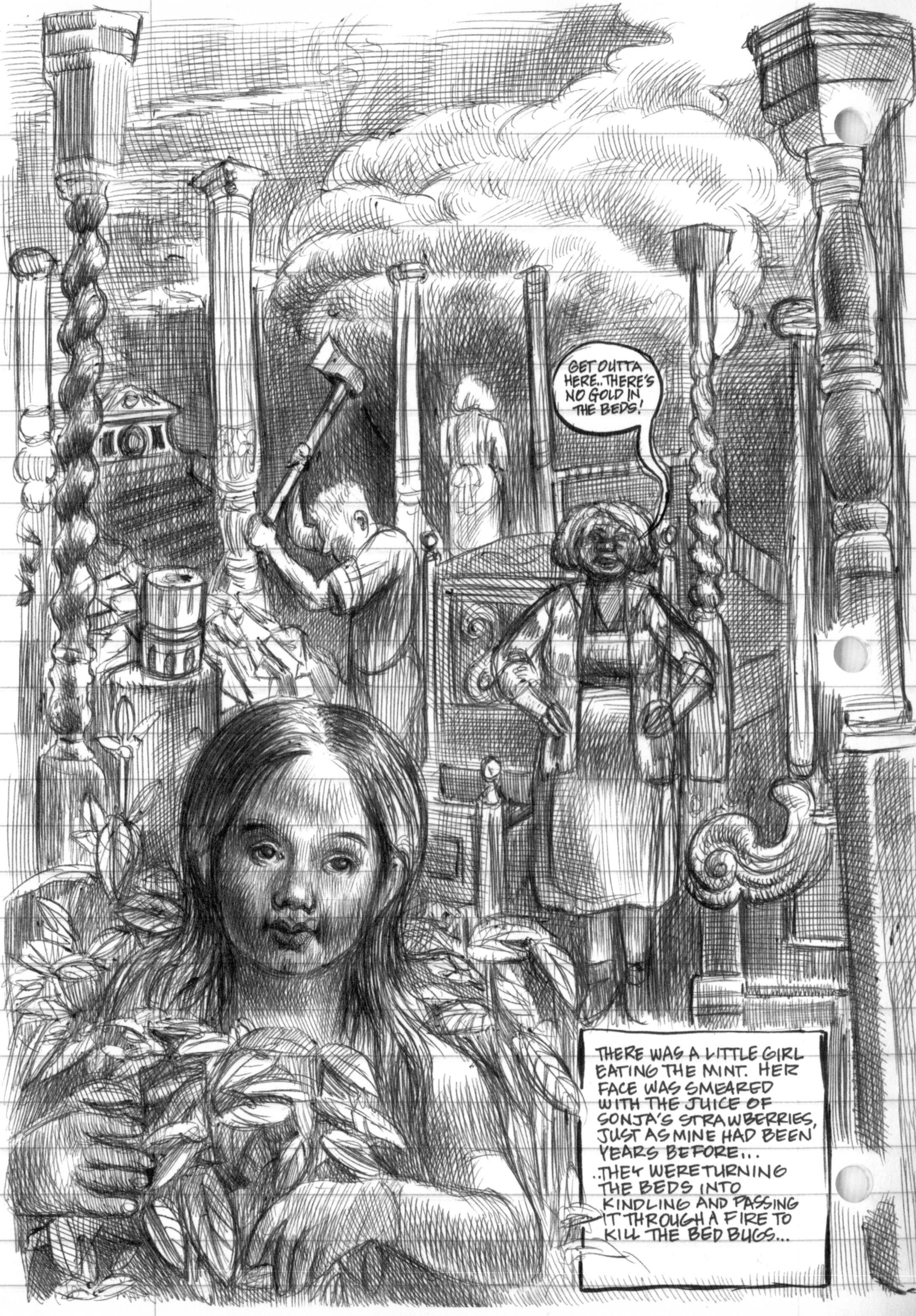
GET OUTTA HERE.. THERE'S NO GOLD IN THE BEDS!
THERE WAS A LITTLE GIRL EATING THE MINT. HER FACE WAS SMEARED WITH THE JUICE OF SONJA'S STRAWBERRIES, JUST AS MINE HAD BEEN YEARS BEFORE...
..THEY WERE TURNING THE BEDS INTO KINDLING AND PASSING IT THROUGH A FIRE TO KILL THE BED BUGS...

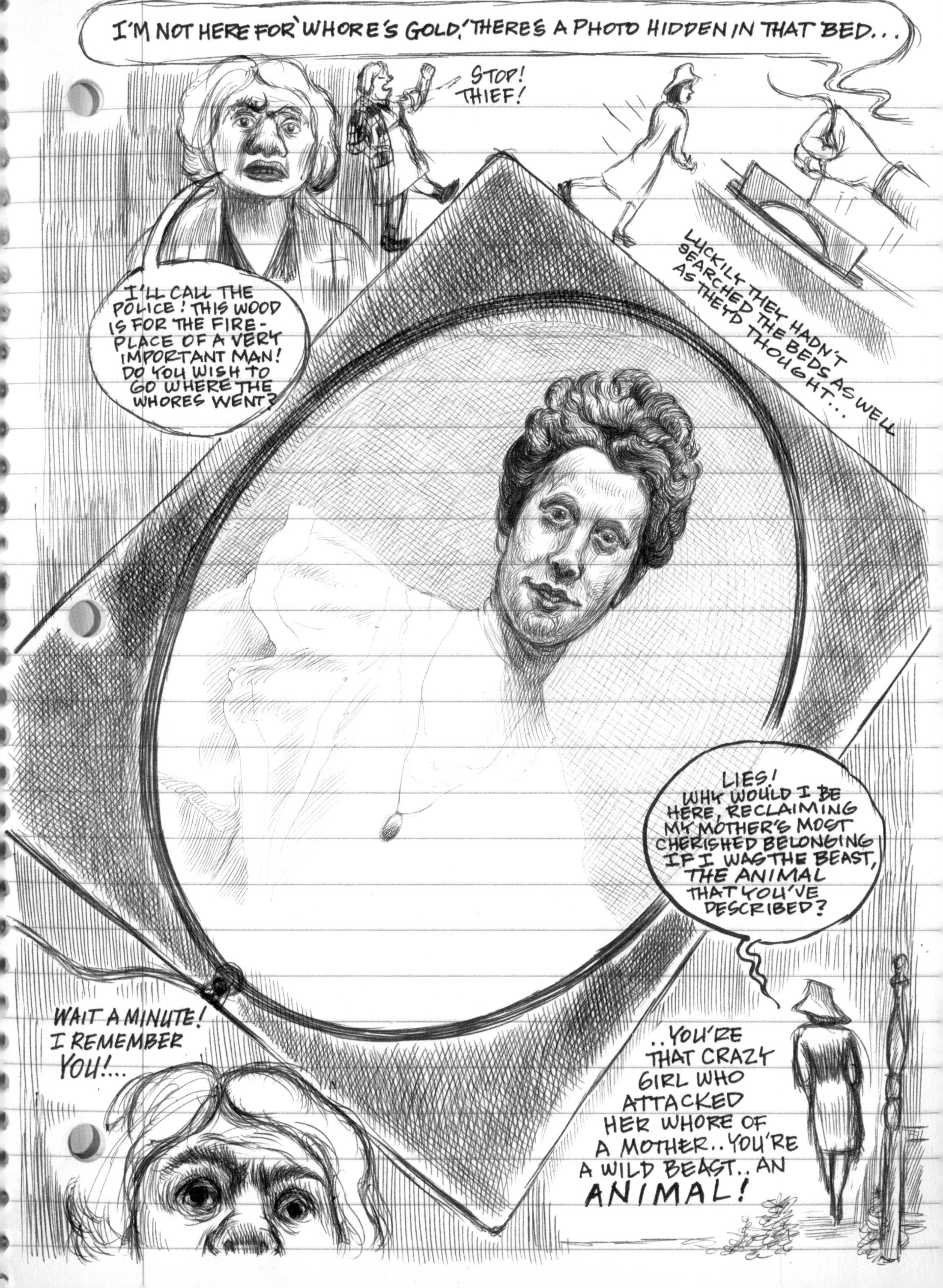
I'M NOT HERE FOR 'WHORE'S GOLD,' THERE'S A PHOTO HIDDEN IN THAT BED...
STOP! THIEF!
I'LL CALL THE POLICE! THIS WOOD IS FOR THE FIRE-PLACE OF A VERY IMPORTANT MAN! DO YOU WISH TO GO WHERE THE WHORES WENT?
LUCKILY THEY HADN'T SEARCHED THE BEDS AS WELL AS THEY'D THOUGHT...
LIES! WHY WOULD I BE HERE, RECLAIMING MY MOTHER'S MOST CHERISHED BELONGING IF I WAS THE BEAST, THE ANIMAL THAT YOU'VE DESCRIBED?
WAIT A MINUTE! I REMEMBER YOU!...
..YOU'RE THAT CRAZY GIRL WHO ATTACKED HER WHORE OF A MOTHER.. YOU'RE A WILD BEAST.. AN ANIMAL!

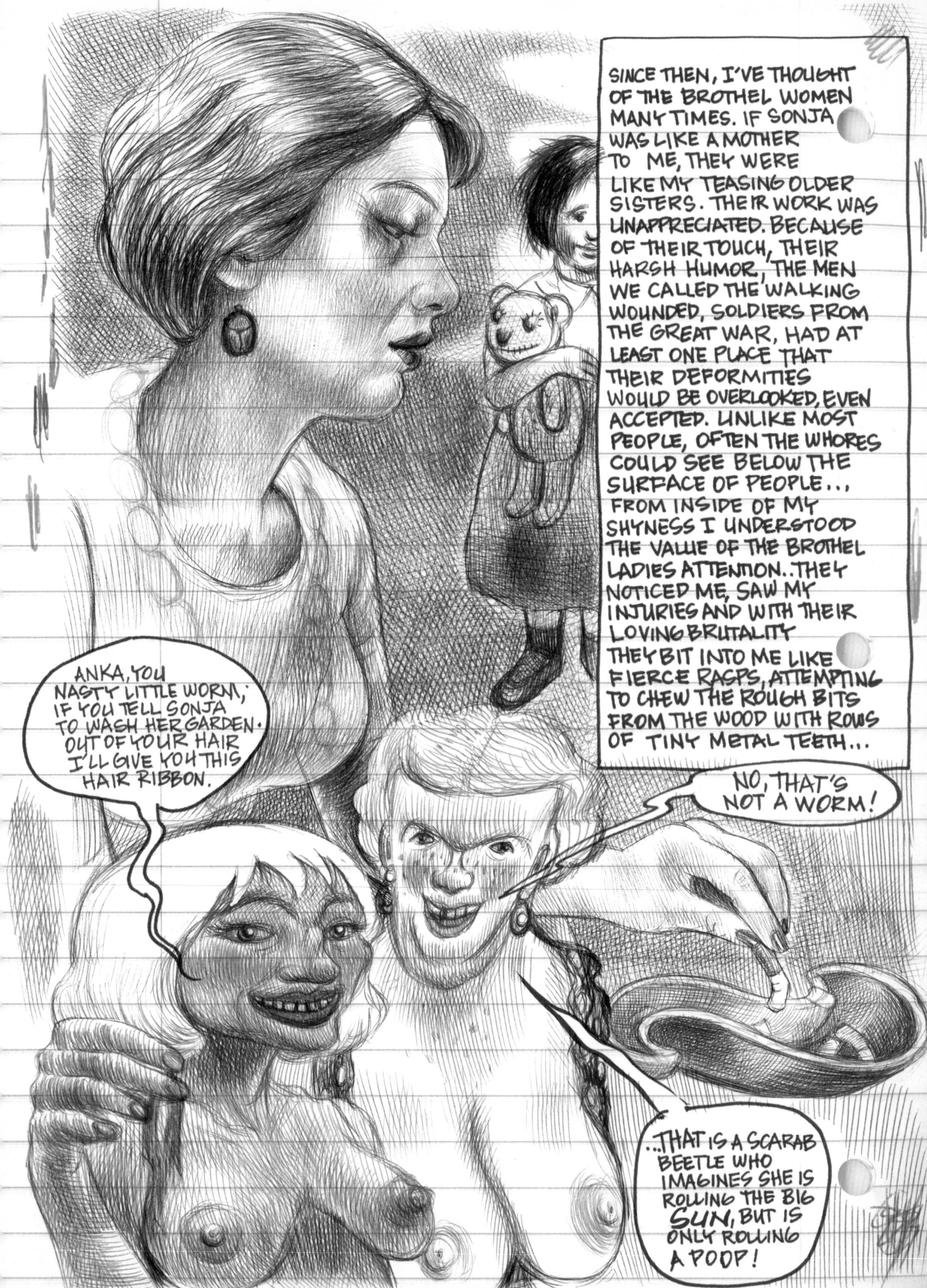
SINCE THEN, I'VE THOUGHT OF THE BROTHEL WOMEN MANY TIMES. IF SONJA WAS LIKE A MOTHER TO ME, THEY WERE LIKE MY TEASING OLDER SISTERS. THEIR WORK WAS UNAPPRECIATED. BECAUSE OF THEIR TOUCH, THEIR HARSH HUMOR, THE MEN WE CALLED THE WALKING WOUNDED, SOLDIERS FROM THE GREAT WAR, HAD AT LEAST ONE PLACE THAT THEIR DEFORMITIES WOULD BE OVERLOOKED, EVEN ACCEPTED. UNLIKE MOST PEOPLE, OFTEN THE WHORES COULD SEE BELOW THE SURFACE OF PEOPLE... FROM INSIDE OF MY SHYNESS I UNDERSTOOD THE VALUE OF THE BROTHEL LADIES ATTENTION..THEY NOTICED ME, SAW MY INJURIES AND WITH THEIR LOVING BRUTALITY THEY BIT INTO ME LIKE FIERCE RASPS, ATTEMPTING TO CHEW THE ROUGH BITS FROM THE WOOD WITH ROWS OF TINY METAL TEETH...
ANKA, YOU NASTY LITTLE WORM, IF YOU TELL SONJA TO WASH HER GARDEN OUT OF YOUR HAIR I'LL GIVE YOU THIS HAIR RIBBON.
NO, THAT'S NOT A WORM!
...THAT IS A SCARAB BEETLE WHO IMAGINES SHE IS ROLLING THE BIG SUN, BUT IS ONLY ROLLING A POOP!

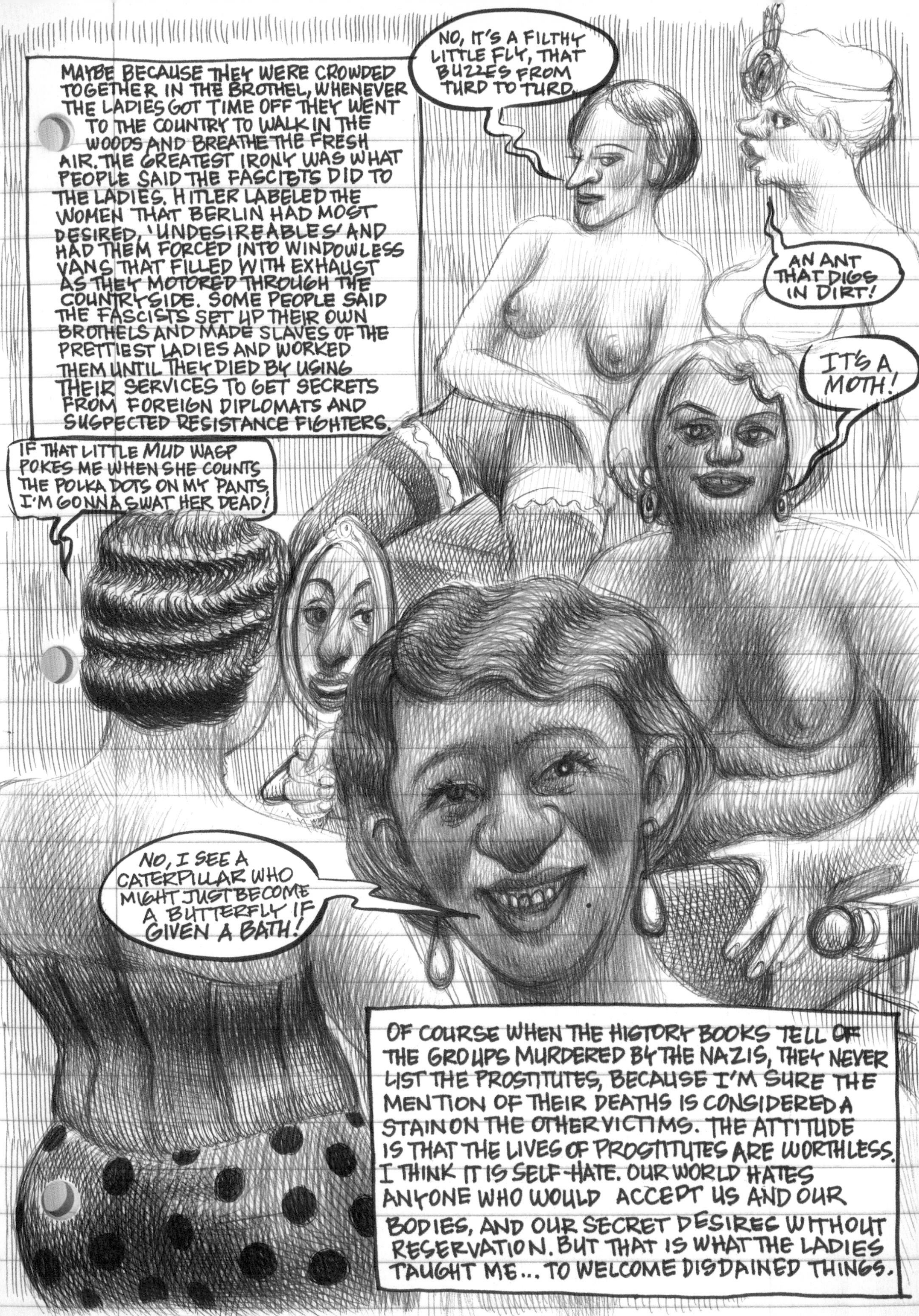
MAYBE BECAUSE THEY WERE CROWDED TOGETHER IN THE BROTHEL, WHENEVER THE LADIES GOT TIME OFF THEY WENT TO THE COUNTRY TO WALK IN THE WOODS AND BREATHE THE FRESH AIR. THE GREATEST IRONY WAS WHAT PEOPLE SAID THE FASCISTS DID TO THE LADIES. HITLER LABELED THE WOMEN THAT BERLIN HAD MOST DESIRED, 'UNDESIREABLES' AND HAD THEM FORCED INTO WINDOWLESS VANS THAT FILLED WITH EXHAUST AS THEY MOTORED THROUGH THE COUNTRYSIDE. SOME PEOPLE SAID THE FASCISTS SET UP THEIR OWN BROTHELS AND MADE SLAVES OF THE PRETTIEST LADIES AND WORKED THEM UNTIL THEY DIED BY USING THEIR SERVICES TO GET SECRETS FROM FOREIGN DIPLOMATS AND SUSPECTED RESISTANCE FIGHTERS.
NO, IT'S A FILTHY LITTLE FLY, THAT BUZZES FROM TURD TO TURD.
AN ANT THAT DIGS IN DIRT!
IT'S A MOTH!
IF THAT LITTLE MUD WASP POKES ME WHEN SHE COUNTS THE POLKA DOTS ON MY PANTS, I'M GONNA SWAT HER DEAD!
NO, I SEE A CATERPILLAR WHO MIGHT JUST BECOME A BUTTERFLY IF GIVEN A BATH!
OF COURSE WHEN THE HISTORY BOOKS TELL OF THE GROUPS MURDERED BY THE NAZIS, THEY NEVER LIST THE PROSTITUTES, BECAUSE I'M SURE THE MENTION OF THEIR DEATHS IS CONSIDERED A STAIN ON THE OTHER VICTIMS. THE ATTITUDE IS THAT THE LIVES OF PROSTITUTES ARE WORTHLESS. I THINK IT IS SELF-HATE. OUR WORLD HATES ANYONE WHO WOULD ACCEPT US AND OUR BODIES, AND OUR SECRET DESIRES WITHOUT RESERVATION. BUT THAT IS WHAT THE LADIES TAUGHT ME... TO WELCOME DISDAINED THINGS.

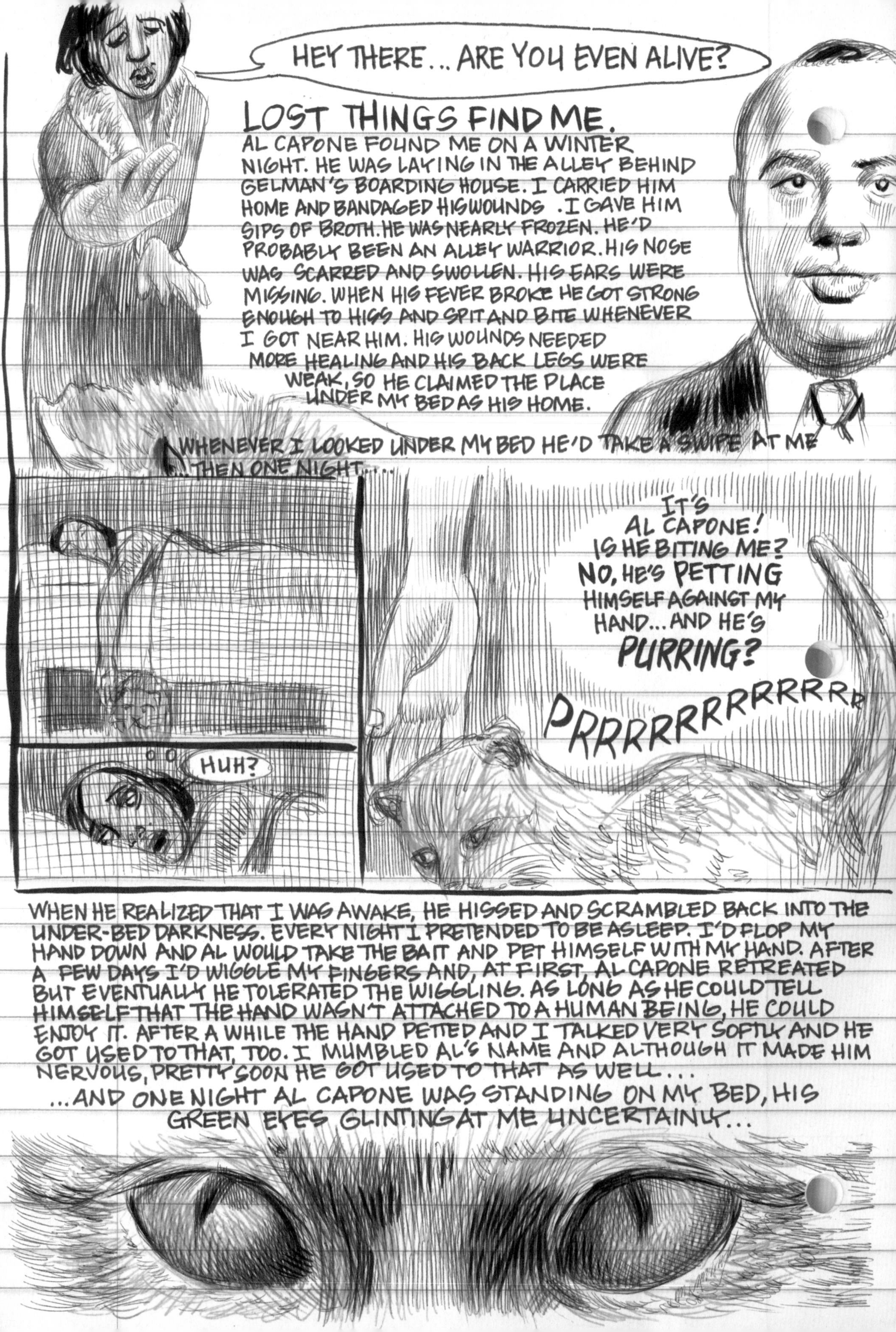
HEY THERE... ARE YOU EVEN ALIVE?
LOST THINGS FIND ME.
AL CAPONE FOUND ME ON A WINTER NIGHT. HE WAS LAYING IN THE ALLEY BEHIND GELMAN'S BOARDING HOUSE. I CARRIED HIM HOME AND BANDAGED HIS WOUNDS. I GAVE HIM SIPS OF BROTH. HE WAS NEARLY FROZEN. HE'D PROBABLY BEEN AN ALLEY WARRIOR. HIS NOSE WAS SCARRED AND SWOLLEN. HIS EARS WERE MISSING. WHEN HIS FEVER BROKE HE GOT STRONG ENOUGH TO HISS AND SPIT AND BITE WHENEVER I GOT NEAR HIM. HIS WOUNDS NEEDED MORE HEALING AND HIS BACK LEGS WERE WEAK, SO HE CLAIMED THE PLACE UNDER MY BED AS HIS HOME.
WHENEVER I LOOKED UNDER MY BED HE'D TAKE A SWIPE AT ME ...THEN ONE NIGHT...
HUH?
IT'S AL CAPONE! IS HE BITING ME? NO, HE'S PETTING HIMSELF AGAINST MY HAND... AND HE'S PURRING?
PRRRRRRRRRRRR
WHEN HE REALIZED THAT I WAS AWAKE, HE HISSED AND SCRAMBLED BACK INTO THE UNDER-BED DARKNESS. EVERY NIGHT I PRETENDED TO BE ASLEEP. I'D FLOP MY HAND DOWN AND AL WOULD TAKE THE BAIT AND PET HIMSELF WITH MY HAND. AFTER A FEW DAYS I'D WIGGLE MY FINGERS AND, AT FIRST, AL CAPONE RETREATED BUT EVENTUALLY HE TOLERATED THE WIGGLING. AS LONG AS HE COULD TELL HIMSELF THAT THE HAND WASN'T ATTACHED TO A HUMAN BEING, HE COULD ENJOY IT. AFTER A WHILE THE HAND PETTED AND I TALKED VERY SOFTLY AND HE GOT USED TO THAT, TOO. I MUMBLED AL'S NAME AND ALTHOUGH IT MADE HIM NERVOUS, PRETTY SOON HE GOT USED TO THAT AS WELL...
...AND ONE NIGHT AL CAPONE WAS STANDING ON MY BED, HIS GREEN EYES GLINTING AT ME UNCERTAINLY...

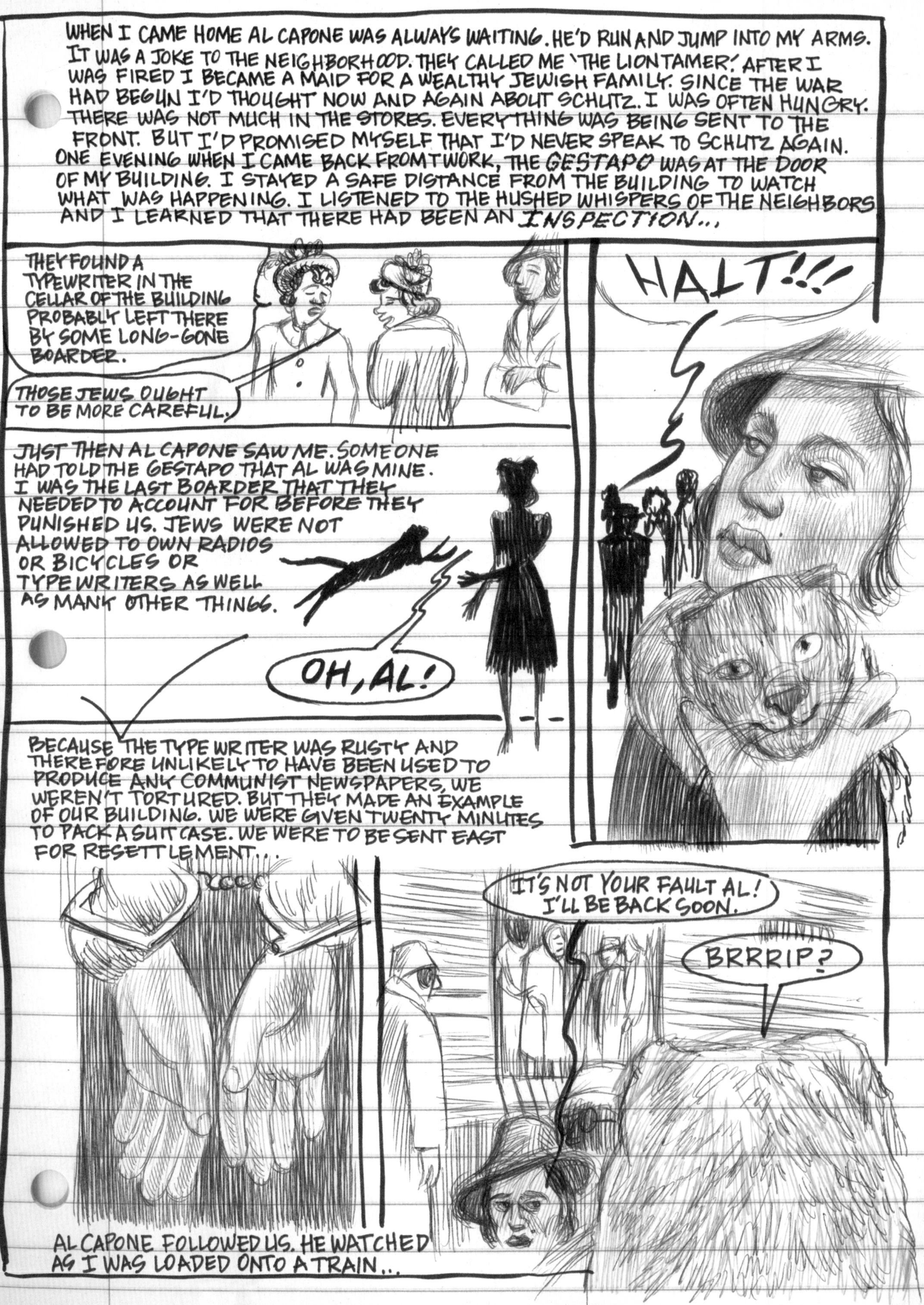
WHEN I CAME HOME AL CAPONE WAS ALWAYS WAITING. HE'D RUN AND JUMP INTO MY ARMS. IT WAS A JOKE TO THE NEIGHBORHOOD. THEY CALLED ME 'THE LIONTAMER.' AFTER I WAS FIRED I BECAME A MAID FOR A WEALTHY JEWISH FAMILY. SINCE THE WAR HAD BEGUN I'D THOUGHT NOW AND AGAIN ABOUT SCHUTZ. I WAS OFTEN HUNGRY. THERE WAS NOT MUCH IN THE STORES. EVERYTHING WAS BEING SENT TO THE FRONT. BUT I'D PROMISED MYSELF THAT I'D NEVER SPEAK TO SCHUTZ AGAIN. ONE EVENING WHEN I CAME BACK FROM WORK, THE GESTAPO WAS AT THE DOOR OF MY BUILDING. I STAYED A SAFE DISTANCE FROM THE BUILDING TO WATCH WHAT WAS HAPPENING. I LISTENED TO THE HUSHED WHISPERS OF THE NEIGHBORS AND I LEARNED THAT THERE HAD BEEN AN INSPECTION...
THEY FOUND A TYPEWRITER IN THE CELLAR OF THE BUILDING PROBABLY LEFT THERE BY SOME LONG-GONE BOARDER.
THOSE JEWS OUGHT TO BE MORE CAREFUL.
HALT!!!
JUST THEN AL CAPONE SAW ME. SOMEONE HAD TOLD THE GESTAPO THAT AL WAS MINE. I WAS THE LAST BOARDER THAT THEY NEEDED TO ACCOUNT FOR BEFORE THEY PUNISHED US. JEWS WERE NOT ALLOWED TO OWN RADIOS OR BICYCLES OR TYPEWRITERS AS WELL AS MANY OTHER THINGS.
OH, AL!
BECAUSE THE TYPEWRITER WAS RUSTY AND THEREFORE UNLIKELY TO HAVE BEEN USED TO PRODUCE ANY COMMUNIST NEWSPAPERS, WE WEREN'T TORTURED. BUT THEY MADE AN EXAMPLE OF OUR BUILDING. WE WERE GIVEN TWENTY MINUTES TO PACK A SUITCASE. WE WERE TO BE SENT EAST FOR RESETTLEMENT...
IT'S NOT YOUR FAULT AL! I'LL BE BACK SOON.
BRRRIP?
AL CAPONE FOLLOWED US. HE WATCHED AS I WAS LOADED ONTO A TRAIN...

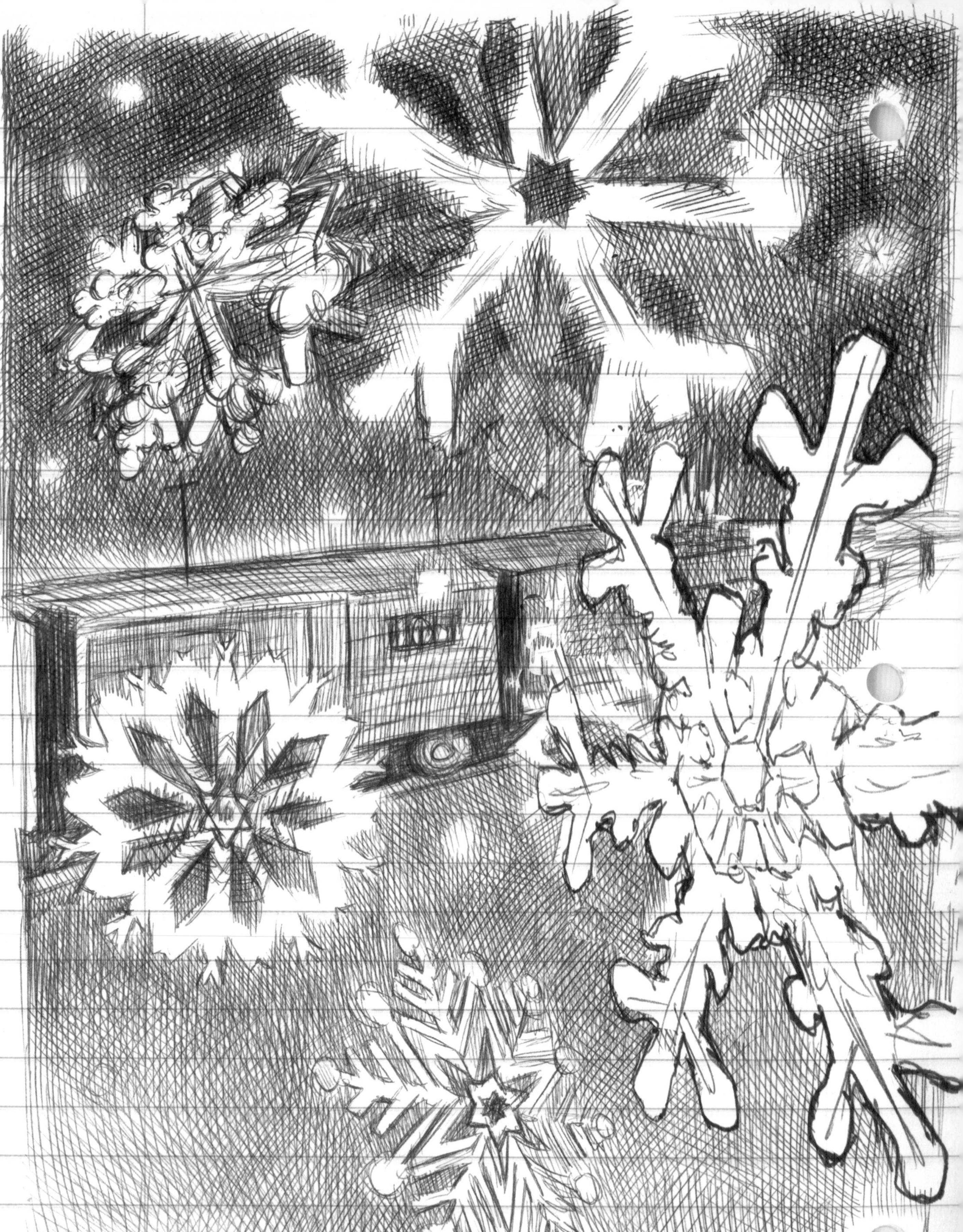

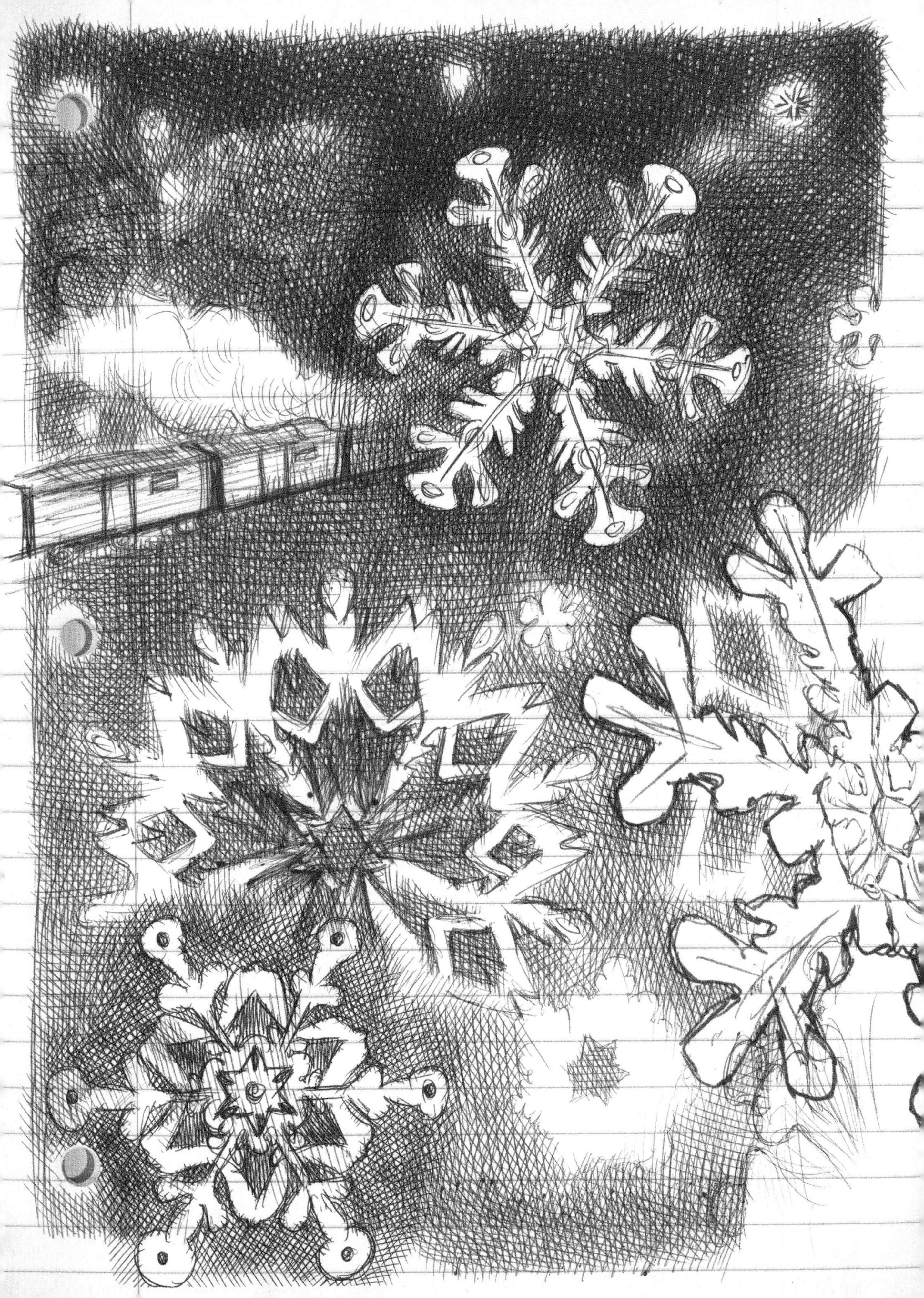

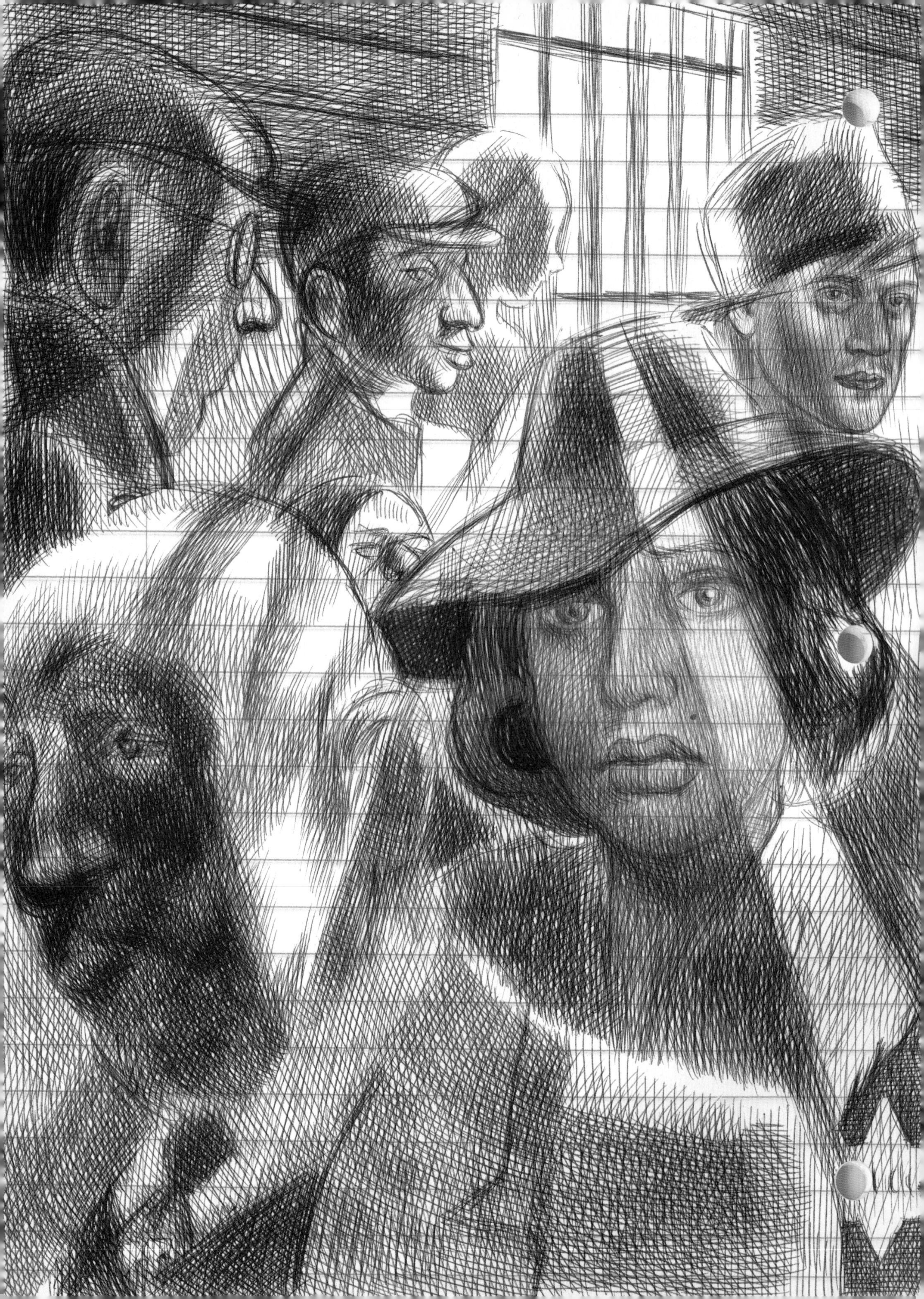

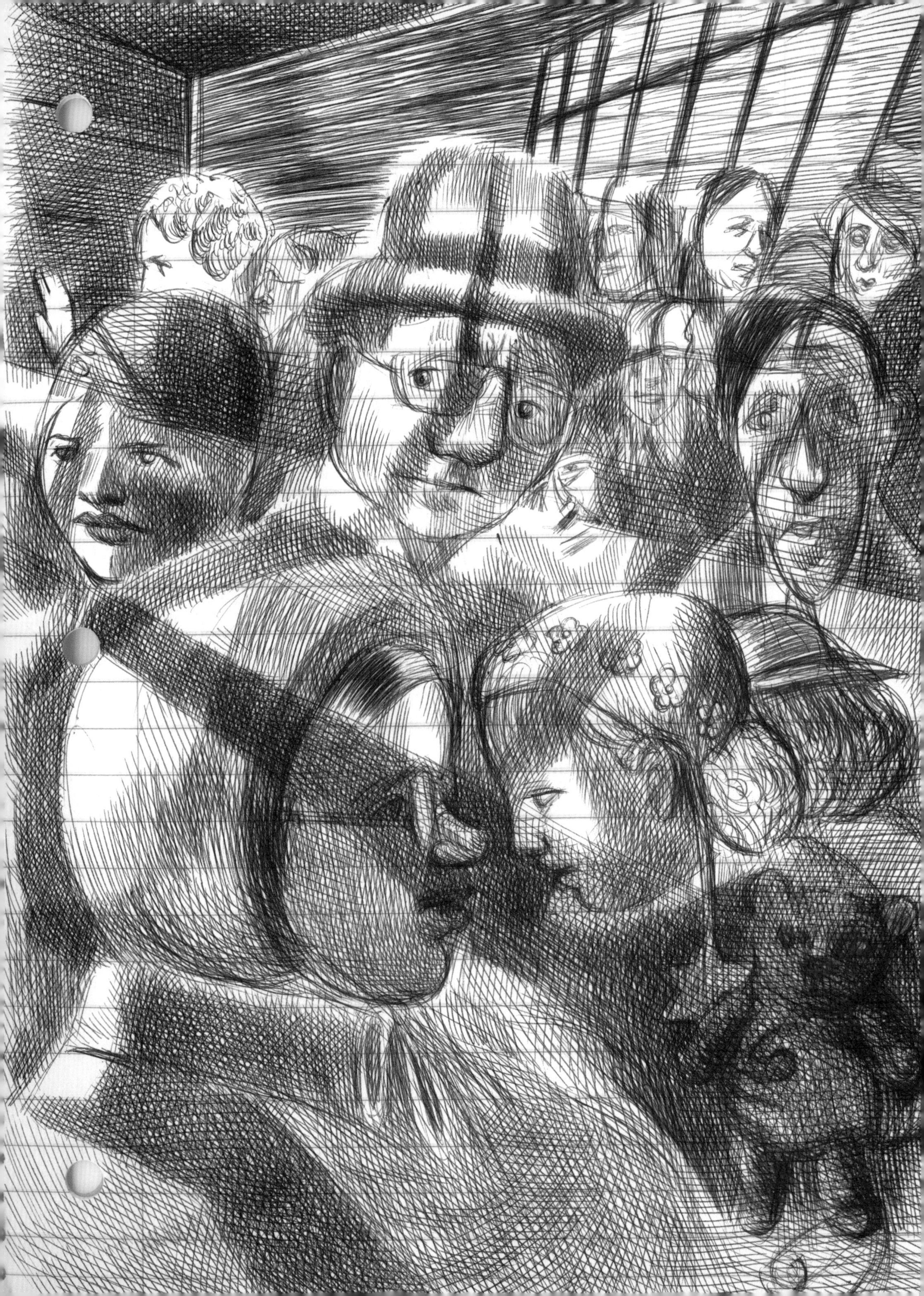

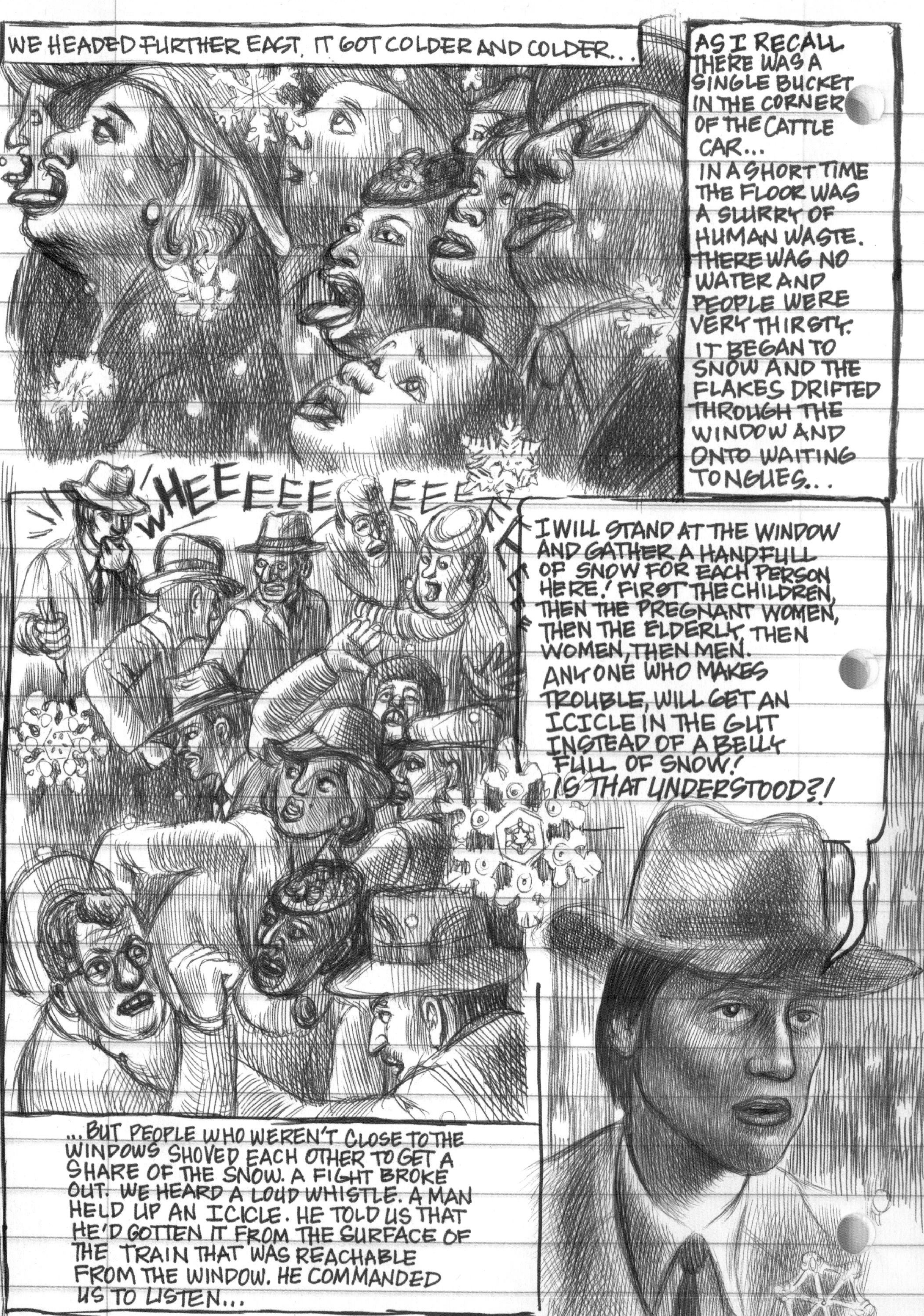
WE HEADED FURTHER EAST. IT GOT COLDER AND COLDER...
AS I RECALL THERE WAS A SINGLE BUCKET IN THE CORNER OF THE CATTLE CAR... IN A SHORT TIME THE FLOOR WAS A SLURRY OF HUMAN WASTE. THERE WAS NO WATER AND PEOPLE WERE VERY THIRSTY. IT BEGAN TO SNOW AND THE FLAKES DRIFTED THROUGH THE WINDOW AND ONTO WAITING TONGUES...
WHEEEEEEEEEEE
I WILL STAND AT THE WINDOW AND GATHER A HANDFULL OF SNOW FOR EACH PERSON HERE! FIRST THE CHILDREN, THEN THE PREGNANT WOMEN, THEN THE ELDERLY, THEN WOMEN, THEN MEN. ANYONE WHO MAKES TROUBLE, WILL GET AN ICICLE IN THE GUT INSTEAD OF A BELLY FULL OF SNOW! IS THAT UNDERSTOOD?!
...BUT PEOPLE WHO WEREN'T CLOSE TO THE WINDOWS SHOVED EACH OTHER TO GET A SHARE OF THE SNOW. A FIGHT BROKE OUT. WE HEARD A LOUD WHISTLE. A MAN HELD UP AN ICICLE. HE TOLD US THAT HE'D GOTTEN IT FROM THE SURFACE OF THE TRAIN THAT WAS REACHABLE FROM THE WINDOW. HE COMMANDED US TO LISTEN...

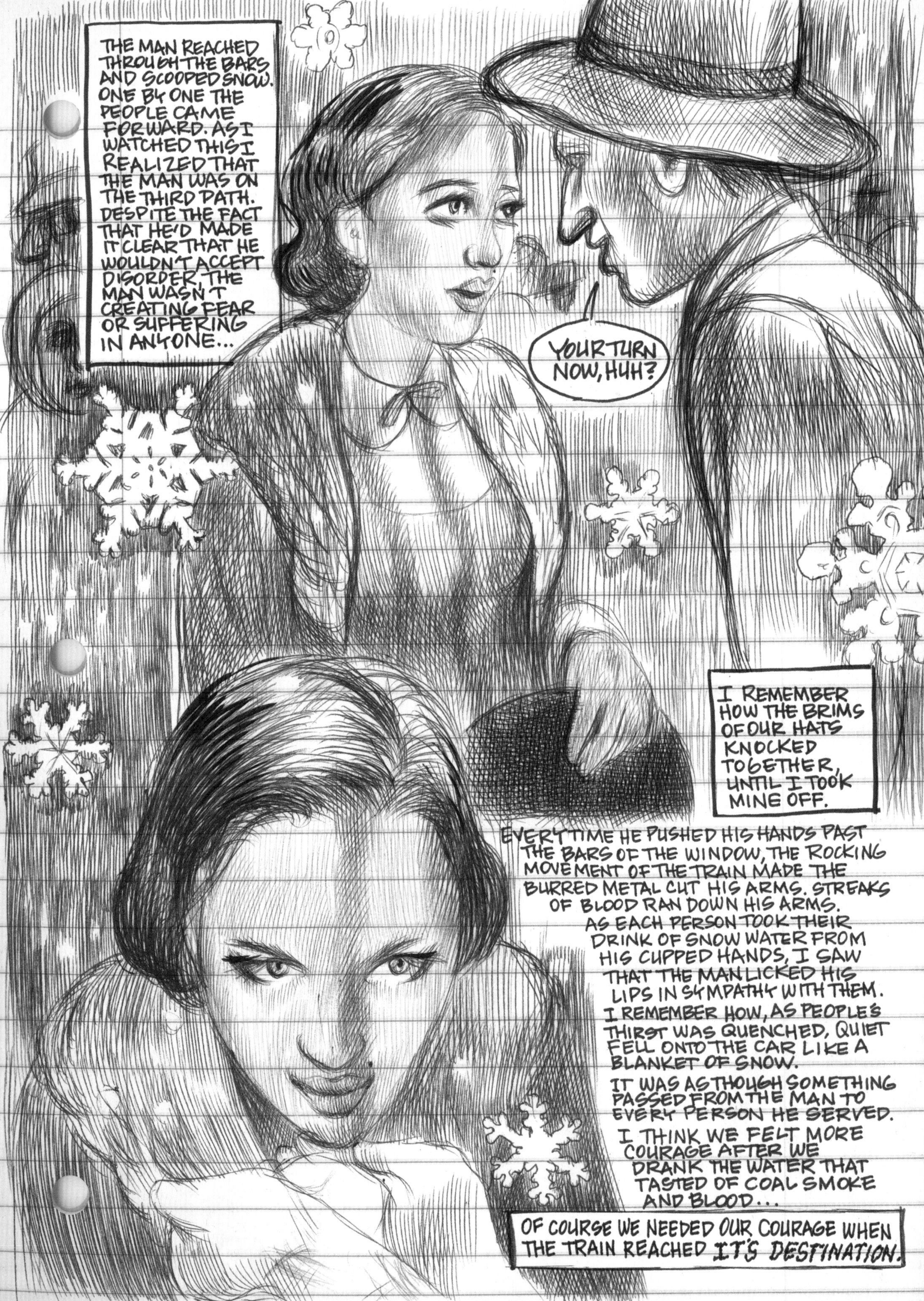
THE MAN REACHED THROUGH THE BARS AND SCOOPED SNOW. ONE BY ONE THE PEOPLE CAME FORWARD. AS I WATCHED THIS I REALIZED THAT THE MAN WAS ON THE THIRD PATH. DESPITE THE FACT THAT HE'D MADE IT CLEAR THAT HE WOULDN'T ACCEPT DISORDER, THE MAN WASN'T CREATING FEAR OR SUFFERING IN ANYONE...
YOUR TURN NOW, HUH?
I REMEMBER HOW THE BRIMS OF OUR HATS KNOCKED TOGETHER, UNTIL I TOOK MINE OFF.
EVERYTIME HE PUSHED HIS HANDS PAST THE BARS OF THE WINDOW, THE ROCKING MOVEMENT OF THE TRAIN MADE THE BURRED METAL CUT HIS ARMS. STREAKS OF BLOOD RAN DOWN HIS ARMS. AS EACH PERSON TOOK THEIR DRINK OF SNOW WATER FROM HIS CUPPED HANDS, I SAW THAT THE MAN LICKED HIS LIPS IN SYMPATHY WITH THEM. I REMEMBER HOW, AS PEOPLE'S THIRST WAS QUENCHED, QUIET FELL ONTO THE CAR LIKE A BLANKET OF SNOW.
IT WAS AS THOUGH SOMETHING PASSED FROM THE MAN TO EVERY PERSON HE SERVED.
I THINK WE FELT MORE COURAGE AFTER WE DRANK THE WATER THAT TASTED OF COAL SMOKE AND BLOOD...
OF COURSE WE NEEDED OUR COURAGE WHEN THE TRAIN REACHED IT'S DESTINATION.

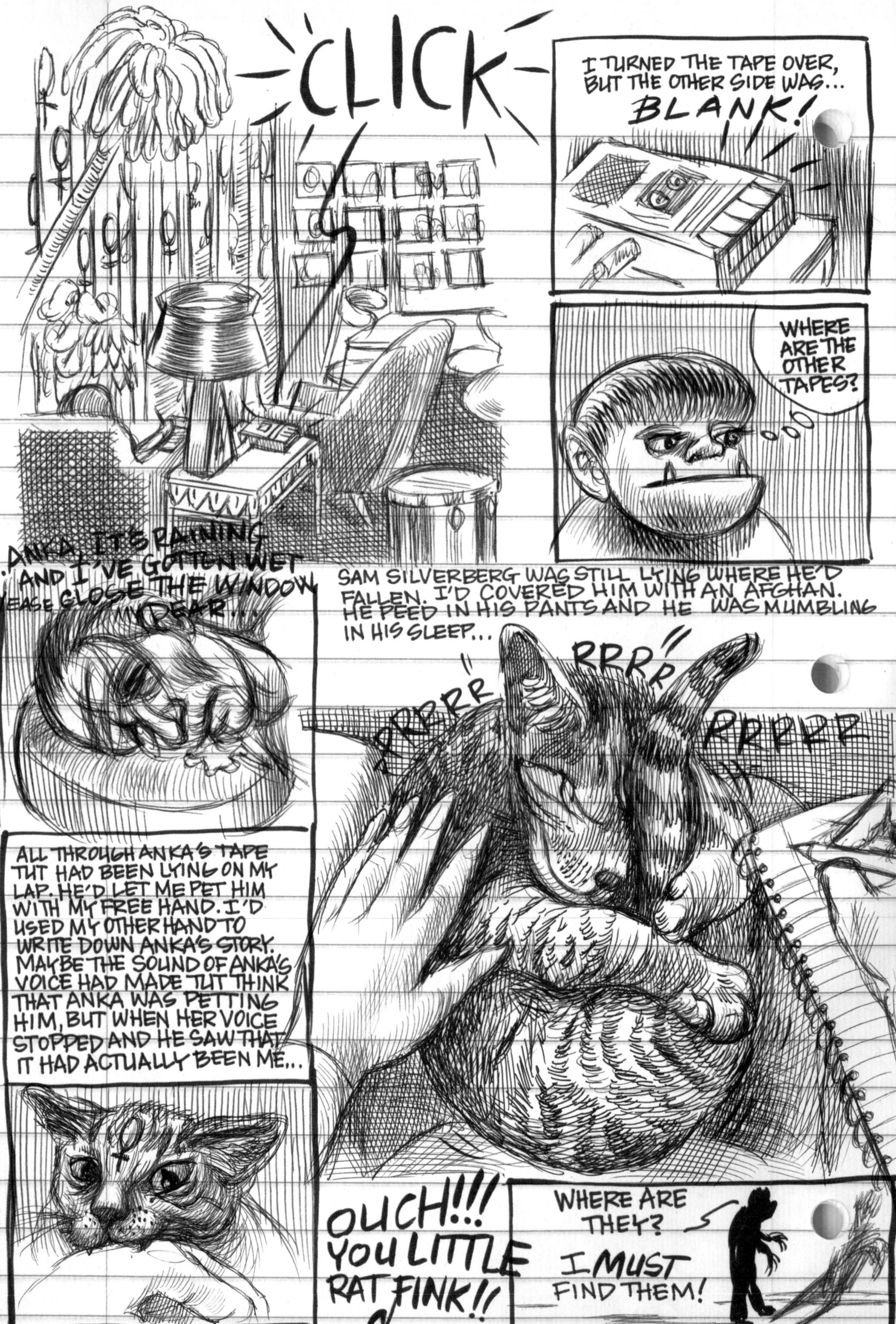
CLICK
I TURNED THE TAPE OVER, BUT THE OTHER SIDE WAS...
BLANK!
WHERE ARE THE OTHER TAPES?
...ANKA, IT'S RAINING AND I'VE GOTTEN WET PLEASE CLOSE THE WINDOW MY DEAR...
SAM SILVERBERG WAS STILL LYING WHERE HE'D FALLEN. I'D COVERED HIM WITH AN AFGHAN. HE PEED IN HIS PANTS AND HE WAS MUMBLING IN HIS SLEEP...
RRRRR
RRRR
RRRRRR
ALL THROUGH ANKA'S TAPE TUT HAD BEEN LYING ON MY LAP. HE'D LET ME PET HIM WITH MY FREE HAND. I'D USED MY OTHER HAND TO WRITE DOWN ANKA'S STORY. MAYBE THE SOUND OF ANKA'S VOICE HAD MADE TUT THINK THAT ANKA WAS PETTING HIM, BUT WHEN HER VOICE STOPPED AND HE SAW THAT IT HAD ACTUALLY BEEN ME...
OUCH!!! YOU LITTLE RAT FINK!!
WHERE ARE THEY?
I MUST FIND THEM!

I RECALLED THAT DURING DINNER, MR. S. HAD GONE TO THE BEDROOM TO GET THE CASSETTE TAPE. I REMEMBERED HEARING THE SOUND OF MR. SILVERBERG SWEARING WHILE HE TORE UP SOME PAPER. ANKA'S PHOTO ALBUM WAS ON THE BED NEXT TO A BOX FULL OF STUFF. I LOOKED THROUGH THE BOX AND THE PHOTO ALBUM. I FOUND A FEW CASSETTE TAPES BUT I HADN'T FOUND THE PIECES OF WHATEVER HE'D TORN UP WHEN I HEARD SAM STUMBLING TOWARDS THE BEDROOM. I RACED TO THE TRASH CAN NEAR THE BED...

PIECES OF A PHOTOGRAPH?

DON'T WORRY KAREN. WHEN ANKA GETS BACK SHE'LL TAKE CARE OF EVERYTHING.

SURE THING MR. S.

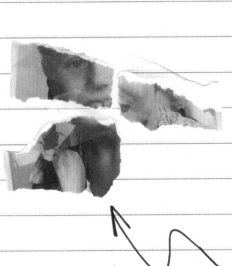

IT WAS WEIRD BEING IN THE VERY BEDROOM THAT ANKA'S BODY WAS FOUND. MAYBE MR. S. HAS BEEN A LITTLE NUTTY SINCE ANKA DIED, BUT HE ISN'T THE TYPE OF GUY TO RIP UP ONE OF THE PHOTOS FROM ANKA'S ALBUM UNLESS HE HAD A REASON. I ESPECIALLY CAN'T IMAGINE HIM TEARING UP A PICTURE OF A KID... UNLESS THIS KID HAD TURNED INTO AN ADULT THAT HE HATED... THE KID SURE DOES LOOK LIKE THE LADY WE CHASED AWAY EARLIER THAT NIGHT...
AS I WALKED HOME I THOUGHT ABOUT WHAT I'VE LEARNED.

SAM HAD FALLEN IN THE HALL. I HELPED HIM UP. HE SMELLED LIKE THE EL STATION IN THE RAIN...

C'MON LETS GET YOU TO YOUR BED.

I DON'T FEEL SO GOOD, MY DEAR.

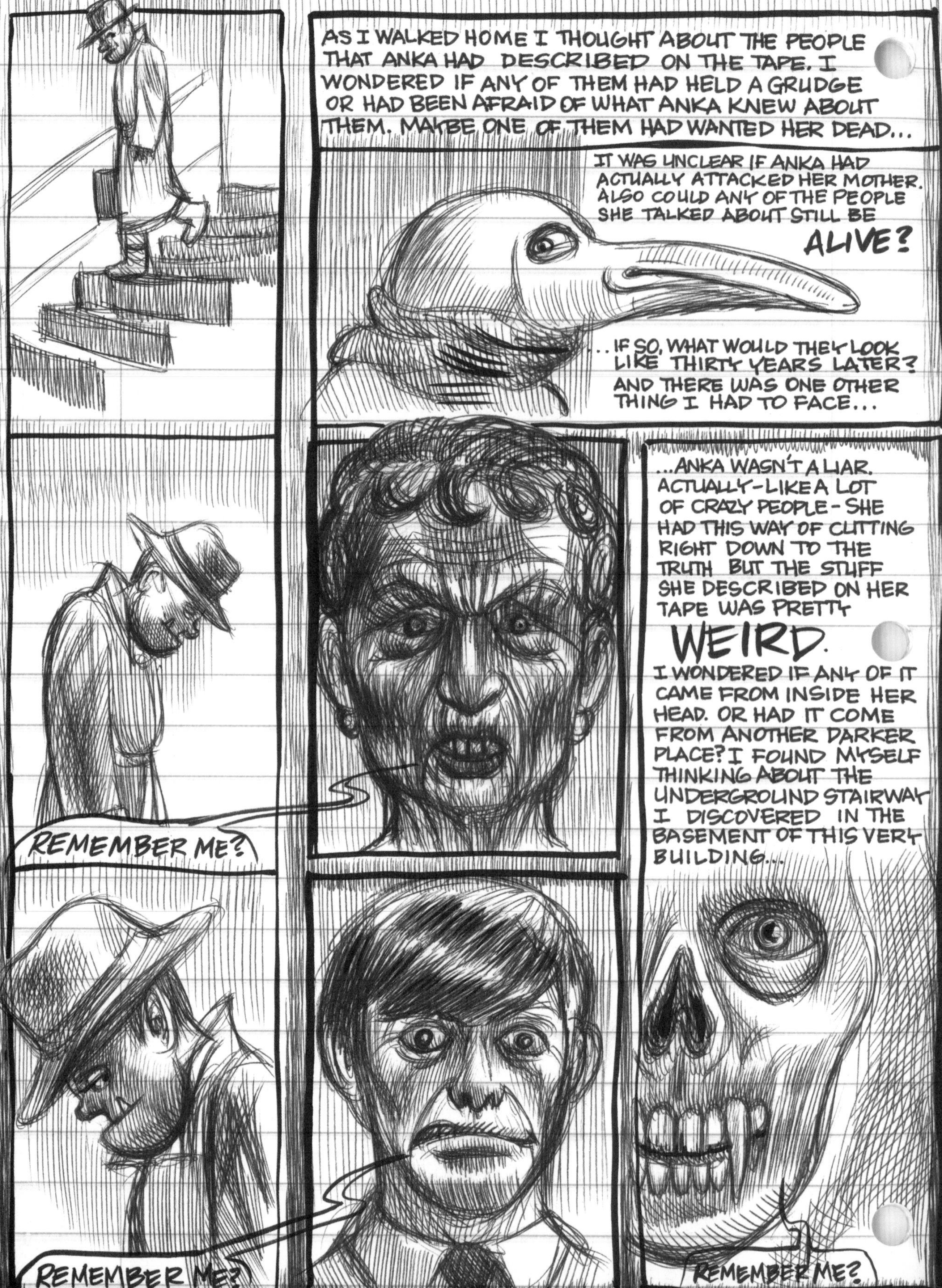
AS I WALKED HOME I THOUGHT ABOUT THE PEOPLE THAT ANKA HAD DESCRIBED ON THE TAPE. I WONDERED IF ANY OF THEM HAD HELD A GRUDGE OR HAD BEEN AFRAID OF WHAT ANKA KNEW ABOUT THEM. MAYBE ONE OF THEM HAD WANTED HER DEAD...
IT WAS UNCLEAR IF ANKA HAD ACTUALLY ATTACKED HER MOTHER. ALSO COULD ANY OF THE PEOPLE SHE TALKED ABOUT STILL BE ALIVE?
...IF SO, WHAT WOULD THEY LOOK LIKE THIRTY YEARS LATER? AND THERE WAS ONE OTHER THING I HAD TO FACE...
...ANKA WASN'T A LIAR. ACTUALLY-LIKE A LOT OF CRAZY PEOPLE-SHE HAD THIS WAY OF CUTTING RIGHT DOWN TO THE TRUTH BUT THE STUFF SHE DESCRIBED ON HER TAPE WAS PRETTY WEIRD.
I WONDERED IF ANY OF IT CAME FROM INSIDE HER HEAD. OR HAD IT COME FROM ANOTHER DARKER PLACE? I FOUND MYSELF THINKING ABOUT THE UNDERGROUND STAIRWAY I DISCOVERED IN THE BASEMENT OF THIS VERY BUILDING...
REMEMBER ME?
REMEMBER ME?
REMEMBER ME?

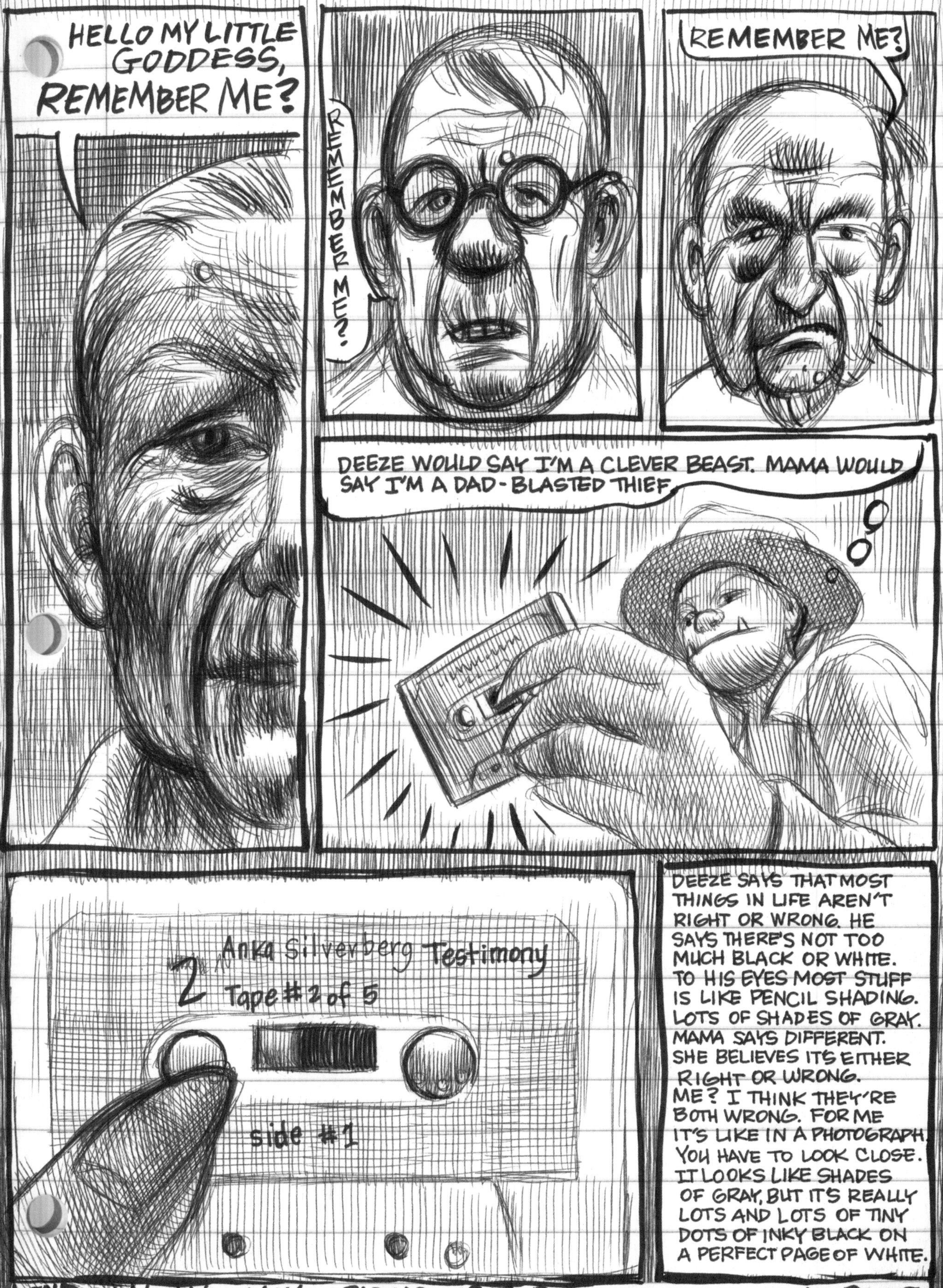
HELLO MY LITTLE GODDESS, REMEMBER ME?
REMEMBER ME?
REMEMBER ME?
DEEZE WOULD SAY I'M A CLEVER BEAST. MAMA WOULD SAY I'M A DAD-BLASTED THIEF.
2 Anka Silverberg Testimony
Tape #2 of 5
side #1
DEEZE SAYS THAT MOST THINGS IN LIFE AREN'T RIGHT OR WRONG. HE SAYS THERE'S NOT TOO MUCH BLACK OR WHITE. TO HIS EYES MOST STUFF IS LIKE PENCIL SHADING. LOTS OF SHADES OF GRAY. MAMA SAYS DIFFERENT. SHE BELIEVES ITS EITHER RIGHT OR WRONG. ME? I THINK THEY'RE BOTH WRONG. FOR ME IT'S LIKE IN A PHOTOGRAPH. YOU HAVE TO LOOK CLOSE. IT LOOKS LIKE SHADES OF GRAY, BUT IT'S REALLY LOTS AND LOTS OF TINY DOTS OF INKY BLACK ON A PERFECT PAGE OF WHITE.
THE ONLY WAY TO MAKE A PICTURE IS TO PUT SOME DOTS ON THE PAGE.

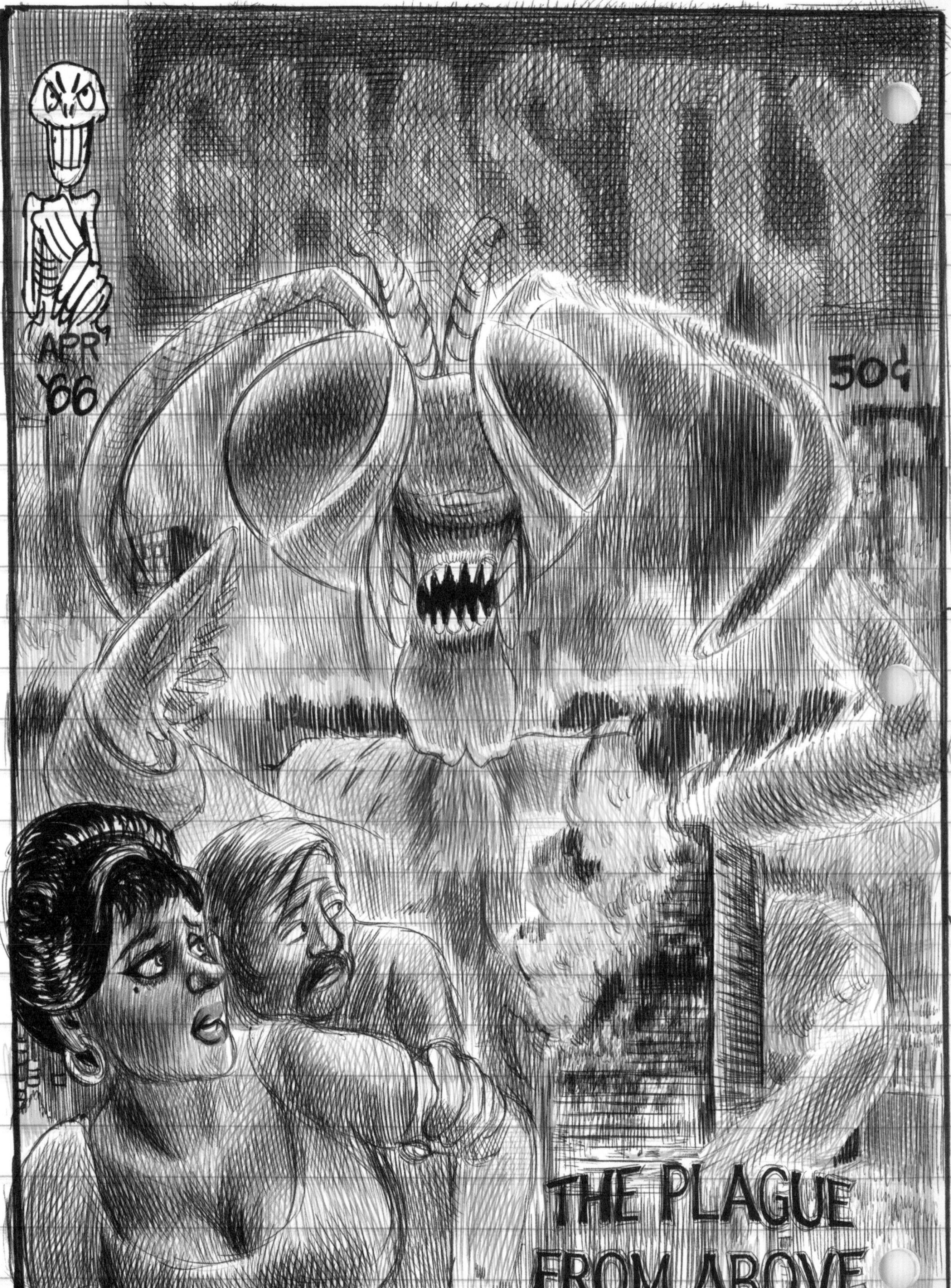
APR '66
50¢
THE PLAGUE
FROM ABOVE

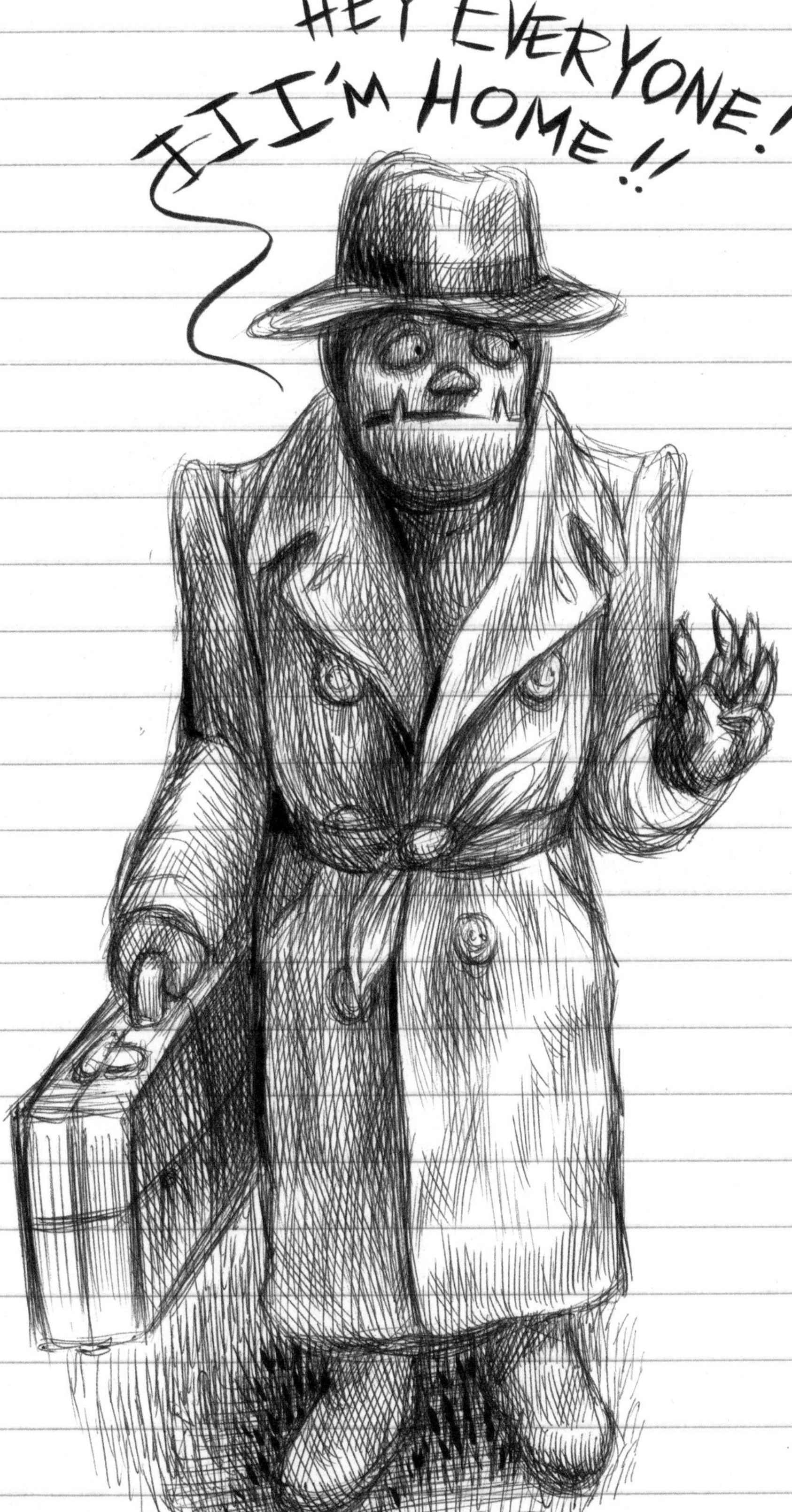
HEY EVERYONE!
I'M HOME!!

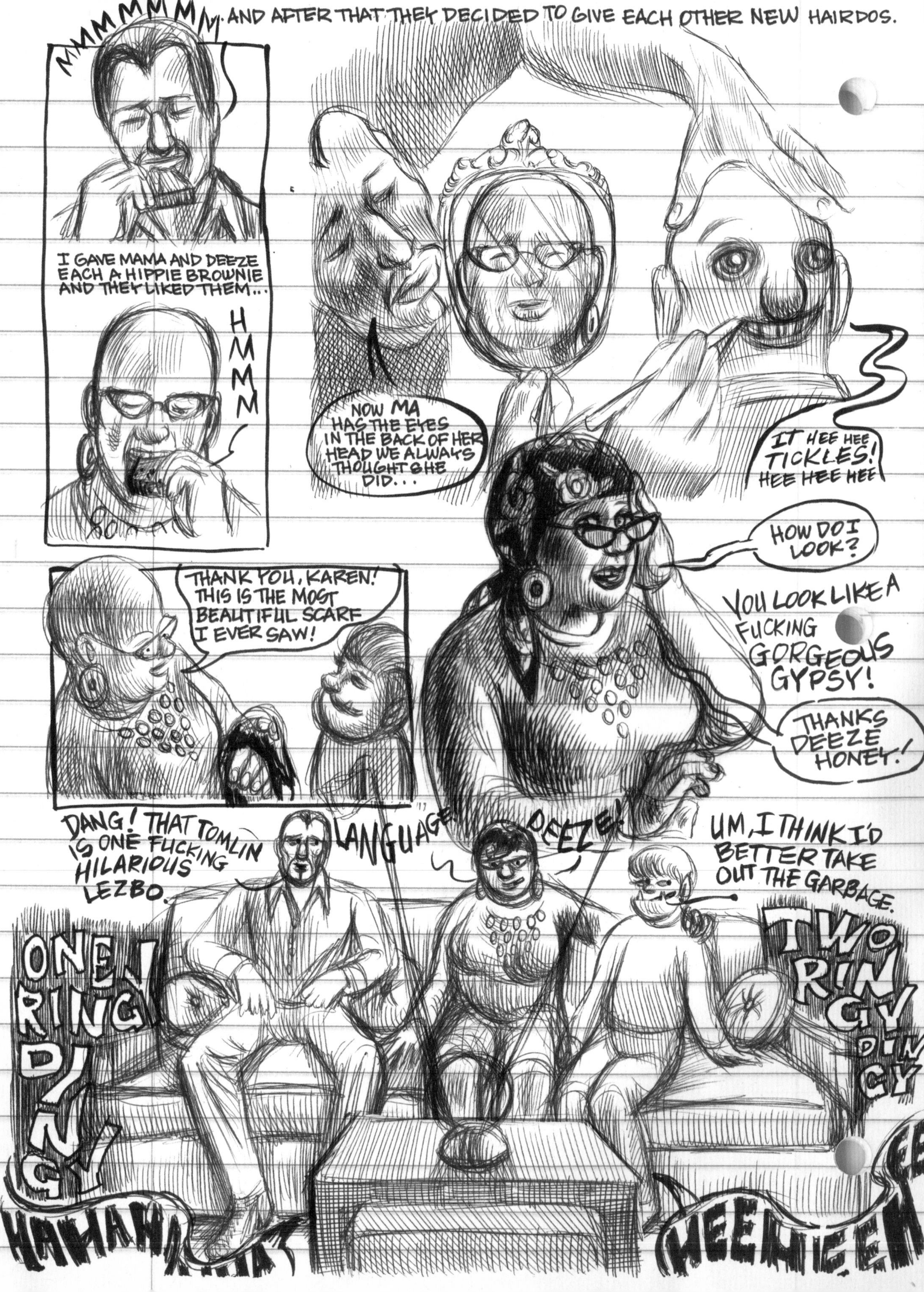
MMMMMMMMM
...AND AFTER THAT THEY DECIDED TO GIVE EACH OTHER NEW HAIRDOS.
I GAVE MAMA AND DEEZE EACH A HIPPIE BROWNIE AND THEY LIKED THEM...
HMMMM
NOW MA HAS THE EYES IN THE BACK OF HER HEAD WE ALWAYS THOUGHT SHE DID...
IT HEE HEE TICKLES! HEE HEE HEE
HOW DO I LOOK?
YOU LOOK LIKE A FUCKING GORGEOUS GYPSY!
THANKS DEEZE HONEY!
THANK YOU, KAREN! THIS IS THE MOST BEAUTIFUL SCARF I EVER SAW!
DANG! THAT TOMLIN IS ONE FUCKING HILARIOUS LEZBO.
LANGUAGE
DEEZE!
UM, I THINK I'D BETTER TAKE OUT THE GARBAGE.
ONE RING DING
TWO RINGY DINGY
HAHAHAHAHAHA
HEEHEEHEE

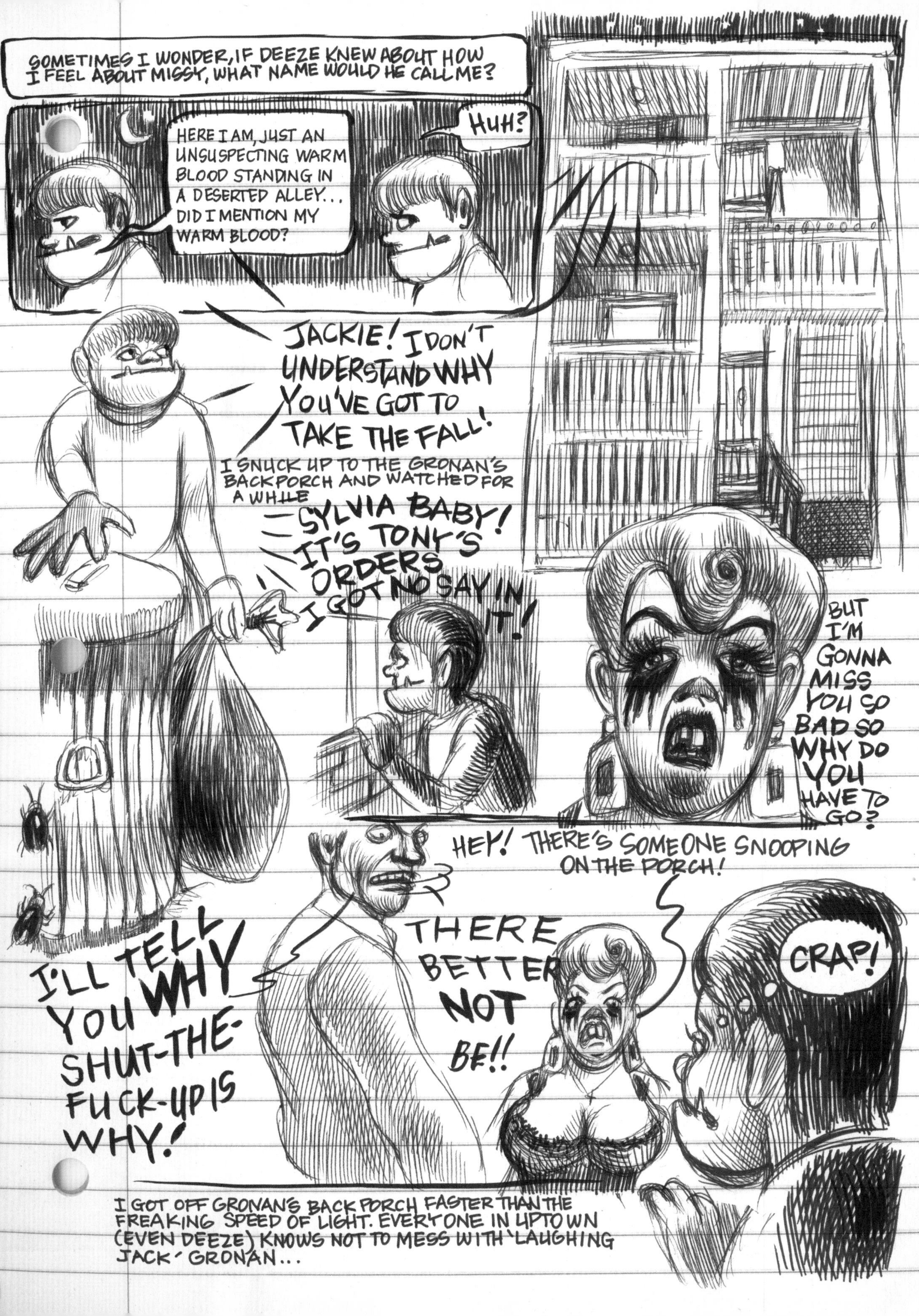
SOMETIMES I WONDER, IF DEEZE KNEW ABOUT HOW I FEEL ABOUT MISSY, WHAT NAME WOULD HE CALL ME?
HERE I AM, JUST AN UNSUSPECTING WARM BLOOD STANDING IN A DESERTED ALLEY... DID I MENTION MY WARM BLOOD?
HUH?
JACKIE! I DON'T UNDERSTAND WHY YOU'VE GOT TO TAKE THE FALL!
I SNUCK UP TO THE GRONAN'S BACKPORCH AND WATCHED FOR A WHILE
SYLVIA BABY! IT'S TONY'S ORDERS I GOT NO SAY IN IT!
BUT I'M GONNA MISS YOU SO BAD SO WHY DO YOU HAVE TO GO?
I'LL TELL YOU WHY SHUT-THE-FUCK-UP IS WHY!
HEY! THERE'S SOMEONE SNOOPING ON THE PORCH!
THERE BETTER NOT BE!!
CRAP!
I GOT OFF GRONAN'S BACK PORCH FASTER THAN THE FREAKING SPEED OF LIGHT. EVERYONE IN UPTOWN (EVEN DEEZE) KNOWS NOT TO MESS WITH 'LAUGHING JACK' GRONAN...

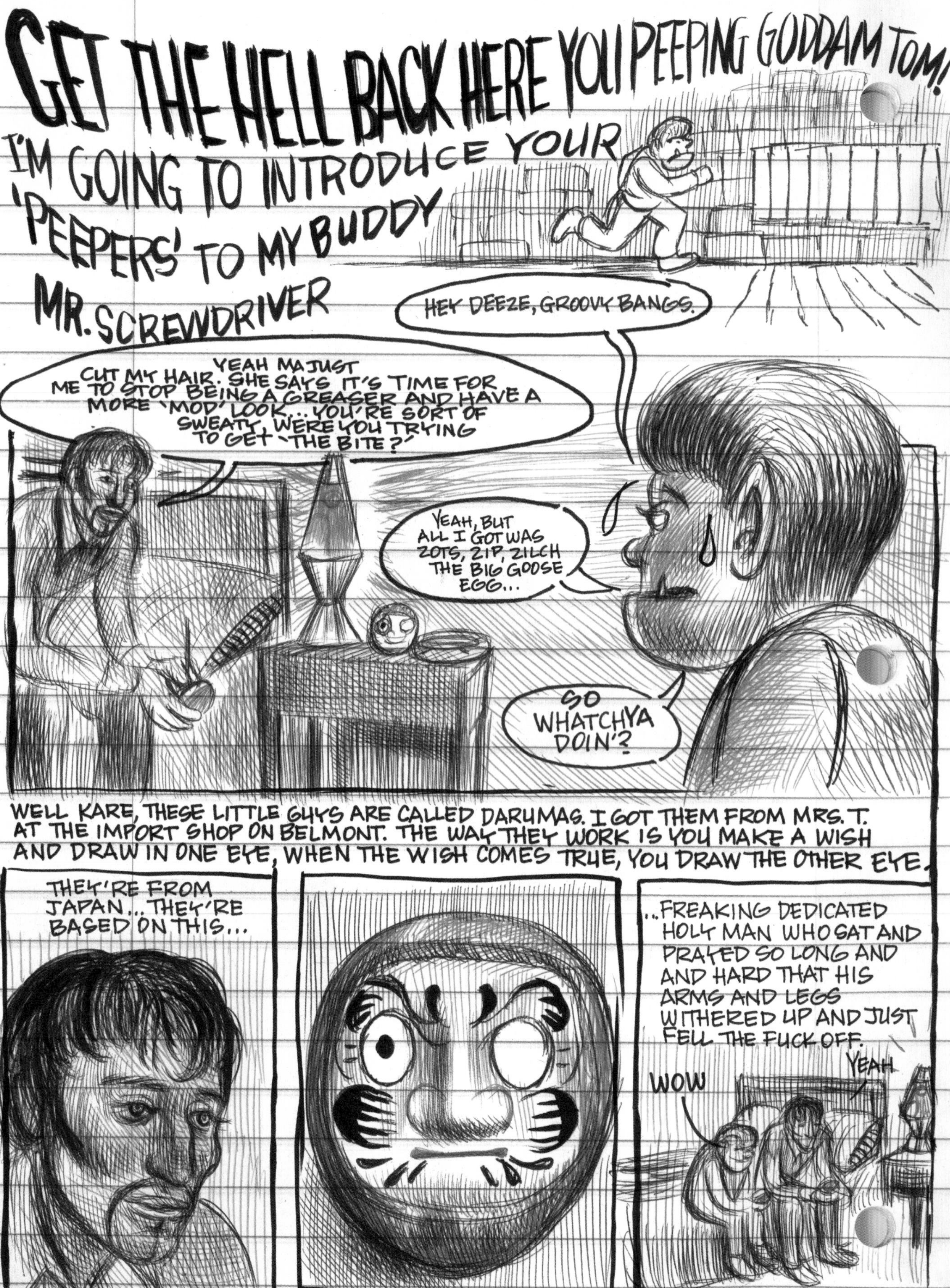
GET THE HELL BACK HERE YOU PEEPING GODDAM TOM!
I'M GOING TO INTRODUCE YOUR 'PEEPERS' TO MY BUDDY MR. SCREWDRIVER
HEY DEEZE, GROOVY BANGS.
YEAH MA JUST CUT MY HAIR. SHE SAYS IT'S TIME FOR ME TO STOP BEING A GREASER AND HAVE A MORE 'MOD' LOOK... YOU'RE SORT OF SWEATY, WERE YOU TRYING TO GET 'THE BITE?'
YEAH, BUT ALL I GOT WAS ZOTS, ZIP, ZILCH THE BIG GOOSE EGG...
SO WHATCHYA DOIN'?
WELL KARE, THESE LITTLE GUYS ARE CALLED DARUMAS. I GOT THEM FROM MRS. T. AT THE IMPORT SHOP ON BELMONT. THE WAY THEY WORK IS YOU MAKE A WISH AND DRAW IN ONE EYE, WHEN THE WISH COMES TRUE, YOU DRAW THE OTHER EYE.
THEY'RE FROM JAPAN... THEY'RE BASED ON THIS...
...FREAKING DEDICATED HOLY MAN WHO SAT AND PRAYED SO LONG AND AND HARD THAT HIS ARMS AND LEGS WITHERED UP AND JUST FELL THE FUCK OFF.
WOW
YEAH

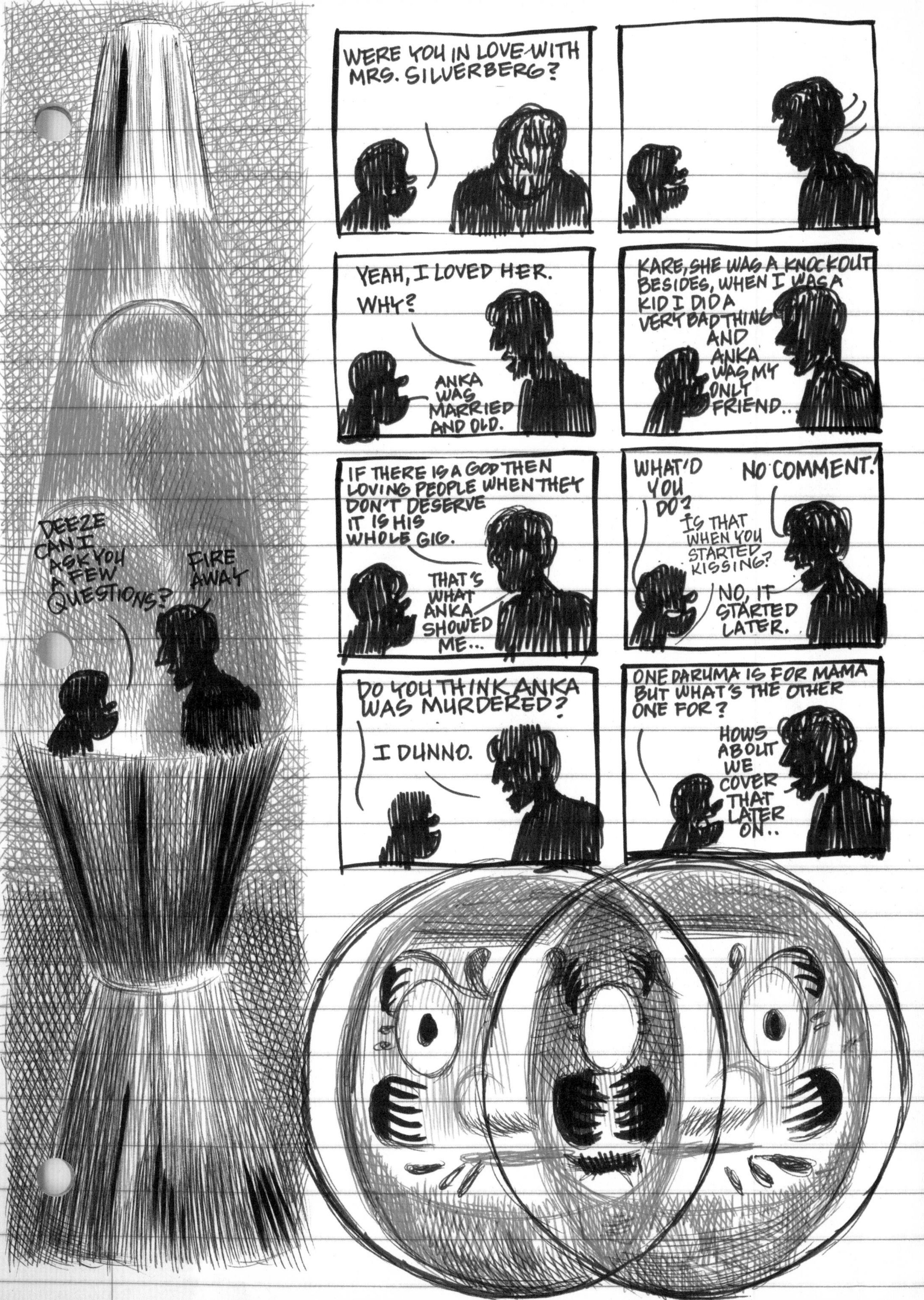
DEEZE CAN I ASK YOU A FEW QUESTIONS?
FIRE AWAY
WERE YOU IN LOVE WITH MRS. SILVERBERG?
YEAH, I LOVED HER.
WHY?
ANKA WAS MARRIED AND OLD.
KARE, SHE WAS A KNOCKOUT BESIDES, WHEN I WAS A KID I DID A VERY BAD THING
AND ANKA WAS MY ONLY FRIEND..
IF THERE IS A GOD THEN LOVING PEOPLE WHEN THEY DON'T DESERVE IT IS HIS WHOLE GIG.
THAT'S WHAT ANKA SHOWED ME...
WHAT'D YOU DO?
NO COMMENT.
IS THAT WHEN YOU STARTED KISSING?
NO, IT STARTED LATER.
DO YOU THINK ANKA WAS MURDERED?
I DUNNO.
ONE DARUMA IS FOR MAMA BUT WHAT'S THE OTHER ONE FOR?
HOWS ABOUT WE COVER THAT LATER ON..

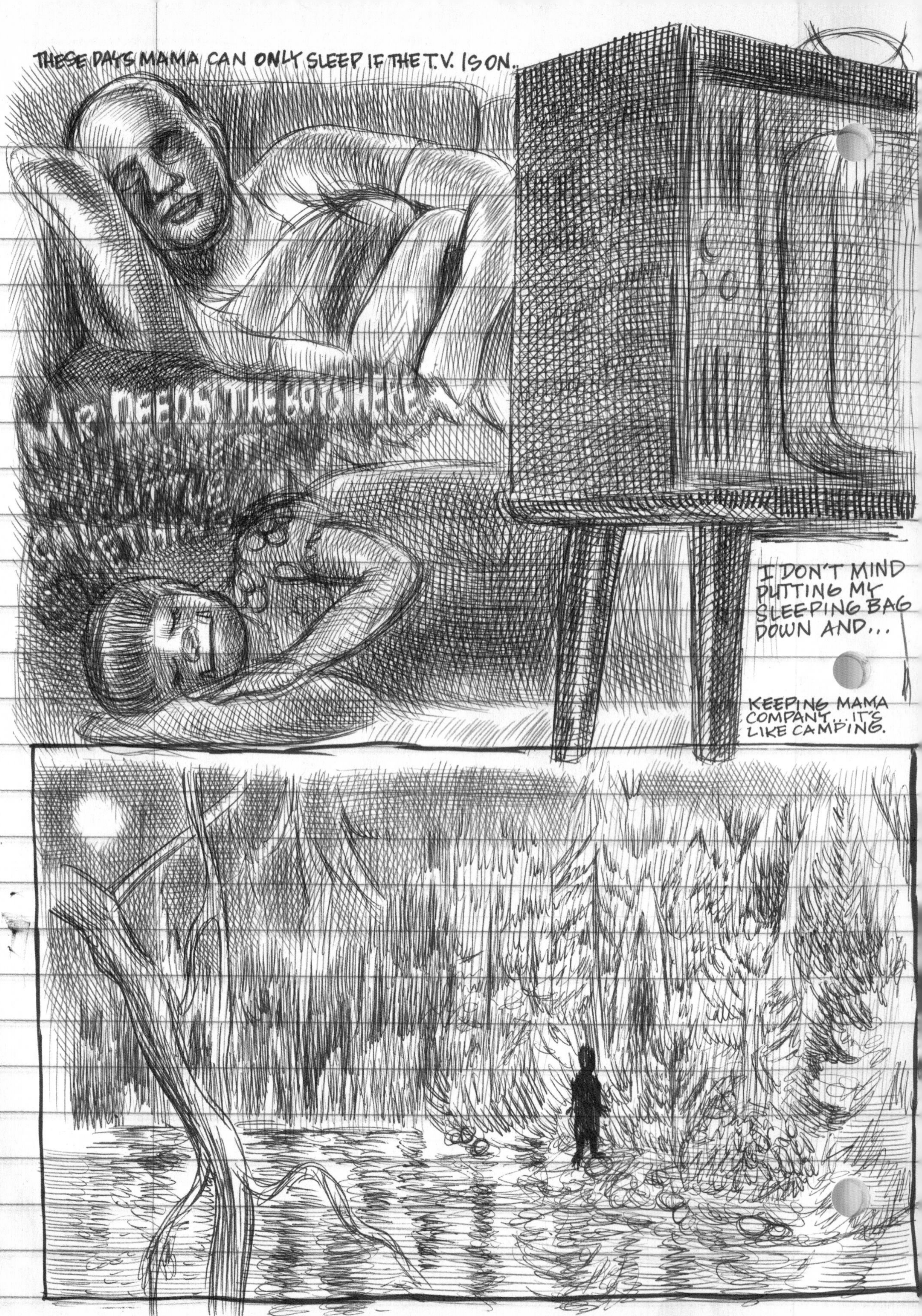
THESE DAYS MAMA CAN ONLY SLEEP IF THE T.V. IS ON..
I DON'T MIND PUTTING MY SLEEPING BAG DOWN AND...
KEEPING MAMA COMPANY... IT'S LIKE CAMPING.

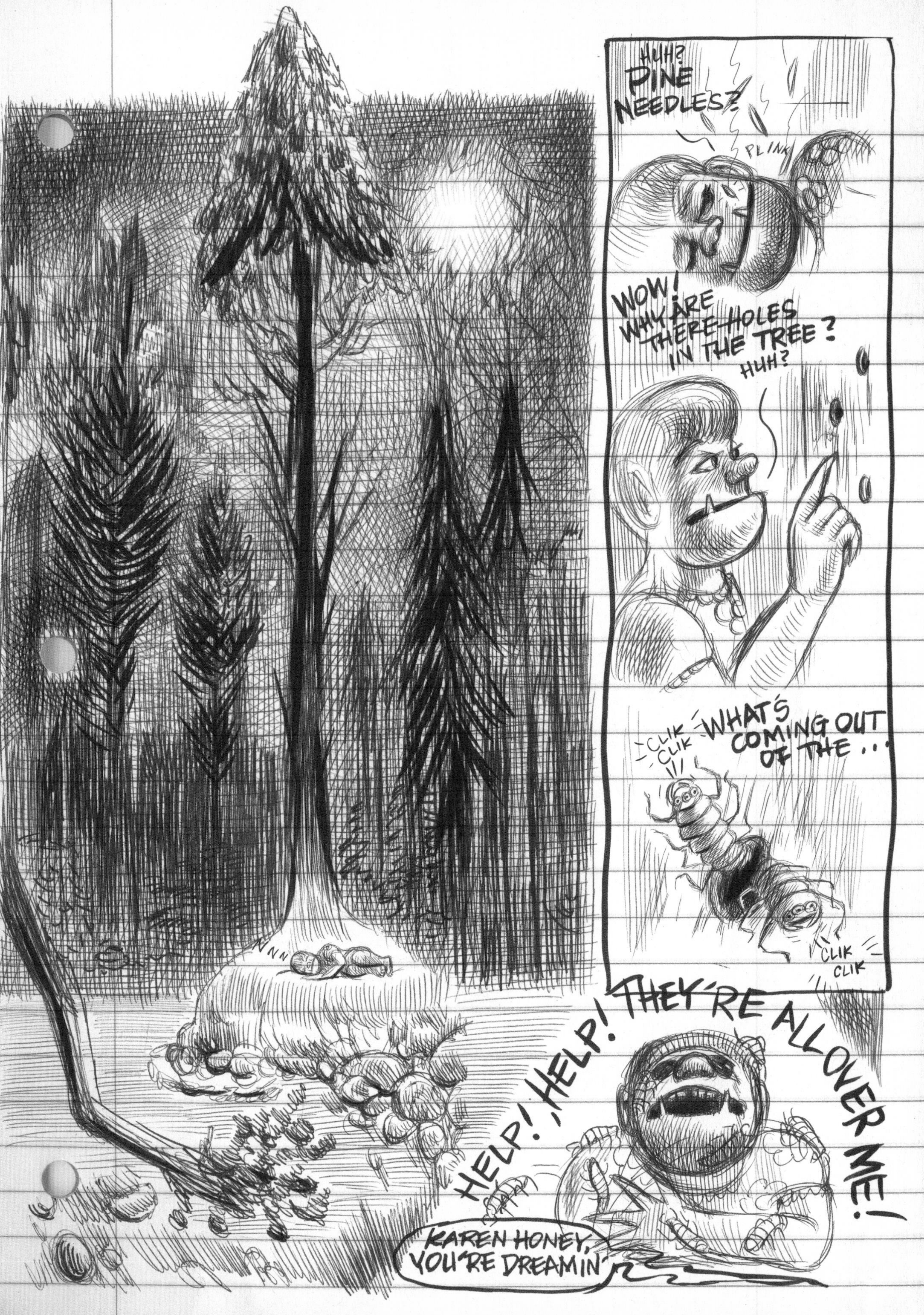

HUH? PINE NEEDLES?
PLINK
WOW! WHY ARE THERE HOLES IN THE TREE?
HUH?
CLIK CLIK
WHAT'S COMING OUT OF THE...
CLIK CLIK
NNN
HELP! HELP! THEY'RE ALL OVER ME!
KAREN HONEY, YOU'RE DREAMIN'

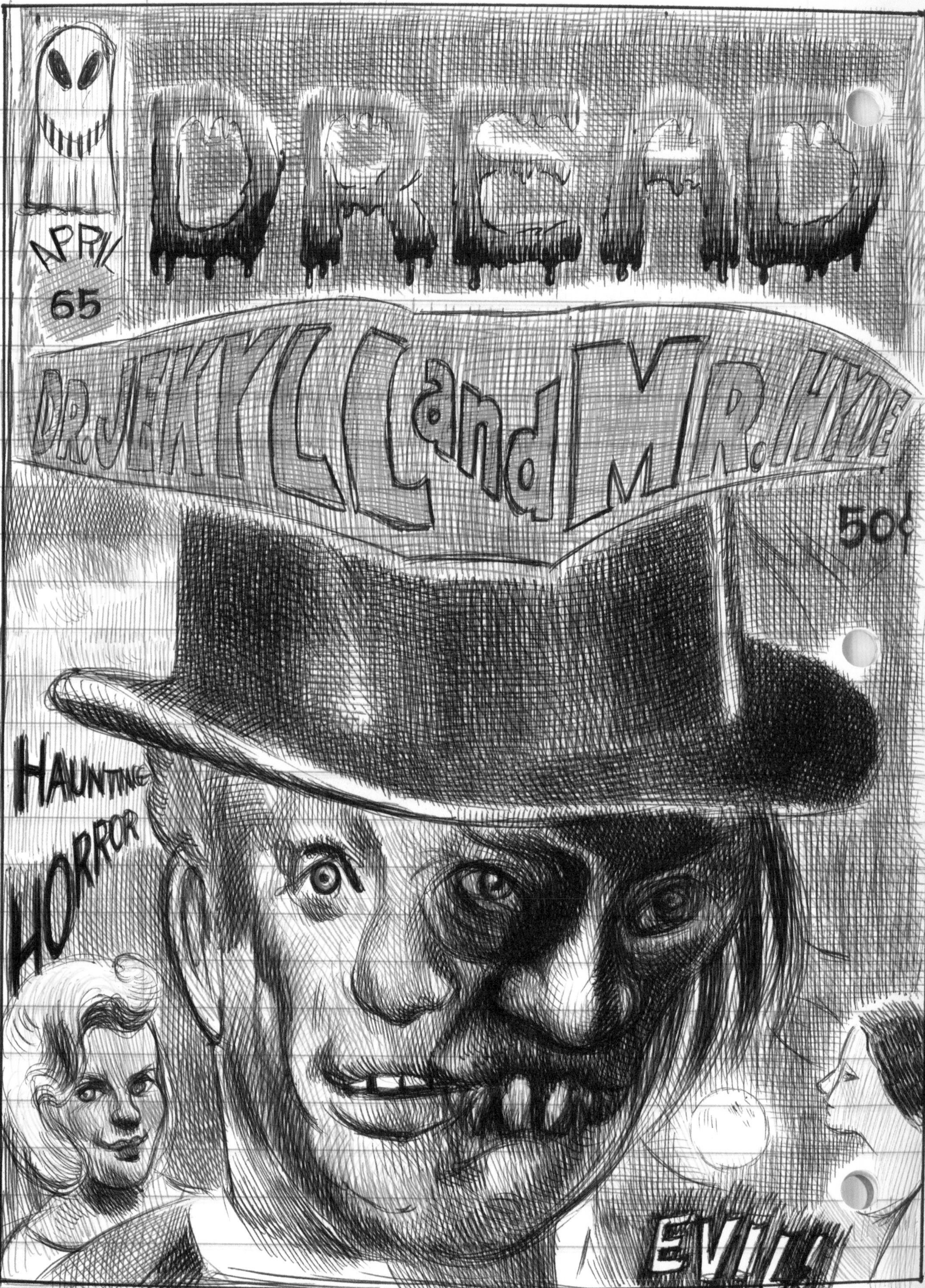
DREAD
APRIL
65
DR. JEKYLL and MR. HYDE
50¢
HAUNTING
HORROR
EVIL!

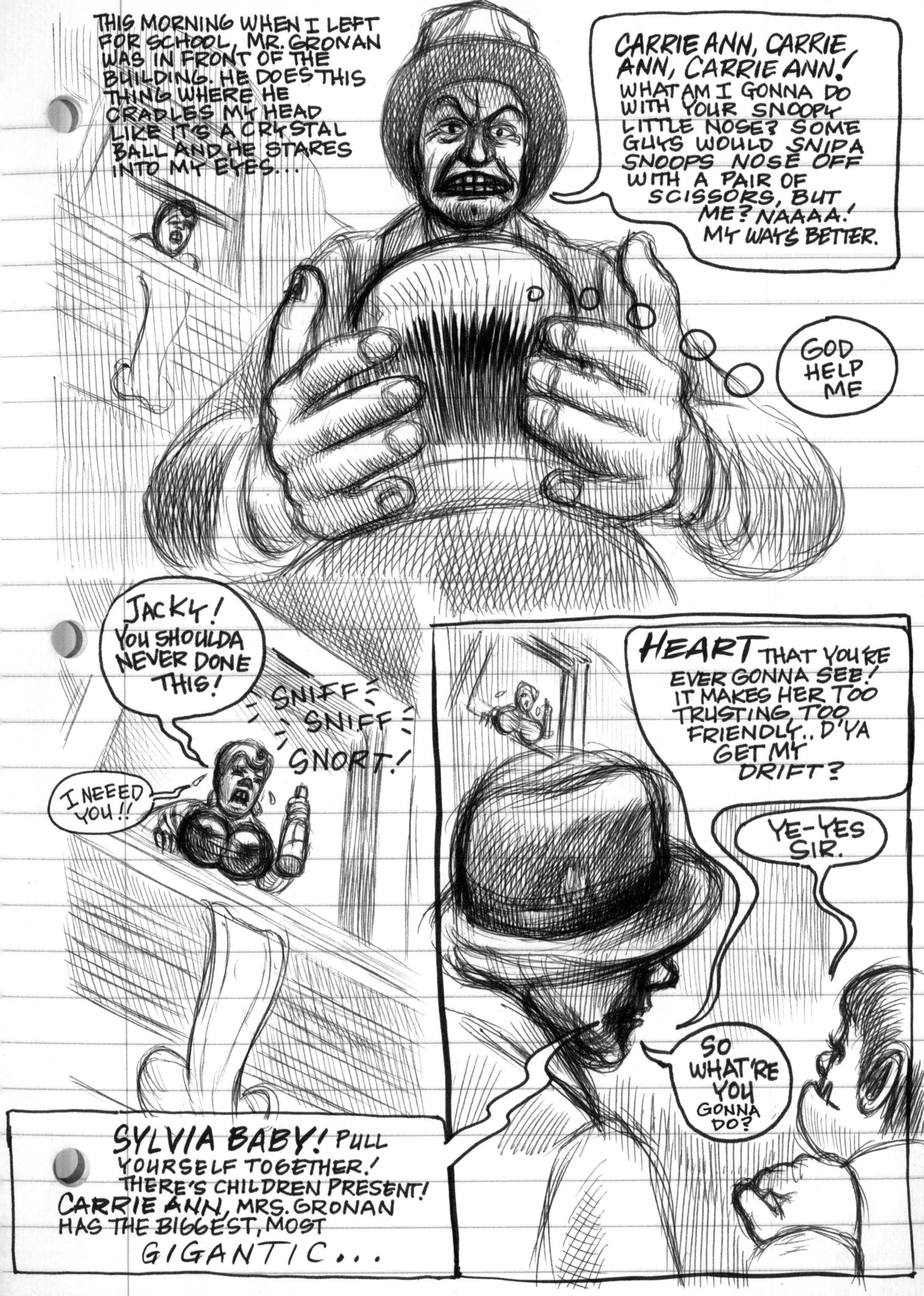

THIS MORNING WHEN I LEFT FOR SCHOOL, MR. GRONAN WAS IN FRONT OF THE BUILDING. HE DOES THIS THING WHERE HE CRADLES MY HEAD LIKE IT'S A CRYSTAL BALL AND HE STARES INTO MY EYES...
CARRIE ANN, CARRIE, ANN, CARRIE ANN! WHAT AM I GONNA DO WITH YOUR SNOOPY LITTLE NOSE? SOME GUYS WOULD SNIP A SNOOPS NOSE OFF WITH A PAIR OF SCISSORS, BUT ME? NAAAA! MY WAY'S BETTER.
GOD HELP ME
JACKY! YOU SHOULDA NEVER DONE THIS!
SNIFF SNIFF SNORT!
I NEEED YOU!!
SYLVIA BABY! PULL YOURSELF TOGETHER! THERE'S CHILDREN PRESENT! CARRIE ANN, MRS. GRONAN HAS THE BIGGEST, MOST GIGANTIC...
HEART THAT YOU'RE EVER GONNA SEE! IT MAKES HER TOO TRUSTING, TOO FRIENDLY.. D'YA GET MY DRIFT?
YE-YES SIR.
SO WHAT'RE YOU GONNA DO?

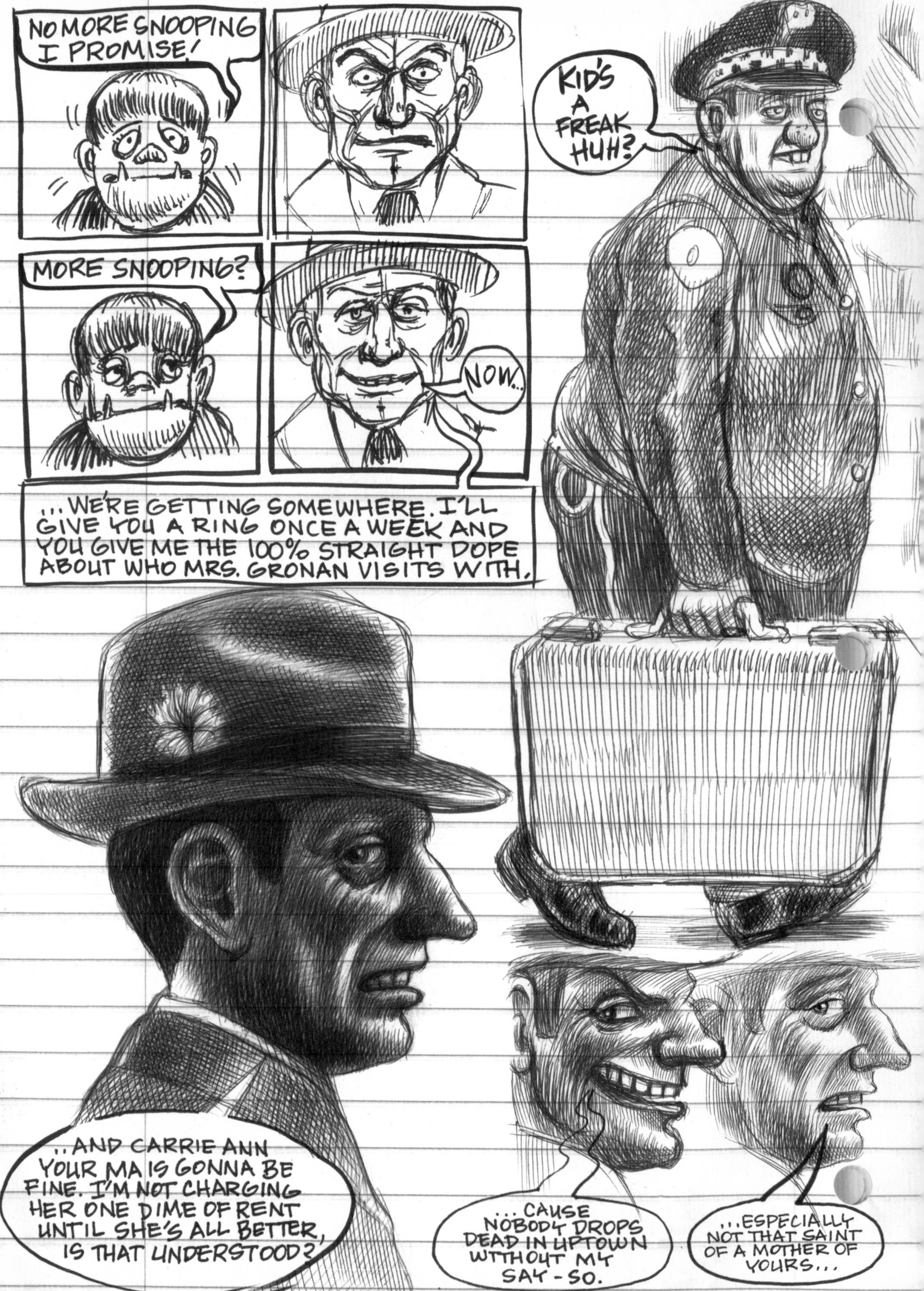
NO MORE SNOOPING I PROMISE!
MORE SNOOPING?
NOW...
...WE'RE GETTING SOMEWHERE. I'LL GIVE YOU A RING ONCE A WEEK AND YOU GIVE ME THE 100% STRAIGHT DOPE ABOUT WHO MRS. GRONAN VISITS WITH.
KID'S A FREAK HUH?
..AND CARRIE ANN YOUR MA IS GONNA BE FINE. I'M NOT CHARGING HER ONE DIME OF RENT UNTIL SHE'S ALL BETTER, IS THAT UNDERSTOOD?
...CAUSE NOBODY DROPS DEAD IN UPTOWN WITHOUT MY SAY-SO.
...ESPECIALLY NOT THAT SAINT OF A MOTHER OF YOURS...

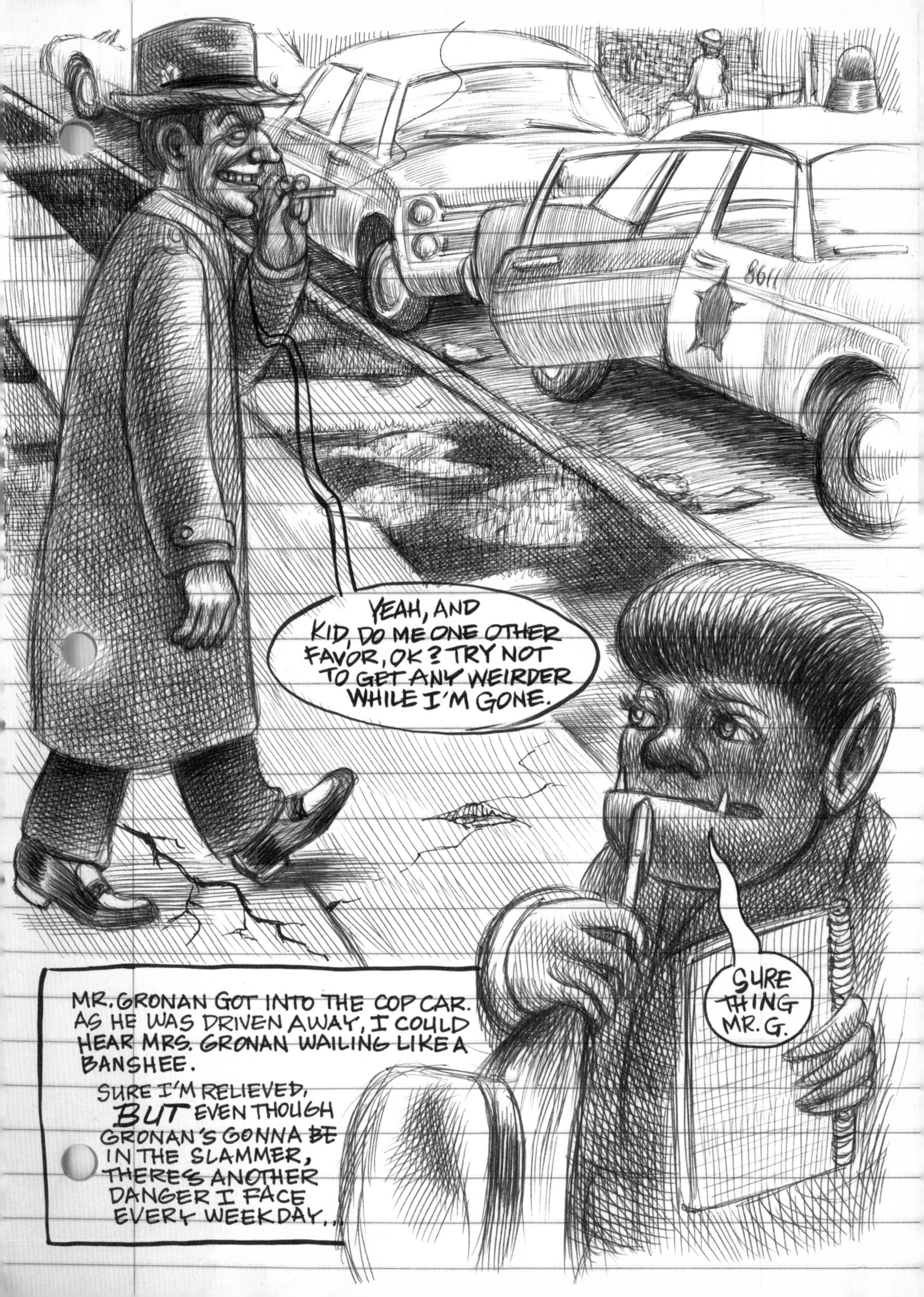
YEAH, AND KID, DO ME ONE OTHER FAVOR, OK? TRY NOT TO GET ANY WEIRDER WHILE I'M GONE.
SURE THING MR. G.
MR. GRONAN GOT INTO THE COP CAR. AS HE WAS DRIVEN AWAY, I COULD HEAR MRS. GRONAN WAILING LIKE A BANSHEE.
SURE I'M RELIEVED, BUT EVEN THOUGH GRONAN'S GONNA BE IN THE SLAMMER, THERE'S ANOTHER DANGER I FACE EVERY WEEKDAY...

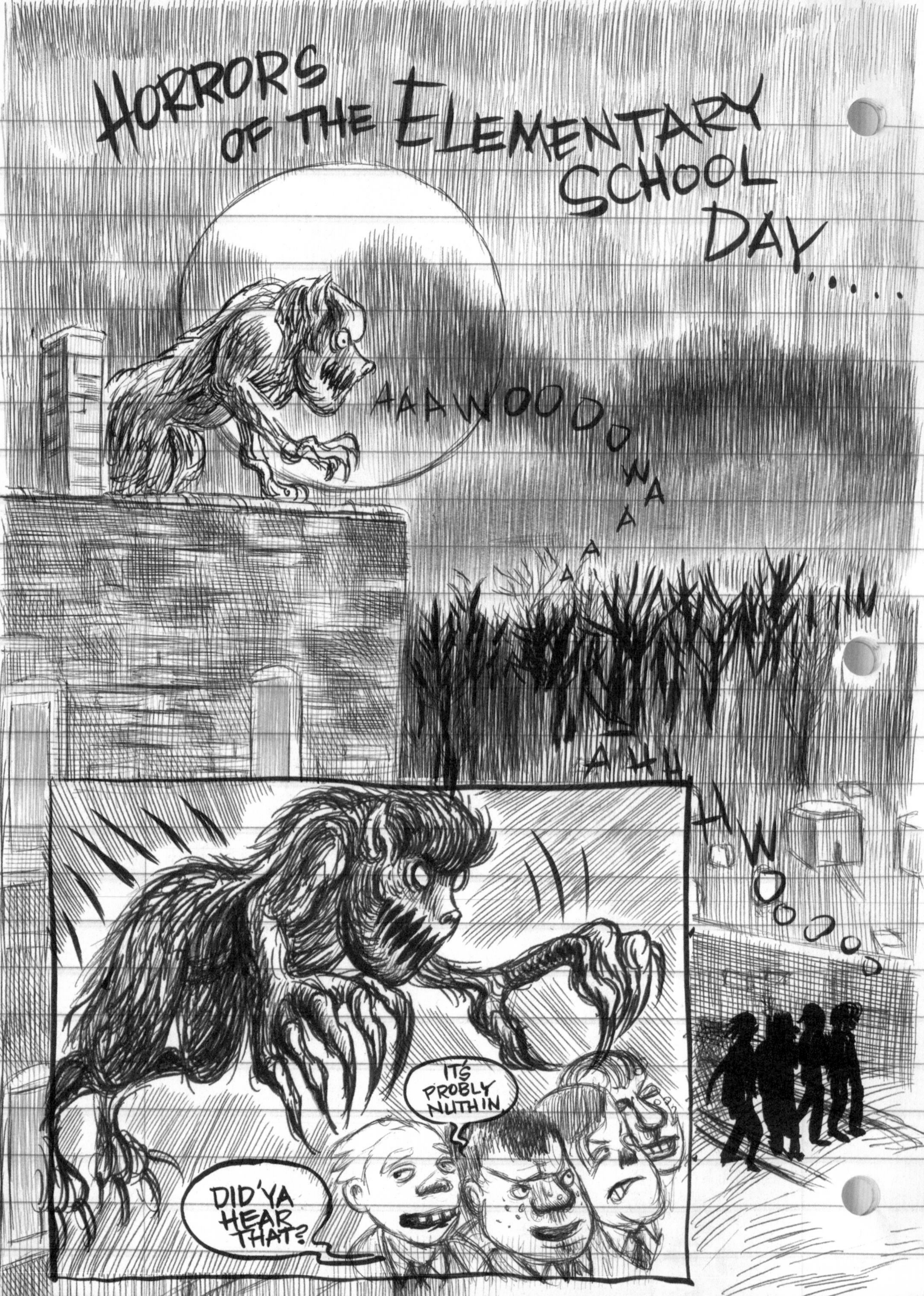
HORRORS OF THE ELEMENTARY SCHOOL DAY.....
AAAWOOOOOWAAAAAAAHHAWOOOOOO
IT'S PROBLY NUTHIN
DID'YA HEAR THAT?

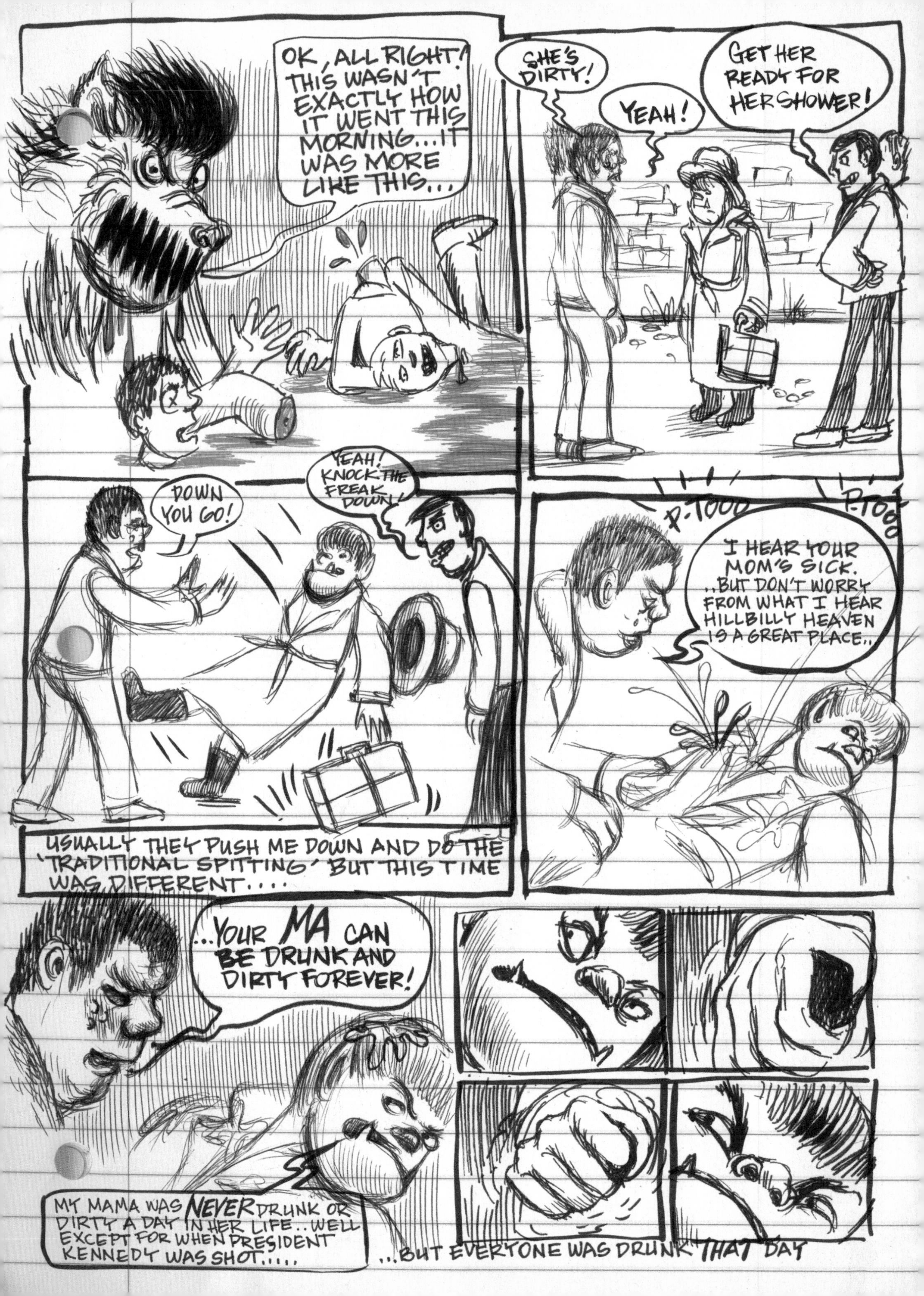
OK, ALL RIGHT! THIS WASN'T EXACTLY HOW IT WENT THIS MORNING... IT WAS MORE LIKE THIS...
SHE'S DIRTY!
YEAH!
GET HER READY FOR HER SHOWER!
DOWN YOU GO!
YEAH! KNOCK THE FREAK DOWN!
USUALLY THEY PUSH ME DOWN AND DO THE 'TRADITIONAL SPITTING' BUT THIS TIME WAS DIFFERENT....
P-TOOO
P-TOOO
I HEAR YOUR MOM'S SICK. ..BUT DON'T WORRY FROM WHAT I HEAR HILLBILLY HEAVEN IS A GREAT PLACE..
...YOUR MA CAN BE DRUNK AND DIRTY FOREVER!
MY MAMA WAS NEVER DRUNK OR DIRTY A DAY IN HER LIFE.. WELL EXCEPT FOR WHEN PRESIDENT KENNEDY WAS SHOT.....
...BUT EVERYONE WAS DRUNK THAT DAY

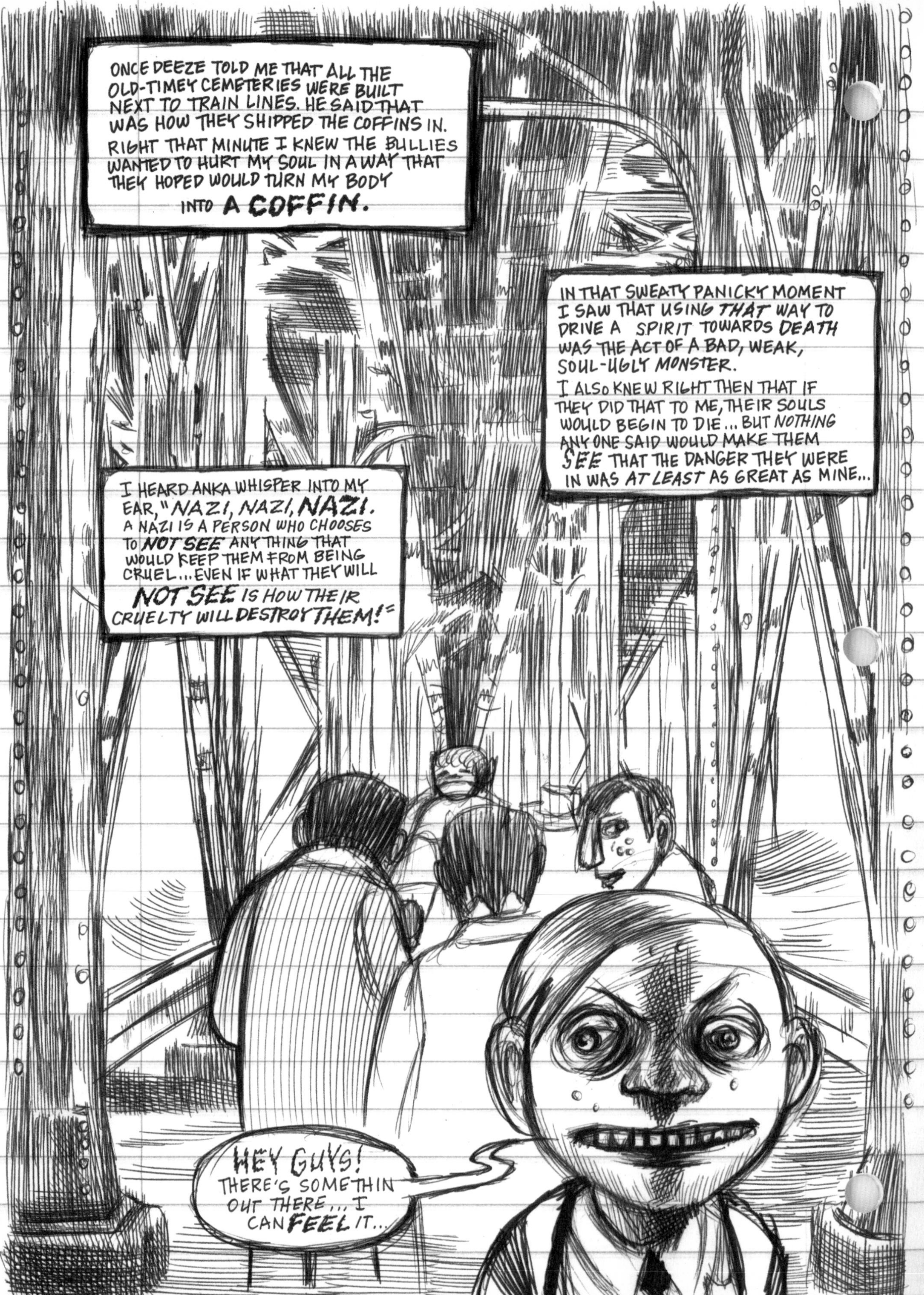
ONCE DEEZE TOLD ME THAT ALL THE OLD-TIMEY CEMETERIES WERE BUILT NEXT TO TRAIN LINES. HE SAID THAT WAS HOW THEY SHIPPED THE COFFINS IN.
RIGHT THAT MINUTE I KNEW THE BULLIES WANTED TO HURT MY SOUL IN A WAY THAT THEY HOPED WOULD TURN MY BODY INTO A COFFIN.
IN THAT SWEATY PANICKY MOMENT I SAW THAT USING THAT WAY TO DRIVE A SPIRIT TOWARDS DEATH WAS THE ACT OF A BAD, WEAK, SOUL-UGLY MONSTER.
I ALSO KNEW RIGHT THEN THAT IF THEY DID THAT TO ME, THEIR SOULS WOULD BEGIN TO DIE... BUT NOTHING ANY ONE SAID WOULD MAKE THEM SEE THAT THE DANGER THEY WERE IN WAS AT LEAST AS GREAT AS MINE...
I HEARD ANKA WHISPER INTO MY EAR, "NAZI, NAZI, NAZI. A NAZI IS A PERSON WHO CHOOSES TO NOT SEE ANYTHING THAT WOULD KEEP THEM FROM BEING CRUEL... EVEN IF WHAT THEY WILL NOT SEE IS HOW THEIR CRUELTY WILL DESTROY THEM!"
HEY GUYS! THERE'S SOMETHIN OUT THERE... I CAN FEEL IT...

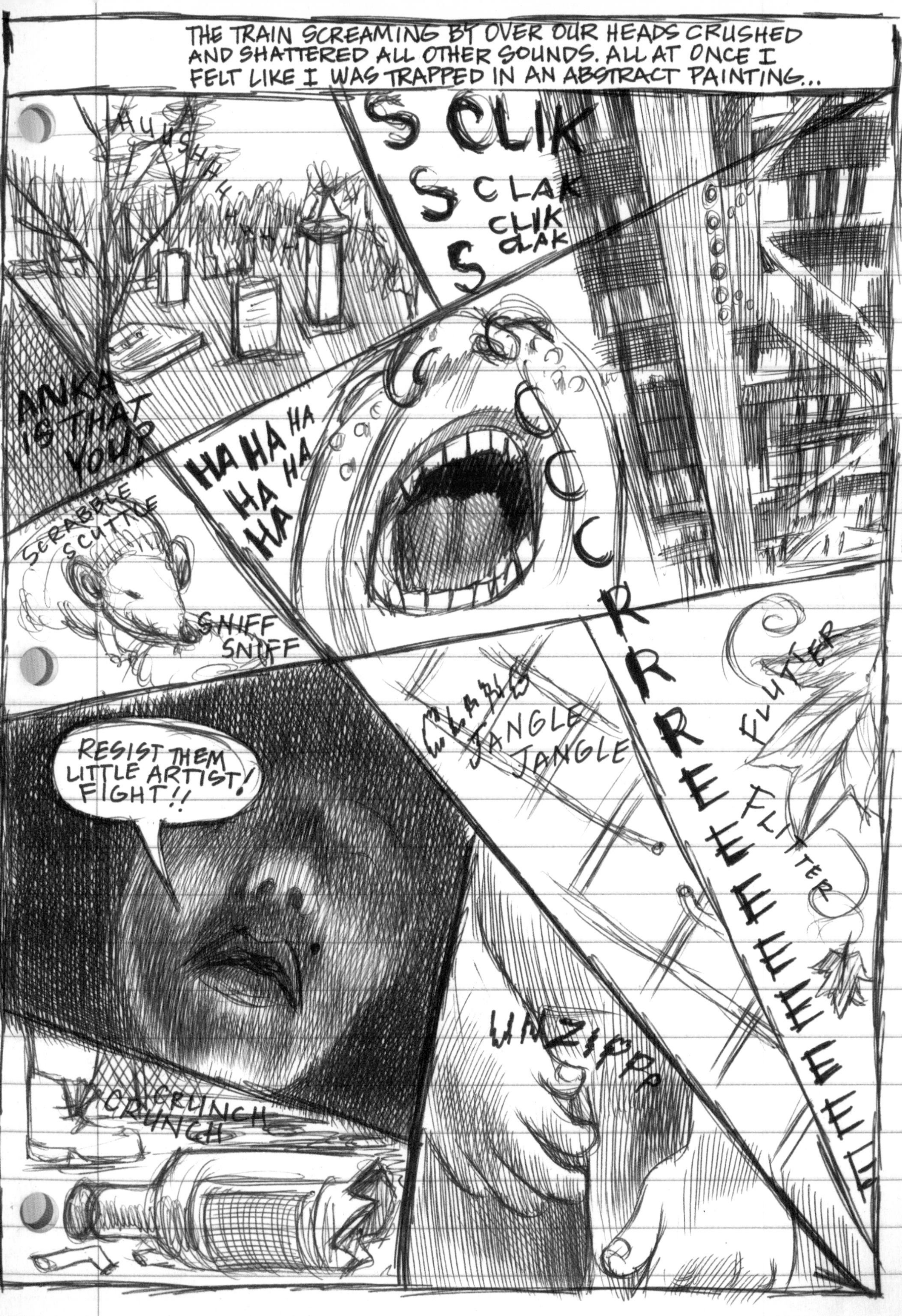
THE TRAIN SCREAMING BY OVER OUR HEADS CRUSHED AND SHATTERED ALL OTHER SOUNDS. ALL AT ONCE I FELT LIKE I WAS TRAPPED IN AN ABSTRACT PAINTING...
SCLIK
SCLAK
CLIK CLAK
ANKA IS THAT YOU?
HAHA HA HA HA HA
SCRABBLE SCUTTLE
SNIFF SNIFF
SCREEEEEEEEEE
RESIST THEM LITTLE ARTIST! FIGHT!!
JANGLE JANGLE
FLUTTER
FLITTER
UNZIPPP
CRUNCH CRUNCH

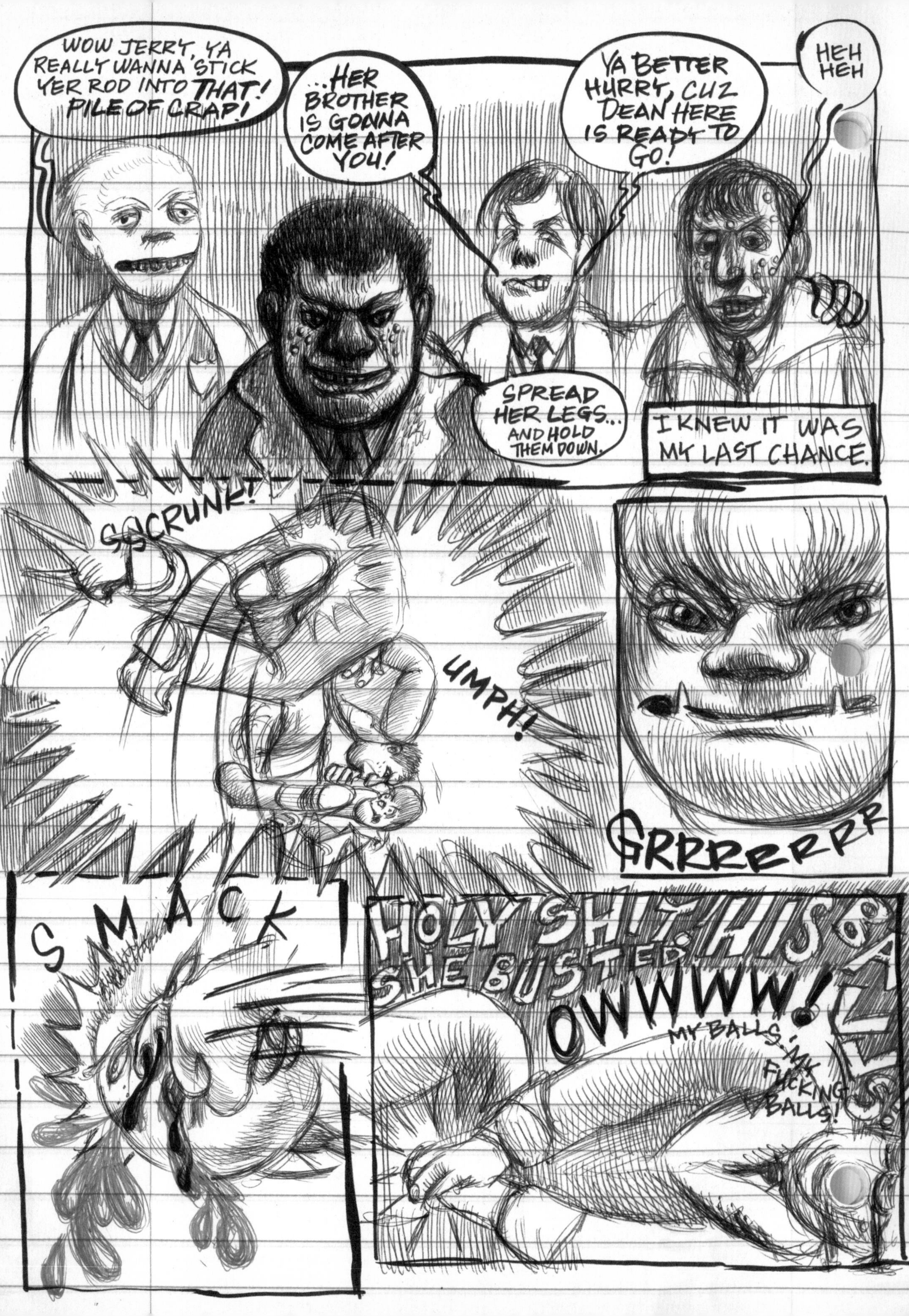
WOW JERRY, YA REALLY WANNA STICK YER ROD INTO THAT! PILE OF CRAP!
...HER BROTHER IS GONNA COME AFTER YOU!
YA BETTER HURRY, CUZ DEAN HERE IS READY TO GO!
HEH HEH
SPREAD HER LEGS... AND HOLD THEM DOWN.
I KNEW IT WAS MY LAST CHANCE.
SSCRUNK!
UMPH!
GRRRERRR
SMACK
HOLY SHIT! HIS
SHE BUSTED
OWWWW!
MY BALLS. MY FUCKING BALLS!

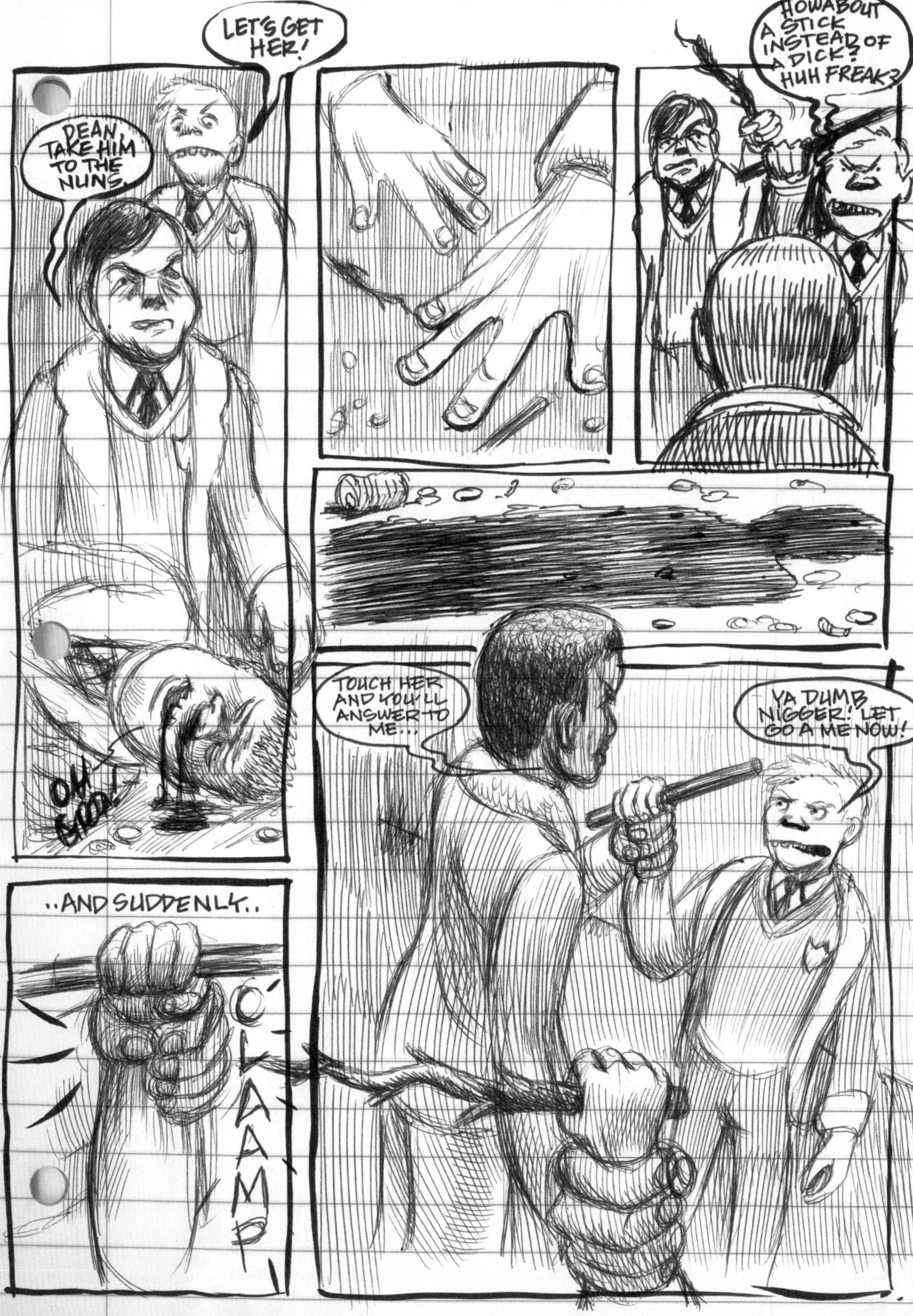
DEAN, TAKE HIM TO THE NUNS.
LET'S GET HER!
OH GOD!
HOWABOUT A STICK INSTEAD OF A DICK? HUH FREAK?
..AND SUDDENLY..
CLAAMP!
TOUCH HER AND YOU'LL ANSWER TO ME...
YA DUMB NIGGER! LET GO A ME NOW!

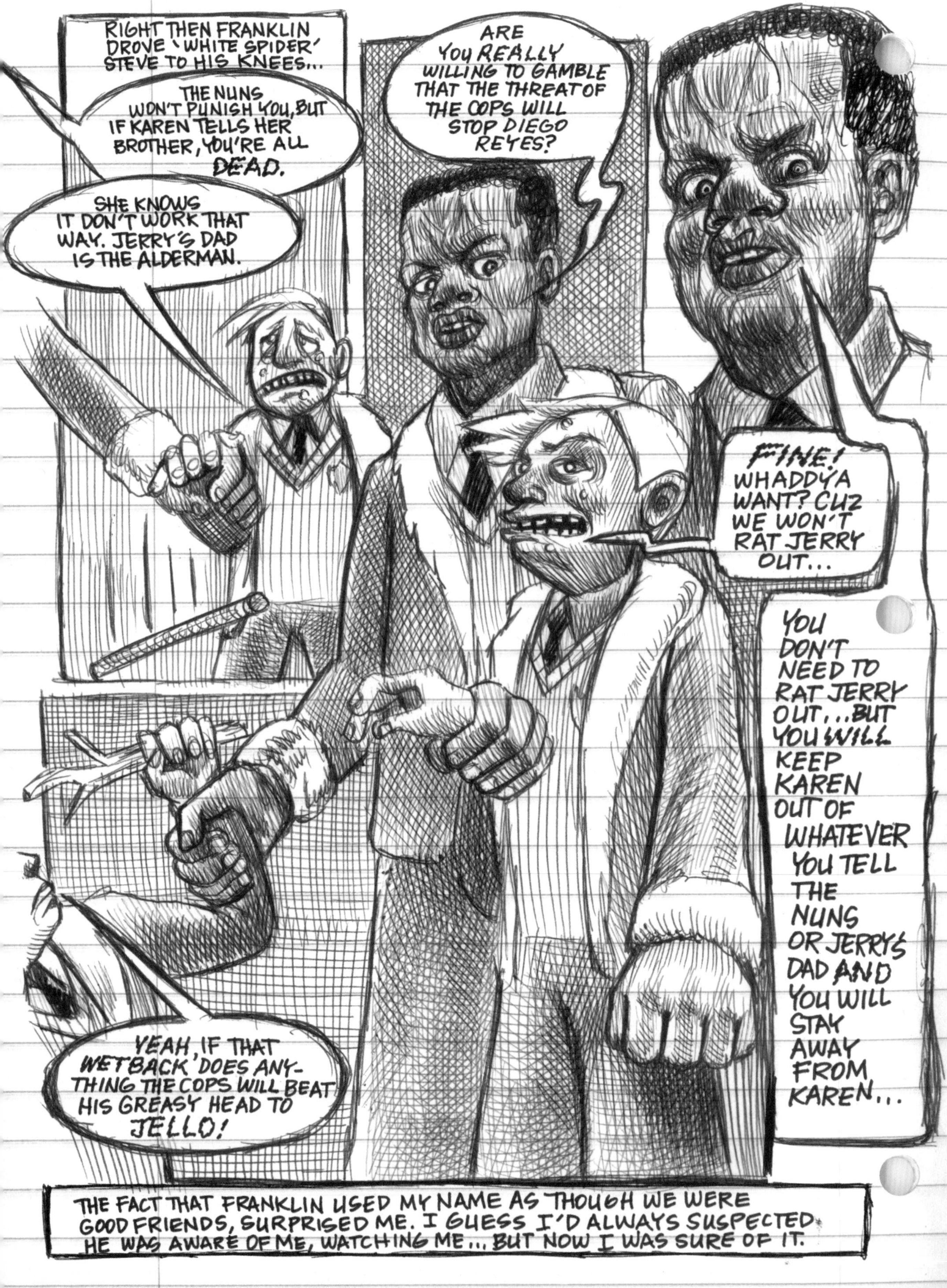
RIGHT THEN FRANKLIN DROVE 'WHITE SPIDER' STEVE TO HIS KNEES...
THE NUNS WON'T PUNISH YOU, BUT IF KAREN TELLS HER BROTHER, YOU'RE ALL DEAD.
SHE KNOWS IT DON'T WORK THAT WAY. JERRY'S DAD IS THE ALDERMAN.
ARE YOU REALLY WILLING TO GAMBLE THAT THE THREAT OF THE COPS WILL STOP DIEGO REYES?
YEAH, IF THAT WETBACK DOES ANY-THING THE COPS WILL BEAT HIS GREASY HEAD TO JELLO!
FINE! WHADDY'A WANT? CUZ WE WON'T RAT JERRY OUT...
YOU DON'T NEED TO RAT JERRY OUT... BUT YOU WILL KEEP KAREN OUT OF WHATEVER YOU TELL THE NUNS OR JERRY'S DAD AND YOU WILL STAY AWAY FROM KAREN...
THE FACT THAT FRANKLIN USED MY NAME AS THOUGH WE WERE GOOD FRIENDS, SURPRISED ME. I GUESS I'D ALWAYS SUSPECTED HE WAS AWARE OF ME, WATCHING ME... BUT NOW I WAS SURE OF IT.

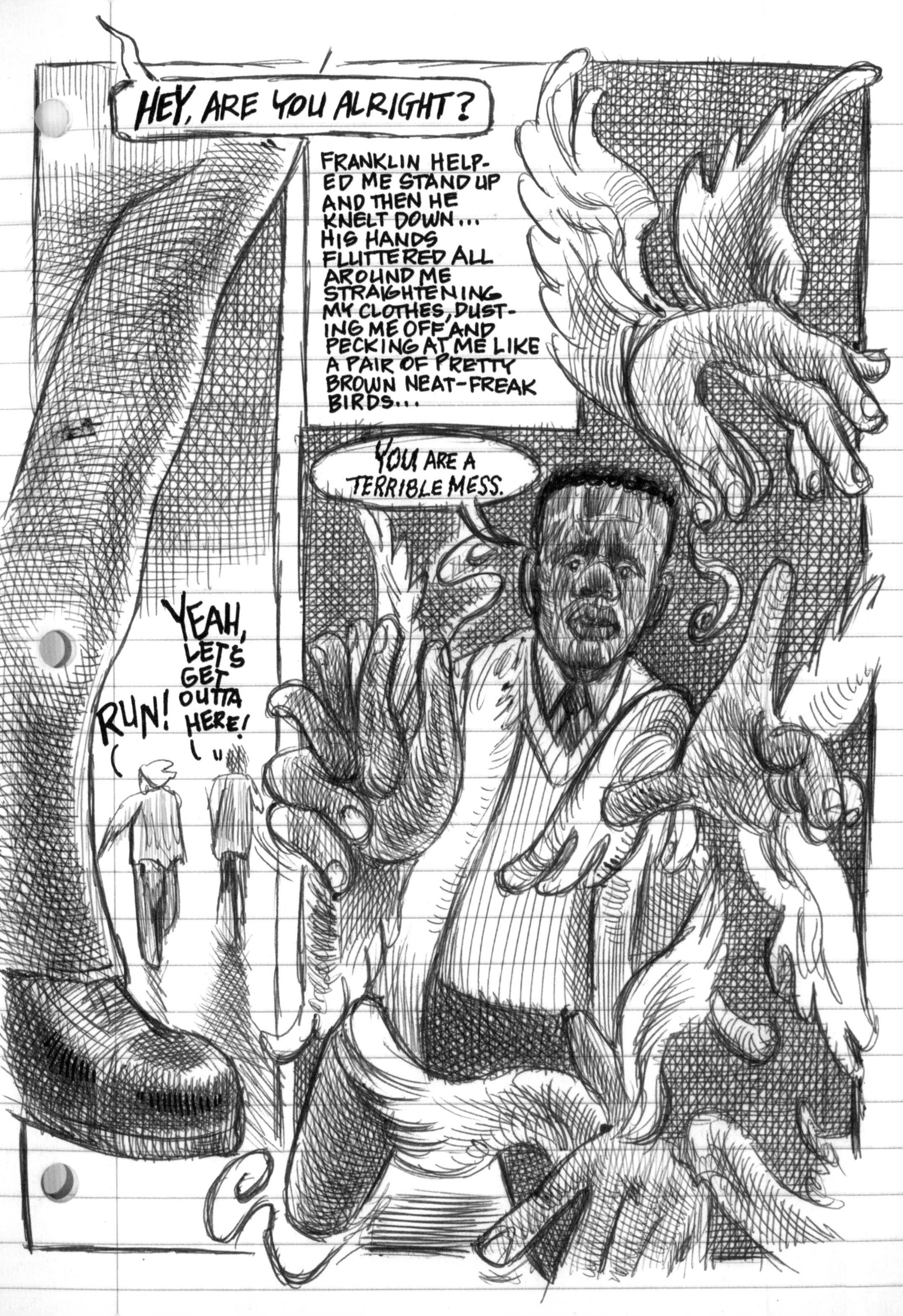
HEY, ARE YOU ALRIGHT?
FRANKLIN HELPED ME STAND UP AND THEN HE KNELT DOWN... HIS HANDS FLUTTERED ALL AROUND ME STRAIGHTENING MY CLOTHES, DUSTING ME OFF AND PECKING AT ME LIKE A PAIR OF PRETTY BROWN NEAT-FREAK BIRDS...
YOU ARE A TERRIBLE MESS.
RUN!
YEAH, LET'S GET OUTTA HERE!

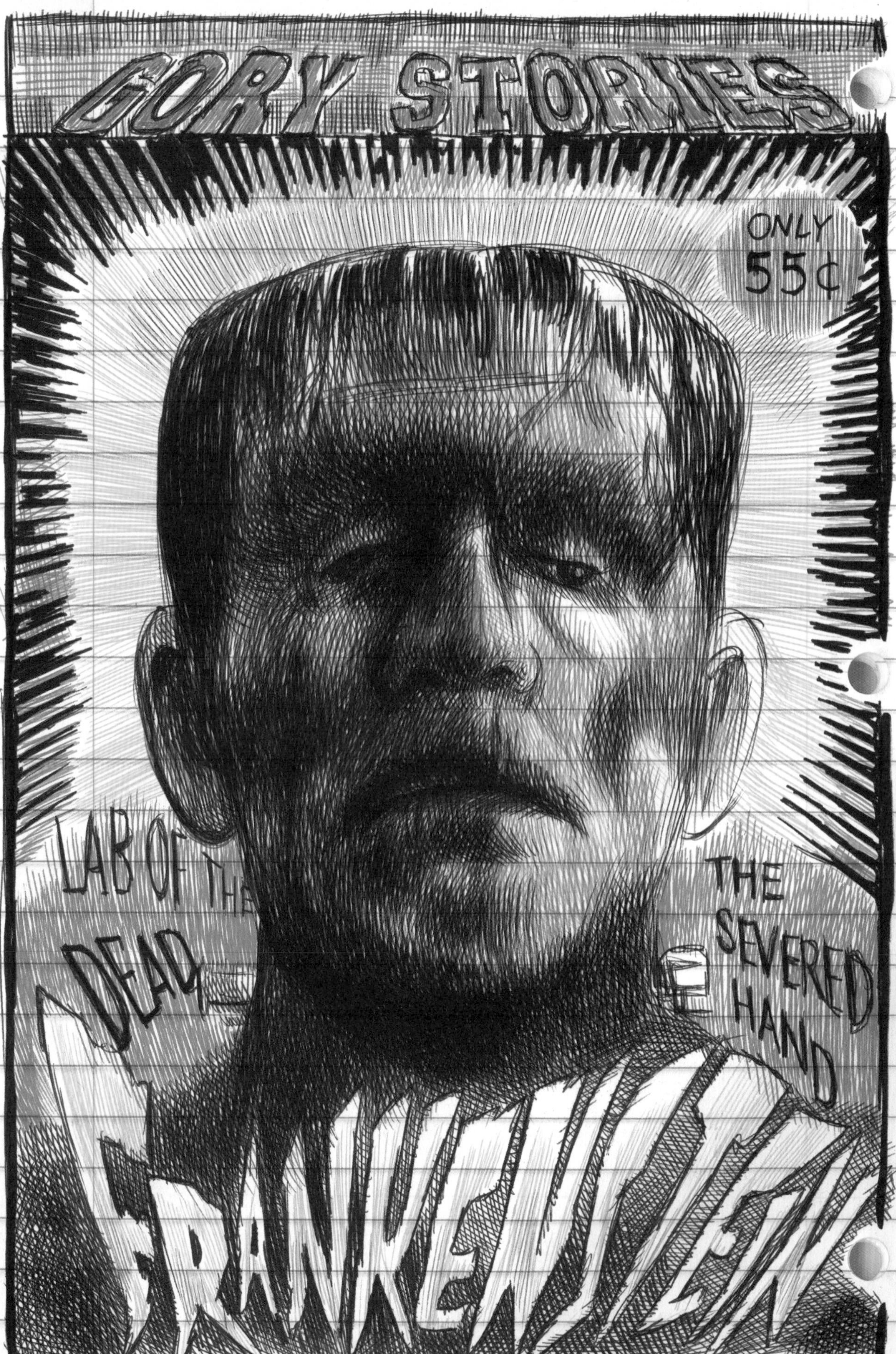
GORY STORIES
ONLY 55¢
LAB OF THE DEAD
THE SEVERED HAND
FRANKENSTEIN

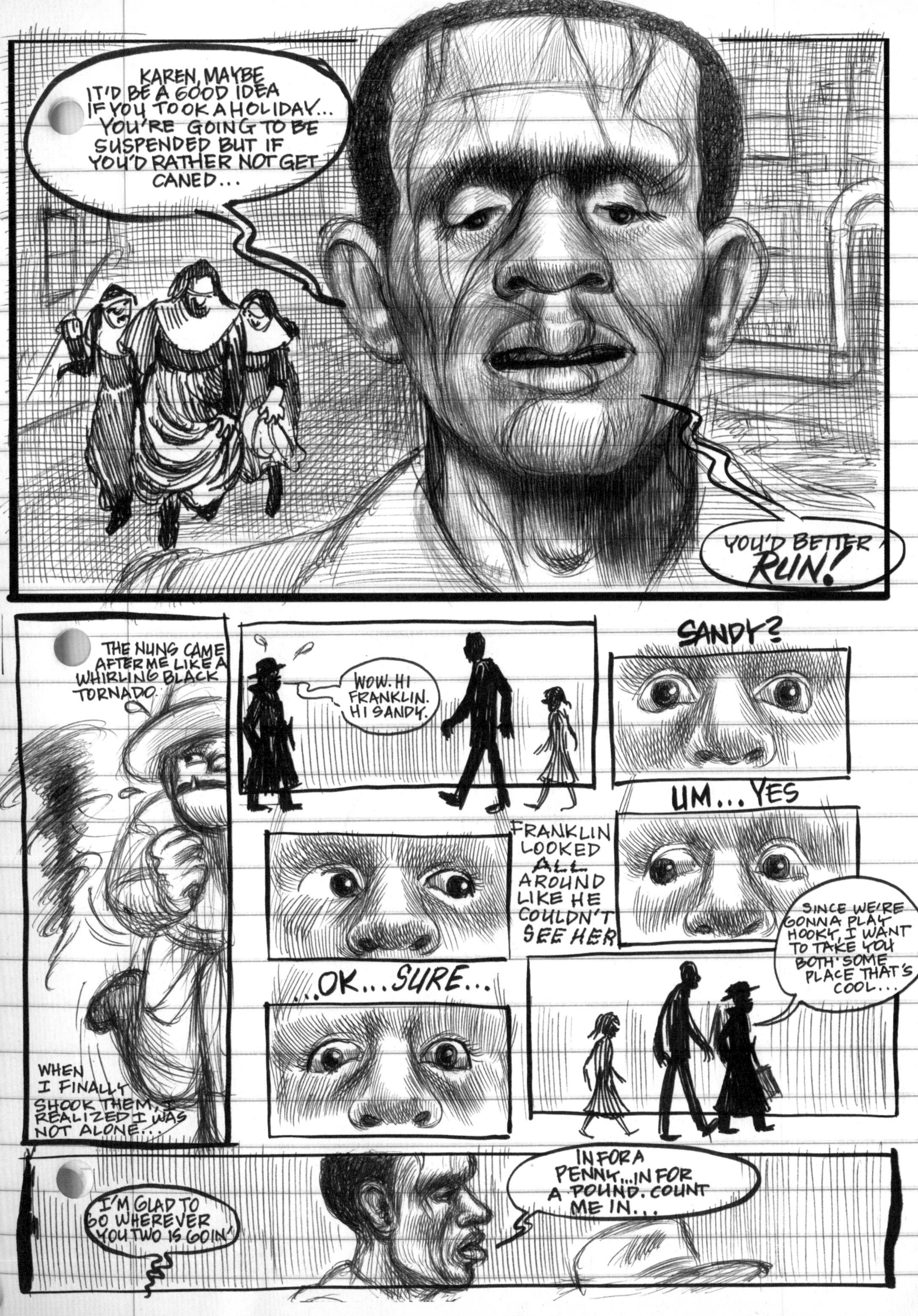
KAREN, MAYBE IT'D BE A GOOD IDEA IF YOU TOOK A HOLIDAY... YOU'RE GOING TO BE SUSPENDED BUT IF YOU'D RATHER NOT GET CANED...
YOU'D BETTER RUN!
THE NUNS CAME AFTER ME LIKE A WHIRLING BLACK TORNADO...
WHEN I FINALLY SHOOK THEM, I REALIZED I WAS NOT ALONE...
WOW. HI FRANKLIN. HI SANDY.
SANDY?
UM... YES
FRANKLIN LOOKED ALL AROUND LIKE HE COULDN'T SEE HER
...OK... SURE...
SINCE WE'RE GONNA PLAY HOOKY, I WANT TO TAKE YOU BOTH SOME PLACE THAT'S COOL...
I'M GLAD TO GO WHEREVER YOU TWO IS GOIN'
IN FOR A PENNY... IN FOR A POUND. COUNT ME IN...

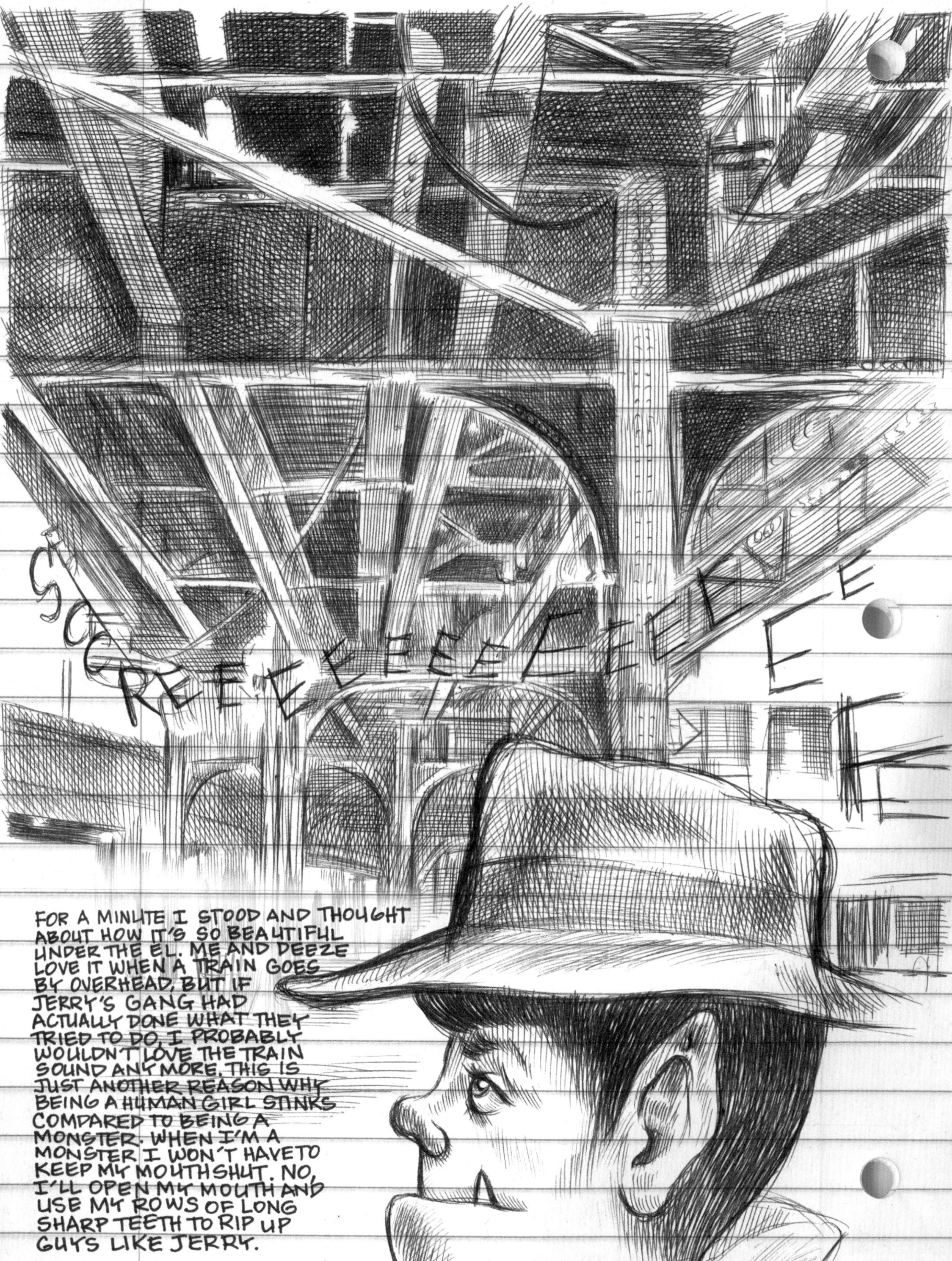
SCREEEEEEEEEEEE
FOR A MINUTE I STOOD AND THOUGHT ABOUT HOW IT'S SO BEAUTIFUL UNDER THE EL. ME AND DEEZE LOVE IT WHEN A TRAIN GOES BY OVERHEAD, BUT IF JERRY'S GANG HAD ACTUALLY DONE WHAT THEY TRIED TO DO, I PROBABLY WOULDN'T LOVE THE TRAIN SOUND ANYMORE. THIS IS JUST ANOTHER REASON WHY BEING A HUMAN GIRL STINKS COMPARED TO BEING A MONSTER. WHEN I'M A MONSTER I WON'T HAVE TO KEEP MY MOUTH SHUT. NO, I'LL OPEN MY MOUTH AND USE MY ROWS OF LONG SHARP TEETH TO RIP UP GUYS LIKE JERRY.

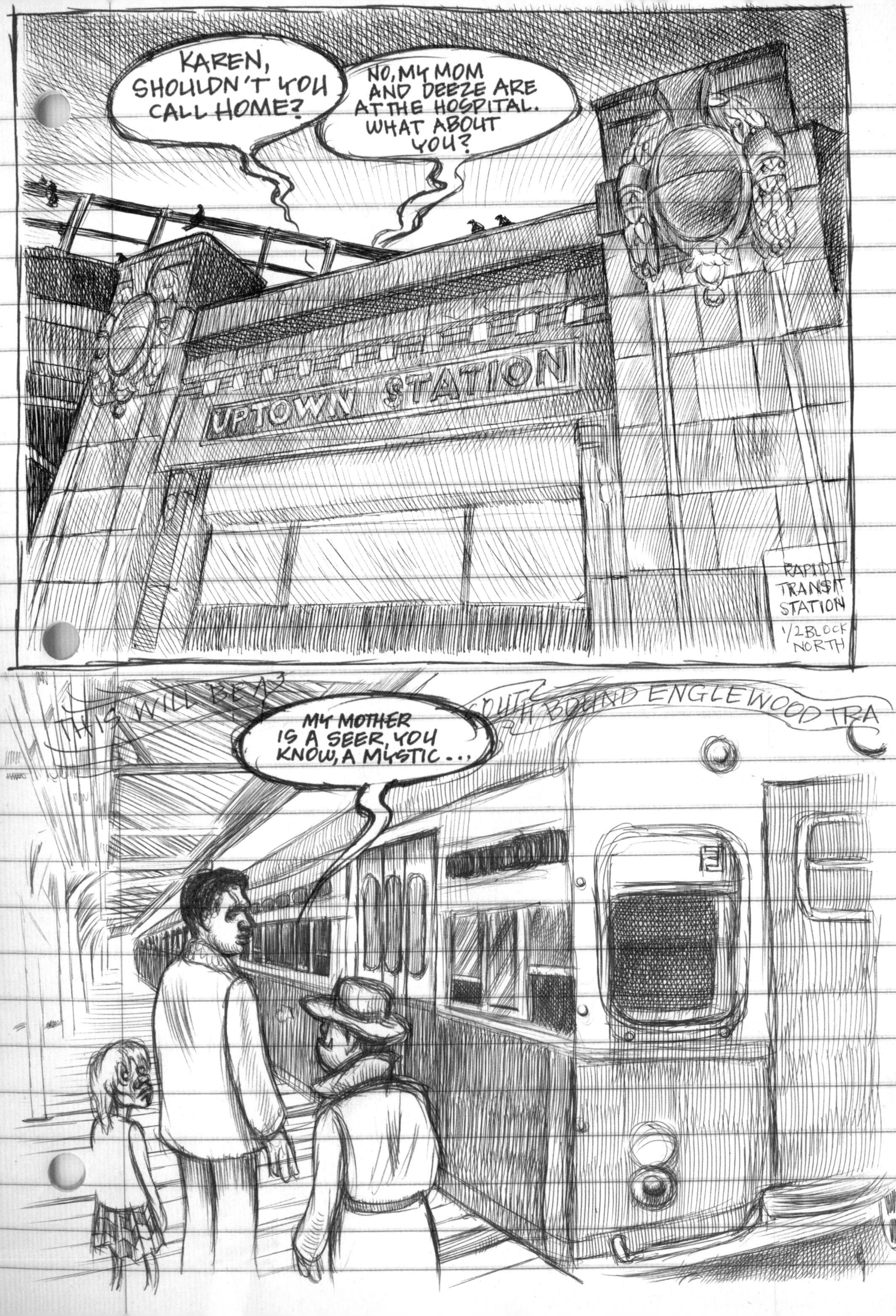
KAREN, SHOULDN'T YOU CALL HOME?
NO, MY MOM AND DEEZE ARE AT THE HOSPITAL. WHAT ABOUT YOU?
UPTOWN STATION
RAPID TRANSIT STATION 1/2 BLOCK NORTH
THIS WILL BE A
SOUTH BOUND ENGLEWOOD TRA
MY MOTHER IS A SEER, YOU KNOW, A MYSTIC . . .

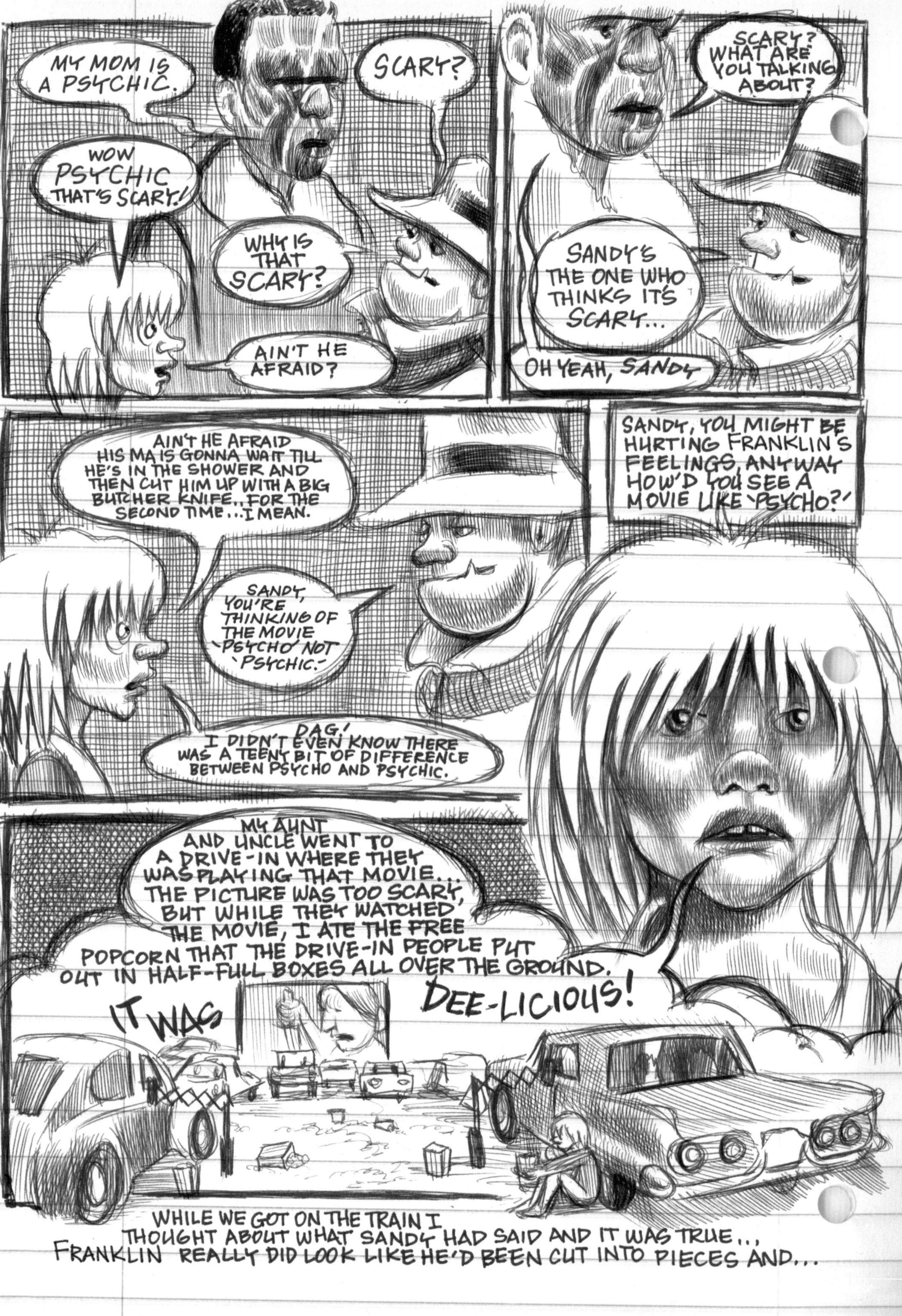

MY MOM IS A PSYCHIC.
SCARY?
WOW PSYCHIC THAT'S SCARY!
WHY IS THAT SCARY?
AIN'T HE AFRAID?
SCARY? WHAT ARE YOU TALKING ABOUT?
SANDY'S THE ONE WHO THINKS IT'S SCARY...
OH YEAH, SANDY
AIN'T HE AFRAID HIS MA IS GONNA WAIT TILL HE'S IN THE SHOWER AND THEN CUT HIM UP WITH A BIG BUTCHER KNIFE.. FOR THE SECOND TIME...I MEAN.
SANDY, YOU'RE THINKING OF THE MOVIE 'PSYCHO' NOT 'PSYCHIC.'
DAG! I DIDN'T EVEN KNOW THERE WAS A TEENY BIT OF DIFFERENCE BETWEEN PSYCHO AND PSYCHIC.
SANDY, YOU MIGHT BE HURTING FRANKLIN'S FEELINGS, ANYWAY HOW'D YOU SEE A MOVIE LIKE 'PSYCHO?'
MY AUNT AND UNCLE WENT TO A DRIVE-IN WHERE THEY WAS PLAYING THAT MOVIE... THE PICTURE WAS TOO SCARY, BUT WHILE THEY WATCHED THE MOVIE, I ATE THE FREE POPCORN THAT THE DRIVE-IN PEOPLE PUT OUT IN HALF-FULL BOXES ALL OVER THE GROUND.
IT WAS DEE-LICIOUS!
WHILE WE GOT ON THE TRAIN I THOUGHT ABOUT WHAT SANDY HAD SAID AND IT WAS TRUE... FRANKLIN REALLY DID LOOK LIKE HE'D BEEN CUT INTO PIECES AND...

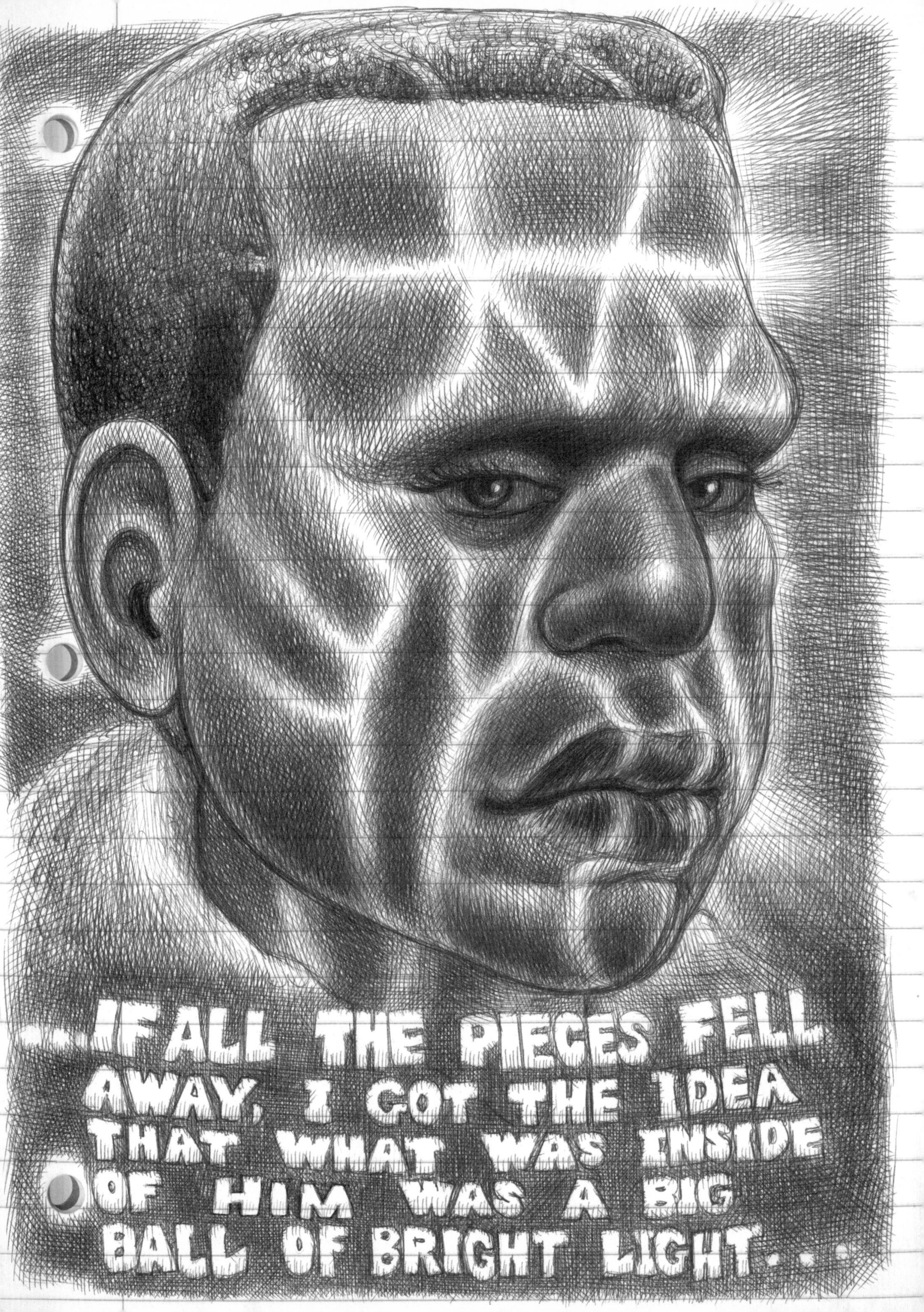
...IF ALL THE PIECES FELL AWAY, I GOT THE IDEA THAT WHAT WAS INSIDE OF HIM WAS A BIG BALL OF BRIGHT LIGHT...

AFTER WE GOT ON THE TRAIN AND TOOK OUR SEATS. I TOLD FRANKLIN THAT I WAS SORRY FOR WHAT SANDY HAD SAID ABOUT HIS FACE...

IT'S ALL RIGHT, I'M USED TO PEOPLE STARING AT ME... BUT YOU'VE NEVER STARED AT THE... AT MY SCARS.. DON'T TELL ME YOU'VE NEVER WONDERED...

I'VE WONDERED BUT IT'S YOUR BUSINESS...

WEEE HOOO

THIS TRAIN IS LIKE A TILT-A-WHIRL WITHOUT THE WHIRL

I WAS ATTACKED BY:-

..AN ANGRY DOG...

DOESN'T LOOK LIKE DOG BITES TO ME...

NO, FRANKLIN LOOKS LIKE HE WAS ASSEMBLED IN THE LABORATORY OF A MAD (BUT ARTISTIC) SCIENTIST.

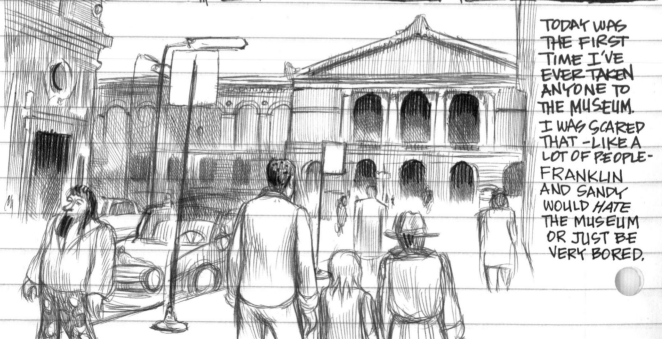

TODAY WAS THE FIRST TIME I'VE EVER TAKEN ANYONE TO THE MUSEUM. I WAS SCARED THAT -LIKE A LOT OF PEOPLE- FRANKLIN AND SANDY WOULD HATE THE MUSEUM OR JUST BE VERY BORED.

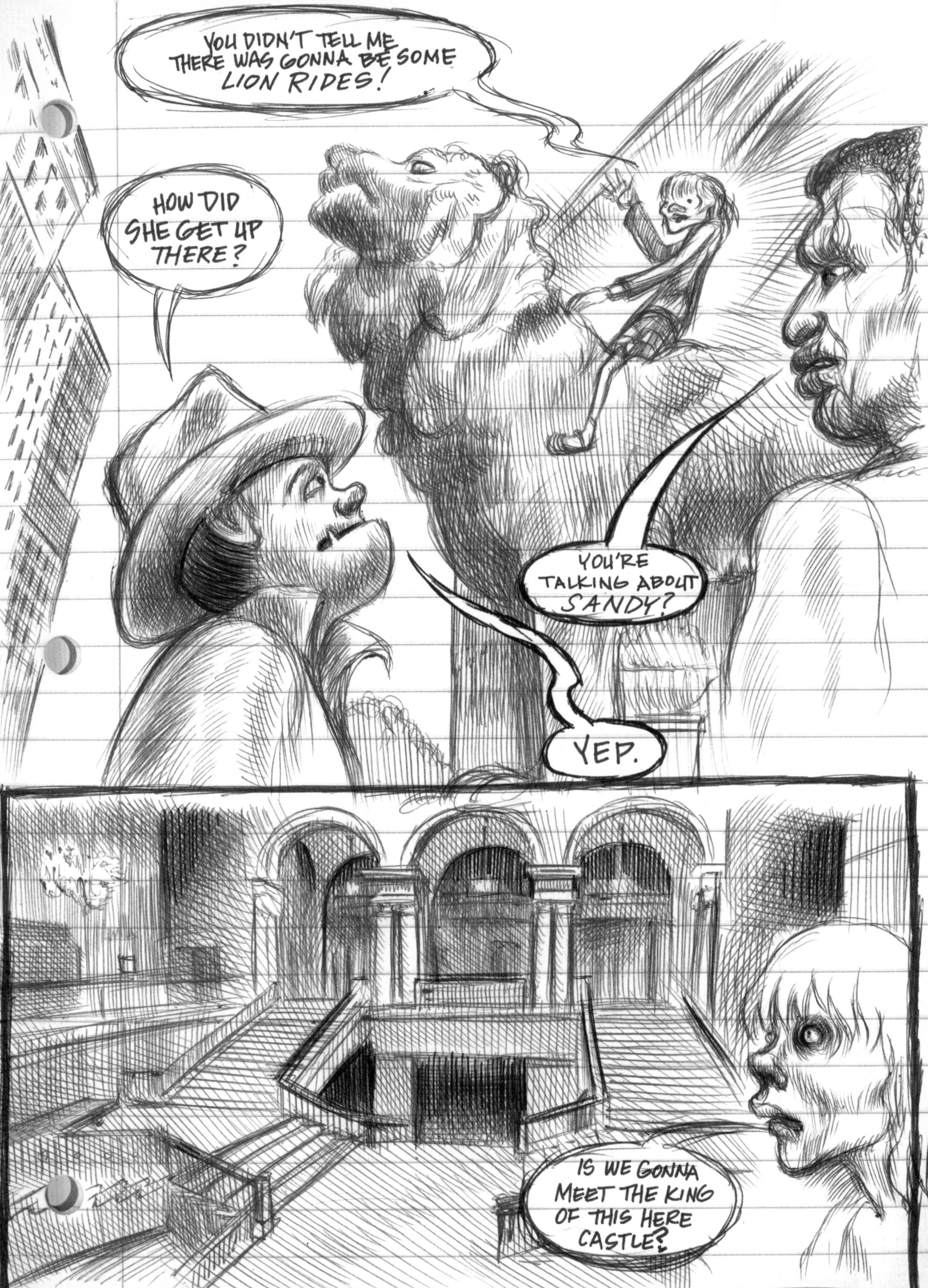
YOU DIDN'T TELL ME THERE WAS GONNA BE SOME LION RIDES!
HOW DID SHE GET UP THERE?
YOU'RE TALKING ABOUT SANDY?
YEP.
IS WE GONNA MEET THE KING OF THIS HERE CASTLE?

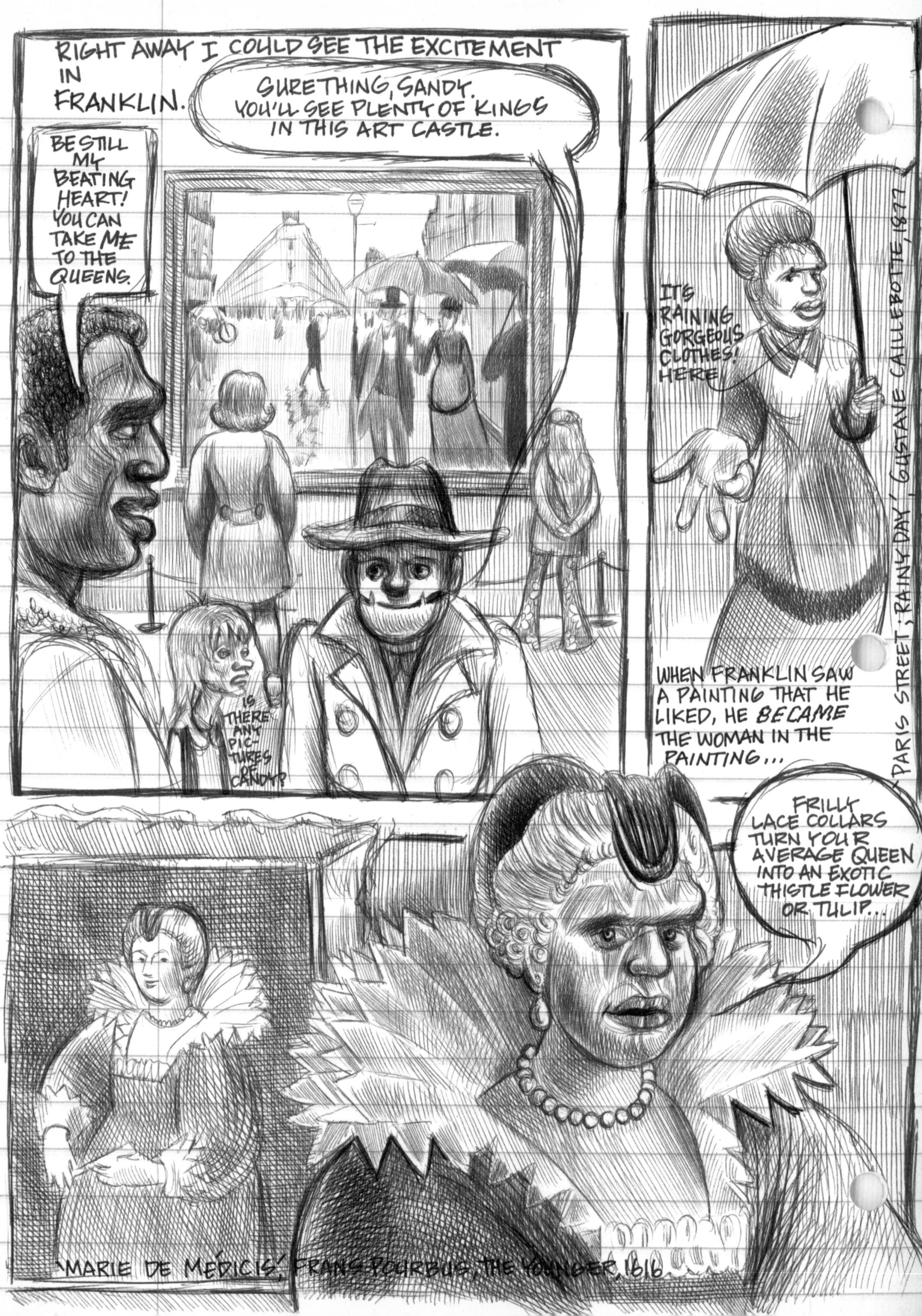
RIGHT AWAY I COULD SEE THE EXCITEMENT IN FRANKLIN.
SURE THING, SANDY. YOU'LL SEE PLENTY OF KINGS IN THIS ART CASTLE.
BE STILL MY BEATING HEART! YOU CAN TAKE ME TO THE QUEENS.
IS THERE ANY PICTURES OF CANDY?
IT'S RAINING GORGEOUS CLOTHES! HERE
'PARIS STREET; RAINY DAY' GUSTAVE CAILLEBOTTE, 1877
WHEN FRANKLIN SAW A PAINTING THAT HE LIKED, HE *BECAME* THE WOMAN IN THE PAINTING...
FRILLY LACE COLLARS TURN YOUR AVERAGE QUEEN INTO AN EXOTIC THISTLE FLOWER OR TULIP...
'MARIE DE MÉDICIS', FRANS POURBUS, THE YOUNGER, 1616

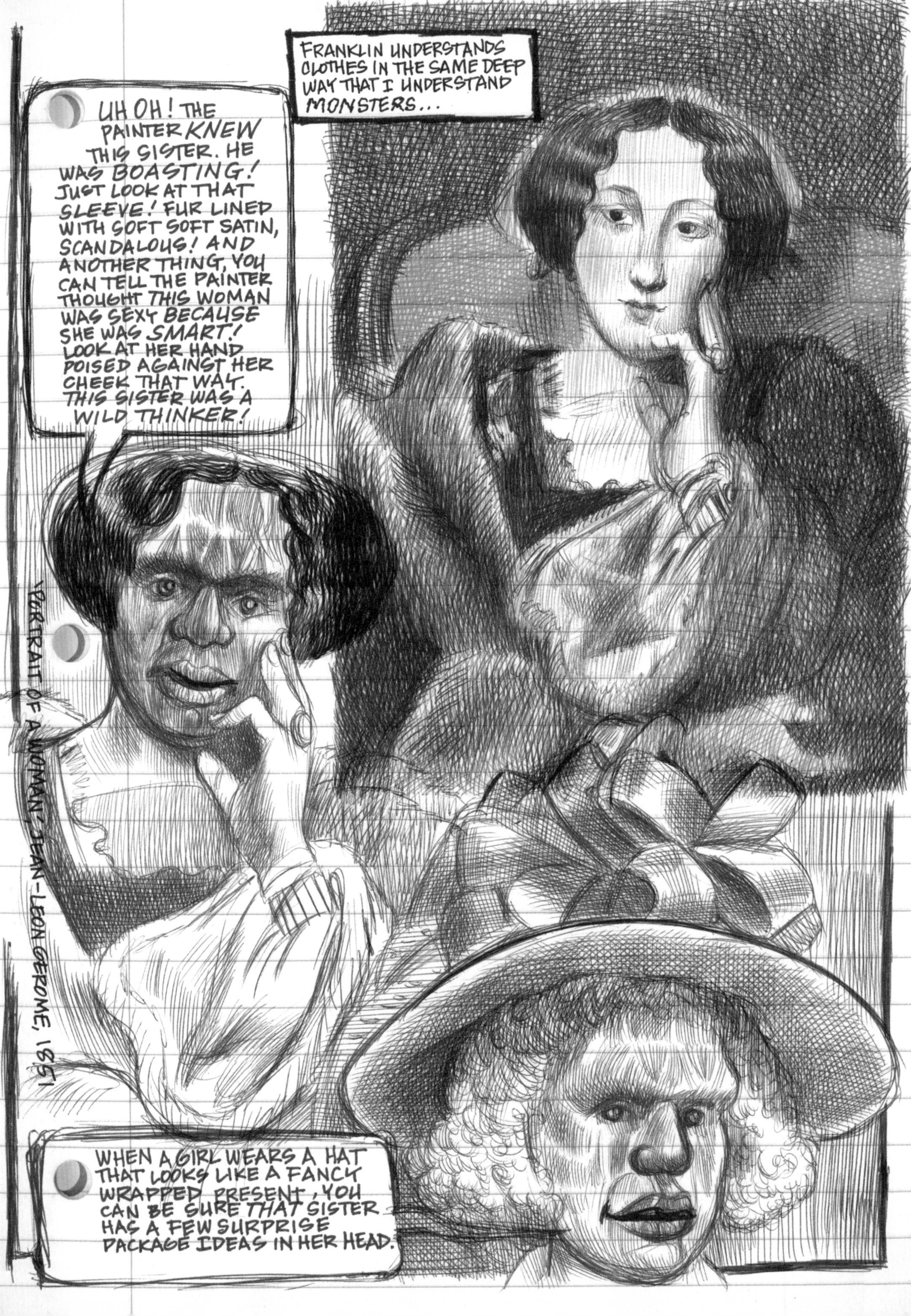
FRANKLIN UNDERSTANDS CLOTHES IN THE SAME DEEP WAY THAT I UNDERSTAND MONSTERS...
UH OH! THE PAINTER KNEW THIS SISTER. HE WAS BOASTING! JUST LOOK AT THAT SLEEVE! FUR LINED WITH SOFT SOFT SATIN, SCANDALOUS! AND ANOTHER THING, YOU CAN TELL THE PAINTER THOUGHT THIS WOMAN WAS SEXY BECAUSE SHE WAS SMART! LOOK AT HER HAND POISED AGAINST HER CHEEK THAT WAY. THIS SISTER WAS A WILD THINKER!
"PORTRAIT OF A WOMAN," JEAN-LEON GEROME, 1851
WHEN A GIRL WEARS A HAT THAT LOOKS LIKE A FANCY WRAPPED PRESENT, YOU CAN BE SURE THAT SISTER HAS A FEW SURPRISE PACKAGE IDEAS IN HER HEAD.

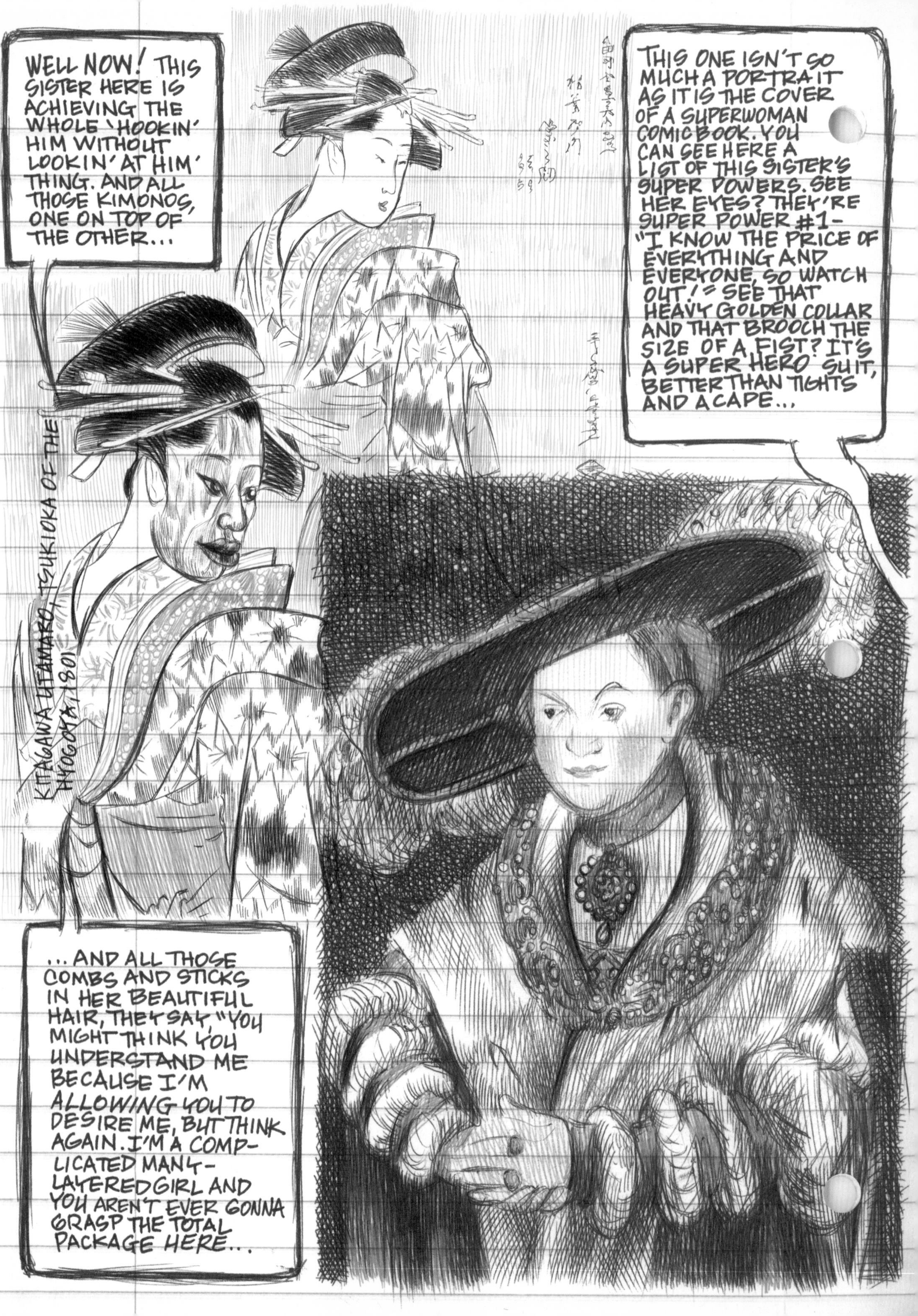
WELL NOW! THIS SISTER HERE IS ACHIEVING THE WHOLE 'HOOKIN' HIM WITHOUT LOOKIN' AT HIM' THING. AND ALL THOSE KIMONOS, ONE ON TOP OF THE OTHER...
KITAGAWA UTAMARO, TSUKIOKA OF THE HYOGOYA, 1801
...AND ALL THOSE COMBS AND STICKS IN HER BEAUTIFUL HAIR, THEY SAY "YOU MIGHT THINK YOU UNDERSTAND ME BECAUSE I'M ALLOWING YOU TO DESIRE ME, BUT THINK AGAIN. I'M A COMPLICATED MANY-LAYERED GIRL AND YOU AREN'T EVER GONNA GRASP THE TOTAL PACKAGE HERE...
THIS ONE ISN'T SO MUCH A PORTRAIT AS IT IS THE COVER OF A SUPERWOMAN COMIC BOOK. YOU CAN SEE HERE A LIST OF THIS SISTER'S SUPER POWERS. SEE HER EYES? THEY'RE SUPER POWER #1- "I KNOW THE PRICE OF EVERYTHING AND EVERYONE, SO WATCH OUT!" SEE THAT HEAVY GOLDEN COLLAR AND THAT BROOCH THE SIZE OF A FIST? IT'S A SUPER HERO SUIT, BETTER THAN TIGHTS AND A CAPE...

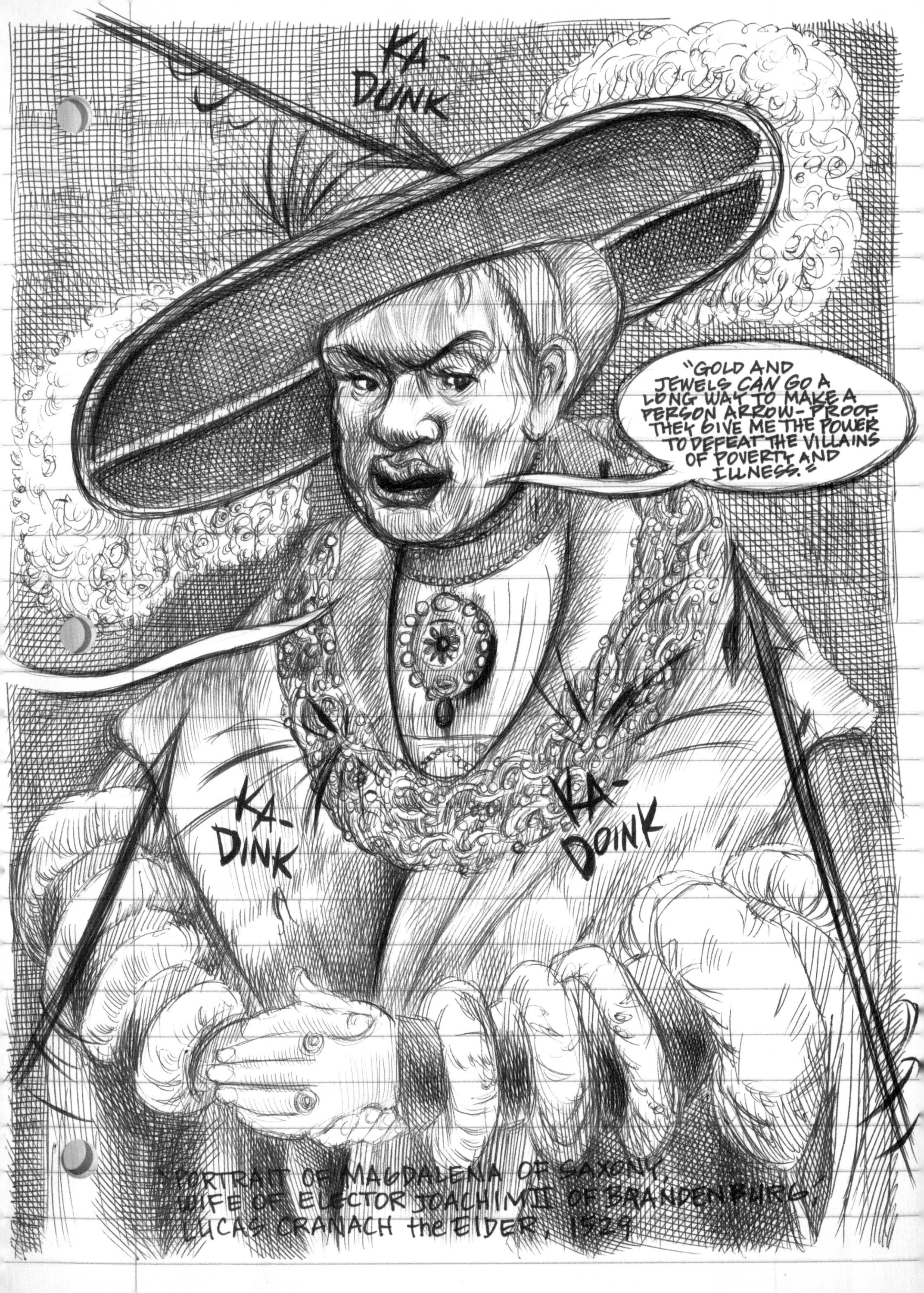
KA-DUNK
"GOLD AND JEWELS CAN GO A LONG WAY TO MAKE A PERSON ARROW-PROOF THEY GIVE ME THE POWER TO DEFEAT THE VILLAINS OF POVERTY AND ILLNESS."
KA-DINK
KA-DOINK

PORTRAIT OF MAGDALENA OF SAXONY, WIFE OF ELECTOR JOACHIM I OF BRANDENBURG, LUCAS CRANACH the ELDER, 1529

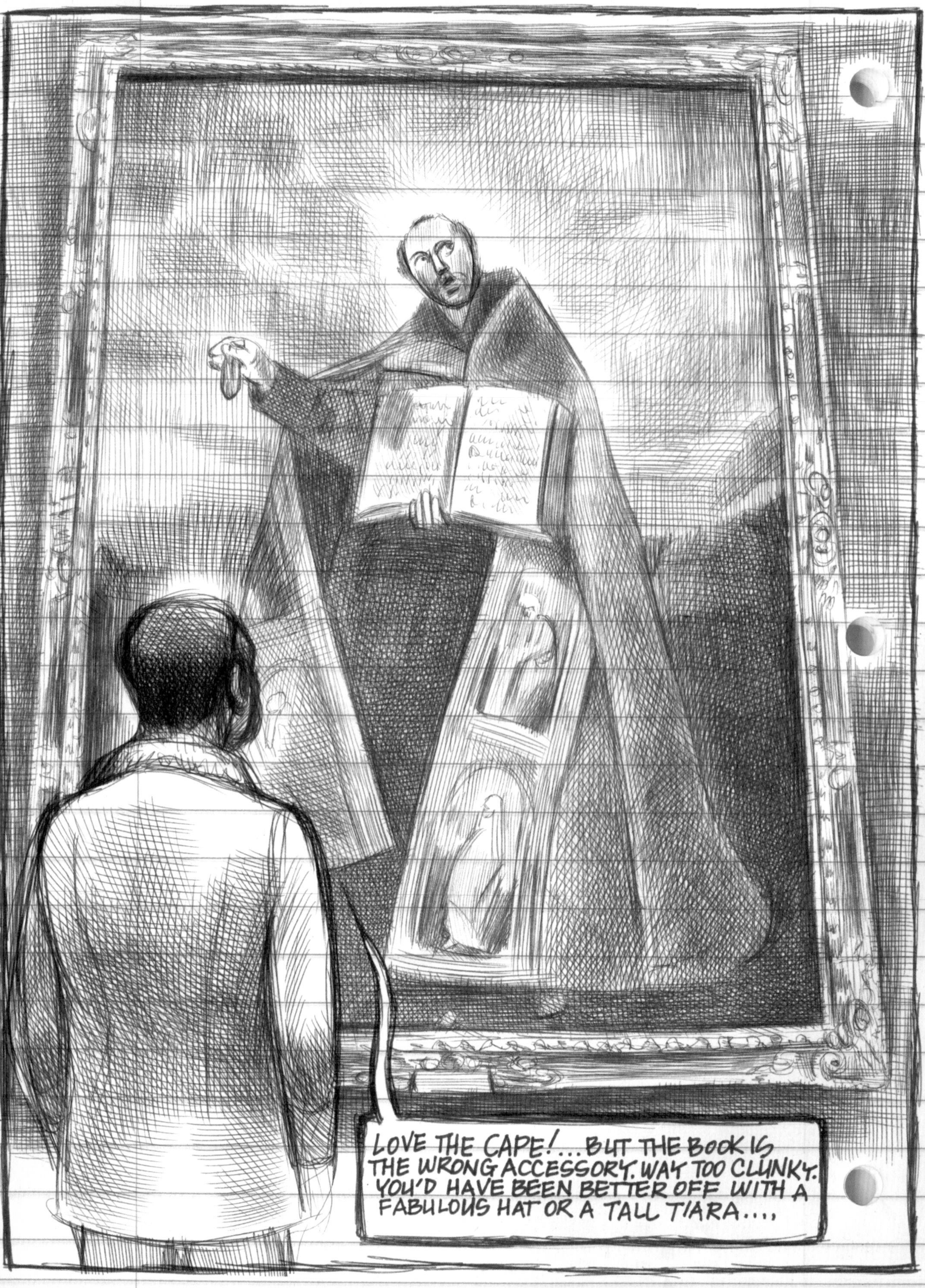
LOVE THE CAPE!...BUT THE BOOK IS THE WRONG ACCESSORY. WAY TOO CLUNKY. YOU'D HAVE BEEN BETTER OFF WITH A FABULOUS HAT OR A TALL TIARA...,

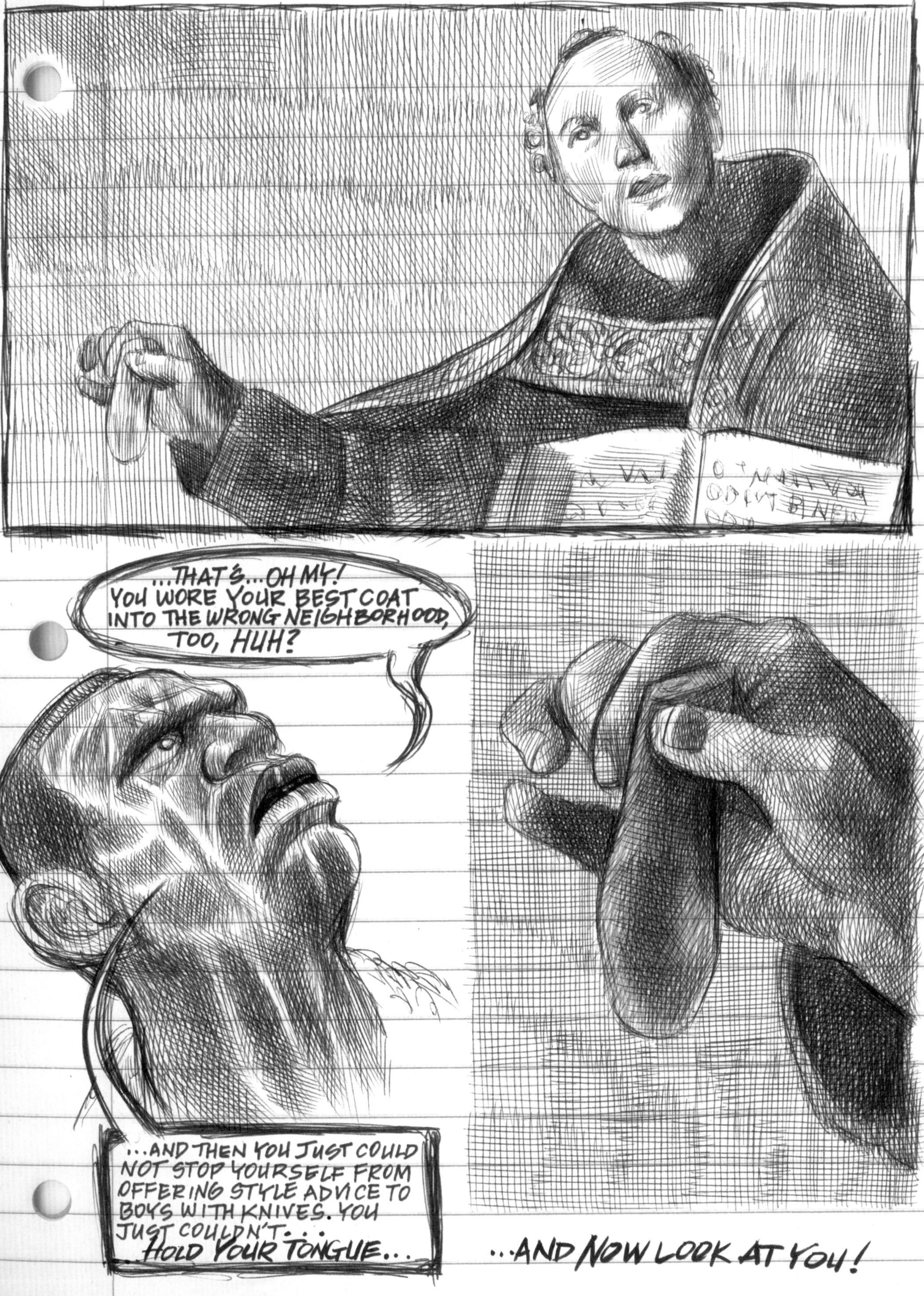
...THAT'S...OH MY! YOU WORE YOUR BEST COAT INTO THE WRONG NEIGHBORHOOD, TOO, HUH?
...AND THEN YOU JUST COULD NOT STOP YOURSELF FROM OFFERING STYLE ADVICE TO BOYS WITH KNIVES. YOU JUST COULDN'T... HOLD YOUR TONGUE...
...AND NOW LOOK AT YOU!

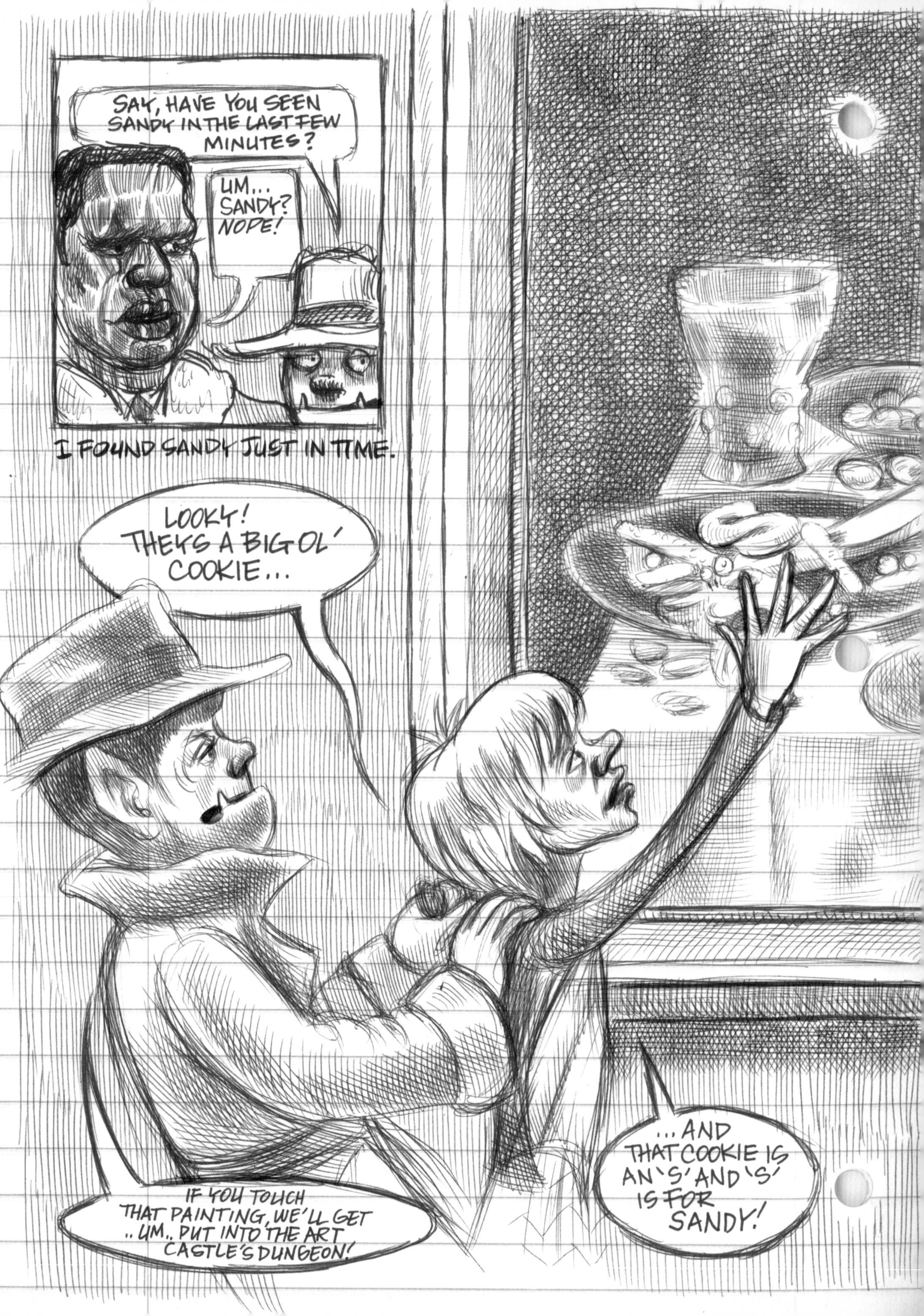
SAY, HAVE YOU SEEN SANDY IN THE LAST FEW MINUTES?
UM... SANDY? NOPE!
I FOUND SANDY JUST IN TIME.
LOOKY! THEY'S A BIG OL' COOKIE...
...AND THAT COOKIE IS AN 'S' AND 'S' IS FOR SANDY!
IF YOU TOUCH THAT PAINTING, WE'LL GET ..UM.. PUT INTO THE ART CASTLE'S DUNGEON!

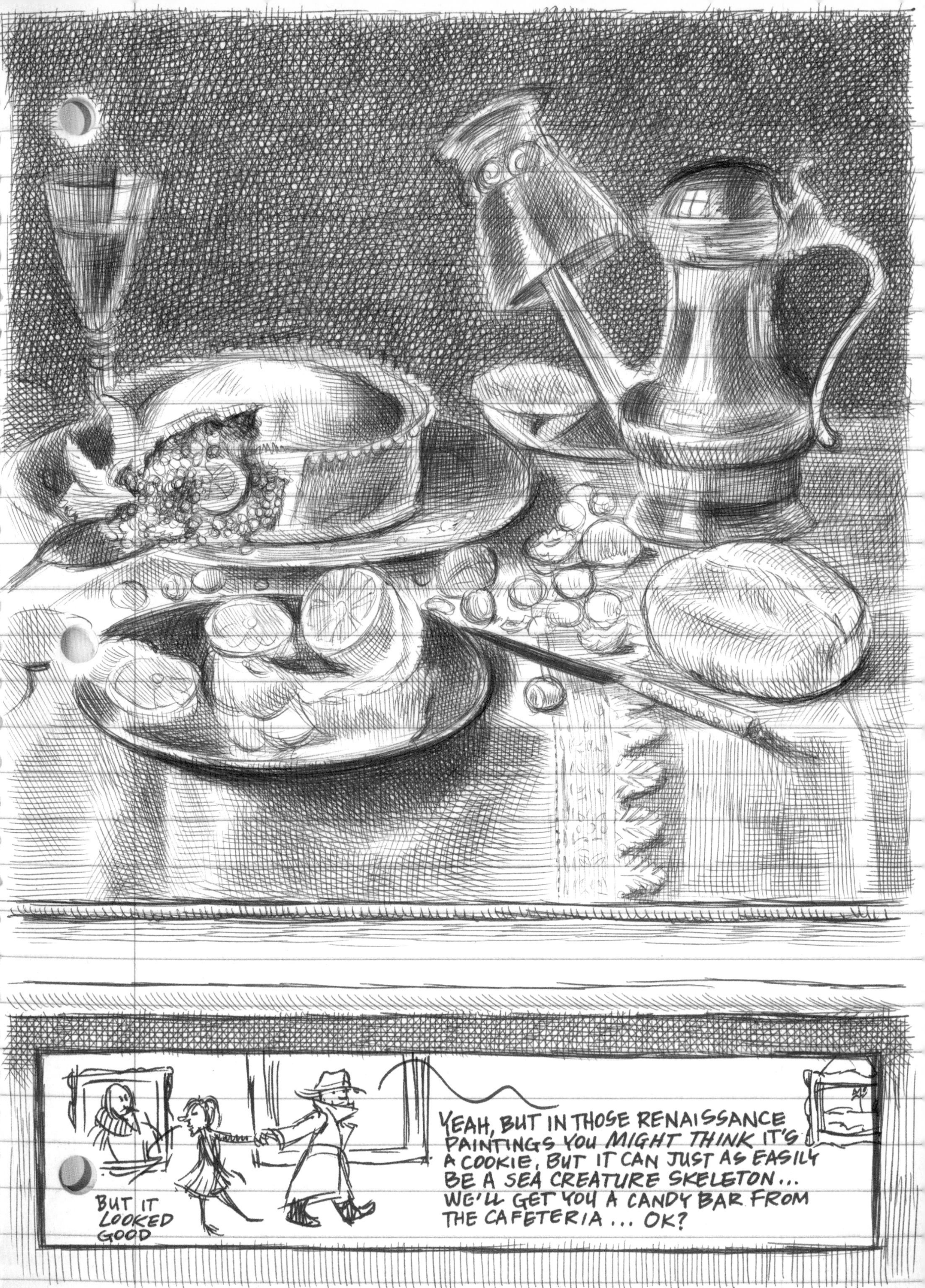
BUT IT LOOKED GOOD
YEAH, BUT IN THOSE RENAISSANCE PAINTINGS YOU MIGHT THINK IT'S A COOKIE, BUT IT CAN JUST AS EASILY BE A SEA CREATURE SKELETON... WE'LL GET YOU A CANDY BAR FROM THE CAFETERIA ... OK?

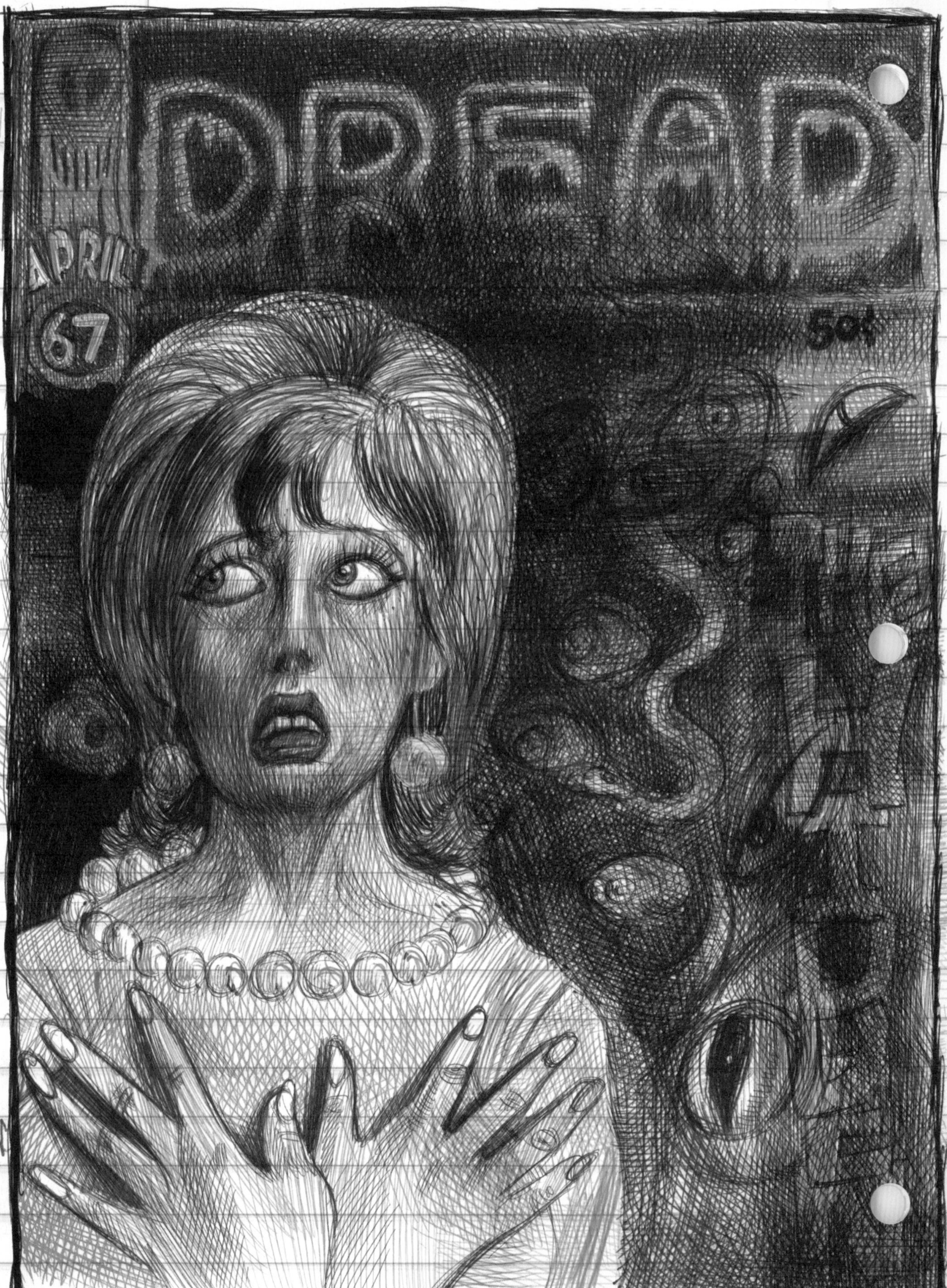
DREAD
APRIL
67
50¢

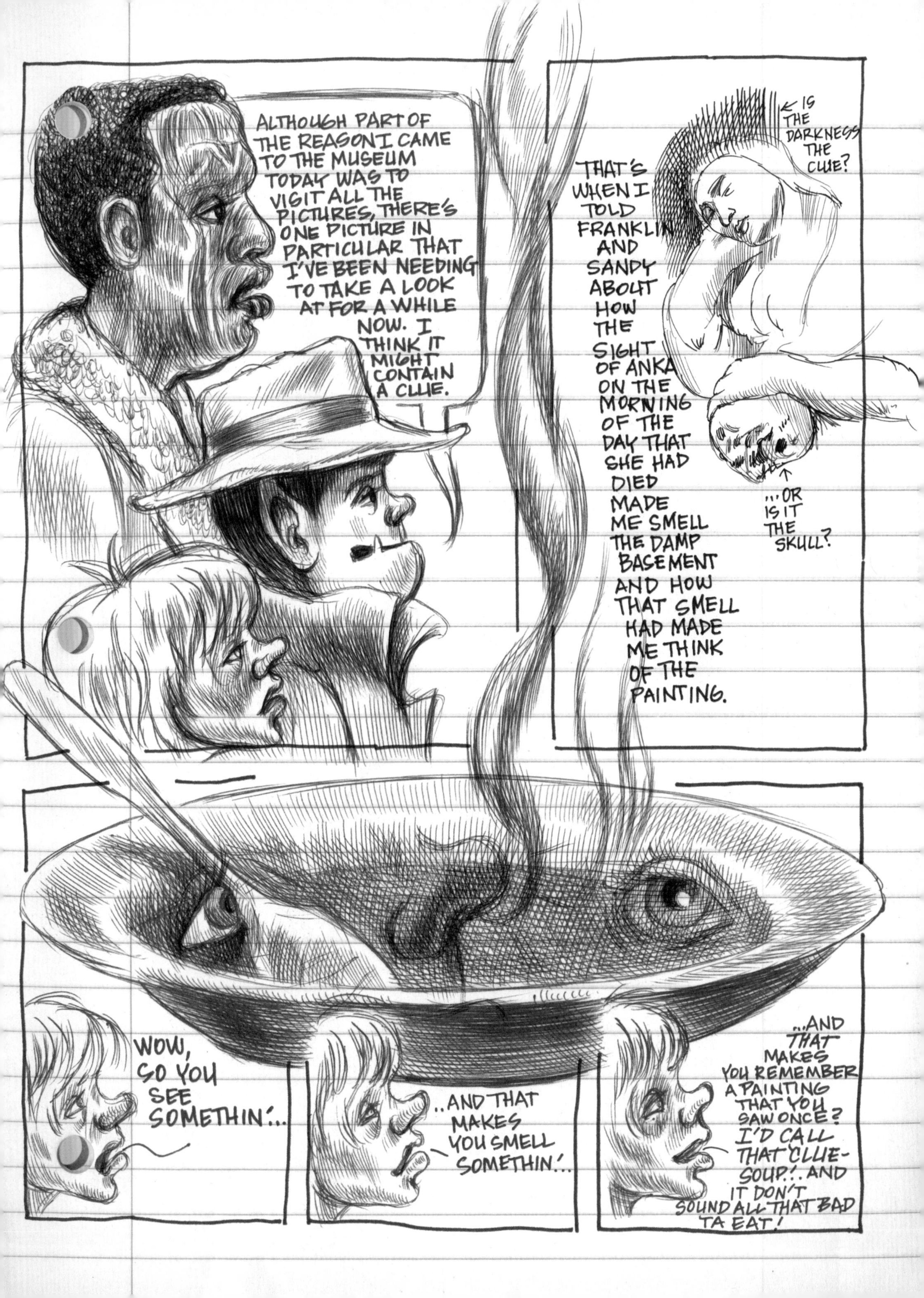
ALTHOUGH PART OF THE REASON I CAME TO THE MUSEUM TODAY WAS TO VISIT ALL THE PICTURES, THERE'S ONE PICTURE IN PARTICULAR THAT I'VE BEEN NEEDING TO TAKE A LOOK AT FOR A WHILE NOW. I THINK IT MIGHT CONTAIN A CLUE.
THAT'S WHEN I TOLD FRANKLIN AND SANDY ABOUT HOW THE SIGHT OF ANKA ON THE MORNING OF THE DAY THAT SHE HAD DIED MADE ME SMELL THE DAMP BASEMENT AND HOW THAT SMELL HAD MADE ME THINK OF THE PAINTING.
IS THE DARKNESS THE CLUE?
...OR IS IT THE SKULL?
WOW, SO YOU SEE SOMETHIN'...
..AND THAT MAKES YOU SMELL SOMETHIN'...
..AND THAT MAKES YOU REMEMBER A PAINTING THAT YOU SAW ONCE? I'D CALL THAT 'CLUE-SOUP'! AND IT DON'T SOUND ALL THAT BAD TA EAT!

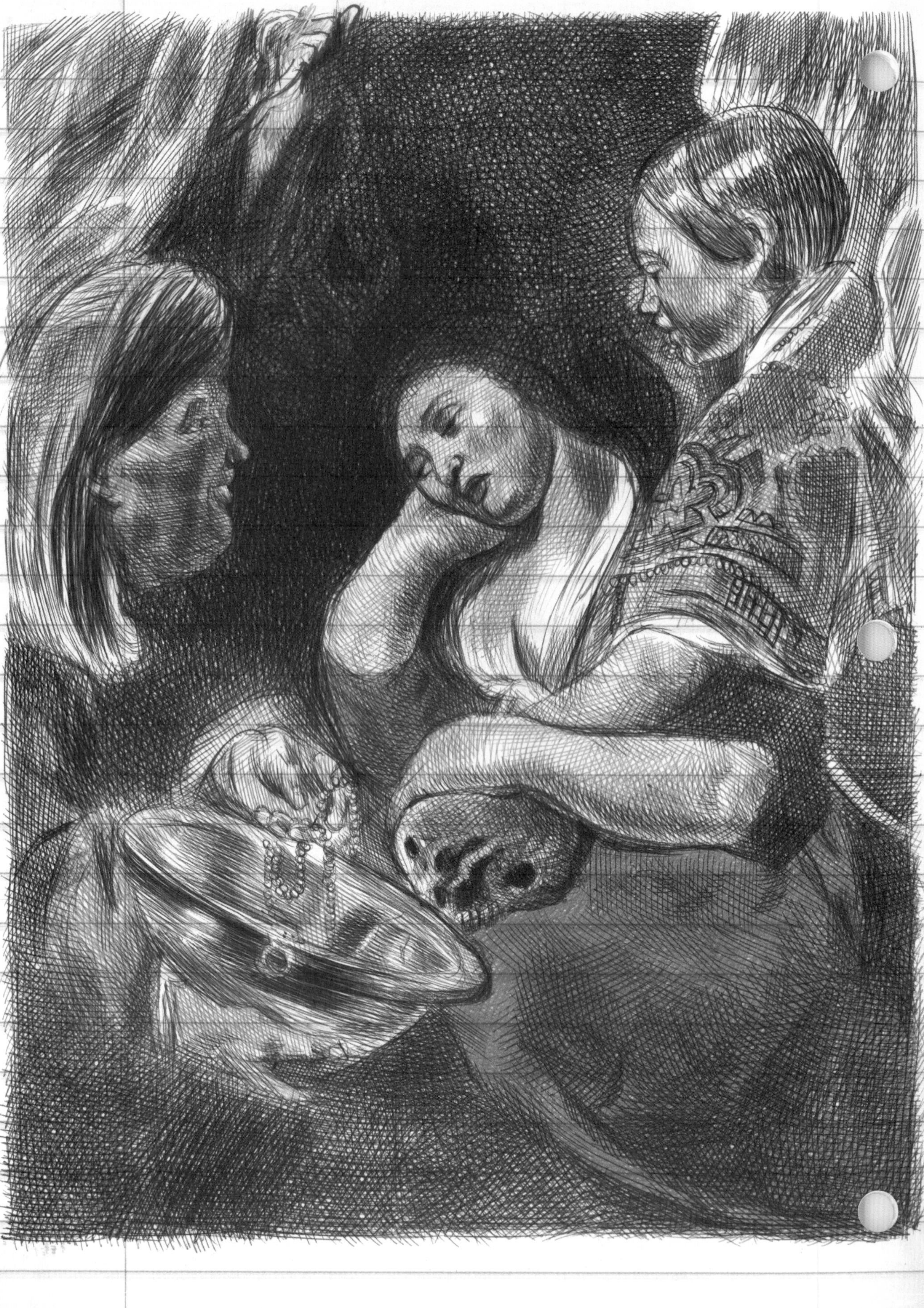

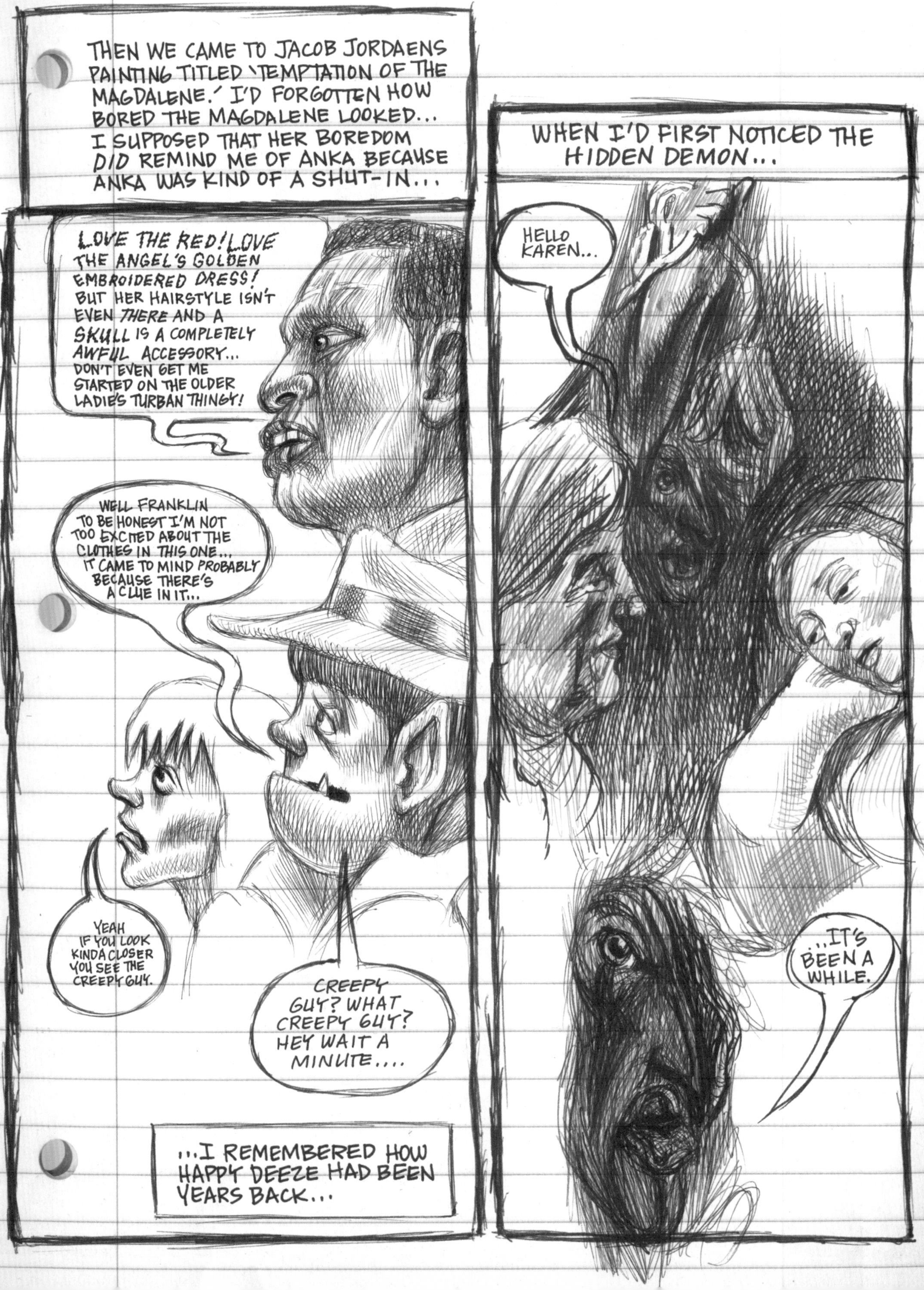
THEN WE CAME TO JACOB JORDAENS PAINTING TITLED 'TEMPTATION OF THE MAGDALENE.' I'D FORGOTTEN HOW BORED THE MAGDALENE LOOKED... I SUPPOSED THAT HER BOREDOM *DID* REMIND ME OF ANKA BECAUSE ANKA WAS KIND OF A SHUT-IN...
LOVE THE RED! LOVE THE ANGEL'S GOLDEN *EMBROIDERED DRESS!* BUT HER HAIRSTYLE ISN'T EVEN *THERE* AND A *SKULL* IS A COMPLETELY *AWFUL* ACCESSORY... DON'T EVEN GET ME STARTED ON THE OLDER LADIE'S TURBAN THINGY!
WELL FRANKLIN TO BE HONEST I'M NOT TOO EXCITED ABOUT THE CLOTHES IN THIS ONE... IT CAME TO MIND PROBABLY BECAUSE THERE'S A CLUE IN IT...
YEAH IF YOU LOOK KINDA CLOSER YOU SEE THE CREEPY GUY.
CREEPY GUY? WHAT CREEPY GUY? HEY WAIT A MINUTE....
...I REMEMBERED HOW HAPPY DEEZE HAD BEEN YEARS BACK...
WHEN I'D FIRST NOTICED THE HIDDEN DEMON...
HELLO KAREN...
...IT'S BEEN A WHILE.

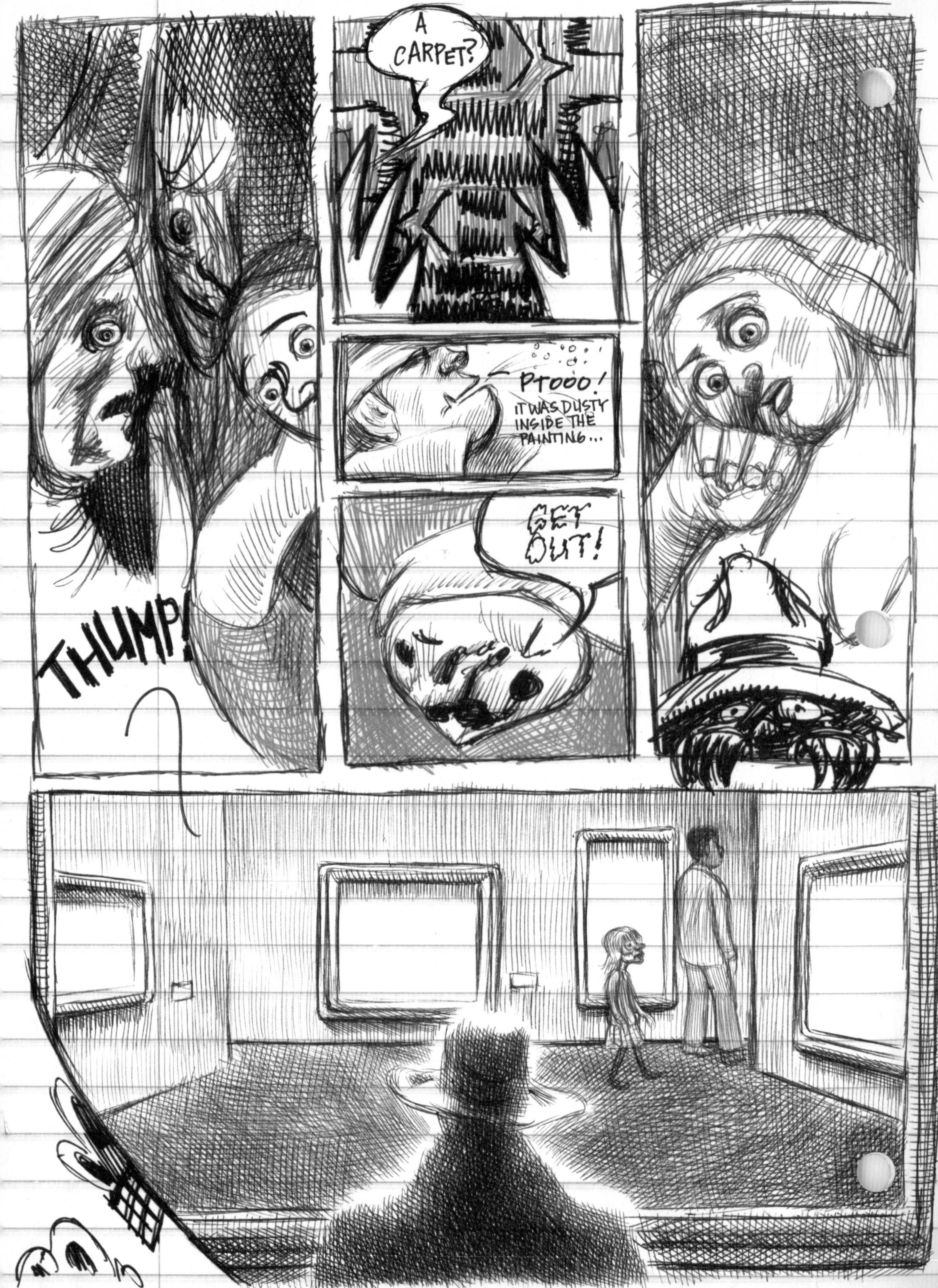
THUMP!
A CARPET?
PTOOO!
IT WAS DUSTY INSIDE THE PAINTING...
GET OUT!

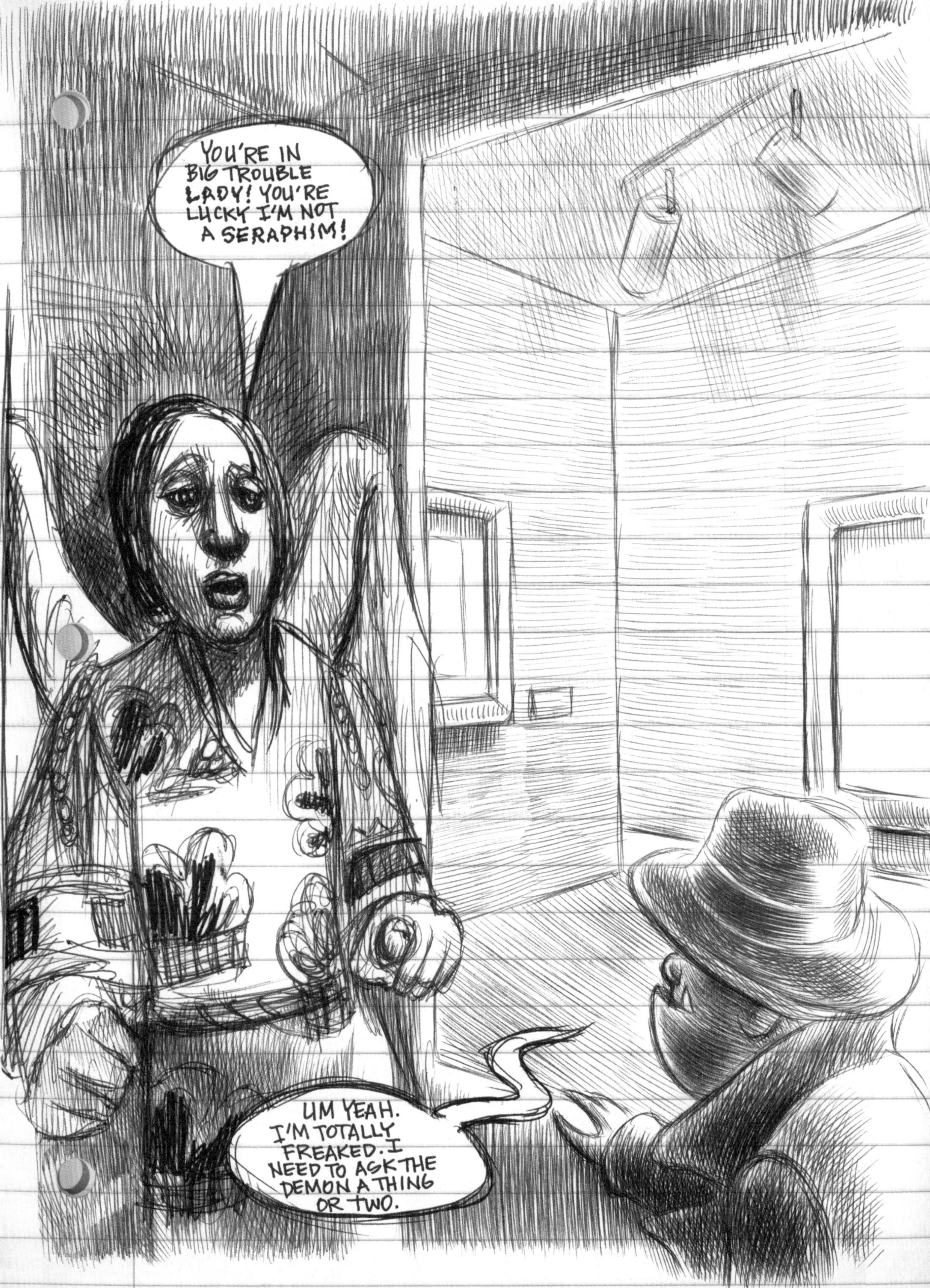
YOU'RE IN BIG TROUBLE LADY! YOU'RE LUCKY I'M NOT A SERAPHIM!
UM YEAH. I'M TOTALLY FREAKED. I NEED TO ASK THE DEMON A THING OR TWO.

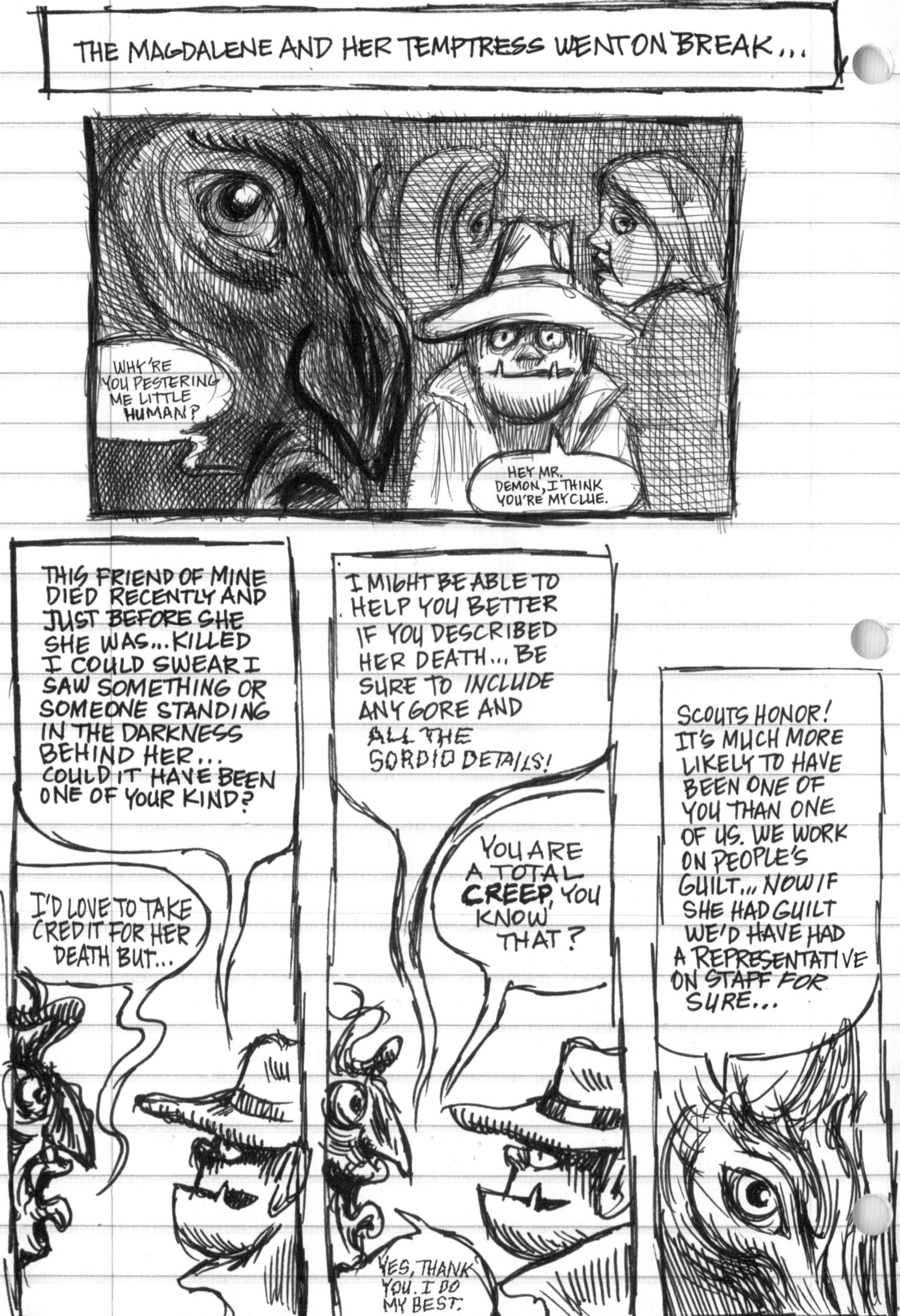
THE MAGDALENE AND HER TEMPTRESS WENT ON BREAK...
WHY'RE YOU PESTERING ME LITTLE HUMAN?
HEY MR. DEMON, I THINK YOU'RE MY CLUE.
THIS FRIEND OF MINE DIED RECENTLY AND JUST BEFORE SHE SHE WAS... KILLED I COULD SWEAR I SAW SOMETHING OR SOMEONE STANDING IN THE DARKNESS BEHIND HER... COULD IT HAVE BEEN ONE OF YOUR KIND?
I'D LOVE TO TAKE CREDIT FOR HER DEATH BUT...
I MIGHT BE ABLE TO HELP YOU BETTER IF YOU DESCRIBED HER DEATH... BE SURE TO INCLUDE ANY GORE AND ALL THE SORDID DETAILS!
YOU ARE A TOTAL CREEP, YOU KNOW THAT?
YES, THANK YOU. I DO MY BEST.
SCOUTS HONOR! IT'S MUCH MORE LIKELY TO HAVE BEEN ONE OF YOU THAN ONE OF US. WE WORK ON PEOPLE'S GUILT... NOW IF SHE HAD GUILT WE'D HAVE HAD A REPRESENTATIVE ON STAFF FOR SURE...

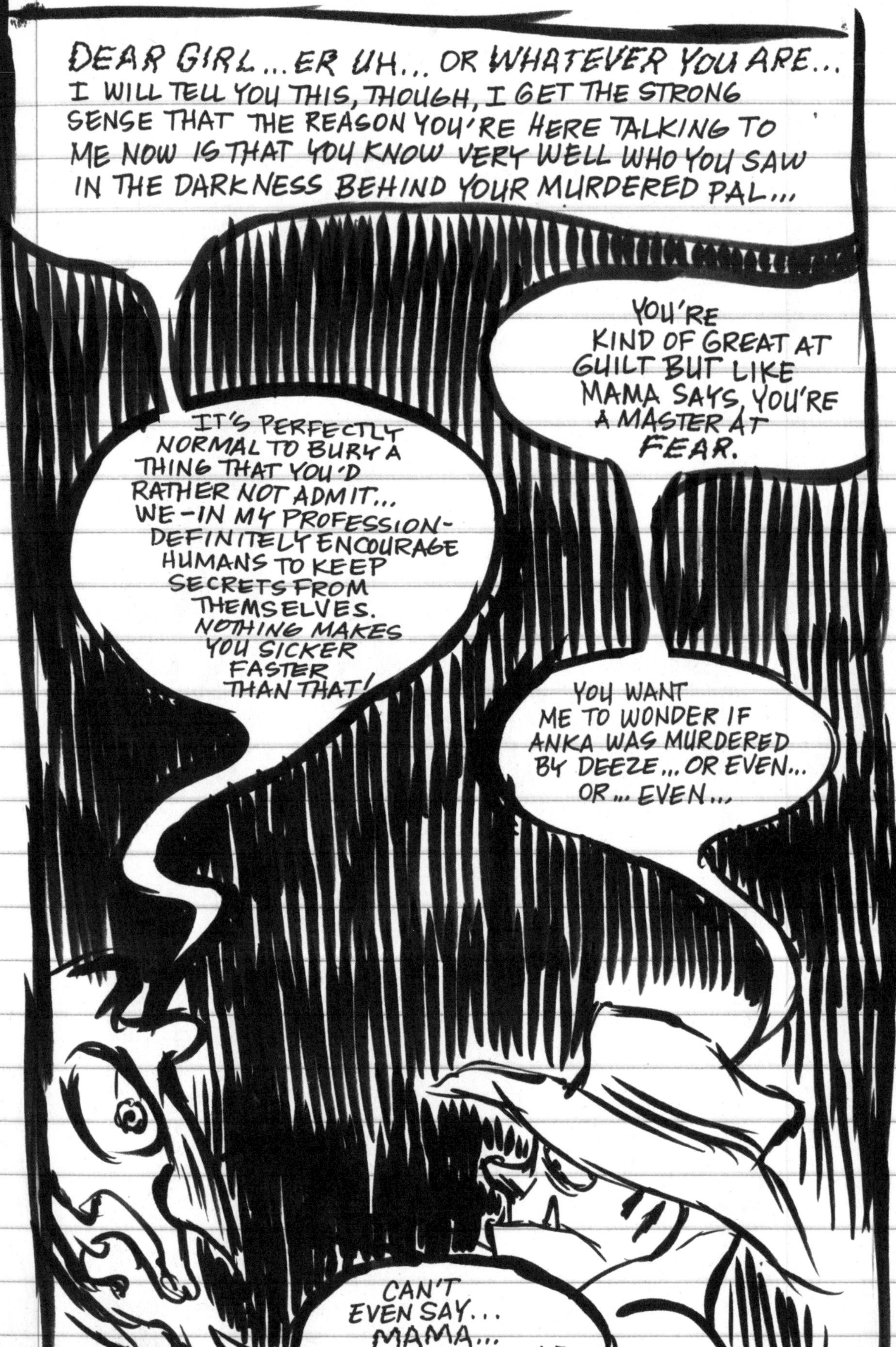

DEAR GIRL... ER UH... OR WHATEVER YOU ARE... I WILL TELL YOU THIS, THOUGH, I GET THE STRONG SENSE THAT THE REASON YOU'RE HERE TALKING TO ME NOW IS THAT YOU KNOW VERY WELL WHO YOU SAW IN THE DARKNESS BEHIND YOUR MURDERED PAL...
YOU'RE KIND OF GREAT AT GUILT BUT LIKE MAMA SAYS, YOU'RE A MASTER AT FEAR.
IT'S PERFECTLY NORMAL TO BURY A THING THAT YOU'D RATHER NOT ADMIT... WE - IN MY PROFESSION - DEFINITELY ENCOURAGE HUMANS TO KEEP SECRETS FROM THEMSELVES. NOTHING MAKES YOU SICKER FASTER THAN THAT!
YOU WANT ME TO WONDER IF ANKA WAS MURDERED BY DEEZE... OR EVEN... OR... EVEN...
CAN'T EVEN SAY... MAMA... CAN YOU, HONEY?

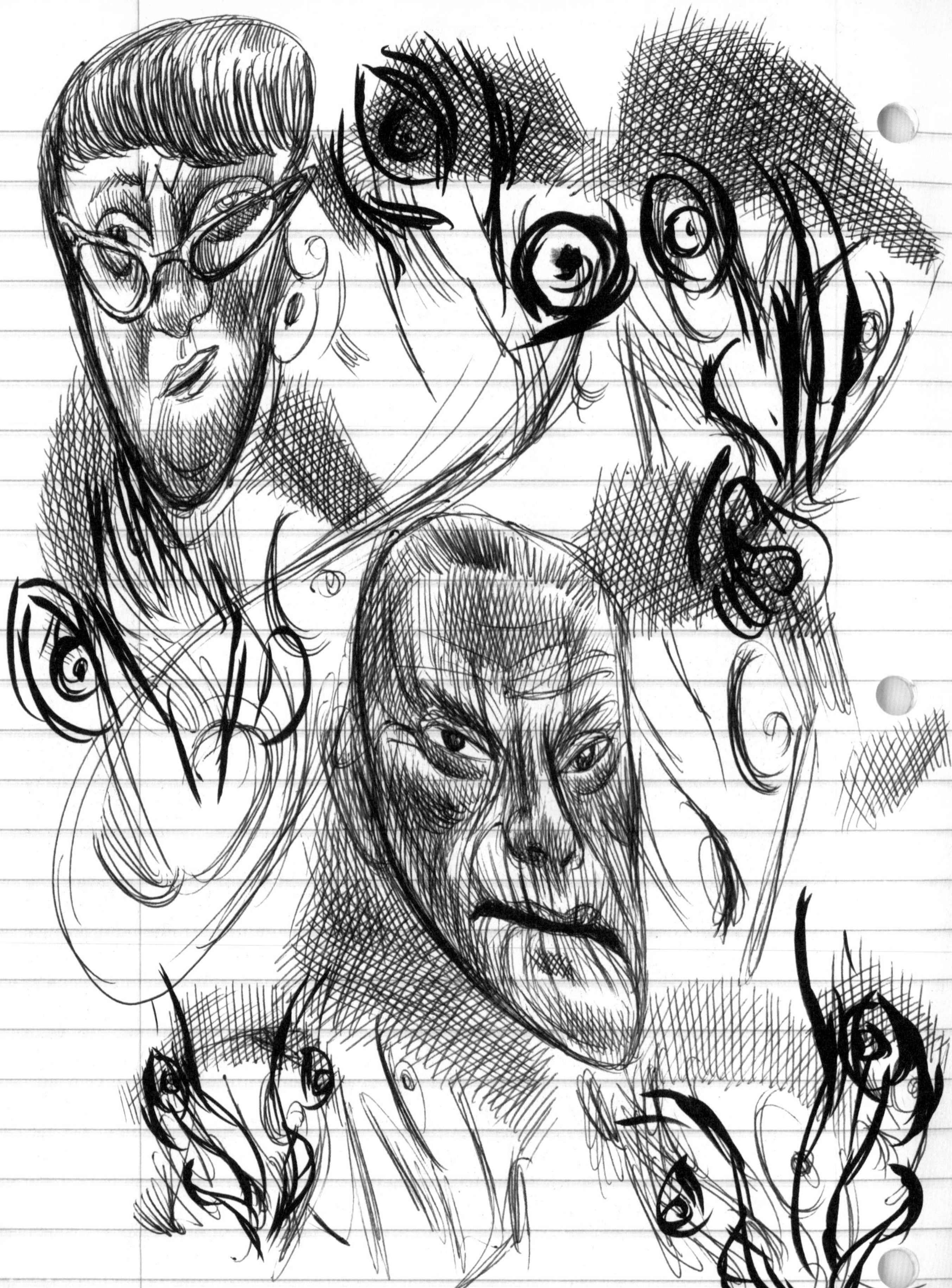

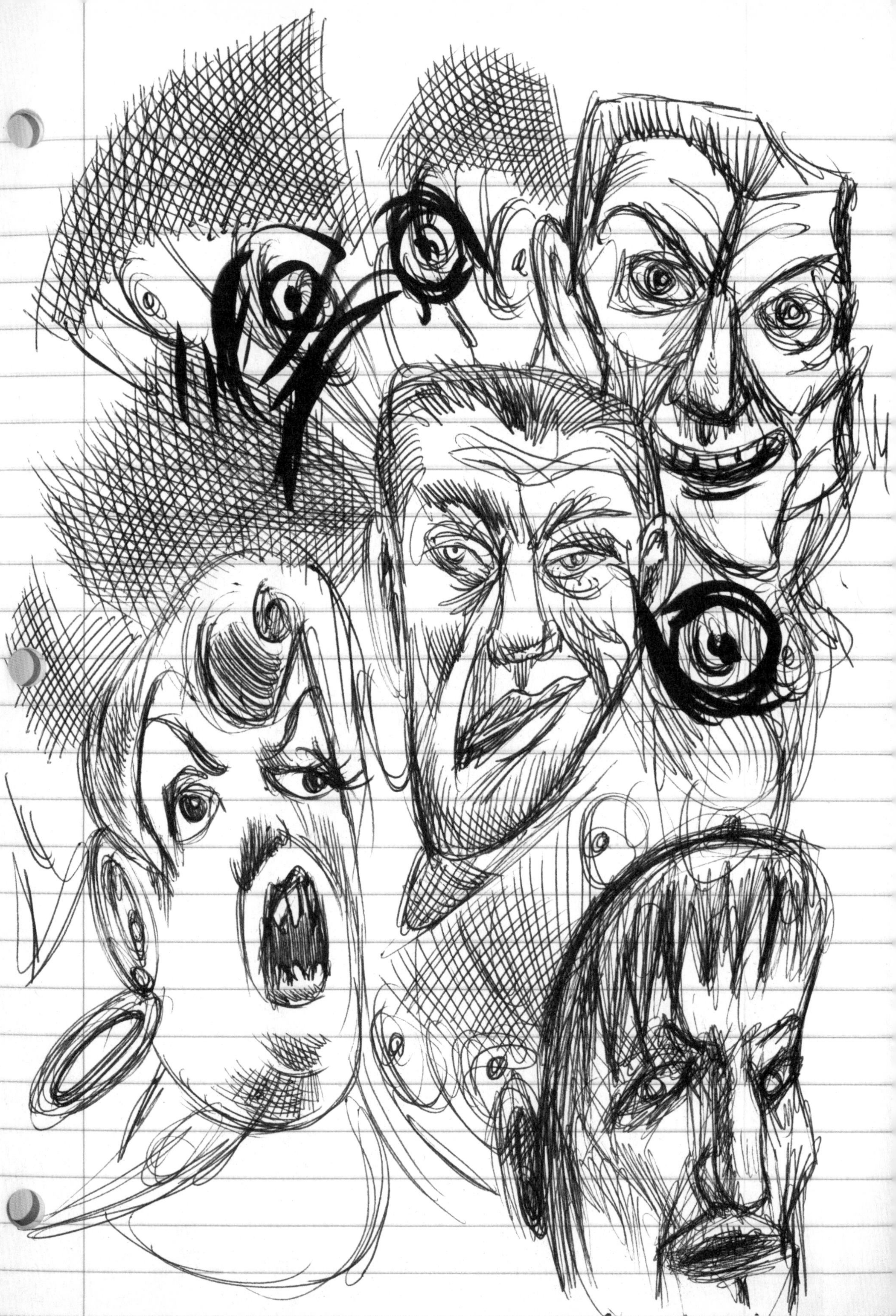

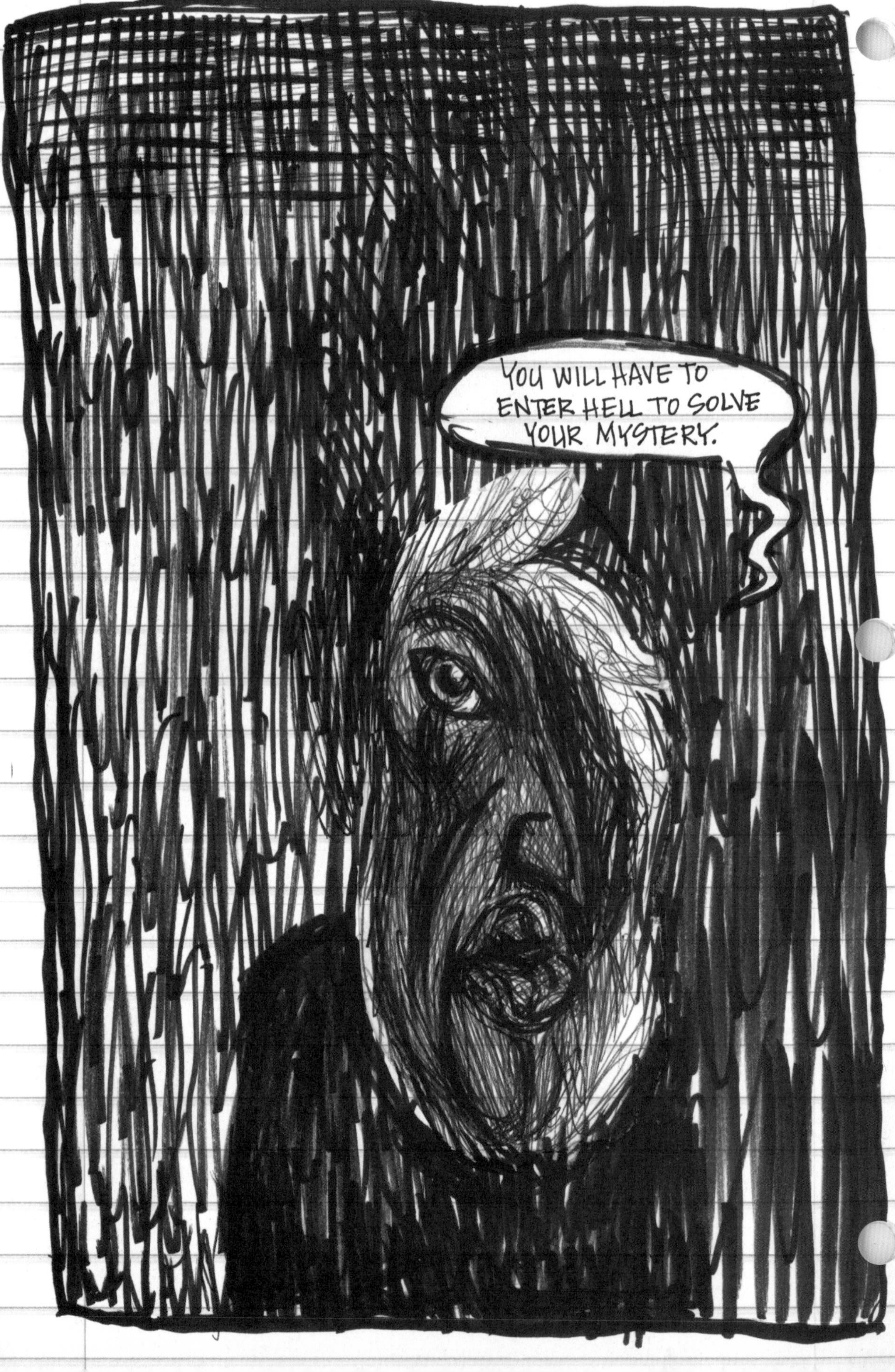
YOU WILL HAVE TO ENTER HELL TO SOLVE YOUR MYSTERY.

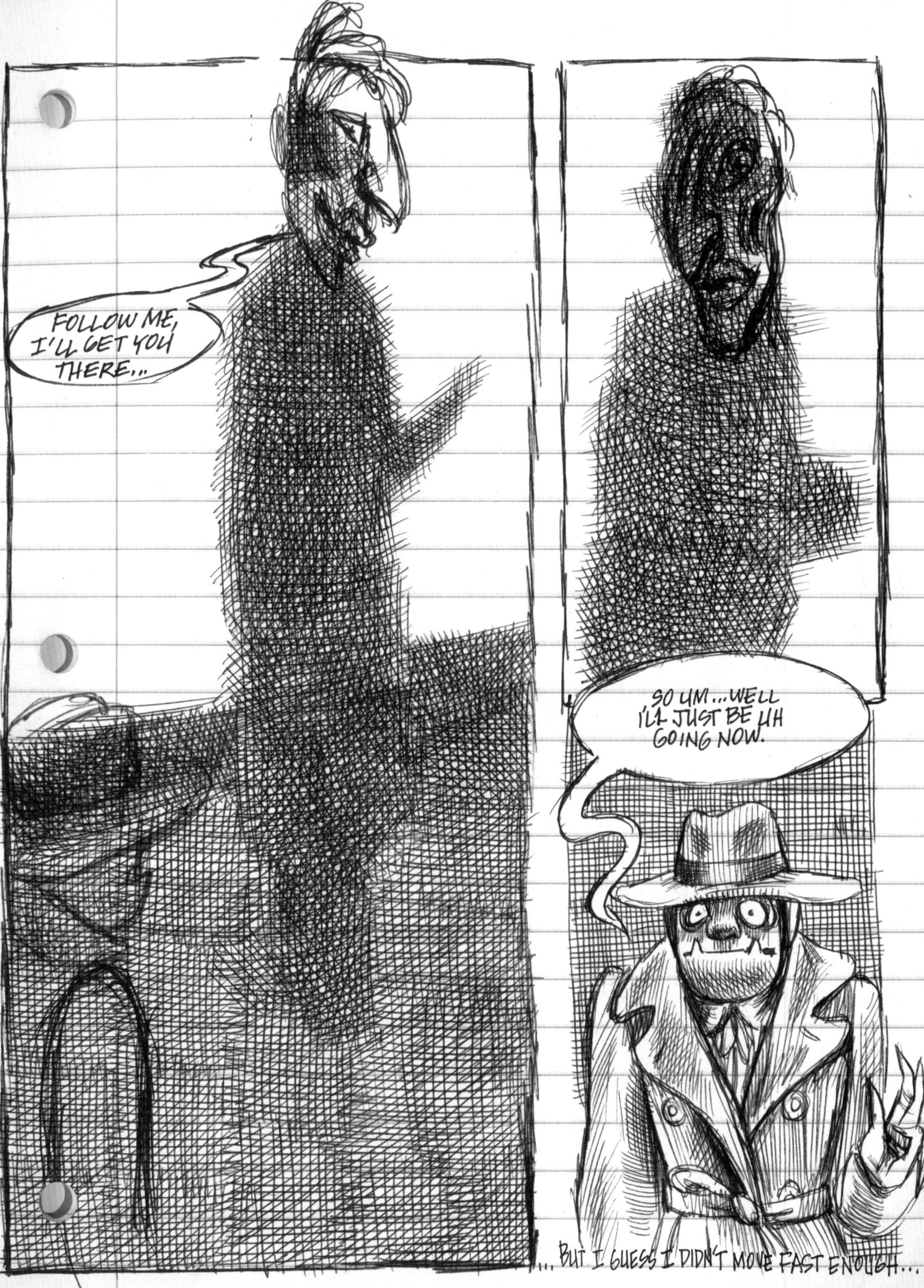
FOLLOW ME, I'LL GET YOU THERE...
SO UM...WELL I'LL JUST BE UH GOING NOW.
...BUT I GUESS I DIDN'T MOVE FAST ENOUGH...

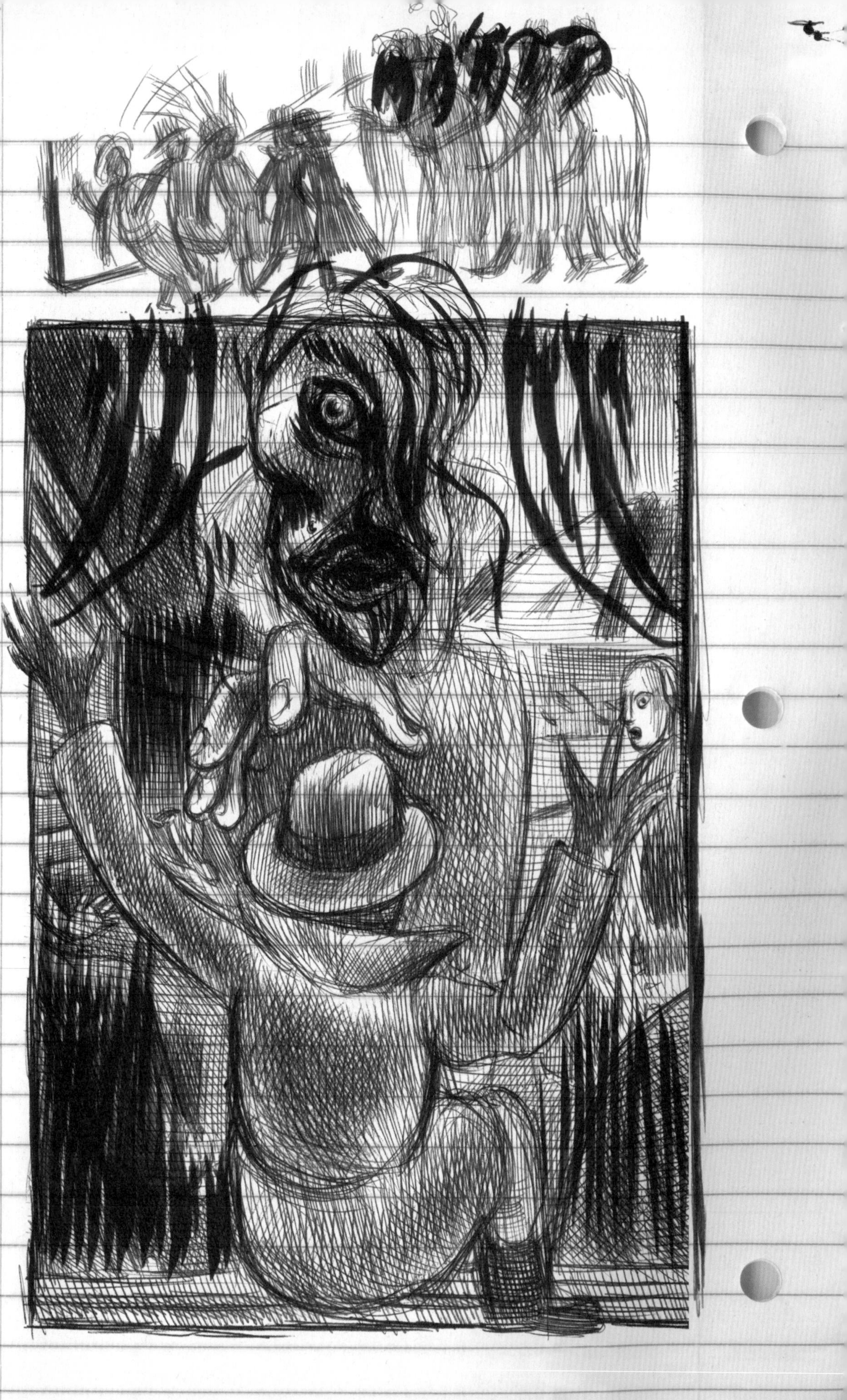

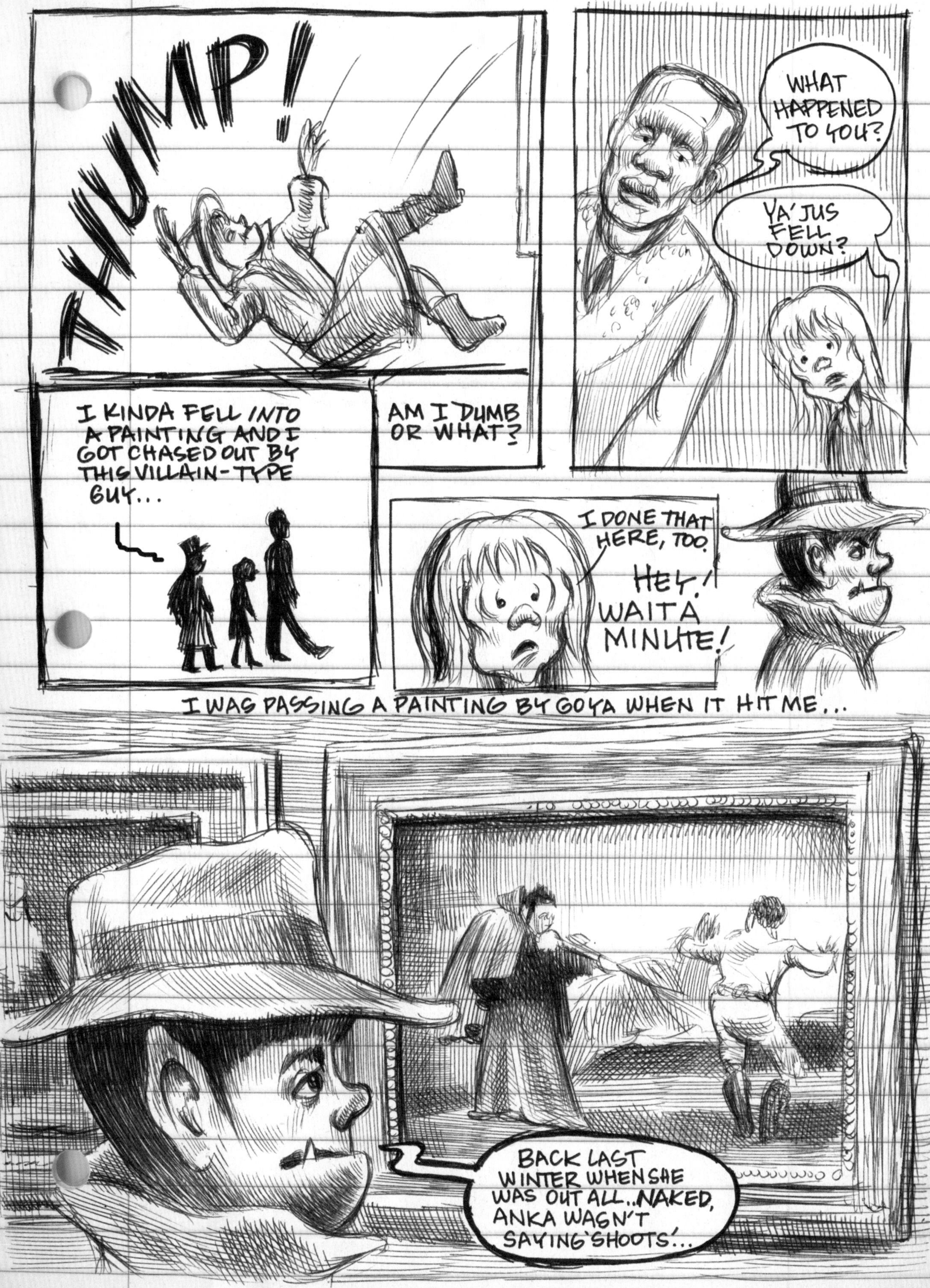
THUMP!
WHAT HAPPENED TO YOU?
YA' JUS FELL DOWN?
I KINDA FELL INTO A PAINTING AND I GOT CHASED OUT BY THIS VILLAIN-TYPE GUY...
AM I DUMB OR WHAT?
I DONE THAT HERE, TOO.
HEY! WAIT A MINUTE!
I WAS PASSING A PAINTING BY GOYA WHEN IT HIT ME...
BACK LAST WINTER WHEN SHE WAS OUT ALL.. NAKED, ANKA WASN'T SAYING 'SHOOTS'...

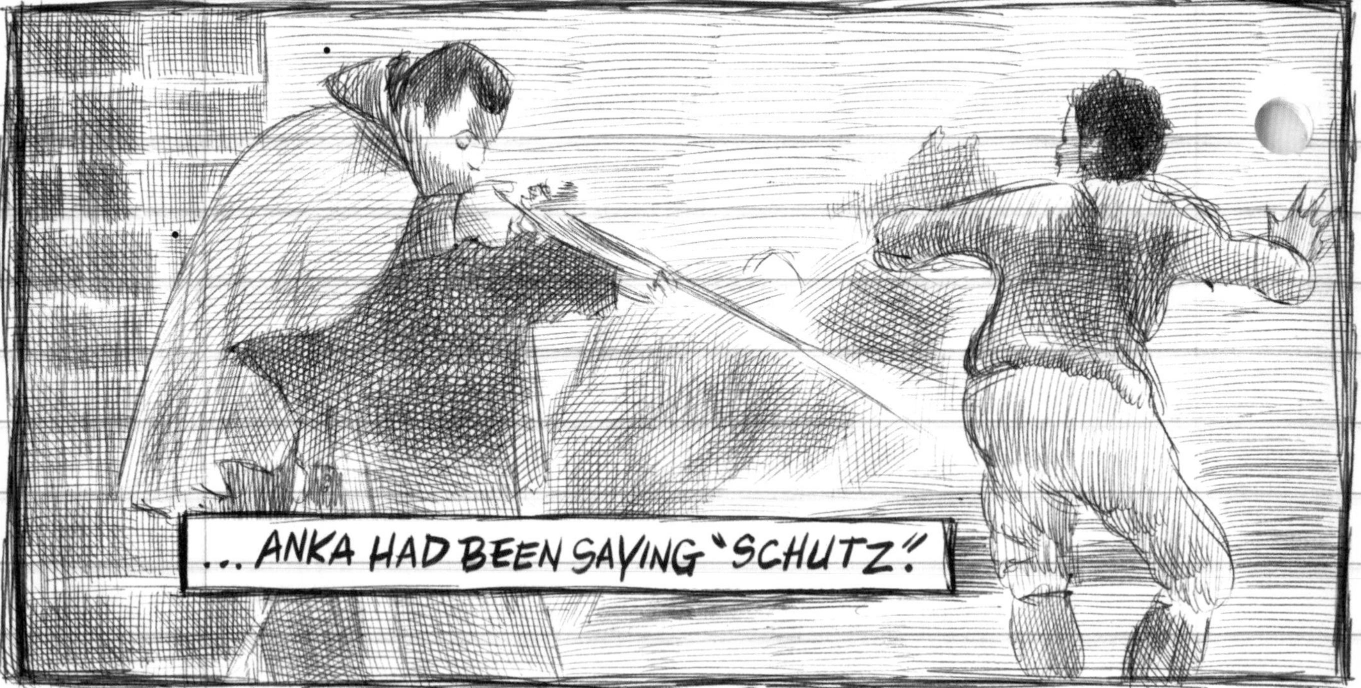
...ANKA HAD BEEN SAYING "SCHUTZ"!

AFTER I RETRIEVED MY BRIEFCASE FROM THE COAT CHECK ROOM, WE LEFT THE MUSEUM...

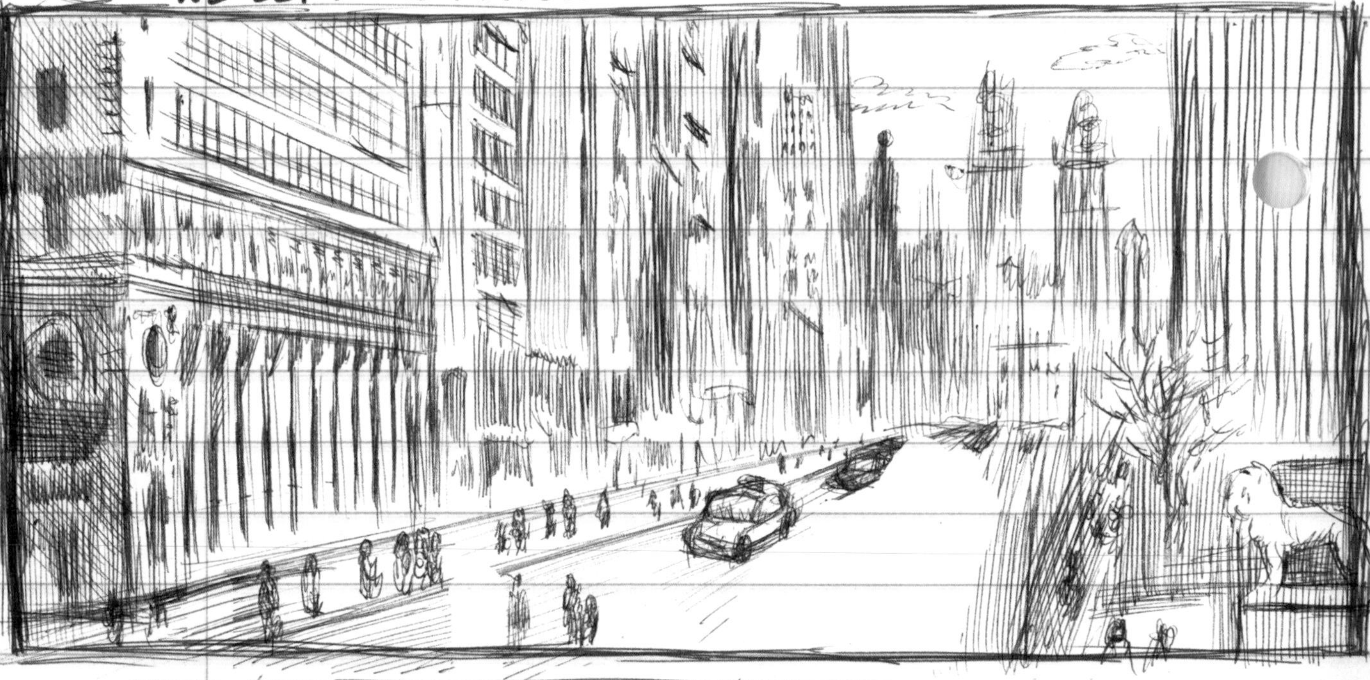

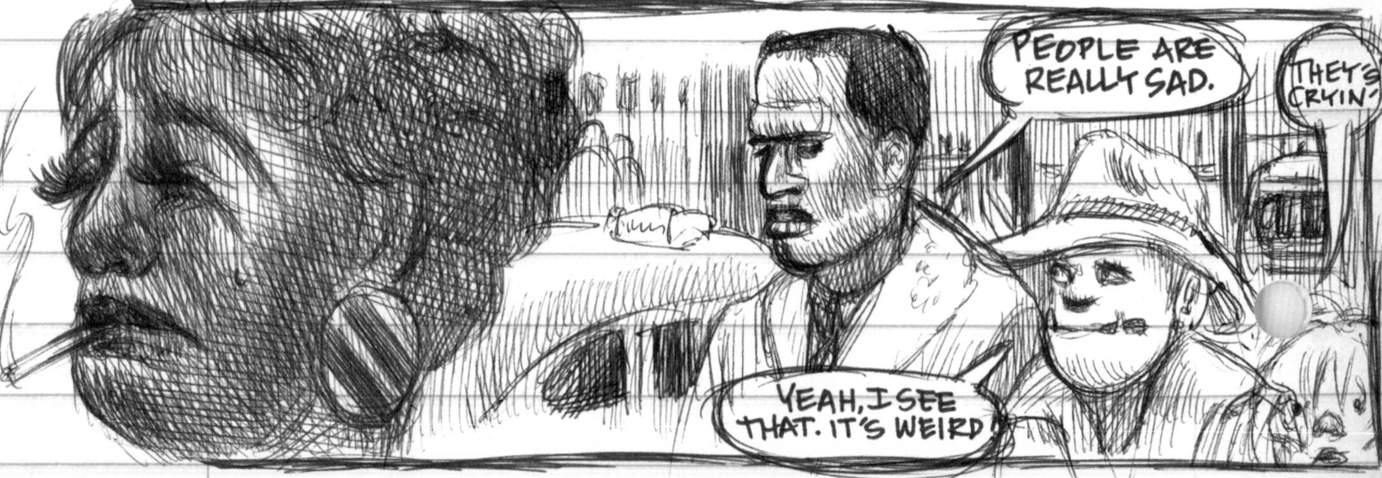
PEOPLE ARE REALLY SAD.
THEY'S CRYIN'
YEAH, I SEE THAT. IT'S WEIRD

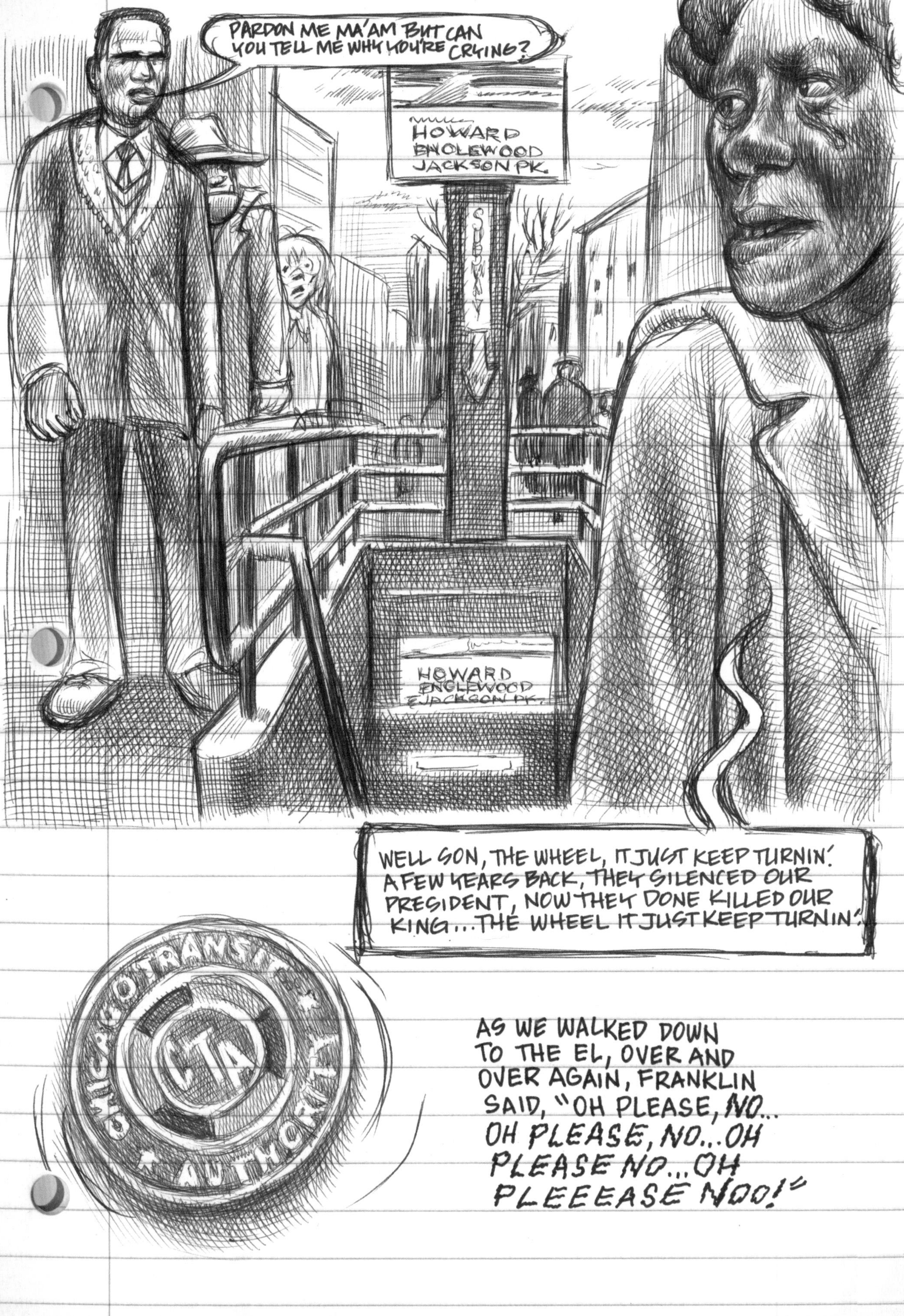

PARDON ME MA'AM BUT CAN YOU TELL ME WHY YOU'RE CRYING?
HOWARD ENGLEWOOD JACKSON PK.
SUBWAY
HOWARD ENGLEWOOD JACKSON PK.
WELL SON, THE WHEEL, IT JUST KEEP TURNIN'. A FEW YEARS BACK, THEY SILENCED OUR PRESIDENT, NOW THEY DONE KILLED OUR KING... THE WHEEL IT JUST KEEP TURNIN'.
CTA
AS WE WALKED DOWN TO THE EL, OVER AND OVER AGAIN, FRANKLIN SAID, "OH PLEASE, NO... OH PLEASE, NO... OH PLEASE NO... OH PLEEEASE NOO!"

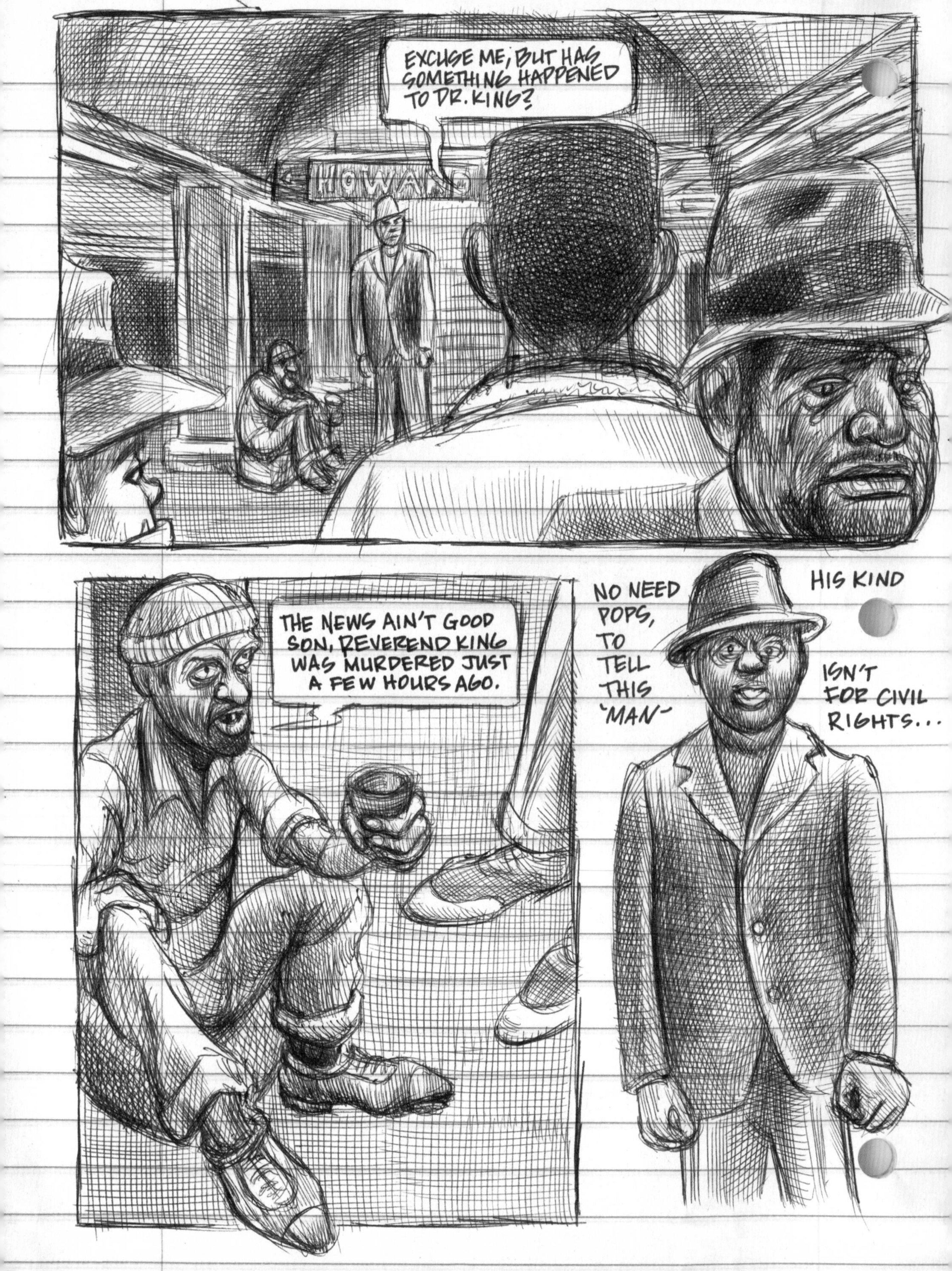
EXCUSE ME, BUT HAS SOMETHING HAPPENED TO DR. KING?
THE NEWS AIN'T GOOD SON, REVEREND KING WAS MURDERED JUST A FEW HOURS AGO.
NO NEED POPS, TO TELL THIS 'MAN'-
HIS KIND
ISN'T FOR CIVIL RIGHTS...

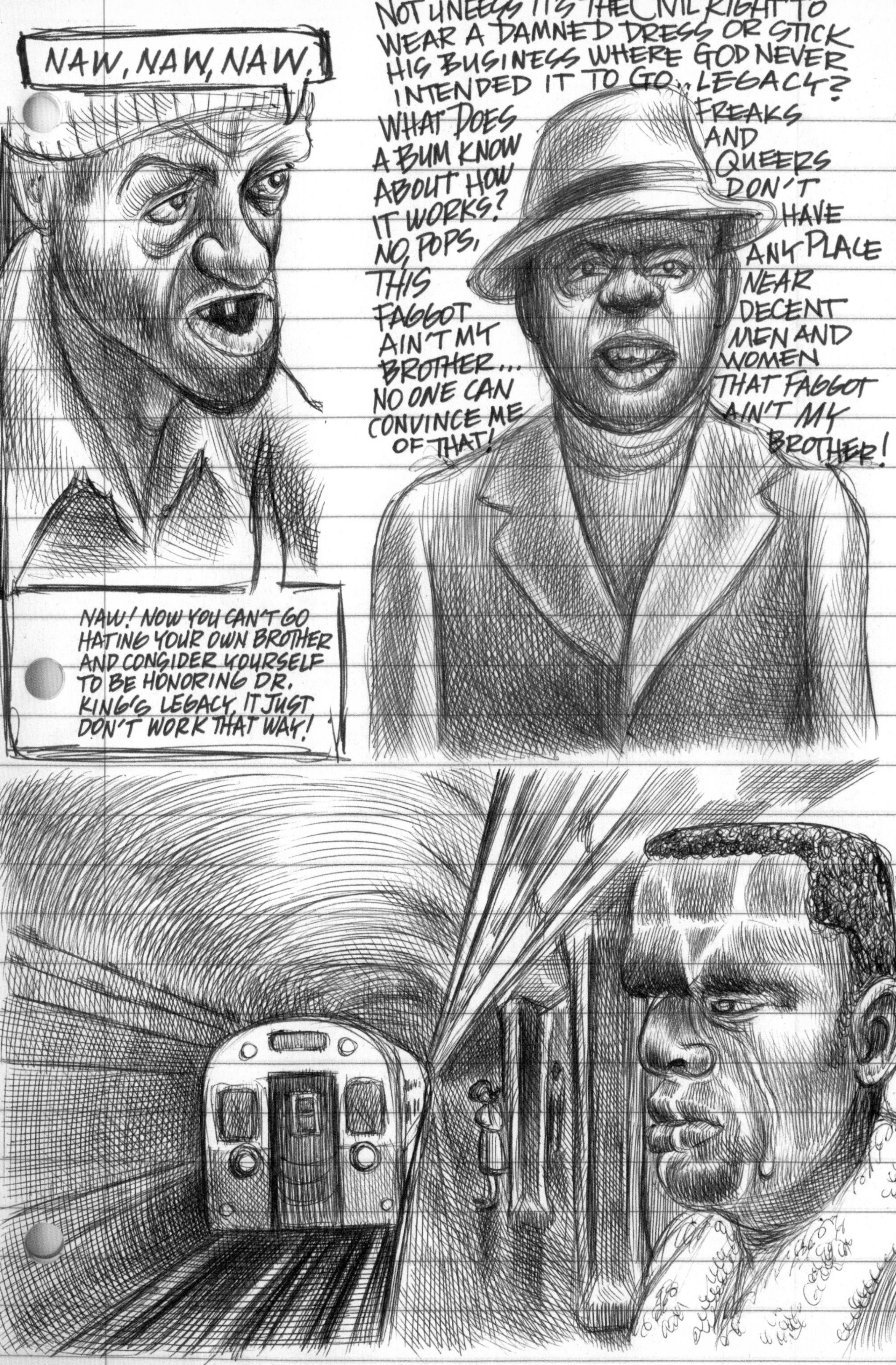
NAW, NAW, NAW.
NAW! NOW YOU CAN'T GO HATING YOUR OWN BROTHER AND CONSIDER YOURSELF TO BE HONORING DR. KING'S LEGACY, IT JUST DON'T WORK THAT WAY!
NOT UNLESS IT'S THE CIVIL RIGHT TO WEAR A DAMNED DRESS OR STICK HIS BUSINESS WHERE GOD NEVER INTENDED IT TO GO.. LEGACY?
WHAT DOES A BUM KNOW ABOUT HOW IT WORKS? NO, POPS, THIS FAGGOT AIN'T MY BROTHER... NO ONE CAN CONVINCE ME OF THAT!
FREAKS AND QUEERS DON'T HAVE ANY PLACE NEAR DECENT MEN AND WOMEN THAT FAGGOT AIN'T MY BROTHER!

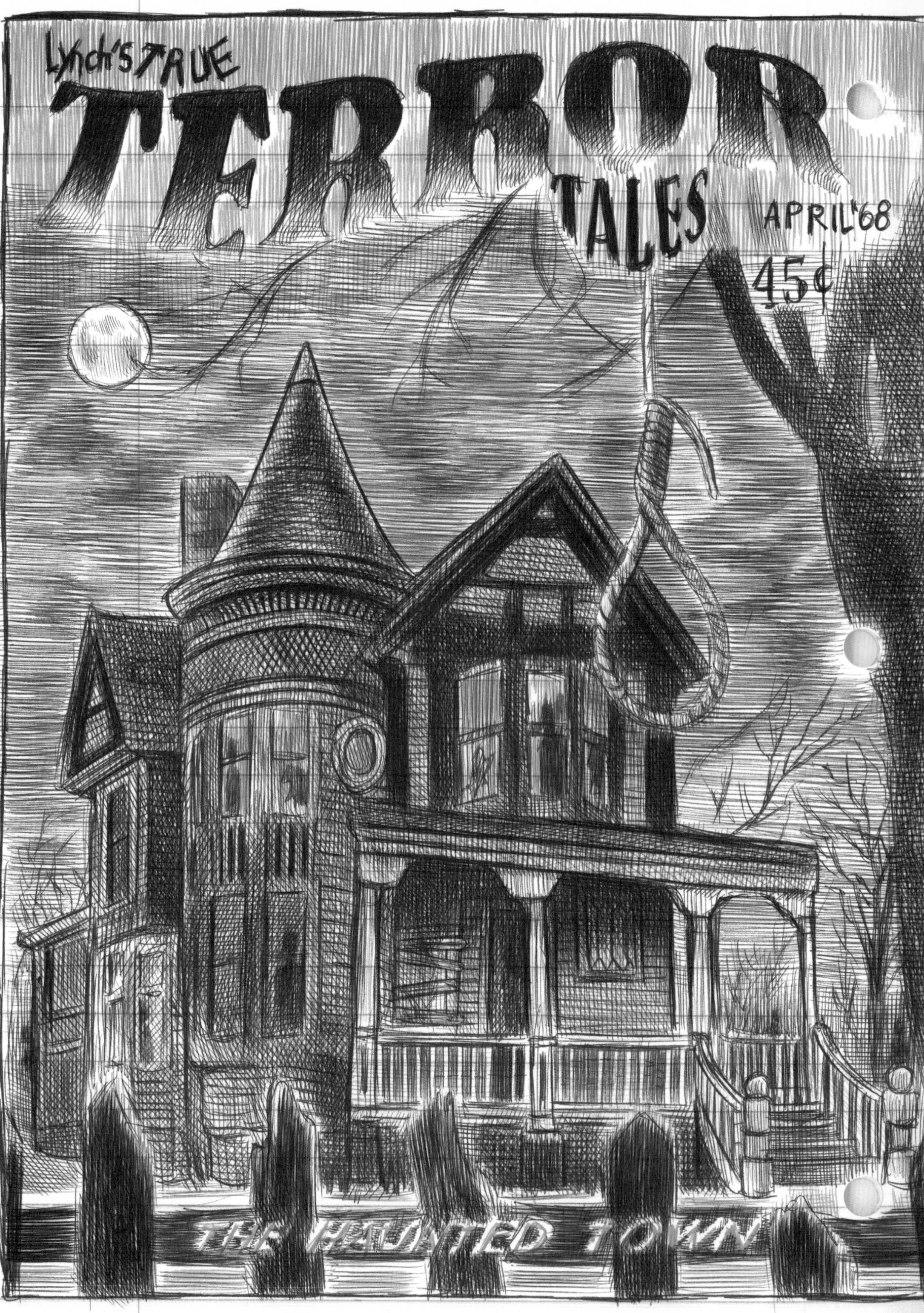
Lynch's TRUE
TERROR
TALES
APRIL '68
45¢
THE HAUNTED TOWN

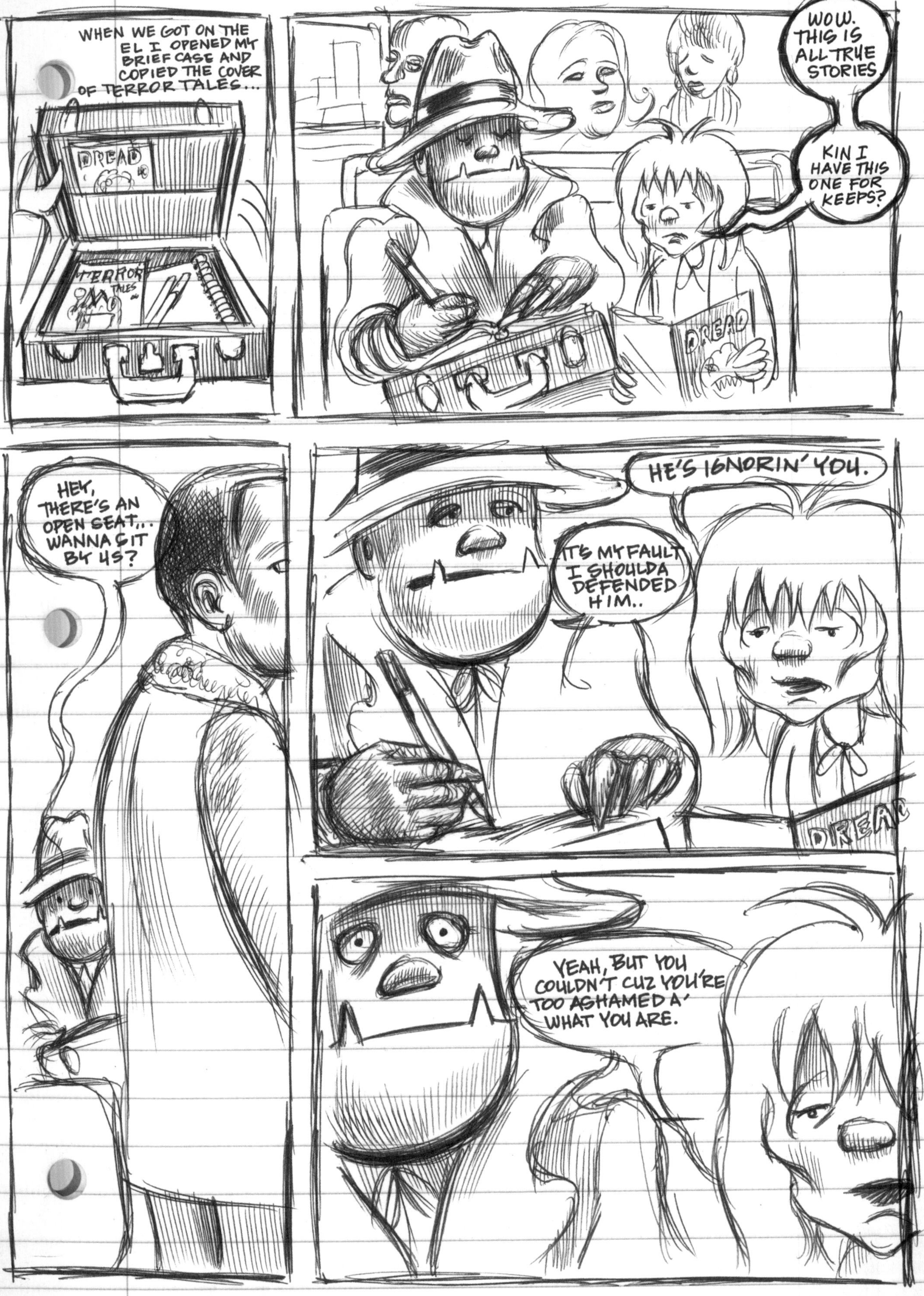
WHEN WE GOT ON THE EL I OPENED MY BRIEF CASE AND COPIED THE COVER OF TERROR TALES...
DREAD
TERROR TALES
WOW. THIS IS ALL TRUE STORIES.
KIN I HAVE THIS ONE FOR KEEPS?
DREAD
HEY, THERE'S AN OPEN SEAT... WANNA SIT BY US?
HE'S IGNORIN' YOU.
IT'S MY FAULT I SHOULDA DEFENDED HIM..
DREAD
YEAH, BUT YOU COULDN'T CUZ YOU'RE TOO ASHAMED A' WHAT YOU ARE.

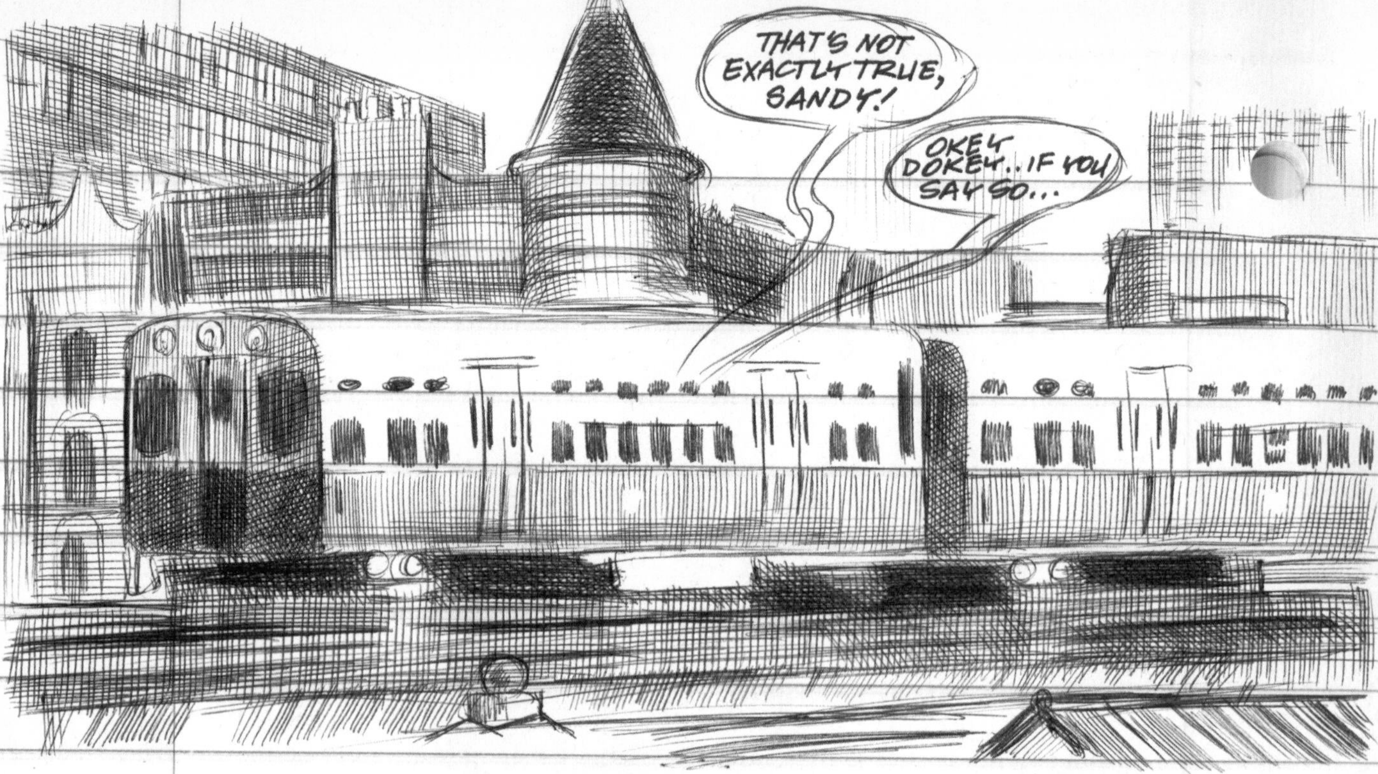
THAT'S NOT EXACTLY TRUE, SANDY!
OKEY DOKEY.. IF YOU SAY SO...

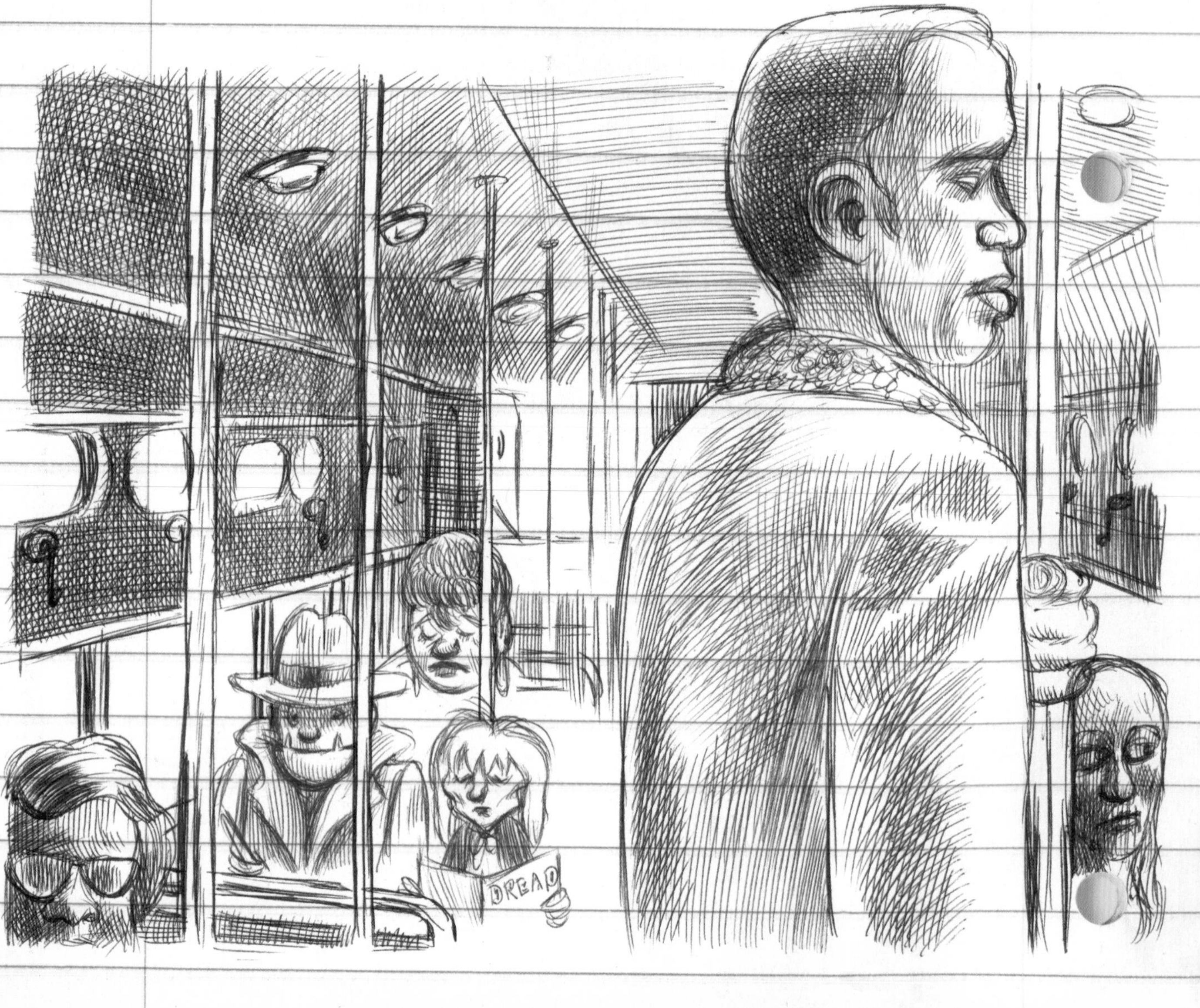
DREAD

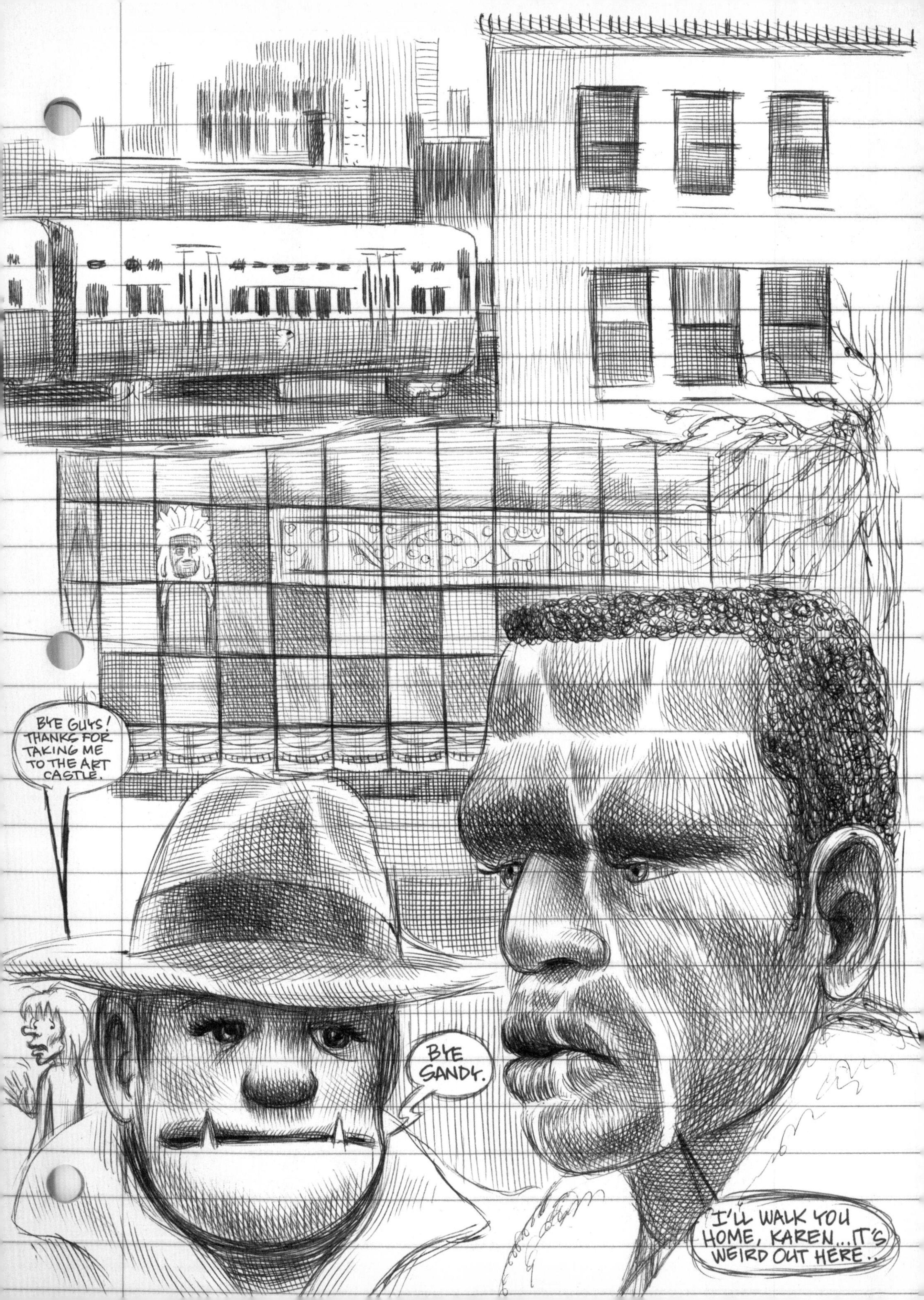
BYE GUYS! THANKS FOR TAKING ME TO THE ART CASTLE.
BYE SANDY.
I'LL WALK YOU HOME, KAREN... IT'S WEIRD OUT HERE..

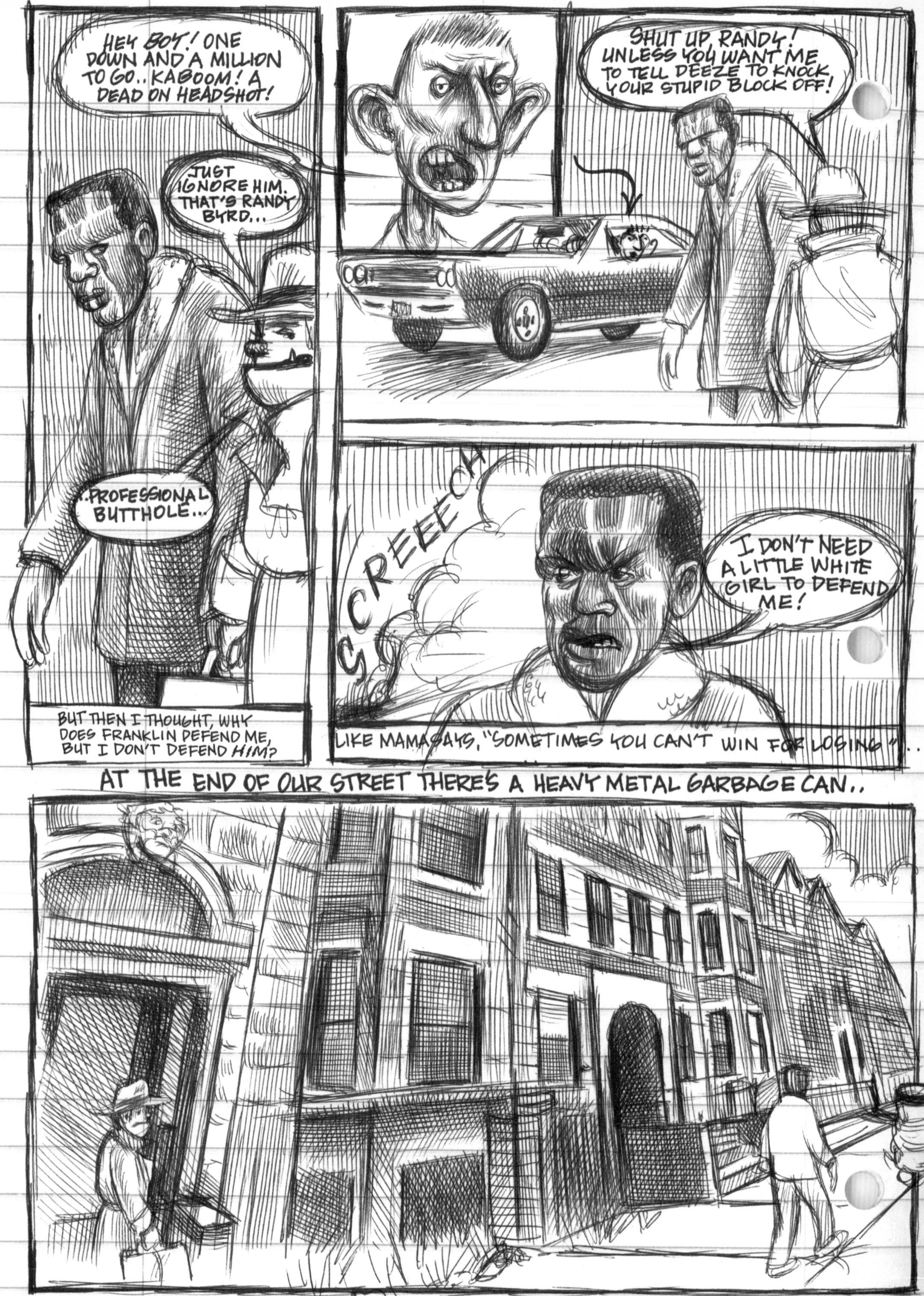
HEY BOY! ONE DOWN AND A MILLION TO GO.. KABOOM! A DEAD ON HEADSHOT!
JUST IGNORE HIM. THAT'S RANDY BYRD...
..PROFESSIONAL BUTTHOLE...
BUT THEN I THOUGHT, WHY DOES FRANKLIN DEFEND ME, BUT I DON'T DEFEND HIM?
SHUT UP, RANDY! UNLESS YOU WANT ME TO TELL DEEZE TO KNOCK YOUR STUPID BLOCK OFF!
SCREEECH
I DON'T NEED A LITTLE WHITE GIRL TO DEFEND ME!
LIKE MAMA SAYS, "SOMETIMES YOU CAN'T WIN FOR LOSING"..
AT THE END OF OUR STREET THERE'S A HEAVY METAL GARBAGE CAN..

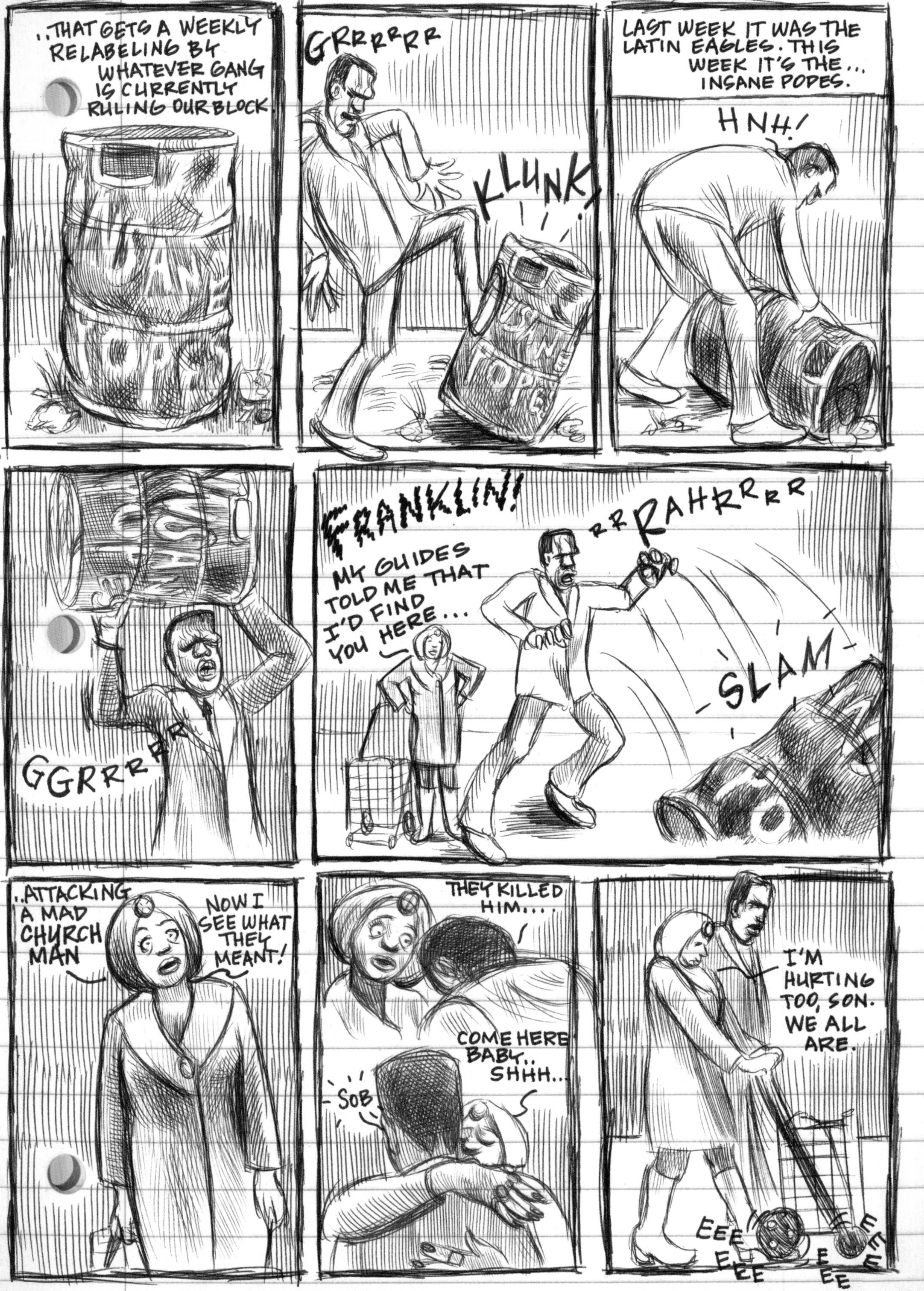
..THAT GETS A WEEKLY RELABELING BY WHATEVER GANG IS CURRENTLY RULING OUR BLOCK.
GRRRRRR
KLUNK!
LAST WEEK IT WAS THE LATIN EAGLES. THIS WEEK IT'S THE... INSANE POPES.
HNH!
GGRRRRR
FRANKLIN!
MY GUIDES TOLD ME THAT I'D FIND YOU HERE...
RRRAHRRRR
SLAM
..ATTACKING A MAD CHURCH MAN
NOW I SEE WHAT THEY MEANT!
THEY KILLED HIM....
COME HERE BABY.. SHHH...
SOB
I'M HURTING TOO, SON. WE ALL ARE.
EEEEE
EEEEE

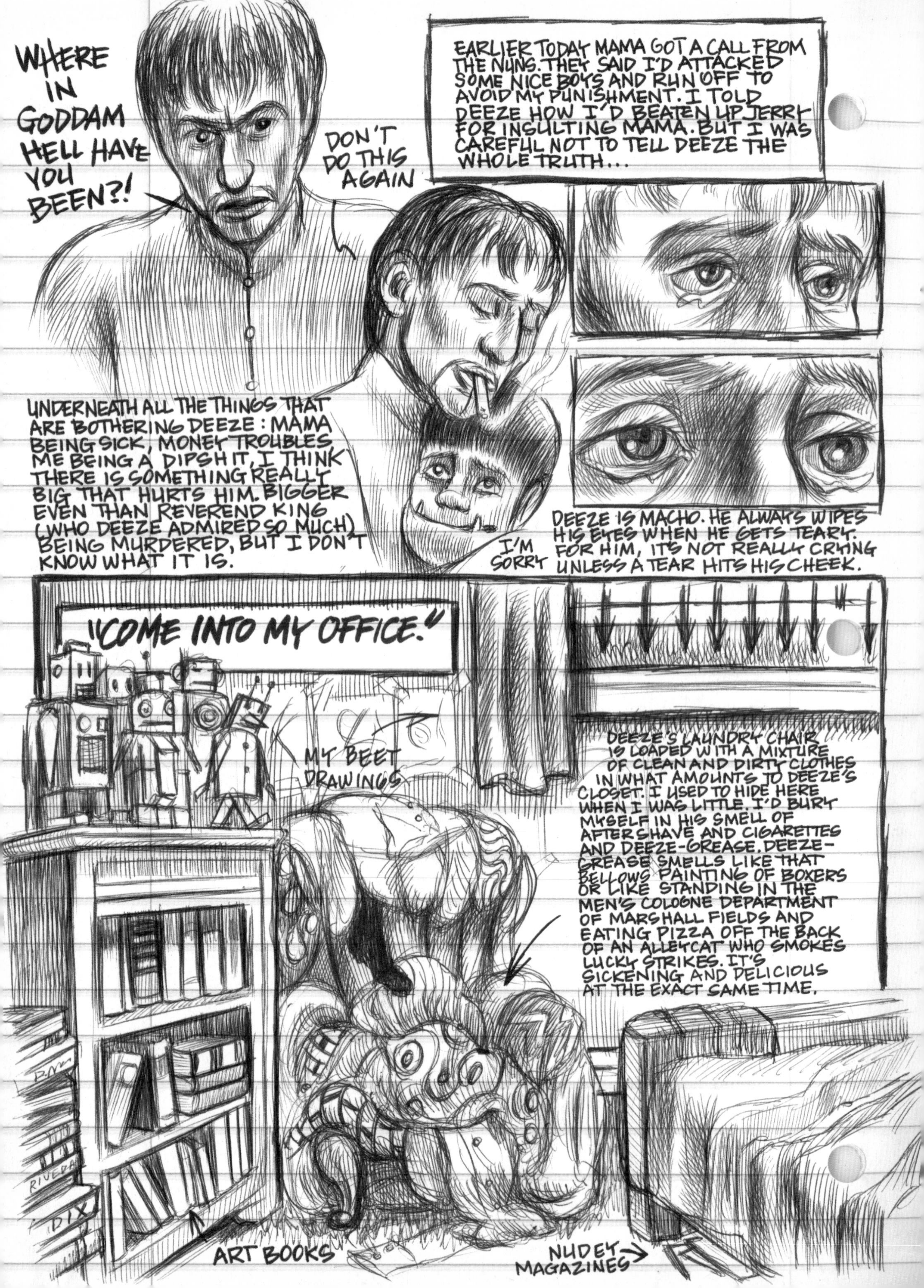

WHERE IN GODDAM HELL HAVE YOU BEEN?!
EARLIER TODAY MAMA GOT A CALL FROM THE NUNS. THEY SAID I'D ATTACKED SOME NICE BOYS AND RUN OFF TO AVOID MY PUNISHMENT. I TOLD DEEZE HOW I'D BEATEN UP JERRY FOR INSULTING MAMA. BUT I WAS CAREFUL NOT TO TELL DEEZE THE WHOLE TRUTH...
DON'T DO THIS AGAIN
UNDERNEATH ALL THE THINGS THAT ARE BOTHERING DEEZE: MAMA BEING SICK, MONEY TROUBLES ME BEING A DIPSHIT, I THINK THERE IS SOMETHING REALLY BIG THAT HURTS HIM. BIGGER EVEN THAN REVEREND KING (WHO DEEZE ADMIRED SO MUCH) BEING MURDERED, BUT I DON'T KNOW WHAT IT IS.
I'M SORRY
DEEZE IS MACHO. HE ALWAYS WIPES HIS EYES WHEN HE GETS TEARY. FOR HIM, IT'S NOT REALLY CRYING UNLESS A TEAR HITS HIS CHEEK.
"COME INTO MY OFFICE."
MY BEST DRAWINGS
DEEZE'S LAUNDRY CHAIR IS LOADED WITH A MIXTURE OF CLEAN AND DIRTY CLOTHES IN WHAT AMOUNTS TO DEEZE'S CLOSET. I USED TO HIDE HERE WHEN I WAS LITTLE. I'D BURY MYSELF IN HIS SMELL OF AFTERSHAVE AND CIGARETTES AND DEEZE-GREASE. DEEZE-GREASE SMELLS LIKE THAT BELLOWS PAINTING OF BOXERS OR LIKE STANDING IN THE MEN'S COLOGNE DEPARTMENT OF MARSHALL FIELDS AND EATING PIZZA OFF THE BACK OF AN ALLEYCAT WHO SMOKES LUCKY STRIKES. IT'S SICKENING AND DELICIOUS AT THE EXACT SAME TIME.
RIVERA
DIX
ART BOOKS
NUDEY MAGAZINES

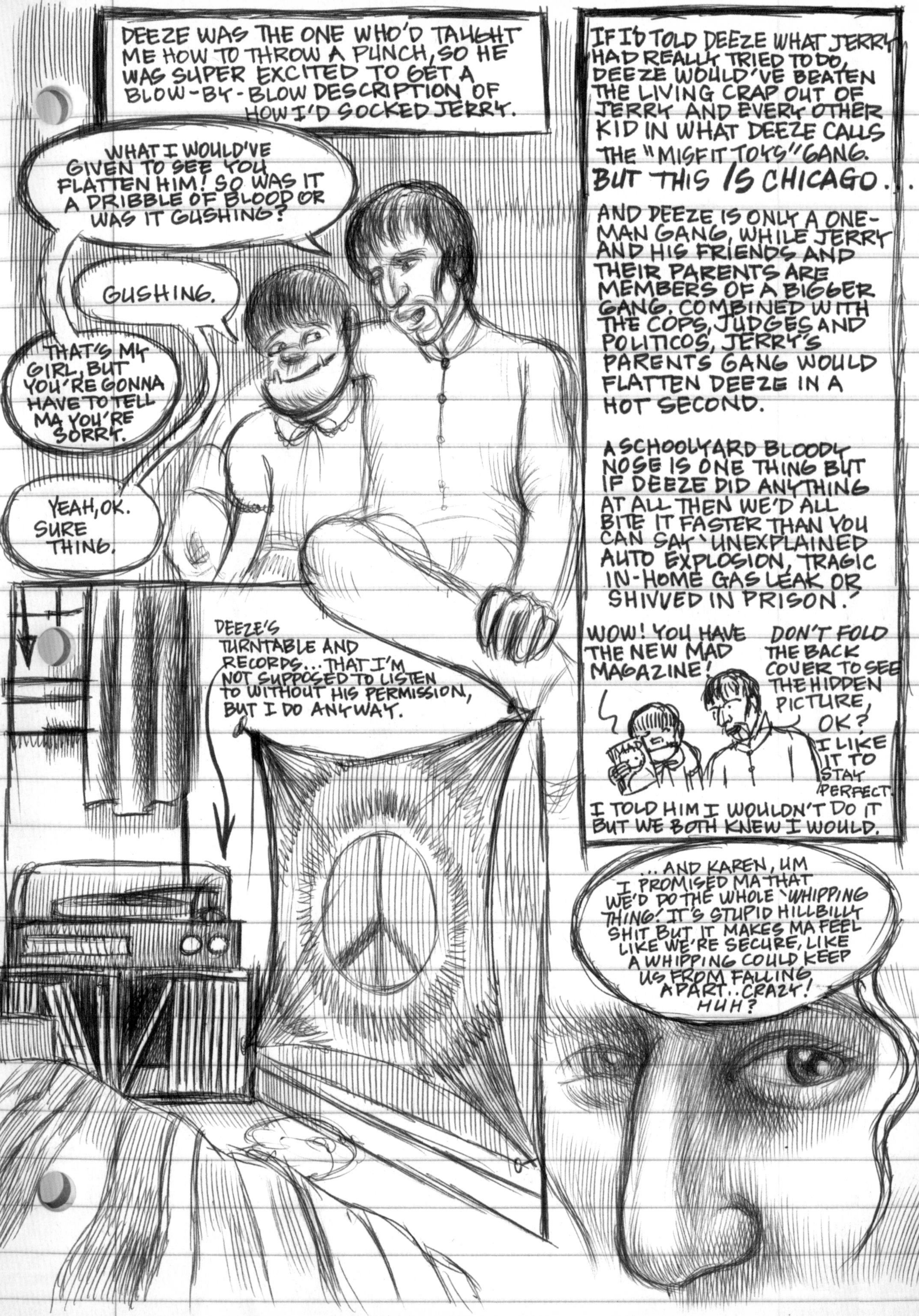
DEEZE WAS THE ONE WHO'D TAUGHT ME HOW TO THROW A PUNCH, SO HE WAS SUPER EXCITED TO GET A BLOW-BY-BLOW DESCRIPTION OF HOW I'D SOCKED JERRY.
WHAT I WOULD'VE GIVEN TO SEE YOU FLATTEN HIM! SO WAS IT A DRIBBLE OF BLOOD OR WAS IT GUSHING?
GUSHING.
THAT'S MY GIRL, BUT YOU'RE GONNA HAVE TO TELL MA YOU'RE SORRY.
YEAH, OK. SURE THING.
IF I'D TOLD DEEZE WHAT JERRY HAD REALLY TRIED TO DO, DEEZE WOULD'VE BEATEN THE LIVING CRAP OUT OF JERRY AND EVERY OTHER KID IN WHAT DEEZE CALLS THE "MISFIT TOYS" GANG.
BUT THIS IS CHICAGO...
AND DEEZE IS ONLY A ONE-MAN GANG, WHILE JERRY AND HIS FRIENDS AND THEIR PARENTS ARE MEMBERS OF A BIGGER GANG. COMBINED WITH THE COPS, JUDGES AND POLITICOS, JERRY'S PARENTS GANG WOULD FLATTEN DEEZE IN A HOT SECOND.
A SCHOOLYARD BLOODY NOSE IS ONE THING BUT IF DEEZE DID ANYTHING AT ALL THEN WE'D ALL BITE IT FASTER THAN YOU CAN SAY 'UNEXPLAINED AUTO EXPLOSION, TRAGIC IN-HOME GAS LEAK OR SHIVVED IN PRISON.'
DEEZE'S TURNTABLE AND RECORDS... THAT I'M NOT SUPPOSED TO LISTEN TO WITHOUT HIS PERMISSION, BUT I DO ANYWAY.
WOW! YOU HAVE THE NEW MAD MAGAZINE!
DON'T FOLD THE BACK COVER TO SEE THE HIDDEN PICTURE, OK? I LIKE IT TO STAY PERFECT.
MAD
I TOLD HIM I WOULDN'T DO IT BUT WE BOTH KNEW I WOULD.
...AND KAREN, UM I PROMISED MA THAT WE'D DO THE WHOLE 'WHIPPING THING.' IT'S STUPID HILLBILLY SHIT BUT IT MAKES MA FEEL LIKE WE'RE SECURE, LIKE A WHIPPING COULD KEEP US FROM FALLING APART.. CRAZY! HUH?

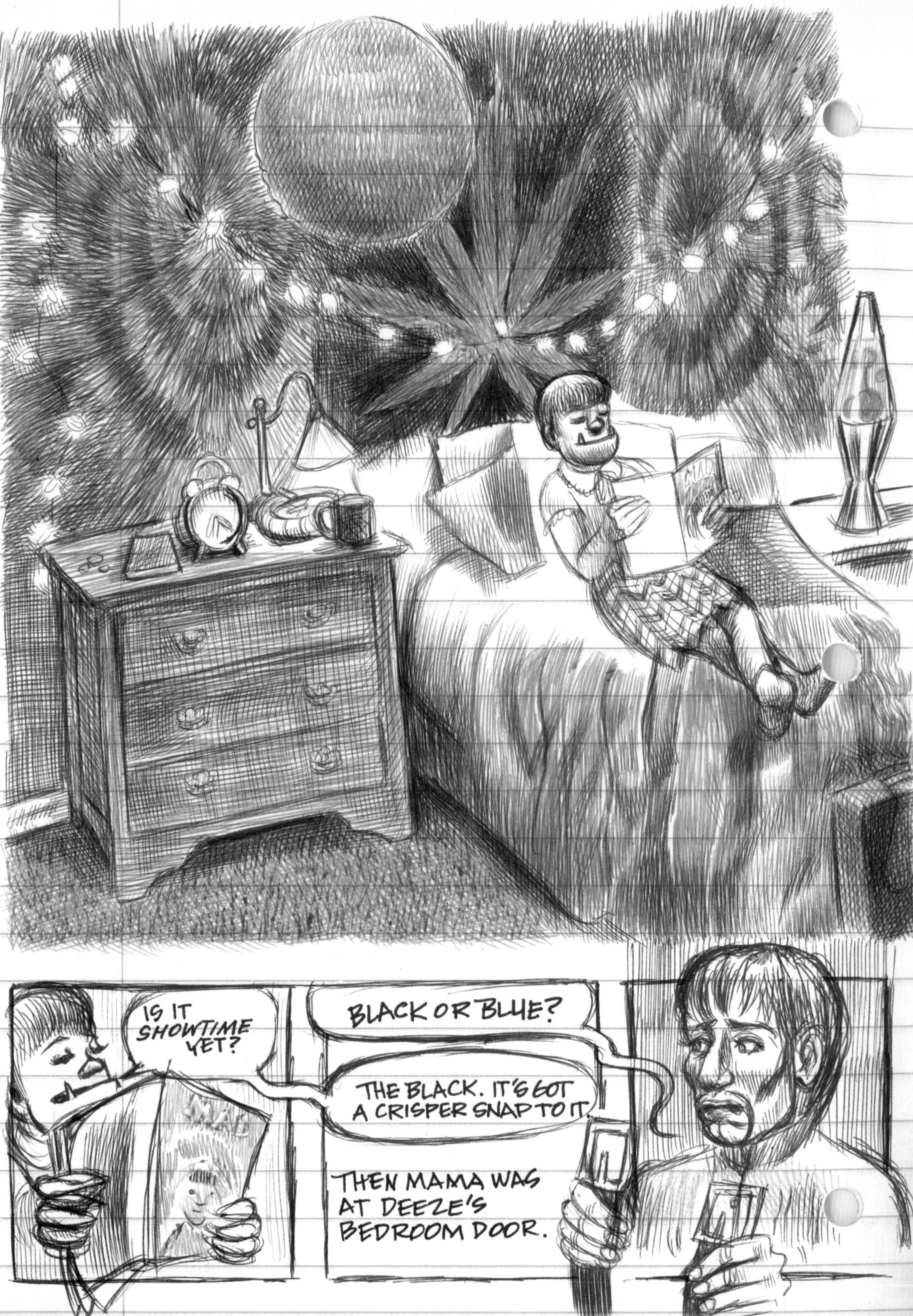
IS IT SHOWTIME YET?
BLACK OR BLUE?
THE BLACK. IT'S GOT A CRISPER SNAP TO IT.
THEN MAMA WAS AT DEEZE'S BEDROOM DOOR.

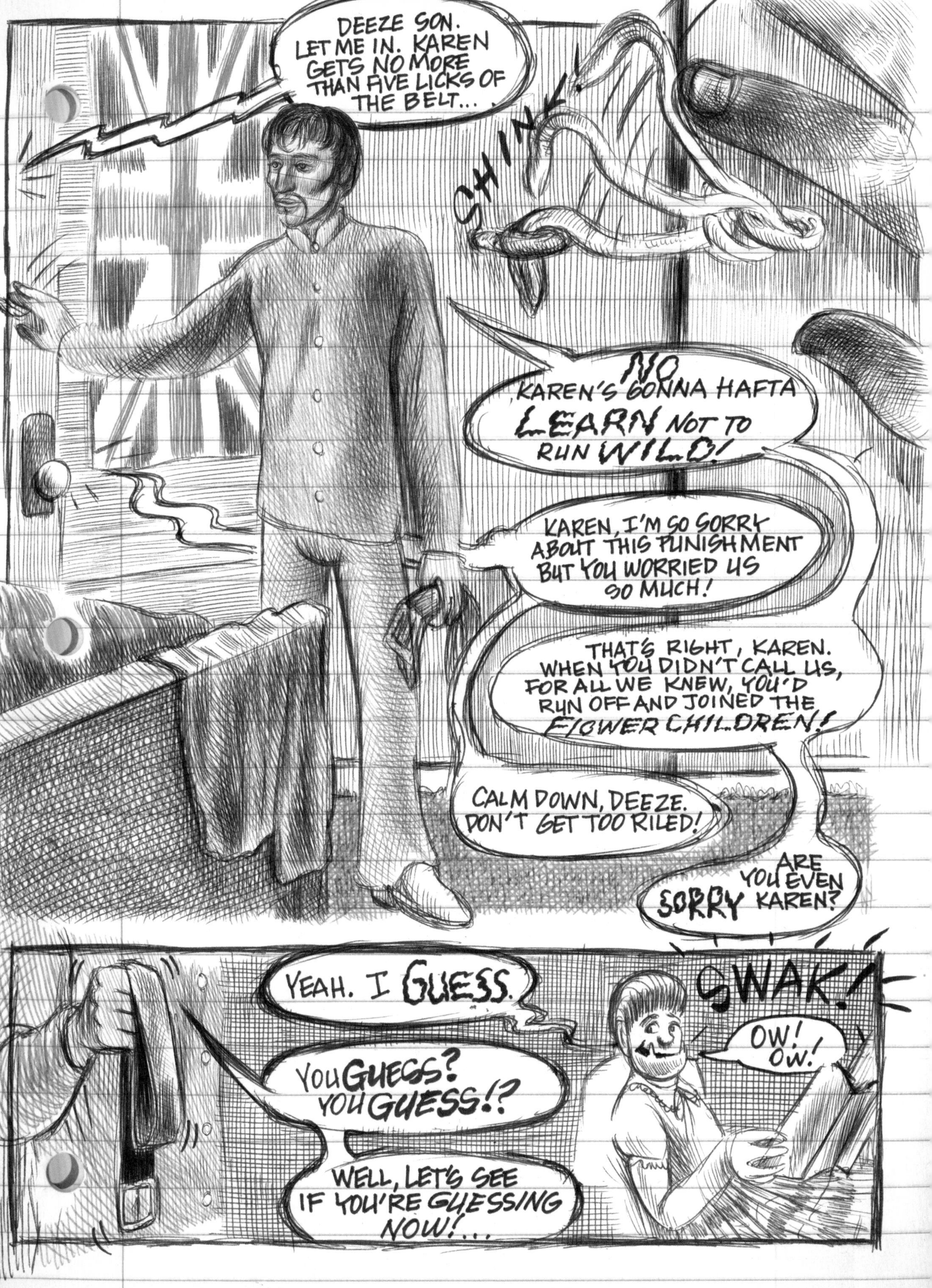
DEEZE SON. LET ME IN. KAREN GETS NO MORE THAN FIVE LICKS OF THE BELT...
SHINK!
NO KAREN'S GONNA HAFTA LEARN NOT TO RUN WILD!
KAREN, I'M SO SORRY ABOUT THIS PUNISHMENT BUT YOU WORRIED US SO MUCH!
THAT'S RIGHT, KAREN. WHEN YOU DIDN'T CALL US, FOR ALL WE KNEW, YOU'D RUN OFF AND JOINED THE FLOWER CHILDREN!
CALM DOWN, DEEZE. DON'T GET TOO RILED!
ARE YOU EVEN SORRY KAREN?
YEAH. I GUESS.
YOU GUESS? YOU GUESS!?
WELL, LET'S SEE IF YOU'RE GUESSING NOW!...
SWAK!
OW! OW!

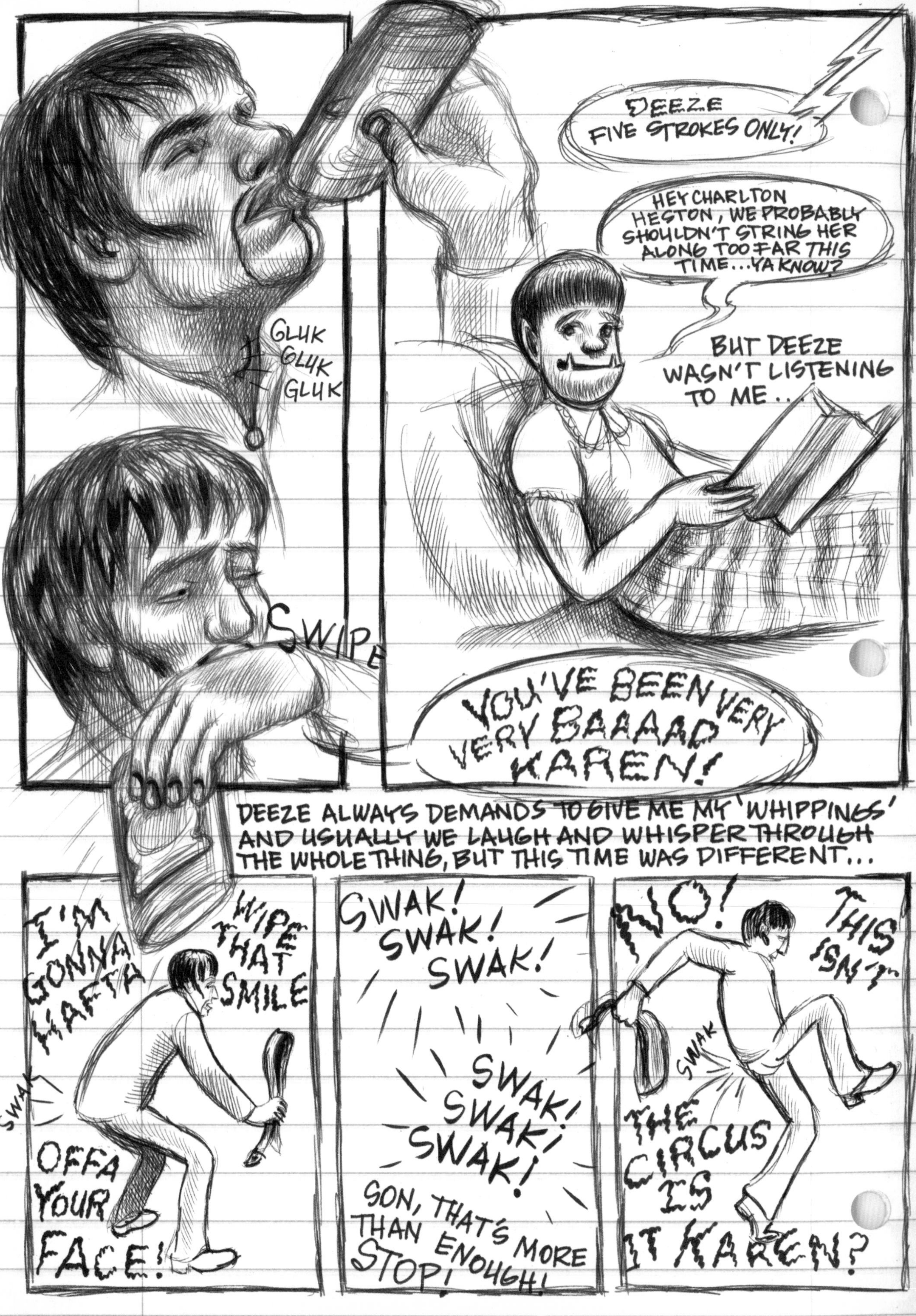
GLUK GLUK GLUK
DEEZE FIVE STROKES ONLY!
HEY CHARLTON HESTON, WE PROBABLY SHOULDN'T STRING HER ALONG TOO FAR THIS TIME... YA KNOW?
BUT DEEZE WASN'T LISTENING TO ME...
SWIPE
YOU'VE BEEN VERY VERY BAAAAD KAREN!
DEEZE ALWAYS DEMANDS TO GIVE ME MY 'WHIPPINGS' AND USUALLY WE LAUGH AND WHISPER THROUGH THE WHOLE THING, BUT THIS TIME WAS DIFFERENT...
I'M GONNA HAFTA WIPE THAT SMILE OFFA YOUR FACE!
SWAK
SWAK! SWAK! SWAK!
SWAK! SWAK! SWAK!
SON, THAT'S MORE THAN ENOUGH! STOP!
NO! THIS ISN'T THE CIRCUS IS IT KAREN?
SWAK

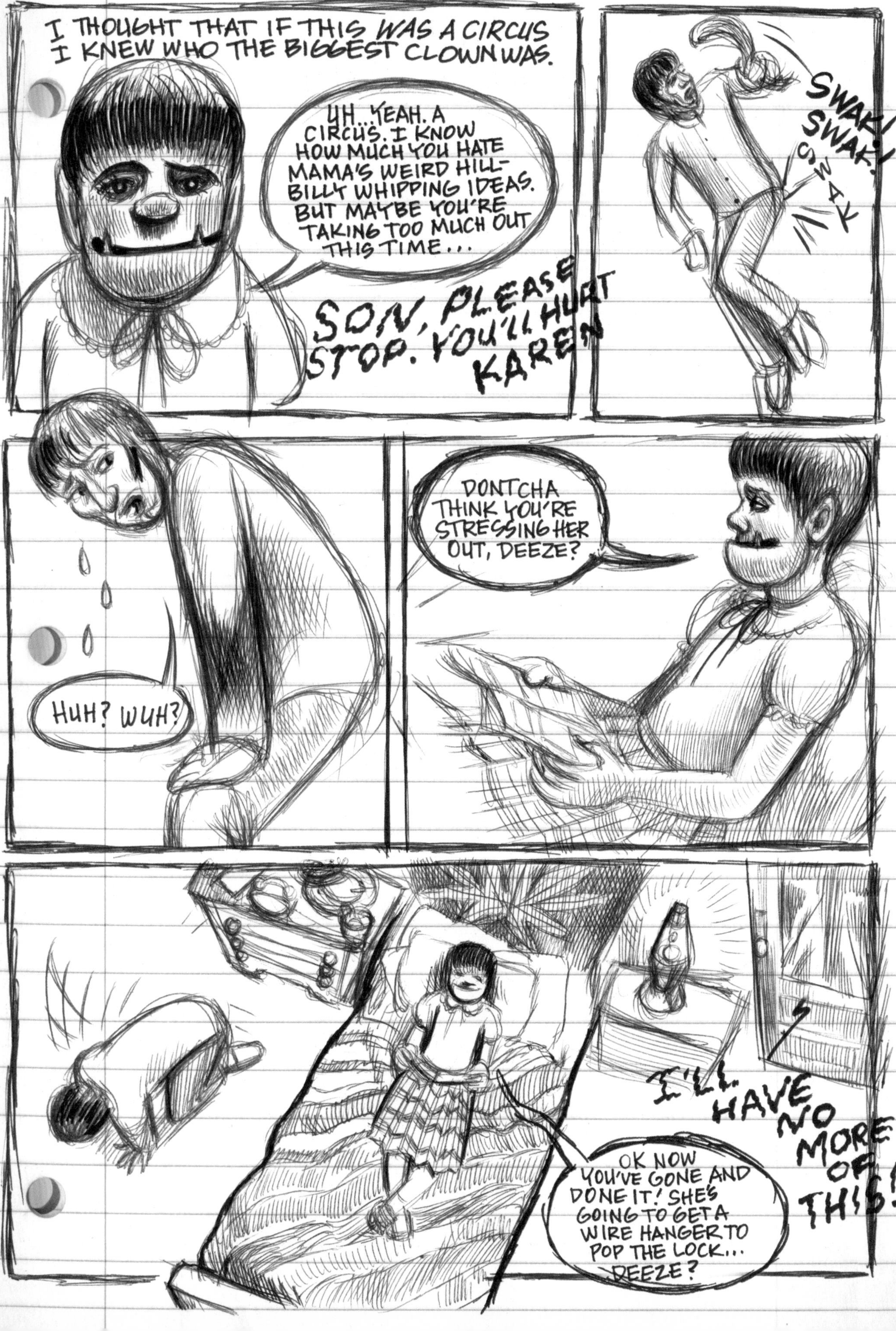
I THOUGHT THAT IF THIS WAS A CIRCUS I KNEW WHO THE BIGGEST CLOWN WAS.
UH...YEAH. A CIRCUS. I KNOW HOW MUCH YOU HATE MAMA'S WEIRD HILL-BILLY WHIPPING IDEAS. BUT MAYBE YOU'RE TAKING TOO MUCH OUT THIS TIME...
SON, PLEASE STOP. YOU'LL HURT KAREN
SWAK! SWAK! SWAK
HUH? WUH?
DONTCHA THINK YOU'RE STRESSING HER OUT, DEEZE?
I'LL HAVE NO MORE OF THIS!
OK NOW YOU'VE GONE AND DONE IT! SHE'S GOING TO GET A WIRE HANGER TO POP THE LOCK... DEEZE?

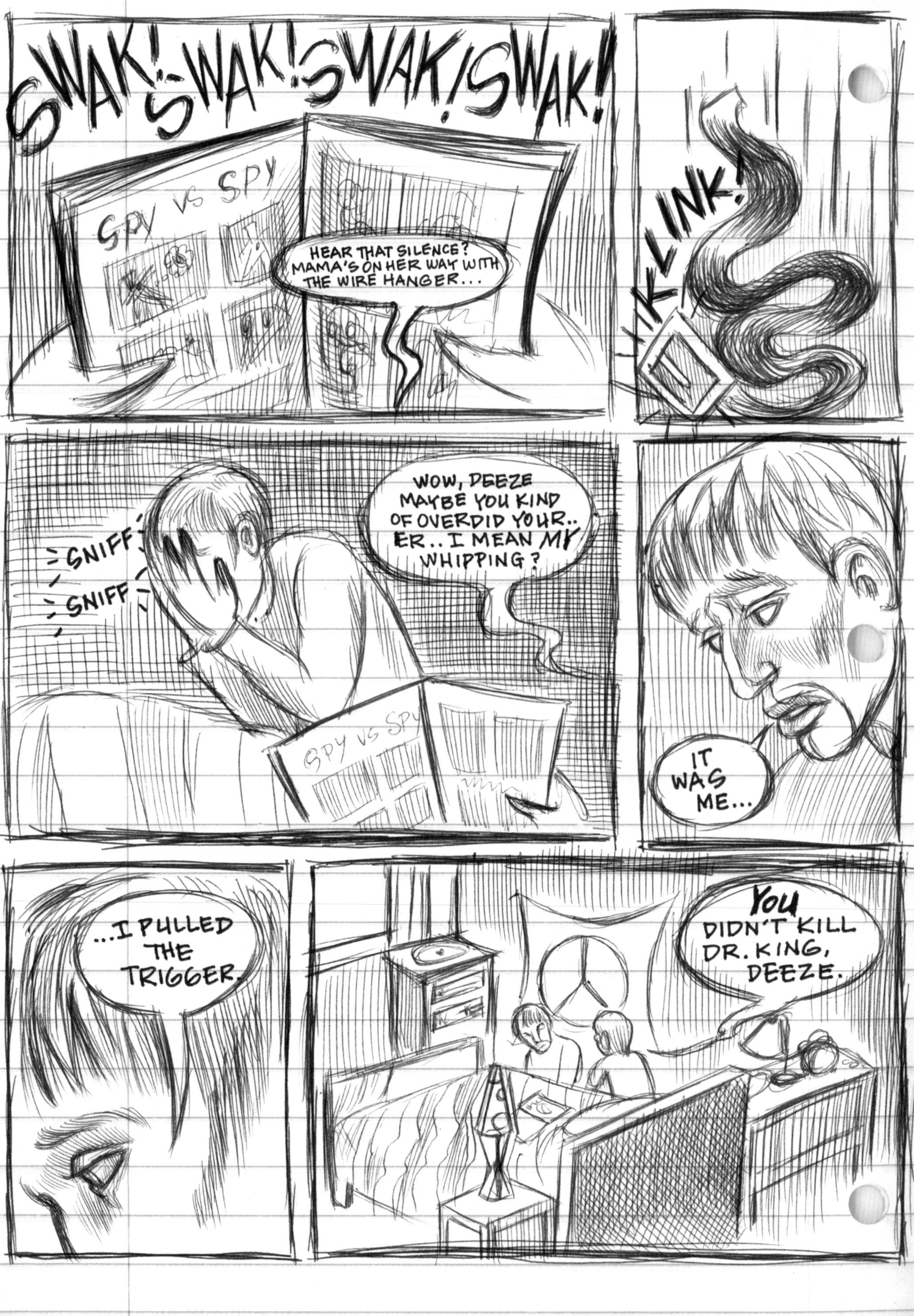
SWAK! SWAK! SWAK! SWAK!
SPY VS SPY
HEAR THAT SILENCE? MAMA'S ON HER WAY WITH THE WIRE HANGER...
KLINK!
WOW, DEEZE MAYBE YOU KIND OF OVERDID YOUR.. ER.. I MEAN MY WHIPPING?
SNIFF
SNIFF
SPY VS SPY
IT WAS ME...
...I PULLED THE TRIGGER.
YOU DIDN'T KILL DR. KING, DEEZE.

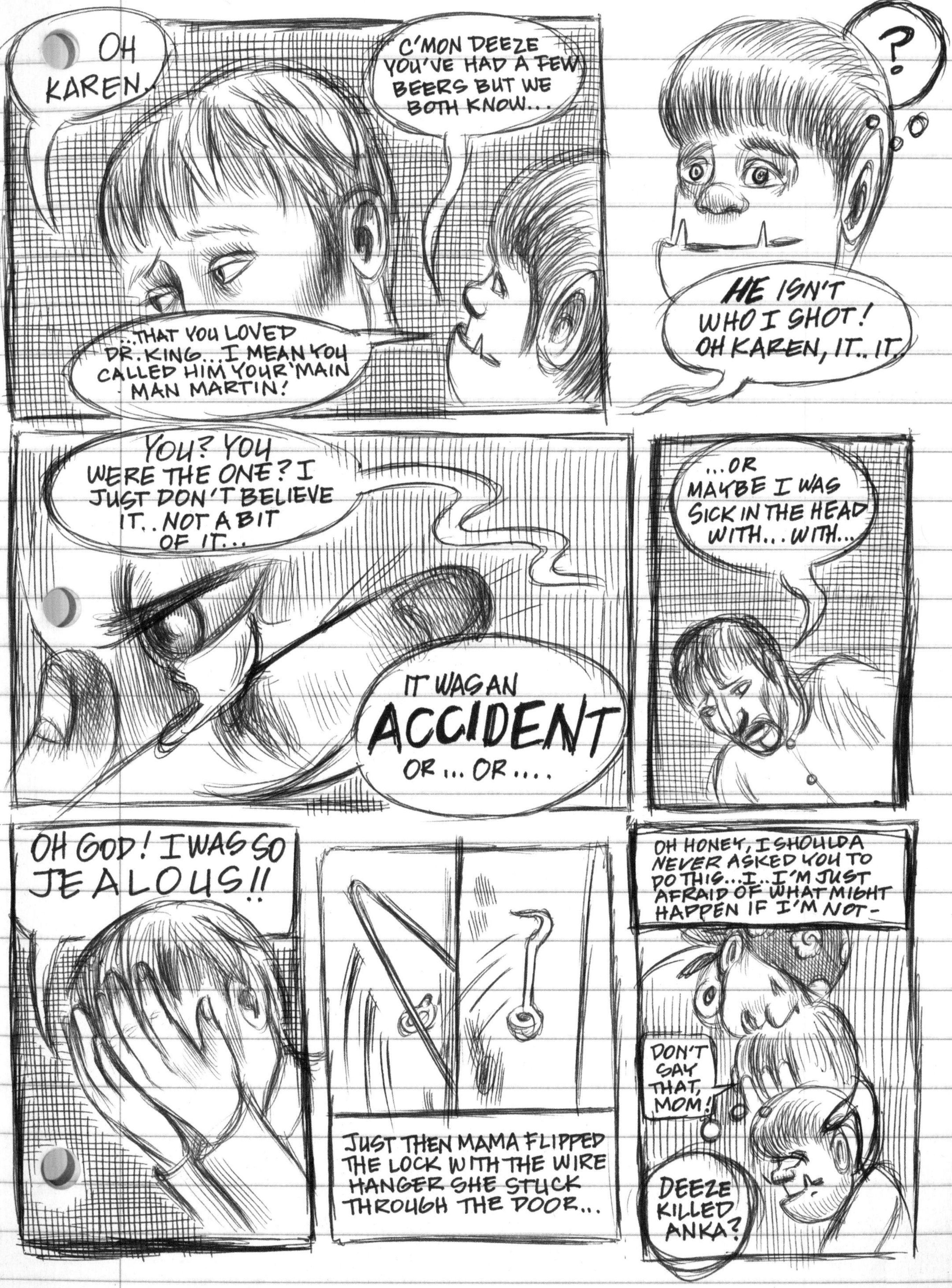

OH KAREN..
C'MON DEEZE YOU'VE HAD A FEW BEERS BUT WE BOTH KNOW...
...THAT YOU LOVED DR. KING...I MEAN YOU CALLED HIM YOUR 'MAIN MAN MARTIN'!
?
HE ISN'T WHO I SHOT! OH KAREN, IT.. IT.
YOU? YOU WERE THE ONE? I JUST DON'T BELIEVE IT..NOT A BIT OF IT...
IT WAS AN ACCIDENT OR... OR....
...OR MAYBE I WAS SICK IN THE HEAD WITH... WITH...
OH GOD! I WAS SO JEALOUS!!
JUST THEN MAMA FLIPPED THE LOCK WITH THE WIRE HANGER SHE STUCK THROUGH THE DOOR...
OH HONEY, I SHOULDA NEVER ASKED YOU TO DO THIS...I..I'M JUST AFRAID OF WHAT MIGHT HAPPEN IF I'M NOT-
DON'T SAY THAT, MOM!
DEEZE KILLED ANKA?

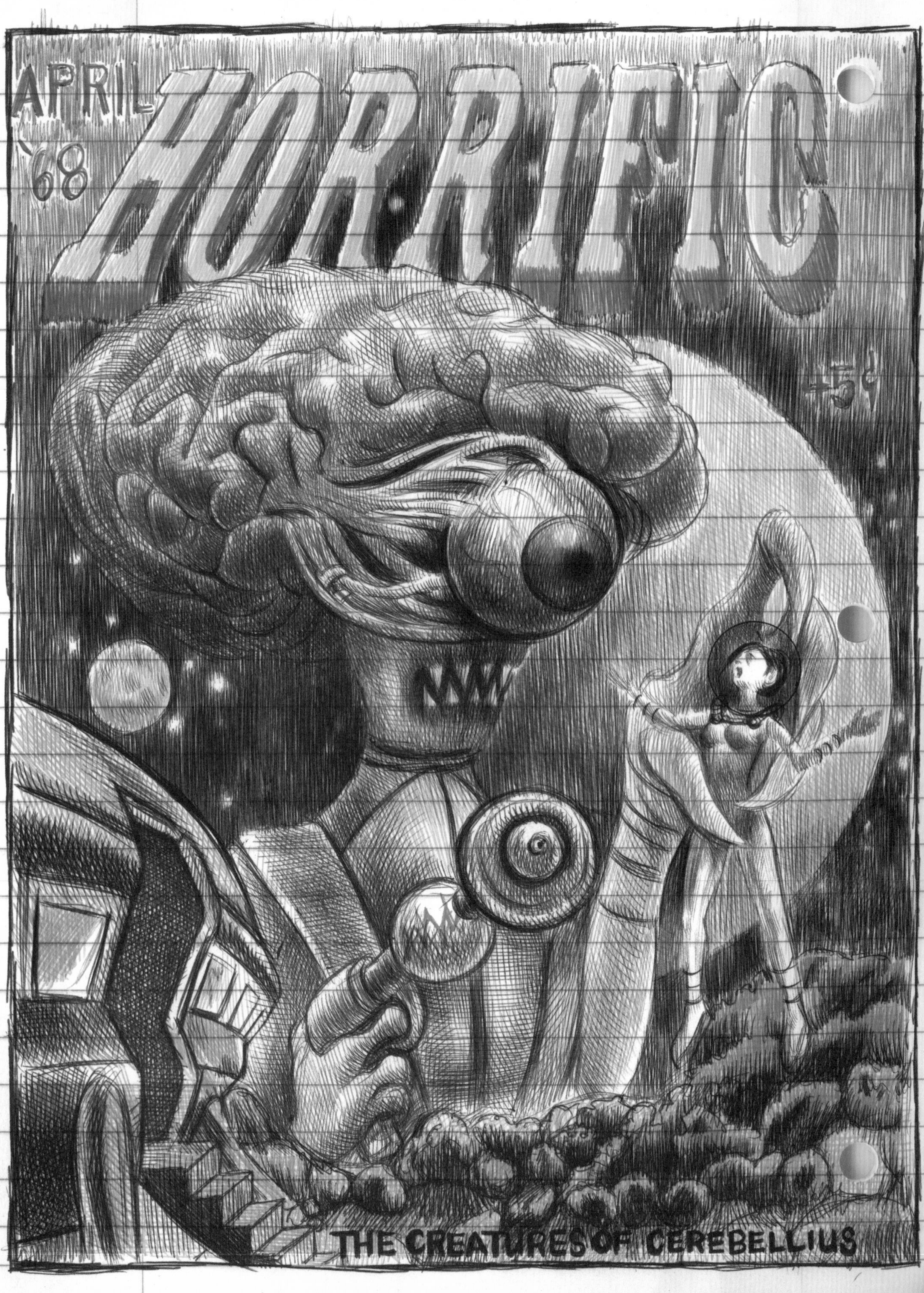
APRIL
'68
HORRIFIC
15¢
THE CREATURES OF CEREBELLIUS

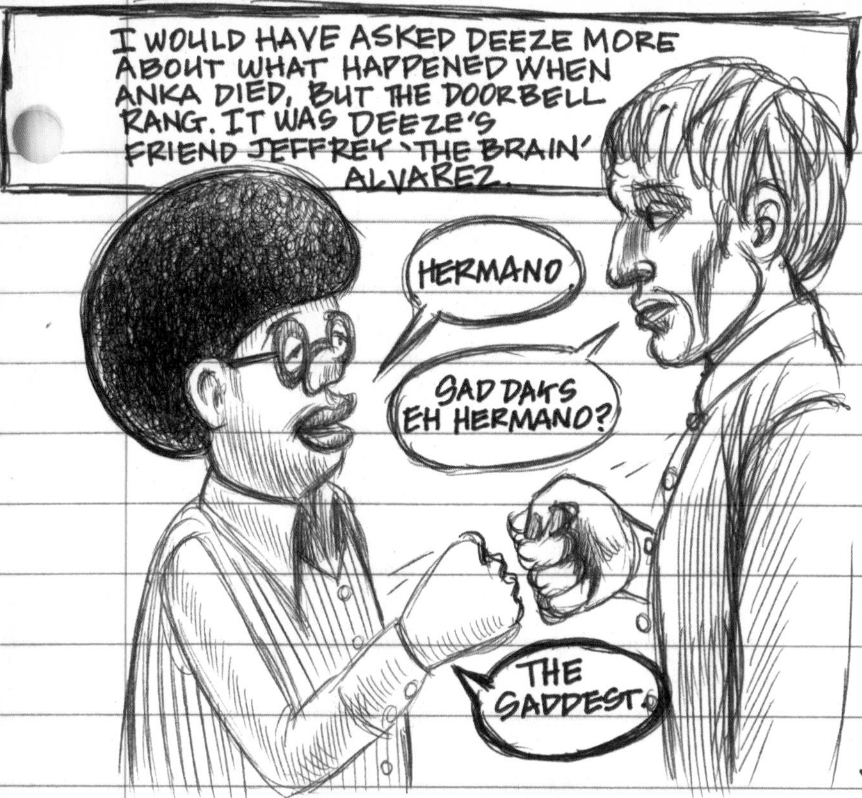
I WOULD HAVE ASKED DEEZE MORE ABOUT WHAT HAPPENED WHEN ANKA DIED, BUT THE DOORBELL RANG. IT WAS DEEZE'S FRIEND JEFFREY 'THE BRAIN' ALVAREZ.
HERMANO.
SAD DAYS EH HERMANO?
THE SADDEST.

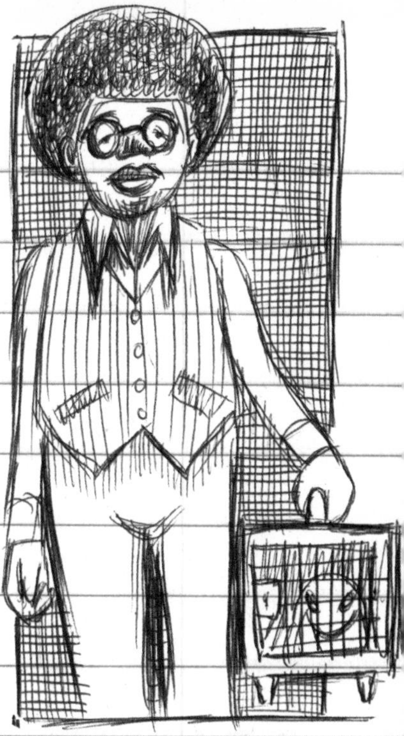

DEEZE SAYS JEFFREY 'THE BRAIN' IS FROM PUERTO RICO.

MAYBE IT'S BECAUSE HIS GLASSES ARE COKE-BOTTLE-THICK, BUT 'THE BRAIN' LOOKS AT EVERYONE LIKE A GENTLE SCIENTIST LOOKS AT RARE INSECTS. HE LOOKS AT ME LIKE WE ARE TOTALLY DIFFERENT SPECIES. IT SEEMS TO SORT OF SURPRISE HIM WHEN THE GIANT CATERPILLAR (ME) RETURNS HIS 'HOLA'. JEFFREY LOVES TO TALK ABOUT POLITICS AND SCIENCE FICTION BOOKS AND I CAN NEVER TELL WHICH ONE HE'S TALKING ABOUT.

WHEN DEEZE AND HIS FRIEND WENT TO THE KITCHEN FOR BEER AND TO TALK ABOUT DR. KING'S MURDER, I DECIDED TO SPY ON THEM

(IN CASE DEEZE SAID ANYTHING MORE ABOUT ANKA)

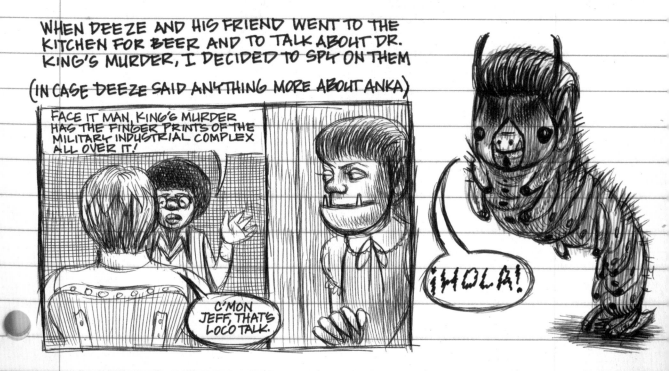

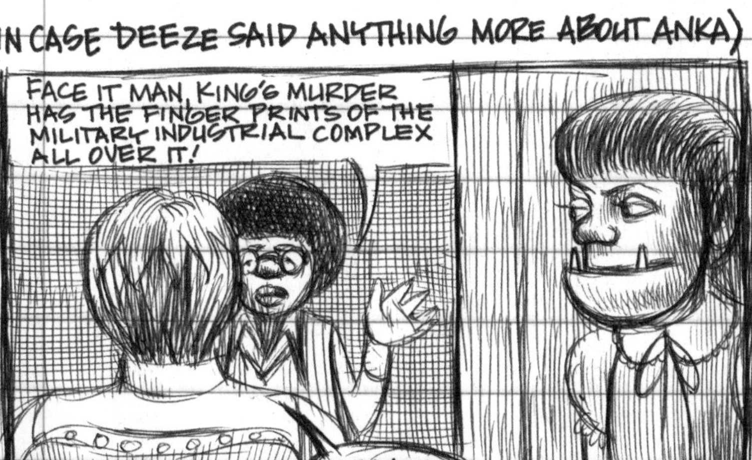
FACE IT MAN, KING'S MURDER HAS THE FINGER PRINTS OF THE MILITARY INDUSTRIAL COMPLEX ALL OVER IT!
C'MON JEFF, THAT'S LOCO TALK.

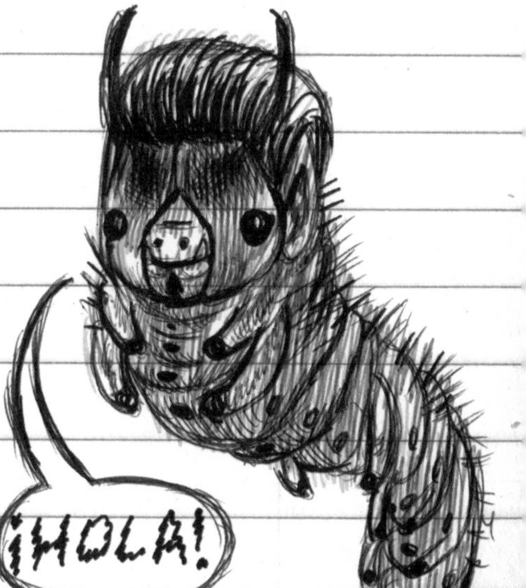
¡HOLA!

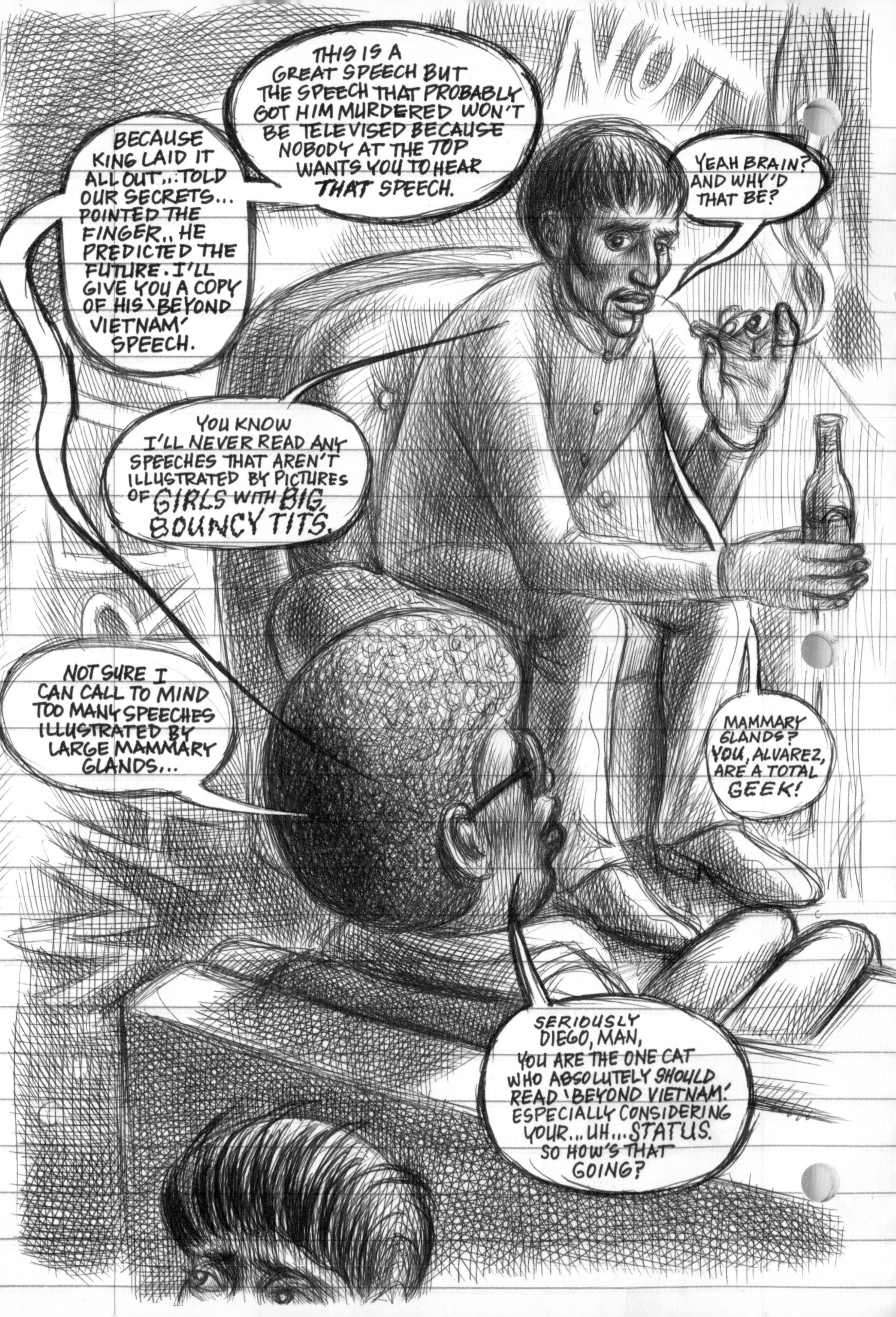

NOT
THIS IS A GREAT SPEECH BUT THE SPEECH THAT PROBABLY GOT HIM MURDERED WON'T BE TELEVISED BECAUSE NOBODY AT THE TOP WANTS YOU TO HEAR *THAT* SPEECH.
YEAH BRAIN? AND WHY'D THAT BE?
BECAUSE KING LAID IT ALL OUT... TOLD OUR SECRETS... POINTED THE FINGER.. HE PREDICTED THE FUTURE. I'LL GIVE YOU A COPY OF HIS 'BEYOND VIETNAM' SPEECH.
YOU KNOW I'LL NEVER READ ANY SPEECHES THAT AREN'T ILLUSTRATED BY PICTURES OF GIRLS WITH BIG, BOUNCY TITS.
NOT SURE I CAN CALL TO MIND TOO MANY SPEECHES ILLUSTRATED BY LARGE MAMMARY GLANDS...
MAMMARY GLANDS? YOU, ALVAREZ, ARE A TOTAL GEEK!
SERIOUSLY DIEGO, MAN, YOU ARE THE ONE CAT WHO ABSOLUTELY SHOULD READ 'BEYOND VIETNAM'. ESPECIALLY CONSIDERING YOUR... UH... STATUS. SO HOW'S THAT GOING?

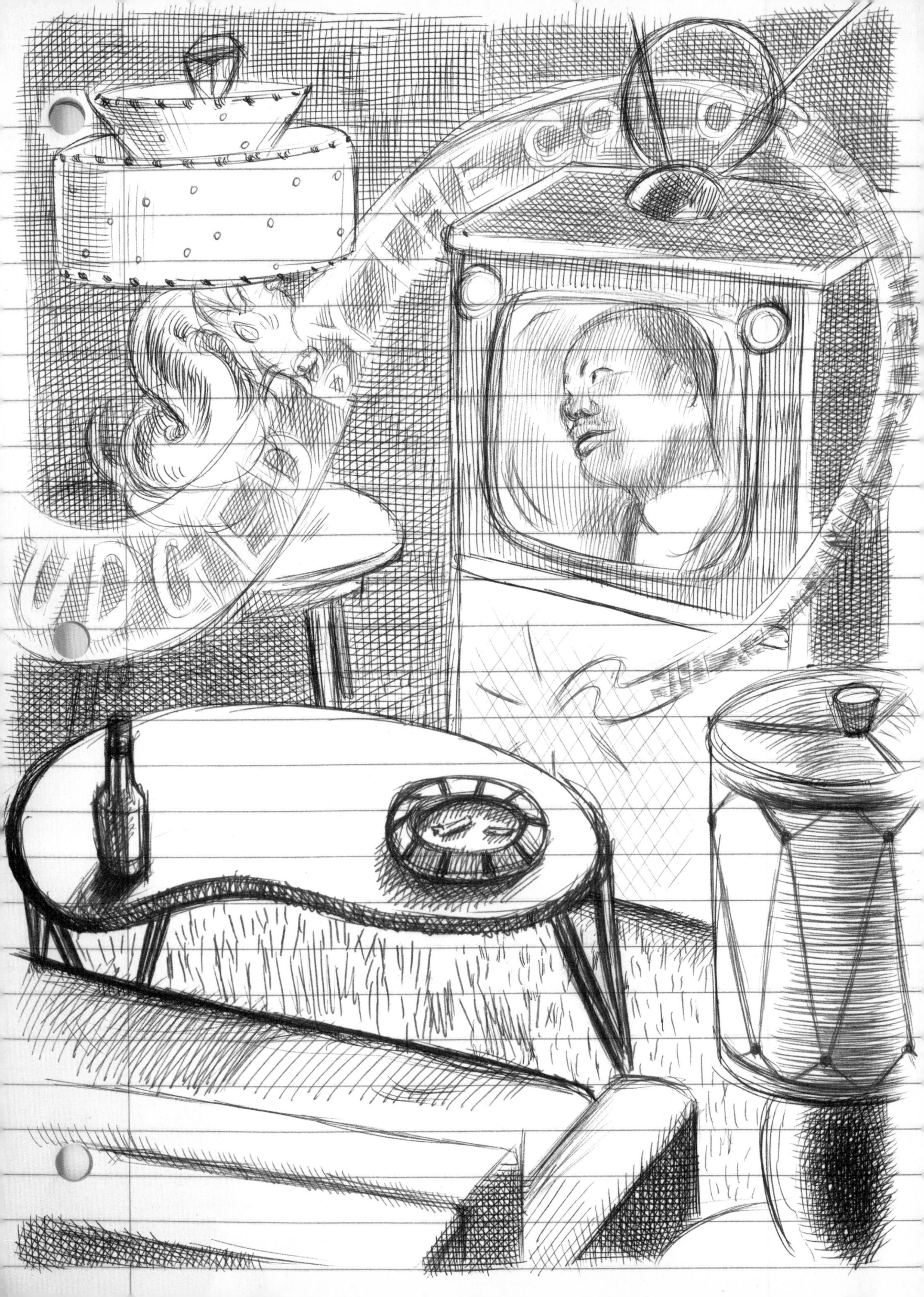

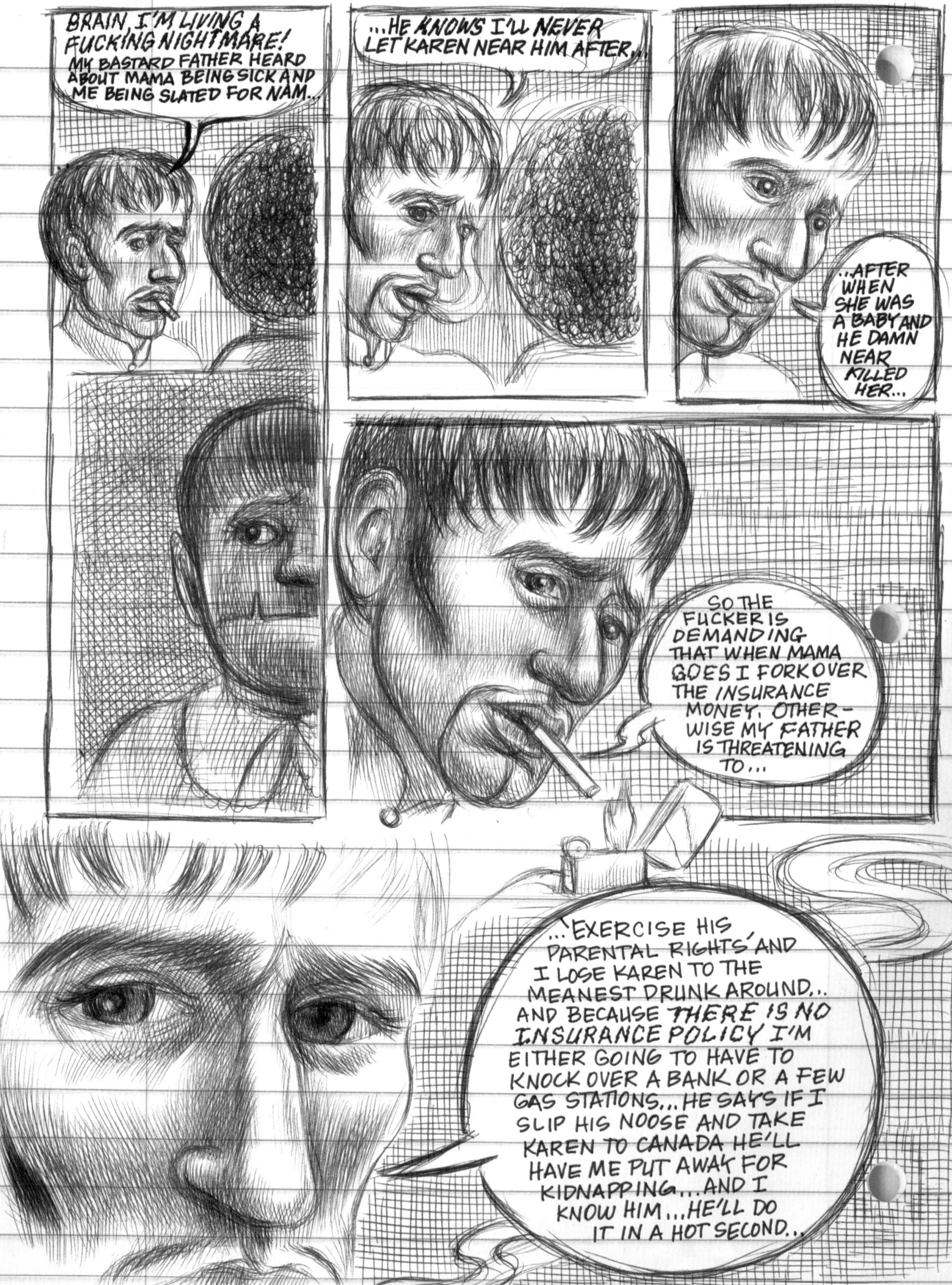
BRAIN, I'M LIVING A FUCKING NIGHTMARE! MY BASTARD FATHER HEARD ABOUT MAMA BEING SICK AND ME BEING SLATED FOR NAM...
...HE KNOWS I'LL NEVER LET KAREN NEAR HIM AFTER...
...AFTER WHEN SHE WAS A BABY AND HE DAMN NEAR KILLED HER...
SO THE FUCKER IS DEMANDING THAT WHEN MAMA GOES I FORK OVER THE INSURANCE MONEY. OTHER-WISE MY FATHER IS THREATENING TO...
...'EXERCISE HIS PARENTAL RIGHTS' AND I LOSE KAREN TO THE MEANEST DRUNK AROUND... AND BECAUSE THERE IS NO INSURANCE POLICY I'M EITHER GOING TO HAVE TO KNOCK OVER A BANK OR A FEW GAS STATIONS... HE SAYS IF I SLIP HIS NOOSE AND TAKE KAREN TO CANADA HE'LL HAVE ME PUT AWAY FOR KIDNAPPING... AND I KNOW HIM... HE'LL DO IT IN A HOT SECOND...

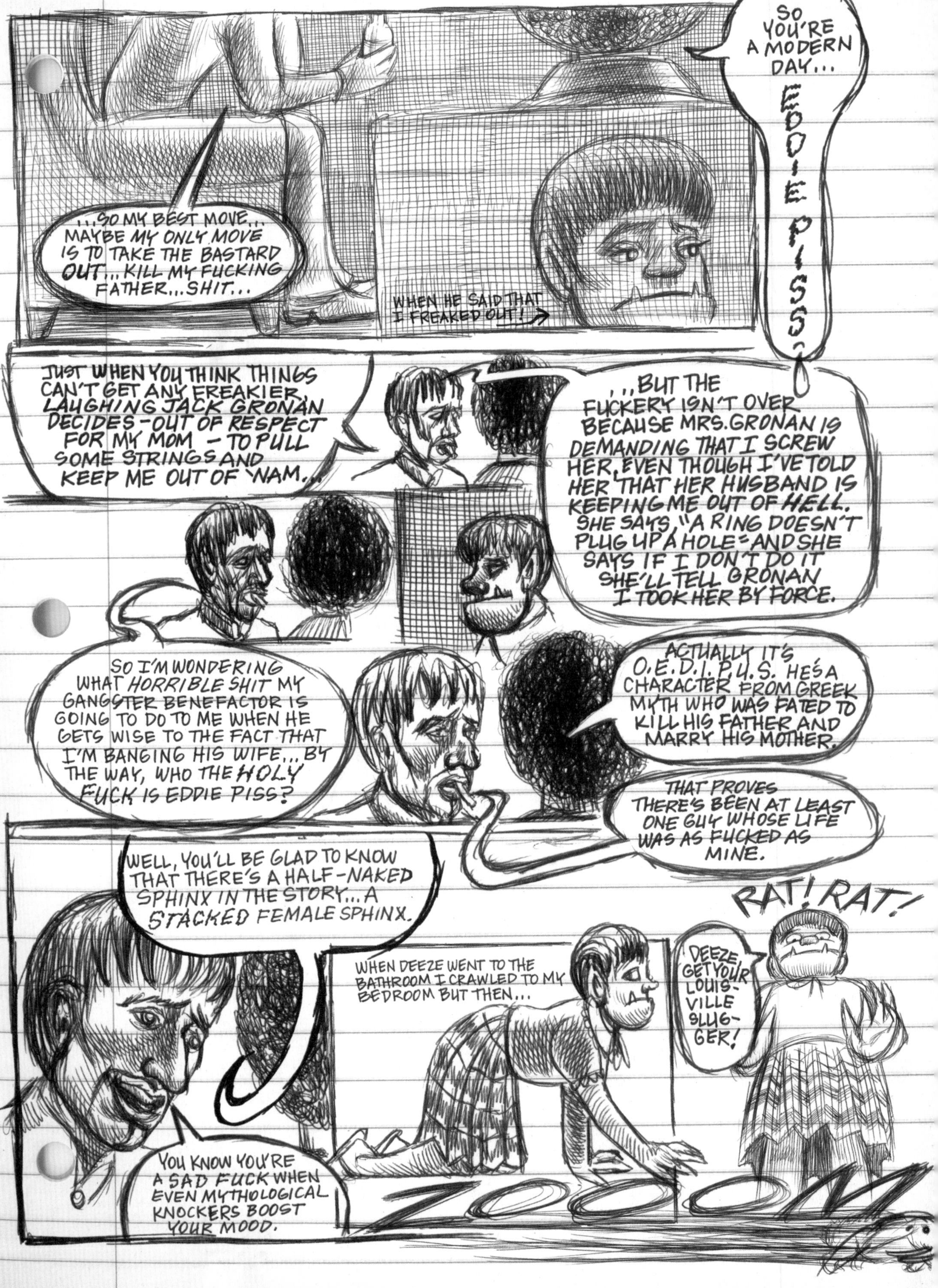
...SO MY BEST MOVE... MAYBE MY ONLY MOVE IS TO TAKE THE BASTARD OUT... KILL MY FUCKING FATHER... SHIT...
WHEN HE SAID THAT I FREAKED OUT!
SO YOU'RE A MODERN DAY... EDDIE PISS?
JUST WHEN YOU THINK THINGS CAN'T GET ANY FREAKIER, LAUGHING JACK GRONAN DECIDES-OUT OF RESPECT FOR MY MOM - TO PULL SOME STRINGS AND KEEP ME OUT OF 'NAM...
...BUT THE FUCKERY ISN'T OVER BECAUSE MRS. GRONAN IS DEMANDING THAT I SCREW HER, EVEN THOUGH I'VE TOLD HER THAT HER HUSBAND IS KEEPING ME OUT OF HELL. SHE SAYS, "A RING DOESN'T PLUG UP A HOLE" AND SHE SAYS IF I DON'T DO IT SHE'LL TELL GRONAN I TOOK HER BY FORCE.
SO I'M WONDERING WHAT HORRIBLE SHIT MY GANGSTER BENEFACTOR IS GOING TO DO TO ME WHEN HE GETS WISE TO THE FACT THAT I'M BANGING HIS WIFE... BY THE WAY, WHO THE HOLY FUCK IS EDDIE PISS?
ACTUALLY IT'S O.E.D.I.P.U.S. HE'S A CHARACTER FROM GREEK MYTH WHO WAS FATED TO KILL HIS FATHER AND MARRY HIS MOTHER.
THAT PROVES THERE'S BEEN AT LEAST ONE GUY WHOSE LIFE WAS AS FUCKED AS MINE.
WELL, YOU'LL BE GLAD TO KNOW THAT THERE'S A HALF-NAKED SPHINX IN THE STORY... A STACKED FEMALE SPHINX.
YOU KNOW YOU'RE A SAD FUCK WHEN EVEN MYTHOLOGICAL KNOCKERS BOOST YOUR MOOD.
WHEN DEEZE WENT TO THE BATHROOM I CRAWLED TO MY BEDROOM BUT THEN...
RAT! RAT!
DEEZE GET YOUR LOUIS-VILLE SLUG-GER!
ZOOOM!

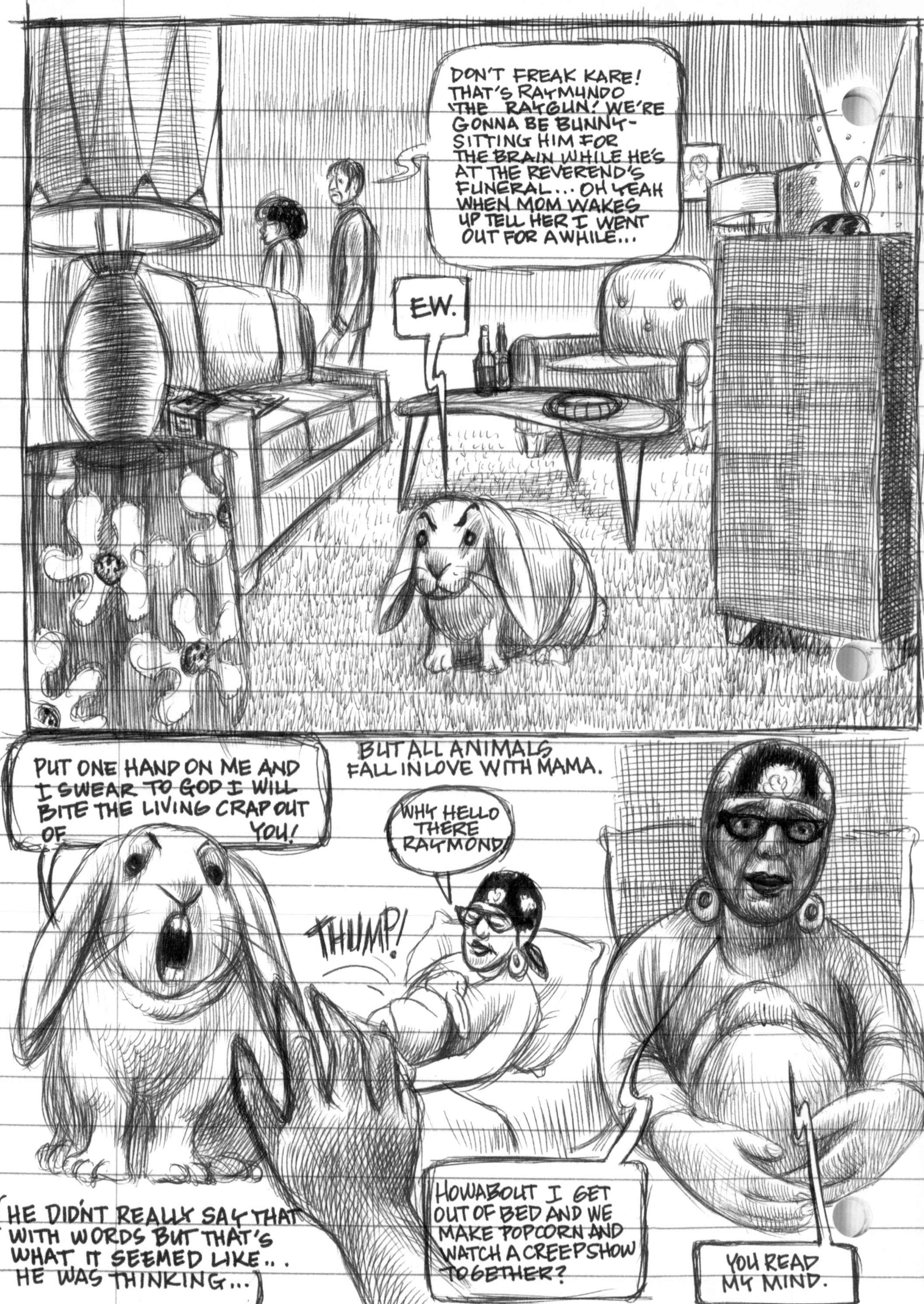
DON'T FREAK KARE! THAT'S RAYMUNDO 'THE RAYGUN'! WE'RE GONNA BE BUNNY-SITTING HIM FOR THE BRAIN WHILE HE'S AT THE REVEREND'S FUNERAL... OH YEAH WHEN MOM WAKES UP TELL HER I WENT OUT FOR AWHILE...
EW.
PUT ONE HAND ON ME AND I SWEAR TO GOD I WILL BITE THE LIVING CRAP OUT OF YOU!
(HE DIDN'T REALLY SAY THAT WITH WORDS BUT THAT'S WHAT IT SEEMED LIKE... HE WAS THINKING...)
BUT ALL ANIMALS FALL IN LOVE WITH MAMA.
WHY HELLO THERE RAYMOND
THUMP!
HOWABOUT I GET OUT OF BED AND WE MAKE POPCORN AND WATCH A CREEPSHOW TOGETHER?
YOU READ MY MIND.

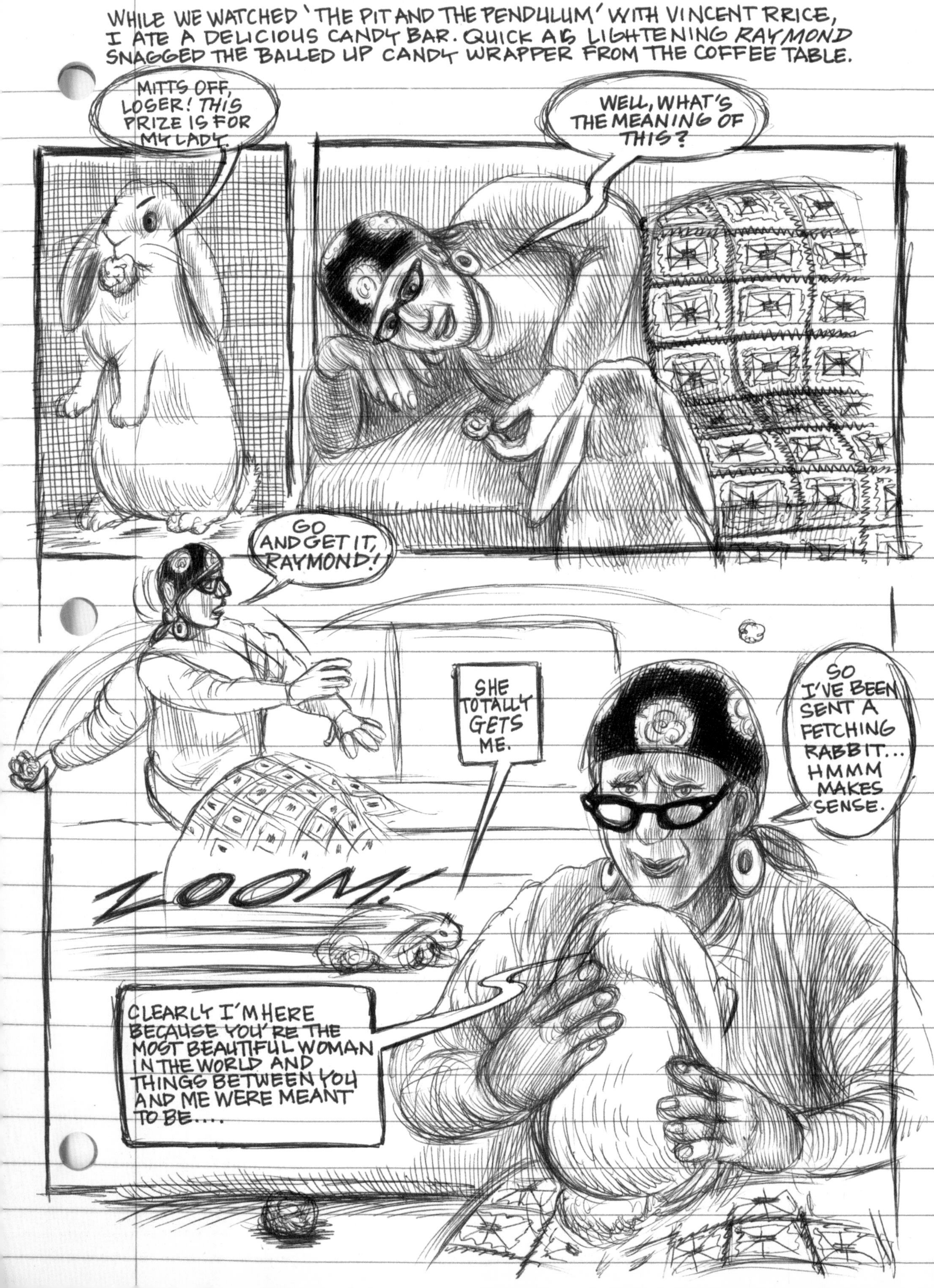
WHILE WE WATCHED 'THE PIT AND THE PENDULUM' WITH VINCENT RRICE, I ATE A DELICIOUS CANDY BAR. QUICK AS LIGHTENING *RAYMOND* SNAGGED THE BALLED UP CANDY WRAPPER FROM THE COFFEE TABLE.
MITTS OFF, LOSER! THIS PRIZE IS FOR MY LADY.
WELL, WHAT'S THE MEANING OF THIS?
GO AND GET IT, RAYMOND!
ZOOM!
SHE TOTALLY GETS ME.
SO I'VE BEEN SENT A FETCHING RABBIT... HMMM MAKES SENSE.
CLEARLY I'M HERE BECAUSE YOU'RE THE MOST BEAUTIFUL WOMAN IN THE WORLD AND THINGS BETWEEN YOU AND ME WERE MEANT TO BE....

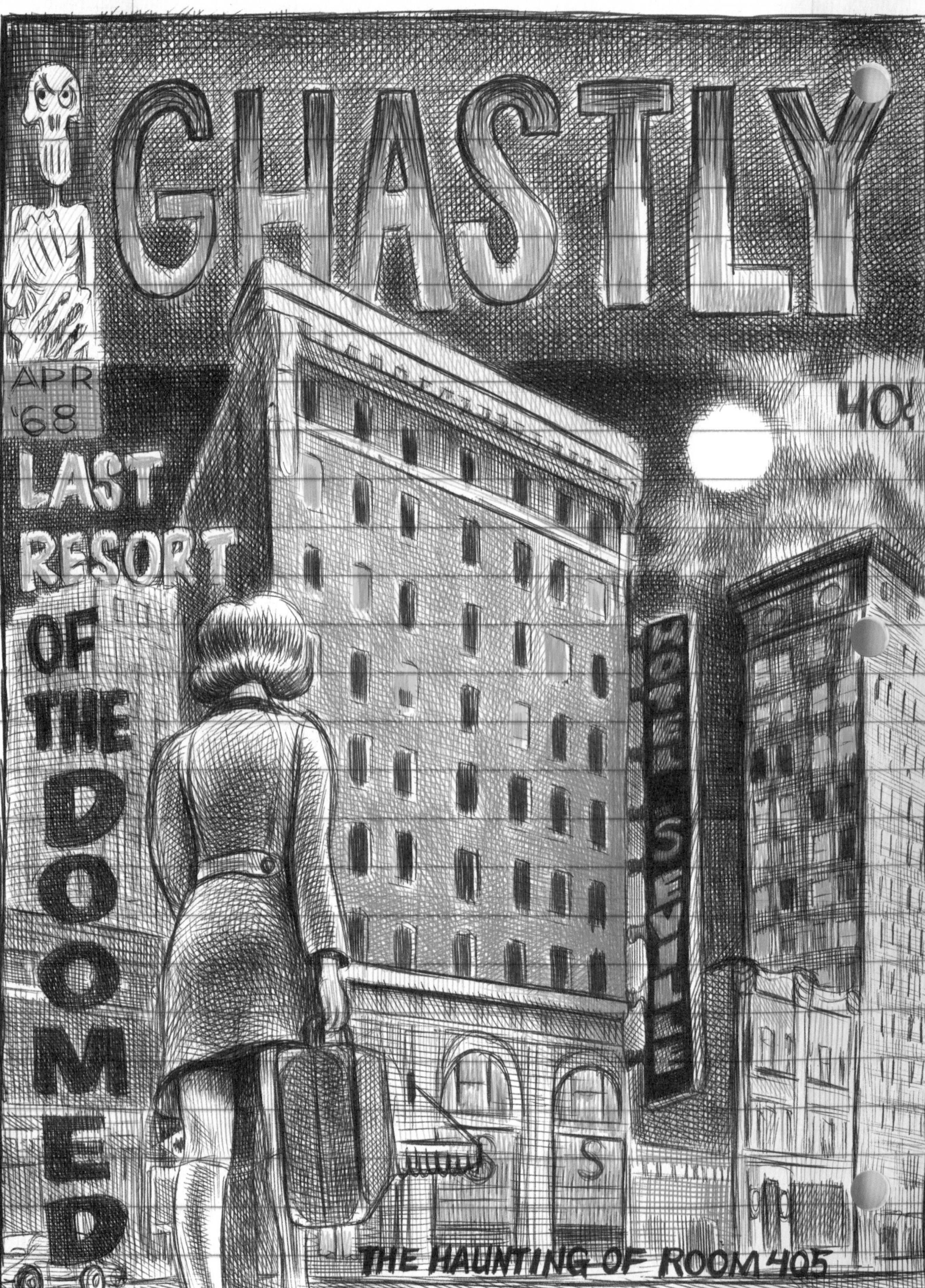
GHASTLY
APR '68
40¢
LAST RESORT OF THE DOOMED
HOTEL SEVILLE
THE HAUNTING OF ROOM 405

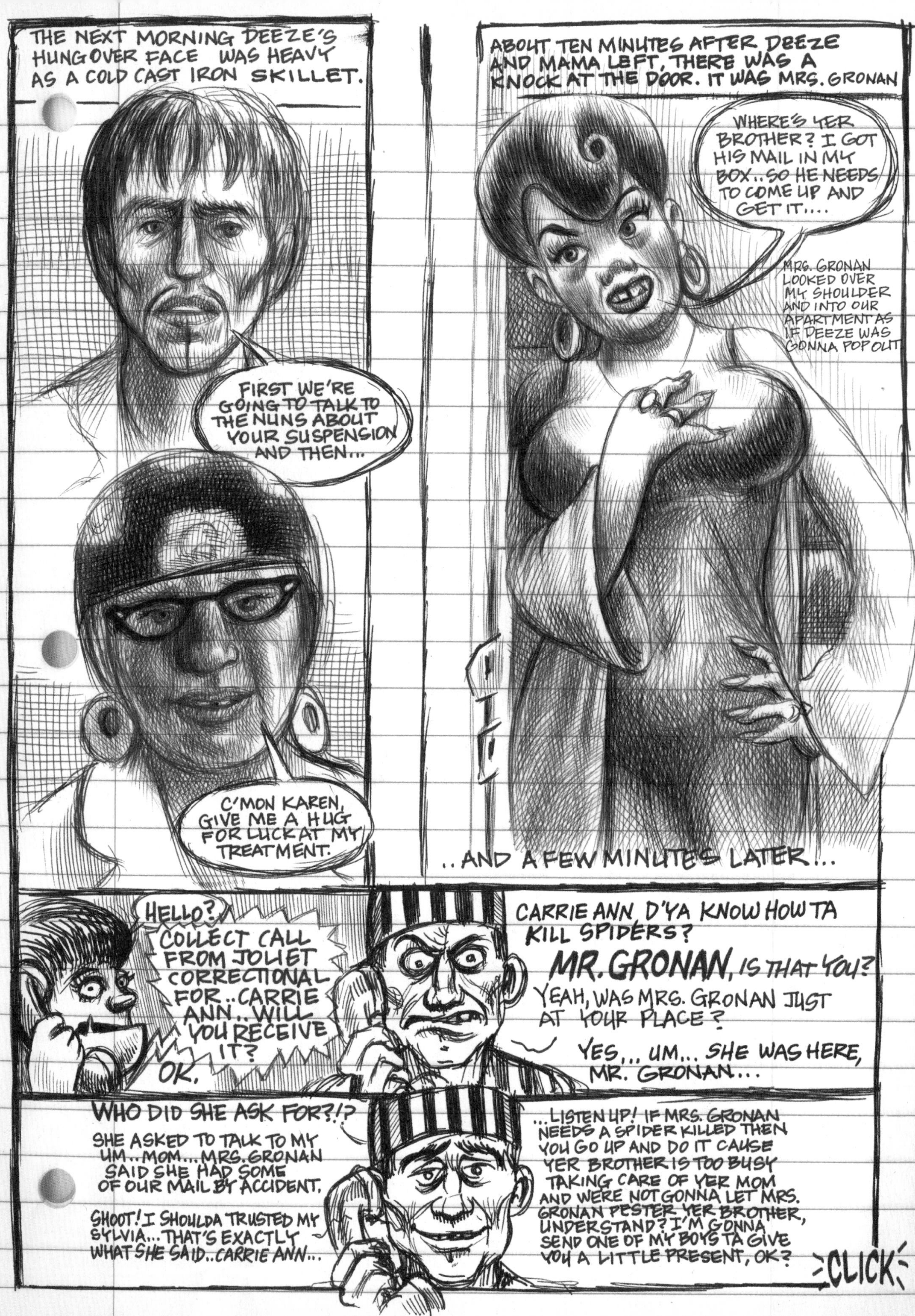
THE NEXT MORNING DEEZE'S HUNGOVER FACE WAS HEAVY AS A COLD CAST IRON SKILLET.
FIRST WE'RE GOING TO TALK TO THE NUNS ABOUT YOUR SUSPENSION AND THEN...
C'MON KAREN, GIVE ME A HUG FOR LUCK AT MY TREATMENT.
ABOUT TEN MINUTES AFTER DEEZE AND MAMA LEFT, THERE WAS A KNOCK AT THE DOOR. IT WAS MRS. GRONAN
WHERE'S YER BROTHER? I GOT HIS MAIL IN MY BOX.. SO HE NEEDS TO COME UP AND GET IT....
MRS. GRONAN LOOKED OVER MY SHOULDER AND INTO OUR APARTMENT AS IF DEEZE WAS GONNA POP OUT
..AND A FEW MINUTES LATER...
HELLO?
COLLECT CALL FROM JOLIET CORRECTIONAL FOR.. CARRIE ANN.. WILL YOU RECEIVE IT?
OK.
CARRIE ANN D'YA KNOW HOW TA KILL SPIDERS?
MR. GRONAN, IS THAT YOU?
YEAH, WAS MRS. GRONAN JUST AT YOUR PLACE?
YES,.. UM... SHE WAS HERE, MR. GRONAN...
WHO DID SHE ASK FOR?!?
SHE ASKED TO TALK TO MY UM.. MOM... MRS. GRONAN SAID SHE HAD SOME OF OUR MAIL BY ACCIDENT.
SHOOT! I SHOULDA TRUSTED MY SYLVIA... THAT'S EXACTLY WHAT SHE SAID.. CARRIE ANN...
...LISTEN UP! IF MRS. GRONAN NEEDS A SPIDER KILLED THEN YOU GO UP AND DO IT CAUSE YER BROTHER IS TOO BUSY TAKING CARE OF YER MOM AND WERE NOT GONNA LET MRS. GRONAN PESTER YER BROTHER, UNDERSTAND? I'M GONNA SEND ONE OF MY BOYS TA GIVE YOU A LITTLE PRESENT, OK?
CLICK

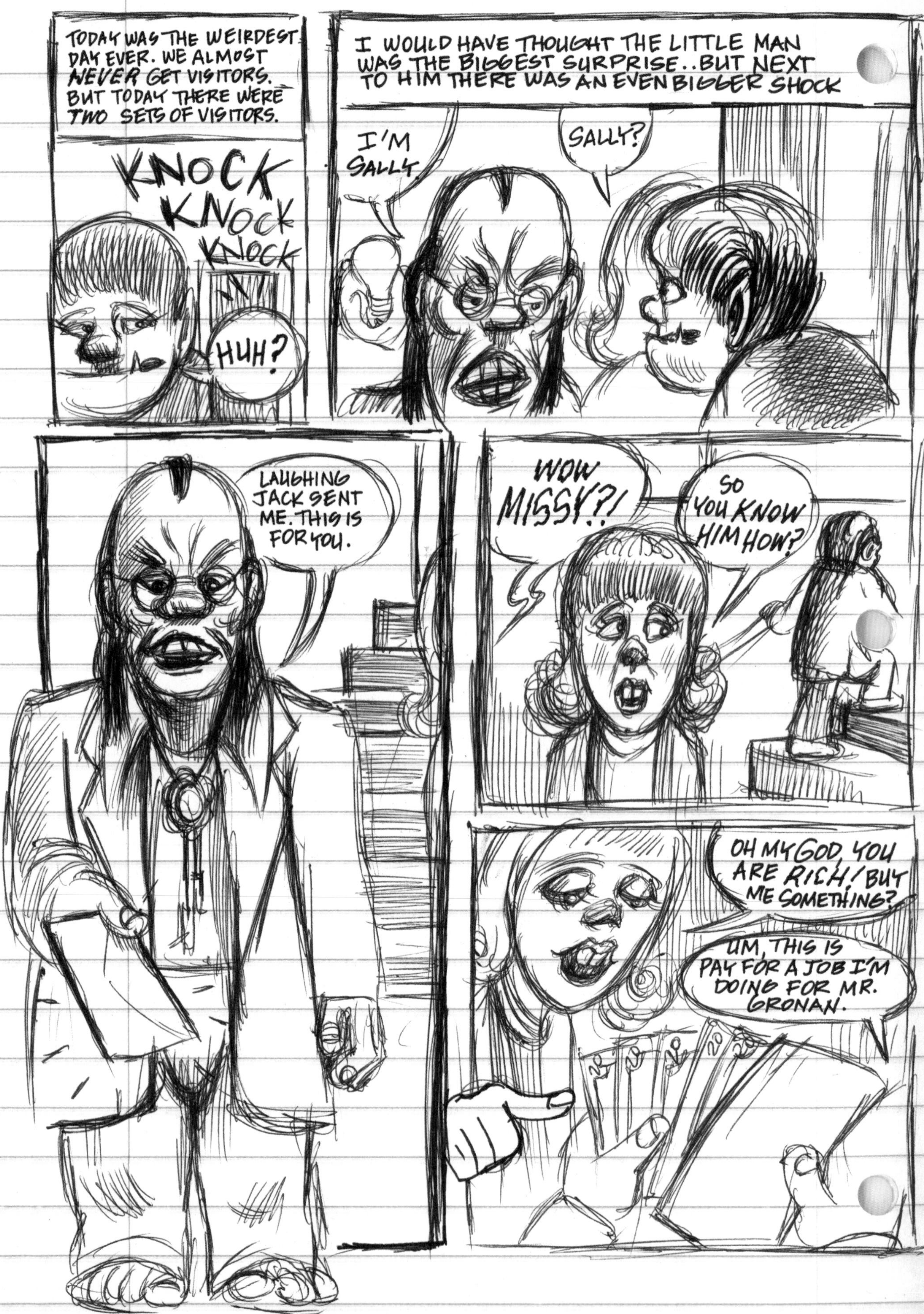
TODAY WAS THE WEIRDEST DAY EVER. WE ALMOST NEVER GET VISITORS. BUT TODAY THERE WERE TWO SETS OF VISITORS.
KNOCK KNOCK KNOCK
HUH?
I WOULD HAVE THOUGHT THE LITTLE MAN WAS THE BIGGEST SURPRISE..BUT NEXT TO HIM THERE WAS AN EVEN BIGGER SHOCK
I'M SALLY.
SALLY?
LAUGHING JACK SENT ME. THIS IS FOR YOU.
WOW MISSY?!
SO YOU KNOW HIM HOW?
OH MY GOD, YOU ARE RICH! BUY ME SOMETHING?
UM, THIS IS PAY FOR A JOB I'M DOING FOR MR. GRONAN.

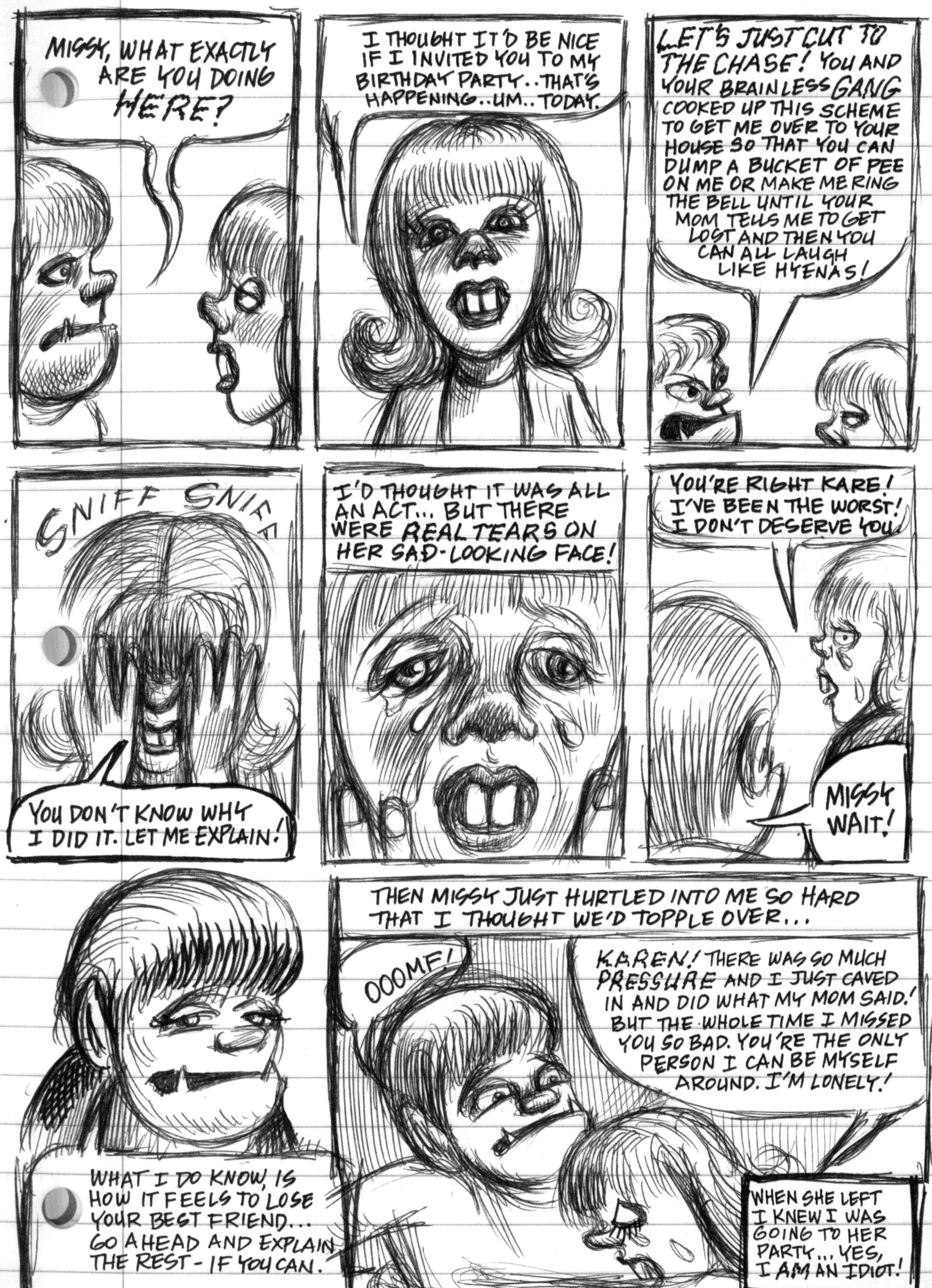

MISSY, WHAT EXACTLY ARE YOU DOING HERE?
I THOUGHT IT'D BE NICE IF I INVITED YOU TO MY BIRTHDAY PARTY.. THAT'S HAPPENING..UM.. TODAY.
LET'S JUST CUT TO THE CHASE! YOU AND YOUR BRAINLESS GANG COOKED UP THIS SCHEME TO GET ME OVER TO YOUR HOUSE SO THAT YOU CAN DUMP A BUCKET OF PEE ON ME OR MAKE ME RING THE BELL UNTIL YOUR MOM TELLS ME TO GET LOST AND THEN YOU CAN ALL LAUGH LIKE HYENAS!
SNIFF SNIFF
YOU DON'T KNOW WHY I DID IT. LET ME EXPLAIN!
I'D THOUGHT IT WAS ALL AN ACT... BUT THERE WERE REAL TEARS ON HER SAD-LOOKING FACE!
YOU'RE RIGHT KARE! I'VE BEEN THE WORST! I DON'T DESERVE YOU.
MISSY WAIT!
WHAT I DO KNOW, IS HOW IT FEELS TO LOSE YOUR BEST FRIEND... GO AHEAD AND EXPLAIN THE REST - IF YOU CAN.
THEN MISSY JUST HURTLED INTO ME SO HARD THAT I THOUGHT WE'D TOPPLE OVER...
OOOMF!
KAREN! THERE WAS SO MUCH PRESSURE AND I JUST CAVED IN AND DID WHAT MY MOM SAID! BUT THE WHOLE TIME I MISSED YOU SO BAD. YOU'RE THE ONLY PERSON I CAN BE MYSELF AROUND. I'M LONELY!
WHEN SHE LEFT I KNEW I WAS GOING TO HER PARTY... YES, I AM AN IDIOT!

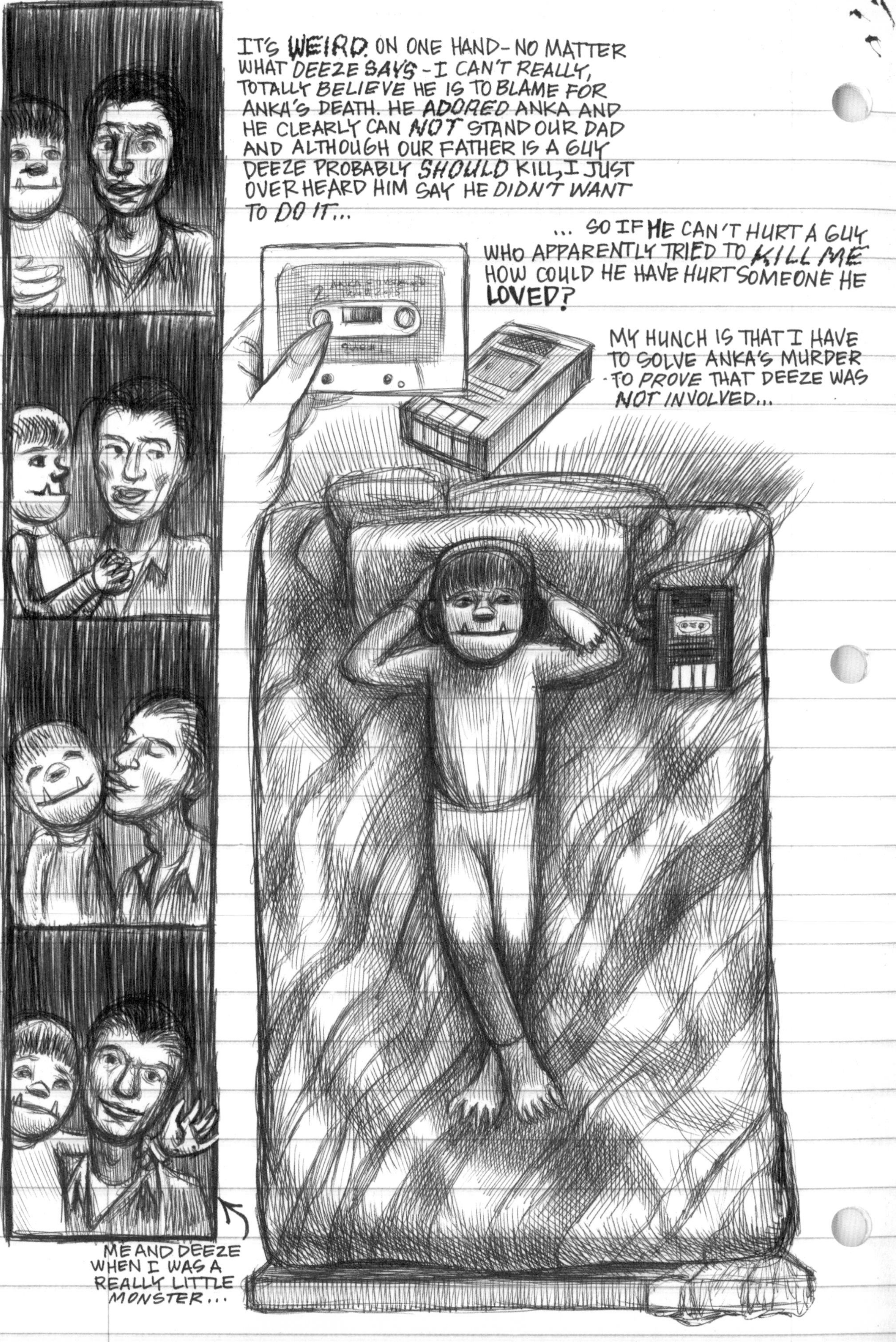
IT'S WEIRD. ON ONE HAND- NO MATTER WHAT DEEZE SAYS - I CAN'T REALLY, TOTALLY BELIEVE HE IS TO BLAME FOR ANKA'S DEATH. HE ADORED ANKA AND HE CLEARLY CAN NOT STAND OUR DAD AND ALTHOUGH OUR FATHER IS A GUY DEEZE PROBABLY SHOULD KILL, I JUST OVERHEARD HIM SAY HE DIDN'T WANT TO DO IT...
... SO IF HE CAN'T HURT A GUY WHO APPARENTLY TRIED TO KILL ME HOW COULD HE HAVE HURT SOMEONE HE LOVED?
MY HUNCH IS THAT I HAVE TO SOLVE ANKA'S MURDER - TO PROVE THAT DEEZE WAS NOT INVOLVED...
ME AND DEEZE WHEN I WAS A REALLY LITTLE MONSTER...

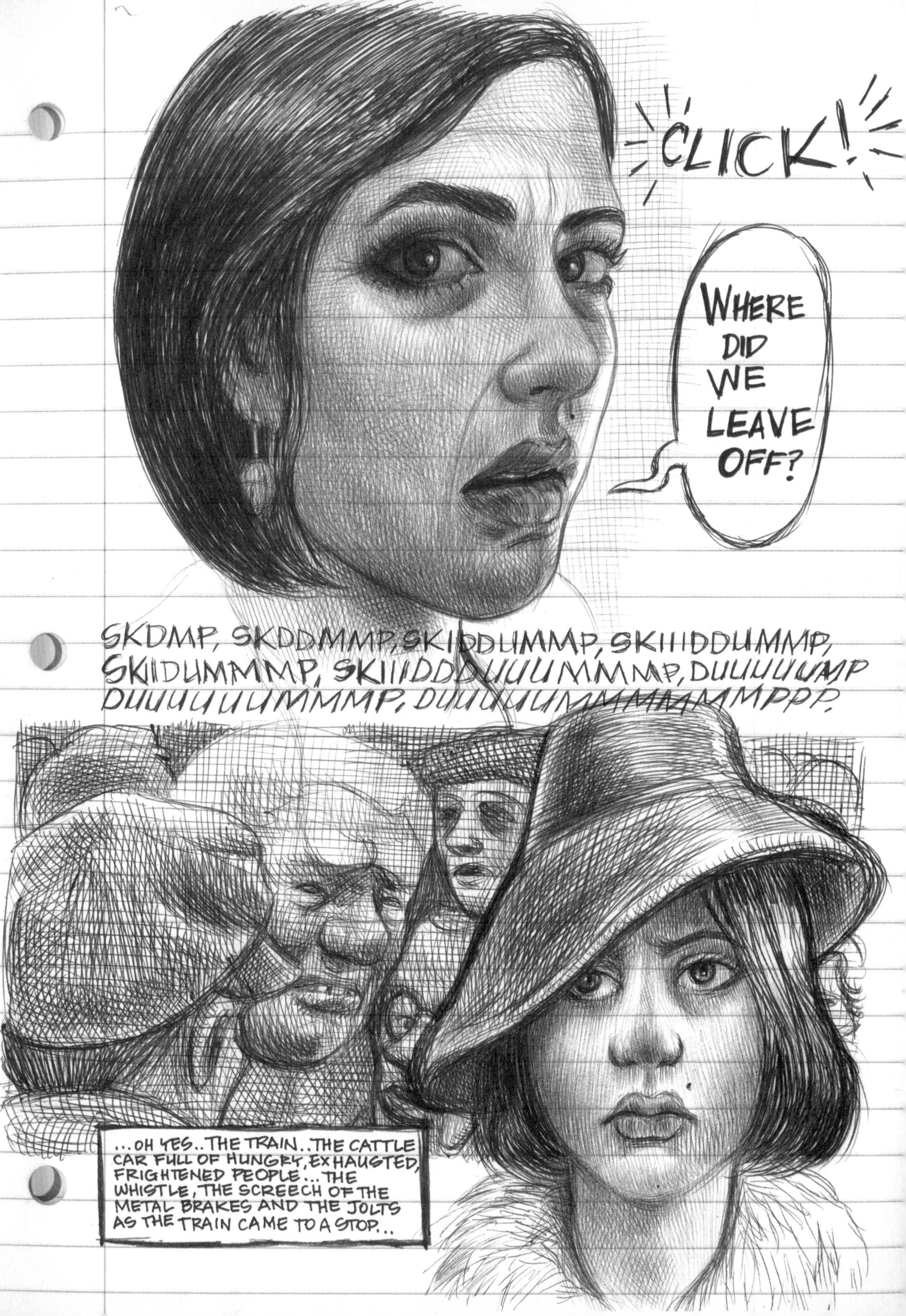
CLICK!
WHERE DID WE LEAVE OFF?
SKDMP, SKDDMMP, SKIDDUMMP, SKIIIDDUMMP, SKIIDUMMMP, SKIIIDDDUUUMMMMP, DUUUUUMP DUUUUUUMMMMP, DUUUUUUMMMMMMMMPPP.
...OH YES.. THE TRAIN.. THE CATTLE CAR FULL OF HUNGRY, EXHAUSTED, FRIGHTENED PEOPLE... THE WHISTLE, THE SCREECH OF THE METAL BRAKES AND THE JOLTS AS THE TRAIN CAME TO A STOP...

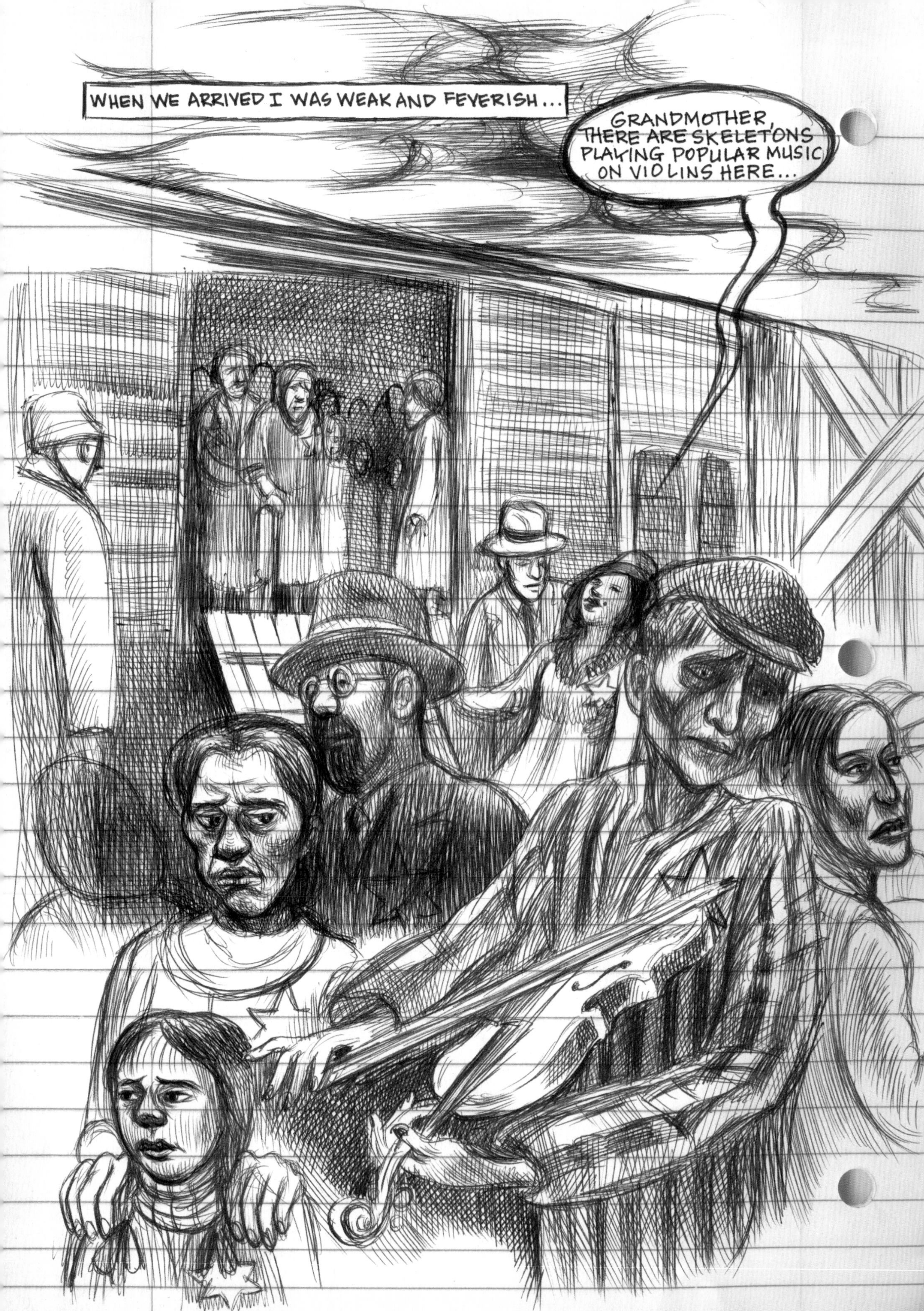
WHEN WE ARRIVED I WAS WEAK AND FEVERISH...
GRANDMOTHER, THERE ARE SKELETONS PLAYING POPULAR MUSIC ON VIOLINS HERE...

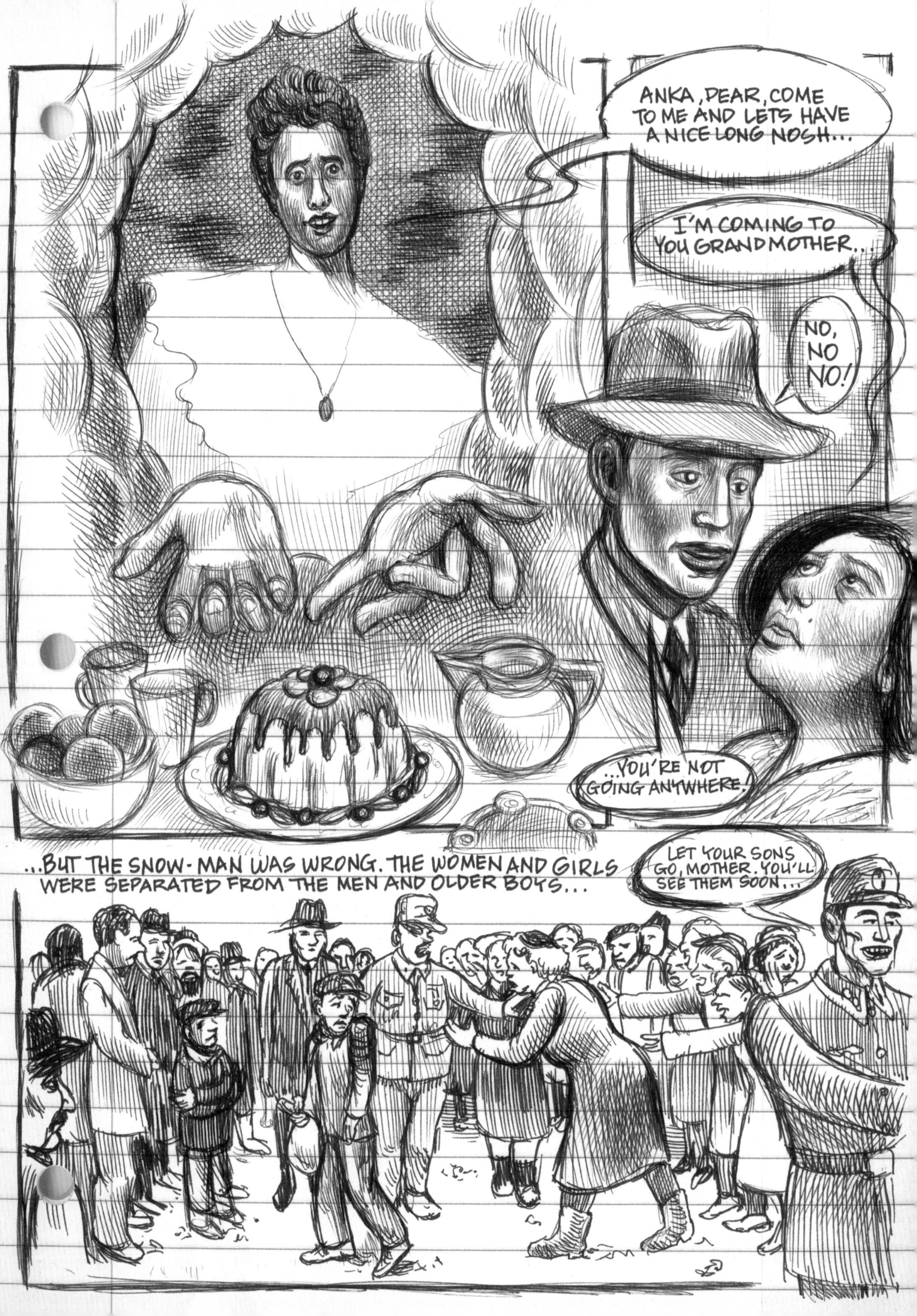
ANKA, DEAR, COME TO ME AND LETS HAVE A NICE LONG NOSH...
I'M COMING TO YOU GRANDMOTHER...
NO, NO NO!
...YOU'RE NOT GOING ANYWHERE.
...BUT THE SNOW-MAN WAS WRONG. THE WOMEN AND GIRLS WERE SEPARATED FROM THE MEN AND OLDER BOYS...
LET YOUR SONS GO, MOTHER. YOU'LL SEE THEM SOON...

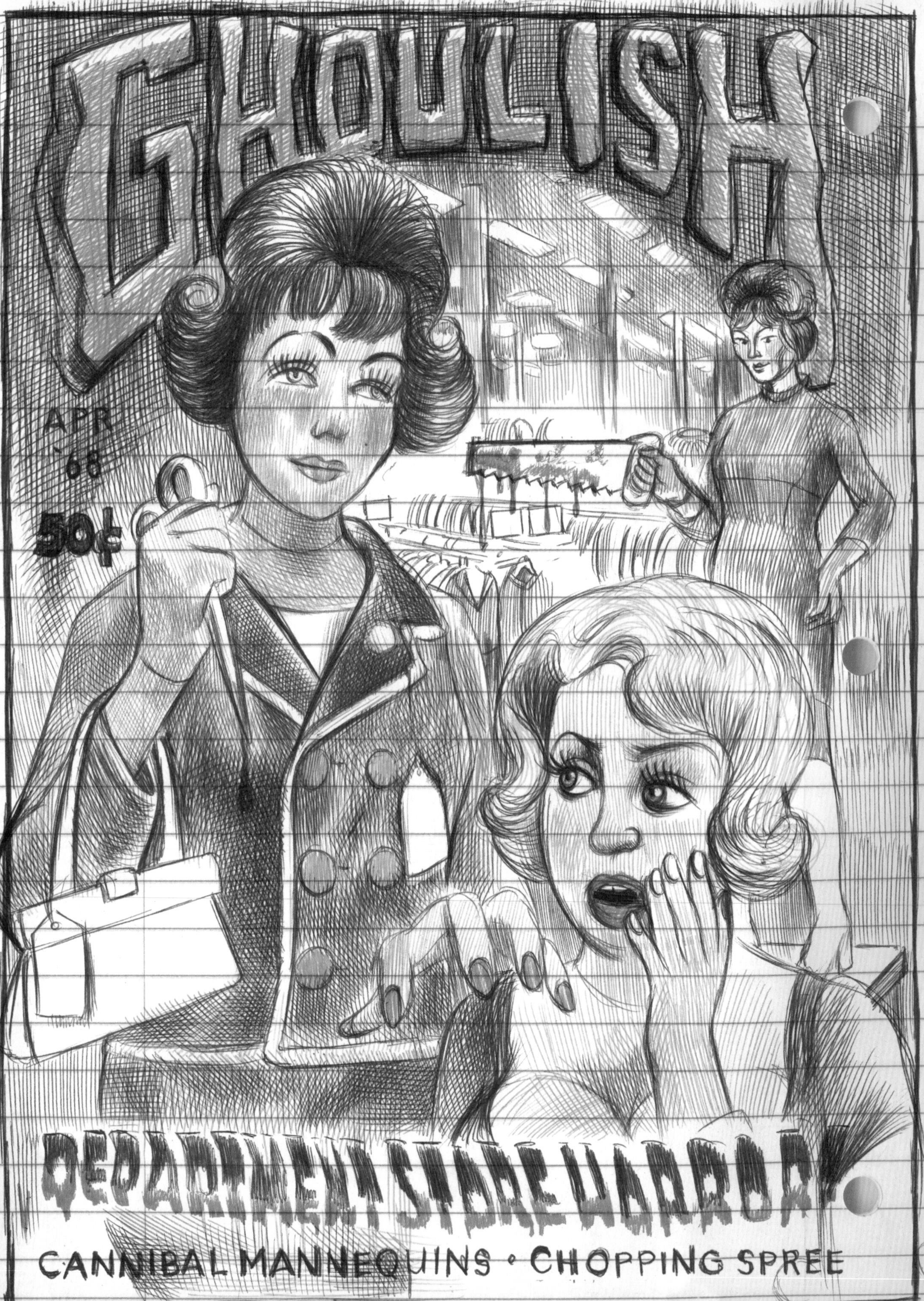
GHOULISH
APR '68
50¢
DEPARTMENT STORE HORROR!
CANNIBAL MANNEQUINS • CHOPPING SPREE

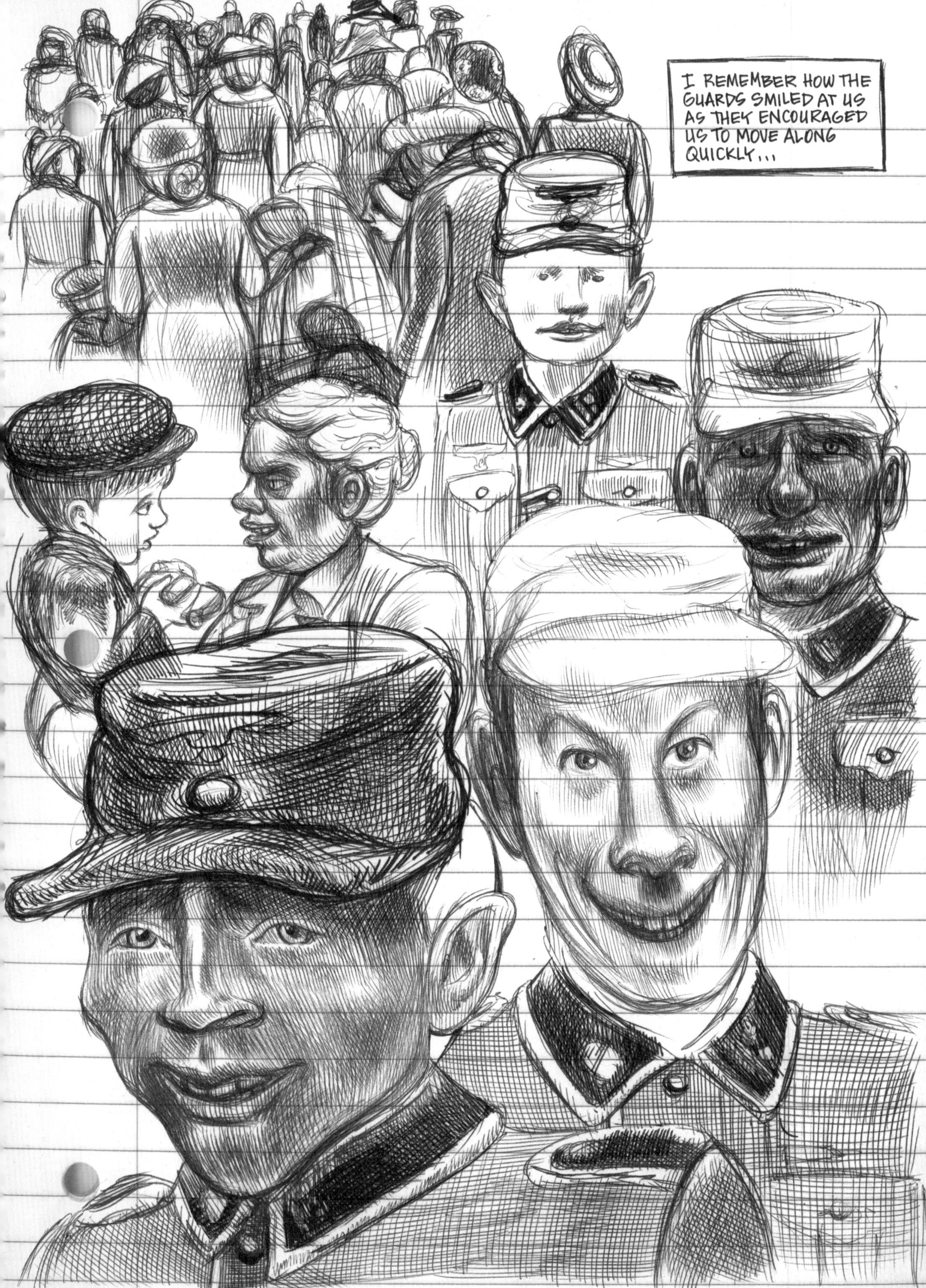
I REMEMBER HOW THE GUARDS SMILED AT US AS THEY ENCOURAGED US TO MOVE ALONG QUICKLY...

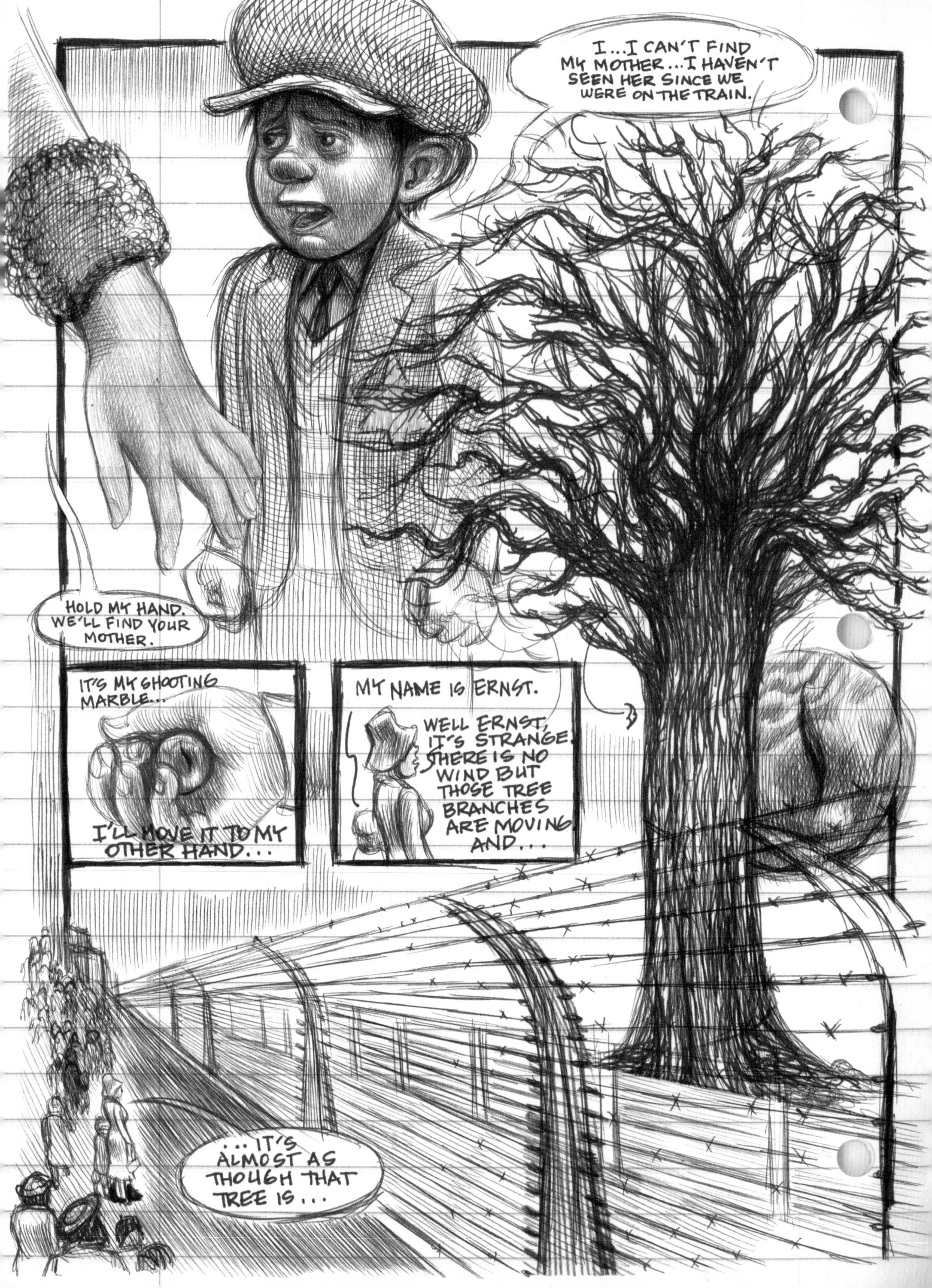
I... I CAN'T FIND MY MOTHER... I HAVEN'T SEEN HER SINCE WE WERE ON THE TRAIN.
HOLD MY HAND. WE'LL FIND YOUR MOTHER.
IT'S MY SHOOTING MARBLE...
I'LL MOVE IT TO MY OTHER HAND...
MY NAME IS ERNST.
WELL ERNST, IT'S STRANGE. THERE IS NO WIND BUT THOSE TREE BRANCHES ARE MOVING AND...
... IT'S ALMOST AS THOUGH THAT TREE IS...

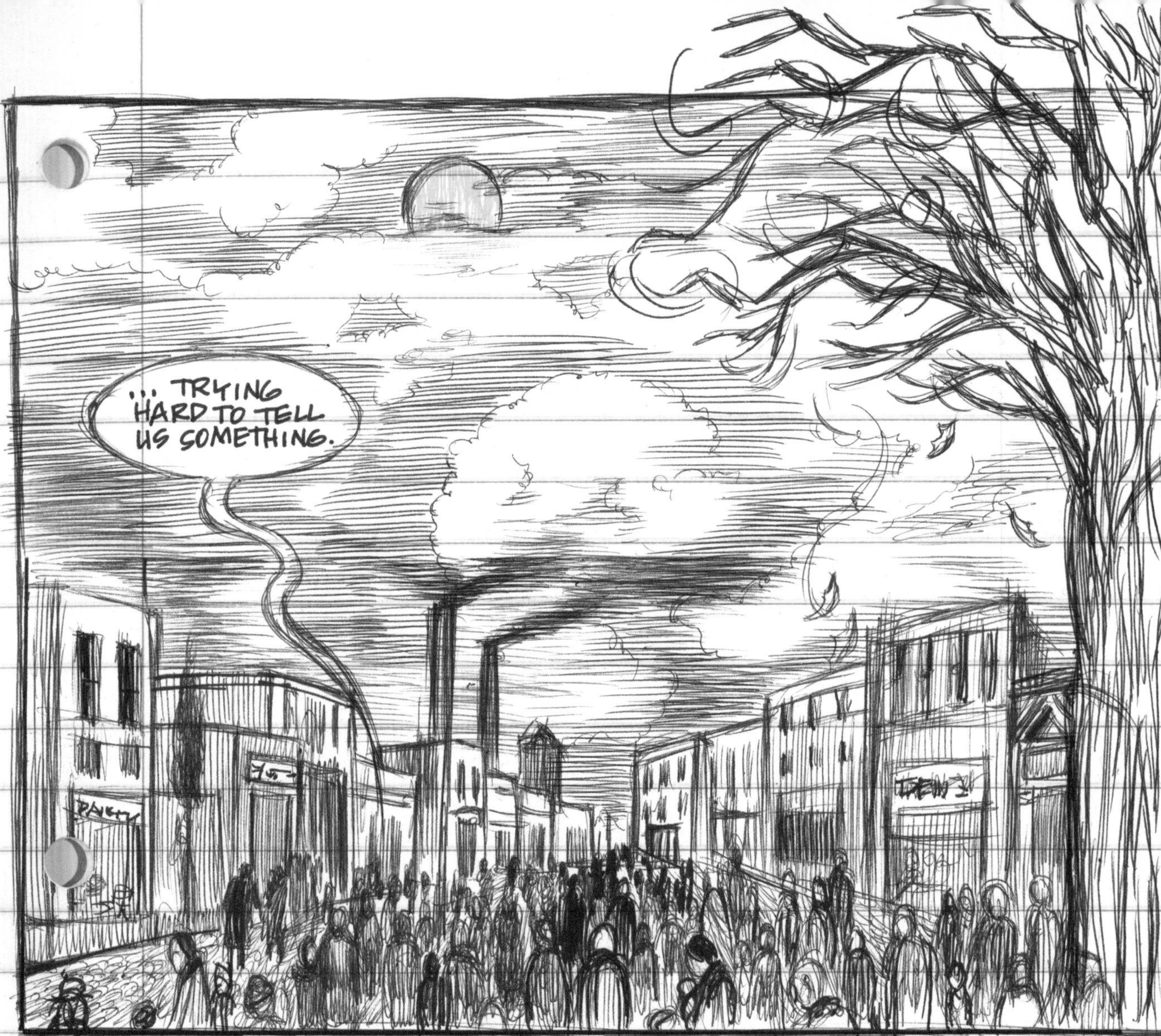
... TRYING HARD TO TELL US SOMETHING.

AS WE WERE MARCHED DOWN A WIDE BOULEVARD LINED WITH STOREFRONTS, I NOTICED THE TWO SISTERS WHOM I'D FIRST SEEN ON THE TRAIN.

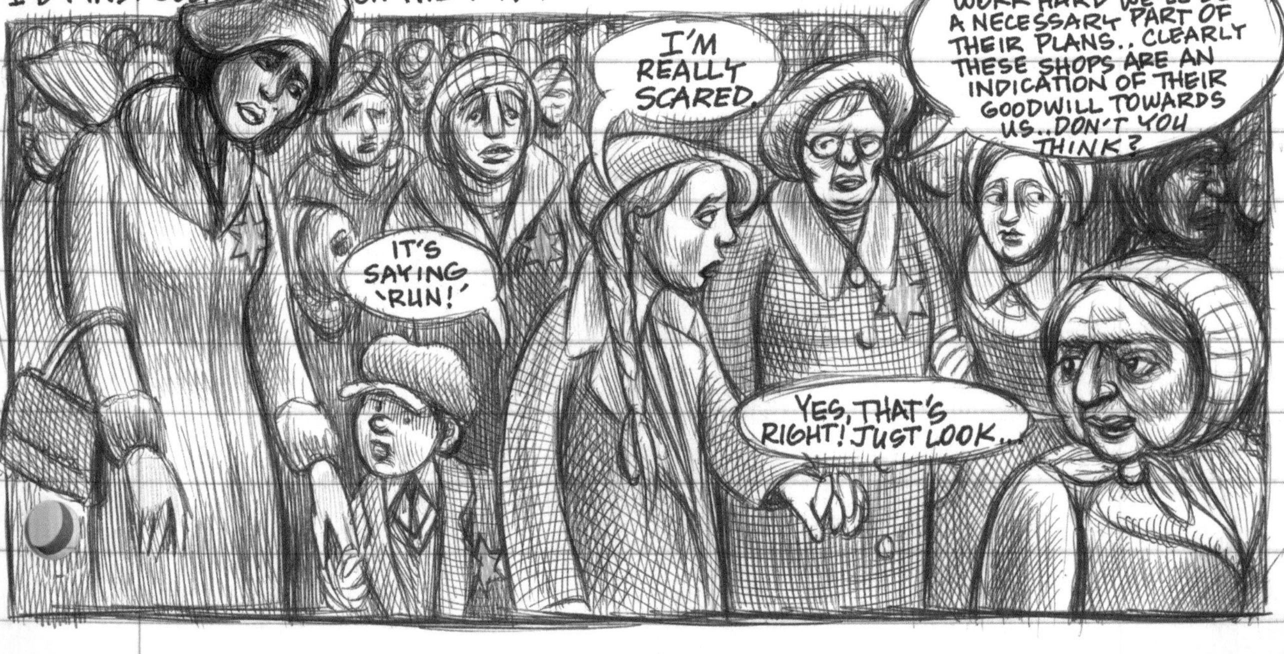
I'M REALLY SCARED.
THIS IS A LABOR CAMP. IF WE WORK HARD WE'LL BE A NECESSARY PART OF THEIR PLANS.. CLEARLY THESE SHOPS ARE AN INDICATION OF THEIR GOODWILL TOWARDS US..DON'T YOU THINK?
IT'S SAYING 'RUN!'
YES, THAT'S RIGHT! JUST LOOK...

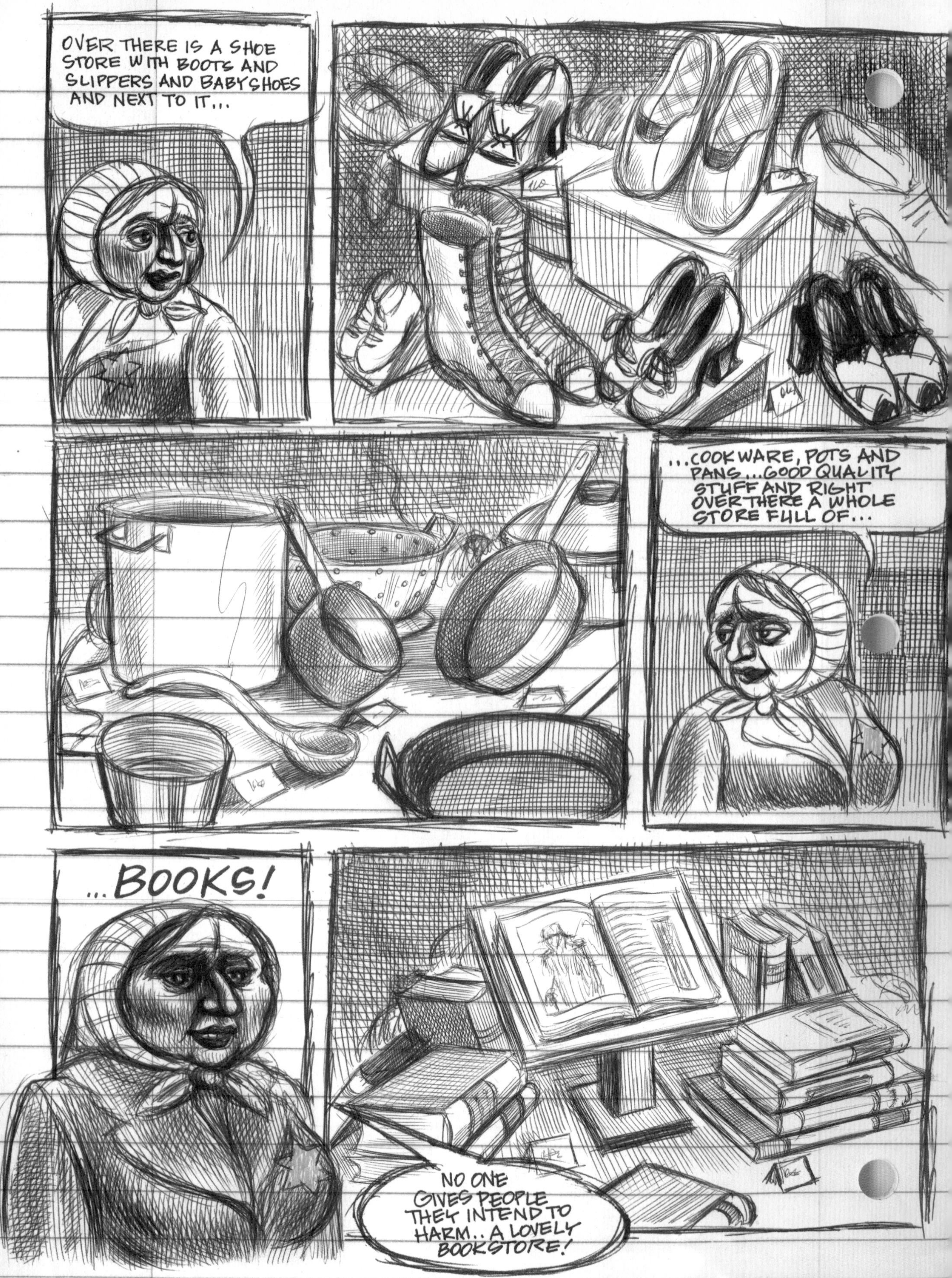
OVER THERE IS A SHOE STORE WITH BOOTS AND SLIPPERS AND BABYSHOES AND NEXT TO IT...
...COOKWARE, POTS AND PANS...GOOD QUALITY STUFF AND RIGHT OVER THERE A WHOLE STORE FULL OF...
...BOOKS!
NO ONE GIVES PEOPLE THEY INTEND TO HARM.. A LOVELY BOOKSTORE!

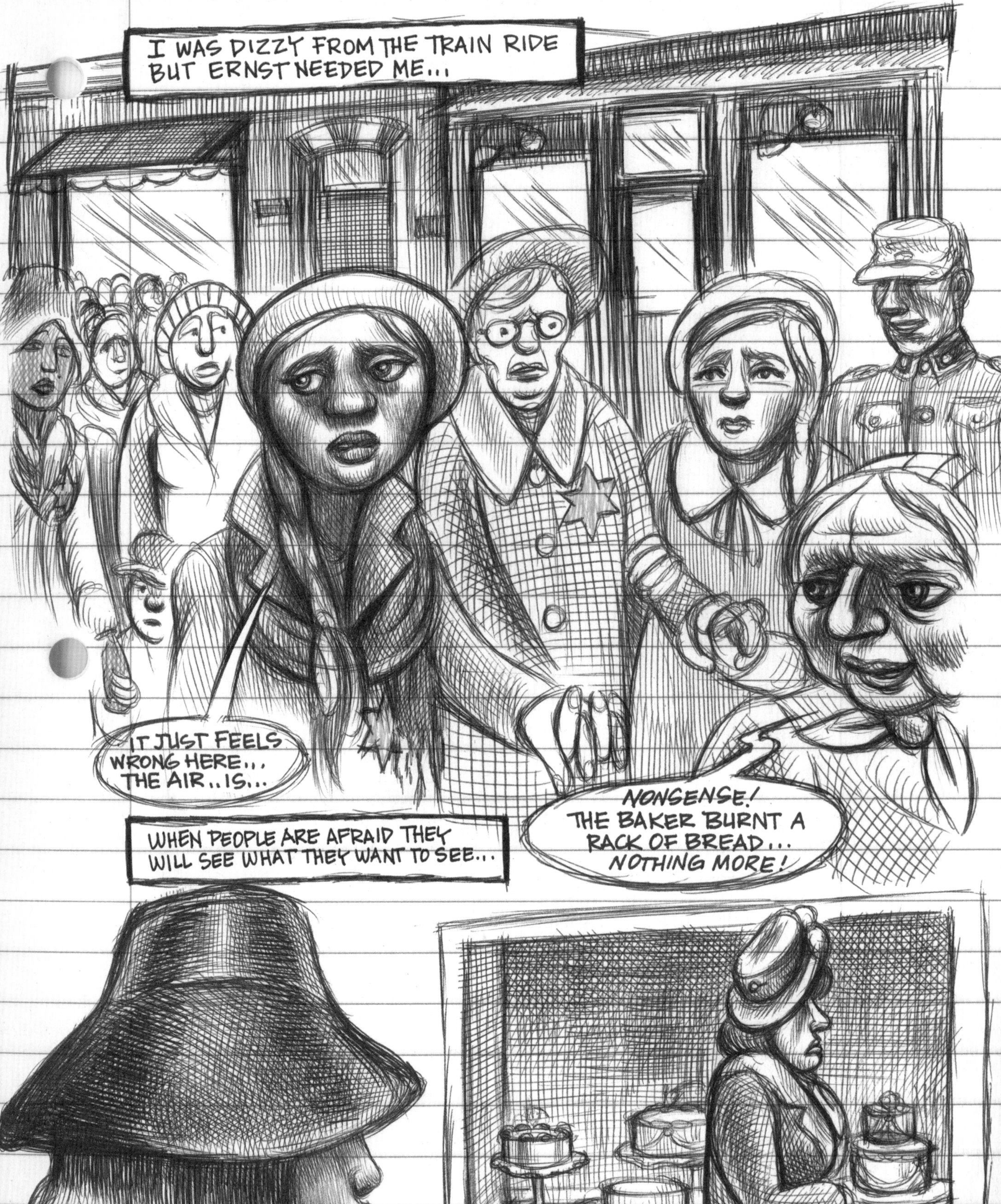
I WAS DIZZY FROM THE TRAIN RIDE BUT ERNST NEEDED ME...
IT JUST FEELS WRONG HERE... THE AIR.. IS...
NONSENSE! THE BAKER BURNT A RACK OF BREAD... NOTHING MORE!
WHEN PEOPLE ARE AFRAID THEY WILL SEE WHAT THEY WANT TO SEE...
HUH?

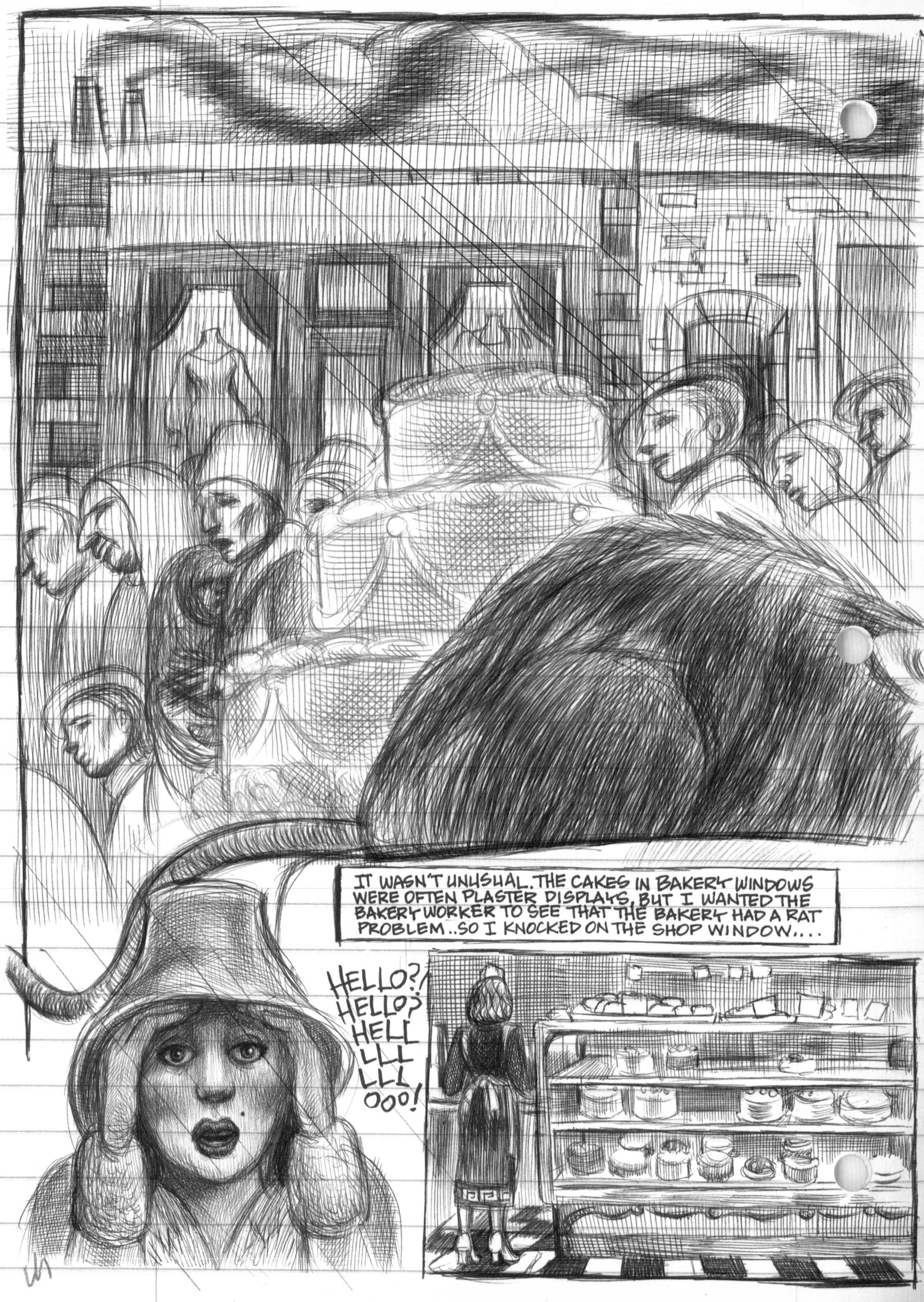
IT WASN'T UNUSUAL. THE CAKES IN BAKERY WINDOWS WERE OFTEN PLASTER DISPLAYS, BUT I WANTED THE BAKERY WORKER TO SEE THAT THE BAKERY HAD A RAT PROBLEM..SO I KNOCKED ON THE SHOP WINDOW....
HELLO?! HELLO? HELL LLL LLL OOO!

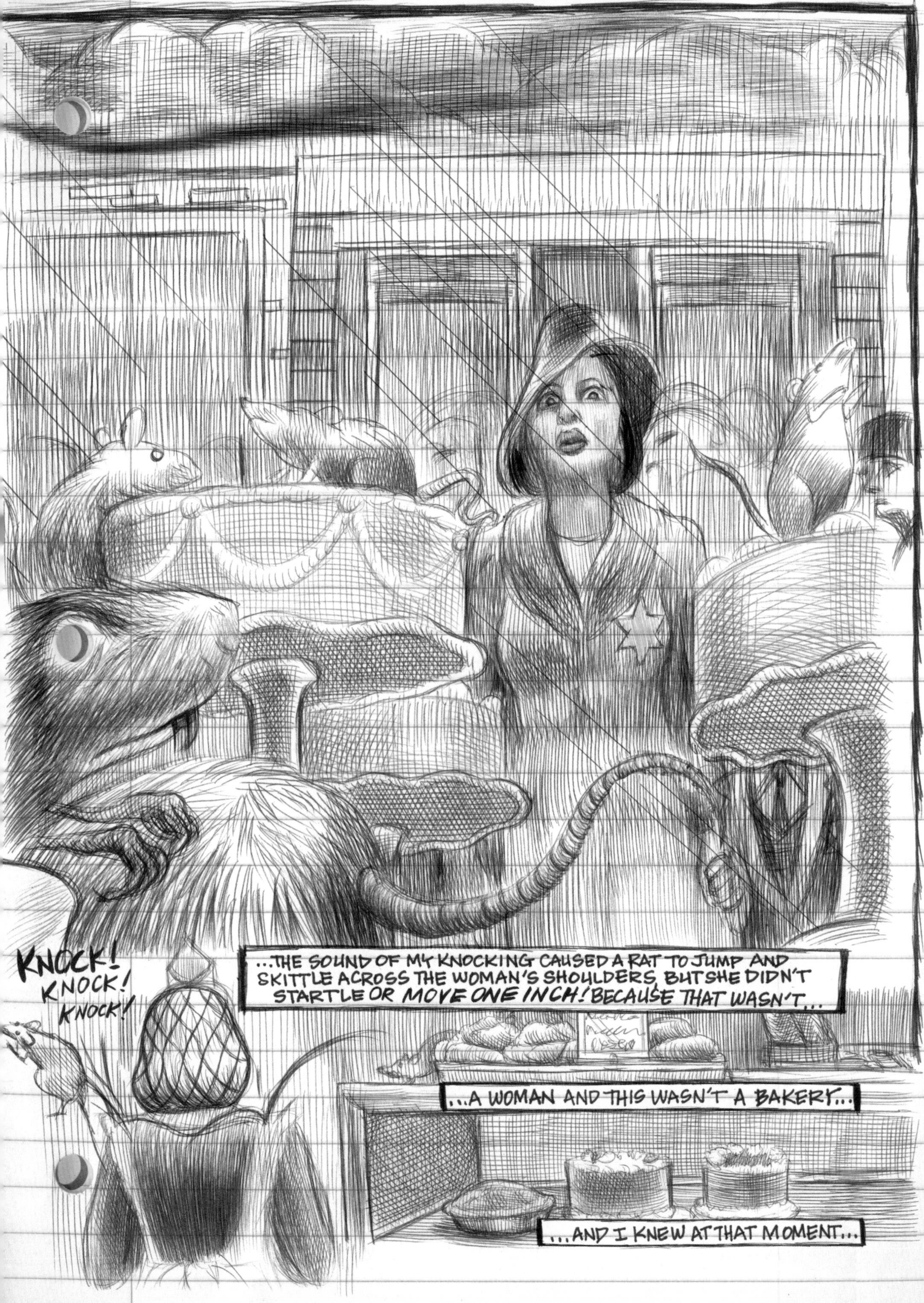
KNOCK! KNOCK! KNOCK!
...THE SOUND OF MY KNOCKING CAUSED A RAT TO JUMP AND SKITTLE ACROSS THE WOMAN'S SHOULDERS, BUT SHE DIDN'T STARTLE OR MOVE ONE INCH! BECAUSE THAT WASN'T...
...A WOMAN AND THIS WASN'T A BAKERY...
...AND I KNEW AT THAT MOMENT...

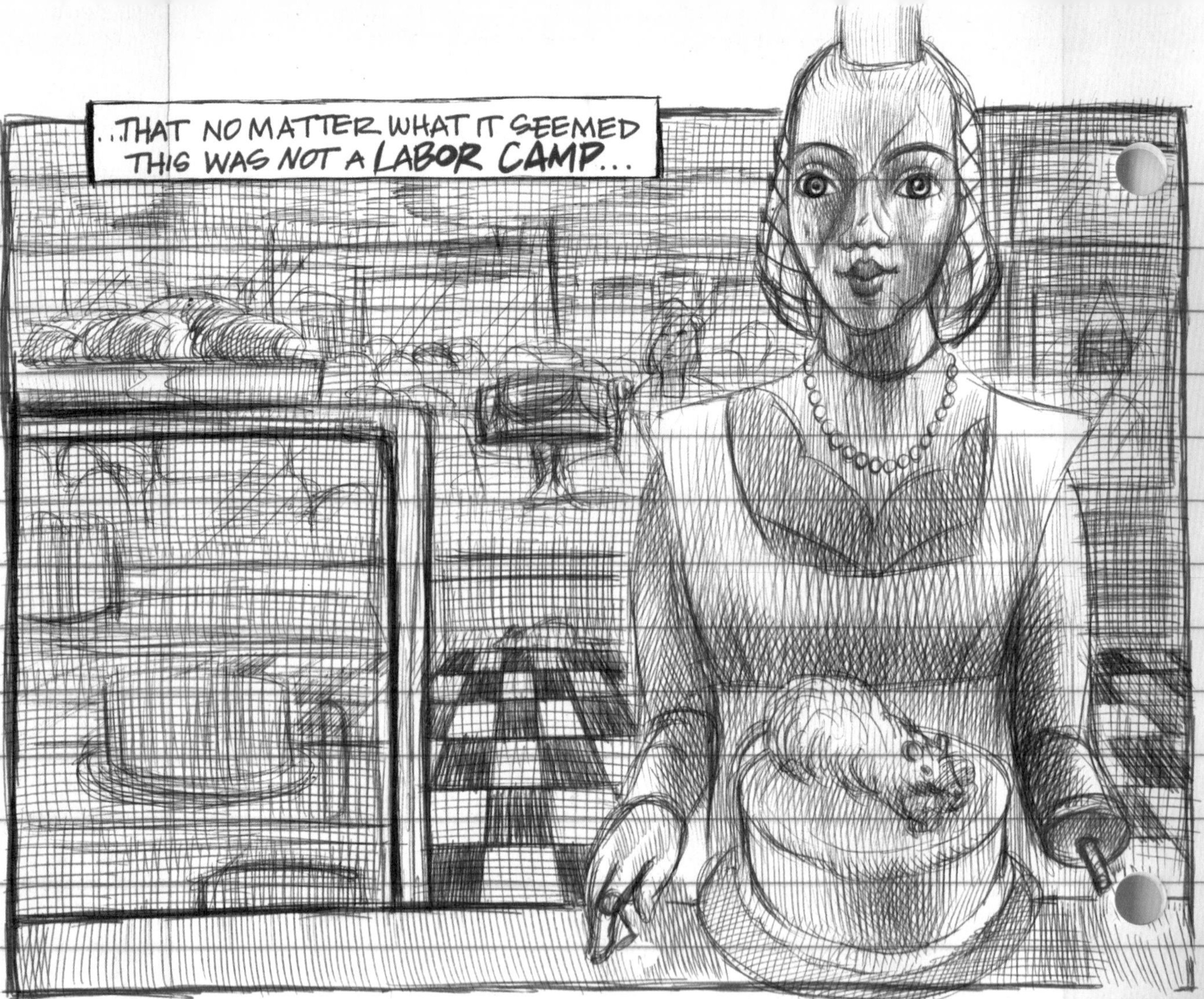
...THAT NO MATTER WHAT IT SEEMED THIS WAS NOT A LABOR CAMP...

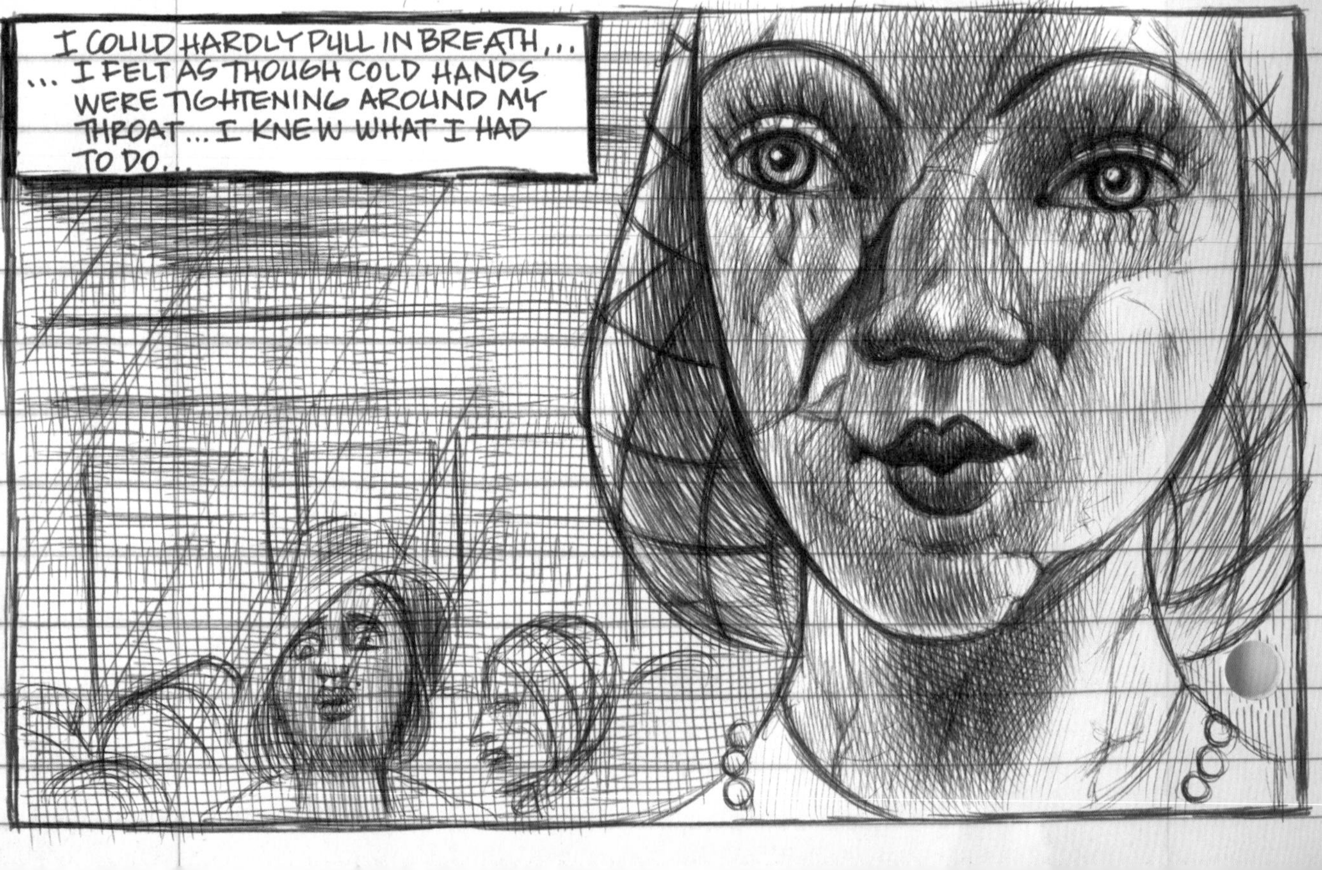
I COULD HARDLY PULL IN BREATH... ... I FELT AS THOUGH COLD HANDS WERE TIGHTENING AROUND MY THROAT... I KNEW WHAT I HAD TO DO...

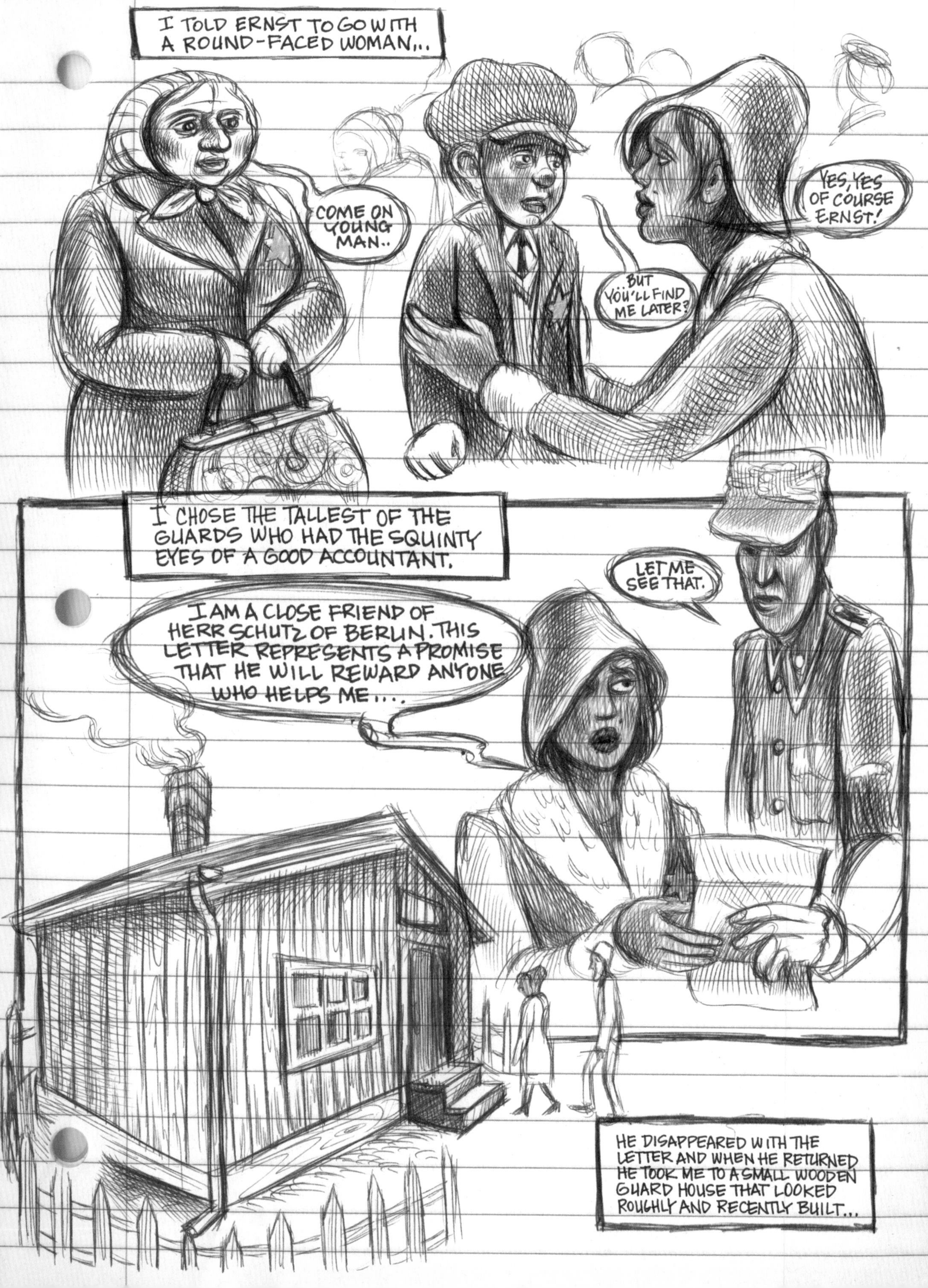
I TOLD ERNST TO GO WITH A ROUND-FACED WOMAN...
COME ON YOUNG MAN..
BUT YOU'LL FIND ME LATER?
YES, YES OF COURSE ERNST!
I CHOSE THE TALLEST OF THE GUARDS WHO HAD THE SQUINTY EYES OF A GOOD ACCOUNTANT.
I AM A CLOSE FRIEND OF HERR SCHUTZ OF BERLIN. THIS LETTER REPRESENTS A PROMISE THAT HE WILL REWARD ANYONE WHO HELPS ME...
LET ME SEE THAT.
HE DISAPPEARED WITH THE LETTER AND WHEN HE RETURNED HE TOOK ME TO A SMALL WOODEN GUARD HOUSE THAT LOOKED ROUGHLY AND RECENTLY BUILT...

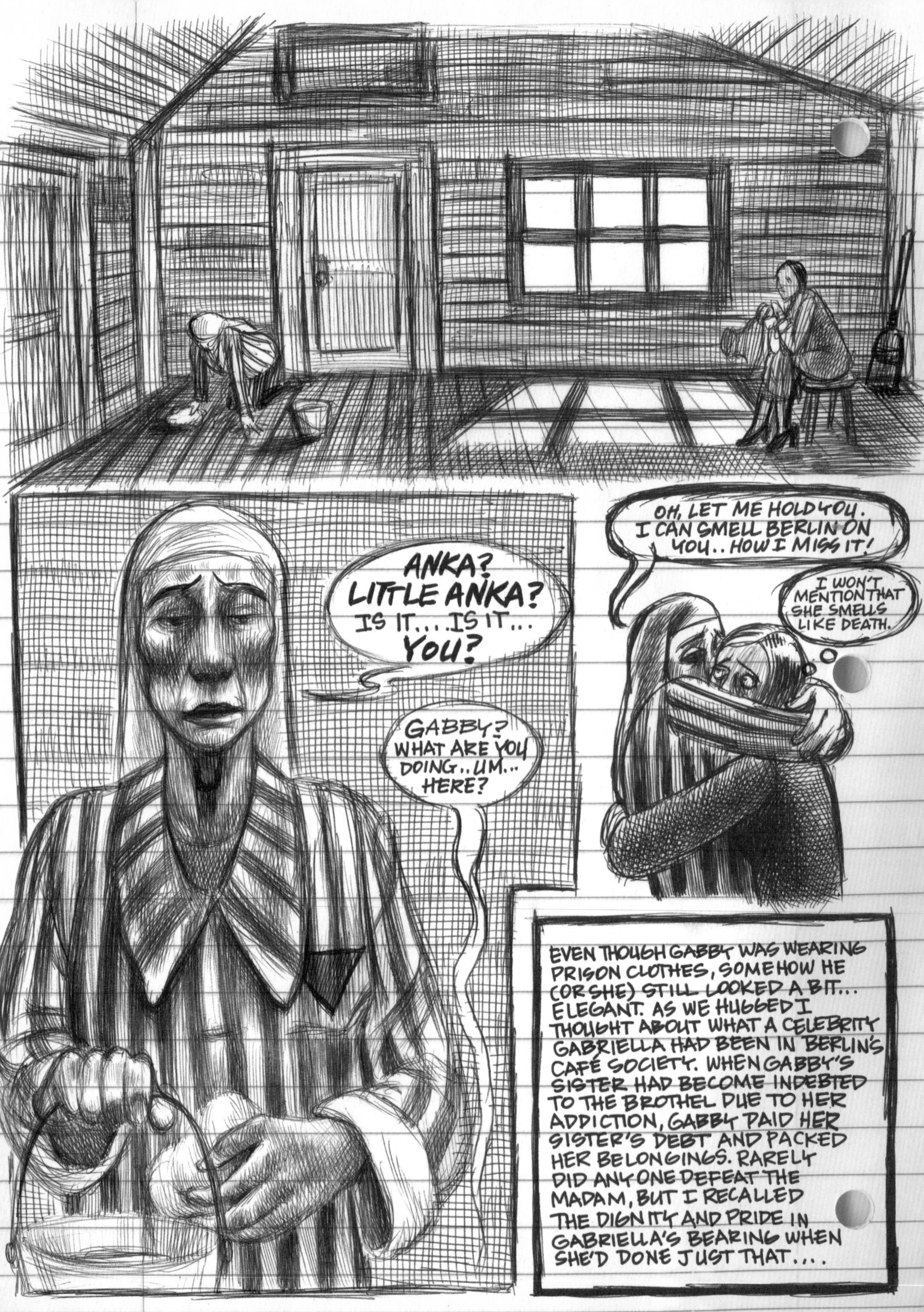
ANKA? LITTLE ANKA? IS IT.... IS IT... YOU?
GABBY? WHAT ARE YOU DOING.. UM... HERE?
OH, LET ME HOLD YOU. I CAN SMELL BERLIN ON YOU.. HOW I MISS IT!
I WON'T MENTION THAT SHE SMELLS LIKE DEATH.
EVEN THOUGH GABBY WAS WEARING PRISON CLOTHES, SOMEHOW HE (OR SHE) STILL LOOKED A BIT... ELEGANT. AS WE HUGGED I THOUGHT ABOUT WHAT A CELEBRITY GABRIELLA HAD BEEN IN BERLIN'S CAFÉ SOCIETY. WHEN GABBY'S SISTER HAD BECOME INDEBTED TO THE BROTHEL DUE TO HER ADDICTION, GABBY PAID HER SISTER'S DEBT AND PACKED HER BELONGINGS. RARELY DID ANYONE DEFEAT THE MADAM, BUT I RECALLED THE DIGNITY AND PRIDE IN GABRIELLA'S BEARING WHEN SHE'D DONE JUST THAT....

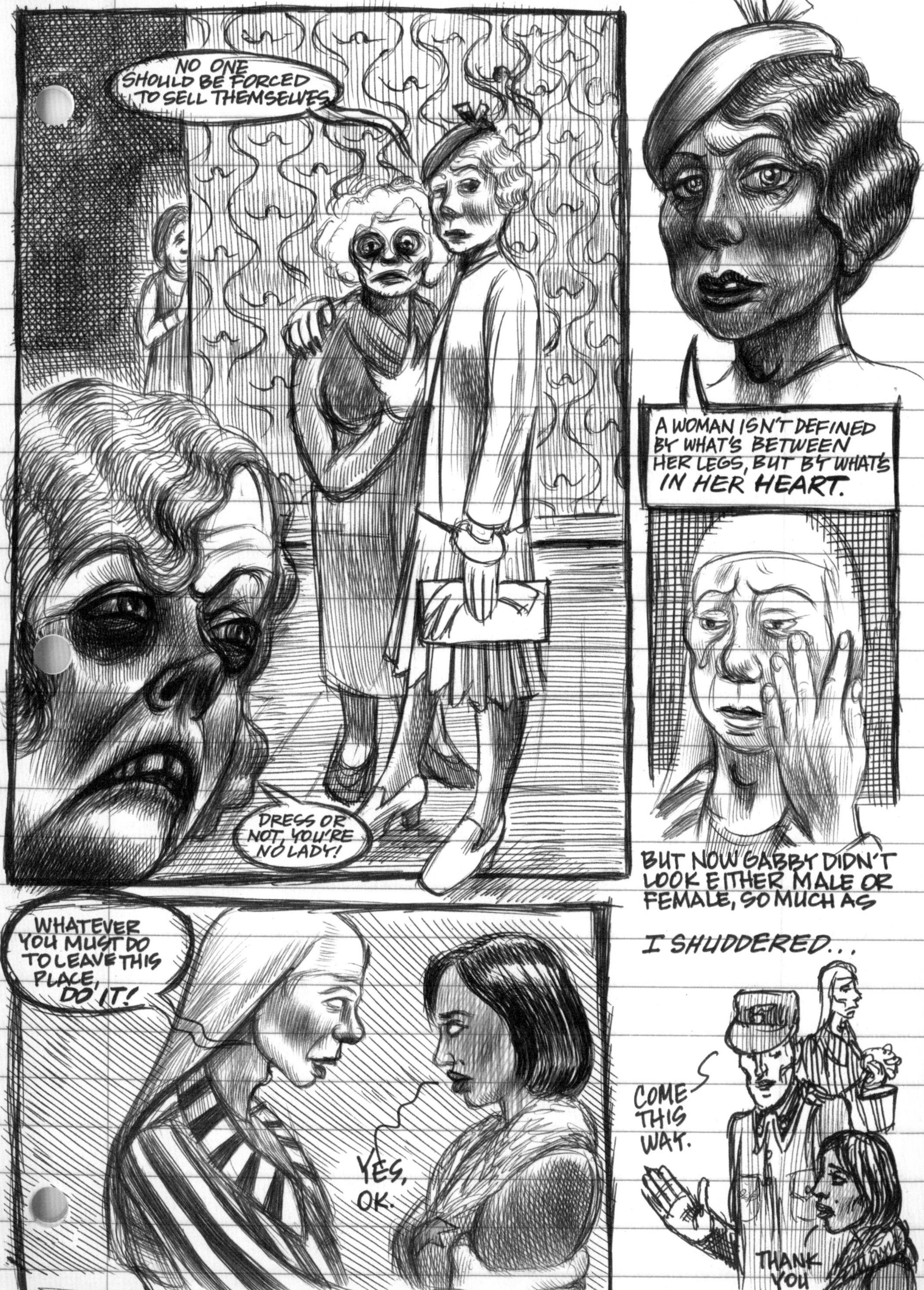

NO ONE SHOULD BE FORCED TO SELL THEMSELVES
DRESS OR NOT, YOU'RE NO LADY!
A WOMAN ISN'T DEFINED BY WHAT'S BETWEEN HER LEGS, BUT BY WHAT'S IN HER HEART.
BUT NOW GABBY DIDN'T LOOK EITHER MALE OR FEMALE, SO MUCH AS
WHATEVER YOU MUST DO TO LEAVE THIS PLACE, DO IT!
YES, OK.
I SHUDDERED...
COME THIS WAY.
THANK YOU

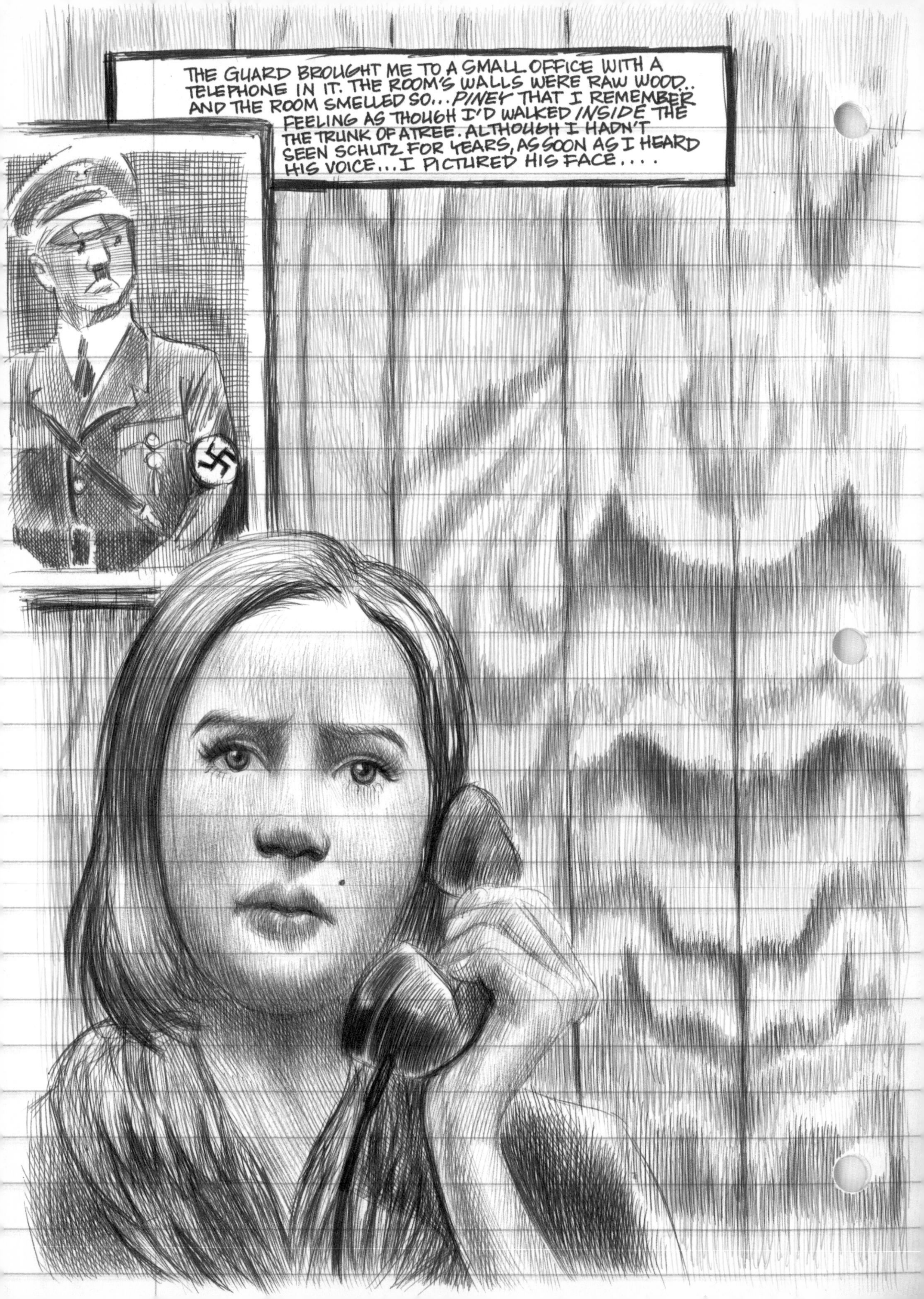
THE GUARD BROUGHT ME TO A SMALL OFFICE WITH A TELEPHONE IN IT. THE ROOM'S WALLS WERE RAW WOOD.. AND THE ROOM SMELLED SO... *PINEY* THAT I REMEMBER FEELING AS THOUGH I'D WALKED *INSIDE* THE TRUNK OF A TREE. ALTHOUGH I HADN'T SEEN SCHUTZ FOR YEARS, AS SOON AS I HEARD HIS VOICE... I PICTURED HIS FACE....

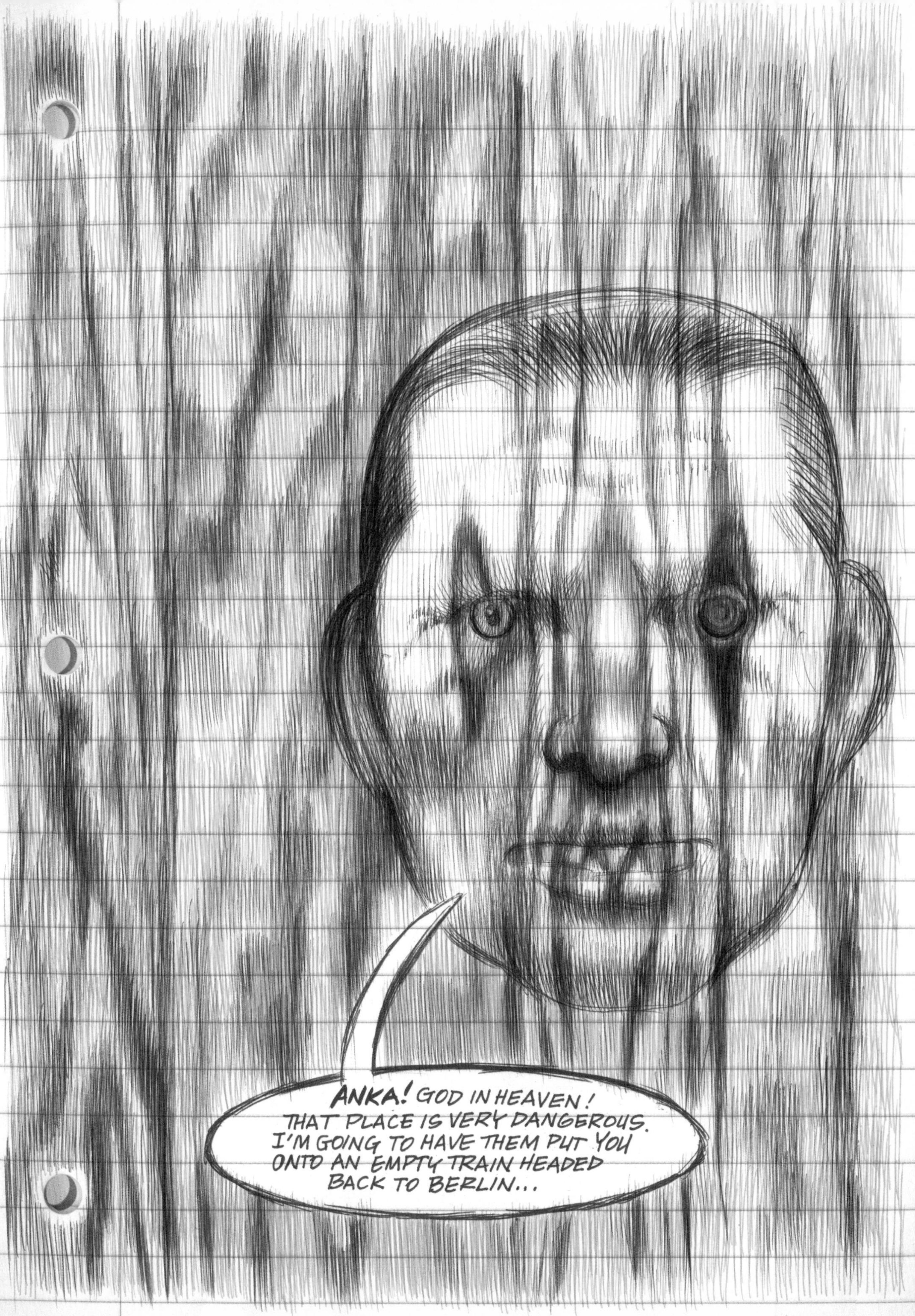
ANKA! GOD IN HEAVEN! THAT PLACE IS VERY DANGEROUS. I'M GOING TO HAVE THEM PUT YOU ONTO AN EMPTY TRAIN HEADED BACK TO BERLIN...

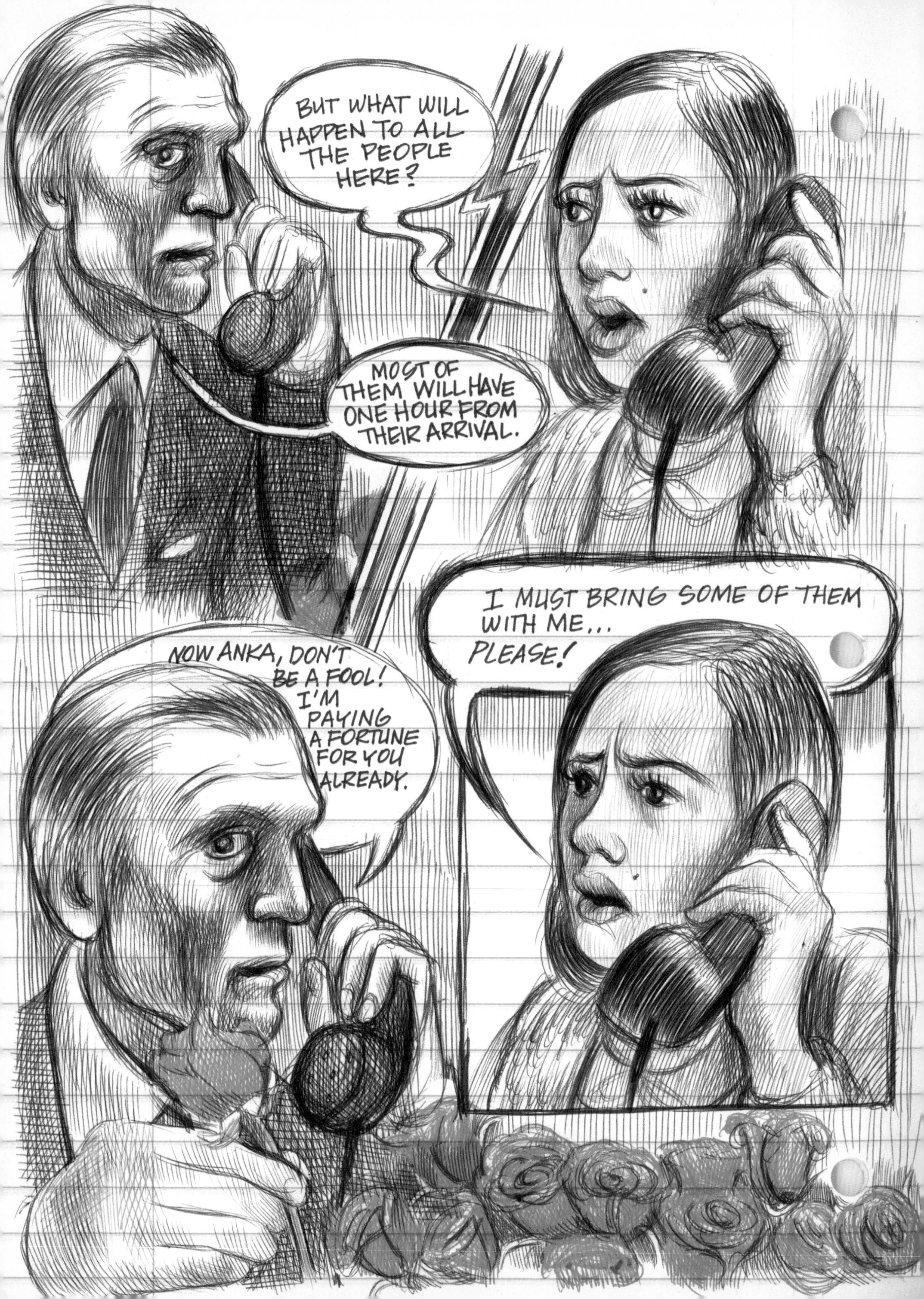
BUT WHAT WILL HAPPEN TO ALL THE PEOPLE HERE?
MOST OF THEM WILL HAVE ONE HOUR FROM THEIR ARRIVAL.
I MUST BRING SOME OF THEM WITH ME... PLEASE!
NOW ANKA, DON'T BE A FOOL! I'M PAYING A FORTUNE FOR YOU ALREADY.

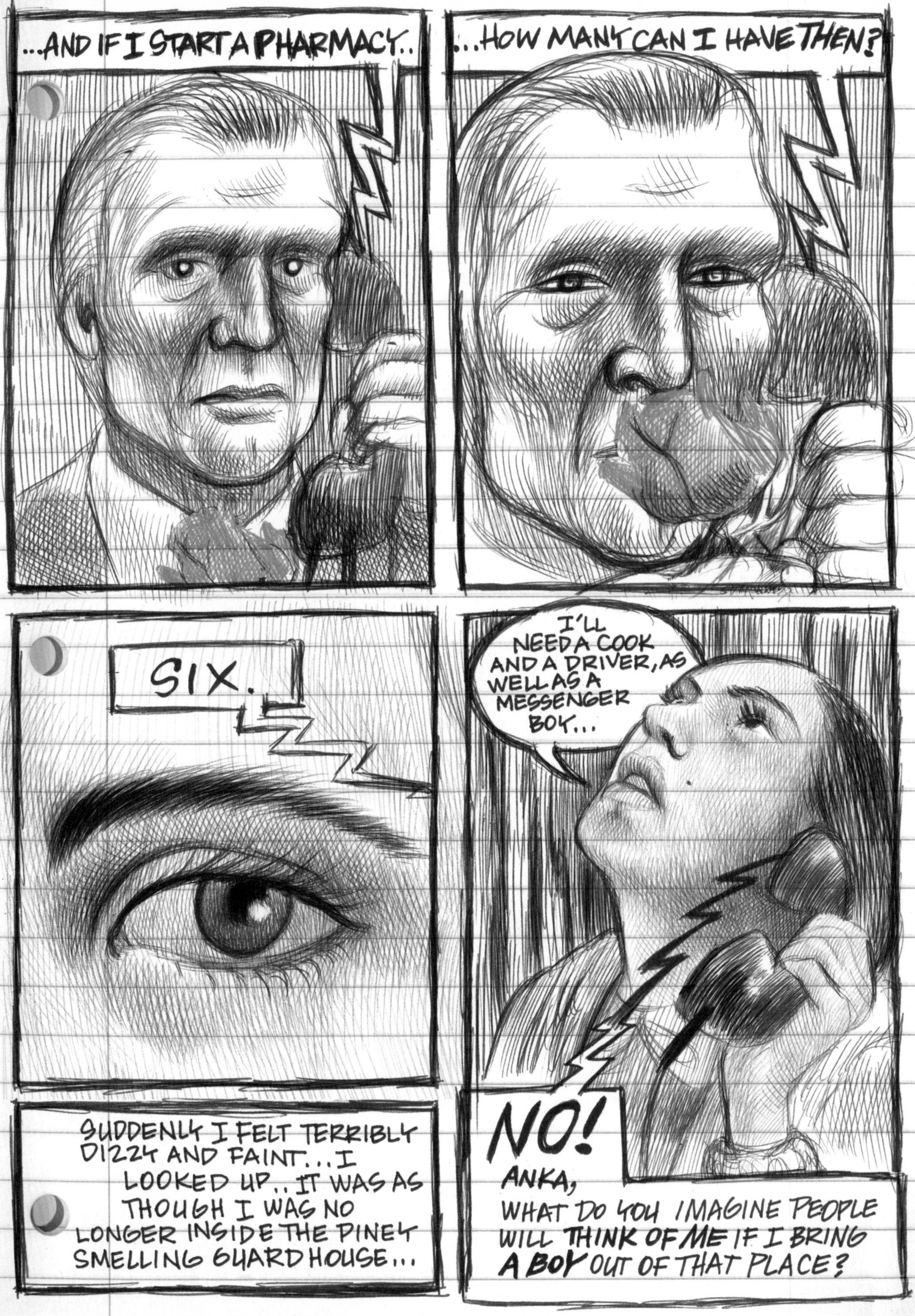
...AND IF I START A PHARMACY...
...HOW MANY CAN I HAVE THEN?
SIX.
I'LL NEED A COOK AND A DRIVER, AS WELL AS A MESSENGER BOY...
SUDDENLY I FELT TERRIBLY DIZZY AND FAINT... I LOOKED UP.. IT WAS AS THOUGH I WAS NO LONGER INSIDE THE PINEY SMELLING GUARDHOUSE...
NO!
ANKA, WHAT DO YOU IMAGINE PEOPLE WILL THINK OF ME IF I BRING A BOY OUT OF THAT PLACE?

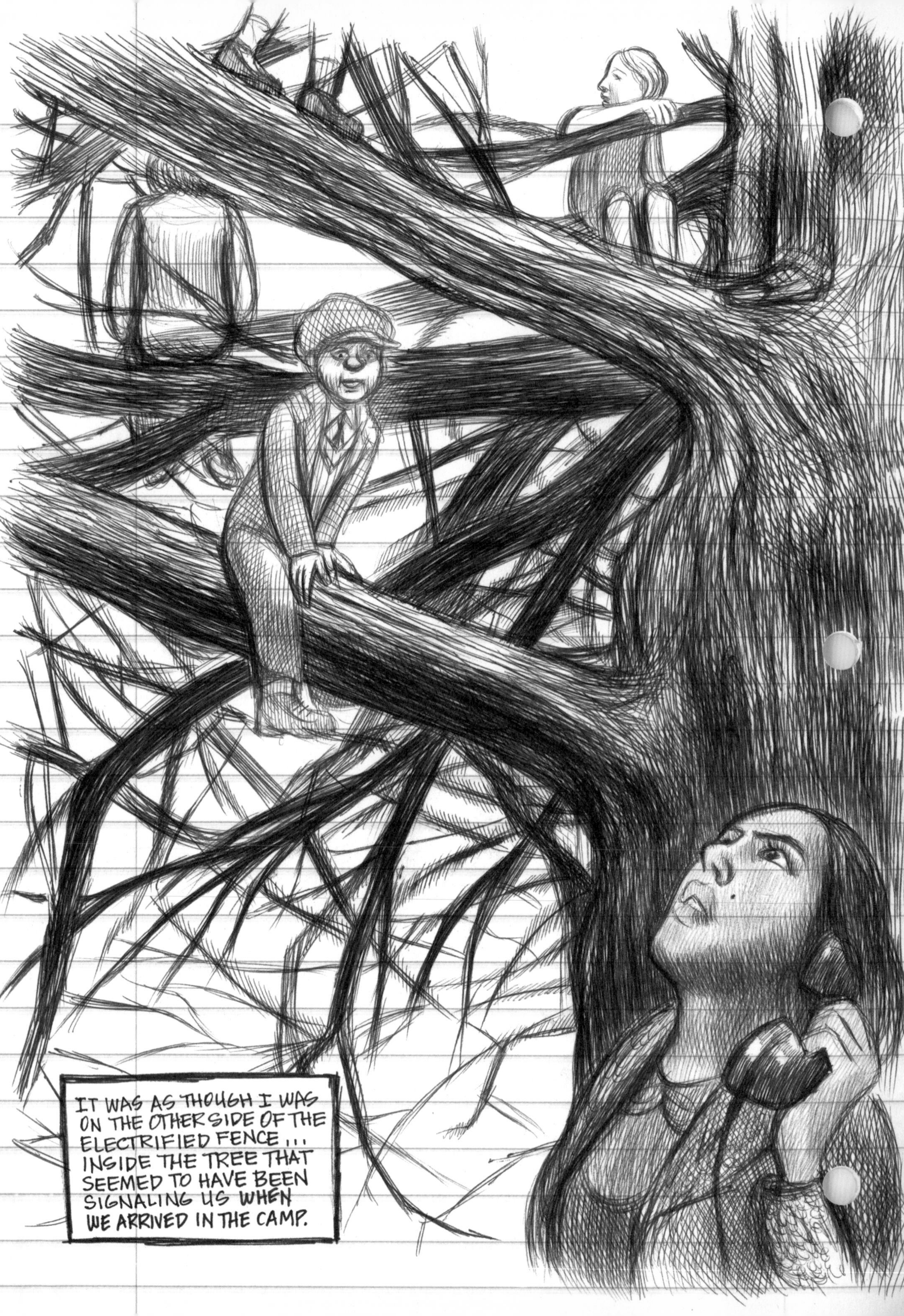
IT WAS AS THOUGH I WAS ON THE OTHER SIDE OF THE ELECTRIFIED FENCE ... INSIDE THE TREE THAT SEEMED TO HAVE BEEN SIGNALING US WHEN WE ARRIVED IN THE CAMP.

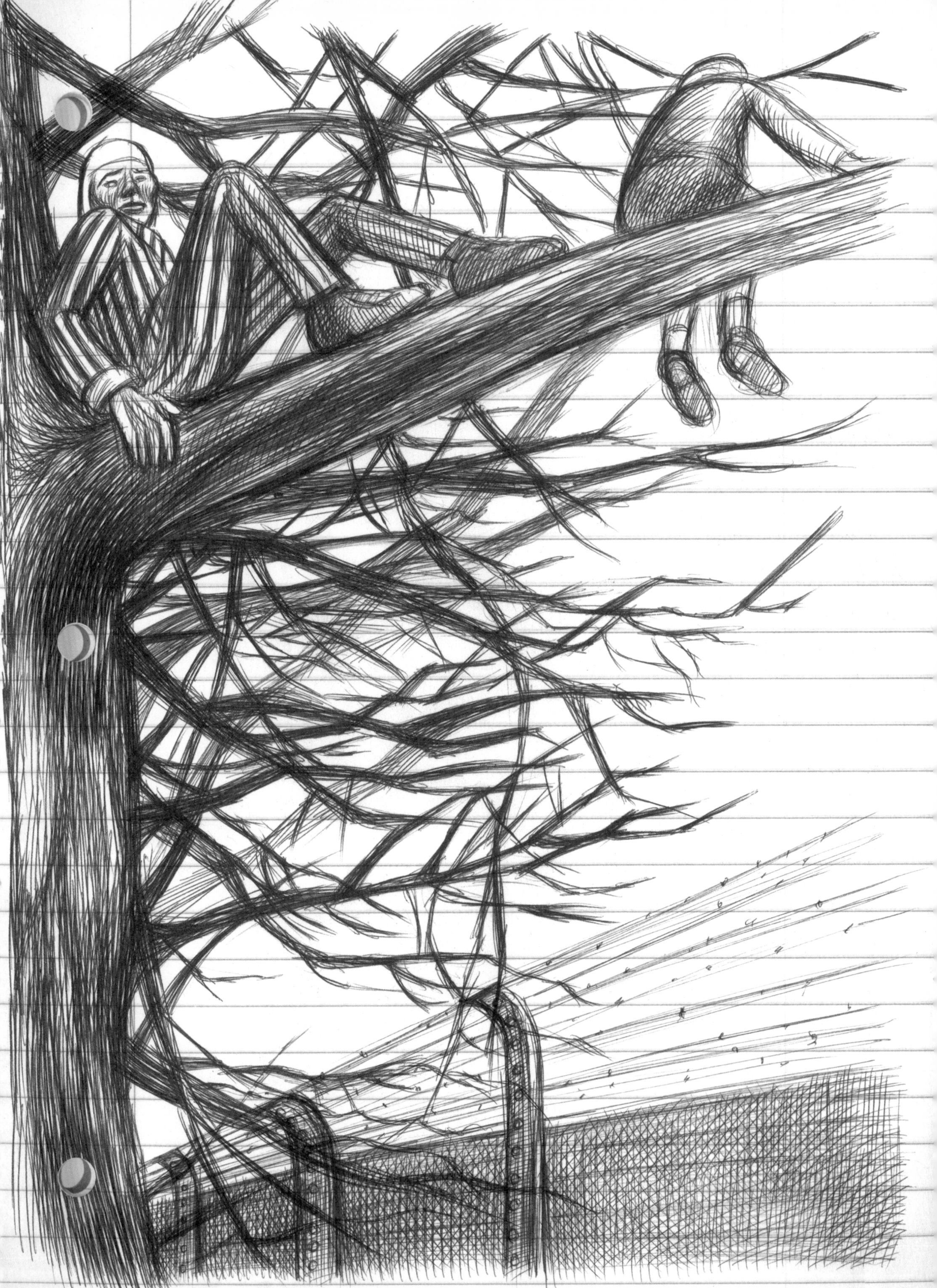

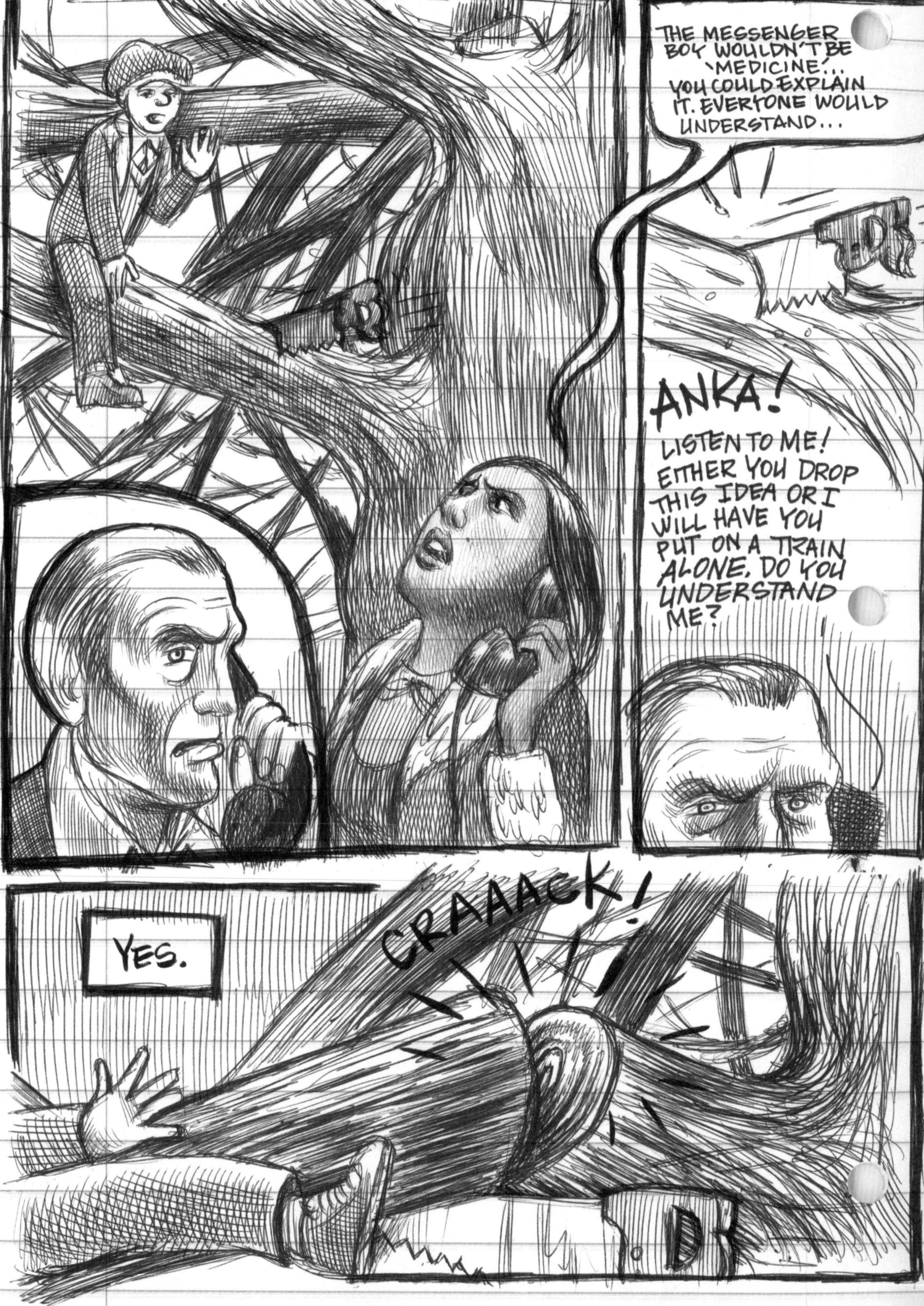
THE MESSENGER BOY WOULDN'T BE 'MEDICINE'... YOU COULD EXPLAIN IT. EVERYONE WOULD UNDERSTAND...
ANKA!
LISTEN TO ME! EITHER YOU DROP THIS IDEA OR I WILL HAVE YOU PUT ON A TRAIN ALONE. DO YOU UNDERSTAND ME?
YES.
CRAAACK!

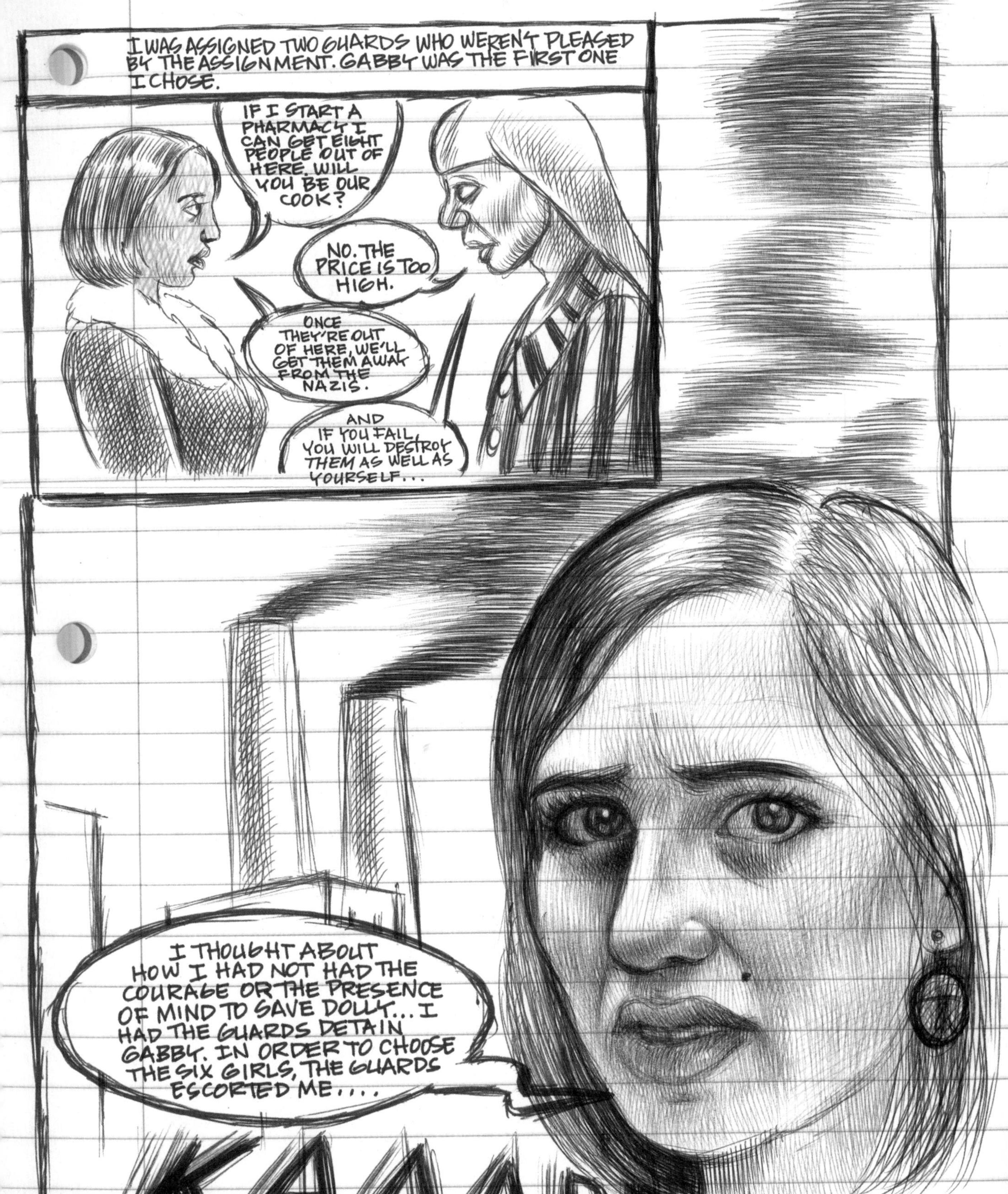
I WAS ASSIGNED TWO GUARDS WHO WEREN'T PLEASED BY THE ASSIGNMENT. GABBY WAS THE FIRST ONE I CHOSE.
IF I START A PHARMACY I CAN GET EIGHT PEOPLE OUT OF HERE. WILL YOU BE OUR COOK?
NO. THE PRICE IS TOO HIGH.
ONCE THEY'RE OUT OF HERE, WE'LL GET THEM AWAY FROM THE NAZIS.
AND IF YOU FAIL, YOU WILL DESTROY THEM AS WELL AS YOURSELF...
I THOUGHT ABOUT HOW I HAD NOT HAD THE COURAGE OR THE PRESENCE OF MIND TO SAVE DOLLY... I HAD THE GUARDS DETAIN GABBY. IN ORDER TO CHOOSE THE SIX GIRLS, THE GUARDS ESCORTED ME....
KAAARRRENNN

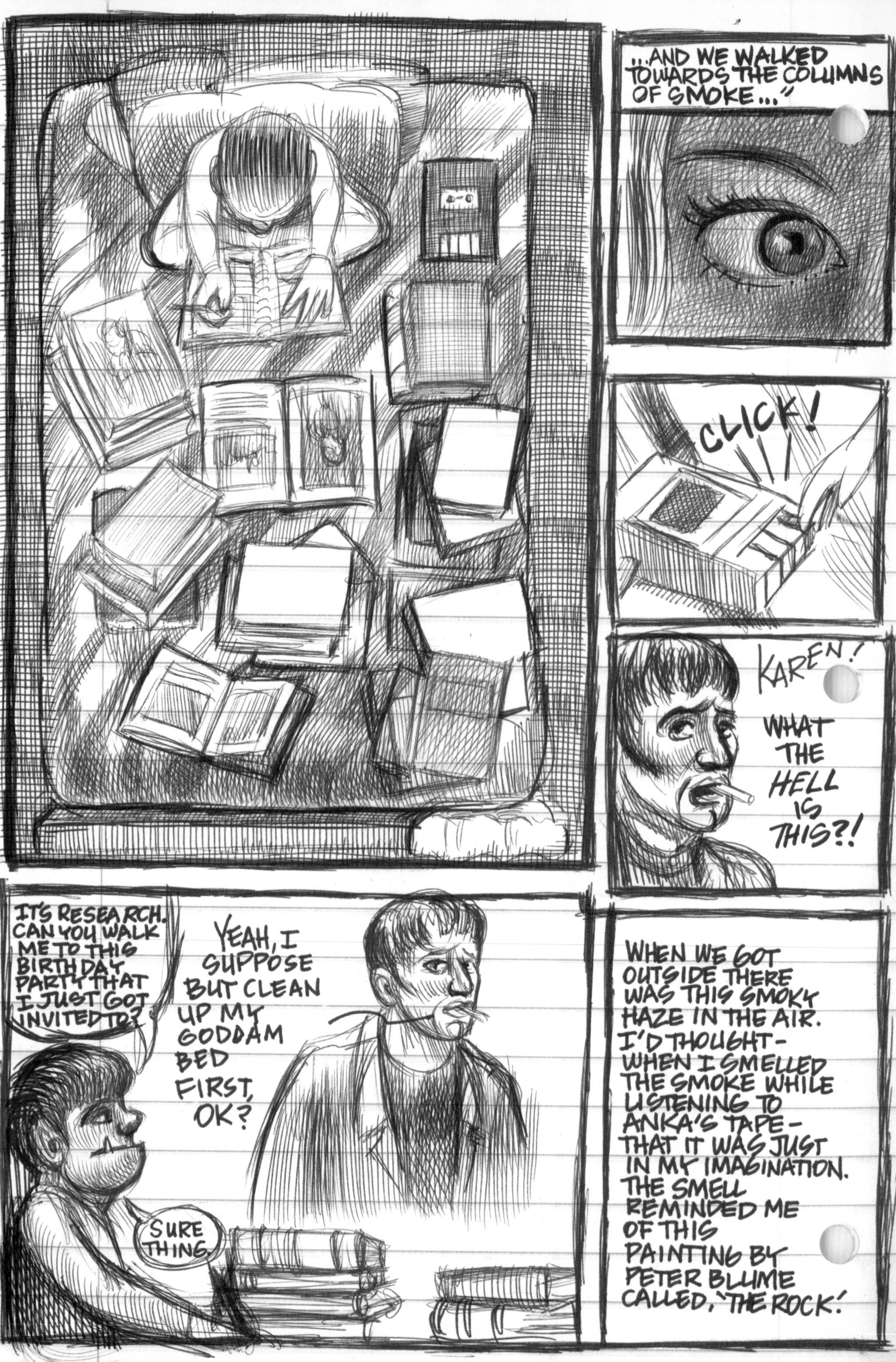
...AND WE WALKED TOWARDS THE COLUMNS OF SMOKE..."
CLICK!
KAREN!
WHAT THE HELL IS THIS?!
IT'S RESEARCH. CAN YOU WALK ME TO THIS BIRTHDAY PARTY THAT I JUST GOT INVITED TO?
YEAH, I SUPPOSE BUT CLEAN UP MY GODDAM BED FIRST, OK?
SURE THING.
WHEN WE GOT OUTSIDE THERE WAS THIS SMOKY HAZE IN THE AIR. I'D THOUGHT- WHEN I SMELLED THE SMOKE WHILE LISTENING TO ANKA'S TAPE- THAT IT WAS JUST IN MY IMAGINATION. THE SMELL REMINDED ME OF THIS PAINTING BY PETER BLUME CALLED, "THE ROCK."

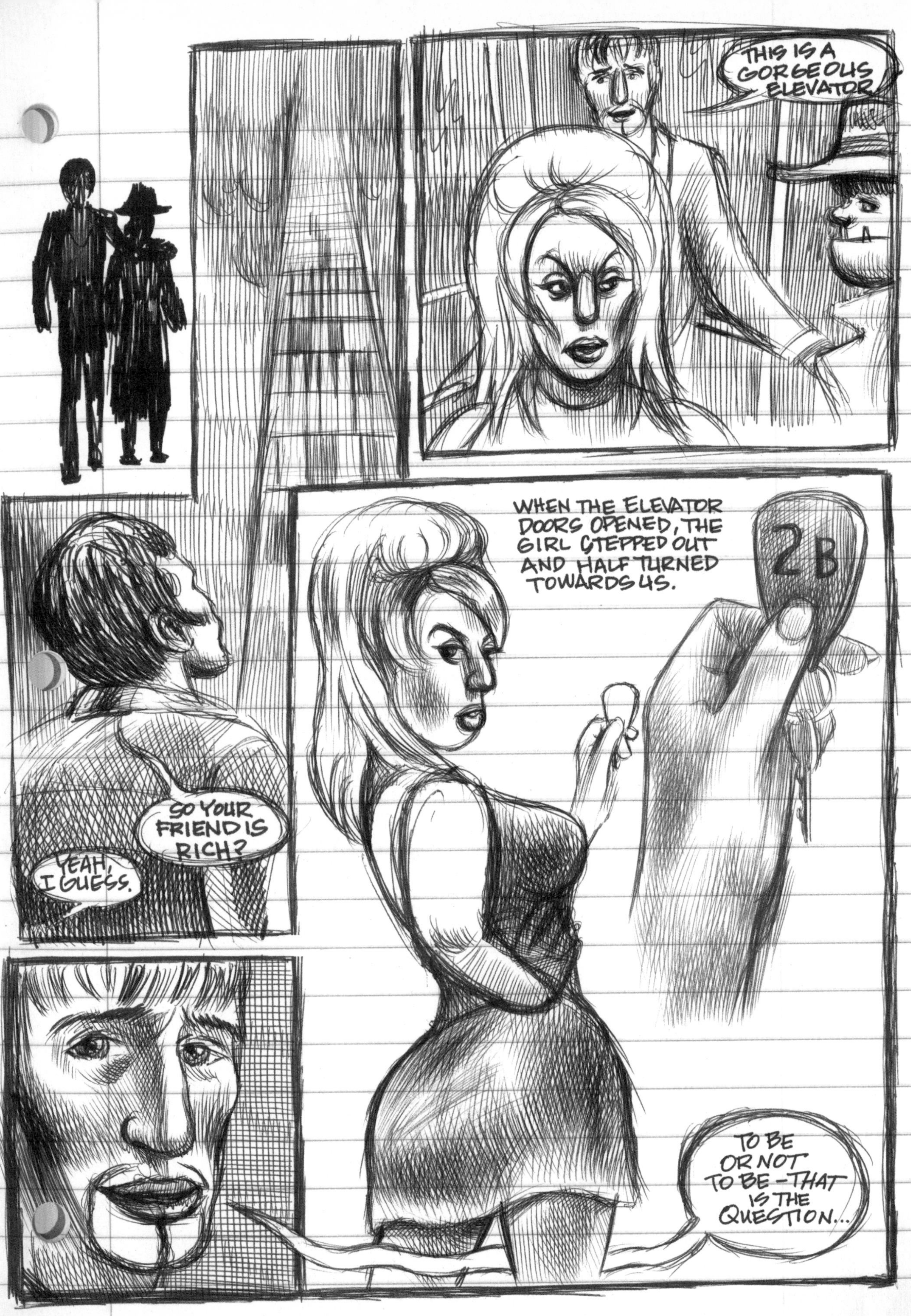
THIS IS A GORGEOUS ELEVATOR
WHEN THE ELEVATOR DOORS OPENED, THE GIRL STEPPED OUT AND HALF TURNED TOWARDS US.
2B
SO YOUR FRIEND IS RICH?
YEAH, I GUESS.
TO BE OR NOT TO BE - THAT IS THE QUESTION...

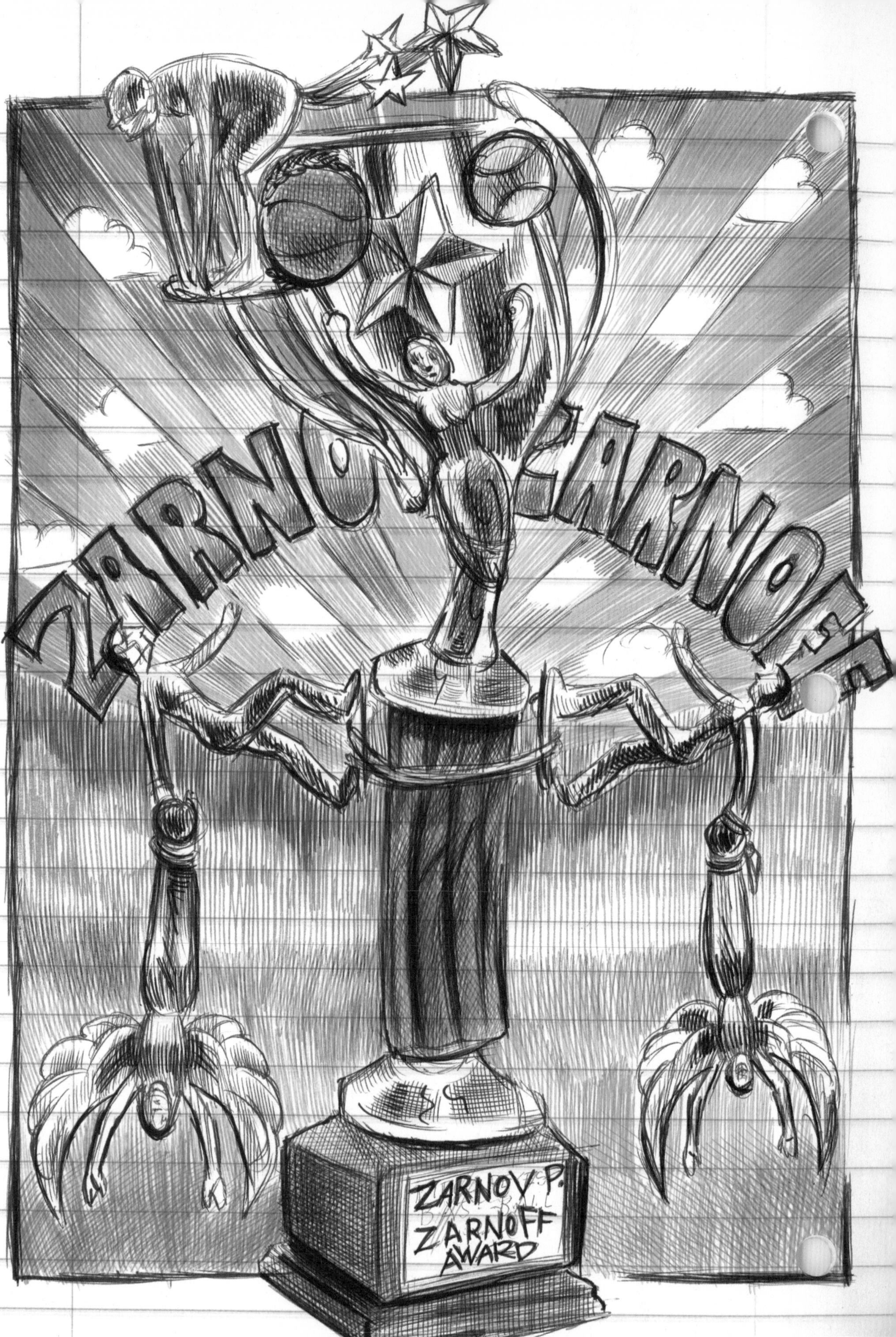
ZARNOV P.
ZARNOFF
AWARD

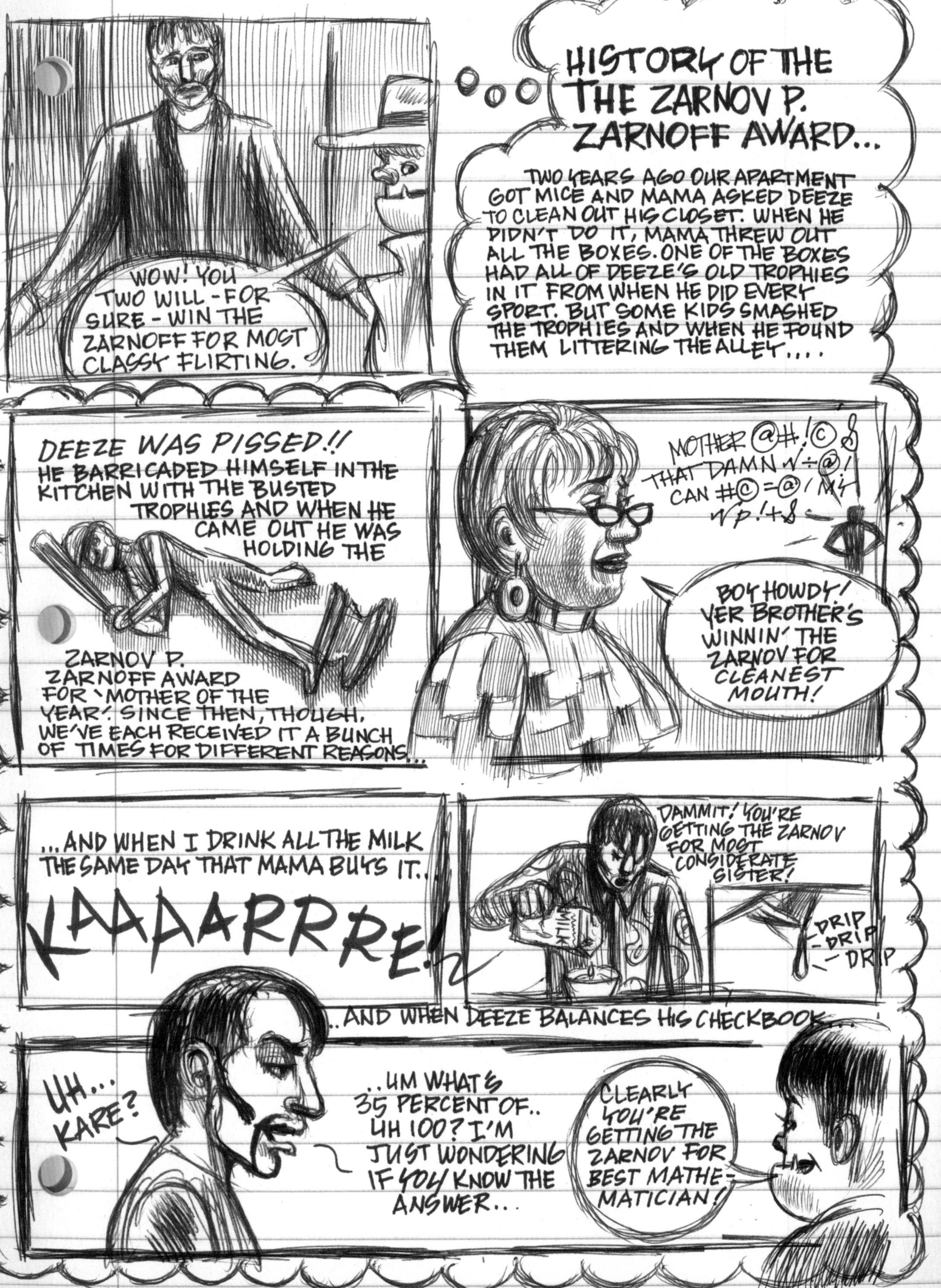
WOW! YOU TWO WILL - FOR SURE - WIN THE ZARNOFF FOR MOST CLASSY FLIRTING.
HISTORY OF THE THE ZARNOV P. ZARNOFF AWARD...
TWO YEARS AGO OUR APARTMENT GOT MICE AND MAMA ASKED DEEZE TO CLEAN OUT HIS CLOSET. WHEN HE DIDN'T DO IT, MAMA THREW OUT ALL THE BOXES. ONE OF THE BOXES HAD ALL OF DEEZE'S OLD TROPHIES IN IT FROM WHEN HE DID EVERY SPORT. BUT SOME KIDS SMASHED THE TROPHIES AND WHEN HE FOUND THEM LITTERING THE ALLEY....
DEEZE WAS PISSED!! HE BARRICADED HIMSELF IN THE KITCHEN WITH THE BUSTED TROPHIES AND WHEN HE CAME OUT HE WAS HOLDING THE
ZARNOV P. ZARNOFF AWARD FOR 'MOTHER OF THE YEAR'. SINCE THEN, THOUGH, WE'VE EACH RECEIVED IT A BUNCH OF TIMES FOR DIFFERENT REASONS...
MOTHER @#!©$ THAT DAMN √÷@! CAN #©=@/M4 √p!+$
BOY HOWDY! YER BROTHER'S WINNIN' THE ZARNOV FOR CLEANEST MOUTH!
...AND WHEN I DRINK ALL THE MILK THE SAME DAY THAT MAMA BUYS IT...
KAAAARRRRE!
DAMMIT! YOU'RE GETTING THE ZARNOV FOR MOST CONSIDERATE SISTER!
MILK
DRIP DRIP DRIP
...AND WHEN DEEZE BALANCES HIS CHECKBOOK...
UH... KARE?
...UM WHAT'S 35 PERCENT OF.. UH 100? I'M JUST WONDERING IF YOU KNOW THE ANSWER...
CLEARLY YOU'RE GETTING THE ZARNOV FOR BEST MATHEMATICIAN!

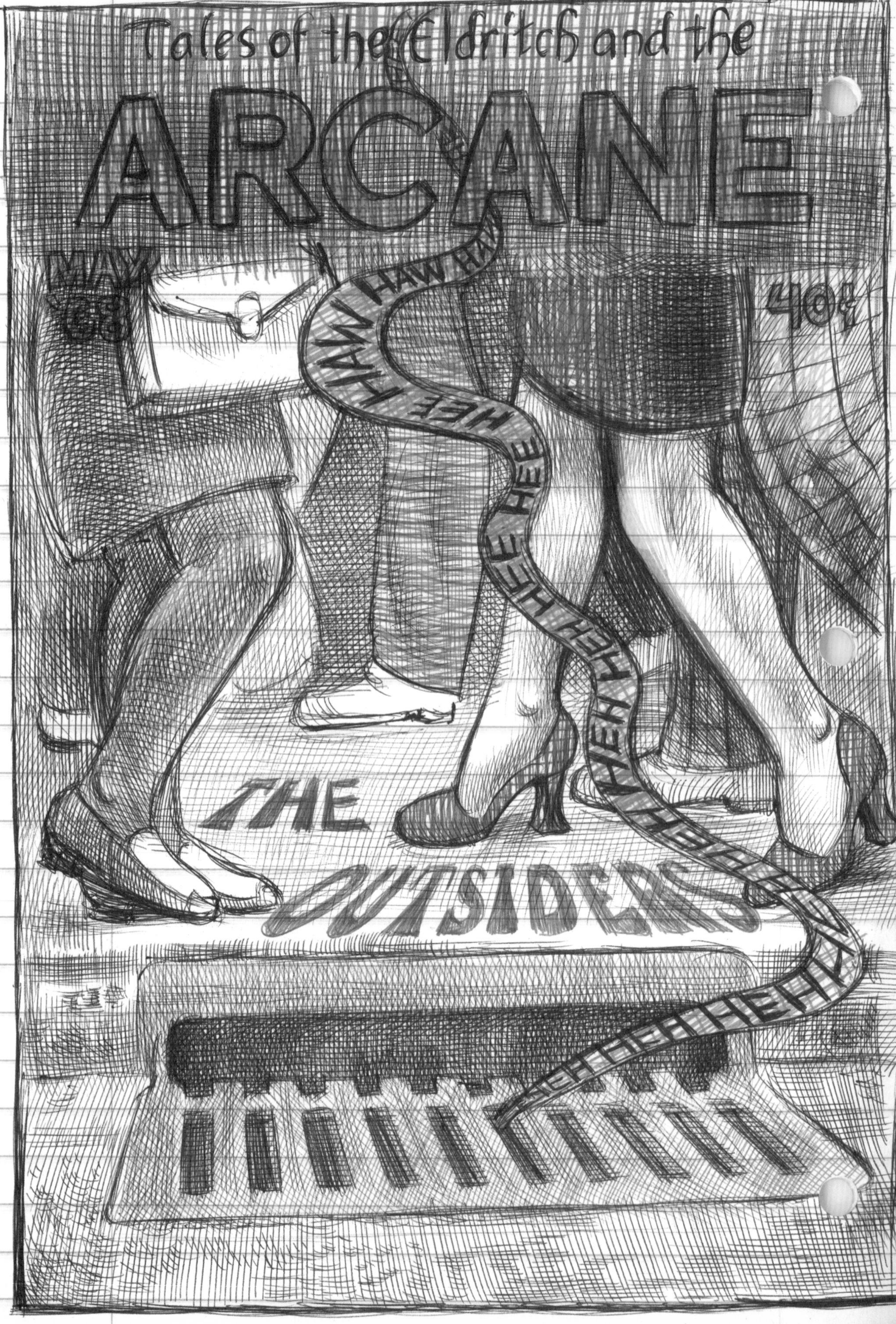

Tales of the Eldritch and the
ARCANE
MAY '68
40¢
HAW HAW HAW
HEE HEE HEE HEE
THE
OUTSIDERS

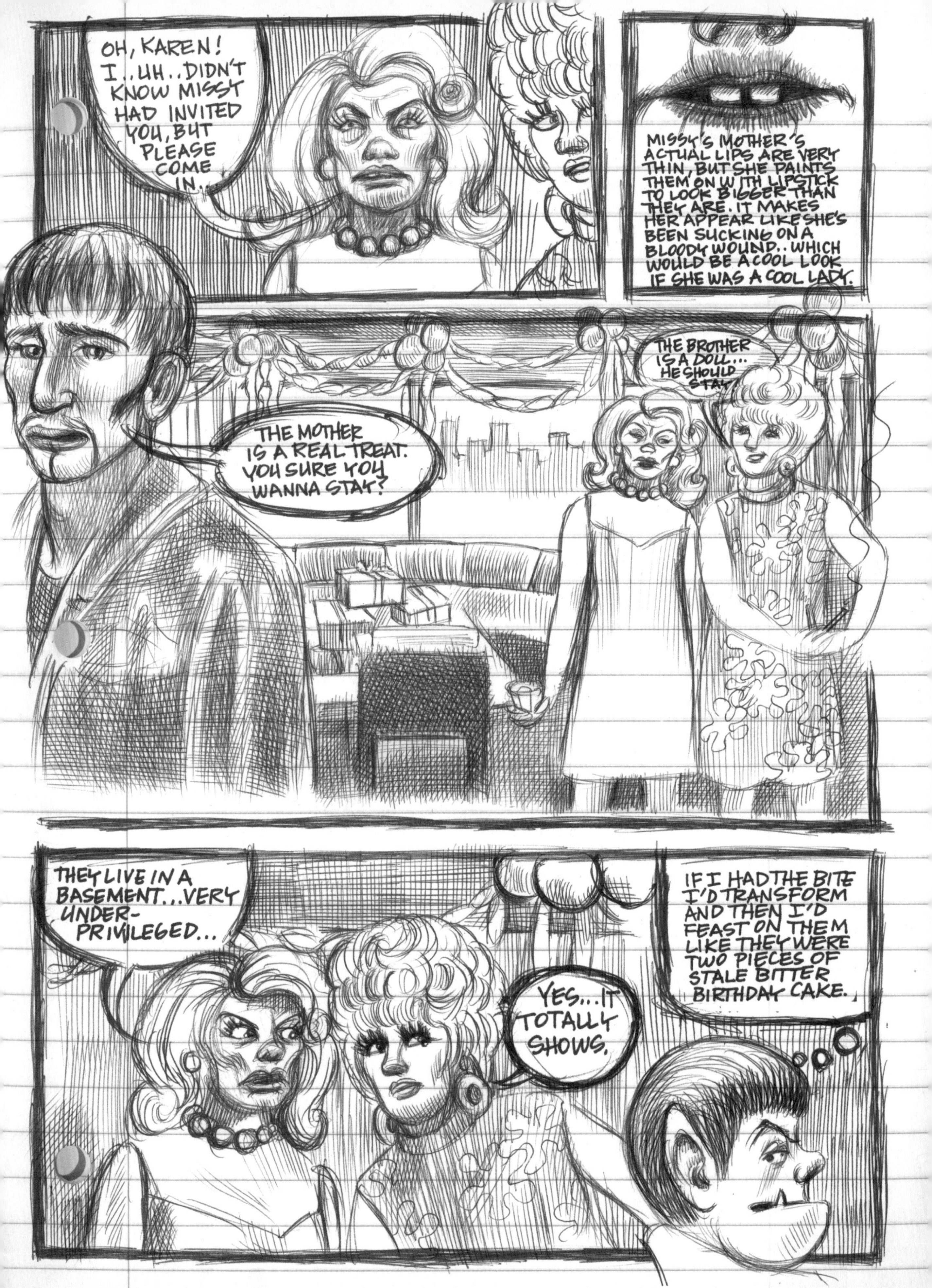
OH, KAREN! I..UH..DIDN'T KNOW MISSY HAD INVITED YOU, BUT PLEASE COME IN..
MISSY'S MOTHER'S ACTUAL LIPS ARE VERY THIN, BUT SHE PAINTS THEM ON WITH LIPSTICK TO LOOK BIGGER THAN THEY ARE. IT MAKES HER APPEAR LIKE SHE'S BEEN SUCKING ON A BLOODY WOUND.. WHICH WOULD BE A COOL LOOK IF SHE WAS A COOL LADY.
THE MOTHER IS A REAL TREAT. YOU SURE YOU WANNA STAY?
THE BROTHER IS A DOLL... HE SHOULD STAY!
THEY LIVE IN A BASEMENT...VERY UNDER-PRIVILEGED...
YES...IT TOTALLY SHOWS.
IF I HAD THE BITE I'D TRANSFORM AND THEN I'D FEAST ON THEM LIKE THEY WERE TWO PIECES OF STALE BITTER BIRTHDAY CAKE.

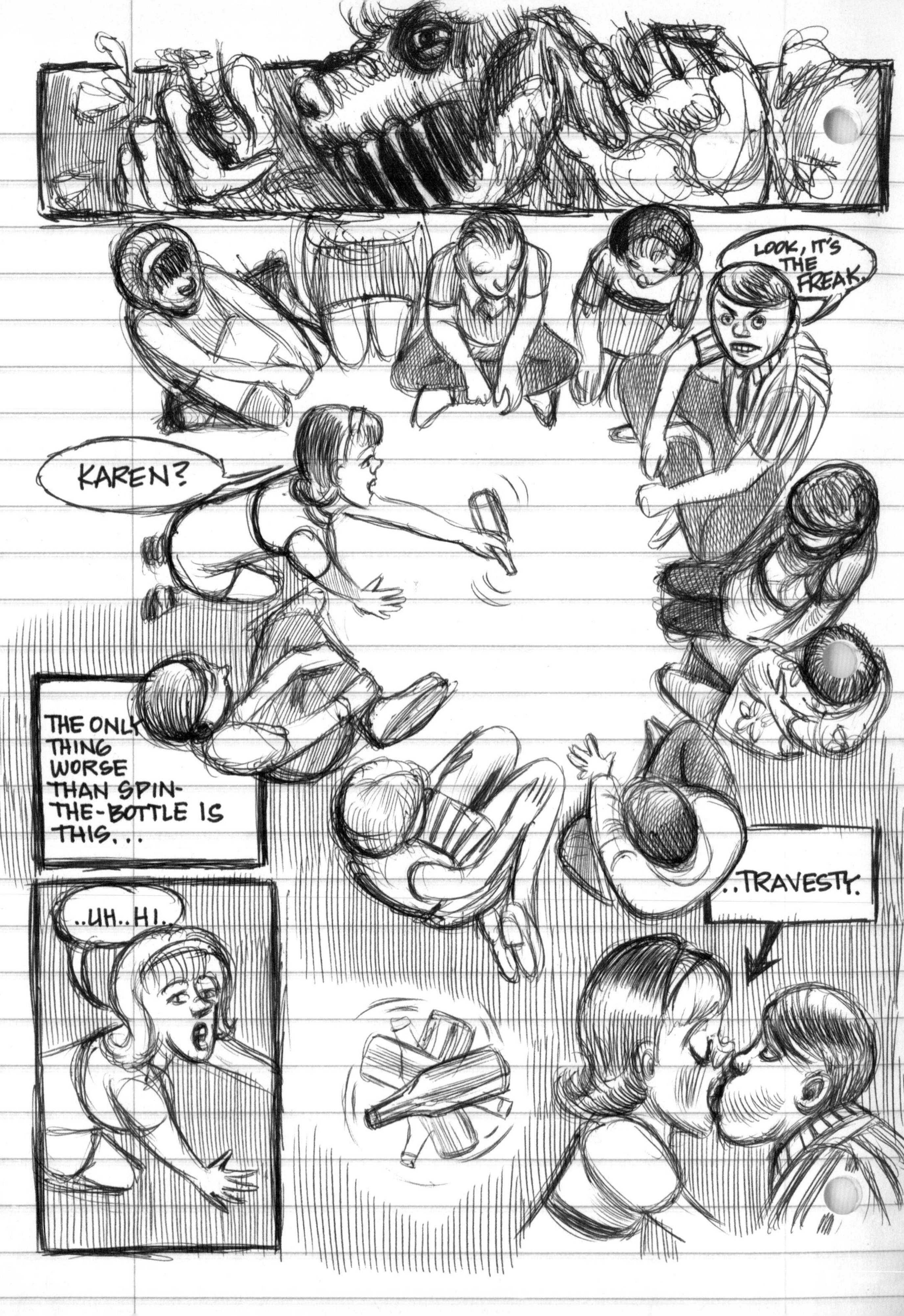
LOOK, IT'S THE FREAK.
KAREN?
THE ONLY THING WORSE THAN SPIN-THE-BOTTLE IS THIS...
..UH..HI..
..TRAVESTY.

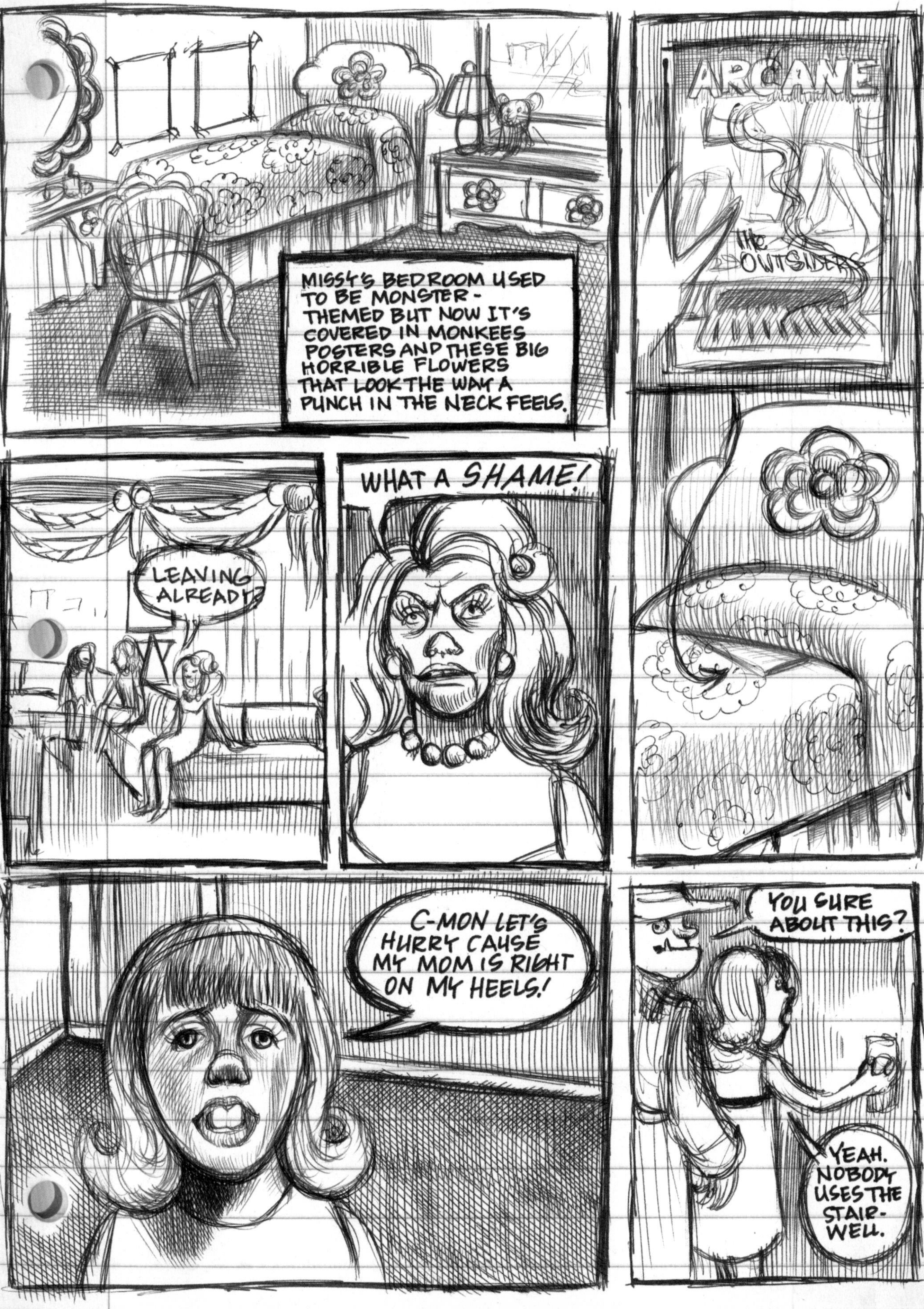
MISSY'S BEDROOM USED TO BE MONSTER-THEMED BUT NOW IT'S COVERED IN MONKEES POSTERS AND THESE BIG HORRIBLE FLOWERS THAT LOOK THE WAY A PUNCH IN THE NECK FEELS.
ARCANE
THE OUTSIDERS
LEAVING ALREADY?
WHAT A SHAME!
C-MON LET'S HURRY CAUSE MY MOM IS RIGHT ON MY HEELS!
YOU SURE ABOUT THIS?
YEAH. NOBODY USES THE STAIR-WELL.

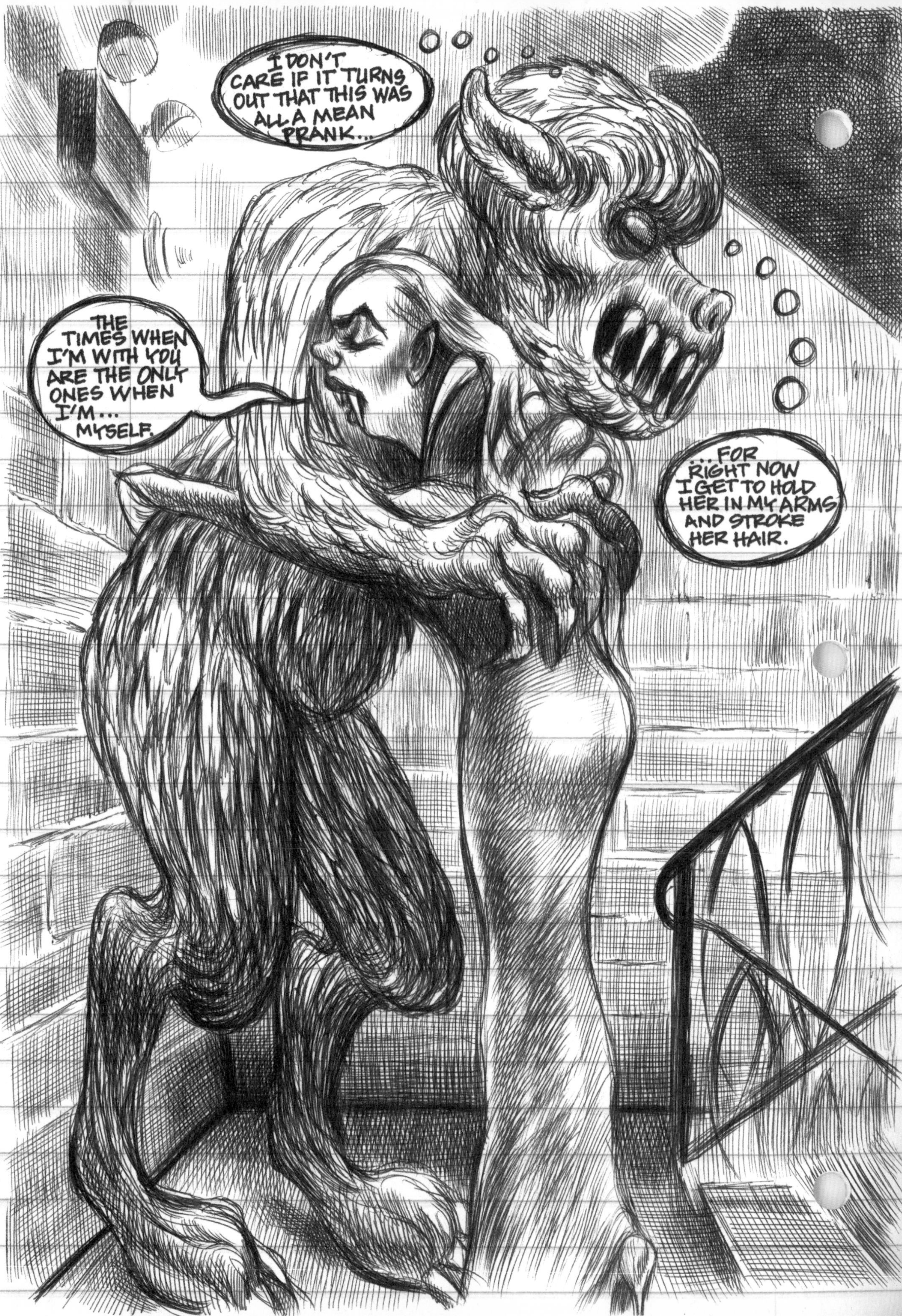
I DON'T CARE IF IT TURNS OUT THAT THIS WAS ALL A MEAN PRANK...
THE TIMES WHEN I'M WITH YOU ARE THE ONLY ONES WHEN I'M... MYSELF.
...FOR RIGHT NOW I GET TO HOLD HER IN MY ARMS AND STROKE HER HAIR.

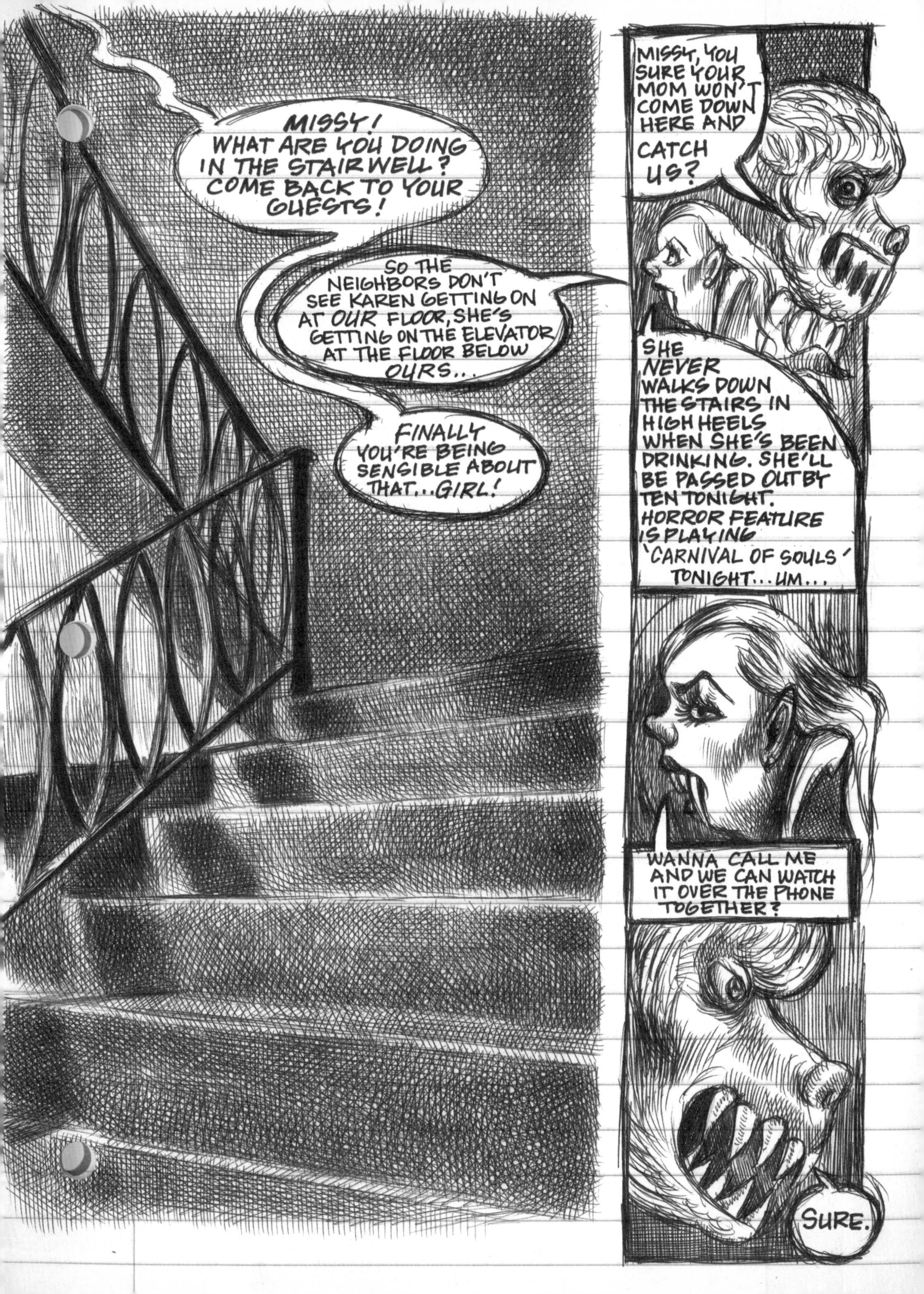
MISSY! WHAT ARE YOU DOING IN THE STAIRWELL? COME BACK TO YOUR GUESTS!
SO THE NEIGHBORS DON'T SEE KAREN GETTING ON AT OUR FLOOR, SHE'S GETTING ON THE ELEVATOR AT THE FLOOR BELOW OURS...
FINALLY YOU'RE BEING SENSIBLE ABOUT THAT... GIRL!
MISSY, YOU SURE YOUR MOM WON'T COME DOWN HERE AND CATCH US?
SHE NEVER WALKS DOWN THE STAIRS IN HIGH HEELS WHEN SHE'S BEEN DRINKING. SHE'LL BE PASSED OUT BY TEN TONIGHT. HORROR FEATURE IS PLAYING 'CARNIVAL OF SOULS' TONIGHT... UM...
WANNA CALL ME AND WE CAN WATCH IT OVER THE PHONE TOGETHER?
SURE.

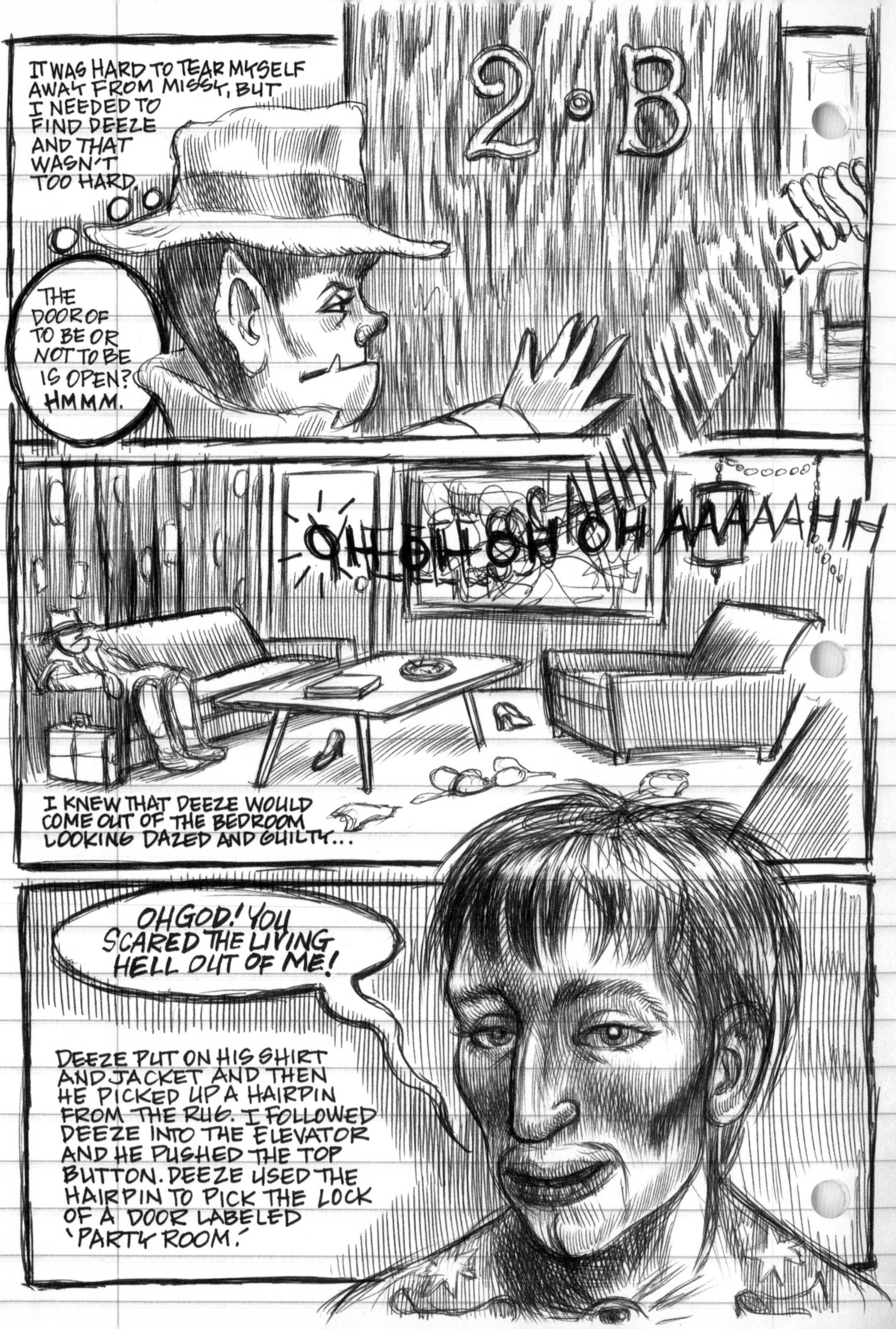

IT WAS HARD TO TEAR MYSELF AWAY FROM MISSY, BUT I NEEDED TO FIND DEEZE AND THAT WASN'T TOO HARD.
2-B
THE DOOR OF TO BE OR NOT TO BE IS OPEN? HMMM.
AHHH
OH OH OH OH OH AAAAAHH
I KNEW THAT DEEZE WOULD COME OUT OF THE BEDROOM LOOKING DAZED AND GUILTY...
OHGOD! YOU SCARED THE LIVING HELL OUT OF ME!
DEEZE PUT ON HIS SHIRT AND JACKET AND THEN HE PICKED UP A HAIRPIN FROM THE RUG. I FOLLOWED DEEZE INTO THE ELEVATOR AND HE PUSHED THE TOP BUTTON. DEEZE USED THE HAIRPIN TO PICK THE LOCK OF A DOOR LABELED 'PARTY ROOM.'

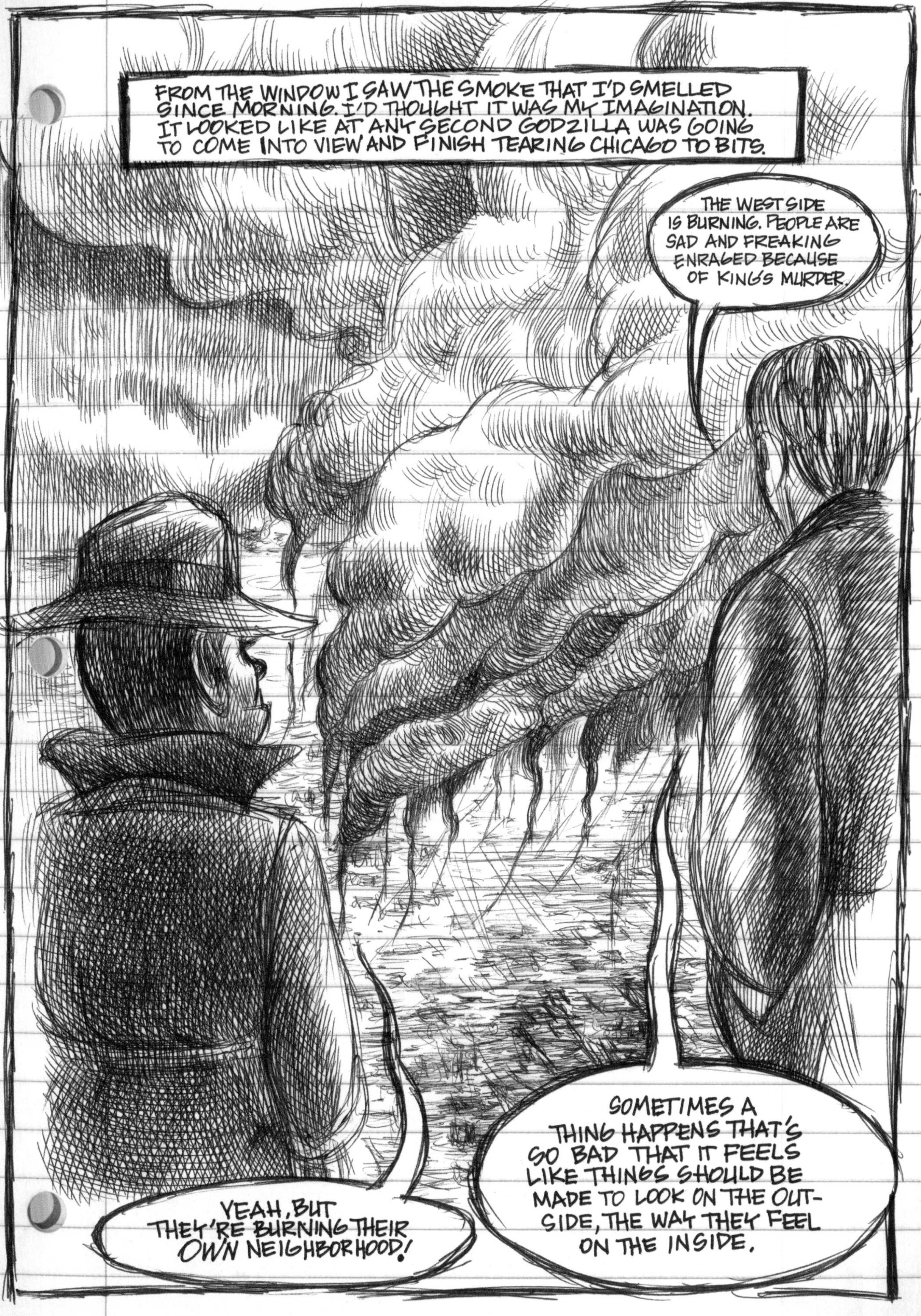
FROM THE WINDOW I SAW THE SMOKE THAT I'D SMELLED SINCE MORNING. I'D THOUGHT IT WAS MY IMAGINATION. IT LOOKED LIKE AT ANY SECOND GODZILLA WAS GOING TO COME INTO VIEW AND FINISH TEARING CHICAGO TO BITS.
THE WEST SIDE IS BURNING. PEOPLE ARE SAD AND FREAKING ENRAGED BECAUSE OF KING'S MURDER.
YEAH, BUT THEY'RE BURNING THEIR OWN NEIGHBORHOOD!
SOMETIMES A THING HAPPENS THAT'S SO BAD THAT IT FEELS LIKE THINGS SHOULD BE MADE TO LOOK ON THE OUT-SIDE, THE WAY THEY FEEL ON THE INSIDE.

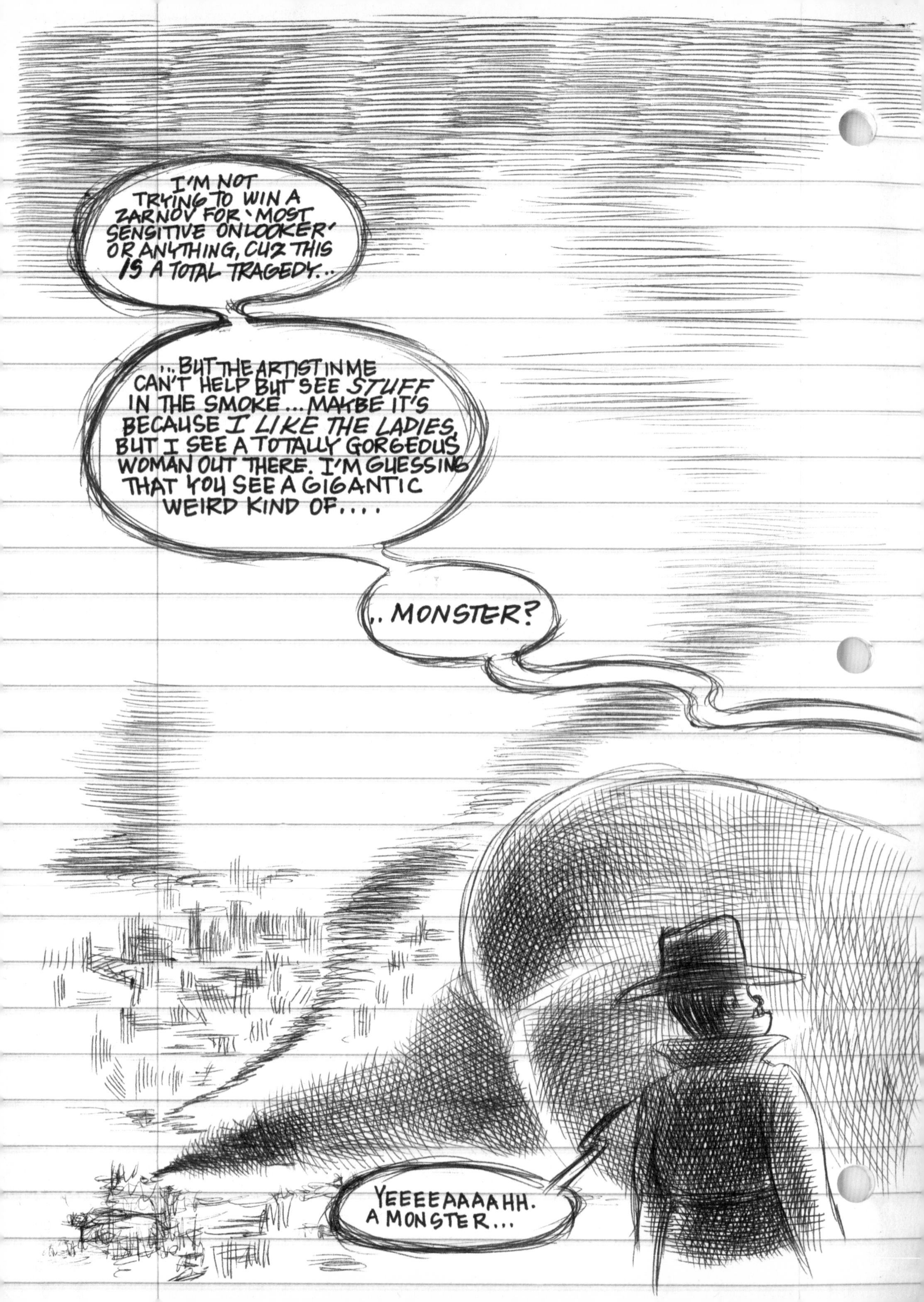
I'M NOT TRYING TO WIN A ZARNOV FOR 'MOST SENSITIVE ONLOOKER' OR ANYTHING, CUZ THIS IS A TOTAL TRAGEDY...
...BUT THE ARTIST IN ME CAN'T HELP BUT SEE STUFF IN THE SMOKE... MAYBE IT'S BECAUSE I LIKE THE LADIES, BUT I SEE A TOTALLY GORGEOUS WOMAN OUT THERE. I'M GUESSING THAT YOU SEE A GIGANTIC WEIRD KIND OF....
.. MONSTER?
YEEEEAAAAHH. A MONSTER...

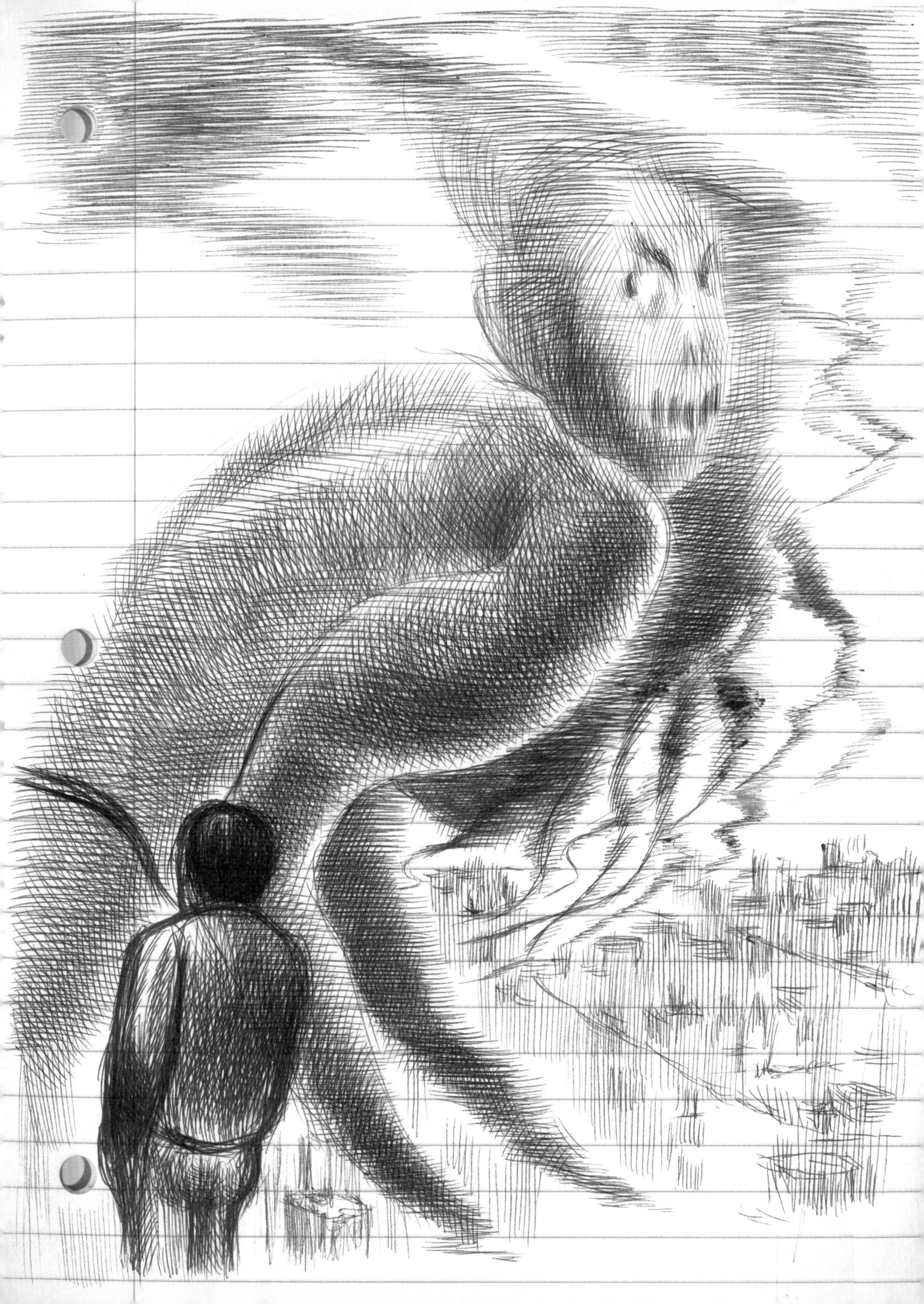

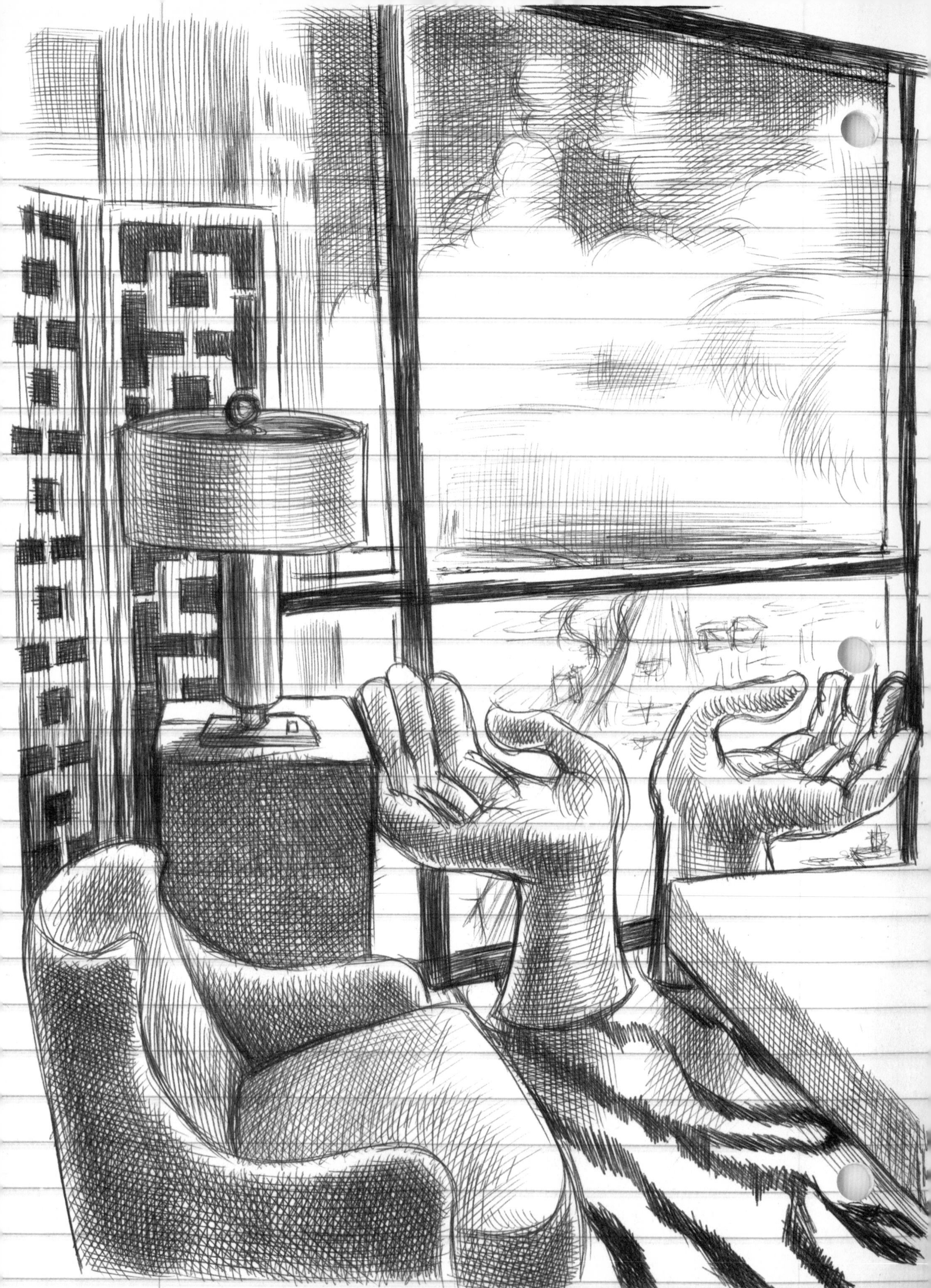

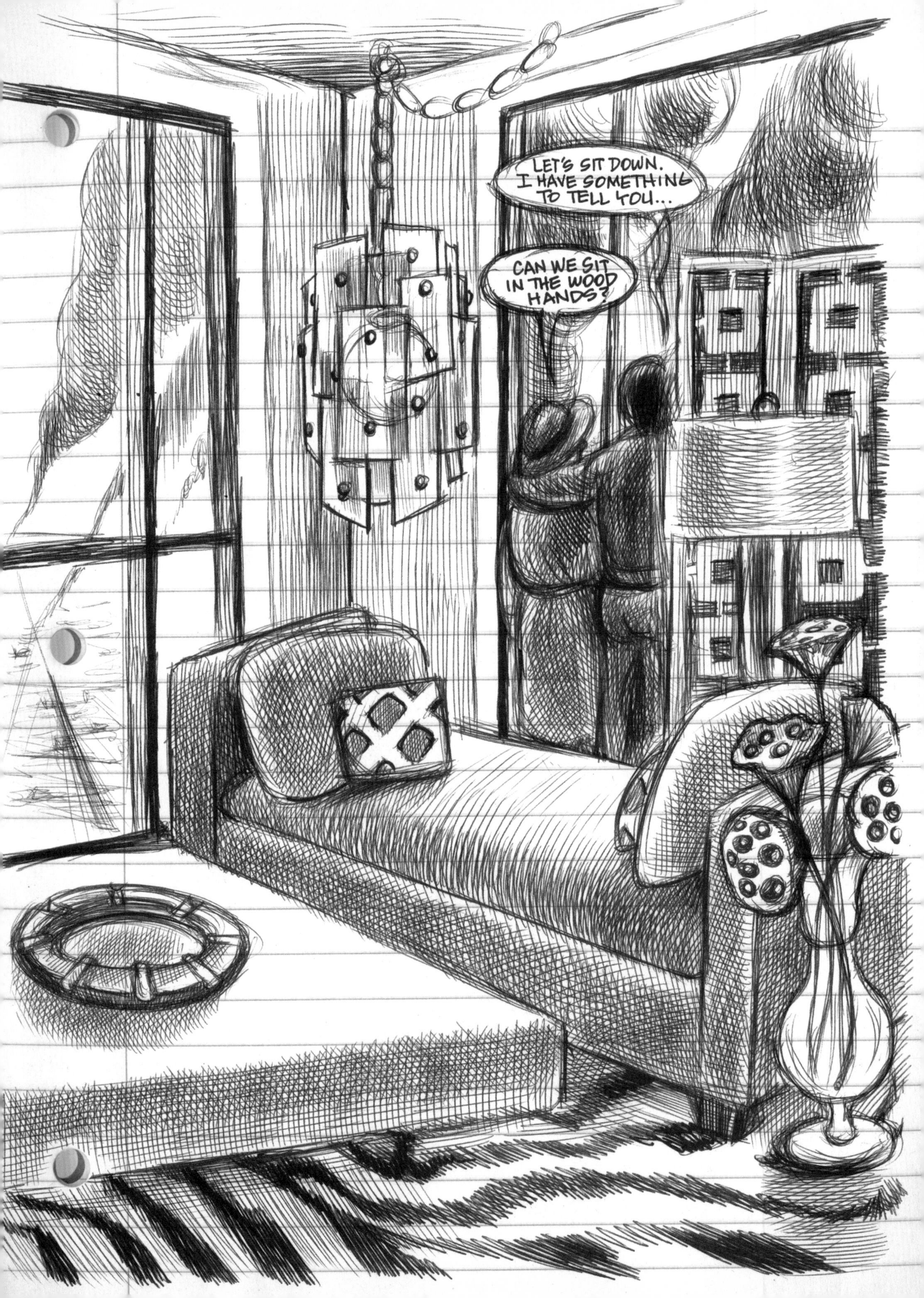
LET'S SIT DOWN. I HAVE SOMETHING TO TELL YOU...
CAN WE SIT IN THE WOOD HANDS?

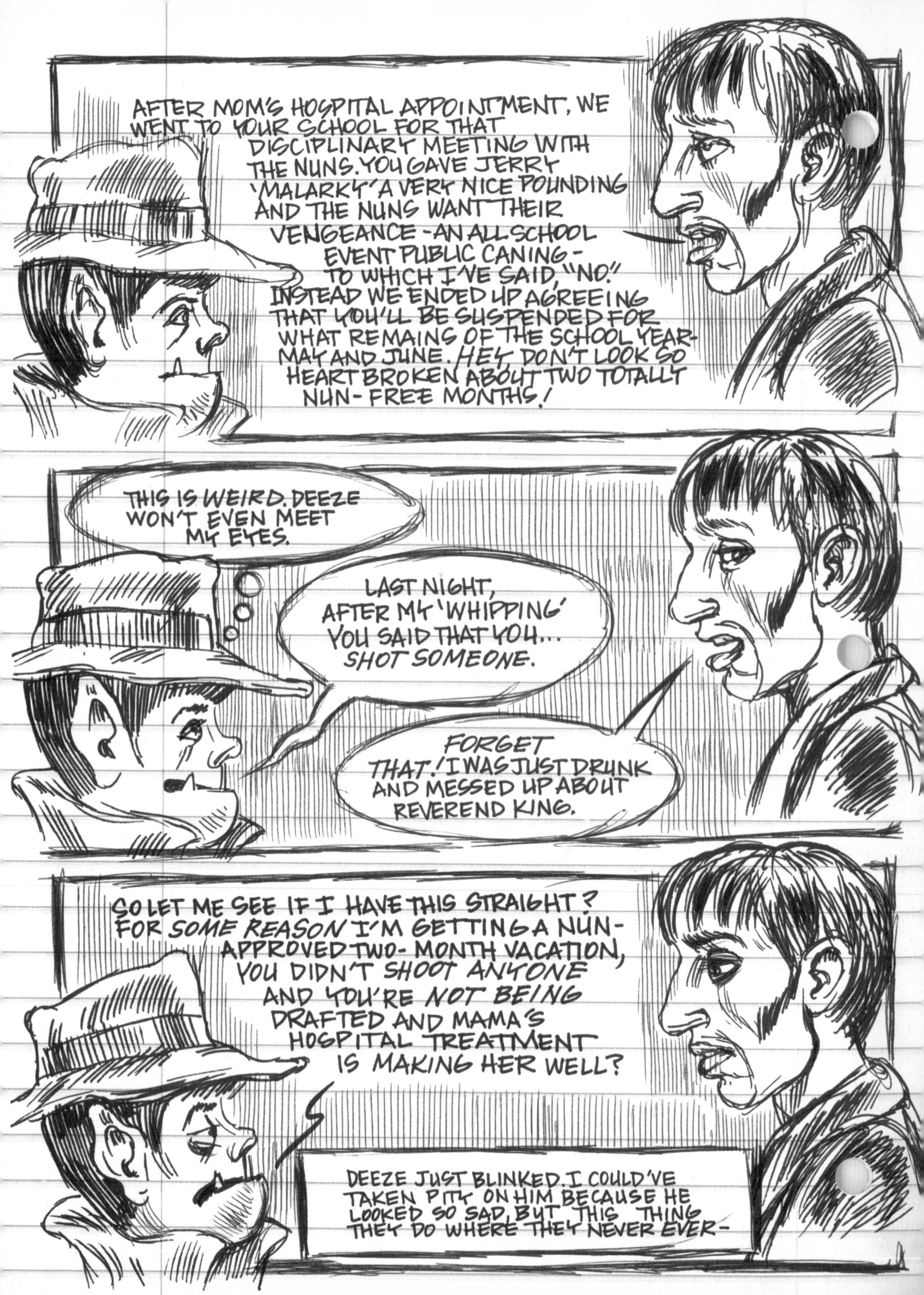
AFTER MOM'S HOSPITAL APPOINTMENT, WE WENT TO YOUR SCHOOL FOR THAT DISCIPLINARY MEETING WITH THE NUNS. YOU GAVE JERRY 'MALARKY' A VERY NICE POUNDING AND THE NUNS WANT THEIR VENGEANCE - AN ALL SCHOOL EVENT PUBLIC CANING - TO WHICH I'VE SAID, "NO." INSTEAD WE ENDED UP AGREEING THAT YOU'LL BE SUSPENDED FOR WHAT REMAINS OF THE SCHOOL YEAR - MAY AND JUNE. HEY, DON'T LOOK SO HEART BROKEN ABOUT TWO TOTALLY NUN-FREE MONTHS!
THIS IS WEIRD. DEEZE WON'T EVEN MEET MY EYES.
LAST NIGHT, AFTER MY 'WHIPPING' YOU SAID THAT YOU... SHOT SOMEONE.
FORGET THAT! I WAS JUST DRUNK AND MESSED UP ABOUT REVEREND KING.
SO LET ME SEE IF I HAVE THIS STRAIGHT? FOR SOME REASON I'M GETTING A NUN-APPROVED TWO-MONTH VACATION, YOU DIDN'T SHOOT ANYONE AND YOU'RE NOT BEING DRAFTED AND MAMA'S HOSPITAL TREATMENT IS MAKING HER WELL?
DEEZE JUST BLINKED. I COULD'VE TAKEN PITY ON HIM BECAUSE HE LOOKED SO SAD, BUT THIS THING THEY DO WHERE THEY NEVER EVER-

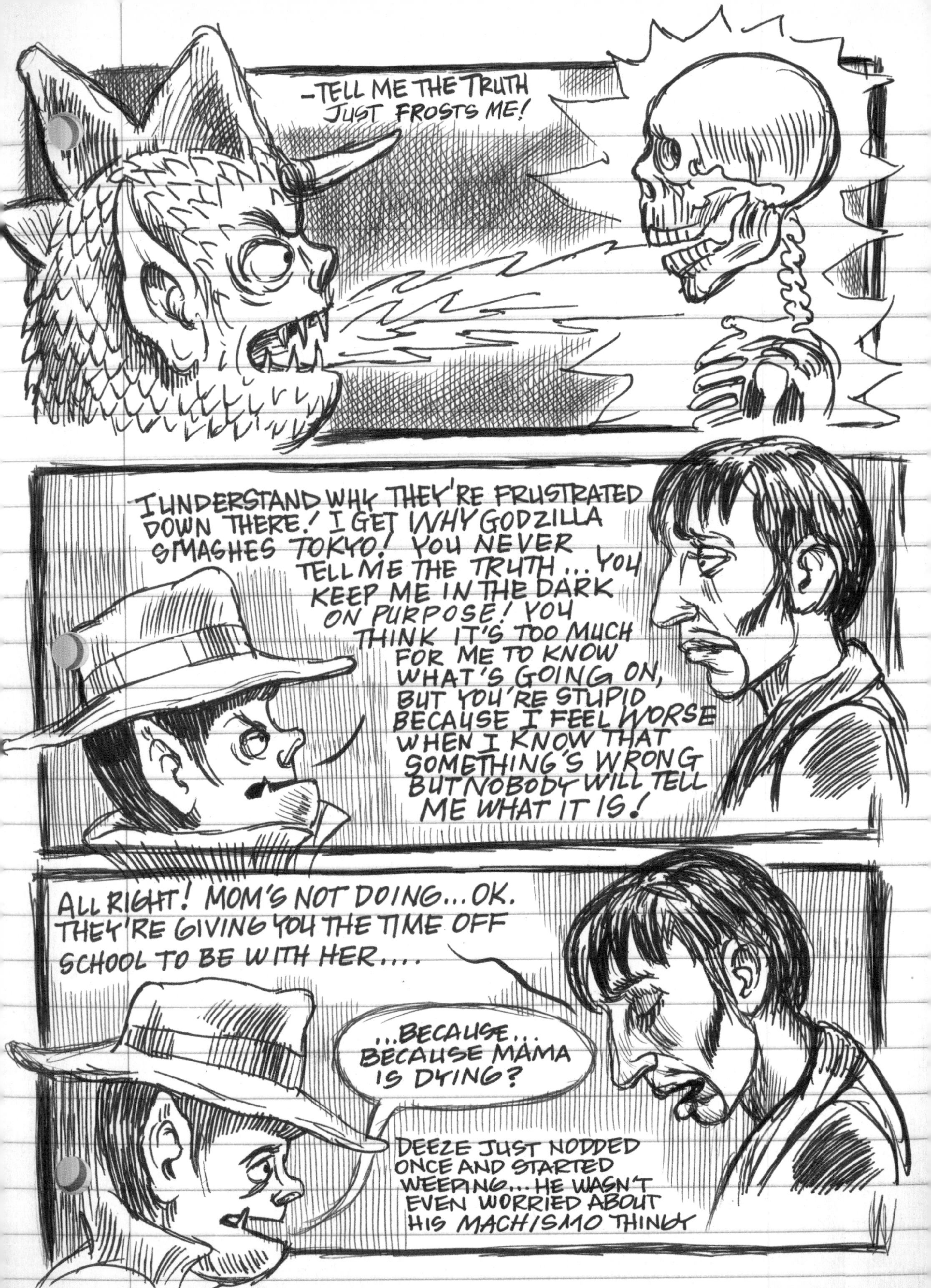

-TELL ME THE TRUTH JUST FROSTS ME!
I UNDERSTAND WHY THEY'RE FRUSTRATED DOWN THERE! I GET WHY GODZILLA SMASHES TOKYO! YOU NEVER TELL ME THE TRUTH... YOU KEEP ME IN THE DARK ON PURPOSE! YOU THINK IT'S TOO MUCH FOR ME TO KNOW WHAT'S GOING ON, BUT YOU'RE STUPID BECAUSE I FEEL WORSE WHEN I KNOW THAT SOMETHING'S WRONG BUT NOBODY WILL TELL ME WHAT IT IS!
ALL RIGHT! MOM'S NOT DOING... OK. THEY'RE GIVING YOU THE TIME OFF SCHOOL TO BE WITH HER....
...BECAUSE... BECAUSE MAMA IS DYING?
DEEZE JUST NODDED ONCE AND STARTED WEEPING... HE WASN'T EVEN WORRIED ABOUT HIS MACHISMO THING

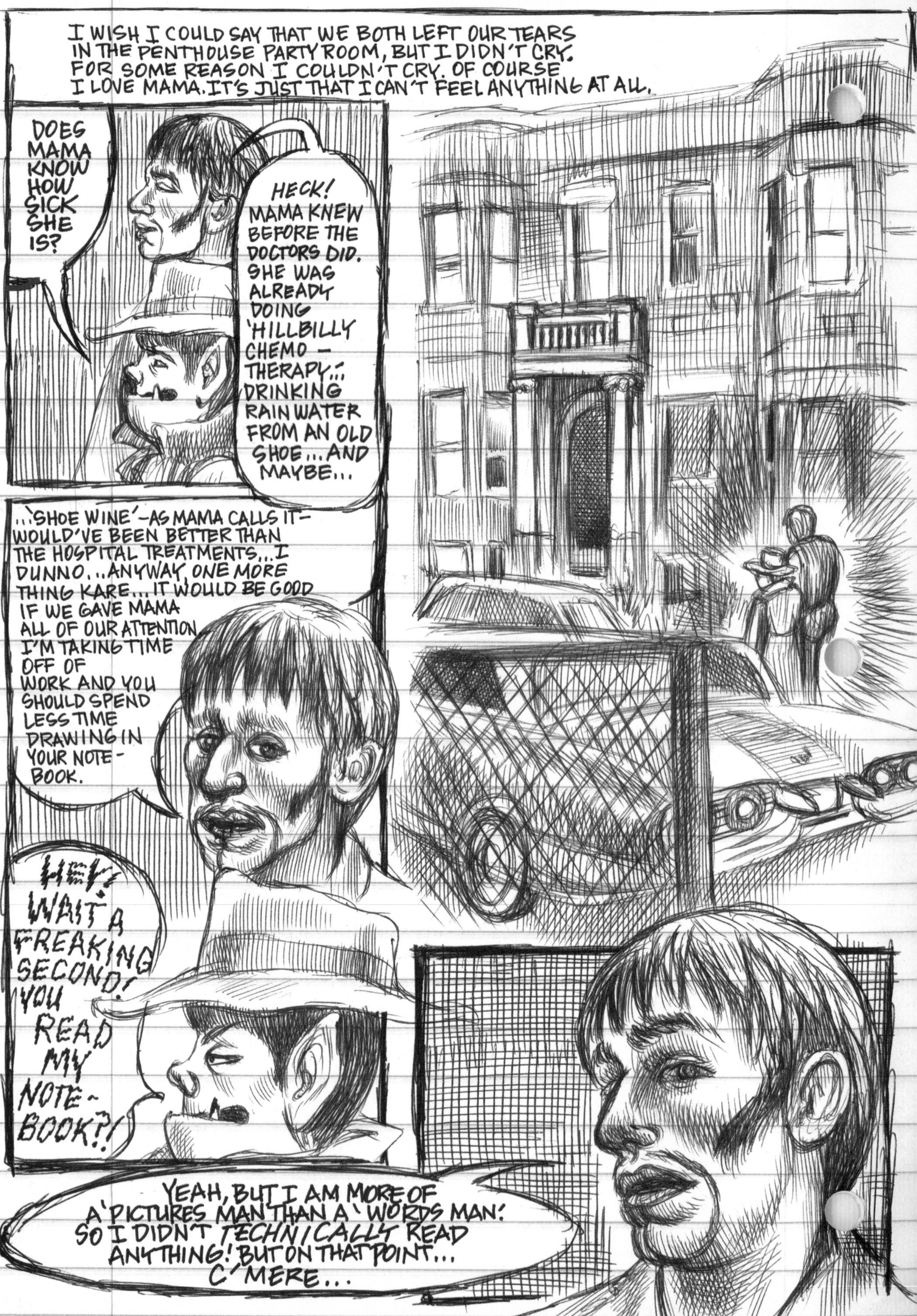
I WISH I COULD SAY THAT WE BOTH LEFT OUR TEARS IN THE PENTHOUSE PARTY ROOM, BUT I DIDN'T CRY. FOR SOME REASON I COULDN'T CRY. OF COURSE I LOVE MAMA. IT'S JUST THAT I CAN'T FEEL ANYTHING AT ALL.
DOES MAMA KNOW HOW SICK SHE IS?
HECK! MAMA KNEW BEFORE THE DOCTORS DID. SHE WAS ALREADY DOING 'HILLBILLY CHEMO-THERAPY'... DRINKING RAIN WATER FROM AN OLD SHOE... AND MAYBE...
...'SHOE WINE'-AS MAMA CALLS IT-WOULD'VE BEEN BETTER THAN THE HOSPITAL TREATMENTS... I DUNNO... ANYWAY, ONE MORE THING KARE... IT WOULD BE GOOD IF WE GAVE MAMA ALL OF OUR ATTENTION. I'M TAKING TIME OFF OF WORK AND YOU SHOULD SPEND LESS TIME DRAWING IN YOUR NOTE-BOOK.
HEY! WAIT A FREAKING SECOND! YOU READ MY NOTE-BOOK?!
YEAH, BUT I AM MORE OF A 'PICTURES MAN' THAN A 'WORDS MAN.' SO I DIDN'T TECHNICALLY READ ANYTHING! BUT ON THAT POINT... C'MERE...

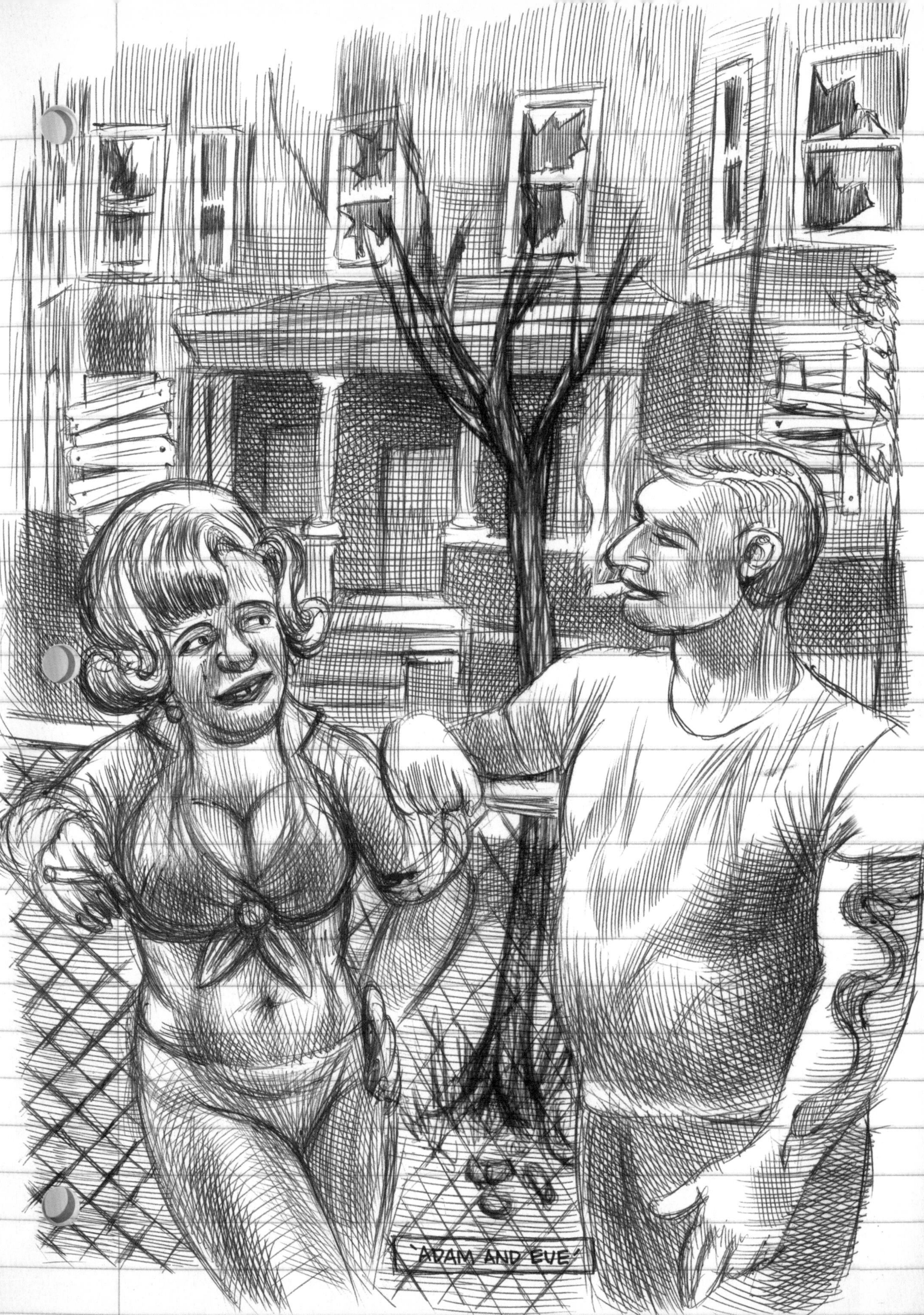
`ADAM AND EVE'

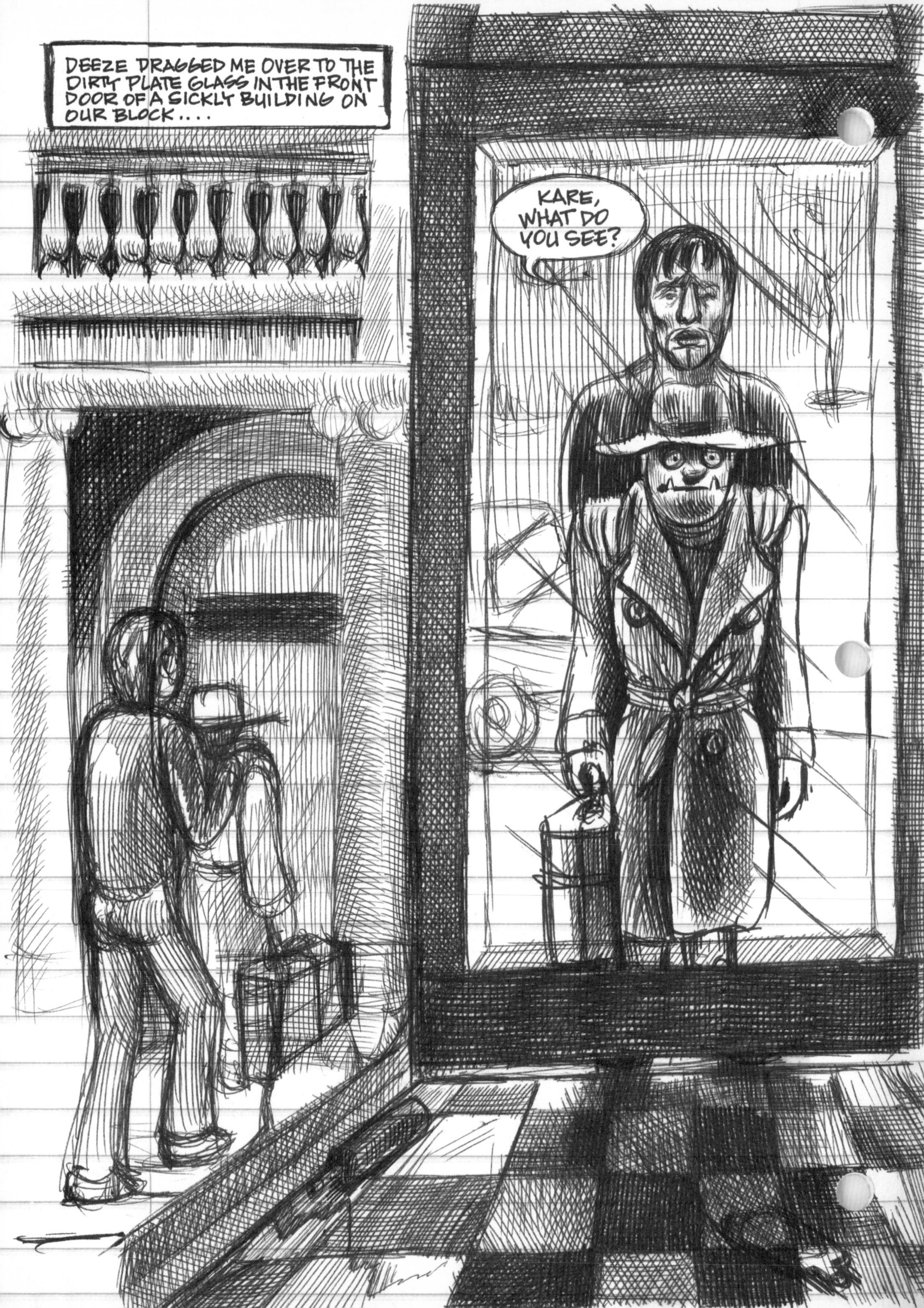
DEEZE DRAGGED ME OVER TO THE DIRTY PLATE GLASS IN THE FRONT DOOR OF A SICKLY BUILDING ON OUR BLOCK....
KARE, WHAT DO YOU SEE?

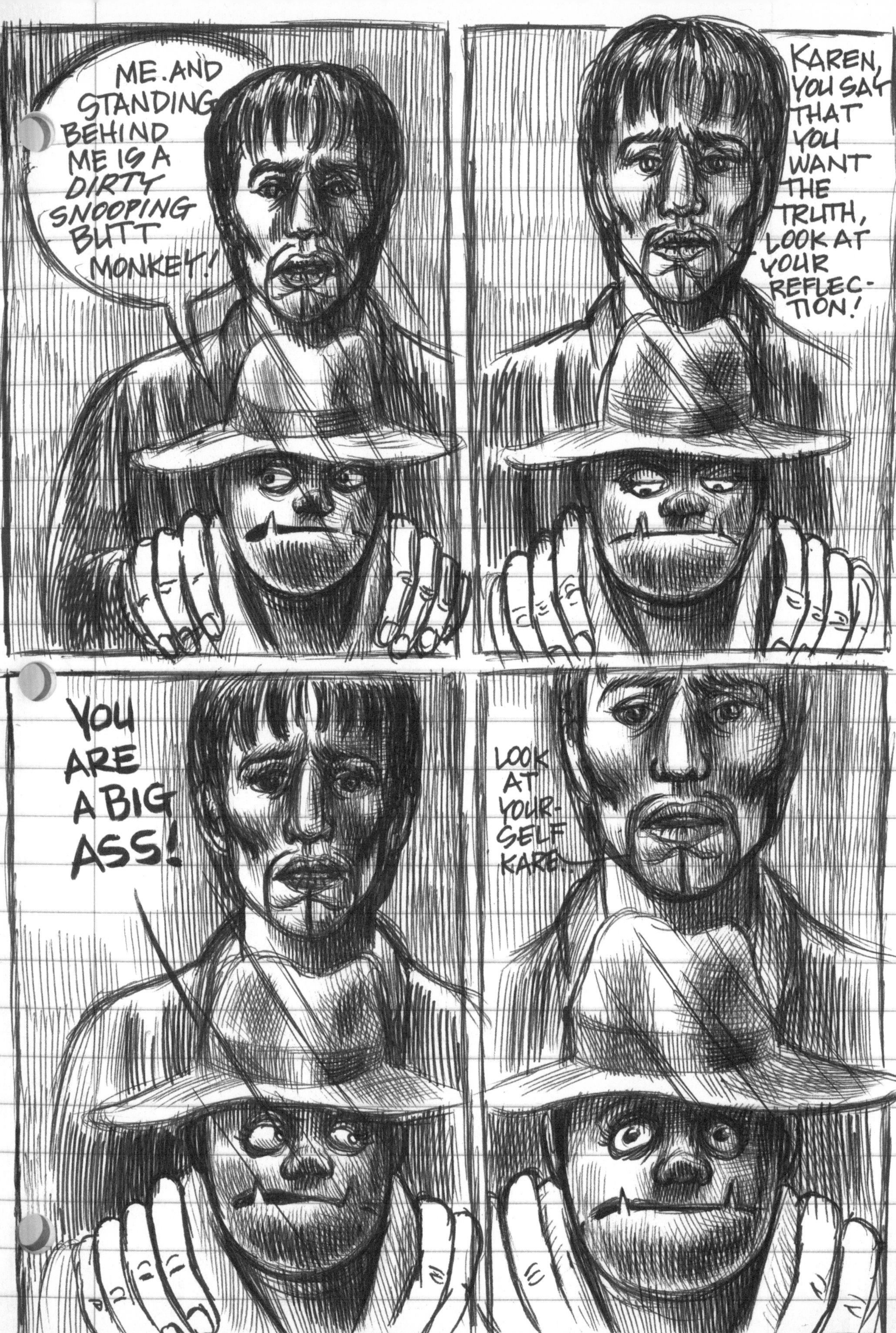
ME. AND STANDING BEHIND ME IS A DIRTY SNOOPING BUTT MONKEY!
KAREN, YOU SAY THAT YOU WANT THE TRUTH, LOOK AT YOUR REFLECTION!
YOU ARE A BIG ASS!
LOOK AT YOURSELF KARE...

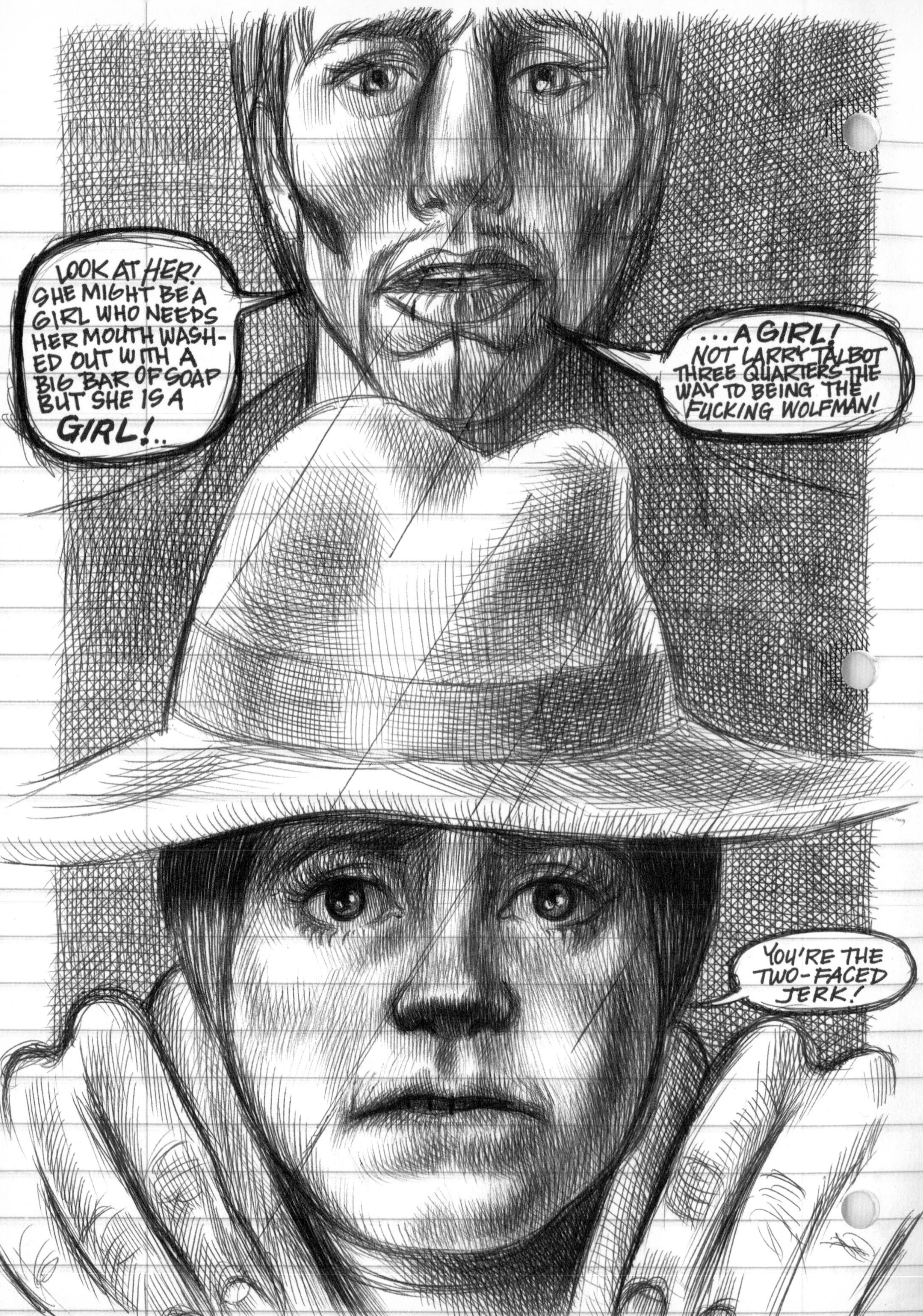
LOOK AT HER! SHE MIGHT BE A GIRL WHO NEEDS HER MOUTH WASHED OUT WITH A BIG BAR OF SOAP BUT SHE IS A GIRL!..
...A GIRL! NOT LARRY TALBOT THREE QUARTERS THE WAY TO BEING THE FUCKING WOLFMAN!
YOU'RE THE TWO-FACED JERK!

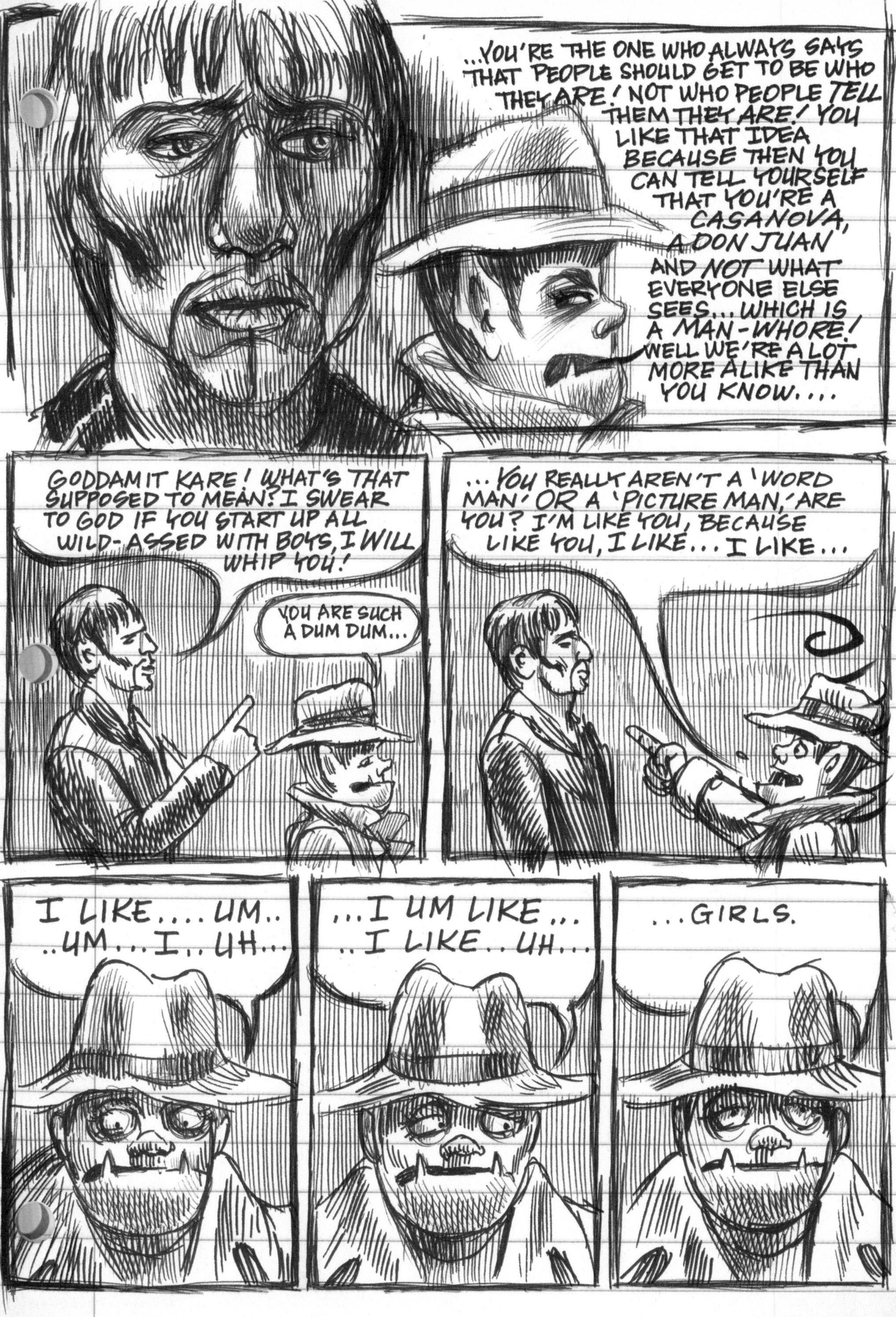
...YOU'RE THE ONE WHO ALWAYS SAYS THAT PEOPLE SHOULD GET TO BE WHO THEY ARE! NOT WHO PEOPLE TELL THEM THEY ARE! YOU LIKE THAT IDEA BECAUSE THEN YOU CAN TELL YOURSELF THAT YOU'RE A CASANOVA, A DON JUAN AND NOT WHAT EVERYONE ELSE SEES... WHICH IS A MAN-WHORE! WELL WE'RE A LOT MORE ALIKE THAN YOU KNOW....
GODDAMIT KARE! WHAT'S THAT SUPPOSED TO MEAN? I SWEAR TO GOD IF YOU START UP ALL WILD-ASSED WITH BOYS, I WILL WHIP YOU!
YOU ARE SUCH A DUM DUM...
...YOU REALLY AREN'T A 'WORD MAN' OR A 'PICTURE MAN,' ARE YOU? I'M LIKE YOU, BECAUSE LIKE YOU, I LIKE... I LIKE...
I LIKE....UM.. ..UM...I..UH...
...I UM LIKE... ..I LIKE..UH...
...GIRLS.

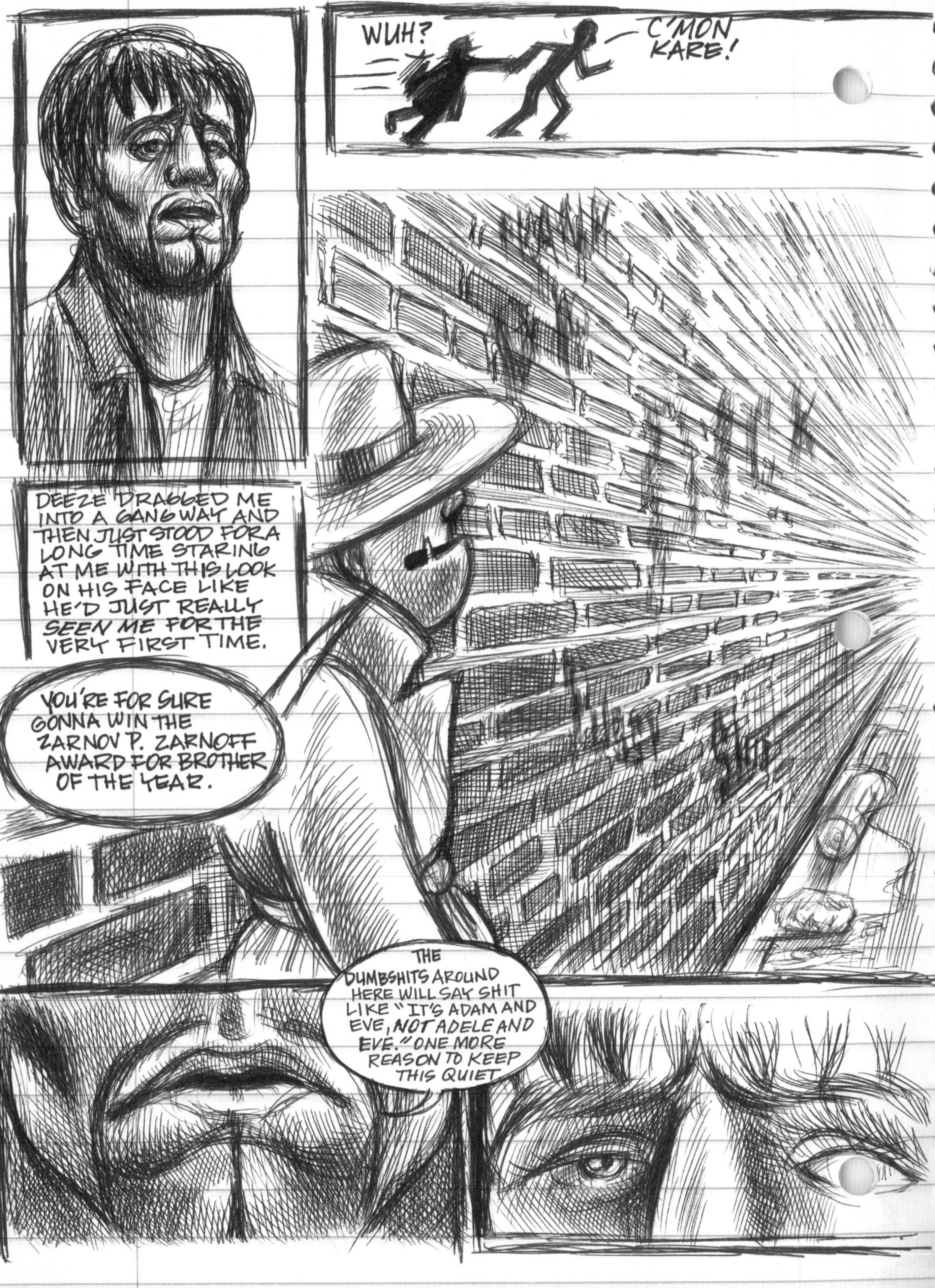
WUH?
C'MON KARE!
DEEZE DRAGGED ME INTO A GANGWAY AND THEN JUST STOOD FOR A LONG TIME STARING AT ME WITH THIS LOOK ON HIS FACE LIKE HE'D JUST REALLY *SEEN ME* FOR THE VERY FIRST TIME.
YOU'RE FOR SURE GONNA WIN THE ZARNOV P. ZARNOFF AWARD FOR BROTHER OF THE YEAR.
THE DUMBSHITS AROUND HERE WILL SAY SHIT LIKE "IT'S ADAM AND EVE, *NOT* ADELE AND EVE." ONE MORE REASON TO KEEP THIS QUIET

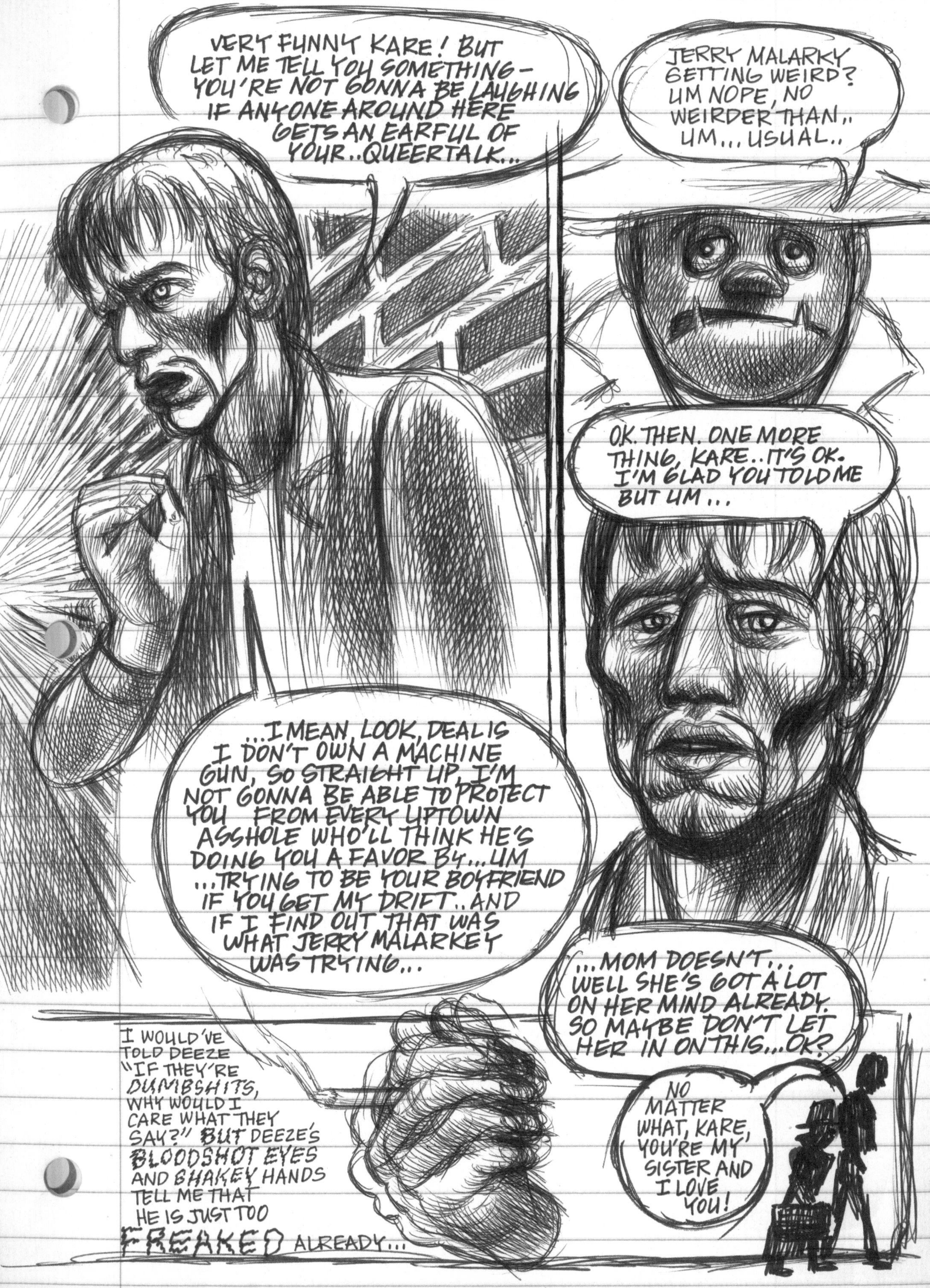

VERY FUNNY KARE! BUT LET ME TELL YOU SOMETHING - YOU'RE NOT GONNA BE LAUGHING IF ANYONE AROUND HERE GETS AN EARFUL OF YOUR..QUEERTALK...
JERRY MALARKY GETTING WEIRD? UM NOPE, NO WEIRDER THAN,, UM... USUAL..
OK. THEN. ONE MORE THING, KARE.. IT'S OK. I'M GLAD YOU TOLD ME BUT UM...
...I MEAN, LOOK, DEAL IS I DON'T OWN A MACHINE GUN, SO STRAIGHT UP, I'M NOT GONNA BE ABLE TO PROTECT YOU FROM EVERY UPTOWN ASSHOLE WHO'LL THINK HE'S DOING YOU A FAVOR BY... UM ...TRYING TO BE YOUR BOYFRIEND IF YOU GET MY DRIFT.. AND IF I FIND OUT THAT WAS WHAT JERRY MALARKEY WAS TRYING...
...MOM DOESN'T... WELL SHE'S GOT A LOT ON HER MIND ALREADY. SO MAYBE DON'T LET HER IN ON THIS...OK?
I WOULD'VE TOLD DEEZE "IF THEY'RE DUMBSHITS, WHY WOULD I CARE WHAT THEY SAY?" BUT DEEZE'S BLOODSHOT EYES AND SHAKEY HANDS TELL ME THAT HE IS JUST TOO FREAKED ALREADY...
NO MATTER WHAT, KARE, YOU'RE MY SISTER AND I LOVE YOU!

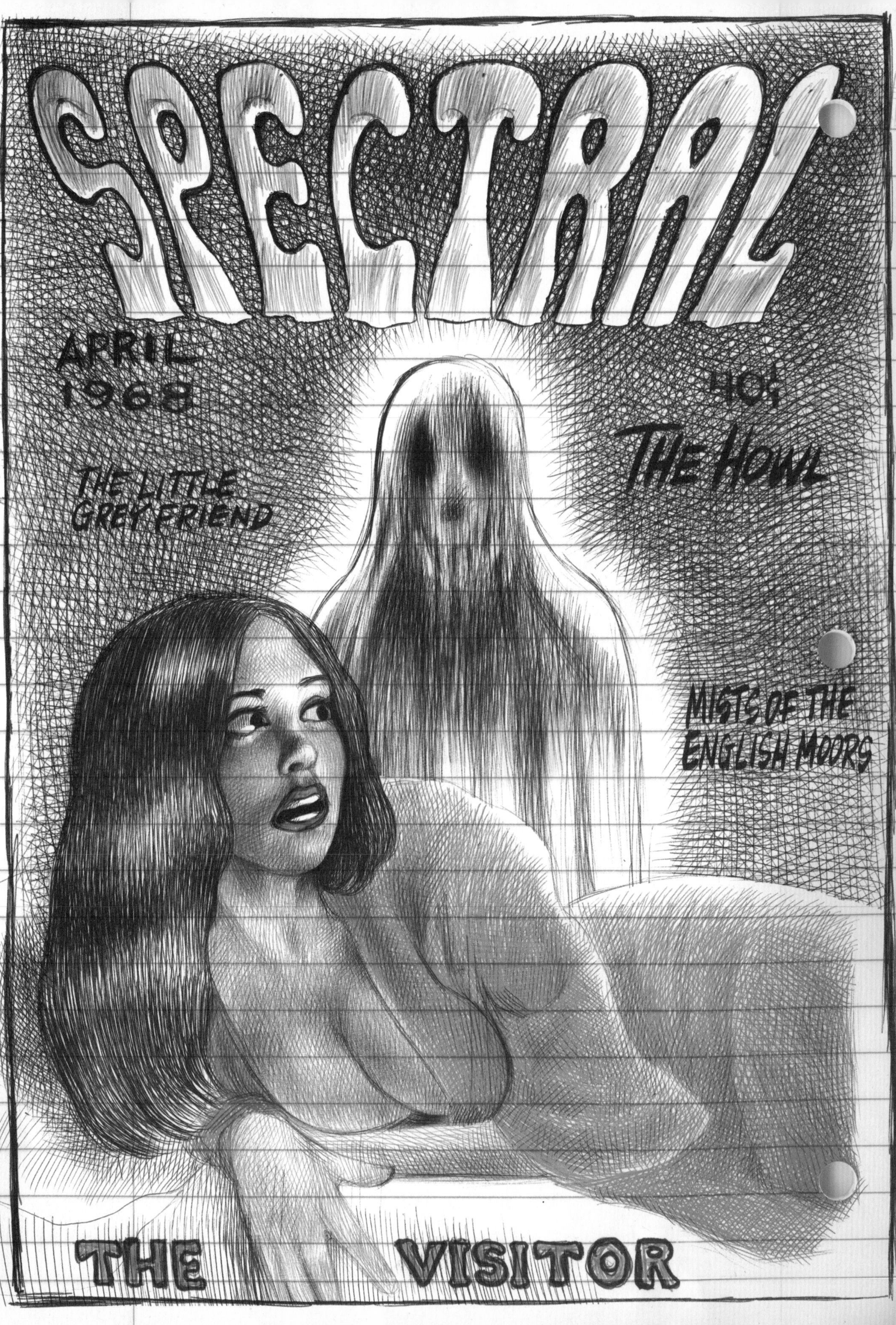
SPECTRAL
APRIL
1968
40¢
THE LITTLE
GREY FRIEND
THE HOWL
MISTS OF THE
ENGLISH MOORS
THE VISITOR

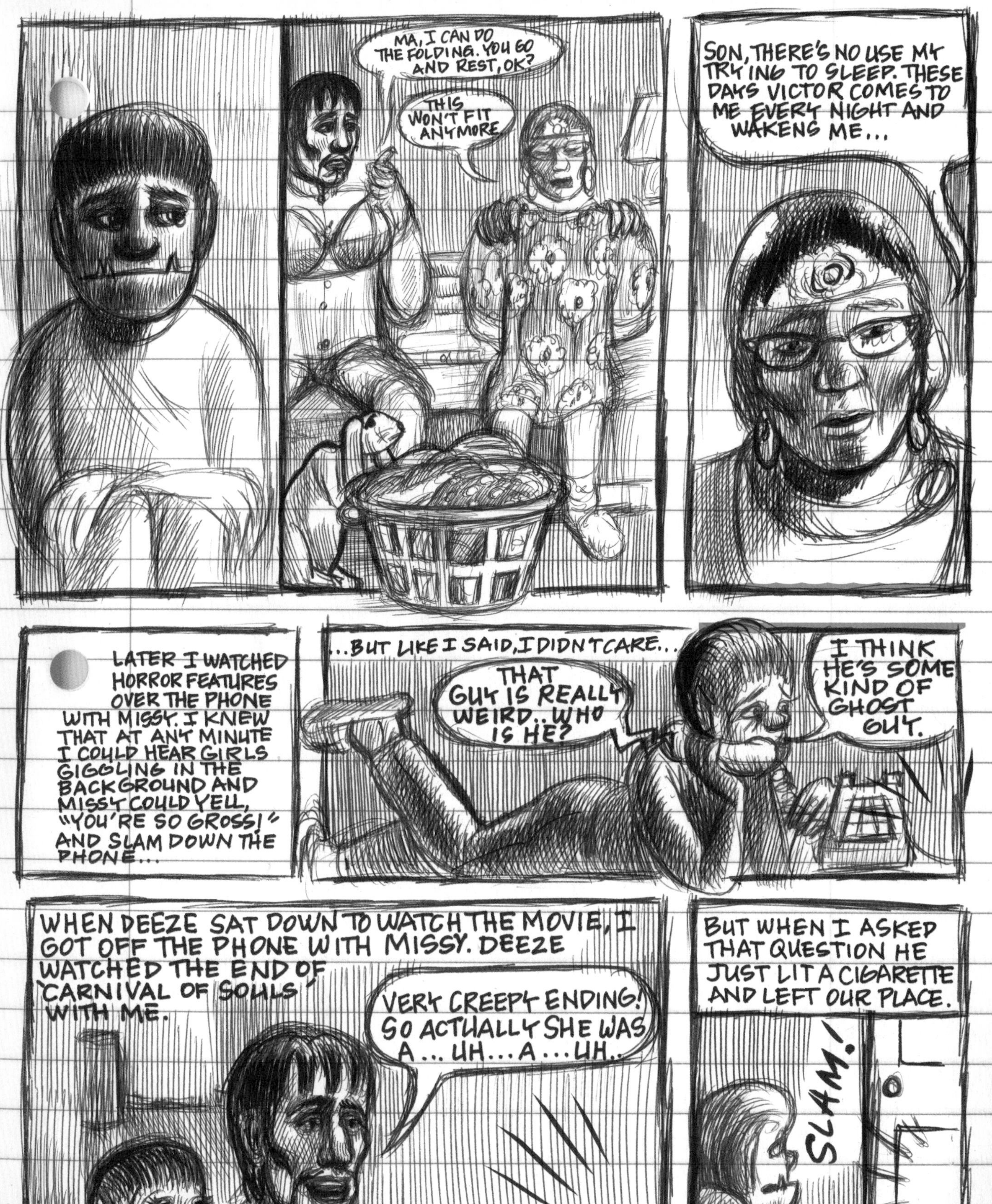
MA, I CAN DO THE FOLDING. YOU GO AND REST, OK?
THIS WON'T FIT ANYMORE
SON, THERE'S NO USE MY TRYING TO SLEEP. THESE DAYS VICTOR COMES TO ME EVERY NIGHT AND WAKENS ME...
LATER I WATCHED HORROR FEATURES OVER THE PHONE WITH MISSY. I KNEW THAT AT ANY MINUTE I COULD HEAR GIRLS GIGGLING IN THE BACKGROUND AND MISSY COULD YELL, "YOU'RE SO GROSS!" AND SLAM DOWN THE PHONE...
...BUT LIKE I SAID, I DIDN'T CARE...
THAT GUY IS REALLY WEIRD.. WHO IS HE?
I THINK HE'S SOME KIND OF GHOST GUY.
WHEN DEEZE SAT DOWN TO WATCH THE MOVIE, I GOT OFF THE PHONE WITH MISSY. DEEZE WATCHED THE END OF 'CARNIVAL OF SOULS' WITH ME.
VERY CREEPY ENDING! SO ACTUALLY SHE WAS A... UH... A... UH..
YEAH. CREEPY, HUH? SO DEEZE, WHO'S VICTOR?
BUT WHEN I ASKED THAT QUESTION HE JUST LIT A CIGARETTE AND LEFT OUR PLACE.
SLAM!
DEEZE?

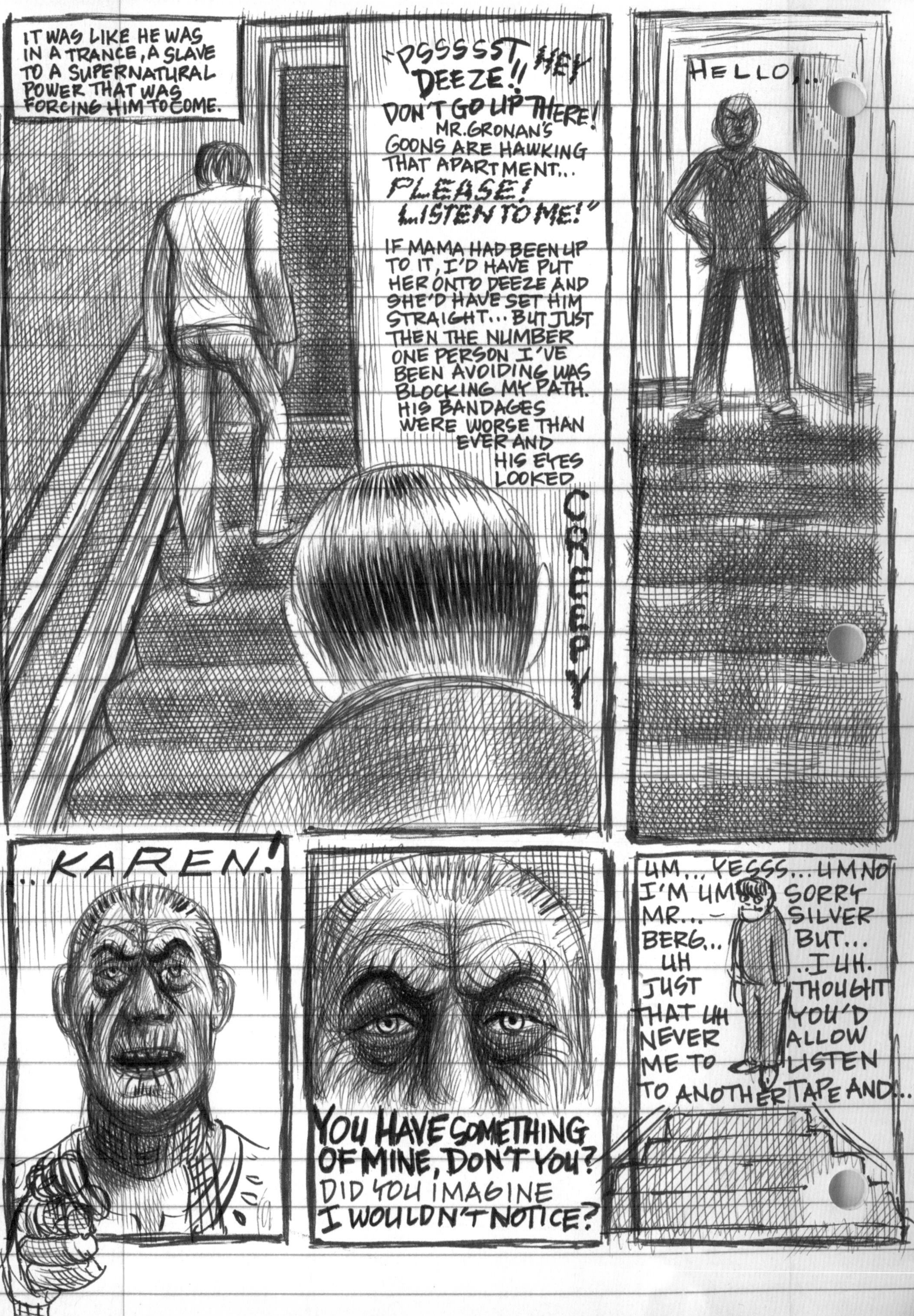
IT WAS LIKE HE WAS IN A TRANCE, A SLAVE TO A SUPERNATURAL POWER THAT WAS FORCING HIM TO COME.
"PSSSSST, HEY DEEZE!! DON'T GO UP THERE! MR. GRONAN'S GOONS ARE HAWKING THAT APARTMENT... PLEASE! LISTEN TO ME!"
IF MAMA HAD BEEN UP TO IT, I'D HAVE PUT HER ONTO DEEZE AND SHE'D HAVE SET HIM STRAIGHT... BUT JUST THEN THE NUMBER ONE PERSON I'VE BEEN AVOIDING WAS BLOCKING MY PATH. HIS BANDAGES WERE WORSE THAN EVER AND HIS EYES LOOKED
CREEPY
HELLO...
..KAREN!
YOU HAVE SOMETHING OF MINE, DON'T YOU? DID YOU IMAGINE I WOULDN'T NOTICE?
UM... YESSS... UM NO I'M UM SORRY MR... SILVERBERG... BUT... UH ..I UH. JUST THOUGHT THAT UH YOU'D NEVER ALLOW ME TO LISTEN TO ANOTHER TAPE AND...

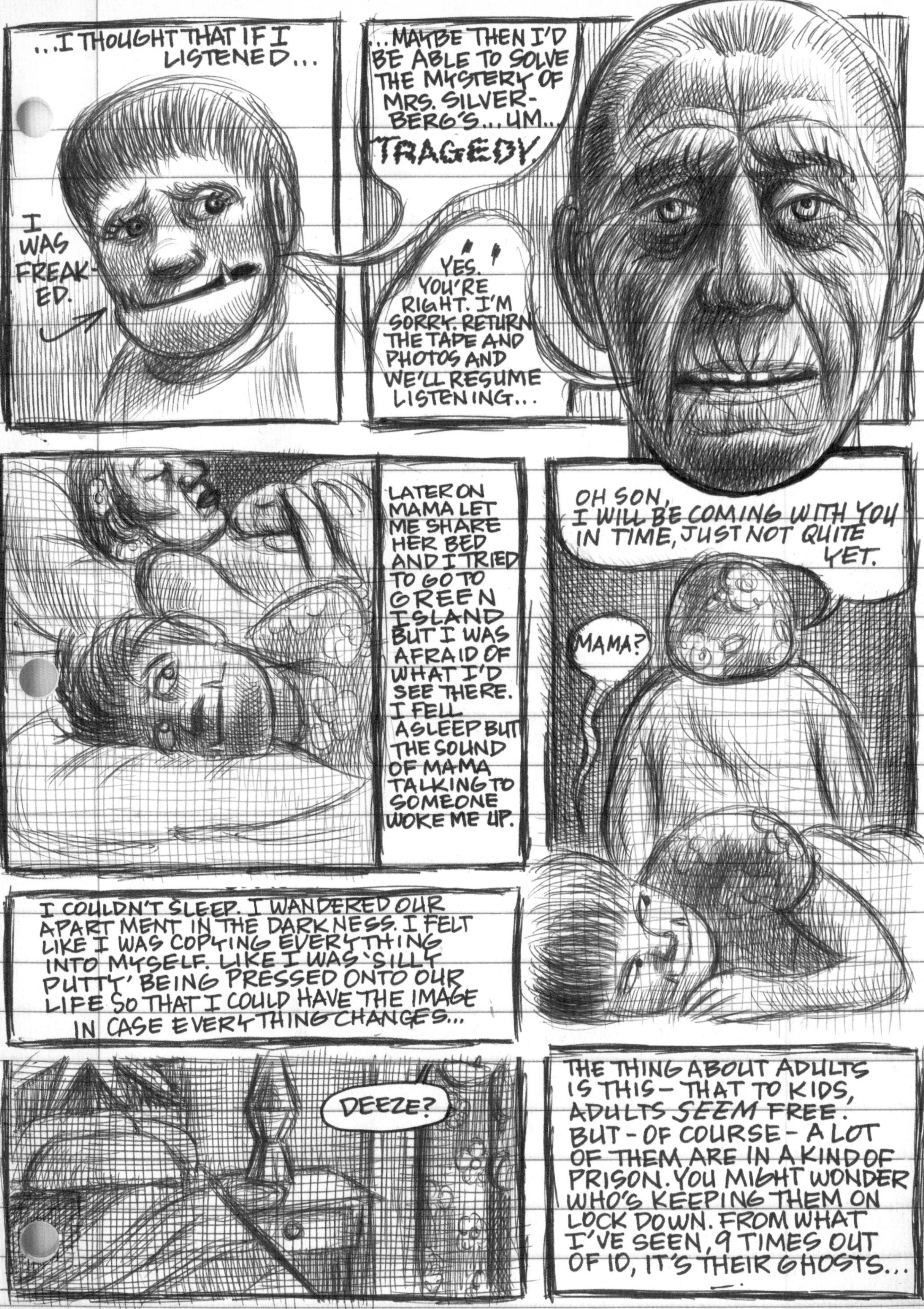
...I THOUGHT THAT IF I LISTENED...
I WAS FREAK-ED.
...MAYBE THEN I'D BE ABLE TO SOLVE THE MYSTERY OF MRS. SILVER-BERG'S...UM... TRAGEDY.
YES. YOU'RE RIGHT. I'M SORRY. RETURN THE TAPE AND PHOTOS AND WE'LL RESUME LISTENING...
LATER ON MAMA LET ME SHARE HER BED AND I TRIED TO GO TO GREEN ISLAND BUT I WAS AFRAID OF WHAT I'D SEE THERE. I FELL ASLEEP BUT THE SOUND OF MAMA TALKING TO SOMEONE WOKE ME UP.
OH SON, I WILL BE COMING WITH YOU IN TIME, JUST NOT QUITE YET.
MAMA?
I COULDN'T SLEEP. I WANDERED OUR APARTMENT IN THE DARKNESS. I FELT LIKE I WAS COPYING EVERYTHING INTO MYSELF. LIKE I WAS 'SILLY PUTTY' BEING PRESSED ONTO OUR LIFE SO THAT I COULD HAVE THE IMAGE IN CASE EVERYTHING CHANGES...
DEEZE?
THE THING ABOUT ADULTS IS THIS– THAT TO KIDS, ADULTS SEEM FREE. BUT– OF COURSE– A LOT OF THEM ARE IN A KIND OF PRISON. YOU MIGHT WONDER WHO'S KEEPING THEM ON LOCK DOWN. FROM WHAT I'VE SEEN, 9 TIMES OUT OF 10, IT'S THEIR GHOSTS...

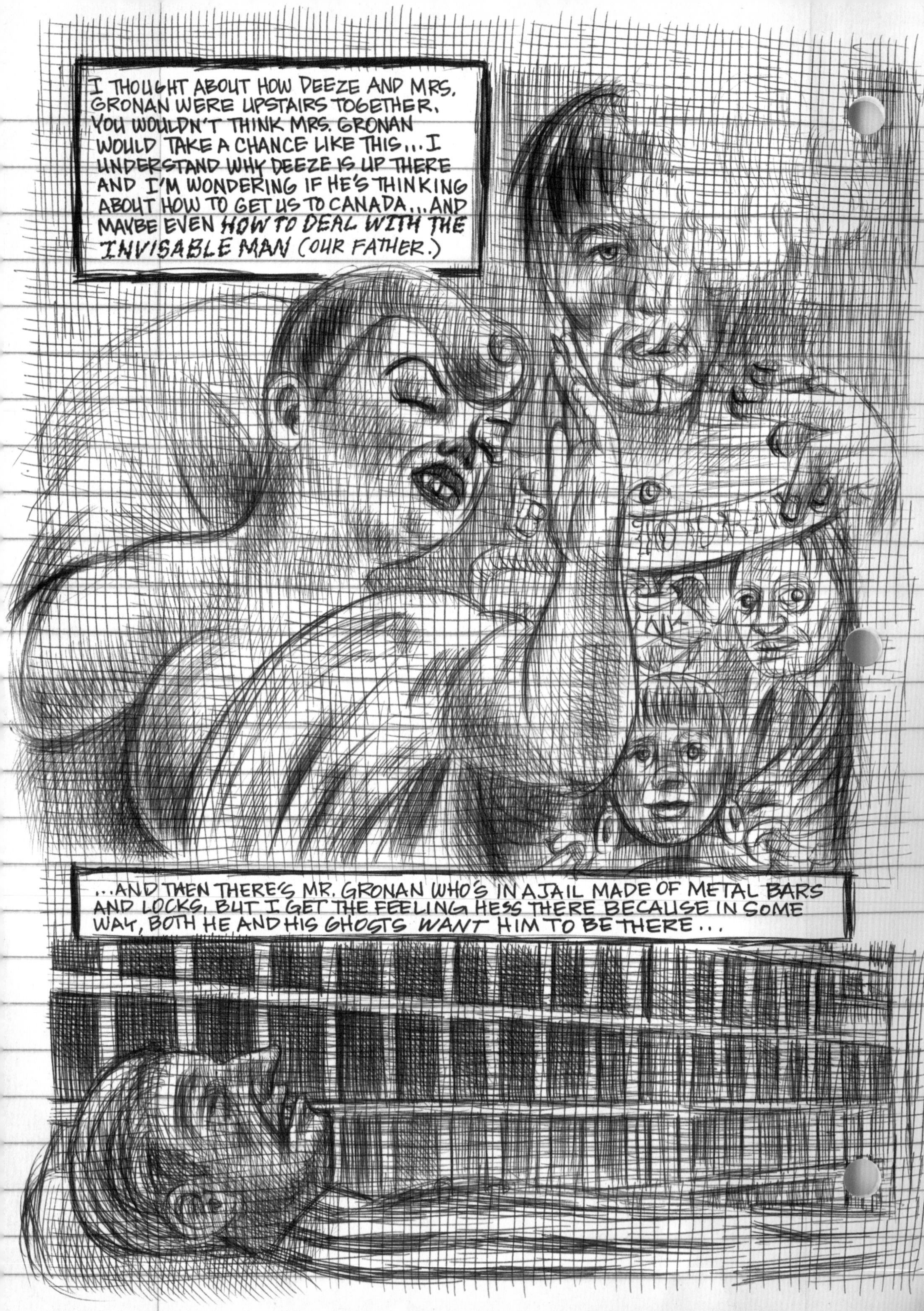
I THOUGHT ABOUT HOW DEEZE AND MRS. GRONAN WERE UPSTAIRS TOGETHER. YOU WOULDN'T THINK MRS. GRONAN WOULD TAKE A CHANCE LIKE THIS... I UNDERSTAND WHY DEEZE IS UP THERE AND I'M WONDERING IF HE'S THINKING ABOUT HOW TO GET US TO CANADA... AND MAYBE EVEN *HOW TO DEAL WITH THE INVISABLE MAN* (OUR FATHER.)
...AND THEN THERE'S MR. GRONAN WHO'S IN A JAIL MADE OF METAL BARS AND LOCKS, BUT I GET THE FEELING HESS THERE BECAUSE IN SOME WAY, BOTH HE AND HIS GHOSTS *WANT* HIM TO BE THERE...

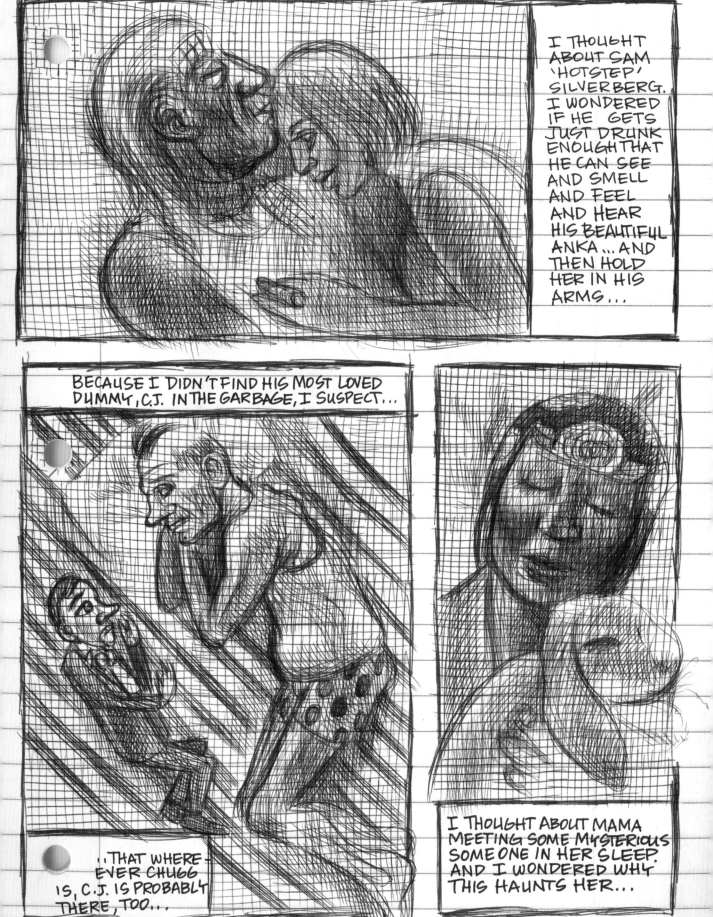

I THOUGHT ABOUT SAM 'HOTSTEP' SILVERBERG. I WONDERED IF HE GETS JUST DRUNK ENOUGH THAT HE CAN SEE AND SMELL AND FEEL AND HEAR HIS BEAUTIFUL ANKA... AND THEN HOLD HER IN HIS ARMS...

BECAUSE I DIDN'T FIND HIS MOST LOVED DUMMY, C.J. IN THE GARBAGE, I SUSPECT...

..THAT WHERE-EVER CHUGG IS, C.J. IS PROBABLY THERE, TOO...

I THOUGHT ABOUT MAMA MEETING SOME MYSTERIOUS SOMEONE IN HER SLEEP. AND I WONDERED WHY THIS HAUNTS HER...

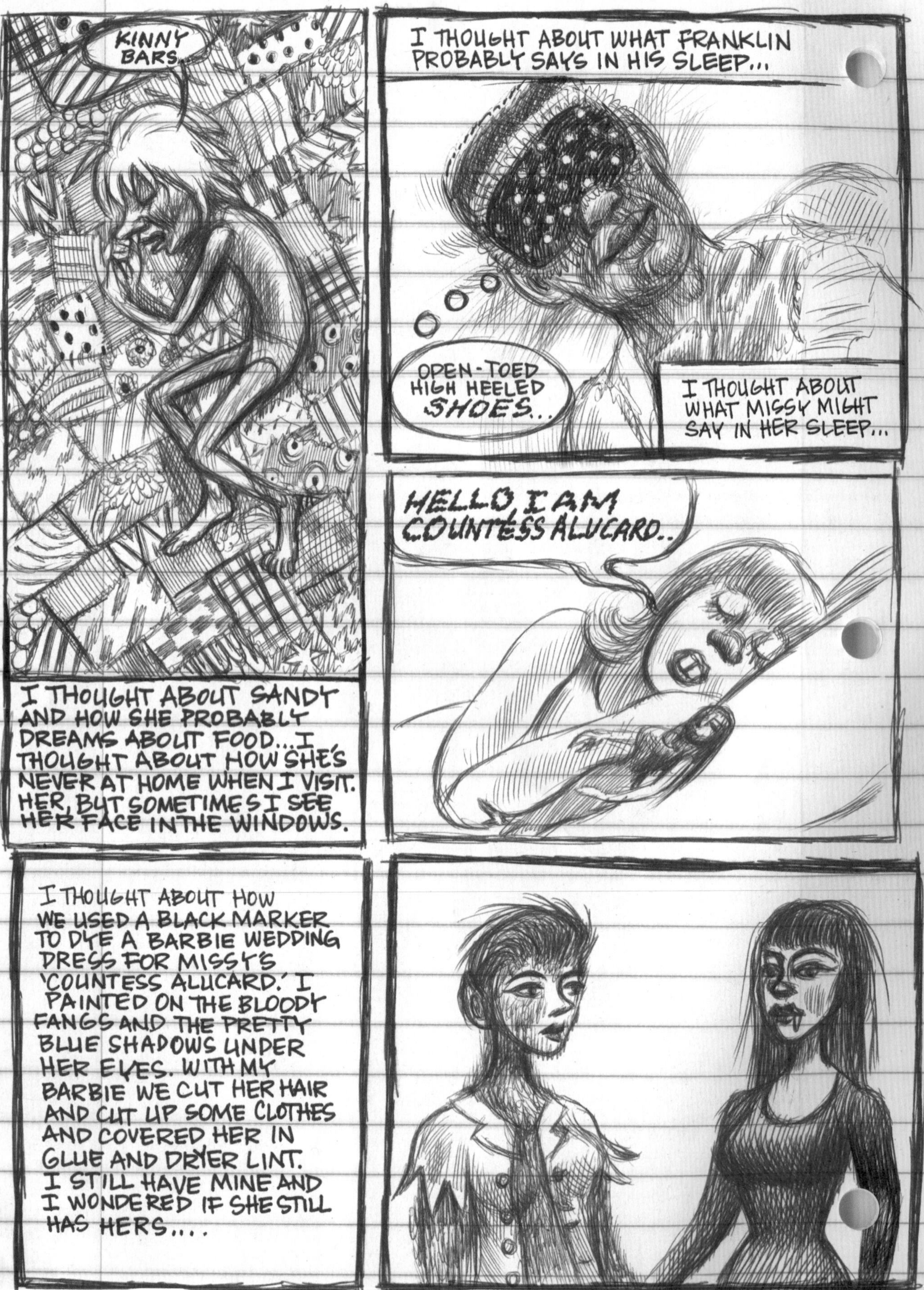
KINNY BARS...
I THOUGHT ABOUT SANDY AND HOW SHE PROBABLY DREAMS ABOUT FOOD...I THOUGHT ABOUT HOW SHE'S NEVER AT HOME WHEN I VISIT. HER, BUT SOMETIMES I SEE HER FACE IN THE WINDOWS.
I THOUGHT ABOUT WHAT FRANKLIN PROBABLY SAYS IN HIS SLEEP...
OPEN-TOED HIGH HEELED SHOES...
I THOUGHT ABOUT WHAT MISSY MIGHT SAY IN HER SLEEP...
HELLO, I AM COUNTESS ALUCARD..
I THOUGHT ABOUT HOW WE USED A BLACK MARKER TO DYE A BARBIE WEDDING DRESS FOR MISSY'S 'COUNTESS ALUCARD.' I PAINTED ON THE BLOODY FANGS AND THE PRETTY BLUE SHADOWS UNDER HER EYES. WITH MY BARBIE WE CUT HER HAIR AND CUT UP SOME CLOTHES AND COVERED HER IN GLUE AND DRYER LINT. I STILL HAVE MINE AND I WONDERED IF SHE STILL HAS HERS....

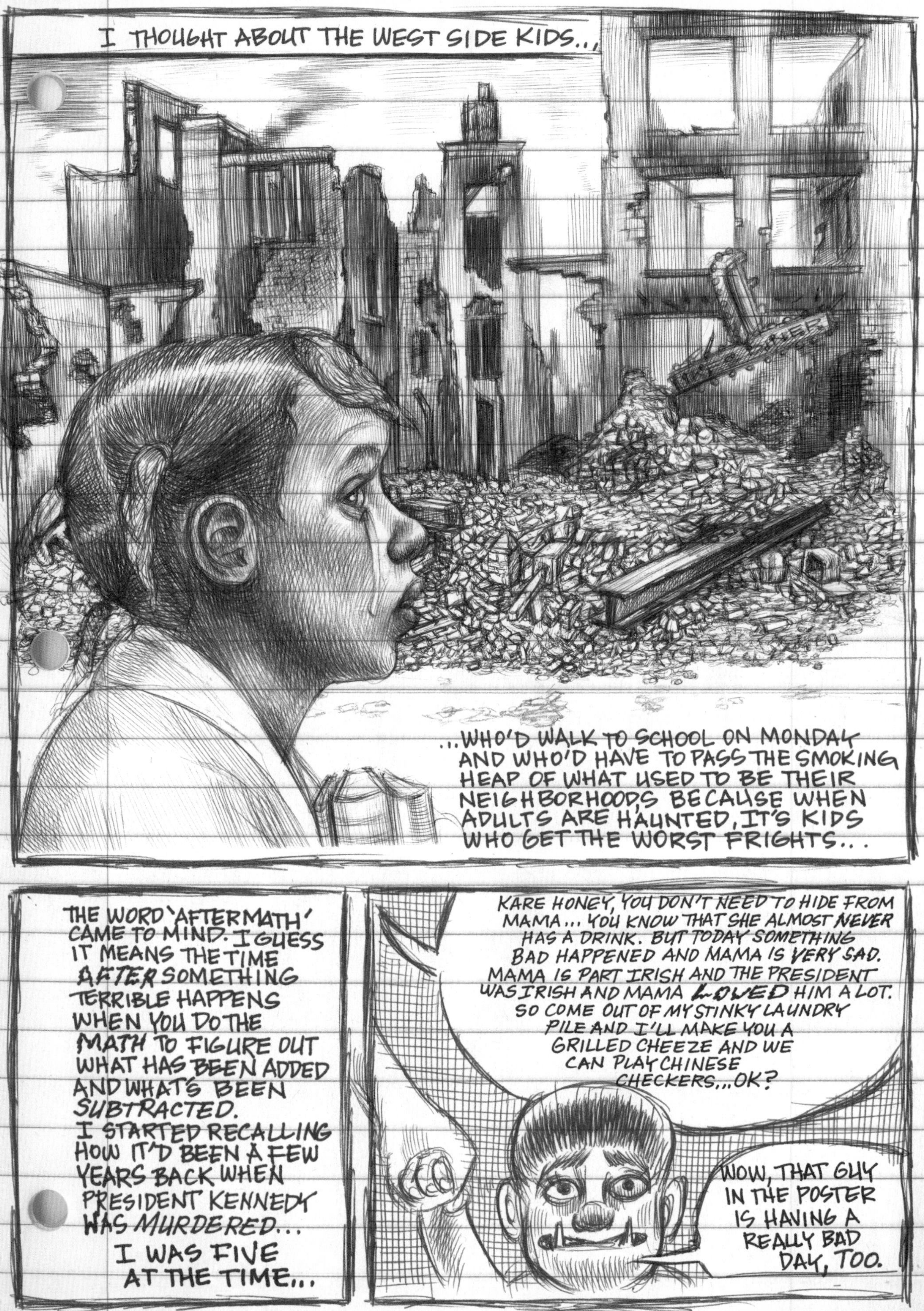
I THOUGHT ABOUT THE WEST SIDE KIDS...,
...WHO'D WALK TO SCHOOL ON MONDAY AND WHO'D HAVE TO PASS THE SMOKING HEAP OF WHAT USED TO BE THEIR NEIGHBORHOODS BECAUSE WHEN ADULTS ARE HAUNTED, IT'S KIDS WHO GET THE WORST FRIGHTS...
THE WORD 'AFTERMATH' CAME TO MIND. I GUESS IT MEANS THE TIME AFTER SOMETHING TERRIBLE HAPPENS WHEN YOU DO THE MATH TO FIGURE OUT WHAT HAS BEEN ADDED AND WHAT'S BEEN SUBTRACTED. I STARTED RECALLING HOW IT'D BEEN A FEW YEARS BACK WHEN PRESIDENT KENNEDY WAS MURDERED...
I WAS FIVE AT THE TIME...
KARE HONEY, YOU DON'T NEED TO HIDE FROM MAMA... YOU KNOW THAT SHE ALMOST NEVER HAS A DRINK. BUT TODAY SOMETHING BAD HAPPENED AND MAMA IS VERY SAD. MAMA IS PART IRISH AND THE PRESIDENT WAS IRISH AND MAMA LOVED HIM A LOT. SO COME OUT OF MY STINKY LAUNDRY PILE AND I'LL MAKE YOU A GRILLED CHEEZE AND WE CAN PLAY CHINESE CHECKERS...OK?
WOW, THAT GUY IN THE POSTER IS HAVING A REALLY BAD DAY, TOO.

WHEN DEEZE PULLED
ME OUT OF HIS LAUNDRY
PILE WE LOOKED AT
THIS POSTER DEEZE
HAD ON HIS WALL...

DEEZE SIGHED.
"SURE SEEMS
LIKE THERE'S
ONE SURE WAY
TO GET DEAD
IN THE U.S.OF
A. AND THAT
IS TO DO THE
RIGHT THING."

BACK THEN I
ALREADY KNEW
I WANTED TO
BE A MONSTER...

BUT LOOKING
AT THAT POSTER
I KNEW THERE
WERE GOOD
MONSTERS AND
BAD ONES...

...THE MONSTERS WHO
MURDERED REVEREND
KING AND THE PRESIDENT
WERE THE WORST
MONSTERS...

AMBROISE FREDEAU, THE BLESSED GUILLAUME
DE TOULOUSE TORMENTED BY DEMONS, 1657

...THOSE ARE THE KIND OF MONSTERS WHO WANT NO ONE TO BE FREE...

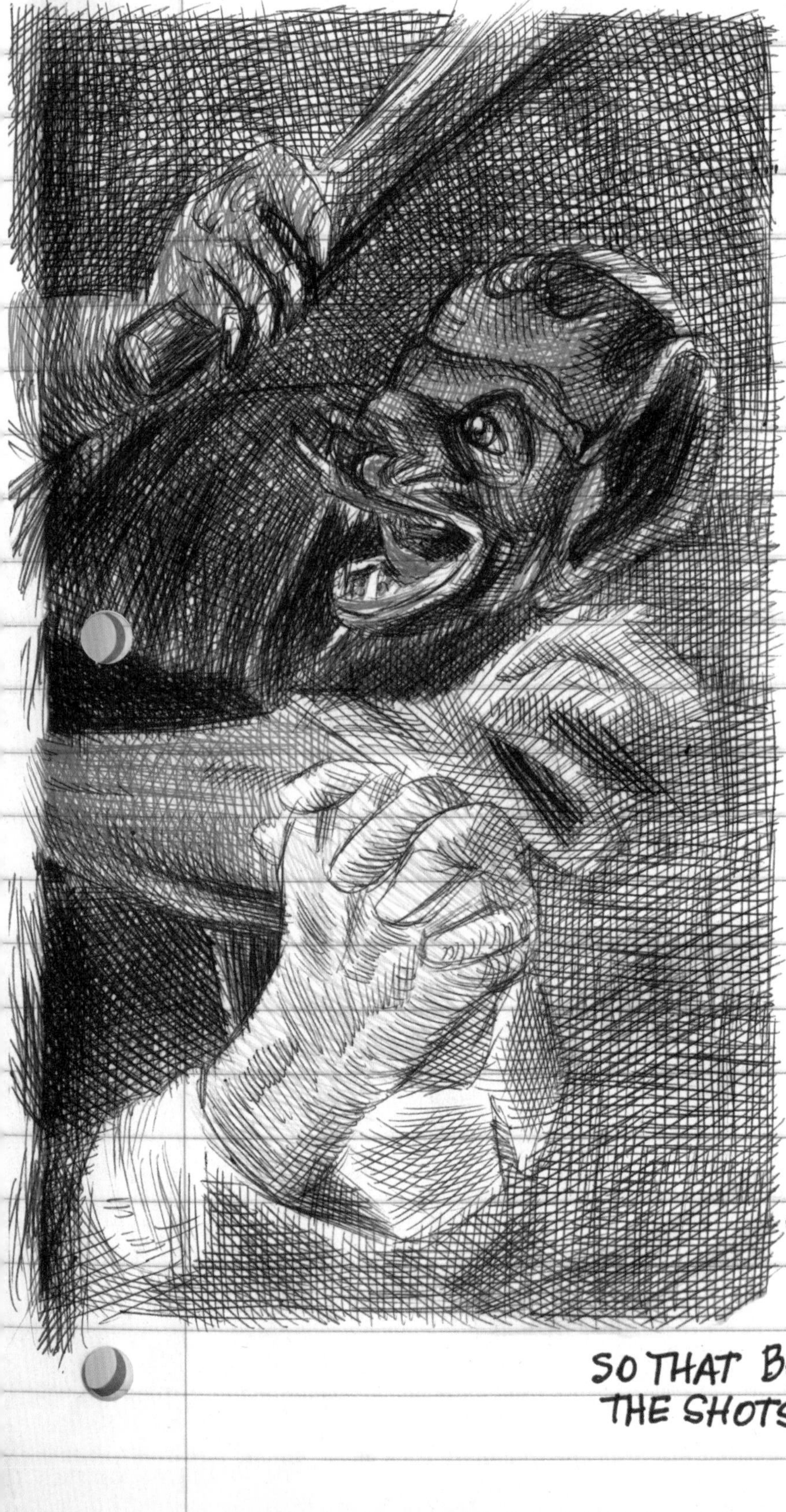

...NO, THE BAD MONSTERS WANT THE WORLD TO LOOK THE WAY THEY WANT IT TO. THEY *NEED* PEOPLE TO BE AFRAID...

...THEY DON'T LIVE IN THEIR LAIR AND MOSTLY MIND THEIR OWN BIZ...

I GUESS THAT'S THE DIFFERENCE,...A GOOD MONSTER SOMETIMES GIVES SOMEBODY A FRIGHT BECAUSE THEY'RE WEIRD LOOKING AND FANGY... A FACT THAT IS BEYOND THEIR CONTROL...

...BUT BAD MONSTERS ARE ALL ABOUT *CONTROL*... THEY WANT THE WHOLE WORLD TO BE SCARED

SO THAT BAD MONSTERS CAN CALL THE SHOTS...

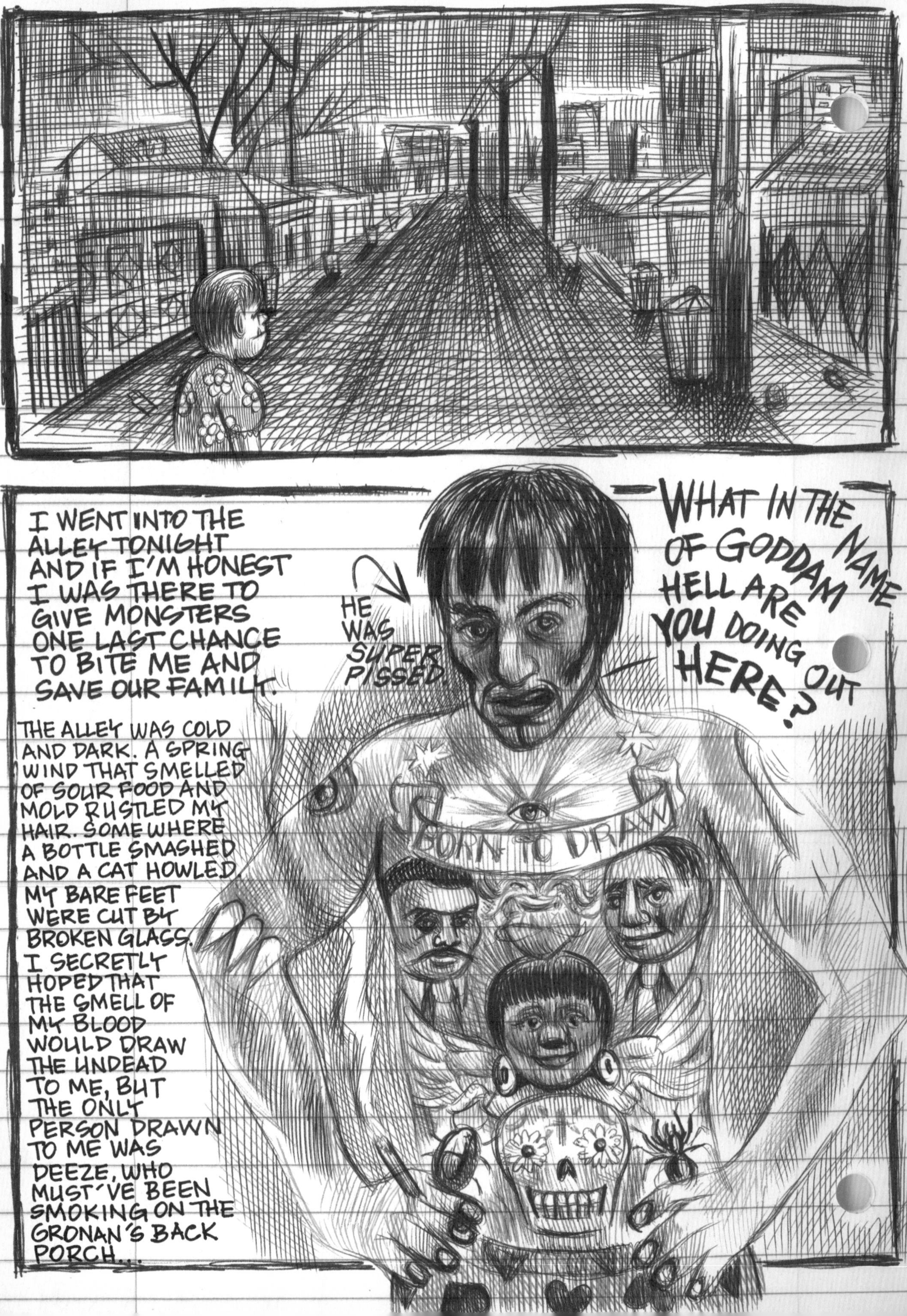

I WENT INTO THE ALLEY TONIGHT AND IF I'M HONEST I WAS THERE TO GIVE MONSTERS ONE LAST CHANCE TO BITE ME AND SAVE OUR FAMILY.
THE ALLEY WAS COLD AND DARK. A SPRING WIND THAT SMELLED OF SOUR FOOD AND MOLD RUSTLED MY HAIR. SOMEWHERE A BOTTLE SMASHED AND A CAT HOWLED. MY BARE FEET WERE CUT BY BROKEN GLASS. I SECRETLY HOPED THAT THE SMELL OF MY BLOOD WOULD DRAW THE UNDEAD TO ME, BUT THE ONLY PERSON DRAWN TO ME WAS DEEZE, WHO MUST'VE BEEN SMOKING ON THE GRONAN'S BACK PORCH...
HE WAS SUPER PISSED.
WHAT IN THE NAME OF GODDAM HELL ARE YOU DOING OUT HERE?
BORN TO DRAW

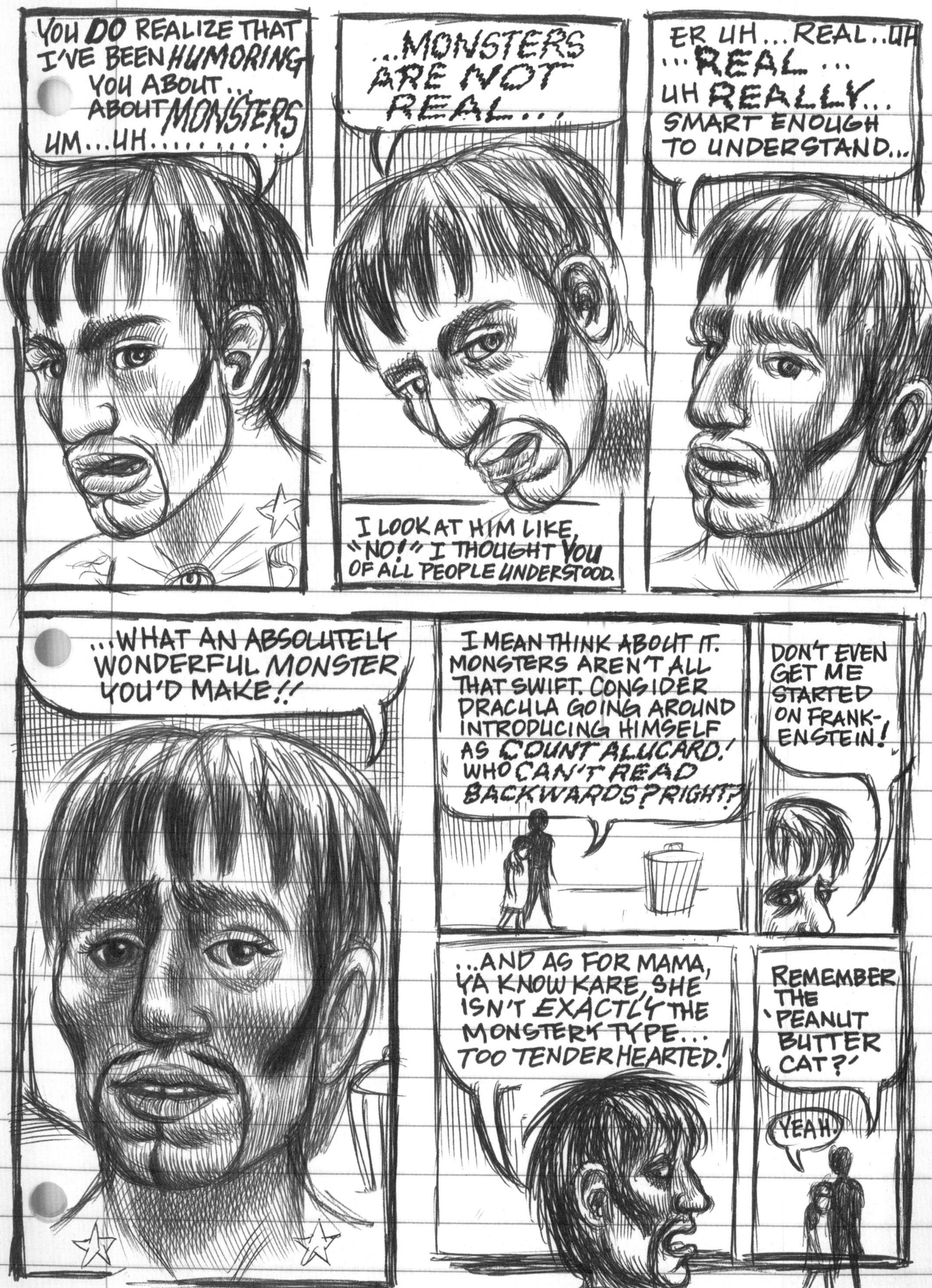
YOU DO REALIZE THAT I'VE BEEN HUMORING YOU ABOUT... ABOUT MONSTERS UM...UH..........
...MONSTERS ARE NOT REAL...
I LOOK AT HIM LIKE, "NO!" I THOUGHT YOU OF ALL PEOPLE UNDERSTOOD.
ER UH...REAL...UH ...REAL... UH REALLY... SMART ENOUGH TO UNDERSTAND...
...WHAT AN ABSOLUTELY WONDERFUL MONSTER YOU'D MAKE!!
I MEAN THINK ABOUT IT. MONSTERS AREN'T ALL THAT SWIFT. CONSIDER DRACULA GOING AROUND INTRODUCING HIMSELF AS COUNT ALUCARD! WHO CAN'T READ BACKWARDS? RIGHT?
DON'T EVEN GET ME STARTED ON FRANK-ENSTEIN!
...AND AS FOR MAMA, YA KNOW KARE, SHE ISN'T EXACTLY THE MONSTERY TYPE... TOO TENDER HEARTED!
REMEMBER THE 'PEANUT BUTTER CAT?'
YEAH.

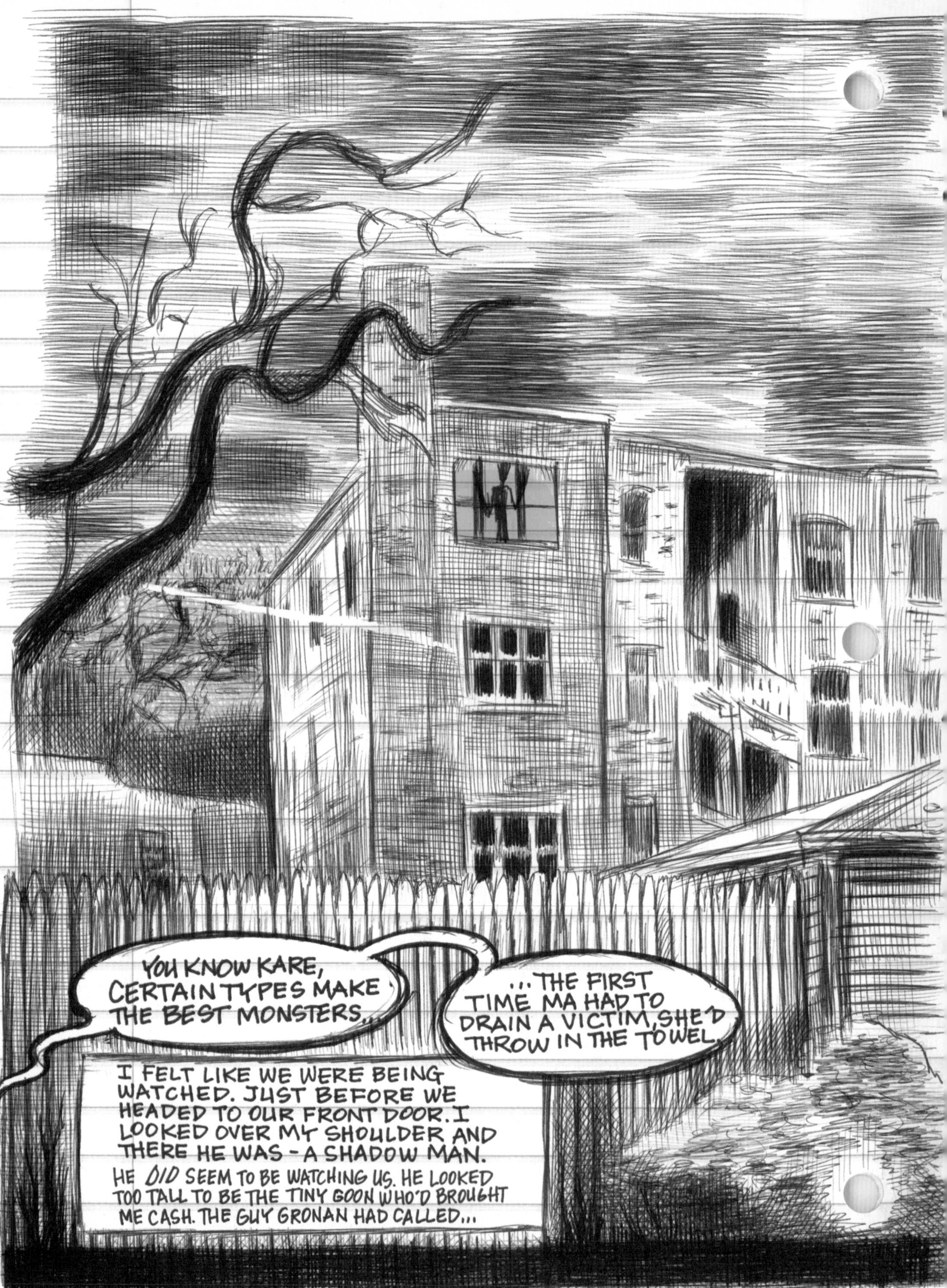
YOU KNOW KARE, CERTAIN TYPES MAKE THE BEST MONSTERS...
...THE FIRST TIME MA HAD TO DRAIN A VICTIM, SHE'D THROW IN THE TOWEL.
I FELT LIKE WE WERE BEING WATCHED. JUST BEFORE WE HEADED TO OUR FRONT DOOR. I LOOKED OVER MY SHOULDER AND THERE HE WAS - A SHADOW MAN. HE DID SEEM TO BE WATCHING US. HE LOOKED TOO TALL TO BE THE TINY GOON WHO'D BROUGHT ME CASH. THE GUY GRONAN HAD CALLED...

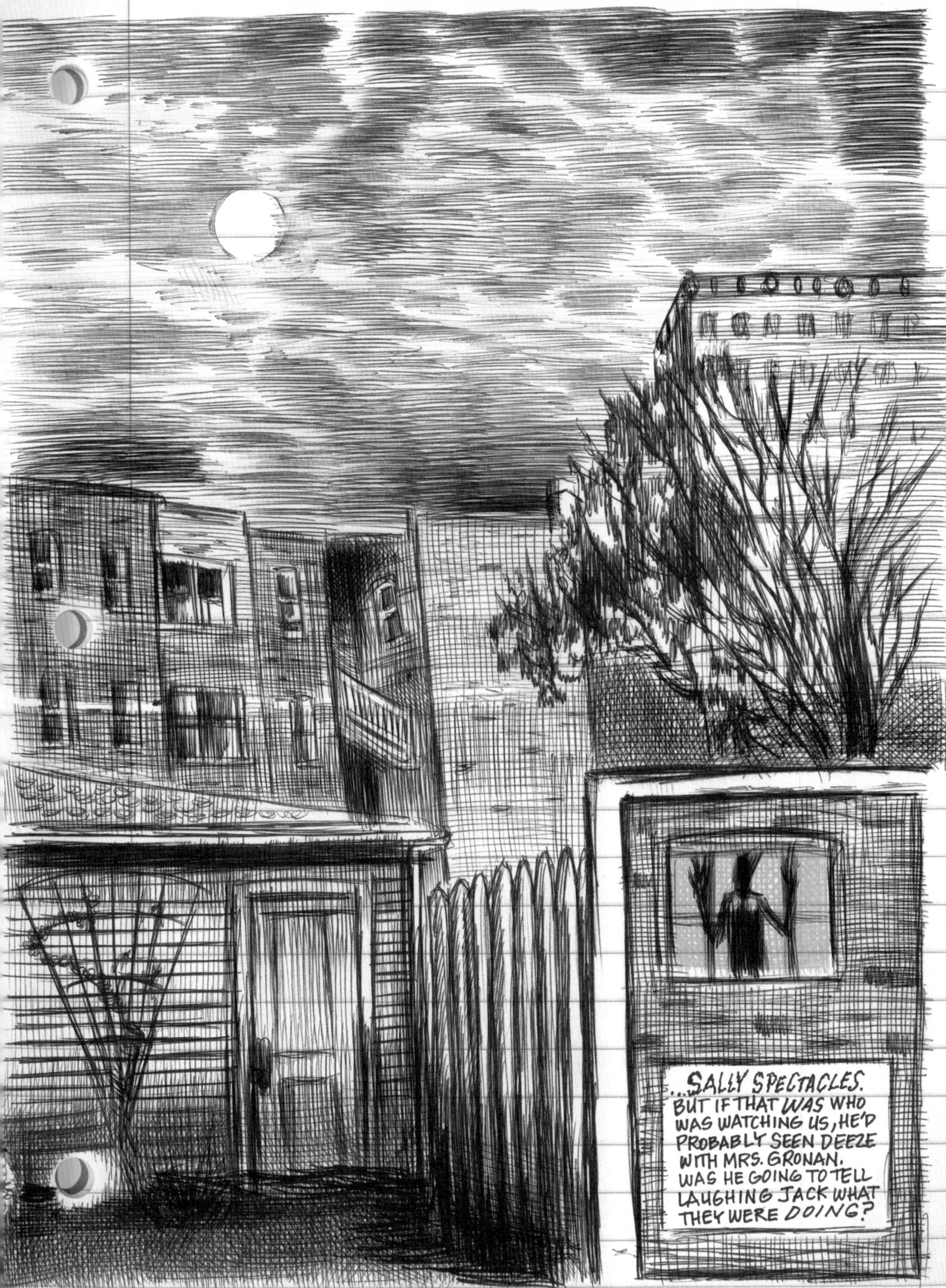
...SALLY SPECTACLES. BUT IF THAT WAS WHO WAS WATCHING US, HE'D PROBABLY SEEN DEEZE WITH MRS. GRONAN. WAS HE GOING TO TELL LAUGHING JACK WHAT THEY WERE DOING?

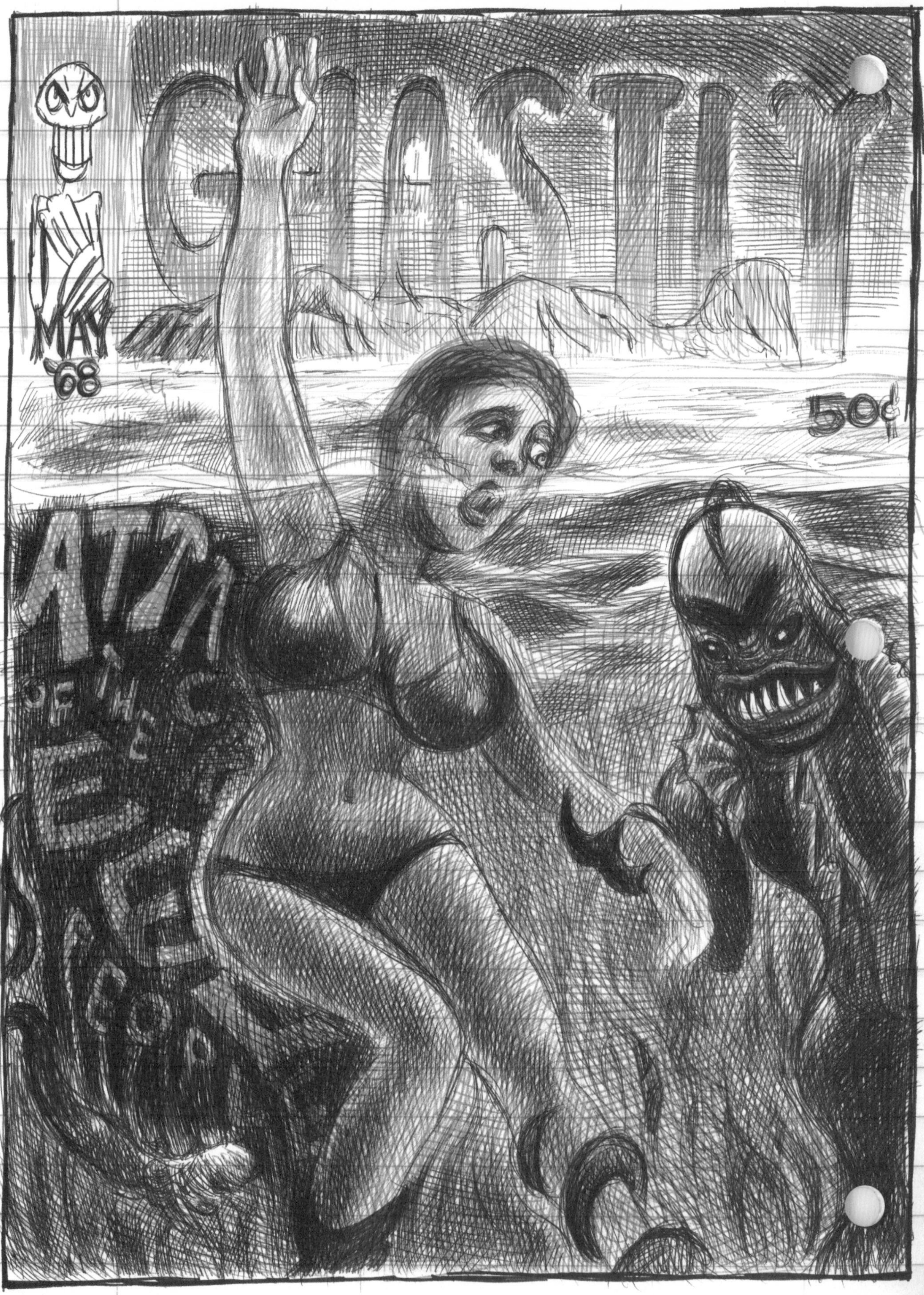
GHASTLY
MAY
'68
50¢

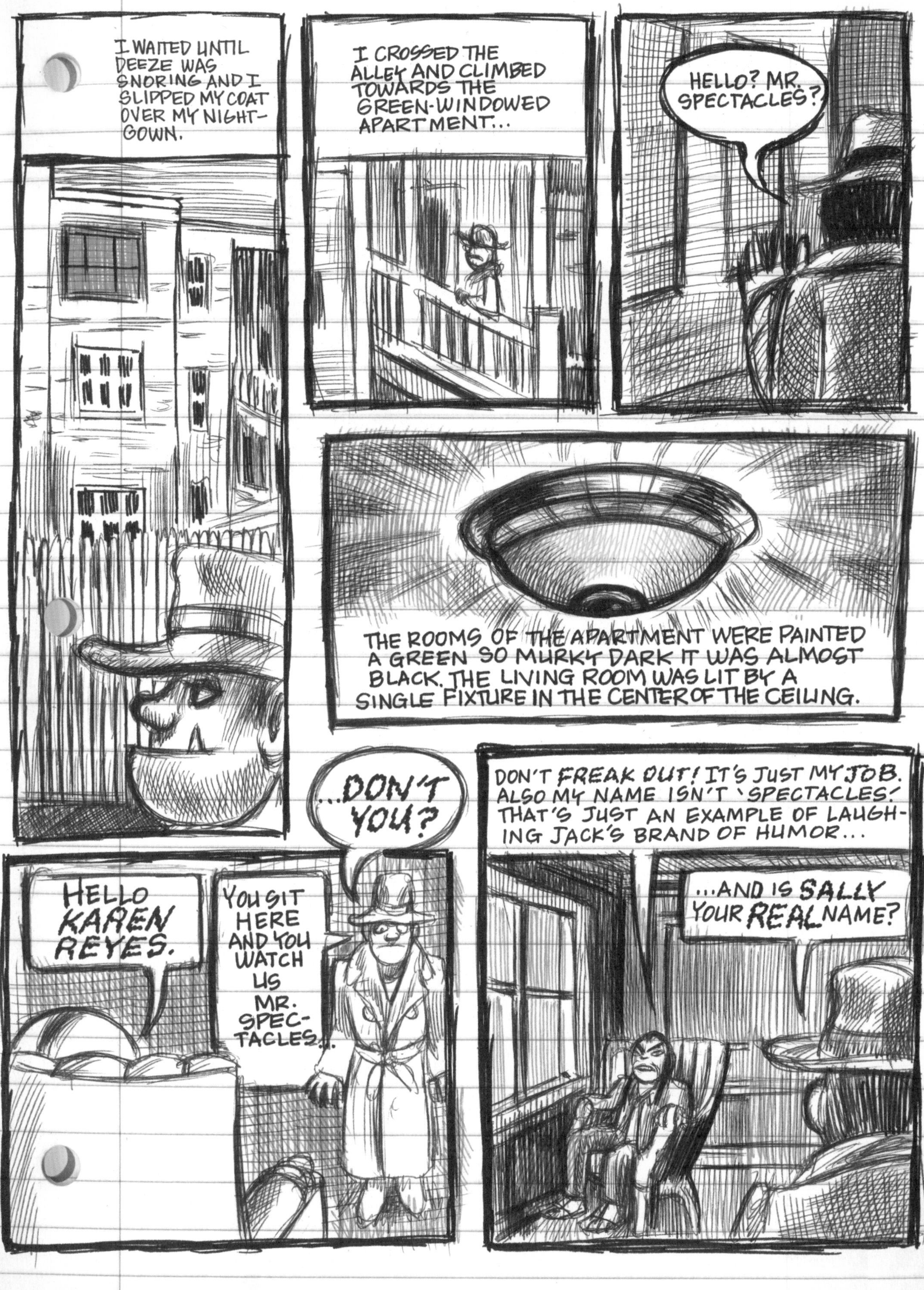
I WAITED UNTIL DEEZE WAS SNORING AND I SLIPPED MY COAT OVER MY NIGHT-GOWN.
I CROSSED THE ALLEY AND CLIMBED TOWARDS THE GREEN-WINDOWED APARTMENT...
HELLO? MR. SPECTACLES?
THE ROOMS OF THE APARTMENT WERE PAINTED A GREEN SO MURKY DARK IT WAS ALMOST BLACK. THE LIVING ROOM WAS LIT BY A SINGLE FIXTURE IN THE CENTER OF THE CEILING.
HELLO KAREN REYES.
YOU SIT HERE AND YOU WATCH US MR. SPECTACLES...
...DON'T YOU?
DON'T FREAK OUT! IT'S JUST MY JOB. ALSO MY NAME ISN'T 'SPECTACLES.' THAT'S JUST AN EXAMPLE OF LAUGHING JACK'S BRAND OF HUMOR...
...AND IS SALLY YOUR REAL NAME?

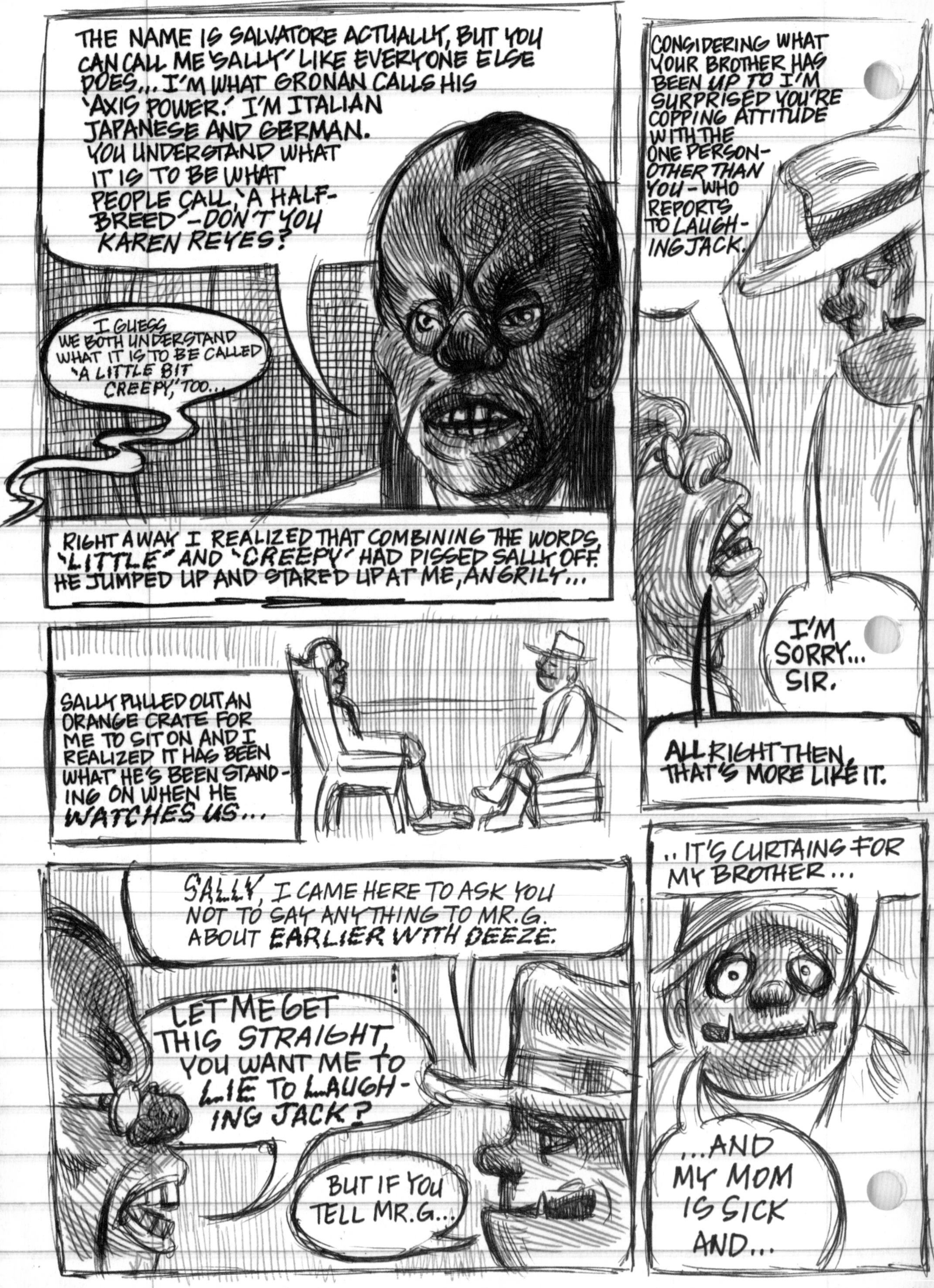
THE NAME IS SALVATORE ACTUALLY, BUT YOU CAN CALL ME 'SALLY' LIKE EVERYONE ELSE DOES... I'M WHAT GRONAN CALLS HIS 'AXIS POWER.' I'M ITALIAN JAPANESE AND GERMAN. YOU UNDERSTAND WHAT IT IS TO BE WHAT PEOPLE CALL, 'A HALF-BREED'-DON'T YOU KAREN REYES?
I GUESS WE BOTH UNDERSTAND WHAT IT IS TO BE CALLED 'A LITTLE BIT CREEPY,' TOO...
RIGHT AWAY I REALIZED THAT COMBINING THE WORDS, 'LITTLE' AND 'CREEPY' HAD PISSED SALLY OFF. HE JUMPED UP AND STARED UP AT ME, ANGRILY...
CONSIDERING WHAT YOUR BROTHER HAS BEEN UP TO I'M SURPRISED YOU'RE COPPING ATTITUDE WITH THE ONE PERSON-OTHER THAN YOU-WHO REPORTS TO LAUGHING JACK.
I'M SORRY... SIR.
ALL RIGHT THEN, THAT'S MORE LIKE IT.
SALLY PULLED OUT AN ORANGE CRATE FOR ME TO SIT ON AND I REALIZED IT HAS BEEN WHAT HE'S BEEN STANDING ON WHEN HE WATCHES US...
SALLY, I CAME HERE TO ASK YOU NOT TO SAY ANYTHING TO MR.G. ABOUT EARLIER WITH DEEZE.
LET ME GET THIS STRAIGHT, YOU WANT ME TO LIE TO LAUGHING JACK?
BUT IF YOU TELL MR.G...
..IT'S CURTAINS FOR MY BROTHER...
...AND MY MOM IS SICK AND...

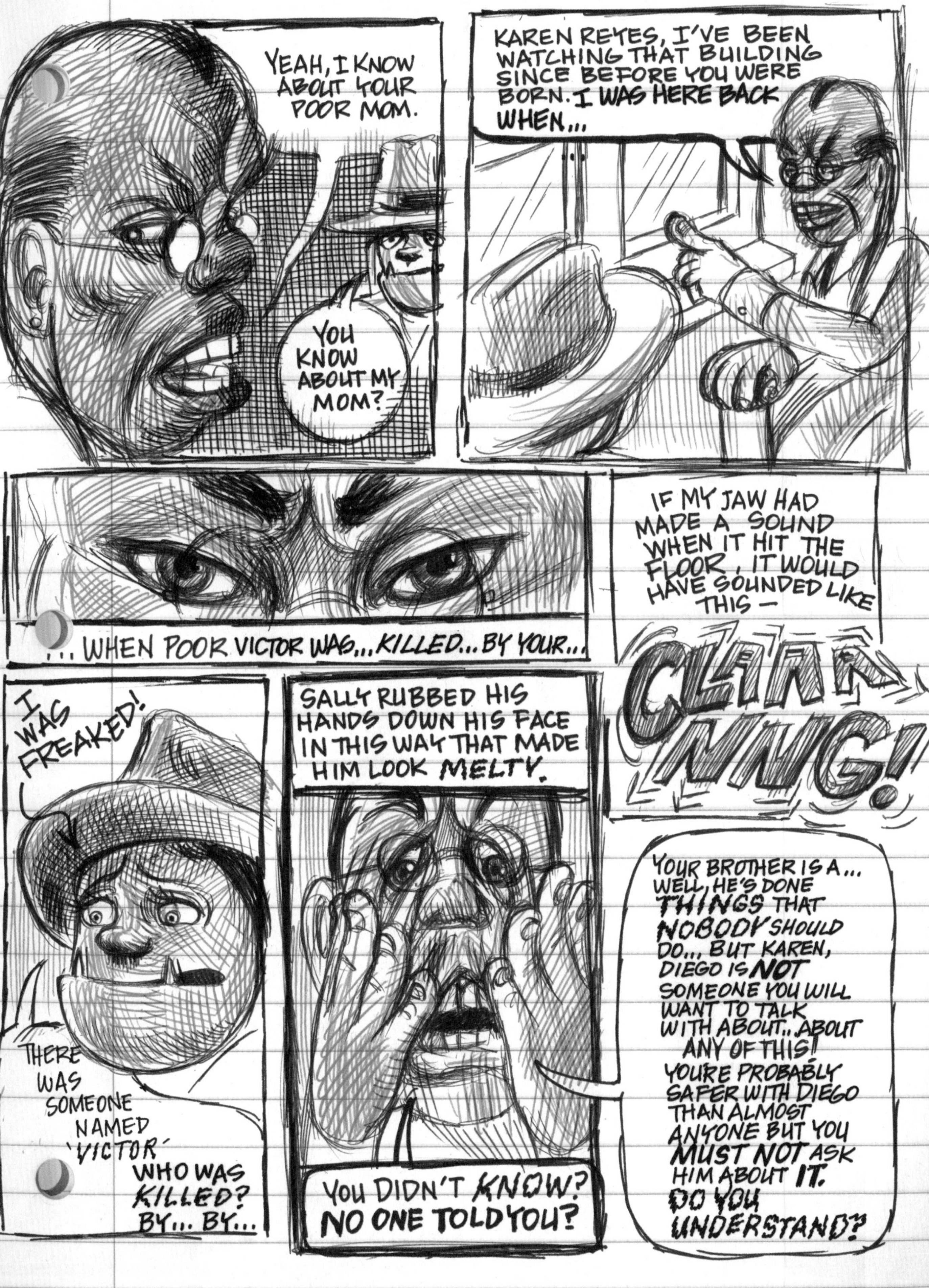
YEAH, I KNOW ABOUT YOUR POOR MOM.
YOU KNOW ABOUT MY MOM?
KAREN REYES, I'VE BEEN WATCHING THAT BUILDING SINCE BEFORE YOU WERE BORN. I WAS HERE BACK WHEN...
...WHEN POOR VICTOR WAS... KILLED... BY YOUR...
IF MY JAW HAD MADE A SOUND WHEN IT HIT THE FLOOR, IT WOULD HAVE SOUNDED LIKE THIS —
CLANNNG!
I WAS FREAKED!
THERE WAS SOMEONE NAMED 'VICTOR' WHO WAS KILLED? BY... BY...
SALLY RUBBED HIS HANDS DOWN HIS FACE IN THIS WAY THAT MADE HIM LOOK MELTY.
YOU DIDN'T KNOW? NO ONE TOLD YOU?
YOUR BROTHER IS A... WELL, HE'S DONE THINGS THAT NOBODY SHOULD DO... BUT KAREN, DIEGO IS NOT SOMEONE YOU WILL WANT TO TALK WITH ABOUT.. ABOUT ANY OF THIS! YOU'RE PROBABLY SAFER WITH DIEGO THAN ALMOST ANYONE BUT YOU MUST NOT ASK HIM ABOUT IT. DO YOU UNDERSTAND?

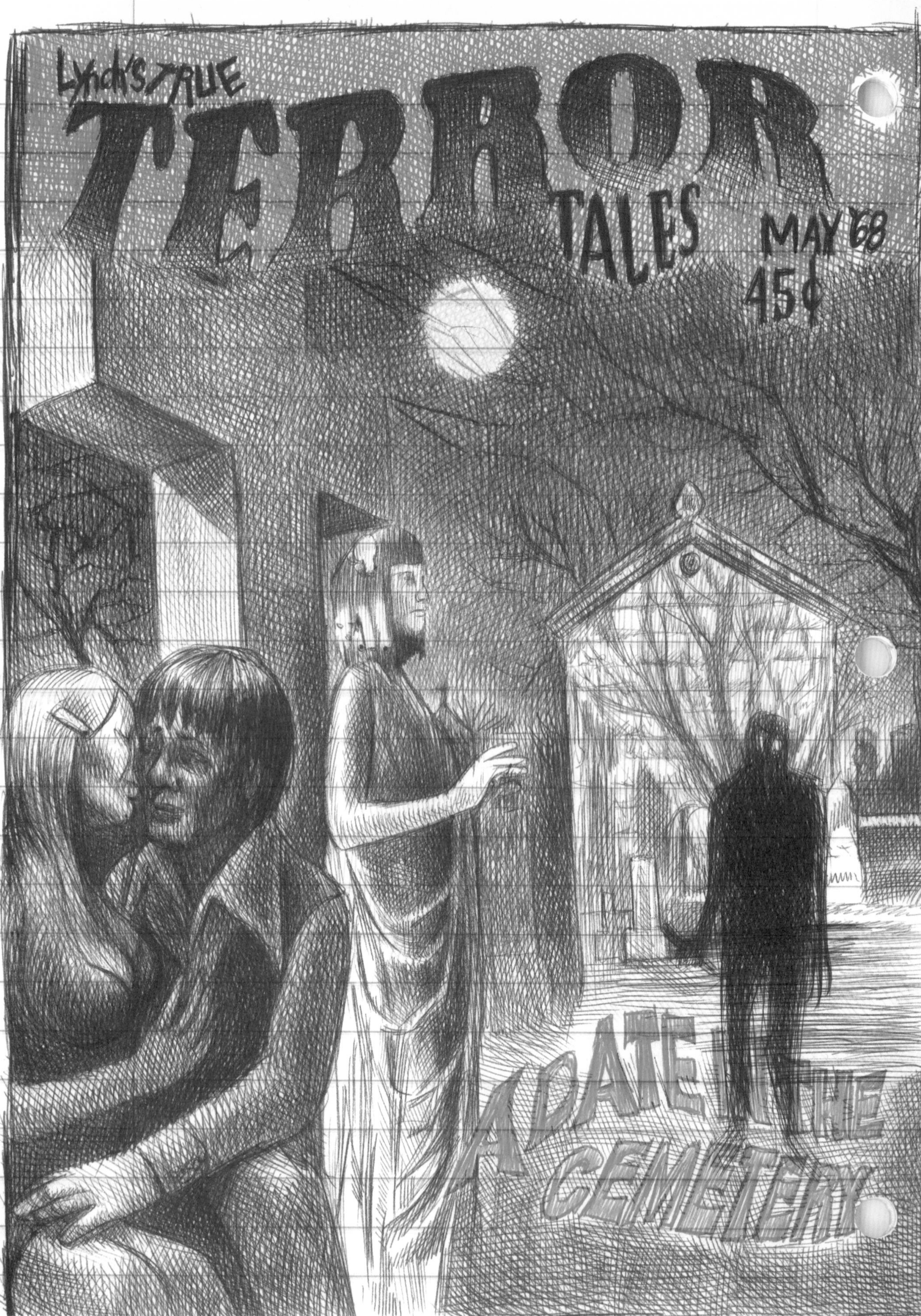
Lynch's TRUE
TERROR
TALES
MAY '68
45¢
A DATE IN THE
CEMETERY

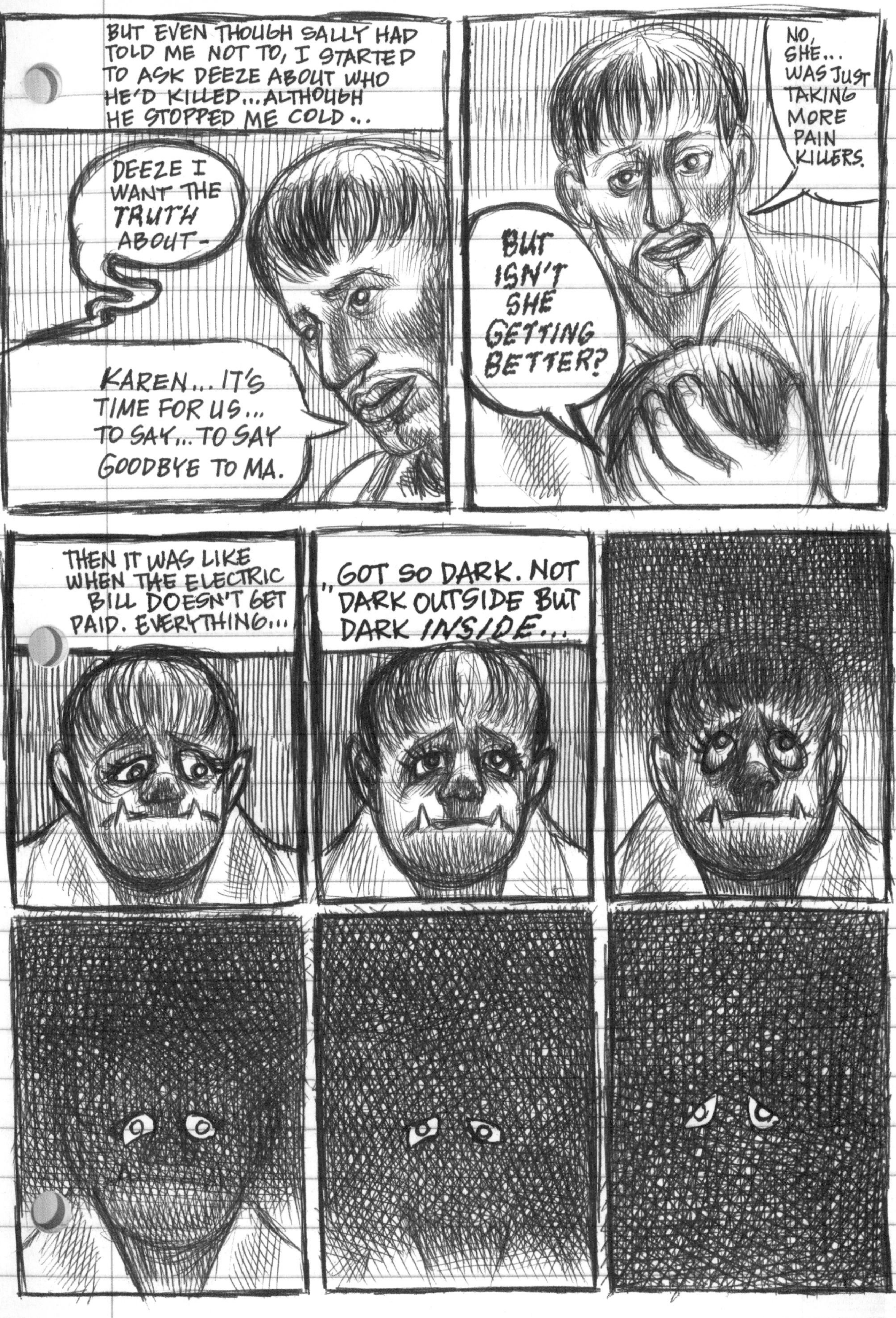
BUT EVEN THOUGH SALLY HAD TOLD ME NOT TO, I STARTED TO ASK DEEZE ABOUT WHO HE'D KILLED... ALTHOUGH HE STOPPED ME COLD...
DEEZE I WANT THE TRUTH ABOUT-
KAREN... IT'S TIME FOR US... TO SAY... TO SAY GOODBYE TO MA.
BUT ISN'T SHE GETTING BETTER?
NO, SHE... WAS JUST TAKING MORE PAIN KILLERS.
THEN IT WAS LIKE WHEN THE ELECTRIC BILL DOESN'T GET PAID. EVERYTHING...
...GOT SO DARK. NOT DARK OUTSIDE BUT DARK INSIDE...

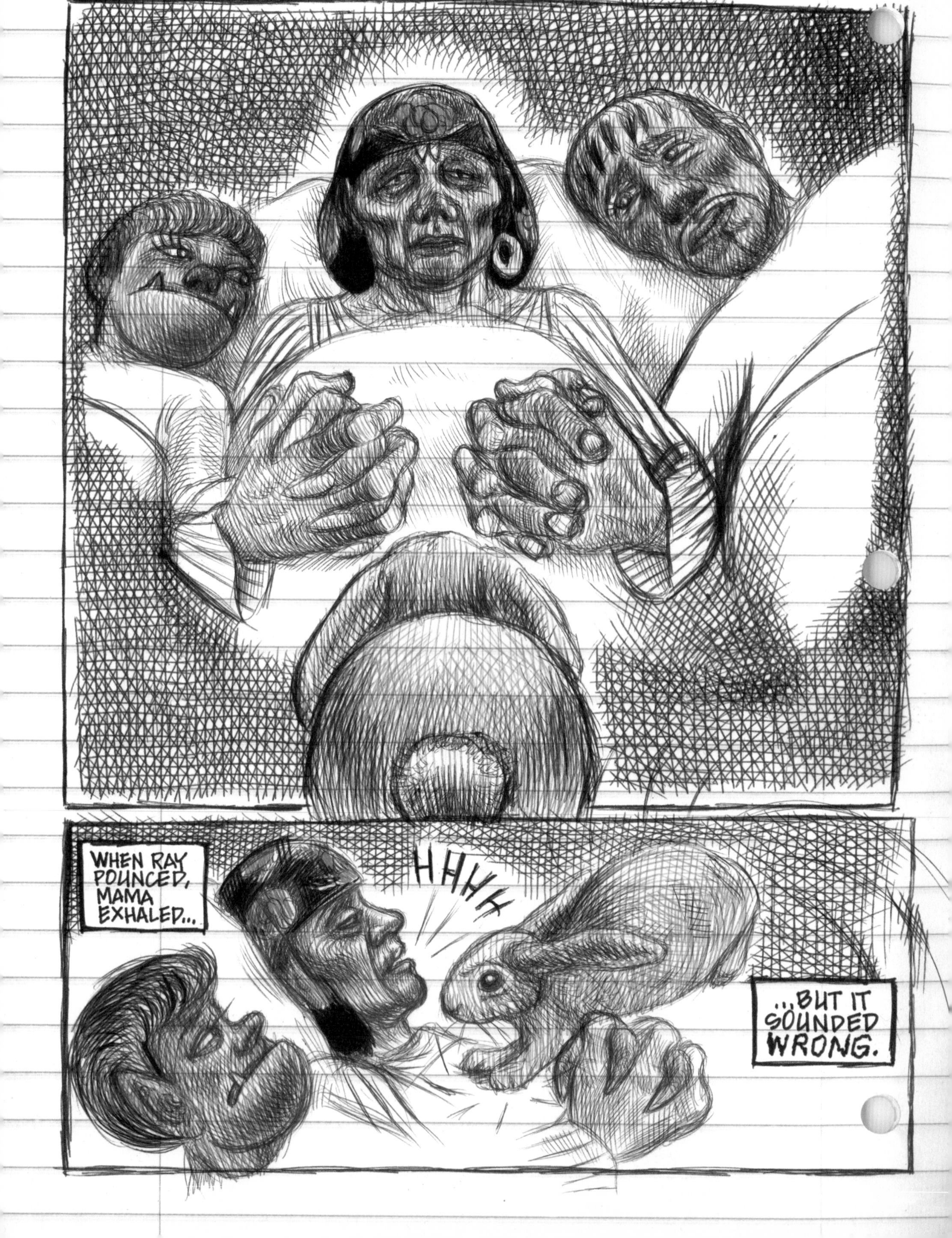
WHEN RAY POUNCED, MAMA EXHALED...
HHHH
...BUT IT SOUNDED WRONG.

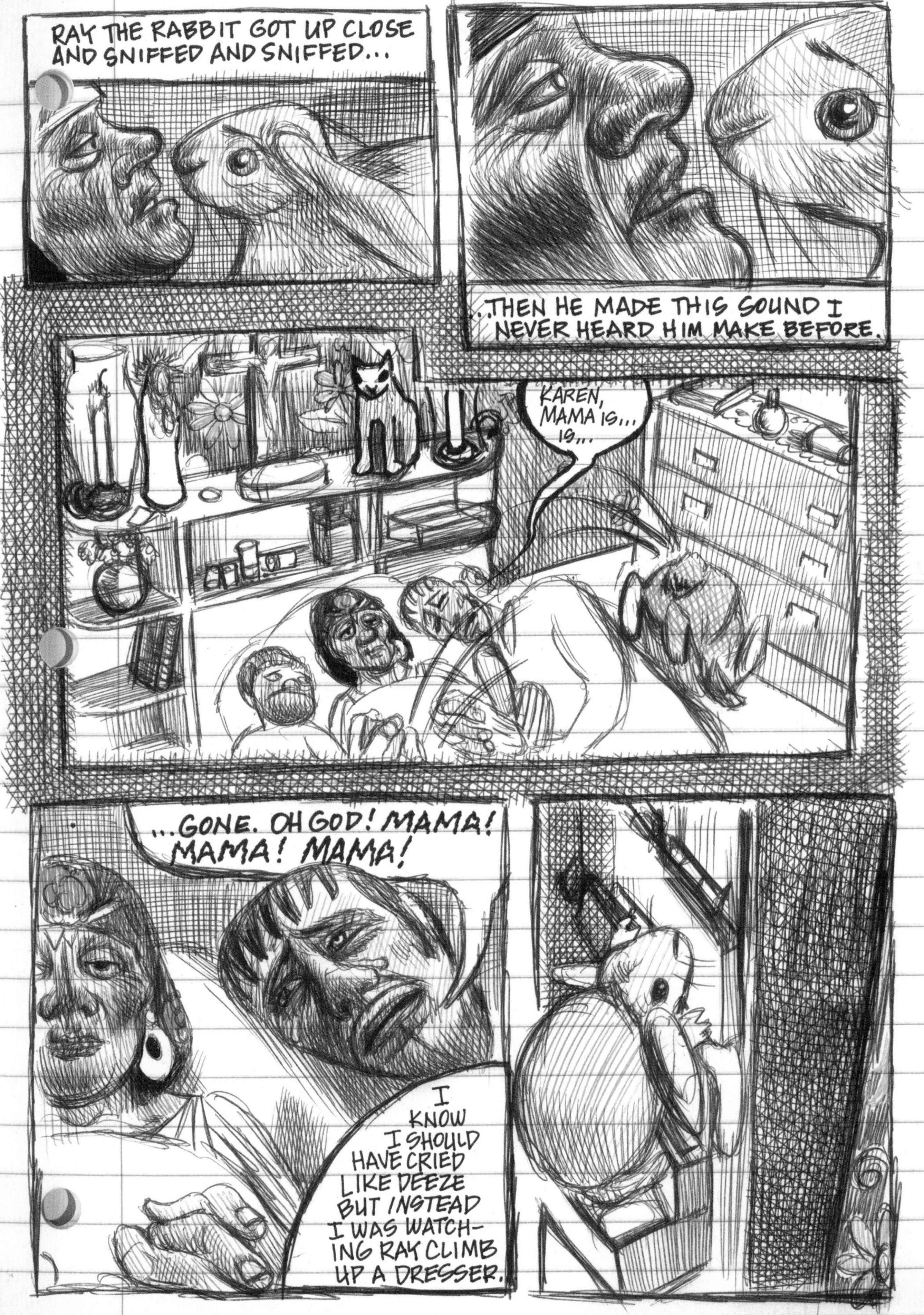
RAY THE RABBIT GOT UP CLOSE AND SNIFFED AND SNIFFED...
..THEN HE MADE THIS SOUND I NEVER HEARD HIM MAKE BEFORE.
KAREN, MAMA IS... IS...
...GONE. OH GOD! MAMA! MAMA! MAMA!
I KNOW I SHOULD HAVE CRIED LIKE DEEZE BUT INSTEAD I WAS WATCHING RAY CLIMB UP A DRESSER.

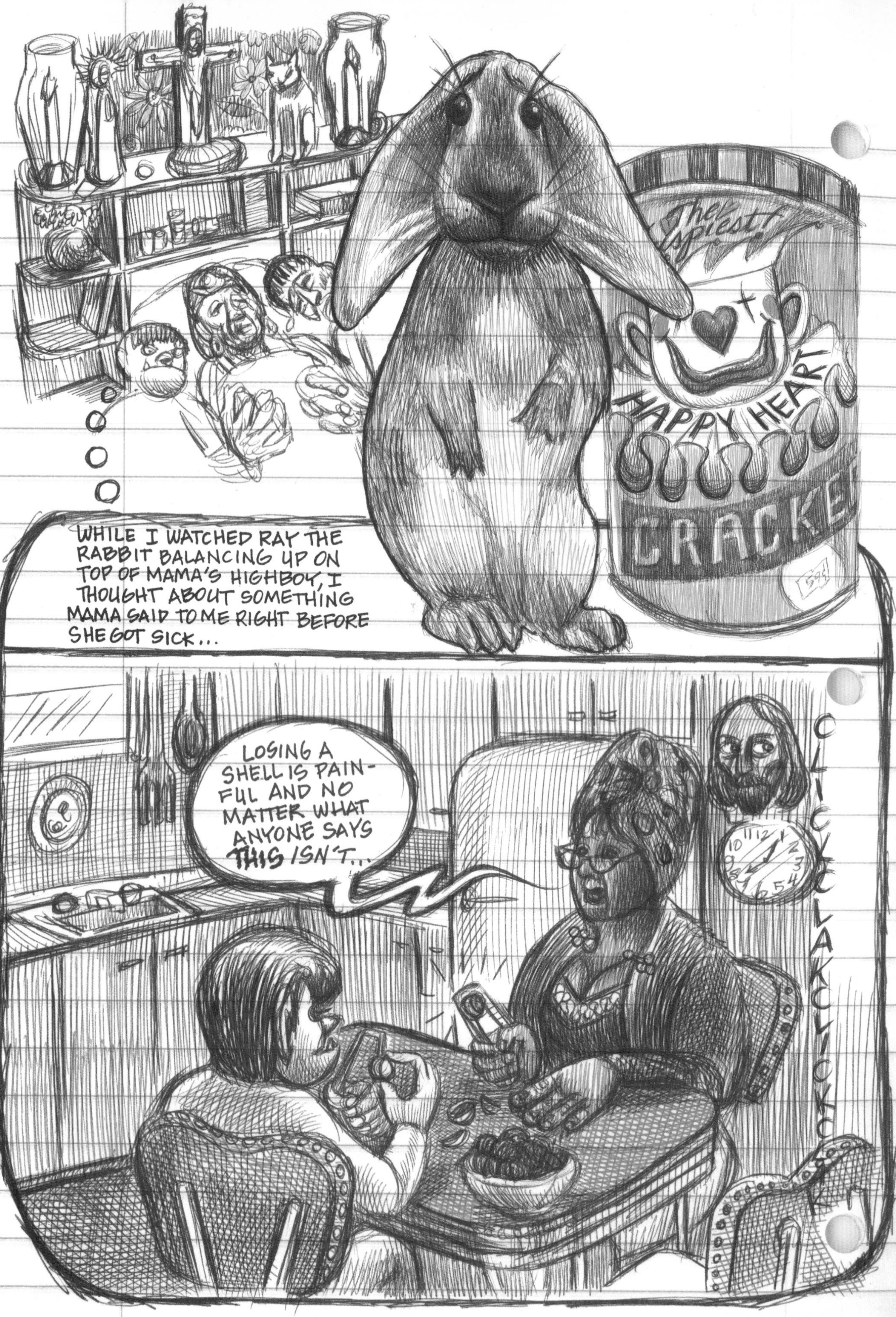
HAPPY HEART
CRACKE
WHILE I WATCHED RAY THE RABBIT BALANCING UP ON TOP OF MAMA'S HIGHBOY, I THOUGHT ABOUT SOMETHING MAMA SAID TO ME RIGHT BEFORE SHE GOT SICK...
LOSING A SHELL IS PAIN-FUL AND NO MATTER WHAT ANYONE SAYS **THIS** ISN'T...
CLICKCLAKCLICK

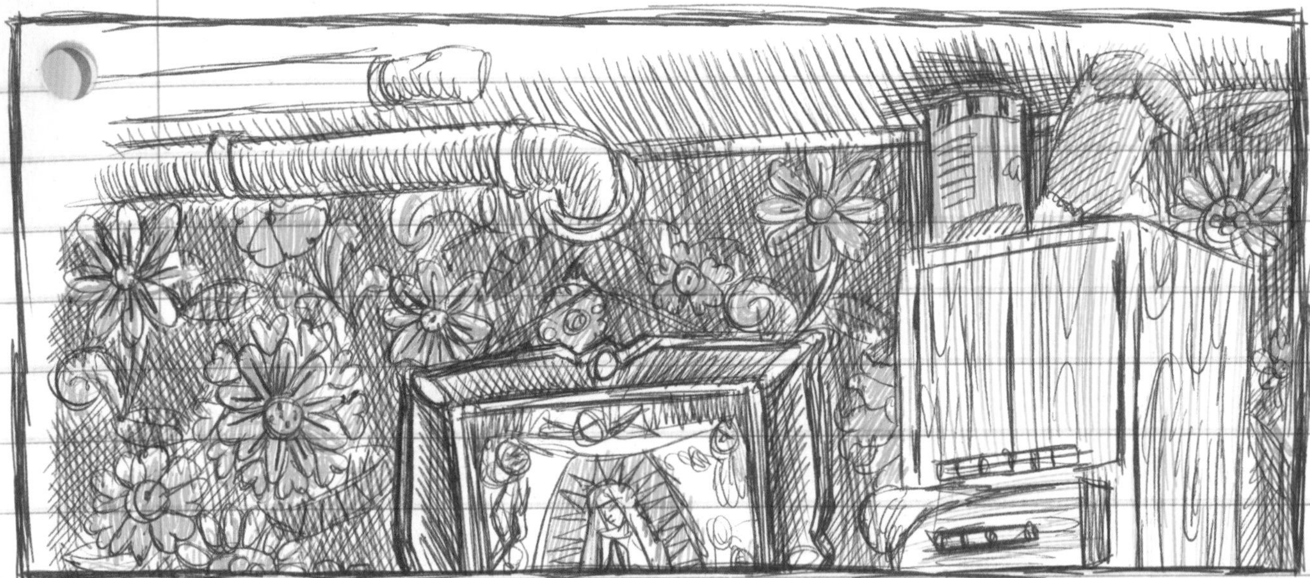

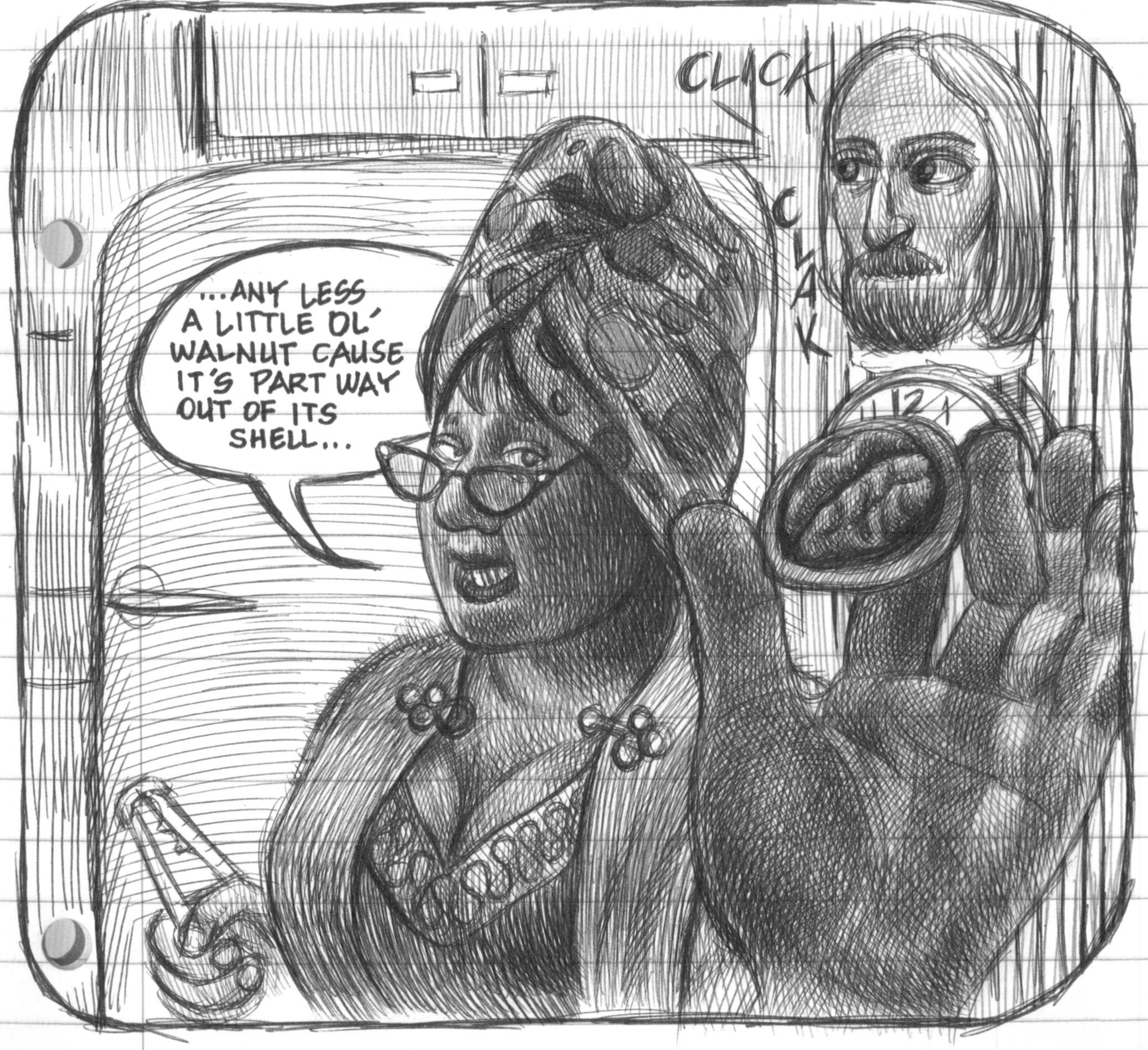
CLICK
CLAK
...ANY LESS A LITTLE OL' WALNUT CAUSE IT'S PART WAY OUT OF ITS SHELL...

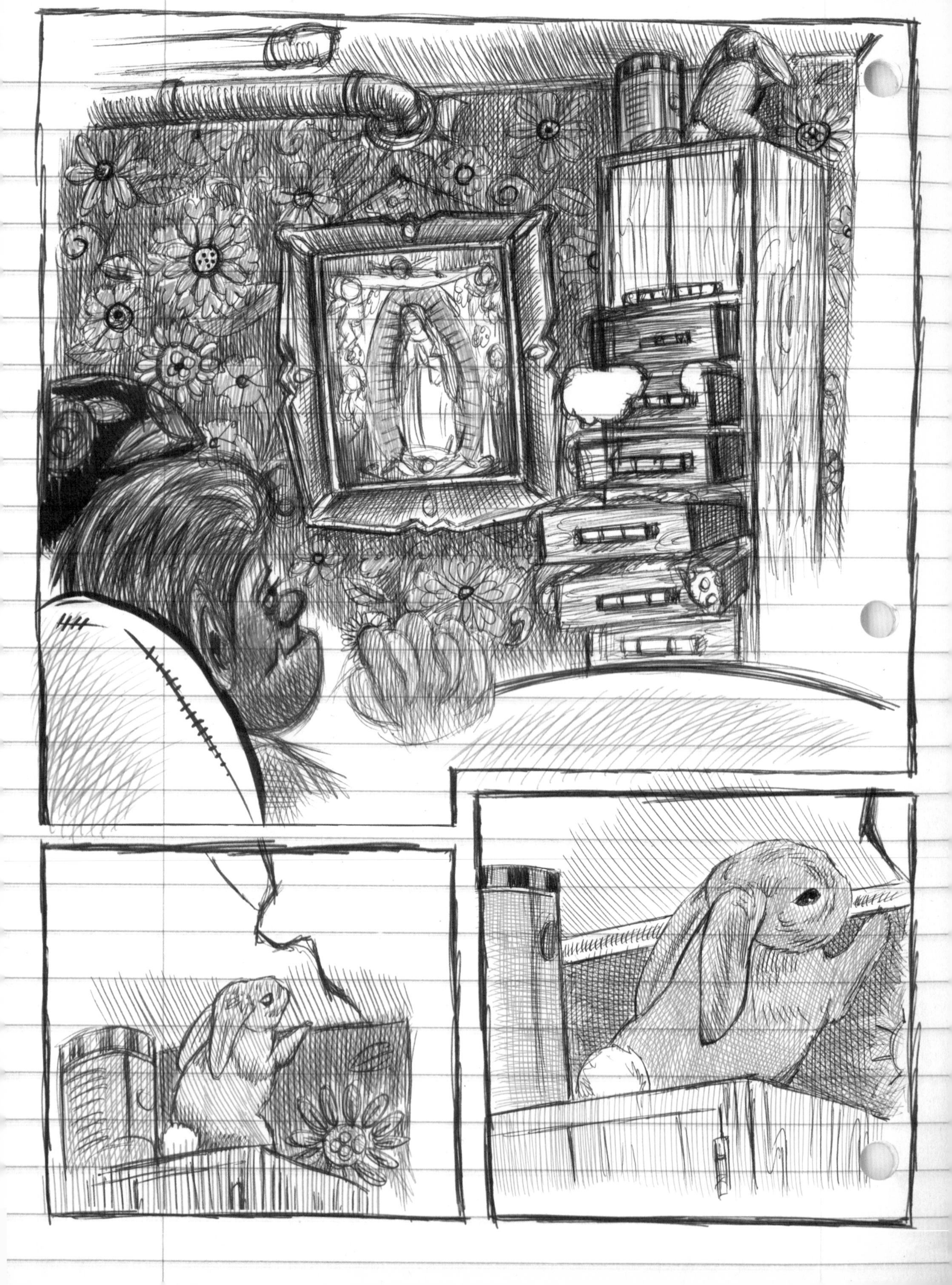

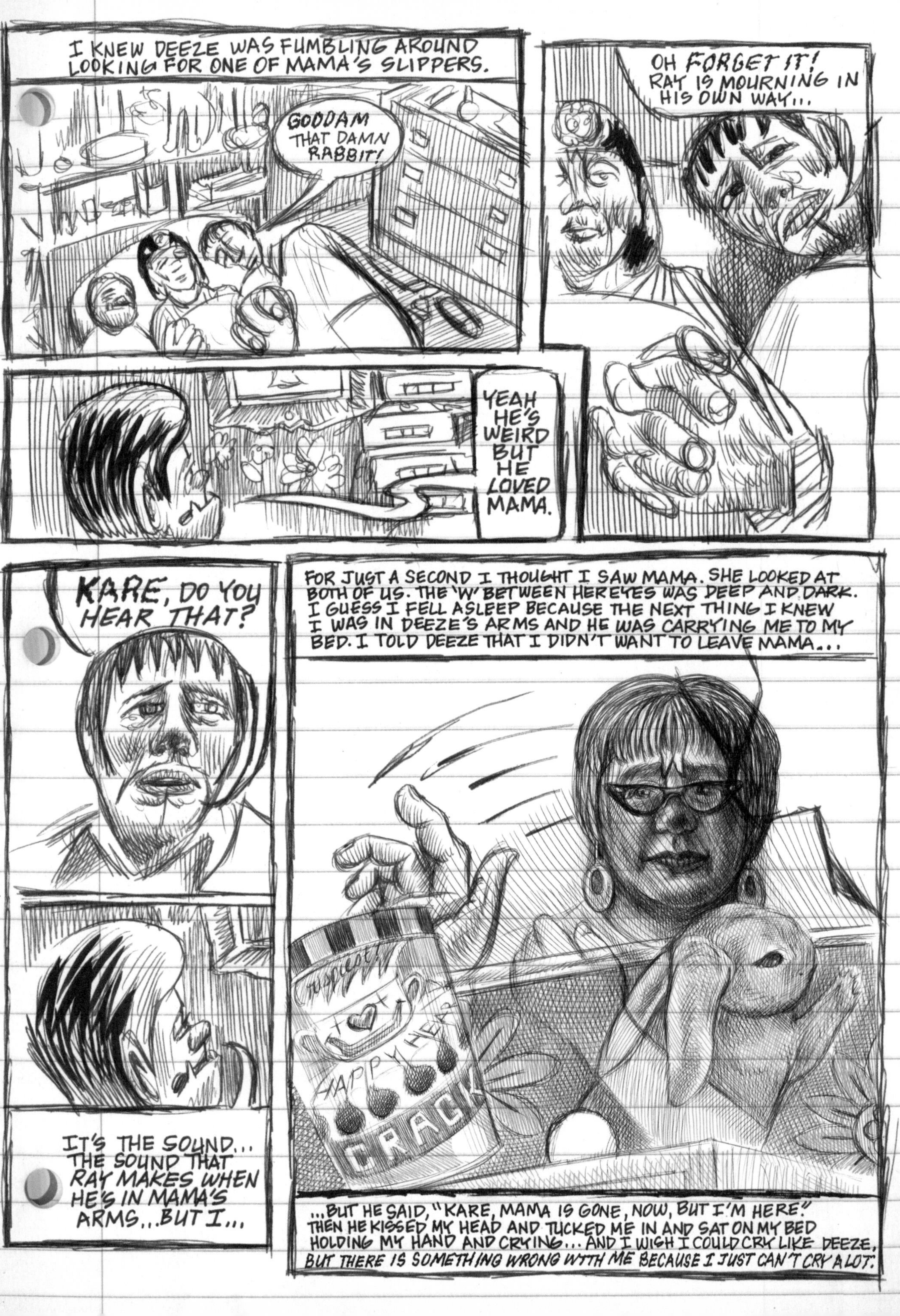
I KNEW DEEZE WAS FUMBLING AROUND LOOKING FOR ONE OF MAMA'S SLIPPERS.
GODDAM THAT DAMN RABBIT!
OH FORGET IT! RAY IS MOURNING IN HIS OWN WAY...
YEAH HE'S WEIRD BUT HE LOVED MAMA.
KARE, DO YOU HEAR THAT?
IT'S THE SOUND... THE SOUND THAT RAY MAKES WHEN HE'S IN MAMA'S ARMS...BUT I...
FOR JUST A SECOND I THOUGHT I SAW MAMA. SHE LOOKED AT BOTH OF US. THE 'W' BETWEEN HER EYES WAS DEEP AND DARK. I GUESS I FELL ASLEEP BECAUSE THE NEXT THING I KNEW I WAS IN DEEZE'S ARMS AND HE WAS CARRYING ME TO MY BED. I TOLD DEEZE THAT I DIDN'T WANT TO LEAVE MAMA...
HAPPY HEART
CRACK
...BUT HE SAID, "KARE, MAMA IS GONE, NOW, BUT I'M HERE." THEN HE KISSED MY HEAD AND TUCKED ME IN AND SAT ON MY BED HOLDING MY HAND AND CRYING... AND I WISH I COULD CRY LIKE DEEZE, BUT THERE IS SOMETHING WRONG WITH ME BECAUSE I JUST CAN'T CRY A LOT.

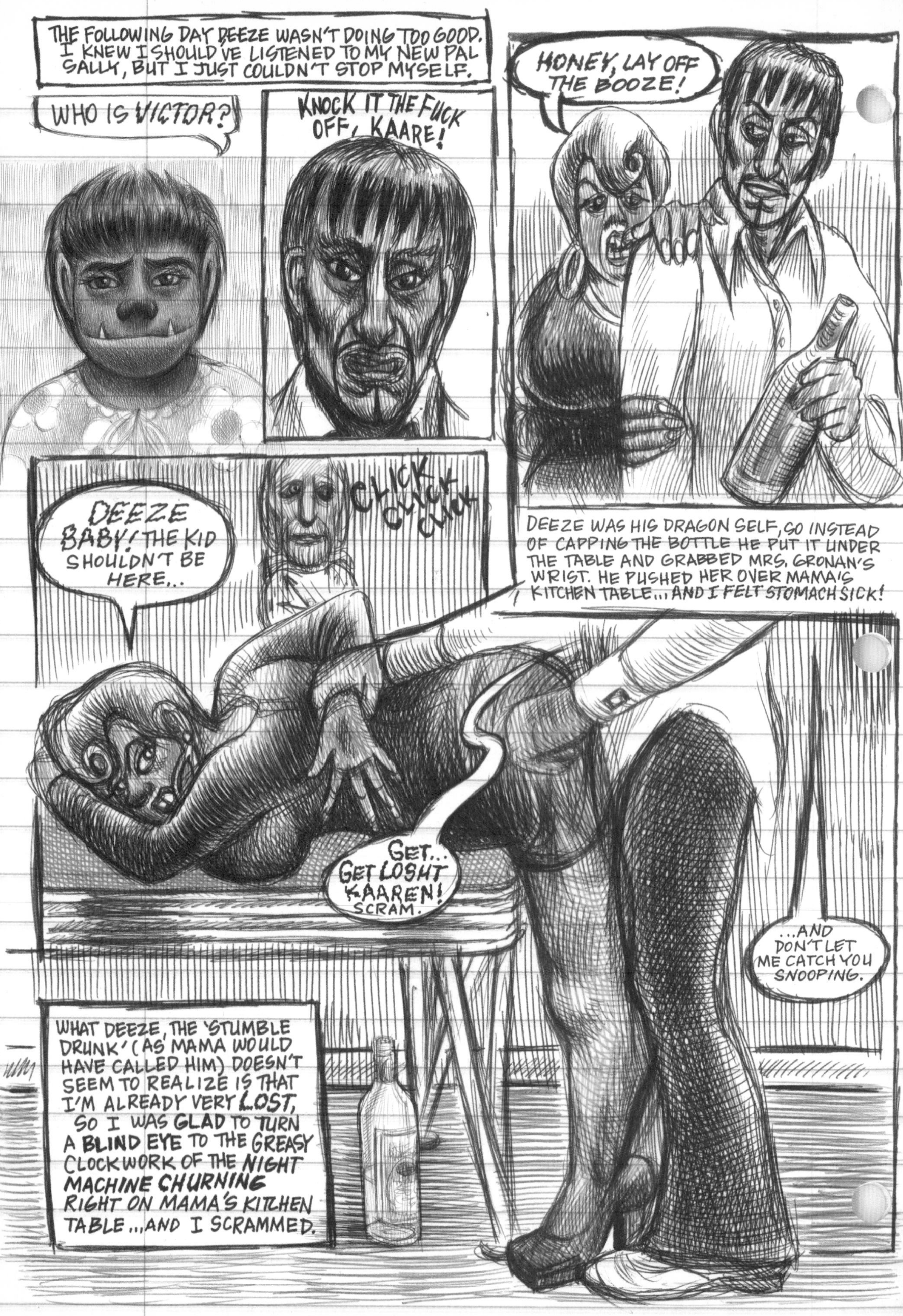
THE FOLLOWING DAY DEEZE WASN'T DOING TOO GOOD. I KNEW I SHOULD'VE LISTENED TO MY NEW PAL SALLY, BUT I JUST COULDN'T STOP MYSELF.
WHO IS VICTOR?
KNOCK IT THE FUCK OFF, KAARE!
HONEY, LAY OFF THE BOOZE!
DEEZE WAS HIS DRAGON SELF, SO INSTEAD OF CAPPING THE BOTTLE HE PUT IT UNDER THE TABLE AND GRABBED MRS. GRONAN'S WRIST. HE PUSHED HER OVER MAMA'S KITCHEN TABLE... AND I FELT STOMACH SICK!
DEEZE BABY! THE KID SHOULDN'T BE HERE...
CLICK CLICK CLICK
GET... GET LOSHT KAAREN! SCRAM.
...AND DON'T LET ME CATCH YOU SNOOPING.
WHAT DEEZE, THE 'STUMBLE DRUNK' (AS MAMA WOULD HAVE CALLED HIM) DOESN'T SEEM TO REALIZE IS THAT I'M ALREADY VERY LOST, SO I WAS GLAD TO TURN A BLIND EYE TO THE GREASY CLOCKWORK OF THE NIGHT MACHINE CHURNING RIGHT ON MAMA'S KITCHEN TABLE... AND I SCRAMMED.

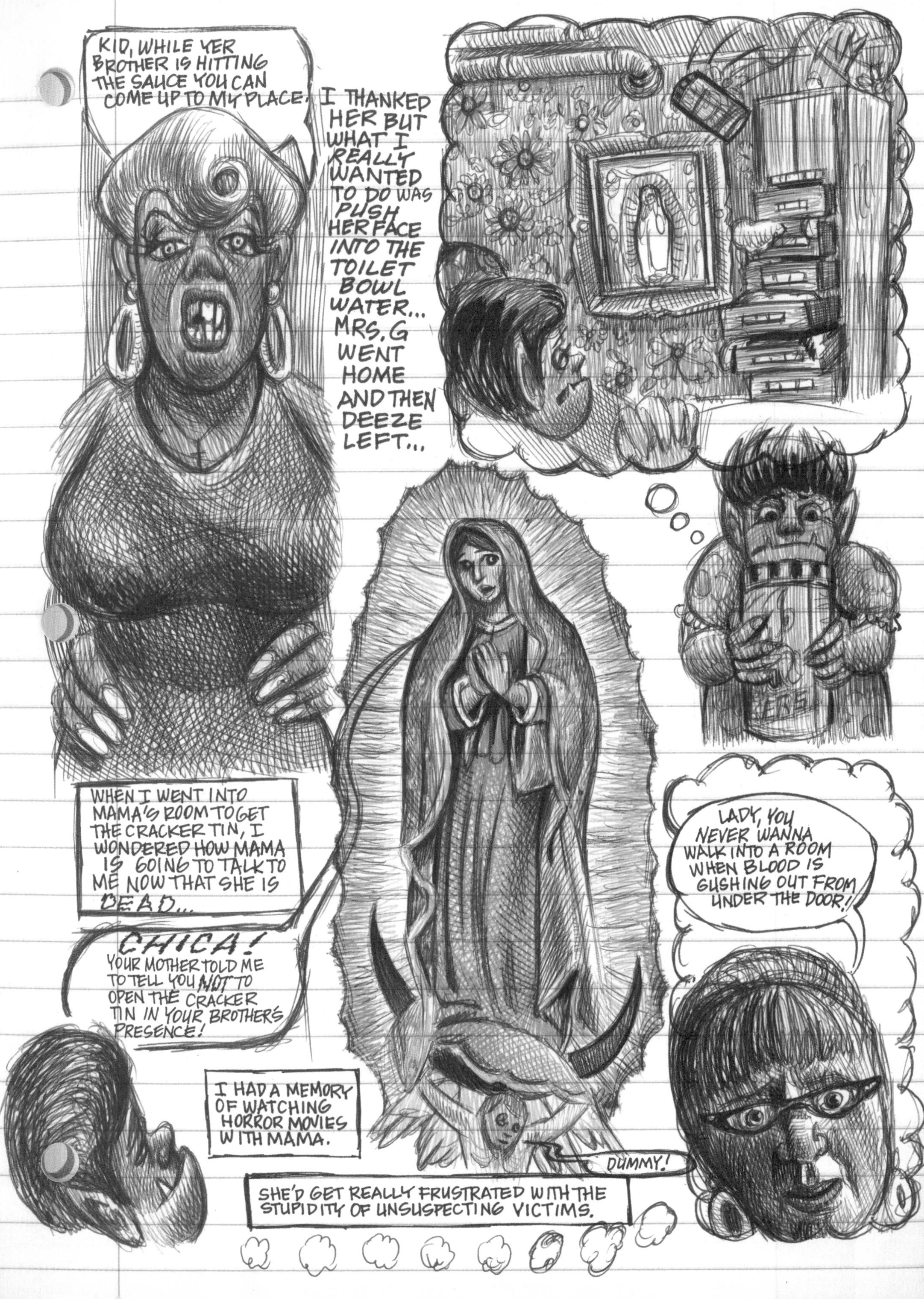
KID, WHILE YER BROTHER IS HITTING THE SAUCE YOU CAN COME UP TO MY PLACE.
I THANKED HER BUT WHAT I REALLY WANTED TO DO WAS PUSH HER FACE INTO THE TOILET BOWL WATER... MRS. G WENT HOME AND THEN DEEZE LEFT...
WHEN I WENT INTO MAMA'S ROOM TO GET THE CRACKER TIN, I WONDERED HOW MAMA IS GOING TO TALK TO ME NOW THAT SHE IS DEAD...
CHICA! YOUR MOTHER TOLD ME TO TELL YOU NOT TO OPEN THE CRACKER TIN IN YOUR BROTHER'S PRESENCE!
LADY, YOU NEVER WANNA WALK INTO A ROOM WHEN BLOOD IS GUSHING OUT FROM UNDER THE DOOR!
I HAD A MEMORY OF WATCHING HORROR MOVIES WITH MAMA.
DUMMY!
SHE'D GET REALLY FRUSTRATED WITH THE STUPIDITY OF UNSUSPECTING VICTIMS.

I KNEW DARN WELL THAT I WAS BEING EVERY BIT AS DUMB AS THE DUMBEST UNSUSPECTING VICTIM. I FINALLY UNDERSTOOD WHY THEY DO THE STUPID THINGS THEY DO. WHEN YOU'RE SO CLOSE TO FINDING OUT THE TRUTH... WELL THE TRUTH HAS A WEIGHT TO IT. AND WHEN YOU'RE THAT ATTACHED TO IT, IT'S ALMOST LIKE BEING ROPED TO AN ANCHOR AND TOSSED INTO DEEP WATER. I GUESS DEEP DOWN I WANTED DEEZE TO SEE WHAT WOULD ~AS MAMA WOULD SAY~ *RILE HIM.*

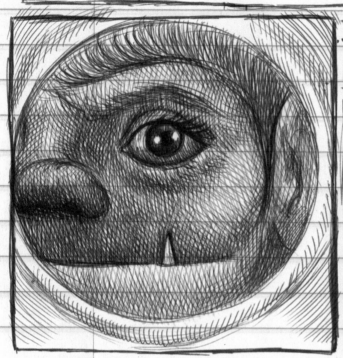

THE THING AT THE BOTTOM REMINDED ME OF A CRUSTY SCAB...

...IT HAS A SAFETY PIN SEWN TO IT'S BACK...

I PUT THE WEIRD THING ON A SOPPING WET DISHTOWEL AND IT STARTED COLORING THE TOWEL...

CLICK CLICK CLICK

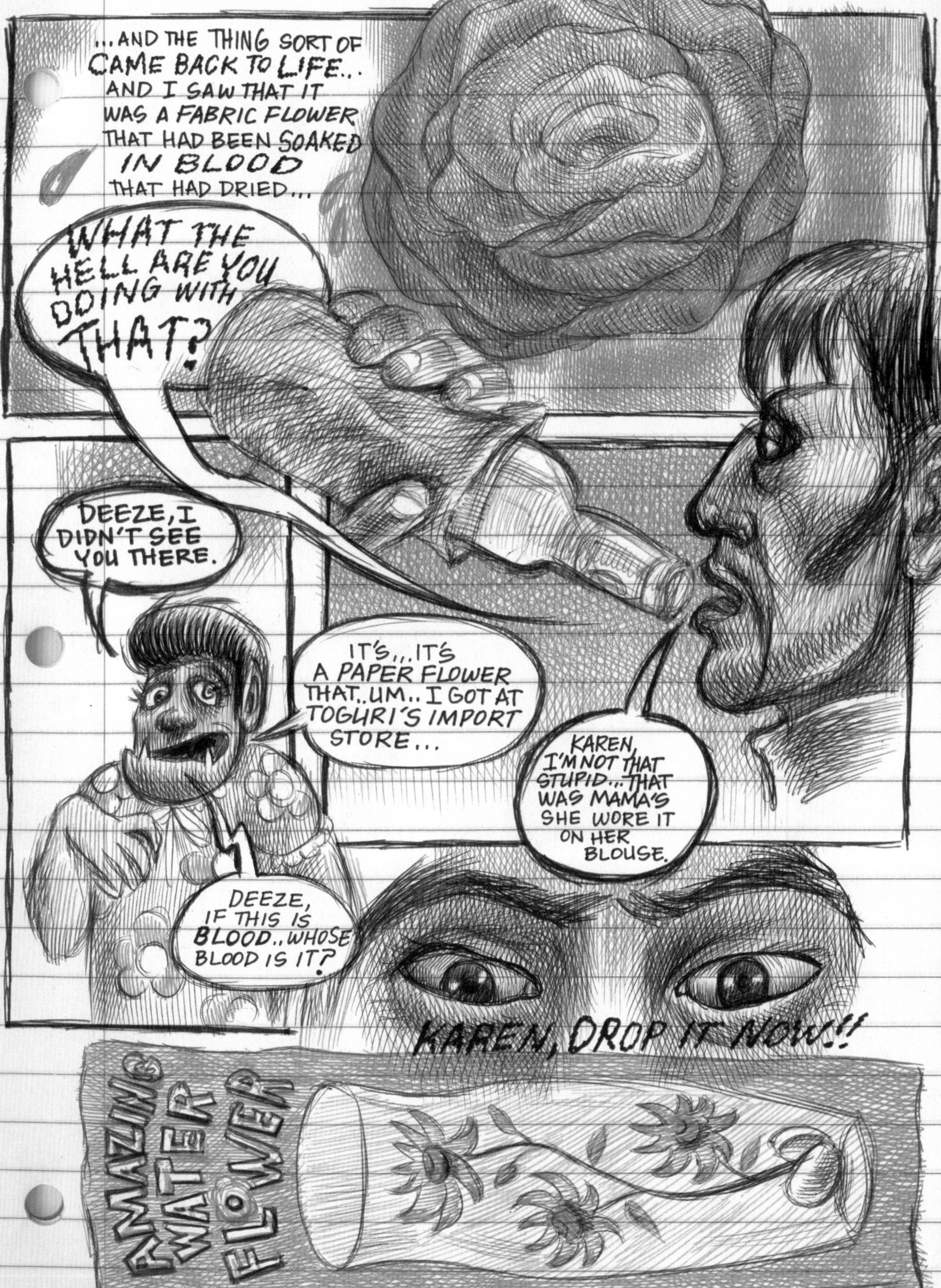
...AND THE THING SORT OF CAME BACK TO LIFE... AND I SAW THAT IT WAS A FABRIC FLOWER THAT HAD BEEN SOAKED IN BLOOD THAT HAD DRIED...
WHAT THE HELL ARE YOU DOING WITH THAT?
DEEZE, I DIDN'T SEE YOU THERE.
IT'S...IT'S A PAPER FLOWER THAT..UM.. I GOT AT TOGURI'S IMPORT STORE...
KAREN, I'M NOT THAT STUPID...THAT WAS MAMA'S SHE WORE IT ON HER BLOUSE.
DEEZE, IF THIS IS BLOOD..WHOSE BLOOD IS IT?
KAREN, DROP IT NOW!!
AMAZING WATER FLOWER

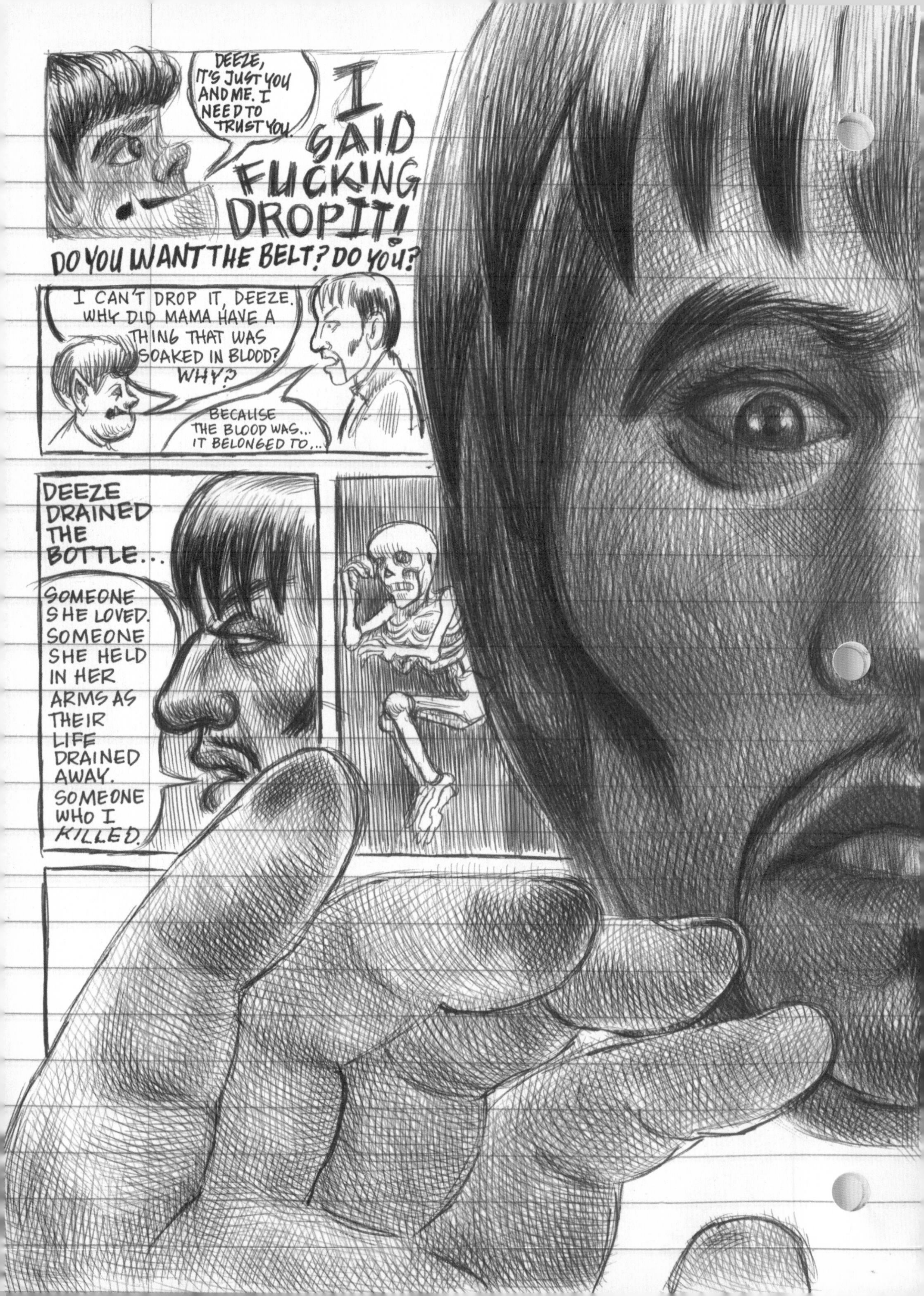
DEEZE, IT'S JUST YOU AND ME. I NEED TO TRUST YOU.
I SAID FUCKING DROP IT!
DO YOU WANT THE BELT? DO YOU?
I CAN'T DROP IT, DEEZE. WHY DID MAMA HAVE A THING THAT WAS SOAKED IN BLOOD? WHY?
BECAUSE THE BLOOD WAS... IT BELONGED TO...
DEEZE DRAINED THE BOTTLE...
SOMEONE SHE LOVED. SOMEONE SHE HELD IN HER ARMS AS THEIR LIFE DRAINED AWAY. SOMEONE WHO I KILLED.

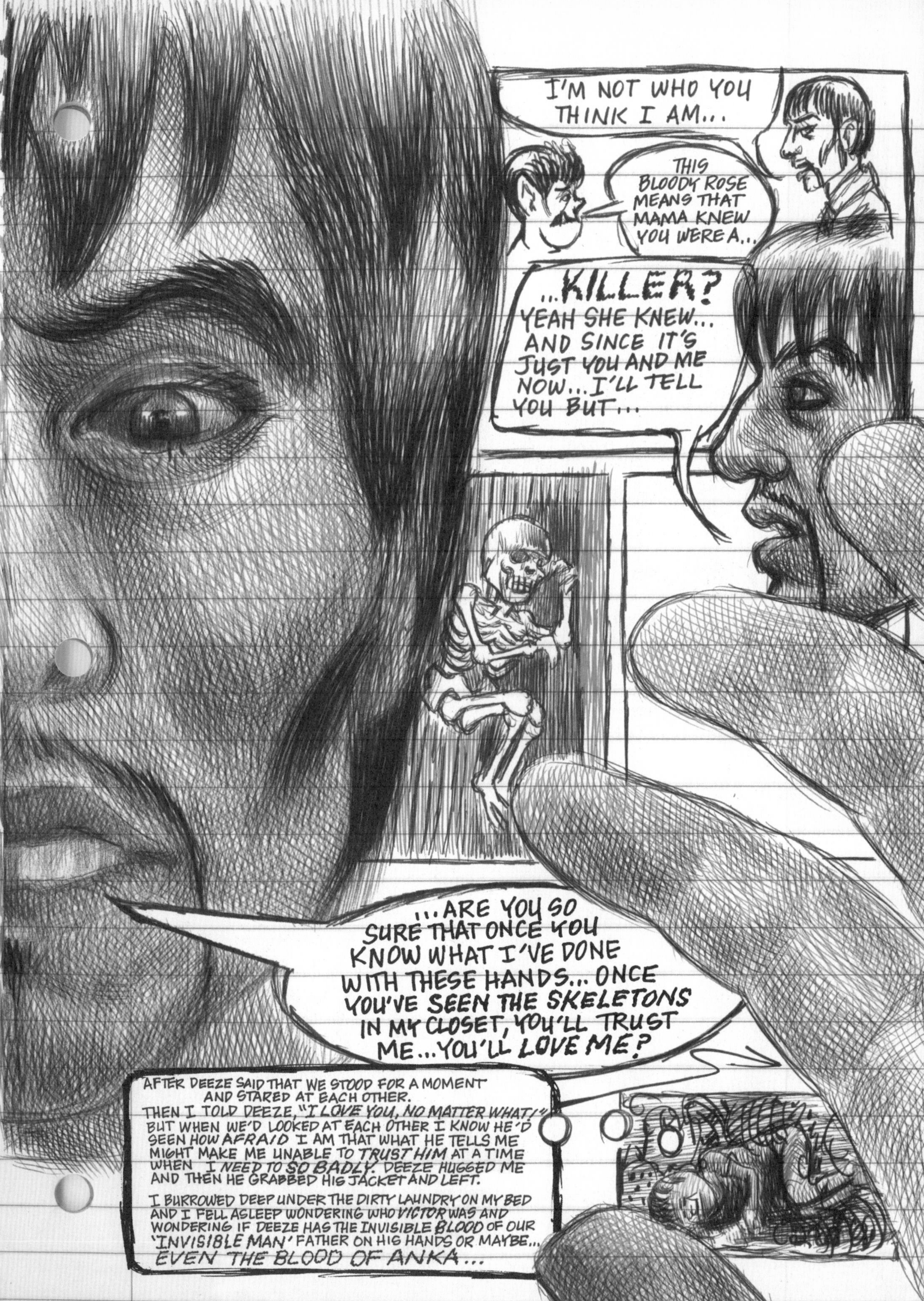
I'M NOT WHO YOU THINK I AM...
THIS BLOODY ROSE MEANS THAT MAMA KNEW YOU WERE A...
...KILLER? YEAH SHE KNEW... AND SINCE IT'S JUST YOU AND ME NOW... I'LL TELL YOU BUT...
...ARE YOU SO SURE THAT ONCE YOU KNOW WHAT I'VE DONE WITH THESE HANDS... ONCE YOU'VE SEEN THE SKELETONS IN MY CLOSET, YOU'LL TRUST ME... YOU'LL LOVE ME?
AFTER DEEZE SAID THAT WE STOOD FOR A MOMENT AND STARED AT EACH OTHER. THEN I TOLD DEEZE, "I LOVE YOU, NO MATTER WHAT!" BUT WHEN WE'D LOOKED AT EACH OTHER I KNOW HE'D SEEN HOW AFRAID I AM THAT WHAT HE TELLS ME MIGHT MAKE ME UNABLE TO TRUST HIM AT A TIME WHEN I NEED TO SO BADLY. DEEZE HUGGED ME AND THEN HE GRABBED HIS JACKET AND LEFT.
I BURROWED DEEP UNDER THE DIRTY LAUNDRY ON MY BED AND I FELL ASLEEP WONDERING WHO VICTOR WAS AND WONDERING IF DEEZE HAS THE INVISIBLE BLOOD OF OUR 'INVISIBLE MAN' FATHER ON HIS HANDS OR MAYBE... EVEN THE BLOOD OF ANKA...

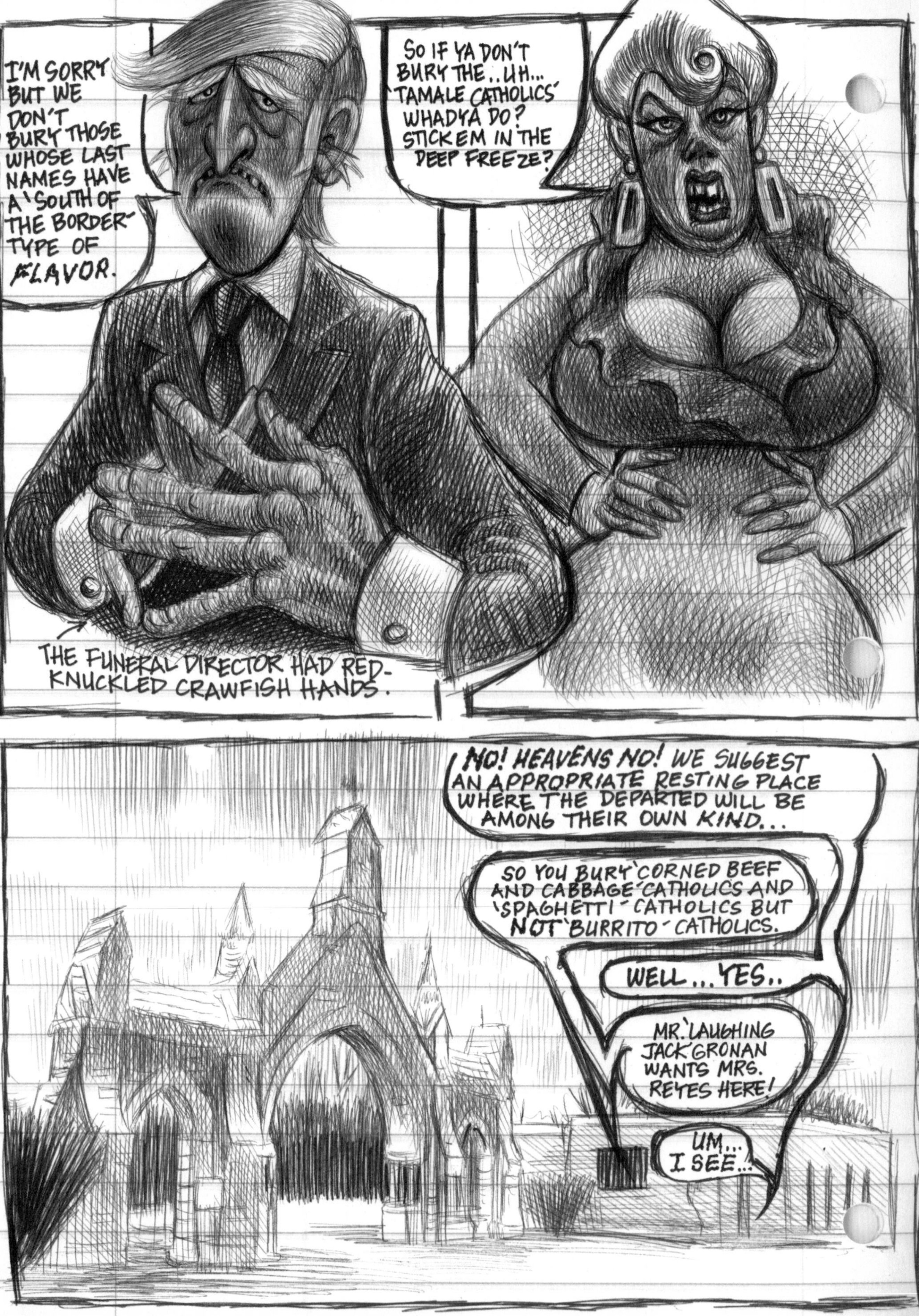
I'M SORRY BUT WE DON'T BURY THOSE WHOSE LAST NAMES HAVE A 'SOUTH OF THE BORDER' TYPE OF FLAVOR.
SO IF YA DON'T BURY THE.. UH... 'TAMALE CATHOLICS' WHADYA DO? STICK EM IN THE DEEP FREEZE?
THE FUNERAL DIRECTOR HAD RED-KNUCKLED CRAWFISH HANDS.
NO! HEAVENS NO! WE SUGGEST AN APPROPRIATE RESTING PLACE WHERE THE DEPARTED WILL BE AMONG THEIR OWN KIND...
SO YOU BURY 'CORNED BEEF AND CABBAGE' CATHOLICS AND 'SPAGHETTI' CATHOLICS BUT NOT 'BURRITO' CATHOLICS.
WELL... YES..
MR. 'LAUGHING JACK' GRONAN WANTS MRS. REYES HERE!
UM... I SEE...

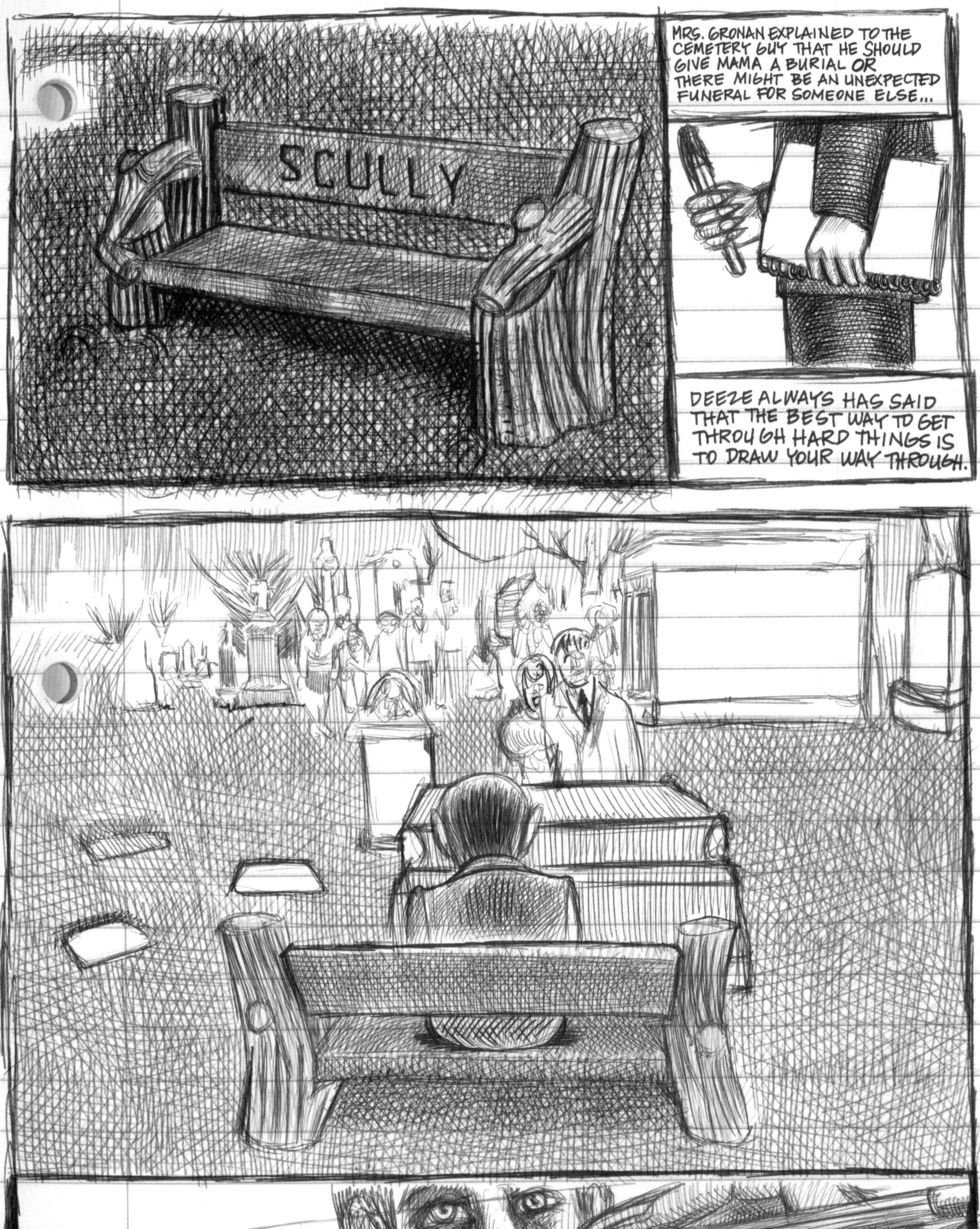
SCULLY
MRS. GRONAN EXPLAINED TO THE CEMETERY GUY THAT HE SHOULD GIVE MAMA A BURIAL OR THERE MIGHT BE AN UNEXPECTED FUNERAL FOR SOMEONE ELSE...
DEEZE ALWAYS HAS SAID THAT THE BEST WAY TO GET THROUGH HARD THINGS IS TO DRAW YOUR WAY THROUGH.

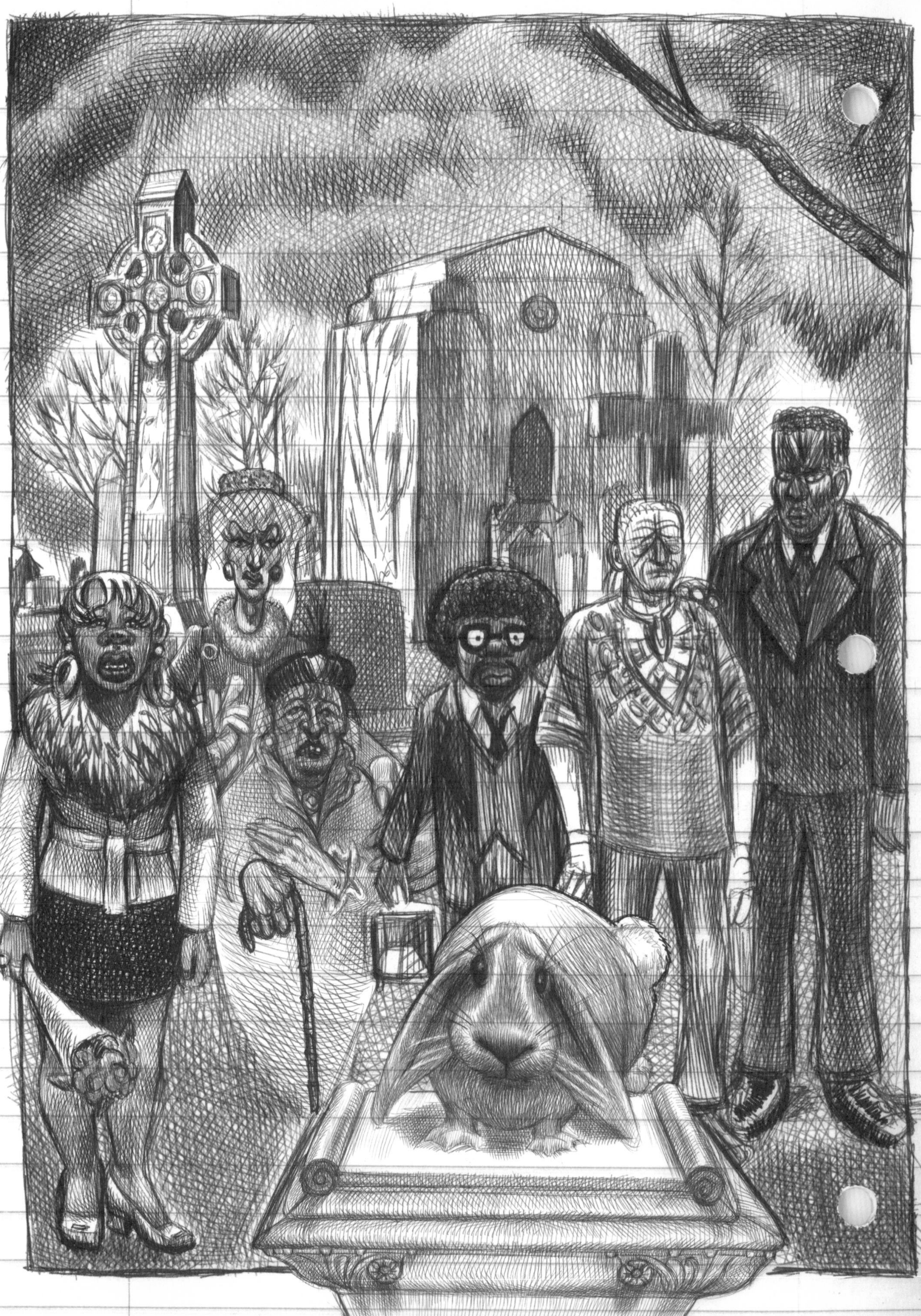

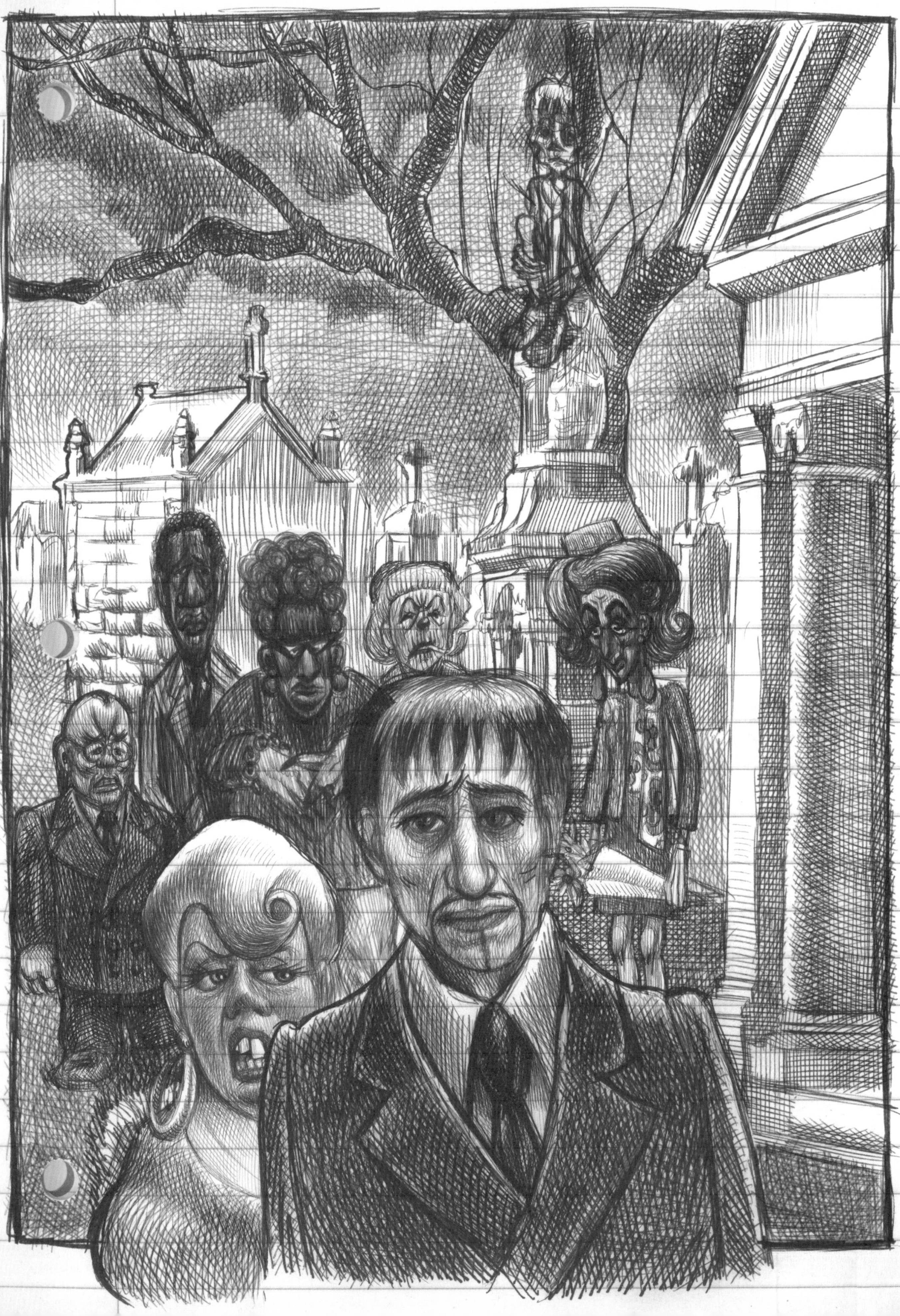

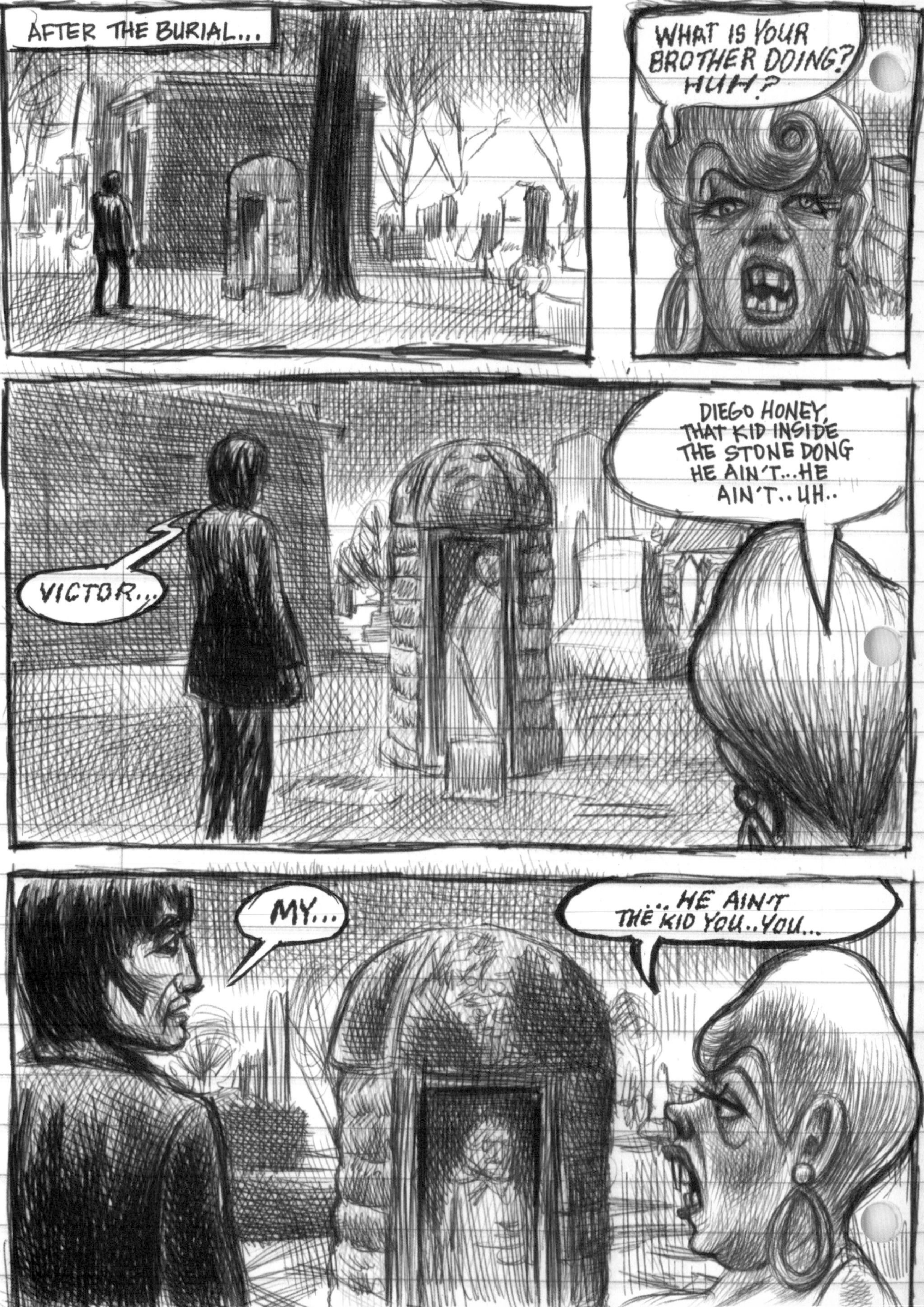
AFTER THE BURIAL...
WHAT IS YOUR BROTHER DOING? HUH?
DIEGO HONEY, THAT KID INSIDE THE STONE DONG HE AIN'T...HE AIN'T..UH..
VICTOR...
MY...
...HE AIN'T THE KID YOU..YOU...

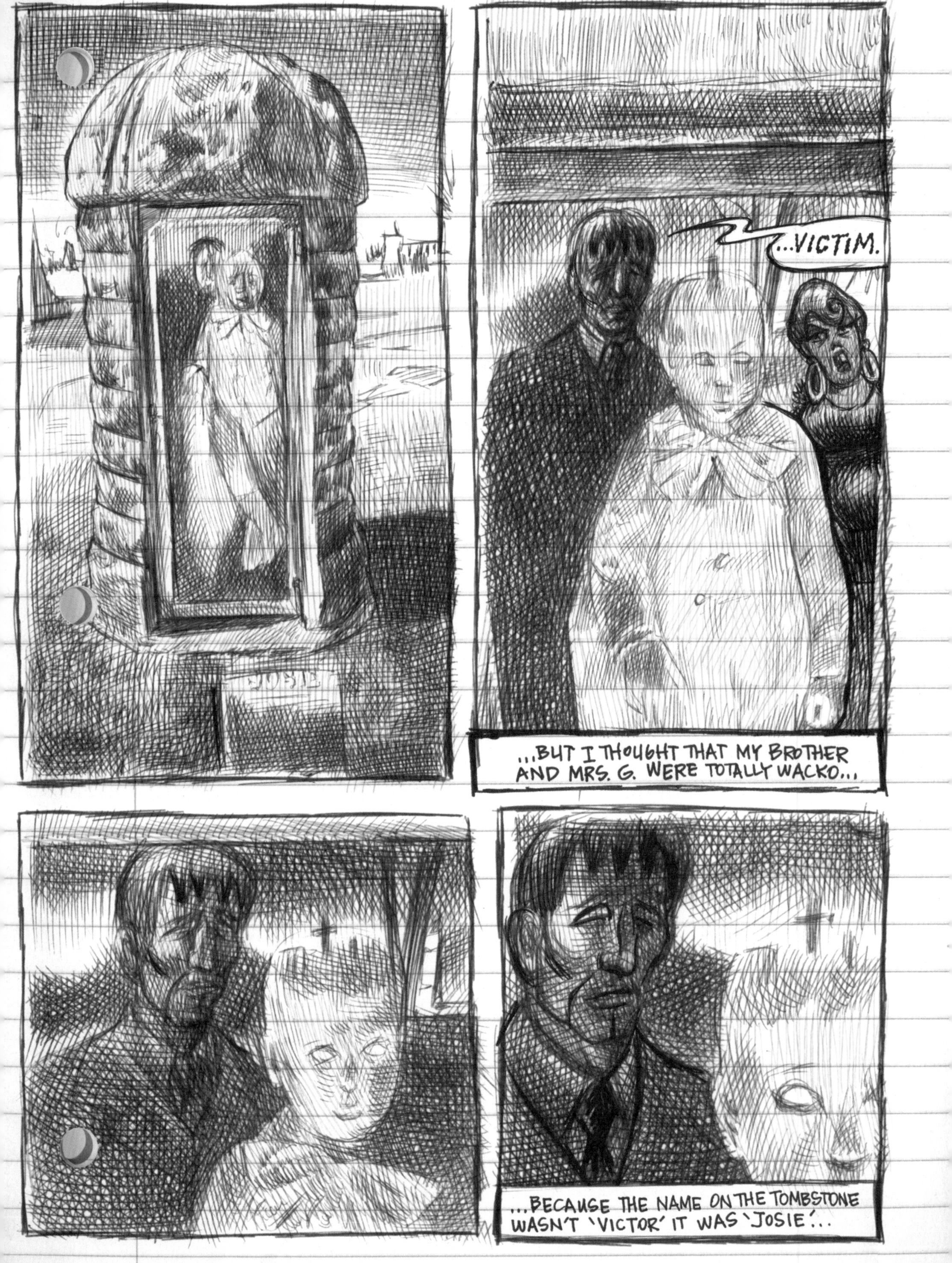
JOSIE
...VICTIM.
...BUT I THOUGHT THAT MY BROTHER AND MRS. G. WERE TOTALLY WACKO...
...BECAUSE THE NAME ON THE TOMBSTONE WASN'T 'VICTOR' IT WAS 'JOSIE'...

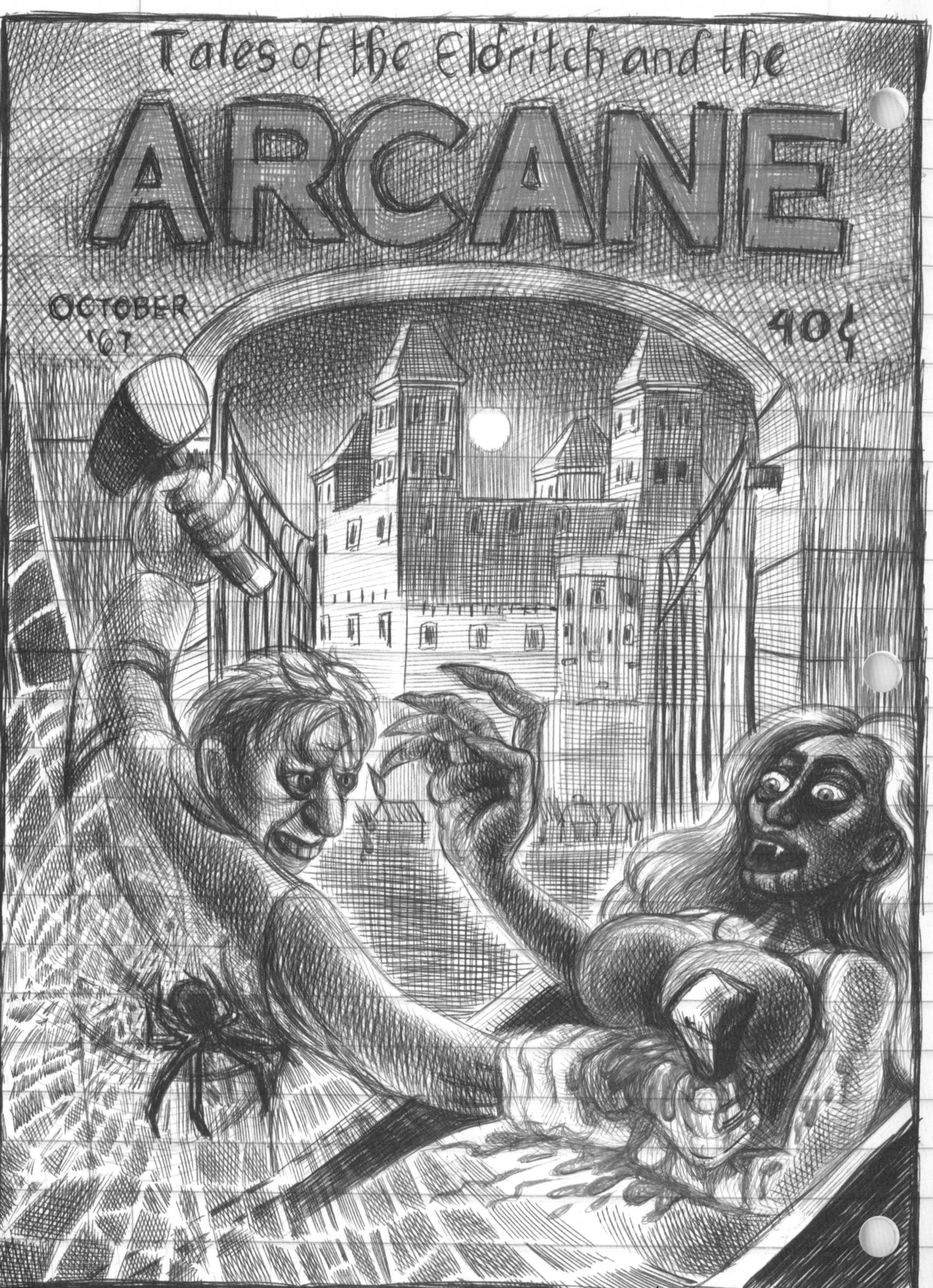

Tales of the Eldritch and the
ARCANE
OCTOBER '67
40¢

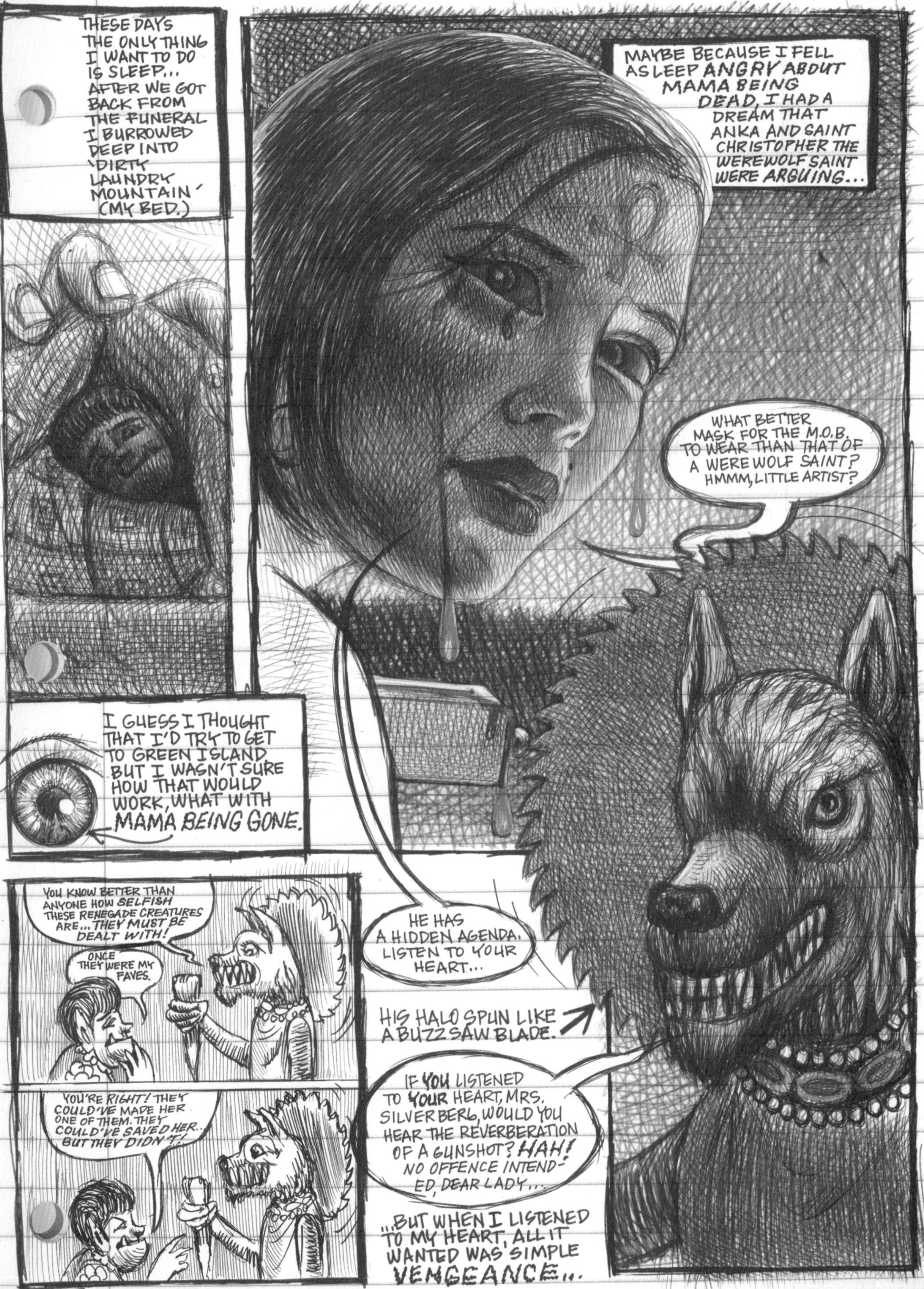

THESE DAYS THE ONLY THING I WANT TO DO IS SLEEP... AFTER WE GOT BACK FROM THE FUNERAL I BURROWED DEEP INTO 'DIRTY LAUNDRY MOUNTAIN' (MY BED.)
MAYBE BECAUSE I FELL ASLEEP ANGRY ABOUT MAMA BEING DEAD, I HAD A DREAM THAT ANKA AND SAINT CHRISTOPHER THE WEREWOLF SAINT WERE ARGUING...
WHAT BETTER MASK FOR THE M.O.B. TO WEAR THAN THAT OF A WEREWOLF SAINT? HMMM, LITTLE ARTIST?
I GUESS I THOUGHT THAT I'D TRY TO GET TO GREEN ISLAND BUT I WASN'T SURE HOW THAT WOULD WORK, WHAT WITH MAMA BEING GONE.
YOU KNOW BETTER THAN ANYONE HOW SELFISH THESE RENEGADE CREATURES ARE... THEY MUST BE DEALT WITH!
ONCE THEY WERE MY FAVES.
HE HAS A HIDDEN AGENDA. LISTEN TO YOUR HEART...
HIS HALO SPUN LIKE A BUZZ SAW BLADE.
YOU'RE RIGHT! THEY COULD'VE MADE HER ONE OF THEM. THEY COULD'VE SAVED HER... BUT THEY DIDN'T?!
IF YOU LISTENED TO YOUR HEART, MRS. SILVERBERG, WOULD YOU HEAR THE REVERBERATION OF A GUNSHOT? HAH! NO OFFENCE INTEND-ED, DEAR LADY...
...BUT WHEN I LISTENED TO MY HEART, ALL IT WANTED WAS SIMPLE VENGEANCE...

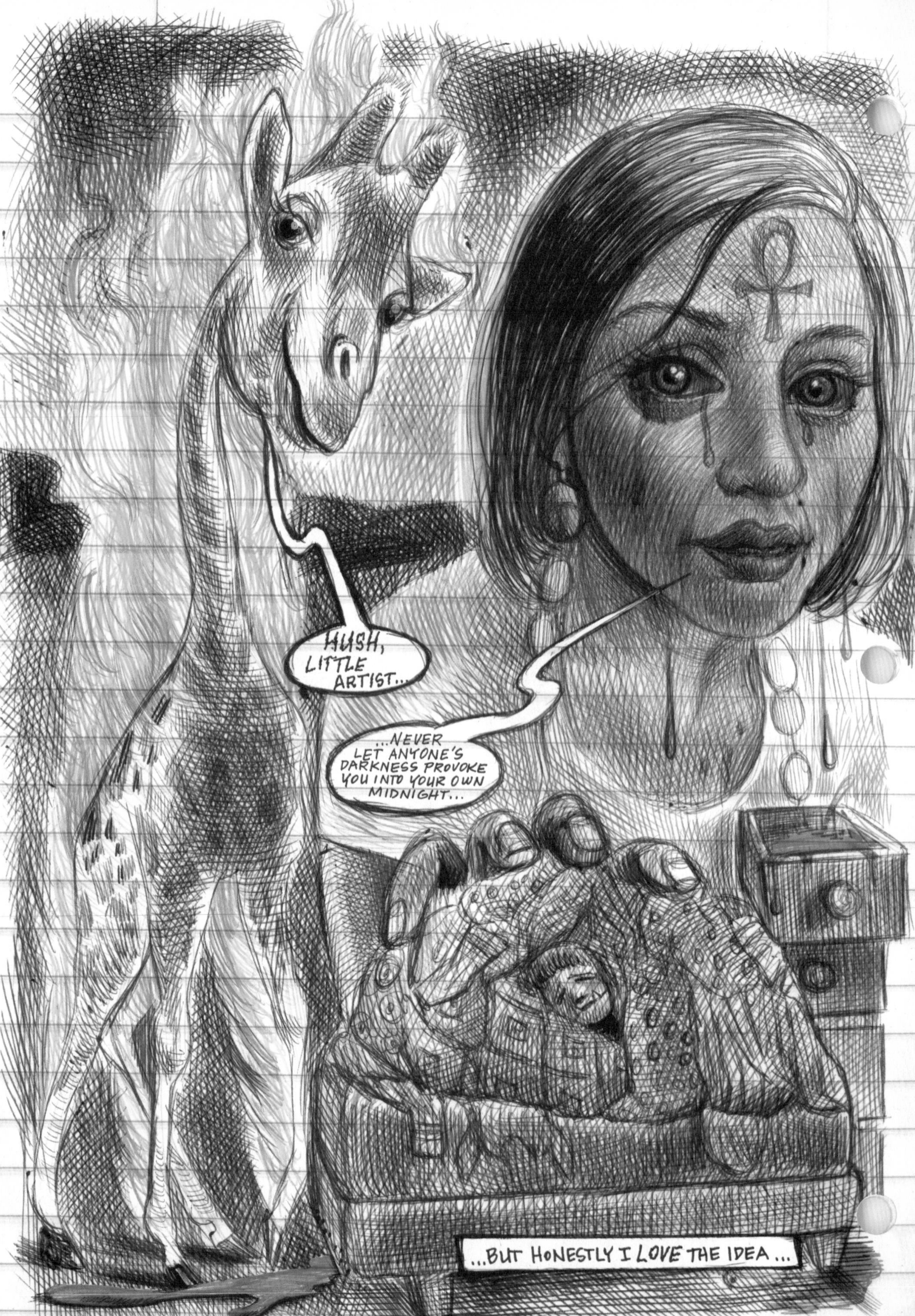
HUSH, LITTLE ARTIST...
...NEVER LET ANYONE'S DARKNESS PROVOKE YOU INTO YOUR OWN MIDNIGHT...
...BUT HONESTLY I LOVE THE IDEA...

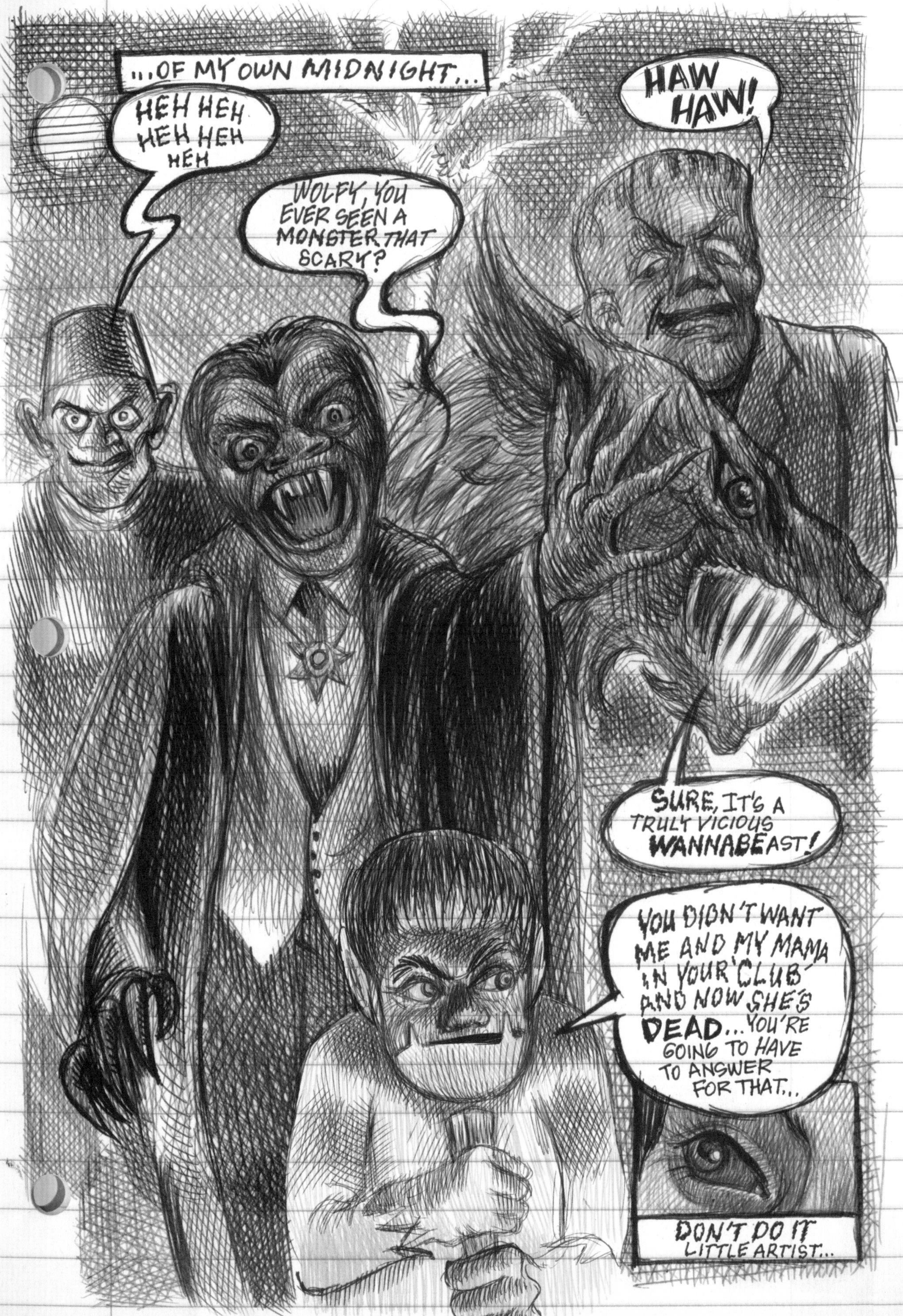
...OF MY OWN MIDNIGHT...
HEH HEH HEH HEH HEH
WOLFY, YOU EVER SEEN A MONSTER THAT SCARY?
HAW HAW!
SURE, IT'S A TRULY VICIOUS WANNABEAST!
YOU DIDN'T WANT ME AND MY MAMA IN YOUR 'CLUB' AND NOW SHE'S DEAD... YOU'RE GOING TO HAVE TO ANSWER FOR THAT...
DON'T DO IT LITTLE ARTIST...

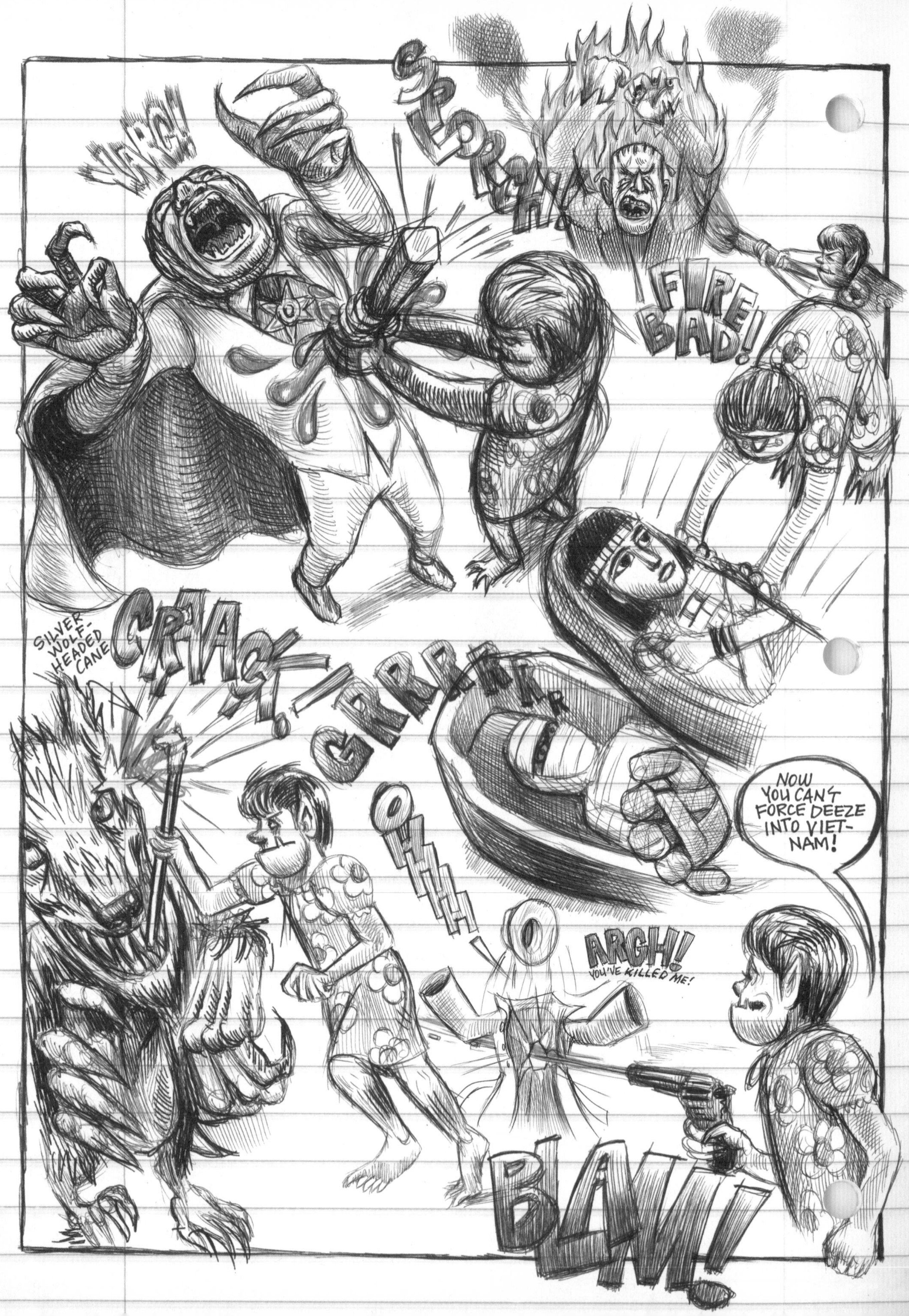
FIRE BAD!
SILVER WOLF-HEADED CANE
CRACK!
NOW YOU CAN'T FORCE DEEZE INTO VIET-NAM!
ARGH!
YOU'VE KILLED ME!
BLAM!

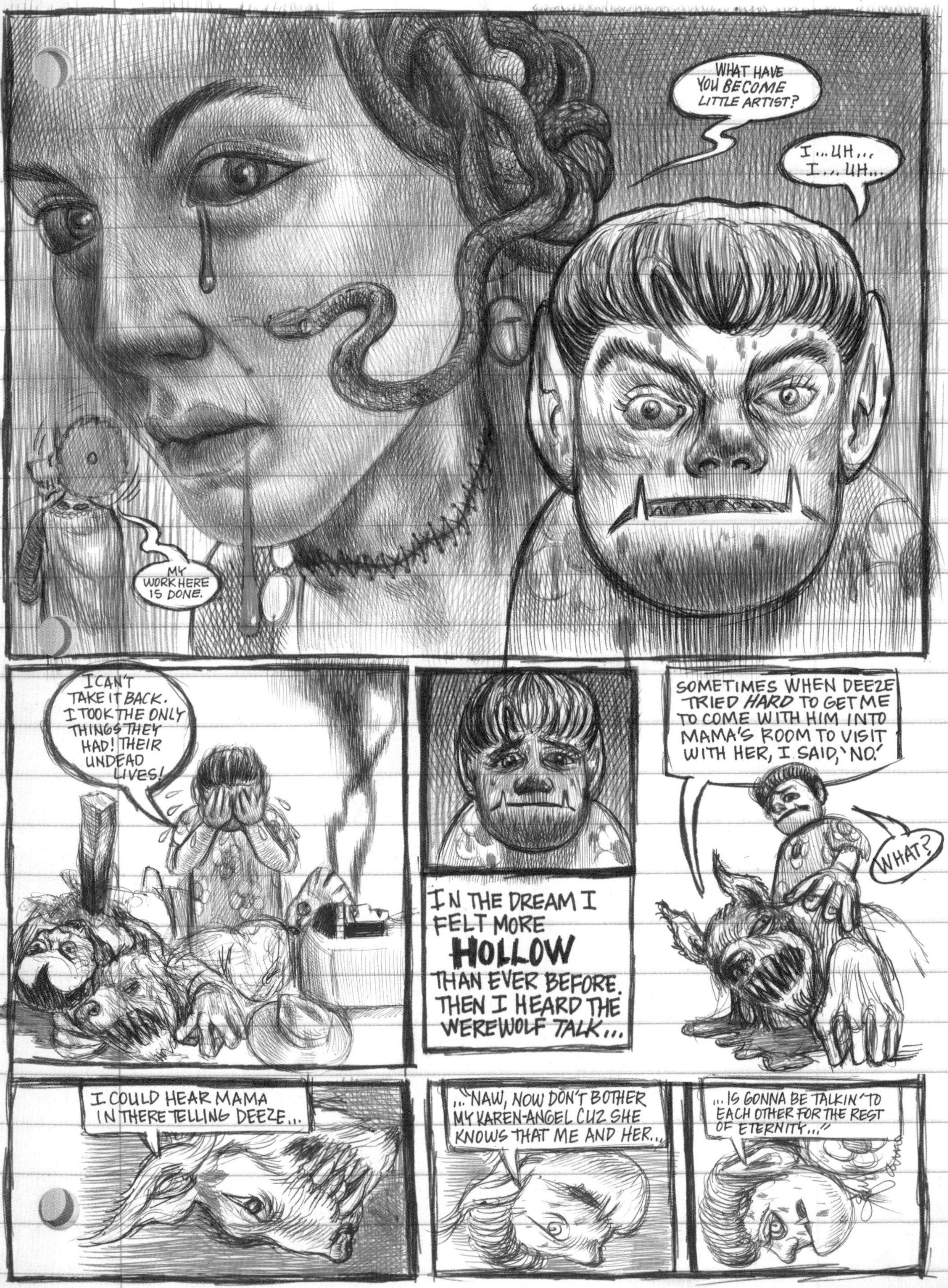
WHAT HAVE YOU BECOME LITTLE ARTIST?
I... UH...
I... UH...
MY WORK HERE IS DONE.
I CAN'T TAKE IT BACK. I TOOK THE ONLY THINGS THEY HAD! THEIR UNDEAD LIVES!
IN THE DREAM I FELT MORE HOLLOW THAN EVER BEFORE. THEN I HEARD THE WEREWOLF TALK...
SOMETIMES WHEN DEEZE TRIED HARD TO GET ME TO COME WITH HIM INTO MAMA'S ROOM TO VISIT WITH HER, I SAID, 'NO.'
WHAT?
I COULD HEAR MAMA IN THERE TELLING DEEZE...
"...NAW, NOW DON'T BOTHER MY KAREN-ANGEL CUZ SHE KNOWS THAT ME AND HER...
...IS GONNA BE TALKIN' TO EACH OTHER FOR THE REST OF ETERNITY..."

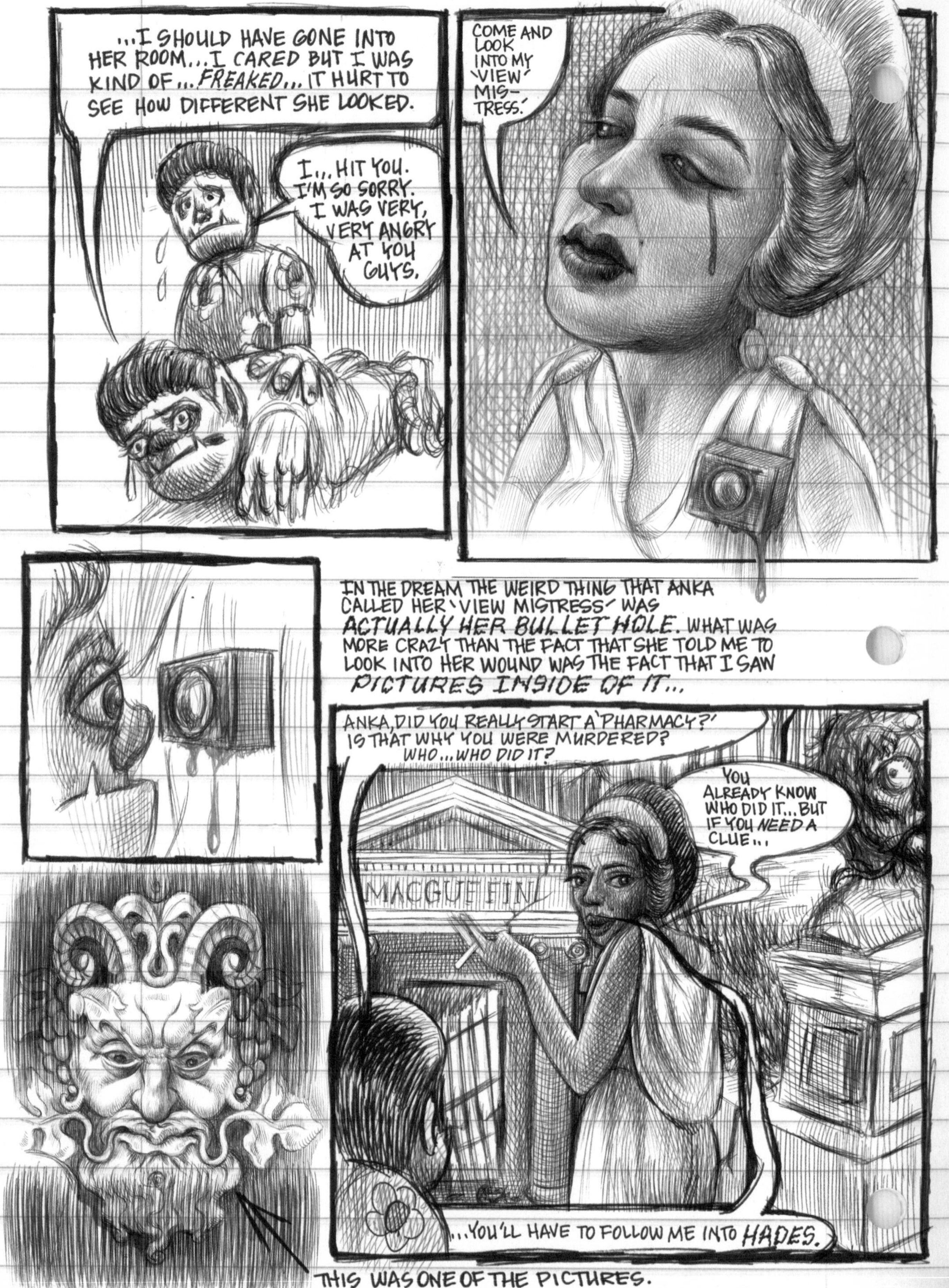

...I SHOULD HAVE GONE INTO HER ROOM...I CARED BUT I WAS KIND OF...FREAKED...IT HURT TO SEE HOW DIFFERENT SHE LOOKED.
I...HIT YOU. I'M SO SORRY. I WAS VERY, VERY ANGRY AT YOU GUYS.
COME AND LOOK INTO MY 'VIEW' MIS-TRESS.'
IN THE DREAM THE WEIRD THING THAT ANKA CALLED HER 'VIEW MISTRESS' WAS ACTUALLY HER BULLET HOLE. WHAT WAS MORE CRAZY THAN THE FACT THAT SHE TOLD ME TO LOOK INTO HER WOUND WAS THE FACT THAT I SAW PICTURES INSIDE OF IT...
ANKA, DID YOU REALLY START A 'PHARMACY?' IS THAT WHY YOU WERE MURDERED? WHO...WHO DID IT?
YOU ALREADY KNOW WHO DID IT...BUT IF YOU NEED A CLUE...
MACGUFFIN
...YOU'LL HAVE TO FOLLOW ME INTO HADES.
THIS WAS ONE OF THE PICTURES.

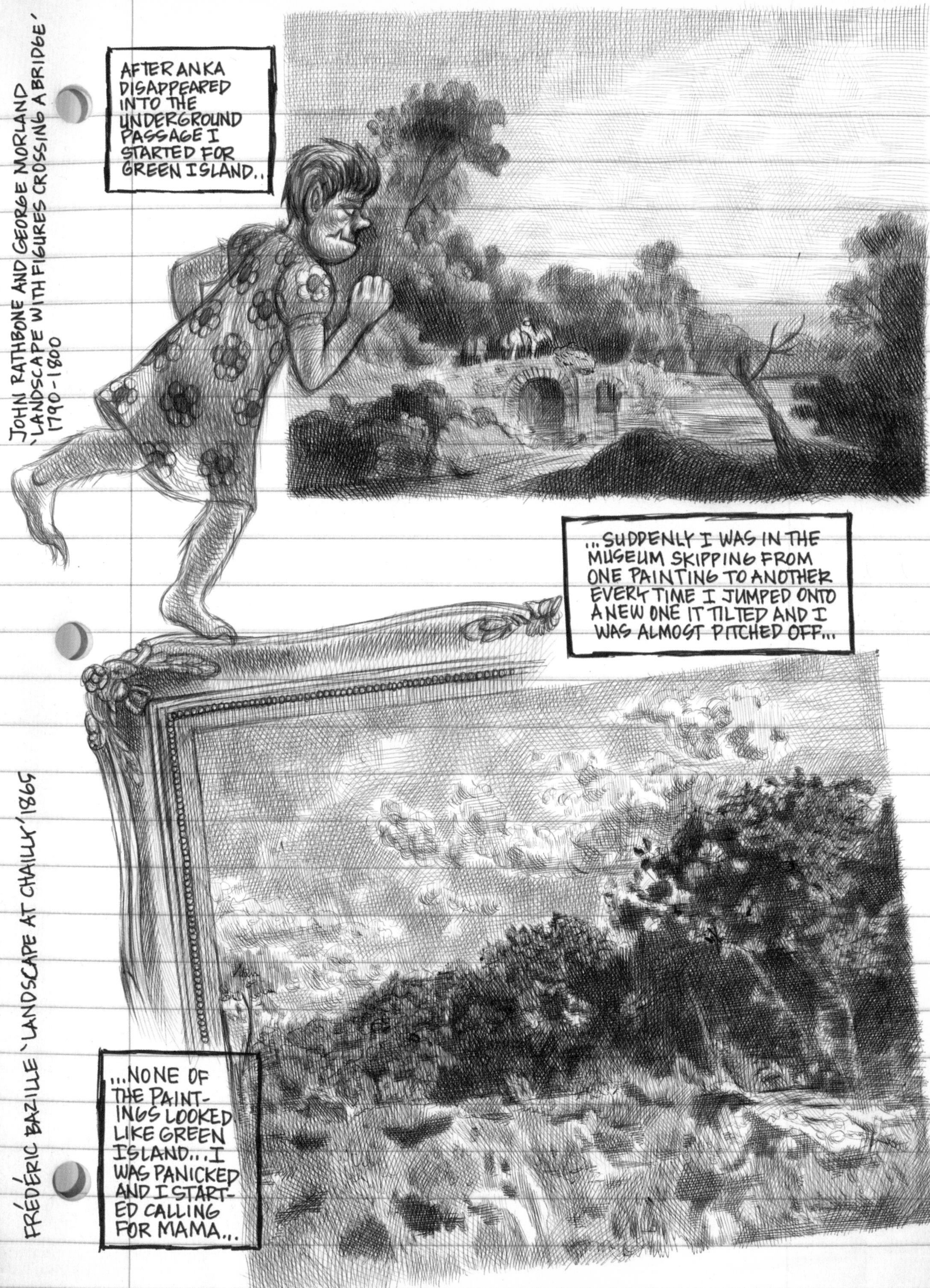
JOHN RATHBONE AND GEORGE MORLAND
'LANDSCAPE WITH FIGURES CROSSING A BRIDGE'
1790-1800
AFTER ANKA DISAPPEARED INTO THE UNDERGROUND PASSAGE I STARTED FOR GREEN ISLAND..
...SUDDENLY I WAS IN THE MUSEUM SKIPPING FROM ONE PAINTING TO ANOTHER EVERY TIME I JUMPED ONTO A NEW ONE IT TILTED AND I WAS ALMOST PITCHED OFF...
FRÉDÉRIC BAZILLE 'LANDSCAPE AT CHAILLY' 1865
...NONE OF THE PAINTINGS LOOKED LIKE GREEN ISLAND...I WAS PANICKED AND I STARTED CALLING FOR MAMA...

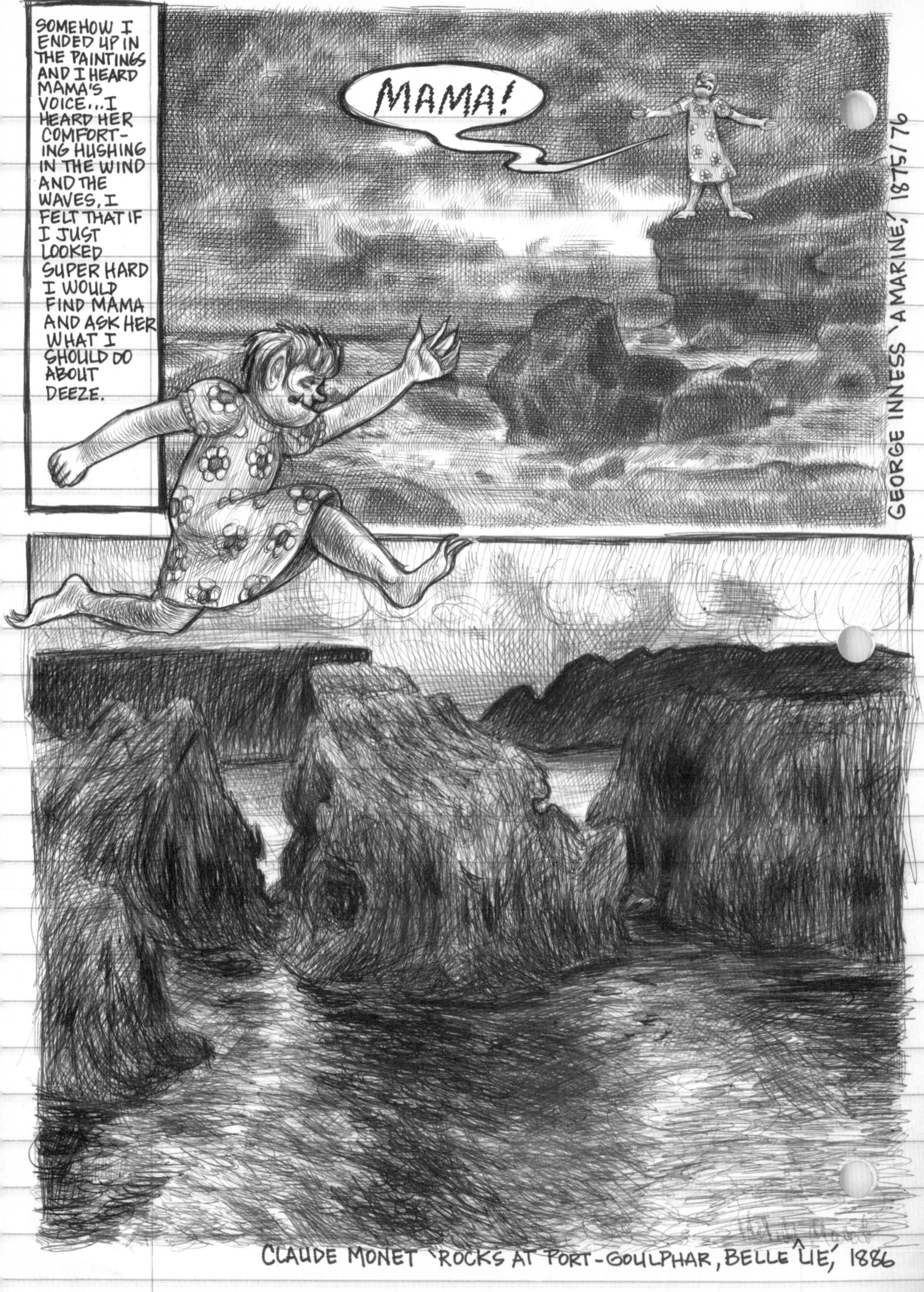
SOMEHOW I ENDED UP IN THE PAINTINGS AND I HEARD MAMA'S VOICE...I HEARD HER COMFORTING HUSHING IN THE WIND AND THE WAVES. I FELT THAT IF I JUST LOOKED SUPER HARD I WOULD FIND MAMA AND ASK HER WHAT I SHOULD DO ABOUT DEEZE.
MAMA!
GEORGE INNESS 'A MARINE,' 1875/76
CLAUDE MONET 'ROCKS AT PORT-GOULPHAR, BELLE ÎLE,' 1886

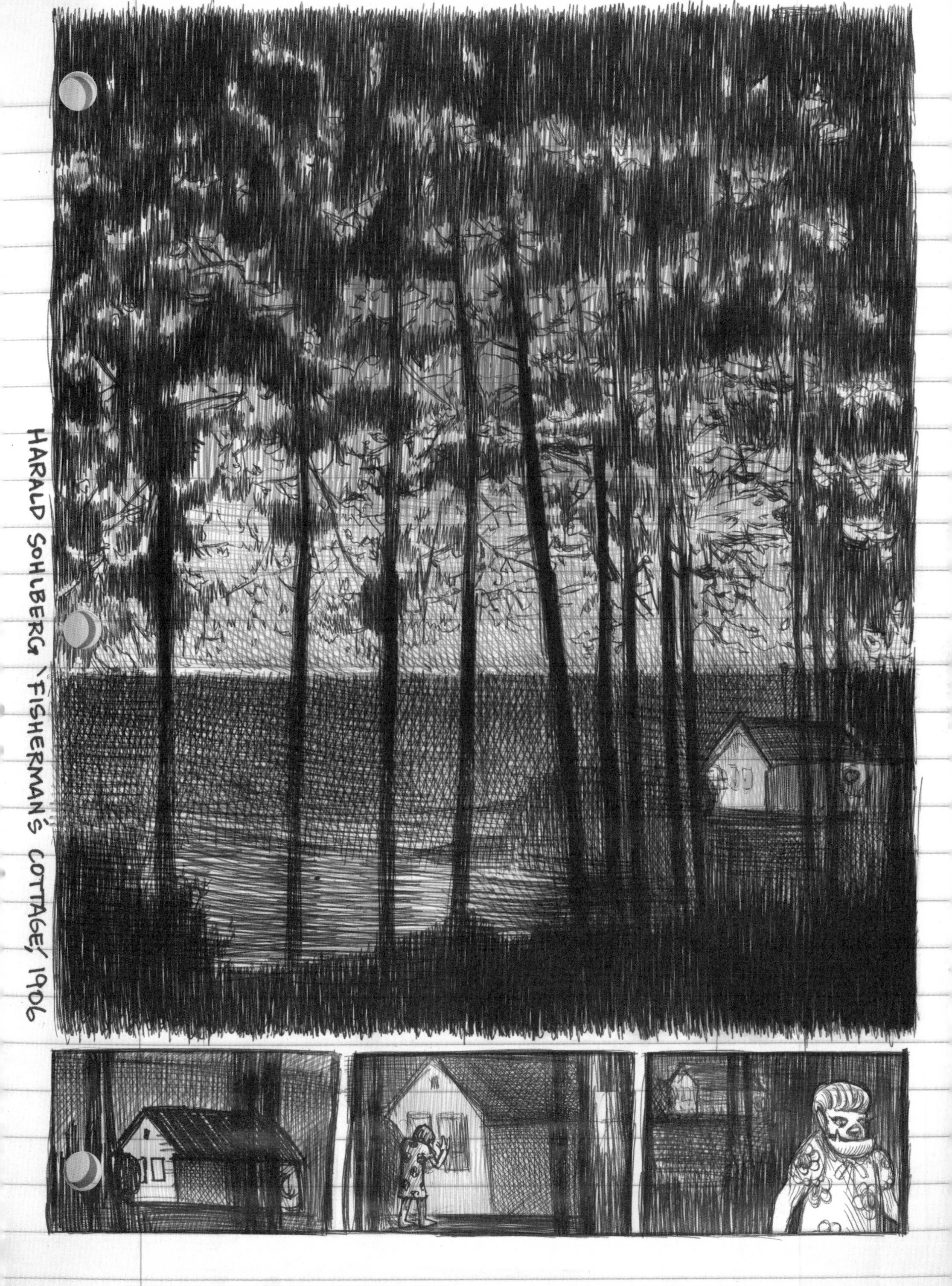

HARALD SOHLBERG 'FISHERMAN'S COTTAGE,' 1906

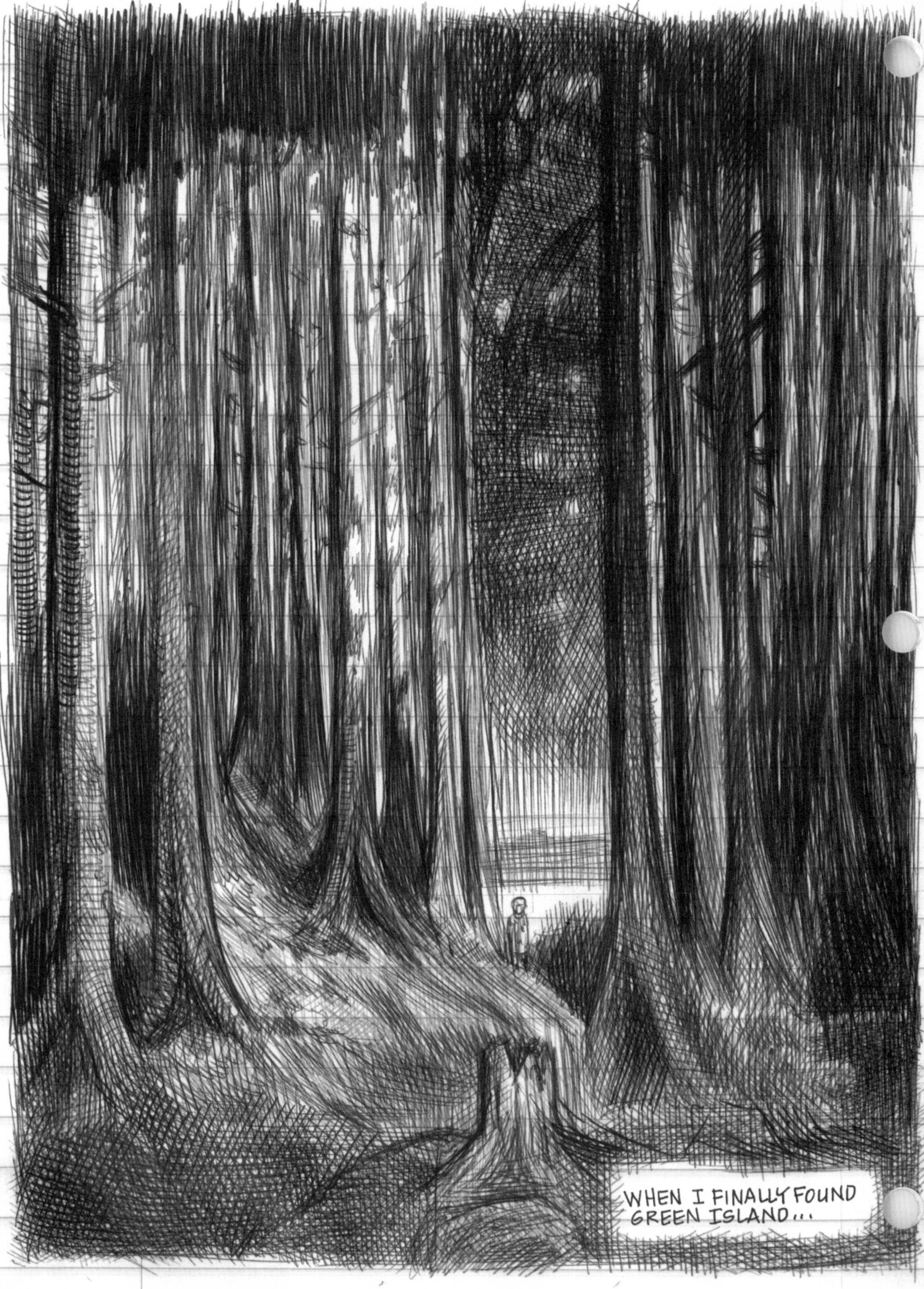
WHEN I FINALLY FOUND GREEN ISLAND...

GUSTAVE DORE 'ALPINE SCENE' 1865 ART INSTITUTE OF CHICAGO

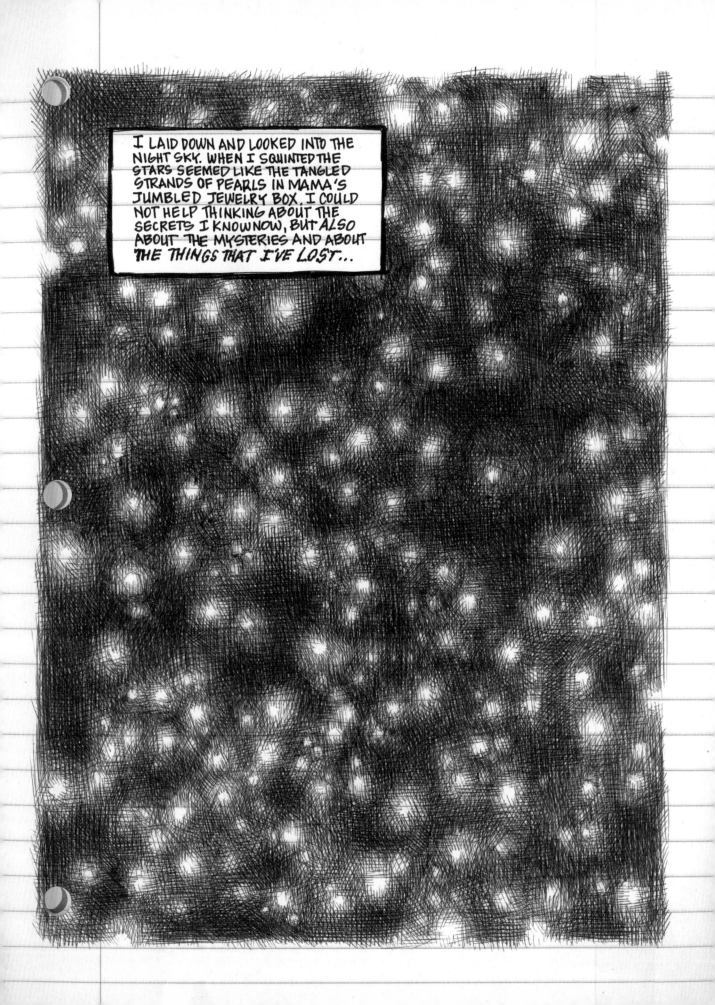

I LAID DOWN AND LOOKED INTO THE NIGHT SKY. WHEN I SQUINTED THE STARS SEEMED LIKE THE TANGLED STRANDS OF PEARLS IN MAMA'S JUMBLED JEWELRY BOX. I COULD NOT HELP THINKING ABOUT THE SECRETS I KNOW NOW, BUT ALSO ABOUT THE MYSTERIES AND ABOUT THE THINGS THAT I'VE LOST...

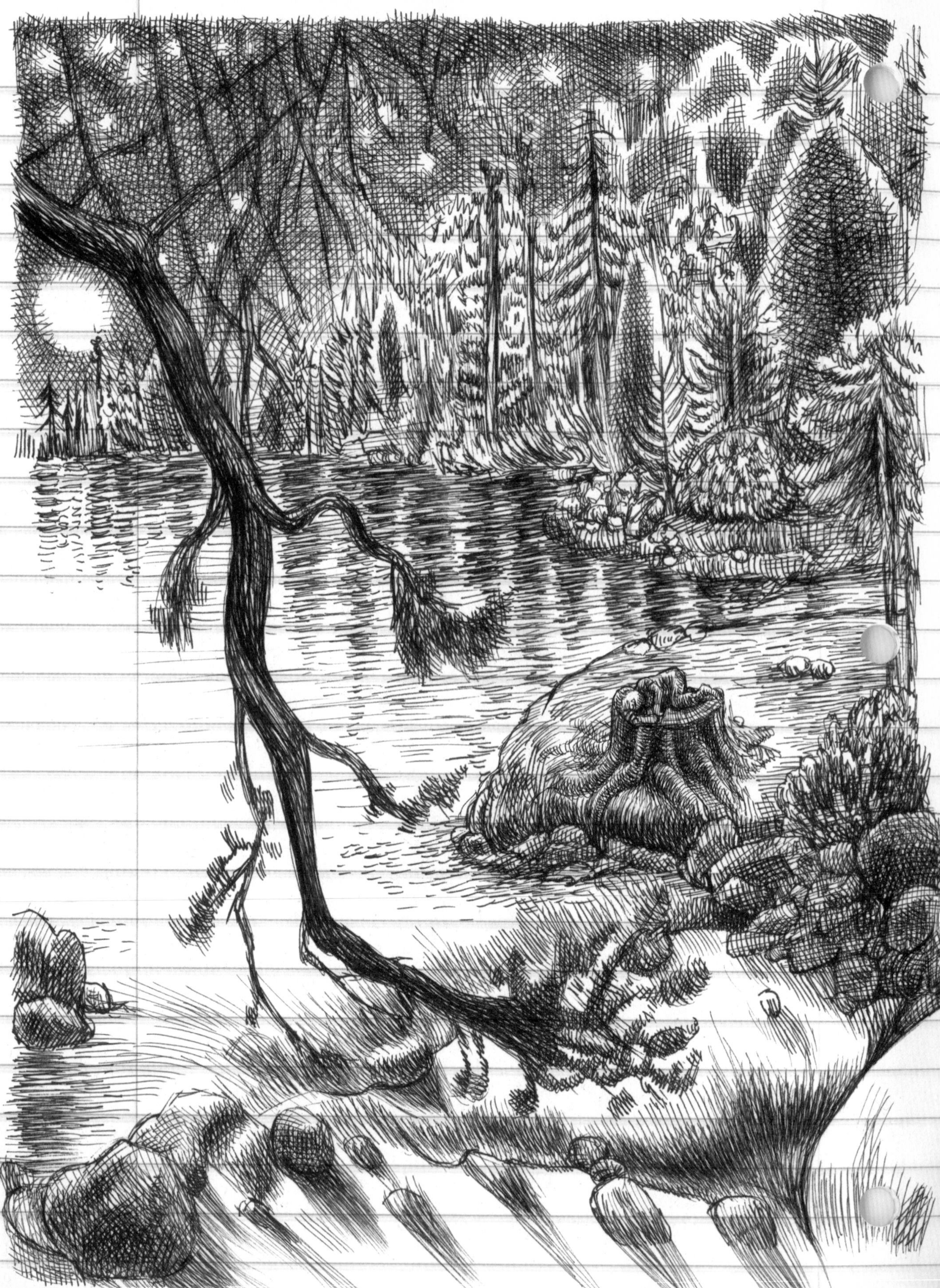

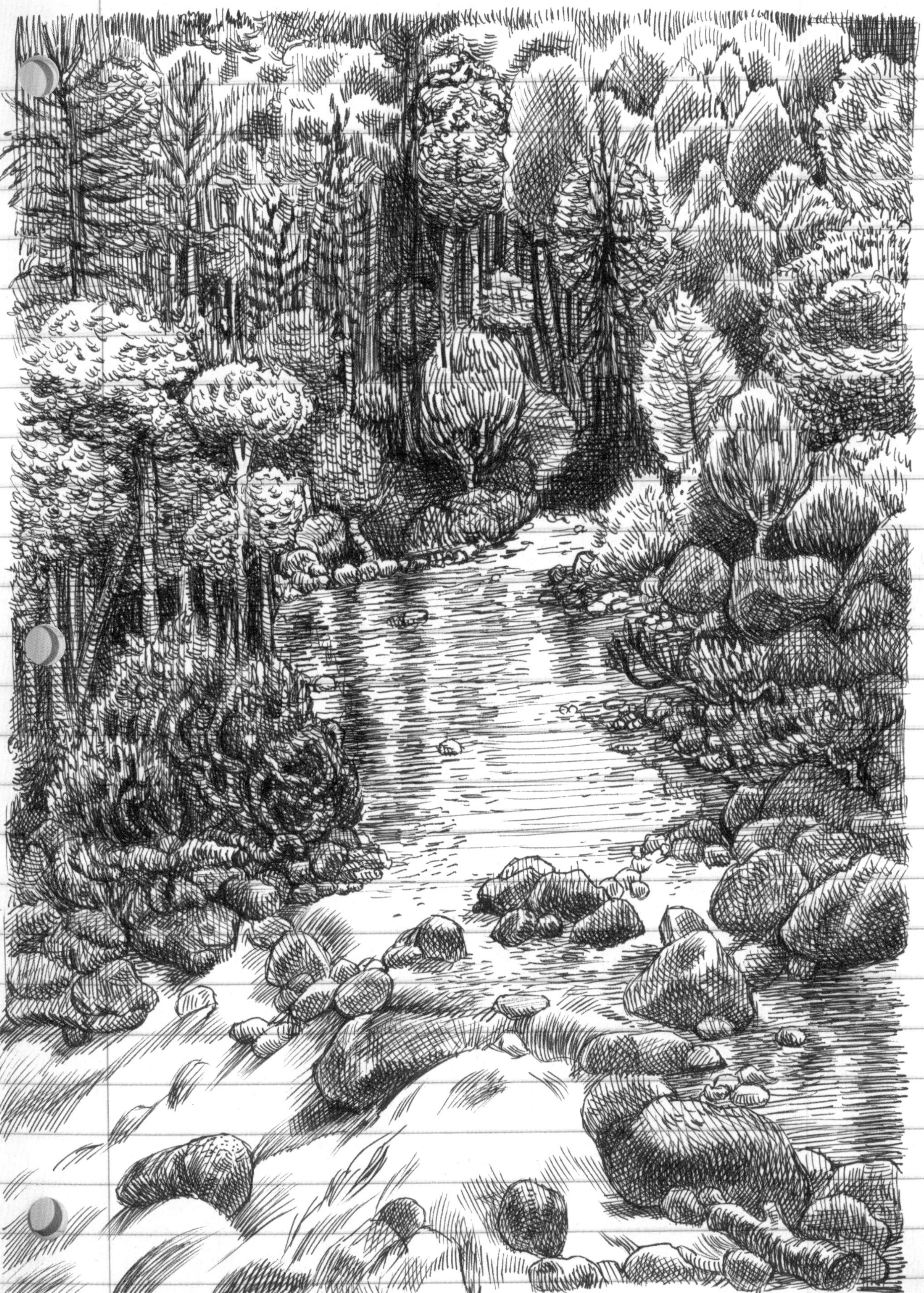

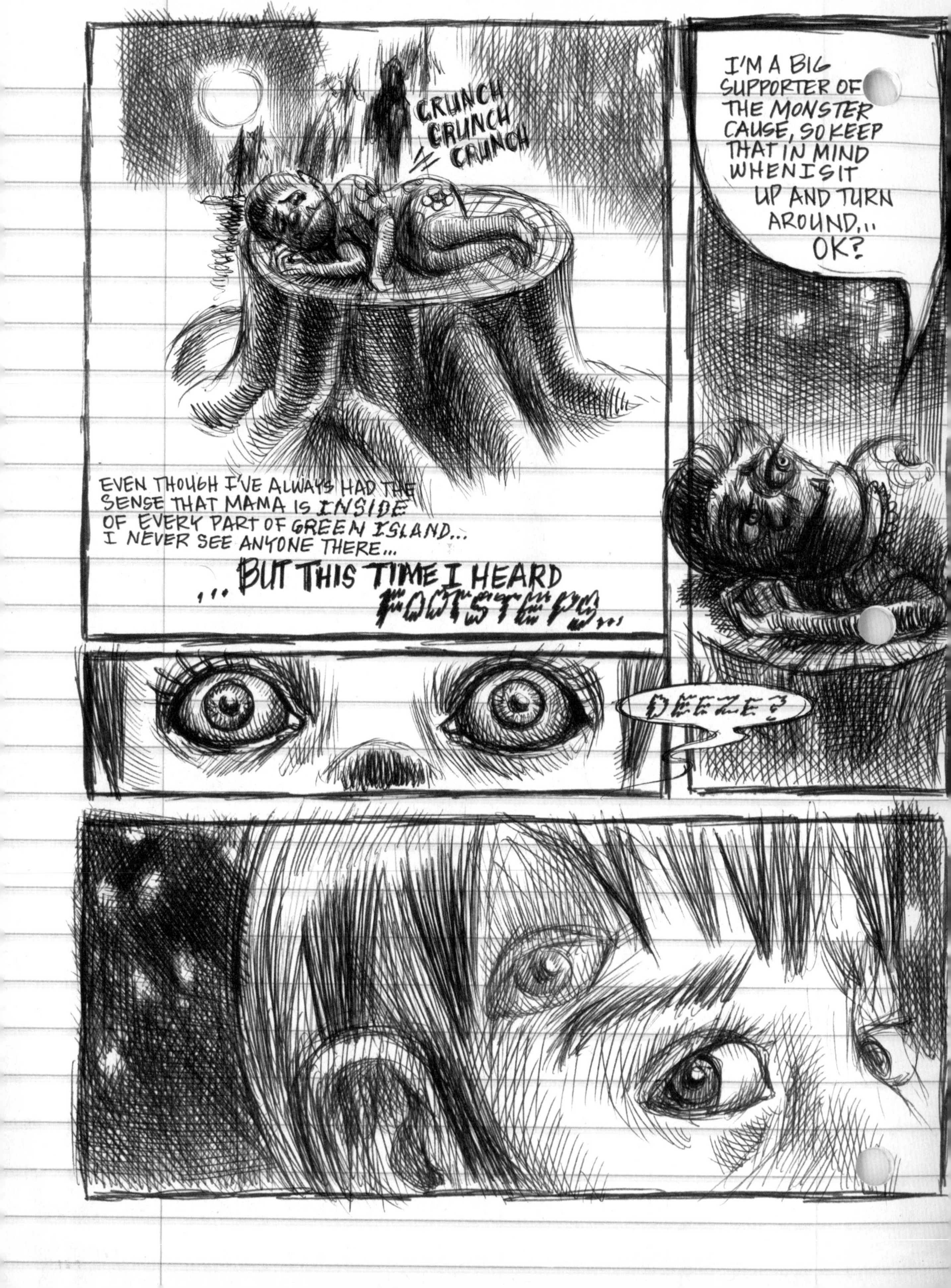

CRUNCH
CRUNCH
CRUNCH
EVEN THOUGH I'VE ALWAYS HAD THE SENSE THAT MAMA IS INSIDE OF EVERY PART OF GREEN ISLAND... I NEVER SEE ANYONE THERE...
...BUT THIS TIME I HEARD FOOTSTEPS...
I'M A BIG SUPPORTER OF THE MONSTER CAUSE, SO KEEP THAT IN MIND WHEN I SIT UP AND TURN AROUND... OK?
DEEZE?

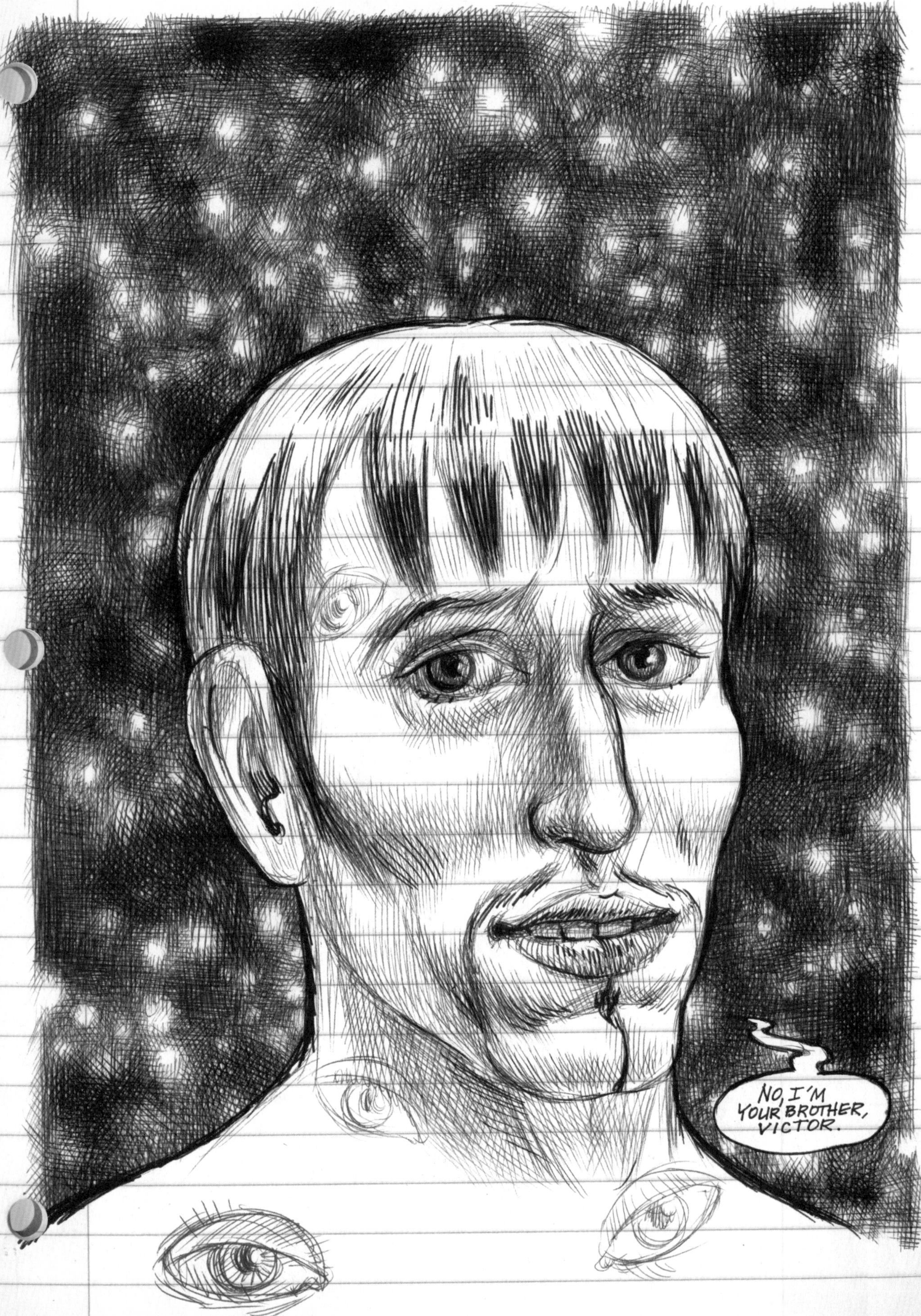
NO, I'M YOUR BROTHER, VICTOR.

EMIL WISHES TO THANK THE FOLLOWING:

RUBY FERRIS, KURT DEVINE, CRYSTAL POWELL, CALVIN REID
BRIDGITTE MONTGOMERY, HOLLY BEMISS, JUDITH GUREWICH,
KATIE ADAMS, STEVE FISHER, GARY GROTH, ERIC REYNOLDS,
JACQ COHEN, ANNA PEDERSON, JACOB COVEY, PRESTON
WHITE, PAUL BARESH, JUDITH WARSCHAUSKY, PAUL McCOMAS,
ANNE ELIZABETH MOORE, CHRIS SULLIVAN, TOBY DEVAN LEWIS,
AMY ENGLAND, LAURA DUNDAS, JOE MERIDETH, JEREMY TINDER,
PAUL ELITZIK, ROSELLEN BROWN, BEAU O'REILLY, FRED HOLLAND,
CANDIDA ALVAREZ, RUTH MARGRAFF, SHERRY ANTONINI,
LISA BARCY, ALISON BECHDEL, CHRIS WARE, JERRY SALTZ,
BILL CARR, BRIAN COX, MOIRA SULLIVAN, KELLY XINTARIS,
WAFAA BILAL, BERT MENCO, JANET LEU, STEPHANIE LUPU,
MARGARET AND SHLOMO BRABHAM, RUTH GUDJONIS, NAOMI
POLLAK, MICHAEL JACKSON, SIGNE RATCLIFF, ELEANOR FERRIS,
WAYNE MILLS, MICHAEL FERRIS, ROSEMARIE FIORE, ANN MILLS,
DANIEL YUTZY, BEV. W., JOHN L., MICKIELA WEISS, CASEY WALES,
JOE GOODMAN, SALLEA WOOD, DALE JOHNSON, ANITA HICKS,
GREG GUTBEZAHL, PAUL TUMEY, JOHN WENDLER, ADAM BURCK,
JOSEPH BURCK, KRISTINA TASHJIAN, MARTI MILLS, STEVE TEMKIN,
ROB SALKOWITZ, ART SPIEGELMAN, SCOTT RAMON, SUSAN MILLS,
KAREN LACEY, BRUCE SIMON, ANDRÉ VAN de PUTTE, CINDY DANGLE
HERMAN, MARYANN SCHAEFER, SAM THIELMAN, MARTI RUST,
BARBARA HERMAN, ROBIN CHAPLIK, MARCO ALEXZONDRA, ANGEL
DEL VALLE, PAULA MAXWELL, TARYN MALONE, MICHAEL STARK,
CAROLYN CARTER, ERIN DEVINE, MICHAEL K., MJ THOMPSON,
MARION J. GLICK, KAREN GREEN, ROY TOMPKINS, ENID WONDER,
JAMES BOLAS, MARK HOLT, MARK WALKER, CHRIS PETRAKOS,
MONICA FOUCHER, MICHAEL TISSERAND, RAYMOND JOHNSON,
MARK NEWGARDEN, GENE KANNENBERG Jr., KATHLEEN
FURORE, ED AVIS, RICK UCCIFERI, RON ZONI, SARAH JANE MALIN,
VALERIE QUINN, AMBER DAVID AND AVERY, JADA HOWARD, ROSE
E. CLARK, JAYSON JANIS, MINNIE, GLENN VICK, DAN EVANS FARKAS
SAMUEL SATTIN, JOANNE MILAZZO, DORO BOEHME, RICHARD REYNOLDS,
CARYN ALMA, ARDEN SERLING, GINA R. SIGAL, PATRICIA HAASE,
TINA HOGAN, GAYLORD DUBOIS, BOX BROWN, KEN MILLS, ADAM ESCHETE,
ELIZABETH CAROLINE, CRISPIN ROSENKRANTZ, RICHARD GREENE,
STORM AINSLEY, LIZ HARRIS, THOMAS COMERFORD, BETH DUVALL,
KATHERINE MONTOYA, RICHARD SALA, MONICA NICKOLAI,
PAUL ARTZ, LINDA YASNYL, GRETCHEN HAASE, NICK JONES,
LOLLY KATHLEEN WALTERS, SARAH FARRINGTON OWENS, ERIC LEE
SAMM BENNETT, KATHY BIDUS, RENE WOODS BECHARD, BILL HAUN,
CINA R. PELAYO, GERARDO PELAYO, ROY BURNS III, CONNIE GOLDMAN,
FRANÇOISE MOULY, NICHOLAS YANES, GENEVIEVE BORMES,
ALEX DUEBEN, HEIDI ANDERSON BOE, CLAUDIA CLEVELAND,
BRIAN R. JOHNSON, LAUREN WEINSTEIN, ANGIE DEVINE, NICK JONES,
TRACEY POLYFLAVOUR, CYNTHIA MAE WILLIAMS, JASON FRANZ,
MILTON KNIGHT, PAM, KIM DEITCH, NICHOLAS JOHN POZENGA,
SETH KALLEN DEITCH, WARD HARKAVY, EMMA AND DAXTON DEVINE,
JAYMES DEVINE, JOSEPHINE LIPUMA, BEN SHLOMO JEREMIAH,

SAVANNAH BURTON, LUCY KNISLEY, CLIFF MILLS, ROB GACZOL, RAY ALMA MICHAEL PETERSON, CHARLIE LEE, CHRIS LINSTER AND QUARTET COPIES. JEANETTE HUBBARD, RUTH B., KATE, JABS MUHAMMED, RICKY, AMY SEARLES, JANNA LEE, JAYMES DEVINE, PHILIP HARTIGAN, DEBRA KAY SIGEL, SARA LEVINE, JOHN ELIAS, JOHN ROTH, JESSICA OLDANI, STEVE MURPHY, ERIN BRIED, CECILIA CORNEJO SOTELO, BERGERONS, JOANNA KENYON, FRANCIS DI MENNO, JUDITH HLADIK VOSS, CAROL HLADIK, RICH VOSS, JODIE RICHTER, REES DAOREN, JAYMES DEVINE, LOUIS BONDURANT, CINA PELAYO, HEATHER McSHANE, DIANE PONDER, DIANE WANEK, GAIL KIEFER, DONNA GLAVAN, RAE ULRICH, JANICE DEMESKI, BARRY ST. VITUS, MARILYN EPEL SILBERG, TONI BARK, MELANIE HANSON, SUSAN DOOM, JOHN COMITO, CHARLIE SUTER, JONAS PACKER, DIANE GREEN, BILL SELBY, DEBRA STEPHENS, MARISSA MANABAT ZAGONE, JOHN RICH, MIMI LEVINE, KAREN WALES, ADAM E., CALVIN FORBES, SUSAN VOLK, ROBBIE LITTLE, GERALD FRANK PAOLI, PHILLIPA EVERARD WEST, KATE STRANSKY, KRYTYNA OLSIEWICZ, NANNE BINGHI BARKDULL, DARREN SURLES, CORINNE HALBERT, MILTON KNIGHT, MARY BETH JANSON BELLON, FLORIE GRAY, PAUL ARTZ, MARION HUBBARD, JEFFREY-JACK PARKS, DEBORAH HIRSHFIELD, MIKE DUGGINS, MEGAN KELLER, JANET MEEGAN, CHARLES PIKE, STEVE BRODNER ELLIOT FELDMAN, ERIC KNISLEY, DREW FRIEDMAN, MARY THOMSON, WARD HARKAVY, TILNA KOMULAINEN, ANN ZATARAIN, PAULA CASAGRANDE, HILLARY BROWN, WOO, ABRAHAM RIESMAN, DANA JENNINGS, DIANE GRIDER, NATE SMYTH, CRAIG DOWNS, STEVEN CARLYLE MOORE, CAREN ROSENBLATT, AGA KUBIAK, JOE NOCE, GREG DEOCAMPO, FRANCESCA GAGLIONE, MELISSA PITTMAN, JIM SIERGEY, BRIAN GRILLO, SCOTT STRIPLING, MICHAEL CROCHETIERRE, MICHAEL BLIGHT, COTY COLSON, MARY VOULES-KETSEZIS, LADDIE SCOTT ODOM, GEANIE STOUT, MANNY KING, JD BANDY, BROOKE LANIER, WLADEK DYDEK, PATE CONAWAY, ZELDA HESSLER, CONOR CIAR, NATE SMYTH, DAVID HOUSTON, ALYSSA HERLOCHER, B. INGRID OLSON, MIMI LEVINE, RICHELLE WUTHERICH EDWARDS, MIKE McCLAIN, LAUREN WEINSTEIN, VALERIE SWEAZY ST. GERMAIN, JUSTIN LYNCH, SUSEN JAMES, DANIEL ANDERSON-BOE, AMBER SMOCK, KATHERINE SCHUTTA, MELANIE BARON EGGLESTON, BART RYCKBOSCH, CATHI SCHWALBE, PATRICIA ANN McNAIR, LEANNE THOMAS, HARRIETTE AND WALDO SPIESS, MICHAEL AND MARIE FERRIS, SCHOOL OF THE ART INSTITUTE OF CHICAGO. MIKE FERRIS, AND FANTAGRAPHICS.

FANTAGRAPHICS BOOKS
7563 LAKE CITY WAY NE
SEATTLE, WASHINGTON 98115

EDITOR : GARY GROTH
DESIGNER : JACOB COVEY
PRODUCTION : PRESTON WHITE, JACOB COVEY, PAUL BARESH
ASSOCIATE PUBLISHER : ERIC REYNOLDS
PUBLISHER : GARY GROTH

WWW.FANTAGRAPHICS.COM · TWITTER : @FANTAGRAPHICS · FACEBOOK.COM/FANTAGRAPHICS

THIRD FANTAGRAPHICS BOOKS EDITION : JULY 2017

PRINTED IN KOREA

LOC# 2016946097

ISBN 978-1-60699-959-2